THE DRAGONRIDER HERITAGE

FIRST SERIES COLLECTION

BOOKS 1-4

BROADFEATHER BOOKS
www.AuthorNicoleConway.com

AVORA

FORRAN PLAI[N]

HOL'RADIX

TIBRUS

VOCRAN OCEAN

BRASKOL

NOLTHAM

ELONDIA

LUNTHARDA

MALDOBAR

[S]OUTHERN SEA

ELONDRAN OCEAN

RIENKA

NAR'HALEEN

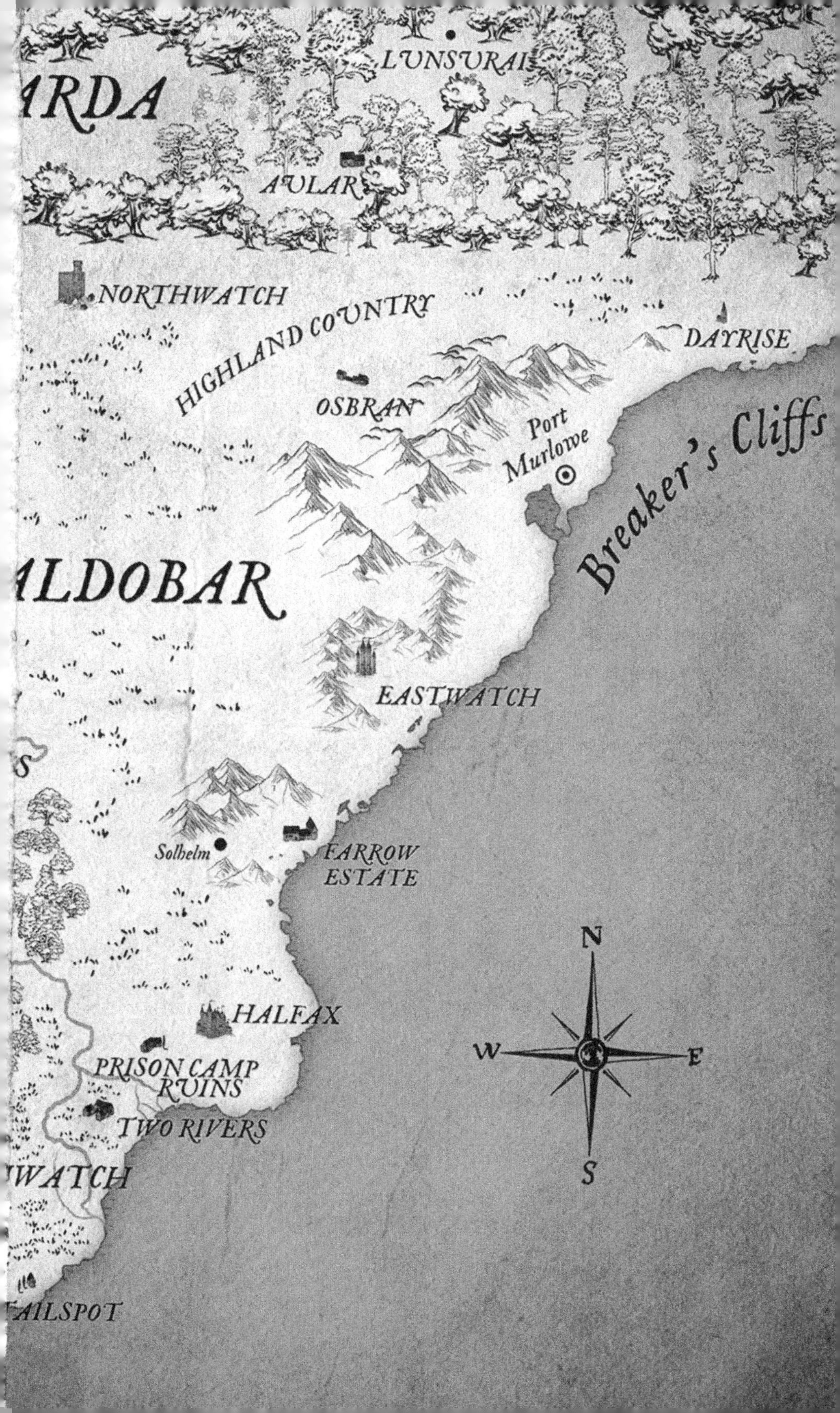

Map

- LUNSURAI
- A'ULAR
- ARDA
- NORTHWATCH
- HIGHLAND COUNTRY
- DAYRISE
- OSBRAN
- Port Murlowe
- Breaker's Cliffs
- ALDOBAR
- EASTWATCH
- Solhelm
- FARROW ESTATE
- HALFAX
- PRISON CAMP RUINS
- TWO RIVERS
- ...WATCH
- ...AILSPOT

N / W / E / S

This book is a work of fiction. Names, characters, places, and incidents are either products of the author's imagination or used fictitiously. Any resemblance to actual persons, living or dead, business establishments, events, or locales is coincidental. The author makes no claims to, but instead acknowledges the trademarked status and trademark owners of the word marks mentioned in this world of fiction.

Copyright © 2022 by Nicole Conway

All rights reserved.

No part of this book may be reproduced in any form or by any electronic or mechanical means, including information storage and retrieval systems, without written permission from the author, except for the use of brief quotations in a book review.

Title and cover design by Covered by Nicole

For Ashlynn & Braeden

THE PANTHEON OF MALDOBAR

THE FOREGODS

God of Was: Itanus
God of Is: Enais
God of Still to Come: Milontos

THE OLD GODS

God of Earth: Giaus
Goddess of the Sky: Astaris
The Fates: Viepol

THE LESSER GODS

God of Life & Nature: Paligno
Goddess of Death & Decay: Clysiros
Goddess of the Sea: Undae
Goddess of the Moon: Adiana
Goddess of Mischief: Iskoli
God of War: Proleus
Goddess of Love: Eno
God of Luck: Tykeron
God of Mercy: Ishaleon

HUNTER

THE DRAGONRIDER HERITAGE BOOK ONE

1
CHAPTER ONE

I startled awake to the smell of smoke and my father gripping my shoulders, shaking me.

"Thatch, get up!" he shouted over me. "Hurry!"

I fell out of bed, tripping over my own feet as I scrambled to yank on my boots. "W-What's going on?"

He didn't have to reply—the answer was written all over his face. With his eyes wide and face blanched with panic, my father shoved a lumpy saddlebag into my hands and spun me around, roughly steering me out of my tiny bedroom and into the hall. "Go to the stable! Run!"

Terror sent a jolt through me like a lightning strike. What was happening? Was it the Tibrans? Were they attacking the city?

For the last few months, our kingdom of Maldobar had been under attack by a foreign enemy. The Tibran Empire had come with war machines and soldiers beyond counting, and they only had one goal—to conquer and kill. So far, they'd done a good job of it. City after city fell to their hordes of soldiers. Not even our prestigious dragonriders, the finest knights in the king's entire army, had been able to hold them off.

Not yet, anyway.

"Go!" Father roared at my back.

I took off at a sprint. Pumping my legs as fast as I could, I darted down the hall to the narrow staircase that led into the stable below. We'd lived in the loft directly above it for as long as I could remember.

The horses were panicking. They whinnied and bucked, kicking at their stalls as smoke and embers swirled in the air. Gods, was the stable on fire?

My legs locked up, bringing me to a screeching halt before the open door. No—it wasn't just our stable.

Outside, every building up and down our street glowed red, swallowed in roaring flames that licked and crackled against the night sky. Men shouted. Women screamed. Children wailed. Horses ran wild in the streets, dragging burning wagons as they searched for a way out.

Gods and Fates, what was happening?

My father appeared as though he'd materialized out of thin air. He gripped the reins of our buckskin mare and snatched the saddlebag out of my hands to fling it over her back. "Get on, now."

"What about you?" I slipped a foot into one of the stirrups and swung my other leg over the saddle.

His eyes squeezed shut, jaw clenched as he shoved the reins into my hand. "I'll be right behind you. Go. Ride to the North River Bridge and take the river road through the marshlands. Head for Mithangol. Don't stop. Do you hear me, Thatch?"

"B-But, Father—"

He grabbed the sides of my face, yanking me down close enough to press his mouth to my forehead. "Do as I say, Son. *Go!*"

My father smacked the mare on the rump. She reared and pawed at the air before she bolted out of the stable at a frantic gallop. We burst into the fire-lit streets, hooves thundering over the cobblestones.

I gripped the reins for dear life. My heart thrashed in my ears as I leaned down against her neck. My body shook and my mind blurred, tangled up in wild panic. What was going on? Why wasn't Father coming with me? We should have left together! How would I ever find him again?

There were burning heaps of something—maybe debris—piled on the streets and sidewalks. My mare skirted around them and jumped the ones she couldn't avoid. It was only when we rounded a corner, heading for the North River, that I realized those heaps weren't debris.

They were people.

A dark shape appeared through the smoky gloom, blocking the path ahead. A barricade? Had someone blocked the street?

As I got closer, I could pick out the shapes of people—men dressed from head to toe in heavy bronze-colored armor. They brandished swords that dripped with fresh blood. Their broad, round shields were spattered with it, too. Marching shoulder-to-shoulder, the soldiers at the front of the line held up torches. Occasionally, they would toss them through the window of a building they passed, setting fire to whatever was inside.

Terror hit me like a fist to the throat.

Tibrans.

I sank my heels into my horse's flanks. She shrieked and poured on more speed. We charged through the plumes of black smoke that poured from buildings on either side of the street.

They spotted me immediately. My muscles seized up as my blood froze in my veins. No stopping now.

I pulled hard on the reins, bringing my mare around in a sharp turn that nearly sent me flying out of the saddle. Arrows zipped past my head, pinging off the cobblestones all around me. We bolted back the way we'd come, zigzagging through narrow alleys and avenues. I had to find another way out of the city—now.

My horse puffed, her mouth dripping with foam and her flanks shining with sweat as we crested a steep road into a small square. Here, nothing was on fire yet, but people still rushed out of every building in droves. They fled toward the North River, toward the bridge. It was our only way out.

Hope gave me new strength. I squeezed the thick leather of the reins harder. We could make it. Just a bit further.

I heard the *twang* of a bowstring. Wait, no, not a bow. Something else. The sound was much sharper and more abrupt. But what would make a sound like—?

A short, thick-shafted arrow caught right in my mare's chest. She crumpled, legs instantly buckling.

I didn't even have time to scream.

I flew over my fallen horse's head and hit the street hard, bouncing like a stone across a pond. My head cracked off the ground, and my arms and legs flailed until I finally landed in a heap, sprawled on my back.

For a moment, all I could do was lie there. My vision faded in and out. My ears rang.

I couldn't pass out. Not now. Up—I had to get up. I had to get out of here.

I clenched my teeth and forced myself to move. Rolling over onto my stomach, my arms shook as I pushed myself to my hands and knees. Something hot and wet drizzled down my face, making my shaggy hair stick to my cheeks and forehead.

My mare lay on her side a short distance down the street, but she wasn't moving. The arrow had hit with so much force, it was buried in her breast all the way to the black-feathered fletching. She was gone.

I'd have to run on foot.

S̲h̲a̲m̲b̲l̲i̲n̲g̲ ̲t̲o̲ ̲m̲y̲ ̲f̲e̲e̲t̲, I staggered toward the nearest alleyway. My head spun, and bright spots winked in my vision. I stumbled and caught myself against the side of one of the buildings. Maybe, if I could just rest for a moment, my head would clear and I could—

"He went this way," a man's throaty voice growled. "I already winged him for you. He won't get far. Best hurry, before those Tibran dogs steal the kill."

Spinning around, I met the glittering eyes of two men as they stepped into the alley behind me. Their dark silhouettes loomed over me, ominous against the faint moonlight and orange glow of distant flames.

Oh no.

I backed away. Run—I had to run!

The heel of my boot snagged on an uneven stone. I staggered, arms flailing as I fell backwards and landed on my rump.

One of the men barked a laugh. He was shorter and huskier than the other, and his dark eyes glittered with primal malice as he studied me. "There's an easy mark for you, pup. Look at him, helpless as a newborn fawn. Pathetic."

My whole body shook. I sat, totally paralyzed, as I watched them prowl closer and closer. They wore the same clothing—matching black leather armor, cloaks, and boots. Something like soot was smeared across their faces, just a single swipe over their eyes.

The shorter one of them carried a large, black crossbow slung over his shoulder. He stroked the trigger with one finger and grinned wickedly down at me, still chuckling under his breath.

The other man was taller, with wide shoulders and a leaner, more efficient build. He had a black handkerchief tied over his nose and mouth that covered most of his face. I couldn't see much more than the whites of his eyes and some of his dark hair poking out from under his hood.

He stalked toward me, his polished black boots crunching on the gravel. Reaching for the hilts of two long, slightly curved scimitars, he drew them from the sheath across his back. The metal hummed, singing in the dark as he spun them over his hands.

Oh gods. He ... he was going to kill me.

Every alarm in my head wailed at once. *Get up! Go! Get out of there, stupid!*

But fear turned my muscles to mush. I couldn't move. I could barely breathe. I trembled as I sat, staring up at the man brandishing those flawless scimitars.

Tears welled in my eyes. I-I didn't want to die. Who were these people? They weren't Tibrans, were they? Where was Father? What was happening?

"Hurry it up! We don't have all night. The Tibrans will be here any minute. We've got orders, you know," the man with the crossbow snarled.

"P-Please, I just want to go home." My voice came out in a broken, breathless sob. "Y-You don't have to do this. You don't have to hurt me or ... or anyone else. You can make a different choice. You don't have to be like them!"

The warrior in black tightened his grip and raised one of his blades. His eyes narrowed into lethal, emotionless slits.

I sucked in a breath and waited for that blade to fall. For pain. For death. Maybe it wouldn't be so bad. Maybe I'd finally meet my mother.

But he didn't move.

The hand gripping that raised blade began to shake. His eyes went round, brow skewing with an expression I didn't understand. What was he waiting for?

The other man yelled louder, his voice cracking over us like the snap of a whip. "Hurry it up, you useless mutt!"

In one fluid motion, the guy brandishing the scimitars whirled into a spin and hurled one of his weapons through the air. It sailed down the alleyway, wind howling over the blade.

I squeezed my eyes shut.

There was an awful gurgling sound like someone choking on water.

Only, it wasn't water.

Peeling my eyes open, I sucked in a gasp. My heart sank to the soles of my feet. The other warrior in black dropped to his knees, crossbow clattering to the ground. His body hit the street, limp and lifeless, with the scimitar sticking straight up out of his chest.

I gagged. Bile burned in my throat as my eyes watered. I couldn't bear to look anymore. If I was next, I didn't want to see it coming. But I couldn't tear my eyes away.

The remaining warrior stalked toward his fallen comrade, wrenched his blade free, and tucked both weapons back into the sheaths strapped between his shoulders. Then he grabbed the crossbow and whirled around.

He stormed straight for me, eyes ablaze.

Oh ... oh no.

I drew back, shaking as I gaped up at him. Was he going to shoot me instead? He thrust the crossbow out toward me—almost like he wanted me to take it. What ...?

"Take this and go," he commanded, his deep voice muffled by the handkerchief covering his mouth. He sounded young, like maybe he wasn't much older than I was.

I eyed the weapon. I didn't want to touch that thing. I'd never held a sword, crossbow, or any other kind of weapon in my life! I was a farrier's son—not a fighter. I didn't even know how to shoot it! "B-But why?"

"Listen to me, kid," he growled as he seized the front of my nightshirt and dragged me to my feet. "Your home is gone. Your family is most likely gone, too. The Tibran army is moving on the royal city of Halfax tonight. So you have two choices: you either run and maybe you get out of here alive, or you stay and die. What's it going to be?"

My pulse roared in my ears as I stared at the crossbow, then back up at the guy holding it out to me. Why was he doing this? He could have killed me—he was supposed to, wasn't he? But he'd saved my life instead. I didn't understand it.

"Why didn't you kill me?" I managed to wheeze.

One of his eyes twitched. "Are you dense? I said get out of here, *now*."

"What about you? Where will you go?"

His brows snapped together into a sharp scowl. He shoved the weapon against my chest hard enough to make me stagger and almost fall over. Then he turned and began to leave.

"Hey! Wait up!" I wobbled after him, my knees still shaking.

He didn't look back or slow down. "Get away from me. I told you to run."

"But I don't have anywhere to go. If the Tibrans are attacking Halfax tonight, then—"

He stopped so suddenly that I crashed into his back.

"Don't you get it? This is it. This is the end. The Tibran Empire is going to raze this whole kingdom to the ground. There won't be anything left. And if you stay here, you'll end up dead in a ditch somewhere, along with everyone else." He barked each word as though it tasted bitter on his tongue. "The king is making his final stand at the royal city right now, but it won't matter. A few dragonriders against the entire Tibran army? They won't last the night. By morning, Tibran banners will hang over every city in Maldobar."

It was true, then. The Tibrans really were going to destroy us.

I shivered, staring down at the sleek, elaborate crossbow in my arms. It was heavy. The wood was stained black. Someone had even taken the time to cover it with intricate silver scrollwork and designs. It was wickedly beautiful—you know, in a "murdered-my-favorite-horse-in-a-single-shot" kind of way.

But I didn't want this thing. I hated it.

"You don't know that," I heard myself mutter. My face was so numb I couldn't feel my lips moving. "The dragonriders could still win."

"Don't be stupid," the warrior in black snapped. With a growling curse under his breath, he started off toward the street again.

Then he froze.

More of those soldiers in bronze armor were storming the streets directly in front of us. There must have been hundreds of them. The noise of their synchronized marching filled the night like the droning rhythm of war drums. It thundered in my ears until I could feel my teeth rattle. The only other sound, the one that never stopped, was the screaming. Townspeople—the ones who hadn't run when they had the chance—were being dragged from their homes.

Suddenly, the warrior slammed an arm across my chest. He flattened me against the side of the nearest building and stood with his back to it, completely motionless. A group of soldiers passed right in front of the alley where we hid in the shadows. One of them glanced right at me.

My heart stopped.

I held my breath.

The soldier paused, blinked twice, and then glanced away, moving along with the rest of his group without ever looking back.

He hadn't seen us.

As soon as they were gone, I sagged back against the wall. I wheezed and fought for breath, wiping away some of the blood that still dripped down my face from the deep gash on my forehead.

"It's too late," the warrior growled quietly under his breath. "They're patrolling the streets, so they've got the city surrounded. There's no way to get past them now without being seen."

"So what do we do?" I whispered, almost falling over as he moved his arm away.

The warrior pulled the black handkerchief down away from his face, revealing his surprisingly young features. I'd been right. He really wasn't much older than me. Taller, sure, but maybe eighteen at the most. His thin mouth was set in a grim, focused frown, and his gaze darted around the alley. Every move he made seemed so quick, sharp, and aggressive, as though he were ready to cut off someone's head at a moment's notice.

Gods, I just hoped it wasn't mine.

"Come on." He pushed away from the wall, quickly moving to the far end of the alley.

I ran after him, lugging the crossbow with me. "Where are we going?"

He glanced back at me, but only for a second or two. The glow of the fires caught his sharp features, revealing bands of gold and green hidden amid his amber eyes. "I know a way out."

2

CHAPTER TWO

My father had always joked that I was a terrible judge of character. He'd said that I only saw what I wanted to see in people—good things—even if they weren't actually there. He'd warned that I couldn't believe every sob story someone told me. If I did, I'd wind up swindled, robbed, and left for dead on the side of the road someday.

As I watched the warrior in front of me, dressed in black leather armor with his blood-spattered weapons sheathed at his back, I wondered if this was that day. I had absolutely no reason to trust this guy. He'd murdered someone, most likely one of his own comrades, right in front of me. And if his skill with those blades was any kind of evidence, then it was a safe bet that this wasn't the first time he'd killed someone.

But right now, he was my only shot of making it out of the city alive.

A few old, wooden crates were scattered around the back of the alley, empty and long forgotten. He stacked them one on top of the other until he'd made a teetering tower. It was just tall enough to reach the eaves of the roof.

If you jumped for it, that is.

He scurried up first, scaling the tower in an instant and springing like a cat to catch the edge of the slanted roof with his fingertips. In one smooth motion, he hoisted himself over the ledge and crouched on the rooftop—all without making a single sound.

Wow.

I swallowed hard.

"Come on. Hurry up." He turned around, holding out a hand.

I took a few steps back, trying to mentally prepare myself for what I was about to do. Right. Okay. This was fine. I could handle it. I could make the climb. I might even be able to catch the edge of the roof when I jumped.

But hoisting myself up like that? Not a chance.

This guy, whoever or whatever he was, had clearly gone through some rigorous physical training. My physical training amounted to moving boxes of supplies for my father around the stable, trimming hooves, and occasionally weeding the garden. Not good.

Gods help me.

Threading the thick leather strap on the crossbow over my shoulders, I took a deep breath and charged forward, clamoring up the tower of crates. At the last second, I jumped. My arms stretched, reaching for the roof. The air rushed out of me as my fingers brushed the edge.

Then I started to fall.

Before I could scream, the warrior lunged out and caught me by the wrists. With his heels braced on the edge of the roof, he cursed through his teeth and steadied himself with my weight.

I dangled over the alley, helpless, staring up at him with frantic desperation. It took everything I had not to yell or freak out. Oh gods, if he dropped me, it was all over. The soldiers would hear it when I crashed into the crates.

"You are useless," the warrior grumbled under his breath as he dragged me up. With one last, incredibly powerful yank, he hauled me over the edge and dropped me onto the roof next to him.

I lay there sprawled on my stomach, panting, trying to figure out why I wasn't dead.

The reason was simple, though ... and currently glaring down at me with his lip curled.

"Get up," the warrior commanded.

Shakily, I shambled to my feet again and took off after him. We ran the lengths of the rooftops, racing up and down the sloped pitches and leaping the gaps between buildings. Every step made my arms and legs burn with fatigue. My lungs ached, and my heart felt like it might punch right out of my chest. Where were we going? I couldn't keep this up for much longer.

All around us, the city blazed in the night. The air was filled with smoke, flames, embers, and screams. Occasionally, the ringing and clanging of metal on metal, the clashing of swords and shouts of combat, broke over the noise. Some of the townsfolk were resisting. But it wasn't enough.

As we skidded down another steep incline, the warrior cut a path to the right, sprinting all the way to the very end of the narrow ledge. He kept stealing quick glances back at me, as though making sure I hadn't fallen behind. Or maybe he was hoping I'd fall and die, so he wouldn't have to worry about me anymore. Seemed like a toss-up, honestly.

I tripped and flailed after him, barely able to keep up with his swift, soundless pace. Every move he made was so solid, sharp, and precise. He never stumbled, never lost his balance. When we got to the end of the roof, he jumped, executing a perfect spin in the air to catch the ledge with his hands. He dropped into a crouch on the balcony below.

Nope. I couldn't do that. Not going to happen.

Shambling to the edge, I sat down and eyed the drop to the balcony where he had landed. It had to be ten or fifteen feet, at least.

Oh, gods.

"Don't go stiff. Land on your feet. Keep your legs loose, bend to adjust for impact," he called up to me. "And quit stalling. The longer you wait, the more you give yourself a chance to panic."

Right. Okay. But I was *already* panicking.

I set my jaw and tried to focus. Concentrate. I could do it.

Maybe if I just eased down slowly ...

My hands slipped. I lost my grip on the roof. I fell, kicking and flailing, as I dropped like a rock toward the balcony.

THUD!

I landed flat on my stomach—right on top of my warrior-guide-sort-of-friend.

"I hate you," he groaned, his voice muffled as he lay facedown beneath me.

"S-Sorry," I wheezed as I scrambled off him.

He muttered a few more curses as he got to his feet and dusted off the front of his black silk tunic and elaborate leather breastplate. Everything he wore seemed to have been made specially to fit his tall, wide-shouldered frame, crafted with excruciating care and detail. Every piece matched seamlessly. The only thing that wasn't black was the single silver-plated cuff he wore over the vambrace on his right arm. It shone like platinum in the pale light of the moon, the relief of a snarling wolf's head engraved into its surface. Odd. The wolf had a third eye right in the middle of its forehead. What sort of symbol was that?

It was a little strange that he only had one of those vambraces, too. He wore a black leather vambrace on his other arm, but there was no cuff to match. Had he lost the other one?

There wasn't time to ask about it then.

We continued above the chaos-filled streets. I tried not to look down or listen to the shouts and screams echoing from the dark. I just wanted it to stop—to wake up in my bed and for all of this to be a terrible nightmare.

But I wasn't that lucky.

Ahead of me, my new warrior friend came to a halt. I crashed into his back, rocking onto my heels and flailing to keep my balance. "Okay. You know what? You're going to wait right here."

Panic ripped through me and I took a reflexive step closer. "What? Wait, please don't—"

He turned and shot me a glare of warning. "I'll get this done faster on my own. Just wait here. I'll be back."

There was no arguing with him.

The warrior unclasped his black cloak and threw it in my face before he prowled to the edge of the balcony. "Stay down. Don't make a sound," he ordered as he crouched low and sprang over the railing. He must have landed somewhere below, but I never heard it. His clothes didn't even rustle.

Draping his black cloak around my shoulders, I sat down to wait. There was nothing else I could do. The balcony itself was about four stories up, and the house it was attached to seemed like it had already been abandoned. At least it wasn't on fire, though. I decided to count that as a good sign.

My mind immediately circled back to my father. Where was he? Was he still alive? Had he made it out of the house? Why hadn't he come with me?

I had no answers. No chance of getting them at the moment, either. My only hope for even living to see daylight again was that warrior in black, somewhere in the city.

That was if he actually came back for me at all ...

MINUTES PASSED. About the time I'd made up my mind that my mysterious warrior-friend had left me for dead, the clatter of metal against stone made my whole body go rigid. I peeked out from under the cowl of the cloak, shaking as my heart pounded in my ears.

The warrior had returned with an armload of what looked suspiciously like blood-spattered Tibran armor.

"Here," he said as he shoved a breastplate and helmet in my direction. "Put this on."

"Where did you get this?" I squinted at the crimson speckling the metal. "Is this *blood*?"

"It's tomato juice."

I blinked. "It is?"

He cut me another exasperated glare. "Of course it's blood, you idiot. Put it on. Now."

I tried. Sliding the crossbow off my shoulders, I picked up the breastplate first. My shaking fingers fumbled over the clasps and buckles. I'd never put on armor before. I'd never had a reason to. Being a farrier's son meant I was a commoner. I ran errands and helped my father around the shop. I looked after horses, swept the stables, mucked stalls, and cleaned hooves. Nothing about my life had ever been violent. I'd never fought anyone, or even wanted to.

Now, I sort of wished I had. Maybe then I wouldn't be so useless, or I could at least put on a breastplate without looking like a complete moron.

I knew that it was a sloppy job. The straps weren't right. The metal front of the breastplate hung off me crookedly. I looked like a poorly dressed scarecrow.

With a grumble and a huff, the warrior stomped over to help. He'd already buckled his own outfitting into place right over the leather armor that he already wore. Breastplate, pauldrons, gauntlets, even greaves—he'd put them on in a matter of seconds.

"For crying out loud," he hissed through his teeth as he began roughly adjusting all the straps. "What good are you?"

"Not much," I admitted quietly. "Not when it comes to things like this. I-I'm sorry. You spared my life, and I can't even ..." My voice died in my throat. I couldn't look him in the eye as shame bore down like a lead weight on my back, making my shoulders droop.

He puffed a tight sigh and stood back, giving me one last appraising look from head to toe. "Look, not everyone is cut out to be a fighter. But if you want to survive this, then you're going to need to do a good job of faking it. The Tibrans have the city locked down. They've closed off the bridge and roads to everyone except their own forces. If we want to get across, then we have to look like them. Got it?"

I nodded.

He didn't look convinced. "What's your name?"

"Thatcher," I replied, swallowing hard. "Thatcher Renley."

His eyes narrowed, studying me for a second before he gave a satisfied nod. "I'm Murdoc."

"No family name?" I asked.

He turned away. "No."

Okay, that was a little odd. Then again, he wasn't exactly normal. In size and age, we didn't seem to be all that far apart. He was taller and obviously a few years older, but standing next to him somehow made me feel like a frightened little kid by comparison. I didn't know how to handle anything that was happening. If he left me behind, I wouldn't last five minutes. Better—I had to pull myself together and do better than this.

"We're going into the street now. You need to prepare yourself. It's bad out there," he warned. "Try not to look. Just keep your eyes on me and do what I do. We'll get out of here and make a break for the marshes."

I stared back at him, silently wondering why my arms and legs had begun to feel so cold and heavy. My ears were ringing again. Oh Fates, what was I doing?

"Hey!" He snapped his fingers in front of my nose.

I cringed back.

"Stay with me, Thatcher." Murdoc handed me the Tibran helmet. I tried not to notice how much blood was on it. "Stay close. Keep the visor down, and don't look anyone in the eye."

Swallowing against the growing tightness in my throat, I forced myself to nod. Then I slipped the helmet over my head and pulled down the visor so that it covered my face. The long, narrow slit cut across the face of it gave me a limited view—but it was enough. I could follow him. I could do this.

Picking up the crossbow again, I held it tight against my chest. I didn't even know how to fire or load it. But Murdoc was right; if I at least looked the part, maybe I stood a chance.

Maybe I'd get out of here alive.

CHAPTER THREE

L eaving that house was like walking into the darkest pits of the abyss. Everywhere I looked, Tibran soldiers marched in small groups, searching the rubble for survivors. Anyone they found was either slapped in chains or murdered on the spot if they were too old or wounded to be useful as one of their slave-soldiers. The horizon glowed red against the night because of the fires still swallowing up block after block, spreading fast over the straw-thatched rooftops. The air was thick with the smell of smoke, and blood ran in the streets like rainwater.

Gods and Fates, how were we ever going to get by without someone noticing we weren't actually Tibran soldiers?

"Stay right with me," Murdoc whispered suddenly, jostling me to get my attention. "If anyone stops us, let me handle it. They are only looking for civilians now. And with the bulk of their forces being slave-soldiers, you can bet they aren't trained thoroughly enough to second-guess anyone wearing their armor."

I met his fiercely determined stare through the eye-slit in my helmet. How did he know all this?

"Who are you?" I whispered.

He turned his gaze away and didn't reply.

I tried to tell myself that it didn't matter. He was helping me. I shouldn't question him. He could have left me on that balcony or killed me on sight, but he hadn't. I should just be grateful.

Murdoc led the way through the war-torn streets, stepping smoothly into formation with a group of soldiers marching past. I scrambled in beside him. We kept with that group until we reached another city square. Then, as quick as a shadow, Murdoc whirled out of the line and into a darkened corner between two shops. I clambered after him, almost tripping over my own feet.

His eyes panned the square like a hawk surveying its territory—fast and focused. He nodded toward another group of the Tibran soldiers approaching. They weren't marching, just strolling along casually while leading a string of captured Maldobarian townsfolk all tethered to a heavy iron chain.

I tried not to look at their faces, afraid I'd recognize someone.

What if...what if I saw my father?

With one wide step, Murdoc assumed a position at the end of the line of prisoners—as though he were making sure none of them escaped. I jumped in after him. As we rounded the square, the formation departed down a large avenue to the right. We veered to the left, making our way toward the northern side of the city.

Step by step, minute after grueling minute, we moved in and out of Tibran formations like phantoms. I was getting better at marching like they did, with my shoulders back and my head high, hand resting on the grip of the crossbow like I actually knew what to do with it. But if someone had actually confronted me, I'd have probably resorted to hurling the whole weapon at them rather than actually firing it. Or throwing up on their boots in terror.

Thankfully, neither happened.

The bridge wasn't far now. We were only a mile or so away when we stopped in another darkened alley to wait for a chance to join another formation. Reaching under my helm, I wiped the sweat from my forehead. It kept running down, mixing with the blood dried onto my skin and dripping into my eyes.

"Almost there," Murdoc whispered.

I nodded.

A thundering roar shook the ground under my boots and rattled the cobblestones like chattering teeth. I knew that sound.

Murdoc and I glanced skyward just as two huge, scaly bodies zoomed past. They were flying low, barely above the rooftops. I sucked in a breath. My pulse raced, thrumming wildly in my ears. Just the sight of them set my blood ablaze with awe.

Dragons.

Outside our hiding place, crowds of Tibran soldiers began running past with their weapons drawn. Suddenly, a column of fire exploded through the street before us. It blasted through the ranks of soldiers and sent them flying in every direction. The wave sizzled over my body, stinging my eyes through the slit of my helmet. Something reeked like acid.

Dragon venom.

Murdoc and I staggered back as two more dragons whooshed overhead. I spotted the glint of firelight off the armor of a rider. It wasn't just a lone dragon—others zoomed by, scales flashing in the night. The Dragonriders of Maldobar had come. But weren't they supposed to be defending the royal city? What were they doing here?

"The tide has turned." Murdoc's voice was low and ominous as he ripped off his helmet and threw it aside.

"What?"

"They must have overtaken the Tibrans at Halfax. They're winning. That's the only reason they would split their forces and mobilize elsewhere."

"T-That's good, though, isn't it? That means they've come here to retake the city."

His expression darkened, hard lines creasing across his brow. Something was wrong. I didn't understand at all.

Then, it was too late.

"You there! Drop your weapons and get down on your knees!" an enraged voice shouted from the street.

I looked up, straight into the faces of two Maldobarian soldiers. They advanced toward us with their blades drawn.

Murdoc bristled, baring his teeth like a wild animal. What was he doing? These guys were on our side, right?

Behind the soldiers, a large scaly head suddenly blocked the entry to the alley, leering at us with huge, piercing green eyes.

I froze. Everything below my neck went numb. The crossbow slipped out of my hands and clattered to the ground at my feet.

The dragon snarled, its lips curling back over jagged black fangs and cat-like pupils narrowing to slits. Its huge body rumbled with a growl and its ears slicked back.

"You won't be given another chance! Surrender now or face our flame!" From the dragon's back, a figure dressed out from head to toe in gleaming battle armor barked down at us.

I dropped to my knees immediately.

Next to me, Murdoc bit angry curses under his breath as he unbuckled his scimitar sheaths and tossed them aside before coming to his knees as well. He put his hands behind his head in a gesture of surrender and shot me a meaningful look. I quickly did the same.

None of it made any sense. Why were they treating us this way? They were our allies. Why would they ...?

Oh gods—the *armor*! Murdoc and I were still dressed like Tibran soldiers. We looked like the enemy.

"We aren't Tibrans!" I cried as the two soldiers stalked toward us, one holding the point of his blade at our faces while the other roughly bound our hands behind our backs. "Please, you have to believe me. We're from Maldobar. We were just trying to—"

"Silence!" The soldier tying my hands planted a boot right in my back and kicked me the rest of the way to the ground.

I lay, wheezing and coughing under my helmet, as they dragged Murdoc toward the street. They didn't forget about me, though. After snatching me to my feet and ripping off my helmet, they patted me down for any more weapons before shoving me forward. As I staggered ahead of them, my eyes locked upon the dragon still crouching right outside the alleyway entrance. Its huge green eyes followed me, tracking me for any false moves, as its snout twitched in a challenging growl.

The dragons of Maldobar had quite a reputation. They were powerful and highly intelligent creatures, but also notoriously spirited and temperamental. And while their lean, muscular bodies weren't much larger than a big draft horse, they had strong, leathery wings attached to their front legs like those on a bat. They also breathed plumes of flame—or rather, they could spray sticky acidic venom from their mouths. The venom caught fire whenever it was exposed to the air and couldn't be doused by water. I'd only heard about them from stories I'd heard around the city. I'd never seen one so close before. We were miles away from Southwatch, the nearest fortress where the dragonriders were posted, so they didn't come around this area very often.

The sight of the creature made my whole body shake with primal fear. Every shred of sense in my brain begged me to run—not that it would have helped. You didn't run from dragons. All it would take was one wrong step, one breath, and my life would be over. I'd be nothing but a black scorch mark on the ground.

"Wait," the rider sitting astride the creature's back called out.

The soldiers paused, jerking me to a halt between them.

The dragonrider dismounted with a flourish of his long, dark blue cloak. I'd heard they all wore cloaks like that; it was part of what distinguished them on the battlefield if they weren't in the saddle. The edges of it were trimmed with gold and a thick mane of white fox fur lined the collar.

I'd never owned anything that nice. And at this rate, I never would.

The dragonrider stalked toward me, a towering man in full battle dress, with his cape rustling at his boot heels. He slid the visor of his helmet back, revealing a scrutinizing scowl. "You're sure this is a Tibran?" He didn't sound convinced. "He's hardly more than a child."

"They've been taking locals from every city they conquer and slapping them in armor. They force them to fight under threat of death or torture," one of the soldiers explained. "No doubt these are two of them."

"They didn't even take the time to brand or shave these," the other soldier scoffed. "That tyrant Argonox must have thought hurling every fighter he had at us would help tilt the odds in his favor."

The dragonrider's frown deepened as his gold-toned eyes looked me over from head to toe. "Put them with the others, then, and see they're sent to Halfax. We'll let the king sort them out." He waved us off.

I started to protest—to insist they had it wrong. We weren't Tibran soldiers. We were just pretending so we didn't get killed!

No one listened.

"You're wasting your breath," Murdoc grumbled as they tossed us into the back of a large armored wagon. The door was barred and locked tight with a thick iron crossbar. You couldn't hope to open it from the inside.

I floundered around to sit up, which wasn't easy with my hands still tied. "What'll they do to us?" I panicked.

He snorted. "If we're lucky? Lock us away as traitors with the rest until we rot in some prison cell."

"A-And if we're not lucky?" My voice hitched with terror. I'd never been an exceptionally lucky person.

He flashed me a meaningful glance, his jaw cocked as though he were gnawing on the inside of his cheek. "They put us to the sword along with the rest of the Tibrans."

My stomach dropped, and I lost my breath again. I stared at him, praying for some sign of hope. There had to be something we could do—some way we could prove we weren't really Tibrans or traitors.

Through the bars of the prison wagon, I watched the dragonrider climb back into his saddle. His beast, a powerful monster with black stripes mottling his turquoise scales, gave another bone-rattling roar before it launched into the sky. The blast of wind from its wings stung my eyes.

I sat back, watching them soar away and join with another formation of riders cruising over the city. Murdoc was watching them, too. I noticed his sharp features were drawn into a grim, almost resolved frown when his gaze panned back to me. "Do you know anyone here who could vouch for you?"

"I don't know. My father is ... he, uh, he stayed behind. I don't know if he's still alive."

"What about in Halfax?"

I shook my head.

He let out a sigh. "Then we'll just have to wait."

The wagon lurched into motion, rumbling over the uneven stones and taking us out of the city. It joined with other wagons, packed with the blood-spattered faces of Tibran soldiers. Some of them were even younger than me.

I tried forcing myself not to look for too long at all the carnage we passed. I was afraid I'd see my father amidst the flames and tangled bodies. But I never did. I couldn't decide if that was a good or bad thing. If he was dead, then I'd lost all that was left of my family. If he was alive, he might never find me. I doubted he'd ever think of looking for me in a prison camp.

Resting my head against the bars, I let my eyes roll closed as I listened to the *clop, clop, clop* of horse hooves and the groaning of the wheels. My chest ached as my heart wrenched. Part of me kept hoping this was a nightmare. Maybe I would wake up back in my bed to the smell of hay, oats, and the musk of the horses from the stable below. Father would scold me for sleeping late. I'd get to work with my daily chores. None of this awfulness would be real.

But the pungent stench of battle, shouts of men, crackle of flames, and roar of dragons was all too real.

And I had a feeling that the worst was yet to come.

CHAPTER FOUR

I'd heard stories from years ago about a large prison camp that once stood outside the royal city of Halfax. Back then, during the Gray War when Maldobar fought against the elven kingdom to the north, that's where many of the captured elven warriors had been taken. But after King Felix took the throne, he'd ordered it to be torn down. He'd even built a monument in its place to honor all who had died there.

I'd never seen it, of course. I'd never left the tiny city of Thornbend in my life. The farthest I'd ever gone was across the bridge when Father and I went to work with some of the horses at the farms outside of town.

When the prison wagon rolled over a steep hill, leaving the farm country and the smoldering remains of Thornbend far behind, my muscles tensed. I cringed back away from the bars. My home, everything I'd ever known, was gone. And I was headed for a prison cell somewhere in Halfax.

Not exactly how I'd imagined my first trip to the royal city would go.

Murdoc and I sat close together, staring in mute awe, as we crossed the open country toward Halfax. Carnage and destruction stretched as far as the eye could see. The rising sun revealed plumes of dark smoke still rising from the battlefield outside the city from miles away. The closer we got, the worse it became.

The battle for our kingdom was over. By the look of things, the Tibran Empire had thrown everything they had at Halfax. Trebuchets and catapults sat in embers. Monstrous war beasts lay dead—creatures I'd never dreamt of in my wildest nightmares. Fallen dragons lay alongside their riders, motionless. The bodies of soldiers from both sides lay in numbers beyond counting, thousands upon thousands as far I could see in every direction. The coppery flavor of blood and acrid stench of dragon venom hung like fog in the air.

I blinked back tears and swallowed hard. We'd apparently won the war somehow.

Maldobar was free from the threat of Tibran invasion. But the cost of that victory? It lay scattered around us like a field of charred corpses.

And in the thick of it all, men and women wearing the white and gray robes of healers searched for anyone who might still be alive.

Our line of wagons rolled and creaked past the monument where the old prison camp had once stood—directly into a new one. Granted, this one was probably only temporary.

Maybe. Hopefully.

The prison camp was not very large and looked as though it had been built in a rush. The walls were made of stacked sandbags and ropes that had been coated with resin and rolled in crushed glass. Inside, several lines of canvas tents gave soldiers somewhere to get out of the elements. But as far as comforts went—there weren't any.

I stayed as close to Murdoc as I dared. I didn't know what else to do. He was the only person I knew here.

If it bothered him, he didn't say. In fact, he didn't say anything at all as we were marched into the camp along with the rest of the captured Tibran soldiers.

The Maldobarian guards manning the only entrance checked each new prisoner thoroughly, taking their time as they stripped away every bit of armor and clothing we had. I stood shaking in nothing but my smallclothes until they herded me to an open-air washing station. I was given a bar of lard soap and a bucket of water to wash myself off before they handed me my boots and a new set of clothes to wear—a coarse, crudely sewn prison uniform that amounted to a bright red pair of pants and tunic. I wondered if those color choices made us easier to spot in case anyone tried escaping.

Beside me, Murdoc's face was the picture of grim focus, eyes blazing like cold steel behind dripping wet bangs and jaw set in a firm line. Standing nearly naked, I tried not to look at anyone else for too long. It was humiliating. But before I could stop myself, my gaze caught on a strange mark that marred Murdoc's throat. A raised band of gnarled, scarred flesh went all the way around the base of his neck. I'd seen the same kind of marks left behind when someone left a collar on a dog or a halter on a horse for far too long—until the flesh was forever disfigured. I hadn't noticed that scar before because the collar of his tunic covered it. He had the same marks around his wrists, as well, as though he'd worn shackles.

I cringed as his eyes suddenly flicked in my direction, catching me staring. I swallowed against a hard knot that rose in my throat, and I looked back down at my red and white clothes. I was a prisoner now. How, by all the gods, had this happened?

My hands shook as I hurried to get dressed. The rough, burlap fabric of the tunic itched something awful, and the sleeves were a little too long, too, so I rolled them up so they didn't get in the way. The pants, unfortunately, weren't much better.

The sun was setting by the time we were finished being processed. Murdoc and I were assigned to the same tent at the furthest corner of the camp, handed a bedroll, and sent on our way. My stomach growled as I staggered after my silent companion. Stealing a glance his way, I got my first good look at Murdoc's face without darkness, blood, and black war paint disguising his features.

Somehow, he didn't look nearly as menacing now. Angry, yes. Miserable, oh yeah. But significantly less like he might murder me in my sleep than when we'd first met.

Murdoc's clean-shaven jaw was sharply angled and he had a thin, frowning mouth. His pitch-black hair hung in a silky, fine mop over his brow, veiling his dark hazel-amber eyes and brushing at the collar of his tunic. He had an efficiently lean build, which was something I couldn't relate to at all. Not that I was pudgy, but when it came to corded limbs and chiseled pectorals, mine ... er, well, they needed some work.

Okay, a *lot* of work.

I was shorter, skinnier, and my light blond hair was a shaggy mess. My father liked to say it looked like a rumpled haystack. I'd let it grow out a bit, which helped because then I could tie it back in a short ponytail at the base of my neck. At least then it didn't stick up everywhere.

Our tent was only big enough for about six people to sleep comfortably stretched out on the floor, but there were about ten of us packed inside. Of them all, it seemed like Murdoc and I were the only ones who weren't actual Tibran soldiers. The others had all the telltale signs: shaved heads, the Tibran symbol branded into the sides of their necks, and that dead-to-reality glazed look in their eyes. They didn't even glance up when Murdoc muscled his way in, staking out a place for us in the corner of the tent. He threw his bedroll down first and then yanked mine from my grasp to toss it down nearby.

"Get some sleep," he commanded.

I blinked at him owlishly. What? Was he insane? I couldn't sleep here. Not after what had happened. Gods—*what was happening?*

His jaw clenched as his eyes narrowed, staring me down for a few uncomfortable seconds. Then he let out a deep, growling sigh. "What's wrong with you?"

I gulped and hung my head. "I-I'm sorry. I know I'm not much help. I'll try harder, I promise. I'll do whatever it takes. Just please don't ditch me. If you do, I'll be alone, and I ... I won't ..." My voice caught and I ducked my head lower. My ribs seemed to squeeze around my lungs, making it harder to breathe and putting a sharp pain in my chest.

Murdoc didn't reply.

When I dared to look up at him again, his mouth had scrunched into a sour frown and his brow was skewed as though he were utterly bewildered. He rubbed the back of his neck and glanced away. "Fine." His tone softened some, as though he was making a conscious effort to keep his temper in check. "Look, there's nothing we can do about our situation right now. They think we're Tibrans, and we have no way of proving otherwise. But the good news is they aren't planning on executing anyone outright. So, until we come up with a better idea on how to get out of here, we have to focus on surviving. So sleep. I'll keep watch. Then we'll swap."

He was right. Our situation was bad—worse than bad, really. I couldn't come up with a single good idea of how we could ever prove we weren't traitors. They'd caught us in Tibran armor.

But there had to be a way. I just hadn't thought of it, yet.

Sitting down on my bedroll, I stayed awake for a long time while Murdoc settled in beside me. He didn't lie down or try to get comfortable, though. Instead, he sat with his legs crossed and his elbows on his knees, his gaze fierce as he panned the other pris-ners around us—as though silently daring one of them to make a false move. He reminded me of a guard dog on patrol.

Curling up on my side, I shut my eyes tightly. I couldn't sleep. Even with Murdoc standing guard, I jerked at every sound. My stomach ached and growled, feeling like it was scraping up against my spine. I couldn't stop shaking, and I didn't know if that was because I was cold or still terrified. My mind raced, blitzing between wondering where my father was and wondering if I was going to die in this prison camp. How could I prove I wasn't a Tibran?

There had to be a way.

DAYS TURNED INTO WEEKS. Then months. And after the second month came to an end, I started to wonder if we would ever leave this place. Or would I be a prisoner here forever?

The prison camp was packed tight with former Tibran soldiers—some of them recruited straight from our own kingdom. Most, however, had been brought over during the initial invasion when the Tibran Empire's hundreds of ships had first struck our shores. There were people from corners of the world I hadn't even known existed. They didn't speak our language and seemed to regard one another like starving jackals rather than former comrades.

They all had one thing in common, though. Every one of them had the Tibran symbol, a letter T with a serpent wrapped around it, branded into the side of their neck. Not all of them had been shaved bald, I discovered. That was usually only done to the most recent recruits, to humiliate them and make them more obvious to the Tibran officer who was in charge of watching them. They fought over everything—food, water, sleeping space, and anything else they'd managed to get their hands on. Murdoc didn't seem nearly as shocked by it as I was. Maybe he'd seen more of that kind of thing in his life.

The fights over food were a problem, though. Many of the former Tibran soldiers were severely malnourished. And even though there was plenty of food to go around, they scrapped like wild dogs every time the Maldobarian prison guards came through to dish out our daily meals. That was when you were most likely to get attacked, beaten within an inch of your life, and left for dead while someone made off with your dinner. More Maldobarian guards had to step in with long, leather whips to drive them back and keep them in line, but it didn't always work.

Because of that, I didn't get much to eat at first. Throat-punching strangers over loaves of bread didn't come as naturally to me as it did to some. But Murdoc could hold his own in a brawl, and he wasn't afraid to deliver whatever physical force he deemed necessary to keep what was his.

The first two fights were the worst by far, and it gave me a new, healthy respect for my sort-of friend. Our first week at the camp, a much bigger, older man prowled over to try intimidating us into handing over our rations. Murdoc, well, he did give the guy a chance to walk away. When the guy tried to grab Murdoc by the neck, I stood in frozen horror while my friend broke both his arms, his jaw, one of his legs, and left his face a purple, bleeding mess—all in the span of about ten seconds.

The second fight took longer. A group of four guys cornered us after we'd gotten our evening rations. I guess they thought their numbers would tip the odds in their favor. It didn't help. Murdoc wrecked every last one of them with systematic precision, his expression never changing from its usual look of cold, distant thought. I didn't know for sure, but I heard that one of the guys had died from his injuries. Regardless, that fight had sent a clear message to the rest of the camp: Murdoc was not a guy you wanted to mess with. By the end of the first month, the other prisoners were so scared of him that they never challenged him over anything he claimed.

Once again, I owed him my life. He always got enough food for both of us. He took the first shift to keep watch while I slept. Without him there, I wouldn't have lasted three days.

Apart from that, life in the prison camp droned on and most of the days were relatively uneventful. The Maldobarian officials running the prison camp were at least making an effort to give their Tibran prisoners some basic human comforts. It was probably more than the Tibran Empire had given to any of their own soldiers; it helped keep everyone calm, for the most part.

Once a week, we got shuffled through the bathing line. Men, women, old, young, it didn't matter. We stripped down to our smallclothes and took our turn with buckets of water and soap. After a while, you quit caring if anyone saw you standing there in your underwear. You were just happy to get the grime off your skin and the grit out of your scalp ... especially if you were one of the unlucky prisoners selected for clearing the battlefield.

We all had jobs assigned to us during our first week in the camp. Some portioned out the food, washed the clothes, or cleaned out the chamber pots. But there was one job no one wanted to do—so naturally, that was the one I wound up with.

Murdoc and I were in a group of over a hundred other prisoners who got up at dawn to help clear the battlefields. We left the camp at sunrise, led by a company of guards in full battle armor. They loomed close by, always watching, as we loaded the bodies of the dead soldiers onto wagons. We sorted them according to armor—Maldobarian and Tibrans.

There were so many Tibrans they had to be buried in mass graves. The soldiers from Maldobar, however, were laid out so families that were still looking for their loved ones could come through and identify them. If they were too badly decomposed or unfit to be seen, we would wrap them in clean sheets and load them onto a separate series of wagons. Those soldiers would have unmarked graves and be given proper burial rites, even if there was no one there to mourn them. I decided that was better than being tossed into a mass grave ... if only a little.

At first, the job made me sick. I threw up at least twice every single day. The smell was terrible, and I knew I must have reeked like death all the time, even after bath day.

But after a while, I learned not to look at the bodies any longer than necessary. The smell quit bothering me so much. Moving around to the various wagons became more mechanical, although it still made my chest grow tight and my eyes water sometimes. It was hard to get over the sheer number of dead left behind by the battle for Halfax. There were thousands of fallen soldiers lying out in the open fields around the royal city; so many lives cut short because of one tyrant's cruelty.

It wasn't right.

After three months, I'd quit expecting to be summoned for my chance to prove that I wasn't a Tibran soldier. Very few from the prison camp ever were. Murdoc suspected that the royals were trying to decide what to do with all of the prisoners. There were so many, and most weren't in Maldobar by choice. Still, letting them all go might not go over well with the citizens of Maldobar, and keeping them locked up like this was an expensive, temporary solution. No doubt it cost a lot to keep us all fed and contained.

Sooner or later, they'd have to come up with something more permanent.

"You think they'll kill us?" I asked around a mouthful of bread.

Murdoc shrugged, still chewing on his own ration. He had secured enough for both of us to have a decent dinner, so we sat in the shade of our tent and ate.

I still knew basically nothing about my grim-faced companion. And honestly, what I did know about him was a little disturbing. I knew that he was strong; the sight of death and gore on the battlefield didn't seem to bother him in the slightest; he refused to talk about himself; and he could knock a full-grown man unconscious with one well-aimed punch. He'd demonstrated that skill several times over the past three months.

After seeing how he could fight and climb the night we met, I had no doubt that Murdoc could have escaped if he really wanted to. Even the Maldobarian guards would likely have a hard time taking him down. But for whatever reason, he stayed. I tried not to get my hopes up that I might be that reason. It seemed stupid to think he'd want a friend like me dragging behind him like a panicky goat—clumsy, noisy, and always in the way. He didn't seem like the kind of guy who cared if he had friends or not.

He'd certainly made a habit of looking out for me, though.

I'd just crammed my last bite of bread into my mouth when a commotion in the narrow aisle between the tents made me stiffen. Fights were still common, especially around mealtime. But this didn't sound like a fight.

Murdoc got up, his expression going colder than usual as he rounded the corner to investigate. A few tents down, a small company of guards came our way. They stopped at every tent, peered inside, and occasionally dragged someone out to get a better look. The man at their forefront wasn't dressed like a common prison guard. He wore the outfitting of an infantry officer and kept one hand resting on the pommel of the sword belted at his hip.

My stomach dropped—this was new. What did it mean? Were they beginning executions to get our numbers down?

"What's going on?" I whispered, glancing sideways at Murdoc.

His mouth twisted into a pensive frown. "I don't know. Let's go."

He didn't have to tell me twice. I turned on a heel, ready to find a good place to hide, when a booming man's voice shouted down the line.

"You there! Hold your position!"

Murdoc and I halted, turning around to face the infantryman as he stomped toward us, his heavy armor clunking with every step. "These are the ones?" He motioned at us to the group of guards following him.

A few of them nodded.

The officer's eyes narrowed as he stopped right in front of me. He stood so close I could see my own reflection in his bloodshot eyes. After studying me for a moment, he took a step over to Murdoc and did the same thing.

Then he gave a huff and snapped his fingers. "These two, then. Take them away."

At once, four of the guards began slapping heavy chains on our wrists and ankles.

I trembled with fear as I stared, wide-eyed, at Murdoc. He wasn't resisting. Why? What was happening? Were we about to be put to death? Hung? Beheaded?

Tears flooded my eyes and ran down my face as they shoved us away from our tent, forcing us to walk side-by-side toward the exit of the prison camp. I didn't want to die, but I was too scared to even attempt begging for my life. I choked on every word, barely able to draw a breath.

Taking one last look over my shoulder, I noticed a small crowd of prisoners had gathered to watch us being marched away. Maybe they were as surprised as I was that Murdoc had surrendered without a fight. Their expressions were a mixture of confusion and fear.

Farther away, the infantry officer had already moved on to the next row of tents. He never even looked our way again as we staggered out of the prison camp's gate. It shut behind us with a sharp, final *clang*.

CHAPTER FIVE

By nightfall, Murdoc and I were sitting in a prison cell in the dungeon of the royal castle. I still didn't have a clue why we were here. If they were going to execute us as traitors, why would they bring us here? Wouldn't they have just marched us somewhere outside the camp and gotten it over with? This didn't make any sense. Was this part of a public demonstration? To make an example of us?

Then again, this was my first experience as a convict in the royal prison system. Maybe this was normal. Maybe our execution would be public, right in the middle of the royal square.

Chained beside me, Murdoc stared listlessly ahead into the gloom. He hadn't said a word all day. I couldn't think of anything to say, either. Only the faint crackling of the torches mounted to the walls filled the heavy silence. They cast a warm, orange glow through the darkness.

The distant creak and groan of rusted hinges and approaching footsteps made my body tense and my back straighten. I held my breath. It was probably nothing—just a prison worker bringing us something to eat or drink. No reason to panic.

It wasn't a prison worker.

A man stepped before our cell, eyeing us through the bars. He looked a good bit older, maybe in his thirties, with wavy dark blond hair that came almost to his shoulders. His blue eyes were flecked with gold that caught in the gleam of the torches as he looked us over.

Who was this guy? What was he doing here? He didn't have the armor of a guard or an infantry soldier. He wasn't wearing fancy noble clothes, either. If anything, his attire had a very efficient, no-nonsense look about it. He had a sword on his belt and a single golden clasp on his cloak in the shape of the royal eagle. A knight, maybe?

"Well, you two look awful. Like death warmed over," he mused as he crossed his arms. "But you don't look like Tibran soldiers, and I've seen enough of them to be able to tell the difference. You." He pointed at me. "You're not even a soldier, are you?"

I shrank back and hung my head like a scolded puppy.

"And you." He panned his gaze to my friend. "You may be a fighter, but you don't look scared enough to be Tibran."

Murdoc snorted and snapped a defiant look away.

"And yet, I'm told you were found in Thornbend, near Two Rivers, wearing Tibran armor." The leather gloves on his hand squeaked as he rubbed at his lightly stubbled chin. "Care to explain?"

"Will it make any difference?" Murdoc's tone was sharp and defensive.

"It might. Tomorrow, you'll be taken before the Queen of Maldobar. She'll give you a chance to explain yourselves, plead your case, and then she will decide your fate," he explained with a strange little smile playing over his lips. "I'm here as a courtesy—to investigate whether or not you are Tibrans or more common folk caught up in the fray. There's been quite a lot of that. No surprise, really, since the Tibran Empire seized almost every major city on our coastline. If you can convince me that you aren't traitors to the Tibrans, maybe I can bend my sister's ear in case she doesn't believe you."

"We're not Tibrans or traitors," I blurted, before I realized two very important things. One, that's exactly what a traitor would say if he were trying to save his own neck, and two, I didn't know for sure that Murdoc *wasn't* a Tibran. He'd been fighting alongside them before, and that's why he'd been ordered to kill me. He hadn't gone through with it, though, and that's all I cared about. Regardless of what he'd been doing up to that moment, he wasn't a Tibran anymore.

That's what I told myself as I stared back at the man through the prison bars, doing my best to look brave.

Then it hit me.

S-Sister? He'd said sister, hadn't he? Did that mean …?

"You're Prince Aubren," I gasped aloud.

He chuckled. "A bit slow, aren't you?"

I blushed and ducked my head again. "Please, Your Highness, I—we—we're not Tibrans. My name is Thatcher Renley. My father was a farrier in Thornbend. And this," I hesitated as I looked at Murdoc. "This is my cousin."

"Cousin?" Prince Aubren arched an eyebrow as though he weren't buying that.

I nodded. "Murdoc Renley."

"Cousins with the same last name?"

"Well, not originally, of course. His parents died when we were little, so we took him in."

"You're not a very good liar either, boy." The prince rubbed his chin again.

I struggled to keep my expression steady.

"I'm not his cousin, or any relation," Murdoc murmured suddenly. "I found him hiding in an alley while Thornbend was under siege. He's an idiot and would have died quickly left on his own, which I'm sure you can now understand, so I took him with me."

The prince pursed his lips, his sharp gaze halting on Murdoc. "Now *that* sounds a bit more like the truth."

"I killed a couple of Tibran soldiers and stole their armor, hoping to get us out of the city after they'd overrun it," Murdoc continued. "It would have worked if the tide hadn't turned before we were clear of the river bridge. The dragonriders found us, and we were detained."

"You've been at the prison camp all this time?" the prince asked.

Murdoc and I nodded in unison.

"All right," he sighed. "I'll have a word with my sister regarding your hearing. Try to get some sleep."

"Wait!" I called out as he began to turn away.

"Yes?"

"Do you ... do you think you could find out if my father is still alive? He might be in another camp or still in Thornbend." Saying it out loud like that made me realize how small the chances probably were. I'd looked for Father in our prison camp for weeks after we first arrived. He wasn't there. None of the guards would tell me anything about Thornbend, either, but I got the impression there might not be much left of it.

Prince Aubren's steely eyed expression slackened a bit and his mouth opening slightly.

"His name was Cohen Renley," I added. "If he escaped the city, then he might've gone to my grandfather's in Mithangol. That's where I was supposed to go. My grandfather is Bren Renley; maybe you can find him, too."

"I'll make an inquiry." He nodded, and then he disappeared into the gloom.

The night passed slowly. I couldn't sleep—even if the accommodations in this cell were a bit better than in the prison camp. We at least had cots to sleep on. Murdoc stretched out on his and was still, although I couldn't tell if he was sleeping or not. It was too dark to see his face.

I lay on my cot, too, staring up at the ceiling where the torchlight cast flickering shadows over the stones. My thoughts raced, drifting back to my father and those last few seconds before he'd sent me away to escape. If he'd survived and somehow made it to Mithangol, he would come for me. I knew he would. Providing, of course, that the prince really did make an inquiry. I'd never met my grandfather—there was a lot of bad blood on that side of the family. But I could still hope.

Hope was all I had now.

EARLY THE NEXT MORNING, Prince Aubren returned with a couple of royal guards. They shackled us before leading the way from the cell up into the halls of the castle itself. I'd never felt so out of place in my life. Walking across the polished marble floors in my filthy boots and prison uniform, I stared around in amazement at all the cavernous halls and rooms. Iron chandeliers shed sparkling light over vaulted ceilings and grand foyers. The walls were adorned with portraits of past kings and queens, their haunting gazes seeming to leer down at me with disgust and disapproval. I did *not* belong here.

At the end of a long hall, the doors of the throne room opened before us. Inside, a strip of royal blue carpet trimmed with swirling gold designs led the way to the raised platform where two thrones stood, bathed in the light of bronze braziers in the shape of crouching dragons.

The Queen of Maldobar sat on the largest of the two thrones. The seat next to her was empty, although a much older man stood beside it clad in a noble tunic, intricate ornamental breastplate, and familiar blue cloak with a white fur collar. A dragonrider's cloak. But the man wearing it seemed too old to be a dragonrider. His shaggy, dark-gold hair fell to his shoulders, mottled with silver, and his neatly trimmed beard was completely gray.

"Sister, I present to you Thatcher and Murdoc Renley, formerly of Thornbend." Prince Aubren stepped forward and gave a formal bow. "I've brought them for your consideration because Sergeant Lamlock didn't believe either of them are Tibran sympathizers. After speaking with them, I tend to agree."

"Is that so?" The queen leaned forward in her seat, resting her chin on her fist. She sounded young, although I didn't dare look her in the eye to see.

To be honest, I hadn't even known we had a queen now. I'd heard about Princess Jenna before, sure. She was the younger of the king's two children, one of the few female dragonriders to ever take the saddle, and supposedly a brilliant fighter. Still, it came as a shock to most everyone in Maldobar when King Felix had announced she would be his heir, not his firstborn son Prince Aubren. No one understood why, except that it may have had something to do with her being a dragonrider like her father. Aubren had opted for infantry and specialized in cavalry, instead.

With her on the throne now, I wasn't sure what to expect. She must have been crowned right after the end of the war while Murdoc and I were still in the prison camp. I had no idea if she'd be understanding of our bizarre situation or not.

"Explain yourselves, then," Queen Jenna demanded. "If you were imprisoned, I can only assume you were doing something to get yourselves mistaken for Tibrans. My men are not idiots—for the most part, anyway. So? What happened?"

This was my chance. I had to make it count. If I was as bad at lying as Prince Aubren said, then surely his sister would be able to see that I was telling the truth.

With my gaze trained upon the floor at her feet, I told Queen Jenna everything. Well, except for the bit where Murdoc stabbed someone through the chest after being ordered to kill me. I left that detail out, for his benefit. I didn't want them to think he had anything to do with the Tibrans. He'd saved my life so many times over—I owed him this much.

"I see," the queen mused after I had finished. "Look at me, Thatcher."

I gulped and slowly raised my eyes to meet hers. She was every bit as beautiful as I'd heard, with eyes of cornflower blue and hair like bolts of spun golden silk. A curious hint of a smile caught at the corner of her lips.

"Gods, boy. You can't be more than fourteen." She shook her head slightly, as though in pity.

"Uh, I-I, uh, I'm sixteen, actually," I rasped, my throat going dry as my cheeks burned with embarrassment.

She looked genuinely shocked. "Sixteen? Then you've got a face like a cherub."

Ugh. There it was—the curse of the baby-face, back to ruin me again. My mouth mashed into an uncomfortable frown as I looked back down at the toes of my boots. The other guys in our neighborhood had teased me mercilessly ever since I hit puberty. The only thing that hadn't matured, apparently, was my face. I still looked like a kid.

"Oh, don't worry too much about it, Thatcher Renley." There was a flavor of gentle teasing in Queen Jenna's voice. "Girls like that sort of thing."

Even my ears were burning now. "T-They do?" No one had ever mentioned that. I was terrible with girls. In my experience, they preferred guys like Murdoc—strong, dark, brooding, and practically oozing that vibe of potential danger.

I had none of that. According to my father, I was about as dangerous-looking as a dandelion puff.

She laughed and motioned to the royal guards. "Let him go. This boy is not a Tibran. Although he may be the cutest thing I've ever seen."

Great—I was "cute." In my experience, that word was the kiss of death. I hated it. Somehow, it always felt patronizing even when it was probably meant as a compliment.

The royal guards unlocked the shackles on my wrists and ankles. I rubbed gingerly at the places where the metal had bruised my skin. "Thank you, Your Majesty."

"What about this one?" Prince Aubren tipped his head toward Murdoc, who had yet to say a word.

Queen Jenna's eyes narrowed slightly as she studied him. "Normally, I wouldn't smile upon murder. But I'm not sure that killing Tibran invaders qualifies as murder. Besides, if this boy is willing to risk his life vouching for you, I can only assume you've done something to earn such loyalty. See that you don't betray it." She motioned to the guards again. "Let him go, as well."

6
CHAPTER SIX

By dinnertime, Murdoc and I were free men. The queen was generous, and she even apologized for what we'd been through in the prison camp over the last three months. She gave us both a fresh change of clothes, new shoes, a place to stay, and jobs in the royal stable—which was a relief since I had nowhere else to go. I struggled to wrap my mind around our good fortune as Murdoc and I walked out of the throne room without shackles or a death sentence.

According to Prince Aubren, my hometown of Thornbend had been left in shambles, which wasn't hard to believe considering how things were going when we were taken away in the back of a prison wagon. The Maldobarian infantry was still going door-to-door looking for survivors or remains and trying to make things safe for townspeople who wanted to return to their homes. I wanted to go back immediately. I wanted to find my father. But Prince Aubren insisted I should wait until he had some definite information on my father's location.

Honestly, I think he just didn't want me to be the one to find my father's body in the ashes of our home.

At any rate, I didn't have much of a choice except to stay put for now. Other than striking out on foot over the open prairie, vulnerable to every highway gang and thief in a ten-mile radius, I had no way of getting back to Thornbend. Making that long journey, only to find I had nothing but a pile of ash and charred wood left of my home, would not be ideal. I needed a better plan.

Fortunately, I was used to being in a stable and dealing with horses.

I'd worked with my father all my life. I could muck stalls, groom the horses, clean and clip their hooves, and even shoe them. It came easily to me, and the royal stable was home to some of the finest stallions and mares I'd ever seen. There were robust chestnuts whose coats had been groomed until they shone like polished copper, and sturdy dapple grays the color of ominous storm clouds. Proud white stallions stamped and tossed their heads, their flowing manes and tails neatly combed and arranged in braids tied off with blue and gold ribbon. These were completely different from the plow nags and merchant horses I'd worked with before.

But the royal stable didn't just keep horses.

At the far back of the royal castle's well-guarded grounds, a large, circular building stood off away from the others. They called it the Deck. Five stories tall with each level holding dozens of stalls that faced inward and no exterior wall to block them off, the Deck dwarfed any stable I'd ever seen before. And its tenants were every bit as monstrous. A broad, paved courtyard of white stone in the center of it was open to the sky above—a landing pad for the leathery-winged monsters that came and went with booming roars. It was like a ring-shaped beehive, only these stalls weren't for bees.

The royal family could easily house over a hundred dragons there, and the Deck was always buzzing with activity. The other stable hands liked to reminisce about what chaos it had been when the king recalled all the able-bodied dragonriders in the kingdom there. They'd run out of room and been forced to begin housing some of the dragons in the undercrofts of the castle itself. Feeding so many of those scaly beasts had been a struggle—one I didn't envy in the slightest. I'd only been into the Deck once to run an errand for the stablemaster, and I didn't plan on making a habit of strolling through that place. Too many huge creatures that might try to eat me packed into one space. No thanks.

Needless to say, I didn't go out of my way to get assigned to work the Deck. Dragons were considerably more dangerous than horses, what with the fire and all, and I had no experience with them beyond getting snarled at once. That was more than enough to make me steer clear. Just the sight of them zooming over the castle grounds, sun glimmering off their scales and horns, made my knees want to buckle. They were beautiful, magnificent, impressive, and powerful—and they also scared the crap out of me.

So when I was assigned to an entire *week* of feeding duty in the Deck, I briefly considered running from the room screaming. My stomach hit the soles of my boots. I must have angered one of the gods. That was the only reason I could think of that I'd gotten chosen for this.

Well, that and Stablemaster Godfrey liked to taunt me about my dislike of dragons. I didn't get the impression he was doing it to be mean, though. Godfrey teased everyone, and sometimes the other stable workers—the ones who had been there a lot longer—would tease him back. He was a towering man, nearly seven feet tall, with big hands that could have crushed my head like a walnut. The other workers had mentioned in passing that Godfrey had once been a knight, a member of the infantry cavalry. But a wartime injury left him with a limp and a crippled knee. He couldn't fight after that. Rather than retire a man with his experience, the royal family offered him a job managing the royal stables.

He was gruff, intimidating, and had one of those steely gazes you only saw in men who had been on the battlefield. I'd never seen him raise a hand to anyone in anger, though, and he always saved working with the more spirited, aggressive horses for himself rather than putting one of his workers in danger.

"Get used to it, boy. We've got nobles coming in by the dozens for the Court of Crowns, and we're already shorthanded. Everyone's got to do a shift rotation at the Deck. Pull your weight or find another job." Godfrey gave a throaty cackle as he hobbled by me in the servant's dining hall.

I stared after him, holding a tray of my empty breakfast dishes. He was almost out of the hall by the time I remembered to call out, "Y-Yes, sir!"

Murdoc snorted, appearing beside me so suddenly it was as though he'd materialized out of thin air. He had a habit of doing that—coming and going like a phantom. I still wasn't used to it.

"It's not that bad," he murmured.

I sighed, dragging my feet as I went to return my tray of dirty dishes to the kitchen. "Maybe not for you. You're not afraid of anything."

"Don't be such a baby. I'll be there to make sure you don't get eaten." His thin mouth split with a dark, almost mocking smirk. "Or scorched."

"You're on Deck duty, too?"

He gave one of his classic noncommittal shrugs and looked away. "I swapped with someone else."

I tried not to read too much into that. Murdoc wasn't the kind of guy who called anyone his friend, not even me. But for whatever reason, he'd hung around even after he was offered a better position inside the castle. His almost brotherly interest in my survival made absolutely no sense, and he'd brushed off all of my attempts to get him to explain why he cared what happened to me. Whatever. I was just glad to have him around. It'd be nice to see a familiar face in all this strangeness—especially when there were dragons involved.

Uggggh. Dragons. I shuddered at the thought. Why me?

"Let's go; move your feet." Murdoc gave me a shove as he started off for the Deck. "Best not to keep hungry dragons waiting."

I groaned and jogged to catch up.

FEEDING dragons turned out to be exhausting, dirty work. And that was without the threat of being snapped in half or burned to a crisp if I didn't move fast enough.

When we arrived, Murdoc and I were given long, leather aprons and gloves that came up to our elbows because of the, er, blood. We filled two wheelbarrows full of big slabs of freshly cut meat while another stable worker talked us through the process. It wasn't complicated. We had to make sure each dragon was fed and, of course, not get killed or maimed in the process. Simple.

Except for all the teeth.

And the fire.

Gods, help me.

"Just be fast about it. They're interested in the meat, not you, so toss it in the trough and get out. Don't antagonize them. Don't try to touch them. And for the love of the Fates, remember to lock the door when you leave. Oh, and when you get to the stall marked number four, do *not* try to open it. That one only gets it through the window. Understand?" the young female worker huffed, her eyes lingering on Murdoc for a couple of seconds longer than they did on me.

He got looked at like that a *lot*—not that he seemed to notice or care. I got a twinge of jealousy as I pushed my wheelbarrow toward the door. Girls never looked at me like that. Was it because of the baby-face thing? Or because I wasn't as muscular? Maybe I could start doing pushups every morning ... Hm. But that might make me late for breakfast.

Murdoc took one side of the circular building while I took the other. That was how we were going to do every floor, working half and meeting up on the other side to reload our wheelbarrows for the next level. Easy, right?

Right.

At the door of the first stall, I brought my wheelbarrow to a halt. I took a few deep breaths, mentally preparing myself. No big deal. Just a big, hungry, possibly angry dragon. I could do this.

My pulse thrummed in my ears as I unbolted the lock and rolled the heavy wooden door open a few feet—only far enough to stick my head through. I peeked inside, squinting into the sunlight that poured in from the stall's open exterior wall. There, curled into a massive heap of gleaming yellow and black scales, was a dragon. A real, actual, hungry dragon.

It cracked a big eye open and stared straight at me.

Oh, gods. They were even bigger than I remembered.

"R-Right," I choked under my breath. "You just, uh, just ... stay right there."

The dragon raised its head, ears perking as it gave a wide yawn. I got a great up-close view of every one of its jagged, dagger-sized teeth. I gulped. Just one of those fangs was about the length of my finger.

Ducking back out of the stall, I picked up two huge hunks of meat from my wheelbarrow. I made a point not to look at the dragon again as I dashed over to the trough, flung the meat inside, and blitzed back to the door. All told, it took about three seconds. Then I pushed the door shut and threw the bolt back into place.

Done.

But that was just the first one. I had about fifty more to go before I was finished. Sweet Fates. Why? Why me?

It got easier with every stall I finished. Granted, I never stopped shaking. But I did get faster. I deliberately ignored the dragon that was usually snoozing or preening itself somewhere nearby as I rolled the door open and deposited the meat in the trough. It was better not to look. I decided that if I was about to get my head bitten off by a hungry, impatient dragon, then at least I wouldn't see it coming. That was bound to be better, right?

Everything went smoothly ... right up until we got to the very last level of the Deck.

"Looks like I'm short a few pieces," Murdoc called as he exited a stall not far down the curved hall. "Be right back."

I nodded, watching as he wheeled away back toward the supply room.

We were almost finished. The last level of the Deck wasn't fully occupied like the others had been. There were more than a handful of empty stalls, so we could skip over those. Only three left to go, then this would all be over. Well, for today, anyway. We still had to keep doing this all week.

I tried not to think about that as I came to the very last stall on my side, armed with two slabs of meat and a mission to get this over with as soon as possible. My clothes stuck to my skin, damp with sweat underneath the heavy leather apron, and my hair kept falling in my eyes. I didn't dare wipe it away, though, not while I was wearing gloves smeared with blood. Gross.

I didn't care what the others said—this was *way* worse than working in the horse stables. I'd take shoveling horse dung over this any day. At least horse manure was basically just a bunch of chewed up grass.

Stopping before another stall door, I seized the slabs of meat in one hand and steeled my nerves for my last feeding. Just one more, then I was out of here. I tried not to think about it too much as I reached for the bolt to unlock the door. The metal mechanisms groaned. But the door didn't budge.

I tried it again with a little more force.

No luck.

Standing back, I peered up at the huge door. It must have been eight feet tall and half a foot thick—which was fairly standard. It was large enough to keep an angry dragon from being able to slam through it. But this one was different than the others. All of the other stall doors I'd worked with that day were wooden. But this door had been plated with solid metal. Nearly every part of it was made from thick, black iron, as though it were meant to withstand much more abuse from whatever was on the other side. The bolt mechanism keeping the door locked was larger, too. Weird.

A big number four was painted onto the door. That's when I remembered; this was the one stall we weren't supposed to open. Chills crept up my spine. What could possibly be in there? It had to be a dragon, right. So why was this one locked up? Was it more dangerous than the others?

A single sliding panel blocked off a narrow window at the far end of the door. It wasn't very big, hardly wide enough for me to cram the slabs of meat through even if I opened it all the way. Was that where I was supposed to put them? I couldn't remember.

I glanced around. There was no one in sight—no one to ask what I should do. Murdoc wasn't back yet. And this stall was the only thing standing between a well-earned bath and me.

I set my jaw and made up my mind. Time to get this done.

Sliding the panel open, I peered inside, just to make sure there was actually something in there. The interior of the stall was pitch black. More chills prickled along the back of my neck. That meant the exterior wall wasn't open to the courtyard like the other stalls. Whatever was inside there, it was *not* free to come and go like the other dragons were.

I took a step back.

A low rumbling sound echoed from inside the stall, bouncing off the metallic walls from somewhere in the dark.

I tensed, blood running cold as I stared into the blackness beyond the window. Where was it? I couldn't see a thing except—

An enormous green eye opened right in front of the window.

I stumbled back another step, sucking in a sharp breath.

The eye was as big as a dinner plate and so close I could see my reflection in the wide, cloudy silver pupil. I'd never seen a dragon with eyes like that. The colored part of its eye was strange, too—like milky jade rather than a sharp, focused color.

The eye moved, darting around as though it were looking for something, and never focusing on me.

Wait—couldn't it see me?

I held perfectly still, watching as the eye continued to search until, at last, it blinked and moved away. A loud snort blasted against the door. I cringed, my heart hitting the back of my throat.

Maybe I was wrong—maybe that wasn't a dragon at all. It could have been anything, really. The Tibrans had brought all kinds of horrible creatures with them when they invaded. It could have been one of their monstrous hounds or one of those venomous felines the traders talked about.

I glanced down to the hunk of meat on the ground at my feet. My pulse raced. Gods and Fates. Maybe I should just ask Murdoc to feed this one.

No. I had to pull it together.

Steeling my nerves, I picked up one of the slabs of raw meat and moved quietly back to the window. My hands trembled as I crammed it through the opening, giving it a few good punches just to make it fit. It left bloody slime all around the edges of the window and made a wet smacking sound as it hit the ground on the other side. Yuck.

"Dinnertime." My voice squeaked with anxiety. "Er, I mean, breakfast."

Nothing—no sound.

My shoulders relaxed, and I started to turn away.

Suddenly, the entire iron-forged door shook with a powerful *BOOM*.

CHAPTER SEVEN

I staggered back, tripping over my own feet and landing right on my rear.

A thundering roar rattled the ground and made the ironwork groan. Something huge wailed against the door, slamming it hard enough to make the ground flinch underneath me. My body flashed cold, every muscle drawing tense. Merciful Fates, what was that thing?

The eye reappeared in the window, staring out and blinking like a huge milky green moon.

I stared back.

Before I could even think to move or scream for help, someone stepped swiftly past me and right up to the door. A man? Where had he come from?

Without a word, he shut the sliding panel over the window, sealing that creature back in the dark. Then he turned to stare at me over one of his broad shoulders, his expression severe. "Who are you?" he demanded, his pale eyes narrowing.

I'd never met this guy before in my life. I knew that. And yet, as soon as I saw his face, something about it struck a chord in my panic-addled brain. I'd seen him, or maybe just his face, somewhere before. But where?

He was a halfbreed, I could tell that much, and he was probably close to Murdoc's age. Halfbreeds were a mix of human and elf, and they weren't common around Thornbend. So I could be pretty confident I hadn't seen him around back home. My father had done some work for Gray elf merchants in the past, so I at least knew what they looked like. But halfbreeds? Not so much.

All Gray elves came from the mysterious kingdom to the north. They called it Luntharda—the wild jungle. As strange as they were mysterious, their hair was always as white as snow and their skin was a much deeper, warm bronze hue. They all had the same eyes that shimmered in a thousand different colors, changing with the light like opals. It was bizarre but undeniably beautiful. No human had eyes like that.

This guy was somewhere in between human and elf. He had the sharp, distinctly Gray elven features—complete with sloping pointed ears and darker toned skin. But his jawline was wider, more square, and his eyes were an icy shade of blue instead of multicolored. His ash-gray hair was cut shorter than the Gray elves usually wore it, and he had the distinct royal blue, black, and gold uniform of a dragonrider. He even had a breastplate buckled over his torso and a pair of polished metal greaves fastened to his shins. Weird.

As far as I'd heard, no full-blooded Gray elf had ever sat in a dragonrider's saddle or worn their cloak before. Not because it was forbidden, of course. Not anymore. Rather, my father had told me the Gray elves held dragons in the highest esteem above all other animals. They feared them like vengeful gods and kept a healthy distance from their nesting areas. I had to agree with that philosophy, honestly.

"Are you all right?" he asked, turning away from the door.

"I-I, uh ..." I wheezed as I scooted back farther away from the door. "What is that thing?"

"He's not a *thing*," the man corrected, his tone calm as he offered a hand to help me up. "He's a dragon. His name is Fornax."

I glanced between the man and the door. Booming roars still raged on the other side. The massive door flinched and rattled on its hinges every time the beast wailed against it, almost as though he were throwing himself into it over and over, trying to break free. Okay, thing or not, that creature was absolutely terrifying.

"Are you his rider?" I took the man's hand and got back to my feet. My knees shook as I dusted off the back of my pants.

"No." His glacier-colored eyes narrowed slightly as he looked me over from head to foot. "He doesn't have a rider."

"I-I wasn't ... I mean, I was just supposed to feed the dragons. I wasn't going to mess with him," I tried to explain.

"I see." The man's expression relaxed some and he turned away to face the stall door again. His pensive gaze focused on the door with an uncertain frown. There was something quietly dignified about him, something beyond just your average dragonrider. I saw plenty of those guys coming and going from the Deck, and they all had that somber, battle-hardened look to them. This guy, though. He was different. I caught a glimpse of a faint scar over one of his eyes. It ran from his eyebrow all the way down to his cheek.

That look. And that scar ...

My stomach fluttered with nervous energy. I *knew* I'd seen him somewhere before. But where? I didn't know any dragonriders personally. At least, not that I was aware of.

"Is he wild? The dragon, I mean. I, um, I thought it was against the law to capture wild dragons now."

"It is," he replied. "Fornax isn't wild. Or at least, he wasn't. Not before."

I knew I shouldn't ask. I was just a stable hand. It wasn't any of my business and this man, a real dragonrider, was so far above me in the social pecking order it was hilarious to think he'd even answer any of my questions. What did I know about dragons, anyway? Nothing, that's what.

But I couldn't help myself. I had to know. "What do you mean? What happened to him?"

The dragonrider slid a sideways glance down at me again, almost like he was sizing me up. "His spirit is broken."

I frowned, gaping up at the rider, who must have been about half a foot taller than I was. What kind of an answer was that? "What do you mean?"

"He was one of many dragons who fought bravely to defend this city from the Tibran Empire. And like many others, he was also one who lost his rider in combat," he answered in a low, quiet voice. "But Fornax lost much more than that."

My gaze locked back on the stall. The roaring and banging had begun to grow quieter, as though maybe the beast on the other side was getting tired ... or simply giving up. Maybe both.

"What do you know about the Tibrans?" he asked.

I stiffened. "They're evil."

"Are they?" One corner of his mouth quirked slightly, hinting at a bemused smile. "That does seem like the easiest explanation. But what's easiest isn't always right. And in the case of the Tibrans, most of them are not evil. Most of them are people just like you and me. The Tibran Empire invaded their kingdoms, but they weren't as fortunate. They lost their wars, and the Tibran Empire enslaved them, took them far from their homes, and forced them to fight to invade other kingdoms. That cycle continued, on and on, until they came here."

"And we defeated them," I finished for him.

"Yes," he agreed. "Therein lies the problem. Now, we have thousands of former soldiers with nowhere to go and no means of getting back to their homes. They were forced to come here to fight a war that wasn't theirs against their will, and now they're stranded. Many of them have been enslaved to the Tibrans since they were children." A hint of sorrow crinkled his brow as he looked away. "As much as many people here in Maldobar would like to see them all killed or imprisoned, it simply wouldn't be right, would it?"

"No," I said, sinking back on my heels. "I ... I guess it wouldn't. But what does this have to do with Fornax?"

The dragonrider straightened somewhat, letting out a heavy sigh, as though this issue was just one of many weighing on his mind. "Fornax was struck by a Tibran weapon; an orb of burning oil. It killed his rider, scarred his face, and has left him permanently blind."

My stomach twisted like it was winding up into knots. I had been right—that dragon was blind. "But you said his spirit is broken."

"Even in that state, gravely injured and blind, Fornax protected the dead body of his rider until the battle was over. He wouldn't let anyone come near him, even other dragons. I suspect that because of his injuries, he couldn't tell that his partner had already died." The man's eyes closed as he bowed his head slightly. "Even now, he won't let anyone touch him or even come close. It's as though, for him, the battle still isn't over. Fornax is lost in the dark, so full of directionless rage and fear that his soul itself is fractured."

I couldn't speak. For a moment, I stood there beside the dragonrider, staring at the iron door as the sounds of the dragon's struggle finally faded away to silence. That's when I realized I was breathing fast. My heart was racing, too. "What's going to happen to him?" I asked, my hands curling into fists at my sides.

"I'm not sure," the rider admitted. "No one can touch him, so he cannot be ridden. He attacks anyone or anything that comes close, including other dragons, so he cannot be released back into the wild. The only solution anyone has been able to come up with is condemning him to that cell."

"But that's not—!" I started to shout. Catching myself, I set my jaw and shot the dragonrider a challenging glare. "That's not a solution. It's torture! He can't live in that tiny box forever!"

"I agree." He stared back, his piercing gaze seeming to cut straight through to the very depths of my soul. "So, what are *you* going to do about it?"

I DIDN'T HAVE AN ANSWER. Even hours later, while sitting outside the royal stable while the swollen orange sun sank below the distant mountains, I still had no idea what I could do. I wasn't a dragonrider. I was a stable hand. I was nobody—the nobody of all nobodies. I couldn't even handle a sword, let alone ...

The whoosh and rumble of a dragon passing low over the castle drew my gaze up. The creature was enormous, bigger than any of the other dragons I'd ever seen, with scales of deep blue. His spines and horns were as black as obsidian and sparkled in the light of the setting sun. With a few mighty wing beats, the dragon disappeared above the clouds, as swift and silent as the east wind.

I knew that dragon right away. There was no mistaking him—not if you grew up in Maldobar hearing all the stories of the Gray War. That was Mavrik, the king drake. He reigned as the dominant male over all the dragons in Maldobar. He was also the dragon who'd belonged to the famous war hero Jaevid Broadfeather.

My father had told me stories about Jaevid when I was little, about how he'd been chosen by that dragon and fought to stop a long and brutal war between the humans and Gray elves long ago. He'd been able to use divine magic and speak to animals, and had even fought alongside the former king.

Only ... Jaevid Broadfeather had died at the end of all those stories. He'd sacrificed himself to appease the ancient gods and basically saved the whole world. There were mosaics, statues, and paintings of him everywhere. You couldn't walk a mile in any city in Maldobar without seeing his face, with his sharp halfbreed features and that scar over one of his—

Realization hit me like a punch to the gut. I choked and wheezed out loud, making Murdoc glance over from where he was stretched out on the grass next to me.

"What's wrong with you?" he mumbled.

"J-Jaevid," I gasped. "Jaevid Broadfeather!"

"What about him?"

"I-I-I think I saw him in the Deck today!"

Murdoc rolled his eyes. "Hallucinations don't count, you know. Jaevid's been dead for forty years. Everyone knows that."

"I wasn't hallucinating. At least, I don't think I was." I sank back, trying to wrap my mind around it. Was that really him? Jaevid was the most famous dragonrider to ever take the saddle. His magical powers had been what ultimately ended the Gray War. He was more than just a hero—he was a legend.

And he was here in Halfax—*alive*.

Gods, no wonder his face looked so familiar. Granted, he looked a lot younger in person. But still, there was no mistaking that scar. It was him; it was really Jaevid!

"No." I set my jaw. "I did see him. He talked to me. He's back."

"Well, some of the other workers were talking about him passing through now and again. Supposedly, he's in charge of the Dragonrider Academy now, when he's not helping to sweep up the rest of the Tibran mess, that is." Murdoc plucked a long strand of sweet grass and stuck it in the corner of his mouth.

I cast my *friend* a smoldering glare. "But you just said he was dead."

One corner of Murdoc's mouth quirked into a smirk.

"You were teasing me?!"

"A little. I'm not sure it even counts with you. People do it all the time, and you rarely notice."

"Great. Good to know I'm everyone's favorite mockery punching bag." I fumed in silence for a minute, glaring at the horizon again.

"Oh, relax. Usually, it's girls doing it, which I can only assume is because they think you're 'cute' or something," Murdoc said, still nibbling on the sweet grass.

I groaned and flopped back onto the ground next to him. "Why does it always have to be cute? I *hate* being called cute."

He shrugged. "Well, if it's any consolation, I think you're ugly."

"Thanks."

"Anytime." He folded his arms behind his head, still smirking to himself as he asked, "So, what did the famous Jaevid Broadfeather say to you?"

What had he said? I gnawed on the inside of my cheek while I thought it over. He'd said a lot, actually. And I hadn't been able to get that last question out of my head. What could I do about Fornax? Nothing, really. I wasn't even allowed to open the door to his stall.

I closed my eyes and tried to imagine what it was like. This dark, empty, nothingness was all Fornax ever saw now. His whole world had gone up in flames during the battle. According to Jaevid, it was still burning.

But what could I possibly do about that?

"Nothing important," I lied quietly. "Jaevid ... just wanted to know my name."

CHAPTER EIGHT

I was about to do something stupid.

Er, well, stupider than usual, anyway.

Nothing I did, nothing I thought about, could get Jaevid's words out of my head. I didn't know him beyond stories of all the amazing things he'd done in the war. And he didn't know me. But something about the way he'd looked at me—something about that question—stuck in my brain like a thorn. I couldn't shake it.

Days passed, and I kept going to Fornax's stall, opening that tiny window, and feeding him like I was supposed to. But the question remained. Every time I stood before his stall, I could practically hear Jaevid's voice still ringing in my ears.

"What are you going to do about it?"

I raised my gaze to the iron-plated door of Fornax's stall. No—not a stall. That was a prison cell.

What was I going to do about it? Something stupid and potentially life-threatening. I was going to help him. I was going to save him.

I was going to find Fornax in the darkness.

Easier said than done, though. While Murdoc probably thought I was a complete idiot, I wasn't dumb enough to jump into that dark metal box without a plan. I needed information. I needed to know more about Fornax and his former rider if I was ever going to stand a chance of gaining his trust. I had to start at the beginning.

I had to learn about dragons.

"Finicky beasts," Stablemaster Godfrey warned when I asked him what he knew about his largest, carnivorous wards. "As temperamental as house cats and stubborn as mules. They're hard to work with, and I've never had a hand for it, myself. You can't outthink them. They're smarter than most people are."

"Ah." I tried not to sound too interested. I didn't want anyone to know what I was up to. They'd probably try to stop me because, well, it was basically suicide. "What about the saddles? What do they look like? I've never seen one up close."

"You wanna see a saddle, boy? There are plenty of them in the Deck. Check the tack room on the first level, if you want, but don't touch any of them," he warned. "Do it on your own time, though. Don't you have horses to feed?"

I did. And it took the rest of the day to finish all my work before I had any time to slip away. Feeding dragons in the morning and working with the horses the rest of the day usually left me exhausted. But I had a new goal to focus on now.

The sun sank over the royal castle's grounds as I slipped into the Deck and crept around to the tack room. There was no one in sight as I shut the door behind me. So far, so good.

Inside the tack room, the strong smell of freshly oiled leather reminded me a little of home. It put a pang of pain through my chest. I set my jaw and pushed those memories away. Now wasn't the time.

Saddles were set up on sawhorses all around the broad room in organized rows. I walked slowly past each one, my eyes scanning for some idea of which dragon they belonged to. Then I noticed each sawhorse stand had a number burned into it—a number to match each stall in the Deck.

I already knew Fornax's stall number. I'd been there to feed him several times now. Walking past row after row of saddles, I stopped in front of one with a big number four burned into the wood. My gut tensed.

This was his saddle—the one his rider had died in.

Like all the others, it was bigger than a regular horse's saddle, and it had a sloped, sleek shape crafted from layer upon layer of molded black leather. The buckles and decorative tacks were all plated in bronze, and the saddle's two large handles looked like they were solid bronze, as well. I couldn't resist. I ran my hand along the side of it, tracing the swirling design work pressed into its glossy surface. It was like a piece of art. The only flaws were a few areas around the seat that had been burned or melted away.

My fingers stopped short of one of those marks. My mouth scrunched. Was that left from the burning oil that had blinded Fornax and killed his rider? Just the thought made my heart pound harder.

Shutting my eyes tightly, I took a few steadying breaths. This wasn't why I came here. I needed to find a way to reach Fornax in the darkness. I needed to figure out how his rider had communicated with him. I could use that information and then, with an insane amount of luck, I might be able to help him adjust to being around other dragons. Or at least get him calm enough to let Jaevid work with him. Then he might have a real chance at being released into the wild. He could have a normal life or, at the very least, a happy one. Anything was better than living in that tiny iron box for the rest of his life.

I studied the saddle over from one end to the other, exploring the design and trying to understand it. From the look of things, the saddle had been made to mold against the dragon's back, fitting snugly over the ridge of horns that ran down his spine. The rider sat on a padded seat shaped into the leather and slid his legs down into the two deep pockets on either side. That must have been what kept him anchored to the saddle during flight.

Steering was a little harder to figure out. This wasn't anything like a horse's saddle. There was no bit, bridle, or reins to guide the dragon. So how did they do it?

The answer was simple, and it gave me an idea.

The two brass handles on the front of the saddle weren't just for holding on. They were fixed to a pair of rotating discs built right into the leather itself. When I twisted one of them, a smooth metal plate about eight inches across descended from underneath the bottom of the saddle. It would put pressure right up against the dragon's side—a gesture the beast could feel against his scales. Twisting the handle the other way retracted the plate and removed the pressure.

I sat back with a satisfied grin. *That* was how they did it. They used those rotating handles to give signals. Twisting them in various combinations would be easy to translate into a language of commands, not totally unlike reins on a horse.

They communicated using touch, and that was something I could use. Fornax was blind, but I was willing to bet he could still feel things well enough. He'd lost his visual language, so he needed a new one. A language of touches, just like this saddle provided. Maybe sounds, too. Now, I just had to figure out how to make one for him.

Oh, and somehow teach it to him without being burned to a crisp first, of course.

THIS WASN'T GOING to happen overnight. I understood that. I'd seen my father work with hundreds of horses throughout my life. He'd taught me a lot about how to approach the skittish, high-spirited, or even aggressive ones without getting trampled to death. It was like a dance, a complicated conversation of touches and sounds, body language and energy. I hadn't mastered it yet, and it was quite a stretch to think I could translate any of that training into dealing with a dragon. Horses and dragons couldn't have been more different.

But fear was fear, anger was anger, and the energy was the same. Those were my obstacles. I just had to learn a new dance.

I had to learn to dance with a dragon.

I started simple. With a few coins from my paycheck, I took an afternoon walk down into the royal city marketplace. Murdoc didn't come—he never wanted to leave the castle grounds. Good thing, too. I didn't want to explain to him why I was buying a small brass whistle intended for training dogs and horses. The pitch was too high for most people to hear it, but animals could. I was willing to bet Fornax could, too.

Whenever I came to Fornax's stall to feed him, I stood before the door and made a trill of two short blasts on the whistle. That was going to be the first word in our language—a request for his attention. Then I opened the sliding window, dropped his dinner inside, closed the window, and backed off.

He was a fast learner. By the third day, I could hear his heavy breaths sniffing around the door when I blew the signal notes.

On the fourth day, I took it a step further. I blew the signal and stepped to the window. Standing before it, I held my breath and stared straight ahead into the darkness of the stall. His breathing echoed off the metallic walls. Then I saw his eye appear, staring straight at me. His growl rumbled like thunder; a warning. He couldn't see me, but he could smell me ... and probably hear my pulse thrashing wildly.

Yeah, I was scared. Terrified, actually. He could still scorch me through that window. One blast of burning venom and I wouldn't have a face—or an entire head—anymore.

I blew the signal again, asking for his attention, but then I added another command. Three short blasts this time. This would be our second word.

"Ease off." I commanded, keeping my voice low and firm.

Fornax blasted a snort that rattled the door. His huge eye blinked.

I did it again. Three short blasts on the whistle. "Ease off, Fornax."

His eye shrank, as though he were moving away from the window. Whether intentional or pure luck, he'd done what I wanted; he'd moved away from the window. I rewarded him with his supper and quickly shut the window.

A few feet away from the door, my knees almost buckled. Gods and Fates, what was I thinking? Was I losing my mind? Or ... were we actually making progress?

It was too soon to celebrate. I had his attention. Now I had to keep it. I had to keep building our language.

After three more days, I was pretty-mostly-almost sure he understood the "ease off" command. But there was only one way to be certain.

Aaand this was where my plan went from somewhat reasonable to downright stupid.

I only had one day left with Fornax. Stablemaster Godfrey had tacked on a few extra days to our duty in the Deck, claiming we were still shorthanded. This was my last try before I'd have to start coming at night, sneaking in when no one was watching, to keep working with him. It would be way riskier. If something went wrong, no one would know until the next morning when they found a Thatcher-shaped scorch mark or headless corpse on the floor.

Today would determine if that was even an option.

Jaevid had said no one could get close to Fornax. No one could even go in his stall. Time to see if that was really true or not.

My hands shook as I stood before the door, prepared but not exactly ready. My knees shook and my heart pounded so fast I thought it might launch right out of my chest. Sweat ran down the back of my neck as I sucked in a deep breath.

This was it—do or die.

I murmured a quiet prayer to the gods, hoping they might let me survive this, before I took a deep, steadying breath. Then I put the whistle to my lips and blew the attention signal.

Immediately, Fornax gave a huff and snort from the other side of the door. He was already waiting. I opened the window and gave him half his portion of raw meat as usual.

Then I went to the door.

I'd figured out how to work the heavy-duty locking mechanism on the stall's reinforced door days ago. It worked like a vault, with a twisting wheel in the center studded with bars. If you turned it just right, the lock would activate and retract the two heavy bars that were anchored into holes cut into the stone floor and ceiling.

I set my jaw and started to crank. I cringed every time the ironwork groaned and creaked, giving me away. With two complete turns, the door was unlocked. I pushed it open, only two feet—just far enough that I could slip inside.

Armed with my whistle and the other half of Fornax's dinner, I stood shaking in the doorway. My legs were so numb they felt like two columns of jelly. Any second now I'd faint, collapse, and that would be the end of Thatcher Renley—idiot extraordinaire.

The light from the hall spilled into the gloom, revealing ... nothing. Just old hay and the smell of animal musk, old blood, and dung. Hmm. That couldn't be right. Where was he?

Something moved off to my left and it took everything I had not to scream and bolt. No—I had to hold my ground. No fear. No negative energy.

A deep, rumbling growl and hiss made my blood freeze in my veins. I stiffened and slowly turned to face the direction of the noise. My heart pounded in my ears as I gave the signal again—three short blasts of the whistle.

Immediately, the growling stopped.

The silence made my skin crawl. Gods, what was he doing? I couldn't see anything except for a few feet in front of me thanks to the light spilling in from the hallway.

I tossed the hunk of raw meat onto the ground about four feet away from where I stood. It hit the ground with a smack, lying barely within the shaft of light. He'd have to come close to get it, close enough that I could see him.

Scrapes like claws over stone and the rustling of something huge stirred in the dark. Strange clicking, popping sounds echoed off the walls. He sniffed loudly, blasting snorts that sounded closer and closer. At last, the light caught over the gleam of scales.

My heart stopped.

Fornax's head appeared in the light, his scales gleaming in a rich, vivid orange color adorned with stark black stripes. Black horns swept back from his head and ran along the ridge above his eyes. Gods and Fates. He was *incredible*; the most beautiful dragon I'd ever seen.

Opening his mouth revealed rows of those jagged teeth as he unfurled his long black tongue, snaking around the meat and drawing it into his mouth. He chewed it, bones and all, crunching the last of his meal in a few bites. He licked at the blood on the ground where the meat had been and then looked directly back up at me.

I let out a slow, shaking exhale. Steady—I had to be steady. No sudden moves. No freaking out. Calm energy.

His small ears swiveled, probably picking up on my frantic pulse and tight, shallow breaths. He'd be able to tell I was afraid, no matter how I tried to hide it. His milky jade eyes blinked. He let out a low, rumbling growl again as his lips began to twitch into a snarl.

This was it. The moment of truth.

I gave three short blasts of the whistle. The ease off command.

His eyes blinked, huge nostrils puffing and ears swiveling.

"Ease off," I said.

Fornax hissed, scaly little ears slicking back.

"I said, ease off, Fornax," I warned, keeping my tone steady. "Ease off."

He stopped growling. His ears kept moving, listening, until ... at last he moved away. His vivid orange scales disappeared back into the darkness of the cell.

I didn't waste a second. As soon as he was gone, I stepped back out of the stall and scrambled to shut and lock it. With the iron door securely back in place, I slowly backed away. I made it about four steps before my knees buckled. I collapsed onto my rear in the middle of the hall, gaping up at the door.

I-I'd done it. I'd stood in the same stall with Fornax, only feet away. Not even Jaevid had been able to do that. But Fornax had *listened* to me.

He wasn't beyond saving.

I coughed a breathless chuckle, still trying to shake off the tremors of adrenaline as I staggered back to my feet. Pumping a fist in the air, I allowed myself one quick shout of victory before whipping around—

—and almost crashing right into Murdoc.

He stared down at me with his mouth hanging open and his face pasty with horror.

Oh no. How long had he been there? Had he seen me?

"Tell me you did *not* go in there with that monster," he whispered, his eyes wide and chest heaving with panicked breaths.

Yep. He definitely saw.

9
CHAPTER NINE

"I can do this, Murdoc! You don't understand," I shouted as Murdoc shoved me out of the Deck and into the cool early morning air. "Just please, let me explain. He's starting to trust me!"

"*No!*" Murdoc thundered back. "You know we aren't supposed to open that stall. You may be thick in the head, but I'm sure you heard the same instructions I did."

"Murdoc, listen," I tried to reason.

He cut me off, grabbing the collar of my tunic and shoving me backward so hard I nearly tripped. "*No*, you listen to me, idiot! That dragon trusts the smell of fresh meat. That is not some feral dog you can tame. That animal will kill you, and I'll end up scraping whatever's left of you off that stall floor."

I stood up straighter to face him, balling my fists as I shouted back, "You don't know that. You didn't see what happened. He listened to me. I can help him. I *will* help him!"

"No, you *will* end up a smoldering corpse," he snarled. "You don't get it. There are some things you can't fix, no matter what you do—some people can't be helped. They're just … too broken. Too far gone." Murdoc's expression darkened. His jaw clenched and his mouth screwed up as he looked away, breathing hard through his nose. "You don't know what it's like to be in real combat or what that kind of violence does to a person's mind."

"Oh, but you do?" Crap. I regretted those words immediately.

I knew Murdoc had a past. I wasn't the brightest guy, sure, but that much wasn't hard to figure out. He knew his way around his blade. I'd seen him kill that man in black, his former partner with the crossbow, the night we met. He'd done it so fast and without any hesitation. I could only guess that meant it wasn't the first time he'd put a blade through someone else. And then after everything that happened at the prison camp, beating those people and possibly killing another with only his bare hands, there was no denying it. It couldn't have been the first time he'd done that, either.

All around us, the dawn wind rustled through the trees and shrubs. The sound filled the tense silence while Murdoc glowered at me, his hazel eyes smoldering with quiet rage in the moonlight. Little by little, the anger drained from his features. His expression went cold and he looked away again, as though dismissing my existence altogether.

"Fine. Go back in there and die if you want." He waved a hand at me dismissively. "I don't expect some soft, squishy, baby-faced little kid from Thornbend to understand."

"I-I'm sorry. I didn't mean that," I stammered as I followed.

"Stay away from me," he warned without looking back.

"No, Murdoc. It was out of line. You're my friend, and I shouldn't have—"

He spun suddenly, seizing the front of my shirt again and dragging me closer. He snatched me up onto my toes and snarled down into my face, baring his teeth like an angry wolf. "We are *not* friends."

Fear crept up my spine like a harrowing chill. I couldn't speak. All I could do was dangle there in his grip, staring back into the utter darkness of his eyes. Wrath and chaos crackled there, spinning like a vortex from somewhere deep within his soul.

"You're a nuisance. And I'm sick of it. Stay away from me," he snapped coldly, dropping me back to the ground.

I landed in a heap. Before I could get back on my feet, Murdoc had already disappeared—as though he'd simply vanished into the night without a trace. I spun around, searching the gloom of the perfectly manicured royal grounds. I called his name.

There was no answer.

In a matter of seconds, Murdoc, my only friend, was gone.

After a few weeks and not a single sign, Stablemaster Godfrey finally quit asking me where Murdoc was. He never returned to the servant's quarters. His bunk was directly across the aisle from mine in the men's sleeping quarters, but it remained empty every night.

Guilt gnawed at my insides. I shouldn't have said that to him. I shouldn't have lost my temper. But then again, how was I supposed to know it would make him this angry? I didn't know any of the details about his past or what he'd been through before we met. He'd refused to tell me anything about himself. We'd known each other for six months and he was still basically a stranger to me. How was that fair? Was I just supposed to continue that way? Stumbling along in his shadow, never knowing who he really was?

Unfortunately, he was also the closest thing to a friend I had. Now, he was in the wind, and I had no idea where to even begin looking for him. All I could do was hope he'd come back. That hope kept me awake at night, watching the door and starting at every sound. My home was gone. My father was probably dead. Any family I might have left in Mithangol—if any of them had even survived the Tibrans—wouldn't want anything to do with me.

Without Murdoc, I had no one. I might as well have been alone in the universe.

On the other hand, when it came to Fornax, now I had nothing left to lose.

No one even cared if I was alive. It didn't matter what happened anymore. So why not? Why not risk it all and find out if I was right—if Fornax could be saved?

It's not like anyone would miss me if I was wrong and he roasted me.

On a clear autumn morning, I stood outside the stables watching the other stablehands bring out the horses to be groomed. I breathed in that first, delicious hint of crisp frost in the air. And I decided it was time to find out, once and for all.

I'd still been working with Fornax with the signals and whistle, using short commands. Now that we'd established a foundation, I didn't worry as much about working with him at night. So far, the most he had done was growl and hiss when I was with him. Granted, I hadn't tried to touch him yet. Breaking that barrier with him would require substantially more trust on both our parts. Now seemed like as good a time as any to determine if we had finally reached that point or not.

Stablemaster Godfrey made a face when I didn't complain about being assigned to feeding duty at the Deck again. I guess he probably thought I was still upset about Murdoc leaving. I was, of course, but today I had other things on my mind. I focused on my plan, forcing all my fears and anxieties to be silent. It didn't matter what happened to me now. Fornax was the only thing that mattered.

I kept my head down and worked through my shift, feeding all the other dragons in the Deck with another stable hand. Only—I skipped Fornax's stall.

After our rounds were finished, I hung back and offered to wash off the wheelbarrows, aprons, and gloves by myself. My partner, a younger girl with short black hair, was more than happy to pass that chore off to me without any protest. Washing blood off our gear wasn't a job anyone wanted, and I was counting on her taking the opportunity to duck out early.

Once I'd finished, I filled a small bag with little chunks of meat, each one about the size of my fist. Then I snuck down to the tack room and pulled Fornax's saddle off the stand. No one asked any questions as I walked down the hall, lugging the massive saddle over my back. I was just another stable worker moving gear around. Nothing strange about that.

At the door of stall number four, I dumped the saddle onto the floor and studied the lock. My body flashed hot and cold and my skin prickled with a shiver. This was a bad idea. Probably the worst of my life. It was reckless. It was risky.

I was totally going to die.

I gave two short blasts into the whistle. Inside the stall, Fornax stirred. He made musical clicking, popping, and chirping sounds almost like a greeting. That was how he'd begun acknowledging me, as though letting me know he heard me.

Gripping the door's studded wheel, I cranked the lock open and pushed the door ajar. This time, however, I pushed it open halfway. All the stagnant, smelly air inside the stall rushed out. Gods, it had been almost a year since anyone cleaned that stall. Not that I blamed them. They probably thought it wasn't worth dying over.

Hopefully, after today, that wouldn't be a problem anymore. I'd even clean it out myself, if I had to.

Fornax's sounds became more anxious, higher pitched, and unsure. He was probably confused. I'd never opened the door this far before.

I gave the attention signal again and then added our latest verbal command. "Ease off."

He obliged, staying in the far corner of the stall, still hidden in the darkness.

I stepped over the threshold and tossed a few of the chunks of meat down not far from my feet. "Okay. Come up."

On cue, Fornax unfurled from his corner and moved into the light.

My breath caught at the sight of him. I'd never seen his whole body before. He was big, even for a male dragon, but his body was sleek and streamlined. His brilliant orange scales shimmered the same color as flame. The same black stripes that adorned his head also covered the rest of his body and reminded me of a jungle cat. The black spines that ran down his back were long and lethally sharp like barbs of solid obsidian.

He blinked at me, nostrils puffing as he homed in on the scent of the meat at my feet. He gobbled it up quickly, and I gave him a few more just for good measure. After all, this next part was bound to be tricky.

I made a long blast with the whistle, going up in pitch at the end. Fornax grumbled with uncertainty as he pointed his snout toward the open door behind me. No doubt he could smell the fresh air coming in from outside. I gave the signal again.

This time, he chirped and lowered his head before flattening out against the ground. The spiked end of his long tail swished, eyes tracking the sound of my footfalls as I walked a complete circle around him. That was our most recent accomplishment, and frankly, it still terrified me. One wrong step, one bad second, and he could end me. But we had to build trust—*mutual* trust, that is.

It was nothing compared to what came next, though.

I rewarded him with a few more scraps of meat, and then gave the signal for him to lie down again. While he was busy eating, I moved slowly back out into the hall. Hefting his saddle onto my back, I approached and laid it out on the floor next to him.

Fornax's nostrils worked furiously as he drank in the familiar scent of the leather. I wondered if it still smelled like his rider ... or his blood. Fornax's ears slicked back and his scaly hide began to shiver as a low growl kindled in his throat.

"It's okay," I said, keeping my tone calm.

His growling quieted a little.

I couldn't rush this part. He had to become calm again in the presence of that saddle before I could do anything else. After nearly an hour and several more chunks of meat, his growling finally went silent. He was back to chirping and yipping, eager to do more tricks in hopes of another bite.

Only ... now it was time for a completely new one.

Taking a step closer, I gave the lie down command once more, just to be sure he remembered what I wanted. I clenched my teeth, squeezing my hand into a fist to try to stop it from shaking as I reached out toward his head. The wind of his breath blasted through my fingers as I inched closer. Five inches.

Then three.

Then one.

My fingertips brushed his snout.

I resisted the urge to scream or cringe away. I had to be steady. No fear. Good energy.

Fornax's ears turned back a little as he pulled back from my touch. He gave a soft, half-hearted growl. Not like a warning or a threat—more like a reflex.

I took another step and touched his nose again. I eased my palm down onto the smooth surface of his scaly head. A ragged breath slipped past my lips. Gods and Fates. I-I ... I was *touching* him.

He didn't feel at all like I'd imagined a dragon would. His scales weren't rough or slimy or cold. They were solid, strong, soft like leather, and warm with life. A smile tugged at the corner of my mouth. Keeping all my movements slow, I ran my hand gently over the gnarled, scarred areas where his face had been burned. Those scales were slightly discolored compared to the others.

His body tensed and shivered. His breathing quickened. He was afraid, but he wasn't growling or snarling. He was trusting me.

"I won't hurt you," I promised in a soft voice. "And I won't let anyone else hurt you, either. Got it?"

He didn't make a sound.

Standing in the glow of the light that poured in from the hall, I kept my hand on his head and let my eyes roll closed. I tried to pour calm energy into my touch, to reassure him that it would be okay. He had to get used to being handled again, if only long enough to be reintroduced to the wild. It would be enough to show the dragonriders he wasn't a lost cause. Then they'd let him out of this cell. He didn't have to spend the rest of his life in this stinking dark hole. He could be saved. He could be free.

A loud scream tore through the peaceful silence.

My eyes flew open and I whirled around just in time to see the dark-haired girl I'd been working with earlier standing in the hallway, staring at us with her eyes as wide as moons. Her face went pale.

She screamed again.

"No!" I tried to shush her, to get her to calm down. It was fine! I had it under control! And then, suddenly ... I didn't.

10
CHAPTER TEN

With a screeching roar and spray of burning venom, Fornax burst from his stall like a phoenix from the ashes.

I dove out of the way and immediately sprinted for the girl. She stood in the hallway, frozen in terror, as Fornax rose up onto his hind legs and spread his black leathery wings wide. His ribs expanded, sucking in another breath for a second shot of flame.

I smacked headlong into the girl, wrapping my arms around her as we went flying across the hall. We rolled, finally coming to a halt with me on top of her to shield her from the blast. Fire flashed in the hallway as Fornax unleashed another spray, painting the wall and ground around us with burning venom. I hunkered down, pressing us both down as flat on the floor as I could.

The acrid smell of the venom stung my eyes and burned my throat. When it stopped, I dared to look up. Fornax let out another panicked roar as he tossed his head wildly.

This was it—my chance.

"Get out of here! Now!" I yelled as I sprang off the girl and ran straight back toward the raging dragon.

Fornax floundered wildly, bellowing in a wild frenzy of confusion and fury. His tail smacked against the walls as his wings and head bashed the ceiling. His sightless eyes searched wildly, his mouth agape and jagged fangs dripping with crackling venom. He yowled as he pitched, lashing out with razor-sharp talons that sparked as he clawed at the stone floor.

I blew the attention command on my whistle.

His head swung around, ears perked and scaly hide shivering with fear. Through the inferno, his ears swiveled and his nostrils puffed deeply, almost like he was searching for something.

Gods—it was *me*! He was looking for me!

I ducked and dodged through the flames as I ran toward him, blowing the attention command again.

He made a desperate bleating sound, like a fawn crying for its mother. It made my brain scramble. He wasn't enraged. He wasn't even angry—not really. He was terrified.

"I'm here," I called. "I'm right here! It's okay!"

Less than a yard away, I stretched out my hand to touch his snout again. He needed to smell me, to feel my touch. He needed to know I was here. I hadn't left him.

Out of nowhere, pain exploded in my arm. My vision went white and my ears rang. I stumbled and fell flat onto my back.

Had he bitten me? Snapped off my whole arm?

I forced myself to look, squinting through the agony.

My arm was still there. Thank the gods for that, I guess. But there was an arrow sticking straight through my bicep. Blood soaked my tunic and puddled on the floor.

Someone had *shot* me. Who? Why?

Hazily, I searched around for whoever was responsible. That's when I saw them: a group of soldiers and stable hands running toward me down the curved hallway. The guy at the front of the group, though ... he wasn't a soldier or a stable hand. He wore the armor and cloak of a dragonrider.

I glimpsed his face through the wavering heat and flashing flames, his sharp features framed by ash-colored hair.

Jaevid!

Wait—had someone seriously *shot* me while trying to aim at Fornax? Whose brilliant aiming was that? I'd about made up my mind to get up and yell at the lot of them, but suddenly the air was snatched out of my lungs.

Two massive, scaly feet grabbed me by the legs and dragged me, bumping and scraping along the floor. I screamed, struggling and pulling at the big orange toes wrapped around my thighs. What was he doing? Where could we possibly go?

Unless ...

Oh no.

If all those people, including Jaevid, had just come inside the Deck through the front entrance, then surely they remembered to close the main door. Right? I mean, Fornax couldn't see it, but it wasn't that far. He would certainly be able to smell the fresh air blowing in.

I yelled for help as Fornax bolted for the exit, his wings flopping and flapping wildly. He smacked into the ceiling and skidded over the floor—dragging me the entire way down to the bottom level. I clawed at the ground, the wall, anything I could get a grip on. My fingers slipped over the worn stones and I left a trail of fresh blood from the arrow sticking out of my arm.

With a triumphant booming roar, Fornax found the door. He burst out of the Deck and into the open air, spreading his black leathery wings wide. Then he shot upward with one powerful flap. The ground fell away. My heart hit the back of my throat, choking out my screams for help.

More arrows whisked past me, one punching straight through my tunic but thankfully missing my flesh. What the heck was going on down there? Didn't they see me?

Through the flailing chaos, I spotted Jaevid running across the royal courtyards, waving his arms. His mouth moved like he was shouting, but with the wind howling in my ears, I couldn't make out what he said.

Suddenly, the arrows stopped buzzing past me. Something else barreled past us, instead, enormous and brilliant blue. Dangling upside down, it was hard to be sure at first. Then I got a good look. Another dragon—a *much* larger one—wheeled around us. Was that ... Jaevid's dragon?

The huge blue drake let out an ear-splitting roar, dipping in dangerously close and snapping his jaws. Oh gods, were they going to fight? Was I about to be dragged into the middle of a dragon aerial duel?

I yelled at the top of my lungs.

Without his sight, Fornax struggled to orient. He probably had no idea where he was. But he heard the blue drake's cry and immediately dove downward, back toward the royal city below. He glanced off the castle's ramparts, smacking me against them, too. My head cracked off the stone, sending everything into a whirling haze. For a second or two, my vision went gray, tunneling in and out of darkness as I clung to consciousness.

I dangled limply from Fornax's claws as he struggled to regain enough speed to stay airborne. His wings pumped erratically, floundering in the air. Behind us, the blue dragon roared again.

Panic made my eyes snap back into focus. Jaevid's dragon was coming back in for a second assault.

Oh no, not again. I had to get free—now!

I writhed my legs in Fornax's grip and tried to kick my way free. He bore down harder, gripping me so tightly my bones creaked, threatening to snap. It was no use.

Fornax wasn't going to let me go.

W ARNING horns wailed in the city below as we smacked against steeples and bounced off bell towers. Fornax obviously couldn't see any of that stuff. He was flying blind, spurred on by panic and fear. Every time we hit something, he shot a plume of white-hot flame and swung his head wildly, leaving a trail of fire behind us. People screamed and fled into the streets.

All of a sudden, something slammed into us from above. It sent Fornax plummeting, twisting and rolling in the air as he fell back to earth. The world spun. Everything was a blur of color and chaos.

We smacked into the ground with a *BOOM*.

Fornax hit first, sprawled on his back, with me still dangling from his grip. Dust, debris, and chips of stone filled the air.

At first, he didn't move. His grip on my legs went slack, and I dropped to the ground like a sack of turnips.

This was my chance. I staggered away, managing to weave and limp a few yards away before I dared to look back.

We'd landed right in the middle of a large city square, cracking a big marble fountain in half and leaving a sizable crater in the middle of the street. People ran in every direction, scrambling to get away. They pushed and shoved past me, dropping their shopping or leaving their wagons and carriages behind.

In a matter of seconds, I was the only one left standing there. Gripping my injured arm, I stood frozen in place with the arrow still sticking out of my flesh. Blood soaked through my shirt and oozed down my arm to drip from my fingertips.

I watched Fornax. My heart thudded hard, clashing in my ears. Get up—he had to get up. It was a bad fall, sure. But he wasn't dead ... right?

I took a step toward him.

Fornax shifted. He growled and snapped his jaws, kicking back over onto his belly and shaking the debris off his back. The sun danced off his brilliant orange and black scales, his powerful shoulders rippling as he flared the ridge of spines that ran down the length of his back. He bellowed, snout working furiously at all the smells. It must have been confusing. He didn't know where he was.

Suddenly, Jaevid's massive blue dragon landed in the courtyard. He was easily twice Fornax's size, with sweeping black horns and eyes that glowed like two yellow moons. No doubt he'd been the one who had knocked us out of the sky. Now he seemed ready settle this, dragon-to-dragon.

I expected him to lunge, to attack Fornax outright and turn this city square into an arena for an all-out brawl. Instead, Mavrik chirped and made a sequence of low popping, chattering sounds, puffing furious snorts and snapping his jaws.

Was he ... *talking* to him?

Fornax replied with a snarl, baring his teeth and flatting his ears. His tail lashed and coiled around his legs as he hunkered back, curling into a defensive ball and hissing like a frightened cat. His whole body shivered as he lowered his head, growling deep in his throat.

Terrified—he was utterly terrified. Any sudden move might set him off again. He would try to run again, blasting fire and trashing buildings again.

I-I had to do something.

I'd barely taken another step when a strong hand grabbed my shoulder. I yelped and jerked away, spinning to find a familiar grim, brooding presence looming over me.

"Murdoc?" I gasped in relief. "What are you doing here? I thought you—"

He shook his head, his voice barely above a whisper. "No sudden moves. He's cornered and he knows it. But any of us try to get close, he'll attack."

I stole a glance back over my shoulder at Fornax, who was still growling and shivering. "It's ... it's my fault. He wasn't ready for this yet. I pushed him too far."

"It doesn't matter now. You can bet coin the city guards are on their way right now. If he's not willing to go with them peacefully by the time they get here, it could get ugly."

I ground my teeth as I cradled my injured arm. Warm blood oozed down, soaking through my tunic and spotting the ground at my feet. "You mean that they'll kill him," I guessed.

"If it comes to that. He's already caused a lot of damage. People could get hurt." Murdoc's eyes went cold, narrowing upon the two dragons. "Who shot you?"

I didn't know. And right then, I didn't care. I shambled toward Fornax, leaving a trail of fresh blood drops with every step.

"Are you insane? What are you doing?" Murdoc shouted, seizing the back of my shirt and yanking me to a halt. "He's not in his right mind, Thatcher. Right now he can't tell friend from foe. He *will* kill you."

"I have to try." My voice shook with the desperation that rose in my chest like a gathering storm. "I won't abandon him. Maybe he doesn't want me. Maybe he never will. But right now, he needs me. Can't you understand that?"

I glanced back to find Murdoc's expression fractured. His eyes went wide, his mouth screwing up as though he'd tasted something bitter. Slowly, my tunic slid out of his grip until his arm dropped back to his side.

"Go, then," he murmured.

I did.

Tripping and stumbling over the rubble, I struggled to make my way toward Fornax. My arm burned, throbbing with agony where the arrow still stuck through my bicep. He'd smell it. He'd know it was me.

Or so I hoped. With my good arm, I pulled the whistle out from under the collar of my tunic and put it to my lips. I gave the attention signal.

Fornax's ears shot forward. His nose pointed straight toward me, cloudy green eyes blinking and searching the dark. His body still trembled and rumbled with an agitated growl as I came closer and closer.

I blew a long blast, going up in pitch at the very end.

His snout wrinkled with a snarl. Fornax snapped his jaws and turned his face away, toward Mavrik, slicking his ears back in defiance.

"Hey." I was close enough to talk to him, only a few yards away, without having to shout. "Don't worry about him. Listen to me, Fornax."

He clicked and hissed, still focused on Mavrik.

I blew the attention signal. "Hey! Focus, okay? I know you can hear me, big guy."

The orange dragon finally turned to stare in my direction again.

"Good," I breathed. "Listen to me. *Me*—no one else. I won't let them hurt you; I won't let anyone hurt you ever again. Okay? I swear it."

I shivered, my body going strangely cold as I took a few more steps. Blowing the lie down command again, I tried to shake off the bright spots winking in my vision. My head swam, making it harder and harder to stay upright. My head lolled as everything started to go dim.

One of my feet snagged on a crack in the street and I fell, dropping like a stone, toward the ground. I couldn't stop it. I couldn't even catch myself. My eyes wouldn't focus. My body, especially my injured arm, throbbed with an itchy pain like I was being pricked with a thousand cold needles.

Something warm and solid broke my fall, catching me before I hit the street. I lifted my head shakily, staring through the dark spots winking in my vision ...

... right into Fornax's milky jade gaze.

He'd caught me.

With a low whine, he breathed in deeply, sucking up the front of my shirt as I lay draped over the end of his snout.

"I-I'm sorry," I rasped, rubbing his scaly cheek with my good hand. "You weren't ready. I pushed too hard. But we can go slower, if that's what you need. We can figure this out together."

Fornax gave a low, musical chirping sound and closed his eyes. Every muscle in his entire body seemed to relax at once. He made a deep, vibrating, popping sound in his throat. It made me smile. I'd never known dragons could purr.

"They've gotta come take us back. But they won't put you back in that cell. I won't let them. You'll get a proper stall from now on." I rubbed his bony brow, running my fingers over the smooth, satin-soft surface of his scales. His hide was like warm, polished marble under my fingertips. Something about it felt familiar, comfortable, and calming.

"I'll take care of you. We'll watch out for each other. That's what ... friends do, right?" I slurred between painful breaths. My eyelids grew heavy. The tingling numbness in my arm had spread through the rest of me, making it harder to breathe. "Just don't cause any trouble when they come, okay? Promise me?"

He snorted.

I took that as an agreement. It would have to do. There wasn't time to double-check to make sure he understood.

The world around me went dark, snuffed out in an instant like a candle in the night.

11

CHAPTER ELEVEN

When I opened my eyes again, I found myself staring up at an intricate bronze chandelier hanging overhead. It had at least a dozen candles fixed in it, their wax dribbling down to cool and harden in bizarre shapes.

Somewhere nearby, the faint melody of a song hung in the air. A lullaby? Was someone whistling? I couldn't tell.

My head pounded like my brain was being squeezed inside a giant fist. Every heartbeat sent sharp throbbing pain across my forehead. The soft sunlight seeping through the drapes only made it worse. I groaned and tried to turn my face away.

The soft whistling of the lullaby stopped.

"Try not to move around much," Murdoc grumbled from somewhere nearby. I squinted into the light, picking out the foggy shape of my friend sitting in a chair at my bedside. He was thumbing through a book, his sharp eyes darting over the thick, yellowed pages.

"W-Where am I?" I asked hoarsely. "What happened?"

"Prince Aubren's wing of the royal castle, in one of the guest suites," he replied with a yawn. "They brought you here after you passed out. Apparently, you cracked your head off one too many buildings while dangling around under that dragon. The healer expects you'll live, though."

"Where is Fornax? Is he all right? They didn't hurt him, did they?" The more I talked, the more my head began to clear.

Murdoc shook his head. "He's back in the Deck—in a normal stall, this time. They've got a few seasoned dragonriders and that blue king drake keeping an eye on him. At first, he wouldn't let anyone get close enough to help you. But Jaevid was able to talk him down. As it turns out, he's been watching your little training exercises with the dragon from the beginning."

I let out a ragged sigh of relief, closing my eyes and relaxing back into the bed. "Good."

"They're saying he chose you, you know."

My eyes popped open wide again. "W-What? Who?"

"Fornax," he clarified. "They're saying he chose you to be his next rider."

My breath caught. "T-That's ... I mean, I can't ... I'm not ... I'm not dragonrider material."

"I agree." He gave a shrug.

"Wait, who said that?" I was hoping it was just a rumor—something started by the guards or other stable hands after hearing what happened. It was an easy conclusion to jump to, and they liked to gossip, anyway.

"Jaevid," Murdoc replied.

Well, crap. If *he* was saying it, then it must be true. He knew more about dragons than anyone.

I slowly sank down into the mattress, staring vacantly up at the ceiling. "I can't be a dragonrider. I don't even know how to fight. I just ... I just wanted to make things better for Fornax. I wanted to help him get better so he could be released back into the wild. I never intended for this to happen."

"That's how life goes, kid." Murdoc snapped the book shut and put it back on the bedside table. Out of the corner of my eye, I spotted a symbol leafed into the front in shining gold. It was the shape of a dragon with a sword in its teeth. The titled pressed into the spine was so worn it was almost indecipherable: *The Dawn of Flame—A History of Dragonriders*.

"I have to go to work. The only way Stablemaster Godfrey would give me back my job is if I promised to cover both our shifts until you're fit to work again," he announced, standing. "Try not to do anything else stupid while I'm gone."

I managed a weak smile. "No promises."

He didn't answer. Striding out of the room, my only friend in the entire world shut the door with a soft *click* and vanished into the royal castle.

With him gone, I felt that crippling sense of loneliness creep back into my mind. The room was so quiet. Too quiet. I probably should have slept, but hearing that Fornax had chosen me as his rider spun my brain into a frenzy. What did that even mean? Could Fornax fly in battle again?

And ... what about me? I wasn't a warrior. Gods, I'd be lucky if I managed to grip a sword from the right end.

Outside the door, the muffled sound of footsteps and voices approached. I recognized one of them right away—mostly because his words had been ringing in my head for a while now. Those same words had been what spurred me into helping Fornax, and had almost gotten myself and a lot of other people killed in the process.

"You're sure he'll be alright?" Jaevid asked, his footsteps stopping right outside the door.

"Positive," another guy's voice retorted casually. "You do realize I do this for a living, right?"

"There was a lot of blood, Reigh," another voice interjected. This one sounded older but familiar, as well. Prince Aubren? I hadn't seen or spoken to him in months.

"Look, the arrow got him in the soft tissue of his arm, through-and-through, nice and clean. If you're going to get shot, that's the way you want it. Trust me, it was way easier to remove than if the arrowhead was still stuck inside." The guy, who must have been the healer, breathed an annoyed sigh. "I stitched it up and gave him a little something for the pain, so he'll be fine. In a few weeks, he'll be back to shoveling dragon dung or whatever he was doing before all this." He chuckled a little and added, "Honestly, I was more worried about the crack to his head. If he hit the ramparts as hard as you said, he probably has a concussion. I won't be able to tell for sure until he wakes up, though."

"I think his shoveling days are over," Jaevid pronounced, his tone softer, as though he were still thinking it over. "Fornax chose him. There's no denying it. I'm not sure I would have believed it if I hadn't seen it with my own eyes. This means he has a place among the dragonriders."

The healer scoffed. "Fornax is blind, you do realize that, don't you? How do you fly with a blind dragon?"

Jaevid didn't answer for a few seconds. "The bond with a dragon is far more than just a relationship between rider and mount. It's soul-deep—you know that. What tethers those two together now is more profound than anything our normal senses can perceive. If they can tap into that and learn to communicate with it, Fornax's lack of sight might not be a limitation."

"Or it could be a danger to them and other riders counting on them for support in aerial combat," Prince Aubren countered. "And not to be cruel, but I've had my eye on this boy for sometime now, and I've seen more fight in half-stuffed scarecrows."

My heart sank at those words. A half-stuffed scarecrow? Ouch. Accurate, probably, but still hurtful.

There was something faintly nostalgic in Jaevid's voice. "They said that about me, too. I had no business being a dragonrider. They thought that my being chosen was a fluke—a mistake. I almost believed them." He paused, letting a heavy silence wash over the debate. "We can't see what lies at the end of our journey. All we can do is take that next step."

"What are you gonna do?" the healer asked. "It's something insane, isn't it? Oooh yeah, it totally is. You've got that look. Poor kid. Someone should warn him to take off now and get a head start."

"Whatever you do, Jaevid, don't even think of trying to duck out on the Court of Crowns," Prince Aubren warned. "Jenna might actually throttle you if you vanish now."

Footsteps, probably Jaevid's, began to retreat, moving away from the door. "I'm curious about something," he said. "There's someone I need to speak to, first. Watch over the boy. I'll be back."

I'd just let my eyes fall closed again when the bedroom door opened. Prince Aubren entered first, his brow rumpled with an anxious frown. Behind him, a shorter, younger guy strode in carrying a tray of medical supplies.

I did a double-take, just to make sure I wasn't hallucinating. He was dressed from head to toe in colorful, Gray elf-styled clothes. Only ... he wasn't a Gray Elf. His long, fiery red hair was pulled back into a messy braid, exposing rounded, human ears. He seemed like he might be about my age, sixteen or seventeen, and there was a very distinct scar slashing from one cheek to the other right across the bridge of his nose.

"Hey, you're alive after all." The redheaded guy laughed when he caught me staring. He plopped the tray of supplies onto the bed beside me and pulled up a chair. "I'm here to change your dressings. Maybe you don't remember, but one of the castle guards patrolling the Deck turned your arm into a skewer yesterday."

"I-I remember," I groaned.

"Well, that's a good sign. We were a little afraid you might have some brain damage after getting towed around by your dragon." He scooted closer and pulled the blankets down to my waist.

I winced as he lifted my injured arm and began unwrapping the gauze. "Who are you?"

"Reigh," he replied, his light brown eyes sharp and focused on the two small puncture wounds on either side of my bicep.

"Prince Reigh Farrow," Aubren corrected.

The redheaded healer rolled his eyes and sighed. "Yeah, yeah. But please don't call me that. Reigh is fine."

My brain scrambled for a moment. Everyone knew about Prince Aubren and Princess Jenna, but I'd never heard of this guy before. Since when did the king have *two* sons?

Reigh must have noticed the total shock and confusion on my face because he gave a shrug and a wry smile. "It's a long story. The short version is, yes, I'm a legitimate Prince of Maldobar—but without all the stuffy clothing and complete lack of common sense."

Aubren swatted him on the back of the head.

"Hey! Working with a wound, here," Reigh growled.

"And you're a healer?" I was still trying to figure out why a prince was treating injuries for commoners while dressing like a Grey elf.

"Among other things," he confirmed. "Jaevid insisted you get the best care. Naturally, they called for the best healer." He puffed his chest a little, shooting his elder brother a challenging look.

Aubren's eyes narrowed. "Hurry it up, Reigh. I know you've got business elsewhere." He folded his arms across his broad chest. I noticed he was only wearing one long, black, leather glove covering his right hand. Weird. Last time he'd been wearing two. So ... either this was a strange fashion choice, or he was trying to hide something. Hmm.

Reigh worked quickly, cleaning the areas where he'd stitched the punctures left behind from the arrow and then smearing them with a smelly green paste. He wrapped my arm in a few layers of clean white gauze and stood up, sighing and rubbing the back of his neck. "Looks like your arm will be fine. Just try not to lift anything heavy for a week or so, eh? How's the head?"

"Hurts," I confessed, using my good arm to rub my forehead with the heel of my hand.

"Unfortunately, that's to be expected. As long as you don't have any vision loss, bizarre mood changes, or memory lapses, there's not much we can do besides wait and see. Until then, get some rest." He patted the edge of the bed before picking up his tray of supplies. "You'll need it. Sounds like Jaevid is going to have a full schedule lined up for you once you're on your feet again."

I still didn't quite understand that. I was supposed to be a dragonrider? How? Fornax couldn't see. I'd never ridden him—unless you counted being dragged through the royal city like a garden plow behind a cow. Not to mention ... Murdoc and Prince Aubren were right; I wasn't a fighter. I'd never make a good warrior.

Reigh left without another word, closing the door and leaving me alone in the room with Aubren. Still standing at the foot of my bed with his arms crossed, he stared down at the floor with his expression shadowed in grim concentration. After a few uncomfortable, silent seconds, he finally spoke. "Thatcher, I'm not sure how to tell you this."

My stomach dropped. Oh no. This wouldn't be good news—I could hear it in his voice.

Aubren hesitated, drawing in a deep breath. "I dispatched men, people I know I can trust to give me results, to search for your father in Thornbend. They investigated, talked to every survivor and soldier they could find. No one has seen or heard from him since the night the city was invaded."

Slowly, he lifted his gaze to meet mine. There was genuine sorrow in his eyes, crinkling his brows, and drawing his mouth into a strained frown. "Your family home, the farrier's shop, was burned to the ground along with nearly every building on that street. They're still working on cleaning up the damage but ... several bodies were found in the debris in that area. They couldn't be identified because of how badly they were burned. But it's believed one of them might be your father." His voice softened to barely a whisper. "I am so sorry, Thatcher. I wish I had better news."

I stared back at him and only managed to swallow stiffly.

"I'm still waiting to hear back from your extended family in Mithangol," he added. "If you want to go and be with them, or if they want to come here and retrieve you, I'll help make sure that happens." He walked around the edge of the bed, slowly making his way over to put a hand on my shoulder. "I will let you know as soon as I hear anything."

"Thanks," I rasped quietly. "You know, for trying."

"What about your mother? Is there no one else we can try to contact for you?"

I shook my head. "My mother disappeared when I was a baby. Father searched for years, but he never found a trace of her."

Aubren didn't reply.

"It's ... it's okay. I sort of had a feeling, you know?" I cleared my throat, trying to keep my voice steady. It didn't work. Tears filled my eyes, blurring my vision. I swallowed hard, trying to keep it in.

"It's all right to grieve for him, Thatcher," Aubren said calmly.

"Y-Yeah," I sniffled, wiping my face on the sleeve of my good arm. "But it's not very warrior-like, is it?"

"You think hardened warriors don't weep for their loved ones?"

I blinked up at him, surprised to find a thin, almost painful smile ghosting over his features.

"Feeling things doesn't make you any less of a warrior. It doesn't make you less of a man," he explained, his voice quieter. "Apathy is something all warriors should fear more than anything else. It's the silent enemy, Thatcher, and the most formidable of all. Because if you lose that ability to feel, to experience grief over loss and compassion for the less fortunate, it means you've lost yourself. Losing yourself like that will tear a person apart from the inside out. It will split your soul. And wounds like that ... well, sometimes they never heal."

CHAPTER TWELVE

I lay in silence—not moving or blinking. I didn't even know if I was still breathing. Aubren's words replayed in my head over and over hours after he left.

Alone in the room, I honestly didn't know what to feel. Father was gone. He hadn't made it out. I couldn't understand why—why hadn't he left with me? Why send me ahead alone? We could have ridden out together. Why would he stay behind? What was he thinking? It made no sense.

The questions swirled and stirred in my head, rising and falling like the swell of stormy ocean tides. There were no answers. Maybe there never would be. Even if Prince Aubren managed to find some of my family members still living in Mithangol, I didn't know if they'd want me to come stay with them. I barely knew them, anyway. Did I even want to go? It would feel like living with strangers, and I wasn't sure if that was what I wanted.

Honestly, I wasn't sure what I wanted, at all.

At some point late in the evening, a servant came in to deliver my dinner. The platter of roasted lamb, small baked potatoes topped with rosemary-infused cream, and a slice of baked bread smelled incredible. My stomach growled and cramped at the smell of it. I just couldn't bring myself to actually pick up the fork.

Pushing the blankets off my legs, I sat up and stared at the door. It was late. I hadn't heard anyone walk by my room in hours. Murdoc had said this was Prince Aubren's wing of the castle. I had no idea where that was exactly. It didn't matter, though.

I spotted my small bronze whistle sitting on the bedside table. It still hung from the long chain I'd worn around my neck.

Suddenly, I knew what I wanted. I grabbed the whistle and strung it back over my head so that it hung against my chest.

There was a new change of clothes and a new pair of boots waiting for me folded neatly inside the large mahogany wardrobe on the other end of the room. I hissed and cursed through my teeth as I worked the tunic over my head, trying not to mess up the bandaging on my bicep. It burned like fire to move my arm—not that I had much of a choice. I couldn't go out in my underwear.

Once I was dressed, I crept out into the dimly lit hallway and started walking. A full moon hung in the clear night sky, casting eerie silver shafts of light through the massive windows of the castle. Huge portraits hung in intricate golden frames, the ghostly faces seeming to watch me as I went past. It took a long time, but eventually I found my way outside.

The cool night wind rustled in my shaggy hair, blowing it around my face and over my eyes as I walked toward the Deck. It was probably getting close to midnight, so I doubted I'd see anyone else around. Inside, the Deck had been secured for the night.

I went to stall number four first—the iron cell where I'd found Fornax.

It was empty.

My shoulders sagged with relief. Thank the gods they hadn't put him back in there.

After searching nearly every other stall, I finally found Fornax on the top level of the Deck, curled up on a bed of clean hay. They'd given him a regular stall, just like I promised. The interior door was closed to the hall, but the one that faced the courtyard below was open. He wasn't a prisoner anymore.

I left the stall door standing open a little as I went inside, putting the whistle to my lips and blowing a soft attention command. Fornax lifted his head, his cloudy emerald eyes staring in my direction, but not seeing me. I was sort of glad he couldn't. I probably looked like a total wreck. Or, that's how I felt, anyway.

"It's me," I said as I walked toward him slowly.

His nostrils flared as he breathed in my scent. His ears swiveled, snout following the sound of my footsteps as I came to stand in front of him. He chirped and clicked curiously.

"Are you okay?" I asked, stretching out a hand to lightly touch the end of his nose. "They didn't hurt you, did they?"

Fornax closed his eyes, his chest thrumming with a deep purr as he pressed his head into my hand.

My breath caught. I set my jaw, gritting my teeth against the emotion that rose up from somewhere deep inside. My eyes welled up again. My chin trembled. Before I could stop it, a gasping sob leaked past my clenched teeth.

Father was gone, and somehow, deep down, I'd known that for a while now. It just hadn't felt real until Aubren said it out loud. Now, it was a fact. I was alone. I didn't have a family or a home anymore.

Fornax was all I had.

"There you are," someone muttered from the doorway. "I've been looking everywhere."

Murdoc leaned against the frame, his thumbs hooked on his belt and head tilted to the side slightly, as though trying to figure out what I was doing here. "You're not supposed to be walking around yet, you know."

I tried to be discreet as I wiped my face on the sleeve of my shirt again. I didn't want him, or anyone else, to see me losing it like this. Maybe Aubren was right. Maybe it was good to let it out. But I couldn't handle anyone teasing me about it—not right now. Murdoc already thought I was weak and pathetic. This wouldn't exactly help my case.

"I just wanted to see him," I mumbled back.

"Prince Aubren told you, didn't he?" He cut straight to the chase.

My mouth screwed up and I looked away.

"You okay?"

"Yeah," I lied in a hoarse, cracking voice. Pathetic. No way he'd buy that.

Murdoc's eyes narrowed like he didn't believe me. Thankfully, he didn't push it. "Let's go back, then. I'm starving."

I gave Fornax one last pet on the nose before closing the stall door and following Murdoc back out into the night. I stared at his back as I trudged along behind him. Before I could think it over, a question rose up in my throat. "Why do you care what happens to me?"

Murdoc stopped.

"Do you want me to leave?" he asked without looking back.

"N-No, that's not what I meant," I stammered. "I just ... you said before we weren't friends. And we don't really know anything about one another. Then you disappeared and ... and I guess I thought you were probably relieved that you didn't have to put up with me anymore. I'm just trying to figure out why you came back."

His broad, powerful shoulders dropped slightly. Turning, his piercing hazel gaze caught mine under the wash of sterling moonlight. "You're a good person, Thatcher. You're naïve, overly trusting, and impulsive—which is a ridiculously dangerous mix, by the way—but you're good. You mean well. And I know it doesn't make sense to you, but believe me when I say that I am *not* someone you should want to be your friend."

It took me a moment to realize that wasn't exactly an answer. "So why did you come back?"

He looked away again so that I could only see the side of his face as his expression dimmed, tightening with a guarded scowl. "Because ... I suppose, even demons dare to dream of being something better, sometimes."

AFTER NEARLY A WEEK of staying in the royal guest room, I finally convinced Reigh that it was okay for me to go back to the servant's quarters. Even though he only dropped by every so often to check my healing process, he didn't like the idea of me being out of his direct supervision. According to him, if I didn't wait for my arm to heal, I could do permanent damage to it.

It took me repeatedly promising not to overdo it for him to finally groan, roll his eyes, and give me a nod of approval. I could go, so long as I stuck to the lighter jobs like feeding and grooming until I was back to my old strength.

He threw his hands up and growled in exasperation as I sat on the edge of the bed, lacing up my boots. "Fine. Suit yourself. You wanna go play with horses, I'm not gonna try to stop you."

I didn't stick around for him to change his mind.

Not that I wasn't enjoying the plush bed, downy-stuffed pillows, silk sheets, hot baths with fancy soaps, and delicious meals—but I didn't belong there. The other servants doing the cleaning and daily chores wouldn't talk to me, as though progressing from a fellow worker to a royal guest meant we spoke a different language now. I didn't like it. Not to mention I still had to sneak out to see Fornax. It felt wrong leaving him out there by himself. I tried to see him every day, but my visits were always short. I didn't have time to work with him on any new commands.

Murdoc only came by every other day to make sure I wasn't getting into trouble. I hadn't seen Jaevid at all, and—frankly—I was pretty sure Prince Aubren was avoiding me altogether. That, I suspected, was because of our last conversation. I couldn't blame him, really. I didn't know what to say, either.

Gathering up my work clothes and belongings, I struck out through the main foyer of Prince Aubren's royal wing. Reigh followed not far behind, carrying a leather shoulder bag full of his medical supplies. I wasn't sure what to make of him. He certainly didn't act like a prince. I hadn't had a chance to ask him about that because he wasn't as chatty as he had been the first time we met. If anything, he seemed angry about something. I didn't know him well enough to ask what it was, though.

Still, my curiosity about him made it hard not to stare. Why would the king have a secret son? By the look of him, Reigh had spent a lot of time in Luntharda, the wild jungle of the Gray elves. He dressed in their style and spoke with their accent sometimes. He even wore his hair in their long, traditional style, although it was a vibrant auburn red instead of white.

I'd almost made up my mind to finally ask him about it when a familiar figure stepped into my path.

"Reigh, Thatcher, could I borrow you both for a moment?" Prince Aubren offered a thin, veiled smile. Dressed out in formal court attire, complete with decorative silver breastplate, pauldrons, and bracers, I wondered if he'd just come from an official meeting.

Reigh stopped beside me and stiffened, his light amber eyes glittering with suspicion like a wary fox as he studied his brother. "Uh oh. You've got your fancy pants on. What's this about?"

The elder prince shook his head, making his feathery golden hair swish across his brow. "I'm not at liberty to say. Her Majesty insisted she be the one to have this discussion with you—*both* of you."

"Great," Reigh grumbled. He threw his head back with an exaggerated sigh. "Fantastic. Why do I have a feeling this is going to end badly for me? Because it always does, that's why. Held hostage by Tibrans, tortured, strapped to the front of a war chariot like an ornament, dragged through a battle ..." He began counting on his fingers. "What could possibly go wrong this time?"

A challenging smirk crept over Aubren's features. "Well, if you'd rather tell our beloved sister no—"

"Hey!" Reigh cut him off with a panicked yelp. "I said '*what could possibly go wrong,*' not '*I wonder how many of my bones Jenna can break in ten seconds.*' I don't have a death wish. Of course I'm going."

Aubren's smirk broadened, dimpling his cheeks at the corners of his mouth. "What a shame. I was hoping for a good show."

Reigh didn't answer, but he gave Aubren a solid punch in the arm as he swaggered past. He waved in my direction, gesturing for me to follow.

I swallowed hard and hesitated. What did this have to do with me? I wasn't a royal. I wasn't even a noble. I was a servant, the son of a commoner. What could I possibly contribute to this meeting? Advice on how to properly muck a horse stall?

Shifting uneasily, I stole a glance up at Prince Aubren. "I-I'm sorry, Your Highness, but ... but I don't understand. Why would Queen Jenna want to see me?"

He lifted an eyebrow. "I believe she plans on asking for your help."

I choked and sputtered. "M-My *help?*"

"Whether you realize it or not, being chosen by a dragon is going to change things for you. Simply having the options you now have is something many young men work their entire lives for. I would consider your next move very carefully, Thatcher. You don't have to become a dragonrider. It's not a requirement. But rejecting it is not something you should do lightly. Listen to her offer. Think it over. Then do what feels right. I have faith you'll make the right choice." He gave me a friendly pat on the shoulder before striding away, his long blue cape licking at his heels.

13
CHAPTER THIRTEEN

Her Royal Majesty, Queen Jenna, waited in a private parlor off from the grand throne room. But she wasn't alone.

Reclining on one of the sofas close to the crackling granite hearth, Jaevid Broadfeather was dressed out in his formal dragonrider armor. I stared in silent awe at the single scimitar belted to his hip—the one with the head of a stag engraved on the pommel. That legendary weapon had been in every story my father had told me about him. Now I was seeing it in the flesh.

Jenna sat across from him, her long royal blue gown the same color as Jaevid's cloak. It even had a bodice made of solid gold crafted to mimic the style of a knight's breastplate, although it stuck out a bit around the bottom, like she'd stuffed a pillow or something under it. Weird.

She looked up when we entered, her keen blue eyes studying us carefully, one at a time. Her lovely face practically glowed when she smiled at me. It made my stomach flutter and my face flush with embarrassed heat. I never knew how to act around pretty women, so I usually wound up acting stupid.

"Welcome. I'm glad to see you're on the mend, Thatcher," she said as she motioned for us to sit. "Make yourselves comfortable."

Reigh plopped onto the sofa next to Jaevid, crossing his legs with an ankle over his knee as he lounged back and sighed. "So? How was the meeting?"

Jaevid's expression tensed. "It's not going to be easy—not that we expected it would be. There's still a lot of fear. Lord Argonox carved a meaningful mark upon the world. It won't be soon forgotten."

Jenna dipped her head in agreement. "But we're beginning to move in the right direction. That's what counts."

Sitting down in a chair beside Jenna, I shakily raised my hand—which made Reigh snort. "Uh, I-I, um ... I'm sorry, but what's going on?"

Jenna shot Reigh a glare as he began choking, suppressing laughter. Jaevid elbowed him in the ribs, hard enough to make him nearly fall over sideways.

"Maybe it's best to start at the beginning." Jenna sat straighter as she stared into the flames dancing in the large, intricately carved fireplace. "You know that the Tibran Empire invaded our kingdom. You know that the war was costly. We nearly lost everything. The leader of the Tibrans, Lord Argonox, was not easily overthrown. Many good soldiers died ensuring that Maldobar would not be added to his empire." Her eyes fell closed. "But I'm afraid we only glimpsed the surface of his cruelty. The Tibran Empire was enormous, far larger than we ever anticipated. So far, we have counted eight other kingdoms that fell to his invasions. All of them were crushed, forced into submission. Their native cultures and traditions were torn apart. Their people were enslaved as soldiers or worse. Their royal families were either publicly executed or forced into exile. It's been a struggle to lure the ones who survived out into the open. They still fear Argonox, even after his death. I suspect many of them also fear me—as though I might try to take up his sword and seize control of his empire."

"We are hoping that, by inviting some of those royals here to meet with us and discuss the future of our kingdoms, they will spread the word to the rest who are too afraid to come right now," Jaevid added. "But we've also begun learning more about Argonox, himself, too."

Jenna's expression darkened, her brows knitting as she opened her eyes again. They flashed like cool blue steel in the light of the flames that licked in the hearth. "We only knew him for half the monster he truly was."

Reigh wasn't laughing anymore.

"Indeed. And one thing we learned very quickly about Lord Argonox is that he had a special appetite for experimentation when it came to people with magical or divine talents," Jaevid added, his tone heavy. "Powers like that were uncommon here, but that was not the case for everywhere else in the world. Some kingdoms have entire races of people endowed with magical abilities."

"And Argonox was fond of taking such people prisoner and torturing them." Jenna's voice halted, and she looked to Reigh for a brief instant. "Some, he killed outright. Others he subjected to ... unspeakable tests. It seems he had an obsession with learning how these magical or divine abilities worked. He wanted to learn to use them for his own gain or how to transfer them between hosts. In most cases, he wasn't successful. But in some cases ..."

"He was," Reigh finished for her, his jaw skewed to one side as though biting back anger. His brow hardened into a wrathful scowl, glowering down at the floor.

"After we defeated him here at Halfax, Lord Argonox's forces dispersed. Some surrendered, but others have fled into the general population where they are now trying to hide. Most are common soldiers, former slaves just trying to find a new way of life in a foreign land," Queen Jenna explained. "We aren't too concerned with them causing trouble. In fact, we intend to extend an offer to help them return to their homelands, if they wish, and rebuild what Lord Argonox destroyed. I expect many will take that deal." She fidgeted with the voluminous skirt of her gown, locks of her long golden hair spilling over her bare shoulders. "That's part of the purpose of the Court of

Crowns—we hope to help these other kingdoms reestablish stability. Then we can forge a unified network between all of our nations, working together to ensure something like this never happens again. It will benefit everyone. New trade routes will open, which will give lots of these now freed slave soldiers jobs and a means to return home."

"Court of Crowns?" I'd heard that phrase tossed around before, but I still wasn't sure what it meant, exactly.

"It's my solution," Jenna explained. "Or, at least, I hope it will be. Since a lot of the issues on the proverbial table involve kingdoms and families far beyond the borders of Maldobar and Luntharda, I want those places and their ruling monarchs to have a say in what happens to their people. I also want to assure them that I have absolutely no intention of laying claim to their lands now that Argonox is defeated. I've invited one representative from each kingdom conquered under the Tibran Empire to come to Maldobar and be a part of the Court of Crowns. Some of the key figures from Argonox's forces will be tried for their crimes, and we will deliberate together to determine the fate of many others. Hopefully, we'll also form a stronger alliance between our kingdoms."

"There are just a few problems." Jaevid sat back, rubbing his chin. "Not that we were expecting it to all go off without a hitch, but tracking down some of these notorious figures from Argonox's army is proving difficult. The war nearly broke Maldobar in more ways than one. We're low on manpower. Supplies are scarce. We have to plan each move down to the last detail because we don't have any time or resources to waste."

"As you know, Reigh, Jaevid has agreed to take on the post of Academy Commander at Blybrig, teaching a new generation of dragonriders the way of the saddle." There was a flavor of satisfaction and pride in Jenna's voice as she regarded Jaevid with a thankful smile. "More riders will help extend our reach and provide security to the four watches again. But they won't be ready soon enough to help with tracking down any of these war criminals for trial."

"And?" Reigh asked, eyes narrowing suspiciously.

"And some of those people I mentioned before—the one's Lord Argonox experimented on—have the potential to be extremely dangerous. There is one, in particular, who is of great concern to us." Jenna's expression went steely, her gaze panning to me with what I sincerely hoped wasn't expectation.

Oh gods. It was. It had to be. That was the same look father gave me when he discovered I hadn't finished my chores before sitting down to supper.

"We know her as Devana. According to our sources, she was one of the first magically gifted subjects Argonox ever imprisoned. It's been extremely difficult to track down any record of her, but we have reason to believe she came from the kingdom of Nar'Haleen. It's a very long journey from our shores, and we've yet to receive any word or ambassadors back from our attempts to make contact. However, if our accounts of that kingdom are correct, and if Devana survived the battle and is now loose in Maldobar, we could be dealing with a potential threat capable of unspeakable violence. Nar'Haleen is said to have a very prominent population of people with magical abilities."

Reigh leaned forward, his shoulders tensed and hunched defensively. "I'd ask which 'source' gave you all that information, but that would be the stupidest question of all, wouldn't it? You've got a professional snitch now, right?"

Jenna flashed him an irritated glare. "She wants to help, Reigh. And we need help like hers. If you have another suggestion for how we can learn about the inner workings of Argonox's forces, by all means, share it now."

He looked away in silence, his features tense with a defiant scowl.

"We *must* find out what happened to Devana," Jaevid spoke up, getting back to the point. "The kingdom of Nar'Haleen was home to a race of elves called the Lunostri—moon elves, in the common tongue. Very little is known about them, but they are said to be descended directly from the moon goddess, Adiana. *Pre-stone* magic, Reigh. Not like us. Direct blood descendants. You know what that means, don't you?"

Reigh didn't answer.

"I, uh, well, um ... what does that mean?" I dared to ask.

Jaevid's eyebrows drew together as he clasped his hands. "To defeat Lord Argonox, I struck a deal with the ancient gods. The result meant that people like Reigh and myself, who were given our abilities because of being chosen by a patron god, would lose those powers forever. I can't bend nature to my will or speak telepathically with animals anymore. Reigh also lost his control over the forces of death and decay. But my pact with the gods wouldn't apply to those with inborn magic. Someone like Devana would still be capable of an alarming amount of destruction. She could hurt a lot of people."

"Who's saying she hasn't already and we just don't know about it?" Reigh countered, his tone still edged with rebellion.

"No one," Jaevid admitted. "But I'm fairly sure we'd have heard about it if she were on a killing spree already. We should count ourselves lucky."

"But who knows how long that luck will last? I can't afford to wait and see. We need to find out if she's still alive, and if she is, where we can find her," Jenna insisted. "As quickly and as discreetly as possible. We don't want to cause a panic by making all the other former Tibran soldiers think we are going door-to-door, rounding them up. After carefully considering our approach, Jaevid and I have come up with a solution we think might work. Reigh, I want you to lead a small group of people to help track Devana down and bring her back here to Halfax for trial—by whatever means necessary."

Reigh dropped his head into his hands and scratched at the top of his head, mussing up his already ragged braid even more. "I *knew* it—I knew this would happen," he muttered through clenched teeth.

"I'm sorry, Reigh. Truly, I am. I know what I'm asking, but we don't have a choice," Jenna pleaded. "Jaevid already has his hands full at the academy—not to mention his wife is in a delicate state. He can't go off chasing down shadows and rumors for months on end. I'm stuck here for obvious reasons. Someone has to manage these incoming royals and bring them up to speed. Aubren and Phillip are too conspicuous, and both of them are busy helping our noble courts here recover and rebuild. There is no one else I can ask to do this."

"Eirik?" Reigh suggested.

"He's taken on a job as a combat instructor at Blybrig Academy training new recruits to help replenish the ranks," Jaevid replied.

"Haldor?"

"He's taken over as Southern Sky General," Jenna answered. "He's been leading the efforts to stabilize the southern coast."

"Aedan?"

"Phillip has been working nonstop to help mentor him as he adapts to his position as the new Duke of Barrowton and rebuilds the city. It's been an uphill battle. Aedan is clever, but he is young. It's taking time for him to earn respect among the noble houses, even with Phillip's support."

"Judan?"

"He's agreed to help supply you with any relevant information his network of spies might uncover, but he's already stretched thin helping us track down other prominent Tibran officials who scattered to the wind. We should have some useful information in the coming weeks—at least enough to get you started." Jenna shook her head, her lips thinning as she studied her younger brother. "Please, Reigh. You have unique knowledge that will help. Kiran trained you to be a proficient scout and hunter. You might be able to reason with Devana. You aren't just the best choice for this—you're the *only* choice."

The crackle and pop of the flames filled the heavy silence. After nearly a minute, Reigh sat back and breathed a deep, defeated exhale. "Fine," he relented. "I'll look for Devana. But I can't do this by myself, you know. I don't have Noh running point for me anymore."

"I know," Jenna agreed, her gaze shifting to me.

Jaevid stared at me, too.

Oh ... oh no.

I stiffened. "B-But I'm just a stable hand! I don't know how to—" I began to protest.

"Yes, you are a stable hand," Jaevid interjected. "But this moment, right now, is your chance to change that. You were chosen by a dragon, and by law, that permits you to enter the ranks of the dragonriders. You have a chance to make a difference. You can help your queen and your kingdom. So, the question is now, what do *you* intend to do with that opportunity?"

My thoughts raced, whipping around in my head like leaves in a hurricane. Once again, Jaevid Broadfeather was asking questions I didn't have the answers to. On the one hand, I wasn't a soldier—I wasn't even a fighter. But on the other hand, Fornax needed me. He trusted me. If I stayed here, working as a servant, I didn't know what would happen to him. I didn't have the money to take care of him, and I didn't know how long he'd be able to stay at the Deck on charity.

Besides, that wasn't any kind of life for him. He needed to get back out into the world and learn to be a proper dragon again, either in the wild or in the dragonrider ranks.

"What, it's not enough to send me off on a potential suicide mission looking for someone with unknown magical abilities armed with nothing but my winning smile? You gotta drop this in my lap, too? You said it yourself, it's not like I can use my power anymore, Jae." Reigh flashed me an irritated glance. "I'm not interested in babysitting a tourist and his useless blind dragon."

Anger flared in my gut, sparking out of nowhere and rising in my throat before I could stop it. "I'm not a tourist," I snapped back. "And Fornax may be blind, but he's not useless."

Reigh narrowed his eyes. "You've flown together *once*. Which, by the way, amounted to him dragging you around by the legs while crashing into every bell tower in the city."

"I know that!" I shouted, snapping to my feet. My hands curled into fists as I glared down at him, pulse thrashing in my ears. "I know I'm not a warrior. And I'm probably an idiot, too. My family's gone, my home is gone, and I don't even own the clothes I'm wearing. But Fornax is all I have, and he chose me. He thinks I'm worth something. I need ... I need to figure out if he's right."

Still reclined on the sofa, Jaevid stared at me with his pale, glacier-colored eyes catching in the light of the hearth. "Well, then." His smile was cryptic. "I suppose you'll need a patron."

"No." Reigh snorted and rolled his eyes. "He'll need a miracle."

14
CHAPTER FOURTEEN

"You did *what*?" Murdoc's head popped off his pillow to glower at me from across the bunkroom.

"I took their offer. I'm going with Reigh. We leave in three weeks. Jaevid needed some time to get our gear together, so—"

A shoe whizzed past my head, smacking against the far wall and leaving a dent.

"Are you completely brain-dead?" Murdoc snarled, brandishing his other shoe like a weapon. "You can't even fire a crossbow. You can barely run without tripping over your own feet. But you want to go riding off into battle against some Tibran witch?"

I ducked as the second shoe hurtled over my shoulder, missing my face by an inch. "It's not a battle, Murdoc! We're just looking for her. We don't even know if she'll want to fight us or not. She might come peacefully."

"Tibrans *DO NOT* come peacefully, you idiot!" he fumed.

"Look, I know it seems bad but ... Jaevid said he'd start helping me learn to fight. And the Gray elves trained Reigh. He was the queen's honored scout in Luntharda, so he's a master with a blade. He has a dragon, too. It's okay, I'll be fine."

"You'll be dead!" He stormed across the room to grab a fistful of my shirt and jerk me up onto my toes. His earth toned eyes glittered with wrath as he mashed his lips together, as though he were having to physically restrain himself from throttling me. "Being chosen by a dragon doesn't instantly gift you with the ability to wield a blade or any weapon, for that matter. Dragonriders undergo years of brutal training. Not to mention, you have about as much ferocity as an overcooked noodle. You are talking about stepping into the path of someone who will *kill* you."

"I know." My tone didn't sound nearly as certain and defiant as I'd hoped. More like someone had stepped on a mouse.

His tone was almost as unsettling as his expression as he leaned in to whisper, "So please explain to me, if you can, how this is a good idea."

"W-Well, I was sort of hoping you might help me, too."

Murdoc blinked. "What?"

"You're good with a blade, right? Couldn't you teach me?"

"You want me to teach you the intricacies of bladed combat in three weeks?"

"Um, well, maybe not all of it. Just the basics?"

Murdoc dropped me like a newborn foal. I hit the floor on my rump with a *thud*. "You're an idiot," he growled under his breath as he went to retrieve his shoes.

Getting back to my feet, I dusted myself off and watched him angrily slamming his boots back down at the foot of his bunk. "Or you could come with me!"

He paused, his shoulders tensing. "And why would I do that?"

I didn't have a good answer. The longer I thought about it, the dumber the idea sounded. Why would he want to tag along on this mission? According to him, we weren't even friends, so basically it was like asking him to babysit me.

"I ... I don't know," I finally admitted under my breath. He was right. I was being an idiot. But I couldn't shake the feeling—the sense that I was meant to do this. And more than that, I *wanted* to do it. I didn't want to be the guy people felt sorry for. I'd only survived in Thornbend because Murdoc took pity on me. I only had a job and a place to sleep now because Queen Jenna and Prince Aubren felt sorry for me, too. I didn't want that to be my life's only legacy. I wanted to be able to stand on my own. To fend for myself. To be someone worthwhile. I couldn't do that if I kept relying on Murdoc to be there in case everything went wrong.

Unfortunately, I didn't know how to tell him any of that. And I wasn't sure he'd even care.

Leaving Murdoc behind, I stormed out of the men's bunks in the servant quarters without saying anything else. I wandered back through the stable and out into the open royal grounds. The cool evening air tingled over my flushed face and neck as I let out a heavy sigh. Autumn already had the kingdom of Maldobar firmly in its grip. Soon, frost and snow would dust the open plains like a sheet of sparkling white. It hadn't snowed all that much in Thornbend. I wondered if I would see a lot of snow this year.

Before I knew where I was going, I looked up and realized I'd wandered all the way out to the Deck. Fornax was probably asleep. Even so, I wanted to see him. Maybe ask him if he was sure he really wanted me as his rider. This was his chance to reconsider. Someone like Murdoc would have been a much better choice. At least he already knew how to fight.

A commotion echoed down the curved hall to my left. Rounding the corner, I noticed the door to the tack room was cracked open. Warm light spilled out into the dark, cold hallway. Was someone messing around in there? At this hour? Most of the servants had finished their shifts hours ago and were getting ready to go to bed. Who else would be out here this late?

Creeping toward the open door, I held my breath and dared to lean around and peek inside.

I ALMOST DIDN'T SEE her.

She was crouching down in front of one of the saddle stands, leaning all around it and scribbling in a small notebook. I noticed her hair first. It was a riot of fluffy, ginger-colored curls that hung all the way down to the base of her back. Those wild curls swished and bounced when she moved, catching the light from the candelabra nearby like spools of copper. She wore a plain, teal blue dress and a long leather-working apron that looked as though it had been tied up in every possible way to fit her tiny frame without dragging the ground.

When she turned around, she immediately froze in place. Her big, periwinkle-blue eyes widened. The odd-looking quill she'd been holding in her lips rolled out as her mouth opened in surprise.

I froze, too. Heat rose in my cheeks and blazed all the way down to the center of my chest. Suddenly, my shirt collar felt too tight. I'd never been good at talking to pretty girls. I could have sworn it was like they enjoyed watching me squirm and choke on myself whenever I tried. Not fair.

"Oh, I'm so sorry, I didn't realize anyone else was still here," she blurted quickly, ducking to chase down her quill as it rolled away across the floor. "I won't be long, I promise. I just have to get a few more measurements and sketches of the handle mechanisms. Are you here to lock up?"

I tried to talk. My mouth moved, but nothing would come out. Oh gods. What was happening? *Talk, stupid! Use your words!*

"Is everything okay?" She stood up again, those chaotic curls framing her small, heart-shaped face. It was difficult to tell how old she was. She was tiny, not an inch over five feet, and so petite she made even me seem like a big guy. But her delicate features were a little too mature for her to be any younger than fifteen or so.

"No—yeah, um, it's fine. I wasn't, I mean you're not bothering me," I choked and stammered like a complete idiot. Crap. Why couldn't I say just one intelligent thing at times like this?

Her whole face brightened with a broad smile. "Are you one of the stable workers?" She tipped her head to the side slightly, making all those pretty red curls swish around her.

"No. I mean, I was, but not now." I cleared my throat and stood a bit straighter. "I'm going to be a dragonrider." That wasn't a lie, right? I was, eventually. Hopefully.

Okay, so I hadn't exactly thought it through. And if Murdoc was right, I probably wasn't dragonrider material anyway.

"Oh, I see." She sounded impressed. "You're very lucky, then. They're magnificent animals. It's been exhilarating to observe them in such close proximity. They demonstrate intelligence that far surpasses any other species I've studied before. Truly impressive." She stopped suddenly, drawing back slightly and curling her shoulders up. "I-I apologize. I ramble sometimes. I don't get out much. I work—a lot. And when I start on a new project like this, I tend to get hyper focused. Sometimes, I forget to eat or sleep for days. Then I fall asleep at my desk, or in the middle of reading, or making notes, and I'll wake up with blotches all over my face because the ink hasn't dried yet. Once, I—" She stopped short and cowered again, dipping her head with an embarrassed little grin. "Sorry. I did it again."

I couldn't stop myself from smiling back at her as I stepped into the room. "It's okay. I don't mind."

Her slender brows shot up as though she were genuinely surprised. "Really? Most people find it ... annoying. Or they just stop listening, but they keep smiling and nodding, you know, to make it seem like they're still paying attention. You can tell they're not, though. Their eyes get all glazed and it's like they're silently wishing you'd just shut up—" She halted again. "Sorry."

"Don't be. My name's Thatcher." I stretched out a hand toward her. "You can call me Thatch, if you want."

She beamed. Standing that close, I could see the faint dusting of hundreds of tiny freckles that dotted every inch of her fair skin. She slipped her small, dainty hand into mine and shook it. "Phoebe. It's a pleasure to meet you, Thatch. So which dragon is yours?"

"Oh, good. You two already know one another," a deep voice suddenly spoke from the doorway.

I cringed, whipping around to find Jaevid leaning in with a bemused grin glinting in his frosty colored eyes. Until tonight, he'd always been sporting some manner of dragonrider armor. Now, all he wore was a plain, black tunic with a little gold trim, dark gray pants, and tall leather boots that matched the bracers on his forearms. A white, bone-carved necklace hung around his neck on a woven cord. The design looked like something crafted by the Gray elves, with intricate details etched into the pearly white surface. I wasn't used to seeing him dressed so informally. Somehow, it made him seem younger—like he might be in his early twenties.

Heat crept into my face as he cast me a knowing look and tipped his head toward Phoebe. "Clever, isn't she?"

"I-I, uh ..." My brain scrambled as I glanced back and forth between them. I honestly didn't know. We'd only just met. "I guess so?"

"Phoebe is an artificer. One of the finest this kingdom has ever seen. She's in charge of making your new saddle," Jaevid explained.

"Oh." I looked back to find her beaming up at me again, eyes as wide as saucers.

"You mean, it's *you*?" she gasped. "You're the one the blind dragon chose?"

"I ... um ... well, yes."

She squealed with delight, bouncing up onto her toes and clenching her fists under her chin. "Why didn't you say something sooner? That's incredible! I'm *so* excited to work with the two of you! I've never made a dragon saddle before, but I promise I'll work extra hard to make a very special saddle that you'll love!"

I couldn't reply. Not while she was grinning and gawking at me like that. My face burned, and all I managed was a stiff little nod. It was embarrassing to have anyone stare at me like that, but when it was a girl, it was a thousand times worse.

"As long as we're all here, we should talk about designs and get his measurements." Jaevid chuckled.

"Right!" Phoebe agreed, producing a spool of measuring tape from one of the pockets of her apron and holding it up proudly. "Don't worry, Thatch. I know this won't be easy, but I promise I will make you a saddle that will allow you to communicate with your dragon just as well as any other rider. It'll take some practice, but if everything goes according to my schematics, then this saddle will allow you to be his eyes."

"You ... you really believe we'll be able to fly like the other dragonriders?"

"That's our hope," Jaevid added with a sigh. "But she's right, it will take a *lot* of practice. The dragonrider code demands that anyone chosen by a dragon be given the opportunity to become one of our brotherhood—but it doesn't guarantee anything more than that chance. You'll still have to complete the same training as any other rider. It's not easy, even for dragons with sight and young men who have trained from childhood to handle a blade. I barely survived it, myself."

My stomach sank and my shoulders drooped. Jaevid Broadfeather, the legendary war hero, had barely survived dragonrider training? Great. I stood no chance, then.

He seemed to notice my deflated hopes and dreams. "Don't lose spirit just yet." He gave my shoulder a consoling pat. "You're still too young to start official dragonrider training. Most incoming fledglings start at eighteen. And this mission with Reigh will be an excellent time to build your bond with Fornax and learn some basic swordplay."

Wow. He really was counting on this being a non-violent retrieval mission, after all. Somehow, hearing that made me a little more confident. If this was just to get some flying experience, then maybe I didn't need Murdoc's help after all.

Phoebe nodded in agreement. "Exactly! You've already laid down a good foundation of trust with your dragon. Now, you just need to hone it. And that's where *I* come in!"

CHAPTER FIFTEEN

Three weeks—according to Jaevid and Queen Jenna, that was how long it would take to get everything ready to begin our search for Devana. We had to wait for an informant from the Gray elf spy network to give us a place to start searching, and there were a lot of important details to be sorted out before we could begin. Not to mention, I had a lot of work to do learning some basic combat moves and how to fly with a dragon.

I swallowed hard, standing in the royal garden right outside the Deck while Jaevid said his farewells to Prince Reigh. Checking over the saddle straps and bags fixed to the back of a sleek, lime green dragoness, Reigh shouted back at me, warning me not to try anything dumb while he was gone since he was the only half-decent medic in the kingdom. His dragoness snapped her jaws in agreement, swishing her long tail and flexing broad, leathery wings. Somehow, I got the feeling she wasn't thrilled that I was going to be tagging along on their quest, either.

"Say hello to Kiran and Enyo for me," Jaevid called as Reigh climbed into his saddle. "Jace and Araxie, too, if you see them."

"Are you kidding me? The word's out now. I can't walk a block in Luntharda without being harassed by people trying to give me stuff," Reigh grumbled as he crammed his riding helmet down over his head and buckled himself into his saddle. "Kiran is inches from a nervous breakdown because of it. I keep expecting him to banish me to live in the palace."

A wry, knowing grin curled up Jaevid's face as he stood back to give them space to take off. "Don't fall for that act. He's so proud of you that he can barely stand it."

Reigh barked a laugh that echoed from under his helmet and gave Jaevid a thumb's up, then leaned down against his dragon's neck. With a thundering roar and a rush of wind off powerful wings, Reigh was gone—making steam toward the wild jungle of Luntharda. He wouldn't be back until it was time for us to leave on our hunt for Devana.

"So, Prince Reigh is from Luntharda?" I dared to ask as Jaevid walked back toward me. "But he's human? And I thought he was a Prince of Maldobar?"

He gave a heavy, exhausted sigh and combed a hand through his shaggy, ash-gray hair. "Well, that's ... sort of a long story. The short version is, yes, Reigh is a Prince of Maldobar. He is Queen Jenna's youngest brother, but he wasn't raised here. He grew up in Luntharda among the Gray elves."

"But why? I didn't even know there was another prince besides Aubren."

"No one did," he replied. "Not even Reigh. It was kept a secret from everyone because of his birthright."

A secret birthright? Geez, I hadn't heard about any of this. Not surprising, really. I was a nobody from nowhere and by the sound of it, these were the secrets and scandals of royals. Not exactly any of my business, right?

I guess my bewilderment was obvious because Jaevid paused, his glacier-eyed stare boring into me for an uncomfortable moment. "What do you know about me, Thatch?"

Oh gods. Why did this feel like a test? I was awful at tests. "Um, well, everyone thought you were dead. You, um, you were the hero of the Gray War forty years ago. You're a halfbreed, but they let you become a dragonrider even though it was against the law back then. And you wound up battling ancient gods and basically saving the world, right?"

His piercing gaze softened, and he laughed under his breath. "I didn't battle gods. Is that really what they're saying?"

My face burned as I ducked my head. "I, uh, well, yes."

He muttered something I couldn't understand and shook his head. "I suppose it doesn't matter what happened back then—not right now. That's a story for a different time. What you need to understand, Thatch, is that up until a few months ago, Reigh and I were the hosts of two ancient gods. I was the chosen one of Paligno, the god of living things, and Reigh was chosen by Clysiros, the goddess of death and decay. That's how it had been for as long as anyone can remember, honestly. The gods were unable to physically manifest in this world, so their essence was contained within two artifacts and normal, mortal people like Reigh and me were selected to guard them and wield some of that god's power."

I tried to process that without bleeding from the ears. No one talked about the old gods much anymore. Their stories had become nothing but ancient myth—so distant that no one took them seriously.

"This was meant to create a balance between the forces of life and death within the mortal world," he continued. "But the problem was that it was far too easy for incredible divine power to fall into the wrong hands. Men filled with malice and greed, like Argonox, came searching for it. They killed many innocent people trying to claim it for themselves. That was why Reigh was sent away in secret to Luntharda as an infant—it was the royal family's hope that he would be protected there and that no one would try to force him to use his power for evil purposes. It worked, but only for a while. When the Tibrans came here, it became clear things would have to change."

Gesturing for me to follow, Jaevid started for the broad, open doorway of the Deck. I fell in step beside him as we passed through the cavernous front entry. "I had to make a bargain with the old gods," he continued. "I had to strike a new balance to make it safer for everyone."

"What was the bargain?" I asked before I could stop myself.

"First, like I mentioned before, Reigh and I surrendered all the divine power we'd been given. Neither of us serves the gods anymore. Not like that, anyway."

"But I thought you said that's how things were kept in balance?"

"It was. Now, however, the gods themselves have returned to the mortal realm. They can walk among us as they did at the dawn of time."

Chills crept up my spine, making my pulse skip and race. "Isn't that dangerous?"

He gave a shrug as he stopped in front of the round, open courtyard in the center of the Deck. "Maybe. Time will tell. At least this way, we won't have to worry about anyone stealing and abusing divine artifacts ... or the people bound to them. Reigh suffered a great deal at the hands of the Tibran Empire. He was tortured and forced to use his power for despicable things."

I hesitated, stumbling to a halt. "Why are you telling me all this?"

Jaevid didn't answer right away. He stood with his back turned, hands in fists at his sides as though he were searching for the right words. "Because Jenna and I are asking a *lot* of him by sending him to hunt down Devana, probably more than we should be. And I honestly don't know if he's up to it. This will most likely bring back a lot of bad memories for him." He fell silent for a moment, keeping his back turned like he wanted to avoid my gaze. "He doesn't want to go, and he's well within his right to refuse. If this gets hard for him, or if you notice him struggling, please ... try to help. Think of it as a favor to me. I'll owe you one."

I scratched at the back of my neck and stared down at the toes of my boots. "Okay, but you don't have to owe me anything. Really, I'm just happy to help. And, you know, to not be living on the streets or still stuck in that prison camp."

A heavy, warm hand landed on my shoulder. Lifting my gaze, I met Jaevid's relieved smile as he gave my shoulder a light squeeze. "You have a good heart, Thatch; I could tell it the first time we met right here in the Deck. That's why Fornax decided to trust you."

For a moment, with the great Jaevid Broadfeather looking at me like that—like I was someone he truly believed in—I almost believed I could actually pull this off. I could be a dragonrider. I could prove myself and maybe even honor my father's memory. I could make him proud.

Too bad it didn't last.

My mouth scrunched and my stomach squirmed. "But, Jaevid, I'm not like you guys. I'm not a fighter. I don't want to hurt anyone. I've never even handled a blade. And this one time, when I was about ten, I got beat up by a girl who lived down the street, and all the guys in my neighborhood made fun of me for months, even though my father told me I should never raise a hand to strike a girl even if she—"

"Thatcher," Jaevid warned. His tone had taken a sharp edge of seriousness.

I snapped my mouth shut and straightened.

"Being a dragonrider doesn't mean you like fighting or that you enjoy hurting people. In fact, it's the opposite of that. We fight so that others don't have to. We carry that burden for them. We're warriors, yes. However, we are guardians—first and always. We protect each other and the people of Maldobar. That's what the dragonrider brotherhood is built upon. That's what you would be a part of. Fornax has already decided that you're worthy of that honor, but you have to decide for yourself if that's the life you want."

My stomach clenched as my brain struggled to process all that. Being a guardian didn't sound so bad, honestly. But I still wasn't sure I was really cut out for that. Fornax couldn't even see me—how could he possibly know if I was the right person for this? What if we couldn't work out a way to fly together? What if I lost my nerve at the wrong moment and someone got hurt because I didn't—

"Where's your whistle? The one you've been using with Fornax?" Jaevid asked suddenly.

Reaching into my pocket, I pulled out the slender brass whistle and held it out for him to see.

Without a word, Jaevid swiped the whistle from my palm. Then he took the strange, elven-styled necklace from around his neck and threaded the whistle onto the woven resin cord. It hung right next to the white, bone-carved pendant as he held the necklace out to me. "Here."

"B-But that's, I mean, isn't that necklace something the Gray elves made? Isn't it special to you?"

A hint of sadness flashed over his features as he stared down at the pendant. "It was a gift from my mother a long time ago. Wearing it always made me feel closer to her, like I wasn't alone in the world. It kept me going until I was able to make a family and a life of my own. Now that I have, it's ... become more of a sad reminder of what I lost. But years ago, it did make me feel braver. Perhaps it'll do the same for you. Consider it a gift of good faith."

I eyed the necklace, watching the sunlight glint off the polished white pendant. It wasn't much bigger than my thumb and had been shaped into a sleek pointed oval with a twist on one end. The tiny etchings on its surface made swirling designs and spelled out words in the elven language that I couldn't read.

Slowly, I reached out and took it from Jaevid's hand. "Thank you."

He smiled, although there was still a hint of sorrow in his pale eyes as I put it around my neck. "If you ever begin to question whether or not you have a place among the dragonriders, look at it. Remember your dragon believes that you do ... and so do I."

MY HEARTBEAT THUNDERED in my ears. Sweat dripped from my brow, stinging my eyes as I raised the tip of the blunted practice sword and sank into a defensive stance. My palms ached, making my grip on my sword clumsier than usual. They were so tender from where the hilt had bruised my skin from day after day of practice that I'd spent the last three nights sleeping with hunks of ice wrapped in a thin cloth in my hands.

Across the sparring circle, my opponent narrowed his eyes. They shone like two icy stars in the dim light. With his mouth set in a hard line, he spun his long, curved scimitar over his hand with effortless speed I could only envy.

Murdoc didn't even want to try to teach me the basics of combat. Jaevid, however, was relentless. He waited for me every morning so we could begin running drills—set after set of strikes, parries, and spinning attacks with several different kinds of weapons. He let me try a scimitar, a halberd, a big two-handed longsword, and finally a regular straight-bladed sword like the infantry soldiers used. Of them all, it felt the least awkward, although not by much.

We spent the days drilling, working on hand-to-hand and weapon-based combat techniques. He claimed he was only showing me the fundamentals of each. It didn't feel like it, though. My brain scrambled to remember where to put my feet, when to swing, how to move, and the names of each maneuver. I ached from pushups and sit-ups—which Jaevid insisted needed to become a part of my daily routine.

"You need to work on building your strength," he'd insisted as he wrapped my tender hands in bandaging to help with the bruises. "And eventually, before you begin formal training, you'll need to take up running. Three miles a day, at least. Start off without armor, then work your way up to full battle gear."

So I tried. I didn't make it half a mile before I collapsed into a sweating, wheezing heap outside the Deck. Fortunately, I'd fallen in the shade of a tree, hidden by a few large bushes, so no one could see me as I lay there and suffered quietly for a few minutes.

After a week, I began to understand why my request had made Murdoc so angry. He was so good with a blade—he'd probably spent most of his life learning this stuff, honing every skill, and sculpting every muscle until he was the perfect killing machine. Asking him to somehow transfer all those years of knowledge into my mushy, useless body had probably sounded like an insult to him. I also realized I was either going to finally start improving ... or die.

Probably die.

"Don't stop moving, boy! And don't lock your knees!"

I shot a glare over my shoulder at the grim-faced man Jaevid had asked to help with my three weeks of basic combat training. He came around every few days, barking orders and growling curses under his breath as he watched me flail through all my drills.

Something about him was strangely familiar—I just couldn't figure out why. It wasn't his face. His dark skin, pitch-black hair, and vibrant, golden eyes were foreign in Maldobar. Maybe I wasn't the brightest guy in Halfax, but even I recognized that much.

Across the sparring circle, Jaevid paced the inner perimeter like a powerful jungle cat. Every movement was smooth and calculated, his scimitar raised and poised to strike. He darted in fast, swinging wide into an attack he'd used before.

I raised my sword to deflect, teeth clenched as I cringed and waited for our blades to clash. My arm shook as pain shot through my hand, flaring up around every tender place where my flesh was bruised. At the last second, my eyes pinched shut, and every muscle flinched up solid, bracing for contact.

It never happened.

I dared to crack open one eye. Still cringing, I squinted up to find Jaevid standing right before me, his mouth skewed with exasperation and the blade of his scimitar about two inches from my nose.

Crap.

"Gods, Fates, and all things divine!" the golden-eyed man roared in frustration. He growled curses in some foreign tongue as he stomped over and gave me a punishing smack over the back of the head. "Quit flinching up like that! Are you thick in the head? You don't shut your eyes during a fight—not unless you *want* to die, that is!"

Jaevid sighed and shook his head, stepping away to slip his scimitar back into the sheath at his hip. "You can't fight what you can't see."

"I know," I murmured. "I'm sorry. I can't help it."

"Reset. Let's do it again," the man grumbled. He halted only a few paces away, just long enough to cast another glare of warning in my direction. "And so help me, if you do it again, I will glue your eyes open."

"I have glue. I just made a fresh batch this morning," Phoebe offered from where she worked nearby, tweaking my saddle and watching us practice. Queen Jenna had given her a large section of the undercrofts to use as a workshop. The cavernous place was lit with hundreds of torches and seemed to go on for miles underneath the castle foundation. With high ceilings and lots of wide-open space, it also made a pretty decent place to practice swordplay.

I was just glad there was no one else down here to watch me make an idiot of myself. It was bad enough to have Phoebe observing this pathetic charade. My stomach soured at the idea of what Murdoc might say if he witnessed any of it.

"Haldor, I think he's had enough. Maybe we should call it a day." Jaevid rubbed his chin, his gaze drifting toward Phoebe with a thoughtful glint.

"Maybe we should call it finished altogether. This boy has no fight in him at all. Unless you'd like to set him up against a squirrel or a stuffed animal, I don't think he'll ever—"

"That's enough." Jaevid's tone cracked off the stone walls of the undercrofts like the bite of a whip.

Haldor's mouth snapped shut. His keen eyes shimmered like an eagle on the hunt, considering me for another second or two before he bobbed his head. "Fine." He combed his fingers through his shoulder-length hair with a ragged sigh. "My apologies. I should take my leave. It's getting late, and I've still got a meeting with Her Majesty and the High Commander. The southern coastline is a mess. Southwatch is still in shambles; I'm at my wit's end with the Merchants' Union. They expect me to be lenient and let their price-gouging slide."

"Because of your family's business?" Jaevid guessed, genuine concern crinkling his forehead as he studied the older man.

Haldor nodded, pinching the bridge of his nose right between his eyes. I'd already guessed he was a dragonrider. After all, he wore their signature blue and white cloak fastened to the pauldrons of his decorative armor. It wasn't the same kind of armor they wore in battle. With only a breastplate, vambraces, pauldrons, and greaves, it seemed a lot thinner and lighter than the battle armor I'd seen other dragonriders wear around the castle grounds. The silver metal was polished till it shone like a mirror in the torchlight, and it was covered in extremely detailed engravings of serpents. Maybe it was only for special occasions.

"My father wants me to retire and take over the fleet," he muttered. "Why, by all the gods, he won't just pass it to my sister, I cannot even begin to understand."

"You mean, you're a dragonrider *and* the heir to a merchant family?" I wondered if that was why he looked so different—if his family were merchants from another kingdom.

"One of the finest," Jaevid answered for him, a knowing grin on his face. "He's the Southern Sky General in charge of all the dragonriders and watches south of Halfax."

"Hah! Flattery will get you nowhere, Broadfeather," Haldor barked and turned away. "Call me whatever you like, I'm fully aware of the monumental catastrophe I've just been handed like it's supposed to be an honor. Rebuilding the watches, moving the dragonriders in, managing the merchants to resupply and restore commerce—not to mention weeding out the occasional Tibran fanatic—all while trying to put the port cities back into full operation. It's like trying to shovel snow with a spoon in a blizzard."

Jaevid chuckled and gave him an appreciative nod. "And you're doing a marvelous job at it."

Haldor rolled his eyes, waving a hand dismissively at us before he turned to leave. "Admit it, you're just glad it isn't you. At any rate, I've got to return to Saltmarsh in the morning. I won't be able to come back for a week or so. You'll have to find someone else to yell at the boy until then. Perhaps Her Majesty would enjoy a turn. I understand this is partially her fault."

"Only partially." Jaevid laughed softly under his breath. "I appreciate you lending us some of your time."

He didn't reply. At least, not until he was nearly to the large, rounded doorway leading into a steep stairwell that wound back up into the castle. Haldor glanced over his glittering pauldrons and narrowed his golden gaze upon me one last time. "You're the same boy I found in Thornbend, aren't you?"

My lungs seized and I choked out loud. *That* was where I'd seen him before! He was the dragonrider who had found Murdoc and me while we were trying to escape the city. Now that he was wearing different armor and not seated on the back of an enormous, snarling dragon, only his voice and strange eyes had struck a chord in my memory. There was no mistaking them now, though.

I nodded shakily. "I-I ... uh, yes. I am."

One corner of his mouth turned up in a half-smirk. "Then you weren't a Tibran, after all. What about the other kid? Is he dead?"

"No, Murdoc is fine. He, uh, he works in the stables now. We both do, er, did. I guess I don't anymore."

"Interesting." Haldor arched an eyebrow. "Is he some relation to you?"

"No. He's my friend," I admitted, fighting back a sheepish look. I had lied about Murdoc's connection in the past—unsuccessfully, of course. But the truth was out. They knew Murdoc wasn't my cousin, even if he'd begun using my last name. What they didn't know was that Murdoc had originally intended to kill me, and I'd sworn to myself I wouldn't tell anyone about that. Not even Jaevid. It didn't matter now.

"Well, keep practicing," Haldor said at last. "When I come back, I want to see improvement. And no more cringing or shutting your eyes during a fight. I mean it. Dragonriders *never* flinch, boy. We stare death in the eye and dare it to come for us."

I straightened and gave him what I hoped was a convincingly serious expression. "Yes, sir. I'll do my best."

16
CHAPTER SIXTEEN

The days passed in a long, painful, exhausting blur. If I wasn't working in the stables alongside Murdoc, then I was training with Jaevid or testing the saddle Phoebe was working on for Fornax. According to Jaevid, having Fornax's old saddle was a stroke of luck. It meant Phoebe didn't have to start from scratch by making a wax mold of Fornax's back to make sure it fit properly. All dragon saddles fit basically the same, sliding into place against their spines in the spot right between the base of their neck and the shoulders of their wing arms. He said that was the most stable place to be during flight.

Jaevid seemed to know a lot about making saddles, so he and Phoebe talked a lot about the design as she drew up her plans. According to them, Fornax should already know the basic steering commands commonly used by dragonriders in combat—which was good.

The problem, as usual, was me. I didn't know any of the commands. I was starting from scratch. Jaevid had spent the last few evenings with me sitting in his saddle while it was propped up on sawhorses, teaching me how to buckle myself in correctly and how to work the handles so I could memorize the basic commands: turning left or right, ascending or descending, and, of course, breathing flame.

There was a lot to remember, and that was the main reason my stomach felt like a sloshing, churning pit of muck as I stood before Jaevid's huge, blue king drake. Mavrik was easily twice as large as any of the other dragons in the Deck. His long, curved black horns jutted from the back of his head, matching the spines that ran down his back, barbed the backs of his legs, and studded the sides of his head like jagged shards of obsidian. He eyed me with what I could only assume was curiosity and gave an unimpressed snort.

I tried not to take that personally.

"You'll be riding in front." Jaevid climbed down from where he'd been adjusting the special extra seat that fit onto the back of his regular saddle. Apparently, it was something new Phoebe had whipped up upon his request. It clipped into place with three big metal buckles and an additional girth strap for stability so Mavrik could carry an extra rider safely.

Jaevid turned to me with a brow arched expectantly. "Ready?"

I bit back the urge to vomit. "S-Sure."

"What about the armor? How's the fit?" He stepped around me, inspecting the new armor he'd ordered piece by piece. He grabbed the front of the breastplate and gave it a swift, hard jerk, as though he were checking to see if I'd buckled it on properly.

I staggered, nearly falling over. "It's okay, I think."

"Too tight?" he questioned. "Move your arms. Does it restrict your swing?"

I waved my arms around, mimicking a few of the new steps and sword-swings he'd taught me earlier that week. The breastplate fit snugly, but not too tight. It hugged against my chest, covering from my collarbone down to the base of my ribs. I could sit up and move, twist, or bend over, and it wasn't all that heavy. Crafted from a single piece of bronze, the front had been adorned in a detailed design of Maldobar's royal seal—an eagle with its wings spread wide, gripping swords and spears in its claws.

"What about your helmet?"

I handed it over so Jaevid could inspect it. There wasn't anything especially unique about it, either. Dragonrider helmets were usually grand, and each one was different, crafted to suit the style and taste of the rider. Mine was plain, although it did have the slender glass window in the front of the visor. Jaevid had already explained that was so I could see out without having the wind in my eyes during flight—a handy detail you wouldn't find on infantry armor.

Slipping the helmet down over my head, I practiced opening and closing the visor, peering through the window, and buckling the chinstrap.

The only other pieces of armor I had now were two vambraces that strapped over a pair of elbow-length riding gauntlets. The palms of the gauntlets were coated with a thick layer of rough resin. According to Jaevid, this was to give me an extra firm grip on the saddle handles.

"It looks good. Well, good enough for training, anyway. You'll need something heavier when it comes time for battle outfitting. You'll have all new armor and gear made during your avian year of training," he said, crossing his arms with a nod of approval. "But this will get you by until then."

"Thank you," I managed, hoping I sounded less terrified with my helmet to muffle my voice. Jaevid had insisted on becoming my patron—meaning he was sponsoring my training. He would personally pay for all my outfitting until I graduated from the academy and made money on my own.

Knowing I was still surviving on grace and charity made my mouth scrunch like I'd bitten into a spicy pepper. Not that there was anything I could do about it, but my dad had always said I should never accept charity if I had a strong back and was able to work to earn a living honestly. Armor was expensive, though. Weapons were, too. Dragon saddles probably cost more than my own life was worth. And paying for a bunk in the servant's quarters within the castle already absorbed my salary almost entirely.

"I, um, I really appreciate you doing all of this for me." I stumbled over my words, too embarrassed to look him in the eye. "I promise I'll pay you back for all of this as soon as I can."

Something almost nostalgic sparkled in his pale eyes as I stole a glance up at his gentle smile. "Work hard, honor your bond with your dragon, and stay loyal to your dragonrider brothers—that is the only payment I want back from you. Understand?"

I gulped against the hard knot of embarrassment still throbbing in the back of my throat. "Yes, sir."

He pointed to the front seat of Mavrik's saddle. "Good. Now, get up there."

My hands shook as I wobbled toward the huge scaly blue beast like a newborn fawn. Since I was shorter than Jaevid, I needed an extra boost to get up onto the dragon's back. It took a minute or two to get myself situated with my legs, boots and all, secured down inside the deep pockets on either side of the saddle.

"Repeat the commands out loud," Jaevid ordered as he slid his own helmet down over his head.

I sucked in a shaky breath and opened my mouth to begin. Before I could even get a word out, Mavrik's body rippled underneath me, making me acutely aware of the sheer size and strength of the dragon I was straddling. I gripped the saddle handles with all my strength, terror turning every muscle to quivering mush.

Suddenly, the huge dragon's black leathery wings flared open wide. He let out a thundering roar of defiance and sprang skyward, leaving Jaevid—shouting and flailing his arms in frantic desperation—behind on the ground far below.

THIS WASN'T SUPPOSED to happen.

Jaevid and I were supposed to be riding together so he could make sure I got the commands right. This was my first real, actual flight on a dragon ever.

I was *not* supposed to be doing it alone.

But as Mavrik made steam, blitzing higher and higher into the cloud-covered sky, I couldn't do anything except hang on for dear life. The earth fell away, every building and person nothing more than a speck dotting Maldobar's weathered landscape far below.

I squeezed my eyes shut and hugged the dragon's scaly neck with all my might. I couldn't even feel my own heart beating anymore. Die. I was going to die.

And for what? Why? Why was Mavrik doing this? How did I get him to land? What was the command for descending? Gods, I couldn't remember any of them now.

We burst through the clouds, sending swirls of glittering white mist in every direction. As Mavrik finally leveled off, I got a good view of the ground ... thousands of feet below. The earth slid by slowly beneath a loose patchwork of fluffy clouds. Sunlight filled the clear air above, revealing a sky of endless, perfect blue, and the cold air squeezed at my lungs with every rasping, panicked breath.

"W-Why are you doing this to me?" I shouted up to the beast.

He tilted his massive, horned head to shoot me an annoyed glare with those vivid yellow eyes.

"Jaevid is going to be really angry, you know."

Mavrik snorted like that wasn't a threat he was worried about at all.

"I-I can't do this," I wheezed through chattering teeth. "P-Please ... let's go back. I'm begging you. I-I'm not ready for this. I ... I think I'm gonna vomit."

The king drake snapped his jaws in defiance and veered sharply to the left, slinging me against the restraints of the saddle. I screamed and fell back against his neck, clinging for dear life like a scared baby squirrel. Hugging his body like that, however, made me realize something—I could feel every time he beat his wings. There was a rhythm to his flight; a definite pattern to the way his muscles tensed, rolled, flexed, and flowed. It reminded me of learning the gait of a horse. The more I fought that rhythm, the rougher and more terrifying the flight was.

I had to stop fighting it—I had to move my body in complement to that cadence.

Pushing shakily away from Mavrik's neck, I slipped my hands back onto the saddle handles and tried to sit the way Jaevid had showed me. I flexed my legs against the boot sheaths, using that leverage to balance myself and lean into the steep turns. It was much more natural, as though we were two parts of the same powerful creature.

I couldn't fight the smile that tugged at my lips.

Okay, this was *way* better than riding a horse. This was ... absolutely incredible.

Little by little, I got braver. I turned the right saddle handle. Mavrik responded immediately, arching his back and tail to angle his wings into a right turn. A twist of the left one, and he veered in that direction. If I twisted both handles inward, the dragon snapped his wings in close to his body and dropped into a steep descent. Turning them outward made him pump his powerful shoulders harder, breaking upward into a sharp ascent.

There was just one command left to try.

Clenching my teeth, I twisted both handles inward with two, sharp jerks. Mavrik's small ears slicked back. His sides swelled, pressing against my legs as he drew in a deep breath. His maw opened, and he spat an explosive plume of his burning venom into the sky. It burned white-hot, filling the air with an acrid smell. My pulse thundered in my ears, chest swelling at the sight of that raw, primal power.

It was like waking up after a lifetime of sleeping.

In that saddle, moving in unison with a dragon's rhythmic flight—feeling his power as my own—I was truly alive for the first time.

I had no idea how long we'd been flying when Mavrik and I finally landed back at the Deck. He curled his huge body gracefully, his leathery wing membranes spread to catch the wind and soften our descent. He touched down as elegantly as a swan landing on the surface of a pond. For a moment, all I could do was sit there, my pulse booming and my breath coming in frantic wheezing puffs.

"Of all the stupid, idiotic, reckless creatures crawling on this soggy earth, Mavrik, you are the *worst!*" Jaevid shouted as he ran out to meet us, flinging his helmet aside. His face had turned an alarming shade of beet red and his lips curled back into a furious snarl.

Mavrik gave an indignant snap of his jaws as he flattened out on the grass, twitching his tail and looking away in complete defiance to his rider's scolding.

"What did you do to him? You better not have been doing barrel rolls up there. Look at me when I'm talking to you, Mavrik—I mean it! He's not ready for those maneuvers! Gods, is he even conscious?" Jaevid scrambled up onto Mavrik's back, making his way toward me with genuine concern crinkling his brow. "Thatcher? Are you alright? Can you hear me?"

My hands shook as Jaevid pried them off the handles, finger by finger.

"It's all right. You're safe now." He spoke softly as he unbuckled my helmet and slid it off my head. "Let's get you down."

"Wait," I panted hoarsely. "A-Again."

Jaevid paused, blinking in confusion. "What?"

"I ... I want to do it again." I leaned back to meet his utterly dumbfounded stare, still trying to catch my breath. "Is that okay? Can I go again?"

His mouth fell open, but no sound came out. After a few awkward seconds, he gave a slight nod. "I, uh, I suppose. If you're sure."

I was.

"I need my helmet back, please." I held out my hand.

He passed the helmet over, and I slid it down over my head, swiftly refastening the chinstrap. Then I gave him a nod and thumbs up. I was ready to fly again.

Jaevid grinned and shook his head as he climbed back down from Mavrik's back. "Just ... try not to overdo it on your first day. I don't want any vomit on my saddle."

17
CHAPTER SEVENTEEN

Riding Fornax was *not* going to be that easy or that simple—I knew that. With only a limited number of days left to prepare, I poured myself into learning to ride Mavrik as often as Jaevid would allow. He wanted to be present every time I buckled in, probably to make sure I didn't fasten something incorrectly and fall off during flight. A valid concern, given my experience level ... which was currently level zero. After all, I'd only been at this for a few days. I was bound to make a few stupid mistakes. Okay, maybe more than a few.

Jaevid stood by every time we flew, offering instructions or corrections after he'd watched us wheel around the castle grounds a few times. As the days passed, I got to know him better, and it became harder and harder to see him as the grand, heroic, epically powerful demigod hero of the Gray War like in the stories my father had told. Not that he wasn't a good person or a talented fighter. Jaevid was older than me, but he didn't look as old as he did in a lot of the sculptures and paintings I'd seen. He seemed to be about twenty at the most—which made absolutely no sense considering the Gray War had been *forty years* ago.

It took a little explaining from Jaevid for me to figure that one out. Apparently, he hadn't actually *died* at the end of the war like everyone thought. He'd been in a divine sleep, lying in wait until the right person came along to awaken him so he could fight for Maldobar once again. That person had been Reigh.

Physically, Jaevid hadn't aged much at all since the end of the Gray War, but he still had a weird air of quiet nobility about him. Sometimes he just stood there, arms crossed over his chest, and watched me with a faraway look in his eerily pale eyes—as though mentally he was a thousand miles away. I guess he had a lot on his mind these days.

According to Queen Jenna, Jaevid was going to be taking over as Commander of Blybrig Academy, the official training school for dragonriders. He'd start as soon as Reigh and I departed on our mission. Technically, I was his first, albeit unofficial, student. Maybe that was why he wanted to be extra sure I didn't do something stupid to get myself killed during my crash-course lessons in riding a dragon. It probably wouldn't look great if his first student died before he ever started his job training others.

The actual flying part wasn't what worried me anymore. Memorizing things wasn't my strong suit, so I worked at it whenever I had a spare second. I knew I had to make the most of the time I had left. I stayed awake every night, squinting by candlelight with my nose pressed to the sheets of paper where I'd begun working out different whistle signals and commands to go along with the saddle Phoebe was making. I had to memorize it all perfectly.

Then I had to teach it to Fornax with our new saddle, which was the real challenge.

I'd already begun working on some of the new commands with him, using the ones we'd already established as a foundation. He caught on quickly, and I could sense our bond growing stronger every day. Translating our new commands to the feel of the saddle would be difficult, though, and the only way to be sure it was working was to actually fly with him.

Of course, that might also get me killed.

Flying with Mavrik gave me more appreciation for what I was really up against. With their large, highly sensitive eyes, dragons were primarily visual hunters. Jaevid suspected that was why losing his vision had caused Fornax to become so feral and afraid. Luckily, their senses of smell and hearing were strong, too. He'd have to rely on those—and trust me when I gave him commands—if we were ever going to be able to fly together.

"I've added more mechanisms to the saddle so that you can communicate more complex signals to Fornax during flight." Phoebe gestured to where my new saddle was on display in the middle of her workshop, a proud spring in every one of her bouncing steps as she guided me around it. "There are metal pedals inside the boot sheaths, one at the toe and another at the heel. Applying a firm amount of force to either will apply pressure to his sides underneath the saddle at various points, just like the handles but in different locations. So at least it will be a sensation he's familiar with. I thought you might be able to use these to indicate speed. Of course, that's entirely up to you. There's also an additional handle in the center of the saddle. It's smaller, set right between the two." She spun to face me, her face lit with a wide, excited smile. "What do you think?"

What did I think? Gods and Fates ...

As I stepped around the sawhorses, my eyes roamed over the sleek, streamlined design. She'd completely refinished the outside of it. The new black leather was polished and oiled to perfection, studded with silver-plated nailheads and pointed, cone-shaped spikes. The seat was padded, meant to fit me perfectly, and the back had been altered so that there was a storage compartment built right in. A few flourishes of silver-inlaid details adorned the sides. They caught and sparkled in the torchlight, practically begging me to run my fingers over them.

"It's incredible," I breathed shakily. "Is it really mine?"

"Of course, silly." She giggled and gave me a playful swat on the arm before she clasped her hands behind her, still grinning. I wondered if she knew she had a big smudge of something, soot or maybe grease, right across her forehead.

"Thank you." I managed what was probably the dorkiest, painfully awkward smile I'd ever given anyone in my entire life. "It's perfect."

Phoebe nibbled her bottom lip, not even looking my way as she planted her hands on her hips. "Let's just hope it works. Are you ready for a test drive?"

"Honestly? No," I confessed. "But we're out of time. Reigh's coming back in three days. We should hear from the Gray elf informant any day, too. So that's all the time I've got left to work on perfecting these aerial commands. It's now or never, right?"

She rocked up onto her toes, making her wild ginger curls bounce and shine like spools of copper ribbon in the dim light of her workshop. "If it's any consolation, I have complete and total faith in you, Thatcher Renley."

I ducked my head, hoping to hide the way my cheeks suddenly flashed with tingling heat. Great. Now I really couldn't afford to screw up. I didn't want to disappoint her. She'd worked so hard making this for us.

"We should probably get to the Deck. Jaevid will be ready for us, and we'll want to get in at least a few hours of practice before nightfall." She blinked up at me, her delicate features drawing up into a look of concern. "Are you okay? What's the matter? Your face is really red. Do you feel sick?"

"I-I, uh, no, I'm good. It's nothing." My voice caught, squeaking and probably betraying what a nervous wreck I was. "Let's get going."

A SMALL AUDIENCE had gathered in the wide courtyard right outside the Deck to watch my first flight with Fornax. Jaevid, Queen Jenna, Prince Aubren, and Southern Sky General Haldor had all come to see whether or not Fornax really could be salvaged as a usable mount. Even Stablemaster Godfrey and a few of the other servants I'd worked with in the stables stood by.

Well, at least if I died, there would be plenty of people around to tell the tale of my final moments.

My heart sank as I continued to search the crowd, hoping to see one face in particular. But Murdoc wasn't there. I hadn't spent a lot of time talking to him outside of our work shifts, and I'd rushed through those as quickly as possible so I could get back to training and practicing. To be honest, we hadn't spoken much at all. And our last real conversation hadn't been a good one. We'd argued, and I'd asked that moronic question about him training me to fight. Guilt soured in my gut as I realized I'd never apologized to him about that. I should have looked for him and tried to make amends, especially if this ride didn't go as planned. I didn't want that conversation to be our final one.

It was too late to go looking for Murdoc now, though. All eyes were on me as I approached the gathering, my heart lodged somewhere in the back of my throat. I tried to breathe through the panic that squeezed at my lungs. Now wasn't the time to lose it.

"I thought I'd let you bring him out while we prep the saddle." Jaevid stepped out to greet me with a tense smile that never reached his eyes. "Ready for this?"

No. Of course I wasn't. I was never ready whenever Jaevid asked me that question, usually because it came before me doing something incredibly dangerous—like riding a blind, formerly feral dragon in a new, experimental saddle neither of us had used before.

"Yep," I lied as I bit down hard against the scorching heat that burned at the back of my throat. "Could we maybe ask the audience not to make any loud noises? Just for this first flight? I don't want to spook him any more than necessary."

Jaevid's sharp features softened and he gave a nod. "Of course. Take it slow, Thatch. Don't rush. You've got all the time you need."

Riiight. All the time I needed. I took a small amount of comfort in the fact that I wasn't the only one fibbing my way through this potential disaster just to make everyone feel better. I had no doubt that Jaevid knew our time was limited as well as I did. We had to get this right. Every extra day we spent training would be a day Devana roamed free, potentially harming innocent people. We had to be ready.

I left Phoebe and Jaevid to begin prepping the saddle and went into the Deck, keeping my head down and avoiding eye contact with any of my audience as I passed by. I didn't see any of their expressions—good or bad.

I found Fornax snoozing in his stall, nestled into a mound of hay like a chicken on a nest. His milky jade eyes opened when I entered. He lifted his head, nostrils puffing in deep breaths as he made popping, clicking sounds. That was his usual greeting now. He was probably hoping I'd brought him a special treat.

"Hey, buddy," I mumbled as I reached under the collar of my tunic for the whistle. It still hung on Jaevid's necklace, clattering against that white bone pendant. Seeing it made my jaw clench and my stomach swirl with anxiety. What was I doing? If my father could see this, he'd probably be laughing his head off. His son, Thatcher Renley, a *dragonrider*? Hah! I had no business at all wearing this armor ... or trying to ride dragons or fight with swords.

Right?

Fornax chirped, tilting his head to one side and swiveling his ears as though waiting for me to give him a command or at least some clue as to why I'd come.

"I don't know what I'm doing anymore," I confessed. Closing a sweaty hand around the whistle, I gripped it tight and shut my eyes. "I don't understand why you picked me. I'm not brave like Jaevid. I'm not a good fighter like Murdoc and Reigh. I'm not even smart like Phoebe. Jaevid thinks it's because I'm a good person or something. I don't even know what that means. It feels like a nice way of saying I'm too dumb to know any better."

The hay crunched as Fornax moved around in his stall. When I opened my eyes again, I found him standing right in front of me, the end of his snout nearly touching my head. A blast of his hot breath blew my bangs back.

"I don't know what you think you sensed in me, but I really hope it's there—for both our sakes." I gently ran a hand over his scaly head, tracing the black markings that striped his deep orange hide. "Today's a big day. We've got to try something new. I need you to trust me, okay?"

Fornax bumped his nose against my chest. A deep purr rumbled in his throat when I scratched at his ears.

"Just stay close to me. I'll look after you."

"Do you even realize the irony of saying that to a two-thousand-pound, fire-breathing dragon? Even if he is blind," a voice scoffed from the doorway.

I knew who it was before I ever looked up.

Murdoc was leaning against the entrance of the stall, his arms crossed and one eyebrow arched like he expected an answer.

Relief hit me like a punch to the chest. Before I could stop myself, the words spilled out in a rush. "Murdoc, I'm really sorry about what I said before when I asked you to teach me how to fight. It probably sounded like I was dismissing how hard you've worked and trained to be able to fight as well as you do. And that's not what I meant, not at all. I ... I just have a lot of respect for you. I guess I thought if I could fight more like you, then maybe I'd stand a chance."

His brow snapped into a flat, deeply furrowed frown that made his eyes flash like cold steel in the dim light. "No."

"No?"

"No, you still wouldn't stand a chance. Even if you knew every single combat technique known to man, you'd stand no chance whatsoever," he growled as he pushed away from the door and walked closer. He stopped only a foot or two away, glowering down at me with his jaw tense and his eyes narrowed. "Because you're not like me. Jaevid's right—you are a *good* person. You want to know what that means and why this dragon chose you? It's simple. You're the first person who treated him like he wasn't a burden or a lost cause. You're the first person to show him patience and understanding. You went looking for him in the darkest part of his own mind, something no one else even wanted to attempt. And then there's that *kindness*—it's the most annoying, relentless, infuriating kindness anyone has ever been subjected to." His lip curled and he glared away, as though trying to contain his disgust. "Ugh. It's like a fly landing in sap. The more you struggle and try to get away, the more stuck you get. You're relentless. No one should be that nice. It's absolutely nauseating."

I wasn't sure how to take that. It kind of sounded like a compliment, but Murdoc's tone was sharp and furious as he bit down hard on every word. "Well, I think you're a good person, too." I tried to match his scowl with one of my own.

I guess it wasn't very convincing because Murdoc's fierce expression cracked. He rolled his eyes, throwing his hands up in the air and turning away. "See? That's what I mean. The fact that you'd even consider me that way is ... *insane*. Before I just assumed you were being naïve and that's why you wanted to stick around me. Now I'm sure you really must be brain damaged or something."

"Why? What's so terrible about you?" I countered.

Murdoc stopped and seemed to freeze in place for a moment. Then, without ever looking back, he bowed his head and murmured, "You'll figure it out eventually. And when you do, you'll wish you'd never said any of this. You'll wish we'd never met, and you'll never want to see me again."

Silence hung in the air so thick it was hard to breathe. I didn't understand what any of that meant—only that it seemed like he was hiding something. Murdoc had never been honest with me about who he really was. He'd never talked about his past. I'd always assumed he just didn't trust me enough. But now, I had to wonder if there was another reason. He guarded that secret so fiercely, like his life depended on it.

Maybe it did ...

"So, are you going to watch me get myself killed trying this?" I asked, hoping it would sound like a joke. It sounded more like a pathetic whimper, unfortunately.

When he glanced back my way, one corner of his mouth curled into a smirk. "Are you kidding?" he chuckled darkly. "Stablemaster Godfrey was taking bets all day yesterday about whether or not you'll crash, get eaten alive, or be incinerated. I'm betting good coin that you'll actually pull this off. I wouldn't miss it for the world."

CHAPTER EIGHTEEN

With my hand resting on his neck to guide him, Fornax followed me out of the Deck and into the broad, open courtyard. Everyone still stood waiting, and they all fell completely silent as we passed. I could feel the pressure of their eyes watching us, as though waiting for my dragon to make a wrong move.

Only Jaevid was smiling as we stopped, and I gave the whistle command for Fornax to lie down. Fornax stretched out on the ground, lowering his head and twitching the end of his tail. His big nostrils flared as he took in the smells of the outside world, the crowd watching, and Mavrik. The king drake lurked close by, already outfitted for flight. The plan was to have Jaevid join us in the air—just in case something went wrong.

Not that there was much he would be able to do about it, really. If the saddle didn't work or Fornax panicked, I was on my own. No one would be able to save me.

I tried not to dwell on that as I walked all the way around my dragon, rubbing his shoulders, side, flanks, and tail with my hands. I'd been working on getting him used to human contact again—to trust that no matter where I touched him, I wouldn't hurt him. That was going to be especially crucial now.

We'd spent a lot of time practicing our new whistle commands. One for turning left, another for right, and so on. It was difficult to gauge how much of what I said Fornax actually understood, but he caught on to the new commands quickly. I sincerely hoped he'd figured out, or at least suspected, what I was up to by now. Everyone kept telling me how smart dragons were. I really hoped they were right.

Regardless, this was the moment of truth.

Stepping around to stand in front of Fornax's head, I went on rubbing his snout and scratching his ears as I nodded to Jaevid.

Immediately, he and Phoebe moved in, carrying the saddle into position. Without a word, they lifted it and slowly settled the weight into place on my dragon's back. The molded underside of the saddle slid down over his spines, fitting to the contours of his body like a glove.

Fornax's ears slicked back. His body tensed, muscles going rock solid underneath his plated scales as his claws dug into the dirt. A low growl started in his throat.

"Hey, it's okay." I put a hand over his nostrils so he could breathe in my scent. "I'm right here. No one's going to hurt you, I swear. But if this is going to work out, if we're ever going to be able to fly together, then you have to wear a saddle again, buddy."

His growl softened a little, but his body stayed stiff, and his muscles began to tremor with anxious energy. This wasn't going to work. Suddenly, I knew what I had to do.

"Step back," I commanded, keeping my tone soft so I didn't spook my already anxious dragon.

Jaevid and Phoebe froze where they were preparing to fasten the girth straps and safety belts. They both gaped at me with similar expressions of confusion and concern.

"He's fine, but he doesn't trust your scents yet. He doesn't know your touch. Let me do it."

Jaevid's mouth scrunched. It didn't take divine power to tell he didn't approve of this idea. But there was no other choice. It had to be me.

Step by step, Jaevid and Phoebe backed off to stand with the rest of the crowd. I waited until everything was quiet and calm and Fornax's growling had finally gone silent. Then I ran a hand down his side, making him aware of where I moved, as I started working where Jaevid and Phoebe had left off.

With a whistle signal, Fornax rose to his feet. I crawled all around him, wriggling underneath, so I could fasten his saddle into place. Jaevid had taught me how to do this with Mavrik, but I'd never actually done it with Fornax's saddle. Thankfully, it wasn't all that different—just a few extra straps and a broader, thicker main girth belt.

When I was finished, I stood back and glanced over my shoulder to Jaevid. He gave me a nod. I'd done it right.

So far, so good. Now I just had one last hurdle to leap. Too bad it was the biggest and most dangerous one of all.

No one had been able to sit on Fornax's back since his last rider had been killed in combat. I hadn't even tried it, yet. I knew that sensation—the weight of a person against his body—might be a difficult one for him. It could bring back all that fear, snatching him back into that whirling chaos of memory in an instant. Only, this time, I'd be caught right in the middle of it.

My palms were clammy and slick with sweat as I fumbled through putting on the last few bits of my armor. I'd opted to keep it light this time, wearing only my breastplate, gauntlets, and helmet. It's not like any of that extra armor would help if Fornax flung me out of the saddle and I plummeted from the sky like a stone from a sling. I'd die on impact no matter what I wore.

I hoped the thick, resin-coated palms of my riding gauntlets would disguise how my hands shook as I touched his head again. Fornax's ears swiveled, his breaths coming in short bursts as his cloudy green eyes searched all around. I wondered if he was able to sense my fear or smell it somehow. Horses could, so it wasn't so far fetched to imagine he could, as well.

"O-Okay, buddy." My voice hitched, echoing from under my helmet as I eyed the saddle—so close but so far. "Let's do this. It's just you and me."

I blew the down command. Fornax hesitated, his hide shivering as though he knew what was coming. Uh oh. Not good.

I blew it again.

Reluctantly, my orange dragon sank slowly back down to the ground. I stepped in, patting his neck and side before I grabbed onto the saddle. It had to be fast. I wouldn't have much time to prepare if he panicked. Sucking in a deep breath, I steeled my nerve one last time. Then I swung a leg over and pulled myself up onto the saddle in one, fluid motion.

Fornax jolted, snapping to his feet and bristling his spines. I gripped the saddle handles, panic stealing the breath from my lungs in an instant. One frantic glance at Jaevid through the glass slit in my helmet made me stop. He shook his head, a determined frown creasing his brow. Now was *not* the time to lose focus. Fornax was feeding off my energy. If I panicked then so would he.

I had to be steady. Calm. Collected.

Grabbing the whistle around my neck, I blew a trill of three short blasts—our signal for attention.

Fornax stopped. His mouth gaped as he panted, still tense and breathing hard.

"Take it easy, boy. It's me. You're not in any danger." I forced my voice to stay calm as I slipped my boots down into the pockets on either side of the saddle. Each one gave a distinct, metallic *click* as I positioned my boots over the mechanisms Phoebe had crafted into them.

I took my time, easing down into position with my hands on the saddle handles. Holding that position, I gave Fornax a couple of minutes to acclimate to that sensation again. His sides swelled with rapid, nervous breaths, pressing against my legs and making the new leather of the saddle squeak.

"Listen to me, okay?" I said, "Listen and remember."

I blew the signal for left and, at the same time, gave the handles a twist for that command. Fornax tensed, snorting a blast of breath through his nose and swishing the end of his tail. But he swung his head to the left.

Excitement sped my pulse into overdrive. He was getting it! I tried it again with the right. He obeyed right on cue, bringing his head to the right. So far so good.

Looking off to my captive audience, I gave Jaevid one of the hand signals he'd taught me. "*Taking off.*"

We were going to do one, slow, circular pass over the castle and land right back here. Nothing fancy—not yet—just enough to let him get a feel for carrying a rider again. That was the plan, anyway. Oh, and not getting killed in the process was also an added bonus.

My stomach flipped and twisted as I gave Fornax's neck a reassuring pat. "Let's try it in the air. Sound good?"

He perked his ears, shifting and flexing his wing arms against the feel of the saddle, as though he knew what was coming. I took that as a good sign. He was ready.

And so was I.

Spitting out the whistle, I twisted both handles outward in the command to rise—one I hoped he might remember from his rider before. It's not like he'd be able to hear the whistle in flight over the rush of the wind anyway. We'd have to rely primarily on touch.

Fornax lifted his head to the sky and unfurled his wings. His leathery membranes stretched and filled with wind like two black sails as he kicked back onto his hind legs and sprang upward. His back arched. His wing arms flexed, strong and steady. In three mighty beats, we were gone—roaring into the clear morning sky like an orange shooting star.

IT TOOK ABOUT five minutes to do two passes around the castle grounds. And all the while, I couldn't stop smiling. I grinned until my cheeks hurt. Flying with Fornax felt nothing like it did with Mavrik. Fornax was smaller, and his wing beats were smooth and sure as they propelled us forward with incredible speed. I ran him through dips and ascensions, testing out all the basic commands I'd learned on Mavrik. He hit every mark perfectly. But it wasn't enough.

More—I needed *more*.

I coaxed him faster and pressed my left toe down on the mechanism inside my boot sheath. We hadn't practiced this much. I'd only been able to simulate the feeling of using that mechanism by tapping him with the end of a long mop handle. But instead of having him roll over like a trained dog at that sensation on the ground, Fornax snapped his strong wings in close and whipped into a barrel roll. He stopped back upright again, and I couldn't hold it in. A wild scream of exhilaration tore out of my chest.

I worked the saddle handles again, driving him downward into a steep dive before repeating the barrel roll command. I leaned down, flattening against his body as we shot toward the earth, spinning like an arrow. Every beat of my heart kicked hard against my ribs. My muscles shook, vibrating with pure adrenaline as I steered him upward again. I howled in wild excitement as we burst through the clouds, climbing so high the air grew thin and cold.

Suddenly, a massive blue shape blurred past us, zipping in the opposite direction with a jolting burst of wind that nearly knocked us for a loop. I whipped around just in time to see Jaevid, seated astride Mavrik, give me a sarcastic little wave and waggle of his fingers.

Wait, was that ... a *challenge*? My mouth curled into a smirk. Game on, old man.

Fornax snapped his jaws and I clenched my teeth, quickly bringing him around to take up the chase. Mavrik might have been bigger, but that size slowed him down. We tore past them at a blistering speed, and I mimicked that sarcastic wave as we went by. It was impossible to be sure over the constant rush of the wind past my helmet, but I could have sworn I heard Jaevid laugh.

Then, out of nowhere, a third dragon appeared. Queen Jenna fell into formation beside us, seated confidently on the back of her mount. Phevos was about the same size as my dragon, and his dark purple scales were striped with teal markings—a little like

Fornax's, only in different colors. He considered us with intelligent, yellow eyes before giving an unimpressed snort and veering away, his long tail grazing the tops of the clouds so that it left a curling trail behind him.

Before I could decide whether or not to chase them next, another dragon broke from the clouds right in front of us, pitching into a roll and taking off after her. I knew that beast right away, mainly because he'd been the very first one I'd ever seen up close. Haldor's dragon, Turq, was named for his rich turquoise coloring. His only marking was a faint yellow blaze down the ridge of his back from his nose to the tip of his tail.

With the sunlight gleaming off their scales, Jenna and Haldor's dragons soared together in perfect unison. Jenna and Phevos took the lead, her position slightly ahead of Turq, as they rose and fell, cruising through the air like two mighty scaled eagles. It was exactly as Jaevid had described—only a thousand times better in real life.

I couldn't fight the way my heart wrenched with an insatiable need to follow them. I had to. I was *meant* to.

Mavrik and Jaevid appeared just in time for us to follow them through dips and dives, swirling ascents and wide loops. With every passing moment, Fornax's body relaxed. His movements were confident and smooth. He didn't fight my commands even once, and never hesitated to respond to any of the gestures of the handles. He trusted me completely.

And in that moment—I felt it. It shook the very foundations of my being, digging into my soul like roots that tethered us together. Fornax and I were one. Our bond was strong.

He was my dragon, and I was born to be his rider.

19

CHAPTER NINETEEN

"Thatcher, that was incredible!" Phoebe bounded forward, ahead of the rest of the group, with her red curls flying. She threw her arms around me as soon as I stepped out of the saddle, nearly knocking me over. "Absolutely brilliant! You did so well! How did the saddle feel? Was the strapping too tight? How about the mechanisms; did they feel loose or too sensitive? I can make any adjustments you need right away!"

"Maybe give him a second to catch his breath, eh?" Jaevid called down from where he still sat in Mavrik's saddle. He slid his visor back, revealing his broad grin. "You alright there, Thatcher?"

As he spoke, the other two dragons flared their wings, flapping vigorously as their hind legs stretched out to touch down right behind him. Turq and Phevos landed with an earthshaking *boom*. Their colorful scales flashed and their long tails whipped as they snapped playfully at one another. They growled and clicked, chirping and crowing at one another until Mavrik gave them a silencing snarl.

It ... it didn't seem real. It couldn't be. Was it?

I staggered, my legs like jelly as I backed away from Fornax. My heartbeat roared in my ears. My head swam and I couldn't seem to clear the blurriness from my eyes, either from doing so many flips or from sheer excitement—I couldn't tell which. And it didn't matter.

I fell flat on my back and lay sprawled on the grass. My wheezing, panting breaths echoed under my helmet. Whenever I closed my eyes, everything seemed to spin, as though I were still in the saddle, whirling with the wild energy of my dragon's flight.

Suddenly a familiar face appeared right over me ... and another ... and another.

"Oh no, did he pass out?" Phoebe asked, her lovely freckled face the picture of genuine concern.

Murdoc's mouth flattened as he reached down and pulled my helmet off. "No. He's just being melodramatic, as usual. Get up, Thatch."

"He didn't throw up in that, did he?" Jaevid's expression skewed with a grimace. His lip curled as he eyed my helmet.

Murdoc glanced down to check. "No."

Laughter broke out past my lips in breathless, rasping bursts. I couldn't stop. The more I tried, the harder I laughed. I cackled until I couldn't breathe and tears were streaming down my face.

"He's lost it," Murdoc pronounced as he shot Jaevid a suspicious glare. "What exactly did you do to him up there?"

"I-I'm okay," I wheezed.

"That's debatable." Murdoc frowned.

"No, really, I'm fine." Sitting up, I struggled to catch my breath as I took off my riding gauntlets and wiped my face on my sleeve. "I just ... I've never felt anything like that before."

"Like what?" Murdoc squatted down in front of me, offering my helmet back with a suspicious frown.

I shook my head, unable to reply. The words hung in my throat, choking me until my eyes watered again every time I tried to speak. There was nothing I could say to describe it so he'd truly understand. The speed. The power. The absolute freedom. There weren't words for how a dragon's—*my* dragon's—flight felt. That feeling of rightness and belonging was beyond anything I'd ever even dreamed of, as though a huge hunk of my soul had been missing until that moment. Now that I'd found it, I couldn't live without it. I'd rather die than ever say goodbye to Fornax.

"You'll have to keep practicing," Jaevid reminded me. "But I'd say you're off to an excellent start."

"Now, let's see if he fares any better with a blade," Haldor chimed in, appearing beside him with his helmet under his arm. "I better not see any cringing or closing your eyes this time, boy."

"He cringes?" Queen Jenna stopped beside them, the wind catching in her long golden hair and rustling the sleeves of her billowy, dark blue tunic. It practically swallowed her tall frame, gathered at the waist for the fitted breeches she wore underneath.

Her brother, Prince Aubren, wasn't far behind. Adding them to the group standing around me, I found myself enclosed in a full circle of curious, brooding, or dubious expressions.

"Every time," Haldor confirmed.

Jaevid was quick to take up my defense. "It'll just take practice."

"Practice takes time, which we don't have." Prince Aubren rubbed his chin with one of his gloved hands. "Maybe this isn't such a good idea."

"We can discuss it again when Reigh returns." Jenna wafted a hand as though she wasn't concerned. "Until then, we've enough to keep us busy. The first official trial in the Court of Crowns is tomorrow morning, and I need to prepare my notes. I promised Reigh we would hold this one before he returned, and we're already cutting it closer than I'd hoped."

The color drained out of Phoebe's face so suddenly I thought she might faint. Her brow crinkled at the same time her slender shoulders drew up to her ears. She pressed her lips together, ducking her head as though she wanted to hide behind her mane of wild ginger curls.

Before I could ask, Prince Aubren put a hand on her shoulder and offered a reassuring, brotherly smile. It didn't seem to help, though. She wouldn't even meet his gaze as she, Aubren, and Jenna walked away back toward the castle together. What was going on with them? Did that trial have something to do with Phoebe?

"Is she okay?" I looked to Jaevid, hoping for an explanation.

His expression had grown dim and cryptic as he shook his head slightly. "I think it would be better if she told you herself."

I NEVER GOT the chance to ask.

When Murdoc and I returned to Phoebe's workshop later that afternoon, carrying my saddle so she could make a few tweaks before our departure, she was nowhere to be found. The coals in her small forge were out, and all her crafting tools had been packed up and placed neatly in a pile off to the side—as though she were planning on leaving. But where? And why now? We'd spent a lot of time chatting while she worked on my saddle, and she'd never once mentioned going anywhere.

My gut clenched, hardening around the suspicion that there was something going on with her no one had warned me about.

"She was the one who made your saddle?" Murdoc mumbled as he thumbed through one of her old, leather-bound books. It was practically bursting with drawings, diagrams, scribbled notes, and scraps of paper.

"Yeah." I sighed as I stared around her empty workshop. She'd always seemed so cheerful and carefree—right up until they mentioned that trial. I was convinced that had to have something to do with it. Somehow, it was all connected.

"Interesting. I'd never peg her as an artificer. But it seems she's quite clever when it comes to—" Murdoc stopped short, his hand halting on a page of Phoebe's book. His brows snapped together, locking into a hard frown as his sharp eyes scanned the contents of that page as though he were reading it again and again.

"What?" I started toward him. "What is it?"

Murdoc turned the book around so I could see.

I stopped. My mouth fell open, and for a few seconds, my mind went completely blank.

No ... it couldn't be ...

Etched onto the thick, yellowed paper of that journal was a very detailed drawing of a Tibran trebuchet. There was no mistaking it. Murdoc and I had seen them dozens of times while clearing the battlefield during our time in the prison camp. Their design was unique and notoriously efficient—something never seen in Maldobar before the war began. Those machines had killed thousands upon thousands of Maldobarian soldiers.

And this was ... well, it looked like a diagram and instructions on how to build one.

"That can't be." My brain throbbed, not wanting to accept what I was seeing. There had to be some other explanation.

Then Murdoc turned the page.

The next one bore another detailed drawing. This one came complete with dimensions and notes on materials for construction. It was a Tibran net-thrower. Those machines had been built after the war began, designed specifically to shoot down dragonriders.

I took a staggering step back, biting back the urge to gag. Phoebe was a *Tibran*? How? That didn't make any sense. She was only fifteen! She was so nice, and ... and she'd made a special saddle just for Fornax! How could she be designing weapons and machines for the Tibran Empire?

"Jaevid knew," I realized aloud. "He knew the whole time. And he never said anything."

"Seems she's been keeping a big secret." Murdoc's tone carried an edge like bittersweet amusement. He snapped the book shut and placed it back on the worktable. "Probably afraid of what you'd think if you knew the truth. Understandable, considering she's essentially responsible for the deaths of countless Maldobarian soldiers and civilians, not to mention anything that might've been used in other kingdoms across their empire. There are probably a lot of people who would love to see her put to the sword. She must be the one standing trial tomorrow morning before the Court of Crowns."

It took a few breaths for me to calm my racing heart and scrambling thoughts. Phoebe was going on trial as a war criminal? Gods and Fates. No wonder she'd looked so terrified.

"I ... I ..." I stammered quietly, my thoughts racing. "Murdoc, she's my friend."

His gaze snapped up to meet mine, that scowl sharpening on his brow once again.

"We have to help her."

His eyes narrowed. "Even though she's a Tibran?"

No. That wasn't right; it couldn't be. Maybe Phoebe had designed these things for Lord Argonox and the Tibran Empire, but that couldn't be the whole story. The girl I knew—my friend—wouldn't hurt anyone like that. Phoebe was a lot of things, but she couldn't be a murderer. I refused to believe that.

"Yes," I replied at last as I set my jaw.

He snorted and crossed his arms. Tilting his chin up, he shot me a challenging glare down the bridge of his nose. "You're talking about defying an entire courtroom of kings and queens."

"I know."

"That's utterly insane, you do realize that."

I clenched my fists. "I don't care. Maybe she was before—I don't know—but I know Phoebe isn't a Tibran anymore. I won't let them kill her, Murdoc."

"If we get caught, they'll put you to the sword, too—dragon or no dragon."

"I said, *I don't care*."

Murdoc tipped his head to the side, a strangely cold smirk spreading over his features. "Very well. Let's crash a royal trial, then."

20

CHAPTER TWENTY

"Are you sure about this?" I whispered up to Murdoc as we shuffled along through a dark, narrow corridor outside the grand throne room. Passages like this were only used by servants to navigate through the rooms without causing a disturbance.

Murdoc didn't answer, and I didn't dare ask him about it again ... or about how he had gotten two elite, royal guard uniforms for us. I hadn't found any traces of blood on them when I got dressed, and that was all I cared to know. Ignorance was bliss when it came to Murdoc acquiring stuff like this.

With my face hidden behind a golden mask, the dull roar of the crowd inside made my stomach flutter. Hundreds of royals, nobles, and aristocrats had gathered from the far corners of the world. They all had one thing in common: Lord Argonox had conquered their land and forced them to submit to the authority of his empire. Now, they had come here to see his key officials answer for their crimes.

And Phoebe was going to be the first person put on the block to be judged.

We slipped into the throne room at the very back, creeping out of the servant's passage and joining a group of other royal guards who marched single file down the length of the long, blue-carpeted aisle. The room had been entirely redecorated for the trial. Heavy draperies were pulled over all the tall windows, blotting every view of the outside world. The room was lit only by the warm glow of flames burning from a series of bronze braziers that stood about twenty paces apart down each side of the aisle. Each one had been crafted in the shape of a dragon so that the flames licked from their open jaws.

The crowds of nobles stood on either side of the divided aisle, speaking softly while we made our way to the front of the room. There, Queen Jenna's throne stood atop a raised platform and was flanked by a dozen other, smaller thrones. The top of each throne was adorned in a different coat of arms—the emblem of the kingdom where that royal held power. Unfamiliar faces sat in attendance there, but each person wore some sort of crown and long, billowing cloak.

The only other feature in the room was a small square pedestal that stood right below the panel of royals. I didn't have to guess what that was for ... because Phoebe was already standing there. Her wrists and ankles were shackled, tethering her with heavy chains to a pair of iron loops on either side of the pedestal.

A hush fell over the room as we stopped, holding a formation on either side of Phoebe. I could see her shaking out of the corner of my eye, her eyes wide and terrified as she stared across the panel of kings and queens that leered down at her from their lofty seats. Her freckled cheeks were swollen as though she'd spent the whole night crying.

I clenched my teeth behind my mask. This wasn't right.

"I call this Court of Crowns to order," Queen Jenna spoke in a smooth, composed voice as she rose from her seat. "May our verdicts bring justice to heal our broken lands."

There was a murmur of agreement through the room as she sat down again and raised a hand, gesturing toward Phoebe. "Before us stands Argonox's own artificer, who goes only by the name Phoebe. She is the creator of his war machines, which is her highest crime, and has assisted in the torture and defilement of countless others during his conquest. It should be noted that while her offenses are severe, she was one of his most valued and closely watched slaves. Every task she performed for Argonox was done under threat of torture and death. Such is her plea for mercy from our court. Let her now be questioned."

I could hear my own heart pounding in my ears as heavy silence hung over the room. No one seemed eager to say anything, at first. Then, from the far end of the line of thrones, an older woman with the same copper-colored hair rose slowly. Her face was creased with age, and her intricate clothes were made with fur and leather, giving it a more rustic and natural style than what people usually wore in Maldobar.

"What is your family name, child?" the old queen asked.

Phoebe's wide blue eyes filled with tears, her lip trembling as she spoke. "I-I don't know, Your Majesty. I was taken when I was barely four years old. I don't remember very much about my family before."

One of the kings seated on Jenna's left sat forward in his seat, his expression cold. "And you expect us to believe that you became Argonox's artificer at so young an age?"

Phoebe blinked, visibly rattled, as though she didn't know how to answer that. At last, she ducked her head slightly, tears dripping from her chin. "T-There were a lot of children like me who were taken to be slaves. We didn't have anything but the rags we wore and whatever tools we were given to work or clean. I-I made little toys out of scraps and bits of garbage for the younger ones. Eventually, some of the officers noticed." Her body trembled harder, rattling the chains as her head bowed lower and lower. "They put me in the armory division and made me fix armor and weaponry. I worked hard because they fed me better when I finished more. Lord Argonox saw me one day while I was repairing the broken axle of a transport wagon—designing a better one. I think I was about eight or nine years old by then. He told me if I was good, if I did what I was told and made more new things for him, then I wouldn't go hungry again. The officers wouldn't be allowed to beat or touch me anymore."

Looking up suddenly, Phoebe's face skewed with a look of absolute terror. "P-Please, I ... I didn't want to do any of it! The first time I refused one of his orders, he ... he ..." Her mouth clamped shut as she gasped and sobbed.

My body jerked forward, pulled by a building fire that scorched through my chest. I *had* to go to her. She was scared and they were making her out to be some kind of a monster, but that wasn't true!

Murdoc planted a firm grip on my arm, forcing me to stay put. Through the eye holes in his mask, he shot me a harrowing glare.

We couldn't do anything. Not yet.

"Show them," Queen Jenna said, her voice gentle as she motioned to one of the guards. "Show them what he did to you when you refused."

Blinking hard against the tears that still streamed down her face, Phoebe stood trembling as one of the elite guards from our formation stepped up to unlock the shackles from her arms and unfasten the buttons on the back of her dainty little gown. Then he moved aside. Phoebe held her dress against her chest, but let the back fall loose all the way to her waist. As she turned to expose her bare back to the panel of royals, a collective gasp and rush of whispers hissed through the room.

Phoebe's back was *covered* in scars, the same branded mark all the Tibran slave soldiers had on their neck. There had to be at least fifteen of them, maybe more. Some were old and had healed into rough, gnarled patches, while others were fresh, probably done not long before Argonox's forces were overthrown. Those marks were still pink and swollen.

"Silence! Silence, please!" Queen Jenna stood, raising her hands to call the company back to order. "Thank you, Phoebe. That's enough."

In an instant, Murdoc's grip on my arm was gone—and so was he. He broke away from our formation and approached the pedestal where Phoebe stood, muscling his way past the other guard. He took off his cloak and wrapped it around her. He held it there while she shakily fixed her dress so that no one would be able to see if she accidentally exposed herself.

With his face obscured by that golden mask, it was impossible to see the look on his face. But I'd known him long enough now that I recognized the way his eyes focused on her, earnest and intense, the way they had been when he had first spared my life in the alleyway at Thornbend.

What the heck happened to staying put and waiting?

"I have talked with Phoebe at length about her involvement in the Tibran invasion. She does not deny or excuse anything that happened, and she has been utterly remorseful," Queen Jenna proclaimed as she turned to face the other royals. "I know her crimes are severe; my own family members were victims of Tibran experimentation. I held one of my dearest friends in my arms while he died because of injuries from Tibran catapult fire. So I do not say this lightly when I urge this court to pardon her crimes under special circumstances—I believe she should remain here, in Maldobar, under my supervision and custody until her family is found. If they wish to reclaim her, then I will gladly send her to them."

Another wave of unhappy murmurs rushed over the crowd. Even many of the royals sat back, their expressions stricken with shock.

"First and foremost, we are a court seeking justice for our kingdoms and peoples. That is why you came here, and why I am appealing to you for this girl's life." Queen Jenna glanced back toward Phoebe, her gaze earnest. "Argonox tainted and twisted so many good people. He broke their minds and spirits, turning them into monsters that thrived only on death and destruction. So many of them, as you will see in the coming months, may very well be beyond saving. But not this one. She is still young. She has a gentle heart. And I believe she is worth saving."

QUEEN JENNA'S APPEAL WORKED. Maybe it was that the other royals in the court found her intimidating, or maybe they were moved by Phoebe's testimony—whatever it was, they all agreed to let Maldobar have custody of Phoebe. The only one who seemed uncertain in her decision was the older, copper-haired woman dressed in fine furs. She watched Phoebe with a glint of pain in her wide blue eyes, and I couldn't help but wonder if they might have something more in common than the color of their hair. If that were the case, however, the old queen never said it out loud. She gave her answer quietly, relinquishing Phoebe to Queen Jenna's supervision, and that was it.

Phoebe was free to go.

As soon as they took the shackles off her ankles, she doubled over with her face in her hands, still choking back sobs. Murdoc moved quickly, sweeping her up into his arms. She gripped his shoulders tightly as he carried her away, striding steadily down the aisle and out of the throne room. No one tried to stop him or even questioned it, so I stepped in right behind him like I knew what I was doing and followed them outside. I could have sworn I saw a hint of a knowing smile in one corner of Queen Jenna's mouth, but I didn't dare to look back to be sure. I kept my gaze fixed straight ahead, focused on Murdoc's back.

That is, until a glimmer in the crowd of nobles caught my attention. Amidst all the fineries, glittering jewels, velvet, satin, and silk clothes, a pair of eyes stood out from behind a deep red face shawl that covered everything else. Those eyes—I couldn't look away. Their peculiar, vivid green irises were ringed with a bright yellow band.

A warm little chill climbed my spine and made all the hairs on my arms prickle. I blinked hard, trying to shake it off. But a strange heat tingled in my chest. What ... what was this feeling?

The eyes vanished, as though that person had just evaporated into thin air.

I let out a shaking breath. Had I just imagined that?

There wasn't time to figure it out.

Beyond the closed doors of the throne room, Murdoc carefully put Phoebe back on her feet and stood back. I paused next to him, watching as Phoebe wiped her face and tried to rake her unruly curls away from her eyes. She peered up at us anxiously, as though unsure what she should do now.

Murdoc jabbed an elbow into my side.

Oh, right, we were still wearing our masks.

Sliding mine off, I gave her what I hoped would be a reassuring smile. "Oh, um, hey."

Her mouth popped open, eyes going wide with sudden realization. "Thatch? You're an elite royal guard?"

"You've got to be kidding me," Murdoc snorted as he took off his own mask. "Who would hire him to guard anything?"

I shot my *friend* a poisonous look. "Gee, thanks."

He shrugged. "It was his idea to rescue you. Thankfully, it wasn't necessary. You've apparently found favor with a new crown."

Phoebe's bright, sky blue eyes danced between us for a moment before she drew back a little, her shoulders flinching up as she bowed her head again. "I-I'm sorry. I should have told you before ... about who I really am and why I've been working for Queen Jenna. She said I could stay here and keep working, make good things again, for as long as I wanted. I don't have anywhere else to go, so I agreed. When I was with the Tibrans, I never got to say no when they asked me to make something. I never had a choice about what I wanted or where I went. I did terrible, horrible, unforgivable things. And I know I can't make any of it right. I-I ... I'm so sorry ..."

I opened my mouth to answer, but Murdoc beat me to it. He stepped past her in one smooth stride, letting one of his hands fall on top of her head, fingers nestling amidst her red-orange curls. He turned her head back so she was forced to look up at him. "Stop that. Don't apologize," he ordered, his voice deep but strangely soft. "You didn't have a choice before. You did what you had to in order to survive. It's over. It's in the past. You survived. And you do have a choice now, so choose to be better and let the rest go."

Phoebe stood completely frozen. I couldn't even tell if she was still breathing. She stared up at him, mouth slightly open, while rosy color crept into her cheeks and made all her freckles disappear.

That's when I noticed Murdoc wasn't staring back at her. He wouldn't even look at her. Instead, he kept his face angled away, almost like he was trying to hide. It didn't work, though.

I caught a glimpse of his face as he pulled away and began to leave. His mouth was locked into the usual grim, brooding frown he always wore—but his face had turned bright red all the way down to his neck.

No. Way. I was hallucinating. I had to be.

"Um, Thatch, who is that?" Phoebe whispered, her expression still captivated as she watched him walk away.

Gods and Fates, I wasn't sure I knew anymore. Murdoc didn't *blush*. He rarely even smiled, unless it was at my expense. It couldn't be. There had to be some kind of mistake. A trick of the light or something.

Just in case this was real, I decided to wait until he was too far away to hear me before I answered that. You know, cause he might come storming back to break some of my limbs.

"An idiot. The biggest idiot to ever walk the earth," I replied with a grin. "And my best friend."

CHAPTER TWENTY-ONE

"Shield up! Block! Boy, don't make me come over there!" Haldor was yelling at me again. It might have hurt my feelings a little, or at least stung my pride, except ... he was right.

Reigh had returned. There were only two days left until we were supposed to depart on our hunt for Devana, and I was no better at fighting than when we'd started. Not for lack of trying. Or yelling, for that matter.

Even Jaevid seemed to be losing hope for me now. He'd tested me with so many different tactics and weapons, but nothing worked. His last-ditch effort had been to hand me a shield—probably with the hope that if I couldn't make myself a real threat in combat, then at least I'd be able to keep from getting hacked in two before Reigh could save my useless butt.

"Try not to take it too personally, Thatch," Jaevid had attempted to console me while demonstrating how to strap the small, circular shield onto my forearm. "Fledgling students get this training for an entire year. You're trying to learn it in a few weeks. It doesn't mean you won't make a good fighter. You should have seen me when I first started—this shield probably weighs more than I did at the time. I was a slow learner, too."

Fine. So Jaevid had struggled with this, as well. Big deal. That didn't do anything to help my current situation, though. Reigh had called me a tourist, like I was just tagging along on his mission to sight-see. So far, it seemed like he would be right. I'd end up being more of a hindrance than a help if things went badly and we had to fight.

And speaking of Reigh ...

I could feel his glare on me like the heat of the sun. He stood next to Haldor with his arms crossed and his dark red hair blowing over his narrowed eyes. His mouth hadn't moved from where it was set into a disapproving, unimpressed frown. So far, this demonstration of my "improved" skills wasn't going well at *all*.

I staggered back, out of breath and trying to raise the shield back up to my shoulder the way Jaevid had taught me. My arm shook under the weight. Sweat drizzled down the sides of my face. Come on. Why couldn't I just get it together? What was wrong with me? I had to get this. I had to be *better*. I couldn't let Jaevid and Fornax down.

"Let's try it again," Jaevid called from across the sparring circle. We'd moved our practicing outside this time, using a corner of the Deck's central courtyard where the dragons usually landed. We'd even brought along an assortment of practice weapons, and Jaevid had erected a wooden practice dummy for me to use.

"What's the point? He's not getting any better," Reigh snorted, shaking his head. "He might even be worse than when you started. I didn't know that was possible."

Jaevid's expression hardened, eyes flashing with quiet rage as he shot Reigh a meaningful look. "Care to test yourself against me, then, *fledgling*?"

The redheaded prince raised his hands in surrender. "No, thanks. I know you could slice me up like warm butter, Jae. You're missing my point. Someone like Devana presents a *real* threat, not a practice one. So he can ride the blind dragon—that's all well and good—but this kid's about as dangerous as an angry squirrel and we're talking about sticking him in front of an unpredictable, extremely dangerous enemy for his first real fight? If we had a few months to prep, maybe we could make him a shield guard, but there isn't time. I don't want to be responsible if this kid makes a wrong move and winds up dead. The last thing I need is more blood on my hands."

Jaevid's aggressive scowl softened into a thoughtful frown. "I suppose you're right. Here, you take a turn with him." Slipping his scimitar back into its sheath, he strode past me and gave my shoulder a reassuring pat.

It didn't help or make me feel any less like crap. Fornax had made a mistake in choosing me. Sure, I loved the feel of being his rider. I'd never felt more right in my entire life than I did when we flew together. But clearly I wasn't cut out to be a soldier in any capacity. I was a lost cause.

My arms dropped back to my sides and I stood watching as he spoke quietly to Haldor. Meanwhile, Reigh was rolling up the baggy, bell sleeves of his black silk tunic and drawing two strange, sickle-shaped blades from where they hung at his hips. Each one was as white as bleached bone with a leather-wrapped hilt and brutal, curved points. They must have been a Gray elf weapon—I'd never seen human warriors fight with anything like them before.

"Stop thinking about what you're supposed to do. You won't have time to think in a real fight. You have to feel it. It's got to become instinct," Reigh growled as he spun each of the weapons over his hands with blitzing speed. He whipped them through rhythmic patterns, the hooked blades practically singing as they flashed in the air. "Ready?"

I nodded shakily.

Without any more warning, Reigh rushed me like a striking viper. He was every bit as fast and efficient with his strikes as Jaevid, but his style was different—less straightforward. He feinted and spun, moving so fast I barely had time to bring my shield up to block as he made a strike at my chest.

The impact rocked me back onto my heels, my vision scrambling for a moment as his blades clanged against my shield.

There was no time to recover.

Before I could blink away the spots in my eyes, Reigh had whipped around to aim another lightning-fast strike for the side of my neck. I raised my sword, hoping to block as I dropped my footing back to put some distance between us again. I couldn't handle it. Reigh moved too fast. His strikes came in a constant flow, not letting up. I scrambled to respond, to stop from overthinking, to block every blow.

Suddenly, the heel of one of my boots snagged on an uneven spot on the ground. I stumbled, arms flailing wide, and fell back onto my rear end. My sword clattered away, far out of reach.

"See? This is what I mean!" Reigh snarled, bearing in hard with a downward strike. "You're one trip away from death."

I flung my shield-arm up, barely managing to block in time. His blades hit hard enough to make my teeth rattle.

"It's bad enough Jenna is making me do this in the first place; I'm not interested in lugging you around as a burden, too!" Reigh blurred through another maneuver, snapping angry words as he twisted the hooked end of one of his blades around the edge of my shield.

In a matter of seconds, he had me pinned flat on my back, a foot planted firmly on my shield arm. The curved edge of his weapon hovered at my throat. My eyes squeezed shut and I cringed away as the razor-sharp blade grazed my skin with a cold scrape.

Reigh's voice hissed angrily through his teeth, biting hard on every word. "You think it's okay to expect me to babysit you when there could be innocent civilian lives on the line?"

My heart sank. He was right. I ... I shouldn't be going. Dragon or not, I still wasn't a fighter; I was a liability.

Opening my eyes, I slowly raised my gaze to meet his. I couldn't keep a look of desperate anger from skewing over my face, making my mouth screw up and my chin quiver. But I wasn't angry with him. I was mad at myself. Why couldn't I get this? What was wrong with me?

"Reigh, I—" I started to speak, but out of nowhere, something small whizzed through the air right past my face. A rock?

It hit Reigh on the wrist so hard he immediately dropped his blade and drew back with a yelp. Hissing curses under his breath, he glared around in search of the culprit. "What the—who threw that?"

Reigh froze suddenly, his mouth snapping shut and eyes narrowing on something, or someone, directly behind me. "Who are *you*?" he demanded.

"The babysitter," a deep voice replied evenly.

Wait ... I *knew* that voice.

Oh no.

Sitting on my rear in the middle of the sparring circle, I whipped around to see Murdoc striding toward us. The wind teased through his shaggy dark hair, blowing it loosely over his brow and the bridge of his nose. A dark, bitter coldness churned in his hazel eyes. Something about that look on his face reminded me of a prowling wolf on the hunt—relentless and utterly wild. His gaze never left Reigh's as he reached out to draw one of the practice blades from our collection without ever slowing his pace.

"Is that supposed to be a challenge?" Reigh tapped his fallen blade with the toe of his boot, flipping it into the air. He snatched it by the handle in the blink of an eye, whipping it around into a defensive pose.

Murdoc looked down at me for a brief instant, as though he were doing a quick check to make sure I wasn't hurt. Then he stepped past me without a word.

My stomach dropped. Bad—this was *so* bad. Something in Murdoc's face and body language was off. I'd seen him fight before plenty of times when we were in the prison camp, but this time was different. It was as though all the light in his eyes had been snuffed out as he stretched his arm out wide, hand gripping the blade's padded hilt until his knuckles blanched. "It's whatever you want it to be, *Your Highness*," he replied with a menacing smirk curling over his sharp features.

Reigh's eyebrows shot up. "Uh, you do realize I'm a Gray elf scout, right? Title aside, I was trained by one of the best fighters in Luntharda."

Murdoc's chilling smile broadened. "Really? That's cute. Do they hand out ribbons for that in Luntharda? Or trophies?" He tipped his head upward in a quick, nodding gesture, as though inviting Reigh to make the first move. "Training means nothing if you can't control your emotions. So try me, little prince. Let's see what you're really made of."

Murdoc and Reigh battled like demons in the middle of the Deck's courtyard. They filled the air with the scrape, clash, and hum of blades dancing in the sunlight as they blitzed through strikes and parries. Reigh was fast, and he was able to keep pace with most of Murdoc's blurring assaults.

But Murdoc was absolutely brutal. Every move he made was efficient, ruthless, and impossibly perfect. His reflexes were ridiculously fast, and his patterns were unpredictable. That seemed to throw Reigh off his game right away. He couldn't settle into a rhythm when Murdoc kept changing up his approach. One second, he was raining down lightning-fast strikes. The next, he was whirling through complex swings, ducking and rolling, and forcing Reigh to retreat.

Standing between Jaevid and Haldor, my heart hammered in my chest as I tried to track their movements. I'd only had a small taste of the true complexity of swordsmanship, but even I could appreciate the near inhuman speed and strength of Murdoc's assaults. He hit so hard that Reigh rocked back onto his heels, baring his teeth and snarling more curses under his breath. His face dripped with sweat. His swings became slower.

Murdoc, on the other hand, was smirking as he breezed through complex strikes, bearing in hard and forcing Reigh into one frantic, defensive block after another. It was as though he could sense Reigh's moves beforehand or predict them somehow. If I had to guess, I would have thought Murdoc wasn't even trying that hard—like he was just toying with Reigh.

That realization made a cold chill prickle up my spine. My stomach flipped. Maybe my best friend wasn't just a guy who happened to be a good fighter. After all, when we met, he'd been dressed in all that strange black clothing. And then there was that vambrace, the silver cuff engraved with the head of a snarling wolf.

"Is that the young man from Thornbend?" Haldor asked. "The one we found you with?"

My hands curled into sweaty fists as my stomach did another erratic flip. "Yeah, that's him."

"He's quite a fighter." He chuckled as though he were impressed. "I've never seen anyone move that fast."

"I have." Jaevid's voice rumbled low, deep and soft like the growl of distant thunder. One glance at his face made my gut wind into knots. His brow was locked into an ominous stare that was fixed right on Murdoc. His mouth and jaw were set so tightly it made a vein stand out against the side of his neck. He stood tense and disturbingly still, watching the fight with his pale eyes tracking every movement.

"Really?" Haldor sounded surprised. "Where?"

Jaevid didn't answer. Instead, his piercing gaze snapped over to me so suddenly it made my heartbeat skip. "How much do you know about that friend of yours?"

"I-I uh ... um, well ..." I took a small step away from him, anxiety swirling in the pit of my stomach. "Not much."

"Does he have any scars?"

"S-Scars? I, uh, I'm not sure what you mean." Honestly, I'd almost forgotten all about Murdoc's scars. I'd only spotted them once, while we were at the prison camp. He pretty much always wore sleeves or tunics that covered those areas.

How could Jaevid possibly know about them?

"Have you ever noticed any scars on him?" he repeated, moving in closer. "Specifically, are there any marks on his wrists or neck that you've seen?"

Murdoc did have gruesome marks around his wrists and the base of his neck; it was a fluke that I'd even seen them in the first place. I didn't want to lie to Jaevid. He was the only reason I had a real shot at being a dragonrider in the first place. But ... something about that tense look of suspicion on his sharp, half-elven features made me hesitate. How had he known Murdoc might have scars exactly like that?

I could have fallen to my knees and thanked the gods when Haldor butted in again, successfully distracting Jaevid from finishing his interrogation. "What about it, Jae? What would scars like that mean?"

Jaevid Broadfeather's expression went dark, closing up as he regarded Murdoc one last time with a steely glare. "It's ... Hmm. I'm not sure." He shook his head and turned away. "It might be nothing. Don't let it go too far, will you? I need Reigh in one piece."

Haldor arched a brow. "And where are you going?"

Jaevid was already walking away, back toward the castle, with determination in every step. "There's someone I need to speak to."

22
CHAPTER TWENTY-TWO

Reigh and Murdoc dueled for almost half an hour before Murdoc finally gave a yawn, rolling his eyes as though Reigh's efforts were a complete bore. In an instant, he swept in with a series of brutal assaults that caught Reigh completely by surprise. Murdoc wrenched both of those curved, white blades out of his hands before delivering a punishing knee to the gut. Reigh crumbled to his knees, gripping his middle and wheezing through what I suspected were a few Gray elf curses.

With the point of his practice sword aimed right at Reigh's throat, Murdoc gave an unimpressed snort. "You fight well, but not well enough. Your attacks come from emotion. You react purely on feeling. It's reckless, not to mention stupid. Drawing your strength from your feelings will only leave you exhausted and outmatched."

Reigh shot him a poisonous glare, his lip curled in a snarl. "Who are you?" he demanded again.

"Murdoc. I'll be joining you on this ridiculous hunt."

Reigh's expression skewed with a mixture of pain, anger, and confusion. "What? There is no freaking way I'm letting you—"

Murdoc's arm flexed as he added a little more pressure to the blade, making the point press harder against Reigh's neck. "With all due respect, Your Highness, I wasn't asking for your permission. If Thatcher goes, I go. It's as simple as that. The way I see it, if you really intend on apprehending this Tibran witch, then you're going to need actual, competent help, anyway. You should be begging me to go, not refusing my offer out of some ridiculous sense of pride."

As much as it hurt to admit, he did have a point. I still didn't understand why Jaevid wanted me to go on this mission. I could fly with Fornax. But if it came down to a fight, I'd only recently graduated from the "running around screaming and flailing like a panicked chicken" level of combat training. Still, I wanted to prove myself. I *needed* to. I also hoped I could continue to build my bond with Fornax so we stood a chance when we joined the other dragonriders at Blybrig Academy. The idea that I'd show up there and embarrass Jaevid and myself by failing was unbearable. I had to do this ... somehow.

Looking away, Reigh clenched his jaw in defiance. "Fine."

"Excellent." Murdoc withdrew his sword and tossed it aside. "We'll be ready at your request."

Reigh didn't say another word as everyone began to disperse. I waited until Murdoc and the others had gone, and Reigh was left working alone to pick up the training equipment, to approach him. He snatched his blades up out of the dirt and clipped them back to the belt strung around his hips. When he noticed me approaching, his eyes narrowed and his nose wrinkled, as though he'd smelled something awful.

It might've hurt my feelings, but I'd gotten used to people—especially the girls my age in Thornbend—looking at me that way.

He turned his back to me, fiddling with the rack of practice swords like he was searching for some excuse not to talk to me. Not that I blamed him. Jaevid had warned me about the toll this mission might take on Reigh. I didn't understand why he was so upset, but I wanted to help. Or at the very least, I didn't want him to hate my guts. The first time we met, when he'd treated my injuries after I was dragged through Halfax by my dragon, Reigh had seemed like a nice guy. A little weird, maybe, but still friendly.

"H-Hey, uh, I ..." My voice caught as I stumbled over my words, trying to decide where to begin. "I wanted to say that I'm sorry for causing you any trouble. And I promise I'll keep practicing. And I'll stay out of your way and do whatever you tell me to, okay? I just want to help."

Reigh's shoulders slumped as he let out a deep sigh. He turned around and shook his head. "Look, I know you probably think I'm being a huge jerk about all this. And I guess you're right. I am kind of a jerk. But you really have no idea what you're getting yourself into. Jae and the others act like it's not a big deal, but it is. I've seen—and *felt*—what the Tibrans can do. The kind of cruelty they're capable of is not something anyone can explain to you. It's been months since we defeated Argonox, but sometimes I can still feel his presence. Something will set me off, a sound or a smell, and then I feel it like a cold breath on the back of my neck. Suddenly, I can't move. I can't breathe. I can't think. It all comes flooding back, and I'm helpless to stop it. I don't know if that feeling will ever go away. And I wouldn't wish it on anyone else, least of all someone like you." He hung his head so low his shaggy, dark red bangs hid most of his face from my view. "Now, Jenna's asking me to track down this Tibran witch. She's demanding that I take you with me. And I can't say no."

I shifted uncomfortably, not sure what to say to any of that.

"I don't like the idea of getting innocent people killed," Reigh continued, his voice tight with frustration as he clenched his fists. "They're sending us out there with no real idea what we'll be up against. I have no divine power to protect myself or anyone else. If something happens, if it all goes bad and you get killed, then I'm going to have to live with that. Your death will be my fault. And I ... I can't go through that again. I've killed enough good people."

I wasn't sure what Reigh meant by that. Maybe he was a little hotheaded, but he didn't seem like the kind of guy to go on a killing spree. There had to be more to it than that, some reason he'd killed before. "It won't be your fault," I assured him. "It's my choice to go."

A sudden, humorless laugh broke past his lips. When he looked my way again, there was a glint of something like exasperation in his expression.

I leaned back a little, just in case this was the beginning of a nervous breakdown and he started swinging his fists next.

"Well, maybe that friend of yours can teach you a few sword tricks. Who is he, anyway? I've never seen anyone move like that."

I sighed, unable to keep my expression from falling at the mention of Murdoc. Everyone kept asking me that question—and I still had no answer. Not a good one, anyway. I'd never told anyone about how Murdoc and I had actually met. Part of me was afraid of how they might react. But Reigh was about to be alone on a dangerous mission with both of us. Maybe he deserved the truth.

"I don't actually know much about him," I admitted quietly. "Please don't mention this to Jaevid and the others, but ... when we first met in Thornbend, while it was still under attack by the Tibrans, Murdoc ... tried to kill me."

Reigh's eyes went wide. He stood still, studying me carefully with his mouth open. "You mean he was a Tibran?"

"No," I answered quickly. "I don't think so. He wasn't dressed like they were. He was traveling with another, much older man. They were dressed in the same black leather armor, and they both had this silver cuff on their arm—like it was part of a uniform. It had the head of a wolf on it, a wolf with three eyes." My head dipped lower and lower as I tried to explain. "The older man told Murdoc to kill me, and I think he was going to, but ... then he didn't. I'm not sure why. He turned on his companion instead and then tried to help me escape the city. That's when the dragonriders caught us."

I was already dreading what I might see in Reigh's expression before I looked up again. He still stared at me, his expression stricken and shocked, and his mouth hanging open.

"He hasn't tried to hurt me since," I added. "I don't think he will. We're friends now. So it's okay."

Reigh arched an eyebrow like he wasn't so sure about that. "So let me get this straight. First, you make friends with a guy who tried to murder you in the street, then you train a dragon who tried to eat you before dragging you around the city by your feet like a sack of potatoes, and *then* you volunteer to go hunt down Tibran witches despite having no combat training whatsoever. Are you suicidal or something? Or do you just have a habit of making friends with things that want to kill you?"

I laughed. When he said it like that, I guess it did sound pretty stupid. "Maybe I just have bad luck."

"That's an understatement."

"My father used to say I'm a terrible judge of character, too."

"Obviously."

"Regardless, I ... I want to help. I want to help Murdoc, Fornax, and you, too."

He blinked, his expression twitching in bewilderment. "Help *me*? With what?"

I gave a shrug. "To find Devana. Maybe that will help you with your other problem—you know, to have some closure."

He looked away again, brows snapping into a guarded frown. "I don't know if it's that simple, Thatcher."

"I don't, either. But we might as well give it a try, right?"

"Yeah. Sure." He still didn't sound convinced.

We parted ways after I helped him finish cleaning up our practice gear. Knowing he didn't hate my guts made the idea of leaving with him in a day or two slightly less terrifying. His anger was justified; he didn't like being forced to face the demons of his past before he felt ready. And even more, he didn't like the idea of Fornax and me tagging along. I just hoped this wouldn't be the complete disaster Reigh expected it to be. I'd already endured more disasters than I ever wanted to.

THE NEXT DAY passed with quiet tension, like everyone was holding their breath in suspense for the Gray elf spy to arrive and give us information on where to begin our search. Jaevid kept glancing skyward while we were training, as though searching for something or someone. Reigh didn't talk much, and Haldor had already departed to continue his work elsewhere in the kingdom. Murdoc stood silently by the sparring circle where we practiced, watching our every move with sharp eyes and disapproving scowls.

I continued to work with a sword and shield, pushing myself as hard as I could to match Jaevid's blurring strikes. I scrambled to remember all the complicated footwork. My technique was improving—or so Jaevid claimed. I couldn't tell it, though. It still felt clumsy and awkward as I slung the heavy metal shield around, stumbling and trying not to trip over my own feet. I had no control over it. I wasn't strong enough, and I was out of time.

By nightfall, I was exhausted and filthy again from training. My mind raced, blurring with doubt and worry as I took my turn bathing in the servant's washroom. Staring at the mirror behind the dressing table, I searched through all my soft, "cute" features for some sign of a warrior hidden underneath. There wasn't one—not that I could see, anyway.

Maybe I really wasn't cut out to be a fighter. If so, then I was wasting everyone's time. I was trying to cram myself into a mold that didn't fit.

Combing my damp, light gold hair out of my face, I tied it back into the short ponytail at the base of my neck and finished getting dressed. Back out in the cold night air, I made my way across the royal grounds toward the Deck. I wanted to say goodnight to Fornax and admire my saddle one more time before going to bed. My gaze wandered up to the canopy of brilliant stars glittering in the moonless sky—just in time to see something blur across it. A shimmering shape hummed over the castle like a silver comet, making a wide pass and weaving around a few of the tall spires before it made a sharp turn back in my direction.

I lurched to a halt, my heart hitting the soles of my boots as the creature landed on the open grassy area right in front of the Deck. From less than fifty yards away, I could barely make out its shape. Lean and powerful, it had six muscular legs and a long, lashing tail. Its body shimmered as though it were made of diamond, covered in thousands of tiny scales that reflected the starlight like chips of mirror. Its thin, translucent wings reminded me of an insect's because each of its feathers were clear, or very faintly colored, as though they were cut from glass.

I'd heard of animals like this, although only in stories about Jaevid or the Gray War. Shrikes didn't live in Maldobar. They were creatures of the wild jungle of Luntharda, and they almost never came this far south. That is, unless they were carrying a Gray elf rider.

And this one was.

The beast snapped bony jaws and hissed, fluttering those wings as a hooded figure climbed down from its back. Bolts of long, silvery white hair blew freely in the night wind as a young Gray elf brushed back his hood and stared right at me. He couldn't have been much older than I was—seventeen or eighteen, probably, but there was a stern sharpness in his gaze that made me want to stand up straighter.

"You there," the elf called out as I started hedging closer. "Are you a servant of the castle? Do you know where I can find Reigh Farrow?"

"I-I, uh, maybe." I honestly wasn't sure about that. At this hour, everyone was probably asleep, right?

The Gray elf considered me with a few quick glances, his eyes catching like starlit opals in the darkness. "I need to speak with him immediately. There is an urgent message for him. I will wait here," he announced in a thick accent.

"Oooh." The realization hit me so suddenly I stumbled and almost tripped over my own feet. "Wait, you're ... I mean, are you the messenger? The spy who's supposed to tell us about Devana?"

The elf pursed his lips, eyes narrowing as he let out a deep, annoyed breath. "I would appreciate some discretion. Or an attempt at it, at least."

"O-Oh, um, right. Okay. Yeah, I can do that."

He forced a thin smile. "Why don't you take me to Master Reigh. Quickly, please."

I nodded and led the way toward the castle. Leaving his glistening mount behind, the Gray elf followed me through the servant's quarters up into Prince Aubren's wing. The royal guards keeping watch along the halls paused at the sight of us, eyeing the Gray elf visitor suspiciously as we moved through the lavish chambers of the castle. I guess they recognized me from my stay here, so they didn't question us.

Eventually, an older servant was the one who finally stopped to ask where we were going and what we were doing here. My answer made the old woman flush a bit, and she hastily showed us to a large parlor deeper in Prince Aubren's chambers.

Reigh, Queen Jenna, Prince Aubren, and Jaevid were all sitting around a large, crackling hearth, speaking quietly when we entered. Reigh stood first, smiling broadly at the elf who offered a brisk salute and bow to the royal company.

"Hakan," Reigh chuckled. "*You* made it into Judan's spy network? How? Who recommended you? Your grandmother?"

The elf rolled his eyes and shook his head, making his long, white hair swish over intricate robes of deep blue, green, and gold. "Now is not really the time. If you don't mind, I need to deliver this information and take my leave as quickly as possible. We are tracking suspicious caravan movements to the west through the marshes."

"Slavers?" Queen Jenna's expression practically sizzled with quiet fury.

Hakan nodded. "We suspect so. Tibran deserters make for easy prey. No one reports them missing."

The queen muttered a curse under her breath, her brow crinkling as she gazed toward the flames licking in the hearth. "I would like a word with you about that once our business is finished here. Prince Judan should have more support tracking them down. It took my father twenty years just to stop them from crossing into our borders before the war. I won't have them returning now."

The spy nodded. "Of course, Your Majesty. Let us begin."

HAKAN WAITED until everyone was settled, sitting around a marble-topped coffee table, to start telling us what he knew. "First, allow me to offer Prince Judan's highest compliments to ..." He hesitated, multihued eyes darting around the room as he blushed all the way to the tips of his pointed ears. "... the, um, the '*most enchanting woman in our known world*' were his exact words."

Prince Aubren made a noise, but I couldn't tell if it was a laugh or him clearing his throat. He covered his mouth as he bowed his head.

Queen Jenna, on the other hand, rolled her eyes and leaned forward to rest her chin in her palm. "Would you mind skipping ahead to the part where you tell me what you know about Devana?"

He nodded, wincing a little. "Yes, of course, Your Majesty. I only wish I had better news to provide." He shifted uneasily. "Tracking down any word of her has been a most dangerous and costly ordeal. We lost several of our best agents in the attempt. That woman, Devana, is no mere bumbling hedge-witch. The power she commands is unlike anything we have ever seen. As we feared, there is convincing evidence that she did survive the retaking of Northwatch by our soldiers after Argonox fell. Many of his warriors deserted immediately and fled into the tunnel system beneath the city. But we strongly suspect Devana remained there."

"Gods and Fates," Prince Aubren murmured as he rubbed his jaw. "That place is an absolute nest of filth and evil. Our forces are still struggling to regain a foothold there. It's riddled with tunnels that we've only just begun to map, so it's become a hive for every Tibran scoundrel, thief, and slaver this side of the Marshlands. They know the tunnels far better than we do, unfortunately, and vanish like phantoms in an instant. I have to ask, how by all the gods can you be sure she really is there?"

Hakan's demeanor darkened, his mouth drawing into a grim frown. "It would have taken months to search for her outright, and we would have lost many more good agents in the process. But we had a stroke of luck. We questioned several former Tibran soldiers eager to give up what they knew in exchange for a fresh start and recommendations for honest work. They pointed us to a man by the name of Dethris. He was one of the Tibran High Guards in charge of overseeing the security of Argonox's most prized captives. He had fled to the city of Osbran, and once we finally tracked him down, he was absolutely terrified to even speak of that woman."

"I'm beginning to sense that's a trend with her," Reigh mused. "So? What *did* he say?"

"He insisted that out of all the captives Argonox kept, Devana was the most unstable and by far the most dangerous," Hakan replied, his voice becoming softer. "Hers was a power not even Argonox fully understood. Her abilities allow her to infiltrate the minds of others, bend them to her will, manipulate them, or ... even destroy them entirely. It is a natural-born talent, he said—not the result of divine interference. Raw magic."

Jaevid's brow creased with deep, worried lines. That was exactly what he'd said before. Magic without a divine source wouldn't be affected by the deal he'd struck. Devana would still be as powerful as ever.

"Dethris reported that Argonox had intended to use her against his enemies, to coerce surrender or control their troops, but Devena was so unstable and immensely powerful that no one was able to successfully control her. She had a taste for violence and enjoyed watching others suffer—even if they were Tibran. After a disaster early in his campaign for world-sovereignty, Argonox ordered that her head be locked inside a heavily-warded mask because that was the only barrier her powers couldn't penetrate. She was never to be released, never to see daylight, and kept more as a prize or weapon of last resort, cut off from any human contact." Hakan's face paled a bit. He swallowed hard, stealing another look around the room as we all sat in silence. "That was when she was ... four years old."

"How long ago was this?" Queen Jenna asked.

"According to Dethris, about twenty years ago. She would be twenty-four now, and seeing daylight for the first time in a very long while."

"Gods," Jaevid breathed in horror. "She was locked in that thing for twenty years?"

"That's what he said. In truth, we don't know much about her current state of mind, although we can guess it is ... highly unstable. It's as though she's experiencing the outside world for the first time. We have no idea what she'll do. But if Dethris's story is true, we should prepare for the worst."

"*Prepare for the worst?*" Reigh repeated, shooting his older sister an appalled stare. "You are hearing this, right? And yet you want to send me in to do what? Try to *reason* with her? She's probably insane, and if she really is some kind of mind-reader or mind-manipulator, what chance would I stand?"

"There is ... some evidence that suggests her abilities were tested upon dragons," Hakan interjected, his voice still tinged with apprehension. "According to Dethris, anyway. He said the last time there was any interaction with Devana, it was because Argonox wanted to see if she could manipulate dragons the same way she could humans and other beasts. He said it was the first time she had been unable to breach another being's mind. Dethris also suggested that she might have difficulty with the minds of those chosen by dragons, as well, since the bond between them is so unique."

"If it's true and she can't control dragonriders, then you and Thatcher might actually be the only chance we have of catching her." Queen Jenna cut her eyes challengingly at Reigh. "Unless you'd rather sit this one out? Northwatch is awfully close to Luntharda, and there are no other dragonriders there to defend the people. Dragons can't even breach the jungle canopy. If she found her way there, no one could catch her. No one could stop her."

Reigh stiffened. Sweat glistened on his forehead as he sat eerily still, fists resting on his knees. His light amber eyes glinted with racing thoughts as he stared into his sister's eyes. "Does ... does anyone in Luntharda know? About her, I mean?"

"Warning has already been sent to King Jace and Queen Araxie," Hakan answered quickly. "But since Devana has been locked inside that magic gilded mask for so long, no one knows what Devana looks like. We can't give the border scouts a description of someone to look out for. It is vital that she be captured or killed as soon as possible."

I could hear my own heart pounding in the heavy silence that settled over the parlor. It kicked and floundered against my ribs like a wild horse bucking in a stall. My hands tingled with panicked cold as I stared across the marble coffee table to Jaevid. The look of earnest desperation twisting at his sharp, angular features caught me off guard.

"Well, then." Reigh sat back with a slow, shuddering breath. "Jae, if you've some hidden divine secret tucked up your sleeve, now's the time to share it."

Jaevid's expression turned wrathful. "My wife lives less than a day's flight from Osbran. She is only weeks away from giving birth to our child, and you honestly think I'd be holding back secrets that could keep her safe? You know as well as I do all my powers are gone. I can't even speak to Mavrik with my thoughts anymore."

"So why not come with me, then?" Reigh countered.

"Because I need him here," Queen Jenna snapped. "These trials have been a complete wreck from the start. We almost had a riot on our hands just this morning. Jaevid's presence is the only thing keeping these people in their seats. If he goes, it'll be chaos and people beating one another up like thugs in my throne room. Not to mention if word gets out about this Tibran witch. It would be complete mayhem. I can't have that. This has to work, Reigh. Dozens of kingdoms and thousands of lives depend on it."

The silence resumed, and once again, my heart thundered in my chest. Despair filled the air like a foul stench as, one by one, every person around that table began to bow their head as though in surrender.

"We'll do it." The words broke past my lips before I could stop them. "We'll find a way to catch her."

Lifting her tired gaze to stare at me, a faint smile ghosted over Queen Jenna's beautiful face. "Thank you, Thatcher. I promise, I will send out word and try to find anyone I can to help you. I've already made contact with a noble family in Eastwatch—dragonriders by trade. They're very experienced and willing to help you prepare for Northwatch."

"This is way beyond my normal level of stupid, you know," Reigh grumbled as he crossed his arms and scowled down at the floor. "But I guess there's no other choice, right?"

Jaevid buried his face in his hands, massaging his temples. "Reigh, if I could, I would go and—"

"Save it, Jae. I know you're jealous you don't get to be the hero this time," Reigh murmured. His smirk was painfully forced as he winked. "It's your own fault you have to stay here and keep the royal heads from butting. Just do me a favor, okay?"

Jaevid gave a solemn nod, returning that half-hearted smile. "Of course. Name it."

Reigh tipped his head toward me. "Make sure Mr. Courage and I get a proper funeral. I mean mountains of flowers, music, a full honor guard of dragonriders, little fancy cakes—I want the works."

HAKAN'S WORDS still hummed in my head, drawing every nerve as tight as bowstrings as I kicked out of bed in the darkness of early twilight. The Gray elf spy had given us lots of information, and not all of it was good news. Okay, actually most of it had been bad—way worse than Queen Jenna or any of us had anticipated.

My stomach flipped, fluttering like crazy while I crammed my few belongings into a bag, laced up my boots, and buckled on the armor pieces Jaevid had gotten for me. I reached down to grab my sword belt, but a hand suddenly shot forward and snatched it up before I could even touch it.

Murdoc stood before me, already dressed to go. There were a set of slender, curved scimitars belted across his back. Where had he gotten those? I didn't dare ask, though, as he went on inspecting my sword, sheath, and belt before handing them over with a grunt of approval. "Didn't think you were going to slink out of here without me noticing, did you?"

I swallowed hard as I took my blade and buckled the belt around my hips. I missed the loop a few times because my hands wouldn't stop shaking. "You don't have to do this," I murmured, biting down to keep my teeth from chattering.

He shot me a suspicious look. "What is that supposed to mean? You don't want my help?"

"No, it's not that."

"Then what is it?"

I shifted and chewed on the inside of my cheek. How was I supposed to tell him? Murdoc hadn't been in the meeting with Hakan, the Gray elf spy, so he didn't know. This was going to be way worse than any of us had imagined. Devana wasn't just some clever Tibran witch. If Hakan was right, then we might be in for a much bigger fight than we anticipated, and we were beginning our search at one of the most dangerous places in Maldobar.

I knew Northwatch had been the Tibran's base of operations during the war. Everyone in my hometown had talked about it during the war. Apparently, the city had once been inhabited and guarded by dragonriders, but after it was conquered, the Tibrans had warped it into their own private hive for every horrible, nightmarish thing you can imagine. Now, it seemed the networks of tunnels surrounding and delving under the city were packed full of leftover traps, monsters, and the occasional group of crazed Tibran soldiers hoping to avoid capture. Oh, and then there were the other usual vandals using those tunnels as a hideout: slavers, thieves, and the occasional mercenary band.

But that was where they believed Devana might be hiding, too. So that was where we had to start our hunt.

"Out with it, kid. We don't have time for you to overthink this," Murdoc pressed.

I rubbed the back of my neck and shuffled my feet—anything to keep from looking him in the eye. "Northwatch," I admitted, mumbling the words and half hoping he wouldn't hear. "We have to go to Northwatch. That's the last place anyone saw Devana. They think she might still be hiding there."

Murdoc's earthy-hued eyes went dark. His expression closed, becoming steely and eerily calm as his posture stiffened. It was the exact same look Reigh, Jaevid, and the others had given when Hakan mentioned that city.

"That place is a deathtrap," he rumbled quietly.

"Queen Jenna said she's got a plan for how to get us in there safely, Murdoc. And it's not like we have a choice. If what the spies found out about Devana is true, then ... she *has* to be caught."

I let my hand rest on the pommel of my sword. Having it there, knowing what I might be about to face, didn't make me feel any more confident. Once again, I couldn't stop asking myself what I was doing. Why was I getting involved with this? Just because Jaevid said I should? Or believed I could be of some value? Gods and Fates, I was not the right person for this job.

My friend didn't move for a few long, uncomfortable seconds. At last, he pressed his mouth into a grim frown and glanced over his shoulder, toward the door. "We should get going, then. I'm curious to hear what the queen has in mind."

I ducked my head and didn't reply. A heavy hand landed on my shoulder. Reluctantly, I met Murdoc's half-cocked smirk.

"Come on then, Thatcher. There are dragons to ride, witches to kill, people to save—don't want to be late for all that, do we?"

My voice squeaked with terror as I followed him to the door. "Y-Yeah, sure."

CHAPTER TWENTY-THREE

The Deck was quiet and all but abandoned at this hour. Only Jaevid and Reigh stood waiting, talking quietly in the pale glow of dawn. Large, wrought iron torches around the interior of the courtyard gave off just enough warm light to see that everything was ready to go. The dragons were saddled, and Reigh's bags were already loaded.

Fornax crouched low alongside Reigh's sleek, green female dragon. They sniffed at one another curiously, ears back and tails swishing. Fornax cringed away whenever she got too close, hissing but never showing his teeth. The dragoness, on the other hand, hedged in closer and chirped softly—almost like she was trying to reassure him as she nudged her snout against his. She must have been younger, because she was smaller than Fornax and had fewer horns and spines along her head and legs. Regardless, he regarded her with tense apprehension, growling and leaning farther away.

Both dragons swung their heads around as Murdoc and I arrived, bags in hand. Fornax chirped and chattered musically, his ears swiveling in my direction as I walked past. I let my hand brush the end of his nose, just to let him know I was close by.

Jaevid waved us over, his smile fading as he noticed Murdoc striding smoothly right beside me. "Feeling alright this morning?" he asked.

Great. Was it that obvious I was on the verge of throwing up from nerves? "Sure. Yeah. Never felt better," I lied.

"Just remember to breathe," Jaevid laughed, giving my shoulder a sympathetic pat. "As one of Queen Jenna's prestigious *'hunters,'* you've got to look the part—not like you're about to run away screaming."

Well, he had me there. I gulped against the burn of bile rising in my throat and tried to put on a fierce face.

Out of the corner of my eye, Murdoc smirked and gave a snorting chuckle under his breath.

"We won't be making the whole push to Northwatch today." Reigh wandered over to console me, as well. "We're making a stopover in Eastwatch. Apparently, there's a noble house taking us in for the night. I don't want to try to storm Northwatch after a full day of riding in the cold wind. I prefer to be fresh-faced and well-rested before I make my grand gestures of suicidal bravery."

"I had hoped that Mavrik and I would be riding with you as far as the Farrow Estate in case anything goes wrong with your first real flight, but there's another trial today," Jaevid added, his expression creased with a few more tired lines than usual. "Jenna expects this one will be unpleasant because the man on trial is a former Tibran General. She thinks my presence will help keep things from devolving into an open brawl in the throne room. They're checking every noble and royal in attendance for weapons as they enter so no one tries to execute him prematurely." He groaned and rubbed the bridge of his nose. "Why do people always assume I'm good at diplomacy?"

"Well, you did end two wars, fight a few gods, and save the world a couple of times." Reigh snorted, biting back a laugh.

Jaevid shook his head, his shoulders rising and falling with a heavy sigh. "Don't remind me."

"So, is it ok if Murdoc rides with me?" I dared to change the subject—especially since Jaevid didn't seem all that happy talking about dealing with nobles.

Reigh opened his mouth to answer, but Jaevid beat him to it. "Yes. Phoebe should be here with the passenger seat any minute."

All the color drained from Reigh's face. His brow twitched, and his light brown eyes widened with confusion, panic, and realization that seemed to make him stop breathing altogether. Once again, he opened his mouth to speak, but he never got the chance.

"Sorry we're a bit late!" a warm female voice called out to us from across the Deck's circular courtyard.

We all turned to look.

Queen Jenna and Phoebe walked side-by-side, lugging bags of equipment toward us. The queen's billowy dress blew around her tall frame, and I could have sworn I saw a hint of a large, rounded belly hidden by the voluminous lengths of her skirt. No way. I'd imagined that, right? She wasn't ... you know, *pregnant*. Right?

As soon as Jaevid spotted them, his face went pale and he took off at a jog to insist on taking the heavy bags from Jenna. The queen scowled and resisted, at first, but a few whispered words made her lips purse sourly and she surrendered the bags. Weird.

Phoebe smiled broadly and waved when she spotted me, her chaotic mane of copper curls framing her face as usual. Although, instead of her usual leather-working apron and dress, today she wore a long, mint green tunic underneath a dark leather vest, tool belt, and wool leggings. Her tall boots came to her knees and were the same deep, chocolate brown color as her vest.

"There were a few things I wanted to prepare before we got going," Phoebe announced as she dropped a big canvas bag right in front of us with a loud *thunk*.

Wait—Phoebe was going, too? No one had mentioned that before now. A smile spread over my face, and I couldn't resist sneaking a glance up at my silent companion. Murdoc stood stiffly, watching her with a convincingly calm expression like an eagle from a perch. Too bad I could still see him rubbing his fingers together furiously behind his back. A nervous habit, maybe?

"*No*," Reigh snarled suddenly, his voice a deep, rumbling growl.

Everyone froze.

Across from Phoebe, Reigh stood with his fists clenched so hard his entire body shook.

Jenna's gaze went steely. "I know how you feel about this, but we don't have a choice, she is—"

"*Not going*," Reigh snapped, biting hard on every word. "There is *no* way. It's not happening."

"Reigh." Jenna's voice had an edge of warning.

"Jenna," he repeated, mimicking her tone.

The queen crossed her arms, taking a defensive step in front of Phoebe. "This isn't up for debate. You need a safe path into Northwatch; you need someone who knows the tunnels and, more importantly, understands what Devana is capable of. Phoebe is the only one with first-hand experience."

"Because she's a Tibran!" he roared like an enraged king drake. "Are you being intentionally dense? She's the one ... the one who ruined my life! She tortured my dragon. Experimented on Aubren. She's a *demon*, and I'm not going anywhere with her!"

Reigh's chest rose and fell with slow, furious breaths as his face flushed almost as red as his hair. Nearby, his green dragoness let out a barking cry and slicked her scaly ears back as she snarled. All the spines along her back bristled as she scooted over closer to her rider.

Her reaction made Fornax growl, too. He flared his own spines and backed away, baring his teeth as his milky, sightless eyes darted in every direction as though he were looking for me.

Okay, this was getting out of hand—fast.

"Reigh, please, just listen." Jenna's expression softened as she regarded her little brother. I guess seeing his eyes well up with tears while his expression twitched with panicked rage was more of a reaction than she'd anticipated from him.

"I said *no*," he repeated. "You know what you're asking. I ... I can't believe you'd even think I would ever be okay with this." His mouth screwed up a few seconds before he threw his hands up, turned on a heel, and stormed away toward the Deck's main entrance.

"Wait a minute! Please!" Jenna took off after him, leaving Jaevid, Phoebe, Murdoc, and me to stand in awkward silence trying not to make eye contact. In the distance, I could hear them shouting back and forth until someone—probably Reigh—slammed a door.

I wasn't sure what to think or say. What was going on here? What had happened between Reigh and Phoebe? When I dared to glance at her, however, it didn't seem like a good time to ask her about it. Her whole demeanor drooped, her slender brows drawn into a look of anguish as she stared down at the toes of her boots.

"It'll be okay," Jaevid assured us with one of those tense, thin smiles that never reached his eyes. "Let them have a minute. If anyone can talk him around, it's Jenna."

Hunter

It took a lot longer than a minute.

Nearly an hour later, Queen Jenna and Reigh returned, trudging toward us with similar expressions of exhausted, frustrated misery. The queen murmured something to him, speaking so quietly I couldn't tell what she said. Whatever it was, it made Reigh nod and they exchanged a brief, stiff hug before she gestured for Phoebe to follow her.

No one said a word as we all watched Queen Jenna and Phoebe walk a short distance away to speak in hushed voices. Phoebe's curly hair hid her face like a curtain, but I could see her trembling as she slowly raised her head to meet the queen's gaze. Finally, Queen Jenna pulled her into a quick hug before walking away and leaving Phoebe standing alone—yards away. When she finally turned to walk back toward us, her face had gone pale. She fidgeted, shifting her weight and wringing her hands as she glanced between everyone. Like a doe caught out in the open, it was as though she couldn't decide if she should run or hold still.

"She's riding with you," Reigh commanded, growling under his breath as he brushed past, letting his shoulder bump mine. One glimpse at his face and it was easy to tell—he was *not* okay. I'd seen him angry and upset before, but this was different. The churning darkness in his eyes reminded me of a gathering storm as he looked back over his shoulder, past Jaevid, Murdoc, and me, to Phoebe. His mouth twisted, and he turned away sharply to adjust some of the straps on his saddle.

"Right. Well, this is sure to be fun." Murdoc licked his teeth behind his lips as he went to join Reigh.

"Thatcher, wait." Jaevid seized my arm before I could follow. "Do you remember what I said? This ... this is not going to be easy for Reigh."

For the first time, a twinge of real, earnest confidence rose in my chest as I leveled a smile back at him. "I know. It's okay, Jaevid. I can handle it."

He blinked in surprise. "You're sure?"

"It's like my father used to say. You can't dwell in the past, no matter how much it may have hurt you. If you spend your whole life looking back, you'll trip over something right in front of you. Reigh just has to figure out how to look forward again." I jostled my canvas bag, rebalancing it on my shoulder. "I'm going to try to help him. Even though he complains a lot and sometimes acts like a jerk, I think it's just because he's overwhelmed and he's carrying a lot of guilt. He's not a bad person. He just doesn't know how to let all that stuff go."

Jaevid blinked a few times, as though he weren't sure what to say. Then he squeezed my arm tighter. "Take care of yourself. Remember what I taught you."

"I will," I promised. Reaching under my shirt collar, I took out the necklace—the one he'd given me that held the white bone pendant and Fornax's whistle. I grinned as I held it up. "I'll make you proud, Commander. I swear it."

The morning wind rustled in his ash gray hair as he studied me, blowing it over his icy-hued eyes and stern, sharp features. Finally, without saying a word, he gave a nod and stood back to watch as we prepared to leave.

I had to help Phoebe drag the rest of her bags over and buckle them to the saddle.

One of them contained two extra seats that buckled onto the back of our saddles so that she and Murdoc could ride safely. My heart pounded, making my blood run with wild, excited energy as I did my final saddle checks and helped Phoebe climb into her spot. She wouldn't look me in the eye as I checked her safety straps. Whatever had happened between Reigh and her, I'd have to get to the bottom of that later. I'd already known about Phoebe being a Tibran. But now I also understood that she hadn't been involved because she wanted to. Lord Argonox had been holding her prisoner and forced her to do all those things. I wasn't sure if Reigh knew that, too, or even if it would make any difference. But I had to hope. Hope was the only thing I had now.

Well, hope ... and a dragon.

CHAPTER TWENTY-FOUR

We left the Deck as the sun rose, painting streaks of warm lavender and soft orange across the horizon. The earth slipped away, spreading out in every direction like a patchwork tapestry of open plains, dense forests, white-crested mountain peaks, and the distant, silvery glimmer of the ocean. Through the glass visor of my helmet, I saw the horizon stretching out before us, and my heart jumped into the back of my throat. Fornax couldn't see this anymore. But, Gods and Fates, I wished he could. I wondered if he could remember it or if all his good memories of flying with a rider on his back had been wiped away—lost forever in the toiling storm of war.

To my left, far off to the west, the jagged Stonegap Mountains thrust up toward the sky and followed the curving edge of Maldobar's coastline. It was said they also hid the dragonrider academy, Blybrig, somewhere in their rocky wilderness. They were a long way off, farther than I'd ever dreamed I'd go, and my pulse surged to think that someday I'd be flying that way to start my own training.

To my right, the eastern coast was much closer. The ocean that lapped at the steep cliffs was dark, cold, and foaming, and I knew that if I followed that coastline south far enough, I'd reach Two Rivers. That city wasn't far from where I'd grown up.

Thinking about home put a hard, cold knot in my stomach. I couldn't bring myself to look back in that direction. If smoke still rose from its burning remains, I didn't want to see it. I didn't want to think about Father, my home, or how my life would never be the same again. Forward—that was where my path lay now. I had to keep my gaze fixed there.

With a beat of his strong wings, Fornax caught the rising wind and soared north. I leaned down closer to his neck, letting him feel my body heat against his hide as I moved the mechanics at my feet and twisted the saddle handles, giving him subtle directions. We chased the long tail of Reigh's green dragoness. I didn't know her name yet, but she slipped so easily through the sky with the smooth, agile strokes of her slender wings, I had to wonder how Reigh had found her. Had it been anything like when Fornax and I first met?

For his sake, I hoped not.

We cruised the open sky with Reigh in the lead, following the coast north. We passed cities and villages far below, their streets bustling in the middle of the day. We soared high over roads that wound with the contours of the landscape and zoomed by rolling farms. Flocks of sheep wandered like drifting puffs of white cloud. Horses whinnied and galloped at the sight of us, while cows just glanced up and chewed lazily.

The sun had begun to sink behind the mountains when I finally spotted a larger city nestled in the middle of steep, sloping hills. The sight of a single, tall spire that loomed over the city like a silver spike sent a pang of anxiety through my gut. I'd never seen one in person, but people talked about the watches all the time in the markets. That fortress had been built specifically to house dragonriders. Eastwatch was one of the four big posts where all dragonriders were sent when they left their formal training. There were a few smaller posts scattered around the kingdom, but the watches were by far the largest and most impressive. They stood like monuments; massive stone and iron guardians looming over the landscape as if to dare any imposing army to challenge their might.

Too bad we couldn't stay there now, though.

The city fanned out around the tower with streets patterned like threads on a spider's web. Most of the thatched and clay-shingled rooftops looked new—probably thanks to being burned during the Tibran invasion. But like the rest of Maldobar, Eastwatch was hard at work rebuilding everything Lord Argonox had destroyed.

From his saddle, Reigh gave a hand signal to get my attention and gestured to an estate on the eastern edge of the city. The noble house stood away from everything else —a big chateau of gray stone and broad, open grazing lands flecked with more white spots that I could only guess were sheep. Nothing out of the ordinary there, really. Nobles usually had a business of some sort to keep their pockets lined with fresh coin.

The four large barns positioned right behind the estate were unusual, though. I'd never seen anything like them. They were long and narrow, with walls and roofs made of metal instead of wood. What would nobles keep in barns like that? Surely not horses or cattle.

We landed in the avenue right in front of the grand old house. The narrow glass windows and the tall granite pillars reflected the orange glow of the setting sun. My back ached and my legs and arms throbbed from sitting in the saddle so long. It took me a minute to climb down off Fornax's back first. Then I offered Phoebe a hand getting out of the saddle. She gripped me tightly, her fingers cold and expression still tinged with apprehension as she stuck close to my side. Not that I blamed her. I had no idea what to expect from this noble family that was supposed to be helping us. I didn't even know their names.

There were candles lit in the windows and smoke rising from many of the tall stone chimneys. Someone was home. Gods and Fates, I hoped they had dinner on. My stomach writhed, growling anxiously at the thought of a hot meal.

Fornax was anxious, too. He growled and sucked in deep breaths of the strong wind, hunkering closer to the ground. His ears perked and swiveled in my direction as I took off my riding gauntlets and let my bare hand rest against his snout. "It's okay," I murmured gently.

Fornax gave another low growl, as though he weren't convinced. He nipped at the back of my head as I walked away, suddenly snagging me to a choking halt by my cape. "Come on, Fornax. Don't be like this. Just stay here. I'll be right back. You'll be fine."

He finally let my cape go, smacking his lips defiantly.

Phoebe and I had to work together to carry our things toward the front door. I'd only brought one bag, but she had two that were almost as big as she was. I couldn't help but wonder what she'd brought so much of. Blacksmithing or crafting equipment, maybe?

Reigh and Murdoc led the way while our dragons stayed crouched down in the avenue to wait. Everywhere I looked, there was nothing but rolling, windswept grassland. The city was miles away, and between the dreary stone mansion, small bare-limbed shrubs, and blank landscape, there was something undeniably bleak and lonely about the whole place.

The cold air whipped at my bangs and stung in my eyes as I made my way along the front drive to the manor's doors. It smelled strongly of sea salt, a subtle reminder of just how close we were to the seaside cliffs—less than five miles, probably. My skin prickled at the thought. I'd always heard those cliffs were wild dragon territory.

No sooner had we reached the front steps of the manor than the large, double doors groaned open and a single man stepped out to meet us. His powerful build and tall stature were emphasized by an intricate brown leather doublet and matching belt, boots, and vambraces laced along his forearms. He regarded us with a half-cocked smirk and tilt of his head, amusement twinkling in his eyes.

"You kids lost or something?" He laughed and rubbed his stubble-flecked jaw as he studied each of us one at a time. "I was expecting soldiers, not a batch of urchins."

Reigh frowned. "Excuse you, but Queen Jenna said—"

The man's smirk stretched wider, dimpling one corner of his mouth. "Relax, Red. No one likes a sour grape—or a rotten tomato, in your case, I guess. Come on in, my staff will see to your mounts." He tipped his head back in the direction of the open door. "Duke Ezran Cromwell, for whatever it's worth, is always at Her Majesty's service. And yours, too, as it were."

"I-I ... um, my dragon will need some extra help." I dipped my head. "If you don't mind, My Lord, I should probably be the one to help him settle in. He, um, he gets scared easily and ... uh ..."

Duke Cromwell looked over our heads to where our dragons were still crouched nearby. His dark brown eyes glittered as he studied them, the pensive furrow in his brow drawing attention to a small scar flecked across his right eyebrow. He seemed to be somewhere in his mid-twenties, and his shaggy, deep brown hair blew casually over his rugged features as he stared back down at me. "Fornax is yours now?"

My mouth fell open. For a second, all I could do was make surprised choking sounds. "Yes, My Lord," I finally managed to rasp.

"I see." The duke's mouth quirked thoughtfully. "And he's blind now, I hear. Yet you're flying him? Impressive. Last word out of Halfax was they might be shipping him back here because he'd gone feral."

"Back?"

He nodded and stepped aside so we could go in. "Of course. Fornax was bred here. He was sired by one of our prized family drakes, Demos, and hatched right out there in those barns. We've been breeding dragons for nearly a hundred years. Don't worry about it, kid. Despite recent events, we are still fully equipped and can handle any dragon—even a blind one."

When I looked back, I noticed four men in dark blue uniforms already approaching our dragons. A few were carrying buckets while others blew into long, thin whistles. But those slender instruments didn't sound like the one I used to communicate with Fornax. In fact, they sounded a lot like the chirping, chittering sounds the dragons made. Fornax's response was immediate. His head lowered, ears perking and nostrils puffing toward one of the men carrying a bucket. The man reached in and tossed something to the ground in front of him—a big slab of raw meat.

The smell made Reigh's bright green dragoness crawl over to investigate, sniffing excitedly as she made eager popping, squeaking sounds.

"They'll be fine," Duke Cromwell said again as he waved us inside. "Let's get in. I have a feeling we'll be getting a storm tonight. Wind's too restless."

Phoebe's cheeks had gone as rosy as ripe apples. "Do you really *breed* dragons here?" she asked breathlessly.

A roguish grin returned to Duke Cromwell's expression as he gave her a wink. "You know it. Come on, Freckles; I'll give you the tour."

THE CROMWELL ESTATE WAS IMPRESSIVE, even if it was a lot less grand and ornate than the royal palace had been. The inside of the manor was cavernous, with bare stone walls, large hearths with roaring fires, floors lined with furs or woven wool rugs, and high ceilings with exposed wooden beams covered in engravings of dragons. Something about the place felt solid, warm, and comfortable. It put my nerves at ease as soon as the door closed behind us.

Before us, the entryway was lined with dozens of suits of armor, each more detailed and incredible than the last. The breastplates, gauntlets, and pauldrons were studded with spikes, engraved with the same design of a crest of a dragon in a circle of flame, and inlaid with flourishes of gold or silver.

But these weren't just fancy suits of armor. The narrow, glass-covered slits cut into the helmets were a dead giveaway. Each one of those amazing ensembles was a set of dragonrider armor.

"I thought dragonriders were buried in their armor?" Reigh asked as he stepped over to get a better look at one.

"They will be. I have six brothers, nine uncles, and gods only know how many cousins. Most of them either are or were dragonriders. After they retire from service, they leave their armor here to be displayed at the family estate. When they die, they'll be buried in it," Duke Cromwell explained, waving a hand at them dismissively. "If they haven't gotten too fat for it, anyhow. Dragons are ... something of a family business for us."

"Are you a dragonrider, too?" Phoebe asked, her eyes practically sparkling at the sight of so many fine designs.

"*Was*," the duke corrected with a sigh. "The estate took a beating during the war, thanks to the Tibrans, and the family line is running thin. Of eight brothers, only six survived. Even more were wounded such that they were honorably discharged from Her Majesty's service. After my dragon fell at the battle for Southwatch, I returned here to try to ensure my family home survived. We took in as many women and children from the city as we could and blockaded and boarded up every point of entry. There was never any doubt that the Tibrans would come, so the best we could do was try to outlast them. It worked, for the most part. This old place stood against the Tibran ranks like a lighthouse in a hurricane, and we were able to endure until reinforcements arrived to help us evacuate to Halfax."

He paused, turning a curious look back at Reigh. "After you lot ended the war, I had a lot of dead relatives to bury and an estate in ruins. Some of my elder brothers still have dragons, and it's a Cromwell tradition to stay in the saddle as long as we're able. Since I no longer have a mount, the family agreed that I should be the one to take over the estate and hatchery, even if I'm not the oldest. I think they feared losing the prestigious title of Duke we were awarded during the Gray War more than the idea of me running things." His expression dimmed as he rubbed at the back of his neck. "Although they likely regret that decision now. It's taken months to get everything up and running again, but the gods have been kind. Despite all the new laws about the breeding of dragons, we can still breed our mounts and sell their eggs. The money has helped the rebuilding process, and I'm able to extend some aid to the city, too."

Phoebe whirled around to face him suddenly, her bright blue eyes as wide as saucers. "Are there any here? Now? Hatchlings, I mean."

Duke Cromwell nodded, grinning as though he found her enthusiasm endearing. "Of course. I've got hatchlings from summer, and a handful of yearlings not yet big enough to be tested to a rider."

Her face flushed almost as red as her hair, hands clenched under her chin as she bounced up onto her toes. "Could we see them? Please? Just one quick look?"

The duke seemed to be enjoying her excitement. He flashed another charming smile and shrugged. "As you wish, Freckles." Turning away, he continued into the estate, leading us down long halls and elegant, grand staircases. Our footsteps echoed off the stone walls and high ceilings, and heavy shadows seemed to choke out all but the meager light of the torches.

"Business has been good, although I've made some changes to the selling process— much to the dismay of my family," he continued. "Disfiguring dragons or cutting their wing tendons to make them more manageable for breeding is no longer allowed by law; a change that, in my opinion, should have been passed long ago. Beyond that, I no longer allow bidding before the eggs have hatched. I don't want to sell any mounts that aren't fit for battle both in health and temperament. Before, we could correct some behavioral problems with bridles and pinch-girths. But I've stopped using any of that gear. If a dragon's spirit is set against taking a rider, who are we to force him?"

"What about the ones who aren't healthy?" Phoebe trotted along, having to skip a little to keep up with the duke's much longer strides.

"If it's a matter of personality, I'll give them a few years to see if their moods even out. If not, they'll be released back into the wild. The ones that aren't healthy are culled in as humane a way as we can manage."

"Wait, you mean you kill them?" I interrupted. Somehow, that just didn't seem right.

"The same thing would happen to them in their natural habitat, boy. I can guarantee that our methods are much kinder than the fate they'd suffer in the wild, though. Sick and deformed hatchlings either die of starvation or because something else eats them. It's nature's way of keeping bloodlines clean and offspring healthy. Only the strong survive."

My mouth scrunched, mashing into a hard line as I thought it over. What did that mean for a dragon like Fornax? He wasn't a hatchling—but Jaevid had said he wouldn't be able to survive in the wild without his sight.

Duke Cromwell stopped at the top of a sloping staircase that led up to a large iron-plated door. It must have been over ten feet tall, and the engravings in the metal wound into the twisting shapes of dragons with their necks and tails intertwined. Right above the huge handle was the image of a dragon's head, cut from solid bronze, with a keyhole right in the center of its open mouth.

"This is the hatching room," he announced as he pulled a large brass key cut in the shape of a dragon out of his pocket. He slipped it into the keyhole, and one twist of it made mechanisms inside the giant door groan and clunk. "Keep your voices down. They've just eaten, and the mothers tend to be grumpy when you wake up their young."

CHAPTER TWENTY-FIVE

Duke Cromwell showed us through each of the four barns on his estate, guiding us from room to room. He offered casual explanations of how the dragons were kept, the eggs were handled, and the hatchlings were raised. If there was one thing I knew, it was good stabling, and the place seemed well organized and clean. The air smelled of animal musk, fresh hay, and the faint, acidic tinge of dragon venom. The new hatchlings, the duke explained, liked to test out their fire-spitting abilities from time-to-time. That's why the interior of the barns had been completely lined in the only thing their acidic venom couldn't burn through—dragon hide. He insisted the hides were harvested only from dragons that had either died of natural causes or fallen in battle.

"It came in especially handy when the Tibrans decided to try using those clay orbs filled with dragon venom against us. Metal works well enough for a while, but it will melt eventually. But dragon hide? Not a chance," the duke added as he led us along the narrow passages that ran between the separated stalls. Each one was stocked with fresh hay and boulders, which he explained made the mother dragons feel more at home. "In the wild, they nest in the caves and ledges along the cliffs right off the seashore. Since fish are their favorite meal, it allows them to feed without having to go far from their nest. A female dragon will lay three or four eggs in a clutch, raise them in that cave, and then, one by one, the hatchlings disperse as they reach adolescence. They may stick close by their mother for the first year, learning how to hunt and assimilating into their social group. After that, they're on their own."

"And their venom is for protection, right? Not for hunting purposes?" Phoebe stared up at him, still hanging on his every word.

For whatever reason, that seemed to be putting an annoyed crinkle in Murdoc's brow. He scanned the interior of the barns without ever saying a word, but his gaze always returned to her.

"That's right. Dragons spray a jet of highly acidic venom. It catches fire with explosive force as soon as air touches it. But they don't use it for hunting—it's more of a weapon of last resort. On the ground, they don't move very fast. If a dragon is cornered or dealing with an enemy it can't fly away from, his venom is his primary means of defense. That's why it takes so much training to teach them to use it as a weapon from the air. It's not something they'd typically do in the wild." The duke flashed that crooked smile again. "Clever one, aren't you, Freckles?"

I spotted Murdoc working his jaw as he studied the duke, almost like he was debating something violent. He didn't, thank goodness. We really couldn't afford to upset our noble host.

Knowing this was where Fornax had come from made my stomach flutter as I stared through the narrow slats cut into each stall. Inside, I could barely make out the big, scaly shapes of dragons curled up in the gloom. They liked their caves warm and dark, according to the duke, and the mothers would wrap themselves around their eggs to incubate them for months. I couldn't help but wonder which stall Fornax had been hatched in.

The next barn held the hatchlings Duke Cromwell had mentioned before. The stalls were larger, with only three in the entire barn, and there were a lot more rocks scattered around to give the young dragons places to play, explore, and test their wings. Behind the protective barrier of iron bars that ran from the stone floor to the metal ceiling, eight young dragons fluttered from rock-to-rock, wrestled in the hay, or lay sleeping in a scaly heap. They squawked and chirped, bounding and gliding low over the ground when they saw us.

Phoebe barely managed to slap a hand over her mouth to stifle her squeal of delight.

The duke laughed and patted the top of her head. "Cute for terrors, aren't they? Just don't ever put your hand near their mouths. Little devils can take off a finger in one bite." He nodded toward the hoard of dragonlings as they surged toward us, clambering over one another and yipping with excitement. With big eyes glittering hopefully, they snapped their jaws and stood up on their hind legs, craning their necks as though looking for any sign that we'd brought something for them to eat. Their heads and feet seemed a bit too large, though, and their wings much too small to allow them to fly for more than a second or two. Although most of the baby dragons already had vibrant colors mottling their scales, they didn't yet have horns on their heads or spines along their backs. Maybe that was something they had to grow into.

An affectionate smile brushed the duke's features as he crossed his arms and stood back, allowing us to take a closer look. "Each one weighs about fifteen pounds at hatching, but they grow fast. These hatched over the summer, and they're already over a hundred pounds each. We separate them from the mother once they can eat without needing her to pre-chew their food for them. It helps make them accept a rider later on if they get used to human scent and being touched as early as possible. It also makes things go easier when we let people in to see if anyone is chosen voluntarily. Anyone is permitted to come and try, and if they're lucky enough to have a dragon choose them, they can take it as soon as it's old enough—free of charge—as long as they can prove they've a way to care for it appropriately. The rest we sell after I've interviewed and vetted the intended rider."

"Questions." Phoebe breathed shakily. She turned slowly back around to face us with her eyes still wide and mouth hanging open. "I have so many *questions, My Lord!*"

"Ask away, then. And call me Ezran. Seems a little ridiculous to continue with those formalities with a Prince of Maldobar present." He cast Reigh a knowing grin. "Especially considering I was warned you don't care much for the social prestige your title grants you."

"No," Reigh replied with a sulky frown aimed squarely at Phoebe. "I don't. And we're not here for tours. We've got real work to do."

"Is that so? Well, then, let's finish up, and I'll show you to the dining hall. I was asked to make certain Her Majesty's hunters had a good meal before you depart tomorrow. For whatever I lack in courtly manner, I know how to provide a decent banquet. Stay close, though. This next barn has the yearlings, and they're a bit more temperamental. Hormones, you know." He tipped his chin toward Murdoc, who still hadn't spoken at all. "That seems like something you can probably relate to, right, Broody?"

If that was meant to be bait to get Murdoc to talk, it didn't work.

"You know what they say about boys who are too serious?" Ezran asked as he began to lead the way again.

"No, what?" Phoebe asked.

"They grow up into seriously boring old men."

Phoebe giggled as she bounced after him like a little kid in a candy shop. I guess for an artificer, getting to see young dragons and learn about how they were bred was basically the same thing. It was not something most people got to see in their lifetime.

Too bad she was the only one who seemed to be having fun. Regardless of how awesome the tour was, Murdoc glared daggers at our host's back as we entered the next barn. Broodiness aside, I got the feeling he was *seriously* contemplating putting a blade through the duke's neck.

Great. Between Reigh's simmering fury about Phoebe and Murdoc's usual moodiness, I was officially on damage control.

THE CROMWELL DINING hall was a long, narrow room with huge, arched windows down one side. They looked out over the dreary, rolling grassland that seemed to glow blood red under the last few rays of the setting sun. Ezran had been right about the weather. The sky was choked with dark clouds, and strong winds rippled the tall grass like waves on the ocean.

Inside the hall, however, we were warm and safe. Huge, wrought iron chandeliers hung over the longest dining table I'd ever seen. There must have been thirty seats in all, but only one end of it had been set for our meal tonight. Platters of baked vegetables surrounded racks of roasted lamb, stuffed turkey, and boiled eggs. Small loaves of fresh, dark bread were arranged beside trays of creamy cinnamon butter, cranberry jams, and huge wheels of cheese. Apple and peach pies sent up curling wafts of steam as they sat, their flaky golden crusts gleaming in the candlelight.

Gods and Fates—I'd never seen that much food in my life. My mouth watered as I stumbled for my chair, shakily tucking my napkin into the front of my shirt as I seized a fork and prepared for an epically delicious battle.

Dinner passed with an uncomfortable tension in the air. Reigh stabbed at the food on his plate like he was trying to murder it while Phoebe asked dozens of questions about the dragons, hatchlings, and eggs. Murdoc sat beside me and ate without speaking, as usual. That part, at least, wasn't out of the ordinary.

At the head of the table, Ezran talked casually about his work here at the estate as we stuffed our faces. Apparently, due to the damage done by the Tibran invasion, only a few portions of the manor were habitable. For that reason, he hadn't hired on a full staff of servants yet—just a few to take care of the basic day-to-day needs. He seemed very particular about the people he hired on to work with the dragons, and he claimed it took a specific kind of personality to be able to deal with the young dragons when they were broken to a saddle.

Hearing him talk about it called back memories of my childhood and watching my dad work with horses. I sat, enjoying the mouth-watering food spread out in front of me, as more and more of those flashes blitzed through my already exhausted brain. It wasn't the first time I'd missed home, but—for whatever reason—thinking of it now hurt more than ever.

"So," Ezran murmured around the end of a long wooden pipe. He held it between his teeth, puffing occasionally as he lit the wad of tobacco at the other end. It smoldered, filling the air with a soothing fragrance. "My sources tell me you'll be heading for Northwatch. They didn't say why, and I don't intend to ask, but if you're going there I can only assume it's serious. That place might as well be a portal to the abyss."

"Trust me," Reigh sighed as he sat back in his chair. "We aren't going there on vacation."

"No doubt. But you should know, word coming out of Osbran is that the Ulfrangar have moved into Northwatch now, too. It's not even safe to walk the streets in broad daylight anymore. The merchant caravans won't go anywhere near it. It's cut off trade from that end of Luntharda completely."

Next to me, Murdoc went completely still. He sat, gripping his fork until his knuckles blanched, his eyes fixed on his plate.

"Ulfrangar?" Reigh asked. "I thought they were a myth? A scary, human bedtime story?"

Ezran shrugged as he puffed at his pipe for a few seconds. "Can't say for sure. It could just be people's imaginations running wild. The war is over, but there's still so much fear in the air. Hard to pick apart truth from rumor anymore."

"What are they?" I managed to pry my eyes from the disturbing way Murdoc seemed to have stopped breathing. "The Ulfrangar, I mean?"

"Supposedly, they're a league of assassins—more beasts than men," Ezran explained. "It's hard to tell if they truly exist, though. Tales of them have been around for ages. The story goes that the only time you see them is when they've come for you. No one meets them and lives to tell of it, but the wealthy and desperate might hire them to … make *problems* disappear." He scoffed and blew a smoke ring into the air that drifted slowly and silently past us down the table. "Convenient when you're dealing with a story that sounds a little too unbelievable, eh? To my knowledge, no one has ever seen one, and there's never been any hard evidence that the Ulfrangar really exist. It would've been impossible not to stumble across them during the Tibran War, right? People always want a scapegoat, a demon in the dark to blame when bad things happen. I doubt there's anything more to them than stories and myth."

"Unfortunately, the demon we're hunting in Northwatch is all too real. And frankly, I'm short on theories of how we are going to apprehend her," Reigh growled under his breath, sliding Phoebe a threatening glare. "A lot is riding on whether or not our little Tibran rat can contain her."

The unmistakable, venomous shade of hate in his tone made Phoebe flinch again. She lowered her head, avoiding his eyes like a guilty puppy.

My hands curled into fists under the table. I understood why he was angry with her. There was bad blood between them—anyone could sense it. Something bad had happened. But he was just being cruel. She wasn't a traitor. She was with us right now, going on this insanely dangerous mission, because she wanted to help.

I opened my mouth, intending to take up her defense. This had to stop. We stood no chance of finding Devana if he couldn't swallow his anger long enough for us to work as a team. Before I could get a word out, an elbow jabbed me in the ribs so hard all I could do was wheeze.

On my right, Murdoc shook his head slowly and mouthed three silent words. "*Leave it alone.*"

Leave it alone? Seriously? Didn't he get that this kind of attitude out of Reigh was going to wind up sabotaging our whole mission? If we couldn't work together, then it was basically moot. We were counting on Phoebe to help us defeat or maybe even capture Devana. We *needed* her.

If Duke Ezran noticed the tension in the air, it didn't show. He glanced my way casually and asked, "So now that you're riding Fornax, I take it you'll be heading to the academy for training?"

"O-Oh, um, well," I panicked aloud. "I-I think so, sir."

"*Pfft*, maybe, if they can find a weapon he doesn't suck at," Reigh grumbled.

I struggled to swallow my embarrassment, but it didn't work. My face burned with total humiliation as I avoided looking toward our host again. I was terrified of what I might see there—like a look of disapproval. What if he thought I wasn't good enough to be riding on one of his dragons?

"Indeed," Murdoc agreed. He'd gone back to eating with his usual, grim, utterly bored expression. "With any luck, he'll practice a bit and then only suck as badly as you do."

Phoebe choked suddenly, nearly spitting hot apple cider into her plate.

Meanwhile, Reigh glared across the table, his eyes flashing like there were tiny, burning villages in them. His jaw clenched. One of his brows twitched. But he didn't say a word.

I tried not to enjoy that too much.

"And what are you, exactly?" Ezran interrupted with a curious glance to my sullen friend. He tipped the end of his pipe to the others one by one, "Red's a prince, whether he acts likes it or not. Freckles was apparently a former Tibran of some kind. Blondie seems like he might be some baker's boy—or at least he eats like one. But you ..." The Duke's eyes narrowed ever so slightly. "You're something else, aren't you?"

Murdoc froze again. He locked gazes with our host from down the table, sitting rigidly without ever saying a word. It reminded me a little of a deer caught out in the open, trying to decide whether or not to flee. Second by second, the atmosphere grew thick and tense. No one said a word.

So I had to. "He's my friend. And he's with us. Right, Murdoc?"

My so-called friend stared at me like I'd smacked him across the face. The way he was looking at me, I started to wonder if I'd spontaneously grown a third eyeball or something.

Great.

After a long, uncomfortably silent moment, Ezran cleared his throat and shifted in his seat. "I suppose it's none of my business, anyway. Her Majesty's hunters were hand-chosen for a reason, and you're all welcome here. I've opened up a couple of rooms on the fifth floor. You'll have to excuse the debris—we're still doing repairs. But the rooms should be clean and comfortable enough for a night."

"Is there a place where I can work a little?" Phoebe asked, hesitantly raising her small hand. "You see, I'm an artificer, and I need to check the devices I've brought to make sure they weren't damaged on the journey. Then I've got to prime them. It's going to take a few hours, and I'll need a large table."

Ezran gestured unceremoniously to the one in front of us. "As soon as the servants clear it, you can help yourself, Freckles."

She beamed and bounced to her feet, wild coppery curls framing her face. "Thank you!"

Leaning far back in his chair, the young duke rested his boot heels on the table and crossed one leg over the other. "As for the rest of you, if there's anything else you need tonight, my staff will be happy to see to it."

CHAPTER TWENTY-SIX

Dinner ended late, and despite a belly of warm food and spiced apple cider, I couldn't stand still. Nerves made my hands twitch. I jerked at every sound as I followed Reigh to our room. The rest of our group had their own agendas, I guess. Murdoc practically evaporated the instant we left the dining hall. He had a knack for that, and I'd become used to him slipping around like my own personal phantom—popping up when I least expected it. Phoebe was already unpacking her bags onto the table when we left, drawing Duke Ezran's attention with each new, strange object she produced.

"She really has a plan for catching Devana?" I dared to ask once I was sure we were out of earshot.

Reigh stomped up the grand staircase ahead of me, his head down and gripping his bag in a fist. "So she claims. And she sold my sister on that idea. I guess we'll see," he mumbled. "What you should really be asking yourself is who she will side with if Devana offers her an alliance? I don't care what she says—that girl is a Tibran. If this mission fails and we all get butchered, you can bet it'll be her doing. Don't say I didn't warn you."

I clamped my mouth shut, throat squeezing around what I really wanted to say. He had every right to be upset—angry, even. But he wasn't giving Phoebe a fair chance. Somehow, they had to get through this. They had to work it out. Otherwise, the biggest threat to my life wasn't Devana; it was getting caught in the crossfire if things between Reigh and Phoebe ever came to blows. Based on what I'd seen, I was pretty confident Murdoc wouldn't stand by and watch that happen. I wouldn't, either. Someone would get hurt. Probably me.

Yeah, definitely me.

Our room wasn't nearly as bad as the duke had made it sound. Three single beds stood beneath canopies of draped red velvet, spaced far apart down the length of a broad room. The one large window at the end revealed a toiling night sky lit by the occasional flash of lightning. Rain peppered the glass and thunder rumbled in the distance.

A large hearth had already been lit with a fire that filled the rest of the room with a warm, golden light. It made things seem more comfortable as I sank down onto one of the beds, running my hands over the plush blankets. It was still bizarre to be around luxurious things like this. My gaze roamed the tall oil paintings of dragons and knights that hung on the stone walls, the animal skin and wool rugs on the floor, and the tall, engraved door that led to what I suspected was a private washroom. I wondered what my father would think about me staying in so many fine noble homes.

If things kept up this way much longer, I'd get to ask him personally in the afterlife after Reigh accidentally murdered me, a dragon burned me to a crisp, or an evil Tibran witch turned my brain to goo.

I shuddered and stood, fidgeting with the pommel of the sword that still hung in a sheath from my belt. "Hey, uh, I think I'm gonna go walk around for a while."

Reigh glanced up from where he was unlacing his boots. "Everything all right?" He actually sounded concerned.

No, of course it wasn't. He had to know that. All I could do was shrug as I started for the door. "Fine. I just want to check on Fornax. I'll be back."

"Say hello to Vexi for me," he replied as he flopped back onto his bed.

Okay, so it wasn't *all* a lie. I wanted to untangle the rat's nest of questions tangling in my brain. But I also wanted to check on Fornax and make sure he was settling in okay. Nothing was on fire, and no one had come screaming from the stables, so it was a safe bet they'd managed to get him into a stall. But I didn't like the idea of him feeling scared and alone—like I'd abandoned him.

Luckily, finding Fornax wasn't all that hard.

The Cromwell estate might have been half in ruins, but it had plenty of room for dragons, and ours had been set up to stay together in a spacious, shared stall in the largest barn. Curled up in the far corner on a bed of hay, Fornax lifted his head when I pushed the door open and slipped inside, giving him a whistle to let him know it was me.

Reigh's dragoness, Vexi, lay curled up nearby, busily preening her bright green scales. Her big blue eyes gleamed like sapphires, considering me for a second or two before she gave a wide yawn and went back to grooming herself. I guess I wasn't that interesting to her.

"Hey there, big guy." I ran my hand over the side of Fornax's scaly head, letting my fingers trace the warm, smooth, leathery surface of his hide. His milky jade eyes blinked, tracking my sound and smell as I went to lean against his side. "My friends are a bunch of jerks sometimes," I whispered with a smile.

He made a low chirp of agreement.

Friends—I had more than one now. Well, sort of. I wasn't sure if Reigh and Phoebe thought of me that way, yet. But maybe after a while. A guy could hope, right?

"So, you're the one Fornax chose to replace my brother." The silhouette of Ezran's tall frame filled the open doorway. With his head tilted to the side, he gripped a half-empty wine bottle in one hand. I couldn't make out his face for the glare of the lights from outside the stall. It didn't matter, though. I could hear the confused disappointment in his voice all too clearly. "I suppose he can tell more about you than I can. Come on, kid. Let's take a walk."

Oh ... oh no. Fornax's old rider, the one who'd been killed in combat, was Ezran's *brother*? My heart hammered as I stumbled back to the doorway, following him wordlessly out into the passage between the stalls. Ezran was a lot taller than I was, and every step he took oozed with confidence, control, and smooth prowess—something I chalked up to being a seasoned dragonrider. Jaevid, Haldor, and even Jenna walked that way too, like lions prowling the battlefield with their shoulders back, heads high, and body braced for whatever dared to cross their path. It made them seem powerful in ways I didn't know if I could be.

"Jaxon was my oldest brother, you know. He was the one who flew Fornax before you. If he had survived the war, he'd be the one sitting on his hands here at the family estate, not me." Ezran led the way up a wooden staircase to the second story, casually making his way along the network of catwalks that went around the perimeter of the stable. "I'm supposed to be grateful. I'm alive. I survived the war. But my dragon is gone. My utility is reduced to getting married and having as many children as possible to continue the family name before I go senile. My adventure is over." He cast me a forced, empty smile that never reached his eyes as he took a swig from the wine bottle. "And now, I hear Fornax actually *chose* you, despite being blind and nearly feral. Freckles said he only trusts you, and that's why you're able to fly together."

I rubbed the back of my neck and looked away. "Well, um, yeah, he ... uh, he did choose me. But I don't really understand why. Reigh is right; I'm not a good fighter."

"And? Did you think this whole destiny thing was going to be easy? That you'd just pick up a blade and everything would just magically fall into place?"

I blushed. "Well, no, of course not. I didn't think it would be easy, but I was hoping it would at least feel right."

A weird, almost sarcastic smile spread over his face and he paused, leading me out a side door from the stable into a wide, open loft room. The pitched, steeply slanted ceiling and windows along each end made the space feel like a triangular tunnel. If not for the gloom of the stormy night, it probably would have offered a sweeping view of the estate's sprawling, bleak landscape. Right now, all I could see was the occasional tongue of lightning pop off the ground or ripple from cloud to cloud like grasping claws of light. Thunder rumbled in the distance, rattling the windowpanes as the rain poured in sheets, streaming down the glass.

"This is one of the training rooms where we practice hand-to-hand combat. When my brothers first started to train me, they kicked my butt all over this room. Jaxon most of all. He was bigger and stronger than I was. He could do things with a blade that seemed to defy the laws of nature. I just assumed he was born with that kind of skill." Ezran chuckled, but it was an empty, hollow sound—more ironic than genuine. "My family is steeped in the legacy of the dragonrider. It's in our blood—that's what my father told me. Nearly a hundred members of our family have sat in a dragonrider's saddle and gave their last breath defending this kingdom. But I remember looking at my brothers, at that wall, and feeling nothing except ... misplaced. I wasn't like them."

Ezran paused as he strolled over to stand right before a space on one of the slanted walls that was covered in dozens of rust-colored handprints. He took another long drink from his bottle and sighed. "It's a Cromwell tradition that when you graduate from the dragonrider academy and earn your Lieutenant's cloak, you put your mark on this wall in blood. And when I was about your age, maybe a little younger, I wanted nothing more than to put mine here. I'd already had some instruction in basic swordplay and grappling, of course. But it didn't matter. My brothers fought like demigods, and I spent hundreds of hours with my face being ground into that floor. I felt like an utter failure. I was ready to tell my father that I didn't want to join the dragonrider academy. I didn't want to embarrass my family by failing."

I chewed on the inside of my cheek, watching as his expression steeled, his gaze narrowing on one spot on the wall—one handprint in particular. He stepped closer and pressed his palm against it. It was a perfect match.

"The biggest lie we tell ourselves is that our failures are final," he said, his voice carrying over the muffled growl of the thunder. "Just because you're destined to do something doesn't guarantee you won't have to work for it. And it doesn't matter how many times you fail at it, kid. It just matters that every time you do land with your face in the dirt, you get back up."

My heart was pounding as he turned to face me, holding out the bottle of wine with a wide, crooked grin. I took it, cringing as I took a sip of the bitter, dark purple drink. It burned all the way down, leaving behind a warm trail along the back of my throat to my stomach. I coughed and quickly handed the bottle back.

"Trust me," he laughed. "Anything in life worth having is worth eating a little dirt for. And you've got a chance to be a dragonrider—that's as good as it gets, so long as you've got the guts to see it through. I suspect you do. A Cromwell dragon chose you, after all. My dragons don't pick losers. Get out there and keep being the worst fighter Maldobar has ever seen. Perhaps, one day, you'll do something great."

ALL I COULD FIGURE WAS that Phoebe must have put Ezran up to giving me this little pep talk or at least mentioned how I was struggling with my training. Maybe he'd even asked her more about it after Reigh brought it up at dinner. As embarrassing as it was, I had to admit I did feel a little better as we left the sparring room.

My mind buzzed just thinking about that wall of handprints, of how many Cromwells might have felt like they would never be able to earn their place there. Ezran was right. I couldn't help failing. That wasn't anything I could control. All I could control was what I chose to do next—to stay down or keep fighting.

The storm raged on against the roof directly above us as we continued through the stables back toward the main house. Every crack of thunder made my heart jump in my chest. The flashes of lightning were nearly constant. It had stormed sometimes in Thornbend, but never like this. The chaos outside sounded as though the sky was breaking apart, unleashing the abyss upon the world.

Ezran didn't seem bothered by it, though. As we made our way through the network of catwalks, I glanced down into the stalls below. The strobing flashes of lightning cast eerie shadows through them. At first, I thought I'd just imagined it, or the flashing of the stormy light was playing tricks on me. Then a pair of bright blue eyes blinked up at us from the back of one of the stalls. A dragon?

I squinted to be sure, but the eyes had already disappeared back into the stormy gloom.

"Whose dragon is that?" I tugged on the back of Ezran's tunic to get his attention.

He paused just as he was opening a tall door that would take us back into the manor. Glancing back, he opened his mouth to reply—but never got a word out.

A frantic scream tore through the hall beyond the door.

My heart jolted in my chest.

Ezran and I spun just as two maids scrambled up the grand staircase before us. Their faces were pale and their expressions twisted with terror as they darted past, tearing away down the hall in a mad sprint to get away.

But from what?

Ezran shouted after them, trying to get them to stop, come back, and explain what was wrong. But they were long gone.

We exchanged a wide-eyed look. What the heck was going on?

Back down the staircase, another scream echoed through the manor's gloomy halls.

"Stay here," Ezran ordered as he started for the stairs.

What? Was he kidding? No way I was just going to stand around like an idiot when my friends were out there. I set my jaw and ran after him, gripping the hilt of my sword like I actually knew what to do with it.

I caught a glimpse of a disapproving frown when he glanced back and realized I was still following him. There wasn't time to argue. I had to find the others and figure out what was going on.

CHAPTER TWENTY-SEVEN

Ezran led the way, darting through the manor like a startled stag. He dodged through dark parlors, sprinted down vacant, gloomy halls, and zipped along narrow servant's passages that led from room to room. And the further we ran, the more I began to notice ... there was no one else in sight. The house seemed like it'd been swallowed in darkness. Not a single candle or torch was lit anywhere. Only the occasional flash of lightning through the windows lit our path as I chased after Ezran's heels.

My heart thrashed wildly, booming in my ears in time with the thunder as I ran. Questions blurred through my mind. What was happening? Who had doused all the lights? Where was Murdoc? Reigh? Phoebe?

Screams echoed in the distance, seeming closer than before. Oh, gods. That ... that wasn't Phoebe, was it?

Dread and panic twisted in my gut as we made our way toward the dining hall. There was still no one in sight. No servants. No maids. No sign of my friends anywhere.

At the end of a broad foyer, Ezran and I skidded to a halt before a huge set of wooden doors. He immediately lunged forward, seizing the handles and giving them a violent shove. The doors groaned, shuddering on their hinges. But they didn't budge. Yanking and cursing, he fought with the heavy brass handles until, at last, he stood back. Breathless and red-faced, Ezran turned to me with a fierce snarl on his lips. "They're locked. Someone must have tied them from the inside."

"Locked? By who?" The only person who had been inside was Phoebe, right? But why would she lock herself in there?

He didn't answer, storming past me with wrath in every step. "Come on. There's another way in."

With Ezran still in the lead, we sprinted back down the hall. He zigzagged through his darkened manor, stealing through hidden passages as quick as a fox. In a shadowed corner between two more grand displays of dragonrider armor, he pressed both hands against a section of the mahogany wall paneling. I cringed back as he gave the baseboard a swift, meaningful kick, and the section of paneling popped out into his hands. Ezran lowered the hidden trap door down slowly, revealing a steep staircase tucked into the wall behind it.

"Whoa." I leaned in closer to get a better look. "What's up there?"

"It's the passage to the ceiling. We only use it when the servants change out the candles in the chandeliers. Or to hide from Tibrans. From up there, we should be able to see what's going on in the dining hall." Ezran leapt for the stairs, then waited for me to slip past him before he closed the trapdoor behind us. "Keep your voice down until we figure out what's going on here."

I nodded, mashing my mouth shut.

From the very first step, the smell of smoke stung my eyes. It brought back flashes of memory that had been burned in my brain from the night Thornbend had fallen to the Tibran Empire. I'd lost everything to their flames.

Was it happening again?

No. It couldn't be … the Tibrans had been defeated. This had to be something else.

The further up the steep, winding staircase we ran, the thicker the smoke became. I could taste ash in my mouth with every breath. It burned in my throat as I gasped and wheezed, coughing and trying to blink through the growing haze.

At the top of the stairs, Ezran stopped suddenly and I flailed to keep from crashing into him. Before I could recover, he grabbed me by the collar and jerked me closer, dropping to a knee and yanking me down behind him as a burst of roaring flames rose up before us. He cursed through gritted teeth, his body stiffening as he tried to shield me from the inferno.

Gods, what was happening?

I squinted through the blistering heat, leaning around Ezran to steal a glimpse. Beyond the top of the staircase, a network of heavy wooden beams spread out across the width of the grand hall. Three huge iron chandeliers hung from them, suspended over what had once been the dining hall—the same one where we'd all eaten dinner earlier. Now, it looked more like the frothing maw of hell.

Far below, the whole room was engulfed in flames. The fire crackled and roared, climbing the drapes and licking greedily up the walls. Black smoke boiled up to the ceiling, carrying a whirlwind of embers and ash with it.

Then I heard it: a muffled sound barely rising over the chaos.

Through the heat and flash of fire, I spotted a small female shape squeezed into the only corner that wasn't ablaze yet.

My heart dropped. Oh gods.

"Phoebe!" I yelled at the top of my lungs.

Her eyes darted up, searching the rafters until she saw me. Her expression collapsed into desperate terror. Tears made clean streaks in the ash on her cheeks. She tried to call out, but couldn't do more than make a few strangled, muffled cries against the gag that was tied over her mouth. Someone had bound her by the wrists, too.

My gut clenched, hardening around the realization that someone had tried to kill her. They had tied her up and set fire to the dining hall, locking her inside so she would burn alive.

No way. Not on my watch.

I shoved away from Ezran and started for the nearest beam. It was broad enough you could walk along it without too much wobbling. The only problems were the roaring inferno below and the twenty or thirty feet of empty air between the ground and me. That didn't matter now, though. I had to get to Phoebe. I had to find a way to rescue her.

"There!" Ezran shouted behind me, pointing over my shoulder to one of the large chandeliers. The ends of the long, heavy ropes that suspended it in the air were coiled to the side. All that extra rope was most likely used to raise and lower the fixtures when needed, so there should be plenty to let them down to the floor.

One glance at Ezran, and I knew. We had the same insane idea.

He followed me along the lofty beams, halting and dashing around plumes of flame, until we reached the chandelier closest to where Phoebe was cowering. Ezran immediately began untying the rope from where it held the heavy iron fixture suspended. Together, we hoisted it up higher—close enough that someone might be able to climb on.

That would be me.

"Can you lift us both with this?" I called out to him.

"Probably, if the rope holds. It wasn't made for this kind of weight!" Ezran shouted back. "Don't you dare die on me down there, kid! Grab her and get out!"

When the chandelier reached the beam before us, I set my jaw, leaned out, and seized the curled iron frame. The fixture must have weighed three hundred pounds or more, and Ezran shouted and cursed as I climbed out onto it. His arms shook. Sweat beaded on his brow and trickled down his cheeks and nose as he strained to slowly let the chandelier descend.

Foot by foot, the ground crept closer. My heart pounded, thumping against my ribs and lodging in my throat as I clung to the warm iron fixture. Close by, Phoebe was swooning on her feet. With her mouth gagged, she probably couldn't breathe well in the first place, and the smoke wasn't making it any easier.

I was running out of time.

As my feet touched the ground, Phoebe tumbled forward. With her arms still bound, she couldn't even catch herself. She collapsed into a heap, lying on her side.

I bolted straight for her, scooping her tiny frame up in my arms and pulling the gag out of her mouth so she could breathe. Her eyes fluttered, blinking up at me hazily for an instant before rolling back. Thank the gods, she was still alive.

"It's gonna be alright. I've got you," I panted as I steadied her weight. Now I just had to get back to the chandelier and—

I jumped as Ezran shouted suddenly, yelling my name at the top of his lungs.

CRASH!

An explosion of sparks and smoldering splinters rocketed in every direction. Oh no.

The chandelier lay, smashed into a million pieces on the marble floor below. Overhead, Ezran stared down at us, still gripping a piece of the rope, his face blanched in shock and terror.

The rope ... it had snapped. Or burned through. Either way, my escape route was gone.

No. I would not let us die here. There had to be some other way out.

Peering through the rippling heat and flashing fire, I could barely make out a path through the debris back to where the doors should be—the same ones we had tried to enter through earlier. The area around them still looked mostly clear, and Ezran had said they were only locked from this side. If I could get Phoebe and reach them quickly, maybe I could get us both out.

I had to try.

I squeezed Phoebe closer against my chest to shield her from the falling bits of ash that rained down from the walls as I started for the doors. It wasn't that far. I could make it.

The heat made every nerve scream in protest. My eyes watered as I squinted through the smoky haze. Close—we had to be getting close. The scorching air seared my throat, and the waves of heat blasted my face and singed my clothes as I ran.

Faster. Nearly there. Just a little further.

I coughed and wheezed. My lungs burned with every smoke-filled breath as I staggered to a halt in front of the tall double doors.

My heart stopped.

Ezran was right; someone had tied them shut. But it wasn't rope, chains, or something I might be able to break. A metal bar as thick around as my wrist was bent through the door handles, binding them closed.

All the blood drained from my face and hands. I stood, frozen in dumbfounded shock. Oh, gods. I couldn't break that. How was that even possible? It would've taken someone incredibly strong to bend metal like that. And how had they gotten out?

Turning around, I stared out across the crumbling, burning dining hall. There had to be some other way. Unless ... whoever had done this was still in here with us somewhere. But everywhere I looked, there was only smoke and flame, cinders and chaos. I couldn't even see Ezran anymore.

There was no way out. No way to break down the door. Not even Ezran could help us now.

The roaring inferno closed in, growing hotter by the second. Another rope holding a chandelier burned through, dropping the huge metal frame onto the ground with a clang and a crash.

I moved away, pressing my back against one of the doors. I shut my eyes tightly, bowing my head and clutching Phoebe closer. We ... we were going to die.

Not even a dragon could save us now.

28

CHAPTER TWENTY-EIGHT

The door flinched behind me an instant before the metal bar wound between the two knobs began to glow bright blue. The light cut through the glare of the flames, going white hot in a matter of seconds. I staggered back, my pulse racing out of control as the light began to spread, cracking out across the doors like jagged fractures in a mirror. More blue light bled through, and I turned away to shield my eyes.

A sound like the low tolling of a bell pierced the air. Blinding light seared over me like a star had settled to the earth only a few feet away. Gods and Fates, what was happening?

I dared to look back—directly into the piercing gaze of a creature I had no name for.

My breath caught. I held perfectly still. With a body like a sleek, powerful tiger, the beast stood less than five feet away. It towered over me, coal-black fur adorned in spiraling stripes and designs of brilliant silver. They glimmered in the glare of the flames, highlighting beautiful swirling patterns.

A flex of the beast's powerful shoulders made a pair of wide feathery wings spread out to fill the now empty doorway, catching in the light in hues of deep purple, dark green, and royal blue. The motion sent out a sudden rush of forceful wind. It snuffed out the flames that licked closer and closer to my heels.

I couldn't resist a gasp. What was this thing?

The great cat crouched low, regarding me with a cautious glare and a twitch of its long tail. I sprang back further, stumbling and nearly falling with Phoebe still in my arms as the animal prowled toward me until it stood so close I could see my own reflection in its wide, strangely colored eyes. They had brilliant bands of golden yellow around the outside of the irises that faded gradually into an electric shade of green at the very center.

The longer it studied me, the more it felt like the creature was trying to peer straight into my soul. Every move of its head made the thin, sterling-colored stripe across the cat's forehead glisten. In the very center, a crescent-shaped mark caught the light like it had been painted there with liquid silver.

My heart thumped wildly. I'd never seen a cat so big. It was almost the size of a horse. It probably could have taken my head off in one chomp. But it was so ... *beautiful*.

"A-Are you a god? Or some kind of spirit?" I'd heard of foundling spirits before, creatures that haunted the wild places of the world. They were said to be tricksters, the first children of the old forest god Paligno, and they often took the shape of animals.

The creature slicked its rounded ears back, curling a lip down at me with a disapproving snort. I decided to take that as a no.

"Uh, well, um, thank you," I remembered to add.

The cat gave another unimpressed puff and turned, brushing me with a feathery wingtip as it strode proudly away into the dark hall beyond. "I suggest saving your thanks for after you have found the rest of your companions."

I jogged after the creature, steadying Phoebe's weight in my arms. "Yeah, that's probably true. Wait—" I almost tripped over my own feet. "Did you just *talk*?"

The creature regarded me with a roll of its eerie, yellow-green eyes. "A bit slow, aren't you?" it replied in a smooth, feminine voice.

I blushed. "I-I, uh, well..."

"Stay close to me. You are in far more danger than you realize, boy." The sleek cat bounded ahead, her paws totally silent on the stone floor.

My mind stalled and started, circling around the possibility that I might be losing it. Or dead. Maybe both. Still, something about that creature felt oddly familiar. Had I seen those bizarre green eyes somewhere before?

I shook my head. No, I had to get it together. The girl in my arms, the house burning down, my two other friends who might also be trapped somewhere inside—that was more important right now.

Dashing out of the doorway, I ran headlong down the hallway after the creature. "Why are you helping us?" I panted.

She gave me what seemed like a feline version of an irritated scowl. "Because you lot are blundering headlong into a fight you barely understand and cannot hope to win," she snapped. "Now keep close and stay silent."

I bit down hard. Who was this person—animal—thing? What fight was she talking about? Did this have something to do with Devana? Or did someone have a grudge against the Cromwells?

The clashing of swords, the scrape and squeal of metal against metal, cut through the eerie silence of the hall nearby. We rounded a corner, almost back to where that hidden staircase had been, and my blood ran cold. I lurched to a halt.

Ezran was locked in combat, whirling a sword he must have swiped from one of those stands of dragonrider armor nearby. The enemy before him moved with a level of ruthless speed and lethal grace I'd only ever seen once before.

I squeezed Phoebe closer.

Dressed from pauldron to boot in intricate black leather armor, the dark figure bore in hard, raining down punishing blows that had Ezran on the defense. A sudden, spinning assault made a glimmer of silver on the warrior's arm catch my eye. I recognized that silver-plated vambrace immediately. It had the same image of a snarling wolf's head engraved into it that I'd seen Murdoc wearing the night we first met.

My heart dropped to the soles of my boots.

Oh gods. There were *more* of them?

EZRAN HAD ALREADY TAKEN several blows. The warrior spun on him again and again with vengeful, blurring speed. Ezran made frantic parries and desperate strikes, staggering on a deep gash in his leg that left a smear of blood across the floor.

I took a shaking step back, my skin tingling with a frenzy of terror. Flashes of memory sizzled across my brain. The look on my father's face the last time I'd seen him. The horses crying out in the stable, trying to escape. Our home burning like a torch in the night. Panic clamped over my throat like a cold stone hand.

On my right, the feline creature surged forward with a sudden, thundering cry. With her ears pinned back and her teeth bared, she spread her darkly colored wings wide. A flash of blue light bloomed in the hallway, making my vision go white. I ducked, turning away and squeezing my eyes shut as I tried to shield Phoebe from whatever was happening.

The light faded, and I dared to glance back.

Through the spots swimming in my vision, I found the figure of a young woman where the feline creature had been only seconds before. Her athletic frame stood in stark silhouette against the lightning that flashed in the narrow windows of the hall. My breath caught. With deep purple robes flowing over her ebony skin, she strode forward on bare feet, gripping a long staff in one hand.

Her staff was unlike any weapon I'd ever seen before. One end was tipped with a spiraling, tri-edged spear, and the other was fixed with a gleaming crystal. Spinning the weapon with incredible precision, the girl dropped into a crouched stance and stole a scowling glare back at me over her shoulder.

I forgot how to breathe again.

Even in the dim hall, her yellow-green eyes seemed to glow, catching every stray bit of light like a cat's. "You stay back," she warned.

I nodded, unable to make a sound except for a few choking noises. Who the heck was this girl?

The warrior in the black leather armor seemed to have forgotten all about Ezran. He spun to face us, leaving the wounded duke to hobble back against the wall, his expression skewed in pain. Ezran's chest heaved with halting, shuddering breaths as he reached down to clamp a hand over his side where another cut in his doublet oozed with fresh blood. Oh no. He was hurt worse than I thought.

The warrior's gaze narrowed over the edge of the black shawl wrapped over his mouth and nose as he whirled a pair of long, curved knives over his hands. They were already wet with Ezran's blood.

Lightning flashed again. Thunder growled, rolling through the sky right over our heads and making the windowpanes rattle like chattering teeth. Then it began.

One second, the girl and the warrior were squaring off, sizing one another up from only a few yards away—and the next, they were tangled in a blur of rolling strikes, feinting slashes, rolls, leaps, and the sparking contact of the daggers against the staff. Their quick, ruthless assaults were so fast, I could barely keep up. Like a cat and a serpent, they rushed in to exchange rapid blows, only to dance back and circle again without ever breaking eye contact.

"You hounds aren't half bad," the girl taunted as she stepped lightly, tossing some of her black hair over her shoulder with a sneer. Each lock fell in loose, glossy coils, framing her soft features and long pointed ears. "Why not take the one you came for and go? Or was this the payment *she* demanded—that you kill all of the queen's hunters, too?"

The warrior didn't reply.

He darted in again, as fast as a shadow, with his blades catching in the storm's strobing light. The elf girl threw up her staff, deflecting his blow in a whirling motion that sent him staggering.

"Too slow," she scolded as she sprang over him in one bound, cracking the crystal-end of her staff over the back of his head before landing back in a low crouch. One hand gripped the shaft of her weapon, knuckles flexed and her expression as cold as a deep winter's night, as she watched her enemy stagger. "Assassin or not, I expected more from a fellow elf-blood."

He turned on her again, his eyes bloodshot and wide with rage. He surged forward, rushing in an angry frenzy. It was no good. She had him off balance, either by taunting him or dancing just out of his reach. He pressed in, swinging wildly, and she zipped under him in an instant. Sliding across the marble floor right between his legs, all it took was one swift jerk of her staff as she passed to knock him off his feet.

The girl was up and on the offensive before I could blink twice. She blitzed into a pinning stance over him, knocking away both his weapons with her bare feet pinned on his shoulders. He started to reach for what was probably another blade hidden in his complex leather ensemble.

"I really wouldn't, if I were you," she hissed as she pressed the spiraling spear-tip of her weapon against the end of his nose. Slowly moving it along his head, she pushed his cowl back to reveal his long, silvery white hair and pointed ears. My heart sagged in my chest, going slack with relief. He was a Gray elf, but he was not anyone I recognized.

Most importantly, he wasn't Murdoc.

I let out a shuddering breath I hadn't even realized I was holding in.

"Goddess take you," the girl murmured through clenched teeth, her eyes going cold again as she abruptly leaned down into her staff, driving it toward the floor in one ruthless motion.

I squeezed my eyes shut and looked away, swallowing against the urge to gag. It wasn't the first time I'd seen someone murdered right in front of me. It probably wouldn't be the last. But that didn't make the sight any easier to stomach.

"Are you mad?" Ezran yelled suddenly. Pushing away from the wall, he staggered toward them with his blade still in one hand and the other gripping his injured side. "Now I'll never know who he is or why he's tried to burn my house down!"

The girl fixed him with an earnest, almost bewildered glare, as though she didn't understand why that was such a big problem. Her bright, intelligent eyes darted between us for a moment, and then she gave an exasperated sigh. Stepping off her fallen enemy, she strode smoothly over the floor with her staff resting against her shoulder. "I would have thought it was obvious. But I suppose it can't be helped. You are Maldobarian, after all."

Ezran's face flushed as red as a ripe tomato, twitching as he glowered back at her. "What is that supposed to mean?"

"It means that *you* have a problem, dragonrider," the girl retorted, tipping her head back to where the assassin lay dead in the middle of the hall. "There are Ulfrangar in your little castle."

"W-What?" he rasped. "That's ... impossible. The Ulfrangar are just a myth. And, even if they were real, what would they want with me?"

"Nothing. They aren't here for you," she replied as she turned to face me with her mouth quirked into a dazzling little grin. "It seems they came for *him*."

CHAPTER TWENTY-NINE

"M e?" I sputtered, nearly dropping Phoebe in surprise. "B-But why?!"

"Why, indeed." The elf girl's gaze darted past me and she leaned around as though someone else might be coming down the hall after us. "I knew they wanted the other one. But you? Hmm. We can discuss this later. The Ulfrangar have sent many agents, and your old friend is wounded. We must retreat."

"*Old?*" Ezran barked angrily.

The elf girl didn't even acknowledge him as she strode between us. Seeing her up close made my stomach flip as our gazes met for an instant. Even in this form, she still had that thin silver line across her forehead, shining like liquid silver against her flawless dark skin. The crescent shape was still there, too. It shone right between her eyes like a tiny moon. She was shorter than me, although only by an inch or two, and her robes were draped around her leanly sculpted frame. The purple linen was so thin it was nearly transparent; giving only glimpses of the intricate leather corset and leggings she wore beneath it.

I swallowed hard. I'd never seen a girl dress like that before. Sure, I'd heard that Gray elves sometimes dressed in vivid colors and expensive silks, and that sometimes the women wore more revealing dresses, but never anything like this. It was a far cry from the heavy wool gowns Maldobarian women usually wore, too. She had the same long, pointed ears, but her hair and skin were totally different from the Gray elves. Gods, who was this girl? Where on earth had she come from?

"Staring is considered rude in some cultures, you know," she noted as she passed.

"I ... I'm sorry. But we can't just leave," I protested, planting my feet firmly. "What about Murdoc and Reigh?"

The elf girl stopped.

"I won't leave them behind."

Slowly, she turned enough to stare back at me. Her expression softened as she searched me, her lips parting slightly. "Reigh," she repeated the name. "Is he a human boy with red hair?"

I nodded. "He's got a scar on his face, right over his nose. Do you know him?"

Her mouth pressed into a firm, uncomfortable line as something like guilt crept over her features. For a few seconds, she didn't move or make a sound. Then, at last, her shoulders dropped. "If he is here, then we will find him. But these two cannot go with us." She gestured to Phoebe and Ezran.

My heart sank. I glanced down at Phoebe, still unconscious with her head lulled against my chest, her clothes singed, and her face smudged with ash. The elf was right; I had to get her somewhere safe.

"Hand her over," Ezran growled as he hobbled toward me, throwing down his sword. "We'll make for the dragon stables. No assassin in his right mind would challenge a dragon, Ulfrangar or not. Meet us there."

Reluctantly, I passed her over into his arms. "Are you sure you can carry her that far? Your leg is—"

"Worry about yourself, kid," he interrupted. "You wanna prove you've got what it takes to be a dragonrider? Now's the time. If this place is going up in smoke, I won't let the dragons or hatchlings in my stable burn with it. I have to get them out. I'll see if I can get your mounts into their gear; we're all going to need a way to get out of here fast."

Realization settled over me like someone had dropped a heavy yoke over my shoulders. Ezran was right. Oh gods, what was I about to do? I couldn't fight like either of them. I couldn't do this, I couldn't—

"Come." The elf girl put a surprisingly gentle hand on my arm. "We must hurry."

The instant she touched me, a strange, lukewarm calm began to seep into the corners of my mind. I took a deep, steadying breath. As I stared into her eyes, my pulse slowed. It thumped hard and loud, like the beating of a war drum, deep in my chest.

Something about this girl made me feel braver.

I set my jaw. "Right. Let's go."

The last place I had seen Reigh was in our room on the fifth floor, so that seemed like the best place to start looking. With me in the lead, the elf girl and I took off into the dark mansion, retracing our path as best I could recall. Now was not the time to get lost, but the shadows hung heavy and thick, ominous against the occasional snap of lightning and rumbling growl of thunder. Rain poured in sheets against the glass windows. Were we going the right way? I couldn't be sure, not with it so dark.

But there was no time to second guess it. I had to trust my gut.

Up another flight of stairs, I coughed and wheezed at the sudden smell of smoke. It stung my eyes, making them water. We passed open doorways and hallway entrances glowing with red light. Someone was setting fires everywhere up here. But why? Was it the Ulfrangar? Ezran and Reigh had sloughed off that they were even real. But it couldn't be a coincidence, right?

I put my head down, dashing past the waves of heat and rolling black smoke as fast as my legs could go. Those men were dressed in the same black armor and silver vambrace that Murdoc had worn when we first met. There was no denying it.

Did that really mean he was an Ulfrangar, too?

My brain scrambled at the idea. For as long as we'd been together, surviving the prison camp and working at the royal stable, I still didn't know much about Murdoc. I didn't even know where he was right now. I had to find him.

And Reigh, too.

Gods, I hoped we weren't already too late.

"Wait!" my new elf companion called out as we passed another long corridor lined with arched windows that spanned from floor to ceiling. There wasn't much to see outside. The stormy night was chaos, and sheets of pouring rain pounded against the glass. Then, another tongue of lightning popped off the steeply pitched rooftop just outside.

My pulse skipped, breath catching in my throat as I spotted a group of figures dueling out there—on the peak of the roof!

It only lasted a second, just as long as the lightning lit up the sky. Two figures locked in combat, their blades clashing. I could have sworn one of them had red hair.

That had to be Reigh.

"We have to get out there!" I panicked. "There must be a door or a passageway out onto—"

A flash of blue light and a yowl were my only warning.

Out of nowhere, a huge furry head shoved between my legs and tossed me upward like someone flipping a pancake. I flailed and landed like a scared baby squirrel on the back of the winged cat, my arms hugging around her neck. In an instant, she had changed forms again.

"*What* are you?!" I rasped between breaths as I gripped fistfuls of her silky black fur.

"Nothing you Maldobarians would understand," she hissed, ears flattening as she crouched. "Keep your head down!"

I realized what she was about to do half a second before she swished her tail, snapped her feathered wings in tight against her sides, and sprang straight at the window. I bit back hard against a scream, burying my face against her fur as we burst through the glass. Jagged shards zipped in every direction. A swipe of something across my cheek left a burning train behind.

The stormy wind blasted us head-on, snatching my hair and stinging my eyes. The pouring rain was bitter cold, and every pounding drop felt like icy needles pricking my skin. Looking up, I squinted through the chaos to where the two figures were still dueling on the ridge of the roof. One of them was definitely Reigh. His long red braid whipped and the two white, sickle-shaped blades he always used flashed against the churning sky.

"We've got to help him!" I shouted.

Beneath me, my feline companion braced against the storm and spread her wings. "Hang on tight." She broke skyward, conquering the rushing winds with each stroke of her powerful wings.

We zoomed up the steep side of the roof toward the ridge at the very top. I could tell Reigh was losing ground. He fought against another assassin in black, another Ulfrangar, but each desperate attack cost him. They were almost to the edge, and the assassin was bearing in hard. Reigh had to fall back. In a few more feet, there'd be nothing between him and the ground but five stories of empty, stormy air.

His foot slipped.

Reigh wobbled, arms waving as he teetered on the edge. His eyes went wide with sudden realization. His guard was down. He couldn't defend himself. Quick as the lightning that split the boiling skies, the assassin broke forward and planted a boot right in the center of Reigh's chest with one final kick.

Reigh fell.

His scream pierced through the howling winds. Fear and panic crushed at my chest like icy hands squeezing my lungs. Oh gods. We weren't going to make it in time!

Reigh's arms shot out suddenly, digging his curved blades into the side of the mansion's outer wall. They sparked as they scraped across the stone, until at last one caught on a ledge. His body jerked to a halt, and he hung, dangling over the staggering drop.

Still perched on the edge, the assassin looked down to where Reigh was hanging, clinging desperately to the hilt of his white blade. He reached beneath his long black cloak and drew another weapon. The familiar silhouetted shape of a large, ornate crossbow cut me to the marrow. It was an easy shot, especially for a trained assassin. Reigh couldn't dodge or even try to escape.

Snatching the necklace from under my shirt, I put Fornax's whistle to my lips and blew. We were a long way from the stable. The noise of the storm was overwhelming, and I honestly didn't know if he would even be able to hear me.

But I needed him—I *needed* my dragon's help.

Beneath me, my feline friend cringed and shrieked in dismay as I blasted the whistle again and again. She glanced back long enough to shoot me a venomous glare and snarled, "What are you doing?"

There wasn't time to explain. A familiar roar boomed in approach. I pushed back away from her neck. "Get Reigh! You're the only one who can reach him in time!" I yelled ... right before jumping out into the open air.

CHAPTER THIRTY

I hit the steep side of the roof hard. The impact knocked the breath from my lungs and made my vision spot as I slid to a halt on the slick, rain-soaked clay shingles. But I was close. I could make it.

I clenched my teeth against my whistle and climbed. My fingers slipped, clinging to the slick shingles as I flailed, pawing wildly to find good places to hold. Faster—I had to move. There wasn't much time.

I scaled the side of the roof inch by inch until, at last, I heaved myself up onto the ridge. It was only about two feet wide—barely enough to stand on. Breathless and squinting through the squinting downpour, I shambled to my feet.

The assassin was only a few yards away. With one last blast on my whistle, I drew my blade and gave a challenging shout, "Hey! Over here, moron!"

The assassin spun. Even with the black shawl hiding half of his face, I could see shock, confusion, and anger gathering over his expression. He raised his crossbow and took aim.

I braced, resisting the urge to cringe away, as I kept my glare leveled on the dark figure before me.

A low *boom, boom, boom* thrummed over the commotion of the storm.

Fornax rose like an orange and black demon, dawning over the edge of the roof behind the assassin. He hovered, his powerful wings pumping under rippling scales, and let out another belting roar of fury. Lightning snapped in the air behind him, glittering over his curved horns and jagged teeth as he searched with his cloudy green eyes.

He was looking for me.

The assassin whirled back around to face my dragon. He took a staggering step backward and raised his crossbow, taking aim at Fornax's head with his hands shaking.

Panic hit me like a punch to the neck. Too late, I remembered ... while a normal bow might not be able to pierce a dragon's hide, a crossbow probably could. If I gave him the signal to breathe fire, he'd scorch me right along with the assassin.

But Fornax had no idea he was in danger.

Rage like hellfire rose in my chest. It burned white-hot over my brain, sizzling across my tongue as I squeezed the grip of my sword. I didn't know who he was behind that shawl. Right then, I didn't care. He wasn't going to shoot *my* dragon.

I lunged with my blade in hand, closing the distance in one bounding leap. Swinging down with all my strength, I rammed the sharp end of my weapon into the assassin's back. We collided, tumbling forward in a tangled heap. I let out a yelp as my blade was ripped from my hand, still lodged deep in the Ulfrangar's body.

Together, the assassin and I rolled off the end of the roof and into the empty air.

Lost to the whipping winds, I fell—tumbling end over end. Blurred glimpses of the ground, the side of the mansion, and the assassin's body twisting only a short distance away, flashed before my eyes. I yelled, crying out with every bit of my strength. Somewhere nearby, Fornax let out an answering shriek of dismay.

Oh gods. I ... I didn't want to die. Not like this!

A strong, scaly foot wrapped around my waist. I wheezed and gasped as Fornax snagged me right out of the air. He'd found me! Probably tracking my screams through the air.

I clung to his big foot, looking up through the rain and soggy hair that blew in my eyes to see him peering down at me, chirping worriedly.

"Thanks, buddy," I coughed as I patted one of his toes. Then I glanced back down. The assassin had hit the muddy ground far below, but I couldn't see any sign of Reigh. My heart pounded out of control as Fornax slowly circled in descent. He landed not far from where the assassin's body was sprawled, motionless with my blade still sticking out of him.

I sucked in a hard, shuddering breath.

I had to know.

Shambling to my feet, I edged closer to where the body lay, the shape of my sword still sticking out of his back. My knees wobbled, unsteady as my head swam from my near-death dive off the top of the mansion. Grabbing the hilt of my blade, I shakily tugged it free before rolling the assassin's body over. Sprawled on his back and slathered in mud, the black shawl over his nose and mouth still covered most of his face. The pouring rain made fresh clean streaks in the mud and black war paint smeared over his eyes and brow.

I swallowed hard, crouching down beside him and wiping my soaked hair away from where it stuck to my face. I had to see this clearly—I had to be sure. My hands shook as I reached to pull the shawl away.

I didn't know him. This assassin wasn't Murdoc.

Cold relief made my shoulders go slack, and I gasped in another unsteady breath. The eerily blank expression on the dead assassin's face bored into me, a little oozing trail of crimson seeping from the corners of his mouth.

I didn't know this man and yet I ... I had killed him. I'd murdered someone.

The blade slipped from my hand, landing with a *squish* in the mud at my feet.

"Thatcher!" someone yelled to me over the storm.

I stood, peering through the gloom and rain to see Reigh running toward me. Right on his heels, the elven shapeshifter had already changed back into her humanoid form. She and Reigh wore similar expressions of worry, their footsteps sloshing in the mud and their clothes and hair drenched.

"Are you all right?" Reigh stumbled to a halt over the assassin's body. "What in the abyss is going on? Why are the Ulfrangar attacking the Cromwell estate?"

My gaze dropped, staring down at the assassin's lifeless body in front of me. I knew why. Or at least, I had a pretty good idea. But I didn't want to say it until I was absolutely sure.

I had to find Murdoc, first.

Glancing back up, I met the piercing, yellow-green stare of our newest ally. She studied me, her brows drawn into a look of suspicion and her lips settling into an uncomfortable frown. Maybe she could sense I was holding back—hiding a truth I wasn't ready to admit. If she could, however, she didn't mention it. Her expression softened slightly as she held my gaze and waited.

"Phoebe and Ezran are hiding out in the barn with your dragon. They're both injured, so you've got to help them get somewhere safe. I know you don't like Phoebe, Reigh, but this isn't about whatever bad blood or old grudges you guys haven't sorted out yet. This is about survival. If you fall back to the city now, maybe you can get some of the dragonriders at Eastwatch to help drive the Ulfrangar out," I said at last, casting Reigh a hard look. This wasn't up for debate.

Reigh's mouth fell open. He made a few unhappy choking sounds, as though he couldn't find words.

"You intend to stay and fight the Ulfrangar alone?" The elf girl gestured to the dead assassin with the spear end of her staff.

"I'm a dragonrider. I'm never alone."

Fornax gave a snort of agreement. He lowered his head to let his chin brush my shoulder.

"Excuse me, kid, but last time I checked, *I* was the one leading this hunting party. There's no way I'm leaving you here," Reigh began to object. "You won't last five seconds. We're going—together—right now. That so-called friend of yours is already long gone, too, if he's got half a brain."

"He wouldn't do that!" I shouted suddenly, anger swelling like a burst of dragon flame in my chest. "He would *not* abandon us like that! Murdoc is still in there. I can't explain how I know that, I just ... do." The words tasted bitter on my tongue, and doubt crept into every corner of my heart. I cringed and looked away.

Did I *really* know that? Murdoc had disappeared sometime after dinner. What if he had known the Ulfrangar were coming? What if he'd fled without warning any of us? Or worse, what if he had been the one who led them here in the first place?

None of it felt right, and every question pricked at my mind like bee stings. I trusted Murdoc.

Reigh took a step closer, his tone heavy as he started to protest. "Thatcher, this isn't—"

"I'll be fine," I cut him off quickly. "It's not like I'm going to storm the front door. Regardless of what you probably think, I'm not *that* stupid. I'll be quick and quiet. Once I find him, we'll get out and meet you at Eastwatch."

Reigh and the elf girl exchanged a grim look, as though they might be wondering the same thing—probably whether or not I'd hit my head or completely lost my mind because, well, this did sound a lot like a suicide mission.

Finally, they both nodded in agreement. Reigh managed a painfully forced smile as he patted my shoulder. "We'll send reinforcements as soon as we can. Hang in there."

"Don't worry about me." I clenched my fists at my sides, forcing my tone to stay steady. I didn't want him to know how terrified I was. "Just take care of the others. He wouldn't admit it, but I think Ezran's hurt badly, and you're the best healer in Maldobar, right?"

Reigh gave a snort. "Yeah, but I'm no miracle worker. Not anymore. So just try not to push your luck too much, okay?" With a nod to the staff-wielding elf girl, he turned to start for the dragon stables.

She hesitated, glancing between Reigh and me for a few seconds before darting off after him. It was obvious that they had some kind of a history. When I'd mentioned his name before, she had seemed to recognize who Reigh was immediately.

Whoever she was, at least she seemed to be on our side. I'd have to get to the bottom of that later. Right now, the clock was ticking. I had to find Murdoc before the Ulfrangar did.

Bending down, I reached for the hilt of my sword again. I needed a weapon. But my hand hesitated inches from the leather grip. A glimmer in the dark, half buried in the mud, caught my eye. I moved closer, digging it free.

This crossbow felt as heavy as the last one had. Holding the finely crafted weapon brought back more of those memories. A coppery flavor in my mouth made my tongue writhe uncomfortably as I stared at it, the rain cleaning away the mud from the silver detailing on the polished black wood. This must have been a common weapon for the Ulfrangar—a favorite of theirs. It was compact, precise, and lethal. But it was also straightforward, uncomplicated, and efficient. There was an arrow still locked in place, ready to fire, and the long leather strap made it easy to sling it over my shoulder.

When I faced Fornax again, his foggy jade eyes seemed to study me with a soft growl of approval even if he couldn't actually see me. I wasn't much good with a sword. I'd been worse with a shield. But maybe this would be different.

Either way, I had to try.

Ezran must have been able to get both our dragons back into their saddles on his own. Thankfully Fornax was wearing his. I climbed up into the seat, the cold rain still pricking at my cheeks like tiny daggers of ice. Slipping my feet into the specialized boot-pockets, I leaned down against my dragon's neck, gripping the handles until my knuckles were white. I shivered, every muscle shaking and humming. I couldn't tell if it was from the cold or the fresh terror coursing through my veins.

Through the storm, the shapes of Reigh and our new shapeshifting friend sloshed their way toward the nearest barn. At last their silhouettes vanished, blurred into the dark and sheets of falling rain. They'd make it. They'd rescue Ezran and Phoebe, and the dragon hatchlings, too—I had to believe that. Reigh seemed like the kind of guy who didn't know how to fail. At the very least, he wouldn't go down without a fight.

I waited, shivering and gritting my teeth, to give them as much time as I dared to get safely inside, then I'd—Gods, I didn't even know what I was going to do.

Die, probably.

My stomach clenched and rolled until bile burned at the back of my throat. How could I find Murdoc? Half of the mansion was ablaze, and flames glowed through the windows on three floors. If he was really still in that place, he wouldn't be able to stay there for long.

Not even the Ulfrangar would be able to—

Then it hit me like a rock to the temple.

I knew what I had to do—how to find Murdoc. I couldn't go searching the manor room by room. I had to get him to come to me. The only problem was, of course, if I gave away my position to Murdoc, then all the Ulfrangar would know where to find me, too.

It was a risk I'd have to take.

Gulping against the terror that rose like icy water all the way up to my neck, I forced my breathing to slow as I gave Fornax the signal to take off. We rose into the air, defying the wild winds of the storm to circle around the mansion. From a few hundred feet overhead, the flash of red flames in the tall windows on four floors was clear now, and the fire was climbing higher by the minute. It wouldn't be long before the whole place went up. If Ezran was right about the special, dragon-hide fortifications holding up to fire, then only the barns might survive this.

As we soared over the four large buildings, the broad door to one rolled open and Vexi burst out. Her vibrant green scales flashed in the night as she shrieked and surged forward through raging winds. Behind her, a blur of silver against the gloom and the faint glow of two yellow-green eyes was the only glimpse of my new shapeshifting friend I could catch. She was a lot smaller than Vexi, but she seemed to match the dragoness's speed easily as she flew through the night in her feline form like an onyx arrow.

They moved fast, zipping by and making steam toward the distant speckling of light on the horizon. Eastwatch wasn't far. Ezran had been a dragonrider, and Reigh was a prince, so there was no way the dragonriders at the tower would turn them away. They'd be safe.

Hopefully.

As we wheeled in for our final approach, anxiety settling into my chest like a cold stone lodged where my heart should have been, another dark shape erupted from the open doorway of the barn with a shrieking, barking cry.

A bolt of lightning cut right over my head. I jolted in terror, flattening down against Fornax's neck as the sizzle and pop rang in my ears. The flash revealed the dark shape of a dragon crawling out into the stormy night, its hide glittering with scales like polished onyx. A single stripe of electric red color ran from its snout, down its back, all the way to the very tip of the dragon's lashing tail.

I sucked in a sharp breath, my heart seizing in my chest as the dragon's big sapphire blue eyes blinked up at us curiously. That was the dragon I'd seen in the barn, locked away by itself. Had Ezran let it out? Or had it broken free on its own?

With another trumpeting cry, it flexed powerful wing arms and spread leathery, dark crimson membranes into the churning air. My heart pounded in rhythm with its wing beats as the dragon took to the air, forging away into the toiling night until it disappeared.

I let out a shuddering breath. At least it hadn't attacked us.

"All right," I muttered as I steered Fornax back into a descent, aiming right for the front door of the Cromwell mansion. "No turning back now."

CHAPTER THIRTY-ONE

Fornax flared for landing, cupping his wings and stretching his hind legs to grip the soggy earth. I braced. At the last second, his ears slicked back, nostrils flaring as his horned head swung with a screech of alarm.

I looked, too—less than a second before it hit.

In an instant, my vision scrambled and my body sprawled through the air like a rag doll as I was thrown from the saddle. I hit the mud and rolled. Fornax let out a startled yelp. My arm popped strangely, and a burst of pain sizzled over every nerve.

Landing on my back, breathless and dazed, I blinked up into the falling rain and toiling skies. Gods, what just happened? Had something crashed into us?

The sound of my dragon shrieking and snarling made everything snap back into focus. I rolled over, forcing myself up onto my knees. My whole body tingled and my lungs spasmed as I fought to get in a good breath. One of my arms felt numb and hung limply at my side. Was it broken? I couldn't tell. Trying to wiggle my hand sent another jolt of pain through me. I bit back a groan, the metallic flavor of blood fresh on my tongue as I looked up through the gloom.

Only a short distance way, Fornax brawled in the mud like an angry lion fending off a pack of jackals. He kicked, clawed, and snarled, slinging sludge and spitting short blasts of burning venom that crackled even in the rain. Dragon venom couldn't be doused with water.

With the chaos of the storm whipping around me, I couldn't see what he was fighting at first. I wiped the rain and my bangs from my eyes as I shambled to my feet, clutching my injured arm.

Then I saw them, blurring against the downpour and glowing heat of Fornax's flames like living mirages. Shrikes—*three* of them. They were hard enough to see during the day; on a night like this, they were all but invisible.

They nipped and circled my panicked dragon, as fast as shadows. Fornax couldn't see them, regardless. He didn't need to.

Whipping around, he snagged one shrike by the tail and flung it to the ground, planting a hind foot onto its body to pin it down with a rumbling snarl. I cringed away as Fornax's sides swelled and he took a deep breath. An explosion of dragon flame sent a wave of heat over my face and drowned out the shrike's desperate cries.

One down.

The last two shrikes hissed, scattering from the flames and pacing in a circle around my dragon. Their mirrored scales glittered, rippling like blankets of diamond as they prowled, translucent wings flared and bony jaws snapping. With a chorus of eerie yipping howls, they rushed Fornax at once. He reared back into his hind legs, spitting blasts of flame. The shrikes dove, darting in to bite and claw at any vulnerable spot.

Fornax roared in defiance. He swung the spiked end of his long tail like a flail. A lucky hit sent one of them skidding across the ground with a gory smack and yelp. Fornax turned, his sides swelling in another blast of flame to finish it.

Suddenly, the last shrike surged in with a piercing cry like the screech of an eagle. It latched onto Fornax's neck as though trying to bite through his scales at his throat. My dragon pitched backward with another booming cry of fury.

Gods, I had to help him.

With my good arm, I pulled the crossbow off my shoulder and raised it. I couldn't stop my hands from shaking. It made the small, silver aiming circle mounted on the crossbow's wooden frame bounce around as I struggled to find a good shot. Sucking in a breath, I struggled to hold the weapon up and slide my finger onto the cold metal trigger. I only had one arrow. One shot. One chance.

Out of nowhere, my vision went dark.

White-hot pain exploded in the back of my head. My knees buckled, and the crossbow slipped from my hands, landing in the mud with a *splat*.

I crumpled forward, my face meeting the cold soggy earth. I tried to call out for help as I rolled onto my side. But every breath was agony. I couldn't make a sound. "Fool. You should have run when you had the chance," a man's deep, rumbling voice spoke over me.

Someone grabbed a fistful of my hair, jerking my whole body up out of the mud with one tug. I slurred and groaned, trying again to call out for help. But my eyes—my mouth—nothing worked. With my last bit of strength, I managed to stare groggily into the face of one ... man? Everything was so fuzzy. My vision tunneled in and out and I tried to focus.

No ... not one man. There were two.

One of them wore the same black leather garb and war paint smeared over his eyes as the other Ulfrangar. But the other one—the one holding me off the ground like a rabbit by the ears—didn't look human. He leered at me with eyes that gleamed like molten silver in the dark. His graphite skin was flecked with tiny shining spots, like a field of stars against slate-colored stone. A menacing smile curled slowly over his lips, revealing pointed canine teeth like fangs.

Fear like a cold dagger pierced my chest. My heartbeat seemed to go silent. This man

*—creature—*whatever he was, there was nothing in his gaze but pure malice. Cruelty. Bloodlust.

Whatever he was ... he was pure evil.

PAIN SPLIT my throat with a broken, muffled cry as I stammered awake in the gloom of a dimly lit room. Someone had tied a gag over my mouth. My hands were bound at my back, making my injured arm throb with agony. My ankles were tied so tightly it made all my toes tingle from lack of circulation.

Gods and Fates, what was happening? Where was I? Where was Fornax? Was he okay?

I struggled, pitching and flailing as much as I could. Every movement was torment. I could barely breathe. Lying on my back, spots winked before my eyes as I tried to get my bearings. The bare wood catwalks far overhead and the smell of smoke mingling with the earthy musk of hay were vaguely familiar through my delirium.

Ezran's dragon barn? Why had they brought me here? Why was I still alive at all? Didn't the Ulfrangar want me dead?

"He's awake," a quiet but firm male voice announced.

"Good. Make him squeal a little," another deep, growling voice cackled. "Nothing brings a wolf in like the sound of wounded prey."

Dread swirled through my gut and sent pangs of cold panic up my spine. I writhed on the cold, damp earth as the figure of a tall man in black Ulfrangar armor prowled toward me, brandishing a long silver dagger in his hand. He spun it through his fingers with incredible speed, making the polished metal flash and sparkle.

In one smooth motion, he bent down and slipped the cold point of the knife behind my ear. Oh gods—was he going to cut my ear off?

I squirmed and whimpered, trying to call out for help.

"Don't be stupid," the firm voice scoffed, and I caught a glimpse of another man standing back with his arms folded, his multihued eyes glinting like warm opals in the dim light. He wore the Ulfrangar armor, too, although I noticed instead of one silver vambrace, he had two. Did that mean he was a leader or something?

The assassin holding the knife to my ear stopped, glancing back. In all there were five of them: four Ulfrangar and one monstrous looking man who stood head and shoulders over the rest.

He was the one who had picked me up outside—the one with skin like dark stone and fangs like an animal. But those weren't the strangest things about him. At well over seven feet tall, he balanced himself on the balls of two paw-like feet, complete with a claw on each toe. He had a long, feline tail that swished and lashed and two pointed ears that were different from those I'd seen on the elves. His silver eyes appraised me with wicked excitement, shining like two moons and he still wore that cruel smirk on his lips.

Whoever or whatever he was, he wasn't wearing the same armor the rest of the assassins were. Did that mean he wasn't Ulfrangar? Or maybe they just didn't have any boots on hand that would accommodate his weird feet or any of their fancy black leather armor to fit his immense frame. What he did have on looked expensive, though, even if it was tattered in some places. A fine jerkin of leather and soft green velvet hugged his lithe, muscular torso, but the sleeves of the shirt he wore beneath had been torn away. Likewise, the breeches he wore were ripped off at the knees—probably to give him more freedom to move those bizarre legs.

"*You* are not of the pack. You do not give us commands." The assassin leader snorted, his lips curling back into a snarl as he pulled the shawl down from his face. I got a much better look at his sharp, distinctly Gray elven features. His golden-brown skin was flecked with scars over nearly every inch of his face, and his white hair had been cut short into a more human style. The crossbow he wore slung over his back looked a lot like the one I'd been using earlier. There was still mud caked on the stock. "We've already lost three of our finest for this one whelp. Zuer will not be pleased. So hold your tongue and wait. You'll get your prize once our payment arrives."

Prize? Was he talking about me? But why? I was a nobody. And I'd never seen anything like him before. What could that monster possibly want with me?

The beastly man dipped his head slightly, his glare smoldering behind a shaggy veil of jet-black hair that was cut off right at his shoulders. "And if he doesn't come?"

The elven Ulfrangar's opalescent eyes narrowed dangerously, his features sharpening into a knowing grin that made my blood go cold. "He will. He was Zuer's favorite from the beginning—the most brutal of her pups. He will fight to his very last heartbeat. Do not doubt his appetite ... or his pride." The elf gestured to the assassin still holding the knife against the side of my head.

The cold scrape of the knife disappeared as the dagger-wielder withdrew. My head spun as I lay, staring groggily up at the group of assassins gathered before me. My gaze caught the ornate silver cuffs they all wore. The engraving of the snarling wolf's head, with a third eye right in the middle of its forehead, seemed to leer back at me spitefully. They were talking about Murdoc, right? He had been an Ulfrangar. That's why he had been dressed in the same armor, wearing that same vambrace, the night we met. That's why he could fight better than anyone else. He was a trained assassin.

My stomach rolled. I felt sick. Biting down on the gag in my mouth, I squeezed my eyes shut.

"This is taking too long," the beastly man muttered. "We're wasting time. Every second we waste here gives the dragonriders a chance to respond. Have you considered that perhaps he's hoping for that? To wait us out until the dragonriders arrive to do his work for him?"

"A fair point," one of the other assassins agreed. "We cannot risk exposure."

The Gray elf's expression tightened. His mouth scrunched. At last, he gave his accomplice a nod.

A muffled scream tore from my throat as the assassin standing over me seized the front of my tunic, flinging me over onto my stomach so he could ram his knife through the back of my shoulder. My spine stiffened. I struggled to breathe around the gag as he gripped my neck, forcing me to stay still with his knife embedded in my body. Tears blurred my vision as my body trembled out of control.

Seconds dragged by. After a few minutes, the elf's expression darkened with a sense of cold impatience. "Again."

The knife twisted inside my shoulder with a sudden jerk, sending another wave of pain through me. My eyes went wide. For an instant, I couldn't hear anything over the ringing in my ears. I screamed again as the the world around me spun out of focus.

"Do you enjoy having that hand?" Out of nowhere, a familiar growling tone cut through the pain sizzling over my brain. "If you do, then I suggest you step away from him."

I lifted my head shakily.

Murdoc strode from the gloom like a prowling wolf, every step effortlessly smooth and calculated. He stopped only a few yards away from where I lay and the rest of the assassins were gathered, his broad shoulders back and head held high. Panning his gaze across the crowd, Murdoc slowly tilted his head to the side as he considered the men in Ulfrangar armor—his former comrades.

His face drew slowly into an ominous scowl as his eyes blazed with a cold fury like star fire on a winter's night. One corner of his mouth twitched, and his arms flexed as he curled his hands into fists. Then his harrowing glare settled squarely on me.

"You should have left with the others," he said quietly. "This was not supposed to be your fight."

I couldn't reply.

"Murdoc." The assassin let go of my shirt, dropping me back onto the ground. Nearby, his companion drew the crossbow, a new arrow already fitted to fire as he aimed right for Murdoc's head with a finger poised on the trigger.

"Blackridge." Murdoc didn't even blink. "Let him go. He has nothing to do with this."

"You're not in a position to be making demands. Did you really think you could turn your back on the Ulfrangar? That you could just skip away into the sunset, lost to the fall of Thornbend, and no one would be the wiser?" The assassin holding me chuckled and gave the knife in my shoulder another sudden jerk.

I bit down against the gag in my mouth, resisting another scream, as I shuddered with pain.

"You should know better. The pack sees all."

Murdoc's mouth twitched again, hinting at a snarl. "Release him now, and perhaps I'll make your death quick—instead of forcing you to *beg* me for it."

"Killing us won't change anything. You know we are oath-bound to hunt anyone who betrays the pack. No one leaves the Ulfrangar except in death. Your blood, like your life, belongs to the pack." The Gray elf took a daring step closer. "All that remains within your power now is how many of your pack-brothers will die along with you."

"And yet the Zuer sent only novice deltas to bring me in? I'm insulted." Murdoc's lips slowly curled into a wide, wicked smirk. His glare flashed to the beastly man standing silently by, watching without moving a muscle. "Did you think allying with more Tibran-bred scum would better your odds?"

The Gray elf tipped his head slightly, gesturing to the rest of his company—including the guy who still had the knife embedded in my shoulder. "She sent us as a courtesy with the hope that you still had some sense of honor to the pack that raised you. The Tibran isn't with us. His score is with this whelp." His finger brushed the trigger again. "This is your only chance to surrender, Murdoc. Come back now, and you will be given an honorable death."

With his smirk fading, my friend stood in uncomfortable silence as though considering his options.

"Very well," he agreed at last, his eyes never leaving mine. For the briefest instant, that icy, fierce exterior cracked. I saw the faintest hint of regret leak through, his brows rumpling and his lips thinning.

My heart thrashed in my ears. Gods and Fates, Murdoc was just going to give up? No! He couldn't! He had to fight—*we* had to fight! How could he just surrender?

Murdoc shut his eyes tightly and turned away. His shoulders tensed. His features snapped back into a scowl that was nearly hidden beneath the lengthy black bangs that fell over his face.

Standing before the Gray elf assassin, he slowly raised his hands in surrender. "I am ... sorry, Thatcher. I'm not who you think I am."

CHAPTER THIRTY-TWO

I jerked in wild desperation, trying to get to my feet. Sorry? He was *sorry*? No! I wouldn't let him do this!

With fresh agony, confusion, and terror turning my brain to mush, I almost missed it. One of Murdoc's hands twitched, blurring through a gesture that lasted only a fraction of a second as he stared down at me. Something about it immediately struck a chord in my frazzled memory. I'd seen that signal before hadn't I?

Then I remembered. It meant "stay down" in the dragonrider code. Was he ... trying to tell me something?

A fraction of a second later, a chorus of thundering roars shook the barn around us. The assassin holding the blade in my back jumped. He yanked the dagger out of my shoulder, leaving me breathless on the floor as a wave of fresh pain scalded every nerve. My vision went black and my breath caught in my chest as my throat closed. I couldn't move. I couldn't think.

All around me, men shouted, metal rang and clashed, dragons bellowed war cries, and the beastly man screeched in fury. Footsteps shuffled by. The pungent smell of dragon venom stung my eyes. I couldn't see what was happening. I was slipping, second by second, losing my consciousness as the back of my tunic became hot and wet.

"Phillip Derrick!" someone's booming shout echoed above all the chaos. "What have you done?"

Gods, I *knew* that voice. It made my heart twist with hope as I strained to make my eyes focus. Stepping over the fallen bodies of Ulfrangar assassins, Jaevid Broadfeather advanced with his scimitar firmly in hand. His gaze fixed in a smoldering glare straight ahead.

I tried to cry out. Help—someone had to help Murdoc! He couldn't fight this on his own.

And Fornax, where was my dragon? Was he all right? If I didn't make it, if I died here, then someone had to look after him. Fornax couldn't be alone. He needed me.

The harder I struggled to make a sound, the darker my vision became. Slumping onto the floor, my mind spiraled into foggy silence. I was ... fading.

"I found him!" someone else called right over me. This voice was softer, more feminine. Warm hands touched my face and gently patted my cheeks. "It's all right, you're safe now," she whispered as she brushed soft fingertips along my chin. "Foolish, silly boy. What if I had been too late?"

"Is he alive?" Reigh's voice shouted over the chaos.

A second before the pain swallowed me again, dragging me under to a frigid, numb abyss, I saw them. It was only a glimpse, but I knew that strange elven girl's wide yellow-green eyes, smooth ebony skin adorned in silver runes, and deceptively delicate features right away. Behind her, Reigh stood with his blades drawn and his teeth bared.

My friends ... they'd come back for me.

"HOLD HIM STEADY!" Reigh shouted over me.

On either side, two men I didn't know—dragonriders—held me down while Reigh prepared to snap my elbow back into its socket. They'd cut my blood-soaked shirt away already, trying to bandage the deep puncture in my shoulder, but there was fresh crimson smeared all over the place as I struggled.

"Let me go! I have to see him! You have to let me see Murdoc!" I snarled in defiance. "They'll kill him, and it's not his fault! Just let me talk to him!"

"If you keep this up, you'll tear something permanent, you moron!" Reigh snapped in reply. "Ready?"

The two men grunted in agreement.

Without warning, Reigh wrenched my arm. I let out a howling scream as my elbow popped, and pain shot through me like I'd been lit on fire. Just as quickly as the sound left my lips, the tingling discomfort in my arm vanished. So did the numbness. I could feel my fingers and move them again.

I let out a shuddering breath, falling back limp on the bed as the dragonriders let me go.

"You're an idiot," Reigh growled under his breath as he sat back, wiping his hands and glaring daggers at me. "But you're a lucky one—lucky it was only dislocated instead of broken. Geez ... and people call *me* reckless. You're in a league all your own."

I didn't feel very lucky. My heart sat like a stone in my chest, heavy and fractured. Somewhere, Murdoc still owed me answers.

"Here, drink this," Reigh murmured as he held a cup of something warm in front of my lips.

The sharp, spicy smell of it made me cringe back.

"Relax, it's just tea, and it tastes better than it smells. Chaser root tea helps with pain," he explained as he began gathering up his tray of medical supplies sitting on the table beside my bed. The two dragonriders left without another word.

With every sip of the warm, peppery tea, my head grew heavier and my eyes wouldn't stay open. I sat back, trying to think past the haze that crept over my brain.

"It's strong, so don't try walking," Reigh warned. "You'll sleep like a log though, and maybe give those wounds a chance to heal before you do something else stupid."

"Maybe pass some this way, then," Ezran fumed from a bed on the other side of the room. Propped up on a few white pillows, he sat scowling down into the bowl of potato stew we'd been given for lunch. Tired lines creased his face and dark shadows under his eyes betrayed the fact that he hadn't slept much. Not that I blamed him.

Physically, he seemed to be doing better. All his injuries were bandaged. Mentally, however? Well, I guess he had a lot to work through. Most of his home had been in flames the last time we'd seen it. Even if his barns and the dragon hatchlings survived, the rest of the manor was probably little more than a heap of charred rocks and cinders at this point.

I slumped into the pillows, barely able to put the cup on the nightstand before my arms went slack. "I ... I feel ... weird," I managed to slur.

"Good. I've got other patients to see." Reigh rolled his eyes as he stood. "Only a few members of the Cromwell serving staff made it out alive, but they've all got burns—Some that'll take months to heal. It's gonna be a long day, so just go ahead and pass out already, would you?"

I obliged. The tea didn't give me much of a choice. My eyes drooped. My body went slack. As my last few shreds of willpower dissolved, I tried to piece together what had happened.

After being rescued from the estate by the dragonriders of Eastwatch, I remembered being taken immediately to the infirmary at the fortress. Jaevid and a company of dragonriders had stayed behind, determined to do an intense search of what was left of Cromwell manor for any more survivors.

Gods, what was Jaevid even doing here? Wasn't he supposed to be back at Halfax helping Queen Jenna?

I wondered if I'd even get a chance to ask.

By morning, the tea had worn off enough that I could at least sit up. Too bad my legs still felt like two heavy logs. I couldn't stand let alone walk. The storm had long passed, giving way to an oddly calm sunrise. The skies were quiet, smeared in soft hues of lavender and pink. Lying on my bed and staring out the window nearby, I could still feel the nervous energy of that storm in my veins. Echoes of thunder rippled from the corners of my mind.

No one seemed willing to fill me in on exactly what had happened to Murdoc. They were probably suspicious of me, too, since he was my best friend and ... well, an Ulfrangar assassin.

Fine. Fair enough.

Lucky for me, dragonriders gossiped like a bunch of clucking hens. I overheard them talking about how the Ulfrangar who weren't killed in the initial assault had fled, vanishing like phantoms into the city. There wasn't much hope of ever tracking them down.

Well, save for one.

According to them, Murdoc had surrendered to the dragonriders without a fight. In fact, he'd been the one to tip them off about what was about to happen at the Cromwell estate in the first place. That must have been where he had gone after he'd vanished after dinner—straight here to Eastwatch to give the dragonriders all the information he had. Now, I didn't know where he was or what would happen to him.

I swallowed hard. Murdoc's last words were still boring into my brain like a worm into an apple. He was right—he wasn't at all who I'd thought he was. But did that really change anything? I'd always known he was good with a blade, and I'd suspected that he was a hired mercenary or maybe even a Tibran defector. Now that I knew the truth, I wasn't sure what to think of him. All I knew was that I didn't want the dragonriders to put him to death or toss him into some abyssal dungeon.

I wanted to talk to him. No, I *needed* to.

But the tea Reigh kept giving me made my breathing and pulse slow. If Reigh had his way, I probably wouldn't be moving for a while. I had no choice but to wait.

Wait—and hope.

Maybe Jaevid wouldn't let them kill Murdoc just yet. Maybe giving away the assault on the Cromwell estate would be enough to buy him some small amount of mercy.

All I could do was pray to whatever gods might be listening that I'd get to see him again.

REIGH'S CHASER root tea kept me lulling in and out of consciousness for what felt like an eternity. My mind stayed hazy and my body felt heavy, numb, and stiff. I slept, but it wasn't restful. My thoughts were caught, tangled up in nightmares wreathed in flame, Tibran armor, and that monstrous man with fangs and claws like a beast.

When I finally woke up, I had no idea how much time had passed. Lying on my back, I stared around the quiet, nearly dark infirmary room. With the streams of sterling moonlight ebbing through the window, I could see Ezran's bed was empty. I was the only one there.

Or so I thought—until movement in the doorway caught my eye and made me jolt upright.

The elf girl leaned sideways, one shoulder resting against the doorframe, and her hips cocked at a confident angle. When our eyes met, a knowing smile curved over her lips. It made my heartbeat skip and stall, thumping wildly in my chest. Girls didn't usually look at me like that.

"You're alive after all," she murmured quietly. "Reigh said your injuries weren't that serious, but I was beginning to wonder."

I blinked a few times just to make sure I wasn't hallucinating. Nope. She really was there, the soft celestial light glimmering over the silver marks on her forehead.

"Where's Ezran?" I groaned as I rubbed at my eyes. "Is he okay?"

She took a few careful steps into the room. Her bare feet didn't make a single sound on the wooden floorboards. "Recovering well enough to sift through the wreckage of his estate, or so I'm told. How are you feeling?" A few locks of her long, loosely curled black hair spilled over her shoulder as she tilted her head to the side.

"Okay," I muttered as I rubbed the back of my neck. The area around the deep puncture in the back of my shoulder was stiff, sore, and throbbed when I moved too suddenly.

"You don't have to lie, you know," she said, finally crossing the distance and spinning around to sit on the edge of my bed. "Not to me."

I dared to meet her intense, yellow-green eyes again. Something about them seemed to peer right past my flesh and bone and straight into the deepest depths of my soul. That probably should have terrified me—or at least freaked me out—but it made it hard to look away from her. I wondered what she'd find down there. Maybe she could tell me why Fornax had chosen me as his rider.

"I should be asking who you are," I realized aloud. "You saved my life twice, but I don't even know your name."

The elf girl's expression tensed some and she blinked rapidly as she stared down to the staff in her hand. Her fingers drummed on the smooth shaft as the moonlight caught over the misty, multicolored stone fixed to the top. "My name is Isandri," she replied at last, her voice so quiet I could barely hear her. "But some used to call me Isa. As for who I am ... it's probably best that you know as little as possible right now."

"Is it alright if I call you that? Isa, I mean."

Another faint smile brushed her features. Her long, dark lashes fluttered as she glanced my way. "I suppose. Reigh mentioned your name is Thatcher?"

I nodded. "Or just Thatch, if you like."

"Very well, Thatch."

"Why can't I know who you are?"

Her enchanting smile faded. "It's not easy to explain. There's something I must do—something no one else can, even if Reigh disagrees. Many lives hang in the balance. But to do this, I have to stay hidden. No one can know where I am or where I'm going." Her vividly colored eyes dimmed with a sadness I didn't understand. "What I can tell you is that I am Lunostri, brought here as a captive by Argonox."

Something about that word—Lunostri—struck a chord. I'd heard it before. But with my mind still hazy from the tea, I couldn't remember. "So ... how, uh, how do you know Reigh?" I had to know. It was obvious they knew each other.

She squared her shoulders a bit and tucked some of her hair behind one of her pointed ears. "It's complicated."

Complicated? Oh ... Yikes. I may not have been very well versed in the nuances of the female mind, but "complicated" usually meant, you know, *romantically* complicated. Even I knew that.

"I-I see. Right. Of course. Sorry." My voice cracked and I deflated. "I didn't know it was like that."

"What is that supposed to mean?" She arched a brow.

"Well, I mean, you're incredible, and Reigh is a prince, right? Plus he knows a lot about elven culture. It makes sense that you two would be—"

"Oh, goddess, no!" she interrupted. "I did not mean like *that*."

My face flushed until I could feel heat practically hissing out of my ears like steam from a kettle. "I-I'm sorry. I just thought, well, you guys seemed to know each other pretty well. I just didn't realize—"

"Stop." She put a hand over my mouth. That's when I noticed her cheeks seemed a little rosier, too. "Listen, Reigh and I met only once before this. It was during the Tibran War. Lord Argonox had held me prisoner for ... a very long time. Reigh was the one who set me free. We struck a deal, but things took a bad turn. I wasn't able to keep up my end."

"Is that why you've been helping us now? To make it up to him?"

She gave a slight shrug. "It was one of many reasons." Her vibrant eyes darted back to me, searching me with sudden intensity. "Now, I have to ask: why are *you* here, Thatch? War and chaos don't seem to be things that you're ... made for, necessarily."

When I opened my mouth, nothing would come out. It was hard enough just to remember how to breathe with her staring at me like that. "I, uh, I was sent here."

"By Jaevid Broadfeather?"

I shook my head. "No. Well, not *only* by him. The Queen of Maldobar chose a few of us to be her hunters. We are supposed to be tracking down a Tibran witch named Devana." Too late, I realized that I probably wasn't supposed to be telling everyone that. Oops.

Isa's expression closed as she drew back slightly, still studying me carefully. "She sent *you* to hunt Devana?"

"Um, well, yes." Great. Well, it'd been a few days since someone last pointed out how badly I fought. I guess that meant I was overdue.

"Thatch, I believe it is best that your quest ends here," she said quietly. "You should go back to your home and stay where it is safe."

Any other time, I would have protested. After all, she didn't know me. Who was she to tell me what was best? I didn't have a home to go back to. But that guarded look jarred something loose in my memory. It was just a second, a single glance, but it rushed back so suddenly all I could do was stare back at her for a moment with my mouth hanging open.

"You ... you were at the castle in Halfax." The words slipped out before I could stop them. "In the Court of Crowns. I saw you standing in the crowd."

The faintest trace of fear crept over her face as she held my gaze.

"Have you been following us all this time? Why?"

She looked away, her mouth clamped into a tense frown, and didn't answer.

Then I remembered. The Lunostri—Jaevid had said they were from a kingdom called Nar'Haleen. Moon elves. And ... Devana was one of them. Did that mean Isandri knew her? Or ... was it possible .... I mean, what if *she* was ...?

My mind spun, reeling as a new tidal wave of questions swarmed my already frazzled brain. No. That didn't make any sense. Why would she help us if she was somehow associated with the Tibran witch Jenna and Jaevid had described?

"Does this have something to do with Devana?" I finally dared to ask. "Do you know her?"

No reply. Isandri sat completely still, staring at the floor without a single word. Her slim fingers gripped the shaft of her weapon tightly.

I let out a sigh. "All right, then. You don't trust me. Fair enough." Rubbing at the back of my neck again, I tried not to think about the pain in my elbow. "Can you at least tell me if my dragon is all right?"

She dipped her head. "He fought bravely. Now, he rests with the other dragons here at the tower. His injuries were minor."

"What about Phoebe?" I hadn't seen any sign of her since I'd arrived here.

Isa paused, her expression darkening again for the briefest second. "She breathed in too much smoke but has already recovered. Now she's gone with Jaevid and the others to see if any of her artifacts can be salvaged from the fire."

Well, that was a relief, at least. "And ... Murdoc? Have you seen him? Do you know where he is?"

She glanced back over her shoulder, arching a brow suspiciously. "And if I do?"

"I need to talk to him."

"That would be a feat. The dragonriders have already questioned him. But he won't say much. Other than offering a brief account of himself to Jaevid, your friend seems determined to go to his death in silence rather than beg for his life." She gave a snort and shook her head slightly, making her long dark hair swish along the base of her back. "I can't decide if that's foolish or brave."

My heart sank. For all the answers I'd finally gotten about Murdoc, I now had twice as many questions. Why had he betrayed the Ulfrangar? Why had he spared my life in the first place? Why had he given himself up to the dragonriders now? Why, why, why ...

"You should try to get some rest," Isa murmured as she stood and strode smoothly across the room. "I expect you'll have a lot to answer for very soon. This has stirred up noble courts and crowns far beyond your borders. If you can manage it, I ... I would appreciate it if you didn't mention my presence to anyone else here. I'd prefer to remain anonymous for as long as I can."

"What? You mean you aren't going to stay with us?"

Her bemused smile reminded me of how other, usually much older women looked at me when they crooned about my "baby face" and how cute I was. It felt patronizing and stung my pride a little. She was about my age, wasn't she?

"You're too kind, Thatcher," she said softly. "I might not be a very good addition to the queen's hunters, though. I've already stayed here too long. Helping you at the estate was a calculated risk on my part. I owed Reigh a great debt, and I ... I couldn't bear watching you suffer. But as I said, there's something I have to do."

"So you're leaving? Just like that? If you're after Devana, we could work together." I argued. "We *should* work together."

Once again, Isa stared at me like someone admiring a puppy. For crying out loud, why did girls always look at me like that? Maybe if I tried growing a beard? Would that help make me look older?

Probably not. Then I'd be cute *and* furry. Ugh.

"Don't worry, you'll have plenty to keep you busy. Reigh says that the Ulfrangar have been nothing but a nasty rumor for centuries. And yet, you've just confirmed that all those awful bedtime stories might actually be real. Whispers in the ranks say that a man, King Jace of Luntharda, has come here personally to question you. The dragonriders hold him in high esteem, even if he is no longer of your country."

My stomach did a frantic backflip. "M-Me? He wants to question *me*?" That didn't make sense. Why in the world would the king of the Gray Elf kingdom want to talk to me? I'd never even been to Luntharda.

She shrugged as she paused in the doorway to cast me one last, meaningful look. "I can only assume he worries about how much of a hold the Ulfrangar may have in his kingdom, as well. Especially since a Gray elf was found among their dead." Her lips pursed, expression becoming thoughtful as she began to turn away. "Take care of yourself, Thatch. There is a darkness coming, a power unknown to even Jaevid or your queen. They foolishly hurled you into its path, but you have a chance to escape. I strongly recommend that you take it. Go home."

"Stop saying that," I snapped, my tone sharp with an anger that rose up so suddenly it left me dizzy. I took a few deep breaths, trying to calm down before I started over. "I don't have a home anymore. It's gone. This—Fornax and my chance at being a dragonrider—is all I have now. Jaevid and Queen Jenna gave me that chance. Now, they've asked for my help."

"No," she corrected, her voice hushed and her expression more guarded than ever. Gazing into her eyes felt like staring into an ever-changing maze, as though her mind were a living labyrinth I might get lost in forever. "Whether they realize it or not, they've asked for your death."

CHAPTER THIRTY-THREE

By morning, I felt more like myself. Still sore, of course, and Reigh insisted I use a sling for my injured arm for a few weeks while my elbow healed, but I could manage. At least, I could manage well enough to have a chat with King Jace of Luntharda.

Politics were *not* my area of expertise. You want to know how to properly trim hooves, hitch up a carriage, or shoe a horse? I'm your guy. But the delicate intricacies of international royal courts?

Forget it.

Honestly, I was counting on what Ezran had told me about the King of Luntharda to be my only saving grace. According to him, King Jace hadn't always been royal. In fact, he hadn't even been a noble until after the end of the Gray War, forty years ago. Before that, he was a dragonrider—a human soldier from Maldobar—and a decorated war hero. He had been Jaevid's instructor at the dragonrider academy and had seen things that people all over Maldobar still told stories about. He had been a commoner just like me. A regular guy. So maybe he would understand why I was a sweaty nervous wreck as I stepped into the finely decorated colonel's office on the top floor of Eastwatch tower.

I managed a nervous glance around at the other men standing around, searching for a familiar face among the soldiers dressed in regal armor who stood waiting for me. Jaevid, Ezran, and Reigh were the only people I recognized out of the crowd. Identifying King Jace wasn't all that difficult, though. I knew exactly which one he was.

Mostly because he started yelling at me immediately.

"*You!*" The old king strode toward me, jabbing an accusing finger at my face. His skin was crinkled with age, and both his hair and short, neatly-trimmed beard were a peppery shade of grayish-white. But he didn't move like an old man *at all*. And the cold fire in his light amber eyes sent chills up my spine as he glowered at me.

"Jace, please, try to calm down." Jaevid stood close by, watching with his expression stern.

"*Calm down?*" The old king balked, spinning on Jaevid with a frenzied scowl. "I am the *only* one giving this the appropriate reaction. There was an Ulfrangar agent in the royal castle—standing in the same room as Jenna, Reigh, and gods only know how many other people you care for. If you had any idea of the risk that situation implies, you'd be losing your mind right along with me." He turned back to me, nostrils flaring as his face flushed beneath that frost-colored beard. 'The gods must have taken a particular liking to you, boy. That's the only reason I can fathom you are still breathing. That, or sheer, dumb luck."

"B-But you don't understand!" I started to protest. "Whatever he was before, Murdoc isn't—"

King Jace surged toward me, moving much faster than I expected a man somewhere in his seventies could. His scorching glare sizzled over me like the heat of a desert sunset, standing so close I could see all the angry little veins on his eyeballs. "You listen to me, boy. Take every ridiculous notion of friendship you have with that thing and forget it—right now. Gods and Fates, you have *no idea* what that creature truly is. He may have been born human, but the Ulfrangar have made an art of stripping away all traces of humanity from the children they obtain. Every breath he takes is a risk that all the malice and cruelty they have poured into his soul will resurface and some poor fool will be standing too close. He cannot be allowed to leave this place alive."

"You don't know him!" I yelled back, trembling with desperate anger as my heart thrashed in my ears. "Who are you to judge? You don't know anything about him! How can you just assume—"

"BECAUSE *I* WAS ONE OF THEM," the king roared back.

I froze. My heart stopped. The room fell completely silent.

What? He ... King Jace ... had been an Ulfrangar assassin? How? When?

One glance over to Jaevid's anguish-ridden face made my blood run cold. He bowed his head, eyes shut tight as he rubbed his forehead. Wait, had he known all this time?

King Jace took a step back, his chest puffing with furious breaths under his long, sweeping robes and golden decorative armor. His light brown eyes searched me, consumed with a fury I didn't understand. As suddenly as I saw it, though, that anger began to fade. His shoulders dropped. His head bowed slightly, and he stared down at the floor.

"It's all right, Jace," Jaevid whispered, his expression still grim.

The older man cringed. His expression fractured, and he buried his face in his hands. "No, Jae. It isn't. For years, I've dreaded the moment when *they* might find some way back into my life." He took in a shuddering breath, as though trying to steady himself. "I was ... abducted by the Ulfrangar as a child. Unlike that monster you call a friend, I had a family before that. I had good memories from before the torment they call training. I understood the difference between right and wrong. That understanding was the only thing that kept their teachings from consuming my soul entirely. But there were many others who were trapped with them just like I was, and they weren't so lucky. I saw the innocence die in their eyes. Their souls were snuffed out like candles in the night. They were alive, but only in body. Their minds and souls belonged to the Ulfrangar. They became cold. The only language they knew was one written in blood."

When he turned to look at me again, the anger was gone from the old king's face. In its place, something like grief made all the hard lines around his eyes and mouth deepen.

That rawboned expression cut me right to the core. I sucked in a sharp breath as he loosened the collar of his finely embroidered silk tunic, pulling it down so I could see the old, gnarled scars around his neck. He pushed back his sleeves to reveal more on his wrists. The marks were faded, but they were thick and still plainly visible.

They looked exactly like the scars I'd seen on Murdoc.

"This is what they do to all their new recruits—children bought or stolen. They call them pups, and from the time they're able to walk, those children are shackled like animals and beaten into submission, tortured, and starved until they obey without question. You have to earn your freedom from those bonds," he explained, his voice broken with anguish and regret. "But to earn that freedom, you have to surrender your soul. You have to prove your loyalty. You have to kill. You have to become one of them."

Looking at those marks made my insides writhe and twist into knots. Had Murdoc really been tortured like that?

"That boy didn't have the influence of a family. He claims he doesn't remember a life before the Ulfrangar—and *that* is what makes him so dangerous. Most likely, he was bought as an infant, so they scorched every trace of mercy and love from his soul before he ever knew he had it. Whether you choose to believe it or not, I know the horrors he's had to endure to survive among them. I know what they've made him do to earn his place. He can't be like us. Like a dog that's learned the taste of blood, he will always be drawn to the taste of it."

"He saved me." My voice faltered, cracking over the doubt that seeped into the corners of my mind.

"He *used* you," King Jace corrected. "Trying to leave the Ulfrangar immediately earned him a death sentence. No one leaves the pack. It's part of the blood oath you take when the order recognizes you as a true member. The only way out is in death. You were nothing but a shield to him; a smokescreen to give him a new identity and chance at escaping their grasp. Don't try to make it more than it was. It wasn't friendship, loyalty, or some desire to be good—it was a survival tactic."

I bit down hard against the hot, stiff, painful sensation that rose in the back of my throat. I ... I didn't want to believe that. Murdoc had come back for me in the end, just like I'd known he would. If that was true, if he didn't care about our friendship at all, then why hadn't he just run away when he had the chance? Why come back to the estate —back to the one place where his former comrades were sure to find him?

"So how did you escape them, then?" Reigh asked, sitting forward to rest his elbows on his knees.

King Jace's brows knitted together, his jaw stiffening as he flashed a look at all the men in armor standing around us. "It was during the Gray War. The Ulfrangar thrive on war. It presents many opportunities to kill for profit—which has always been their primary function. Hired assassins, you see. They pull at the hidden strands between kingdoms like spiders on silken threads, invisible until it's too late. But with business booming, it became harder and harder for Ulfrangar agents to communicate without risking exposure. Many of us were dispatched in small strike forces of one or two members so we could work more efficiently and complete jobs faster. I was sent with two others to eliminate some noble brat. It was supposed to be an easy job. Cut his throat while he slept and vanish—simple."

King Jace rubbed at his beard, avoiding our stares while we waited for him to finish. "But when I got there, something about the job just ... threw me off. It became harder and harder to justify what I was doing. Memories of my family haunted me nearly every night. So when I looked down at that kid, sound asleep in his bed, I couldn't do it. I sabotaged the mission, tipped off the city guards, and let them arrest me. As far as the Ulfrangar knew, I was put to the sword. Executed by order of the crown. But in truth, someone in the royal castle got wind of what I really was—Ulfrangar and not just some flea-bitten, mercenary mongrel. I was a top pedigree killer."

"The King of Maldobar offered you a fresh start," Jaevid finished for him, recognition dawning over his face. "Hovrid offered you a dragon."

"Yes. But with strings attached," King Jace agreed. "He'd send some other poor fool to the sword in my place, and I would be sworn in as a dragonrider. In return, I had to make it my mission to eliminate every member of Luntharda's royal household I could on the battlefield. If I accomplished that, I would be given a lavish retirement to live out the rest of my days in comfort and peace. I was almost successful, too." A strange, nearly sad smile brushed over his lips. "And then I lost my wingend in battle and was sent to the academy to teach and scout for a new partner. I met my very first student, a pitiful little halfbreed and his wild dragon. Nothing was ever the same after that."

Jaevid and King Jace stared at one another for a moment. The silence between them was like standing in a room choked with steam, uncomfortable and heavy. The old king was the first to look away, shifting his stance and muttering under his breath.

"Are you sure you just want to kill this guy without even hearing him out?" Reigh asked. "I've traveled and dueled with him. He's the best swordsman I've ever seen. In case you've forgotten, there's a Tibran witch out there still twisting in the wind. He could be an incredible asset to bringing her down."

King Jace hesitated. "Jaevid, ultimately, this is your decision. But if you don't hear anything else I say, at least hear this: the Ulfrangar *will* come for that boy again, regardless of what you choose to believe about where his allegiance lies now. They will never forgive his desertion, and there is no corner of this earth they won't raze to the ground in search of him." He sighed, readjusting the collar of his tunic to cover his scars. "Their network is vast—larger than you can comprehend. Their coffers are deep. There's nowhere they can't go and nothing they won't do to get what they believe they're owed. Keeping that boy alive or letting him travel with Jenna's agents will only put more people in danger. Whatever you decide to do with him, be sure the outcome is something you can live with."

I DIDN'T KNOW what to believe anymore. After the meeting was finished, I left the Colonel's office with Reigh on my heels. My head spun, swarming with questions, worries, and doubts. The evidence was overwhelming. Murdoc was an Ulfrangar assassin. And while I'd suspected from the beginning there was a lot more to him than he would ever admit, I now had to come to terms with that ugly truth.

Strangely enough, what bothered me the most now was that he'd never told me. Didn't he trust me at all? Or was I really just a smokescreen? A human shield to keep the Ulfrangar thrown off his scent?

When we reached the top of a staircase leading down into the depths of the dragonrider tower, Reigh put a hand on my shoulder. "Hey, Thatch, hang on a second."

I bowed my head to look down at my boots.

"Are you okay?" He sounded sincerely concerned. "I know that got a little heated back there."

Gnawing on the inside of my cheek, I tried to think of something to say. "My father used to say I was a terrible judge of character. I guess he was right," I confessed. "And now I just feel sick. People died. Phoebe was hurt. Ezran, too. You were almost killed. And it's because of me."

"Hey, stop that, okay? I don't have any hard feelings about what happened. Neither does Ezran or Phoebe. We know it wasn't your fault."

Somehow, I couldn't agree.

"I'm sorry about Murdoc," Reigh murmured. "And for doubting you before. You saved my life on that roof."

"No. Isa was the one who caught you," I objected.

"Yeah. That's true. But that assassin was gonna shoot me. All Isandri would have rescued was a corpse full of arrows if you hadn't climbed up there to stop him." He cleared his throat, lowering his voice as though he didn't want anyone else to overhear. "I'm probably in the minority of opinions here, but I don't think you're a bad judge of character. A little naïve, sure, but ... Murdoc came to Eastwatch and tipped them off about the attack and how to take the Ulfrangar out. He tried to save us as soon as he sensed what was about to go down. And when we landed here without you, he lost it. He wasn't going to let anyone stop him from going back for you. Jaevid got him to agree on a compromise, working with the dragonriders, to get you out safely. Deadly assassin or not, there's still something good in him—something the Ulfrangar didn't destroy."

I bit down hard against the tightness that crushed at my chest. "I ... I want to talk to him."

Reigh gave a solemn nod. "Yeah. Me, too."

"I do, as well," someone spoke up from behind us.

Together, Reigh and I turned to see Jaevid striding down the hall in our direction, concern still sharp upon his features and his long cloak fluttering at his boot heels.

"See?" Reigh gave my shoulder a squeeze before brushing past me down the stairs. "We've all got questions. Now, let's see if that friend of yours is up for a chat. I have a feeling that if anyone can get him to talk, it's you."

34
CHAPTER THIRTY-FOUR

Murdoc was probably the most dangerous criminal ever held in custody at Eastwatch tower—and maybe in all of Maldobar, too. And since this place had already weathered the Gray War and the Tibran War, that was saying something. They had him under tight security, locked in a cell in the dungeon beneath the tower.

It took a long time for us to get down to the bottom levels. The elevator shaft that ran through the center of the structure from the fiftieth floor at the top all the way down to the ground wasn't meant to carry people. Jaevid warned that it was far too dangerous. Instead, we took the seemingly endless stairwell that wound through every floor.

Jaevid led the way, leaving Reigh and me to follow along behind in silence. The farther we descended, the faster my heart raced. I tried to breathe through the panic rising in my chest. My mind raced, blurring between my need for answers and wondering if I was really ready to know the truth. What if Murdoc refused to say anything to me? What if the dragonriders decided to put him to death? Would I have to watch him die?

Walking beside me, I noticed that Reigh seemed to be breathing hard—too hard for someone just going down steps. His face had gone pale. His mouth locked shut, and his gaze focused straight at Jaevid's back. A vein stood out against the side of his neck, as though he were gritting his teeth.

When we were nearly at the bottom of the staircase, Reigh halted suddenly. His chest heaved, mouth gaping as he sucked in shallow, frantic breaths.

I stopped, reaching out with my one good arm to steady him. "Hey, what's wrong?"

His eyes darted around, wild and confused, as though he couldn't see me at all. What was happening? He'd seemed just fine a few minutes ago. His forehead beaded with sweat as his legs suddenly buckled and he sank into me. I staggered, shouting to get

Jaevid's attention while trying to ease Reigh into a sitting position on the floor with only one hand.

"Reigh!" Jaevid called as he jogged back up the steps. "What happened?"

I gaped up at him in shock. "I-I don't know. He just collapsed."

All but shoving me out of the way, Jaevid dropped to his knees in front of him. Reigh was still breathing hard. Beads of sweat rolled down the sides of his face as he stared back at us, eyes wide and pupils dilated.

"Is he going to be okay?" I panicked.

Jaevid's expression went steely. He grabbed Reigh's face in his hands and forced him to make eye contact. "Reigh, you need to listen to me. Calm down. You're not at Northwatch. The war is over. Argonox is gone. I know what you're seeing looks real. I believe that you're seeing it and I know it seems like it's really happening. But it's not. The war is over. You're safe."

Reigh's light brown eyes welled, his expression skewing with pain. He blinked back at Jaevid, body trembling as his gaze suddenly seemed to focus. "J-Jae," he stammered hoarsely. His hands shot out to grip the front of Jaevid's breastplate like a drowning man clinging to a life raft.

"It's not real, Reigh. Think—try to remember what happened. We defeated Argonox together. You're not at Northwatch anymore," Jaevid repeated, his tone softer. "The war is over. You're safe now."

I stood back, not sure how to help. I wasn't a medic or a healer by any stretch, so it was probably best to give them some space. Jaevid continued to talk to him in a gentle, soothing tone as Reigh gradually calmed down. After a few minutes, he looked much less pasty and seemed to be breathing normally again, although he still hadn't stopped shaking.

Gods and Fates, what happened? Was he sick? Was it some kind of fit or attack?

"Go on ahead of us," Jae ordered without ever looking my way. "We'll catch up."

"No," Reigh snapped, his voice still weak. "If he's gonna be stuck with me fighting witches and monsters, he should know what he's really in for." He paused and muttered what I suspected were a few curses in elven under his breath as he lurched back to his feet. His hand still shook as he raked some of his lengthy red hair away from his face.

I glanced between them, confused. Reigh had mentioned that he was having issues with what had happened to him during the war. But this was a lot more serious than I'd expected.

"I ... I've been having flashbacks more often," he confessed quietly. "At first, it was just at night. You know, nightmares. I'd wake up soaked in sweat. But lately, it happens even when I'm awake. Something sets it off, a sound or a smell, and it's like I'm back there. It's been a lot worse since I came back to Maldobar."

Jaevid's frown darkened. "How often?"

Reigh avoided eye contact as he dipped his head in shame. He closed his eyes to take a few deep, stabilizing breaths. "Uh, well ... almost every day. Three times since we got here. Funny how all the dragonrider watches look exactly the same on the inside, right? I think this is the first time I've been inside one without someone trying to kill me." He barked a thin, uncomfortably forced laugh.

No one else was laughing.

"Lighten up. I'm fine."

The look on Jaevid's face was almost unreadable. Empathy laced with something darker—a grim understanding. I wondered if he ever had flashbacks. He'd been a soldier too, right? He'd probably seen his fair share of gruesome things.

Jae's pale, aquamarine eyes tracked Reigh as he started down the stairs again, his brow still creased with concern. Then he looked back at me, pinning me under a tense, disapproving stare.

I nodded slightly. It didn't take a genius to see that Reigh was trying to slough this off like it wasn't a big deal. But it was, and that awkward laugh wasn't fooling anyone. If something set off a flashback at the wrong time, like when we were fighting, things could go bad in a hurry.

"Stop it, Jae. I can feel you caring from way over here. Knock it off," Reigh shouted back as he stomped away down the stairs. "I'm fine. I mean it."

Only he wasn't—I knew that now. No wonder Jaevid had wanted me to look after him.

WE FOUND Murdoc chained to the center of a cell in what felt like the deepest, darkest corner of the Eastwatch tower dungeon.

My breath caught as we stepped around the corner, approaching the thick iron bars that separated the cell from the rest of the cavernous stone corridor. There were rows of cells on either side, lit by crackling torches that made the shadows dance, but the one where Murdoc was held lay at the very end of the hall.

Kneeling on the cold stone floor, Murdoc was bound with iron gauntlets clamped over his hands so that he wouldn't be able to use his fingers. The gauntlets were tethered with taut, heavy chains that held his arms out to the sides. A heavy metal collar was locked around his neck, and there were shackles on his feet that clamped them to the floor.

Four armored guards surrounded him, their swords drawn and leveled at his neck just in case he made a false move. When we walked up to the cell door, they didn't move an inch. They might as well have been statues. It took Jaevid clearing his throat a few times before one of them even looked our way.

While he conversed quietly with the guards, I stared at Murdoc and tried to remember how to breathe. My stomach twisted and wrenched, squirming like I'd swallowed a live eel. My heart pounded, and I clenched my teeth to keep them from chattering.

The young man kneeling on the ground in that cell barely resembled my friend now. He was filthy, his skin smeared with grime, soot, and dried blood,. His dark hair hung in a shaggy, tangled mess that hid his face from our view. Gods, was this really him?

They'd stripped him down to his smallclothes, revealing every horrific scar on his body. Hundreds marred nearly every inch of him. Most looked old and faded, but many more were still raised and obviously recent.

"I do apologize, Lord Broadfeather, but we were given explicit orders not to let this criminal out of our sight," the leader of the guards argued. "I cannot let you speak to him without supervision."

"And who gave you those orders?" Jaevid demanded.

"They came straight from Colonel Haprick," the guard replied with a faint tremor of nervousness.

"Yeah? Well, now you have orders straight from his Highness, Prince Reigh of Maldobar, to take your men and get out of here." Reigh stepped in between them with a harrowing glare. "*Now*. Before I lose my patience."

The guard blinked, shocked and uncertain for a moment, and then bowed swiftly and gestured to the other guards. Immediately, they all sheathed their blades, opened the cell door, and marched down the hall without another word.

Impressive.

"You enjoyed that," Jaevid mumbled as he stepped into the cell.

Reigh shrugged and followed. "Only a little."

Standing outside the bars, I tried to will my feet to move. I needed to go in. I had to talk to Murdoc. But the longer I stared at him, the more it felt like I was slowly drowning in lukewarm water. I didn't know this person. Not really. The realization made my gut clench.

I was ... *afraid* of him. I didn't know what to say. Frantically, I tried to remember all the things I'd wanted to ask him before. My mind had gone completely blank.

"Thatch?" Reigh had paused to stare back at me, an eyebrow arched expectantly.

I swallowed hard. Squeezing my eyes shut, I forced myself to move. I crossed the threshold into the cell, my teeth still chattering as I stood right in front of where Murdoc was chained. He never moved. Never said a word. He didn't even look up. If not for the way his ribs pressed against his skin as he breathed, I might have thought he was unconscious or dead.

For a few long, agonizing minutes, we all stood in silence around him.

Finally, words tore out of me I couldn't repress. "Why didn't you tell me who you really were?"

Murdoc didn't respond at first. Then, slowly, he lifted his head to stare up at me. His earth-toned eyes, a mixture of browns, greens, and flecks of gold, caught in the warm torchlight. They hadn't lost any of their sharp, smoldering intensity.

"Because you would have forgiven me for it," he replied quietly.

"What?"

"I am what I am, Thatcher—what *they* made me. But I know you don't understand what that really means. You would have forgiven me out of ignorance. No Ulfrangar deserves that kind of mercy."

"You judge yourself very harshly," Jaevid said. "Even though you spared his life twice. Once at Thornbend. And again by coming here with your warning. That was the only thing that saved any of the lives at Cromwell estate."

Murdoc's calculating stare snapped away to meet Jae's, his mouth twitching with withheld fury. "Is that enough to atone for the hundreds of others I've killed already?"

My thoughts scrambled at those words. Hundreds? He'd killed *hundreds* of people?

"Whatever good you think I've done is nothing. It's an insignificant speck of dust compared to what came before."

Reigh crossed his arms. "So we should just kill you and be done with it? Is that what you're saying?"

Murdoc's head bowed slightly, an ironic smile ghosting over his lips. "If you're smart. And I'd suggest making it a public event, or else you risk the Ulfrangar not hearing of it before they torture and butcher your little band of hunters in search of me. As I hoped, the arrival of so many dragonriders caught them off guard. They don't wage open warfare. But trust me, they won't make the same mistake twice. They'll come again. And they'll make sure their work is accomplished."

"No," I snarled suddenly. Heat rose in my veins, scalding under my skin and drawing every muscle tight. It made my injured elbow throb, but I didn't care. Hearing him talk like that—like one of those assassins—made my blood boil. "I won't let you die."

Murdoc snapped a defiant glare up at me, his mouth twitching with a snarl. "Stop it. You're acting stupider than usual. If I'm publicly executed, then you and the others won't be targeted any further. But if you spare my life out of some ridiculous notion of friendship and loyalty, you'll ensure that all of us meet a gruesome demise. The Ulfrangar *will not* let me go, Thatcher. And if you try to stand in their way, they will cut you down, too."

"I DON'T CARE!" I yelled into his face. My heart pumped wildly, anger scorching my throat as I bit back the urge to punch him. "Calling you my friend isn't ridiculous. It isn't stupid, and neither am I. If anything, you're the stupid one here. You think dying is going to make up for all the bad things you did? It won't. It just makes you a coward who's too afraid to face his own past. If you really wanted to make up for that, if you really wanted to change, you'd be standing with us instead of hiding down here like some self-loathing, little child."

Murdoc flexed against his bonds, making the chains groan as he glared back at me.

A strong, steady hand came to rest on my shoulder. "Calm down, Thatcher," Jaevid urged.

I tried. But my vision blurred with rage as I took a step back, away from my so-called friend. "Just stop this. Stop running and hiding. Stop pretending like your fate is already written. Dying doesn't make the pain go away—not for anyone. It just makes it someone else's burden. *My* burden. Don't you get it? You and Fornax ... you're the only family I've got now."

Silence hung heavy in the air until Jaevid spoke up again. "Murdoc, there is a chance that even if you forfeit your life, the Ulfrangar will keep pursuing Thatcher and the others, anyway."

He blinked, obviously confused. "They'd have no reason to—"

Jaevid didn't let him finish. "The man that was with them, the one who looked more beast than human, was he Ulfrangar, too?"

Murdoc hesitated. His eyes darted between us as though he were thinking it over. "No," he replied at last. "He wasn't. At least, not to my knowledge."

With his mouth setting into a hard, grim line, Jaevid turned away to pace the length of the cell. "So Phillip has betrayed us, but not for the Ulfrangar. Gods and Fates, what is he doing?"

"Who?" I'd heard them talk about a man named Phillip while we were meeting with Queen Jenna. Surely this wasn't the same guy, though ... right?

"Phillip Derrick, formerly Duke Phillip Derrick of Barrowton," Jaevid confirmed.

"He is, or was, my sister's fiancée," Reigh added. "It's kind of a long story, but he was held captive by the Tibrans for a while, too. They experimented on him with something called switchbeast venom, and it transformed him into that monster. We, uh, well we *thought* his mind was still intact. His personality didn't seem any different. I thought he was supposed to be at Barrowton helping Aedan?" His expression crinkled with uncertainty as he glanced Jaevid's way. "He wouldn't betray us, not in a million years."

"Something must have happened," Jaevid insisted. "Phillip loves Jenna. I spent hours scouring his mind when we first rescued him from the Tibrans. He wouldn't turn on us; he wouldn't betray *her*. Not even if his life depended on it."

"I agree." Reigh was rubbing at his neck and chin thoughtfully. "Can we really be sure that was him? I didn't get a good look, and there may have been others who suffered that same kind of torture, right?"

"Ulfrangar don't hunt with anyone outside the pack," Murdoc countered. "You must be mistaken."

"I *saw* him." Jaevid's jaw locked, his brow drawing into a grimace of rage and anguish. "It was Phillip. He was with the Ulfrangar at the estate."

Reigh's expression was riddled with concern, as well. "Is it possible his mind is slipping? From the venom?"

"I don't know." Jae rubbed his face with his hands, groaning between his fingers. "I can't sense those things like I did before. All I know is what I saw, and there's no mistaking him. I ... I called out to him, but he didn't even look my way. It was like he didn't know me. As though it were his body, but it was not his mind—not the Phillip we know. Gods, how am I going to tell Jenna? She thinks he's still in Barrowton."

I cringed. Unfortunately, I remembered that monstrous guy clearly, too. He'd seemed set on kidnapping me, although I didn't understand why. "They, uh, they mentioned something about me being a prize. It sounded like that monster ... er ... man, Phillip, wanted to abduct me. Like maybe he was working with the Ulfrangar, or they had some kind of deal worked out that involved handing me over as payment."

"Who would want you?" Reigh paused, flashing me a roguish smirk. "No offense."

"Could it be Devana?" I guessed.

All three of them stared at me with similar expressions of bewilderment.

"Well, it's just that we know she can manipulate people's minds, right? What if she's manipulating Phillip somehow?" I tried to sound convincing or, at least, like I wasn't a complete moron.

Jae's eyes went wide. "Maybe. If that's true, then has she left Northwatch? Is she roaming from city to city now? How many more people are in danger?" He strode back toward Murdoc and crouched down before him, balanced on the balls of his feet with his elbows on his knees. The length of his long blue cloak pooled around him and the torchlight danced over the polished surface of his dragonrider armor. "Are you listening, Murdoc? Do you understand what this means? Whether you live or die, the Ulfrangar will come for Thatcher again. And with Phillip on their side, I'm not sure anyone is beyond their reach. As you said before, they won't make the same mistake twice. They'll try to kill Reigh and Phoebe. They'll try to take Thatcher as their prisoner again. And if Devana has allied with them or is using them somehow, then I'm not sure even Reigh or myself could stop her."

"Not that I don't intend to try," Reigh added with a snort of defiance. "It's one thing for her to be some former Tibran agent lurking around, but if she's done something to Phillip? Jenna won't rest until we've got him back—and I wouldn't be much of a brother if I didn't help."

Jaevid slipped a hand beneath his breastplate, reaching into one of the pockets of his tunic. A brass-plated key shimmered in the dim light as he held it up in front of Murdoc's face. "The only question remaining is what do *you* intend to do about it?"

I stiffened. Jaevid had asked me that question once before. Now, it was Murdoc's turn. I held my breath and waited for him to answer.

"You're really willing to risk letting me go?" Murdoc's gaze darted between us, his expression tense and uncertain. "Just like that? After everything I've done? After everything you've seen?"

"I'm willing to give you the same second chance Jace was given," he said firmly. "What you do with it isn't something I get to decide. It's your life, Murdoc. I suggest you choose wisely."

Murdoc's expression had gone cold, his sharp gaze fixed on the key before him with a pensive scowl. Seconds ticked by. Then, with a rumbling growl through clenched teeth, Murdoc answered, "Get these chains off me."

CHAPTER THIRTY-FIVE

"You do realize King Jace is going to lose it when he hears you let Murdoc go, right?" Reigh jogged along after us as we hurried out of the dungeon. "He'll probably spit fire, bleed from the ears, or break someone's neck. Or, you know, all of that. But then again, he is pretty old. He could just have a rage-induced heart attack and die on the spot."

"I'll handle it. Honestly, I'm more worried about telling Jenna that Phillip has gone rogue." Jaevid sounded more annoyed than worried as he handed Murdoc his cloak to wrap up in while we trekked back up the stairs.

"Yeah. She's gonna lose it, too," Reigh agreed. "Make sure you're standing across the room when you tell her. I know she's moving a little slower than usual these days, but you'll still need a head start."

Jaevid shook his head. "Let's just get him some clothes, pack up, and get you moved out of the tower as soon as possible. I've got connections in Dayrise that can provide a place for you to regroup before you head to Northwatch. If Devana is the source of the problem, then it's best that we apprehend her as soon as possible."

"You're still not going with us? After all this?" Reigh chuckled like that was a bad joke. "Come on, you know you miss it. The hopeless odds? The near death experiences? The epic feats of heroism?"

Jaevid snorted and shook his head, his mouth scrunching as though fighting back a smile. "No thanks. I've got to report this to Jenna right away. And then I'm needed at home—which is where I should be now. That was the only reason Jenna would let me out of the Court of Crowns; you know that."

Reigh's brows shot up. "Any day now, huh?"

I could have sworn Jae was blushing as he ducked his head and looked sheepishly away. "The midwife didn't want me to leave in the first place because the baby could come at any time. But once I spoke with Jace about Murdoc, I knew I had to be here."

"You sly dog!" Reigh cackled and smacked him over the back of the head. "You'd rather change diapers than save the world? Fine. I guess I understand."

Jaevid turned red across his cheeks and all the way to the tips of his ears. "I'm sure you can manage well enough without me this time. Besides, this is your chance to pull off the heroic acts without me stealing your spotlight."

"Riiiight," Reigh groaned and rolled his eyes.

"Just ... try not to burn anything else down."

Reigh grinned wolfishly. "I'll see what I can do. No promises, though. Especially if I'm lugging them along." He thumbed over at Murdoc and me. "Buncha walking disasters, these two."

Murdoc snorted, but he didn't retort.

We made our way back to the dragonrider levels of the tower near the top without incident, although I was a winded, exhausted, sweaty mess once we got there. I'd never climbed so many stairs in my life. My calves were howling as I dragged myself the last few feet into the room in the infirmary where I'd been for the last few days. Murdoc sat down on the edge of the bed, and I collapsed into a chair nearby.

"Wait here; I'll see about clothes and get Phoebe up to speed," Reigh said as he and Jaevid paused in the doorway. "Hopefully she's stopped crying about the gear she lost. We salvaged some of it, but most burned to a crisp. She's been working for days to come up with a new plan to contain Devana."

Murdoc glanced up at the mention of her name, his lips thinning. "Was she ... injured?" His voice caught.

That cunning smile curled across Reigh's face again, making his eyes glint with mischief. "Breathed in a little too much smoke, but she's fine."

Murdoc's body relaxed.

"Stay here, would you?" He slipped me a wink. "With the guards out of the way, hopefully we can buy a few hours before anyone—especially King Jace—notices he's gone. But let's play it safe, all right? We need to be long gone by nightfall."

I nodded. "Sure."

Satisfied, he turned on a heel and started away down the hall with Jaevid right behind him. I waited until I heard their footsteps retreat to let out a shaky sigh. Easing back in the chair, I rubbed at my sore elbow through the length of cloth Reigh had tied around it as a sling to keep it held firmly against my torso.

The silence was oppressive. Sitting on the bed, Murdoc stared down at the floor. Jaevid's cloak was still wrapped around him, hiding the scars that marred his body. It didn't do anything to hide the dusky, haunted circles under his eyes, however.

"Thatcher?" He spoke so quietly I barely heard him.

"Yeah?"

"I ... I'm sorry. I should have told you the truth. I guess part of me hoped you'd figure it out on your own so I wouldn't have to."

I picked at the hem of my tunic. "Yeah, well, I'm not that smart, remember?" I couldn't do anything to keep the sarcasm out of my voice.

"I just assumed this time you'd want to walk away. I wouldn't blame you if you did." His expression fractured with raw shame and he leaned forward to bury his face in his hands. "You don't understand what it's like to look at your reflection and see nothing but horror—the pain you've caused so many others. I *hate* what I am, and I'm powerless to change it. I'd rather let them kill me than live another day like this. But I can't let them kill you, too. You don't deserve that fate."

A knot formed in my throat as I watched him break down. Getting up, I moved over to sit down next to him. "I'm not angry, you know. I'm just disappointed. I thought by now you'd trust me—that we could trust each other. It probably sounds stupid, but I really do think of you like family. Like a brother, I guess. I always wished I had one."

"No," Murdoc rasped. "It doesn't sound stupid. But Thatcher, I ... I don't know who I really am. I don't even know my own name."

"Wait, it isn't Murdoc?"

"No. Ulfrangar like to name their pups after the places they get them. That's what they called me."

I scratched at the back of my head. "But I don't know of any cities named Murdoc."

He let out a shuddering sigh and moved to let his chin rest in his palms, still hunched over. "I know. It's probably a street or the name of some orphanage. Sometimes they sell babies to the Ulfrangar when they have too many to care for, which happens a lot during wartime. Too many mouths to feed and not enough to go around."

"That's ... awful."

"The world almost always is," he said. "I tried looking for the place where they got me, somewhere called Murdoc, whenever I could get away with it without someone from the pack noticing. I searched for years. I never found anything, though." His tone was utterly defeated. I saw it in his eyes, too. That look, like hopelessness, regret, and sorrow were all he'd ever known.

"You couldn't just ask someone in the Ulfrangar? They wouldn't tell you?"

"It's not the kind of thing you ask the people training you to become one of the most lethal assassins in the world, Thatcher. Where I came from, who I might have been before they took me, didn't matter. And asking too many questions might taint your reputation before the Zuer—the leader of the pack. Risking her dissatisfaction is potentially lethal," he explained. "Instead, I tried to put it behind me. I tried to believe it didn't matter. But then ..." Murdoc fell silent, his mouth suddenly clamping shut.

"Then what?" I pressed.

"Then I met you." His forehead crinkled as his brows drew up, his expression skewing into a grimace. He dropped his head into his hands again. "I'd never had anyone look at me as anything but a worthless pup, a rival to be eliminated, or a monster that had come to destroy and murder. But that night in Thornbend, you looked at me like I was a person. A real, actual *person*. Then you called me your friend. You trusted me without question. No one had ever done that before. And I started to believe I could be the person you thought I was. Someone better. Someone good. I could leave the Ulfrangar behind and start over. It made me lose sight of the truth."

"What truth?" I had a feeling I knew what was coming—what he would say next. But that didn't matter. He still needed to say it. And more than that, he needed me to hear him say it.

"That it doesn't matter where I go, what I do, or who I'm with, the Ulfrangar will always own me. They will always be there, like a wolf circling in the shadows around a campfire, just waiting for me to set foot back into the darkness of their world." His voice trembled, muffled by his hands. "Waiting to destroy me and anyone I might care about. They won't forgive my desertion. They won't just let me go. Once you are one of them, they own you until you take your last breath in this world. Only death can release you from your oath."

"They don't own you, Murdoc," I declared, trying to sound braver and more confident than I actually felt.

Honestly, I was terrified. He was running from something more dangerous than I could fathom, risking his life to get away. I didn't know if I could help him. But I wanted to try. I had to. Regardless of what King Jace believed about him, Murdoc *was* my friend. I wouldn't turn my back on him. Not now. Not after everything we'd been through.

"We'll figure it out together," I promised, patting him on the back. "And when this is over, we're going to find where you came from—together."

Murdoc raised his head a little. He stared at me through his fingers with wide eyes, and his brow puckered with shock and confusion, like maybe I'd grown a third eyeball or something.

"You know, you're probably the worst friend in the entire world," I added. "Terrible. I mean, you've almost gotten me killed, what, like a dozen times now? You run away whenever I try to have a real, heart-to-heart conversation with you. Not to mention you lied to me about who you really were."

His expression fell into an exasperated scowl. "I really hope there's a point to this little speech you're making."

I stood, straightening my collar with my one good arm before I swaggered to the door. "But I'm the worst fighter in the world, and now you're stuck following me into battle against an enemy I stand no chance of defeating. So, I'd say we're about even."

His mouth scrunched sourly. Murdoc glared at me like he was trying to weigh the risk of drawing attention from the dragonriders in the rooms nearby against how much he might like to hit me.

"Now, if you'll excuse me, I'm going to reserve one of the bathing stalls for you because, honestly, you smell awful and you look like you just got scraped off the bottom of someone's shoe," I announced.

"Thatcher," he growled in warning.

I waved a hand dismissively. "Relax, I'll be stealthy about it. I'll even guard the door so no one comes in."

"You're about as stealthy as a cat with a string of tin cups tied to its tail."

"Yep. And you're about as nice as a rabid jackal. It all evens out."

It happened so fast I almost missed it.

One second Murdoc was leering at me as though trying to decide how many of my fingers he was going to break, and the next ... a broad, genuine, *actual* smile spread over his face.

It only lasted a second or two before he turned away and resumed his usual, brooding frown down at the floor.

"Fine, fine," he puffed. "Just hurry it up."

36
CHAPTER THIRTY-SIX

There was a renewed sense of confidence in my step as I walked with Reigh and Jaevid down the curved hallway that wrapped around one entire floor of the tower. Stalls for dragons lined the walls on either side. As we passed, brightly colored eyes peered at us through the narrow windows. Occasionally, a dragon's snort or curious chirping echoed from the other side of the stall doors. The familiar smell of hay mingled with animal musk hung in the air. Something about that smell made the tension in my aching muscles relax.

Probably because it reminded me of home.

"Check over your saddles quickly," Jaevid advised, his voice low and quiet. We were trying to slip out of here with as little fanfare as possible. "I'll see about getting the doors open to the launch platform. Reigh, you've got the location in Dayrise, right? Think you can find it in the dark?"

Reigh made a scoffing sound in his throat. "Come on, Jae. I'm a Gray elf-trained scout, remember? Have some faith, would you?" He stopped in front of a stall and rolled open the heavy wooden door. His green dragoness, Vexi, poked her head out into the hall and perked her ears. She sniffed and chirped, nipping at the front of his tunic playfully. Reigh let out a yelp of surprise when she grabbed a mouthful of it in her jaws and dragged him into the stall.

Jaevid turned to me with a tense smile, as though he were struggling not to let his apprehension show. I wondered if he was anxious about our mission ... or about his wife. Both, probably. "Are you okay, Thatch? Think you can still ride with that arm?"

I nodded. "Yeah. It'll be fine." I gave it a flex to show him. Reigh had taken off my sling and replaced it with layers of heavy wrapping to stabilize my elbow but still allow me to move and grip my dragon's saddle. It still felt stiff and sore, but I could manage.

"I wish I could go with you," Jae murmured, regret in every word. "I'm afraid of what I've involved you in. I thought this would be simple; that you'd only be acting as courtesy reinforcements if Reigh needed some backup bringing this woman in. I knew it might be risky, but I had no idea it would get this bad."

"I can handle it." At least, that's what I was hoping. Ignoring that little voice of panic and doubt in the back of my mind was getting harder, though. Especially with Isa's warning still hanging over my head. She'd insisted that Jae and Jenna didn't know what was really going on when it came to Devana. All I could do now was pray she was wrong about that.

Jaevid didn't look convinced, though. "Just be careful. Keep an eye on Reigh and Phoebe, and if it gets too dangerous or if you see Phillip again—"

"Then he'll have to get through me." I nearly jumped out of my skin as Murdoc's deep voice growled right behind me.

Looking back, I stared up into my friend's scowling, no-nonsense expression. He seemed more like himself now, dressed out in sleek, dark brown leather armor that fit snuggly to his tall frame. It was much plainer than the stuff the Ulfrangar wore, more understated and straightforward. But it looked comfortable, and with two slender swords belted across his back and a smaller set of dueling daggers at his hips, it suited his fighting style.

"Look after them," Jaevid said as though it were a direct order. "I'm sticking my neck out for you and putting my trust in what Thatcher claims to see in you. Don't make me regret it."

Murdoc answered with a single bow of his head.

Jaevid breathed a small sigh, like he was glad to have that said so we could now move on. "If I'm right, if something's happened to Phillip Derrick, then he's now a threat none of us are prepared to deal with. You all have to be on your highest guard," Jaevid warned. "But if you see him, you *cannot* fight him."

My heart thumped wildly at that thought. I remembered that monstrous guy all too clearly. His strength alone had been incredible. Unbelievable. What else could he do that Jaevid wasn't telling us about?

Murdoc opened his mouth like he might be about to ask, but a cheerful voice from down the hall made all three of us pause.

"Murdoc! Thatcher!" Phoebe ran toward us, her wild mane of coppery curls flying. She hit me at a full sprint like a charging bull, throwing her arms around my neck to squeeze me in a fierce hug. "I'm so happy you're okay!"

"You ... don't ... say," I choked as I tried to pry her arms loose enough for me to wheeze in a breath. She had a strong grip for so small a person.

Pulling back, she put her hands on my cheeks and pulled my head down so she could stand on her toes and plant a kiss right in the middle of my forehead. "They said you were hurt badly. I was so worried. And then they said Murdoc was—" Phoebe suddenly fell silent as she turned to look up at him.

Standing solemnly off to the side, Murdoc regarded her with an awkward, uncertain frown. Everything about him was stiff and uncomfortable. It was painful to watch. We were really going to have to work on his normal social skills.

Suddenly, Phoebe wrapped her arms around his middle and hugged him, too.

His eyes went wide, expression blank as he held perfectly still in her embrace. I couldn't tell if he was even still breathing or not when she pulled back and beamed up at him. "I'm glad you're back with us. It wouldn't be the same without you."

Murdoc opened his mouth, but nothing came out. His face had gone pink around his cheeks and nose. "I-I, uh," he managed to stammer hoarsely. "Thank you."

Her face lit up with a radiant smile. "Do you like the cross-sheath for your blades? I modified the design myself. Oh! We should get going, right? Come look—I made some changes to Vexi's saddle so you can ride more comfortably." Grabbing one of his hands in hers, she began pulling him away down the hall.

With a frazzled, slightly panicked glance back at us over his shoulder, Murdoc staggered along after her. He didn't exactly put up a fight, though.

"For the record," Jaevid chuckled, crossing his arms, "I think you're right about him."

"Y-You do?" I sputtered.

He was grinning from one pointed ear to the other. "Yeah. Maybe Jace knows more about the Ulfrangar than I do, and he might even be right about having memories of a family being what ultimately helped him shake off their teachings. But I don't believe anyone's fate is written beyond our ability to change it, if we choose. Not that it's easily done, of course. But Murdoc has a lot of things working in his favor now." Jae's icy blue eyes glanced my way for an instant. "Still think you're up to being a dragonrider after all this?"

I couldn't fight the smile that spread over my face, making every inch of me feel warmer, stronger, and more alive. "Absolutely."

"Good." He started off down the hallway after Murdoc and Phoebe, waving for me to follow. "No time to waste, then."

FORNAX GREETED me with a blast of hot, smelly dragon breath right to my face. It blew back my hair and made my eyes sting a little from the smell. Yikes.

He kept on bumping me with his nose and sniffing through my hair as I walked around to get a look at the saddle. Finally, I had to stop and give his head a thorough petting before he'd let me work in peace.

Everything was already packed and ready to go. Phoebe didn't have her giant bags of gear anymore—just a small backpack clipped into place right next to mine. Jaevid had already gone off to get the door to the launch platform opened for us. We had to hurry.

Swinging his huge head around, my dragon made low murring, chittering sounds as he continued to sniff me over as though he were checking for damage. I let out a breath that I felt like I'd been holding in since we'd been separated at the Cromwell estate. He'd fought so hard to protect me from the shrikes.

I wrapped my arms around his snout and laid my head against his. "Thanks, big guy."

He grumbled and growled in reply, giving me a swipe up the side of my face with his sticky black tongue. It left a trail of thick, smelly dragon spit on my cheek and forehead.

Gross.

"Okay, we need to have a talk about the licking thing. Because first, it's sticky. It smells awful, then it dries, and it's basically impossible to get off." My hand stuck to my cheek, then again to my shirt as I fought to wipe it away. No luck.

A giggle from the doorway made me look up.

Phoebe came strolling in, carrying a large bundle under her arm as she came to join me at Fornax's side.

"What's that?" I dared to ask.

"A gift," she announced proudly as she held it out. "Murdoc asked me to make it for you before we left Halfax. Luckily, it wasn't destroyed in the fire."

My jaw dropped as she carefully pulled back the black cloth covering it. Gods and Fates. I ran my hands over the dark stained wood and polished brass fixtures that gleamed in the low light of the stall like gold. It was a crossbow—a beautiful, hand-detailed crossbow.

"He was very specific about the design. It took a little time to get all the calibrations right," she explained. "And, don't say anything to him about this, but I made a few tweaks of my own. It will be much more efficient this way."

I stroked the padded brown leather strap, admiring how she'd even taken the time to press some gold-leafed scrollwork into it along the edges. It was incredible. Beyond incredible. It was too much.

"I-I ... I don't ... I mean ... " Words failed me, so I just babbled until I finally gave up.

"It automatically reloads between shots, and the recoil should be minimal so it fires as smooth as silk," she added, standing back with a proud grin on her face. "It holds fifty arrows, ready to fire. What do you think?"

I tried to breathe through the shock, which probably looked a lot like hyperventilating. "What do I think?"

I couldn't put it into words, so instead, I just hugged her. She squeezed me back, ruffling my hair and smiling as she brushed past to climb up into her spot on the saddle behind me. "Now hurry up, dragonrider! We've got to clear out before anyone notices!"

Right. I threaded the crossbow across my shoulders so that it hung against my back. For the first time, it felt like a part of me. It felt *right*.

Climbing up into the saddle, I couldn't get my heart to stop racing. Even after we had made our way out of the stabling area, taking off from the lofty platform all the way at the very top of Eastwatch tower, my pulse roared in my ears as the wind howled over my helmet. We sailed out into the smooth afternoon air, every beat of Fornax's mighty wings sending us surging forward.

Ahead, beyond the steep cliffs and rocky mountain peaks, the city of Dayrise was waiting. It wasn't too far from Northwatch—as long as you didn't have to navigate the steep paths through those peaks and canyons. On foot or riding a horse, it might take two or three days.

For a dragonrider, however, it was easy.

I gripped the saddle handles fiercely, lowering my head and cutting my gaze off to the east through the glass slit in my helmet. In the distance, I could see where the steep cliffs ended and the glittering sea touched the horizon. Smoke still rose from Cromwell manor, curling up like a grim reminder of what would happen if we let our guard down. Good people got hurt and killed.

I set my jaw and looked forward again, feeling the necklace Jaevid had given me under my tunic like an iron weight against my chest. Whatever came next, I couldn't let that happen. When the Ulfrangar came—either for me or Murdoc—I'd be ready for them. When we faced Devana, I would fight.

And this time, Fornax and I would show them all what the queen's hunters were really capable of.

EPILOGUE

A SHORT STORY FROM JAEVID BROADFEATHER

Almost home—just a little farther.

Guilt soured in my gut as Mavrik and I did a low pass over the city of Solhelm, just southwest of our new home. I leaned down against his neck, gripping the saddle handles so tightly my fingers went numb. My ears were still ringing after meeting with Jenna. It had been brief, especially since I didn't have much in the way of hard evidence to provide when it came to Phillip's location. She didn't want to believe he would ever betray her. Honestly, neither did I. But I knew what I had seen through the fray and flames at Cromwell estate. And even if Phillip's mind had been altered either by the switchbeast venom or something else, that had been *his* body. I was sure of it. Those were problems for another time, however.

Right now—right this second—I needed to be at home.

"Faster," I urged as I gave Mavrik's neck a pat. He puffed and grunted, wheeling on powerful black wings above the updrafts and gusts of salty air that blasted in from over the eastern seas.

The rugged landscape below seemed to drag by. The bare rock cliffs, rolling grassland, and swelling hills stretched on to the foothills of a small mountain chain that followed the craggy coastline all the way north, past the boundary of Luntharda. North of Solhelm and the old Farrow estate, I saw it: my home.

It was still strange to call it that. Never in my wildest dreams had I imagined a house like this would be mine. I'd begun my life as a scrawny little halfbreed, unwanted in my father's family and rejected by a world that had a long list of reasons why a kid like myself never should have been born in the first place. Destiny had a different plan, though ... as well as a few deities.

I smiled underneath my helmet and gave Mavrik's neck another pat. It was all thanks to this stubborn dragon that I'd ever become more than that. He'd chosen me as his rider and set my life on a new course—one that had dropped me in the middle of wars, royal courts, and schemes of divine magic numerous times. Now I had people from kingdoms I'd never even been to looking to me for answers. Jenna was still fresh under her crown. With the Tibran War barely ended, she had been dealt a difficult hand. Not that I regretted any of it, but noble life still wasn't something I felt comfortable with.

It would take a while to really feel like this place was home.

The chateau sat on a farm of open prairie, the fields of long, windswept grass flowing and rippling like a golden ocean below. In summer, it would be green, and the stone fences would be mended so we could graze horses or small cattle if we wanted. Although, being this close to wild dragon territory, I wasn't so sure that was a good idea. My dragon being a king drake might discourage them from coming too close, but I wasn't willing to bet on that just yet.

The intricately cut glass on the front windows of the chateau, made in the designs of diamonds, ovals, and interlocked circles, caught the light of the setting sun with glittering perfection. The smooth, sand-colored stone of its sturdy walls glowed with a welcoming hue, reflecting the golden-orange horizon. It was only two stories and twenty-six rooms, in all. I'd been told that was modest for a noble house, but it still seemed huge and excessive to me. After all, as a child, I'd spent most of my life sleeping in the attic of my father's barn.

Now, I had my own barn, and it was more than twice the size of my father's and far better made. The fine stone structure stood stoic against the bitter wind on the far side of a paved courtyard. No doubt it had been built to stable horses, not dragons; even the courtyard was barely big enough for my blue king drake to land. He tucked himself in low against the ground, chirping anxiously as I clambered down from the saddle and took off my helmet. The cold wind blasted through my damp, sweaty hair. I shivered, pulling the fox fur collar of my dragonrider cloak tighter around my shoulders as I ran for the large, arched front doors.

"Master Jaevid!" Our housekeeper ripped the door open before I could even touch the handle. Flushed and breathless, she stared up at me with her long pointed ears peeking out of the silvery white hair that framed her face. Navalie was young, somewhere in her late teens, but had taken over running things around our new home with expert precision. I'd questioned why a girl so young would set off for a kingdom so different from her home with the intention of being a housekeeper. Sitting poised and proud in my office, Navalie had insisted that running noble homes and managing the rest of the staff was her dream. Who was I to question that? Besides, she'd come highly recommended as one of Reigh's childhood friends from Luntharda. So far, it seemed like she and my wife had become fast friends. They shared a distaste for disorder and a liking for archery.

It was a little easier to leave Beckah, my new bride, alone in this place knowing she had a friend here to keep her company. Her two older ... younger ... well, her sisters had come to visit for a month or two while I was gone to court. They'd even brought along her elderly and incredibly feeble mother. Having family around helped somewhat, but that part was complicated for all of us. And I could tell it was still a little awkward for Beckah. She'd only been back about a little more than a year, and so much had happened in that time.

As often as I could bear it, I tried to give her time to herself to reflect and think things through. We'd gone to where her father was buried to pay our respects, and she'd barely made it ten minutes before she broke down. He'd enjoyed a full and rewarding life, but that didn't mean he wouldn't be missed. It had been that way for me, too. Coming back was like waking up from a nightmare and not recognizing where you were anymore. The world was different. We were different. For as many new joys, there were just as many sorrows.

But I still loved Beckah more than anyone—that hadn't changed. I knew it never would. I wanted her to be with me always. While I ran around the kingdom, flailing like a panicked chicken on Jenna's political errands, it became more obvious to me that Beckah was all that really mattered in my life now. So kings, Tibran witches, and whatever new drama Reigh was cooking up would just have to wait.

"How is she? What's happening?" I panted as I hurried inside, spinning in a staggering circle while Navalie helped me out of my cloak. "Where is Beckah?"

Navalie stepped lightly, darting ahead down the foyer with my cloak and helmet in her arms. She still dressed in the traditional Gray elven style, sporting brightly colored, flowing silk robes that were gathered at her wrists and ankles. She'd asked about that when I hired her on—how I wanted her to dress. Honestly, I appreciated the sight of some of my mother's culture in our otherwise Maldobarian home.

Navalie spoke quickly, her tone gentle and, despite her best efforts, still heavy with a Gray elf accent. "Now, Master Jaevid, I don't want to alarm you, but—"

"What?" I shouted in panic. "What's wrong?"

"Nothing! Nothing to panic over," she squeaked in a frantic voice. "I mean, maybe a little. Not really. Mistress Beckah has been having contractions for over a day, so we knew it might progress at any ti—"

"*Over a day*? And no one sent word to me?" I ripped off my riding gauntlets and threw them onto the nearest chair as I raced through the front parlor and up the staircase to the second floor. "Gods and Fates, is she all right? Tell me!"

Navalie was right behind me, still frantically juggling the pieces of gear she picked up off the furniture. "She's doing just fine! Everything is progressing normally. The midwife is here, and her waters came only a few hours ago. We tried sending word, but you'd already left Halfax. We weren't sure where—"

"Can I see her?" I cut her off again.

"You'll have to ask the midwife! I'm not sure if—"

"Where is she?"

"In the bedroom. Oh, but you're still in your armor! Shouldn't you change first?"

There wasn't time for that. My heart pounded, booming in my ears and clashing against my ribs as I scaled the staircase in a mad sprint, taking two and three steps at a time. Navalie couldn't keep up. She kept calling after me even after I was long gone—zipping down the halls to the grand master suite at the far end of the manor.

I hit the door of our private chambers out of breath and seeing stars. Gripping the brass handle, I threw the door open and startled the two servant girls working in the front sitting room. They whirled around, eyes wide until they realized who I was.

"Where is Beckah?" I demanded between rasping, wheezing pants.

"S-She's in the bedchamber," one of the servants squeaked. They'd been busy rinsing clean towels in a basin of hot water, but as soon as I arrived, both packed up their work and prepared to move it into the bedchamber. "Please wait here a moment. I'll get the midwife for you."

Wait a moment? She had about three seconds before I went in there to see what was happening to the love of my life.

Fortunately, it only took about that long for the midwife to emerge. A short, slightly stocky little woman stepped out of my bedroom with a glare that might have singed my eyebrows right off my face if I'd been standing any closer. "Keep your voice down, Master Broadfeather. I won't be asking you again," she commanded in a hushed voice, wagging a promising finger right in my face. It might have been terrifying if not for the way the large bow on the back of her long, white apron fluttered behind her like wings on a fairy. Beneath that, she wore a long, dark blue dress with the sleeves rolled neatly to her elbows, and her ginger-blond hair was bound back in a neat bun.

"But ... but my wife," I protested weakly. Something told me that, despite her stature, I did not want to test this woman's patience.

"A mother *must* have a calm, peaceful environment. I won't have you going in like a tornado of anxiety and disturbing her concentration." The midwife glanced me up and down, her green eyes keen and quick. "Take a few breaths, if you can, and try not to look so pasty." She went back to the door and waved me in, moving fast for so small a person. "Just a few minutes, all right? And then you'll have to wait out here."

I nodded. Then again, I probably would have agreed to anything she told me to do right then. Dance around with bells on my toes? Sure. Right away.

Only a few candles flickered around our bedroom, giving the otherwise spacious room a close, cozy atmosphere filled with soft, warm light. The heavy drapes had been drawn over all the windows, and our large bed was stripped of its usual mixture of fur-lined blankets. It had been neatly arranged with clean white linens, towels, and pillows. The subtle scents of lavender, lemon, and clary sage hung in the air, mingled with the crisp tinge of peppermint—probably coming from the oils one of the midwife's assistants was using to massage Beckah's legs and feet. When I entered, she stopped right away, whispering comforting words to my wife while covering her with blankets again. Then the room quickly cleared out of everyone except for Beckah, the midwife, and myself.

My hands shook, and I struggled to remember how to breathe as I crossed the room and rounded the bed. Propped up on a stack of rice-stuffed pillows, Beckah looked exhausted but strangely blissful as she lay with her hands resting on her round, swollen belly. Her long, dark hair had been woven into a loose braid, and the wide neck of her thin, white nightgown hung off one of her slender shoulders.

Her smile left my mind reeling, completely at a loss for words as her soft green eyes searched mine. Gods, she was beautiful. What had I ever done to deserve someone like her looking at me like that? Like there was no one in the world she'd rather be with?

"Jae ..." She breathed my name like a sigh of relief. "You're here."

"Of course I'm here," I managed, forcing my tone to stay steady as I bent down to kiss her forehead. "Gods, Beckah, I'm ... I'm so sorry. I should have come sooner."

"It's okay, love." She gave a soft, exhausted laugh. "You're the great Jaevid Broadfeather. There's always going to be kingdoms calling for your help now, whether you like it or not."

I eased down onto my knees at her bedside, resting my elbows on the mattress. "Maybe so, but none of that matters. Not compared to this."

Suddenly her face blanched, going so pale that even her lips went white. Her expression skewed, eyes pinched shut as she gripped the blankets and fought to take in slow, steady breaths.

Panic struck me like a white-hot dagger to the gut. Gods, what was happening?

"Focus on your breathing," the midwife reminded from across the room. By her tone, it seemed whatever was happening was normal. "Relax your legs, concentrate on pulling your breaths in, and let it pass."

Beckah didn't reply, but her gaze went steely with focus as she stared straight ahead.

The seconds dragged. I didn't dare to move, even to blink. After what felt like an eternity, she let out a shuddering sigh and went slack against the pillows again.

I tried not to show how petrified I was to see her like this. The last time I'd seen a woman in labor had been her mother, and that hadn't gone well. My divine power had been the only thing able to save her and her baby, but I didn't have those abilities anymore. If something went wrong now ... I wouldn't be able to do anything to stop it.

I was completely and totally helpless.

"Beckah, I—"

"It's okay, Jae. I can bear this," she cut me off like she knew I was about to start apologizing again. "We'll be fine. Don't worry."

I wanted to believe that. Gods, I had to.

From across the room, the midwife gave me a small gesture. I needed to go. There was nothing I could do here, and Beckah needed to concentrate and relax as much as possible. My ears were ringing, and my heart lurched with every step as I got to my feet again. I took her hands in mine and kissed every one of her knuckles.

"If you need me, I'm right here. Okay?" I forced what was probably the world's worst excuse for a genuine smile. "I'll be right outside that door."

Hers was real. It spread over her freckled cheeks and filled my soul like a breath of clean spring air. "I love you, silly man."

I gave her hands one more gentle squeeze. "I love you, too."

Leaving the room was agony. Outside, the servants had laid out a fresh change of clothes from my wardrobe so I could get out of my formal armor. They'd also brought a platter of food. By the time I stepped out into the front sitting room, someone else was already helping himself to my dinner.

"How is she?" Felix Farrow, the former King of Maldobar, Queen Jenna's father and my long-time best friend, was reclining on one of the sofas, stuffing his cheeks with tea biscuits.

My shoulders dropped. I didn't know whether to yell like a maniac or collapse. "She's in pain. But everyone keeps assuring me it's normal," I grumbled as I shuffled over and dropped onto the sofa beside him. "When did you get here?"

"This morning." My old friend scratched at his short white beard and yawned. "I thought I should stay at least until you arrived."

"Thank you." Sitting forward, I started unbuckling my breastplate, pauldrons, vambraces, and greaves. I tossed all my armor, piece by piece, into a stack next to the coffee table.

"Want me to stay? I'd hate to leave you here alone and miss watching you pace ruts in the floor." He flashed me a knowing grin.

"Yeah," I admitted. "I ... don't know what to do."

"Nothing you can do now, Jae. Take it from a seasoned father of three—er, well, four. Sort of. Anyway, the best thing you can do right now is stay out of the way."

"How long does it usually take?" I hated how ignorant and ridiculous I sounded asking something like that. But I honestly didn't know. I'd never been around this sort of thing before.

"Depends." Felix was back to stuffing his face with some of the small, triangular cut sandwiches from the platter. "Somehow, the first time always seems to take an eternity. But Beckah is strong. She'll power through this; I'm sure of it."

Free of my riding gear, I rubbed my face and leaned against the back of the sofa. "It's going to be a long night."

His cattish grin twinkled with delight, like there was so much I didn't know and he couldn't wait to watch me suffer through it. "You have no idea. I hope you enjoyed sleeping at night, cause you're pretty much done with that for a long, *long* while."

"Kiran said babies sleep a lot," I countered.

Felix's grin widened. "Oh, yeah, sure—*they* do. But that doesn't mean you'll get to sleep, too." He kicked back on the sofa, propping his feet up on the coffee table with a satisfied sigh. "So, do I get to know what names you two have picked out if it's a boy or girl?"

I let my eyes fall closed while I focused on slowing my frazzled pulse. "It's bad luck to tell anyone. You know that."

"Just so you know, Felix is an excellent name."

"If we decide to get a dog, maybe."

He punched me in the arm so hard I almost fell off the sofa.

I couldn't help but laugh, even if I'd probably have an enormous bruise on my bicep tomorrow. Having him here to take my mind off what might be happening in the next room, to tease, taunt, and otherwise distract me—well, it was what I desperately needed. I guess Felix had probably known that all along. Without him, I'd spend the night pacing or standing with my ear pressed to the door.

But he was here. I didn't have to go through this alone.

The sun sank beyond the western hills and night closed in, passing quietly with nothing to fill the silence except for our quiet conversation and the crackle of the fire burning low in the hearth. After we finished the platter of food for dinner, Navalie brought in tea and cider. Her features were drooping with the same weariness and distress mine were, but she stayed up through the night. Every few hours, she eased into the bedroom to get a report from the midwife. Then she returned to give us the details—which I only barely understood. Dilating? What did that even mean?

Sometimes, I heard muffled sounds from the bedroom. The soft voice of the midwife. Beckah grunting or whimpering. It made my jaw clench until my teeth were sore.

Felix tried to reassure me that everything was fine. I still had to get up and walk a few laps around the room, though. It didn't help, but it felt better than sitting still. My shoulders sagged, and my back ached. I'd spent so much time in the saddle, and exhaustion made my eyes heavy and my head pound. But I didn't dare fall asleep. Not now. Not until I knew Beckah was all right.

I'd barely sat down on the sofa again when a desperate, high-pitched cry wailed from beyond the bedroom door.

My heart hit the back of my throat. Beckah! Oh gods. I snapped to my feet, starting for the door until Felix's strong grip closed around my arm and yanked me to a halt.

I met his gaze in a fury, ready to punch his lights out.

He raised a hand to put a finger to his lips, gesturing for me to stop and listen.

I froze. Through the heavy silence, the cry continued, muffled slightly by the door. It was so loud. So frantic. But it wasn't Beckah.

It was a baby's tiny, squealing cry.

My heart thumped hard and then seemed to stop altogether. Oh gods, that was ... that was *my* baby.

I stood, afraid to move, straining to hear the sound. My mind blurred through an endless list of questions. Was Beckah all right? Was the baby okay, too? Why hadn't someone come out to get me yet? Gods and Fates, what was happening in there?

Then the crying stopped.

For what felt like a miserable eternity, everything was quiet. Minutes dragged by. Or was it hours? I couldn't be sure.

At last, the door cracked open. I sucked in a sharp breath, holding it as the midwife emerged with a tiny bundle wrapped in soft, white cloth. Felix finally let me go.

I staggered a few steps closer and stopped, freezing solid again as the midwife moved slowly, carefully, toward me. She held the bundle out and guided my arms to show me how to hold it.

A tiny, pink, perfect face blinked up at me with pale green eyes the color of turquoise. They blinked sleepily and slowly closed. The baby in my arms squirmed and grunted, tiny wrinkly fists tucked under a chubby little chin.

"Master Jaevid," the midwife said gently. "You have a daughter."

I made a noise somewhere between a choke, gasp, laugh, and squeak of pure panic. She was the most beautiful, incredible thing I'd ever seen. And so small! I could barely feel her weight in my arms as I held her close. She had a head full of silky hair already, and all of it was the same beautiful dark shade as her mother's. Her teeny ears sloped into delicate points—something she'd undoubtedly gotten from me. Gods willing, that would be all she got from her ridiculous father who couldn't stop the tears from welling in his eyes.

"Congratulations," Felix said with a tired smile. "She's beautiful. Well done, my friend."

"I-Is Beckah ...?" I rasped, looking back to the midwife. I couldn't do anything to hide the tears running down my face.

She wore the same tired but undeniably content smile, her cheeks a bit flushed and her eyes teary as she nodded. "She's doing just fine. Everything went smoothly. It was perhaps the easiest birth I've ever witnessed. We're helping her get cleaned up, and then you can go in. It'll just be a few more minutes." She offered a small bow before returning to the bedroom, leaving me standing there holding my tiny, fragile newborn baby.

Gazing down at her, it was as though the world shifted under my boots. My life, my wants, my needs—nothing in the world mattered more than this child. She *was* my world now. I bit down hard, trying to hold back the tears that welled in my eyes again.

"So." Felix draped an arm around my neck. "What name did you and Beckah choose? Felixine sounds nice. Or Felixiana. So many possibilities!"

If I hadn't been holding the most precious thing in the entire world, I might have punched him, if only for revenge. "Absolutely not."

"What, then?"

When I looked down at her again, I couldn't hold it back. A smile spread over my face. It sent warmth through every part of me. "Maylea," I answered. "Her name is Maylea."

BETRAYER

THE DRAGONRIDER HERITAGE BOOK TWO

PART ONE
MURDOC

1
CHAPTER ONE

Thatcher Renley was, by far, the biggest idiot I had ever met in my entire life—and that's saying something, because I'd also met Prince Reigh Farrow. He was in a close second. But at least he had enough common sense to know that this so-called hunt Queen Jenna and Jaevid Broadfeather had sent us on was essentially a glorified suicide mission. We were charging straight into a fight with a largely unknown Tibran witch, armed with only fragments of information about her abilities and location. And if that weren't enough, there were only three competent fighters among our group—dragons included.

Granted, Reigh could manage decently against common enemies. He'd apparently been trained in combat by the Gray Elves, and their scouts had recently improved in their fighting ability. They must've stumbled across someone with an actual brain who was now training their scouts and warriors. Knowing that, Reigh had probably held his own fairly well in Luntharda. But we were a long way from the wild jungle, and sooner or later, that temper of his was going to cost him.

Phoebe was ... well. Hmm. Perplexing, I guess. She fluttered around with her mad storm of red curls flying, bubbling like an excited child about the projects she was working on, and radiating a relentless optimism that sort of made me sick to my stomach after a while. Not that she annoyed me, really. It was just strange to be around someone that persistently happy all the time. Happiness wasn't something I'd had much experience with.

Which brings me back to the biggest moron of them all who, unfortunately, was now both my primary concern and the bane of my existence. Thatcher was astronomically stupid. Honestly, it was staggering he'd survived as long as he had without someone following him around, smacking his hand whenever he was about to try something dangerous. He'd volunteered for this mission without having any combat training of any kind. He was a farrier's son, for crying out loud, and was essentially the human personification of a dandelion puff. Short, scrawny, wide-eyed, and baby-faced—he didn't have a prayer of surviving this mess unless someone watched over him constantly.

How, by all the Gods and Fates, *I* had wound up being that person was still beyond my understanding.

Ugh. Fine, fine. I'd done it by choice, I suppose. Sort of, anyway. I mean, sure, I could have left him there in that alleyway in Thornbend to die along with most of the other peasants and villagers. Maybe that would've been kinder in the long run—especially if we were all soaring toward a gruesome death right now. Still, in that moment, with all the world swallowed up in flames and that pitiful kid on the ground at my feet, I'd looked into his eyes as he spoke to me, offering me a different path I'd craved for so long. And I'd realized ... no one had ever talked to me that way before. Like I was *someone* and not *something*. No one had ever treated me that way. No one had ever looked at me and regarded me like ... a person.

So, I'd made a rash and irrevocable decision. A mistake, probably. But then again, I'd been swallowing back hopes of escaping that life—the life of an Ulfrangar assassin—for as long as I could remember. That night in Thornbend had been my first real opportunity. The only catch was, of course, keeping the baby-faced kid who kept calling me "friend" alive, too.

Thatcher treated everyone that way, though. It's like there was no room in his mind for the possibility that a person really could be evil. Shocking, considering the vacant way he stared at me sometimes—like you could pass a twig through his ear and it would come out the other side and not hit anything in between.

At first, I'd just assumed he was incredibly sheltered or naïve. Maybe he was. But after our experience with Phoebe, finding out that she had been a Tibran, I'd expected him to reject her entirely. Anyone else probably would have. Whether out of shame or fear, she'd kept that information from everyone.

But Thatcher had insisted on helping her. He'd forgiven her without a second thought. He was stupid, yes. But he was also far kinder than anyone could ever deserve.

Least of all me.

He still called me his friend like it was nothing. He laughed and chatted with me as though he genuinely enjoyed my company and wanted me around. He kept chasing after me whenever I tried to put some safe distance between us. Didn't he get it? Couldn't he sense it at all? I was *not* a good person. I never had been. I'd accepted a long time ago that no matter where I went or what I did, the pack—the Ulfrangar—would always own me. They'd carved their mark upon my soul from the very beginning and nothing could erase it. Deep down, I would always be one of them.

Even now, sitting behind Reigh astride his lithe green dragon, the weight of their presence crushed down over my body from every side. They were everywhere and nowhere. They moved in shadow, lived in anonymity, and thrived on the constant stream of the world's darkest secrets. There was no place I could hide, nowhere I could go that they wouldn't be able to reach.

The more I thought about it, the harder it was to justify why I'd let Jaevid set me free —even if I knew the answer already. Because of Thatcher, the idiot. No one seemed to know what he'd done to provoke Devana and her new monstrous minion, Phillip.

Maybe nothing. And honestly, I didn't care. It didn't matter. They wouldn't put a hand on him if I had anything to say about it. He'd called me a friend—someone who was like a brother to him—and that was enough. It was more than anyone else had ever done for me my entire life.

We cruised, riding the strong winds coming in from the sea along the eastern coastline. The tower of Eastwatch faded behind us, and far below, small villages and towns dotted the hills. Most were a safe distance from the steep cliffs that dropped into the toiling dark ocean—places where wild dragons liked to nest. But the farther we flew to the north, the more the cliffs gave way to rocky beaches. Fishing towns were built right up against the banks amidst the clusters of odd, hexagonal basalt columns and massive trunks of washed-up driftwood from Luntharda's giant trees.

Dayrise stood just a few miles inland, stretching all the way to the sea where a large port was packed tight with big merchant ships. The vessels cruised in from the open sea, white sails puffed and banners fluttering high as flocks of seagulls chased them in. Most were probably owned by merchants happy to be sailing their trade routes again now that the Tibran war was over.

Not that I'd ever been to Dayrise myself, honestly. The Ulfrangar network spanned far beyond Maldobar's borders, but the territory I'd been assigned to work was back down on the southern tip of the kingdom. I'd never had any reason to journey this far north.

Too bad it didn't make me feel the least bit more secure.

A glimmer caught my eye far in the distance off our right side—the tell-tale flash of sunlight over glossy scales. A dragon. He was far off, maybe three miles on our tail, and had been since we left Eastwatch. From so far away, I couldn't tell much else. Maybe it was just a security escort from the dragonriders keeping an eye on us from afar. Maybe it was a curious wild drake that'd caught wind of the dragoness in our group and was interested in her. I didn't know.

And when it came to being followed, I *hated* not knowing.

The sight of those faraway scale flashes and the faint shape of great dark wings flapping put a pang of dread like a cold iron spike in my gut. I looked away and set my teeth against the rush of adrenaline that made my skin tingle and my heart pound like mad. I'd have to mention it to the others eventually. But not yet. I needed more information, first. To be sure this wasn't some arrangement Jaevid had put in place because, well, he now knew what I was. He had every reason to be concerned and to want to keep a close eye on things.

Or on me, rather.

Reigh started our descent as we neared the city's outer limits. I had no idea where we were supposed to go or who Jaevid Broadfeather had waiting for us. Hopefully not another noble with an estate we might accidentally burn down. Well, sort of accidentally, anyway. And technically we hadn't been the one doing the burning, but I digress. Whatever. Burned is burned, I suppose.

Unlike Eastwatch, the city of Dayrise wasn't one visited by dragonriders on military orders on a regular basis. There was no towering spire meant to house soldiers and mounts looming over the rooftops, and no high city walls topped with battlements. Not that we got any strange looks as our dragons circled outside the city's outer limits. In fact, there were more than a dozen sizable inns crowded around the main roads leading in and out of the city's tightly packed streets. Many of them were flanked by massive barns two or three stories tall intended to house dragons.

Reigh chose one closer to the port on the western side of the city and guided his green dragoness into a smooth landing. She cupped her wings and stretched out her hind legs, landing on the grass as elegantly as a swan on a pond.

Thatcher's much larger orange drake landed next to us, shaking his black-horned head and puffing unhappy snorts through his nose. The dragon curled his long, striped tail around his legs and bristled, small ears turned back as those milky green eyes darted around.

I frowned. Thatcher trusted that beast wholeheartedly. But I'd seen it drag him across the horizon like caught prey once already. Thatcher had been lucky to walk away from that ordeal—luckier than anyone else seemed to want to acknowledge.

"Let's get Vexi and Fornax settled here and find our contact," Reigh called back to me as he straightened in the saddle. He pulled off his helmet, nearly slapping me in the face with the end of his long, sweaty braid in the process.

"This is an old city," I muttered as I studied the road ahead that led into the narrow cobblestone streets. "Places like this tend to be dangerous after dark, and there's only a few hours of daylight left. We should go quickly."

He unbuckled and dismounted first, then stood sorting through his saddlebags while I climbed down. "I agree. Which is why I'm leaving you in charge of this." Reigh took out a small drawstring purse, poured a few gold coins into his palm then tied it shut again and tossed it in my direction. "Our contact is supposed to meet us at the sign for the Crosswall Docks. They're probably already waiting on us. Think you can find it? Taverns with dragon accommodations are harder to come by here, and we need to keep a low profile—meaning, we stay away from the ones farther into the city. So, I'll settle up for the dragons here and meet you there."

The purse jangled when I caught it, as though there were still quite a few coins tucked away inside. "You expect that to take a while? We need to stay together." It wouldn't take that long, of course. I knew that as well as he did—meaning he had another motive for wanting a few minutes alone.

"I've got some letters to send back to Luntharda. Shouldn't take me more than an hour," he replied, bowing his head to hide his face as he crammed the handful of coins into his pocket. Reigh's emotions ran so close to the surface, it was ridiculously easy to read him even with his face angled away. Judging by the scarlet color his ears were turning, these must have been personal letters. Letters to a girl, most likely. *Love* letters. Ugh.

He would've made a terrible assassin.

"And who is it that I'm supposedly looking for at the docks?" I pocketed the bag of coins and ran a hand through my hair, trying in vain to get it out of my eyes. Months away from my former life had allowed it to grow out longer than it'd ever been before. I'd have to fix that soon.

Reigh's expression scrunched as though he were trying to think—emphasis on *trying*. Complex thought didn't seem to be one of his stronger qualities. "He didn't say specifically. Just that we're looking for another Broadfeather. His brother, probably. I can't recall his first name, but I met him briefly after the war ended."

"If we go on ahead, how do you intend to find us later?" I arched an eyebrow.

He shrugged. "Looking for someone named Broadfeather at Crosswall Docks? That's plenty to go on. I'm sure someone can point me in the right direction."

Fair point. A last name like that was one people generally remembered, after all.

"Did you see all the ships?" a sing-song voice chimed suddenly. Phoebe practically fluttered over to stand beside me, her red curls bobbing around her and her big, blue eyes shimmering with excitement. "Aren't they beautiful? Can we go see them up close?"

Reigh's entire demeanor soured as he stood straighter. "Didn't see enough of them while you were sailing around with the Tibrans, conquering other kingdoms and slaughtering their people?" He growled every word through his teeth as he leered down at her.

She shrank back some, almost like she might duck behind me if he made a move toward her. "O-Oh, um, well, no. I mean, yes, I did have to sail with them. But Lord Argonox didn't allow me to leave my cell or go up onto the deck during—" She stopped short and went quiet. Her brows drew together as she flicked speedy, nervous glances around everyone. "I-I'm sorry," she stammered at last, as though she couldn't think of anything else to say.

Reigh didn't respond. Instead, he glowered down at her with his mouth mashed into a tight frown. His light amber eyes flashed with a mixture of wrath and what I could only guess was withheld terror.

I'd seen that look before from my Ulfrangar handler whenever I'd challenged or defied him, as though for the briefest instant he wasn't sure if he should hold his ground or flee. And while I could sympathize to a degree—after all, Phoebe had apparently been the one in charge of all the magical experimentation for the Tibran Empire—she was about as threatening as a freshly-cut daisy on her own. She probably weighed seventy pounds to his one hundred and fifty or so.

Awkward silence hung in the air until Thatcher drifted over to join us, sporting his usual, blissfully vacant grin. "Are we staying here for the night?" he asked cheerily. "I've never stayed at an inn before. I thought Jaevid had arranged for us to stay with someone in the city?"

With a tight sigh, Reigh spun on a heel and gestured for Thatcher to follow him. "He did, but we've got to get the dragons settled and I'm betting yours will need extra assistance. So, come with me. Murdoc, you can take *her* and find our host. We'll catch up."

PHOEBE DIDN'T SAY a word for a long time as she followed along close beside me. Lugging her bag of gear over my shoulder, I tried not to look her way more than necessary. According to Thatcher, I gave the impression that I was glaring whenever I stared at someone for too long. No need to make it worse.

Besides, one glance was all it took. The distant fogginess in her eyes as she stared down at the sidewalk put an uncomfortable tightness in my chest. I should say something, right? That was the normal thing to do. Wasn't it? Gods and Fates, how was I supposed to know what normal was?

"You should stop apologizing," I blurted before I could change my mind. My tone came out much harsher than I intended, as usual. Curse it all. I should have kept my mouth shut. Silence was always safer.

Phoebe tripped over an uneven stone. She staggered, and I snapped my free hand out. I seized her arm to hold her steady.

She let out a scream. Not a surprised little yelp—a real, primal, utterly terrified scream. Phoebe went completely stiff in my grasp, blinking up at me with her entire body trembling.

What? Why would she look at me like that—like I was about to do something terrible to her? I'd never raised a hand to her. Was it because she knew I was an Ulfrangar now?

Before I could ask or even say a word, her entire expression suddenly went blank again. Her body relaxed and she glanced around, seeming confused for a moment. "O-Oh! Murdoc! I-I guess you startled me." She blinked up at me, face flushing almost as red as her hair. The forced, twitchy smile on her lips looked almost painful. "I'm so sor—um, I mean, thank you."

I slowly let her go. "I ... I didn't mean stop apologizing in general. I meant stop apologizing to Reigh."

Phoebe swallowed hard. Shifting her weight from one foot to the other, she fidgeted with the embroidered hem of her long tunic as her mouth scrunched up. "I, um, well, I mean he is right to hate me. I did—"

"I know what you did," I interrupted as I began walking again. "Most everyone does now, right? But Queen Jenna forgave you. The Court of Crowns absolved you. You've apologized to everyone over and over, including Reigh. You've made changes to your life to become something better now. No one can ask any more of you than that."

"But he still hates me, doesn't he? He'd probably kill me if you and Thatcher weren't here." She trotted to catch up and fall in step next to me like before.

"There's nothing you can do about that. You can't change your past or erase what you've done. And because of that, some people will always hate you. Even if you do everything right from now on, it still won't matter to them. They will never be able to see you as anything more than what you were," I tried to explain without biting every bitter word through my teeth. "But that doesn't mean you should go on groveling for forgiveness. You've done your part. Forgiving you is Reigh's problem now. So let it go."

She didn't respond right away. For a few more blocks, she followed along in total silence while we wound our way through the city's narrow streets toward the sea. Then I felt the pressure of her wide, blue-eyed gaze on me again. It hit me like the glare of the sun, making my skin tingle. "Aren't you afraid that people won't forgive you for being an Ulfrangar?"

I paused at a corner before a broad, open square. In the center, a white stone fountain sprayed ribbons of water around the bust of a man in battle armor. He stood tall and proud, his eyes seemingly focused right on me, with a helmet under his arm while his other hand rested on the pommel of the sword belted at his hip. A dragonrider, most likely. But not one I recognized.

"That's different. I don't expect them to forgive me, so it would be pointless to ask for it," I confessed as I held the statue's frozen gaze. "The people who know what I've done could never truly forgive me. Like King Jace. And the ones who don't understand only offer their forgiveness because they don't know any better." I flicked a look down at her. "Like Thatcher."

Her mouth scrunched into a dissatisfied little frown. "What about Lord Jaevid, then? He knows, doesn't he?"

I couldn't keep the irony from my tone. "No. Not really. He's gotten a small taste of it, so now he's suspicious. But he doesn't understand the extent of what I am."

"Well, I forgive you, Murdoc," Phoebe announced, a rebellious crease in her brow. "So which am I, then? Someone who understands? Or someone who doesn't?"

I had to think about that.

The Tibran Empire had paid hefty sums to hire out Ulfrangar assassins and spies throughout the war. Phoebe had probably seen others like me before, if only in passing. She'd certainly seen all of the evil and unbridled cruelty that could come from a man like Argonox. In fact, she had probably witnessed and experienced more of it than even she could remember. But did she really comprehend what I was? What I'd done to survive up to this point?

"Could you forgive Argonox?" I countered. "Or any of the soldiers who were in charge of keeping you obedient? What about the ones who put those marks on your skin?"

Her face slowly drained of color. "B-But you didn't do tha—"

"I'm no different from them," I cut her off quickly. "You strip away the emblems and the banners, the flags and the creeds, and you're left with the same thing. At its roots, evil is evil, and it doesn't matter what you dress it up in. That's why deep down, I'll always be what the Ulfrangar made me. I'll carry their darkness in me until the day I die."

"You really think that?" Her voice was hardly more than a whisper. "You truly believe you're evil like Lord Argonox was?"

I set my jaw and looked away. No matter how I turned the words in my head, none of them sounded right. I couldn't bring myself to answer. It wouldn't matter anyway. Clearly, she couldn't understand. We were nothing alike. Phoebe hadn't chosen to become a Tibran. She hadn't chosen to do all of the things Argonox had forced her to do. But there had been moments in my life, a few vile moments steeped in malice and blood, when I had. I could have rebelled then. I could have let the Ulfrangar kill me for my defiance and ended it there. But instead ... I'd accepted that fate. Wanted it. Thrived on it.

Sometimes, I'd even enjoyed it.

That was the part of myself King Jace would never trust—the part Reigh, Thatcher, Jaevid, and Phoebe should have been disgusted by. But they didn't know.

And I had no idea how to tell them.

CHAPTER TWO

Phoebe and I walked on, the ambient noise of the gulls and city folk filling the awkward silence. Friendly, casual conversations weren't exactly one of my finer skills. Thatcher insisted that practice would help. So far, all practicing had done was make me look like a sulking idiot. Ughh.

I stole another quick glance down at Phoebe as we made our way down a broad avenue. Her brow was still creased and her mouth a little scrunched, although she didn't seem as dejected anymore. Thoughtful, maybe. It was hard to tell with her. Ah, well, thoughtful was better than upset, wasn't it?

The street ahead of us had to be the main thoroughfare leading inland from the port. None of the other roads had been so wide—probably to accommodate the amount of wagon traffic that moved through. It sloped down gradually as it led toward the sprawling port, offering a better view of the city with its countless, tightly packed, white stone buildings and thatched roofs. Now and then, I caught glimpses of masts and sails peeking above the rooftops ahead. Every breeze carried the heavy musk of sea salt.

Many of the locals walking past us carried large bags, baskets, or crates filled with things they'd probably gotten at the portside market. Dayrise supposedly had one of the finer trade markets in the kingdom. Granted, it was smaller than the one in Saltmarsh, but still a decent size.

The closer we got to the port, the stronger the aromas of sizzling street meats, freshly caught fish, and imported spices became. All the scents of the market mixed together and stirred up a strange, dull ache in the pit of my stomach I didn't understand. Maybe it reminded me too much of Saltmarsh?

Queasy and distracted, I flinched and almost stepped off the curb and into the street when Phoebe suddenly darted a few steps ahead. "Look! We should check there for the right dock." She pointed ahead to where the road stopped abruptly at a circular intersection. Two other streets split from the circle, leading in opposite directions along the docks. In the center of the circle, a large wooden sign stood alone with a fairly detailed map of all the docks engraved into it.

"We're looking for Crosswall Docks," I reminded her as we stopped to study it.

She nodded. "Wow. There are so many. I hope it isn't too far."

I had to agree. There were fifty or so different docks of varying sizes marked on the map, each one packed into different coves and lagoons tucked amidst the steep, jagged cliffs. Only a small portion of the docks—which happened to be right in front of us—actually sat on an open beach. That area, it seemed, was partitioned off and heavily regulated for public use. Interesting.

Glancing in either direction, I studied the oddly constructed walkways and buildings that hugged against the side of the cliffs like barnacles. Some even passed under enormous sea-arches or connected to sea stacks. Below, the dark, cold ocean rippled and foamed at the hulls of the ships. It growled deeply like a slumbering beast and that odd ache rose in my gut again. Something about this place just felt ... off. Different. Bizarre. I just couldn't piece together why. I'd never set foot in Dayrise before this. Gods and Fates, what was wrong with me?

"Hmm, let's see." Phoebe stood up on her toes to get a better look at the map. "Blatherly, Nocklin, Hamourlow—oh! I found it! Crosswall is this way." She bounced happily and pointed to a small cove to the south. "That's not far, is it?"

I sighed. "No. Let's get going. The sun will be down soon and I'd rather not be stuck out here at night."

Thanks to her constant gawking at all the ships, Phoebe nearly wandered off the walkway, crashed into people, and tripped over her own feet more than a dozen times. Ridiculous. She was almost as troublesome as Thatcher ... *almost*. So far, she hadn't attempted to tame any feral dragons. But the day wasn't over, so I wasn't letting her out of my sight.

Phoebe blushed and pouted when I insisted she walk right in front of me so I could at least steer her in the right direction. It's not like I had a choice if she wasn't going to pay attention to anything except the ships. The pouting stopped when I tugged her out of the way of a line of merchant wagons thundering down the wooden walkway, though. Gods and Fates, it's like I'd been assigned to herd a bunch of kittens.

We pressed on through the crowds of sailors and dockhands rushing to finish their work before dark, passing the warm light glowing through the windows of the portside taverns and inns. City workers lit lamps along the walkways and merchants closed up dockside shops. Fishermen had their nets hung out, ready for an early morning's work tomorrow, and city guards patrolled in groups of two. The low rumble and rush of the ocean kept a deep rhythm as we made our way from one cove to the next. Each one was marked with a rickety wooden sign hanging on rusted chains—some so worn they were barely legible at all. Nothing seemed out of place.

That is, until we reached the sign for Crosswall Docks.

Pausing before it, Phoebe and I exchanged a look. There wasn't a soul in sight. Before us, a network of piers wound around the huge ships that rocked gently at their moorings. Behind us, a row of narrow, weather-beaten buildings stood smashed together like worn old books packed into a shelf. Hmm. Wasn't there supposed to be someone meeting us here? Maybe they'd given up once it started to get dark and—

My entire body went stiff at the all-too-familiar sound of pained grunts and shouts. It was faint, distant, and hard to discern over the rumble of the surf. But there was no mistaking it. I *knew* that sound.

In a single heartbeat, my senses came alive like a fuse in my brain had been lit. I dropped Phoebe's bag of gear. It hit the ground at my feet with a *thunk*.

Everything seemed to slow. I turned to face the line of buildings and studied each one, absorbing every detail, until I spotted it—a narrow alley between a grimy sailor's tavern and a tailor's shop that had already closed for the night.

There.

The noise still echoed from the gloom, but the shadows hung too thick to be sure. I'd have to get closer.

"M-Murdoc?" Phoebe whimpered as I reached back to draw one of my long, slender longswords from the cross sheath at my back.

"Stay here. Don't move from this spot," I ordered.

Forging into the gloom of the alley, I stepped silently past stacks of wooden crates, old barrels, and heaps of trash. My jaw set at the scent of a coppery musk in the air. Blood. The sounds of scuffling, grunting, and breathless cackling grew louder.

"Disgusting piece of horse fodder," a gruff voice snarled. "Think they can just burn our homes and murder our sons and then stay here living off our charity!"

"I say we cut them pointed ears right off his head," someone else sneered.

"Hah! We can nail 'em to that traitor-lovin' hag's front door!"

A chorus of broken, slurring laughs cackled loudly. The faint scrape and hum of a blade leaving its sheath set every nerve in my body on fire. Heat poured into my veins.

I stepped around the last mound of crates and saw them. Three men stood around a quivering mass on the ground. A person. Their prey. Whether it was a man or woman, elf or human, I couldn't tell.

And it didn't matter.

As soon as I came into view, all three men whipped around to face me with their eyes wide and bloodshot. My lip curled. They reeked of fish, sweat, and too much ale. Blood dripped from their knuckles and one of them held a wooden club. Another gripped a long dagger in a shaking hand.

A smirk curled across my lips.

"What're you smilin' at, eh? Get lost!" one of them shouted. I guess brandishing that club made him feel a bit more confident.

His mistake.

I slowly slipped my sword back into its sheath.

"That's right, scum," the man with the dagger snickered. "Put that prissy little sword away and move on. A snot-nosed brat like you probably doesn't even know how to use it."

Reaching into my pockets, I slipped my fingers through the set of thick leather bands that had been shaped to fit perfectly over my knuckles on each hand. Studded with steel spikes that caught in the moonlight, my cestus gloves were one of the few pieces of Ulfrangar gear I couldn't justify parting with.

"I know how to use it," I said as I drew my hands out and curled them into fists, the silver spikes on my knuckles glinting. "It's just much more *fun* this way."

THE FIRST TWO thugs went down easy.

The one with the club rushed me first, staggering forward with a challenging shout. He reared back for a swing aimed at my head.

I ducked in, closing the distance between us in an instant and grabbing the club as it came around. His eyes went wide right before I rammed the club backward in his grip with one brutal shove. The smaller end bashed into his nose with a gory CRUNCH. He floundered backward with a garbled scream, tripped over his own feet, and hit the ground with the club still in his hand. Idiot.

His comrades weren't far behind, though.

The second man dove at me, reaching out like he wanted to seize my shirt collar. I spun and dipped away from his grasp, grabbing his wrist and snatching his whole arm down hard against my shoulder. CRACK! His elbow snapped like a tree branch and he howled right in my ear. An elbow to the gut silenced him, though. I hurled him over my shoulder and slammed him into the ground, delivering one solid punch across his face with my spiked gloves.

Pathetic. What a bore.

The howling hiss of the wind over a blade made my pulse spike suddenly.

I whirled around to find the last guy making a strike at my neck with his dagger. The point barely brushed my skin as I dropped low and kicked into an evasive roll. Landing in a crouch with my fingertips on the ground, I bared my teeth in a snarl. Less than ten feet away, my remaining enemy also sank into an offensive pose with the dagger raised.

This one was smarter. Judging by his footing and the way he held that knife, he must have had a little training in the Maldobarian infantry, too. A former soldier? Interesting —but only a little.

I narrowed my eyes.

He only hesitated for a few seconds. Then he gave a primal shout and lunged straight for me.

I didn't move. Just a bit closer. One more step, and then I could—

The man lurched to a halt. His eyes widened and his voice went silent with a rasping gurgle. He fell forward like a freshly cut tree, hitting the ground with a *thud*, and didn't move.

What the ... ?

Then I saw it—a single, short arrow sticking out of his back. A crossbow bolt?

My gaze darted back up to the gloom of the alley. Thatcher stood shaking like a dead leaf in autumn, his face blanched and his mouth hanging open as he gripped his crossbow.

"H-He was going to kill you," he stammered and wheezed as I got to my feet. "I ... I-I didn't have a choice. I had to do something. I didn't mean to kill him, I just—he was about to attack you!"

I walked over to carefully pluck the weapon out of his stiff, shaking hands. Seemed safer, just in case he panicked and accidentally fired off another shot. "Breathe, Thatcher. You did fine."

"B-But he's dead, isn't he? Oh, Gods and Fates, I didn't mean to!" he fretted as he waved his hands. "I'll be arrested! Someone should find the city guards before—"

"No one's arresting anyone." I sighed and rolled my eyes. "Or getting the city guards involved. Try to calm down. What are you doing here already? I thought it would take hours for you to catch up with us?"

Thatcher opened his mouth, but before he could get a word out, Reigh came striding from the shadows with a suspicious scowl. "What the heck is going on back here? Phoebe said you were fighting someone?"

It took him all of about two seconds to glance between me, the three thugs on the ground, and the person they'd been pummeling still cowering on the ground nearby. Granted, he had no way of knowing that particular individual wasn't one of them.

His shoulders dropped and he let out a heavy, exasperated groan. "For crying out loud. I leave you alone for less than an hour and you're already dueling drunken sailors?" Reigh shook his head as he stomped past us. "Over what?"

"That," I nodded to the shivering heap of a person at the farthest end of the alley. "Figured I would spare them from getting their ears cut off and being beaten to death. I hope you approve, *Your Highness*." My tone sharpened on those last words.

Reigh flicked me a harrowing glare, but he didn't reply. Squatting down, he reached a hand to touch the cowering victim's back. They were still curled into a ball on their elbows and knees, hands covering the back of their head.

I wandered over to get a better look, Thatcher shadowing my every step.

"Hey, you okay?" Reigh used a much milder tone. "We're not gonna hurt you. I'm a healer. If you're injured, I can help."

Slowly, the figure began to unfold from that defensive, fetal position. It—er, well, *he* sat up, looking around at us with one wide, terrified eye. The other one was turning an unsettling shade of purplish blue and had already swollen shut. That paired with the fresh blood smeared over his face from the open gash on his very obviously broken nose made for a gruesome sight.

But that wasn't what made me frown as I studied him more closely. With his impressively brawny frame showing through his tattered, bloodstained tunic, the young man quivering on the ground looked like he could break my neck with one squeeze of his fist. When he stumbled to his feet, he towered over the rest of us like a shepherd surveying his flock. Merciful Gods. Surely a guy that size could hold his own in a brawl. Why hadn't he tried to defend himself?

"I, um, I'm okay. I'll be fine. But, um ... thank you," he mumbled as he dipped his head. The gesture made his mane of dark, russet-red hair shake loose around his wide shoulders. It hung down to the middle of his back in thickly woven locks, each one tied off with a copper bead.

Reigh had to lean back a little to meet his gaze. "I hate to break it to you, but in case you're not aware, your nose is pointing sideways right now. My expert medical opinion is that noses should point forward, so I'm going to go out on a limb here and say that no, you're not fine."

The huge boy—kid—guy blinked his only working eye as though he were surprised. Honestly, I couldn't tell how old he was because despite his stature and severely-beaten face, his voice still sounded young. Bizarre. He probed gingerly at his absolutely broken nose and whimpered. "O-Oh. Well, it's ... it's okay. I'm sure it'll be fine."

Reigh folded his arms and looked at me with an eyebrow arched in disbelief. "Riiight. Well, just who are you, anyway? What's your name?"

The boyish giant hesitated. He glanced around at the three of us again, limping a little as he tried to take a step backward. "It's, um, it's Jondar," he mumbled at last, bowing his head and cringing away. It almost seemed like he expected us to jump him as soon as he answered. "Jondar Broadfeather."

Reigh's mouth fell open. Thatcher choked out loud. My brows shot up.

This guy ... was Jaevid's *relative*?

3
CHAPTER THREE

Still standing obediently where I'd left her, Phoebe yelped in alarm when she saw our towering ... *friend*? Was friend the right word? This trend of meeting people I wasn't supposed to kill still baffled me at times.

Ah, well, despite being well over six feet tall, Jondar didn't seem like much of a threat. If anything, he stumbled over his words and cringed away from every sudden sound, sort of like Thatcher had while we were being held at the prison camp. I had no doubts those long months had been scarring for him. Thatcher hadn't grown up in the same world I had. Violence and survival were foreign languages to him, and unfortunately, I'd been serving as his teacher while we were imprisoned there, so he'd lost out on all fronts.

"I'm guessing you're the one who's supposed to be meeting us, then?" Thatcher asked as we gathered beneath the light of the lantern hanging over the sign for Crosswall Docks.

Jondar gave a hesitant nod, still seeming totally oblivious to the blood oozing from his nose, down his face, and onto the front of his tunic. Granted, he had other injuries to worry about—including his eye. A few cuts on his back were also bleeding through his shirt, and there were some nasty-looking bruises developing on his cheeks and forehead. "I ... I apologize for not being here when you arrived. I, um, I was supposed to wait right here by the sign, I know."

"It's fine. I'm just glad Murdoc found you before those guys finished you off. What'd you do to set them off, anyway?" Reigh asked as he picked up his saddlebags and flung them over his shoulder.

Thatcher and I did the same, picking up the rest of our luggage, Phoebe's bags of supplies, and waiting for Jondar to take the lead.

"O-Oh, well, it's not a big deal, honestly." Jondar's laugh was as awkward as it was strained. His breath caught and he put a hand over one of his sides. Hmm. Broken rib?

One look at Reigh's disapproving scowl verified it; Jondar was hurt far worse than he was admitting.

Now wasn't the time to argue with him about it, though. The giant kid started off down the walkway again, trundling along and occasionally flicking anxious glances back at us over his shoulder like he expected us to all jump him at once. "There's some people here that don't like us—er, well, *me*, specifically. It's fine, though. I understand. I'm ... a bit different."

Understatement of the decade.

"Still, that's no excuse for them to hurt you like this," Phoebe piped up, obviously feeling a bit braver now. She peered up at him with her dainty features crinkled with concern. "It looks so painful. Are you sure you don't want us to take you to a healer?"

"*I* am a healer," Reigh growled at her sharply. "I can take care of it when we get inside."

"Lucky we found a new place to stable the dragons that was much closer by, huh?" Thatcher added as he nudged my arm with his elbow and smiled weakly. "You were in a tight spot there."

"Mm, more like lucky you didn't shoot yourself in the foot instead of that thug," I corrected. He didn't have the combat skills to get smug about it.

He frowned and looked down. "I did okay with it before. I know how to aim."

I snorted, shook my head, and let it go. There wasn't much aiming required in shooting a target only a few feet away. But now wasn't the time for critiquing his fighting abilities—or lack thereof.

Jondar led us away from the walkway, continuing inland for two blocks on a narrow street that wound along the bottom of a steep canyon. Smooshed between the towering walls of dark stone, the air seemed cooler and both sides of the street were packed tight with tall, skinny buildings. Some were shops, while others seemed purely residential. Lights glowed, bright and warm in the windows. At last, he stopped before a three-story home with a green-painted door and heavy drapes pulled closed over all the windows.

Huffing and puffing, Thatcher dropped his bags at his feet and wiped the sweat from his brow with his shirtsleeve. "I hope there's something to eat. I'm starving," he moaned under his breath.

"Me too," Phoebe agreed.

Jondar knocked three very distinct times and stood back. "I'm sure Mum's got something ready for—" He snapped his mouth shut as the door whipped open. Light from inside the house poured over us until a figure stepped into the doorway.

Tall and thin as a reed, a middle-aged woman stared at us. Her brows rose in surprise. Not that I didn't get why—typically, royals sent out warriors, spies, or military emissaries to carry out dangerous secret missions on their behalf ... not a troupe of ragged, squabbling teenagers. But, here we were, as promised.

The woman's pale blue eyes shone like arctic water as she slowly looked each of us over from head to foot. Her lips pursed unhappily. Tossing her long braid of jet-black hair over her slender shoulder, she moved aside and pushed the door open farther to let us in. "Well, then. It seems I'll need to have a word with my dear little brother about the age of the children he's recruiting for his mad adventures these days," she huffed in a smooth voice. She tipped her head in gesture for us to come inside. "In with you. Gods and Fates, are even one of you over twenty?"

Her eyes lingered on me for a second longer—probably because I was the tallest and oldest-looking of the bunch—as though she were aiming that question at me, specifically.

Too bad for her, I didn't know exactly how old I was. Ulfrangar didn't exactly throw birthday parties for the pups they were training to be the deadliest assassins in the world. The best I could do for her was shrug indifferently. Maybe I was? Who knew.

"*Brother?*" Reigh hesitated in the doorway, studying her. "You mean ... ?"

One corner of the woman's mouth quirked into a knowing, almost mischievous little grin. Despite the few wrinkles in the corners of her eyes, she still had a pretty face and just a touch of mischievous energy in her gaze. "Indeed, boy. I'm Lin Broadfeather. Jaevid is my half-brother."

You could have knocked him over with a sneeze. "I ... um, I'm ... No one ever mentioned in the stories what happened to you and ... " Reigh paused, his face flushing almost as red as his unruly curtain of hair. He quickly stepped around her to get inside with the rest of us right behind him. Jondar brought up the rear, his head down and angled away as though he didn't want Lin to see what'd happened to his face.

"My mother and sister?" The woman guessed as she shut the door. When she faced us again, her expression had smoothed into a calm, almost sad smile that never quite reached those pale eyes. "They wouldn't, would they? Ours wasn't exactly a shining role in any of those tales. But it's just me here, now. Well, me and the little ones. And Jondar, of course. He's my—" Lin stopped short and drew in a startled gasp. "Gods and Fates, Jon! What have you been into?! Your face! Your eye!"

The massive, auburn-haired guy shied back some when she stomped over and grasped his chin, tugging him down to her level so she could have a closer look at his injuries. "I-It's nothing, Mum. Really. It doesn't even hurt much."

Lin Broadfeather's face turned an unsettling shade of red. She stroked gingerly at the rising knot on his forehead and the swollen, bloodied bridge of his nose. He'd be lucky if it wasn't broken and crooked for the rest of his life. That was preferable to being dead, though.

It was in my experience, anyway.

"Who did this to you?" she seethed sharply. "Was it those Waverly boys again? I swear by every god that's ever crawled this soggy earth, I will have their hides as draperies if it's the last thing I ever do!"

He squirmed and cringed, but didn't resist. "Mum, please, they—"

"Was it those dockhands from Callivan's? Oh, just wait till I get my hands on him, I'll ram that fancy cravat right down his throat. He'll be tasting cheap lace for weeks!"

"Mum!" Jondar shut his eyes tightly as he shouted over her furious growling. "It doesn't matter!"

Lin leaned back to stare up at her much taller son with a perplexed frown. "What do you mean, Jon?"

"I-I mean ... I mean, *they* already took care of it. That one in the middle, uh, he beat them pretty badly," Jondar stammered as he glanced around, looking pretty much everywhere except back at her. "I don't think they'll bother me again."

"They better not," I muttered. "I'll break worse than a few bones next time."

"Like their necks?" Phoebe asked, blinking innocently up at me like a little spring fawn. Gods preserve me.

I smirked. "Maybe."

"I'm pretty sure I may have—but almost definitely did—kill one of them. On accident. With my crossbow," Thatcher admitted, flinching with every word. "Sorry about that."

Lin gaped at him for a moment. I had to sympathize. Despite looking like a cherub-faced twelve-year-old, Thatcher hadn't hesitated to pull the trigger. There might be something worthy of a fighter buried deep beneath his vacant expression after all. Hmm.

"Did anyone see you do it?" she asked.

Thatcher gulped. "Um, I ... I don't *think* so. There was no one on the street when we left."

She sank back on her heels with a deep sigh. "Well, then, we won't speak another word of it. Those brutes working down at the docks—especially the ones Nathaniel Callivan hires. They're not much better than common highway robbers. They had it coming, if you ask me. Good riddance." She looked back up at Jon's battered face and shook her head. "Boy, you'll be the death of me. If you'd ever just swing back at them just once, then—"

"Then I'd be exactly what they're accusing me of being," he interrupted, his tone stiff and heavy, as though this was an argument they'd had many times before. "I won't be like that. I won't be like them."

Lin didn't push the issue any further. Instead, she brushed an affectionate hand over his cheek and sighed again. "Come on, then. Let's see if we can't clean you up a bit and get our guests settled in for the night."

I'D BEEN in the servant's quarters and even in Prince Aubren's wing of the royal castle in Halfax. I'd stayed in inns, taverns, slept in stables, and camped out in the woods or by the side of the road. But as I stepped through Lin Broadfeather's house, the worn, dark wood floorboards groaning a little under my weight, I realized ... this might have been the first time I'd ever been in someone's personal home. Well, as an invited guest, anyway.

From the front parlor arranged with a well-used sofa and matching set of dark purple velvet chairs, to the small courtyard at the center of the home that was open to the sky above and overgrown with climbing vines—everything about this place felt close and strange. Intimate in a way I wasn't used to. A series of paintings that looked like they'd been done by a child hung on the plaster walls. A big wicker basket overflowing with dolls, little wooden swords, and other toys sat at the base of the steep staircase that led up to the second floor. Soft light flickered from the candles in the iron candle-fixtures mounted to the walls. Everything in the house looked well-used, although still clean and mostly tidy. Not to mention it smelled of ... hmm, was that stew?

My stomach gave a hopeful growl as we followed Lin into the kitchen at the very back of the house.

"Fates, after so many months, I'd hoped those idiots would lose interest and leave us alone," she muttered as she tugged a long apron off a hook by the door and quickly tied it around her waist. "I suppose I shouldn't be surprised, though. Callivan, that pig-faced buffoon, always did like punching down. But giving those animals he hires as dock hands free run to go about beating up children? Despicable!"

She rambled on as she bustled around the kitchen. The fire crackling in the big stone hearth at the far end of the room made all the polished copper pots and pans hanging along the walls shine. A long wooden table stretched nearly the length of the space with eight mismatched chairs of different colors and shapes crowded around it. Dishes, bowls, and cups were stacked neatly on open shelves above a counter that was crowded with big ceramic jars and containers with cork stoppers. Bundles of herbs hung from nails over a big washing basin to dry and hefty sacks of vegetables, flour, and potatoes sat heaped into a corner. A large, half-eaten wheel of cheese wrapped in paper sat on the table along with a stack of bowls and handful of spoons.

Reigh dropped his bag of gear next to one of the chairs and dug out one of his healer's kits. "At the risk of sounding insensitive, why, exactly, are the resident village idiots trying to beat Jondar to death?"

Lin's pale, glacier blue eyes dimmed and she turned away to stir a long spoon in the iron pot hanging over the fire. "I'm afraid it's not a simple problem. And it's not just Jondar. I try to keep the others, the little ones, inside unless I'm with them. We've had one too many close calls. I can't even risk sending them on errands to the market alone anymore." Her slender brows drew together, rumpling with unease. "It's hard enough building a life out of the ash and cinders the Tibrans left behind, but it takes a downright vile soul to torment the children that were left behind. They've already lost everything and been cast out into the streets like garbage."

"You've been taking in the Tibran child-soldiers?" I couldn't hide my surprise.

Lin nodded. "Someone ought to. Some were hardly more than toddlers when they were released. Others might as well have been because they'd been neglected and abused until they didn't even know how to bathe or feed themselves properly. They only taught them how to fletch arrows, sharpen swords, and the like. Jondar and I are fortunate enough to have enough room to house them and a decent enough income to keep them fed and clothed. But I never imagined I'd have to protect them from the city folk here."

"Wait—so Jondar *isn't* one of the Tibran child-soldiers?" Thatcher asked as he glanced between them.

Lin gave a wistful smile over her shoulder. "No. He really is my son. Granted, he doesn't look it. Took after his father. But I suppose simply looking different is the only excuse fools like that need to justify attacking someone."

Thatcher's ears were practically smoking as he kept looking back and forth, as though trying to wrap his mind around how that hugely tall and impressively brawny guy could possibly be related to the slender, willowy woman still stirring her pot of stew. "But ... but he, I mean ... he's ... "

"You're an *elf!*" Phoebe chirped suddenly. She bounced onto the balls of her feet excitedly as she stared at Jondar—who immediately froze where he stood, tucking some of his heavy brownish-red locks behind one very distinctly pointed ear.

"Half-elf," Lin corrected.

"Not a Gray Elf." Now Reigh was staring at him with bewilderment, too.

"Obviously," I snorted. No Gray Elf grew that tall. Jaevid had been extremely fortunate to retain his more human-like stature. Gray Elves seldom stood even an inch over five and a half feet. But Jondar was too monstrous to have even a drop of Gray Elf blood in him.

"No. His father wasn't from Luntharda. Or Maldobar, either, for that matter," Lin confirmed as she began spooning the thick, rich stew from the pot into five bowls. "Kien came from the deep mountains far to the north, beyond the wild jungle. It was years ago, long before the Tibrans ever came here. He'd been forced to leave his homeland and his people behind, and had gotten a job working on one of the merchant vessels. His ship made port here and, at the time, I was serving as a barmaid at one of those rotten dockside taverns, trying to keep my hateful witch of a mother and brat of a sister from starving to death." She hesitated. Emotion flickered in the depths of her eyes, as though the memories had swept her away.

"They met because Father was defending her honor," Jondar piped up, his jade-colored eyes suddenly bright with enthusiasm. "A drunken sailor spanked Mum on the—"

Lin snapped back to reality instantly. "*Jondar!* Let's ... let's not share all those details, dear." She flushed and turned her back to us as she began cutting off slices from a long loaf of bread. "It's all ancient history now, anyway. Kien was a ... large man. Bigger even than Jondar. And that alone was enough to terrify most people. But he also didn't speak the common-tongue well enough to explain himself. So most of the other sailors avoided him. Kien came to the tavern every so often and sat at the back by himself, ate his meal, drank a few mugs of ale, and hardly said a word to anyone. Sometimes other men would stagger up to him, half-drunk, and challenge him to fight. They'd call him all sorts of names, spit in his plate, anything to try and taunt him. But he never fought back. Never even told them off."

"Sounds familiar," I muttered.

Jondar cringed a little.

"Just one good brawl. One solid punch to the face, and I knew those men would never taunt him again." Lin stepped over to slide a bowl of soup in front of each seat at the table. She did the same with plates arranged with a few slices of bread and cheese. "Finally, I couldn't take it anymore. I asked him why he wouldn't put an end to it, why didn't he just give them what they wanted so they'd leave him alone forever. Kien just sat there, giving me this calm smile. That big, wonderful fool—I don't know if he even understood a word I said. He must've worked a little harder at learning our language after that, though, because it wasn't two weeks later that he asked if my father had promised me to anyone yet." Her voice caught, torn somewhere between a laugh and a despaired sigh. "Of course, the only thing I was promised to was a lifetime of being ridiculed while I worked my fingers to the bone."

Heavy silence settled over the room as we stood watching her. I doubted if there were even ten people in all of Maldobar who hadn't heard Jaevid's story. He'd spent most of his adolescent life living with his human father, Ulric Broadfeather, who was well-known to have been cruel and abusive to all of his children—although he'd obviously had a special hatred for Jaevid. I'd never heard much about the other kids, though. Some accounts even claimed that Jaevid's half-siblings had been just as vicious to him as Ulric. But who could say? Tales and legends weren't always reliable. The only one who knew the truth of it all were the ones involved.

Including Lin.

She swallowed thickly, eyes shining with moisture as she put the last plate down and stood back. "Well, don't let it get cold. You must be hungry."

Thatcher didn't need any more encouragement. He immediately dropped his rear end into the nearest chair and pulled the bowl of stew closer. Phoebe did the same, although not as quickly. She eased down slowly into her seat, still staring at Lin with concern riddling her features.

"How did he die? Kien, I mean," she asked hesitantly.

Lin took in a deep, steadying breath and came around the table to sit down at one of the places without any food. "During the war. Things became so desperate here that Baron Weslann sent out a decree for any willing men and women to take up arms and try to hold the port. Of course, since we live portside, Kien volunteered. You should have seen the looks on the Maldobarian infantry officers' faces when he stepped forward—like they couldn't decide if they should be pleased or terrified." Another pained smile ghosted over her features as she stared down at the tabletop before her. "He must have won them over in the end, though. Kien was like that. Once you got to know him, you couldn't help but like him."

"I heard about the battle at Dayrise," Reigh said quietly. "They held out longer than anyone expected."

Lin nodded in agreement. "We don't have an official military post here, but quite a lot of the city folk and workers are veterans who still know their way around a blade. When the battle was over, the few surviving Maldobarian soldiers helped evacuate as many of the citizens still in the city as they could. I overheard some of them talking about Kien. They said he'd killed nearly two hundred Tibran soldiers on his own before he fell."

My mouth opened slightly. Gods and Fates—*two hundred*? Just what exactly had that giant elf been doing before he decided to sail down to Maldobar and tinker around on ships?

"You'd think the folk around here would remember all that when they torment his only son," Lin added with a growling huff. "But people are stupid and their memories are far too short."

No argument there.

"But still," Thatcher protested with a mouthful of food. "He died a war hero. Why wouldn't they remember that?"

"Because there's lots of heroes in wars, boy." She lifted her gaze, staring down the table to where her son sat on the opposite end. "Not all of them carry swords and shields. And not all of them get remembered."

CHAPTER FOUR

"I should have a look at that nose, Jondar. If it's broken, I can set it for you. It won't feel too good, of course, but at least you won't walk around with a crooked face." Reigh spoke up as the rest of us settled in to eat. He'd already spread out his bundle of medical tools. "Could I get some hot water and a rag? I'll need to clean out the blood and see what I'm working with here. Take a seat, Jondar."

Lin nodded and got to work. She poured hot water from an iron kettle hanging over the fire into a large bowl and brought it over.

Meanwhile, the towering elf boy slowly sank into the chair nearest to the hearth, his dark green eyes never leaving the collection of small knives, needles, spools of thread, and vials of strangely colored potions spread out on the table nearby. He went pale when Reigh picked up one of the needles and began inspecting it carefully.

"I-I'm fine, really. It doesn't even hurt that much anymore," Jondar protested weakly, making a sound somewhere between a squeak, a forced laugh, and a suppressed scream.

Reigh didn't even look up as Lin brought over a pile of folded white washcloths. "Relax. It'll hurt when I put it back in place, but only for a few seconds. It'll be sore and tender for a while, though. So, after I stitch up that gash, I'm gonna bandage it tight," he explained as he began sterilizing the needle and threading it. "I've got a few herbal remedies for pain. You can stir them into tea if you want. Makes them taste less disgusting."

Jondar gulped. He didn't look reassured at all.

"Are you hurt anywhere else? Open wounds? Sore spots?" Reigh asked as he carefully placed the threaded needle into the bowl of hot water. "They pummeled you pretty good. We need to be sure they didn't break anything else."

"I-I ... uh ... " He flicked a nervous glance between Reigh and his mother, as though trying to decide what to say. Maybe he was wondering if he could get away with lying or not.

Nope.

"*Jondar*," Lin said his name as though it were a warning, her glacier-blue eyes glittering with maternal force.

He looked down, muttering under his breath. "My left side hurts," he confessed. "Especially when I breathe or move around."

Reigh looked him over thoughtfully. "Sharp or dull pain?"

"Sharp ... sort of. It's sort of just throbbing until I move a certain way or take a breath."

"Hmm. Might be a broken rib. I'll take a look in a minute. Nose first."

A crack, scream, four stitches, and a few bloody rags later, Jondar's face was more or less fixed. I had to give him credit—Reigh was a decent healer. He worked fast, and his stitching job was proficient and neat. Jondar likely wouldn't even have a scar when it finished healing. I'd seen him work before this, of course. He'd taken care of Thatcher multiple times now. For how quickly and easily he lost his temper in every other situation, Reigh seemed to thrive under the pressure of treating medical injuries. He stayed calm. His hands were steady. He even made joking small talk so that Jondar relaxed somewhat.

Well, right up until he cracked his nose back into place, anyway.

After they'd cleared the table and washed the dishes, Lin and Thatcher helped Phoebe spread out her working materials on the long table. Reigh was still busy checking Jondar over for more injuries. He needed help getting his shirt over his head since lifting his arms seemed to cause him even more pain. Not that I was any sort of medic, but judging by the large, swollen, and angry-looking bruise he had along his left side, a broken rib or two seemed very likely. He had bruises all over him, though. Some were purple and blue—fresh. But others had already turned greenish yellow as they healed.

Wounds like that weren't exactly foreign to me. I'd been nearly beaten to death more times than I could count. Sometimes by elder Ulfrangar agents and sometimes by other pups. Seeing him that way gave me a weird sense of grim nostalgia.

"Yeah, something's definitely fractured at minimum," Reigh concluded as he probed around Jondar's ribcage with his fingers. Every poke made the big elf flinch, hiss through his teeth, and shut his eyes tightly. "Unfortunately, when it comes to ribs, there's not much I can do. It just has to heal on its own. Try not to do anything too strenuous, all right? No heavy lifting or stuff like that. If you do, maybe wrap your chest to stabilize it some. I'll leave some of this herbal remedy to help with the pain, too."

"How long will it take to heal?" Jondar mumbled gloomily as he picked up his shirt again.

Reigh made a thoughtful clicking noise with his tongue. "Mm, six weeks or so. But the pain'll get a lot better. If it were winter, I'd say go get yourself a hunk of ice, wrap it in a cloth, and hold it against your side for a few hours. That helps a lot." He turned away, beginning to clean and pack his medical tools back into the leather, roll-up bag. "Honestly, based on how bad they beat you, it's lucky you didn't have anything more serious broken. Or a concussion."

"Well, they were planning on cutting his ears off," I mumbled. "That's when I decided to even the odds a bit."

"And we're eternally grateful you did," Lin added with a smile as she wandered over to stand beside me. "You must be tired now. Why don't you come upstairs and rest? I've got pallets ready in the upstairs drawing room. I'm sorry that it's not a big space, but there are plenty of pillows and blankets to go around. With seven little ones, Jondar, and myself—we're short on beds these days."

"I'm sure it'll be fine." Thatcher grinned at her broadly as he picked up his bag.

"I think I'll stay and work a bit more, if that's okay." Phoebe looked up from where she sat at the table, fiddling with something that looked suspiciously like a pair of spectacles. Weird. What was she making now?

I eased back down into a chair at the table and unbuckled my vambraces to settle in. "I'll stay with her. Someone should keep watch and I don't need much sleep."

"Riiight." Reigh gave a teasing snort. "So, what, assassins are too awesome to need sleep or something?"

I didn't even look his way. "No. It's just that all the frustrated energy from your deeply-rooted insecurities sustains me."

Phoebe did a terrible job playing off a snorting giggle as a cough.

Reigh rolled his eyes as he picked up his own bags and started for the stairs. Maybe he'd gotten used to my comebacks. Or maybe he was too tired to fire back. It'd been a long day, after all.

"You won't stay up all night, will you?' Thatcher asked, his expression the picture of genuine concern. "You were in the dungeon before. How long has it been since you actually got to rest?"

I opened my mouth to reply, but a sudden loud, shrill squeak made us both flinch and glance over at Phoebe. She had her arms stretched over her head and her mouth open wide. Wait a minute, was that ... a *yawn*? Seriously, who yawned like that? It was like someone stepping on a chipmunk.

And cute—sort of.

I smirked and leaned back in my chair, folding my arms over my chest. "Tell you what, when little miss squeaky gives up and goes to bed, I will, too."

"Can't stand to be outdone, can you?" Thatcher laughed.

"Nope. My *awesome* assassin ego forbids it."

EVEN IF I didn't need it, my mind circled around the thought of sleep. Strange. I'd never allowed myself to sleep simply because I felt like it. All these months of eating full meals, sleeping in warm beds, and living normally were starting to make me go soft. That was ultimately Thatcher's fault. If I hadn't spared him that night ...

The memories replayed before I could will them back, taking me instantly back to that night in Thornbend. The smell of the smoke. Flashes of fire and screams in the night. Thatcher sobbing as he looked up at me, smeared with soot and blood. He'd begged me for his life. And in that moment, something deep inside me had snapped, like the last strand in a rope that had been slowly coming undone for years.

Now I had more questions than answers. Why had Jaevid spared me? What motive was he hiding? Was this pathetic attempt at finding another purpose going to wind up getting Thatcher, Phoebe, Reigh, and anyone else who got too close killed? Where could someone like me possibly go to hide from the Ulfrangar? Was I really prepared to spend the rest of my life looking over my shoulder, just waiting for the past to catch up to me? That's what King Jace had done, apparently. I guess he'd assumed that day had finally come when he saw me. Somehow, I doubted finding out the truth about why I was there had brought him any relief.

My mind spun like a dark whirlpool as I sat, watching Phoebe work feverishly by candlelight. Everyone else had already gone upstairs to bed. The house was silent and still except for the occasional crackle and pop of the embers in the hearth.

Now was as good a time as any.

"I'm going to walk the house," I murmured quietly as I stood. "I'd like to know where all the points of entry are."

Phoebe glanced up from where she was still fiddling away with those spectacle-looking things. "Do you think we'll get attacked again?" She sounded worried.

I shrugged. "With the way things have gone for us so far, I believe we can count on it. It might not be tonight, but we might as well be prepared." I decided not to tell her we were already being followed. No need to get her too panicked. Besides, I was fairly sure two out of the three parties doing the following weren't any threat to us ... yet. The dragon seemed to be keeping a wary distance away.

And then there was the girl ...

So far, she had only watched us from afar—far enough I'd almost overlooked her. Fates, I really was getting soft. Granted, she was as stealthy as a cat. I doubted the Ulfrangar trailing me were even aware of her.

Phoebe didn't reply and quickly turned her attention back to her tools, her mouth mashed into a tense, crooked line. That must've been her way of working out her anxiety. That, or she was hoping to finish before everything got lit on fire again.

I moved silently from room to room, slipping through the darkened halls and peering into each room. Everything downstairs had already been locked up for the night. There were three heavy bolts on the front door and a sword hanging on a hook above it—Lin's way of taking measures against the city folk who'd been harassing her family, I suppose. Effective. The windows were all locked, as well, and heavy drapes were pulled over them to keep anyone from stealing a peek inside. The courtyard was a great deal more concerning. Although the opening overhead had been covered by a lattice—something probably put in place to keep birds from making a mess and building nests up there—it wasn't substantial enough to keep a person out. An ideal entry point. I'd have to keep an eye on that.

Upstairs, the second story was nearly all bedrooms now. Two of them had several bunk-style beds where children lay, curled up in blankets, sound asleep. Even in the dark, I could count all seven of them. Four girls. Three boys. All of them were likely under the age of ten, although it was hard to tell without seeing their faces clearly.

I found Jondar's room at the far end of the hall. He lay on his back, feet hanging off the end of his too-small bed, sound asleep like everyone else. Nothing about his room struck me as odd ... except for the sheathed greatsword leaning up against the wall in the far corner. Hmm. Why would a guy who didn't even want to throw a punch be keeping a weapon like that? His father's sword, maybe? Lin hadn't mentioned any specific weapon Kien might have used, though. Interesting.

The drawing room, where our beds had been neatly spread out on a large wool rug for the night, was the only room with windows looking out to the street below. Lin's bedroom and a narrow storage room stacked with crates and trunks were all that lay on the third floor. The storage room had a small escape door that gave access to the roof, however. Probably a safety measure in case of a fire. Unfortunately, it also provided another way into the house. I'd have to keep an eye on that, too.

By the time I got back downstairs, Phoebe had left her work and the rest of the universe far behind. She sat slumped over the table with her head resting on her crossed arms, wheezing softly as she slept. Her eyelids flickered and her wild, gingery curls spilled out over the tabletop where all her pages of sketched diagrams and notes were still scattered everywhere. By the weak light, I could barely make out the images of what seemed to be masks—or rather, the same mask from several different angles. Strange. What could that be for?

I hesitated in the doorway and rubbed the back of my neck. Should I risk moving her? Or was it better to just drape a blanket over her and leave her alone? Sleeping like that couldn't be comfortable. What would Thatcher do?

Gods, I was no good at this—being with people, and all that went along with it.

With a steadying breath, I moved closer and gently slipped my arms under her. She hardly weighed anything as I lifted her up. Her soft curls tickled my neck as she squirmed restlessly. Then she gave a small, breathy sigh and went limp again. Her head lolled against my shoulder as I carried her up the stairs to the drawing room. It made my chest feel strangely tight, having her soft cheek against me like that.

I lurched to a halt as a shadowed figure greeted me in the doorway. My jaw clenched and my mind snapped to the location of every weapon I'd seen stashed around the house. My weapons downstairs. Longsword in Jondar's room. Reigh's scythes on the floor by his pallet. Thatcher's crossbow nearby. The sword above the front door.

"I'll take next watch," Reigh grumbled as he emerged from the gloom.

I let out a deep, controlled breath. Gods. He had no idea how close I'd been to—ugh. It didn't matter. I studied him, my gaze catching on the dark circles under his eyes and the fresh sheen of sweat on his brow. "Aspiring to my level of awesome?"

He gave a snort and shook his head. "You're not the only one who doesn't sleep much," he growled bitterly through his teeth as he walked past, heading for the stairs. I caught a glimpse of his face when his light amber eyes flickered my way. The pasty hue to his skin made the dark, puffy circles under his eyes all the more obvious. I noticed his arms and hands shaking as he locked a stormy glare onto Phoebe for one hard, cold second. "And that ... is *her* fault."

5
CHAPTER FIVE

Sleeping had always been hard, but it was worse now that I was away from the Ulfrangar. I'd developed the skill of being able to "switch off" my brain when I truly needed to rest—only because I knew exactly where the danger was. Usually, sleeping on bedrolls all around me. Now, I had no idea where my enemies were.

Lying on my back in the dark, listening to Thatcher wheeze and Phoebe breathe softly on their pallets, I chased the phantoms in my mind. Memories of early years with the Ulfrangar always vanished like smoke whenever I tried to recall them clearly. But they were always there, lurking and taunting me in these quiet moments. My memories of my later life, after my handler had selected and begun to train me, were much clearer. Part of me constantly wondered where he was. I had no doubt that somewhere out there in the night, Rook was looking for me. I'd fully expected to find him among the other Ulfrangar sent to kill me at the Cromwell estate. He had to. That was his charge as my former handler. If I could not be trained, then I had to be eradicated, and that was his responsibility.

To hunt what he'd essentially created.

I swallowed hard against the rising, burning tightness in my throat. What would Rook say when he did find me? What would he do? Deep down, I'd always had a feeling he suspected that I wanted to find out where the Ulfrangar had acquired me. He might have even known it, himself. But he never spoke a word about it. And I'd never dared to ask. Asking those sorts of questions among the Ulfrangar were a fantastic way to guarantee yourself the beating of a lifetime.

You belonged to the pack. Who you were and where you came from didn't matter.

But ... if I could recall something—*anything*—from before they'd taken me, then maybe I could find my family. Then I could sort out if I'd really been sold off like a spring heifer, stolen from a family that had wanted me, or brought by slave traders from some distant kingdom. My only clue was my name. And so far, I'd found absolutely nothing about it on any map or record within Maldobar.

That void, the deep ache of nothingness that gnawed at my mind, was always there. It never let me rest. It rattled at those chains of memory buried deep in my soul even when I did fall asleep.

Like tonight.

Across the room, Phoebe turned over in her makeshift bed. The motion and rustling of blankets immediately snapped my brain back into consciousness. I lifted my head to peer at her through the gloom. She groaned a little, and I could barely make out the quilts moving as she shivered.

Was she cold? Hmm.

Getting up, I pulled one of the blankets from Reigh's pallet over and prepared to spread it out over her. He was still on his shift of keeping watch, so he wouldn't need it anyway.

One of my hands brushed her shoulder as I tried to carefully tuck the blanket around her. Her eyes flew open suddenly. Her expression twisted, mouth gaping wide open and body shuddering hard as she sat upright in bed.

I jerked back. What the—?

Phoebe screamed.

Her cry ripped through the silence, frantic and desperate, as she kicked and flailed to get all the blankets off herself. I threw my hands up in surrender. Had she mistaken me for an intruder? In the near dark, it certainly seemed possible that she didn't recognize me.

"W-What's going on?!" Thatcher slurred as he bolted upright, too.

I couldn't even begin explaining. Phoebe screamed louder, shouting garbled words in a foreign language as she lunged at me. She clawed and fought, and I had no choice but to seize her by the wrists to keep her from raking her nails over my face.

"Gods and Fates, Phoebe! It's me!" I shouted at last. "Stop that! It's Murdoc!"

She howled louder, staring at me with eyes wide and pupils fully dilated as she fought against my grip. Her rasping, screeching words came faster. Tears ran down her blanched, utterly terrified face.

I set my jaw, forcing her arms down. Curse this. I didn't want to hurt her. But if I let her go now ...

"Thatcher!" I tried to call out over her screaming. "Don't just sit there, idiot, do somethi—"

Out of nowhere, a hand clapped over Phoebe's mouth. She pitched backward, twisting and writhing against the arms that suddenly snagged around her from behind. One kept a firm hold on her face, muffling her cries and keeping her head still, while the other wrapped around her whole body to pin her arms at her sides.

Reigh dragged her back, falling onto his rear and holding her firmly against his chest as she bucked and fought him. "It'll pass. Just give her a few minutes," he murmured as he fixed me with a grimly focused glare.

What? What the heck was going on? What was wrong with her?

"I heard a scream," Lin called from the doorway. The flickering light from the candle she held illuminated her bleary-eyed look of concern. A hint of maternal wrath sharpened her features when she saw Reigh holding Phoebe like that. "What's going on in here?"

"It's fine," Reigh grunted, voice halting and starting as he struggled to speak with Phoebe still writhing and kicking in his grasp. "She's ... having a night terror. Just ... give her a second."

"A night terror?" Thatcher echoed in a breathless whisper.

"It's ... sort of like ... sleepwalking." Reigh growled through his teeth, still fighting to keep her still. "She's not awake. Gotta let her ... work through it ... or she might hurt herself."

Hurt *herself*? Gods, she'd nearly clawed my eyes out.

"Can't you just wake her up?" Lin pressed, crossing the room to stand over us.

The light from her candle revealed Phoebe's feral, tear-streaked expressions as she struggled. Her pupils stayed dilated, even in the light. Fates—she really was asleep.

"Probably not," Reigh managed to huff.

The seconds passed with the muffled sounds of Phoebe's cries filling the dim room. After several minutes, a pair of Lin's children appeared in the doorway, and she left to herd them back to their beds. Once the door shut behind her, Reigh's heated gaze snapped back up to meet mine again. We sat that way for what felt like an eternity until, at last, Phoebe's struggles slowed. Her arms gradually went slack and her head lolled back against his chest. Slowly, Reigh took his hand away from her mouth.

Silence.

She'd gone back to sleep. Although, according to Reigh, she'd never really been awake to begin with. Well, thank the gods that was over.

"Is she going to be okay?" Thatcher asked, still looking worriedly between us.

"She'll be fine," Reigh grumbled. "She probably won't even remember this happened."

"Oh." Thatcher sank back on his pallet, visibly surprised. "Maybe, uh, maybe we shouldn't tell her. It might embarrass her."

No one replied, although I did agree. There wouldn't be much point in telling her, anyway. If episodes like that were really like sleepwalking, then it's not like she could do anything to prevent it anyway.

"I should go tell Ms. Lin everything's fine now. She seemed pretty worried," Thatcher realized aloud. When I gave him a confirming nod, he quickly crawled out of his bed and staggered out the door.

With Phoebe's tiny body still held against him, Reigh sat panting. A few beads of sweat ran down the sides of his face.

"What did she say? She spoke, didn't she?" he asked in a hoarse whisper.

I shook my head slowly. "I couldn't make it out. It was too garbled. But it sounded foreign." I decided not to tell him that, among my many other Ulfrangar-trained skills, training in languages was one of my finer proficiencies. I'd mastered nearly twelve so far. But the one she spoke? That wasn't one I recognized.

His mouth scrunched into a tight, painfully forced frown, as though he were trying to hide his surprise. "I didn't realize she spoke anything except the common tongue," he admitted at last.

Honestly, I hadn't either. But it wasn't a shock. "The Tibrans took people from all over the world as slaves to their banner," I reminded him, keeping my voice hushed. "I was told all their slave soldiers were forbidden from speaking their native languages, and punishments were severe for those who did."

"Probably a nightmare about that, then," he guessed as he shifted his hold to clumsily pick her up. He shuffled over to lie her down on her bed, and she immediately whimpered softly and curled up on her side with her back to him.

"Weird, though," Reigh mused.

"Why?" I had a feeling I knew what he meant, but I decided to give him the chance to explain himself in case I was wrong.

I wasn't.

"Because she wasn't a Tibran slave," he snapped under his breath like it should've been obvious.

I couldn't stop myself. Their relationship was none of my business, and I knew very little about what had transpired between them before the war ended. But still—his willful ignorance had finally worn through all my self-control. Wrath like hot cinders crackled on my tongue as I surged forward, reaching around him to carefully pull down the wide collar of her tunic. It being borrowed from Lin and a bit too big for her helped, too. The gnarled scars left behind from her many Tibran slave-brands marred the fair, freckled skin on her shoulders.

Reigh's expression went blank, face emptying of color for a moment as he stared down at them.

"In case you are confused, this was not something the Tibrans did to reward their volunteers or loyal workers," I snarled through my teeth as I smoothed her tunic back into place and moved away.

He swallowed thickly, but didn't reply.

And I couldn't resist the urge to make one final, brutal hit. "I wonder, how many people have cursed and condemned you for all the good men you slaughtered at Barrowton?"

Reigh's whole body jerked. His head snapped around to stare at me with his eyes as wide as two amber moons and his face the picture of horrified shock.

"Oh, yes. I know all about it. They called you the 'Angel of Death,' didn't they? Word of that massacre reached the Ulfrangar all the way down in my territory in Saltmarsh. You killed lots of Tibrans, yes. But you killed just as many Maldobarian soldiers," I hissed as I stood and went to retrieve my cross-sheaths from a hook by the door. Trying to sleep again would be pointless now, so I might as well keep watch.

Buckling my blades into place across my back, I turned toward the door and flashed a final, parting glance at him over my shoulder. "You didn't even leave corpses behind for their families to bury. There was even a rumor that you'd murdered your own father, that elven man who raised you, in the same battle—a crime only rectified by Jaevid's mercy and a god's divine power," I growled through my teeth. "Tell me, Prince, how that is any better than being a Tibran slave? Is she a monster for accepting the same grace you did? Or are you a hypocrite for condemning her while your own hands still drip with innocent blood? What have you done to atone for all those deaths? Have you been tried by the Court of Crowns? Have you apologized to any of the families of those soldiers you killed? Or does being the chosen one of a goddess justify murder?"

PART TWO
THATCHER

6
CHAPTER SIX

This wasn't good. Not one tiny little bit. Murdoc and Reigh had basically made a sport of picking at each other with snide comments and little insults. Mostly it seemed harmless, like a semi-friendly rivalry. Or, at least, it had before.

But after two days of being trapped in Ms. Lin's house, waiting for word to come from Prince Judan's spy network that would help us in our mission to find and apprehend Devana, I was getting worried things might actually come to blows. The snide comments had become outright arguments, and the insults ... well, they'd gone from mild and taunting to absolutely venomous.

Something had clearly happened after Phoebe's night terror when I had left the room. I'd come back to find Murdoc gone and Reigh sulking on his bed, lying with his back to everyone. Neither one of them had said a single word to one another the whole next day.

But today? Well ...

Sitting in the front parlor, I kept my eyes on the Swords and Crowns board in front of me. A pair of Ms. Lin's adopted children—two little girls who couldn't have been older than eight or so—seemed to enjoy beating me thoroughly at this game over and over. Whatever. It didn't matter, really. I'd never been much good at complicated games like this, anyway. Plus, it was nearly impossible to concentrate on anything with Murdoc and Reigh snarling and hissing at one another again like a pair of angry ferrets. I could hear every word they said, even from the next room.

"We cannot stay here another day," Murdoc snapped. "One was reckless enough. Two was downright stupid. This ... this is just inviting disaster!"

"And where else are we supposed to go, exactly?" Reigh growled back. "The Ulfrangar are everywhere, right? So it doesn't really matter where we go. They'll still be on our heels. At least here we're in the open enough that they'd have to be willing to accept a degree of exposure to make a move, right? No way Phillip can move around this city without being spotted, either. That's why Jaevid had us come here. Out in the open is the safest place for us now."

"Then we should at least insist on moving to one of the dockside taverns." Murdoc's tone hushed somewhat, almost like he didn't want anyone else to hear him. It didn't work. "I'm not sure if you've noticed, but Jaevid essentially has us staying in an orphanage staffed by his own family members. I don't know about you, but I'd prefer not to have the blood of innocent children on my hands if I can help it."

Reigh gave a haughty, snorting chuckle. "Never been sent on the hunt for children, then, Mr. Assassin?"

I winced. Uh oh. Too far below the belt. Geez, it almost seemed like he wanted a fight.

Murdoc's silence was *way* more terrifying than his yelling. A cold sweat prickled over my skin as I glanced over at the open doorway between where I sat in the parlor and where they were in the foyer. Every second of quiet that ticked by made my pulse race faster. What were they doing? Oh Gods, had Murdoc finally lost it and snapped his neck already? Maybe I should go check—

"Look, I get why you're concerned," Reigh spoke up again, his voice much calmer and maybe even a little apologetic. I guess he could tell he'd taken things a step too far. "For the record, I'm not any happier about being stuck here, either. But we don't have much of a choice until Judan's agents give us some direction. Right now, we only have vague ideas about Devana's location, and you have to agree that isn't enough—not for this mission. Northwatch isn't the kind of place you want to storm into unprepared. This has to be a precision strike for it to work. Once we have the information we need, believe me, I'll be the first one in the saddle. Until then, we should use this time wisely. Phoebe's in there doing ... whatever it is she does. Supposedly making tools for us to use to fight and capture Devana."

Murdoc didn't reply right away. Awkward seconds slipped by. Finally, he let out a growling sigh. "If Devana has already gained some cooperation out of the Ulfrangar, that alone proves she's far more cunning and resourceful than anyone has given her credit for. How can we be sure that this Prince Judan fellow can even get close enough to her to find out anything at all? What if he falls victim to her powers, as well?"

Now Reigh was the one being quiet.

"And do I really need to remind you what Phillip could do if ever he did decide to make his move against us? Fates preserve us—if Devana really was using her divine power to control his mind, then what are we even doing trying to reach her at all? Clearly we've been set on a hunt that was doomed to fail from the outset."

"So? What are you saying? You want to give up now and go back to Halfax? Go back to shoveling horse crap and polishing saddle brass?" Reigh demanded, his tone sharp with an edge of defiance. "Because I don't know about you, but the fact that a witch with that kind of power is joining forces with people like the Ulfrangar and Phillip makes me scared enough to puke. I doubt she's gathering them all together for a tea party, right? And as much as it pains me to admit it ... Phoebe might be the only person in the world who can come up with a way to bind her. She did it to me, after all. That's why I'm staying. I'm seeing this through—to whatever end. I don't know what the Ulfrangar do when things get dangerous, but Gray elf scouts *do not* retreat."

After another long, tense pause, the hinges of the door creaked as it opened. "If sitting still is driving you nuts, then maybe you need to focus on teaching Thatcher how to do more than fire off panicked shots with that crossbow, yeah?" Reigh said. "So far, you're the only one who hasn't taken a crack at trying to hammer some actual combat skills into that thick skull of his."

I cringed again. Right. Well, he wasn't wrong. I'd only shot that guy in the alley because I thought Murdoc was in danger. I hadn't aimed—not really. It'd all happened too fast. Even now, I barely remembered doing it.

Reigh gave a resigned sigh. "I'm going to check on the dragons and see if any word has arrived at the inn. Who knows, maybe Jaevid will send someone else to fight with us. Or he'll come up with a better plan than sending a bunch of rookies for this mission. I'll be back in a few hours."

The door shut with a *thud*. I swallowed hard. My stomach twisted as I stared down at the game board before me. Crap. I was already losing this game, too.

One of the little girls gave me a tiny, apprehensive smile as she subtly nudged one of my pieces with her finger. A hint.

I forced a smile back. "I think you two already got me this time. We'll have a rematch later, okay?"

They both beamed, nodding and already setting up the board again to start playing against one another without saying a word. Neither of them talked much. Ms. Lin had mentioned that the Tibrans had forbidden all their captured soldiers and slaves from speaking their native languages. Getting caught doing that would earn them a severe beating, so now several of her children still wouldn't speak much at all—including these two.

I had to hand it to her, Ms. Lin was one of the most patient people I'd ever met. I couldn't help but watch while she gently juggled all of her kids, herding them through meals, baths, and chores throughout the day. She took time to interact with each one, played with them, and had even begun teaching some of the older kids to read and write. All of them had really short hair—probably because the Tibrans had shaved the heads of all their captives. While it'd begun growing back on some of the other kids, the two girls now deeply involved in another game of Swords and Crowns were still almost bald. It made the branded mark on the side of their necks more obvious, too.

Granted, Ms. Lin had given them tunics with high collars to hide as much of it as possible. I could only assume that was to keep anyone from harassing them when they went out into public. Ms. Lin watched over all of them like a mother bear. She was soft, warm, and gentle with them. But one wrong look from someone passing them on the street brought out the fangs. Observing all that put a strange knot of pain deep in my chest. Envy, maybe? I wasn't sure, and thinking about it too much made the feeling even worse.

Getting up, I rubbed at the back of my neck and tried to think of what I could say to Murdoc. Somehow, things still felt ... weird between us. Like he was avoiding being stuck in the same place with me alone. Okay, so, he did have his reasons. I knew his secret now.

Er, well, one of them, anyway. But it's not like that changed anything. We were still friends. He wasn't an Ulfrangar anymore. And I didn't doubt his loyalty for a single second. I knew I could trust him to fight on our side no matter what.

"Hey, uh, Murdoc?" I called out as I stepped into the foyer.

He wasn't there.

I hesitated, glancing back and forth down the foyer. Murdoc was nowhere in sight. But I'd only just heard them arguing. Had he left with Reigh? No, surely not. That would've meant Jondar and I were the only ones left to protect everyone. Hah! As if Murdoc would ever allow that to happen. I didn't need anyone to tell me how bad I was at combat—Jaevid, Haldor, and Reigh had already made that abundantly clear when they tried to train me.

Then where would Murdoc go ... ?

Oh. Right. *There*. Great.

I groaned, dragging my feet as I started for the stairs.

"You know," I grunted as I struggled to heave myself through the hatch door that led out onto the roof of Ms. Lin's house. "Some people might say it's a little cliché that you keep doing this."

"Doing what?" Murdoc mumbled from where he sat on the ridge at the top of the roof.

"Brooding on the rooftop," I wheezed, finally managing to drag a leg out of the opening and crawl out on my belly. Ugh. Not even remotely cool.

He just rolled his eyes and looked away. "Some people would be incredibly stupid, then. I'm not up here for my benefit."

"Oh really?" I'd officially broken a sweat by the time I managed to shakily climb up to the ridge and sit down beside him.

"There's five points of entry into the house. Two on the bottom floor—the door and parlor windows. It's unlikely anyone would try to burst in that way for a surprise attack in the middle of the day. Too much foot traffic on the street. Same with the second-story windows. They all face the street, as well," he explained as he fidgeted with the small, leaf-shaped dagger he usually kept tucked into the side of his boot. Murdoc spun it through his fingers so fast it was like a gleaming silver blur humming around his hand. "That just leaves the fire escape door on the roof and the courtyard. Both are an ideal way in for someone who doesn't want to be spotted from people on the street below."

"I guess that means you're up here standing guard, then?" I guessed.

He nodded. "I can see both from here."

I frowned down at the toes of my boots. It made sense, I guess. He probably had a hard time shutting off that part of his mind that'd been trained to think like ... well, like an assassin. I wondered if that would ever go away. For now, I hoped it wouldn't. That state of mind might be the only thing that kept us from getting murdered in our sleep.

"I don't understand why they haven't already made their move," Murdoc muttered suddenly.

I glanced over to study his fierce, scowling face. "Who?"

"The Ulfrangar. We've been here two days—stationary, without the dragons, only lightly armed, and in a house full of potential hostages. But they're holding back. It's always harder to hit a moving target. We're giving them the perfect opportunity. I don't understand it at all." His piercing gaze narrowed, focused on the other rooftops around us. "Why? Why haven't they made their assault?"

"Maybe it's because of you." I pulled my legs up closer to rest my elbows on my knees.

One corner of his mouth twitched up into a half-smirk. "I doubt it."

"How come? You handled them pretty well before, right?"

"I wasn't alone in that fight, Thatcher," he said. "I mean, yes, before all of this I was considered one of the strongest pups still in training. But at the Cromwell estate, I wasn't fighting them alone. Jaevid and a few other dragonriders had come with me to even the odds. Without their help, I don't think I would have been able to save you." His expression softened some, becoming more thoughtful as he went back to flipping that dagger around. "But we don't have that kind of cavalry at our disposal here. We're backed into a corner, taking cover in what's basically an orphanage. When they do attack us again—if we're still staying here, I don't think we will be able to make a clean escape without someone getting killed."

Somehow, the way he said that ... it made me think he was talking about himself. Like he intended on sacrificing himself so the rest of us could escape. The idea put fury like hellfire in my gut. No way. I was *not* going to let that happen.

I glared at him, trying to come up with the right words. Before I could, however, he let out a deep breath and shook his head. "Part of me keeps wondering if it has anything to do with Jaevid."

I arched an eyebrow. "Jaevid? But he's not even here."

"He doesn't have to be," Murdoc explained. "There's something you need to understand about the Ulfrangar, Thatch—something I'm not sure anyone outside the order itself even truly comprehends. The Ulfrangar didn't start in Maldobar or Luntharda, and they're not limited to the borders or boundaries of any kingdom. Their reach spans the entire known world. Their network is deeper than any trading guild or spy organization ever contrived. They've orchestrated events that have altered the course of history. They've kindled revolutions. Toppled dynasties. There's almost nothing they can't do—and there are only a few people throughout history that have ever given them reason to pause." He glanced my way again, his hazel eyes as sharp as an eagle's. "Jaevid Broadfeather is one of those people. When he came back from the dead, it sent a shockwave through the entire Ulfrangar order. A council was called to decide what should, or even could, be done about him. In the end, though, the Zuer made the decision. There aren't many people in the world the Ulfrangar consider a credible threat, but Jaevid is one of them."

A strange tingle of unease shivered up my spine. I almost didn't want to know—but I *needed* to. "Why?" After all, he is just one man. Dragonrider or not, he couldn't take on an entire global network of assassins by himself ... right?

He gave a hollow, ironic chuckle. "I guess no one wanted to piss off a deity—especially not one that had returned from the dead, bargained with a goddess, and stood against an entire invading empire with only a few dragonriders. All that, and the backing of two prominent kingdoms and a formidable king drake as a mount, makes him untouchable."

Okay. Fair point.

"The world fears what the Ulfrangar can do in the shadows. That's why the stories and rumors about them seem more like scary fairy tales than anything that could ever be real." Murdoc stopped spinning his dagger, angling it perfectly so that it fell squarely into his palm. His fingers slowly closed around the hilt. "But the Ulfrangar fear what someone like Jaevid could do out in the open. And whether he realizes it or not, there were a few fleeting seconds on that battlefield at Halfax when Jaevid had held the power of the mortal and divine worlds in his hands. He could have assumed Argonox's seat of power. He could have crushed the Maldobarian and Lunthardan royal lines, tossed their crowns into the heap with the rest of the kingdoms already conquered by the Tibran Empire, and essentially held absolute authority over the known world."

I swallowed hard. "He didn't, though."

"No," Murdoc agreed. "He didn't. And now that I'm associated with him—now that they've seen us fight side-by-side—who knows? Maybe that's making them cautious."

For whatever reason, that idea made me smile.

"What's with that smug look?" Murdoc snorted.

"I dunno. I guess it's kind of nice to think that we have friends in high places, you know?"

His eyes narrowed upon me dangerously, sending a fresh pang of pure panic through my body.

"The only place you're going to be is in a million bloody chunks all over the ground if you don't get your act together and learn to fight," Murdoc growled as he pointed the tip of his dagger at the end of my nose. "As much as it causes me extreme pain and disgust to admit—Reigh is right. I've wasted enough time standing by watching everyone else flail around trying to teach you. Consider yourself *my* student now."

Dread flushed through my body like someone had dumped a bucket of icy water over my head. Murdoc was going to teach me to fight now?

Oh no. Gods help me.

7
CHAPTER SEVEN

Well. This was it. This is how I would die.

Murdoc paced before me like a caged panther, his expression as cold as a winter's night as he sized me up from across Ms. Lin's small courtyard. Five of her kids were lined up at the windows, their noses mashed against the glass as they watched us.

I had an audience again. Great.

"I thought you were going to teach me to shoot the crossbow?" I mumbled as I looked down at the shortsword in my hand.

"Any moron can shoot a crossbow. You look down the sight, hold your breath to steady your aim, and fire. Even you can't mess that up. Lesson over," he replied sharply. "You need to learn to handle a blade. Ranged weapons like that are not going to be of any use when you have an enemy right in your face."

My shoulders dropped. Not this again. Hadn't I already made enough of a fool of myself trying to learn this? It just wasn't in the cards for me. I wasn't meant to be a swordsman.

"You have three problems," Murdoc growled as he reached back to draw one of his longswords from the sheath at his back.

"O-Only three?" That didn't sound so bad.

"Yes." He glanced down at the weapon as he gave a few artful swipes through the air as though testing the weight. "First of all, you're a coward."

I deflated. "Oh."

"But, ironically, only when your own life is in danger," he continued. "When it comes to fighting for someone else, you're able to focus and act accordingly."

"Is, uh, is that something you can fix?"

He stopped pacing and turned to face me. "No."

Oh. Well, crap.

"But *you* can." He pointed the end of his blade at me. "You need to keep your place in this situation firmly in mind. You need to remember that your life is no longer your own. If you die, your dragon becomes riderless again and likely devolves back into the state you found him in—confined to a dark cell for the rest of his life. Is that what you want for him?"

A little spark of panicked anger flickered to life deep in my chest. Gods and Fates, he was right. What would happen to Fornax if I got killed? Who would take care of him? Where would he go?

"No," I answered at last.

"Then act like it. Fight like it. Convince me and anyone else you cross blades with that you mean it." Murdoc nodded to the sword in my hand. "Your second problem is your choice of weapon."

I blinked down at my sword. This wasn't the right weapon for me? Jaevid tested me on so many. None of them had felt right, honestly. But the short sword had been the least awkward in my grip.

"You're not very physically strong. You're also on the short side. But if your shot the other time was any testament, you seem to have decent reflexes. That means you'll do better with a smaller, shorter weapon that can strike from close range at speed." Murdoc surmised. "A xiphos would be ideal."

"A xiph-what?"

"It's not a common blade here, unfortunately. My handler, Rook, used one as his primary hand weapon. They're nimbler than a shortsword. Lighter, too. The double-edged blade has a more exaggerated leaf-shape and the grips are short and don't have a crossguard on the hilt. Makes for easier handling for quick movements in close combat."

I swallowed hard. "Is there somewhere we can get one?"

He shrugged. "I don't know. Ideally, you'd have one made especially for your height and weight. It doesn't matter now, though. You'll have to keep making do with what you've got."

"I, um, I might be able to help with that." From where he sat on a small bench in the far corner of the courtyard, Jondar cleared his throat and sat up a little straighter. Two days after his near-deadly beating in the alley, his injuries finally seemed to be healing. He could open his bruised-up eye again, although it still looked swollen and painful.

Murdoc stared at him with a brow raised curiously. "Is that so?"

Jondar nodded and stammered, "I-I, well, I work as a swordsmith's apprentice most days. I can't do much until my rib heals enough that I can work the forge again, so my patron told me come back in next week." He flushed slightly and looked down. "When I go back, though, I can probably make something that suits you. Master Porter says I'm fairly skilled. He even lets me fill orders on my own now."

"Interesting," Murdoc mused as he gave him another once-over glance from head to foot. "Is that where the sword in your room came from?"

Jondar's whole head turned as red as a radish—all the way to the tips of his pointed ears. "N-No! That, um, that one was my father's. But I did repair it after some of the soldiers brought it back to Mum after the battle. The blade was battered and bent. It felt wrong to leave it like that."

"All right, then." Murdoc nodded, his lips pursed thoughtfully. Then he turned back to me. "This brings us to your last problem."

I tensed. I was a coward and I was apparently using the wrong weapon—what else could possibly be wrong?

"Put that blade away," he commanded as he did the same with his own longsword.

Huh? We weren't using swords? But I thought we'd come out here so he could teach me combat?

Turning around, Murdoc bent long enough to grab two apples from the basket he'd brought from the kitchen earlier.

I smiled. Wow, was it time for a snack break already? Excellent timing. I'd been too distracted to eat much breakfast after—

An apple smacked me right in the middle of my forehead.

I flailed and staggered back, trying to stay on my feet. What the ... ? Had Murdoc just *thrown* that at me?

"Hey! That hurt!" I fumed as I rubbed at the throbbing place where the apple had hit me.

"Then catch the next one," he warned.

"What?" I'd barely managed to glare back at him when another apple came sailing right at me like a comet. This one smacked me right in the cheek.

"I meant catch it with your hands, not your face."

"Stop that!" I yelled.

"I'll stop when you catch them," he snarled back. "With one hand. Go!"

Another apple rocketed straight for me. Stumbling, I threw up a hand and tried to grab it.

I missed.

The apple cracked me across the nose, making my eyes water as I hissed a few curses under my breath.

"Faster, idiot," Murdoc growled again.

"I-I think you broke my nose!"

"No, I didn't." He sighed and rearmed himself with more apples.

"You're throwing them way too fast! Nobody could catch that!"

"Stop being a baby. Don't try to think, just catch."

Two more apples later—either out of desperation or sheer wrath because of all the times he'd hit me in the face—I finally managed to throw a hand up and snatched one out of the air right in front of my face.

Whoa ... I gaped in surprise as I held it up for him to see.

Murdoc gave an approving smirk. "Again."

He threw them faster. He threw some high so I had to jump and reach for them. Others he spun low so I had to lunge down to grab them before they skipped off the stone floor of the courtyard. It wasn't pretty. Half the time, it felt like I was just floundering around wildly. But I didn't miss a single one.

"Good." He actually sounded pleased as he crossed his arms and nodded to the last apple still resting in my hand. "Now, which hand is that?"

I frowned down at the shiny red apple in my palm. "Uh, my left?" Couldn't he see that from where he was standing? I'd been catching them in that hand the whole time.

"And which hand do you use to grip your sword?" he asked.

I had to think about that for a minute. "My right one." That's the one Jaevid, Reigh, and everyone else had told me to use.

"Exactly." Murdoc's dark, earth-toned eyes glimmered with wicked delight as his smirk broadened. "You've been using the wrong one. You're a left-handed swordsman, Thatcher."

"Sloppy. And you're still too slow. Again." Murdoc's voice snapped over me like the bite of a whip.

Sweat drizzled down the sides of my face and neck as I sprang into a forward strike, my sword—in my left hand—slashing through the air with a deadly hissing hum. My blade clashed with his with enough force to make all my teeth rattle.

"Strike two," he barked. "Stop hesitating."

I whipped around into a tight spin, making another fast, sideways slash. *CLANG!* Our blades met again. I froze in place. My heart pounded and my fingers ached. My shoulders burned. It hurt. But for the first time, everything about this felt so ... *right*.

"Watch your footing. Parry up."

He surged in, as fast as a striking viper. I drew back, moving in perfect sync to shift my balance and angle my blade up to block his attack.

"Still too slow. Disarm."

I twisted my hold, ducking under his next strike as I sidestepped. My blade scraped down his until our hilts bashed together with a *clang*. I wrenched mine sideways with one brutal jerk, yanking his sword out of his grip and sending it clattering across the stones out of reach.

"Now finish it."

I immediately drove my right elbow back into his gut right below his sternum. He sputtered a wheezing gasp and stumbled back, losing his balance just in time for me to hook a toe under his ankle and sweep his leg out from under him. As Murdoc fell back, I ducked into another fast spin. I dropped low, landing on a knee beside him as he hit the ground—the point of my blade poised perfectly over his heart.

We stayed like that for a second or two, panting and staring at one another while I waited for another command. Then, Murdoc's frosty glare cracked. He smiled. Flopping back on the ground with his arms wide, my sword still barely an inch over his chest, he chuckled between gasping breaths.

"Not bad," he rasped.

I was too stunned to make a sound. Or move. Gods and Fates ... he'd managed to teach me all this in *one* lesson?! Jaevid had spent weeks trying to drill combat moves into my head, and none of it had worked. How? How had he known how to instruct me like this? How had he known that I was using the wrong sword-hand? Jaevid was older, wasn't he? He probably had a lot more actual experience in combat, too. So why was Murdoc the only one that could actually teach me anything when it came to swordplay?

I wanted to ask. But as I put my sword aside and dropped back onto my rear end on the ground beside him, the door to the courtyard burst open and footsteps stomped quickly over toward us. I squinted up through my sweat-soaked bangs that were sticking to my face.

Reigh stood over me, his mouth hanging open and his face the picture of complete shock. Er, at least, I thought it was Reigh. Something was off. I narrowed my eyes a little as I studied him harder. Hmm.

Then it hit me. He'd cut all his hair off! His one long rope of dark red, braided hair was gone—lopped off right at his jawline. But, wait, hadn't he worn it long before because it was a Gray elf tradition? I mean, sure, he was a human. He'd been raised in Luntharda, so he still honored a lot of their customs and traditions. So why had he cut it off now?

Before I could think of a good way to ask, Reigh snapped his mouth shut and gave Murdoc a hard look. "You—how did you do that? I sparred with this kid. He was utterly useless."

I set my jaw and tried really hard to get my eyes to smolder like Murdoc's whenever someone annoyed him. "I'm not that much younger than you, you know," I grumbled. The way he kept calling me a kid all the time was like his way of establishing dominance or something. Annoying. And stupid. I mean, yes, I was shorter and scrawnier. But still ...

Reigh held up a finger as though to silence me before I even tried to say another word. "Spill it, Murdoc. How'd you get him fighting like that so fast? I was barely gone for two hours."

My cunning, former-assassin friend didn't move from where he lay on the ground. Instead, he put his hands behind his head and grinned. "I would tell you, but then I'd have to kill you. It's one of those secret *assassin* things, you understand."

"Oh, right, I forgot the part where being a deadly assassin automatically makes you a good combat instructor." Reigh's tone was practically dripping with sarcasm. "Seriously, how'd you do that?"

Murdoc rolled his eyes. "In this case, it does. You were trained by the Gray Elves to become a scout. Jaevid was trained by dragonriders in their style of combat. Both are sufficient for most situations, but neither are meant to do more than keep you alive in the throes of battle. They're also steeped in that mindset of tradition—which is fine, at times, but it can also keep anyone from improving flaws in older techniques."

Reigh's expression tightened, becoming skeptical. "Oh? And the Ulfrangar fighting style has all that solved, right?"

"Yes," he replied evenly. "The Ulfrangar methods have been cultivated over thousands of years and are refined constantly to ensure dominance, stealth, and efficiency. It's an art. A lifestyle. Not a survival measure. Like comparing the techniques of a guard dog to a wolf—that's what our handlers say. Dogs fight well to defend their turf, but they are seldom the aggressors and they know, eventually, reinforcements are coming. A wolf crafts its hunt to be dynamic, considering the opposing threat, and using his pack and the elements of his environment to his advantage. And because Ulfrangar ultimately wind up training one another, knowing how to evaluate and teach is every bit as vital as learning it yourself. The two always go hand-in-hand." Murdoc closed his eyes as he lay there, crossing an ankle over his knee leisurely. "I was still a pup when I defected, but if I'd stayed, I would have ultimately ended up teaching my own pup in ten years or so."

Reigh's mouth scrunched up like he'd bitten into something sour. I guess he didn't have a snappy reply for that.

I, on the other hand, stared at Murdoc in shock. He'd never talked about the Ulfrangar this much before. Granted, I didn't understand half of what he said. What did it mean to be a "pup?" Was that like being an apprentice or something?

"Did that dragon of yours scorch your hair off or something?" Murdoc asked, suddenly changing the subject.

Reigh didn't answer and his expression was still drawn into a dissatisfied scowl as he stalked away, his hands crammed into his pockets. He hesitated at the door that led from the courtyard back into the house and glanced over his shoulder. "We got word from Jaevid. Judan's agent is going to make contact today. I expect we'll get orders to go somewhere else, so pack up. I want to be ready to move as soon as we know what our next move is."

Murdoc's eyes popped open. "To Northwatch?"

"I don't know. Maybe. He wasn't specific," Reigh muttered. "He didn't want to risk giving any detailed information or plans in writing in case our letters got intercepted. So the agent is supposed to meet us at the tavern tonight at dusk."

"Good." Murdoc's tone seemed approving as he sat up and flicked me a quick sideways glance. "There's something else we should address with him."

I scrunched my brows and frowned. Something else? What was he talking about?

"Like what?" Reigh sounded suspicious, too.

"I have reason to believe we are being followed," Murdoc answered flatly as he pushed himself back up to his feet.

Reigh gave an exaggerated eye roll. "Of course we are. I'm surprised we don't have a whole parade of assassins following us around at this point."

Murdoc offered a hand to pull me up, as well. "I'm not talking about them."

"Then who?" I dared to ask.

"The shapeshifting girl, for starters. She's been following us since Halfax, but after our encounter at the Cromwell estate, she's hanging closer than ever. If she's surveilling us for Devana, then—"

"She's not!" I interrupted quickly. "That is, um, I'm pretty sure she's not. She's on our side, I think."

Murdoc's eyes narrowed on me. "You *think*?"

Okay, fine. I didn't know that for sure. I didn't know much about Isandri at all. But after talking with her, I just couldn't imagine that she was working for Devana. If anything, it seemed like Isandri was on her own separate mission—something to do with Devana that she didn't trust me enough to talk about. But she wasn't a bad person. She wasn't our enemy. Somehow, I just *knew* that. After all, she'd fought alongside us at the Cromwell estate. She'd helped us. If she was serving Devana, then wouldn't she want us dead, too?

Right. Well, convincing Reigh and Murdoc about all that was another matter, though. The epitome of futile, probably.

"You're talking about the elf, right?" Reigh crossed his arms and struck a stubborn pose with his chin tipped up slightly.

Murdoc snorted like he found that funny somehow. "Calling her merely an elf is a hilarious understatement. She's obviously a Lunostri. Probably a shalnii from Damaria or Nar'Haleen based on her abilities."

Um, a shal-what? Wait, how did he even know she had abilities? I mean, obviously she did. But he hadn't actually seen her shapeshift, had he? Or maybe he'd seen it when she, Phoebe, and Reigh had arrived at the dragonrider tower?

My brain scrambled as I tried to decide what to ask first. Before I could make up my mind, Reigh spoke up. "Whatever she is, I don't have issues with her following us—not so long as she keeps fighting on our side when it counts. We met before the war ended, and so far, she hasn't given me any reason not to trust her."

Murdoc shrugged. "Fair enough. But then there's the matter of the dragon."

Reigh's eyebrows shot up. "Dragon?"

"It's been following us since the Cromwell estate, too. Granted, it's keeping a wide berth. I've only caught a few glimpses from afar. But it's definitely tracking our movements," Murdoc confirmed. "Believe me, I *know* when I'm being hunted, and that thing is definitely hunting us."

"Could it be a wild dragon? Or ... ?" I looked at Reigh, hoping he had some clue or reason for that—preferably one that didn't involve anyone being maimed or burned alive.

Reigh shook his head and waved a hand dismissively as he turned away to leave the courtyard. "It's probably Jaevid's. Or one of his informants keeping an eye on us. I wouldn't put it past him to set several creatures on our trail like that now that he knows what we're up against."

Somehow, that explanation didn't sit well with me. Jaevid had said before that he couldn't talk to animals anymore. He'd lost all his divine powers at the end of the Tibran War. So how could he use a dragon to keep track of us like that? Unless ... well, he might've had his king drake give the order. But that still didn't make sense. Dragons didn't communicate telepathically, either. It wouldn't be able to tell the king drake anything about us, or even go and get him in time to help us. Hmm. Something about this wasn't right.

And one look at Murdoc's steely, concerned expression told me he must've felt the same way.

8
CHAPTER EIGHT

"Oh! If we're about to leave Dayrise, then maybe we'll have a chance to let you test out my newest piece of gear for you and Fornax!" Phoebe bounced excitedly along beside me all the way to Ms. Lin's front door. "I think you'll like it! Oh, um, at least, I hope you will. It's still a bit finicky. These divine artifacts never like to be tampered with much. But I'm nearly ready for a real test flight!"

I managed a tense, probably painfully forced-looking smile at her and nodded. But I couldn't bring myself to reply. Not when my mind was a literal snowstorm of worries.

We'd hurried through packing our bags and stacking them by the door, ready to grab and go in case we got orders to leave the city immediately. It'd taken a few minutes of yelling and name-calling for Reigh and Murdoc to finally settle on a plan about how we were going to go and meet Judan's agent. Reigh and I were heading out first, going a little ahead of the meetup time to saddle the dragons and prep them for departure in case we needed to leave in a hurry. Meanwhile, Phoebe and Murdoc would come just after dusk so we could all speak to Judan's agent together. It was safer, Reigh thought, for us to split up that way. We'd force our pursuers to split their forces, too, since Murdoc and I were their primary targets. Having us separated meant Phillip and the Ulfrangar would have to track two moving targets instead of just one.

It sounded good to me. Murdoc didn't like it, though. Not one bit. He didn't like having me out of his sight. I guess he wasn't confident at all that if we encountered Phillip or Ulfrangar while we were out, neither Reigh nor I would be able to fend them off.

A valid concern, really, even if Reigh didn't want to admit it.

"Look, if you go with us, we're definitely looking at having the Ulfrangar on our heels," Reigh had reasoned, somehow managing to stare straight into Murdoc's furious glare without spontaneously combusting. Incredible. "If it's just Thatcher here, then we may only have Phillip to contend with. He's strong, yes. But he's just one person. And we'll have the dragons on our side."

"You hope," Murdoc had seethed.

The argument hadn't ended there, of course. But whenever they rolled into one of their venomous snapping matches, it was really hard for me to resist the urge to take a brief, mental break from reality until they worked it out. Eventually, Reigh managed to convince him that this was the best of all our terrible options. Phoebe couldn't fight at all, and having all our bags with us would slow us down.

So off we went.

I tried not to let my anxiety show as I stopped at the door, waiting for Reigh to finish lugging his saddlebag down the stairs. Not that I was nervous about using whatever invention Phoebe had come up with for us. That wasn't it, at all.

With or without a plan, leaving Ms. Lin's house felt like leaving the safety of a hidden bunker in the middle of a battle—even if Murdoc insisted it was riskier to stay here than being out in public. Maybe he was right. The Ulfrangar didn't want to be drawn out into the public eye, and going after us while we were out in the open in a busy city was about as public as you could get.

As Reigh and I stepped out the front door, I couldn't stop myself from searching the sidewalks and alleyways we passed for anyone who looked like they might be an Ulfrangar. Or Phillip. Or Devana.

Not that I even knew what Devana actually looked like, but still.

The tavern where we'd left our dragons stabled wasn't too far from the Crosswall Docks. We kept to the main thoroughfares where the foot traffic was heavier, falling in line with people coming to and from the seaside markets. I stuck close at Reigh's side, my hand resting on the hilt of my shortsword as we wound our way through city squares to a quieter set of streets. With my crossbow slung across my back, I felt a little more prepared this time. At least I had a better idea of what to do if someone attacked me. But after only one lesson, I seriously doubted I would last more than a second or two against someone like Phillip. Or an Ulfrangar. Or basically anyone with actual combat training.

A ragged sigh of release slipped past my lips as I spotted the tavern at the far end of a steep avenue. There weren't all that many taverns around Dayrise that had room to house dragons, but the owner at the first tavern we'd tried had given us directions to this place and insisted they should have plenty of space.

Towering at over five stories, the huge rectangular building was unlike any I'd ever seen before—even in Halfax. It definitely stood out, with an entire top floor constructed sort of like a miniature version of the Deck back at the royal castle. That top level had been built especially to stable dragons, with a series of open stall doorways facing out. Each stall had a small landing platform, and a big door that could be rolled closed from the inside.

I smiled. My dragon was in there waiting for me. I wondered if I blew my whistle from this distance, if he would still be able to hear it. Probably.

Making our way to the front of the tavern, I glanced at the big wooden sign posted by the front steps that was painted so that each letter looked like a little dragon, curling into the right shape to spell out the words: THE DRAGON DEN.

The first floor was exactly what you'd expect from a tavern so close to the port—noisy, smelly, and packed thick with sailors and dockworkers. The clatter of dishware, barks of laughter, and rumble of loud conversation filled the air. The massive hearth at the far end of the room had been made to look like a dragon's open mouth, the flames of a fire crackling inside.

No one even looked up as we passed through the dining area, slipping around the tables crowded with patrons to the stairwell on the other side of the room. The second floor was pretty much the same as the first—just a second sprawling dining area where barmaids in fluffy white skirts and aprons carried trays of mugs and dinner plates. The third and fourth floors were much quieter, and aside from a few private gambling parlors, seemed to mostly be rooms for rent.

The stairwell ended at the door to the fifth floor—which was a bit more substantial, to say the least. It had a massive iron bolt and metal plating, and the huge hinges groaned as Reigh lugged it open and let me go first. Beyond that door, a narrow hall led between the stalls for the dragons. The air smelled thick and musty, like old hay and that unmistakable musk of animals. Bizarre noises beyond some of the closed stall doors made me wonder if there might be a shrike or two in here, as well.

"Get him saddled up and ready for flight," Reigh ordered as he dropped his own bag before the stall door where his sleek, green dragoness was stabled. "Once I'm done, I'll head downstairs and wait for the others. You stay here, eh?"

I nodded and took off for the next stall at a jog.

Throwing open the large bolt, I slipped the whistle that hung around my neck on Jaevid's necklace between my lips and gave a few shrill notes. Beyond the door, I heard something massive moving around. The door rumbled against my hand. I grinned. Fornax.

Rolling the heavy wooden door ajar, I slipped inside—

—and crashed right into a dragon's giant snout.

My massive scaly monster gave a low, vibrating chirp deep in his throat as he took in a deep breath of my scent that sucked up the front of my tunic. His milky, jade-green eyes stared in my direction, not actually seeing me.

I let the whistle drop from my mouth as I rubbed a hand along his snout. "Hey, big guy. Miss me? Told you I'd come back."

His scaly ears swiveled forward, listening as he chirped curiously. Coiled before me in the small stall, his massive orange and black body filled the cramped space like a mountain of shining scales. This wasn't a great place to keep him, and I didn't feel good at all about making him stay packed in here any longer. It was easier on Reigh's dragoness. She was smaller, younger, and didn't have all the muscular bulk he did.

"Don't you worry, it won't be much longer," I promised as I moved around him, running my hands down his thick neck to his side. Whether or not we got orders to leave the city, I'd take him for a flight so he could stretch his wings a little and breathe some free air. "Have they been feeding you enough?"

He gave a low grumbling growl and nipped at my back, still blasting me with his smelly dragon breath as I went to check his saddle. I'd left it hanging off a series of hooks arranged on one of the walls. Not an ideal way to store a dragon's saddle, according to Reigh, but it would work temporarily.

Fornax chirped and chattered as I crawled all over him, slipping the heavy saddle over the ridge of spines that ran down his back. It fit against his body like a glove, formed so that the underside settled perfectly over those spines right between his neck and wing arms. Working in that cramped space left me sweaty and out of breath when I finally stood back to admire my work. I'd done it all just the way Jaevid had taught me, careful to check every buckle three times before I moved on. No doubt it'd taken me a lot longer than Reigh, but he had way more experience doing this.

"How about I open the door and let some fresh air in, eh?" I panted as I wiped the sweat that dripped down my face onto my sleeve. It took all my strength and bodyweight to get the outer door open. Leaning against it fully, I heaved and groaned as I forced it along the rusted metal tracks built into the floor and ceiling. Cool wind rushed in, rustling in my hair and tingling over my face and neck. Much better.

Now for the other one. I went back to the much smaller door that led into the narrow interior corridor. I'd only left it cracked a little—just enough for me to slip inside. It'd feel much better to open it the rest of the way and let the wind blow through, right? Maybe it'd clear out some of that musty smell, too.

Stepping back out into the corridor between the rows of stalls, I set my jaw and braced myself to start dragging the heavy door open the rest of the way. I squared my footing and took in a deep breath. A few good pushes were all it'd need.

A hand clapped down hard over my mouth, crushing my face with incredible force so that I couldn't make a sound.

FEAR SHOT through my chest like an icy arrow.

I pitched and kicked wildly. I clawed at the hand and flailed with all my strength. But it was no use. Someone much bigger and far stronger than me dragged me off my footing and into the stall directly across from mine in a matter of seconds.

Oh gods. Who was this?! Was it Phillip? Was he about to kill me? Reigh! Where was Reigh?!

I reached for my sword. Maybe if I could just—

"I wouldn't recommend that, boy," a deep voice growled quietly right in my ear.

Wait, that ... that wasn't Phillip. It did sound like a man, but the tone was eerily smooth and tinged with an accent I'd knew I'd heard somewhere before. But where?

"Calm down, hold still, and listen. I didn't come for your life, but I may take it just for spite," the man muttered, seeming to bite angrily at every hushed word.

All the blood drained from my face. I went as stiff as a corpse in his grasp, barely daring to blink as my heartbeat boomed in my ears.

"You've no idea the trouble you've caused," he snapped, "the mess you've made. The blood that will now undoubtedly be spilt because of your bumbling ignorance."

W-What? What was he talking about? Maybe he was mistaken. Maybe he thought I was someone else, or—

"Murdoc will die because of you," he fumed, still keeping his voice down so softly that my dragon probably couldn't even hear it. "Because you tempted him away too soon. Calling him friend. Treating him like some feral dog you thought you could tame. You little *fool*. You really have no idea what you've done, do you?"

Okay, nope, he definitely had the right person. But he didn't move his hand even long enough to let me breathe, let alone try to explain myself.

"Things are in motion now that cannot be undone. You've put *my* pup right in her path," he snarled. "So now you are going to do something for me. The only thing that might stop this before it's too late."

Wait a second, did he say ... *his* pup? Did that mean this was Murdoc's handler? The Ulfrangar man who'd trained him?

My brain scrambled, trying to come to terms with that. He'd only mentioned him to me once, and his name ... Gods and Fates, I couldn't remember what it was. R-something. Root? No, that wasn't right. It didn't matter, though. Why did it sound like he wanted to help Murdoc? Wasn't this guy supposed to be hunting him down with the rest of the Ulfrangar?

"They're coming for him. Right now, as we speak. They'll make their move to force him out into the open. They will burn that house you've been hiding in to the ground, staging it as an accident, and take him during the chaos," the man warned. "They'll block all the exits but the roof, and as the spectators and crowds gather to help put out the blaze, they will make their move."

Oh ... oh gods. They were going to burn down Ms. Lin's house? Right now?!

"Murdoc is strong. Before this, such an obvious tactic would have never worked. But now his sight has been clouded by you and the rest of those kids he's herding around. He's not even considering his own survival. He will panic. He'll try to save the others. They're counting on that—on finding him amidst the flames. And he won't escape this time, not unless you intervene first. So you must follow my instructions *exactly*." His tone sharpened, carrying an unspoken threat. Disobeying him would most likely be a deadly mistake for me. "You see that pile of gear there?"

I blinked through the terror that made my vision swim, finally spotting a pile of black cloth tucked into the far corner of the empty stall. I nodded as much as his grip on me would allow.

"That is Ulfrangar gear. You will put it on and leave this tavern alone immediately. Return to the house as fast as you can. Perhaps you'll make it there before the fire starts, but it's unlikely at this point," he explained quickly. "I will make sure that the front door can be opened if you push hard enough at the very base of it. Force your way inside and go to the very top floor. There, we will make certain that *you*—not Murdoc—are taken captive. I have already ensured that the hunters sent for this mission are ones who have never seen Murdoc in the flesh before. They won't question it when I identify you."

I choked and whimpered, my throat closing around a cold, hard knot of fear like I'd tried to swallow a lump of ice. Oh gods. He was going to make sure they kidnapped me instead of Murdoc? But what then? Surely they'd figure it out eventually, right? I didn't look anything like Murdoc, after all. I wasn't even a good enough fighter to pretend for long.

"Just keep your mouth shut as much as you can. The longer we can carry on this ruse, the better Murdoc's chances of escape along with the rest of your little friends will be." His hold on me relaxed ever so slightly. "I'm going to release you now. It would be in your best interest not to turn around. Stay just as you are and do as I've told you." He gave a small, ironic snort of a laugh. "And take heart, boy. Whatever wrathful, violent ideas you have about me likely won't go to waste. Once we are discovered, the Ulfrangar will kill us both. But perhaps Murdoc will have enough time and sense to use this opportunity, while their gaze is averted, to disappear once and for all. It will be his final chance."

I shut my eyes tightly, still struggling to breathe around his hand as my mind raced. Then, suddenly, his hand disappeared. He gave me a violent shove from behind that sent me sprawling face-first into the floor. I landed in a heap, sucking in rasping breaths and spitting out mouthfuls of hay.

"Now," the man growled low as something that must've been one of his boots landed square on my back and pinned me there, lying on my belly. "Do as I say. And see that you don't screw it up. His life depends on it."

CHAPTER NINE

By the time I managed to stagger back to my feet and whirl around, the man—Murdoc's Ulfrangar handler—had vanished like a ghost without a single trace. He wasn't in the stall. He wasn't in the hallway outside. Reigh was downstairs waiting for our contact already so ... it was just me.

A cold thrill of panic surged up my spine all the way out to the ends of my fingers. The Ulfrangar were about to burn down Ms. Lin's house with her and the rest of her family inside. They might be there already. And I was the only one who knew about it.

I was the only one who could save Murdoc.

My hands shook as I scrambled to put on the long dark cloak and all the pieces of Ulfrangar gear stacked in the corner. The black leather vambraces were something I'd only seen Murdoc wear once, back when we first met. They gleamed in the weak light of the stable, crafted from silver and engraved with the relief of a snarling wolf's head. A wolf with three eyes.

Just the sight of that beast made my stomach turn. What was I doing? I... I should tell Reigh. I should go to him right now. But if I did, we might be too late. We might not be able to stop them from taking Murdoc. And it would be my fault.

The pair of gleaming weapons lying at the bottom of the stack were almost exactly like Murdoc's, too. A pair of slender blades fitted into a cross sheath that buckled across my back. My sweaty fingers slipped over the silver-plated buckles as I fastened the straps over my chest. I wouldn't be able to fight with them. I couldn't wield a blade like he could. So even trying to use them was out of the question. They'd know right away I wasn't really an Ulfrangar.

Pulling the hood over my head to cover as much of my face as I could, I took a deep, steadying breath. I could do this. I had to. Murdoc was my friend. I wouldn't let those monsters take him.

"Fornax," I called out as I rushed across the hallway back into his stall.

He met me with a series of low chirps, ears swiveling as he flicked the end of his tail restlessly. I blew a series of commands on the whistle that made him perk up some. He rose up, stirring in his stall and puffing heavy breaths through his nostrils. That Ulfrangar man had told me to go alone. But I wasn't about to go anywhere without my dragon. We were two halves of the same whole. And if I was going to stand any chance at all of coming out of this alive, I would definitely need his help.

After all, I'd already proven once that while Ulfrangar were probably the best in the world at fighting other people—they didn't hold up all that well to dragonfire.

"I'm counting on you, buddy," I said, my voice still trembling a little as I gave him one last, quick scratch under the chin. Then I had to go.

Bending down, I quickly slipped my necklace off and tucked it, whistle and all, into the side of my boot. Maybe the Ulfrangar wouldn't search there.

I ran for the doorway and bolted down the stairs, blitzing right past all the other floors and arriving in the dining hall on the first floor with my head down, hood up, and face turned away. Skirting along the edge of the room, I made a wide berth around where Reigh stood at the bar. With his back turned to the rest of dining area, he didn't even seem to look my way.

My insides stirred and swirled, like I'd swallowed a fistful of live eels, as I ducked out the tavern's front door. Doubt made me stop, but only for a second. No. I couldn't get him involved. Someone had to be here when Judan's agent showed up. Regardless of what happened to me, Murdoc, or anyone else—Devana still had to be caught. That mission had to go on.

As soon as my boots hit the street, I took off in a sprint. Ahead, the setting sun had already begun to sink below the far horizon. There wasn't much time.

My feet flew, heart pumping wildly and lungs burning, as I ducked and dodged through the crowds near the market. I smacked right into a lady carrying a basket full of bread. She screamed and loaves went flying, but I couldn't stop.

Now—I had to get there now!

Skidding around the last corner, I whipped onto the street where Ms. Lin's house stood only a few blocks down.

But it was no good. I could already see it even from that distance.

The glow of flames against the gathering dusk. Smoke boiling up into the blood-red sky. A crowd gathering. Men running with buckets of water. Women screaming. Children crying.

Everything seemed to go numb. I couldn't even feel my own face, or the movement of my mouth, as a sound ripped out of my throat like a primal scream of rage and panic. Ms. Lin's house—it was already on fire!

There wasn't time to second guess it. I had to do this. Now.

Pushing and shoving my way through the crowd, I surged up the steps to the front door. Several big men were already there, trying to force the door ajar so they could get in, but they weren't having any luck. Others had already smashed out the front window and were trying to climb inside.

That man, though. He'd said to hit it low. So, I dropped down and charged straight for it without ever slowing down, slamming my shoulder into the door with a *CRACK*!

The door burst open, popping off the lowest hinge and crashing inward. I crashed with it, tripping and falling into a heap in the foyer. Immediately, the sweltering heat of the flames roared around me. Heat scorched my face and seemed to suck all the air right out of my lungs.

But there wasn't time. I couldn't stop now.

Shielding my face as best I could with one hand, I stumbled through the maze of licking flames and swirling embers. The living room was gone—already consumed. Ahead of me, the hallway leading to the kitchen was like a vortex straight into the abyss, with flames climbing the walls and fanning out over the ceiling. I coughed and wheezed, staggering forward until I reached the staircase. Gods, where was everyone? Jondar? Ms. Lin? Phoebe? Murdoc?

I didn't see any sign of them until I reached the top floor. There, in the narrow hallway choked with smoke, the door to Ms. Lin's room was shut. It looked like someone had stuffed rags along the floor to fill in the gap underneath it.

I halted before it, staring at the door through the inferno and boiling plumes of black smoke. It hurt just to keep my eyes open, and there was no way to be sure, yet ... somehow, I just knew. Murdoc was in there with the others. Probably working out a plan to escape. I could've sworn I heard glass smashing somewhere in there. Breaking out the windows?

Oh no. I had to hurry. If Murdoc was about to go outside, then I had to be sure the Ulfrangar caught me before any of them that might be lurking outside spotted him.

Bolting the distance to the storage room, I threw open the door—

—and came face-to-face with an Ulfrangar assassin.

THE MAN GLOWERED DOWN at me, easily twice my size, with most of his face obscured by smears of black paint. The glow of the flames shone off his dark leather armor and silver-plated vambraces. His eyes shone in hues of deep gold, seeming to reflect the firelight as he took a step toward me.

On instinct, I cringed back. I threw up my hands and nearly tripped over my own feet.

His mouth drew into a snarl, baring his teeth as he lunged suddenly and caught me by the front of my shirt and snatched me back. "Found you," he bellowed.

That voice—there was no mistaking it. This was the man who'd caught me at the tavern. This was Murdoc's handler, the man who had trained him to be an Ulfrangar.

Somehow, I'd expected him to be younger. Maybe closer to Jaevid or Aubren's age. But his short-cut dark hair was speckled with gray and he had deep, weary lines around those piercing golden eyes as he drew me up onto my toes and rumbled right in my face, "You'd better play along, boy."

I nodded frantically. Then, in what I hoped was typical Murdoc fashion, I took a wild swing at him.

He seemed nearly as stunned as I was when my fist cracked over his cheek. It made his head snap sideways, but his vice-grip hold on my tunic didn't slacken at all. Something like infernal wrath danced and flickered in his eyes as he slowly turned his head back to glare down at me again.

I did my best to glare back.

"Rook!" Someone who sounded a good bit younger shouted from behind the man. "We must hurry! They've called for the city guard! Have you found him?"

Rook dragged me the rest of the way into the storage room and slammed the door, closing us both inside. I resisted, even trying a few of the sparring moves Murdoc had shown me, as he tried pushing me toward the small hatch door in the roof. Through that opening, I caught a fleeting glimpse of several other assassins peering down at us from beneath their cowls.

It was no good, though.

As I reared back to take another mad swing at him, Rook blocked easily. He moved as fast as a striking viper and struck me once over the side of the head. My vision immediately went starry and I dropped to my knees. Everything tunneled to darkness as I keeled over sideways.

"Yes," he thundered over me disapprovingly. "Throw down the tethers and send word to our men in the street to depart. I have found our traitor."

PART THREE
MURDOC

10
CHAPTER TEN

Even during the height of my training as an Ulfrangar—when I'd been so deeply consumed in their practices that it wakened a dark and vicious appetite deep in my soul—I had never even dreamed that I might be compelled to murder a member of any royal family. Jobs like that were reserved for the most proficient and experienced hunters from among our ranks, after all, and the very thought of being involved in something that would impact an entire kingdom's worth of people was daunting. I wasn't sure if I wanted that kind of blood on my hands.

Until today.

Reigh Farrow, his royal *highness*, was proving to be a constant pain in my rear end. How, by all the Fates, someone hadn't already paid off an assassin to slit his throat was beyond me. But at this rate, it wouldn't even be necessary. He'd blunder his way right into a gruesome demise all on his own. Probably tonight, at this rate.

Or he'd make another snide comment that finally made me snap, and I'd push him in front of an oncoming merchant wagon.

Either way would've suited me fine, honestly.

The only problem was that, once again, he'd dragged Thatcher off with him. Split up? Divide our forces? Sure, I had my doubts that the Ulfrangar would really work alongside an outsider like Phillip. But I wasn't certain enough about that to hang anyone's life on it.

Unlike Reigh.

"I could go with them," Jondar murmured as he stood next to me in the doorway, watching them disappear into the midafternoon crowds down the street. "But I'd probably draw too much attention, especially at a tavern."

I glanced up at him with a brow arched. "Can you even use that sword you've got hidden away in your room?"

He flushed all the way to the tips of his pointed ears. "I-I, um, well sort of. My father had begun teaching me. You know, before he passed. He wanted me to be able to take care of Mum and protect her if I had to. But I doubt I could hold up against someone like you."

I licked my teeth behind my lips. The son of the warrior who had butchered two hundred Tibrans in the battle for Dayrise couldn't even hold his own in a duel? What a waste.

"Eventually, you'll have to decide if you're going to take up that weapon again and honor your father's legacy, or carry on being a coward," I retorted, maybe a little too harshly.

His head dipped some and he looked away, his brow drawing up into a fretful look of humiliation. As though that dilemma was one he'd already thought about a thousand times. It didn't seem like he was any closer to an answer, though. Especially if he was still getting his nose kicked in by half-drunken thugs in alleyways.

"They'll be okay, won't they?" Phoebe murmured softly. She'd been standing at my side, staying so quiet and still, I'd almost completely forgotten she was there at all.

I turned away to go back into the house. It didn't feel right to even try answering that question. Maybe, by some small miracle, Reigh was right. Maybe splitting up would confuse the Ulfrangar temporarily—force them to adjust plans—and prevent an immediate attack.

But deep down, I knew that wasn't the case. They were already watching us closely. And after our little exchange at the Cromwell estate, I had no doubts they'd bring at least ten hunters. Possibly more, or an elder or two. I'd slipped out of their grasp once. They wouldn't allow for it a second time.

And then there was Phillip—the former duke, or whatever he was. A monster of Argonox's design. He'd apparently been set on Thatcher's trail like a hunting hound. I hadn't crossed blades with him yet, so I didn't know for sure what his strengths and abilities were. But if Jaevid Broadfeather was treating him with caution ... well, let's just say I wasn't going to go into a duel with him pulling any punches.

Anything that frightened Jaevid Broadfeather was enough to make my blood run cold enough to freeze my soul solid.

I couldn't sit still even to eat the delicious-smelling roasted fish Lin served to Jondar, Phoebe, and her other adopted children. They carried on normally, eating their dinner while she fussed over them. I had no appetite, though.

After the meal was over and Lin had begun herding the smallest of her brood through their normal bedtime routines, I finally forced myself to sit down at the table. Across from me, Phoebe still fiddled with a few pieces of her latest invention, adjusting what looked like a leather strap connected to a pair of spectacles. No, it looked more like some sort of mask that would only cover half of someone's face. Interesting. The style was similar to the oddly-detailed, thick leather strap spread out on the table beside her. Was this the piece she'd been working on for Thatcher?

"It'll be dark soon," Jondar said as he settled into the chair next to me.

I nodded. He was right. We'd have to go soon.

"You're sure you don't want me to go with you?" Jondar offered. "Even if I can't manage a blade well, my—er—size is sometimes enough to make people avoid me. Plus, the Ulfrangar don't know who I am, right?"

I gave a snort, flicking him a quick bemused grin. "You're the son of a Broadfeather. They know who you are, trust me."

His eyes widened some. "O-Oh. Really? Just because I'm Jaevid's nephew? I've never even met him. He and Mum mostly exchange letters. They met once, but I had to stay behind and look after the little ones."

I couldn't resist an ironic laugh. "Yes, Jondar. The Ulfrangar would definitely take note of Maldobar's best-known war hero having a nephew. Especially one that looks like you."

"Ah, well, I suppose that won't work, then." He deflated and sank back in his chair.

"Imagine if you did learn to fight well," Phoebe piped up, seeming to suddenly emerge from her work-trance long enough to give him a starry-eyed stare from across the table. "The nephew of Jaevid Broadfeather, a half-elf like he was, and the son of a war hero ... I could craft you some specialized armor, and then—"

She didn't get a chance to finish.

CRASH!

A booming sound like the crunching of wood and smashing of stone shook the kitchen windows behind us. Phoebe screamed, and I sprang from my chair with one of my blades already drawn.

I sprinted for the doorway and paused, gaping for a moment at the roaring flames that already filled the courtyard. Curse it all to the abyss. They ... the Ulfrangar were here. Right now.

They'd come for me.

IN A MATTER OF SECONDS, everything was chaos.

A chorus of screams from upstairs and another *CRASH* jarred me from my daze of shock. I surged up the stairs with Jondar and Phoebe right on my heels. A burst of roaring flames rose up before me as soon as I reached the top of the stairwell at the second floor, stunning me again briefly. The hallway to the left was already consumed, choked with fire and reeking black smoke. They'd used tar bombs—a tactic I knew all too well. I'd been trained to use those fist-sized orbs filled with dragon venom and a dose of paralyzing poison, too.

They were going to try to drive us all out into the open, just like they had at the Cromwell estate.

"Stay with me!" I yelled and seized Phoebe's hand, dragging her along as I rushed for the second stairwell leading up to the third floor. The flames hadn't gone that far yet.

"But my brothers and sisters!" Jondar shouted, still hesitating at the base of the stairs. He stared back at me, his face a blanched, twisted mess of terror and desperation.

I growled curses through my teeth as I sheathed my blade. He was right. We had to find them.

From where I stood, halfway up the stairs to the third floor, it looked like Lin's room was still untouched. A risk. But there wasn't any other choice. I pointed at it and gave Phoebe a shove in that direction. She yelped and stumbled, barely catching herself on the stair railing.

I glared back down at Jondar. "You go with her in there and shut the door, I'll find the others!" I yelled again. "Do *not* open the windows!"

"Murdoc!" Phoebe cried out.

But I didn't stop. Sprinting past Jondar, I forged into the flames toward the bedrooms where Lin's smaller children should have been. The blistering heat and plumes of foul smoke scorched my face and throat. I gagged, barely able to keep my eyes open by the time I reached the first door.

Flinging it open wide sent a surge of fire out around me as the air rushed in. From somewhere in the mayhem, I heard another scream. I whirled around to find four of the children—the girls—cowering together right behind the door. They sobbed and clutched one another, cringing away from me as I pulled the smaller two up into my arms.

"Hang on to me! Come on! We have to run!" I commanded the others as I guided their tiny hands to the hem of my tunic. There wasn't time to be gentle. We had to move—*now*.

Bursting back out into the hall, I basically lugged them all the distance to their mother's bedroom.

BAM—BAM—BAM! I beat on the door with my forearm.

The door cracked open, and I caught it by the handle before Jondar could whip it open all the way. We had to control the airflow. It was our only hope.

Shoving the four, sobbing little girls through the crack in the door, I met Jondar's horrified gaze for a brief instant before I turned and ran back toward the stairwell.

My lungs spasmed. Halfway down the hall, I choked and gagged again. My head swam, eyes searing with pain. The smoke was so thick I could hardly breathe. I couldn't —I wouldn't stop now. Lin might still be somewhere in this hell. And her other three children. They would die unless I ...

I fell against the wall, barely catching myself enough to stay on my feet. The heat. The smoke. It was ... it was too much. I-I wasn't going to make it.

"Do not stop!" a female voice pierced through the ambient crackle, hiss, and rumble of the fire.

My body shuddered as I forced myself to look up, almost collapsing completely. See —I had to see who it was. That voice was so familiar, and yet ...

She appeared before me like a mirage through the flames, a wavering dark figure clutching a toddler against her chest while two other children and a woman—Lin—ran behind her.

The Lunostri elf girl. She'd come to save us once again.

As soon as she spotted me, the elven girl stopped. She whipped around to hand the toddler to Lin and urged her to keep going up toward her room. They dashed past, faces streaked with tears and ash.

But the elf girl stayed behind.

She seized my arm and pulled it over her shoulder, forcing me to stagger at her side.

"Foolish," she scolded. "They only want you, but now everyone in this house will perish in your name!"

My head bobbed and I set my jaw, trying to pull away from her to walk on my own. I couldn't.

The elf girl lugged me all the way to Lin's room and, once we were inside, dropped me onto the floor with a few curses in her native tongue. "Take blankets and push them under the crack of the door," she ordered as she stepped over me and hurried to the windows, snatching back the drapes. "My, my. You lot certainly do cause trouble wherever you go, don't you? You've already burned one noble's home, and now this." She gave a snort and shook her head, making her long, loosely curled black hair swish along her waistline. "Your fire-starting friends have already blocked off all the exits except for this. I suppose they hope to corner you here and take you amidst all the chaos. Clever." She clicked her tongue thoughtfully, "They'll be coming any moment now."

That girl, whoever she was, had obviously learned a great deal about the Ulfrangar because ... she was right. Any second now that door would burst open. The Ulfrangar would arrive. They'd take me and kill everyone else in this room before setting it ablaze, too. It would appear that they'd all just perished in the fire. No one would be the wiser.

Rage stoked in my chest, deep and fierce. It consumed me in an instant. Every muscle drew tight and I shakily lifted my head to meet that elf girl's glowing, yellow-green eyes. The glow of the fire outside the windows put a golden glow across her ebony cheeks as she studied me *hard*—as though she were looking past my flesh and bone and straight down into my soul.

I wasn't giving up. I wouldn't give in. The Ulfrangar might kill me, but I wouldn't let them touch anyone else in this room. Setting my teeth against the pain that split my chest with every breath, I pushed myself back to my feet. "We leave," I rasped, every word agony in my fire-scorched throat. "Now."

CHAPTER ELEVEN

The Lunostri elf girl gave one brisk nod. My decision to move, to resist until the bitter end, seemed to be all the verification she needed. "I can fly with three of the children, at most. But once we break the windows, it will be a race against time. I'll return if I can, but the flames will come swiftly and it is a long way down. Too far to jump, especially with the young ones."

"No one's jumping," I growled as I drew one of my blades and shambled past her. I swung hard, aiming a swift slice along the top of the drapes hanging over the window. "Jondar, rip the blankets off the bed and start tying them together. Lin, bring the children to the window and get ready. We're making a sling. We can lower them to the street. Children first."

I had to give him some credit, in the face of certain disaster and death, Jondar didn't hesitate. His wide-eyed look of terror had given way to something more like grim acceptance. Maybe he assumed that he and I wouldn't be getting out of here alive. I decided not to tell him that he might be right about that. Regardless, he got to work fast.

"M-Murdoc?" Phoebe whimpered, still clutching those few pieces of crafting handiwork against her chest. That sense of knowing in her wide, rain-blue eyes put another pang of dread through my chest as she grasped my arm with one of her small, trembling hands.

I tried to swallow and gagged again as a sharp pain ripped through my throat like I'd swallowed shards of glass. "Y-You'll be fine," I managed hoarsely.

Phoebe's mouth opened, her wide eyes searching me as she squeezed my arm harder and her little ginger-colored eyebrows crinkled together. Then her hand slipped away. She took a few steps back and stood by with Lin and the children, watching while I went on cutting down the drapes and tossing them to Jondar. Even without looking her way, I felt her gaze on me—as though there were something more she wanted to say. Whatever it was, though, she never said it.

"Tie the rest of these off." I dumped the rest of the drapes at Jondar's feet and rushed past. The elf girl had already busied herself helping him, so I got to work on another problem. Any moment now, or possibly already, the Ulfrangar would come looking. We only had seconds—if that—and it would take much longer than that to lower the children down to safety even a few at a time. I had to barricade the door.

Glancing around the room, there wasn't all that much to work with. A bed, dressing table, chair, washstand, and quilt rack. I seized the chair and wedged it under the knob as tightly as I could. It wouldn't stop them for long, but it might buy us a minute or two.

Or so I prayed.

"Ready!" With the last drapery tied off to the end of our makeshift rope, the elf girl sprang to her feet. She bounded toward the window again, her shape shimmering and warping with every step. Her bare feet and slender hands became paws, and a pair of magnificent shining wings unfolded from her back as she sprang forward.

By the time she reached the window, she'd become a creature I didn't have a name for. A massive feline with a pelt like black velvet, striped in silver. A single beat of her deep purple, green, and blue-feathered wings made the windows shudder and burst outward all at once with a deafening *SMASH!*

The night wind rushed in, and almost instantly, the flames that were licking and crackling from the first-floor windows rose higher.

"GO! NOW!" I yelled, seizing two of Lin's older children—a pair of little girls—and all but flinging them onto the elf girl's back. "Hold on tightly! Do not let go!" I commanded as they sobbed.

There was only room for one more passenger, and I was not confident at all that the two little girls would be able to hang on once they took flight, so I seized Phoebe by the arm and dragged her over. Grasping her by the waist, I hoisted her onto the elf girl's back and forced her down so that her bigger, much stronger body was basically pinning the little girls in place.

That was it. That was all I could do.

But before I could take even a single step back, Phoebe whipped around and caught my face in her hands. Her gaze met mine, wild and frantic, an instant before she pressed her mouth against mine.

I froze.

That touch—the desperate press of her warm, soft lips against mine—made everything in the universe seem to fall silent.

W-Why would she ... ? I-I wasn't—that was just—*why*?!

"If you're quite finished!" the elf girl snarled, her feline form slicking back rounded ears as she lashed her long tail.

I pulled away. My mouth still hung open and my lips seemed to hum with tingling energy as I stared at Phoebe.

With a thundering roar and beat of powerful wings, she was gone.

"Murdoc!" Jondar called as he rushed to the window carrying our would-be rope made of tied blankets and drapes.

Right. Now wasn't the time to hesitate.

I took one end of it and Jondar grabbed the other. Together, we spread out the middle portion of one of the segments of drapery like a hammock and tucked two of the smallest children inside. Flames snapped and popped through the shattered windows as we worked together, braced against the wall on either side to slowly lower them down. Below, some of the city folk who'd gathered spotted us and hurried over to catch them as soon as they were within reach. We did the same with two more of the children, and that only left Lin and the youngest, wailing toddler she clutched to her chest.

"Hurry, Mum!" Jondar shouted over her as she hesitated, staring at him as though in petrified awe.

Her expression shattered. She gave a sobbing, screaming cry and threw her free arm around his neck to hug him franticly. It only lasted a moment, and then he put his hands on her shoulders and forced her back. His features stayed locked into that grim, stony scowl as he positioned our hammock-rescue-rope around her and his youngest sibling. He never even said a word as he guided her to the window, showing her how to sit and lean back so she could lie safely in the folds of the fabric.

And working as one, Jondar and I lowered them down. The gathering crowds of city folk on the street below shouted, seeming suddenly panicked. Why? What was happening? I couldn't see from where I was braced against the window's frame and I couldn't make out anything they were screaming. My arms burned and shook, hands aching and lungs spasming as I fought not to gag on every breath I took. I'd breathed in too much of that smoke and probably burned the inside of my lungs. And the poison ... I already couldn't feel my face and fingertips.

But I could make it. Just a bit longer, that's all we needed. Then, if we were lucky, Jondar and I might be able to—

Our makeshift rope snapped.

Lin's scream cut through me like a dagger as the weight suddenly vanished from the rope in my grasp.

Oh gods.

NO!

Whether the fire had burned through our sad excuse for a rope, or one of the knots had finally come unraveled, I couldn't tell.

And it didn't matter.

"*MUM!*" Jondar cried out in a bellowing roar. He dropped his end of it and rushed to lean out the window.

I stood paralyzed and horrified, watching him but not knowing what to do. Had they fallen all the way to the ground? Had anyone in the crowd below been able to catch them? Were they dead, or—

CRACK!

The door burst open with a shower of splintered wood and a whirling storm of embers.

I whipped around, hands snapping up to the hilts of my dual longswords. This was it. They'd come. The Ulfrangar had finally made their move.

As the clouds of black smoke dispersed, filling the room and stinging my eyes and throat again, my heart dropped to the soles of my boots. My gut clenched. The monstrous dark figure looming in the doorway leered down at me with glowing eyes of sterling silver. His lips curled back over fang-like teeth.

It ... it wasn't an Ulfrangar.

It was that beast. The one who'd been a man once.

The one they called Phillip.

"JONDAR!" I gave a shout of warning as I backed away.

Jondar whipped around, gaping up in horror at the encroaching monster of a man prowling into the room. "G-Gods and Fates! What is that?!"

I honestly wasn't sure. Jaevid had attempted to explain the origins of this monster to me once already, and I'd heard chatter among the Ulfrangar that the tyrant Argonox was fond of experimenting with all sorts of twisted and foul magics. But had he truly made this?

Regardless, it didn't matter.

Out—we had to get out. Now. Jaevid had also warned us not to fight this guy, and as he moved into the room, long tail swishing and clawed hands flexing, I began to appreciate why. Wearing nothing but a pair of tattered, torn, and blood-spattered breeches, he considered us with those shining silver eyes. Every controlled, predatory movement made corded muscle ripple along his bare torso and arms. He didn't move like a man at all.

He moved like a beast.

"You?" he hissed in dismay, glowing eyes flicking between Jondar and me. "No! It was supposed to be *him*—not you. Where is he? Where is the godling boy?"

I hesitated, my grip tightening on my weapons. Godling boy? Was he talking about Thatcher?

"Liars! They have betrayed our bargain!" The creature roared, long legs curling an instant before he lunged straight for me.

He was on me before I could blink, crossing the room like a tongue of lightning. I barely had time to throw up a parry as his huge hand darted out as though to grab my throat.

The impact sent me stumbling back. I rocked onto my heels and sank down, ducking sideways and surging back in close for a hilt-strike. The crossguard of my longsword cracked against his cheek.

He drew back slightly, seeming surprised as he blinked down at me for a few seconds.

Curse it all—I had to focus. I couldn't be this sloppy.

"Quick, aren't you?" The beastly man gave a deep, growling chuckle. "They promised me his life, but since our deal has been broken, I believe I'll take yours instead. You're the little whelp that betrayed them, aren't you? I'm sure they hoped to spill your blood as punishment. To make an example of you to their ranks. But that glory will be mine."

He launched forward again, as fast as a nightmare amidst the flurry of embers and churning smoke.

I dodged and feinted, throwing up one frantic, desperate parry after another as he bore in hard. Every impact of his clawed hands against my blades rattled my bones down to the marrow. My longswords they—they weren't even breaking his skin! They didn't leave so much as a scrape as I landed a lucky swipe along his forearm.

It ... it shouldn't have been possible. What, by all the gods, was he? A demon?

I pressed in harder, making brutal strikes as I spun and dipped with his near-chaotic assaults. He sneered suddenly, whipping around and catching the blades of both my weapons in his bare hands. His silver eyes gleamed, reflecting the orange glow of the fire as he focused on me. With one jerk, he cracked both my longsword blades in half.

Then he drove his head down into mine.

Everything went dark. I was moving, falling. But my arms flopped uselessly. My legs wouldn't respond.

I hit the ground on the flat of my back, my ears ringing as the world seemed to spin. No ... No, I couldn't pass out. Not now.

Blinking groggily, a hazy glimpse of fire and shadow flashed before my eyes. I groaned, fighting against the pull of the darkness.

Up—just get up you idiot!

My vision snapped back into focus suddenly as something as solid and unrelenting as iron clamped around my throat. A hand. I wheezed, choked, flailing weakly and pawing at the fist that pinned me to the floor. "Pathetic," Phillip snickered as he crouched over me. "They talk about you like you were some sort of champion among them. Is this the best the Ulfrangar has to offer?"

He bore in harder. Something in my throat cracked. Instantly, I couldn't breathe.

"Like crushing a cockroach," he growled gleefully.

I saw it an instant before it hit—the glint of the firelight off something flying through the air. Something long and pointed.

Phillip let me go. He howled in pain and pitched backward, flailing and trying to reach around as though there were something lodged in his back.

I sucked in a gasp of hot, smoky air and scrambled backward away from him.

But he wasn't worried with me anymore. He whipped wildly and finally managed to get ahold of it—the broken-off end of one of my blades. He ripped it free and flung it away.

Then his cold silver eyes narrowed upon Jondar. "*You,*" Phillip hissed.

The giant of a half-elf balled his fists and took a protective step toward me. "M-Me," Jondar confirmed, his tone still shaking some.

Overhead, the glow of the fire on the roof shone through the rafters and thatching. One of the big timber beams above us cracked. A fresh shower of sparks, splinters of wood, and bits of burning thatching sprinkled over us. Oh, gods. We had to get out before—

CRACK—BOOM!

The beam buckled. Fire and embers filled the air as the ceiling collapsed right overhead, burying all three of us in the roaring inferno.

CHAPTER TWELVE

"Look there. Tell me what you see, pup."

Sitting next to my handler on the eaves of a tall bell tower, I followed the gesture of his hand across the sprawling port below. There, massive merchant vessels swayed at their moorings while crews of sailors moved crates of goods on and off their gangplanks. Gulls fluttered around their towering masts, making mournful cawing sounds and chasing after anyone moving shipments of fish. The docks were packed with people—sailors, dockhands, merchants, and locals who'd come to shop at the fishing market.

But none of that was what Rook had been motioning toward.

"That ship there," I replied quickly, focusing my stare upon another, somewhat smaller ship. It'd anchored farther out in the cove, away from the docks and other ships, as though keeping a cautious distance. "It's a pirate vessel."

"Are you certain?" Rook cast me a sideways glance, one of his bushy dark brows arched. He looked ... younger. Happier than the last time I'd see him. The creases in the corners of his deep, golden eyes weren't so severe. His dark olive skin was smoother, and his closely trimmed beard didn't have nearly as much gray in it.

What was this, then? A dream?

I swallowed hard, staring up at him for a moment. Then I realized—I was a *lot* smaller than him. An eerie prickling sensation fluttered in my gut as I looked down at myself. No, I wasn't just smaller. I was younger. My body was smaller and dressed in the rough, battered leathers of a pup fresh into his training.

A pang of realization hit me square in the chest. This wasn't a dream. It was a memory. Something I hadn't dared to think about in ... *years*.

"Well?" Rook pressed, his tone a bit sharper.

I studied the ship again. "Yes, I'm sure."

"Why?"

"They're staying away from the traffic at the port and accessing the docks by longboat. They want a head start if anyone suspects what they are, and that's why they also haven't packed in their sails," I answered. Even my voice sounded much smaller and younger, but I couldn't tell how old I'd actually been. Maybe eight?

"What else?" Rook didn't sound impressed.

"The hull is low, so they've probably got cargo onboard. But the merchant's mark on the stern is a forgery."

"How can you tell?"

I narrowed my eyes upon the emblem painted in gold upon the very back of the ship; the image of a bird inside a five-pointed star was familiar, but a little off. "The nightingale's head is pointed the wrong way and the tail is too small."

"Good." Rook's mouth quirked at one corner, almost smiling ... but not quite. "A clever attempt, though, wouldn't you say? It likely serves them well to pretend. Blending in with the other merchant vessels that travel these waters probably allows them to get in close to their prey before they strike."

"But doesn't anyone here sail for that merchant? Wouldn't they recognize that wasn't one of their vessels?" I asked.

He made a pleased, thoughtful sound in his throat. "Hmm. I doubt it. Not here, anyway. That merchant line sails out of Rienka, far across the Southern Seas. There are about two hundred merchant companies operating there, each with a fleet of vessels and hundreds of routes. In all that traffic, coming and going constantly, they'd have no trouble slipping through unnoticed."

I sank back some, still studying the ship bobbing in the distance. It rose and fell with the swell of the ocean, its white sails puffed proudly in the late evening wind. "That's what we do, isn't it?" I dared to ask.

Once again, Rook gave me a sideways look. "What do you mean?"

"We hide in the crowds, moving in and out, pretending to be like everyone else until we strike."

He didn't reply. Not for a long, almost uncomfortable moment. Then Rook breathed a heavy sigh and looked away. "I suppose you're right."

I sat up a little straighter, grinning proudly. "But *we* never get caught."

Seconds passed, then minutes, and Rook didn't say anything. His golden gaze stayed fixed upon the horizon, and his expression didn't change from a distant, deeply pensive frown that settled over his stoic features like a steely mask. I'd seen that look before—many times, in fact. As though his thoughts had carried him somewhere far away, somewhere no one else could reach him.

Now, I had to wonder where that was.

"We do get caught sometimes, Murdoc," he said quietly. "And when we do, the pack demands that we speak nothing about who we are. We must go to our deaths in complete silence. That is the only way to retain our honor."

I'd been too young, too stupid, to understand the weight of what I asked him next. Now, hearing it made me cringe. "Have you ever seen anyone get caught?"

Rook slowly panned his gaze down to me, brows drawn up ever so slightly. Then his jawline went hard. His mouth pressed into a grim, stern line. "Yes. Once. When I was a novice hunter, many years ago."

I swallowed hard. "What happened to him?"

There was a cold, bitter finality in the way he spoke every word. "The city guards executed him and burned his body."

"So, then ... he died honorably?"

"No, Murdoc," Rook answered firmly. "That is the lie many men, not just Ulfrangar, tell themselves. Honor is for the living, not the dead."

"I've got him! He's back!" someone yelled right over me. I couldn't force my eyes open to see who it was, but that voice ... something about it annoyed me immediately.

And what was he talking about? I'd come back? Back from where? Had I ... had I died or ... ?

My thoughts scrambled suddenly. White-hot agony ripped through me like my flesh was being peeled right off my bones. My eyes flew open and my body went rigid as a garbled, rasping cry tore from my throat. It hurt—gods, why did it hurt so much?!

"Hang in there, Murdoc. Try not to move, all right? I just need you to focus on breathing. Slow and steady for me." Reigh leaned over me, his face smeared with ash. "You've got some pretty bad burns, but we'll take care of it. Phoebe! Get over here!"

I couldn't answer. I couldn't think or even move. Every gulp of air burned like acid in my throat.

"I've got something in my bag, just try to keep him awake. He's in shock, so just talk to him, and try to keep him focused," Reigh ordered, his voice growing fainter as though he were moving farther away.

Then a small but strong hand grasped mine. Rough palms. Tiny fingers. Warm.

Phoebe.

It took every shred of strength and concentration to will my eyes open, my head lolling to the side so that I could see her. Kneeling close beside me, Phoebe gripped my hand like someone clinging to a life raft in a stormy sea. Her tears had left clean streaks in the ash smeared over her cheeks. Even her dress was blotched with soot.

Gods, what had happened? How had they gotten us out of that hellhole? Where was Jondar? Had Lin survived? And ... and Thatcher. Where was he? Why wasn't he here? Or maybe he was, just not anywhere close by?

Just the thought of his name made my pulse spike again. I clenched my teeth, barely managing to croak out one broken question. "W-Where ... i-is ... Th—Tha ... tcher?"

"Oh Murdoc," she began, but her voice caught. Her eyes welled and her expression crumpled with a sob. "We don't know. He's disappeared. He wouldn't just leave us, would he?"

No. He wouldn't.

As my vision began to dim again, my thoughts went on racing between waves of agony that threatened to stop my heart again. Think—I just had to think. But my mind frayed a little more each second, becoming a sluggish haze. Everything jumbled together, lost in the darkness that consumed me again.

Where would Thatcher go?

That man—Phillip—had come into the room expecting to find Thatcher there instead of us. He'd even said something about a deal he'd struck with the Ulfrangar. I'd never heard of the Ulfrangar working with an outside party like that before. But maybe this Phillip guy was different somehow? Maybe he really was connected to Devana. It seemed like she had a lot more strings to pull within the Ulfrangar than we realized. Somehow, she'd gotten their full attention and cooperation.

But what would they strike a deal with him for, exactly? My life? Thatcher's capture? Or both?

That had to be it.

And if the Ulfrangar had intended to leave Thatcher in that house for Phillip to find, then that must mean ...

Oh gods. Was it possible?

Had they mistaken Thatcher ... for me?

13
CHAPTER THIRTEEN

Time passed. Or at least, it seemed to. I wasn't exactly sure. The concoction of healing remedies Reigh kept funneling down my throat kept me in a state of groggy delirium. My arms and legs flopped uselessly, as heavy as lead. Every time I fought to open my eyes, the room spun and whirled, making my gut clench like I might vomit.

So I had no choice but to lie there ... and wait.

I slept, but not peacefully. Nightmares tugged at my brain like briars—glimpses of my past that seemed to materialize from the darkness, smoke, and crackling flames that still seared my mind. Things I'd buried deep. That night in Thornbend, when I'd first met Thatcher, I'd assumed that my choice to betray the Ulfrangar would eventually kill me. After all, no one just walked away from them. Traitors to the pack were hunted ruthlessly and executed without remorse, so I knew that punishment would catch up to me eventually. But *only* me. Thatcher, Reigh, and Phoebe, and all the others shouldn't have been of any concern to them. I would be the only one to suffer the consequences.

Now I knew just how disgustingly stupid that assumption had been. Thatcher was gone. Missing. Most likely captured. He might even be dead already.

And it was my fault.

More time dragged on. The pain came and went in waves. Sometimes so intense it woke me long enough to gasp for a few breaths and moan a few words. I caught glimpses of a bedroom I didn't recognize and snippets of conversations going on around me. But nothing made much sense.

Then, all at once, it stopped. The hazy chaos broke, fading to silence and stillness. The sound of my own breathing kept a steady rhythm with the beating of my heart. My hands and feet tingled whenever I focused on twitching or moving them. But there wasn't any pain—or at least, not like there had been before.

I opened my eyes, finding myself lying in a narrow bed beneath a wide window with a clean quilt tucked around me. The warm air smelled strongly of herbs, and the room was sparse. Nothing hung on the walls except for a single curtain pulled back away from the window to let the dim light in from outside. The sky beyond the windowpane was stormy and bleak, making it difficult to tell what time of day it was.

Not that it mattered, really.

The clunk and squeak of a door opening made me flinch. I set my jaw, bracing for pain as I rolled my head over to see who'd come in. Only, there wasn't much pain. Soreness, mostly. But nothing I couldn't withstand.

Lying in another narrow bed across the room, I recognized Jondar right away—even with a bedside table blocking my view of his face. His feet hung off the end of the bed, and the blanket had been pulled back from one of his legs to reveal a thick plaster cast that went from his knee to his ankle.

Reigh leaned over his bed, checking him over silently for a minute or two. Even from that distance, I could tell that his features were somewhat ashen and there were heavy, dark circles under his eyes. His whole demeanor drooped, slumped with exhaustion as he went to the foot of the bed and ran a finger up and down the bottom of Jondar's foot, making it flinch a little. Testing for nerve damage, probably. It must've been a bad injury.

Was I any better off? Or worse? With my head still swimming somewhat, I couldn't tell yet.

When Reigh noticed me watching him, he quickly stepped over to my bedside and sighed. "Glad to see you're finally awake." He kept his voice hushed. "You breathed in a lot of that smoke—which, as it turns out, had been spiked with some pretty heavy-duty toxins. Everyone's been feeling the effects, but you and Jondar breathed in a lot more than the others."

Well, that explained why I'd hardly been able to fight at all in my pathetic attempt at a duel with Phillip. Embarrassing. Thank the gods no one else had seen that wreck.

"They only made it out okay because of you two. If the kids had stayed in there any longer, breathing in that stuff, I'm not sure they'd still be alive," he went on as he poured a glass of something—probably water—from the pitcher sitting on the nightstand between our beds.

I swallowed hard, forcing out a few hoarse words. "Lin is all right?"

Reigh nodded. "Fortunately, they weren't that far off the ground when that rope you made broke. Only eight feet or so. There were enough people gathered around to help by then, so they were able to catch her and the kid. No harm done." He helped me sit up a little before pressing the cup into my hand. The movement made me groan through my teeth as every muscle seemed to tremor and ache in protest. "Here, drink this. You scorched your throat pretty badly, but I've been able to get access to some faster-acting Lunthardan remedies. Lucky you."

Lucky? Not the word I would have used to describe any of this. But I didn't have the strength to argue with him. Yet.

"Jondar is probably the worst off. A few of your burns were fairly severe, but he got hit by the beam when it fell. It had him pinned by the legs and broke one of them pretty badly. Compound fracture. He won't be making any swords for a while. The medicines will help to speed things along, but he's still got at least a month of hobbling around with a crutch. Maybe longer if he doesn't take my advice and rest," Reigh grumbled under his breath. "Big moron already took a fall trying to get to the bathroom on his own. He might actually be more stubborn than I am."

I sort of doubted that.

"W-What is this?" I rasped again and took a sip from the cup. The bitter, almost grass-tasting liquid hit my tongue and made me shudder. Ugh. Whatever he'd mixed into the water made it taste horrible. I curled my lip and shot him a dubious look.

He just shrugged. "It's an herbal blend. Manages your pain, speeds healing, and staves off infection. I can try putting some honey in it but, honestly, it won't help much. Just drink it. A few more doses and you'll be well enough to eat something solid."

I grimaced and took another sip. "W-Where are we?"

Rubbing his hand through his now chin-length hair, he glanced me over and seemed to hesitate. As though there was something else he wanted to say but didn't know how. "In one of the city's healing houses. My fath—uh, well the man that raised me, Kiran, he knows the medic running this place. Kiran trained him, actually, I think. Anyway, he's taken good care of us. Lin and the others are staying with Jondar's boss's family. The Porters. They seem like decent enough people." He shifted uncomfortably, lips pursing for a moment as he fidgeted with the pitcher again, adjusting it on the table. "Phoebe's here, though. She didn't want us to be separated any more than we ... " His voice trailed off and he looked away, his brows scrunching together unhappily.

I didn't reply. Sitting up with my back resting against the pillows, I watched the water in the cup ripple as my hands shook. From the medicines, maybe? Or the quiet rage boiling in my veins?

"Listen, Murdoc. I ... there's something I have to confess." Reigh gave another heavy sigh and moved down to the end of my bed to sit. "Thatcher is gone. I left him alone at the tavern for a few minutes. He was with Fornax, and there was no one around, so I thought he'd be fine." He shut his eyes and rubbed at the back of his neck. "I guess I was wrong. Someone must have been waiting for us to separate—someone who wasn't afraid of the dragons. Once I realized he was gone, I looked everywhere. I even flew passes around the area with Vexi, but the only sign I found were a pile of some of his clothes in one of the dragon stalls back at the tavern. It's like he vanished into thin air. Even his dragon is gone."

Wait—what? No. That couldn't be right.

I looked up slowly, focusing squarely on Reigh as my mind whirled with that new information. Why would Thatcher discard his clothes? Or had someone forced him to? But why? Ulfrangar didn't typically strip down our captives or prey. The goal was always to move them outside of the city as discreetly as possible, and there were many rules around that. But forcing him to undress? And then leaving those clothes behind? Sloppy.

It made no sense.

"Isandri is ... well, she's furious. Or terrified. Or maybe both. She went to look for him days ago and I haven't seen her since," he continued, hanging his head some. "You think he would abandon us? Go off on his own? I didn't think he was the type for that, but you know him better than I do."

"No. He wouldn't." Frowning down at my body, bandaged thickly across my chest, one of my arms, and half my leg from my thigh to my knee, it was as though all the anger drained out of me at once. The cold, hollow emptiness left behind made my fingertips tingle like I'd dunked them in icy water. Thatcher would never have struck out on his own like that. He'd done a lot of stupid, reckless things since I'd met him, but he knew the dangers if any one of us got separated. He knew Phillip was looking for him.

"So, then, someone took him. Or forced him to go," Reigh concluded, his voice going quiet. "Apparently not Phillip, since that's who tried to kill you before the house collapsed. Well, according to Jondar's description, anyway."

"It was Phillip," I confirmed. "But he didn't come there looking for us. He wanted Thatcher."

Reigh's gaze snapped back over to me, eyes wide. "So ... he got it mixed up? Or what? That doesn't make any—"

"I know," I interrupted. "Clearly there was some sort of plan between him and the Ulfrangar that went wrong. Someone messed up. They likely thought I'd be the one going to meet Judan's agent with you, and meant to abduct me there instead of Thatcher."

Reigh's mouth mashed up bitterly, seeming deep in thought as he stared back at me. "But ... they know what you look like, right? How could they possibly screw that up? Someone would have to trick them intentionally to ever mistake Thatcher for you."

My heart gave a lurching, frantic *thump* ... and stopped. My mouth fell open, and my entire body seemed to go numb.

Merciful gods. He was right.

For them to mistake Thatcher for me would've required someone deceiving them. Someone who knew how and when to do it—likely an Ulfrangar. After all, few people could dupe the pack like that. Too many of them knew what I looked like. So it had to be someone they trusted enough not to question. Someone with years of experience. Someone who would want me to evade their capture.

"Rook." The name left my lips in a broken whisper.

Reigh frowned hard, light brown eyes narrowing suspiciously. "What?"

I shoved the cup at him, setting my jaw against the aching soreness in every muscle as I threw the blankets off my legs. "I need clothes," I growled through my teeth. "And my weapons. Now."

"Murdoc, what the heck is going on? Who or what is Rook?" Reigh protested as he stood up like he might try to stop me. "And besides, you're in no condition to be fighting anyone yet. You shouldn't even be walking yet. Lie back down before you wreck all my hard work."

I didn't reply as I shakily hauled myself up onto my bare feet.

He lunged forward as though to catch me by the arm. "Hey! Are you even listening to me?"

I shot him a scorching glare, my mouth twitching as I fought to keep some tiny fragment of composure. I must've failed miserably because he stopped short and raised his hands in surrender.

"Rook was my handler," I snarled. "He was the one who trained me. The one who taught me to be one of *them*. And if he has Thatcher now, it can only mean one thing."

Reigh's expression steeled some, his hands curling into fists as he lowered them. "And that is?"

"He's going to attempt to pass off Thatcher as me to the rest of the Ulfrangar," I rumbled, every word burning like dragonfire in my chest. "He's going to try to have him executed in *my* place."

IT TOOK a fresh eternity to wrestle myself into pants, a tunic, and the scorched remains of my leather armor and weaponry. Thankfully, most of it had more or less survived the fire. It all needed a thorough cleaning, and to be re-sealed with the appropriate oils in the usual Ulfrangar method, but it was still usable. Buckling my cross-sheath over my back, I hissed curses through my teeth as I cinched it tight. It put pressure on the burns around my chest, spiking my discomfort level from a tolerable dull ache to a sharp, distracting agony.

I could bear it, though. I had to, for Thatcher's sake.

I willed my hands to stay steady as I laced up a pair of borrowed boots and slipped my hands into my cestus gloves. A flex of my fingers made the silver spines bristling along the knuckles catch in the weak light.

Good enough.

"Murdoc, stop. Look at yourself, would you? How do you expect to fight anyone this way?" Reigh called after me as I staggered down the hallway of the healing house. "It's been three days! They're probably long gone by now. Not to mention, Phillip may be still out there right now. What's to say he won't try to catch you off guard and finish what he started?"

"Back off," I growled through my teeth as I caught the railing at the top of the stairs and steadied myself.

He didn't. Not even for a second. "How do you know they all haven't left the city already?"

"Because I've made sure of it," a smooth, all-too-familiar feminine voice purred from somewhere behind us.

Reigh and I turned in unison, staring at the slender figure lurking in the heavy shadows down the opposite hall.

I narrowed my eyes. That accent was impossible to miss—not something you heard in Maldobar often. But it was the shimmer of those golden markings across her forehead, a band with a small crescent moon right between her eyes, that gave her away. They seemed to glow almost as brightly as her bizarre yellow-green eyes while she stood there, considering us.

Reigh's shoulders slumped and he breathed her name like a sigh of relief. "Isandri."

She didn't seem quite as pleased to see him, though. "That little fire and the appearance of your monstrous friend have put the city guards on edge. They patrol more regularly and keep a vigilant watch at the city gates," she said coolly. Prowling forward, the shadows seemed to slip off her frame like black sheets of silk. "Not vigilant enough, though. So, I've set my wards about the various other exit points. If your fellow hounds step a paw over them, I'll know it immediately." She tipped her head toward the crystalline head of the tall staff she carried.

"You did what?" Reigh asked.

"I told you before, she's a shalnii," I mumbled as I considered her—the purple and green robes that draped off her leanly muscular frame and her long, elegantly pointed ears. No mistaking it now. "They're essentially temple guardians. Holy warriors devoting their entire lives to the service of one of the ancient gods. Judging by that oath mark sealed across her forehead, she most likely serves Adiana, the Moon Goddess."

Isandri's strange eyes narrowed a bit, seeming to consider me with a little more caution. "You know much, hound."

"More than you'd probably like for me to share, *miwos*." I decided to demonstrate that a little, adding in a word from her native language. I didn't know her personally, but I'd seen enough from her now to venture a fairly specific guess as to who she was ... and why she kept coming to help us. Such things were taken to be pagan fairy tales by anyone in Maldobar who'd actually heard of them in the first place.

Now wasn't the time to dive into that, though.

Isandri paused, vividly colored eyes widening for the briefest instant before she gave a snort of amusement. "Very well, then. While I dislike making it a habit to involve outsiders in this, I find myself in need of your ... special knowledge. The hounds are deep in hiding now, some place I cannot find, but I suspect they won't stay that way much longer. If we're going to find Thatcher before they leave this city or realize his true identity, then I suggest we work together. If you're even fit to fight, that is."

"He's *not*," Reigh grumbled.

"Shut up," I snapped. "I've fought with worse."

"Yes, but did you actually win?" Isandri gave me another slow glance from head to foot and arched a brow as though she weren't convinced.

Ugh. I flicked a glare of warning between them and turned away to shamble down the stairs. Arguing about it any further was a waste of valuable time. Clearly neither of them had ever been forced to strangle someone else to death for a few scraps of food after weeks of starvation and brutal beatings from whelpers. Ulfrangar were fond of selecting the harshest from among their ranks to take shifts *breaking in* the new pups—a task they called "whelping." It was the first step upon that dark path; a dark baptism into their world of blood and shadow.

And it'd taken them a lot longer to break me than it had the others. This wasn't going to break me easily, either.

Not until I got Thatcher out.

14

CHAPTER FOURTEEN

"I hope you have some idea of where to begin our search," Isandri huffed as she and Reigh followed me downstairs. "I have already surveyed many of the inns and taverns in the city, but there has been no sign of them."

I gave a bemused snort. As if they would ever stay somewhere so obvious. "Of course there hasn't."

She didn't answer, but I could practically feel the sting of her glare at my back. Heh. I had to give her credit—she handled herself well in combat. That shapeshifting trick was handy, too. But it was time to teach this little priestess a few new tricks.

Isandri opened the door ahead of me, poking her head out and glancing both ways like a nervous cat. The smell of salty sea wind and rain rushed in, rustling in my hair as I muscled in close enough to nudge her the rest of the way outside.

"I can't go with you, you know," Reigh grumbled as he stopped behind us at the front door of the healing house. "When we didn't show for the meeting, Judan's agent left word for us. He'll be making contact anytime now, and without much warning. I guess with Phillip and the Ulfrangar still in the area, they're playing things more carefully. Who knows, with Phillip making an appearance again, Jaevid might decide to come back."

I paused, unable to control how my shoulders tensed up at the mention of his name. His voice lowered, becoming tense. "But, uh, here. Take this with you."

I glanced back, my gaze tracking from his intense, thoughtful frown to his outstretched hands. In one, he held a long black cloak. But in the other, a tiny glass vial about the size of half my pinky finger rested in his open palm.

"What is this?" I asked as I took them both. Stopped on the end with a little nub of cork, the liquid inside the vial sloshed in unsettling hues of yellowish brown when I held it up to look closer.

"Something Kiran has been working on for a while. He calls it 'godsgrave.' He's been trying for years to find a good use for the sap that comes from the carnivorous trees in Luntharda. Greevwood sap on its own is extremely toxic. A few drops would stop your heart in an instant. But mixed with a few other things, he's found it can have some ... pretty potent effects." Reigh cleared his throat and scratched at the side of his neck, eyeing the vial like he half-expected it to explode. "Basically, it's an extremely condensed compound of that sap, a few plant extracts, and a remedy we commonly use for numbing pain."

I eyed the vial dubiously. "And what does it do, exactly?"

"Temporarily shuts off your ability to feel pain. One sip and you won't feel anything. But everything else gets ... intense." Reigh slowly raised his gaze to meet mine with a haunted expression. "It's like the world slows down. You see *everything*. You'll fight like a demon even if they run a pike through your gut. You'll fight until the effects wear off, or you die." He bowed his head and took a step back. "Kiran was hoping to be able to offer it as a mercy to warriors who'd been fatally wounded in battle and had no hope for escape or rescue. But the effects were a lot more extreme than we anticipated. It was too dangerous. And the aftermath, when the compound wears off ... it's enough to make you wish you were dead. So don't take it unless you have no other choice."

I pocketed the vial and gave him a nod. "Thank you."

Waving a hand dismissively, Reigh's mouth scrunched sourly as he turned away to go back inside. Before he shut the door, he hesitated one last time. "She's, uh, she's asleep now, but I'll tell Phoebe you said goodbye. She'd probably want to hear that—and also that you plan on coming back in one piece."

I swallowed hard. "Fine."

"Good. Now get to work."

PHOEBE. My mind seemed to go quiet in the wake of her name. The storm calmed. The rage smoldered down. I just... didn't understand what that meant. She'd always puzzled me. But now it felt different somehow. Why?

Was it because she'd kissed me?

What did that even mean? Was I supposed to respond? To say something to her about it? Or let it alone? What had she even meant by that gesture?

Or did it mean anything at all?

"So, about that clever plan you claim to have hidden up your sleeve," Isandri quipped as she stood by, her staff resting over her shoulders.

I shook my head and rubbed my forehead with the heel of my hand. Right. Now wasn't the time to lose focus.

I buckled the cloak over my shoulders and pulled the hood down low before giving her a challenging glare. "Just try to keep up."

She smirked.

Thunder cracked overhead as we took to the streets, fast and silent. Dark clouds gathered, choking out the afternoon sun and kicking up gusts of wind. It drove most of the common folk indoors, freeing up the narrow backstreets and alleyways so we could move easily without being spotted.

I took point and led the way, my eyes constantly panning the sides of the buildings as we passed through the city like two dark specters. Corners of shops. Hitching posts. Statues. Ugh, nothing.

There *had* to be one around here somewhere ...

There!

I stopped short and quickly sidestepped, seizing Isandri by the arm and yanking her into the small alley with me.

"Don't do that," she snapped as she yanked her arm away.

I pressed a finger to my lips and made a gesture, motioning for her to slowly take a peek around the corner. There, straight ahead, a large white limestone fountain stood in the middle of a round city square. We'd passed around many of those, avoiding them since there was still a few city folk milling around even in this weather. But this one was different. This one stood in the middle of a covered market, where the main streets on all sides were covered by lengths of heavy cloth and crowded with shops, stands, and stalls where vendors sold everything from food, trinkets, tools, clothing, and jewelry.

None of that concerned us, though.

"The fountain at the center. You see it, don't you?" I whispered as Isandri peered around the corner.

"Yes. There's a few men watering horses there. But they don't look like any of your hound friends," she replied quietly.

"They aren't," I confirmed. "Look at the base of the fountain. There's a mark engraved into one of the stones at the bottom left corner. Do you see it?"

Her eyes narrowed a bit. "Yes. I think so."

"What does it look like?"

"I ... hmm. It's difficult to tell from this distance. A curved line like a J. And two shorter lines meeting at a point from the right side of it—like a sideways V," she guessed, quickly flashing me a puzzled look. "What does it mean? What does that have to do with the hounds? Or finding Thatcher?"

"It means we must play this very carefully." I licked my teeth behind my lips and considered her carefully. She wasn't exactly inconspicuous. Lunostri elves seldom left the scorching sands of their homeland. She stood out like a sore thumb. But in this case, that might work to our advantage. She was obviously foreign, a rare sight, and sure to pique their interest.

I turned to put the flat of my back against the wall and held a hand toward her. "You brought a blade, I hope? Something other than that staff?"

There was a challenging glint in her strange, yellow-green eyes as she reached into the folds of her robes and produced a fine, nine-inch dagger. "They aren't my specialty," she warned as she placed it, hilt first, in my hand.

"Good. And a coin?"

Her lips pursed into a suspicious little frown as she riffled through her robes again and finally pulled out a single, golden coin. There was real worry on her face as she reluctantly handed it over. "It's the last I've got."

"You won't need it," I said as I used the point of her knife to etch something into one side of the coin—a symbol just like the one on the side of the fountain. *His* mark. "You're with us now, and between Jaevid and Queen Jenna, we've been given more than enough to pay your way, too."

Her eyebrows rose when I handed the coin back to her, almost like she wasn't sure what that meant.

"Place this coin on the edge of the fountain, etching down, right above the stone with the mark. Move fast and don't linger. Place it there and come immediately back," I instructed. "Keep your head down. Don't make eye contact with anyone. Come directly back this way but don't stop or acknowledge my presence. Walk past and keep going."

"What is this? What are we doing?" Isandri questioned, even as she closed her fist around the coin.

I let out a slow, controlled breath and flipped the dagger over my palm once. Seizing it firmly by the hilt, I set my jaw and flexed against the growing pain in my hands. "Sending a message," I answered.

15

CHAPTER FIFTEEN

Crouching low, I chanced a look with one eye around the corner of the alley where I waited—I had to be sure. There wasn't time for a second try.

Isandri moved lightly on her bare feet, slipping away from our hiding place and crossing the market square. A few patrons milled around the area, not seeming to pay her any mind as they carried baskets and armloads of bought goods and chattered. Two men watering their horses talked, but stopped to stare at her for a second or two as she approached. They quickly lost interest, though.

Without hesitation, Isandri placed the golden coin on the edge of the fountain right where I'd told her to. Excellent. Then she turned around and started back in my direction. So far so good.

As she came my way, a figure stepped away from one of the shopping stalls on the far corner of the square. The young man strolled aimlessly for the fountain, hands in his pockets and expression indifferent. Hmm. His fine tunic and doublet marked him as upper class. Not a noble, but well off. Not local, though. Despite his human features, his deep bronze skin, stark black hair, and deeply-set eyes of burnished gold were distinctly Damarian. Foreign. Probably came and went with the merchant vessels.

He paused before the fountain for less than a second. His hand moved so fast I barely spotted him making a grab for that coin. He slipped it into his pocket and immediately walked after Isandri, keeping a cautious distance behind her.

I ducked back into the alley. My adrenaline spiked, sending shaking, buzzing energy through all my extremities. I gripped the dagger and waited with my back against the wall. Their footsteps approached—Isandri's first and much harder to hear since she didn't wear shoes. Most Lunostri didn't, though. A cultural norm for them.

His boots, however, made much more racket. Easy to track.

Isandri breezed by first, not looking at me or pausing even for an instant.

Then he came.

I surged forward, seizing the man in a hold with my hand over his mouth. A twist of his body, and well-aimed strike to the ribs made him falter long enough that I easily pinned him against the side of the building. I held up the knife, letting him focus on it for a moment before I pressed it firmly against his throat.

"What are you doing?" Isandri fussed in a frantic whisper as she rushed back to my side.

"Getting directions," I growled through my teeth. "Go keep watch. This won't take long." Judging by the pearls of sweat rolling down the man's brow and the way his pupils had gone as tiny as pinpricks, it probably wouldn't take two minutes to get everything I needed.

Isandri hissed a few curses under her breath in her native tongue and stalked by to take up a guarding position at the entrance to the alley.

"Now then, I'm going to make this very simple. Tell me what I want to know, and maybe then I will let you go. Understood?" I seethed, pressing in a bit more with the sharp edge of the dagger.

The man squirmed in my grasp, his desperate whimpers muffled by my hand.

"I'll take that as a 'yes.'" I leaned in closer, staring him straight in the eye from mere inches away. "A group of Ulfrangar are in hiding somewhere in this city—the same ones who burned that house down by the Crosswall Docks. I'm sure your *employer* has made you aware of at least twelve Ulfrangar safehouses in this city, but I don't have the time to search them all myself. I want to know which one they're hiding in—*now*."

I eased my grip off his mouth long enough for him to gasp out a few words. "F-Faregate Crossing! The attic of the public theatre!"

"And how many are there?"

His Adam's apple jumped as he swallowed hard. "Six. But they got a captive with them now."

My heart gave a fierce, hard *thump* that made my whole chest ache. "Alive?"

"I-I think so. They haven't moved in several days. Too much activity in the city guard, so they've stayed low," he stammered quickly. "B-But they likely won't for much longer. Word's come out of Solhelm. Jaevid Broadfeather is coming this way."

My heart gave another painful kick and I set my jaw. This idiot was probably right. Like jackals fleeing the stalking approach of a tiger, if Jaevid was coming, then the Ulfrangar would want to be long clear of the city before he arrived. They'd move soon—maybe even tonight. The storm would give good cover and make it easier to slip past the city guards.

We had to hurry.

A tongue of lightning snapped overhead, sending out a rumbling roll of thunder as I studied the man for a few more seconds.

"I-I'm telling the truth!" he insisted. "I swear it by the gods!"

"I know," I confirmed as I took a step back. "Now go."

He didn't waste any time scrambling past Isandri and me, sprinting out of the alley like a startled cat. I let him get a few yards away, far enough that no one from the market square would find him until morning.

Then I drew my arm back in one fluid, perfect motion ... and threw the dagger.

"He gave you what you wanted," Isandri whispered and scowled at me disapprovingly as we left the alleyway and into the marketplace. "Why did you kill him anyway?"

"He works for a crime lord named Arlan the Kinslayer," I mumbled as I wiped the dagger clean and handed it back to her. "Specifically, he's a messenger, so flapping his tongue earns his living. He would sell us out long before we ever reached that safe house."

"You don't know that," she countered.

I rolled my eyes. "I *do* know it. Anyone who gives up information so quickly in that line of work is either incredibly new, or incredibly stupid. Stupid enough to try meddling with the Ulfrangar. And I'm not willing to gamble Thatcher's life on anyone's mistake."

"Hah." She made a sharp, unconvinced, puffing sound. "You gave him your word, though. You said you'd let him go."

Really? What could a temple priestess possibly know about the dark games of assassins and thieves? "And I did. I said I'd let him go—not that I'd let him live. Further evidence that he was a moron we shouldn't trust."

Isandri's mouth pinched up sourly, probably tasting a few more of those Nar'Haleen profanities she wanted to hurl at me.

"Don't question my knowledge of my trained profession, and I'll extend you the same respect. Fair enough?"

Her expression crinkled slightly, showing the tiniest traces of tension and unease, as though she were considering me a bit more carefully than before. "I suppose."

"Excellent. Now, let's move. We need to reach the safe house before the storm hits."

Isandri didn't say much as we moved on, slipping into the long, cramped avenues lined on either side with dozens of merchant booths that went on for blocks in both directions. Lightning popped and sizzled overhead, and the gusting winds billowed in the heavy tapestries draped over the streets. A sudden *whoosh* of falling rain lashed over my head and shoulders as we moved quickly from street to street.

The rain drove most of the patrons and vendors indoors, but as we neared one of the public map boards, a line of four merchant wagons rattled past. Their tall wheels threw up a spray of muddy water all over a petite figure in a long dark blue cloak standing on the corner ahead of us. A girl? From this distance, I couldn't be sure.

Until I heard her shriek. She cringed back and her foot slipped on the slick stone curb. Her arms flailed, flinging the stack of papers she'd been carrying into the air as she fell backward—directly toward another oncoming wagon.

I moved before I could think. Darting forward, I seized her by the arm and yanked her back onto the sidewalk just as the wagon roared by. Her papers fell in a flurry, tossed and drenched by the stormy winds. They landed in a soggy mess all around us as she thumped hard against my chest.

"O-Oh! Oh no!" She shrieked and dropped to her knees, scrambling to rake the ruined papers back together into a soggy pile.

It didn't work. The rain had basically turned them to mush.

I bent down before her, picking up one and frowning. The ink was smeared and it all but fell apart in my hands, just like the rest of the papers. But it seemed like they'd all been covered in the same thing: a small paragraph beneath a large, bold headline that read *"MISSING BOY – PLEASE HELP."*

That one line was the only part I could still make out on the sheet I held out to her.

Her head lifted slightly, but not enough that I could see her face yet thanks to the hood of her cloak. She reached out to take the paper from my hand. Then, she finally looked up.

Soaked locks of her long black hair stuck to her cheeks and forehead as the woman —not a girl—blinked up at me through the pouring rain. She must've been in her late-twenties, even if she was quite short.

The instant our eyes met, something flickered deep in my mind, a sense of alarm I couldn't comprehend. I'd never seen her before. Had I? So why did seeing her make me feel ... uneasy?

Her brows knitted together as she stared wordlessly, dark hazel eyes studying me for what felt like ... gods, I didn't even know how long. Minutes? Hours?

My mouth opened. I-I needed to say something. To ask who she was.

But I couldn't make a sound.

And neither did she.

"If she's all right, then we should press on, Murdoc," Isandri spoke over me suddenly.

I flinched and nodded. Right.

"S-Sorry," I managed to stammer as I got back to my feet. "I have to go."

The woman didn't reply or even look up again.

I jogged after Isandri as she sped off across the street, grinding my jaw against the urge to look back. Whoever she was, it didn't matter. The storm had moved in. The Ulfrangar would be moving soon. Thatcher was running out of time.

And so was I.

PART FOUR
THATCHER

16
CHAPTER SIXTEEN

Alone—I was alone in the dark. Sitting with my wrists and ankles bound up in cables, I couldn't see anything through the cloth sack pulled down over my head. No light. No movement. Just darkness.

My neck ached where something heavy, maybe a chain or a cable, had been fastened to a pole at my back. That was the only thing that kept me upright as I sagged and weaved, fighting to stay conscious. They hadn't given me anything, no food or water, since I'd been taken from Ms. Lin's house. At first, hunger had gnawed at my gut like someone scraping my insides with sandpaper, and thirst made it painful to swallow. But after a while, those feelings had ebbed away. Now ... I was just tired. So tired I could barely sit up. So tired I could barely focus on anything for more than a few seconds. My thoughts went from racing and frantic, to numb and foggy. From focused and desperate, to a haze that felt more like a dream.

Or a nightmare, I guess.

How long had it been? Days, probably. I had no idea how many, though, or where they'd taken me. Wherever I was, the Ulfrangar must've been keeping me locked away separately from the rest of their group. Probably worried I'd overhear their plans. Or maybe that man, the one who'd attacked me at the tavern and forced me to disguise myself in their armor, was worried one of his comrades might realize I wasn't Murdoc— or an Ulfrangar. For him, there was probably a lot riding on this ruse. What would the Ulfrangar do to him if they found out he'd tricked them? And why was he even doing this in the first place? As far as I could remember, Murdoc had never mentioned any sort of special bond between him and his former handler. Shouldn't he want the real Murdoc to be found and punished for leaving?

None of it made sense. And my thoughts wouldn't stay focused long enough to try figuring it out.

Part of me wondered where Murdoc was now. Had he figured out what happened? Or did he and the others assume I'd run off? Flown away on Fornax and left them all behind?

Not that it mattered, really. Even if they suspected foul play, or that I'd been captured, they'd never be able to find me, right? I was on my own now.

I nodded in and out of consciousness, my head lolling to my chest until the tether around my neck choked me enough that I couldn't breathe. I startled awake, wheezing and shaking, struggling to breathe again through the sack. Gods, when would this be over? Why didn't they just kill me and be done with it? What were they waiting for?

In the distance, the muffled rumble of thunder rattled the floor under me. A storm? It grew louder until the whoosh of rain on the ceiling overhead filled the silence. As my head began to slump toward my chest again, that sound lured out memories from the darkest corners of my mind. Things I'd hoped I'd forget eventually.

But some things stay with you forever, even if you don't want them to ...

"THATCHER! Stay in the house! Don't you dare come outside—I mean it!" my father shouted, his face drawn and pale as he rushed to cram his feet into his boots.

Lightning flashed through the windows, briefly filling our front room with eerie, pale light. Thunder shattered overhead, so loud it seemed like the sky might come crashing down right on our roof. I stood, frozen in terror, wearing nothing but a long nightshirt that came to my knees and gripping an old quilt I'd brought from my bed.

BANG—BANG—BANG!

Someone pounded on the door.

I ducked behind one of the parlor chairs, leaning out to peek when Father opened the door. A man stood just outside our door, his long cloak dripping wet as he held up a lantern of his own. "Cohen, you must hurry! There's some commotion down at the bank," he panted and gasped, "I-I think they've found her!"

"Fates have mercy." Father rushed across the front room and snatched his cloak from the back of the chair where I hid.

I yelped and ducked down, trembling as I felt his gaze fall on me.

"Thatcher," he said my name again, and there was something strange in his tone now. Not anger or frustration. I ... I wasn't sure what it was. But it put a crawling, swirling sensation in my stomach.

I bowed my head low and hedged closer to him while squeezing my quilt to my chest.

He bent down and took my small, four-year-old shoulders in his big hands. "Look at me, Son."

I tried, but I couldn't without my lip trembling and tears welling in my eyes.

"Go back to your room and shut the door. Close your curtains, but do not look outside. Can you do that for me?" he pleaded softly.

"Where's Mother?" I managed to whimper.

His expression shattered, going eerily blank as his eyes searched my face like he was desperately trying to come up with the right thing to say. He swallowed hard, as though steeling himself. When he spoke again, his voice was steady but his hand trembled as he cupped one of my cheeks. "Do as I ask, Thatcher. I'll see that Mrs. Westfield comes over to check on you, all right? Just, please, go wait in your room."

Something about it—that look in his eyes and the tremor of his touch—was all wrong. Why? What had happened? Why was he leaving? Where was Mother?

"Yes, Father." I bobbed my head.

"Good boy." My father stood up quickly, his gaze lingering on me for a moment. Then he flung his cloak over his shoulders, grabbed the lantern from the hook by the door, and rushed outside. The door shut behind him with a *thud*.

I ran for my room as fast as my bare feet could carry me, practically flying to my bedroom and shutting my door. I dashed to the window and threw back the curtains, trying to see something—anything—through the darkness and the raging storm outside. The wind howled and moaned around the corner of our house. Sheets of rain lashed against my windowpane. Every few seconds, a bolt of lightning spread across the clouds like a rippling spider web of light. It illuminated the street below where a group of men gathered around my father. They held up lanterns, the gale snatching at their cloaks and nightshirts.

Then, all at once, they all took off down the street toward the river.

And I waited.

I watched the darkness, feeling every rumble of thunder all the way down to the marrow of my bones. What if Father didn't come back? What would happen to me? Where did he go?

Where was Mother?

It must've taken an hour or two for Mrs. Westfield to arrive. The old woman hobbled into my room, holding up a candle and patting the rain from her frosty white hair. When she spotted me, still crouched at the window, she quickly waddled over to snatch the curtains closed and shooed me back to bed.

I waited for a few minutes, after she left to sit in our front room before I dared to crawl out of my bed again. I crept to the window and ducked under the drapes. It took a few seconds and a little hard blinking for my eyes to adjust to the flashing, blinking bursts of lightning.

Then I saw them.

A group of figures in cloaks moved slowly down the street, flanking a small horse-drawn cart and holding lanterns out to light the way. The little wagon rolled to a halt right outside our house. And from my second-story bedroom, I could see directly down into the back of it—

—Right at the place where my mother sat, half covered by a rain-soaked blanket, limp across another cloaked figure's lap. Her long hair only looked dark when it was wet, like it was now. When it was dry, it was as light, wavy, and golden as mine. But her skin looked as pale as chalk and her eyes...

My heart pumped fiercely when she looked up at the window, at me, and blinked slowly. I could see it, feel it, like the pull of a churning dark vortex. Seeing emptiness in her gaze felt like standing on the edge of a high cliff and looking down at the deadly drop. It made my stomach flip and my body shake.

The cloaked figure holding her in the back of the cart looked up—right at my window. It was my father. His eyes went wide. Whirling around, he snatched the quilt up to cover Mother's head and block her gaze.

But it was too late.

I knew.

She'd tried it again.

I JOLTED back into consciousness as someone smacked my face—*hard*.

My cheek stung and my eyes flew open. The world spun in smeared hues of gray as I gasped and pitched wildly against the restraints still tied tightly around my body.

A hand clamped down over my mouth suddenly, pinning my head back against the post behind me so that I couldn't move it at all. "You need to calm down. Be still. Breathe."

Tears welled in my eyes, blurring my vision as I struggled to focus on the familiar face of an older man. He crouched down right in front of me, golden eyes smoldering with somber intensity as he waited for me to relax.

I-I couldn't.

Was this it? The end? Had he come to kill me? Gods and Fates, I didn't know if I should be relieved or terrified.

"You need to drink this," he whispered as he held out a small waterskin with his other hand. "Ulfrangar are trained to go weeks without needing food or drink while still being able to fight, but you won't last another day at this rate. Now, keep your mouth shut. Make too much noise and we'll both die in this room. Understood?"

I couldn't move my head to even nod. But my look of utter horror must've been answer enough for him.

He slowly moved his hand away from my mouth and held up the waterskin, bringing it to my lips. He let me have small mouthfuls, just a few at a time, until the waterskin was nearly empty. Then he took the last few swigs for himself.

Squinting groggily around the dim room where I sat, I couldn't even begin to guess where we were. There were dozens of old crates, boxes, trunks, and racks of clothing stacked around big pieces of something—maybe furniture—covered in white sheets. Someone's attic, maybe?

An oil lamp burned in the middle of a few small travel bags, the sort you'd wear over your shoulder or across your back. Those were the only things around that weren't covered in a thick layer of dust.

So, where were the other Ulfrangar? There'd been a whole crowd of them there when this guy had dragged me out of Ms. Lin's house. At least three—but probably more.

"They've gone to prepare the way," he murmured quietly like he could read my thoughts. "They won't be gone long. Here, eat this." He held something else up and crammed it into my mouth.

I choked as I struggled to chew. Bread. Hard, dense bread. He fed me bite after bite, pausing to let me chew and swallow, while he studied me closely. Almost like he was trying to figure me out. Yikes. Well, that was bound to be disappointing for him. I'd never been accused of being all that complicated.

"Who are you?" he demanded suddenly, still keeping his voice hushed.

I drew back a little, wary that saying anything might get me hit or worse. Hadn't he told me not to speak?

After a few moments of awkward silence and intense scowling, I finally decided to risk it. "I-I … I'm Thatcher. Thatcher Renley." I wasn't sure what else to say.

His scowl deepened the hard lines around his vibrant golden eyes. "An apprentice to Jaevid Broadfeather?"

I choked again. "N-No. I, uh, I don't *think* so, anyway. I'm not even a dragonrider. Not yet."

"Then you're his relative? Son? Nephew?" he interrogated.

"No. We're not related. At least, not that I know of."

"Then explain this." He held up a finger, dangling something right in front of my eyes. The soft light from the lamp caught over the bone-carved pendant and whistle that hung on the end of a long resin cord. My necklace! He must have found it hidden in my boot.

I stared at it, unable to keep my face from screwing up desperately as I tried to rasp out words. "It was a gift. He gave it to me before we left Halfax."

"Why?"

That question caught me like another blow to the face. "I … I don't know."

The man pursed his lips thoughtfully, considering the necklace again before he tucked it back into his pocket. "The whistle summons your dragon, I assume."

Yikes. Well, so much for that idea.

I bowed my head and looked away. "Why are you asking me all this? Why does it matter who I am if you're just going to kill me later?"

I honestly wasn't expecting an answer. Another smack across my cheek, maybe. Or having that bag crammed down over my head again. Either seemed likely.

But he turned and sat down beside me, his expression still grim and intense as he stared straight ahead into the light of the lamp. "I wanted to know why Murdoc did this. I thought perhaps it was because you were someone of great importance to Maldobar—someone closely tied to Jaevid Broadfeather. That might have at least explained why he turned on us so quickly."

"Would that have mattered?" I asked hesitantly. "If I was someone connected to Jaevid, I mean. Would it make any difference?"

The man gave a heavy sigh that made his broad, powerful shoulders droop some beneath all that black leather armor. "No. I suppose not. But it would have given me some peace of mind. It might have meant … that I was not entirely to blame."

Umm, what? *He* was to blame for Murdoc leaving the Ulfrangar? That didn't make any sense. He hadn't even been there when it happened. Not that I'd seen, anyway.

"I knew he still had doubts. Murdoc still had hesitations. He'd nearly earned back his patronage price, nearly won himself a place among the pack as a hunter. He was at a pivotal stage, and I knew one push in the wrong direction would make him stumble," the man went on, seeming to be talking more to himself than to me now. "But I let him go with Pike, anyway."

My mind reeled, frantically trying to sort out what all of this meant. "Pike ... was that the man with him in Thornbend? The one he killed?"

He nodded once. "One of my former pups. There'd always been a hint of rivalry between them—at least, on Pike's part. Murdoc stood to be the most feared and capable hunter of us all. To be forced to submit to the shadow of a younger, less experienced hunter would be difficult for any Ulfrangar. Within the pack, respect must be earned. Usually that takes time and many hunts." He paused, mouth flattening into a bitter line. "It was my mistake, letting them hunt together. Pike pushed him too hard, and Murdoc was not ready."

Silence settled between us, filled with the rush of the pouring rain and the occasional low boom of thunder.

Finally, I couldn't stand it anymore. I had to ask, even if he killed me for it. "You're ... you're called Rook, aren't you?"

His gaze panned slowly around, landing on me with a look of confused surprise. "He spoke of me?"

I tried to nod, but the chain around my neck clamped down on my windpipe if I moved that much. "Only a little," I wheezed. "When he was trying to teach me how to fight."

His eyes narrowed. "Murdoc attempted to teach *you* swordplay?"

Okay, why did he have to say it like that? Like there was no way anyone would be dumb enough to try teaching me fighting techniques? Ugh.

"He said I'm getting better at it," I grumbled. "I'm left-handed. And I should use a xiphos, like you."

Rook glanced me over again, as though inspecting to see if he'd missed some important detail before. What he saw must've been just as disappointing as before, however, because he gave a sarcastic snort and looked back toward the lamp. "You've got a bit of courage, I'll grant you that. But not much else. It's curious why the witch wants you so badly. I thought perhaps some relation to Jaevid Broadfeather might explain that, too."

My pulse skipped at that word—*witch*. Was he talking about ... ?

"Devana?" I gasped shakily.

His jawline went rigid, making a vein stand out against the side of his neck. The leather of his gloves squeaked as his hands drew slowly into fists in his lap. He didn't have to answer. I could see it written all over his face.

He knew exactly who she was.

"Do you know where she is?" I whispered, feeling every throbbing beat of my heart like someone dropping stones on my chest.

Rook's expression went as cold as a winter's night. His eyes grew distant, heavy brows knitting as he growled out one quiet word.

"Northwatch."

CHAPTER SEVENTEEN

A million thoughts raced through my mind as I sat, staring at Rook. I was still too stunned to make a sound. He knew who Devana was. He knew she was looking for me. And he knew where she was hiding. Or, he knew the general area. But if they had some kind of deal with her, then it was possible Rook knew a specific location we might be able to find her.

Now came the most important question—the one thing no one, not even Jaevid, seemed to know.

"Why?" I struggled to keep my voice quiet and my teeth from chattering. "Why is she trying to capture me? What does she want from me?"

Rook flicked me a puzzled sideways glance, as though he suspected I was taunting him or something. Like it was something so obvious I should've known better than to bother asking. He opened his mouth to reply—

Footsteps approached, growing louder and closer.

He moved as fast as a fox, pulling the cloth sack back down over my head again. That was it. He was gone.

And I had no answer.

"We're ready," a female voice said from somewhere farther away, probably close to where that lamp and those few bags were sitting. "The way is clear, but we must be swift. We've seen no sign of Devana's pet beast since his disappearance at the capture point, but in this weather, it's far more difficult to track him."

"Then pack up," Rook commanded. "I'll cloak the traitor and keep a blade on him. Only a fool would think he can't slip those bonds."

"And what of the beast?" the woman asked, her voice somewhat tense.

I guess dealing with Phillip put them on edge, too.

"He may try to intercept, but if he's got his prize, then there's no reason for him to pursue us any further. Our business is concluded," Rook answered sharply. "Now hurry. Pack what's left and tell the others we're mobilizing now."

Footsteps thumped and bumped nearby. Noises like the shuffling and scraping of stuff being moved around came from the direction of those bags. It only lasted for a minute or two. Then everything became quiet again.

I struggled to keep my breathing slow in the tense, heavy silence. My racing pulse hammered in my ears and throbbed in every one of my fingertips. Were they both gone? Had Rook left with her?

Suddenly, someone grabbed me roughly by the head, holding me down while they fiddled with the chain around my neck. It went slack with a metallic *clink*, and I couldn't resist a deep exhale of relief. Thank the gods for that.

"It will be over soon," Rook said, his voice hushed and somber—almost apologetic. "I will ensure that I am the one holding the blade when it happens. I will make it fast and painless. That is the only comfort I can offer you."

The spot around my throat ached as I swallowed hard. I didn't know what to say. Was I supposed to thank him? Was that his way of showing me mercy? Or trying to make me feel better?

He muttered something else in a language I didn't understand as he let go of my head. Then he seized me by the shoulders and dragged me up to my feet in one swift jerk. I wobbled, almost collapsing as my knees shook.

Rook held me steady and paused for a moment, as though hesitating. The sound of the rain on the roof overhead filled the tense silence. But if there was something else Rook wanted to say, he never did.

Or maybe he just never got the chance.

"We're clear!" the female voice called from somewhere nearby.

Rook moved behind me, throwing a cloak over my shoulder and pulling the hood down low—most likely to hide the fact that I still had a bag over my head. Reaching to discreetly grip one of my arms, he dragged me forward with his side against mine. Something sharp poked at the base of my back. A dagger's point?

I couldn't worry much about it as I stumbled along next to him. It took every bit of focus I had not to trip over my own feet. My head swam and I got a mouthful of the cloth sack every time I wheezed and gasped for a breath.

Rook kept a firm grip on me, guiding me down a steep set of stairs. My boots struck a wooden floor that creaked and groaned under our weight. I caught the faintest whiff of the stormy wind an instant before we moved outside. The rushing *shhhhhh* of the rain on the stone streets filled my ears. It soaked through my cloak, the sack, and seeped cold droplets that ran down my neck and shoulders. My boots splashed and sloshed with every step.

We moved fast, walking briskly for several minutes before Rook suddenly hauled me sideways and stopped.

My heartbeat skipped and stalled. What was happening? Where were we? Was someone close by? If ... if I cried out, would someone hear me?

I bit back the urge to scream. To flail. Yell, wave my arms, and run.

Rook still had my whistle. If I could just get to it. If I could just blow into it once. Fornax might be able to find me.

The clip-clopping of horse hooves moved gradually past—close enough to make my throat go tight. I bit down hard. Quiet. I had to stay quiet.

As the noise of the horse faded in the distance, lost to the rumble of thunder, Rook shoved me forward again. I stumbled, almost tripping, but he yanked me back and I felt the pinch of that dagger's point jabbing right at the base of my spine. A bit more pressure and I might have died instantly.

I couldn't tell how long we went on that way—moving speedily for a few minutes and then ducking, crouching, or holding perfectly still while Rook kept an iron grip on my arm and a dagger at my back. My clothes, my hair, the cloak thrown over me—everything was soaked completely through. My boots slowly filled with water until my toes went numb and I couldn't stop myself from shaking. Violent shivering rattled me down to my bones no matter how hard I tried to hold still.

When we stopped again, Rook took the dagger away and grabbed me roughly by the shoulders. He picked me up and basically tossed me like a sack of old potatoes. I landed face-first in the bottom of what might have been a wagon or a cart. I couldn't be sure with that bag still on my head, but the way the floor bounced a bit and creaked under my sudden weight was familiar. I'd loaded more than my share of work carts for my father, after all.

"Stay down and don't make a sound," Rook growled over me. The floor jostled again as though he were climbing in, too.

He sat down next to me, planting a boot on my back and knocking twice on the floor of the wagon. It lurched into motion almost immediately.

Lying sprawled on my belly, I turned my head to the side just so I could breathe a little easier. Below my ear, the wheels of the wagon ground along the stone streets, jolting whenever we crossed an uneven stone, and the horse's hooves clicked in a slow, steady pace. Minutes passed. Or hours. Or maybe even longer. I honestly couldn't tell.

And it didn't matter.

The longer I lay there, shaking and shivering under that rain-soaked cloak, the more my eyelids seemed to grow heavy and every breath was a fight against a growing sense of sharp, squeezing tension in my lungs.

Finally, I let my eyes fall closed. Maybe it was the cold, or the fact that I hadn't had much to eat or drink, but every part of me felt numb and distant. I'd finally stopped shivering, and every sound seemed to grow fuzzy and faraway. The howling, stormy winds bit right through my soaked clothes all the way to my skin. Gods, the air was so cold. It hurt to even breathe it in—but only a little now. Just a dull, prickly sort of ache that stretched down through my arms and legs.

Hmm. Strange. What ... what was I even doing here? I couldn't remember. And ... where was here, anyway? Was I alone ... or? Oh, right. Rook was here somewhere. But I couldn't feel his boot on my back anymore. I couldn't feel much of anything, really.

Nothing except an uncontrollable urge to fall asleep.

My whole body drooped, gradually going slack against the floor. Too late, I wondered if this was a bad sign. Was something wrong with me? I ... I should tell Rook. Or try to get warm somehow.

But I couldn't.

My breathing came slow and shallow. A strange sort of quiet crept into my soul, like I was drifting in still, dark water. Weightless and alone in the silence, I couldn't feel anything. No pain. No cold. Just ... endless nothingness.

"*Find me.*" A faint whisper echoed like a memory from somewhere deep in my mind. Someplace I hadn't even known existed.

My pulse gave a desperate, loud thump. My face twitched. I knew that voice, didn't I? I could have sworn I did.

"*My heart. My soul.*" The voice cooed softly, sending ripples of warmth through me from my chest all the way to my toes. "*Find me. I beg of you. Find me, my Ishaleon.*"

I wasn't floating.

I was flying—through the air like a ragdoll, to be exact.

I jolted awake as I smacked hard into the side of the wagon. Or maybe that was the ground? I couldn't tell with the bag still over my head. Regardless, the impact jarred my already delirious brain and knocked the breath from my lungs. I wheezed and cried out hoarsely. Just what the heck was going on?

I got about a half a second of clarity—long enough for me to guess that the wagon must have tipped over somehow—before something big and heavy smashed down right on top of me with a loud "*OOF!*"

Rook.

He landed on my chest and immediately began hissing and snapping out sharp words that were probably profanity in some other language. Loud crashing and smashing nearby made me cringe and grunt, wriggling underneath Rook's weight. Were those crates? Or trunks? Whatever they were, I was just glad they hadn't landed on me, too. It was bad enough to have Rook basically sitting on my face.

"Stay here and do not make any sound!" He snarled as he climbed off me and disappeared.

My heart pounded, making my chest thrum with sharp pangs of pain as I kept wheezing and gasping for breath under that stupid sack. Off—I had to get it off. I set my jaw and tried to roll over, to move even just a little. I flopped around uselessly with my wrists and ankles still tied, probably looking a lot like a caught salmon. In the end, the best I could do was roll over onto my side. The shivering returned with a vengeance, making every muscle in my body seize and shake out of control.

Muffled shouts made my eyes search in vain through the darkness. What was going on? What had happened? Was that ... the clashing of swords? Had someone attacked the Ulfrangar? Or the wagon we were hiding in?

Then it hit me.

A sound—I needed to make a sound. A shout or a whimper—anything really. I had to do it right now.

"H-H—" I rasped weakly, my throat closing up as I shivered. I bit down hard, gulping in a deep breath before I threw my head back and shouted as loudly as I could "S-SOMEONE H-HELP!"

Something crunched nearby, coming closer and closer. Footsteps? I jerked and panted, trying to cry out again. But all I managed were a few faint, stammering whimpers.

The footsteps grew closer and closer. Then they stopped. Oh, gods, what if they left? What if they couldn't see me?

Or what if it was Phillip?

That horrible thought hit me like a punch to the throat. Oh no. What if he'd found me? I went stiff and still, straining to hear something—anything. A breath. A muttered word. Just some small clue about who might be close by.

I let out a garbled scream and flailed back weakly as someone suddenly grabbed the bag over my head and swiftly jerked it off.

"Thatcher!" A familiar feminine voice gasped my name in relief.

I blinked up owlishly through the gloom. Lying limp and breathless on my back, I couldn't stop my face from screwing up as I met Isandri's horrified stare. Once again, she'd saved me when I thought no one could.

"Merciful Goddess, you're freezing," she said as she crouched down and threw the soggy cloak off me. "It's all right, Thatcher. You're going to be okay now."

Something in her voice made me wonder if that was actually true, or if she was just trying to make me feel better.

Pulling a dagger from her robes, she quickly cut the bonds on my hands and feet. Then she dragged me in closer, wrapping her arms around me, and hugging my body against hers. Warm—she was so warm. And she smelled of something soft and delicately sweet. Like lilac. Or maybe jasmine. Honestly, it didn't matter which. It was completely wonderful, and I breathed it in deeply as my head lolled against her shoulder.

We couldn't stay that way for long, though.

"We have to move," Isandri urged gently. "He won't last long. This is our only chance."

"H-He?" I slurred groggily as she helped me stagger to my feet.

Her eyes caught in the flash of lightning, reflecting it like two yellow and green mirrors for a fleeting instant. She stood straight as she glared toward the opening of the canvas-covered wagon where she'd found me. Beyond it, the winds still raged. The rain fell in torrents and thunder rattled the sky. Shouts and cries mingled with the chaos, tangled with the *occasional clang, clatter,* and *scrape* of swords. Gods and Fates, it was as though the whole world was being torn apart out there.

"Murdoc." Her tone was solemn as a cold, forbidding sense of determination settled over her beautiful features. "He's come to end it."

18
CHAPTER EIGHTEEN

I froze, staring blankly at Isandri.

Murdoc? He'd come, too? But ... but that meant ...

Oh gods—he was fighting them! Murdoc was fighting the Ulfrangar on his own!

I staggered forward, tripping and nearly falling as I scrambled to the opening at the back of the up-turned wagon. I couldn't let him do this. He'd never be able to take them all without help. Rook, the very man who'd trained him to fight in the first place, was out there. He wouldn't stand a chance!

"Thatcher!" Isandri shouted frantically. "No! We must go now!" She seized the back of my tunic.

I twisted, jerking out of her grasp.

No. Absolutely not.

I would not leave Murdoc behind like this. He'd come to save me. Now it was my turn. I could help him.

I just had to get my whistle.

I bit down hard against the sharp, shooting pain that surged up my legs with every step as I ran out into the storm. The wind snatched at my hair and the rain struck my face like a thousand icy needles. The broad, open sky rippled with waves of snapping, sizzling light, illuminating the battle before me.

All the air rushed out of me at once.

Murdoc stood only twenty or thirty yards away, gripping a blade in each hand, as he faced down a much older man clad in black leather armor. Rook. Even from a distance, I recognized his hard features and salt-and-pepper-colored beard.

He glowered at Murdoc, the silver cuffs fitted into both his vambraces flashing as he spun his short, leaf-shaped blade over his hand. "Look around you, Murdoc. I taught you to know when you are beaten. Surrender honorably. This is the last mercy the pack can offer you." He gave a flourish with it, gesturing to the crowd of other black-clad figures that encircled them. More Ulfrangar. Fates, there ... there must have been twelve of them in all.

But why weren't they attacking me? Why weren't they trying to take me captive again?

Oh. Right. Because *I* wasn't the one they really wanted.

"You also taught me to *never* surrender," Murdoc growled back, his face twisted in a look of reckless, primal rage I'd never seen before. "There is no honor here! There never was! Only death. Only blood and suffering. That was the only reward. You told me to look for more—to find my reason. But there was nothing!"

Rook's brows snapped together, his lip curling in a snarl. "Is that what you've truly come for, then? More blood? More death? To send a few more souls to the afterlife ahead of you?"

Murdoc let out a yell and lunged like a springing panther. Rook met him halfway, moving like a dark shadow over the soggy earth. Their blades flashed in the stormy light, blurring through spinning strikes so fast I couldn't even make sense of them.

Murdoc and Rook dueled like demons amidst the storm, still shouting at one another as they blurred through parries, feints, and slashes. All around them, the circle of Ulfrangar lurked like a ring of ghostly reapers. They never moved. They didn't even draw their weapons.

A few of them already lay in the mud nearby, their bodies twisted and motionless. Dead.

I started for the nearest one and pried the shortsword out of his hand. My heart hammered in my throat, hands clumsy and numb as I whirled around again—

—Just in time to see Murdoc take a hit.

Rook scored his side with a swipe of his blade, slicing open his side and leaving his tunic hanging open. Blood ran from the deep, gaping wound right below Murdoc's ribs, but he didn't falter. He didn't even blink or wince. He dove straight in again, retaliating with a vicious series of strikes that forced Rook back on his heels.

I hesitated, squeezing the hilt of the blade in my hand. S-Something wasn't right. That look on Murdoc's face. That wild chaos in his wide, bloodshot eyes. His expression was empty except for primal wrath, and his pupils were so wide they blotted out all the color of his irises. It's like it wasn't him at all.

"We must not linger," Isandri snapped in my ear as she seized my wrist, probably to try and stop me from actually using that blade.

"W-What's wrong with him?" I stammered, never taking my eyes off the fight. "What's wrong with Murdoc?"

She squeezed my wrist harder. "Thatcher, it isn't something you can—"

"Tell me!" I snatched my arm away and glared down at her.

"He ... took something. Some medicinal potion Reigh gave him," she answered bitterly. "I don't know what it was. But it's not likely he'll survive the effects. His hope was only to provide a diversion long enough that we could escape. That is why we must leave *now*, Thatcher!"

What? Reigh had given him something? I blinked, stunned and struggling to process that as I looked back to where my friend still fought. He bore in hard, his movements an absolute hailstorm of blitzing strikes that Rook struggled to match. That pale, stunned look of confusion on the older man's face said it all.

He'd never seen Murdoc fight like this, either.

I should go. I should run away and not look back. I knew that. It's what Murdoc wanted. It's the whole reason he'd come.

But I couldn't.

I stood locked in place, watching as he dueled like a fiend in the thundering, sizzling chaos of the storm. He dropped low and kicked into a roll, sliding easily under one of Rook's swift assaults. The blade hummed a deadly melody as it slashed through the air, hitting nothing. Rook's eyes went wide, as though he realized his mistake.

Too late.

Murdoc sprang up behind him. In one fluid, perfect step, he whirled both of his longswords through a downward strike—right across the back of Rook's legs.

The man crumpled immediately, falling like a puppet whose strings had been cut. He hit the mud at Murdoc's feet, barely managing to roll onto his back before the point of a longsword pressed threateningly at his throat. He slowly looked up.

My friend stood over him, panting in deep, furious breaths as he held the end of one blade to his former handler's neck. The rain ran down his face and dripped from his chin and the end of his nose as he glared back down at Rook. His expression twitched, but I couldn't tell if it was from rage or ... something else.

Around them, the other Ulfrangar assassins shifted uneasily. A few of them had dared to touch the hilt of their weapons. Crossbows, daggers, swords, and scimitars—each one of them was armed to the teeth.

That's when I realized. Gods and Fates, Murdoc knew he'd never get out of this alive. Even if he beat Rook and took down a few of the others, it wouldn't matter. As soon as he ended it—as soon as the duel was over—they'd converge.

And he'd be overwhelmed in seconds.

I took a staggering step toward him. Whatever potion he'd taken, he was still my best friend. I couldn't leave him like this. "Isandri," I said as Murdoc's arm and shoulder flexed, drawing back and preparing to make that final strike. I wasn't even sure she'd be able to hear me over the wind and thunder.

Her shoulder lightly brushed mine as she stepped in closer to stand at my side, holding her staff tightly in both hands now. "I know," she replied without ever looking my way. "I am with you."

IT ALL SEEMED to happen in slow motion, like the entire universe had suddenly frozen in place.

Murdoc struck, plunging his blade down into the center of Rook's chest. The Ulfrangar converged upon him immediately like a pack of dark wolves. Arrows zipped and hummed in every direction. Blades flashed in the night. Murdoc disappearing into a mob of black-hooded figures.

Isandri and I rushed forward together.

I wouldn't last long. I knew that. I wasn't all that good a fighter anyway, and I'd just spent the last several days bound up and nearly frozen to death. I probably wouldn't last five seconds. But for his sake, I had to try.

I got lucky on my first attack. Rushing for the nearest Ulfrangar, who'd stopped to take aim with his crossbow from a distance, I drove my blade into his back with all my strength. He pitched wildly and dropped his crossbow, crying out before he fell.

I staggered back, half in shock that it'd actually worked, and half completely terrified as two more Ulfrangar whipped around and saw what I'd done. They narrowed their eyes and started for me at a sprint. Oh no.

Before I could react, Isandri sprang past me with the crystalline head of her staff crackling and gleaming like a star in the night. She dodged and wove, locking in combat with the two assassins as though it were as natural as breathing. She moved with a grace and speed that should've been impossible, bending around their attacks with perfect synchronization to dodge every blade that swept by.

CRACK!

She beat one of the assassins over the head with the big crystal-tipped end of her weapon. The blow sent him staggering back in a daze, and she swiftly darted forward to sweep his legs out from under him. He hit the ground flat on his back, and Isandri sprang, jabbing the other end of her staff—the one tipped with a tri-edged blade—into the other assassin's chest as he tried to rush her from behind. She wrenched it out of him in one brutal motion. He dropped immediately, and Isandri landed in a crouch over the first one to finish things with that spear-blade again.

Three down.

But I still couldn't see Murdoc.

Through the fray of combat, I searched for some sign of him as I grabbed the crossbow of the Ulfrangar I'd just cut down and prepared to press my luck again. Gods, where was he?

"Murdoc!" I shouted, but my voice was lost to the roar of the storm and clashing of combat. No way he could hear me.

Suddenly, another sound rose over the rumble and rattle of the fight. A noise I knew well. The high-pitched blast of a whistle.

My whistle.

A tingling rush of confusion and panic rushed through me. My pulse skipped. Had Murdoc found it on Rook's body? Was he calling for Fornax?

"B-Blow it again!" I yelled, my voice cracking and breaking as I surged forward with the crossbow ready to fire. "Don't stop!"

The whistle blared again—sounding over and over like a barely audible scream.

Then, from somewhere amidst the toiling, churning skies, came a booming reply. A bellowing roar that made hope like hellfire burn through my chest. Fornax!

I whirled around, searching the clouds for him. A brilliant tongue of lightning forked out across the sky, revealing the silhouette of a dragon descending toward us with his broad wings stretched wide. His horns flashed and his scales gleamed under the strobing light of the storm.

Only ... it wasn't Fornax. It was a dragon I'd never seen before. And it was headed straight for the middle of our fight.

Straight for Murdoc.

PART FIVE
MURDOC

19

CHAPTER NINETEEN

I hit the ground on my knees and crumpled forward as another Ulfrangar fell to my blade. Landing next to him, I shuddered hard as pain ripped all the breath from my lungs. My arms shook, hands clenched around the mud-caked hilts of my longswords as I pushed away from the ground.

Curse it all. Up—I had to get up. I couldn't quit. Not now. Not until this was done. I had to stand. I had to fight. Every second gave Thatcher and Isandri a chance to …

My elbows buckled.

I hit the mud again. My entire body screamed in protest to every breath I took. Reigh's godsgrave potion had run its course and bought me a lot more time than I'd expected. But now came the end. The agonizing aftermath Reigh warned me about when the potion finally stopped working.

Only four Ulfrangar remained, their blades drawn on me as they hesitated and watched me writhe. Probably wondering why I'd suddenly stopped fighting.

It wouldn't last, though. Even if they were all novices on their first hunt, they'd forget their fear soon. They'd move in to finish this once and for all.

And I couldn't even stand long enough to face them head-on. So much for dying with dignity.

I cried out as my spine thrummed with wave after wave of pain that made my arms and legs convulse. Each breath sent white-hot agony exploding through my chest. Every nerve fired at once, as though I'd been set on fire and left to burn.

Die—I wanted to die. If living hurt this much then, please, just let it end. It would be okay. The others would be fine.

I squinted up at the nearest of my former comrades. Even with his cowl up and his face smeared with a swipe of black paint to hide his features, I could see his eyes studying me. Like he was trying to make up his mind to attack or not. Maybe he thought this was a ruse. A trick to get him to drop his guard.

"H-Hurry up ... a-and ... d-do it!" I spat, tasting blood in my mouth with every halting, broken word.

His gaze narrowed, grip tightening on the scimitar he carried. He took a step toward me.

A sound ripped through the night, making us all pause. A high-pitched screech, like the shrill call of a whistle.

My mouth fell open.

Still sprawled on his back, his body broken and bleeding, Rook stared straight at me as he held an all-too-familiar silver whistle to his lips. That ... that was Thatcher's whistle. The one he used to summon Fornax. He blew it again and again, never blinking as his eyes bored into mine with earnest.

W-What? What was he doing? Had Rook lost his mind? If he kept that up, he'd call that beast down upon us! Why would he *want* to bring the dragon here? It would kill the Ulfrangar—his own men—and then ...

Then, I might escape again.

Gods. No. T-That couldn't be it. That couldn't be why he'd done all this. Why he'd kidnapped Thatcher and forced him to take my place. Why all these Ulfrangar he'd brought with him were ones I'd never met before; people who wouldn't recognize that Thatcher wasn't me.

It couldn't be because he was ... trying to save me.

Could it?

No ... *NO!!*

Something boomed through the dark. The low, rhythmic *thump—thump—thump* of mighty wing beats coming closer. Massive. Powerful.

Fornax.

I couldn't get up or move except to roll onto my back. The rain stung at my face and forced me to close my eyes. But I could still hear the whistle's shrill note screeching in the air.

The earth flinched under my back as the dragon landed. Its angry snarl, and the sudden *WHOOSH* of roaring flames when it breathed fire, drowned out the storm. The few remaining Ulfrangar screamed in terror. Their footsteps sloshed and slurped in the mud as they fled past me. The *twang* of crossbow fire made the beast bellow again, and another burst of flame exploded into the night so close I could feel the heat against my cheek.

Then it all went completely silent. The shouting. The dragon's roaring. Even the rain seemed to have stopped stinging at my face as I lay there, shaking in the cold mud.

Slowly, I forced my eyes to open ...

... and stared straight into the face of a dragon I didn't recognize.

Crouched down low, the beast's wings shielded me from the storm as it craned its large head down and sniffed at my face. Blasts of hot breath stirred in my wet hair and it snuffled all over my head and chest, bumping me with the end of its short, black-and-red-scaled snout. Its scaly ears perked and swiveled as it made low, almost worried murring sounds.

W-What? What was this? Who was this creature? And where was its rider? Had Jaevid sent someone ahead to intercept us?

I kept waiting for someone to appear, a dragonrider in shining armor to clean up any remaining Ulfrangar that hadn't already fled. But no one came. Squinting up at the dragon's back, I couldn't see that it was even wearing a saddle. A wild dragon, then?

No. That didn't make sense. Wild dragons didn't act this way. They avoided people whenever they could. They certainly didn't seek them out in the throes of battle and … save them.

I mean, not outside of old tales and stories, that is.

The beast blinked its large blue eyes, tilting its head to the side. It bumped me with its nose again, as though coaxing me to move. I couldn't. Not much, anyway. Not enough to stand.

It took everything I had, every last shred of strength, to reach a shaking hand up and touch the dragon's snout. Those warm, smooth scales slid under my palm like soft, worn leather. Heh. That still caught me by surprise every time. I'd always imagined they'd be rough and cold to the touch.

The dragon made curious popping and chirping sounds in its throat as I ran my fingers over the ridge of black horns that began at the tip of its nose. They were a stark contrast to the red stripe that ran down its head like a blaze. Larger black horns jutted back like obsidian spikes from over its ears. But from where I lay, I couldn't see much else about it. I couldn't tell if it was male or female, or even judge its size.

Not that it mattered. It wasn't like this was *my* dragon. Any second now, its rider would show up. Maybe they just hadn't had the time to put their saddle on before taking off to our aid.

"T-Thank you," I managed hoarsely before my arm dropped back to my side.

The dragon gave a disapproving, almost panicked bark. It bumped my chest with its nose again, nipping at the front of my blood and rain drenched tunic. But I couldn't respond. Not this time.

My head slumped to the side as everything around me seemed to fade to blurred shades of gray. I … I couldn't do this much longer. Every second, every heartbeat, brought me closer to the end. The edges of my vision began to grow dim.

And that's when I saw him.

Rook lay only a few yards away, motionless and staring straight back at me through the pouring rain, his expression was empty.

He was already gone.

My eyes rolled closed again, and for an instant, I could have sworn I heard something. Distant echoes of someone shouting my name, almost totally drowned out by the raging storm. The shouting grew closer and closer, until I was almost certain I recognized their voice.

That couldn't be right, though. Thatcher was bound to be miles away from here by now. Isandri had sworn she'd take him away as soon as she found him.

So why did that sound so much like him?

Something absolutely reeked of horse. No, not horse. Something else. It had that same heavy, animal musk to it, though. And something else—almost like rotten meat.

I coughed and gagged a little, my face scrunching as I stirred awake. Opening my eyes, I found myself staring straight down the throat of a dragon. The sight of massive fangs and the low rumble of a hungry growl right in my face made my heart hit the back of my throat. Oh gods!

I tried to scrambled back, but every muscle and joint in my body resisted. I could barely move, and I only managed to scoot a foot or so back away from the creature.

Far enough to realize it wasn't growling.

It was *snoring*.

The dragon lay next to me with its tail curled around both of us, sleeping with its head flopped sideways and its mouth hanging open. Its long tongue lolled out as it snored with every heaving breath it took, blasting puffs of its breath right in my face.

Well, that explained the smell.

I stared in shock, struggling to piece together what had happened and how I'd wound up here ... with a dragon. A sort of small-ish one, in fact. It wasn't nearly as big as Fornax, and was even slightly smaller than Reigh's dragoness, Vexi. A young dragon, then? Or a runt?

I frowned. What was it doing here, anyway?

And where, exactly, was *here*?

One look around the place—at the gray stone floor sprinkled with old hay, rough wood walls, tall thatched roof, and line of stalls on the far wall—and as best I could tell, I'd wound up in someone's barn. There weren't any windows, only one large sliding door at the far end that had been drawn closed. The warm, humid air smelled strongly of rain, hay, grain, and that ambient odor of animal musk.

Definitely a barn. But whose?

I tried sitting up again, but every muscle still lurched, spasmed, and throbbed in protest. No luck. The most I could do was lift my head and stare down at my pitiful state. A few quilts had been carefully spread out on top of a mound of hay as a makeshift bed for me, and my clothes were gone. All I wore now were smallclothes and a pair of loose drawstring pants. Most of my chest and torso were wrapped in layers of heavy bandaging, and one of my arms was in a sling that held it firm against my chest.

But I was alive.

I had to remind myself that was a good thing as my head pounded and ached. Lying back on the hay-bed again, I tried to focus and remember what had happened. It was impossible to concentrate with that dragon snoring right in my face, though.

I scowled at it. Why, by all the gods, was it curled up around me like that?

Somewhere out of sight, a door creaked and groaned open, and footsteps shuffled along the hay-strewn floor toward me. I managed to crane my head just far enough to catch a glimpse of Reigh as he strolled my way with a tray of medical supplies in his hands.

He paused when he saw me. Then his shoulders dropped with a relieved sigh. "Oh, good, you're awake. And here I was already trying to think of another excuse to give Phoebe and Thatcher for why they can't come in here to visit you yet."

"W-Where are they?" I grunted as I tried, and failed, to sit up again.

"At the Porter's with Lin and Jondar. Here, let me help you." He set the tray down on the floor nearby and knelt down, putting his arms behind my back and carefully guiding me into a sitting position.

"Thatcher is all right?" I asked, watching his reaction carefully for any signs of distress.

There weren't any. Reigh just shrugged and went on arranging the hay and quilts behind my back so I could rest while I sat. "He was hypothermic, dehydrated, and had taken a few hits. He had some pretty nasty bruises, but he wasn't too bad off considering. Nothing a long soak in a hot bath, a few healing remedies, and a lot of water couldn't fix."

I swallowed hard and looked away. Rook had been very gentle with him. I couldn't help but wonder why. None of what he'd done made any sense, and just trying to think about it put a knot in my throat that pulsed and throbbed whenever I tried to speak.

Fortunately, Reigh didn't seem to notice. He went on chattering as he laid out his medical wares so he could change my bandages. "Isa had a few minor wounds, but she's fine, too. Honestly, I'm not sure Clysiros herself could stand against that girl in a fight. She's scarier than you are sometimes. No offense."

I flicked him a haggard glare.

"You, on the other hand, better keep your butt in this bed for at least the next three days. Seriously, I mean it. You have no idea how close you came to dying, Murdoc. I told you godsgrave is risky enough on its own, but you had sword gashes straight down to the bone. The one on your side nicked your intestines, and the one on your thigh came less than an inch from your artery. If it'd hit, you would have bled out before anyone got to you. Add that to the burns you already had, the scarring in your lungs from breathing in that toxic smoke, and the strain godsgrave puts on your heart and brain—you, my friend, are either the luckiest or unluckiest person I've ever known."

I had a feeling I knew which. "Why aren't we at the healing house?" If my injuries were that bad, I had to wonder why I was being treated in someone's barn.

Reigh's mouth split with a smirk as he began removing the old bandages from around my torso. "Yeeeah, well, big surprise, the medic running this place doesn't want you *or* your dragon at his house—not after the last two places we stayed in, you know, burned to the ground."

Fair enough.

Then it hit me. I shot Reigh a piercing stare. "What do you mean *my* dragon?"

He nodded to the snoring monstrosity stretched out on my other side and laughed like it should have been obvious. "That one. He won't let you out of his sight."

"He?"

"Look at the dewclaws. See how big and pronounced they are? That means it's a male. He's a young one though. Probably only six or seven years old. I don't even know if he's big enough to ride yet."

I glanced back and forth between Reigh and the dragon a few times. "Right. Well. *He* isn't mine."

Reigh gave a smug little chuckle that made me want to punch his face in for some reason. "He is now."

Okay, now I *really* wanted to punch him.

"Look, I get it. When Vexi chose me, it wasn't so different. I wasn't out hunting for a dragon or anything. And she was wild, too. But take it from someone who tried—you can't fight his bond. You can't get him to 'un-choose' you. So you might as well get used to it," Reigh said as he leaned back and stared at my now exposed chest and abdomen. His brows furrowed, as though he were critiquing the gruesome lines in my flesh that had been meticulously stitched closed. The one on my side ran from the back of my ribcage all the way to my hip, and another across my chest slashed right over my collarbone and down to my pectorals. "Looks like we need to up your dosage on the infection remedies. You know, Kiran never finished the research on it, but I'm convinced that godsgrave slows healing. Or at the very least it counteracts some of our usual anti-infection poultices."

He rambled on, talking about medical procedures and his theories behind the side effects of godsgrave, while he cleaned all my wounds and redressed them with clean bandaging. It took a while, and the only thing he relented on was making me put that sling back on my arm.

"Your shoulder had some serious bruising down to your elbow, but I still can't find any traces of a break or a fracture," he resolved aloud. "I guess just try not to overdo it. Lie here, brood, and let yourself heal."

I snorted and shook my head. He never let up with that cocky attitude. Not even for a minute.

"After a few days, when you're feeling more like yourself, there's ... uh, there's something we need to talk about." The reluctance in Reigh's tone made me go tense.

"And that is?"

He rubbed at the back of his neck and lowered his voice, as though he were afraid someone might overhear. "Devana. I finally got information from Judan's agent. Turns out we might need to change our plans up a little. But it can wait until we are all able to sit down and discuss it," he muttered. "Besides, I think Isandri might be holding out on us. You should have seen her face when Jondar told me about Phillip referring to Thatcher as a 'godling.' I could've knocked her over with a feather. She hasn't said much since, but I have a suspicion that she knows what's really going on with Thatcher and Devana."

I sat, paralyzed in thought. After everything that had happened, I'd nearly forgotten about what Phillip had said. I'd heard that term, godling, somewhere before. But it must have been in passing, or so long ago that the meaning hadn't stuck. Hmm.

"We'll figure it out when you're on your feet," Reigh added, already gathering up his supplies. "I'll come back with dinner in a little while. Try to get some sleep. The storm still hasn't let up at all, so it's not like we can go anywhere right away. Flying a dragon in weather like this is miserable. Can't see anything and the winds are terrible." He paused, and I could hear that cunning grin in his voice without needing to see it curl over his stupid face. "Besides, *you* don't have a saddle for *yours* yet."

I lifted my head and gave Reigh a meaningful look. "He. Isn't. Mine," I growled again, louder this time.

Reigh laughed and flapped a hand at me sarcastically as he swaggered out of the barn. "Whatever you say, *dragonrider*."

20
CHAPTER TWENTY

I was *not* a dragonrider.

No. Absolutely not.

I did, however, have a problem. A very big, dragon-shaped problem that seemed to have an obsession with stealing my shoes and licking the insides of them until they were slathered with sticky saliva.

"*YOU!*" I shouted as soon as I heard that tale-tell *sluuuurp* when I stuck my foot down into my boot. I yanked it out, grimacing as my sock dripped with globs of fresh dragon-spit.

Across the barn, the culprit wilted on the spot. His ears drooped and he waggled the end of his tail as he dipped his head. It might've worked to curb my rage ... except that he had my other boot hanging off the end of his snout. It hit the floor with a soggy *slap*.

Gods, Fates, and all things divine. I would throttle that blasted scaly menace if it's the last thing I ever did.

"*NO!* Not again!" I thundered as I started for him. "So help me, I will—"

"Glad to see you two are getting along," Reigh snickered as he stood by the door, watching my struggle with a wry grin on his face.

Maybe I'd just throttle him, too.

I stormed away to retrieve my other boot, muttering curses under my breath the whole way. There was no way I'd *ever* become a dragonrider. Thatcher had been a questionable choice only because of his fighting abilities—or lack thereof, rather. But *me*? Donning shining armor and flying in the shadow of men like Jaevid Broadfeather? Hah! Ridiculous. Stupid. An insult to their legacy, honestly. I was a criminal. Not a knight. Clearly there was something profoundly wrong with this creature because it couldn't have picked a more terrible candidate for a rider in the entire world.

Except for Thatcher, maybe. But he was already taken.

"He must like your foot smell or something," Reigh laughed again when I swiped my boot off the floor and turned it upside down so all the thick blobs of drool could slowly ooze out onto the floor.

Ugh. Why me? Wasn't dealing with Thatcher enough? Or was this the gods' way of punishing me for my lifetime of sin and murder? If so, bravo. Well played. But I would've preferred one of them to just smite me on the spot.

"Have you given him a name yet?" Reigh asked as he wandered over. He still gave me those intense, inspecting looks whenever he thought I wasn't paying attention—as though watching me for any signs of pain or distress.

It'd been four days now, though. And thanks to his medical skills, I could manage well enough. There was still some pain, especially where I'd taken that sword to the side and thigh. But I could bear it, and the wounds were already scarring over. Those foul-smelling elven herbs stank like swamp silt, but I couldn't deny their effectiveness.

"No," I grumbled as I stood there, waiting for the spit to drain out of my shoes.

"Well, you should. He's gotta have a name."

I shot the shoe-thief a glare over my shoulder. He sat there, blinking at me with those wide, vivid blue eyes, his wings folded against his black scaly sides and his ears swiveling curiously in my direction. From what Ezran Cromwell had told us about dragon breeding, I could guess that a coloration like his might be desirable. Most of his scaly body was as black as onyx, all except for a bright red blaze that ran from his snout, down his back, all the way to the end of his tail. A color-combination like that might have made him look menacing ... if not for the absolute air-headed vacancy in his eyes. Gods, it reminded me of Thatcher.

"Naming him would mean I'm keeping him," I muttered. "And I'm not, so there's no point."

"Still going on with that, eh?" Reigh arched an eyebrow. "Well, I guess there's no law saying you have to be a dragonrider if you're chosen, just that you can't be turned away."

"It would be a waste if you didn't, though," a deep voice interrupted us suddenly.

Reigh and I both startled. We whirled around to find a tall, broad-shouldered man standing behind us with a wide, knowing smile on his face. It made the scar over one of his eyes scrunch a little right at his cheek. The tips of his pointed ears peeked through his lengthy ash gray hair—which he'd raked back into a messy ponytail at the base of his neck.

Jaevid Broadfeather.

And he hadn't come alone.

On either side of him, Thatcher, Isandri, and another tall half-elven man I didn't recognize stood looking on with mixed expressions of awkward uncertainty, concern, and amusement. My throat tightened a little, feeling strangely stiff and dry when I noticed that of all of them, the only one who wouldn't look me in the eye was Thatcher. He stared down at the toes of his boots, his brows drawn up worriedly, and didn't say a word.

It was the first time I'd seen him since ... well, since before everything had gone wrong.

I looked down, too. Silence was probably best, for as long as I could manage it.

Although, part of me wanted to ask where Phoebe was. Why hadn't she come with the rest of them? Was she all right? Or was she avoiding me now?

After that, um, *event* during the fire, I wasn't sure what to say to her. Should I even say anything? It might've been better just to act like it never happened.

Figuring that out would have to wait, though.

"It seems there's a lot we need to talk about," Jaevid said as he panned his glacier-blue eyes around at all of us. "But before that, Murdoc, I'd like a moment to speak with you alone."

My pulse instantly jolted into a frenzy, kicking wildly in my chest as I dared to meet his gaze for an instant. Thatcher looked up, too. His look of concern intensified and he opened his mouth like he might protest.

So I spoke up quickly, before he could get a word out. "Fine. If that's what you want."

"How about I take everyone else to the Porters and you two can catch up, yeah?" Reigh offered, seeming to sense the rising tension in the air.

The others agreed and started out of the barn—chatting, laughing, and bickering like a herd of noisy goats. Well, all except for Thatcher. He still didn't speak, although he followed along behind the rest of the group without putting up a fight.

Good. If this conversation was going to go where I suspected it would, then I didn't want him to hear any of it. Despite what I'm sure he would have said to the contrary, I hadn't done much to make myself worthy of being called his friend. I'd put him in danger, almost gotten him killed, hidden things from him, and not been there for him the way a normal person would have.

I'd tried, of course. I just ... didn't know how to *do* normal. It didn't come to me as naturally as I'd hoped. Frankly, so far, it hadn't come to me at all.

Now, I didn't want to have to look him in the eye while I disappointed him yet again.

AT FIRST, Jaevid didn't say anything. He stood there, his brow creased as he focused his gaze upon the floor. His mouth quirked to one side and then the other, as though he were chewing on the inside of his cheek. Probably trying to choose his words carefully.

I decided not to give him the chance. "Listen, if you're about to give me some long-winded speech about destiny and how this is my big chance to become something better—just don't. Save your breath," I blurted quickly, before I lost my nerve. "I *know* I'm not the kind of person the glorious dragonriders of Maldobar would ever want in their ranks."

Jaevid's thoughtful frown smoothed and he gave me a quick, almost puzzled glance. "Actually, I was going to ask if you're all right," he said evenly as he stepped casually past me and approached the young dragon instead.

I blinked. What? He ... wasn't going to try to convince me to join them? Why not? As much as I wanted to know, I didn't dare ask. Otherwise, he might wind up giving me one of those speeches, anyway.

"My wounds have healed enough for me to travel, so I—"

"I don't mean physically," he clarified.

Oh. So *that's* what he wanted to talk about.

I shifted and looked away. "It's not worth discussing."

"I beg to differ. Reigh and Isandri told me about what happened—about how much you risked to save Thatcher. I have to admit, I was surprised. I've wondered if his loyalty in this friendship was a lot stronger than yours. I'm pleased to be proven wrong."

I scowled as I bent down to put on my boots, using that as an excuse not to answer. Not that it was surprising he had wondered about my loyalties. Quite honestly, I was surprised no one else had questioned me more about that. So far, only King Jace had thrown up serious objections to my presence.

Well, him and me. But it seemed like my vote didn't really count in this case.

"And then you had to fight and kill your former trainer; the man that essentially raised you," Jaevid continued as he offered a hand out for the dragon to sniff. "I'm not sure anyone would be all right after that, Ulfrangar or not."

My jaw tensed and my hands halted as I tied my bootlaces. I did *not* want to talk about this. Not with him. "It's fine. I'm fine."

"Is that so?"

"Yes," I growled through my teeth as I stood straight again.

He didn't say anything for a minute or two. Then, while he ran his hand along the dragon's snout and scratched at its chin, he spoke softly. "Did you hate him?"

My breath caught and immediately my mind went blank. I ... I didn't know how to answer that. Did I hate Rook? Was I supposed to? He wasn't my father, even if he had been my handler since I was eight. Yes, he'd taken care of me, fed me, taught me to fight, and overseen my education. But he'd also been the one who beat me whenever I stumbled in my training. The bite of his whip across my back had been my reward if I took a single wrong step during combat drills or got an accent incorrect during my language instruction. The Ulfrangar didn't exactly exist to foster feelings of familial affection. In fact, there were quite a few strictly enforced laws within the order preventing that very thing from taking place. Pack loyalty was one thing. That was expected.

But actual comradery? Empathy? *Love*? No. Those were not beneficial to Ulfrangar. Those were manifestations of weakness. Feelings like that that would threaten the stability and efficiency of the pack, and so they must be culled.

Or so I'd been instructed—by Rook himself.

And yet he'd done all this. Risked and lost everything. None of it made any sense to me, and I stood there with my mind a whirling vortex of uncertainty.

I ... I didn't know if I'd hated or loved him. I didn't even know what those words meant. Not in practice, anyway.

Jaevid must have been able to sense my complete bewilderment because he gave a heavy sigh and finally turned to face me. "I don't know if I should even tell you this. I don't know if he would even want you to know. But I don't like keeping secrets, especially ones like this. You have a right to know it."

My mouth opened, but I couldn't force a single word out. What secret? What was he talking about?

"Rook was the one who asked me to come here. He sent word directly to my estate and asked me to save you. He knew what was coming, that the Ulfrangar would orchestrate another attempt to abduct or kill you, and for some reason ... he thought that if I was the one who intervened on your behalf, they might not pursue you anymore."

My mouth fell open. Rook had contacted Jaevid? To try and save me?! Gods and Fates.

It was one thing to try to thwart their assault—that was dangerous enough on its own. But to completely break the Ulfrangar's oath of secrecy and communicate plans to someone outside the pack? I'd never heard of anyone doing it before. Ever. The punishment for that kind of betrayal was one far worse than death.

And Rook had risked that ... for *me*?

"W-Why?" I rasped weakly. My heart pounded wildly, making my face flush as I took a staggering step toward him. I didn't really expect Jaevid to know or even answer. I couldn't hold it in. "Why would he do that? Why would he—?!"

"I think he must have cared for you quite a lot," Jaevid interrupted, his voice still calm and even. "It seems a great many people do, even if you don't consider yourself worthy."

I snapped my mouth shut.

He looked back over at the dragon, who was still watching us curiously, twitching his little scaly ears, and puffing through his big nostrils. "Including this young one. Amazing, isn't it? How attached they become so quickly."

I bowed my head, hoping to hide the way my face burned with shame. "How can I make him go away?" I begged. "You have to make him go. Please."

Jaevid didn't answer. He didn't have to, though. I could feel his disapproving scowl from ten paces away.

"This isn't over. They'll ... they'll try again," I murmured. "Failing to apprehend me twice is something the Zuer won't let stand. She won't hold back now. Next time they come for me, it'll be worse. It'll be for redemption, not just punishment."

Jaevid's head snapped up suddenly and he met my gaze with a look that made my stomach drop. For an instant, I realized why the Ulfrangar avoided him. Why he gave them pause. It wasn't wrath, rage, or fury that burned in the depths of his glacier blue eyes like cold fire.

It was sheer force of will.

"You're right, Murdoc. It isn't over," he said. "And it won't be until something in this equation changes. You need to consider very carefully what you do and say around the others—especially those who care so much for you. What you choose to do now doesn't just impact your own life."

I swallowed hard. "I-I know."

"No. You don't. Not fully. And that's ... well, it's something else I need to talk to you about." His tone softened and that smoldering intensity in his gaze ebbed away, replaced with something I couldn't quite place. Regret? Sorrow? "It's about Thatcher, actually."

I stiffened. "What about him?"

He shook his head slowly, making a few locks of his ash-colored hair slip loose from its messy ponytail. "His father has been confirmed dead."

I set my jaw. "Yes. He knows that."

"No," Jaevid corrected sternly. "He knew we strongly suspected it, but since we were unable to identify any remains or find someone who'd actually seen him that night, there was still hope. Enough hope that Prince Aubren had continued his search." His chest heaved as he gave a deep, resigned sigh. "But now Aubren finally tracked down someone who saw him during the attack on Thornbend. And, Murdoc, that is where things become complicated. Apparently, Thatcher's father had gone to a house nearby to try and rescue an elderly woman from her home. She was frail and could barely walk on her own, so he was attempting to carry her out. It was someone he must have known—likely a family friend."

I couldn't even feel myself breathing anymore as I asked, "How did he die?"

"A group of individuals wearing black armor and cloaks were seen dragging him and a dozen or more civilians from their homes. They executed him in the street along with all the others, then threw the bodies into the river." Jaevid wouldn't look up at me again. "Murdoc, were you hunting with the Ulfrangar on the eastside streets of the city that night? On the avenues close to the river?"

My heart sat like a cold, frozen stone in the center of my chest.

Oh ... oh gods.

"Yes," I whispered.

He shut his eyes, as though the question was nearly too bitter to speak. "Did you drag any men from the houses there and murder them in the street?"

My mind raced, blitzing over all my muddled memories of that night. The fire in the night. The screams of the dying. The smell of blood and smoke in the air.

The faces of the people I'd slain.

Had any of them looked like Thatcher? Or had Thatcher even resembled his father at all?

I-I couldn't—I didn't—I-I—*CURSE IT ALL!*

"Murdoc." Jaevid's voice was eerily calm as he took a step closer to me. "Did you kill Thatcher's father?"

I ... I didn't know. By all the gods, *I didn't know!*

And the longer I stood there, paralyzed and staring straight into Jaevid's pale, piercing eyes, the more I realized it didn't matter. Even if my hand hadn't been the one holding the blade, it might as well have been. An Ulfrangar had killed Thatcher's father. Another assassin—someone just like me.

I was guilty by association. And that would be enough.

That realization washed over me like freezing rain, slowly numbing every part of me. My shoulders dropped and my head bowed.

"Murdoc?" Jaevid pressed.

I shut my eyes tightly. "Everything about that night went wrong," I murmured. "Rook said it was doomed to be a reckless mess. And he was right. Argonox had a contract with the Zuer that guaranteed Ulfrangar assistance when the final battle for Halfax began. We were to patrol the streets, seeking out and neutralizing any hints of resistance from the Maldobarian infantry ... or citizens. When the order from the Zuer came down that the contract had been activated, Rook and some of the veteran hunters were furious. The requirements of the contract were too vague. What was considered to be 'resistance' from Maldobarian soldiers or citizens hadn't been clearly determined. There was too much room for interpretation. It would be sloppy—and the Ulfrangar *hate* sloppy."

"But it wasn't Rook you hunted with that night," Jaevid pointed out.

I shook my head. "No. It wasn't. Rook didn't want me on the frontlines. He said I wasn't ready, and he didn't want my last hunt as a pup to be something so poorly planned. So he left me with one of his former pups—someone he'd trained years ago. We were supposed to stay at one of the city squares close to the river and keep out of sight, attacking only if we spotted any Maldobarian soldiers moving through the area. But the others ... they got restless. Frustrated. Blood-hungry. They decided to break off into smaller groups and hunt independently. As a pup, I couldn't refuse orders from an elder hunter, especially not the one Rook had put in charge of me. So I had no choice. I couldn't stay behind."

Jaevid sank back on his heels some, his expression creasing with a look of somber understanding. "And that was when you began pulling civilians from their homes."

I couldn't reply. Not when my throat constricted, strangling every word I tried to speak. Seconds passed in silent agony as I looked down, trying to process everything and make sense of it.

"I suppose this explains why Rook felt so responsible for your situation," Jaevid said at last.

"Thatcher won't forgive this," I whispered, unable to hide the brokenness in my voice. "None of them will. They've dismissed everything else, all the horrible things I've done. But they won't be able to overlook this."

Jaevid didn't reply.

So I had to ask. I needed to know. "Are you going to tell Thatcher?"

"Murdoc, I didn't come here to judge or condemn you," Jaevid answered quietly. "But I can't keep this from him. I won't tell him you may have been involved, though. That part should come from you." He took another step toward me and put a hand on my shoulder. "I won't give you false hope, either. I don't know if Thatcher can forgive this. But keeping it from him would be worse, I can promise you that."

My heart thrashed in my ears, a booming rhythm like thunder or dragon wingbeats. I could barely think past it.

"This is the reality of the situation we're all in now: You're absolutely right—things are going to only get more dangerous from here. There are forces at work in this kingdom I'm not sure any of us thought we'd ever encounter, let alone have to fight against. And the only way I can see us even standing a chance at being successful in severing your connection to the Ulfrangar and apprehending Devana, is if you all remain together." Jaevid's gaze drifted back to the young dragon, who still watched us closely. "There's strength in unity. But unity requires honesty. Sooner or later, you'll have to tell him the truth. And Murdoc, I'd strongly encourage you to do it sooner, because the longer you wait, the more it is going to feel like you were deceiving him."

He was right. I knew that. And yet, just the thought of trying to have that conversation with Thatcher made my stomach turn and my breath freeze in my lungs. I'd watch his last bit of faith in me die.

I'd lose the only real friend I'd ever had.

"We shouldn't keep them waiting much longer." Starting out of the barn, Jaevid paused only to pull a necklace out of his pocket. Thatcher's necklace. He put the whistle to his lips and looked skyward. "I have a hunch your dragon will do better if he's not left here on his own. So I promised I'd make sure Fornax was safely secured here for the night."

"He's not *my* dragon," I reminded him again.

Jaevid flashed me a quick, almost patronizing smirk. "I believe he'd beg to differ, but suit yourself. I won't try to sell you any lengthy speeches about the glories and virtues of becoming a dragonrider. But I will say this: You wouldn't be the first Ulfrangar to take the saddle. And I believe in that moment, that man probably felt a lot like you do now—like an unworthy imposter. The funny thing about being a dragonrider, though, is that it's never been about worthiness. It's been about wanting to be something better, not for ourselves, but for others, and being willing to work every day to achieve that. Changing isn't an easy or painless thing. It's allowing yourself to be torn down to the foundations of your soul so that you can be rebuilt into something better."

Jaevid's smile became cryptic and challenging as he held out a hand to me, as though to shake it. "So the question that you have to answer isn't whether or not you're worthy. It's whether or not you can make yourself better, and if you're willing to work hard enough to make it happen—even if it hurts."

PART SIX
THATCHER

21
CHAPTER TWENTY-ONE

Something was wrong with Murdoc.
 As long as I'd known him, he'd been grim, serious, and a generally grumpy person. Most of the time, anyway. He did lighten up every now and then, usually when he found an opportunity to tease me about something.

But as soon as he stalked into the Porter's spacious corner house, I knew something had changed.

His black hair was ruffled, like he'd been running his fingers through it over and over. He followed silently along in Jaevid's shadow with his head down and didn't even glance my way when they came inside. His expression was one I'd never seen before, like mentally he was trapped a thousand miles away with no hope of ever finding his way back. His dark eyebrows were drawn together, furrowed but not in anger, and his mouth was set into a straight, grimacing line.

I waited for him to look up—to acknowledge me somehow—as he lingered in the foyer with Jaevid. We hadn't spoken at all since we'd parted ways at Ms. Lin's house, and there was a lot I wanted, and needed, to tell him. But I wasn't about to bring up any of that stuff in front of everyone.

Not that I didn't expect a little wrath and sulking from him. It was bound to happen. He'd warned us that separating was too dangerous. And then, as soon as we had, everything went wrong. Murdoc had been right all along.

Somehow, though, this didn't feel like his I-told-you-so anger. Now, I wasn't even sure if I should try to talk to him at all. That tension in his chiseled features immediately made my hands shake and my throat go dry—like he might bolt from the room, attack me, or break down screaming if anyone even said "hello" to him.

"I've asked the Porters to remain upstairs with your sister and her children for the duration of our meeting," Prince Judan announced in his heavy elven accent. Standing next to me, he thumbed at the pommel of one of his scimitars anxiously as he exchanged a meaningful glance with Jaevid. "The less they hear of this, the better. There is no need to involve any more innocent folk."

I had to admit, Prince Judan scared me a lot less than the rest of Jaevid's royal friends. He had a much more comfortable, friendly way about him. He regarded the rest of us with a relaxed, almost defiantly casual attitude—like we were all old comrades he'd known for ages.

"Agreed," Jaevid said and rubbed at his brow. "And I apologize for the wait. That young dragon is … incorrigible. It took a while to convince him to stay put in the barn, even after we got Fornax settled in with him." He gave a loud, groaning sigh and reached into his pocket. Drawing out the necklace he'd given me with my whistle still attached to it, Jaevid dropped it into my hand with a tired smile. "But they are both safely squared away for the night. Fornax has already greatly improved with his responsiveness to these commands. I'm impressed."

My face burned a little as I took the necklace. "O-Oh, um, thank you, Sir."

He nodded and his smile immediately drooped with exhaustion as he rolled his eyes. "But that little one—he is *far* too comfortable with swaggering into people's dwellings. I suspect Ezran Cromwell may have had something to do with that. We had to stop that little troublemaker from crawling after us down the middle of the street three times. He nearly spooked a horse into flipping a wagon full of crated chickens and imported honey."

"Sounds like a sticky situation," Prince Judan said, grinning.

"Yes, well, you weren't the one who might've wound up chasing sticky, angry hens through the street. Fates, no wonder Ezran's been pitching such a fit over finding this dragon." Jaevid shot him a withering glare as soon as he trudged past into the Porter's front sitting room. He dropped into one of the blue velveteen armchairs and sighed.

The Porter's had a much larger and intricately decorated home than Ms. Lin's. Not that it was too fancy or intimidating. Sort of the opposite, really. Despite all the nice furnishings, woven wool rugs, and engraved wooden edgings around every doorway, it still felt cozy and homey. Big, bright windows faced the street and a small courtyard out back on all three levels of the house, and each of the spacious rooms had white plaster walls and fine stone fireplaces. There was a large workshop out back where Jondar said he'd been learning their family's craft—swordsmithing.

Business must've been good, and there was no questioning their skill; not when nearly every room had a beautifully crafted weapon prominently displayed somewhere on a fine pedestal or mounted to the wall. The only thing that seemed a little out of place was an old knight's helm set on a small stand at the very center of their hearth's mantelpiece. It looked like it hadn't been touched in years, not even to be cleaned or polished. There were dents and scratches on it in a few places, and the white feather crest was stiff and dusty. Weird. There weren't any other pieces of armor in the home that I'd seen since we'd been staying here, and this one looked like no one had dared to touch it in quite some time.

"Going to send word for Ezran to come fetch the beast, then?" Judan guessed.

Jaevid rubbed his face with his hands, like he was trying to massage some sanity back into his brain. "Given the circumstances, I'm not sure."

"Ezran? You mean Duke Cromwell, right?" I asked, stealing another glance at Murdoc as we all settled in around the sitting room where Isandri, Reigh, and Phoebe were already waiting.

His expression still hadn't changed.

"Yes. It would seem this particular young drake is from one of the Cromwell's most prestigious bloodlines. A descendant of Icarus—perhaps one of the last," Jaevid explained. "Ezran's been searching for him like a madman ever since the estate was attacked, afraid the dragon wouldn't be able to survive on his own in the wild. I guess he's been following you this whole time." He paused, flicking a quick look over to Murdoc out of the corner of his eye. "Er, well, following *one* of you, anyway. Regardless, Ezran will be pleased to know the dragon's been found safe."

"And less pleased that he's been found with us, I assume," Reigh added with a snort.

Jaevid gave a conceding wince and shrug. "True. There is that. But we can work out those details later. For now, we've got plenty of bigger issues to address—starting with what information Judan has found out about Devana, and what this means for all of you."

"Well, that can't be good. You always start with the good news first, so if you're opening with Devana ... " Reigh muttered.

Jaevid gave a conceding nod. "Fortunately, it's not my news to share. Judan, if you'd be so kind."

Reclining casually on the end of a sofa right beside Isandri, the half-elven prince looked up when Jaevid called on him. "Ah, yes. Well, first let me say that finding any information on this girl has been an absolute nightmare. My agents have been pushed far beyond their normal call to duty in order to track down those with any reliable, first-hand knowledge of her. Nearly every Tibran officer we managed to interrogate reacted with sheer terror at the very mention of her name. Many of them would not even speak it aloud."

"What about that guy from before?" Reigh pressed, leaning forward to rest his elbows on his knees. "The High Guard you found?"

Prince Judan shifted uneasily. "Dethris, yes, his information gave us a place to start. After speaking with him, we found another Tibran soldier who became rather talkative when we suggested our intent was to exterminate her. Our sources told us he'd served as a common security guardsman under the Tibran banner, primarily standing outside the cells as reinforcements during any interactions with particularly hostile and dangerous captives. Big fellow. Had an awful scar across his forehead."

"Captain Molivan," Phoebe whispered so quietly I barely heard her from where she sat on a small tufted stool across the parlor.

Everyone looked her way—Murdoc included.

She immediately ducked her head, flushing as scarlet as her hair as she fidgeted with the embroidered hem of her long tunic. "H-He, um, he was posted in my workshop sometimes. He always carried a studded flail on his belt."

Judan's expression tightened with sympathy as he studied her. "He's been hiding out in Cernheist since the war ended, taking jobs as a hired guardsman for the merchant caravans hauling wares out of the mines in the area. We flushed him out rather easily, though."

"I hope you arrested him, at least," Reigh growled bitterly.

"Unfortunately, the purpose of my agents moving within Maldobar is only to acquire information, not apprehend anyone. I passed all the information we got on Molivan to Aubren. What he chooses to do with it from there isn't up to me," Judan replied. "But Molivan was an interesting old dog, I'll grant him that. He was so eager to see Devana killed, I could've recruited him on the spot. I didn't, of course. The information he gave may prove to be quite useful, though. He said he witnessed many of the experiments performed with Devana firsthand. Failed attempts to control her, and the disasters that followed."

Reigh's gaze flashed to Phoebe accusingly. "*Your* experiments?" he demanded.

Phoebe's mouth popped open and she shook her head frantically. "N-No! I never did anything to her. There were other artificers—those who claimed to specialize in divine magic. I'd only ever dabbled with that sort of thing, toyed with some artifacts, before ... " Her voice died in her throat and she snapped her mouth shut.

"Before *me*," Reigh finished for her.

She went pale and quickly looked down at the toes of her shoes, not saying another word.

I had to give him some credit. After a few seconds of the most awkward, tense silence I'd ever endured, Prince Judan cleared his throat and went on talking like nothing had happened. "Molivan confirmed Dethris's report that Devana had been kept with her head locked within an eyeless, magic-infused mask made of solid gold. To 'muzzle her like a wild dog,' were his precise words. Apparently, Devana was unable to use her abilities when she wore it, and making eye contact with her victims intensified her psychic hold upon them."

"Yeah, we already know that," Reigh grumbled under his breath. "And that apparently she doesn't seem to have that same power against anyone chosen by a dragon."

Judan's forced smile was paper-thin and blatantly sarcastic. "I'm aware that you do. But like any half-decent spy, I like to confirm any and all information I'm given with as many sources as possible. It allows for more reliable reports and fewer dead witch-hunters." He flicked his gaze away, focusing on me with a hint of concern. "And this fellow, Molivan, had a bit more to say about the interactions he witnessed with Devana than Dethris did. He said that she would frequently throw fits, or have outbursts of anger that forced them to restrain her further until she calmed. During these episodes, she screamed the same thing over and over—a demand."

I shrank back in my seat, a cold sweat prickling at my brow as my stomach flipped and cramped. "A demand for what?"

"A person—or so they assumed at first. But it was a name the Tibrans didn't recognize," he answered, "Ishaleon."

So far, Isandri hadn't said a word or even moved much as she sat on the sofa right next to Prince Judan. But the instant he said that name—*Ishaleon*—her eyes widened. Her hands clenched in her lap and she shifted a little farther down the sofa, turning her face away.

I went stiff in my seat, too.

I ... I knew that name. Didn't I? Gods and Fates, it seemed like I did. I could have sworn I'd heard it somewhere before. But where?

For the life of me, I couldn't remember. Every time I reached for it, the memory seemed to fragment and scramble, like I was trying to grab a fistful of smoke. Impossible.

If Judan noticed our distress, however, it didn't show. He went on explaining without missing a beat, "The Tibrans have always taken a much different stance on the treatment of the gods within their culture, of course. They tend to not hold them in the same high regard that most of the rest world does. So that name meant little to them. Of course, those from Luntharda know it well."

"Ishaleon," Reigh repeated quietly. "The God of Mercy."

Prince Judan nodded in agreement. "Shepherd of the Lost—or so they call him in the old stories. He is the patron of healers, prisoners, orphans, and widows. He's not one of the more prominent figures within those tales, however, and when the Tibrans finally identified his name as the one Devana cried out for, they just assumed she was pleading for divine deliverance from her fate."

"Because she *was*!" Isandri snarled suddenly, her expression twisted with rage as she glared out across the room.

No one said a single word.

Even Jaevid sat stock-still in his chair. His piercing stare fixed squarely upon her like a powerful bird of prey. Focused. Intense. Unpredictable.

Isandri's face twitched and her mouth screwed up, yellow-green eyes welling with tears as she slowly panned her infuriated glare around at each one of us. Then, without another word, she snapped up from her seat and stormed out of the parlor. Somewhere in the distance, a door slammed hard.

"I-I, um, I really should go and check on her," Phoebe suggested as she slid off her stool. She forced a flustered grimace that might've passed for a smile and quickly ducked out of the parlor, too.

Prince Judan's deep, ivy-green eyes narrowed slightly, tracking her every move until she left the room. "I was not aware you'd collected yet another participant in this mission. Just who is she, exactly?"

Reigh sighed. "It's ... complicated."

"Complicated or not, she clearly knows something significant about Devana—something that could be vital to this entire mission." Jaevid leaned forward, his tone sharp but disturbingly calm. The look of withheld, quietly smoldering wrath on his face was, without a doubt, the most terrifying thing I'd ever seen in my entire life. He made Murdoc look huggable. "Explain it."

Reigh flushed as red as a radish all the way down to his neck. "Y-Yeah. I think she does. But I don't know what, specifically. Look, I only met her once before all this. When we went to Northwatch tower to rescue my brother and sister, we had to split up, remember? You took Jenna up to the rooftop exit so the dragonriders could get you guys out safely. I didn't have it so easy, though." He hesitated and flashed Jaevid a quick, reluctant glance. I guess he was preparing to make a mad dash for the door if Jaevid suddenly lunged at him. "It took me a while to work my way down to the dungeons below the tower where Argonox was holding his high-profile captives. I basically had to carve myself a path there in blood. And once I got there, I'd used so much of my power, I knew my chances of getting out of there alive were slim. But I wanted to make sure Aubren survived. So I, um, I sort of ... recruited Isa. She was in the cell across from his, and I said I'd break her out if she'd help him escape. She agreed."

Prince Judan's brows shot up and he sat a little straighter. "She was a Tibran prisoner?"

"Yeah," Reigh confirmed. "I mean, obviously my plan didn't exactly work. I couldn't move fast enough and the Tibrans were swarming like bees on a hive. I tried opening another portal to send Isa and Aubren through it, but the Tibrans found us first. I was too weak to hold them off, too. Isa was the only one who made it through the portal and, to be honest, I don't even know where she wound up or where she went after that. I honestly wasn't expecting to see her again, let alone at the Cromwell estate."

Jaevid's brows snapped into a frown. "What do you mean? I never saw her there."

Reigh gave a thin, awkward laugh that died in his throat almost immediately. "Heh, um, actually, you ... kinda did."

Now Jaevid and Judan were both scowling at him like a pair of wolves cornering a fox.

But before Reigh could even begin to explain, Murdoc finally spoke up from where he still lurked at the edge of the room. "She's a shapeshifter," he muttered in a quiet, almost completely emotionless tone, almost like he was reciting something he'd memorized. "No doubt you saw her in her beastly form before."

Jaevid's eyes went as wide as two pale blue moons. "She can work magic?"

"Er, well, yes ... sort of." Reigh winced and hedged. He'd gone back to rubbing and scratching at the back of his neck. "I'm not sure if it's actually her doing it, or a power she can draw from that staff she carries, or—"

"It's both," Murdoc interrupted again. "She's a Lunostri elf from the kingdom of Nar'Haleen. She's also a shalnii priestess. The oath mark on her forehead means she serves the moon goddess, Adiana, and the weapon she carries marks her as someone of great distinction within their faith."

Prince Judan blinked at him in shock. "You are remarkably well-informed about her, aren't you?"

Murdoc didn't even look his way. "Any Ulfrangar would be. We're thoroughly educated in the foreign cultures and languages from infancy."

"Then what else can you tell us about her?" Jaevid urged.

"Crystals like the ones on the head of her staff are only given to those charged with overseeing the protection of the temple and its inhabitants. They're powerful artifacts, and it supposedly takes years of ritual attunement and training to be able to use them," he went on explaining. "Taking that into consideration, it's possible that she's a high priestess, although she looks way too young for that. And since she can also shapeshift, I think it's far more likely that she's someone of greater significance to the shalnii."

"Someone related to Devana?" Jaevid guessed.

Murdoc still didn't move an inch or make any expression at all. "Apparently."

"Then we need her to talk to us," Prince Judan insisted, his steely-eyed gaze snapping back to the direction she'd fled. "We need her to tell us everything she can about Devana. If all the information my agents have gathered is correct and Devana has truly broken free from her gilded mask, it may be nearly impossible to neutralize her. We'd run the risk of sharing Phillip's fate."

Reigh drew back in surprise. "You ... you confirmed it, then? That he really is working for Devana?"

Prince Judan didn't answer aloud. He didn't need to, though. His features hardened somberly, riddled with a look of worry and regret I didn't quite understand. Had he known Phillip before this?

"I made contact with Aedan in Barrowton personally," the half-elven prince confirmed at last, his tone heavy. "As I'm sure you're aware, he had been working with Phillip personally over the last few months as he prepared to take on the responsibilities of duke there. There was much concern for the city because of the state of Northwatch. It's overrun with every vile breed of thief, cutthroat, and criminal you can imagine. Phillip was concerned those individuals might migrate to Barrowton, or target merchants and travelers making their way there. A valid concern, to be sure, but he ... insisted on investigating the severity of the situation himself."

"Of course he did," Reigh growled bitterly, his mouth drawing up into a furious, pinched-together pucker as he glared away. "That moron. I bet he insisted on going alone, too, didn't he?"

Prince Judan gave a defeated sigh of confirmation. "Yes. Of course. Given his appearance, he did not believe anyone in Northwatch—be they criminal or otherwise—would want to cross him. They might even assume he was one of them. But Aedan said he never returned."

"Idiot," Reigh fumed under his breath. "If Jenna hears that, she'll be ready to breathe fire herself."

"You mean *when* she hears that," Jaevid grumbled. "And guess whose job it is to tell her?"

"So he likely did come into contact with Devana," Prince Judan concluded, his tone hushed and mournful again. "I can think of no other reason my friend would do such things. Phillip was never a violent person, even when we were children. He cared nothing for violence and war games. To think that Tibran witch has twisted his mind so drastically, gods, it makes me wish I could be the one to put an arrow through her head. She must be stopped. She must pay for this."

"I thought Phoebe had a theory—some way to apprehend her safely?" Reigh asked with a now similarly worried frown. "Isn't that what she's been working on this whole time?"

"She was indeed. But over the events of last few weeks, it seems that most of her supplies and crafting tools have been destroyed." Prince Judan's mouth pinched up sourly, as though he resented every word. "It is a devastating loss. Her theories were solid, and we had great hope of utilizing them to apprehend Devana without causing her any great bodily harm. After all, she's quite young, and has suffered the very worst abuse the Tibran Empire could inflict. But the situation must now change. She's using Phillip as her foot soldier, and perhaps others we don't yet know about. We will have to resort to... *other* methods."

Something about those last words made my heartbeat skip. My hands clenched as my stomach did a fluttering series of flips. Other methods? What exactly did that mean? And why did it make me feel so ... Fates, I didn't even know. Upset? Worried? Angry? Afraid? Sad? The rush of emotions all tangled in my mind, twisting together until I couldn't even speak.

"But why is Devana so fixated on Thatcher?" Jaevid murmured as he eased back in his seat again and combed a hand through his shaggy gray bangs to brush them out of his eyes. "They've never met. If Devana is from Nar'Haleen, then it's extremely unlikely they're related." He glanced my way, as though waiting to see if I had any theories.

Um, no. I absolutely did not. I slowly shook my head. "Maybe she's mistaking me for someone else?"

"Phillip said something during our last encounter," Murdoc spoke up again, although he still didn't look my way for even an instant. "During our fight, he referred to Thatcher as a 'godling.'"

"Godling?" Prince Judan made a scrunched, bewildered face. "Not a term I am familiar with. What does it mean? Is this something you've heard of before?"

Murdoc's brow rumpled as his frown deepened. "No. It sounded familiar at first, but if I have heard of it, I've forgotten."

"We'll have to try to get Isandri to open up to us, then," Jaevid resolved aloud. "She's gone out of her way to be caught up in this—followed you and fought alongside you. It's time to figure out why. Which of you think you can convince her to talk?"

22

CHAPTER TWENTY-TWO

No one said a word.
    Reigh looked down at the floor. I swallowed hard. Murdoc maintained his ominous, broody demeanor without even blinking.
    Great. So none of us were in a good position to be trying to question Isandri for helpful information.
    Jaevid was right, though. Someone had to try. We needed to know why she was fighting with us. But I sort of doubted any of us could actually pull that off, even if we did volunteer. She didn't seem to trust us much at all—which was fair. We didn't know her and she didn't know us. Not really, anyway.
    Things were more uncertain than ever now. More dangerous. And even if Isandri had always kept her distance before, she'd been staying with us at the Porters' house for the last few days. Granted, she hadn't said much in that time, but still. She seemed committed to joining in this messy charade now.
    Reigh might have been the best choice to do the questioning. Isandri apparently knew him from their brief interaction in the Tibran War. But she'd also spoken to me several times, although it sort of seemed like she found me more annoying than trustworthy. And Murdoc? Well, they'd only just officially met. Even Phoebe was basically a stranger to her. So none of us were in a good position to try to talk her into doing anything.
    Several awkward, quiet minutes passed, and when no one volunteered, Jaevid puffed a heavy sigh. "Well, that's ... not exactly encouraging."
    "I-I, um, I'll try," I raised my hand shakily. "I mean, it makes the most sense for me to be the one to do it, right? I'm the one Devana's after, so maybe she'd at least tell me why I'm a target."
    "I hope you're right," Jaevid agreed with an apologetic smile. "But, unfortunately, this brings us to our next problem."

Now Judan was the one shifting uncomfortably in his seat.

"Phillip has tried twice now to abduct you, and we've only barely been able to prevent that from happening. I'm growing concerned that we may not be so successful next time," he said, using that same overly-diplomatic, parental tone my father had whenever he was explaining something to me I didn't want to hear.

Not good.

"Now that we've confirmed that the Ulfrangar are indeed cooperating with Phillip in some capacity, the risk to you has become too great to ignore. It was never my intent to put you in that level of danger, and for that, I must apologize." He sighed, as though bracing himself for what came next. Or maybe my reaction to it. "Thatcher, I'm going to insist that you and Phoebe return to Halfax and leave the remainder of this mission to Reigh, Murdoc, and Isandri. You simply aren't ready for something like this."

My mouth fell open. What?! Jaevid wanted me to just ... run away? After all this? After everything we'd risked? Murdoc had nearly died, for crying out loud!

No—I had to be hearing that wrong or misunderstanding somehow. Devana was using Phillip to find *me*. She'd even gotten the Ulfrangar involved. And I was supposed to just go whimpering back to the castle like a scared puppy while my friends fought this battle for me?

No. I couldn't do that. I wouldn't.

Maybe I wasn't a good fighter. Maybe I wasn't even a real dragonrider. I might even be a naïve, kid-faced, idiot. But I wasn't a coward.

I sat up straighter, leveling what I really hoped was a convincing frown on him. "With all due respect, Sir, I'm not running from this. If Devana has something against me, then I should be the one to help settle it."

"He does have a point." Reigh rested his elbows on his knees and clasped his hands, his light amber eyes flicking up to me. "Devana is after him. Having him with us means we know exactly where her focus will be—where she'll be pointing all her attacks and energy. If Thatcher goes back to Halfax, we lose that focus. We won't know what she'll do next. Will she risk sending Phillip to Halfax? Or will she do something more drastic? Hurt people?"

Murdoc's jawline went rigid and he scowled darkly. "Are you suggesting we use Thatcher as *bait*?"

"No, I'm suggesting that as long as we've got her attention focused on us, her path of destruction is limited to wherever we are." Reigh glared back at him. "I'm also imagining what seeing Phillip like this would do to my sister if he did chase Thatcher all the way to Halfax."

"That's actually part of the reason I'd like to do whatever we must to capture or kill Devana as quickly as possible," Jaevid interjected. "There's been some ... significant developments at Halfax since you left."

Reigh's face drained of all color. "Is Jenna okay?"

"Physically? Yes. But otherwise, I'm honestly not sure. She's a strong person, but she's already been under tremendous strain," he lowered his voice, as though he didn't want anyone outside this room to hear what he said. "I couldn't stay with her long, but she took the news about Phillip as well as you can imagine. She was ready to saddle up her dragon and hunt him down personally. Thankfully, Felix, Haldor, and I were able to talk her out of that. But the shock of that news must have been too much. She finally went into labor right after my departure, I'm told." It was impossible to miss the guilt in his voice, and his mouth pressed into a thin, tense line as he looked down, too.

I blinked, unable to hide my shock. Wait a minute—*what*? Queen Jenna had been *pregnant*? I mean, sure, I'd noticed something seemed a little off about her before. Her gowns had been arranged and tailored to hide it well, so I'd never been sure exactly. But normally, whenever a queen of Maldobar was expecting a baby, the entire kingdom was buzzing about it. Everyone would be speculating about if it would be a boy or a girl, and flocking at the castle gates to catch a glimpse of her at every public appearance to see evidence of her growing belly.

Queen Jenna hadn't even announced that she was expecting a baby. No one had said a single word about it. And now she'd already given birth? Why would she hide it? Didn't she want the rest of the kingdom to know about a new prince or princess? I mean, maybe it was because she wasn't married to Phillip yet, but would that really matter? They were already engaged, right?

It didn't make any sense at all.

It wasn't my place to ask, though. This was a family matter—a royal family matter. And I wasn't family or royal.

Reigh's whole body seemed to sag lower in his seat, his head bowing to put his face in his hands. "Gods and Fates. I-I should have been there. Is ... is she all right?"

"I received word only just this morning. My agents reported that she came through it valiantly," Prince Judan spoke up, his expression sympathetic. "I couldn't be there personally, of course, but Kiran came as soon as he could. He attended to her through most of it. As with the pregnancy itself, it took far longer than normal and caused her great pain. The child finally came on the midnight hour of the moonless night. A prince."

My skin prickled at those words. A prince born on a *moonless* night? Maybe I had my head stuck in all the fairy tales and stories I'd heard as a child, but I'd always heard that royals born on a night like that were cursed. Was that why she'd kept it a secret? No, surely not. Jaevid would've said something if that were the case. Er, maybe, anyway.

Reigh rubbed at his brow and cheeks, as though he were trying to massage the guilt and worry out of his own head. "And the baby? Is it—he—healthy?"

"As far as anyone can tell, despite the extremely odd circumstances of his birth. I suppose congratulations are in order for you, Uncle Reigh." Prince Judan gave a strained smile that never quite reached his eyes. "Jenna has named him Ronan."

Still rubbing at his face, Reigh didn't look up or say anything. It put heaviness in the air like a fog so thick I could've sliced it with a sword.

"Reigh, Jenna is fine," Jaevid insisted gently. "I got another letter from Kiran just this morning. She's recovering well. The baby is doing well, also. But Jenna needs to focus her energy on that right now. She's even called for an intermission of the Court of Crowns under the excuse of giving the attending royals time to communicate with their homelands and begin the process of moving some of their own citizens back there. Your father and brother are helping as much as they can. But Phillip should be there, too. He would want to be—you know that. So we need to end this quickly. We need to restore him to your sister's side as soon as we possibly can."

My hands clenched at my sides. Sitting across from everyone, I looked around the room at all their worried, grim faces, and I just knew. This was it. This was what I had to do.

Before Reigh could answer, the words burst out of me like they'd been launched from a catapult. "Jaevid's right. We can't waste any more time. And that's exactly why we're going to set a trap for him, and you're going to use *me* as the bait."

I'M PRETTY sure that if I'd been standing even half a foot closer to Murdoc, his glare would've scorched me to ash right on the spot. Fortunately, I was across the room, so it just made me wince a little. Lucky me.

Jaevid immediately began to object. "Thatcher, that is not—"

"Hey, I don't like it any more than the rest of you do. But it's the fastest option, and you know it," I pointed out quickly. "We've been on the run this entire time. Running from the Ulfrangar and from Phillip. We set out on this mission as hunters, but we've been running scared basically since the beginning. As long as we keep that up, we're only barely staying a few steps ahead of them, hoping we make it through the next attack. We need to get out in front of this problem. You don't know exactly where Devana is in Northwatch, and trying to storm the city would be a disaster. But I'm betting Phillip knows her exact location. He would have to, right? You said it yourself; he had to have seen her in order to become controlled by her magic in the first place. So he will know where she is. Then we won't have to storm in there blindly with no idea what we're up against."

You could've heard a mouse sneeze as everyone in the room gaped at me like I'd just spontaneously sprouted a second head or something. I tried not to take that personally. Sure, I wasn't usually the plan-maker.

Okay, so I was never the plan-maker.

This time, however, I knew I was right. That feeling burned in my gut as I went on. "Phillip is the key. We find him first, catch him, and we find Devana."

"Devana may just decide to kill him on the spot as soon as we have him in our custody," Prince Judan warned. "Those Tibrans, Dethris and Molivan, both warned that she could break a man's mind once she'd gotten into it. She could drive them insane beyond the point of saving."

"Maybe so," I countered, "But if she's controlling him, then I'm also betting she can hear what he hears and see what he sees. I think I know how I can get her attention and force her to cooperate. I just ... I need to talk to Isandri first. I need to be sure." I glanced around at them, my legs shaking a little as I slowly got to my feet. "So I'm going to go do that now, if you don't mind. And then after I'm not going back to Halfax. I'm staying right here with my friends to see this through."

Murdoc's silent, disapproving glare followed my every move like the glare of a small sun as I hedged out of the room and out into the hall. But he didn't say a word. Neither did any of the others. At least, not while I was still standing there.

I hadn't gotten two feet out the door before I heard Prince Judan whisper, "That boy has lost his mind, hasn't he?"

"Yep," Reigh chuckled back quietly. "It's about time, I guess. And here I thought I'd finally get through one of these little Jaevid-spawned excursions without having to do something insanely dangerous and possibly suicidal. Does it make you nostalgic, old man?"

"Yes, actually," Jaevid's answer came so softly I only barely heard it as I continued walking away. "It certainly does."

CHAPTER TWENTY-THREE

I'd barely grasped the door handle to go out into the back courtyard of the Porters' home when Murdoc's deep voice came from right behind me.

"Thatcher."

I flinched, almost coming up out of my boots in surprise. Slowly, I turned back to see him standing less than three feet away, his grim features drawn taut and stiff in a look of bitter frustration and—wait a second, was that *worry*?

Uh oh. What was this about?

"You don't have to do this," he said firmly, seeming to bite down extra hard on every word.

"Well, sure, but I'm not sure Isandri is going to talk to anyone else abou—"

"You know that's not what I mean." He looked me over and then shook his head with a groan. "Is this about proving yourself to Jaevid? Or trying to look brave in front of everyone else? Is that why you're suddenly doing these things?"

I let my hand slide off the door handle and faced him. "What things?"

He rolled his eyes and gave another exasperated groan. "Ugh, stop playing dense. You're volunteering to step into a dueling arena with Devana and Phillip as your opponents. I'd call it reckless, but at this point, I'm not sure it qualifies for anything short of absolute insanity. And before, when you tried to … take my place with the Ulfrangar … " His voice halted some and he looked away. "Why are you doing all this?"

Okay, to be fair, I didn't exactly have a choice about that whole mess with the Ulfranger. Rook probably would have killed me on the spot if I had refused. But maybe I hadn't put up as much of a fight as I could have.

The reason was simple, though. And it didn't have anything to do with Jaevid or some sad, desperate attempt to look brave.

"I went along with taking your place because you're my friend. Rook said you'd be killed if I didn't, and I couldn't let that happen. And this time I, well, I guess I just want to help."

Murdoc arched an eyebrow as though he weren't buying an inch of that explanation.

I huffed and crossed my arms. "Hey, Reigh's my friend, too. And this is a big deal for him," I protested. "Queen Jenna gave us this mission. She's counting on all of us—now more than ever. And yeah, it would be nice not to look like a complete loser after Jaevid's put so much of his time and faith into helping me. But I guess you can just chalk this up to more of my gross kindness because I'm being a 'good person' again. Whatever that even means."

"You're an idiot," he grumbled.

"Yeah, yeah. I know." That was old news.

"You're going to get yourself killed."

I shrugged. "Possibly."

Murdoc worked his jaw to the side, almost like he was actively resisting the urge to put a fist through my face. Uh oh. I knew that look. I'd seen it a few times right before he went after someone in the prison camp.

In the interest of survival, I took a step back toward the door. "I ... I am sorry, though. For what happened with Rook, I mean."

His face had gone a little pale when he looked back down at me again. "It wasn't your fault," he said, his voice barely more than a whisper.

My heart gave a painful *thud* deep in my chest. According to Rook, it had been my fault. I'd been what made Murdoc stumble and finally fall—the final straw that made him rebel against the Ulfrangar. And now that was why his life was in danger.

Murdoc would never agree with that, of course. He'd say it was his own choice. He'd say I had nothing to do with it. And that would all be a big heap of lies just to keep me from feeling guilty. Or protect me. Or something else really stupid and annoying. He kept on doing that; treating me like his little brother he had to shelter and look after.

It had to stop, preferably before it got him killed.

"No, Murdoc. It *was* my fault. I went with Reigh. I agreed to split our group even after you said it was a bad idea. I chose not to listen. And it almost got all of us killed. It forced you to have to fight and kill someone important to you. I know there's nothing I can do to make up for all that. But I swear it won't happen again. From now on, we're a team. We stick together. Okay?"

He studied me wordlessly for what felt like an eternity. Then he let out a slow, controlled breath and combed his fingers through his hair, brushing some of his bangs out of his eyes. That's when I saw it. In the blink of an eye, something strange twisted his expression. An emotion I couldn't quite place. Hints of it seemed to seep through his usually ironclad mask of steely, grim indifference. It made his eyebrows draw upward as the corners of his mouth twitched downward. His hazel eyes darted around, never focusing, almost like a frightened feral animal. Was that fear? Pain? Grief? What was wrong? Had something else happened? Something I didn't know about?

I wanted to ask, but Murdoc spoke first. "Thatcher, there's something you need to know." His tone, tight and forced, made my stomach clench and my palms go clammy.

Oh no. There *was* something I didn't know—something bad, if his expression was any clue.

I held perfectly still, barely able to breathe.

Murdoc opened his mouth, but another sound suddenly filled the silence between us. A melody. Soft, simple, and sweet, it floated down from the floor above us. Someone upstairs was whistling a lullaby.

In less than a second, Murdoc's face blanched as white as milk. His gaze slowly panned up, mouth still hanging open as he listened.

"It's just Mrs. Porter," I explained. I'd heard her whistling it before, numerous times over the last few days. "Don't worry, it's fine. Jaevid said they're a good family."

Murdoc still hadn't moved. As far as I could tell, he might've stopped breathing, too. That look on his face, like he'd just seen a ghost, froze on his sharp features as his gaze panned quickly back and forth, like he was searching the ceiling overhead.

"It's just them up there. Oh, well, and Ms. Lin, too. And all their kids," I said, hoping it'd reassure him a little in case he was worried that we were about to get attacked again. "You can go up and meet them, if you want. Last chance, probably. Jaevid's been talking about moving us all to the barn where Fornax and your dragon are being kept. You know, in case the Ulfrangar decide to light something else on fire." I turned back to the door and opened it. "I've got to go find Isandri, though."

"I-I ... " Murdoc's voice caught. He blinked hard a few times, then finally shut his mouth and looked back at me. His face was a little less pasty, although not quite back to normal, as he spoke hoarsely. "No, I'm ... I'm going with you."

I couldn't resist a snort. "Gonna try to persuade Isandri with me? Or just watch and make fun of me while I fail at trying to talk to a girl?"

"As entertaining as I'm sure that would be—no," he quipped as he followed me out the door and into the cobblestone courtyard between the Porters' house and their workshop. "There's actually someone else I need to speak to."

I chanced a suspicious glance back at him over my shoulder. Someone else? But there wasn't anyone else from our group out here. Well, except for Phoebe. Was that who he needed to talk to?

And why did his face look so ... red?

I didn't get a chance to ask.

A MOUNTAIN of black and red scales dropped from the sky right in front of me like a boulder crashing to earth.

Murdoc's dragon landed with a *BOOM* that sent me staggering back until I crashed right into him. We both toppled back, landing in a heap on the ground.

We didn't stay that way for long, though.

"*YOU!*" Murdoc thundered as he basically tossed me off him and jumped to his feet. He stormed toward the dragon with his fists balled and his shoulders hunched aggressively. "I've told you a thousand times: I DON'T WANT YOU! Get out of here! Go back to the Cromwells or wherever it is you came from!"

The dragon sank low, cowering and lowering his head to the ground. His scaly little ears drooped as he made a series of low, whining sounds like a cowering puppy.

"No! Stop that!" Murdoc waved his arms as he shouted. "Begging is not going to work. You are an absolute menace! Why won't you just leave me alone?!"

The dragon smacked his lips and curled his tail around his legs, whining and cowering closer and closer to him.

"R-Right," I squeaked, terror still making my whole face numb as I shakily got back up. "I'm, uh, I'm gonna go and let you sort this out."

Murdoc didn't answer. Or he didn't hear me. He went on yelling and scolding the young dragon that kept scooting in nearer to him while it whimpered and chirped hopefully.

Yikes. And I'd thought my first encounters with Fornax were rocky. He really had his hands full with that little drake. Granted, the other dragons had seemed pretty welcoming of him. Reigh's dragoness, Vexi, had immediately taken to wrestling with him, and Fornax accepted the affectionate grooming from both of them with only a little growling.

Leaving my friend to continue his raving fit, I quickly ducked out of the courtyard, and into the workshop. I was willing to bet that was where I'd find Isandri and Phoebe hiding.

There was a small balcony on the second floor of the workshop that overlooked the docks, and Isandri had taken to sitting up there by herself most nights. I guess now that we all knew about her and that she'd been following us, there wasn't much point in her hiding anymore. But for whatever reason, she still didn't seem to want to hang any closer to the rest of us. She kept her distance, held her silence, and watched from afar like a silent guardian.

That couldn't continue on for much longer, though. I knew I'd heard that name—Ishaleon—somewhere before. It struck a chord in my brain, setting my nerves ablaze like someone had prodded me with a red-hot branding iron. Isa had reacted to that name, too. And apparently, it had special meaning to Devana, as well. Somehow, that name was connected to all of us.

I needed to find out how.

"Isa? Phoebe? Are you guys in here?" I called up the stairs as I squeezed through the small opening in the workshop door. I guess that's where they had come in, too.

No answer.

Stepping carefully through the crowded, dark shop, I couldn't help but stare around at all the work areas laid out in a square shape around a small forge right in the center. The faint glow of the smoldering coals inside it filled the air with the faint scent of ash and scorched metal. Familiar smells that put a tightness in the center of my chest I couldn't ignore. It reminded me of home. Father hadn't done a lot of metalworking, but he had a small forge of his own for shaping and fitting horseshoes. He'd shown me how to light it when I was so small I could barely see over into it without standing on a bucket. I hardly weighed enough to even pump the bellows. The sound of his laugh filling our family stable as I struggled to do it on my own, having to hang from the top handle of the large leaf-shaped air pumps in order to pull them down, rose up from some long-forgotten corner of my mind.

It caught me totally off guard.

My throat went tight and my eyes watered. Father was gone. I hadn't gotten to bury him or even say goodbye. I didn't know if anything I was doing now would have even made him proud. He'd never said much about dragons. He'd worked so hard to teach me everything he knew. He was tough when it came to discipline and always demanded my very best when he critiqued my work. But he was kind, too. He'd shown me how to win the trust of the wary and frightened horses. He'd shown me how to be gentle when I worked with them. He smiled and laughed a lot, and when I was small, he'd held me in his lap by the firelight and told me stories—usually about Jaevid. Thinking of him being just ... gone. Gods. Sometimes, it still didn't make any sense. How could he be gone when my memories of him were still so clear?

I couldn't think about any of that now. Wiping my eyes on the sleeve of my tunic, I quickly moved away toward the back of the shop where a wide, sturdy staircase led up to the second level. That was where Mr. Porter, the resident swordsmith, kept all his raw materials packed away neatly. It was also where the small balcony looked out over the harbor several streets away—like maybe this little shop had once been someone's home or carriage house before the Porters had repurposed it for their family profession.

I hadn't even reached the top of the stairs when I heard two feminine voices talking quietly somewhere in the gloom.

"I know I shouldn't have done it. It was completely selfish of me, and I should find some way to apologize. Gods, I'm so embarrassed—what was I thinking?" One of them murmured. Phoebe, probably, because she didn't have the strong, foreign twist to her words Isandri did. "I've never done anything like that before. I've never even wanted to. And now I don't know what to say to him at all."

I stopped and held my breath. Okay, so maybe it wasn't good to eavesdrop on them like this. They were whispering, so it was pretty obvious they didn't want anyone else to hear what they were discussing.

But I couldn't help myself. Who were they talking about? What had Phoebe done?

"Given his past, he probably has no idea how to respond to it," Isandri replied. "Do you truly have *those* kinds of feelings for him?"

"I-I ... I think so. Yes. But I don't want to force this on him."

Okay, now I really wanted to know who they were talking about. Reigh? Murdoc? Jondar?

"How about you? Have you ever, you know, been in love?" Phoebe asked quietly.

Isandri didn't respond right away. And when she did, it was so faint I barely heard it. "Yes."

"Who was it? Someone from your homeland?"

"No," Isa's voice trembled a little. "He was from here, in Maldobar. The Tibrans had captured him, as well. He was forced to serve as a guard, but never stopped working to subvert them and help the Maldobarian forces whenever he could. He snuck letters in and out of Northwatch for months, leaking secrets about Tibran legion movements under the name 'Lamb.' That's what he called himself whenever he was around the captives like me. He was secretly helping a lot of us. He'd sneak us food and water, even medicines sometimes. But he wouldn't tell anyone his real name. Not that I blame him. If Argonox had found out what Lamb was doing, he may have used that secret channel of contact to lure the Maldobarians into a trap."

"Fates," Phoebe gasped faintly. "Right. That makes sense, though. He must've been afraid of anyone giving him away if they knew who he really was. I might have known him—by a different name, of course. Do you know what he looked like? Is he still alive?"

"I only glimpsed his face a few times through my cell door. He was a Gray elf, but didn't speak with their accent." Her tone sweetened, as though she were smiling to herself at the thought of him. "It was foolish, I guess. We never really met. Never even spoke without an iron door between us. But the first time we saw one another through the tiny window in my cell, he just stared at me for a long time without saying a word."

Isandri gave a small sigh, as though she had to collect herself before she went on. "I suppose most people here do that, though. Not that I don't understand why. Lunostri elves don't often leave our homeland, let alone come this far north. But Lamb didn't look at me as though I were a strange spectacle or a puzzle piece that didn't quite fit into the tapestry of society. That's how I've always been treated—even in Nar'Haleen. I wasn't like the others in the temple where I studied and trained as a child. My gifts and powers were far different from the usual children they took in. I was unique. Set apart. I felt it in the way the High Mothers looked at me even on my very first day. I baffled them."

"Sounds familiar," Phoebe said, her tone warmer now, too. "Being the oddity, I mean. I know what that feels like."

"Like a barrier only they can see has been dropped between you and everyone else. Suddenly, you are set aside. You become the *other*," Isandri agreed. "But Lamb looked at me and smiled so warmly. Not like something strange that needed to be figured out. He looked at me like I was something beautiful—something precious that he wanted to draw in closer to himself and embrace instead of put on a pedestal and analyze. I'd never had anyone look at me that way." Her voice hitched a little, as though she were biting back emotion. She hesitated, falling silent for a few seconds. Then she added quietly, "I suppose it doesn't matter now. He likely died during the war."

"Maybe not," Phoebe said encouragingly. "He was very clever, wasn't he? Surely he survived. And if he did, I promise I will help you find him. Prince Judan probably already knows who he is—especially if he was feeding everyone secret information about the Tibrans. You should ask him!"

"I-I ... " Isa stammered as though she were flustered. "Um, p-perhaps. But there's too much to worry with now." Isandri paused again, long enough this time that I had to wonder what was going on.

I'd almost convinced myself it was safe to peek around the corner of the stairwell to check when Isandri suddenly snapped sharply in my direction. "Like the PERSON who is currently EAVESDROPPING on us from the STAIRWELL!"

24

CHAPTER TWENTY-FOUR

I bit back a yelp, nearly tripping over my own feet and falling back down the stairs.

"Thatcher Renley, you stop lurking over there right this instant," Isandri demanded.

Great. Well, that's what I got for snooping, I guess. With my head hung, I trudged out of the stairwell and into the room. Nearby, Isa and Phoebe sat on a few of the crates, frowning at me with their lips pursed and their eyes narrowed.

"I-I'm sorry. I was just, uh, I—I needed to talk to Isandri," I blurted, too embarrassed to look either of them in the eye. "I didn't want to interrupt."

The two girls exchanged a meaningful look, as though neither one of them believed that at all.

My face burned like someone had pushed my whole head into that forge downstairs. Ugggh. So humiliating.

At last, Isa gave a small shrug of her bare shoulders and tipped her head to the side. It made bolts of her long black hair spill out from where she'd tucked it behind her long, pointed ears. "Very well. Phoebe, could you give us a moment?"

Phoebe's big blue eyes glanced between us a few times before she finally bobbed her head, stood, and quickly stepped by me on her way down the stairs. As her soft footfalls retreated, my thoughts tangled around everything I'd wanted to ask. Before, it'd all seemed so clear—what I needed to say and what I wanted her to tell me. Now, my panicked brain scrambled for anything that sounded remotely intelligent.

Ugh. I seriously needed to work on this not being able to talk to pretty girls thing.

"I'm going to assume this is about Devana," Isandri spoke first, her vivid yellow and green eyes catching and reflecting the dim light like a cat's.

"Y-Yeah," I managed to wheeze. "But really, it's more about me. That name they were talking about before, the one that Devana was calling out while she was imprisoned by the Tibrans—I've heard it before. I know I have. I just can't remember where. My parents weren't all that religious. Or at least, my father wasn't. So I don't think I heard it from them. I think ... I think I heard it in a dream."

Her chest rose and fell with a deep, steadying breath. She looked away, as though she were bracing herself. "Ishaleon." She repeated the name so gently, so carefully, it almost sounded like a prayer.

I took a few steps closer to her and slowly sank down onto the crate Phoebe had been sitting on earlier. "What's going on here, Isa? What does all this have to do with me? Why is Devana trying to abduct me? Or does she just want to kill me herself?"

Isandri closed her eyes. "No. She wouldn't kill you. Not on purpose," she answered. "At least, I ... I thought so before. She wanted you to save her. But knowing she's recruited the help of someone like that monstrous man now? I'm not sure what to think anymore."

"Save her?" I choked. "But why? I don't understand. I've never even met her!"

There were tears in her eyes when Isandri opened them again and stared straight at me. "You have, Thatcher. Eons ago, we all knew each other very well. The world was a much different place then, and so were we. Time has passed, and we've lost one another over and over again. But your soul remembers us—remembers *her*—even if your current body doesn't. No matter what happens, we will always be drawn to one another from even the farthest corners of the world."

A sudden rush of chills surged up my spine, spreading through my whole body like a ripple of wild energy. It made my heartbeat skip and stall and my breath catch. My toes curled inside my boots and I couldn't keep my hands from shaking as I stared back at her.

What the heck was she talking about? Eons? My *soul* remembered Devana? What did that even mean? None of this made a single shred of sense.

Isandri must have been able to sense my complete bewilderment, or see it plastered on my face, because she smiled sadly and shook her head a little. "I'd hoped I would never have to tell you this. I thought if I could handle it myself, if I could just keep you at a distance, then it wouldn't have to happen again. You'd never have to—" Her voice caught as her expression faltered, as though she were fighting tooth and nail to keep the emotions controlled.

All I could do was sit and stare at her, hanging on every word while wave after wave of those eerie chills swept through me. Each one grew stronger, making all the tiny hairs on my body prickle and my insides twist up and flutter like I was being stretched from the inside out.

But when she didn't continue, I had to ask. I had to know. "I'd never have to what?"

Isandri shut her eyes tightly again, as though every word were agony. "You'd never have to know ... that you are a godling, like me. Like Devana. Thatcher, you *are* Ishaleon."

I couldn't stop myself from laughing out loud.

Me? A god?! She couldn't be serious. It just wasn't possible. No way was I any sort of god. God of idiots, maybe. Or people with insanely bad luck.

No, this was just a joke or a huge misunderstanding. If I'd had any relation to anything divine, Jaevid would know about it. I mean, he knew everything about the deities, right? So he would have told me already.

Nope. Isandri was mistaken. It was as simple as that.

"Isa, I'm sorry, but there's absolutely no way I'm Ishaleon." I tried to speak without wheezing and chuckling. I didn't do a very good job. "I mean, have you even seen me try to fight? It's pathetic."

She had, of course. Several times, in fact. So I knew there was no way she could deny that much.

Even so, Isandri sat eerily still with her lovely features settling into a cold look of irritation. She didn't find this funny at all, apparently. "I suppose that would be a problem if Ishaleon were a god of war, but were you not listening before? He is the God of *Mercy*. The hand to the helpless. The shepherd of the lost."

"Okay, but he's still divine, right? God of Mercy or not, he'd still be able to defend himself," I argued. "And unlike you and Devana, I don't have any special powers. I can't shapeshift or read anyone's mind. I'm not even all that smart. So just how am I a god of anything?"

"Because it isn't that simple," Isandri snapped, her tone tight and bitter as she glowered at me. "His spirit, his soul, resides within you and always has. You are not merely a spokesman or keeper of his essence like Jaevid or Reigh were. You are *him* reborn. His echo trapped and cursed to resonate forever in this world. That is why Devana called out for him—for *you*—because you were the only one that might be able to save her. That is why you've felt compelled to find her, why you've begun to remember fragments of their past."

I frowned back at her. "That doesn't even—save her from what, exactly?"

Her annoyed scowl faded, gradually becoming something much more frightened and vulnerable. "Herself, I think."

Isandri looked down at her hands, seeming to suddenly notice how they were shaking. Reaching for her staff where it was leaned against the crate next to hers, she gripped it until her knuckles paled some. "I'd hoped I could make it to her in time; that I could get to her before that monster Argonox and the rest of his disgusting minions had defiled her divine soul. But I think it's too late. Thatcher, there is so much more to the younger gods than the world has ever known—knowledge that has been a tightly guarded secret since the time of the old gods because of men like Argonox who would use it to do terrible things. They call us godlings because our power isn't as great as those who came before. But it is still enough to shake mortal kingdoms apart. That's why I've tried to be careful. To do this as quietly as possible. I don't want anyone else to know what we are."

Her eyes welled with tears again and her chin trembled as she stared back at me in earnest, gripping her staff as though it were her lifeline. "We were too late to save her this time. The Tibrans have warped her into something wretched. Love is powerful, Thatcher, even when it's twisted into something evil."

"Devana is ... the Goddess of Love?" I guessed, still frantically trying to decipher what she was talking about.

Isa gave a tiny nod as she sniffled. "She is Eno trapped in mortal flesh. We have endured this way for eons, cursed to be reborn over and over, and never remembering our past selves. Our physical bodies are still vulnerable, still as frail as any other mortal being. We live and die just as they do. But our souls remain immortal, divine, and containing the power of any other god or goddess."

"Is that how it was for Jaevid? After he destroyed Paligno's stone?"

She nodded again. "For a short time, it was similar. But even then, it was only Paligno's essence that Jaevid harbored. His mind and soul were still separate from that of Paligno. We contain every aspect of our deific selves. We are them—their minds, personalities, and feelings—all bound in mortal flesh. It was the price we had to pay to stay here after the Law of the Stones was set forth by the foregods. The rest of our brothers and sisters were banished from the mortal realm, but their essences remained—linked to stones and protected by chosen mortals. Eno ... she would not go. She wouldn't abandon the mortals she'd come to care for so much, even if it meant she would have to suffer a mortal life to remain with them."

I shifted anxiously. "What about Ishaleon?"

Isandri met my gaze again, her voice steadier despite the pain in her eyes. "She was your twin. Your other half. Mercy and love go hand-in-hand. You would not leave her. So you stayed behind, too."

"And ... you?" I almost didn't want to know.

"I was charged by our eternal mother, Astaris, to protect and watch over both of you. You were her youngest children. I was her most beloved. She feared for all of us. She still does. She wants us to stay together as we were intended."

My body went stiff and cold at the mention of that word. *Mother.* It eclipsed my mind like a massive dark storm, consuming my every thought. I swallowed hard as I tried to wrestle those feelings down. The confusion. The anger. The pain. The ... gut-wrenching sadness. Gods and Fates—had it been because of me? Had I done that to her? Was it my fault all this time?

"What, um, what about our mortal parents? Would they, um, be affected by what we are? Would it do anything to them?" My voice caught and I cringed, trying desperately not to let it show. I couldn't let it reach the surface. Not now—not in front Isa. "Would it ... make them go mad?"

Her slender brows crinkled and furrowed slightly. Tilting her head to the side made those silvery painted marks on her forehead gleam in the faint light ebbing through the glass balcony doors nearby. "I don't think so."

A rasping, choking sound slipped past my clenched teeth, somewhere between a sigh of relief and a hollow chuckle. "O-Oh. Okay. That's, uh, that's good." I cleared my throat, trying to collect myself a little. It didn't work. "H-How do you even know all of this? I know you said it's been a secret for a long time, but surely *someone somewhere* has heard of it. I don't get why, if this is what I'm supposed to be, I've never heard of it before now."

A distant, ghost of a smile brushed over her features. "The elder priestesses at the temple taught me, just like all the other hopefuls. In Nar'Haleen, Astaris is held in greater esteem than here in Maldobar. She is their patroness, and they are devoted to her in every way. The temples take in candidates from throughout the region who show any hint of magical gifts, testing them to see if they may have godling potential—searching for her lost children. That's how they found me," she recalled fondly. "I was so little, barely eight, but I could already craft things, little illusions, out of moonlight by then. It terrified my mortal parents, and they were desperate to find help for me. They took me to the great temple of Calo'Luna. I'll never forget the first time I saw it. It felt like a dream. Those alabaster halls rising from the sands, shining like pearl in the moonlight. I'd never seen anything so beautiful."

Isandri sat back some, tucking a few of her runaway dark locks behind her ear. "When the elder priestesses told them what they believed I was, my mother held me and wept. I think she must have known I wouldn't be able to go back home with them. I don't remember feeling sad, though. Even if I couldn't go back home, I liked the temples. It felt like I belonged there."

It was hard for me to visualize any of what she said—priestesses and temples hidden away in the golden dunes so far away. Maldobar didn't have any grand temples or anything like that. I wondered if I'd ever get to see anything like that myself.

"What is it that happened to your family?" she asked, her tone soft and cautious, as though she were choosing her words very carefully. "Did they pass during the war?"

Pain throbbed in the back of my throat like I'd tried swallowing my own heart. "My father did," I answered hoarsely. "But my mother ... "

Heaviness like a lead weight settled over my chest and shoulders. It made me sag forward until my elbows came to rest on my knees. I hadn't even let myself think about Mother in so long, let alone talked about it. Father had told me I could, if I needed to. I could ask him questions about her and what'd happened. I guess he hadn't wanted me to feel like he was trying to pretend like she'd never existed.

But I'd tried not to. The few memories I still had of her weren't exactly good ones. I didn't remember her voice or her smell. I didn't even remember her smile or what it sounded like when she said my name. My mother lingered in my mind only as an indifferent specter. A figure I recognized, but didn't really know.

Isandri sat, silent and still, watching me. Her lips parted, like she might say something or ask another question. She didn't, though.

So I tried to explain. "She disappeared when I was little. She'd done it several times before that—just wandered away in the middle of the night in nothing but her nightgown. My father searched for her a long time. We never found a trace of her." My mouth twisted, skewing to the side as I chewed on the inside of my cheek for a moment. Anything to keep the emotions from reaching the surface. "When I was little, the other kids on our street used to laugh and sneer at me, saying she was crazy. They wouldn't let me play with them because they said I was probably insane, too, and that I might give it to them—like it was a disease or something." I shook my head, making my lengthy pale gold bangs brush the sides of my face. "I pretended not to care, like nothing they did or said to me mattered. But I knew I wasn't like the rest of them. I've always felt ... I don't know, set apart. Different. Like everyone I've wanted in my life, everyone I've wanted to be close to, has kept their distance. Is that because of what I am? Because I'm supposedly Ishaleon? Can they sense it, too?"

Isandri reached out to rest one of her hands on my arm, her deep ebony complexion a stark contrast to my own only sort-of tanned skin. We were so different. She was an elf; a priestess from a kingdom I'd honestly never even known existed. But I couldn't deny how that gentle touch made me feel connected to her in a way I'd never been with anyone else. She understood.

She ... was like me.

"Thatcher, I know this probably sounds unbelievable to you right now. There are still times when I question it, too. Your powers haven't even manifested yet, so it's a lot to take on faith. But it's not like you're at war with some entity inside you, like his will is any different from yours. This is who you are—who you've always been. Whether you believe me or not now, soon it won't matter. Soon you'll know just as I did," she whispered, giving my arm a gentle squeeze. "Difficult things will happen. People won't know what to think. They won't believe you. They won't understand. But I can tell you one thing: Even if I don't know you or your companions very well yet, I can see that they do care for you tremendously."

"I'm still not sure I believe any of this," I confessed. "Murdoc certainly won't."

"That's okay. You will, in time. If you're finally beginning to hear echoes of our past, to feel our bond, then the rest will come. Probably fairly soon."

"What does this mean for our mission? For finding Devana? She's sending Phillip to abduct me, but if it's too late, and she can't be saved, then ... what does she want with me? To kill me?"

Isandri's hand withdrew, falling back to plant a resolute grip on the shaft of her staff. "I ... I don't know, Thatcher. But I've got a very bad feeling. The things she's doing, the people she's involving, I'm worried what else we might face before we can end this. Her gifts have been twisted against their original purpose, poisoned by hate and malice. Her mind and power have been defiled. If it's too late to save her, then all I know to do for her now is to end her suffering. I'd truly hoped there would be another way. I'd hoped I wasn't too late. But she's done all this." Her lips thinned and she leveled a steely, determined stare upon me. "The Law of the Stones has been revoked. This is the last time we will be born within a mortal body. After this mortal life ends, we will return to our true selves, and will no longer be bound by the struggles of a mortal life. That may be the only way to help her now. Are you prepared for that?"

I didn't know. I still couldn't make sense of all this. I needed to think—to try to process it all. Unfortunately, there wasn't much time.

"To even have a chance at doing that, we have to find a way to reach her. We need to catch Phillip first," I countered, arching an eyebrow. "I think I've got an idea how we can do it. Are *you* prepared for that?"

One corner of her mouth bowed into a cunning smirk. "I believe I am."

CHAPTER TWENTY-FIVE

"I said NO!! Go away! I mean it!"
    Murdoc was still howling at his young dragon like a mad man, waving his arms like someone trying to scare crows off their garden. I guess that approach didn't work as well on a two-thousand-pound dragon, though. The drake squawked in protest, slicking his ears back and nipping at the leg of Murdoc's pants. It didn't take much for him to yank my best friend off his feet and hold him upside down for a few seconds before dropping him again. Murdoc hit the ground flat on his back with a *thud*.
    "Doesn't look like he's having much luck, eh?" Reigh chuckled from where he stood beside me with his arms crossed.
    Gathered in an open field at the edge of the city, Isandri, Reigh, and I watched them bicker while we waited for Phoebe to prepare the only pieces of equipment she'd managed to save—something for Fornax and me that she'd been working on. We had to test them out before we finalized any of our plans for catching Phillip, and this was our last chance. If they worked, it might make things a lot easier. If not? Well, we'd figure this out one way or another.
    Fates, I hoped they worked.
    Regardless, there was a lot left to do. Murdoc had a theory about how we could pinpoint Phillip's location. Prince Judan hadn't approved of it at *all*, even if it was the same way Murdoc had tracked down the Ulfrangar that took me prisoner. I wasn't quite sure what all that meant, or why the idea made Prince Judan so uneasy. Something about a crime lord? Anyway, Prince Judan had scowled disapprovingly all the way to his shrike this morning before departing to deliver an update of our progress, or lack thereof, to his father. I wondered how furious King Jace would be about Murdoc this time?
    Yeah. He'd probably be breathing some fire, too.
    At least Jaevid was sticking around to help, although he didn't seem all that happy

about it. I couldn't exactly blame him for that. He had a wife and a newborn baby that needed his attention now, and yet here he was, playing hero again. Er, well, kind of. Today he'd been playing more of the reliable uncle. He'd spent most of the afternoon working out new living arrangements for Ms. Lin and her children until their home could be repaired, but all that seemed to be settled.

Now, Jaevid was bound and determined to bring Phillip in with us. According to him, Phillip wasn't just a former friend he'd helped to save during the Tibran War. Phillip was also his brother-in-law. Yikes. No one had said a word about that to me before. Then again, I was probably the only one who hadn't already known it.

"I have not shared any of what Phillip has done with my wife," I'd overheard Jaevid seething in a deep, ominous growl to Prince Judan right before we'd left for this test. "And I'd appreciate you not letting her hear of it, either. I did not want her fretting over her brother's possible betrayal when she's only just given birth."

Double-yikes. I'd heard stories of Beckah Derrick almost as often as I'd heard them about Jaevid. She'd been another hero in the Gray War, and supposedly every bit the fearsome fighter Jaevid was. She'd also been the first woman ever chosen by a dragon—a king drake. Impressive? Oh yeah.

Jaevid was right, though. If she'd just had a baby a few days ago, she needed to rest. We had to take care of this on our own. But if my suspicions were correct, I might be able to draw Phillip out into the open. Then we could settle this on our terms.

Hopefully, anyway.

Gods and Fates, what was I doing?

"I do not understand why he insists on rejecting the beast. Isn't it a great honor in your kingdom to be chosen by a dragon?" Isandri asked, her expression genuinely puzzled as we all watched them from a distance.

"Yeah," Reigh answered with a sigh. "Buuut he's an idiot."

"A huge idiot," Phoebe mumbled.

"A huge, *stubborn* idiot," I agreed.

Crouched nearby, Fornax and Vexi made a few sulky, chirping sounds like they were in agreement, too.

"Okay, Thatch." Phoebe sprang up from where she'd been crawling all over a blanket spread out on the ground between us. She'd laid out all her tools there so she could make some final adjustments to the gear before we started the test run. "Can you get Fornax to lie down? I'll show you how this works. It's fairly simple. Um, well, in theory. I think it'll work. It should. Yes, I'm fairly certain it'll be fine."

Reigh and I exchanged a worried glance. Uh oh.

"No, no. I'm sure it will all work just perfectly." Phoebe stood back and planted her hands on her hips, scrutinizing all the bits and pieces of equipment arranged before her. Then she looked up at me, the wind catching in her storm of vibrant red curls. "Ready?"

After that little speech? Um, no. I absolutely was not. But there wasn't much choice. We were out of time, and she'd been working on this nonstop basically since we'd arrived at Ms. Lin's house.

"Let's give it a try." I tried my best not to look scared out of my mind and forced a smile back at her. Taking my whistle out, I put it to my lips and blew the command to Fornax.

His ears perked in my direction, nostrils puffing curiously as he slowly sank down to put his belly on the ground. Walking up to my great orange dragon, I ran my hand along the side of his head. He made low, content purring noises when I gave him a scratch here and there behind his ears as Phoebe carried over something with long leather straps that sort of looked like a bridle. It didn't have a bit, of course, and the straps had all been hand-tooled with strange little markings. Weird. What was all this for, exactly?

She talked me quickly through how I could buckle it onto Fornax's head, arranging all the straps comfortably around his horns, and making sure the centerpiece—a hexagonal piece of metal—was over the middle of his snout, right between his eyes. The metal piece had an odd, shiny piece of … well, honestly, I didn't know what it was. It had graining on it like wood, but shone in the sunlight like black opal when you looked at it from certain angles. Something about it made my skin tingle with an eerie little chill.

"Many of the divine artifacts Argonox collected during his conquests were lost or destroyed when Northwatch was retaken," Phoebe explained as she adjusted the straps carefully, her blue eyes as sharp and her tiny hands quick. "But I managed to save a few things. This was part of a device he'd made me experiment with a lot," her voice quieted, becoming hardly more than a whisper. She flicked a fast, almost frightened glance back toward Reigh, as though she didn't want him to overhear. "He called it the Thieving Mask."

"What did it do?"

"It was supposedly a relic borne of Iksoli, Goddess of Mischief. Before I began working with it, putting it on allowed you to see through the eyes of whomever had worn it before you," she said. "According to my research, divine artifacts are nearly always given their power because they contain some fragment of a deity. A drop of their blood, tears, or even a hint of their presence left behind that's imparted itself to the object. The mask was carved from the wood of a tree that the goddess herself bled onto. Something that supposedly happened during a battle between the gods long ago, probably."

My stomach gave a little panicked flutter. I hadn't told any of them about what—or who—Isandri believed I was. Not yet. It wasn't that I thought she was lying to me. She didn't have any reason to, as far as I could tell. But I wasn't altogether convinced she had the right person pegged for being a potential godling.

I'd told them only what was absolutely necessary, and so far, Isandri hadn't pushed me to divulge anything else. They knew Devana was fixated on me. She thought I was someone she knew from a previous life—someone she'd wanted to save her who hadn't. And now, she seemed to want revenge for that abandonment. Clean and simple.

Not.

Murdoc was still suspicious, of course. I guess he'd gotten pretty good at telling when I was holding out on him. Plus, he'd heard Phillip refer to me as a godling, so eventually I'd have to come clean. Or he'd figure it out on his own and break my neck for not telling him the truth sooner.

For now, though, I didn't want to prance around calling myself a god. It still sounded a little too bizarre to be true, and I had nothing to back up a claim like that. No mystical, earth-shaking divine powers. I could barely even hold a sword properly. God material? I think not.

"Anyway, by learning the runic language used to channel and shape that power, I was able to alter its purpose. I've done it before, and this relic is fairly malleable compared to some of the others I've worked with," Phoebe prattled on, sounding quite proud of herself as she stood back to admire the bridle. "It takes on new purposes well. So this seemed like a very practical adaptation."

"Adaptation to what?" I asked, quirking my mouth as I looked it over.

Fornax gave a bored yawn. So far, it didn't seem to be doing anything.

"Here." Phoebe reached into the pocket of her much-too-big leather apron and held out a pair of spectacles with a long, adjustable strap. No, not spectacles. Goggles!

Er, well, sort of. There weren't any glass pieces on the front, just more of that bizarre wood where the lenses should have been.

I held them up, admiring how she'd crafted the frame with little golden accents and more of those tiny, intricate engravings. Runes.

"Beautiful, aren't they?" She beamed, a grin stretching across her face from one freckled cheek to another.

"Yeah, they are." I cleared my throat. "Um, but, I won't be able to see with them, you do know that, right? I can't see through wood."

She gave a melodic giggle and swatted my arm like that was a joke. If it was, I didn't get it. "You're so funny, Thatch! Come on, just put them on. Then you'll *see*."

So I did.

THE INSTANT I slid the goggles down onto my head and aligned them over my eyes, Fornax let out a string of panicked growls and chirps. He stirred beside me, shifting and pitching as he tucked himself up into a frightened, shivering ball.

Phoebe, gods, she was right. I could see. Looking through the wooden lenses, I saw everything as clear as day. Isandri considering us with a wary, anxious frown as the wind stirred in her purple robes. Reigh standing nearby, watching with a skeptical scowl. His green dragoness gazing worriedly at Fornax. Murdoc dangling upside down from his dragon's mouth again. Nothing out of the ordinary there.

I panned my gaze around at all of them, and then settled on to Fornax. He'd gone silent and still, his sides swelling with shallow, panicked breaths and his scaly hide trembling. His head didn't move at all, but his big, cloudy green eyes—they darted quickly back and forth.

Almost like he was seeing something, too.

That wasn't possible, though. Fornax was blind. He had been for almost a year now. Right?

Taking a step closer to him, I reached a hand out to touch his head.

He looked around, meeting my hand as though he'd known exactly what I was about to do. My hand brushed his warm scales and, little by little, he relaxed.

"Is it working?" Phoebe leaned into view, her expression slightly worried.

"I-I'm not sure," I gasped. "I can see, but ... is Fornax ... ?"

All her concern melted away, replaced with an almost teary smile as she bobbed her head. "He's seeing what you do. The Thieving Mask allows two minds to look through one set of eyes. All I did was break it apart and restructure some of the runes. With those goggles, you can share your sight with Fornax. It'll work best during flight, or when you're standing close together. The range isn't that great, unfortunately—the cost of reworking the runes yet again. But at least this way, they've found a much better purpose."

"Phoebe, I-I—" I couldn't speak. The words hung in my throat as I looked around, letting Fornax see it all.

The wide-open fields where tall, golden grass rippled in the wind. The looming city of Dayrise behind us. The blue sky that peeked through big, puffy clouds that slowly rolled over the horizon, probably gathering into another storm.

He made a low, whining, almost desperate sound. He hadn't seen the sky in so long.

I whipped around, quickly climbing up into the saddle on his back without another word.

"Just a test drive, okay! Don't try anything too extreme yet!" Phoebe called after me as she backed a few paces away, giving us plenty of room.

My hand shook as I fumbled with the saddle straps, flailing to buckle myself in as fast as physically possible. I didn't want to waste a moment, not another second.

Then I leaned down to pat Fornax's strong neck. He let out another frantic cry, somewhere between a roar and an eager scream, as he reared back and spread his strong wings wide. His hind legs coiled, preparing for the leap. His tail lashed and his sides flexed against my legs as every thick muscle in his body drew tense.

"Let's go, big guy." I couldn't keep my voice steady as exhilaration buzzed through every part of me. I fixed my gaze upon the horizon. "There's a big world waiting for us out there, and we're going to see it—together."

Then I gripped the saddle handles and gave them a twist.

Together, we surged for the open sky.

SUCCESSOR

THE DRAGONRIDER HERITAGE BOOK THREE

PART ONE
MURDOC

1
CHAPTER ONE

"Widen your feet. Sink lower into your stance. Chin down," I growled through my teeth as my fingers shifted on the soft leather grip of my blade. "Eyes on me. Don't let your focus waver. No emotion. No thought."

Across the sparring circle I'd scratched out in the dirt of the Porter's back courtyard, Thatcher stared at me with sweat drizzling down the sides of his face. That look of steely focus in his light green eyes was new, promising, and hadn't come a moment too soon. We might make a halfway decent swordsman of him, after all.

Eh, well, maybe only a third-way. But at this point, I'd take whatever I could get if it kept him from getting killed instantly the next time we found ourselves in a fight.

It wasn't all good news, though. I could also see his hands shaking from ten paces away. His clothes were drenched and he could barely keep his guard up. We'd been at this since sunrise, and I'd only let him stop long enough to get a few gulps of water. I'd been pushing him hard. Too hard, probably. But with the last few pieces of our plan to capture Phillip now primed and ready, time was of the essence. Now that Thatcher had some fraction of understanding of the basics of bladed combat, I couldn't afford to let him get lazy. He'd been a farrier's boy before all this, after all. The hardest work he'd probably ever done was shoveling horse manure.

I had to give him some credit. He had a stubborn streak that'd begun to surface a lot lately. Whether or not that was a good thing remained to be seen.

Stubbornness at the wrong time got a lot of good warriors killed.

"Now, strike one!" I snapped, and darted in fast and low with my blade swung wide.

Thatcher moved in unison, feinting to the side and throwing up a block. Our blades clashed. The ringing of metal on metal filled the courtyard. Thatcher was younger, smaller, and had a much shorter reach. But he'd learned to handle a small sword decently enough, although I could tell the weapon still didn't suit him.

"Strike two, and stop hesitating," I snapped.

He spun and made a fierce downward strike, forcing me to parry up and rock onto my heels.

"Good." I ordered, "Disarm and end it."

I saw his expression tense, mouth skewing uncomfortably for an instant before he gave his blade an angled twist that interlocked our hilts. As he wrenched my weapon away, he jerked me downward and drove his knee into my gut.

My blade fell, clattering to the ground as I dropped to my knees before him. My vision spotted some and I coughed. I should have felt the point of his sword against my neck. But instead, I saw his feet shuffle a step back. My jaw clenched. He was hesitating *again*.

Gods curse it. *This* was exactly what would get him killed.

Using another rasping cough as a distraction, I sprang forward and seized my blade again. I rushed him in a flurry, easily knocking his desperate attempt at a parry aside. One heel-hook around his ankle swept his legs and Thatcher fell, landing with a *THUD* on the flat of his back at my feet. The impact sent his weapon skidding away over the cobblestones.

He stiffened; eyes wide as I pressed the point of my blade against the hollow of his throat. "Care to guess why you lost this time?" I growled through my teeth.

"I-I—" he began to stammer.

I added a bit more pressure to the blade, and he immediately snapped his mouth shut. "You lost because I told you to end it," I snarled as I glowered down at him. "And instead, you hesitated on the finishing move and refused the kill. How about guessing what happens if you do that in a real fight?"

He swallowed hard and looked away, face flushing with embarrassment. "I die."

"Yes. You die. Maybe think about that instead of whatever is keeping you from taking the final strike." Withdrawing my sword, I stepped back and offered down a hand to drag him back to his feet. "That's enough for now. Jaevid wants us ready to move out by tomorrow night, and you're no good to anyone if you're too tired to lift your blade at all."

He cast me one of those signature Thatcher puppy-eyed looks of shame. Ugh. "I'm sorry, Murdoc. I really am trying."

I sheathed my weapon and shrugged. "I know. But you have to try harder. Your mental state is more important than whatever skill you have. If you go into the fight uncommitted to what you're about to do, then it wouldn't matter if you knew every combat maneuver known to man. You'd still lose."

He bobbed his head like he understood.

Only, I knew he didn't. He'd only gotten a few tiny tastes of real combat now. He'd seen it plenty of times, yes. But actually being on the opposite end of a bladed weapon in a fight for your life? That was completely different. It wasn't even comparable to firing that crossbow of his.

"Let's get something to eat," I suggested as he trudged along after me, still moping. Usually, the mere mention of food was enough to get him to stop that nonsense.

It worked this time, too. His face brightened and he jogged to catch up, bouncing along beside me like an excited rabbit. "Do you think we could go down to one of the street vendors? There's one selling sweetcakes with honey cream inside them, and I—"

He stopped suddenly.

I stopped, too. Before I could stop it, my face drew into a sour frown.

Leaning in the doorway that led back into the house, Jaevid Broadfeather had his arms crossed and a pensive expression as he watched us. The wind stirred in his shoulder-length gray hair, and his thoughtful squint made that long scar over his eye wrinkle along his brow and cheek. I guess he'd been watching our practice the entire time. Great.

"Well, that's quite an improvement over the last time I saw you duel," Jaevid said as Thatcher strolled up to meet him.

His face flushed, making him look like someone had thrown a handful of hay on top of a big beet. "T-Thank you, sir. But it's really all because of Murdoc. He's a good teacher."

"Apparently so," Jaevid agreed, his steely-hued gaze intense and appraising. He studied me for a moment, seeming to measure his words carefully before he straightened and cleared his throat. "Thatcher, could you give us a moment? I need to speak with Murdoc about something alone."

Thatcher glanced between us worriedly as he stammered, "O-Oh, uh, yeah. Sure. I'll just, um, wait out here, then."

Jaevid nodded. "We won't be long. Come with me, please."

I sighed, not meeting any of Thatcher's worried looks as I followed Jaevid into the Porters' house. He might've been confused about what the great Jaevid Broadfeather wanted to speak to me about, but I wasn't. In fact, I had a pretty good idea what he wanted.

Or at least, I thought I did—right up until he glanced back just long enough to mutter, "This isn't about Thatcher."

I blinked. It wasn't? He wasn't going to interrogate me about whether or not I'd explained my ... *situation* on the night Thatcher's father had been killed?

Hmm. All right. Now he had my interest piqued.

Passing through the clean, elegantly furnished halls of the house, Jaevid walked on in silence until we reached the door that led into the dining room. I'd been inside once or twice, but we hadn't spent much time around our mysterious hosts—mostly at Jaevid's request. He didn't want us getting too familiar with them just yet, which was probably a good idea considering what had happened to our last two hosts. I'd only seen or heard the Porters from a distance, and that was enough. They were a well-off family of tradesmen, swordsmiths to be precise, and liked their privacy, as well.

"This way." Jaevid opened the door to the dining room and stepped aside, letting me go in first.

As soon as I'd gone past, he shut the door and followed me down the length of the long room. There was no one else inside, and the curtains were drawn over the large windows to filter the sunlight that usually made the place feel open and airy. The candelabras and lamps weren't lit, and there were no fine place settings spread out in preparation for a meal.

Instead, what lay carefully positioned upon the polished wooden table made me freeze in place. My blood went cold in my veins, sending a chill racing up my spine. I stole a glance back at Jaevid, who stood nearby with his arms crossed again as he watched me.

So ... *this* was what he wanted to talk to me about.

STANDING before the long dining table, my eyes roamed the neatly arranged spread of black leather armor, bracers, vambraces, greaves, and weaponry. Daggers. Small darts. A longbow and quiver. Gloves with knuckles studded with silver barbs. So many relics of a past drenched in blood.

My past.

My gaze halted on one blade in particular, laid out on the far end of the table. Resting in an oiled black leather sheath, the sight of a smaller blade with a fine, straight silver grip and a bird engraved on the pommel made my gut clench and my shoulders tense. I knew that weapon right away.

Jaevid didn't say a word or try to stop me as I reached for it. The dark steel blade hummed a beautiful deadly note as I drew it from the sheath. Slender, simple, and efficient, I'd seen this weapon countless times since I was a child. But this was the first time I'd ever held it.

Rook's xiphos blade.

"Most of the dead Ulfrangar agents had already been stripped of their armor and weapons by the few that managed to escape," Jaevid said quietly. "We salvaged what we could, including that. I understand it may have some ... significance to you."

My jaw clenched. I caught a glimpse of my reflection in the flawless surface of the blade. The image was warped, like a twisted echo of myself was sealed inside that weapon, sneering back at me from a very different life—one where I hadn't defected from the Ulfrangar and instead devoted myself entirely to their world of shadows and blood.

I shut my eyes tightly and turned my face away, forcing a few slow, steadying breaths.

"Murdoc?" Jaevid sounded concerned. "Are you all right?"

I quickly sheathed the xiphos again. "It's nothing. I'm fine."

His lips pursed as he gave me a dubious look. His pale, glacier-blue eyes studied me like an artist scrutinizing his own work. "I take it you haven't had a chance to speak with Thatcher, yet," he guessed.

"No." With everything that'd been happening—and a certain obnoxious scaly menace following my every move—there hadn't been a good opportunity yet. "But I will. I'll see that it's done before we make our attempt at capturing Phillip."

Jaevid opened his mouth to reply, but before he could get a word out, the door at the far end of the dining room opened. We both turned to see Prince Judan striding toward us, keeping pace alongside a much older man dressed in the formal, bell-sleeved robes of gray elven royalty.

Only ... he was not a gray elf.

My hands instinctively drew into fists, gripping the sheath hard. The moment his light amber eyes focused on me with harrowing intensity, I knew exactly who he was.

His features were deeply creased with age, and he was a fair bit shorter than I'd imagined. The last time I'd encountered him, I'd been bound in chains, blindfolded, and had quite a few swords poking at my back as a reminder. But that look—there was no mistaking it.

King Jace of Luntharda, and apparently a former Ulfrangar, had arrived. And somehow, judging by that heated scowl and the sharp urgency in his strides, I doubted he'd come to chat about the weather.

2
CHAPTER TWO

S till standing beside me, Jaevid blinked at him in obvious surprise. So, this part of the meeting wasn't one of his sly plans? Fantastic.

As the angry king drew closer, Jaevid quickly stepped between us and raised a hand. "Now, Jace, please listen. This was my doing, not his. I—"

King Jace stopped, flicking him a glare of warning. "Every due respect to you for what you've done in service to our kingdoms, Jae, but by all the gods, get out of my way. *Now*," he seethed.

Prince Judan put a hand on his father's shoulder. "F-Father, perhaps—"

King Jace shook him off and took another, aggressive step forward. "I want both of you to wait outside while I have a word with this one." He jabbed an accusing finger in my direction. "And if I have to make it by royal command, I will."

"You can't expect me to—" Jaevid began to protest again, beginning what I could only assume would be another speech in my defense.

"It's all right," I interrupted. I couldn't stomach listening to that again. King Jace wanted to have a chat with me? Fine, then.

Jaevid's brows rose as he glanced at me over his shoulder.

I shrugged and looked away.

Footsteps filled the awkward silence as Jaevid and Judan excused themselves from the dining room. The door shut with a soft *thud*. For nearly a minute, I stood facing the old king while I stared at the floor and neither one of us said a word. Any moment now, the yelling would start. The threatening. The inevitable eruption of fury for the danger I was putting Thatcher and the others in. Or maybe he was more worried that I would turn on them myself? It was hard to guess with him.

When I finally lifted my gaze to meet his, I found him staring—not at me—but at the blade in my hand. His eyes narrowed as his brows pulled together, wrinkling his forehead even more, as his mouth pressed into a strangely earnest line. Strange ... What was that look for?

"Let me see that," he demanded suddenly, holding his hand out.

I glanced between him and the blade, and then silently handed it over.

King Jace held it up, examining the sheath and hilt carefully before he let out a heavy sigh. With that one breath, all the smoldering rage and tension seemed to drain from his features. What was left behind ... it almost seemed like sadness. His shoulders went slack. He ran a thumb over the mark on the pommel—the engraving of a raven-like bird.

"They told me that the man who tried orchestrating your escape, the one who abducted Thatcher, was your former handler. But they never told me his name," he murmured, his tone quiet but heavy.

I frowned down at the blade. "His name was Rook."

"I know," the old king said.

My heart gave a frantic lurch. "Y-You do?"

"Yes," he answered, still staring at the weapon in his hands. "Because I trained him. Rook was the first and only pup I ever trained."

All I could do was stand there, my mouth hanging open, as I stared at him. I knew about his past. I knew he'd been an Ulfrangar assassin. But he, King Jace—Ruler of Luntharda, hero of the Gray War, and veteran Dragonrider of Maldobar—had trained *my* former handler? It just didn't seem possible.

"I suppose that would make you my heirling, since he's now dead, wouldn't it?" He gave an empty, humorless chuckle and shook his head. "If I were still with the pack, anyway. You'd become my pup. Finishing your training would be my responsibility."

I didn't know what to say, or if I should even try to speak. I didn't want another handler. And I was fairly sure he didn't want me to be associated with him at all.

King Jace panned his gaze over to stare at me, and this time, there was something anguished and fractured in his expression. A soul-deep weariness that seemed to be the source of all the wrinkles in his skin and the silver mottling his otherwise dark brown hair.

"Rook was not your family. He wasn't your father," he said. "But he was ... as good a person as an Ulfrangar can be. I saw that from the beginning. He had the skill of a true swordsman. Finesse and speed to rival anyone I'd ever fought. But he did not have the heart of a killer. I saw that from the beginning, too. He could fake it well enough to get by without the others noticing. But it was my job as his handler to find such weakness and destroy it."

He stood silently for a moment, expression slackening into something distant, as though he'd become lost in the memories. Then he frowned and cut his gaze back to me. "I never told anyone why I defected during my last mission—why I couldn't slay the young boy I'd been sent there to kill." He held the blade out to me again, offering to give it back. "I'd only just seen Rook earn back his patronage price and take his blood oath, becoming a true pack member. He wasn't my pup anymore. And that boy ... well, they looked a lot alike. Too much, I suppose. It felt like I'd already killed Rook once by letting him fully join the pack. I couldn't bring myself to kill him again."

I stared at the blade, wanting to reach out for it. But for whatever reason, I couldn't will myself to move. I had killed Rook, not him. I had killed the one person in the world who'd even cared if I was alive at all when I was a kid. He'd beaten me, yes. Every pup knew the bite of their handler's whip. But he'd fed me, too. He'd treated my wounds. He'd taught me. And when I needed it the most, he'd ... tried to help me.

Even with his last few breaths blown into that stupid whistle—Rook had tried to save me.

My vision went blurry, forcing me to lose all sight of the blade as tears welled in my eyes. I clenched my jaw, my chest heaving in deep, shaking breaths as I stood stiff. I blinked hard, forcing back the rising tide of heat and tension that swelled in my chest and scorched the back of my throat.

No. I would *not* do that. Not now. Not ever.

Suddenly, a hand fell onto the top of my head. It ruffled my hair before grabbing a fistful of it and jerking my head back. He held me like a dog by the scruff so that I was forced to look at the old king right in the eye. "Zuer is going to come for you now. You know that don't you, pup?"

I glowered back at him, but didn't resist. For a much older man probably somewhere in his late sixties, he still had a grip like solid iron. "Yes."

"There's not a single soul that has crossed blades with her who has lived to tell of it," he growled. "She'll hunt you like a rabid beast and cut the heart right out of your chest. Does that frighten you?"

"No."

A smirk tugged at one corner of his mouth. "Is that so?"

"I accepted that inevitability the moment I decided to leave the pack," I snapped, every word like bitter poison on my tongue. "Just as I'm certain you did. But the dying isn't the hard part, is it? It never is. Living, trying to put it all behind you, trying to learn how to be like everyone else—that is the true battle for people like us."

His hold on my hair went slack as that eerie, haunted smile spread over his face. "It is, but only at first," he said as he stood back. He considered the xiphos one more time before he finally pressed it into my hand. "Soon, you'll find yourself slipping, becoming comfortable, becoming someone else. They have that effect."

I closed my hand around the sheath tightly, still staring at the old king as he began to turn away. "Who does?"

His eyes fell closed, that smile softening into something much more tender. "The people who love you."

My heart gave another uncomfortable twist at those words. The people who *loved* me? For whatever reason, when he said that, the only person I could think about or even picture in my mind was ... Phoebe.

But why? She'd never said anything like that to me. Yes, she'd kissed me before, but I couldn't allow myself to jump to any conclusions or read too much into that. People did strange things when they thought they were about to die, and in that situation, she might've done the same thing whether it was me, Thatcher, or even Jondar who had been standing close by. We hadn't even spoken to one another since that night.

I didn't hold any special significance—not to her. Not like that.

To even assume that was ridiculous.

"Your little plan to capture Phillip isn't going to work, not unless you can be sure about where to find him and when to make your strike," King Jace said as he strode away toward the door.

I frowned at his back. "It's not like we have much of a choice."

"Don't you?" He chuckled and didn't even look back as he made his way out of the dining room. "I think we both know that's not true. But asking for *his* help will be risky ... and expensive. Especially after you killed one of his informants. Still, it might be worth the price. You'll probably only get one shot at this. Best to make it well-aimed and foolproof—if you can."

WITH THATCHER AND REIGH INVOLVED, requiring any plan we came up with to be foolproof was basically impossible. Unfortunately, King Jace was right. We had an idea of how to catch Phillip. But timing and posturing were going to be crucial if this was ever going to work.

Phillip was practically a phantom—no small feat for a man that looked like he did. Granted, he didn't have much of a choice. If he went strolling around the city squares in broad daylight, it wouldn't take ten minutes to find him. Just follow the sounds of common folk screaming in horror. But he wasn't stupid. He was keeping a very low profile. And while being able to use Thatcher as glorified bait to hold his focus was a definite advantage when it came to catching him, it wouldn't be enough. We needed to be ten steps ahead on this. We needed to know his moves even before he made them. No surprises. No foul-ups.

Basically, we needed an expert eye. Or many expert eyes, rather.

But, Gods and Fates, I did *not* want to go down this path. There was a reason the Ulfrangar did not involve themselves with that man. If even half the stories about him were true, then he would turn on us at the first opportunity. He didn't make alliances. He made business agreements, and adhered to them only as long as they benefited him.

Or so I'd been warned.

Slippery as a serpent. Ruthless as a shrike. Arlan the Kinslayer was not a man anyone wanted to cross—not even the Ulfrangar. He'd spun his intricate web across many kingdoms, including Maldobar. It was a vast criminal network that dealt exclusively in the trafficking of information, secrets, and rare or illegal goods.

I'd been told he openly refused to involve himself in assassin-type work, though. His price for hired murder was too high even for kings and queens. And apparently, he also refused to be involved with the highly illicit slave market. I wondered if he considered himself morally above all that. The idea made me smirk. An *ethical* criminal lord? Hah.

Then again, maybe he simply knew where to draw the line when it came to crossing territories with the Ulfrangar. You didn't survive long in a world of cloaks, daggers, danger, and secrets by stepping on the wrong toes.

Honestly, Kinslayer's restraint from that corner of the criminal market was probably the only thing preventing an all-out war between his network and the Ulfrangar. A dispute like that was guaranteed to be long, bloody, and costly for both sides.

King Jace was right again, though. I'd killed one of his agents while I was attempting to track down Thatcher after the Ulfrangar had captured him. So I'd potentially poisoned that proverbial well already. He might refuse to work with us on principle now.

Drifting from the dining room out into the hall, my mind raced with the prospect of trying to work out some sort of deal with Kinslayer. I'd have to do this carefully. There was a small chance Kinslayer might not know I was the one who'd done it. Very small. Hmm.

Without realizing it, my feet carried me down the empty hall of the Porter's home. I wandered past oil portraits hung in fine golden frames arranged along the plaster walls, my footsteps all but silent on the long, woven rugs. Something about the people in those paintings, their expressions stoic and focused, stirred a tension in my chest I didn't understand.

I stopped at last in the front parlor—the same room where we'd met with everyone to decide our next move. It'd only been a week or so, and nothing in the room had changed since then. But as I paused before the mantle, a weight like an iron yoke settled over my shoulders. The family had countless blades on display in nearly every room, like testaments to their family's craft. All were beautifully made, polished to mirrored perfection, and didn't have a single crack, scrape, or smudge on them anywhere.

And yet, set in the place of highest respect on their mantelpiece, an old knight's helmet rested on a wooden stand. It was beaten, dented, and tarnished on every side, as though it had seen countless battles. The white feather crest was frayed, and I knew the small, brown spots speckling it in places were likely old blood. It looked like something you'd dig out of the carnage of an old, forgotten battlefield.

So why did they have it displayed here? And why hadn't they bothered to clean it up or repair it?

And why did it feel so ... *familiar* to me?

It shouldn't. It made absolutely no sense. I'd never even been to this city before, let alone seen a helmet like this one.

A strange, warm chill tingled from the top of my head down to my shoulders as I reached out for it. I couldn't explain it. I ... I needed to touch it. To hold it.

My fingertips had barely brushed the worn metal when a sharp voice barked at my back. "Please, don't touch that."

I tensed, snapping my hand back to my side, and turning to look.

My gaze met hers from across the parlor, and instantly sent a bolt like cold lightning through my body. I froze, staring into the face of a young woman in a dark maroon dress. Her long black hair was wound into a plaited braid that hung down to her waist, although a few locks had slipped free to frame her face.

I had seen her before. I knew it immediately. That day in the city, drenched with rain and all her papers scattered in the street—I'd seen this same woman.

And just like before, the sight of her made my mind go silent, as if everything in the world had stopped around me. Her eyes of deep, earthy hazel studied me carefully from head to foot with a look of similar shock.

But it didn't last.

Her mouth pinched into a tight, small frown as she dipped her head and gave a small curtsy. "It is very important to my family. Please, don't disturb it."

I had to pry my eyes off her to steal another glance at the helmet. Important? Then why leave it in this state?

"Whose was it?" I asked.

She quirked a brow, blinking and drawing back slightly as though it were a ridiculous question. "Lord Broadfeather did not tell you?"

"No."

The young woman's eyes tracked over me again, seeming lost for a moment. Her lips parted, expression hanging on the verge of quiet desperation, almost like she was looking for something—some part of me hidden deep beneath the surface.

Whatever it was, she didn't say.

Instead, she looked down again. "It belonged to our ancestor, Levran Porter."

My eyes nearly bulged right out of their sockets. They were related to *those* Porters? "The first dragonrider?"

She gave a small, cryptic smile. "Yes."

I gaped back at the helmet. This belonged to the very first Dragonrider of Maldobar? It took a few moments for me to wrap my mind around that. I'd read about Levran Porter in a few of the old texts I'd found left lying out in the royal castle. He'd been at the battle with God Bane that had decided the fate of Maldobar centuries ago—the same battle where his dragon had chosen him.

The first dragon to ever choose anyone, actually. That had been the beginning of the dragonriders.

And it had all happened not even ten miles from where I stood.

"You seem surprised," the woman said, taking a few steps closer. "Forgive me, I know Lord Broadfeather would rather that we not become too familiar, but I must ask ... have I seen you before somewhere?"

I nodded slightly. "Yes. In the street. It was raining, and—"

"You helped me pick up my papers," she finished for me, realization making her eyes go wide. "What ... what is your name?"

"Murdoc," I replied. Curiosity flickered like an ember in my mind, getting the better of me once again. "Did you ever find him? The missing boy from your papers?"

Her expression shattered, falling into a look of pure anguish as she bowed her head. "No."

"Who was he? Your son?" After all, she looked somewhere in her twenties. She might've had her own husband and children tucked away in this house somewhere.

"No," she murmured in a quiet, broken voice. "My brother."

Her answer made me pause. The Porters were missing a brother? Not a husband? Was it someone she'd lost in the war, then?

No doubt there were countless young men who'd gone off to fight for Maldobar who had never returned to their families. Then again, maybe that wasn't the case here. The papers she'd been carrying had said it was a boy that was missing. He must have been young, then. Too young to be a soldier.

Still, lots of folk went missing during wartime—young and old alike. When villages and cities saw the arrival of invading forces, families were often scattered, split, and lost forever in the chaos. That's exactly what had happened to Thatcher, after all. And Dayrise had probably seen that same sort of chaos during the Tibran War.

"I am ... very sorry for your loss," I murmured. I didn't know what else to say. Moments like this, when I should have shown compassion and empathy, still felt like I was cramming my left foot into a boot meant for the right. Awkward and strange—as though nothing I said was the right thing.

"Don't be. He's not dead," she corrected me sharply, her gaze lit with heated little fires as she stared me down. "I will never believe he's dead. I will find him. If it takes the rest of my life, I will *not* stop looking for him!"

"Aria!" A voice shouted punishingly from somewhere out of sight.

The young woman winced, sucking her teeth angrily for a moment as her face flushed and her brow drew into a look of fretful anger. "Excuse me," she muttered and whirled around to storm from the room. Her footsteps retreated, thumping loudly up the stairs. Somewhere overhead, a door slammed hard and the sounds of two voices arguing were too muffled for me to make out what they said.

Hmm.

Either Aria Porter was in the minority of opinions when it came to whether or not her brother was still alive, or someone didn't want her talking about it around us. Perhaps both. Interesting.

I took one last look at the helmet resting on the stand. Now all the dents and scrapes made sense. The state it was in now, probably the same as the last time Levran Porter had taken it off his head, meant something. They hadn't restored it because wiping all those marks away would be like erasing the legacy attached to that helmet. And a family history attached to the origins of the dragonriders wasn't one that should ever be erased.

I just wasn't quite sure it should be left, collecting dust on the parlor mantel, either.

3
CHAPTER THREE

"You want to ask *who* to help us track down Phillip?" Jaevid's sharp features drew into a puzzled frown that made his dark eyebrows scrunch together.

"Arlan the Kinslayer," Prince Judan repeated glumly where he sat right next to him, fiddling with his fork.

Gathered around the Porter's dining table for our evening meal, we'd waited until after everyone was finished eating before we talked any business. Frankly, I'm not sure anyone could've pried Thatcher away from his plate before that. He still ate every meal like he'd never seen food before.

Of course, no members of the actual Porter family were joining us. They'd eaten already and gone about their business, so I didn't even catch a glimpse of Aria—not that I was trying to necessarily. There was no point in getting too familiar with any of the members of our host family. We'd be out of here soon enough, and with any luck, they'd never see any of us again for a long while. Or ever.

"And who is that, exactly?" Jaevid asked again. "I've never heard of him before."

"Arlan is a very well-known presence in the criminal world," King Jace explained from where he sat at the head of the table. Having him here changed the whole mood—and not necessarily for the better.

Thanks to my upbringing within the Ulfrangar, I'd done some fairly bizarre things throughout my life, but I couldn't remember ever sitting at a dining table with a king before. And clearly the Porter's two servants didn't have any experience serving royalty, either. They tripped all over themselves serving dinner, and apologized profusely after every course.

Not that King Jace complained. If anything, he seemed to enjoy the food. He even assured them everything was fine, but they still went on acting like they might as well have been serving him pig slop.

"You honestly think we can find him? Let alone get a meeting with him and convince him to cooperate with us?" Judan snorted and dropped his fork onto his empty plate with a clatter. "My agents have only ever been able to glimpse him from a distance. The man is a ghost. He comes and goes like the wind. His informants and associates are fiercely loyal. They'd all rather die than give up anything about him. He's smart, resourceful, and knows how to play the game very well."

"I understand that, but *who is he*?" Jaevid asked once again, his tone now tight and irritated. "I have a hard time believing Kinslayer is his real family name."

"That's part of the problem, no one knows, really," King Jace admitted. "Even when I was an active agent in the Ulfrangar, not much was known about him personally except that he was an elven man, although not from Luntharda, and that he seldom met with anyone in person. We were warned to steer clear of him, and the Zuer at that time wouldn't take any contract against his life."

"The current one won't, either," I added. "It's always been too risky. No one wants an open conflict with his organization."

Isandri gave a wistful smirk over the rim of her teacup. "The wolves would not dare to hunt the tiger? How interesting."

"Is he Lunostri?" Jaevid glanced between us, arching one of his eyebrows.

Judan shook his head. "I doubt it. We don't get many Lunostri traveling this far north, even along the merchant routes. Those that do undoubtedly get noticed."

"Indeed." Isandri gave an exasperated sigh. "You Maldobarians are not very discreet with your amazement."

"And even Holvradix Elves, like Jondar's father, tend to stand out in a crowd, as well. So that means he must look enough like the locals here not to raise any eyebrows when he appears in public," Jaevid mused as he rubbed at his chin. His pale eyes flicked up to King Jace, fixing him with a meaningful look. "Avoran Elf, then?"

The old king nodded slightly. "I would guess so. Which comes with its own constellation of problems, but we can worry about all that later. Right now, we need to sort out if we can even find the man."

They went on debating back and forth, and all the while Prince Judan seemed to get more and more uncomfortable. He squirmed around in his seat, leaning this way and that, and messing with his fork until, at last, he cleared his throat.

"I, uh, I might have a way to locate him. Or at least find out if he's in the area," he confessed without ever looking up.

Everyone fell silent.

Well, except for his father, who had a very expectant frown on his face as he asked, "And would you care to share that with the rest of us, son?"

Judan rubbed the back of his neck. "Not especially, but I'm out of other ideas. During our initial investigations into the remaining Tibran forces hidden away across Maldobar, we found many who were of great importance to Argonox's campaign. Some we allowed to stay in hiding and never even made them aware of our presence. They're being watched carefully, of course, in case they do anything we don't like, but the idea was that these people might come in handy in situations ... sort of like this one."

I crossed my arms and sank back in my chair. "I didn't realize Kinslayer was involved with the Tibrans."

"He wasn't," Judan answered quickly. "But some of his newly acquired informants were. They're desperate for work, after all, he can supply a lot of it. Some of them also have specialized training that makes them particularly useful. They know how to keep their heads down and their mouths shut."

The prince shifted in his seat again, expression drawing tense as he glanced around the table at the rest of us. "I found her quite by accident, though. To be honest, I'm not sure how many of the Tibrans even knew she was a member of their forces. And like so many of them, she's unable to return to her homeland now. She's clever, though, and quite resourceful. I wasn't surprised to find that she'd gone to work for Kinslayer. And after I'd spoken with her a little—you know, assuring her I wasn't about to try to cart her off in shackles—we ... sort of ... struck a bit of a deal. She'd occasionally feed me useful tidbits of information if I were to sometimes ... return the favor."

One of King Jace's eyes twitched. "You've been hiding a contact that's a former Tibran *and* one of Kinslayer's informants?"

Keeping secrets like that from his father—the King of Luntharda—who had once been an Ulfrangar? Impressive. I had to fight the urge to give him a slow round of applause.

"Yes." Judan squared his shoulders and cast his father a hard look. "If you'll recall, I was trained to treat the highly valuable contacts I discover with much more care than the rest. How did you phrase it again? 'When you stumble across a well that draws buckets of wine instead of water, you don't visit it every day. You use it sparingly. Draw from it too often, and sooner or later, someone will notice. Then you'll have a dry well and a village full of drunken idiots.'" He gave a sarcastic flourish of his hand. "Poetry."

Now King Jace's other eye was twitching, too.

So *that's* where Rook had gotten that line.

"All right, fair enough, but I think now might be the time to draw from that well, Judan," Jaevid urged. "Circumstances being what they are. Is she someone you can get in touch with quickly?"

The half-elven prince gave a cringing, shrugging, reluctant nod. "I think so? She ... is close by."

"In Dayrise?" Jaevid pressed.

"Port Marlowe," Judan mumbled like it was a naughty confession.

I gave a snort and rolled my eyes. Port *Marlowe*? Gods and Fates. That place was practically spilling over with pirates, crooked merchants, and all manner of seafaring filth. It'd been a great trade city once, but after being totally decimated in the war with God Bane, most of the commerce was forced to shift to Dayrise. Port Marlowe became a glorified hideaway for the less reputable seafaring vessels—and was undoubtedly a great place for a former Tibran soldier to hide out. We could *not* take Thatcher and Phoebe somewhere like that. Out of the question. It'd be like leading two lambs through an alley of sick, starving stray dogs. They wouldn't last two minutes.

"We leave at sunset, then," Jaevid concluded with a heavy sigh.

"Um, what?" Reigh made a scoffing, disapproving sound. "You can't be serious, Jae. Look at us. We can't all storm in there like a troupe of street performers," he protested. "We'll stick out like an extra toe."

The planets must have all aligned at that exact moment because, for once, I had to agree with him. "No offense to the famous heroes of the Gray War, but both of you are too recognizable."

Jaevid straightened and scowled, puffing up like an angry cat. "I can be discreet."

A bemused grin split over King Jace's mouth. "Jaevid, you are many things, but discreet has never been one of them. Has your memory gone fuzzy again? Do I really need to remind you what you put me through your avian year of dragonrider training?"

Jaevid's eyes narrowed, lips pursing sourly as he sank back into his chair again. I guess he didn't have a retort for that.

Judan countered as he rubbed at his jaw thoughtfully. "You're right, Jaevid can't go anywhere now without being recognized. I could risk taking that one, though. He's decent in a fight." He nodded toward me.

I smirked. "I'm flattered."

Beside me, Thatcher went stiff in his chair. "If Murdoc goes, then so do I," he declared.

I couldn't think of a time when I'd ever wanted to smack him upside the back of the head more than I did right then. But with Jaevid and King Jace both staring at us, I swallowed back that urge and settled for shooting him a scathing glare instead. That idiot. Did he even have a brain at all? He wouldn't last five seconds if he got lost or separated from the rest of us somewhere along the—

"You need to stay here with Jaevid and me," Reigh spoke up again. "Look, I know that's not what you want to hear, but you're the one Phillip is after. You leave this place, and you'll basically be strolling around with a big target on your back, and it could blow our whole plan of luring him out at the right time. Right now, you being here with Jaevid is probably the only thing giving him pause. So, I'm sorry, but it's not up for debate."

Thatcher's face flushed and his mouth mashed up like he'd bitten into something bitter. He panned his gaze around at all of us before settling a look of withheld rage on me. Granted, on his soft-featured face, it sort of looked like he might be about to throw up instead of yell at anyone. But I'd seen that look before enough times to know it for what it truly was.

He was furious.

"Take a breath and relax, would you?" I said with a scowl. "We'll get this done faster with fewer people. And nothing might come of it at all, so there's no point in getting worked up."

"You're in just as much danger as I am because of the Ulfrangar," he growled through his teeth.

"All the more reason to let them go into the city alone," Reigh reasoned. "There may be another way you can help, though. The way I see it, it's only an hour or two to fly there by dragon, and Mavrik's too conspicuous to do a fast drop-off without alerting every thug, thief, and assassin in a ten mile radius. That leaves us. You and I can take them to the outskirts on Fornax and Vexi—but that's as close as we can afford to get to all this."

Jaevid, King Jace, and Prince Judan all nodded in agreement.

I saw the defeat sink into Thatcher's expression like an unwatered plant wilting in a pot. His shoulders sagged and all the rage seeped from his face, his mouth drooping into a dejected frown.

"I ... I guess there's no other choice, then," he murmured quietly.

"No, there isn't. But don't worry. The next time I negotiate a secret and possibly deadly meeting with an infamous crime lord, I have every intention of dragging you there with me ... and possibly using you as a human shield." I gave him what I hoped was a friendly, reassuring gesture and jabbed him with my elbow as I leaned forward against the tabletop. Things like that still felt so awkward and forced. I didn't know how to be that—friendly. Big-brotherly. Family-ish. Or whatever it was called.

Ugggh.

Why did normal interactions have to be so weird? Life was so much simpler when I'd just assumed everyone in the room would kill me the first chance they got. This whole "being nice" nonsense was excruciating.

But it did make Thatcher smile a little, so maybe it worked.

"Well, with that decided, I'll need to prepare for departure back to Luntharda immediately," King Jace announced as he stood, giving his son a quick, meaningful glance. "By shrike would be the fastest, if that can be arranged."

"Leaving so soon?" Jaevid's tone held the tiniest hint of sarcasm. A taunt, maybe?

King Jace scoffed, waving a hand at him dismissively as he started out of the room. "Only temporarily, Broadfeather, don't you worry. I won't be allowing you to steal all the glory again. I will, however, need to fetch my most powerful weapon if we're going to be dancing around Ulfrangar and chancing meetings with crime lords."

I arched an eyebrow. "And that weapon would be ... ?"

The old king smirked widely. "My wife."

CHAPTER FOUR

"We do this fast and clean. In and out, minimal sound," Reigh insisted, keeping his voice hushed as we gathered inside the modest barn roughly three blocks over from the Porters' home. Jaevid had negotiated for a few of the smaller dragons to stay here, stabled and out of sight, until we could move them elsewhere. So far, it'd kept the beasts from causing too much trouble with the local city folk.

Well, most of them, anyway.

I clenched my teeth, biting back a curse as a heavy snout came to rest on my shoulder. I stumbled under the weight of his head and nearly fell over as a blast of hot, smelly breath hit my cheek. Gods and Fates, not this again.

The scaly menace who'd apparently "chosen me" made curious popping and clicking sounds as I tried shoving him off me and turning my back to him. So far, I'd tried sending him away by force. Obviously, that hadn't worked. If anything, it'd only provided a ceaseless source of entertainment for Jaevid and the others to watch me flail. Time to change tactics.

I could only hope that ignoring him entirely would work better.

"We make the drop three miles out of town and immediately turn back," Reigh continued as he flicked a glance at Thatcher. "Then we return here to wait, and go back for the pickup at dawn. With any luck, no one will even know we were in the area."

"Should the unthinkable happen and we find ourselves on the wrong end of a fight, Murdoc and I will take cover in one of my company's safehouses and wait it out until dawn." Judan said quickly. "So if you return to the drop-off point and we aren't there, do a low pass and look for green smoke on a rooftop. You can extract us from there."

Reigh and Thatcher nodded in unison.

"All right." Reigh's chest heaved with a deep, steadying breath. Then he looked squarely at Judan. "And you're sure about this? You can really convince this person to arrange a meeting with Arlan the Kinslayer?"

The half-elf prince winced a little and looked down, shifting his footing. "I can certainly try. Kinslayer is a fickle beast, but there may be something of equal value I can offer him in return for a little cooperation."

A few seconds of tense, heavy silence made it all the more obvious that the young dragon still lurking at my back was noisily preening himself with slurps and smacks. Ugh.

"Well, then. Let's get this done." Reigh concluded at last. "Judan, you're with me. Thatcher, hang off my wing and follow our lead."

It didn't take long to get everyone prepped for departure. I rolled the big barn doors ajar before pausing to check my weaponry one last time. Parts of my body still gave stretching or aching throbs of pain when I moved a certain way—particularly around the deep gash I'd taken to my side. Taking Reigh's healing remedies had now become a part of my daily routine, and I had to admit, they did wonders for speeding the healing process and relieving some of the pain. They might've done more if I had been able to rest and take a break from doing any heavy lifting or combat training. That wasn't an option, though. No rest for the weary—or the injured, in my case.

Stepping back, I gave Reigh's sleek, green dragoness some space as she crawled forward. Vexi shook her great horned head and flexed her wing fingers as she lumbered past. Reigh and Judan already sat in the saddle fixed to her back, and gave me a thumb's up signal that they were ready to take off. They'd hold a circling flight pattern until we joined them in the air.

With a rumbling snarl, the green dragon prowled past and out into the small, empty city square outside. A few wing beats and blasts of wind later, and she disappeared into the dark sky overhead.

Now it was our turn.

I turned back, prepared to get into the saddle of Thatcher's much larger male dragon. But there was a large black and red scaly beast sitting directly in my way, blinking at me with wide blue eyes.

Not this again ...

The young drake smacked his lips excitedly, rump wiggling some as he swiveled his small ears in my direction. He hunkered down, presenting his back eagerly like he wanted me to climb on.

No. Absolutely not.

"We have been over this," I growled. "The answer is no. It's always been no. And it will always be no. And even if it were yes—which it isn't—you're not wearing a saddle. Jaevid doesn't know if you're even old enough to take the weight of a rider in flight."

The black dragon gave an excited snort and hedged a little closer, swishing his long tail.

Great.

"You could just give it a try," Thatcher called to me suddenly. Already sitting comfortably astride Fornax, he peered down through the newly-crafted, enchanted goggles he had already pulled down over his eyes.

I shot him a glare. "No."

"But why not? Who knows, you might actually decide you like it."

Shoving the young dragon's head out of my path, I refused to make eye contact with either of them as I climbed into the back of the saddle. "Because I am *not* a dragonrider," I seethed quietly.

WE SOARED THROUGH THE NIGHT, cruising above a thin veil of clouds and keeping to the coastline. With any luck, we'd be mistaken for a few of the many wild dragons that roamed this area, and no one would give us a second look. Fornax's strong wings caught the rising currents from the sea, leathery membranes filling with the salty wind as he cruised off Vexi's right wingtip. He kept in tight formation, not making a sound beyond the occasional heavy *whump—whump—*of his wing beats.

Far below, the faint lights along the coastline gave away scattered tiny villages and a few ships anchored off shore. Off to the right and far in the distance, a looming thunderhead flashed with lightning. It was too far off to hear the echoing boom of thunder, but the sight still sent a prickle of primal awe and terror up my spine. Storms were frequent this far north, especially at this time of year. But seeing one from the air like that was like staring into the cold, indifferent eyes of an ancient god.

Terrifying ... and somehow exhilarating at the same time.

When the dense cluster of lights marking Port Marlowe appeared in the distance, Vexi dipped into a low approach, barely skimming the tops of the trees. She closed in on a small clearing in the sparse forest not far from the outskirts and swiftly touched down. Fornax ducked in after her, squeezing in just long enough for me to climb off his back. Judan quickly dismounted, as well, and together we sprinted for the cover of the tree line. Hunkered low in the prickly thickets, we held our positions as the dragons took to the air again.

Once the resounding boom of their wing beats had faded into the night, we exchanged a meaningful look. We were on our own now. Time to work.

I let Judan take point as we made our way through the forest, light and fast, until we came to a well-used road that wound off into the distance. Open roads were always a risk, so we stayed within the cover of the trees as we followed it toward the city. No need to announce our arrival, after all.

It took less than a half hour to reach the city limits, and the closer we got, the more intense Judan's gaze became. His sharp features went cold as his dark green eyes moved quickly, scanning the area ahead. He'd pulled his long, brown hair back into a tight, efficient braid that exposed his pointed ears. I had to admit, for someone who was half Gray Elf, he hadn't inherited many of their traits. Usually, halfbreeds tended to look more like Jaevid—er, well, except in height. Jaevid was unnaturally tall, especially for a halfbreed.

But Prince Judan could have easily passed for a human if not for those ears. He looked a great deal more like his father, I guess. Interesting ...

"She'll be at the tavern on the dockside road," he murmured as we halted about a hundred yards from the city's gate. Or rather, the crumbling ruin that had once been its gate. It was little more than an empty archway of stacked dark stone now. No guards. No watchtowers or battlements.

"Keep your hand on your dagger and your guard up, but try not to look too tense," he whispered again. "I've no enemies here, but with the Ulfrangar so hungry for your blood, there isn't much to stop them from confronting us right in the middle of a city square. We should try to appear as casual as we can."

"What about members of your agency? Are there any posted here?" I asked.

His brows furrowed slightly. "A few, yes. It's a good place to pick up information on target movements. Sailors love to gossip, and pirates like to brag." He gave a soft chuckle. "But I suppose I don't have to tell you that, eh?"

True enough. The Ulfrangar didn't specialize in capitalizing on selling or acquiring information, but that didn't mean we had no idea where to get it. We just preferred the point of a blade as a persuasion tactic instead of haggling. "Take lead, then."

He stood and pulled the hood of his cloak down, then paused to cast me a crooked grin. "And if you can manage it, no honorifics. No calling me 'highness' or 'prince' unless you'd like to end the evening sprinting for our lives. In these circles, I go by Bann."

Right. Well, he wouldn't have been much of a spy if he went around calling himself His Royal Highness Prince Judan of Luntharda. Perhaps those muddled, mostly-human features worked to his advantage in this lifestyle.

We stepped into the street side-by-side, making our way down the dark avenues littered with trash, smashed bottles, and the occasional body. It was difficult to tell if those people were dead or had simply collapsed after a night of drinking, but I wasn't about to stop and check any pulses. Judan didn't, either. With his bow and quiver at his back and his thumb hooked through his belt, right at the place where one of his two short-bladed scimitars hung, he kept his focus on the path ahead.

Lit lanterns squeaked in the wind where they hung over the doors of some of the shops and houses, giving off just enough of a weak glow to spot the figures of other people walking the streets. We made a point to avoid them, choosing different routes and back alleys until we reached the wide, dockside road. There, the ambient sounds of music, loud voices shouting, laughing, or singing, and the faint smell of food mixed with soured ale filled the air. It gave me a little shiver of nostalgia—taking me back to my childhood spent walking in Rook's shadow along the harbor roads of Saltmarsh.

I set my jaw and pushed those memories down.

A group of figures stood under the eaves of one of the slump-roofed buildings, smoking on pipes and gulping from glass bottles of liquor. They all seemed to go still and silent as we passed, watching us with eyes shining in the faint light that ebbed from the broad, cracked window panes of the taverns behind them. There were more than a handful of those establishments ahead of us, their windows still glowing brightly against the gloomy night. One glimpse through the windows revealed gruff-looking patrons packed around long tables, drinking from pints, harassing barmaids, and playing card games.

Judan didn't slow his pace until we reached one at the farther end, a shabby looking place with a sign above the door depicting a fat green dragon with tiny wings spilling out of an overturned ale mug. The chipping letters painted under it read: The Wasting Wyrm. Hmm.

Compared to the other taverns on the street, this one seemed to be smaller, although it was clearly the first level of a full-service inn. The floors above were lined with smaller windows, some with candles burning in them, and more than a few people reclined on cramped little balconies overlooking the street.

Basically, the place was every bit the den of debauchery I'd expected to find in a town like this. As soon as we stepped inside, the pungent smell of sweat, old blood, bad ale, and burnt food hit me like a shovel to the face. I blinked hard, resisting the urge to cough as I followed Judan through the grid of crowded tables heaped with pint glasses, ale horns, heaps of coins, and drunken vagabonds who'd passed out in their plates. On the far wall, a heavy-set old man squinted up at us with only one eye from where he was busy wiping the tabletop. His other eye was, well, gone. Nothing left but an empty socket. Not that it looked like a recent injury—clearly he'd been without it for a long while—but he hadn't even bothered to cover it with an eye patch.

He gave a sneering smirk and tipped his head at Judan, then spit on his bar top and went back to wiping it ... with the spit.

I made a mental note not to eat or drink *anything* here.

Judan waved back and carried on, making his way to an area of the tavern where a table had been pulled right to the front of the room before a roaring stone hearth. Beneath the glow of the flames, a pair of figures sat opposite one another, leaning in with their hands locked to arm-wrestle. A small crowd gathered around, swapping handfuls of coins as they placed their bets on who'd win.

On one side, a hulking oaf of a man sat with the sleeves ripped off his sweat-stained tunic and his bald head shown with a sheen of sweat. His neck was nearly as thick around as his entire head, and his massive arms bulged with muscle. He leered at his opponent with bloodshot eyes.

But she didn't so much as blink.

I frowned, staring in silent shock at the very petite young woman who sat across from him. Gods and Fates—she couldn't have been an inch over four foot, six inches. They'd brought out an old crate for her to sit on so she was able to reach the tabletop easily with her elbow.

Was she a ... ? No. No, that couldn't be it. Dwarves never came this far east. They scarcely ever left their massive stone fortresses. I'd never heard of one making an appearance in Maldobar before.

But there she sat.

What the young dwarven woman lacked in height, however, she more than made up for in brawny sculpted muscle adorned in faint, blue tattoos that spiraled over her tanned skin, contouring her shoulders, arms, and disappearing beneath the fitted leather ensemble she wore. Her ginger blond hair was thick and wild, pulled into a pair of braided pigtails, framing her larger-than-normal ears.

She didn't even glance our way as she leveled a wry grin at her opponent, tipping her chin in a subtle taunt.

It worked. The idiot across from her gave a grunting bellow like an enraged bull. The half-drunk Gray Elf who seemed to have established himself as the referee, slapped the table between them—and the fight was on.

CRACK!

In less than a second, the dwarven girl cranked his arm to the side and bashed it so hard into the tabletop it left a dent.

Holy. Gods.

Coins flew through the air as cheers and shouts of dismay erupted through the entire tavern. I ducked as an empty pint glass flew past my head. Judan laughed and applauded, then stood with his arms crossed and his eyes twinkling with delight while she raked her stack of coins into a large leather purse. Then she reached in for a fistful and smacked them down on the tabletop.

"That was a good one, yeah? How about a round for the lot of ya—on me!" She giggled in a merry, sing-song voice. It gave away how young she probably was. Er, well, comparatively, anyway.

Dwarves were something of an oddity when it came to aging. I knew enough about them to understand that they aged far more slowly than humans or elves. So while she might look and sound like a teenager, she was probably far older. Possibly even several decades older. But for a dwarf, a woman of thirty years or so was still *very* young—more like a sixteen-year-old in human terms.

Another chorus of cheers went up through the room, and the now-defeated oaf gathered the shattered remains of his pride and left the table, cradling his arm.

"Good show, Garnett!" Judan called over the noise.

Immediately, her head whipped around to stare straight at us. A huge grin spread over her freckled cheeks and her bright, purple-hued eyes practically glowed with joy. She climbed out of her seat and flung her arms out wide as she strode toward him. "Bann!"

He met her halfway and reached a hand down to shake hers. I could've sworn I saw him wince a little at her grip.

Standing back with her hands planted on her broad, shapely hips, the young dwarven woman beamed up at him and laughed. Her wide grin made the single blue rune tattooed beneath her left eye crinkle a little. "What're you doing here? Not enough trouble for you in those fancy cities these days?"

"Oh, plenty," he confessed. "Can't I come visit just because I miss that beautiful face of yours?"

She wrinkled her small, button nose and stuck her tongue out at him. "Now, you watch that mouth, pretty boy. I'm wise to your tricks." Then her violet gaze flickered to me, looking me over quickly with well-practiced intensity. "And who's this? Friend of yours?"

He shrugged. "You could say that. He's actually the reason I'm here. Is there a place we can have a little chat and maybe I can get you a drink of something decent?"

Her smile faded a bit, replaced by a hint of wary suspicion as she glanced back up to him. "Of course. This way, gentlemen. And step lightly—I think someone must've hit the floor rather than the outhouse over by the stairs."

CHAPTER FIVE

Garnett led us up the steps to the third floor of the tavern, down a narrow hall, and into a small bedroom. It smelled considerably better than the rest of the place—thanks in part to the fact that the big window that faced the street was pushed open to let the cool night wind in. There was only one small leather pack on the floor at the foot of a lumpy bed, and a pair of double-headed hand axes leaned up against the wall beneath the window. The rest of the space looked as though it hadn't been touched.

I guess she wasn't planning on staying here for long.

As soon as we were inside, Garnett quickly shut the door and threw the lock. Then her sturdy shoulders flexed with a heavy sigh. "Why do I have a feeling I'm not going to like this conversation, Bann?"

He smiled apologetically. "You can use my name," he said quietly. "He knows who I am, just as I'm sure you do."

When she turned around, that impish smile played over her lips again as she tilted her head to the side a little. "Hmm, yes, well, I wouldn't be very good at my job if I didn't, now would I, *Your Highness*?"

"What gave me away?" He chuckled softly.

She winked and waggled a finger at him. "Now, see, if I told you that, you'd stop doing it." Her expression cooled some as she glanced my way again. "But this one ... I don't even have to guess who he is. He might as well have it branded across his forehead. So, what're you doing running around with an assassin?"

"*Former* assassin," I corrected her.

Her eyes narrowed a little. "No such thing, I hear. They don't let anyone leave their ranks. Not alive, anyway. So, either you're a liar, or you're a dead man walking. Judging by that desperate look in your eyes and the way you've been tracking every dark corner and exit point since you arrived, I'd bet on the latter."

It was hard not to be impressed. She was sharp, I'd give her that.

"It's not a simple situation, Garnett," Judan admitted as she brushed back the hood of his cloak so she could see his face clearly. "Which is part of the reason I'm here. I know we promised not to impose on one another's business. And believe me when I say, I would not be crossing that line unless I had no other choice. But there's a problem at large in Maldobar that might make things difficult for both of us—and for your employer, as well. I came to ask for his help in fixing it."

Her brows went up and she glanced back and forth between us, seeming to ponder whether or not she should even say another word. Finally, her expression steeled and she licked her teeth behind her lips. "Very well, then. Speak your business and I'll make sure the word is passed along accordingly."

"Garnett, please." His tone was gentle and pleading as he stared down at her. "We've been friends for nearly a year now. I know what you went through before, and I truly don't want to sour things because of this. I wouldn't even dream of asking, but—"

"Ugggh, please, spare me the flowery speeches," she groaned as she rolled her eyes. "Such drama. If you've something that important at stake, then just spit it out, man. We don't have all night." Her expression quirked into a small, suspicious grin as she looked at me again. "Is it a woman? It is, isn't it? His secret lover? You're not his son, are you? My, that would be scandalous!"

I opened my mouth, but the prince beat me to it. "No! Gods and Fates, it's nothing like that."

Garnett looked genuinely disappointed. "Then what is it?"

"It concerns Duke Phillip Derrick," he divulged at last. "I'm sure your employer is aware of the state he's in."

Her lips pursed thoughtfully. "Naturally."

"And that he's been ... missing recently."

She nodded.

"And is now working with the Ulfrangar."

Her violet eyes went wide. I guess that part was news to her. "You're sure? I didn't think they worked with outsiders."

"They don't, normally," I confirmed. "But it seems the Zuer has struck some sort of bargain with him. They want my life for my desertion—and he wants someone else's in return for helping them hunt me down."

"It's making a real mess of things," Judan added. "Stirring up trouble. Drawing a lot of public attention, which is bad for all of us."

Garnett arched an eyebrow, as though silently urging us to get to the point.

"Look, there's a chance that one of Argonox's most strictly-guarded former assets might be involved in all this. She might even be the one pulling the strings." He shifted uncomfortably and rubbed at the bridge of his nose. "I probably don't have to tell you what kind of problems we may all soon be facing if Devana is allowed to run free and unchecked."

Once again, Garnett's eyes went wide. She definitely recognized that name. "Y-You're ... you're sure it's her?" she stammered breathlessly.

"Reasonably," he said. "Enough that I'm here, asking for your help, if that's any evidence. We need to meet with your employer face-to-face. We need to negotiate a way to work together to recapture Duke Phillip. He may be the key to finding out what's really going on between her and the Ulfrangar. We've got the bait and a mad plan for the trap; all we need is the precise timing and location. I'm sure your employer could provide us with both."

She tapped her chin, beginning to pace quickly back and forth in front of us. Finally, she stalked briskly over to her pack and opened it, rummaging through the inside until she drew out a roll of clean parchment, an ink bottle, and quill. "It'll take a few days to get a response, but I'll send this along tonight. I can't promise he'll want to get involved, though."

Judan's eyes fell closed as his entire body seemed to relax with sudden relief. "It's enough that you'd even try. Thank you, Garnett."

"Don't thank me yet," she warned. "You know how he can be—stones know you lot spend plenty of time trying to spy on him. And that one murdered one of our new informants." She jabbed the end of her quill in my direction with a devious little smirk. "Or did you think I didn't know that was you? Tsk tsk. Sloppy, especially for an Ulfrangar. I thought you weren't supposed to leave any traces?"

I couldn't resist returning that smirk. "Like I said, *former* assassin."

She gave a snorting giggle and unfurled her roll of parchment. "I take it you'll be wanting to meet in Dayrise?"

"If possible. We're hunkered down for now, closing ranks as best we can. But time is of the essence, and so long as we have both their targets, I can only assume they'll strike again very soon."

"Naturally," she agreed. "Well, make yourselves comfortable, boys. He'll want every detail you can spare in order to make a decision either way, so I've got to be sure I take this all down correctly."

BY DAWN, we were standing back in the small clearing where Reigh and Thatcher had dropped us off. Just as the first few rays of sunlight began to turn the far horizon the faintest shades of blue and deep purple, the faint booming of dragon wing beats echoed in the distance.

I knew I should be relieved. Satisfied, even. But as I stood watching the two silhouettes of the dragons slowly approach from the north, my mind raced with a flurry of new questions. Had we made the right choice in going to Kinslayer? Involving him might be a huge mistake. It might blow up in our faces, and what then? What if he betrayed us? We'd just given up a lot of valuable information about our situation to that dwarven woman—girl—person. It was hard to tell how old she might be, honestly. Not because of her stature, though. Her soft, youthful features and merry demeanor reminded me a little of Phoebe, although in a much rowdier way.

My mouth scrunched. Why was I comparing her to Phoebe? Gods, why was I even thinking about this at all?

"Don't worry," Prince Judan murmured. He must've noticed my unease. "I know she doesn't seem like it, but Garnett is very careful and discreet. She's one of Kinslayer's chief informants now—most trusted of them all. She knows how to keep her mouth shut when it matters."

"That's ... not ... I wasn't thinking about that," I grumbled back. My cheeks burned, and I looked away so maybe he wouldn't see my face turning red.

"Oh? Care to share, then?"

No. I most definitely did not want to share my thoughts about Phoebe. But the longer he stared at me, those probing half-elf eyes dissecting every tiny move I made, the harder it was not to react.

Then again, maybe it wasn't such a bad idea to ask him. He was an unbiased party in all this. He was also much older, and had a reputation for being popular among the women at court. Surely he could provide some insight.

Clearing my throat, I faced him again and tried to keep my expression as indifferent as possible. "If there were a certain girl who ... who seemed to have particular *feelings* for me, what would you recommend?"

Judan's jaw dropped. For a few seconds, he just stood there gaping at me like a beached fish. "That's, um, quite the question to ask, Murdoc."

"I don't have any experience with this sort of interaction," I muttered. Somehow, saying that out loud was even more humiliating. "I've always made a point to avoid it. But now it's inescapable. And I'm not sure what I'm supposed to do. She's avoiding me, almost like she's afraid to face me now, and ... it seems like I should give her some kind of response."

"Response to what?" He cringed back some, almost like he was afraid of the answer.

"She kissed me."

"O-Oh. I see." He scratched at his throat, gaze wandering back to where the dragons were drawing nearer and nearer to our position. "I suppose that depends on how you feel, boy. But to be honest, I'm probably not the right person to be asking about that sort of thing."

I frowned. "Why not?"

His sharp features softened with a strange, almost mournful smile as he stared up at the sky. "Because I've never been kissed by the woman I love. I doubt I ever will be. I can tell you one thing, though. If I believed for even a second that I had any chance at all at winning her heart, I wouldn't hesitate. I would tell her how I felt, and I would do whatever I could to stay by her side forever. I suppose that's what you should be asking yourself."

I waited, still not sure what he meant by all that.

Prince Judan met my gaze with a brokenness in his eyes I barely understood. "Ask yourself if you can stand watching her be with someone else for the rest of your life."

6

CHAPTER SIX

Jaevid and the others stood waiting in the barn as we landed one at a time and made our way inside. The young drake yipped and fell all over himself as he waddled over to greet us. It made Vexi chirp and chatter back at him, making pleased musical sounds as she rubbed her snout against his. Fornax was less amused, though. He gave a reluctant growl as the smaller dragon approached, and leaned away with his ears slicked back.

It didn't take long for everyone to gather around long enough for Judan to recount what had happened. Only his father, King Jace, was absent. He'd probably already left for Luntharda—which quite honestly, was for the best. Powerful wife-weapon or not, it was risky for him to spend too much time here. Word was bound to get out that a king had taken up residence on the block, and that was exactly the kind of attention we did not need right now.

Judan didn't spare any details as he explained the situation. Not that there was much to tell, really. We'd found his contact and convinced her to reach out to Arlan the Kinslayer. Now, all we could do was wait and prepare.

The atmosphere felt a lot more restless and uneasy than usual as the members of our group began to break off. Jaevid and Judan left together, probably returning to the Porters, and kept their voices low as they spoke. Isandri and Reigh made their way over to where Thatcher was guiding Fornax to a place in the hay so he could lie down. The one person I didn't spot right away was a certain redheaded artificer.

Where was Phoebe?

I glanced around, stopping when I spotted her walking for the barn door by herself. She hesitated in the doorway, looking back at me with an anxious expression. Her lips parted, sky blue eyes searching my face for a moment like there was something she wanted to say. But she quickly looked away, ducked her head, and slipped out the door without ever saying a word.

A heaviness settled in the center of my chest, like someone had pierced my heart with a grappling hook and was pulling it down toward my boots. Judan's words rang in my head like echoes of a tolling bell bouncing off cavernous cathedral walls. If Phoebe eventually chose to be with someone else ... how would that make me feel? Or would I even feel anything at all?

I tried to picture it in my mind—her walking along with another man, holding hands, and swapping affectionate smiles. It might even be someone I knew. Someone like Thatcher, or even Reigh, if he ever decided to pull his head out of his rear. Unlikely.

Before I could stop it, the image of her standing with Thatcher, looking adoringly up at him as he leaned down like he meant to kiss her flashed through my brain.

It made my hands draw into fists as that heaviness in my chest intensified. It grew until I thought my knees might buckle.

I ... I *hated* that idea.

I also now had the sudden urge to punch Thatcher as hard as I could.

Fortunately, that only lasted until I fixed my glare upon him. He was petting his dragon and talking to Isandri, oblivious as usual with that blissfully vacant smile on his face. That idiot ... if I actually hit him that hard, it'd probably break his jaw. Or kill him.

Uggh. Gods and Fates, I had to stop this. *Now.* I couldn't afford to get caught up thinking about things that, for someone in my situation, were completely pointless. It didn't matter how I felt. It was better if she avoided me.

My heart still pounded in heavy, hard thumps as I turned to leave, as well. After all night on my feet, every sore spot on my body where I had wounds still healing ached beneath my leather armor. Maybe I should ask Reigh for a larger dose of that healing remedy before I tried stealing a few hours of sleep. It might give me a much-needed boost of strength in case we were attacked again before we could even meet with Kinslayer.

Or maybe Kinslayer himself would join Devana in contracting the Ulfrangar to be rid of us. It was a toss-up, really.

Before I could even reach the doorway, a large black and red beast appeared in my path, making musical chirping sounds and sniffing at my head.

"You again." My tone didn't sound nearly as forbidding and cold as I'd hoped. Curse it all. I guess the fatigue really was getting to me. "Out of my way, dragon."

A snort from his huge nose blew my hair back. He bumped his snout against my chest and blinked at me with those enormous, vivid blue eyes. I could see my reflection in his dark, vertical pupils as he went on chirping and murring at me. Almost like he was concerned about me.

My hand moved, drawn to the obsidian sheen of his hide. A second before my palm could touch his scaly head, I realized what I was about to do. My jaw clenched and I pulled my hand back, shutting my eyes tightly.

"It's for your own good," I growled through my teeth. "Out of all the people in the world you could have chosen, you've picked the wrong one. Please, just ... go. Go back to the Cromwell's. I'm not going to be a dragonrider."

His little ears drooped, wide eyes blinking slowly as he tilted his head to the side slightly. Gods, sometimes it seemed like he really could understand what I said.

But that couldn't be the case. He was just an animal.

And I ...

My head swam suddenly, making me stumble. I-I couldn't breathe. My chest—it wouldn't move. And my arms, my legs—nothing would respond. I couldn't even catch myself as my legs buckled and I dropped onto the barn floor.

My vision tunneled as I lay on my back, staring up into the worried dragon's gaze as it crowed and yipped in panic. Somewhere nearby, Thatcher shouted my name. Footsteps came closer, rushing over the barn floor.

Then it all began to fade.

And I was alone ... alone in the dark again.

"THAT ONE, that one, and that one there," a deep, rasping voice grumbled past in the gloom. The heavy *thunk—thunk—thunk* of many footsteps passed, coming closer.

My pulse raced wildly as I scrambled back, cramming my small, naked body into the corner of my cell as hard as I possibly could. My bare feet slid over the grime and filth on the floor. Most of it was mine. I didn't have a chamber pot, and the chains only went so far.

The footsteps stopped suddenly, and a light appeared. It glowed like a small star in the dark, stinging my eyes. I cowered back, trying to hide my face against my knees as my body convulsed with terrified shivering.

"What about this one?" the voice asked.

"Not but eight. Too young to come off the leash," another voice replied sharply. "Fights like a demon, though. Ought to be a good show when he does."

The first voice made a deep, thoughtful noise. "Cut him loose," it decided at last. "Let's see what he's got."

"But he's not—"

"Hey! I'm the one who decides when they're ready, not you. I saw him in the last feeding. He killed a boy twice his size. He's young, yeah, but if he's got fight like that in him, he'll do just fine. So, get him up and put him with the others."

No one else argued.

The footsteps came closer. The sound of rusted metal parts moving groaned and squealed. Oh Gods, they ... they were coming. They were coming for me.

Not again. Please, not again.

A sudden yank on the chain connected to my neck sent me sprawling forward. I pitched and flailed, gripping at the tight metal collar around my throat as they wrenched me down. The sharp, jagged edges bit into my skin deeper than ever. But I didn't make a sound. I didn't dare cry out or make any noise. A hard crack over the back of my head made my ears ring and my arms and legs drop limply to the cold, filthy stone floor.

They unlocked the shackles on my hands and feet, but left the one around my neck as they rolled me over. The light of the glass lantern illuminated the faces of two men, glaring down at me with utter disgust as they held me down and fastened a leather muzzle over my face that gagged my mouth.

Then they dragged me out by the ankles. My head thumped over the uneven stone floor until, at last, the men dropped me at the end of a line of other kids. Others like me. They stood, wearing the same wide metal collars around their necks and leather muzzles over their mouths that I did. But not a single one of them dared to even glance my way.

They were all easily twice my size, and likely much older. Probably stronger, too. More desperate. Meaner. Far more lost. Their eyes caught in the weak light from the lantern, dark and empty as they stared straight ahead.

There were girls and boys, elves and humans, and none of us had a single stitch of clothing on. Our bare bodies were so gaunt and drawn we looked like living corpses, and our skin was a patchwork of bruises, cuts, gashes, and scars. The two men hooked us all on a long chain that connected our collars, then stood back to take count.

"How many does that make?" The first voice—coming from a tall man with a long, crooked nose—called down the line.

"Twenty in all," the second voice answered. "That enough?"

"Should be."

I-I had to get up. Now. If I didn't, they'd drag me, and the collar was so tight I'd probably smother to death. My body shook, knees quaking and head lolling, as I managed to get on my hands and knees. I leaned against the wall, digging my nails desperately into the stone to drag myself up. No sooner had I gotten onto my bare feet than the chain tethered to my neck went taut, hauling me forward at the end of the line.

We staggered through the dark, chains rattling with every step as we passed rows of other cells. There must have been hundreds of them lining the twisting, cavernous halls. Sometimes the passing light of the lantern fell across a figure slumped inside, chained by the neck, ankles, and wrists. Some looked old enough to nearly be teenagers. Others were barely old enough to walk on their own.

But I didn't dare to stop and get a better look. I couldn't risk even more than half a second's glance. Ahead—that was the only safe place to look.

The tunnel eventually sloped up, coming to several barred doors that were unlocked and opened for us to pass on. We climbed stairwells, ascending until the air began to smell cleaner, fresher, and faintly of salt.

A sharp right turn led into a much larger tunnel filled with openings in the ceiling that let shafts of brilliant sterling light pour in. Before I could stop myself, I tipped my head back to stare up through one of the openings as we passed beneath it. Through a diamond-shaped hole cut in the stone, the moon hung like a shining white pearl, wreathed in wisps of dark cloud.

A loud *CRACK* was my only warning. An instant later, white-hot pain surged up my back, making my spine go rigid and my eyes well. I knew that feeling all too well, even as it ebbed into a burning, throbbing, crippling agony that nearly made my legs give out again. The whelpers who were in charge of moving us around always carried whips.

"Eyes forward, pup," the man at my back hissed angrily.

Tears slid down my face as I struggled to breathe past the gag in my mouth. Stop—I just wanted it to stop. I'd steal whatever they told me to. I'd kill anyone they wanted. I'd do anything if ... if they would just let me die.

The whelpers led us down another broad hallway, through a pair of massive wooden doors, and into an atrium with a tall ceiling domed in glass. The moonlight pouring through it illuminated a black and gold glass mosaic set into the gray stone floor—the head of a snarling wolf with three eyes.

A symbol I'd seen many times.

Our pattering footsteps echoed through the chamber as we moved on, marching through another massive set of doors and into the glare of bright torchlight. Before us, a huge circular room was arranged like an arena. Its dirt floor was already splashed and spattered with blood, and a massive iron chandelier hung overhead, illuminating the space with wavering, fiery light.

Above the twenty-foot wall that encircled the arena floor, six men in identical black leather armor sat on a balcony in silent observation as we entered. Their eyes searched us one at a time, as though looking for any signs of weakness.

The doors shut behind us with a low *BOOM*.

On a separate, much higher balcony, a figure in a long, hooded black robe stood. It gestured to the whelpers, who immediately began unfastening our collars from the chain.

A shudder of panic and desperation flushed through my body, making my pulse roar in my ears, as I watched that tether fall away. Free—I was free. I could run. I could try to escape. But where ... ?

"Twenty have been brought for your consideration," a breathy female voice spoke from under the hood of those black robes. "But only six shall depart in your charge. Each has been instructed in the basic way of the blade. Each has been trained to obey the will of the pack. Each hold their fate in their hands." She turned, taking up a large, silver-crafted hourglass filled with black sand. She held it up so that everyone in the room could see. "Today, your fate is sealed, pups. Should more than six remain when the last grain falls, then all shall perish. Those who endure to stand as the six will be granted advancement under the charge of a handler. You will no longer know hunger. You will no longer know chains. You will learn to walk with the pack as many have before you, forged forever to the blood oath of the Ulfrangar."

My heartbeat surged, droning in my ears as one of the whelpers suddenly shoved something into my hands. A rusty, dull scimitar already speckled with old, dried blood.

My hand closed around the frayed leather hilt, squeezing hard as all the feeling, all the emotion, seemed to slowly begin to drain from my mind. There was no fear. No panic. Nothing except a numb emptiness.

... And rage like hellfire.

"Fight well, pups," the woman said, turning the large hourglass over. "Tomorrow is your first dawn."

7

CHAPTER SEVEN

"Come on, you miserable grumpy jerk," a familiar voice shouted over me. Was that ... Reigh?

BAM!

Someone smacked me hard over the face. Then I could faintly feel pulses of pressure bearing down on my chest, as though they were trying to restart my heart.

"Isandri! Again!" Reigh yelled.

Fingers pinched my nose closed as a mouth pressed hard over mine, forcing breath into my lungs.

Suddenly, my whole body gave a jolt. My eyes blinked, refocusing as I gulped in a frantic, halting breath.

"There we go, that's it," Reigh panted as he rolled me over onto my side. "Deep breaths, Murdoc. Slow and steady. You're all right."

No, I most certainly was not. What in the abyss had happened? Had I collapsed? Nearly died? Why?

"See, this is why the whole silent brooding thing is so annoying. The pain's been bad lately, right? You should have said something, idiot," he muttered as he watched me lie there and wheeze. "Looks like you've still got some of the godsgrave elixir in your system. Even trace amounts of it can drop you like a newborn faundra. If you'd said something about the pain sooner, I could've given you something to try to counteract the effects so at least it didn't stop your heart."

Great. Now he told me. "W-Would've ... been ... n-nice to k-know that ... s-sooner," I managed to croak.

"I did warn you that stuff was nasty," he reminded me.

"Will he recover?" Isandri asked. Sitting close by, she ran a hand soothingly over my shoulder.

"Yeah, but he needs to take it easy." Reigh sighed. "I guess we all know that isn't going to happen, though, eh?"

Hah. Right.

"*REIGH!*" Jaevid's voice boomed through the barn.

My vision still swerved some as I looked over to find him rushing in with Thatcher right on his heels. I guess he'd immediately dashed off to get help from our resident war hero.

Their shared horror at my state was aggravating, but Reigh eventually talked them down. I'd be fine. I just needed another heavy dose of healing herbs and anti-toxin remedies. Some sleep, too, if I could manage with Thatcher fussing over me like a worried mother hen.

I tried not to think of how undignified it must have looked when Jaevid looped an arm under my shoulders and dragged me up, helping me hobble out of the barn and back to the Porter's house. All the while, Thatcher asked repeatedly if I was going to be okay, and Reigh blathered on about the godsgrave elixir. Part of me wished I was still unconscious.

It wasn't until hours later, while I was lying on a bed in a small bedroom in the Porter house, that I could think at all. The Porters had lent us as much space as they could, and this bedroom had just enough space for Reigh, Thatcher, and myself to sleep. Our things were still scattered all around, and the curtains were drawn over the window to make everything dim. A small shaft of the evening sunlight managed to bleed through, though, and sparkled off the silver pommel of Rook's sword leaning against the far wall.

It was the only piece of the Ulfrangar gear I'd kept.

Reigh had already come and gone after cramming all manner of healing mixtures, salves, and whatnot down my throat. The heavy doses of healing medicines left me feeling relaxed and a little delirious as I lay there, nodding in and out of consciousness.

Staring straight up at the ceiling, I forced my foggy brain to focus on each of my breaths as my mind circled around that dream. I hadn't thought of that day in so long. To be honest, I'd been hoping to never think of it again for the rest of my existence. That was the day I'd first met Rook. The day they'd removed my collar.

My first dawn.

My eyes fell closed. It seemed like so long ago. And now Rook was gone. Now I was trying to stumble through a somewhat normal daily life with Thatcher and the others—doing things like eating full meals, sleeping in beds, and trying to figure out feelings about girls.

Somehow, it still didn't seem real.

And the longer it went on, the more I realized ... I might never feel right in this world. I might never be able to fully shake off that Ulfrangar part of myself.

Part of me might always be that kid, chained naked in the dark.

A soft knock at the door made me open my eyes again. Thatcher stepped in, his smile tense and forced as he closed the door behind him. "O-Oh. Hey. You're awake. Did, uh, did Reigh give you more medicine?" he stammered nervously.

I nodded. "In between calling me an idiot fifty more times, yes."

He let out a shaky, relieved breath as he sank down into the chair at my bedside. "That's good. You, uh, you really scared us there for a minute."

"I'm not going to die yet," I muttered. Too late, I realized I probably should've tried to make that sound more reassuring. Gods, I really was bad at this whole friendship thing. "I'll be fine, Thatcher," I tried again.

"Jaevid's really angry at him for giving you that godsgrave stuff in the first place. But Reigh says as long as you keep taking some of the healing remedies regularly for the next few weeks, you should be fine." He swallowed hard, fidgeting with his hands as he leaned forward to rest his elbows on his knees. "Hey, uh, Murdoc? There's ... there's something I need to talk to you about."

Oh no.

My stomach clenched, seizing into a hard knot so suddenly it made my pulse skip and stall. Had Jaevid gotten impatient and already told him about my involvement with his father's death? Gods and Fates, I was not prepared to have this conversation. Not yet.

But I didn't have a choice.

"Okay," I managed to murmur back, my gaze instinctively drawn away. If we were going to discuss this, I couldn't look him in the eye. It only made that pain in my gut worse.

"You know how I went to try and convince Isandri to tell us what she knows about Devana?" He hedged, pausing to nibble at his bottom lip as his expression skewed with uncertainty. "She knew ... kind of a lot. And I know I haven't really told everyone about it yet, but it just didn't feel like the right time, and I was afraid because ... " His voice trailed off to strained, apprehensive silence.

"Because?" I prodded, looking back at him.

"Because I was afraid no one would believe me. I'm not even sure I believe it. But if there's even a small chance it's true, then someone should know before this goes any further."

"Someone should know what, Thatcher?"

His brows scrunched together and his mouth mashed into a crooked, grimacing line. He sat eerily still; his light green eyes barely visible behind his shaggy blond bangs. And with another deep, unsteady breath, he began to explain.

By the time he'd finished, I understood why Thatcher hadn't said a word about this to anyone until now. My thoughts raced, trying to make sense of it. He and Isandri were some sort of reborn deities in mortal form? *That's* what she had told him? And Devana was supposed to be one, as well?

Gods and Fates ...

We sat in silence for a few minutes while I tried to process all of that. On the one hand, I had heard Phillip refer to him as a 'godling' when I'd faced him last. I'd seen Isandri work feats of magical power many times that, even for an elven priestess, were nothing short of incredible.

But on the other hand ... Seriously? *Thatcher*? I'd never seen him do anything even remotely magical. He could barely hold his own in a fight. And he was supposed to be some sort of reborn god? It sounded completely ludicrous.

"I don't guess she has any proof that this is all true," I muttered as I set my jaw and tried to sit up.

"No," he admitted.

Rubbing at the back of my neck, I stared down at the quilt draped over my legs as I considered it—the entire situation—from every angle I could. "It doesn't matter if you're a god or not," I decided aloud.

He blinked in surprise. "I-It doesn't?"

I shook my head. "No. Because regardless of whether or not any of that is true, Devana believes it. Phillip is doing her bidding, so he believes it. The Ulfrangar have allied with it, so they might as well believe it. So, even if it's a bunch of crap, we are going to be pitted against people who are ready to die for it. They believe you're this Ishaleon. And that may be something we can use to our advantage."

Thatcher sank back into his seat some, staring at me with his expression still tense and uncertain. "I don't understand. How?"

I rubbed my fingers together, unable to resist that old nervous habit as my mind filled with a riot of new ideas. A different plan.

"You were right—you are the only one who can be the bait if this is ever going to work," I said as I looked up at him suddenly. "They already think you're a god. Now, we'll teach them to fear you like one, too."

He pulled a mortified look and leaned away a little. "Uh, Murdoc, I'm not sure if that's, umm—"

"It'll work." A grin curled up one side of my mouth as I glanced sideways at the blade leaning against the wall. Rook's xiphos. "Go tell Phoebe it's time to light the forge. We're going to need her help for this one."

8
CHAPTER EIGHT

Word from Arlan the Kinslayer came late that night, barely twenty-four hours since we'd sent our request with Garnett. Something, or someone, approaching the front door after sunset set off Isandri's protective wards. In an instant, we were all on high-alert.

Unfortunately, by the time Jaevid flung the door open with his scimitar firmly in hand, whoever had come was already long gone. The streets were dark and empty. There wasn't a soul in sight.

The only evidence of their presence left behind was an envelope stuck to the door by a small silver knife.

He pried the knife loose and handed it and the letter over to Judan. Sealed by a signet pressed into a drop of red wax, the fine paper of the envelope shone in pearlescent gold as he held it up. The AK insignia on the signet was unmistakable. This was from Kinslayer.

Everyone gathered in, bunching around Judan as he opened it. His sharp eyes scanned the page before he handed it off to Jaevid, shifting his gaze to where I stood next to Thatcher. He didn't have to say it out loud. I could see it written all over his sharp features. That sense of grim finality and steely determination in his gaze. The way his jawline went rigid as he nodded once.

Kinslayer would meet us.

"It doesn't have a time listed for us to be there," Jaevid pointed out as he handed it to me, next. "What does this even mean?"

I scanned the single line of text printed in a neat, perfectly straight line at the very center of the page:

King's Cross.

I smirked. "It's a location. An inn in one of the city squares not far from here. I spotted it when we arrived. And there's no time because he wants us to come right now."

Judan dipped his head in agreement. "Isandri and Reigh, you're on. Go ahead and stake out an observation point. Hold that position unless you see things take a nasty turn. The rest of you are with me. Gather what you need. We leave this house in sixty seconds."

It didn't take half that for us to strike out into the dark city streets. Isandri and Reigh left separately, moving stealthily ahead along the rooftops until their figures vanished like phantoms in the night.

I'd chosen my weaponry carefully this time. While the remedies had gone a long way in improving my strength and relieving that dull pain left where I'd been wounded before, I wasn't taking any chances. Not with Kinslayer.

I fastened the cross-sheath onto my back and slipped a pair of longswords into it, fitted my cestus gloves into my pockets, and slipped a pair of long daggers down the sides of my boots. With my preferred arsenal in place, I helped Thatcher buckle on the holster Phoebe had made for his crossbow so that it hung at his right hip. He had two of the interchangeable cartridges full of bolts that could easily be swapped out. That just left one last thing.

"Here, put this on your belt." I made a point not to look him in the eye as I handed him Rook's xiphos blade.

I didn't need to see his face to know he was giving me one of his classic, open-mouthed, goldfish-like stares. "B-But wasn't this your handler's? Isn't it special to you?"

I flicked a glance down at the weapon, the moonlight glinting off the raven engraved onto the pommel. "I guess," I muttered low. "But I think he'd want you to have it. Besides, you need a xiphos. And they're not easy to get in Maldobar."

His hands shook some as he took it from me, holding it as though it were made of glass. "Thank you, Murdoc. I'll ... I'll try to take good care of it."

I nodded and turned away, waiting while he raced through buckling it to his belt before we started after Judan and the others.

It wasn't a lie. When Ulfrangar took their oath and became full members of the pack, they were gifted with a weapon that suited their particular fighting style. I'd never received mine since I was still a pup when I left them. But Rook's had been this xiphos. It had been significant and completely unique to him, and was something I'd never even held until Jaevid gave it to me. Weapons like that weren't ones a mere pup would ever dare to touch. And holding it now, even though Rook was gone, still felt ... wrong, somehow. I couldn't put my finger on why, exactly. But the sense that he wouldn't have wanted me to hang onto it wasn't something I could ignore.

Besides, Thatcher did need it. The sooner he could learn to fight with a blade that suited him, the better.

Hopefully tonight wouldn't be his first time using it, though. With any luck, we would get through this without anyone drawing a blade.

Heh. Yeah. Sure.

As if we *ever* had that kind of luck on our side.

To the untrained eye, all was quiet and still as we made our way quickly through the sleeping city. A thin bank of fog drifted soundlessly over the streets, curling in our wake as we hurried along. My eyes saw every fragment of detail, though. The shadowed figure sitting in a darkened window, watching us pass. The scrape on the stone at the corner of an alley, indicating there had likely been a struggle there. My ears picked up on distant footsteps, the faint bark of a dog, and the soft, constant dull rumble of the ocean. For years, my senses had been honed to this, primed for the hunt.

But tonight, I felt more like prey. A skittish deer making a desperate dash across an open meadow.

Judan led the way, guiding our group down the main avenues toward the city's center. A decent tactic. Keeping us in plain sight of all the homes and shops we crossed was safer, even if most of them were closed up for the night. Nearly all the windows were dark, and the tenants inside were probably sound asleep already. Still, this was neutral ground. Anything that happened here would get lots of public attention in a hurry. If the Ulfrangar were watching—and I knew, without a doubt, they were—they'd be less likely to make a strike in the middle of a heavily populated street, even at night. In a place like this, everyone could hear a scream. Help would come running in the form of citizens brandishing pitchforks, gardening tools, and kitchen knives. And then, the city guards would soon follow. In a matter of minutes, the wild fireside tales of the nefarious Ulfrangar assassins wouldn't be mere myths anymore.

Not that they were now, anyway—not since Jaevid Broadfeather and no small number of royals were now aware of them.

Too bad that didn't make me feel any more secure or confident about our situation.

A cold chill rushed up my spine the instant my eyes fell upon the front of the King's Cross Inn. It stood right in the center of one of the largest city squares in Dayrise—one Phoebe and I had walked through when we arrived. The square itself was broad, open, and nearly hexagonal, with tall buildings flanking the central intersection on seven sides. Here, four main streets met and formed a roundabout, with a large fountain right at the center. Radiant moonlight sparkled off the ribbons of water that showered the tall bust of a man dressed in battle armor. Before, his image hadn't meant much to me except that he must be a dragonrider. There were hundreds, maybe thousands, of statues like that in Maldobar honoring various heroes. Now, I recognized the helmet tucked under his arm.

This was a statue of Levran Porter—the very first dragonrider.

The eyes of his massive statue seemed to follow us as we slipped by, skirting around the empty square and making our way to the front of the inn. Most of the fine, stained glass windows on all four floors were still lit, and a pristinely crafted sign hung above the door, depicting a pair of crossed rapiers and the letters K and C in gold paint. This wasn't some grimy pirate tavern. Places like this usually only catered to wealthier guests; merchants, traveling nobility, and the occasional lesser-royal.

An interesting choice of venue for Maldobar's most notorious crime lord to do his illegal business.

A small, thin man peered at us through the large spectacles perched on the end of his long nose as soon as we entered. He scowled disapprovingly as he looked us over, probably figuring out pretty quickly that we weren't here to rent a room. Before he could get a word out, though, Judan stepped over and muttered a few hushed words. The innkeeper's face went pale, eyes wide behind his round lenses as his gaze darted between the prince and the rest of us.

As if on cue, Jaevid brushed back the cowl of his cloak and leveled a somber, forbidding stare upon the man. With his face plastered on tapestries, marble busts, mosaics, and paintings in every city across the kingdom, I doubted he could go anywhere without someone recognizing him.

The innkeeper certainly seemed to. He nodded frantically, tripping all over himself to pull out a ring of polished brass keys from under the long counter where he stood. The keys rattled in his shaking hands as he fumbled through them until he found the one he wanted. He pried it off the ring and handed it quickly to Judan.

Easy enough.

"I'm betting that face of yours guarantees excellent service wherever you go," I muttered quietly.

Jaevid flicked me a look out of the corner of his eye. "I try not to abuse that privilege," he whispered back. "After a while, you get tired of that kind of recognition."

I looked away to hide my smirk. The poor war hero, cursed with fame and adoration.

Judan gave a nod as he led the way toward the grand staircase at the far end of the inn's first floor parlor. Jaevid, Thatcher, Phoebe, and I followed in silence, climbing up to the top floor. Apart from our soft footfalls, not a single sound drifted through the inn's dim halls. Candles flickering in colored glass globes made the shadows seem to dance and waver on the mahogany-paneled walls as we moved quickly. My gaze halted briefly on Phoebe as she walked nearby. She still hadn't said a word to me. Her face looked paler than usual, and her soft blue eyes were wide. Both of her small hands were clenched into shaking fists at her sides.

Hmm.

On pure impulse, I let my arm brush against hers as I slowed my pace and fell to the back of our group where I was supposed to be watching to make sure no one tried to attack us from behind. I still couldn't bring myself to meet her gaze, though. Not when that small, almost insignificant amount of contact made my chest constrict and memories of that night when she'd kissed me race across my brain. I couldn't think about that —not now.

Judan stopped before a lone door at the far end of the fourth-floor hall. As far as I could tell, there were only two rooms on this entire level. Most likely they were the largest, most luxurious suites in the entire inn. Typical.

Jaevid put a hand on the hilt of his scimitar, standing at the ready between the door and the rest of us as Judan slipped the key into the polished brass lock.

I shuddered as a small rush of adrenaline scorched my system, drawing every nerve and muscle tense. I slipped my hands into my pockets to feel my metal spike-studded gloves. If someone rushed us through that door, it'd be close combat. Too close for me to try using my blades with Phoebe and Thatcher there.

It would be ugly.

The lock clicked open, and warm golden light bled through the crack as Judan slowly and quietly pushed the door in. Voices came from inside. Happy, laughing voices. A man's smooth, deep tone and a woman's cheery giggling.

Thatcher and I swapped a puzzled glance.

Judan had barely put a toe over the threshold when the conversation inside grew louder. Footsteps approached. They were coming closer.

"Oh, don't be so modest! If anyone can make sense of these texts, it's you. I have every confidence!" the woman's voice teased.

"I will certainly do my best, Your Grace," the man replied.

"How long will you be in Dayrise? Perhaps we could have dinner?" The air of flirtatious hope in her voice was unmistakable.

And it made me want to gag.

"Only a day more. I've some historical documents to deliver back to Luntharda. Then I must be on my way." The man cleared his throat. "I've much work left to finish before the morning, so I'm afraid I must wish you a good evening, Your Grace."

Judan gave a signal and we all moved at once, ducking to the side to hide in the shadows outside the door. Only Jaevid held his position, hand still resting on the pommel of his scimitar, as the heavy footsteps came closer and closer. They hesitated before the door, and a shadow eclipsed the light that spilled from the room beyond. Someone let out a heavy, almost weary sigh.

Then the door swung open, and a man's tall, lean frame filled the doorway. With the bright light from the room at his back, it was difficult to make out any of the details of his features at first. But his eyes were impossible to miss. They gleamed in the dim light of the hall, glowing like two smoldering coals of golden-orange, as he stared straight ahead at Jaevid.

Gods and Fates—I'd never seen eyes like that.

Without a word, he stepped out into the hall and shut the door behind. More of his features came into view, then. With his wide-shouldered frame clothed in a simple dark red tunic, plain black breeches, and black riding boots—nothing he wore seemed to match the social class of someone staying at a place like this. They weren't peasant's clothes, sure, but they didn't mark him as anyone of nobility. He wasn't even wearing a sword belt.

Not our Kinslayer, then? A scholar, maybe? That would explain why he had two large, leather-bound books cradled carefully under one arm.

His thin, frowning mouth pursed some, almost thoughtfully, as he glanced Jaevid up and down. His long, sharp jawline stiffened, but not with fear or apprehension. His shining, ember-like eyes narrowed and he turned slightly—just enough to flick a look back down at where Thatcher, Phoebe, and I were lurking in the shadows by the door.

"So, you've come. And with so many." His voice was a deep, almost soothing mixture of amusement and precision. "Very well, then. Follow me."

9
CHAPTER NINE

"This isn't him, is it?" Thatcher whispered as we followed the man along the hall and back to the second floor.

I couldn't answer. Even Judan had admitted he didn't know much about Arlan the Kinslayer, and none of his agents had ever gotten close enough to find out much about the man. But this person, whoever he was, didn't carry himself like an accomplished criminal lord—or even like a swordsman. He didn't even have a weapon that I could see, and I couldn't detect any traces of hired guards lurking anywhere in the vicinity when he finally stopped before another door. Here, the rooms were much more modest, smaller, and closer together. The one he unlocked was at the farthest end of the hall, off by itself, and ill-lit for anyone to even attempt keeping watch.

All I could guess was that he worked for Kinslayer as some sort of assistant, bookkeeper, or maybe even a messenger. Maybe a little bit of all three. Regardless, the fact that he'd stopped here, at this door, meant one thing: Kinslayer was waiting for us on the other side of it.

I tensed, slipping my fingers into the spiked gloves in my pockets just in case. Jaevid still hadn't taken his hand off his scimitar, and Judan was watching this guy's every move.

The door swung open, and I held my breath as another swell of adrenaline made my skin prickle. This was it. No turning back now.

As the man moved into the room ahead of us, his boot heels clicking on the wooden floor, Judan and I leaned in to survey our opponent.

Only ... there was no one else in there.

A roaring fire crackling in the hearth against one wall lit the spacious room and revealed a small sitting area with a long velvet sofa and two wingback chairs. The majestic, canopy bed on the other side of the room looked completely untouched. In fact, the only evidence of anyone actually staying in the room was a half-empty wine bottle, crystal glass, and stack of books on a narrow claw-footed desk that sat right beneath the room's only window. The desk itself was covered in an array of paper and parchment, ink bottles, and fine feather quills. The tall man added the two books he carried to a stack of several more leather-bound tomes at one end before he picked up the wine bottle and began to refill his glass.

"If you don't mind, do shut the door. I assume what you've come to say is not something you'd like shared with anyone else listening nearby," he said, sounding almost bored as he sank down into the leather chair behind the desk.

With the light of the fire filling the room, I got a much better look at his face. Pointed ears peeked out from his elbow-length, perfectly straight golden hair, and his long, somewhat pointed features had a predatory look about them as he studied each one of us over the rim of his wine glass.

"A-Are you ... Arlan the—?" Judan stammered in surprise as he lingered at the back of our group just long enough to close the door behind us.

"Just Arlan will do, thank you." The man cast him an irritated glare out of the corner of his bizarre, glowing eye.

My mouth fell open. I frowned. *This* was him? This was the notorious and extremely dangerous man they called Kinslayer? No. It was a trick. A ruse. It had to be.

"And you are Judan, third-born prince of Luntharda," he continued as he slowly panned his eerie gaze around at each of us, one at a time. "Phoebe, formerly of the Tibran Empire. Murdoc, the defected Ulfrangar pup. Thatcher, the farrier's boy from Thornbend. And ... " His gaze halted on Jaevid, who now stood directly in front of his desk. "Jaevid Broadfeather, born in the squalor of a wartime ghetto, raised to might as the champion of the dragonriders, and hand-chosen to speak for the God of Life. Please, do consider me honored. I had rather hoped our paths would cross eventually. And now they say you'll be taking over as the commander of the dragonrider academy? A job like that is a bit beneath a man of your accomplishments, I should think."

"Then we think very differently about the importance of training the future generations that will fight on our behalf," Jaevid countered. "I am honored to hold that station."

The smile that bowed Arlan's thin lips never even came close to reaching his eyes. Those smooth expressions and perfectly chiseled elven features made it difficult to place his age. At a glance, I would've guessed he was somewhere in his mid-twenties. But if he really was an Avoran elf? Fates only knew ...

"Such humility," he mused, seeming almost delighted. Then that smile vanished, and he glanced my way again. "And such ironic company you keep now. My people tell me you pursue the now-fallen Duke Phillip Derrick. If your intent is to solicit my aid in slaying him, I'm afraid you've been misinformed. Arranging murders is not something I care to entertain."

"We don't want to kill him," Judan clarified. "We only want to capture him. It's our hope that whatever magic has been used to turn his mind can be undone. But even tracking him has proven difficult. His movements are nearly impossible to trace, and he's becoming increasingly unpredictable with his attacks. He also seems to be working in alliance with the Ulfrangar."

Arlan's expression creased with a thoughtful frown. "I see. Then you believe he's under the control of a sorcerer of some sort and not acting of his own free will?"

"Not a sorcerer," Thatcher piped up suddenly. "Devana. She's ... not a sorceress. I-I mean, um, not really."

Everyone paused to stare at him, and I got the distinct impression I was the only one who had any idea what he was actually talking about. Judging by the crazed looks of silent rage Judan and Jaevid were giving him, Thatcher still hadn't told the rest of our merry band of misfits about his supposed 'godling' status. Oops.

Arlan's eyebrows rose, as well. And for a few seconds, he sat there staring at Thatcher in complete silence. Then, slowly, that cold smile crept over his face again. "Indeed, she is not."

SOMETHING ABOUT THAT LOOK, like a fox grinning as it considered a mouse, didn't sit right with me. We weren't here to play mind games.

"Look, we need to know about his movements, patterns, or if your network has picked up on any locations where he might be hiding out," I said, half-hoping to divert his attention away from the more vulnerable members of our group. "As I'm sure you already know, we came here with the intent to hunt down and apprehend or kill Devana before this very thing could happen. But now it has, or is beginning to, and this might be our only chance to stop her before she can cause any real damage. Are you willing to help us or not?"

His smile dimmed some, and he glanced me up and down again before looking away almost dismissively. "Yes, I'm aware of the mission Queen Jenna sent you on. However, what you're asking is not so easily accomplished. Especially not when you make a habit of killing my informants in the street like common thugs. That was very sloppy, *pup*."

I tensed, my face twitched as I bit back a snarl. "I don't trust messengers to keep secrets."

"But you should know better than to think I would deliver any sort of aid to the Ulfrangar," he snapped, a hint of anger flashing in his fiery eyes.

"He was wrong to have killed one of your men," Jaevid interjected, as though trying to defuse the pending argument. "It was a misstep on our part, and we apologize for the inconvenience it likely caused you. But the boy is right—we cannot do this without help. We need information and the advantage of knowing where Phillip is hiding, or at the very least, where we might be able to intercept him. Is that something we can negotiate?"

Arlan's wrath seemed to fizzle. His lips pursed thoughtfully as he leaned forward to rest his elbows on his desk. Before him, I recognized the neatly written penmanship on a creased piece of parchment. It was Garnett's letter.

"I'm a businessman, Jaevid Broadfeather. What you ask is within my ability to give, yes. But it will bring substantial risk to my informants," he said at last.

"Name your price." Judan took an earnest step forward, but Arlan's glowing stare seemed to stop him dead in his tracks.

"Be careful saying such things, young prince. You've only glimpsed the cruelty of the world," he warned. "Fortunately, I've no interest in exploiting you—for now. I'll provide what information my men can safely gather to you, and in exchange, I want only a favor."

I balked. "That's it? Just a favor?"

His cryptic expression made my throat go tight as he fixed a meaningful look back upon Thatcher. "Favors can mean many things. For now, I'll bide my time. If this arrangement is satisfactory to you, then go."

No one said anything for a few seconds. Judan stared at him, blinking like he was totally baffled. I had to agree. We were just walking out of here? Without paying him a single coin?

Something about this wasn't right. What favor could we do for him that a man like Arlan couldn't already have done by one of his own people? Hmm.

"Very well," Jaevid agreed with a heavy sigh. "A favor for a favor. It seems fair, right, Judan?"

The prince's mouth scrunched bitterly, as though he was also having a hard time believing it was that easy. "I suppose," he said at last.

"Then the deal is made," Arlan concluded, standing from his desk and stretching a hand out toward Jaevid. "I'll be in touch."

Jaevid grasped his hand and shook it once. "We'll be waiting."

As we all turned to leave, I noticed Thatcher hesitating at the very back of our group. He stopped and turned back, looking at Arlan and chewing at the inside of his cheek as though he were concerned about something.

I stopped, too.

"Uh, Mr. Arlan, sir, there's ... there's something else I wanted to ask, if that's okay." Thatcher faced him, looking downright childish standing before a man who was probably six and a half feet tall.

Gods and Fates, had he absolutely lost his mind? What else could he possibly want to ask this guy?

The elven man's expression softened into something curious and almost amazed. He tilted his head to the side slightly, making some of his long golden hair spill over his shoulders and down his chest. "Yes?"

"You, um, you said you knew Devana wasn't a sorcerer. Or, uh, sorceress, I guess." Thatcher stumbled over his words, occasionally chancing quick, sideways glances in my direction. "Does that mean you know what she really is?"

Arlan's head bowed some, his features seeming to draw into a grim, nearly mournful look. "Yes. As I'm sure you do, as well." He closed his eyes and turned away, beginning to walk toward the window with his hands clasped at his back. "Take courage, young one. The worst is yet to come, I think. There are many enemies in your path, some waiting outside this very building."

My stomach dropped to the soles of my boots. What? There were enemies waiting for us outside? Right now?

"Fight well," Arlan murmured, his shining eyes reflecting in the dark glass of the window like two small flames. "We shall meet again very soon, I think."

CHAPTER TEN

I could already hear the sounds of combat long before we ever reached the first level of the inn. The scrape of metal against metal paired with the occasional sharp cry of pain, and low, concussive *WHOOM* of Isandri wielding her magical staff. Curse it! Was it Phillip? Or the Ulfrangar?

We hit the first-floor parlor at a sprint, darting by the innkeeper who was already cowering behind his counter, and making a break for the front door. Slipping my hands free of my cestus gloves, I whipped my hands back to slide my longswords free of their sheath. Before me, Judan and Jaevid drew their scimitars. Thatcher pulled out his crossbow and set the trigger.

"Stay here," I shouted at Phoebe as Judan flung the door open wide. "Find a place to hide and don't move!"

She blinked up at me, her eyes already brimming with tears. "B-But, Murdoc—!" she began to protest frantically.

There wasn't time.

The scene before us was already mayhem. Isandri's magic filled the night with blooming flashes of white light as she and Reigh squared off with four figures dressed from head to foot in black leather armor. I caught the glimmer off their silver wrist-cuffs. Rage like hellfire roared in my veins, making my vision go red as a coppery flavor hit my tongue.

Ulfrangar.

"Reigh's hit!" Jaevid shouted in warning as he forged forward to join the fray. Almost immediately, another Ulfrangar dropped from the shadows of the rooftop nearby and dashed for him. Their blades locked with a sparking of metal on metal.

Another hidden assassin sprang from the alleyway to our left, making a diving strike at Judan. In one fluid motion, he brought both of his short-bladed scimitars in perfect unison for a cross-parry.

That left me.

I snarled, focusing my wrath upon the two nearest assassins still locked in a duel with Reigh. He and Isandri stood together, cornered at the base of the fountain as the four assassins closed in. I had to give him credit, even with his back bristling with two arrow bolts, the young prince held his guard and deflected their strikes. But his reactions were slow, already desperate. Blood ran from the corner of his mouth, standing out against his ashen skin, as he staggered back and almost lost his footing in the water of the fountain.

No time to second guess it.

"Hold the doorway and cover me!" I shouted to Thatcher as I took off for Reigh at a sprint. Rearing back, I flung one of my swords end-over-end at the back of the nearest Ulfrangar. It howled through the night, spinning and hitting my prey straight through the back. His body immediately stiffened, arms flailing wide with a gurgling cry.

Then his legs buckled. He fell sideways, hitting the ground right as I ran past. I seized the hilt of my blade again on my way by and ripped it free, spinning immediately into a series of strikes against the second assassin Reigh was still struggling to fend off.

TWANG—TWANG—TWANG!

I knew the sound of crossbow fire even over the roar of combat. Arrows pinged off the stone around me, one zipping past my head so close I felt the wind as it ripped past.

"That better not be you, Thatcher!" I roared as I locked in combat with the assassin.

"It's not!" he shouted back angrily. "There's archers on the roof!"

Curse it all to the deepest abyss.

I dipped and feinted, dodging my enemy's brutal wave of assaults as Reigh staggered back, disengaging completely and leaning against the base of the fountain as though he were having to fight for every breath. More arrows zipped by, hitting the stone and water around us.

"I'll handle it," Isandri hissed, landing a successful blow with the tri-dagger end of her staff and ramming it through one of her opponent's torso. She gave the weapon a brutal twist before ripping it free and touching two fingers to the mark on the center of her forehead. The sterling runes glowed brightly against her ebony skin, and sent out a glimmer of silver light that pierced the air around us as she shifted shapes.

Rising up in her feline form, she spread her broad wings to the night and let out a thundering roar before she shot skyward.

The rush of arrows stopped abruptly, following her ascent. But her departure left the one remaining Ulfrangar she'd been fighting to focus back on me. Suddenly it was two against one.

And I liked those odds.

Lights began to flicker to life in the windows of the shops and houses around the square one-by-one as the sounds of combat rang loudly in the air. City folk cracked open their doors to see what was going on. The smart ones quickly shut them again. But others ran out into the night, screaming about Tibrans, and armed with whatever they could get their hands on—rakes, shovels, and hammers. They didn't last long.

These weren't Tibrans we were fighting, after all.

It would be enough to raise the alarm, though. The city guards would come. We just had to hold out until then.

Along the rooftops, Isandri's form shimmered as she streaked from one rooftop to another. With yowls and snarls, she pounced on the Ulfrangar archers posted on the eaves surrounding the central square. Effective—but slow. And as best I could tell by the number of arrows still hitting the stone all around us, they'd brought at least eight archers in all.

It was all we could do to fight while trying to stay out of range, holding our enemies in the shadow of the fountain and under the eaves of the buildings. Blows seemed to rain down against me from every side as I pressed in harder. But in the eye of that storm, caught in the onslaught of spinning blades and slashing strikes, my mind was completely calm. Every thought was controlled. Every movement planned and primed. I'd done this dance a thousand times, and I knew every step.

My blades hummed a deadly melody in the air as I drove the two Ulfrangar assassins before me off the fountain. I forced the fight back out into the open, away from where Reigh still leaned against the statue. If he had any sense at all, he'd use this opportunity to run for cover: the inn where Thatcher still stood in the open doorway. He could make it. But he had to go—*now*.

A hoarse, gasping elvish curse made me turn just in time to see Reigh hit a knee in the shallow water at the base of the fountain. He gripped his chest and wheezed, seeming to fight for every breath. Had one of those bolts sticking out of his back hit a lung? It didn't seem likely. He wore his scout's armor. And while it wasn't made of metal, the layered, hardened hides were enough to keep an arrow from punching too far into the soft flesh of the person wearing it.

That only left one possibility.

As another assassin met the pointed end of one of my swords, I drove it in all the way to the hilt, gave it a final twist, and threw him down on his back. Then I glanced across the chaos for whoever happened to be standing closest. Help—I needed help. If my suspicions were correct, then Reigh had about five minutes before he wouldn't be able to walk on his own.

Judan was closest to where we stood, but he still dueled fiercely, taking on two more Ulfrangar than the last time I'd glimpsed him. They had him on the run. Blood ran from an open gash over one of his thighs, and a blow to the face bled down his brow, over his eye, and drizzled along his cheek. No good.

Jaevid, on the other hand, was just ripping his scimitar free of an assassin's limp body when he whirled around in my direction. His frenzied, wide-eyed stare met mine for an instant.

Before I could get a word out, someone dashed by me—moving fast and low. I gaped as Thatcher ducked around me, his crossbow still gripped in one hand as he scrambled over into the fountain and looped his arm under Reigh's shoulder. Had he seen Reigh go down? Or noticed that he couldn't breathe?

Between the flashing, wild strikes of my own duel with the one remaining assassin before me, I watched as Thatcher hauled him out of the fountain and staggered past me again. He headed straight for the inn's open doorway, Reigh barely able to stand. They were so close. A few yards away. Then only a few feet.

THUNK!

Another arrow caught Reigh in the back of the leg. He went down, and dragged Thatcher with him.

They landed in a heap not ten feet from the doorway. Another cacophony of bow strings strummed in the dark. Another volley of crossbow fire slashed through the night and peppered the stones. And Thatcher had nowhere to hide.

Jaevid cried out, already running for him. He was too far away, though. He'd never get there in time.

Thatcher's gaze caught mine for half a second, terror written in every corner of his face.

No, wait. Not terror.

Gods and Fates, what *was* that look?

His jawline hardened and his eyes narrowed, focusing skyward suddenly as the colored rings of his eyes began to glow. But nothing like Arlan's. No, this was ... a blinding, white-hot light like the glare of the sun. His nose wrinkled and he thrust a hand out, his open palm glowing with that same radiant light.

That one gesture sent out a shockwave that blew Jaevid backward as a rippling current of golden light spread out from Thatcher's open hand. It closed around him and Reigh like a dome of sparking, crackling power—immediately catching every arrow that would've hit them. The arrows hung suspended in the air, trapped in Thatcher's golden shield of light.

It only lasted a second. Maybe two. But for what felt like an eternity, everyone in the city square stared at him in complete awe.

He ... he really was a godling.

And then, with another flash of golden light, it was over. Thatcher's body lurched like a puppet with its strings yanked. His expression went blank. His eyes rolled back. As the protective dome of power around him began to melt away, his body dropped to the ground right next to Reigh's and lay motionless.

Oh ... oh gods. What had happened? Was he dead?!

"*THATCHER!*" Jaevid called out again as he began shambling back to his feet.

At that same instant, a flash of red light followed by the rapid *BOOM—BOOM—BOOM—BOOM* shook the earth under my boots. All four streets went up in flame at once, fire roaring high and closing off all our exits at once. The night filled with the glow of fire, boiling black smoke, and the reek of dragon venom. The Ulfrangar ... they were using death charges. The same foul weapons we'd been instructed to use to herd the panicked crowds of villagers through Thornbend on the night of the final battle for Maldobar.

I screamed in rage as I made a wild, dipping strike at the assassin before me, lunging at him like a maniac. It must've shocked him. We'd been trained to fight without ever losing control of our emotions. Our control is what made us so powerful and efficient.

But I had lost all semblance of it as I sprang through the air, bearing him to the ground with both my swords buried deep in his chest. His eyes went distant as he lay motionless with me still crouched on his chest.

My chest heaved with every manic breath, and I bared my teeth in a feral snarl as I stood and stepped off him, facing the fire-laced square with my blades dripping crimson. Before me, ten more Ulfrangar emerged from the shops and houses all around us. Their hands clenched swords and daggers, or held more crossbows at the ready. And in that moment, I knew.

This was the end.

They would kill me tonight.

But by all the gods, I would take as many of them down with me as I could. They would pay for every drop of blood they'd ever spilt hunting me. Tonight, my name would be carved into the Ulfrangar's memory for all eternity.

I walked out to meet them in the shadow of the fountain, my arms held wide with a longsword in each hand. Before me, ten Ulfrangar formed a semi-circle as they closed in for the final strike. There was no running. No former-handlers to tip the odds in my favor. Not this time.

I was alone with my destiny.

All I had to do now was wait for the axe to drop.

With any luck, I could hold them off long enough to buy the others the time to find some way to escape. But they'd have to hurry. I didn't have any godsgrave coursing through my body, numbing the pain of any injuries and allowing me to fight on. I wouldn't last more than four minutes at the most.

Or ... so I thought.

I stumbled backward, almost falling as a monstrous shape dropped from the sky and hit the earth before me with a bellowing roar. Black and red scales sparkled in the glow of the flames as the young dragon stood between the Ulfrangar and me, unfurling his black leathery wings and bristling all the jagged spines down his back. He curled his long tail around me protectively.

And for a moment, no one moved.

Then one of the Ulfrangar took a calculated step back.

The black dragon's lips curled back in a vicious snarl, revealing rows of fangs that dripped with burning venom that puddled on the ground, crackling and smoldering in the night.

I moved forward, taking up a defensive stance right next to the dragon's head with my blades still drawn.

He glanced sideways at me, bright blue eyes meeting mine in the glow of the flames.

My heart thudded hard, seeming to twist deep in my chest. This creature, however stubborn and ridiculous it was, had found me again. And just like before, he was ready to fight at my side to the bitter end. I'd never accepted him, but he still wanted to help me. He still wanted to save me.

He still ... wanted me to be his rider.

I swallowed hard. Looking forward again, back toward the line of enemies with their weapons still trained upon us, I tightened my grip on my swords.

"I'll make you a deal, dragon," I panted. "If we manage to get out of this alive somehow, I'll ... I'll *consider* letting you stay around. Do we have a deal?"

He gave a deep, snorting growl in reply.

I took that as a yes.

Sheathing one of my weapons, I stepped over and grabbed onto one of the thick black spines that grew down the length of his back all the way to his tail. I swung a leg over and sat, positioned at the base of his neck right in front of his wing arms. He was a lot smaller than Fornax, Vexi, and Mavrik. And as he stood, I could feel that he had to work much harder to bear my weight. But he could do it.

He rose up, tossing his head and giving another booming battle cry.

"All right, just take it easy. You know I'm new at this," I muttered under my breath as I set my glare back down at the line of Ulfrangar assembled before us.

A few more of them took wary steps back. One on the end of the group bolted and ran for cover.

I smirked and gave the dragon's thick, scaly neck a pat. "They like to burn things. So, let's show them what we can do with a little dragon fire, eh?"

PART TWO
THATCHER

11
CHAPTER ELEVEN

Everything hurt. My whole head seemed to vibrate with sharp throbs that made even my teeth ache. Wave after wave of a strange, sharp tingling coursed through every inch of me. But I couldn't move. I couldn't even open my eyes. Or were they already open? I-I couldn't tell. All I could see was empty darkness, and all I could hear was a high-pitched ringing in my ears.

It'd all happened so fast—like a blurry nightmare that replayed over and over. I'd been running, dragging Reigh toward the open door of the inn. He'd been badly hurt already. He needed help. If we could just get there, just get to the safety of the inn, maybe someone could help him before it was too late.

Then they'd shot him again.

Reigh had fallen. And so had I. We were trapped there, sprawled in the open. I couldn't get Reigh to move or get back up. He was fading—dying right in front of me.

So I ... I had done something.

I-I wasn't sure what. It'd come out of nowhere. A presence in my mind like a rush of hot summer wind, filling my lungs and setting my soul on fire. In an instant, relief like a warm, radiant light rose up from somewhere deep inside me—like a breath I'd been holding all my life and could finally release.

Then came power—a force I didn't understand. It'd taken over so suddenly, and all my thoughts went blank.

And I couldn't remember anything else. There was nothing except darkness. Gods, what was happening? Where was everyone? Was Reigh okay?

Was I?

What about Murdoc? And the others?

I-I couldn't stay like this. I couldn't die yet. Not until I knew the others had made it. Up—I had to wake up! Move, stupid! Now!

My eyes flew open and I sucked in a gasping breath. My hand jolted to the pendant and whistle hanging around my neck, gripping them in a shaking fist. My whole body trembled as I sat up and tried to blink the blurriness from my eyes. Everything seemed to be sloshing and swirling, like I was trying to stay upright on a boat in a stormy sea.

"Easy, easy. I'll hold him steady. You've got to try to break them as close to his back as you can." Phoebe's voice came from somewhere nearby, talking quickly.

Still weaving where I sat in the middle of the inn's parlor, I squinted around at all the fine furnishings in a daze. Had someone brought me back inside? That must be it. But who? I looked over to where Phoebe and Jaevid were crouched over something on the floor nearby. No, not some*thing*. Some*one*.

Reigh.

While Phoebe held him on his side, gripping him hard, Jaevid worked. His hands were smeared with crimson as he focused, brow furrowed and pale eyes sharp on Reigh's back.

CRACK!

He held up one blood-soaked end of a crossbow bolt, now snapped in half. The feathered end dripped as he tossed it aside and went back to work.

CRACK!
CRACK!
CRACK!

With every arrow broken, Reigh's eyes went wide as he lay on his side, staring straight at me with Phoebe still pinning him in place. But he didn't scream. He didn't make a sound. His face was completely ashen. Blood seeped from the corners of his slightly blue lips.

Jaevid moved quickly, snapping off the arrows that were stuck into his body and throwing them away.

Gods and Fates. I-I had to help. Reigh was ... he wasn't going to make it. Not at this rate.

My head lolled and my vision swerved as I crawled toward them. If I could just get to him, then maybe I could do something or use that power again somehow.

I set my jaw, fighting for control as I crawled faster. Every movement got easier. My head began to clear. The ringing in my ears faded completely and I could hear the sounds of distant combat still raging outside. The booming of a dragon's mighty roar. The clash and clatter of swords.

Was Murdoc somewhere out there?

No—I couldn't think about that right now. I had to help Reigh, first.

"Take your knife and cut the side lacing of his breastplate. We need to get it off, but don't jar the bolts any more than necessary," Phoebe instructed as she quickly and carefully rolled Reigh over so that she cradled his head in her hands and his chest was draped over her lap. Then her gaze snapped to me, mouth falling open in shock. "Thatcher!"

"I-I'm fine," I slurred through my teeth, reaching the corner of a low coffee table and using it to stagger to my feet. "What can I do?"

Phoebe's look of surprise vanished, turning instantly to firm concentration again.

"Find the innkeeper. Ask him if he has any thistlebriar herbs or lockberry tea. Bring that, clean rags, and as much warm water as you can!"

"Right. Okay. I'm on it." I wheezed as I began to stagger away, leaning heavily on every piece of furniture I could as I rushed to the front foyer of the inn.

IT DIDN'T TAKE me long to find him. There, still cowering and hyperventilating behind his desk, the innkeeper sat cowering in a heap. He slapped at me as I came close, screaming and holding up what was probably the only weapon he had in the entire place: a cheese knife.

"Get up! I need your help!" I barked. "I need all the thistlebriar and lockberry you have! Clean rags and water, too!"

He slapped the air in my direction again. "N-N-No! I'm not moving! Are you insane?! Get away from me! Y-You brought this here! Y-You and that lot of *criminals*!" he wailed.

Argh! We didn't have time for this!

Ripping my new xiphos sword from the sheath, I leveled it right at the man's throat. "*SHUT UP AND GIVE ME WHAT I NEED! NOW!*"

He went stiff with the point of my sword pressed right against his Adam's apple, eyes wide and mortified behind his round spectacles. He scrambled away like a scared rat, tripping all over himself as he ran to a nearby supply closet. He came back lugging an armful of materials—including a tea-kettle still half full of hot water.

Grabbing the supplies, I ran back into the parlor as fast as my wobbly, somewhat numb legs would carry me.

Phoebe didn't waste any time. As soon as I returned and put everything down beside her, she began talking us through what to do as she cradled Reigh's head, her fingers on his neck as though keeping a constant track on his pulse. His expression had gone distant, and his chest spasmed in fast, shallow breaths. Not good.

"Pour out all but about half an inch of the water, then I want you to pour all the tea leaves and herbs in and stir until you make a chunky paste. We have to make a poultice to try and slow the poison," Phoebe said, snapping her gaze up to Jaevid suddenly. "This will buy him some time, but we have to get him to a healer as quickly as possible."

Jaevid nodded and snapped to his feet. "Get him ready to be moved. I'll try to call Mavrik in."

We kept working as he ran from the room—me squashing tea leaves and water into a sticky, gooey paste and following Phoebe's instructions to cram as much of it down into the wounds around the arrow shafts as I could. Fortunately, Jaevid had already cut away Reigh's leather breastplate and clothing, so I had a good view of where the three arrows were still lodged in his back.

He tensed every time I stuck my fingers into one of those wounds, groaning some as the arrow's tip wiggled inside him. Sometimes I could feel it, less than two inches into his body, but Phoebe warned me not to try pulling any of them out.

"Ulfrangar like to use barbed tips. If you pull them out, it'll rip his back apart and spread the poison faster," she murmured.

"What kind of poison is it?" I asked as I used the last of the paste to fill the wound on his leg.

"Bellanarix," she answered quietly. "It comes from Rienka, a kingdom south of here. The Ulfrangar use it a lot when they want to disable their enemies but not kill them right away because it paralyzes first before doing more serious damage. It stops you from breathing. You suffocate unless someone forces air into your lungs. Eventually, though, it stops your heart."

I didn't have to ask how she knew all this. She'd probably been forced to experiment with all kinds of poisons while she worked for the Tibrans. There was no telling what they'd made her do, and I wasn't about to start interrogating her about all that. Right now, I only cared about one thing.

"Is ... is he going to make it? Is any of this going to help him?"

Phoebe's expression was a skewed, anxious mixture of uncertainty and sadness. "I-I don't know," she confessed in a broken whisper. Tears pooled in her eyes as she ran one of her hands through his messy, dark red hair. "I know these herbs can help to neutralize the toxins and even absorb some of them, but I'm not a healer. And there's so much of it. His wounds are so bad already. I-I—"

She gasped, her eyes shutting tightly as she bowed her head. Tears ran down her face, dripping onto his hair. "H-He can't die. Not now. Not like this. Gods, please ... please spare him."

A strange warmth thrummed in my chest again, making my heartbeat skip. I couldn't fight the urge to reach out and put a hand over hers. "Reigh is strong," I reminded her. "He's not going down without a fight. So tell me what to do next; Jaevid will probably be back any second."

Phoebe blinked up at me, her chin still trembling as she nodded slightly. "Okay," she whispered. "Thank you, Thatcher."

After using all of the herbal paste to cake in and around the wounds, I tied the clean washcloths around each of the arrow shafts and fitted Reigh's leather breastplate back around him carefully, using that like a makeshift bandage to hold the arrows still and keep the herbs pressed into place. Since Jaevid had cut the lacing on the sides, I had to rip some of the lacing out of one of his boots to tie it back on. Luckily, since he'd been shot through the calf, too, he had some lacing to spare since we couldn't risk putting his boot back on without jarring that arrow.

I'd barely finished tying his breastplate on before Jaevid and Judan burst in, out of breath and spattered in blood and ash. Granted, Judan was obviously a lot worse off. He limped on his left leg, occasionally stopping to grip at the place where a deep slash cut across the top of his thigh right above his knee. But after catching a quick glimpse of the feral bloodlust still blazing in his eyes, I didn't dare offer to help him. He might lash out and decide to rip my arms off or something.

"Hurry!" Jaevid commanded sharply, waving us to the stairs. "Mavrik is too big to land out there, but Isandri is holding the rooftop. Go!"

I hesitated. Wait a second. We couldn't leave yet. Skidding to a halt at the base of the stairs, I looked up at Jaevid. "Where is Murdoc?!"

"Doing far better than we are, at the moment, I can assure you," Jaevid growled impatiently. "Come on, Thatcher, we don't have time to—"

I didn't stick around to hear the rest. I wasn't leaving Murdoc behind. No freaking way. If he was still out there fighting in the square, then that's where I needed to be, too.

Jaevid yelled my name, but he didn't try to chase me down and stop me as I bolted for the front of the inn. As I crossed through the doorway, I reached beneath my tunic's collar and drew out my whistle. Putting it to my lips, I blew a series of sharp blasts—repeating the pattern over and over. The high-pitched note pierced the night, so high you could barely hear it.

Then I reached around to the back of my belt, unclipping the new goggles Phoebe had made for me and pulling them down over my eyes. I stared at the fountain ahead of me for a few seconds—long enough that Fornax would get a good look at where I was—before I pulled them down around my neck.

Then I ran out into the night like a complete madman.

CHAPTER TWELVE

Dead Ulfrangar lay everywhere. Gods, there must have been dozens of them scattered across the city square. Several had fallen in the fountain, making the water run red with their blood. Some were on fire, their bodies crackling and smoking like cinders left behind on the ground.

Bathed in the glow of red flame coming from all four of the roads that led into the square, I turned in a circle, looking everywhere for anyone who might still be standing.

Murdoc—where was Murdoc?!

There was no one. No Ulfrangar still fighting. No hidden assassins lurking in the dark. No sign of my best friend anywhere.

But Jaevid had just told me he was alive. He had to be here somewhere. Or had he left already when the others did? Met them on the roof, maybe? Gods and Fates, how could I be so stupid!

I whirled back toward the inn. But I didn't make it a single step.

A dark figure loomed before me, silhouetted against the light that gleamed from the open doorway. My stomach gave a painful twist of panic. I knew who he was even before he raised his head to sneer at me with his silver eyes catching in the ambient red glow of the flames.

Phillip.

"Look at the mess you've made, little godling," he chuckled darkly.

I set my jaw, doing my very best to glare back at him as I reached for my xiphos. I pulled it from the sheath at my hip again and stepped back into one of the fighting stances Murdoc had shown me.

His smirk widened, revealing his long, pointed incisors. "What's this? You want to play?" He drew his hands up, knuckles cracking as he flexed each one of his claw-tipped fingers. "I'd expected you to surrender in some idiotic attempt to spare your friends. But I agree; this way is much more *fun*."

"Oh, we'll play, all right," I spat back. I couldn't tell if it was courage, adrenaline, or just full-on insanity that kept my voice steady. But right then, I didn't care. "You may not remember whose side you're really on right now, but that doesn't mean I won't enjoy taking you down. Not after everything you've done. The only way you're taking me to Devana is cold and dead!"

His deep, rumbling laugh echoed across the open square as he took a prowling step forward. "Oh, you little fool, you have *no* idea!"

A thundering roar made us both look up just in time to see a familiar, enormous blue king drake go zooming low over the city square and disappear into the dark. From where I stood, I couldn't tell who might be riding him. Had Jaevid gotten the others out? What about Isandri? And where the heck was Murdoc?!

"Poor little wretch," Phillip purred with delight as he turned his focus back to me. "Looks like all your little friends have left you here to fight all alone."

I swallowed hard and tightened my grip on my sword. "I'm a dragonrider," I whispered under my breath. "I'm never alone."

I heard it only half a second before it happened—the howl of wind over something enormous. Something coming from the sky, hurtling through the dark like a boulder flung from a catapult.

BOOM!

Fornax hit the ground behind me, cracking the stone under his weight and toppling the massive statue as he landed.

I dropped to a knee, using my free hand to pull my goggles back on and focusing right on Phillip. Then I put the whistle to my lips and blew another command.

Dragon fire exploded in the night, blasting right over my head and engulfing the ground where Phillip stood.

I couldn't afford to stand around and wait for the flames and smoke to clear. Whether Fornax's blast had hit him or not, there wasn't time to be sure. I ran for my dragon, ramming my sword back into its sheath and hauling myself up into the saddle.

Grabbing hold of the saddle handles, I wheeled him around, quickly giving him the command to take off. He snapped his jaws and spread his massive wings. His strong hind legs coiled, preparing to spring skyward. Only then, an instant before he launched upward, did I dare to look back.

Through the licking flames and boiling plumes of black smoke, I could barely make out the front door of the inn. But Phillip wasn't anywhere in sight. I couldn't see his body on the ground—or anywhere at all.

Oh gods. How had he managed to dodge the blast? Where was he now?

I whipped around, straining to see as Fornax took to the air like a mighty, scaly eagle. Through the chaos, I almost missed it.

There was someone standing in the inn's doorway.

But it wasn't Phillip. It couldn't have been. The figure was too short, too petite, and almost childlike. Was that ... a little girl?

Standing with her hands on her hips, her entire form seemed to be made of varying shades of eerie bluish light, making her look nearly translucent as she stared straight back at me. Her bobbed-off blue hair blew around her face, almost veiling her wide, delighted grin. She threw her head back, her chest shaking as though she were laughing hysterically.

What the ... ?

I blinked hard. Maybe I was seeing things. I had to be.

But when I looked back down at the doorway, she was gone.

MY MIND TANGLED on every thought, caught in that moment and the sight of that girl standing amidst the flames. Something about her, about that smile and the way she laughed, sent pangs of cold terror through every part of me. Had I just seen Devana? How? Wasn't she supposed to be at Northwatch?

I had no idea. And the more I thought about it as I hugged my body down against Fornax's strong neck, the more I wondered if I'd only imagined it. Maybe it was just a trick of the light, a glare off my goggle lenses, or something my twisted, terrified brain had dreamt up.

I let out what was probably the most undignified scream of my entire life as another dragon suddenly zoomed in beside us out of nowhere. Thank the gods Jaevid wasn't anywhere in sight to have witnessed that. So much for acting brave in front of Phillip.

I recognized the younger, much smaller, red and black drake that had been harassing Murdoc pretty much nonstop as he dipped into formation off our right wingtip. He gave a trumpeting call, seeming to work extra hard for each of his wing beats, almost like ...

Gods and Fates, he had someone on his back!

I squinted through the dark, barely able to make out the shape of a rider clinging to the spines on his neck.

Wait—wait a second. Was that *Murdoc*?!

It was!

My jaw dropped. There was no mistaking it. Murdoc sat on the young dragon's back, holding on tight with one arm and waving at me frantically with the other. It could've been the way he was flinging his arm around while also shouting at me—which I could barely hear thanks to the wind—but I could have sworn he was trying to tell me something.

Also seeing him through the goggles I wore, Fornax gave a low grumbling sound as he slowly stretched his wings out to slow our speed, soaring carefully closer to the drake. As soon as he saw us moving in, Murdoc pushed himself up from the young dragon's neck and gathered his feet under him. Too late, I realized what Murdoc was about to do.

Oh no.

Murdoc sprang through the air, landing with a thud on Fornax's back right behind me. His hand hit the saddle seat attached to the back of mine and he let out a sharp cry, fingers sliding dangerously over the slick, oiled leather.

I whipped around, seizing his forearm. He gripped mine in return, and together, we hauled him up the rest of the way into the saddle. After he quickly buckled himself in, he gave my shoulder a pat to get my attention and pointed off to the left.

In the distance, the dark bluish shape of a monstrous dragon soared about two miles ahead of us. Mavrik.

I gave Fornax a signal, maneuvering the saddle handles and toe-pressure pedals to steer him that way. He immediately gave a few furious beats of his wings and surged into pursuit. Beside us, the smaller black drake could keep up much better now that he didn't have a rider on his back. He darted around us, looking like a streak of red lightning thanks to the scarlet blaze of color that ran from his nose, down his back, all the way to the tip of his tail.

We chased after Mavrik all the way past the city's outer limits. Behind us, the glow of the fires still burning in the city square stood out on the horizon. It put an ache in my chest. How many people had gotten hurt or killed because of us this time? There were dozens of dead Ulfrangar, of course. But what about civilians?

My mouth scrunched bitterly as I turned my gaze forward again. We couldn't go on like this—leaving a path of cinders and destruction everywhere we went. We had to put a stop to this.

As we soared lower, dropping down to only a few hundred feet off the ground, Mavrik led us out across rolling farmland flecked with little spots of light here and there dotting the dark landscape. Farmhouses, probably.

Mavrik gave a few booming roars of warning as we circled wide around one of those spots. Down below, an answering dragon's cry echoed back. I couldn't see where it came from, though. Was that Reigh's dragon?

The big stone house was isolated, standing off by itself probably five or six miles from the nearest neighbor, with a large barn beside it and a paddock likely for small cattle like goats or sheep. Smoke rose from the chimney and lights burned in a few of the first-floor windows. Someone was home and still awake.

But who?

As our dragons flared their wings and made a final approach, more lights lit in the second and third floor of the house. The front door opened, and several figures seemed to crowd into it. One broke out across the front drive, running to meet us as Mavrik and Fornax landed side-by-side. The smaller drake touched down right behind us, blinking and chirping worriedly as our dragons lowered themselves onto the ground so we could dismount easily.

I didn't recognize the much older Gray elven man who sprinted to Mavrik's side, but it was obvious that Jaevid did. They spoke to one another in fast, hushed voices, and I could have sworn I saw the elven man's expression skew with grief and horror at the sight of Reigh's motionless body held firmly against Jaevid's chest.

A sudden, shrieking cry made Fornax tense beneath me. His hide shuddered and shivered, face turning away as the high-pitched, nearly screaming sound repeated, and Vexi scrambled from the cover of the barn nearby. She floundered forward, screeching in alarm as her big blue eyes searched us wildly.

Reigh—she was looking for her rider.

As Jaevid and the Gray elven man worked together to lower him down, moving carefully until the elven man had his full weight balanced over his shoulders, Vexi went on screaming in panic. Her cries echoed through the chilled night like a mother wailing for her lost child. That sound ripped through me like the bite of a cold knife. Beneath me, Fornax's body still shivered and his milky jade eyes shut tightly.

Had he called for his lost rider that way? The one before me, who had died in the battle for Halfax?

When the elven man started back for the door, carrying Reigh as quickly as possible, Vexi followed right up until they disappeared inside. Then she sat back on her haunches and whined, curling her slender tail around her body and tucking her wings in close.

Judan immediately scrambled down to chase after the elven man, and Murdoc and I began unbuckling, too. I pulled my goggles back down around my neck and fumbled with my saddle straps, cursing under my breath as my hands shook with adrenaline.

But Jaevid didn't move. He stared after Reigh, expression torn with worry and regret. Then, he looked right at me. His gaze seemed to turn steely—focused and determined. He gave Mavrik's neck a firm smack, and with a blast of wind off mighty wings, the king drake broke skyward again. He soared back toward the city, the steady, booming rhythm of their flight fading into the distance.

He was going back? But why?

"Thatcher! Murdoc!" Phoebe's voice nearly startled me out of my boots as I hit the ground right next to Fornax.

I turned around just in time to see Isandri landing in her sleek, powerful winged feline form with Phoebe clinging to her back. Isa's dark fur sparkled and shone in the moonlight, striped with silvery markings like those on a tiger as she prowled closer. Swishing her long tail, her ears perked toward the farmhouse before she panned her gaze back in the direction Jaevid had gone.

"Are you okay? Where's Reigh? Why did Jaevid leave?" Phoebe gasped frantically between panting breaths as she scrambled down from Isandri's back. "Whose house is this?"

I only had answers to about half of those questions. But I didn't have any time to reply. Someone called out to us from the doorway of the farmhouse, waving us in.

Murdoc and I exchanged a look. More friends of Jaevid's? At the rate things were going for us, I could not fathom why, by all the gods, he'd want us staying with any more of his friends or family. We were essentially a moving tornado of death and destruction at this point, right?

Then again, this place was pretty remote. And even from a distance, I could tell that the barn next to the farmhouse looked like it hadn't been used in years. The closer we got to the front of the place, the more of that evidence I saw. The front gardens were overgrown with weeds, and the front porch had basically been taken over by a climbing vine dotted in little yellow flowers. Some of the stonework along the steps was cracked and crumbled, and the thatching on the roof looked like it probably needed major repairs. The windows were fogged by a layer of dust, making it impossible to see inside as we made our way up the steps to the front door.

There, standing with her long black hair blowing around her waist while she wrung her hands in her apron, Ms. Lin stared at us with her face pale and eyes wide.

"Merciful Fates," she gasped as she got a good look at Murdoc who—out of all of us —was probably the most horrifying sight.

He was spattered and dripping with blood from head to foot. None of it looked like it might be his own. Or, rather, if it was, I couldn't tell. But he had crimson sprayed over his face and neck, caked onto his hands, and smeared over every inch of clothing he wore.

Yikes.

"Get inside, all of you, and hurry," she urged, her tone quivering with anxiety as she grabbed the front of my tunic and basically dragged me inside.

"Where is Jaevid going?" Murdoc demanded, stopping in the entryway as though he might suddenly change his mind and go charging back out after him.

Ms. Lin's expression was utterly haunted as she looked between all of us as though, for a moment, she was frozen in dumbfounded shock.

"I-I don't know," she whispered at last. "But gods help whoever tries to stop him."

CHAPTER THIRTEEN

Tension like a toxic fog hung thick in the atmosphere as Judan, Isandri, Murdoc, and I took turns in the farmhouse's small washroom on the first floor. Ms. Lin had apparently been in the process of moving her family into this larger, but definitely older home. Some rooms were already spotless and filled with new furnishings. But others were still empty, covered in a thick layer of dust.

Thankfully, the washroom was one of the clean ones. The copper tub also looked new, and had been set up next to a water pump so it could be refilled easily. The small furnace underneath heated the water, and made for instant relief when it was finally my turn to sink beneath the water and wash the blood, grit, and grime off me.

Sitting alone, watching the steam rise off the water's surface, my mind blurred over everything that had just happened ... and everything that still was happening right this second. Phoebe had rushed upstairs to help the elven man—a healer from Luntharda—try and save Reigh's life. Ms. Lin wouldn't say much except that we all needed to ask the gods for their mercy.

Somehow, hearing her say that, made me want to vomit. The mercy of the gods? Was she talking about me? Was I supposed to pray to myself? Or should I go in there and try to work divine magic on him? Could I even do that? Isandri had said that Ishaleon was a god of mercy, but what did that actually mean?

I buried my face in my hands and bit down hard against the urge to scream. What was I supposed to do? What was my role in all this?

I had to re-dress in my sweaty, somewhat bloody clothes when I got out of the bath. Back in the kitchen, I found Judan, Murdoc, Ms. Lin, and Jondar all sitting around the kitchen table staring vacantly at untouched teacups before them. It still seemed like no one had said much of anything, and the creaking of the chair under my weight as I sat down made everyone look at me at once.

I decided to use that opportunity to ask, "Where's Isandri?"

Murdoc was running his fingers through his still-wet hair. "She went to sit outside the door."

He didn't have to explain which one. I'd known that Isandri and Reigh had a little history. They'd met during the Tibran War and seemed friendly enough with one another. She'd been fighting with him in that square when he got shot so many times.

I wondered if she was blaming herself for that.

After a few more minutes of sitting in the kitchen in complete silence, I couldn't take it anymore. This was like slow torture. And ... well, I had to tell them. They needed to know what happened.

"I saw Phillip in the city square," I announced, keeping my tone quiet. "He was there with the Ulfrangar again."

Murdoc's gaze snapped up to me. "What? When?"

"Right before Fornax came." I rubbed the back of my neck, trying to fight the chill that prickled at my skin just thinking about it. "If he hadn't shown up right at that moment, Phillip probably would've killed me. Or abducted me. I don't really know what his motives are anymore."

"Did he say anything?" Judan pressed, his voice tight and hitched with pain. Sitting next to Ms. Lin, his expression twitched and cringed occasionally while she held a cloth over the deep gash on his leg.

"Not anything we haven't heard before. But it was strange, right before I escaped, I saw ... " My voice died in my throat as that memory resurfaced again.

"You saw what?" Murdoc pressed.

"I saw a girl standing in the flames." Gods, it sounded unbelievable, even to me. "She was looking right at me and laughing. And—I mean, I know this sounds insane—but I could have sworn she was made of blue light."

Seconds ticked by. No one said a word.

Great. Now they all thought I was out of my mind.

I shrank down in my chair, wishing I could hide underneath it. "I-I don't know, um, maybe it was just my imagination, or a trick of the light, or—"

"Or Devana," Judan interrupted suddenly.

I gaped at him. Of course, that's sort of what I had been thinking, too. But hearing him say it out loud put a fresh pang of terror in my gut. Could that really be true? Had that been Devana standing in the flames?

"What has Isandri told you about her?" Judan sat up straighter, his breath catching and face skewing with pain at the movement. He put a shaking, clenched fist on the table where everyone could see it. "We've been very patient and let you take your time getting information from her. I understand better than anyone else here that sometimes that can take time. But we are officially out of time, Thatcher. You need to tell us what you know—what Isandri has told you about Devana and why she is hunting you—*right now*."

O-Oh no.

I stole a look over at Murdoc, but he was glaring at me now, too. Crap. Well, so much for having some backup.

Sucking in a steadying breath, I tried to match the intensity in their gazes as I looked between both of them. "It's not my intention to keep anything from you. I told Murdoc some of it already. And I'll tell everyone the entirety of it—but only when Isandri is here, too. This doesn't just concern me. It's her life caught up in it, too. She has a right to speak her truth herself instead of me trying to do it for her."

Out of the corner of my eye, I could've sworn I saw Ms. Lin's mouth tug into a small, almost proud smile. It made my face flush a little.

"I don't think we should discuss any of it until Jaevid gets back and we know if Reigh is all right," I added quickly.

Judan gave a low, growling sigh as his hand relaxed on the table. He shook his head a little, then winced and touched the hugely swollen knot on his forehead. "Fine. We wait until Jaevid comes back."

"And if he doesn't?" Murdoc had gone back to staring grimly at the still-full cup of tea in front of him.

Judan never answered.

Tensions were still high, even after the sun began to rise and almost everyone had drifted off to find a quiet corner to think, sleep, or pray in. I found a spot on the floor in the house's front sitting room, leaning against an old trunk next to the hearth. There wasn't much furniture in this part of the house, yet. Just a sofa, a rocking chair, and an old tea cart. But the floor was clean, and I couldn't stop my head from dropping to my chest, my chin hitting the heavy goggles that still hung around my neck, as I basked in the radiant warmth from the fire.

Ms. Lin managed to urge Prince Judan into stretching out on the long sofa, his injured leg elevated, and a cold rag pressed to the knot on his head. He had a few other cuts and slices, but none of them looked as serious. After a while, he drifted off to sleep.

Murdoc leaned against the wall by the broad front window, staring out through the old, wavered glass. His brow was locked into a deep furrow, his thin mouth frowning so hard it looked almost painful. With his arms crossed over his chest, his hazel eyes caught in the firelight as he watched the horizon—probably looking for some sign of Jaevid.

Jondar still needed a little help managing the stairs with his injured leg, although he seemed to be getting around a lot better on it now. Ms. Lin helped him hobble back upstairs to his room, and after a while, the house grew silent and hauntingly still. Only the crackle and pop of the fire filled the room.

Occasionally, I caught the faintest murmur of voices from upstairs. It was impossible to tell if it was Ms. Lin and one of her kids, or the Gray elven man and Phoebe still trying to help Reigh, though. That sense of not knowing was almost worse than the silence.

At last, my head hit my chest and sleep overtook me. Maybe it was still my body coming off the rush of adrenaline, but every part of me felt heavy and weak. So I didn't resist.

I must've dozed for a few hours because by the time the sound of footsteps and hushed whispers made my eyelids flutter and my body twitch awake, bright sunlight was pouring through the sitting room window, shining right into my face. I squinted, stirring, but immediately went still again as the voices grew closer.

"It's chaos, Lin. Absolute chaos. Felix is coming to personally help deal with the crisis. Mavrik and I must have carried a thousand buckets of water to help stop the blaze from spreading, but that doesn't help much against dragon venom so the damage is still severe." I recognized Jaevid's weary voice murmuring somewhere nearby.

I held perfectly still—doing the very best sleeping act I could.

"You did the best you could, Jae," Ms. Lin consoled softly. "You've been working so hard during all of this. Even finding this house for us. I still intend to find some way to pay you back for it."

He sighed, and I could hear the dissatisfied frown in his voice without ever seeing his face. "Please, Lin, don't. It's the least I can do after what happened, and I promise to see after having everything properly repaired. I wish I could do more right now, but circumstances being what they are—"

"Hush with that now, brother of mine," she scolded him gently. "You ought to get a bath and rest. I can make you some breakfast. You must be starving."

"No, no. I can't. Not yet," he protested, but it was only half-hearted. "Has Kiran said anything about Reigh's condition?"

"Only that he's still in a delicate state. He came down for a bit; just long enough to get clean water and more bandaging," she said. "They managed to extract the arrows, but the poor boy is still as pale as a ghost. They've been taking turns sleeping while the other watches to make sure he keeps breathing. I offered to take a turn, as well. But of course, that stubborn man wouldn't hear of it."

Jaevid chuckled weakly and his footsteps began to move, retreating from the room. "Kiran's always been the 'I'll-do-it-myself' sort. You get used to it."

"I suppose. And I have tried not to nag after him too much. He's done wonders for Jondar's leg, and wouldn't even let me pay him for it. Although, I did manage to force him to eat something and have a few cups of tea. No point in going on like this if he doesn't at least have some energy." Ms. Lin's much lighter footsteps seemed to follow after him. "Come now, Jae. You really should at least sit down and catch your breath. Have something to eat. You look exhausted. Reigh made it through the night, which I would dare to take as a good sign—at least enough to warrant a proper rest for everyone. Perhaps we'll see some improvement today."

Jaevid went on resisting all her attempts to get him to sit down and eat or drink something for a few minutes. But each time, his refusals got less and less convincing. Finally, he agreed to some toast and cheese.

Then they both paused, and I could tell there was something else they wanted to say. Or rather, something Jaevid wanted to say.

"How has Thatcher seemed since he got here?" he whispered, every word careful and hushed.

"Quiet, for the most part. Although the others were trying to bully him into spilling anything he might know about, well, I assume about the ones who've been hunting you. He wouldn't budge on it, though. Not until you'd returned."

Jaevid didn't speak for a few long, horribly tense minutes, and I could have sworn I could feel his stare on me like the glare of a desert sun. "He's brave, I'll grant him that. But what I saw him do ... I have no explanation for it. I expected magic from Isandri. Her people have strong ancestral ties to it. But Thatcher is human. He's a farrier's boy from Thornbend."

"Sometimes destiny chooses the most unlikely of us." Ms. Lin's tone was gentle and strangely cryptic. "Whatever he is, Jae, he trusts you. They all do."

"I know," Jaevid whispered. "I think that's what worries me most of all."

Their voices faded from the room, leaving me again in silence. I waited until I was sure they were gone before I dared to crack an eye open. Judan wasn't on the sofa anymore. Murdoc was gone, too, and the fire in the hearth had burned down to a few smoldering cinders resting in a deep bed of soot. Great. Was I the only one who'd slept in?

I stood up and stretched, trying to rub the stiffness out of my neck from sleeping all night sitting up against that trunk. I could've gone into the kitchen. That's probably where everyone else was—sitting around the table again, staring at cups of tea, and waiting for the world to come to an end. But I wasn't ready for that yet. I needed to think. Moreover, I needed to put some distance between myself and everyone else while I did. I wanted to be somewhere calm. Somewhere private and safe.

So, I went looking for Fornax.

14
CHAPTER FOURTEEN

Moving quietly, I slipped down the hall and out the front door of the farmhouse. The morning air was crisp and chilly, and in the distance, dark clouds gathered over the rolling plains. More storms would come in soon. I could almost taste their chaotic energy in the air as I walked off the front porch and out across the overgrown front garden. Once, it had probably been nice. But the hedges were wild and all the stone bordering the paths were now displaced, cracked, or missing completely.

The barn wasn't much better off. If Jaevid really was going to have this place worked on for Ms. Lin and her family, he was probably better off just demolishing this barn and starting from scratch. Parts of the roof were caving in, and boards were missing from some of the walls. The ones still standing were warped and gray with age, and one of the massive sliding doors on the front was missing completely.

When I stuck my head inside, I took in a deep breath of the musty smell of old, rotting hay. Even if it was falling apart now, this place had probably been really nice when it was built. Why had it been left abandoned for so long?

A mountain of different colored scales shifted in the back of the barn, taking up nearly half of the entire floor space. The heap shifted as I walked closer, the different colors and patterns of scaly hide writhing and coiling together until, at last, three yawning dragon heads emerged to squint down at me.

Vexi smacked her jaws disappointedly before she laid her head back down somewhere in the pile. The smaller drake plopped his head onto her side and gave a few owlish, slow blinks before his ears drooped and he started to snore. Well, then. I guess I'd interrupted a dragons-only cuddle fest? They were packed into the mounds of old hay like a bunch of lazy house cats, probably using their combined body heat to soothe one another.

Fornax was the only one still looking my way, his snout tracking my steps as I wandered over to sit down beside him. He couldn't see me, of course. Without my goggles on, he couldn't see anything at all. But he knew my scent and could follow the sounds of my footfalls easily enough.

"Hey there, big guy. Found a good spot, huh? Did these two finally convince you to get cozy?" I asked as I ran my hand along the side of his neck.

He murred low, sniffing through my hair and pushing his huge nose against my side. I rubbed and scratched around his horned head until he made those deep, purring sounds in his throat.

"And here I was going to see if you wanted to go fly together a little," I muttered as I fiddled with one of his ears. "I guess I shouldn't try leaving, though. Jaevid probably wants us to all stay together. Speaking of which, where's Mavrik? He didn't want to join in?"

Fornax gave a snort, as though he didn't know or care where Jaevid's king drake had wandered off to. His eyes closed and he pushed his head against my hand harder, urging me to keep scratching.

It made me smile. "Thanks for coming to my rescue last night. Looks like we made another big mess, though."

"What happened was not your fault," a female voice spoke up suddenly.

I turned to find Isandri standing in the doorway, her expression cryptic as the breeze stirred in her long, dark hair.

"Is Reigh awake? Is he all right?" I dared to hope.

Her fair brow crinkled in distress. "He hasn't regained consciousness yet," she answered quietly, her voice heavy with guilt. Her bare feet didn't make a sound on the hay-scattered floor as she came closer. The nearer she got, the clearer I could see the exhaustion and absolute anguish that seemed to make her entire body droop.

I knew I should say something. I should try to talk to her, console her, and remind her that, whatever happened next, we were all in this together.

But as soon as I opened my mouth, she blurted, "It was my fault. He ... he took those arrows for me." Her expression skewed, faltering between a fractured mixture of fear and grief. She bit at every word as though it were acid on her tongue. "They outnumbered us quickly. We were not prepared for such an assault. If he had not thrown himself in the path of those arrows, it would be me lying up there clinging to life—not him!"

"Isandri, you can't blame yourself for any of this," I reasoned. Stepping closer, I wondered if I should try to hug her. That frenzy in her eyes was raw and wild. Like she might hit me if I tried to touch her. "It could've just as easily been Murdoc, Judan, me, or any of us lying up there. Frankly, I'm stunned it's *not* me. If anyone was going to get shot full of arrows, I would've sworn it was going to be me."

She shot me a venomous little scowl, like I was not helping at all. It didn't last, though. Little by little, her features fell back to that look of sorrow and regret. She moved toward me a little and let her head slump to rest on my shoulder. "I'm not used to any of this, Thatcher. Being with others. Fighting alongside them. Caring so much. It ... it hurts."

A faint smile brushed my lips as I dared to pat the back of her head. "Yeah. It does."

"At the temple where I was raised, they kept me away from the others. I was always set apart. They said it was because of who I was and what I was ultimately meant for that I should be held in distinction. It was an honor," she murmured miserably. "But it always felt ... lonely. And now it's as though a part of me is broken. I'm not good at this. You make it look so easy. It's not fair. And now I've gone and nearly killed Reigh."

"Okay, well, you make fighting and using your power look easy. So welcome to my world." I smiled a little wider. "That shapeshifting thing is a hard act to follow, you know. But, Isa, I'm certain no one blames you for what happened to Reigh. Please don't be so hard on yourself. I mean it. You're learning the ropes of all this—being a hunter for the queen, fighting the Ulfrangar, and trying to work together—right along with the rest of us. And ... and being what we are, with the power we have, it doesn't make things any easier. Feels like it should, though, huh?"

Isa lifted her head, staring at me with her strange, yellow-green eyes seeming to search me thoroughly. "You believe me, then?"

I shrugged. "I don't have much of a choice now, do I? Even if I don't really understand what I did ... "

She glanced away, her mouth scrunching to the side thoughtfully. "It was a shield of pure, divine power. Very befitting of Ishaleon. I suspect it is only the beginning, though. Now that the connection to your true identity has been made, I suspect more of your powers will now surface more quickly."

What? *More* powers? I couldn't decide if that was awesome or absolutely terrifying—but I was seriously leaning to the latter.

"You know, uh, the others want to talk to you. Er, well, to both of us, I guess. And I think it's time we told them what's really going on here. With us, I mean. You know, that we're reincarnated deities and all that," I said. "Especially since I, um, I'm pretty sure I saw Devana last night."

Isandri's frown became severe. "What do you mean you *saw* her?"

"I saw a girl standing in the flames in the city square. She was smiling at me. Laughing. Her whole body glowed with blue light. It had to be her, right?"

Her expression closed and she seemed to withdraw, leaning back slightly as she stared straight into my eyes. "You're sure you saw this?"

Uh oh. That couldn't be a good sign.

"Yeah. That ... that was her, wasn't it? That's how Devana looks?" Did Isandri even know what she looked like? She acted like she'd known her—and maybe she had. We hadn't exactly gotten to talk much about all this.

She didn't answer. Not out loud, at least. But as she held my gaze, her features slowly changing to a look of confusion and silent mortification, I could tell: Whatever I'd seen in the flames that night ... it wasn't Devana.

So, who was it, then?

I opened my mouth to ask, but Isa spoke first. "Do you really trust him?"

"Trust who?"

Isandri stared back at me, her lovely features still tense with worry. Her lips thinned some and she glanced down at her bare feet. "Jaevid Broadfeather. I know he's had some experiences with the gods. He was hand chosen to speak for Paligno, the god of all living things. But that connection has now been severed. And our situation is very different." She shifted some, making her deep purple, silken robes swish. "He holds great influence in the royal court. His word, his opinion of us, could—it could ... " Her voice trailed off as she bit at her bottom lip, her slender shoulders drawing up slightly. "Thatcher, throughout history, there have been many times when our past-selves have been used, tormented, and imprisoned. They were forced to use their power for vile things. Men like Argonox. And some who were even worse. I don't know your queen. I don't know Jaevid. But I do know the damage that our power in cruel hands is capable of."

Well. That was definitely not something I'd considered before now. But she did have a point. A really good one, actually. Jaevid was probably one of the most influential people in the entire kingdom now, whether he liked it or not. And Queen Jenna was in a unique position of power right now because of the Court of Crowns. Isandri had every right to be anxious about what they might do or say when we came clean about our, uh, *situation*.

But I just couldn't imagine either of them trying to force us to do anything evil with our power.

They weren't like Argonox—I was sure about that.

"Do you trust me, Isa?" I asked.

She looked up at me again, blinking in surprise. "Y-Yes. Yes, of course, I do."

"Good. Because I trust you, too. And that's the only way any of this works, I think. If we trust each other," I said. "Jaevid and Queen Jenna are on our side. I trust both of them, just like I do you, Murdoc, Phoebe, and Judan. We're going to be okay, Isandri. Whatever happens, as long as we keep sticking together, we're going to be okay."

Her eyes welled a little, mouth scrunching as she looked down again. A few locks of her long dark hair slipped from behind her pointed ears, brushing her cheek. "Okay, then. If you're certain," she whispered.

Without looking up again, she turned away and began to walk toward the barn's open door.

Hmm. I'd really been hoping that would cheer her up a little. Then again, I was still figuring out this whole friends-but-also-we're-divine-siblings thing dynamic with her. I needed some serious practice.

Fornax gave me a nudge with his snout, almost knocking me over. I staggered a little and shot him a glare—which, of course, he couldn't see. Maybe he could still sense it, though, because he smacked his lips and gave a stubborn snort. One look at the bridle Phoebe had made, still fitted to his head, gave me an idea.

"H-Hey, uh, Isandri?" I stammered.

She stopped and looked back. "Yes?"

"Before you go, um, would you want to help me out with something?" I slipped my goggles off from around my neck and held them out to her.

She turned to face me, arching one of her eyebrows dubiously as she glanced between the goggles and Fornax. "So long as this is not a request to fly your dragon, Thatcher. I've my own wings and I much prefer them, thank you very much."

"No, no. It's not that," I said. "It's just, well, you know how these work, don't you?" I nodded to the goggles.

"Phoebe said they allow the dragon to see through your eyes," Isa replied as she took a few cautious steps back over and took them. "A sort of shared sight."

I nodded. "Right, yeah. So whoever wears those goggles acts as Fornax's eyes. He can see what they see."

Her mouth quirked to one side as she looked the goggles over. "And what is it you'd like me to do with them?"

"I want you to—I-I mean, I wanted to ask if you would be willing to put them on and ... look at me." I managed a small smile and shrug. "You know, because Fornax chose me to be his rider, and we've been flying together for a while now, but even though we've used these goggles a few times so he can see again ... he's never actually seen ... me."

Isandri's expression went blank for a second or two. Then, little by little, she began to smile. "You want me to wear them so he can see what you look like?" she asked.

"Yeah. You know, I just thought he might want to see who he actually picked." I cast my dragon a sideways look. He'd already begun extracting himself from the big scaly snuggle pile and crouched low beside me.

"Just so you know, it's too late to change your mind," I reminded him. "Just because I look like a shrimp instead of being all big, beefy, and intimidating doesn't mean you get to go shopping for a different rider."

Fornax gave a grumbling, annoyed sound and nipped at my belt.

I gave his big, scaly head a playful shove. "Come on, you know I'm only kidding."

One swing of his massive head and shove of his snout against my side bowled me over, knocking me flat on my rear. I laughed and tried pushing him away as he made low, sulky grumbling sounds and basically put my whole torso in his maw like a mother dog mouthing playfully at her pup.

All of a sudden, he stopped.

Fornax drew back, blinking his big, milky jade-colored eyes down at me slowly. His scaly ears perked, swiveling as he tilted his head to one side and then the other. His nostrils puffed in deep breaths and made long trills of curious, almost mystified chirping sounds.

What? Was something wrong?

Then Isandri moved. She'd come over to stand right beside us, staring down at where I lay through the lenses of Phoebe's specially-made goggles.

My stomach fluttered and spun, seeming to knock the breath out of me for a moment as I slowly looked back over at my dragon. My heartbeat pounded so fast I could hardly feel it, like it was just one long, continuous, blurring thump.

He was ... *seeing* me. For the first time.

"H-Hey there, big guy," I managed to wheeze nervously.

His chirping grew louder. His ears perked straight up and he pushed his nose against my chest, sucking in a deep breath of my scent.

I put a hand on his giant, horned head. "So? Am I worse than you imagined? Or better?" I asked.

"I think he is quite pleased," Isa said with a knowing grin as she stepped a little closer and crouched down, putting her head right beside his. That was probably as close as anyone could get to the same perspective for him.

I looked at her—him—both of them, and tried to blink the tears from my eyes. I pressed my palm against the end of his nose and managed an unsteady smile. "Well, that's a relief. Guess I don't need to worry about you looking for a new rider after all."

Isa giggled some. She gave us a few more minutes with Fornax looking me over thoroughly and snuffling through my hair before she finally slipped the goggles off and handed them back to me.

"Thanks, Isa." I grinned as I put them back around my neck.

"It was my pleasure." She smiled back.

I gave her a challenging little waggle of my eyebrows as I led the way to the barn door. "Now then, feel like telling the rest of our friends our big, bad secret?"

She sighed, but her expression wasn't nearly as tense or upset as it has been before. "No. But it seems we must."

"It'll be fiiiine," I laughed. "No worse than usual. I promise."

She rolled her eyes as she walked right alongside me, her arms crossed into the big, flowy sleeves of her robes. "Given the events of the past few weeks, that is not a very good standard to aspire to."

"Then we'll aspire not to burn anything down. How's that? Sound good?"

"I suppose that'll do." She sighed and shook her head. But I could have sworn I caught a hint of another little grin on her lips.

Striking out across the garden together, Isandri and I made our way back to the farmhouse—fully prepared to deliver the news about our weird identities and everything that went along with them. But as we got closer to the front porch, the sight of someone already making their way up the front steps made me stumble to a halt.

Um. What? I squinted, certain I had to be seeing things. No way that was real. Because from where I was standing, it looked exactly like there was a little girl knocking on the front door of the farmhouse.

A little girl ... with two big, double-headed handaxes hanging from her belt.

CLEARLY I'D TAKEN one too many blows to the head while training with Murdoc. That was the only explanation I could come up with for why I kept seeing little girls doing random stuff—like laughing while standing in flaming wreckage, or knocking on the front door dressed in a sleeveless chainmail shirt and carrying two big axes. Yep. I was finally losing it.

Only, one sideways glance at Isandri's wary scowl sort of made it seem like she might be seeing the same thing I was. So, either this was a shared hallucination, or there really was a very short girl standing on the front porch of the house. I decided to bet on the second.

Isandri and I exchanged a glance as we approached, not saying anything until we'd climbed the steps and stopped only a few feet away from her. Even from this close, I had absolutely no idea who she was. One of Jaevid's friends, maybe? Or another one of Judan's agents?

Surely he wasn't recruiting kids for his secret spy network, though, right?

After almost a minute of standing there in awkward silence, Isandri finally elbowed me in the ribs and tipped her head toward the girl.

"O-Oh! Um, hello there. Are you here to meet Jaevid or ... ?" I choked and stammered like a complete idiot. Ugggh. Why couldn't I pull off at least one confident introduction? I mean, what was I even nervous about? She was just a—

The girl turned around, blinking up at us in delighted surprise.

Okay. She was definitely not a little girl. I mean, not literally. She was little. Er—well, little-r than I was used to seeing. Short. She was really short. But her features seemed much older, like maybe she was somewhere in her late teens. Her tanned skin was freckled across her rosy cheeks, and her ginger-golden hair framed her face in two thick, long braids. Her sleeveless chainmail top revealed the swirling, blue tattoos that contoured her muscular arms, and I noticed a matching single rune on one of her cheeks right below her left eye.

W-Wow. I'd never seen anyone like her before. You know, and not just because of her stature. She was like ... I-I couldn't even come up with the right words.

When our gazes met, and her smile widened until I could see dimples in her cheeks, every thought in my brain scrambled.

I-I couldn't even speak. My mouth hung open, but nothing would come out. Not even a pathetic whimper.

"Well, hello! And here I was wondering if I'd come to the wrong place." She laughed and beamed up at us. "Although, the giant blue dragon guarding the front lawn was a bit of a giveaway. Hard to miss that one, yeah? Is Prince Judan around? I've a bit of information for him."

Heat bloomed in my face like someone had just lit my hair on fire. Oh gods. I had to say something. Speak! Speak words!!

Isandri must have noticed my complete internal breakdown because she puffed an exasperated sigh and spoke up. "And you are?"

"Garnett, at your service!" she answered cheerfully and offered a quick bow. "And you must be the Lunostri that's given my boys such a hassle to follow. Forgive me for not knowing your name; been hard enough just to track your movements let alone get close enough to pick up much information about you. That trick with shapeshifting—absolutely brilliant, by the way. If you've ever a mind to find work here in Maldobar, I'm sure my employer would love to have a chat with you. We could certainly put those skills of yours to use!"

Isandri's brows rose slowly as her mouth opened. Now she seemed to be the one struggling to come up with words. At last, her eyes narrowed a little as her lips bowed into a secretive smile. "It seems you know me well enough, for now. And you are a child of Runeheart, correct? I've read of your people. The dwarves of the Whitecrown Mountains, I believe?"

Garnett clasped her hands at her back and bobbed her head. "Ah, yes. Well, unfortunately, reading about them is about all you can do now. I don't imagine many of them escaped the Tibran scourge. I was lucky. They say knowledge is power, but sometimes it's the only thing that keeps you alive, eh?" She tapped at her temple and winked. "My father was Chief Delver for King Burbrand himself. Basically, the head engineer in charge of planning and constructing new tunnel systems. He taught me quite a lot, and that nasty Tibran lord had a mind to dig tunnels of his own. So he needed my brains—intact, of course."

"You dug all the tunnels the Tibrans used?" I blurted. Oh gods. Why? Why did I have to go and ask her that?! It wasn't any of my business, and her time with the Tibrans was probably a painful memory like it was for Phoebe.

"Ah, well, I didn't dig them personally, of course. But I was in charge of planning them and organizing the workers, the underbeasts, and all that." Garnett's vibrant, lavender-hued eyes darted up to me suddenly. "And you? Hmm." She squinted a little, as though I were a puzzle she was solving at lightning speed.

For a few, truly mortifying seconds, I forgot how to breathe.

"You're one of the boys that's been giving everyone such trouble, yeah?" she asked, although her tone made it sound like she already knew the answer.

I dipped my head some and swallowed hard, trying to scrape together one intelligent sentence. "Y-Yes. I guess I am."

Uggh. Pathetic, even by my standards.

She patted me on the arm consolingly. "Don't fret, love. We've all caused our fair share of trouble, I suspect. And we're about to stir up a bit more! Come, I need to speak with Judan as soon as possible. If you want to catch that slippery beast-man, you're going to have to move fast."

15
CHAPTER FIFTEEN

G arnett entered the old farmhouse like a ray of pure sunlight. Her giggling laughter carried down halls as she met Judan with open arms and another broad smile. The more they talked, the more everyone else began to emerge from all the shadowy corners of the house to see what was going on.

Jaevid and Ms. Lin came from the kitchen, their sharp expressions of confusion eerily similar thanks to their matching pale blue eyes. Jondar shuffled up behind them like a towering, russet-haired giant, still limping with every step. Murdoc stepped in from the front sitting room, scowling suspiciously. Motion from the stairs that led up to the second floor made me glance up just in time to see Phoebe appearing there like a ghost. The sight stole my breath for a second. Gods and Fates, I hadn't seen her at all since we arrived here. There were heavy circles under her wide eyes as she stared around at everyone, like she was hoping for some clue about what was happening. Behind her, the curious faces of a few of Ms. Lin's younger, adopted children peeked down, too.

Garnett had quite the audience. But if it fazed her in the slightest, it never showed. She looked around at all of us, eyes catching like sunlit amethysts, before her gaze seemed to settle back on Judan. "Quite the collection of folk you've gathered here. Not that I came to question your tactics, but isn't it a bit reckless to put yourselves up in another house full of children? You know, given that the last few places you've graced with your presence have wound up a heap of cinders? Granted, having that big blue dragon roosting outside is a definite deterrent."

"He doesn't seem to have slowed you down at all," Jaevid grumbled as he shot an annoyed glare out the front window.

"Aww, don't be too sour with him. I've spent most of my life dealing with beasties that were much bigger and had a lot less sense than that one. You could say I've got a way with them. Runs in the family," Garnett announced proudly as she squared her shoulders and puffed her chest. "All he needed was a little scratch on the chin."

I couldn't tell if the look on Jaevid's face was one of complete horror ... or just pure shock. Maybe both.

Yeah, probably both.

Judan, on the other hand, flushed some as he rubbed a hand along the back of his neck. "Well, you'd be right about this not being the most ideal place to set our proverbial flag. But we don't intend to stay here a second longer than necessary. Which is why I'm praying you've come with the information we need from your employer."

For the first time, Garnett's bright demeanor seemed to dim. Her expression softened to a look of gentle concern as she glanced all around at us again. I could have sworn her eyes seemed to linger on me for a second longer than the rest though.

And I failed miserably at not reading too much into that.

"Yes, well, I do have that," she answered quietly. "Perhaps we should all have a seat, yeah? It could take a while and you're going to want to hear every word."

No one argued, and one-by-one, nearly everyone in the hallway began to make their way into the sitting room. Even Phoebe hedged down the steps, moving slowly and warily, with her pale face locked into a look of concern. She drifted wordlessly over to stand right beside me, seeming to almost weave on her feet—like she might collapse from exhaustion at any second.

Ms. Lin stayed back, hesitating at the threshold with Jondar for a moment. They shared a few whispered words, and then quietly retreated up the stairs and out of sight. I guess they'd decided to give us some privacy. Probably for the best because what we had to discuss now was something that could very well get us all killed.

Or, me, at least. I was going to be the bait, after all.

"I suppose I should clear the air for everyone so we can get down to business," Garnett said as she plopped down on the floor in the middle of the sitting room rug and began unclipping her two double-headed hand axes from her belt. She tossed them one at a time off to the side and then sat back with a sigh. "I'm Garnett. I was formerly a slave-soldier, forced to serve Lord Argonox and the Tibran Empire. But after the war ended, I went to work for the only person I could find who was willing to give me a job with reasonable pay. Not a lot of options around here for a misplaced dwarven woman who specializes in engineering underground tunnels and only has one previous employer that happened to have been a soulless, bloodthirsty tyrant."

She gave a shrug and quirked her mouth to the side thoughtfully. "That said, I've been one of Arlan the Kinslayer's chief informants for about a year now. He recognized I've got skills besides just digging tunnels. I'm especially good at keeping tabs on my *former* coworkers, and watching for when they're about to do something particularly stupid. Ironically, this is the first job he's ever assigned me to that required both my knowledge of digging and Tibran nonsense." She gave a thin, slightly nervous chuckle. "You want to know where your beastly friend has been hiding out—and it took my contacts here in Dayrise less than four hours to find him. Problem is, as I'm sure you can now guess, actually getting to him is going to pose a real challenge ... and no small amount of danger."

"You mean he's hiding out in abandoned Tibran tunnels?" Judan asked suddenly, sitting forward in the wingback chair where he'd settled. "I didn't realize there were any of those even located in this area."

"Oh, yeah, lots." She wafted a hand like that should've been obvious. "Argonox was a monster, but he wasn't an idiot. He wanted tunnel systems constructed to connect every major city in Maldobar. It was a way he hoped to avoid the air-based defenses of its, er, *your* dragonriders. Not a bad plan, but the underbeasts can only dig so fast, and we were losing soldiers by the hundreds to cave-ins because he wouldn't allow me enough time to ensure the stability of the new routes."

From the back of the room, Jaevid had apparently revived from his fit of shock. "I'm sorry—the *what*?"

"Underbeasts!" Garnett replied cheerily. Then she paused, winced a little, and bobbed her head. "Oh, right, you don't have them here. Monstrous mongrels with no eyes, big toothy mouths, and hides like iron plating. They're dumber than a bag of boulders, but they can dig like nothing else. My kin have used them for delving new tunnels and caverns for, gods, probably thousands of years."

"And Argonox brought these underbeasts here? To Maldobar?" Jaevid's entire face had gone frighteningly pale.

"Yes. No small feat, I tell ya." She tapped her chin and quirked her mouth again—to the other side this time. "I think there were five at first, but a few died on the voyage. We came here with three still living. That pigheaded tyrant stole them straight from the heart of my homeland when he conquered it."

Jaevid cleared his throat, shifting his weight from one foot to the other as he studied Garnett carefully. "And ... just how many of them are there left here in Maldobar now? Or were they all killed in the war?"

"Oh, stones, no! Hard to kill those big brutes. They don't do well on the surface, and certainly not on ships, but underground? Well, you'd do better running than trying to hunt them down," Garnett replied quickly and probably too cheerfully for everyone's taste. "I'd wager all three of them are still alive and well somewhere."

Too late, she seemed to notice the mute horror of everyone else in the room.

She immediately put on a pleading smile and waved her hands. "Oh! But, really, it's nothing to worry over. They're content to stay down deep in their tunnels. You shouldn't have any trouble from them. Like I said, they don't do well on the surface."

"But if Phillip is hiding out in these tunnels, or using them to move from place to place undetected, then there's a chance we might run into one of these monsters, correct?" Judan asked, his tone quiet and heavy with concern.

Garnett gave a cringing shrug. "I suppose, but quite honestly I doubt you'd find any this near the surface. Truly, it's nothing at all to fret about. I'd be much more worried about the switchbeasts and war hounds."

Phoebe made a sound like someone stepping on a puppy's paw. Her already pale face seemed to blanch as white as milk. "B-But they were all killed! They were all destroyed in the final battle! Weren't they ... ?"

Several long seconds of uncomfortable silence ticked by before Jaevid finally murmured, "We had hoped many of them were. But with no idea how many of those horrific beasts Argonox actually had at his disposal in the first place, it's impossible to know for certain how many might be left to roam the countryside now."

More silence.

Judan rubbed at his chin and jaw, brow creased as he stared down at the toes of his boots. All around the room, everyone stayed grim and still, as though we were each lost in our own private storm of worry.

"Look, I know that all sounds a bit scary, but from what little Judan has told me about your plan, and what I now know about Phillip's moving patterns, I doubt very much any of us will be battling underbeasts, war hounds, or anything like that," Garnett spoke up suddenly, her smile still as cheery as ever. She peered up at me with her wide, soft lavender eyes brimming with confidence, and I suffered a small heart attack. "I know you intend to act as bait. And given his peculiar fixation on you, that's probably your best bet at luring him into the right spot to spring a trap. But he's a wary devil. Smart, too. He knows you'd all like to catch him and that's going to pose a problem unless we do this just the right way."

Judan sank back in his chair, lacing his fingers together as he studied her through suspicious, narrowed eyes. "Sounds like you've got an idea what way that should be, Dear Garnett."

She grinned broadly and tapped her chin. "I do indeed, Your Highness. You see, you all want to try to lure him to this fellow and catch him as soon as he appears—which is exactly what he's expecting. We've got to be cleverer than that. So I propose, instead, letting him take the bait." She paused and winked at me. "Let him take you hostage and return to the tunnels, confident in his victory."

Murdoc's hard, angular features snapped into a pensive scowl. "You're suggesting we set the trap for him in the tunnels while he's gone, then spring it on him there."

Her impish grin practically glowed with delight. "Precisely! Snare him on his home turf. It's the last place he'll be expecting anyone to strike."

"That could work," Judan agreed. "It's risky, but if he's got no reason to suspect we know about him using the tunnels to move in secret, it's unlikely he'd change those patterns now." He glanced sideways at Jaevid. "This could be the edge we've needed—an element of surprise."

"Phoebe, if I can bring you the supplies today, do you think you can manage to put together a way of binding someone like Phillip?" Jaevid asked. "With his strength, regular chains and shackles won't hold up long. I've seen him break solid iron with his bare hands."

My mouth screwed up as a memory flickered through my mind. I'd seen him do that kind of thing, too. Well, not personally, but I'd certainly seen the evidence of it. When we were fighting the Ulfrangar off at the Cromwell estate, someone had tried to kill Phoebe by locking her in the dining hall and setting it ablaze—and they'd bent a rod of solid iron in order to bind the doors shut. Until that moment, I hadn't thought much about who had actually been the one to twist that thick metal bar that way. Now, just the thought sent a cold pang of dread through my gut.

And I could only imagine how it made Phoebe feel.

Standing between Murdoc and me, all the light seemed to die in Phoebe's eyes as she stared around the room. Her hands trembled as she wrung them behind her back, as she seemed to shrink back, almost like she wanted to hide behind us completely. "I-I can certainly try, Lord Jaevid. But it ... it might require causing him some discomfort. I would ... I-I ... " she stammered until, at last, her expression seemed to collapse entirely into a look of pure terror. Her mouth mashed shut and she swallowed hard, eyes welling as her chin trembled.

I was so busy staring at her, wondering what I could possibly do to comfort her some, that I almost missed it. Another hand appeared at her back, slipping swiftly and discreetly to grasp one of hers and hold it tightly.

It took all my concentration not to smirk as I dared to glance over the top of her head at the only other person standing close enough to her to do something like that.

Murdoc.

He kept his gaze trained straight ahead, looking very convincingly bored and indifferent. That idiot. I mean, did he really think I wouldn't notice that little maneuver? Oh, was he in for it later. I'd seen him go rushing to her rescue more than once now. No way was I letting this slide without finding out what, exactly, his intentions were when it came to Phoebe. He'd probably hit me a few times, sure, but it'd be worth it to watch him blush and deny it.

"We understand that you might have to hurt him in order to restrain him, Phoebe. Just do your best," Jaevid offered consolingly. "Given the circumstances, some extreme measures may be required for all of us. But if we can get Phillip back and restored to his right mind, it will be worth it."

Judan made a disbelieving, snorting sound. "And how do you propose we do that? If Devana truly has him under some manner of divinely-powered mind control, then she could kill him the instant he's caught in our trap. How can we break that bondage without her leaving his mind a pile of quivering mush?"

Jaevid's smile was hauntingly cryptic. "By using a little divine power of our own."

My stomach clenched up and dropped to the soles of my boots like a block of cold lead as everyone in the room suddenly looked right at me. What? Why were they staring at me like I had all the answers to ...

O-Oh. Right.

I guess most of them had seen what I'd done in the city square to save Reigh. And while I couldn't argue that projecting that magical shield wasn't a manifestation of, er, well, my divine power, I had no idea if I could do it again. Was breaking Devana's hold on Phillip even something Ishaleon could do?

Regardless, this seemed like Jaevid's roundabout way of prodding me into talking about my new ability. I guess he knew I was holding back a lot. Isandri, too. And before we made any moves against Devana, we all needed to be on the same page.

Might as well get it over with.

I flicked a quick look of warning over to Isandri before I cleared my throat and stood a little straighter. After all, if I was about to tell them all an outrageous and borderline unbelievable story about ancient gods being reincarnated as regular people like, er, me, then I needed to at least look convincing.

Ugggh. Gods help me.

No one laughed out loud—which, honestly, I took as a good sign.

I finished explaining as much as I could, and then stopped to let Isandri fill in the numerous gaps in my understanding of how this all worked. She knew all the fine details when it came to the actual history of why Ishaleon, Eno, and Adiana were being reborn as mortals. Hearing it again didn't make it sound any more believable, however. I guess the one thing we did have going in our favor was that now I'd proven that working divine magic wasn't something unique to Isa just because she was a Lunostri priestess. If I—the bumbling and mostly useless son of a poor farrier from Thornbend—could work divine magic, then there had to be a good explanation.

"So your projection of that shield is a manifestation of the God of Mercy's power," Jaevid reasoned aloud. His pale, glacier-blue eyes focused on Isandri with an intensity that made me want to melt into a puddle. She didn't seem too intimidated by it, though. "And your ability to change your shape is because you're Adiana?"

She nodded. "Yes. Adiana has been depicted many times as a great black cat—the master of all hunters. I have been able to take on that shape since I was a child. On a moonless night, however, I am unable to do it, and my other powers are greatly diminished."

"And on a full moon?" Garnett asked, her face practically glowing with interest.

Isandri tilted her head to the side, mouth quirking into a bashful side-grin. "I can disappear entirely for short periods of time, if I wish."

Garnett practically squealed with excitement as she bounced a little where she sat. "You can become *invisible*?! That's incredible!"

Isa's ebony cheeks seemed to flush with a hint of deep scarlet. "That is ... well, yes. Thank you."

"Too bad we're not going after Phillip on a full moon, then," Judan sighed, sounding genuinely disappointed. Then his gaze snapped back over to me. "So what else can you do, then?"

I opened my mouth, but the only thing that would come out were choking, sputtering sounds. What else could I do? Sword-fight terribly, muck stalls, weed a garden, and occasionally tame a feral dragon. Other than that, I didn't have any specialized skills, and somehow I doubted any of those were divinely powered.

Hanging my head, I finally managed to answer, "Nothing, I guess. I don't know. Isa thinks my powers have only just started to manifest."

"That's unfortunate," Jaevid muttered, now running his fingers thoughtfully over his mouth. "I'm not sure how well it applies to your circumstances, but when it came to my own magical abilities—the ones I had while I served Paligno—I found that the more I used them, the stronger they became. Perhaps you can find some time to practice here while Phoebe prepares."

"Sure. Yeah, I can do that," I answered.

"You won't have long," Garnett warned as she waggled a finger at Phoebe and me. "My informants are watching your man, Phillip, as best they can. But we can't guarantee he will stay in one place forever. He's probably already on the prowl, trying to find where you're all hiding. It won't take him long to track you here—the Ulfrangar, too, for that matter. What with the blue dragon, and all. Makes you a bit of an obvious target. I wouldn't delay longer than a day, at most. If it's all the same to the rest of you, I'd like to stick around and make sure it all goes to plan. I can help you bring this fellow in, too. I'm decent enough in a fight, should it come to that, so you don't have to worry. I can fend for myself."

"That's an understatement," Murdoc grumbled under his breath.

"I'll say," Judan chuckled. "I don't think we're in a good spot to be turning away potential help, though. Stay if you want, and be sure to report back to Kinslayer how daring, brave, and dangerous we all are."

Garnett laughed as she shot back to her feet, tossing one of her long, gingery-golden braids over her shoulder. "Oh, absolutely. When I'm finished, it'll be a proper ballad filled with tales of your glory."

"Or our deaths," Isandri muttered.

I had to agree. We were all well on our way to winding up a glorious death-ballad, with me in the starring role as the would-be deity who had no powers. Great.

"A day it is, then." Judan stood with a groan, still favoring his injured leg some for his first few steps out of the room. "Perhaps by then, Reigh will be back on his feet, too. In the meantime, I'll send word to my own network. With any luck, tomorrow night, we'll have Phillip back and a much better idea of what sort of enemy we've made in Devana."

16
CHAPTER SIXTEEN

This wasn't going to work.
    That reality settled over my shoulders like a yoke of solid iron. Standing at the far end of the barn, I wiped some of my sweaty hair from my eyes as I stared at the light of the setting sun ebbing in from the open doorway. My skin prickled and I shivered as the chilly wind rustled through my damp tunic. Six hours straight of trying to call forth that shield again, or even find the presence of Ishaleon's power hidden somewhere in my frazzled brain, and I had absolutely nothing to show for it. Well, except for the worst headache of my life.

    I'd tried everything. Meditating, pulling from memories, trying to find that sensation buried somewhere deep inside me again, and even having Isandri try to guide me through her own powers—nothing worked. My brain throbbed and pulsed like it might suddenly explode and come oozing out my ears.

    I ... I couldn't do this.

    "Giving up?" A familiar voice made me look up again. Murdoc swaggered in, surveying me with his piercing hazel eyes. Somehow that look had always reminded me of an eagle on a perch eyeing down potential prey.

    "N-No," I wheezed as I leaned over to rest my hands on my knees and tried to catch my breath. "I-Isandri thought it might help if I put m-my body under intense strain."

    "I see. And you chose pushups to cause your body *intense* strain?" I caught a hint of sarcasm in that question.

    I shot him a glare. Any other time, I might've fired back with a withering retort. But right then it was all I could do to keep breathing. Besides, he was right. What was I doing? This was never going to work. Ishaleon was supposed to be the God of Mercy, so maybe I should try focusing on doing something ... merciful? What did that even mean?

    A loud crow of excitement made us both look up as a familiar young dragon bounded over, galloping awkwardly on his hind legs and wings arms. He coiled himself around Murdoc's stiff, forbidding figure and mouthed at his boots playfully.

And I saw my perfect opportunity for a tiny bit of revenge.

"So, I couldn't help but notice before," I said as I stood up and shook my bangs out of my eyes again.

Murdoc arched an eyebrow. "Notice what?"

"You. Riding a dragon."

He scowled, his face flushing across his nose and cheeks, and gave the young drake's head a forceful nudge with his boot. "I didn't exactly have a choice," he grumbled as he stepped away from the dragon. "It doesn't mean anything."

The drake snapped his jaws. The pupils of his vibrant blue eyes narrowed and he gave a disapproving snort and nipped at the back of Murdoc's tunic as he walked away.

"Hey, I said I'd consider it. And I have. The answer is still no," he growled as he stopped long enough to extract his shirt from the dragon's teeth. "I'm grateful for what you did. You saved my life and probably their lives, too. But this isn't going to work."

The dragon let his shirt go. His big scaly head lowered and his ears drooped. He made a series of low, sad chirping sounds.

Murdoc crossed his arms and looked down, jawline hardening as his dark brows rumpled together.

I frowned. "What exactly is there to consider? I mean it's a job, right? A real one. And a way better one than mucking stalls at the castle. I mean, I get it if you don't want to take another job where you have to fight. But Jaevid is the one who told me that being a dragonrider isn't about the fighting—it's about protecting. Not to mention we would get to go through training together!"

Murdoc didn't answer.

"Hey, are you listening? I just said that you and I would get to go through training at the dragonrider academy *together*. Do you even realize how crazy it is that it's even an option for us?!"

He still wouldn't look up or answer. And after almost a minute of standing there watching him brood, I finally gave up.

Flopping my arms back to my sides, I sighed loudly and shook my head. "Okay. Fine. Suit yourself. But can you at least tell me why? Why don't you want to be a dragonrider?"

"Because it isn't that simple. It will never be that simple," he snapped. Keeping his head bowed hid most of his face behind his lengthy black bangs, but I could hear the anger shaking in his tone plainly enough. "What you and everyone else seem to be forgetting is that, defected from the Ulfrangar or not, I am a criminal. I am a *murderer*, Thatcher. You really think a dragon choosing me is enough to erase all that?"

"Queen Jenna said killing Tibrans wasn't—"

"I'M NOT TALKING ABOUT KILLING TIBRANS!" he roared suddenly as he met my gaze with a frenzy I wasn't expecting. Balling his hands into fists at his sides, he took a step toward me with all his features drawn tense in a snarl.

But as quickly as his rage exploded to the surface, it seemed to fizzle just as fast. He stopped only a few feet away from me, his broad chest still heaving with furious breaths as all that rage in his eyes slowly melted away to something else. Something like ... fear.

What? What would Murdoc possibly be afraid of? I'd never even seen him look that way before—ever. Even when there was a pack of Ulfrangar or a gang of prisoners ready to kill him, Murdoc didn't so much as flinch.

This wasn't right at all.

"I ... I have killed innocent people, too, Thatcher," he said quietly, talking fast and stumbling over his words as though in panic. "Before we met, Rook had taken me on dozens of hunts. A-And ... and on that night, before I found you in that alleyway ... There were so many—I don't even remember their faces. We drug them from their homes. We slaughtered them in the streets. People you probably knew. People ... you might have even loved."

My heartbeat slowed, seeming to drum heavy and hard against my ribs as I stared back at him. "What are you trying to say, Murdoc?"

His mouth opened, but for a few seconds he seemed to falter. At last, he dropped his gaze away and murmured, "Jaevid got another report from Prince Aubren a few days ago. His soldiers have still been interviewing people in Thornbend, probably trying to help families that got separated find one another again. He said ... he said there were a few people who reported seeing your father trying to help an elderly woman escape her house."

What? They'd seen Father?!

Before I could get a word out, Murdoc continued, "He got captured by Ulfrangar who were rounding up victims and killing them in the streets. They killed him, Thatcher. The Ulfrangar killed your father. It ... it might have even been ... me."

Everything stopped. My thoughts. My breathing. My pulse. I stood frozen, staring back at him, trying to understand—trying to make sense of it.

He shook his head a little, still not looking back my way. "I don't know it for sure. They train all pups not to look our prey in the eyes if we can avoid it. Don't look at their faces. Don't listen to anything they say. Focus on the hunt. The hunt is all that matters. I don't remember any of the people we killed in Thornbend. I don't know who held the blade that took his life. But it doesn't matter. It could have just as easily been mine as any other Ulfrangar's blade that ended your father's life that night."

All the feeling drained from my body—like I'd just been pushed beneath the dark, churning surface of an icy river. In the chaos and the cold, I couldn't feel anything.

Except pain.

And *anger*.

"Thatcher, I-I ... I'm—"

I hit him.

One second I was standing there, my ears ringing and my vision swerving in and out of focus. The next, I was on top of him, swinging punch after punch down at his face. I drove my fist across his nose, jaw, and anything else I could make contact with. It should've hurt. I should have been able to feel my knuckles aching with the contact of every blow.

But I couldn't feel anything.

Murdoc didn't even try to fight back. Or if he did, I couldn't tell. I caught only fleeting, blurred glimpses of what happened. The world blurred in and out of focus. My ears rang until I couldn't hear anything else. Blood roared in my veins. Everything went numb as one word vibrated in every corner of my soul:

Father.

Out of nowhere, a pair of strong arms suddenly clamped around my neck and dragged me backwards. I kicked and fought, trying to wrench myself free as someone yanked me off Murdoc. I could barely hear the muffled, garbled voices yelling all around me—like someone had crammed my ears full of cotton.

"Thatcher! Stop it! Calm down!" A voice shouted right in my ear. Was that ... Jaevid? I wasn't sure.

And it didn't matter. I couldn't stop. I flailed and pitched, trying to get back so I could hit Murdoc again. And again. And again until ... until ...

"*THATCHER!*" Jaevid's voice boomed over me so loudly, it sent a jolt of panic through me that snatched me back to reality.

All of a sudden, I could hear myself wheezing out desperate, manic sobs as I sat on my rear with someone grappling me from behind to hold me in place. I could feel my knuckles aching, my body shaking, and my throat burning with every ragged breath. My arms and legs went limp, flopping like overcooked noodles as I sagged back against whoever was still gripping me around my chest and pinning my arms at my sides. Little by little, their grip began to ease. But I couldn't move now.

My head still spun as I stared straight ahead. Before me, Phoebe and Isandri were helping Murdoc sit up. His face was smeared with crimson that oozed from his nose and mouth. He blinked slowly, his expression hauntingly empty as he jerked away from every attempt to inspect his injuries. He didn't look my way—not even once—as he turned and started to stagger out of the barn.

Once he was gone, the person holding me down finally released their hold. But it wasn't Jaevid who scooted over the barn floor to sit beside me. I'd just assumed he was the one pinning me.

Garnett studied me, her strange violet eyes searching my face with concern. She sat close by and didn't say a word.

"Gods and Fates," Jaevid muttered as he appeared right in front of me, eclipsing my view of Murdoc. He crouched down to study me, too. "Thatcher, what happened? Why were the two of you fighting?"

Until that moment, I hadn't realized there were tears running down my face. My chin quivered. I looked down at my battered, bloody knuckles. I didn't even know if that was my blood smeared all over my fingers ... or Murdoc's.

"Thatcher?" Jaevid put a hand on my shoulder.

"H-He said," I started, my voice coming out in a hoarse, broken whisper. "H-He said ... h-he might h-have ... killed ... my father."

CHAPTER SEVENTEEN

"What? Is that true?" Garnett gasped quietly as she looked up at Jaevid for answers. "He was an Ulfrangar before, wasn't he?"

Jaevid didn't reply, though. His expression had gone grim and distant as his gaze drifted from mine to the ground between us. With a heavy sigh, he stood again and ran a hand through his shaggy, ash-gray hair. "Look after him, will you? See if you can get him to calm down. I'll try to get this sorted out."

Sorted out? What could he possibly do to sort any of this out?

Nothing, that's what. No one could fix it. Father was dead—maybe because of Murdoc. No one could just *sort that out*.

Garnett stayed sitting beside me even after Jaevid left to find the others. She didn't say anything, though. At least, not for several minutes. Then, at last, she looked over at me and cleared her throat a little. "I, um, I hope I didn't hurt you before. When I pinned you, I mean. You've got a lot more fight in you than you look—oh, er, I mean that as a compliment, of course."

I buried my face in my hands so maybe she wouldn't see my face screw up or my eyes welling again.

"Oh, love, it's going to be okay," she cooed and put a hand on my back. "You really didn't know your friend was an Ulfrangar?"

"I knew," I muttered—doing my very best not to sniffle where she could hear it. "I just ... didn't know he might've killed my father."

"*Might* have?" She sounded surprised. "So, you don't know for sure that he did?"

I shook my head. "Does it matter? He was in Thornbend that night. That's how we met in the first place. And he was with the same group of Ulfrangar who murdered Father, so it could have just as easily been him—"

"—Or someone else," she interrupted. "Listen, love, you seem like the good sort. And I'll be the first to admit, I don't know what all this about reborn deities means for you.

But you can't get your head caught up in maybe's, might's, and if's. It'll drive you mad," she said as she gave my back a pat. "We were all something else before the war. Good or bad, the war—the Tibrans—changed all of us. That friend of yours *was* an Ulfrangar. I *was* a slave. Jaevid *was* dead. You were, well, based on what the others have said, you were just a regular boy. A commoner, yeah?"

I swallowed hard and looked down. Fine. She did have a point.

But what if Murdoc had been the one to ... ?

"War changes everything," Garnett continued, her voice becoming much smaller and quieter as she looked away across the barn. "I'm not saying you should forgive him or pretend like it didn't happen. Not at all. You should do what you feel is right." She fell quiet again for a minute or two, then glanced over at me quickly. "Need the healer to take a look at you? Did he hit you back anywhere?" She sounded genuinely concerned.

"No." Somehow, admitting that out loud only made it all worse. Murdoc hadn't even tried to defend himself—let alone punch me back. And I knew that had nothing whatsoever to do with my fighting ability or me catching him off guard. Murdoc could've ripped me in half like a piece of wet paper if he wanted to.

He'd *chosen* to lie there while I beat him.

But why?!

I put my face in my hands again. What was I supposed to do? Act like this didn't matter? Go on as usual? Try to find him and ... *talk* about it? It all sounded stupid, even to me. I didn't know what to say, and I didn't want to try to think of anything because then I might wind up forgiving him and ...

"He was your closest friend before, wasn't he? Do you hate him now?" Garnett asked suddenly.

My heart gave an awful, painful lurch in my chest. It made my eyes well up again, and I was glad she couldn't see it.

Did I hate Murdoc now? I-I ... I didn't know. I wanted to. But deep down, gods, I didn't know. None of this was right. None of it was fair. Murdoc was the closest thing to family I had left now. He'd taken care of me, saved my life more times than I could count, and tried to teach me how to fight. Thinking about all of it—about everything we'd been through—made me want to throw up. Or hit him again. Both, I guess.

"I'm so sorry, I know I'm really bad at this. Cheering people up, I mean." Garnett's hand slipped off my back. "And we don't even know one another. But at least I know your name now. It's Thatcher, isn't it?"

I wiped my face on my sleeve a few times before I looked over at her. "Y-Yeah."

"And Jaevid said you're from Thornbend?"

"Yeah. Although, I've heard there's not much left of it now." I sighed. My face still felt hot and flushed as I rubbed my pounding forehead. Ugh. I probably looked pathetic to her. The epitome of childish. Red eyes, swollen cheeks—the whole embarrassing show.

"Ah." She shifted a little where she sat, fiddling with one of the ends of her braids. "Guess we've got that in common, too, then. My father was killed by the Tibrans when they conquered our homeland. That was years ago, though."

I flicked her a sideways look. "Did you hate them for killing him?"

Garnett looked my way with her mouth scrunched up and one eye squinted like she was trying to think back. "Mmm. I guess so, at first. But then I became one of them. And I didn't hate myself, sooo ... " She shrugged and went back to fiddling with her braid. "All the Tibran slave soldiers had stories exactly like mine, you see. They came from somewhere else against their will, left nothing but ash and ruin behind, and lost someone or everyone dear to them. So it was hard to blame them—to stay angry at them for what happened. Because I wound up being forced to do that same thing to other people. Hating the soldiers for the will of their ruler is sort of pointless, yeah? Especially when those soldiers are only fighting under threat of death or torture."

It was impossible not to sit there and draw parallels between her and Murdoc. I tried not to—really, I did. But I knew his situation wasn't much different. He had never had a choice about becoming an Ulfrangar. He'd told me he was taken as a baby, beaten and abused, and forced to learn their brutal ways. Maybe being angry at him wasn't fair. Maybe the one I should have been angry with—the one I should have hated—was the leader of the Ulfrangar. The Zuer, or whatever they called her. That person was the one passing down the orders to kill people to all the assassins who'd been brainwashed and stripped of their humanity so they obey without question.

Only ... Murdoc had questioned them. He'd defected. He was trying to change.

Or at least, that's what I wanted to believe.

"You know, it's weird, but sometimes I actually miss it," Garnett confessed with a strained, sheepish smile. "Not because of what I was forced to do while I was enslaved to the Tibrans, of course. That part was awful. But when I was with them, I knew how to fit in. I knew what was expected of me. I knew what all the rules were. Ever since the war ended and I've been trying to make my way through this new, free life ... it's like the rules constantly change. There aren't many dwarves left in the world—and certainly none in Maldobar. At least, not that I've seen. It's like I'm a piece that's trying to be crammed into the wrong puzzle or something. Sometimes I sort of fit here or there, but it's never quite right. I wonder if it ever will be ... "

Her expression became distant and thoughtful as she let her braid drop and sank back a little. The evening sun shone against her tanned skin, making every freckle on her cheeks and nose stand out. It made the flecks of gold and blue hidden in her light violet eyes shimmer.

Once again, I wished I didn't look so pathetic sitting there like a little kid who'd just gotten in trouble for picking a fight. I wished I looked older and more mature. I wished I had something impressive, meaningful, and good to offer a girl like her.

I almost came out of my own skin when Fornax suddenly flopped his head down onto the ground right between us with a *THUD* and loud dragon sigh. Good grief. I'd almost forgotten he was back there. I managed a weary smile as I ran a hand down his snout. What a ridiculous monster.

"It's quite amazing that these beasties choose to bond with people so closely," Garnett said as she stared adoringly at my massive orange dragon. "Or that they even listen to you at all. Jaevid was able to hold all of them back earlier with just a few words."

"Yeah, he kind of takes the cake when it comes to dragon-handling, I guess."

"It's unbelievable. I heard stories about them when I was little. But I never dreamed

I'd ever see one. Especially not like this." She reached a hand out toward Fornax, like she wanted to pet him, but hesitated at the last second.

So I grabbed her hand and brought it the rest of the way to press against the side of his huge head. She tensed, sucking in a gasp. Then her eyes went wide. Her lips parted. She grinned from ear to ear as she stroked her hand along his bony brow and traced the curves of his sweeping black horns.

"His name is Fornax," I told her.

She looked up and met my gaze. Several locks of her fluffy ginger-gold hair that were too short for her thick braids fell around to frame her face. And, Gods and Fates, I couldn't remember a girl ever looking at me like that. Not in my whole life.

"He's incredible, Thatcher of Thornbend," she declared with a giggle. "And so are you."

Okay, now my entire head was probably red.

I gaped at her, and there was probably smoke coming from my ears as I tried to decide exactly what she meant by that. *I* was incre—no. Definitely not. Not even close. How could she think that? She didn't know me.

I, Thatcher of Thornbend, had been called a lot of things. But no one had ever called me incredible ... until now.

GARNETT and I sat for what felt like hours on the floor of the barn, talking about the dragons, how I'd managed to tame Fornax after he lost his first rider, and what her life had been like as a slave-soldier. She'd been farther in the world than I could imagine, and had seen things I'd never even heard of.

Since her job within the Tibran ranks meant she had spent most of her time in the labyrinth of underground tunnels and caverns they built in each kingdom, she hadn't seen Lord Argonox much. Two or three times in all. The workers who constructed the tunnels had been left to themselves for the most part—with only the occasional visit to see how things were progressing.

Of course, it wasn't all good. Most of it sounded awful, actually. They were locked away in the dark far below the surface. They had to deal with wrangling the underbeasts and the constant threat of cave-ins. Food was scarce, and there was no medical aid for workers who got injured on duty. Workers fell sick a lot, and there wasn't much anyone could do to help them. They didn't breathe fresh air or see the sky for months or even years. Honestly, I didn't understand how she could've lived through that and still be so ... happy.

But Garnett was.

And somehow, listening to her chatter about her life before the end of the war made everything seem less awful—if only for a little while.

I couldn't believe that she'd never met Phoebe before, though. I'd just assumed all of the Tibran engineering geniuses would know one another. But the idea made Garnett giggle and she gave my shoulder a playful shove.

"What? You really think Argonox would have let us mingle and make friends like that? Hah! He was a real blockhead about some things, to be sure, but he wasn't dumb when it came to keeping his soldiers under thumb. He knew mixing too many sharp minds in one place would eventually lead to a successful escape plan. Or a full-blown mutiny. Maybe both!" She patted one of the hand axes she wore threaded through her belt fondly. "And what a glorious mutiny it would have been."

"Did anyone ever try it? To mutiny against him, I mean."

Garnett had gone back to scratching Fornax's head, making my big dragon purr as he lay there with his eyes closed and his tail wrapped around us. "Oh, sure. Several times that I remember. It never worked, of course. Got a lot of people killed, though. The lucky ones died during the actual uprising. The ones who didn't—who were caught and tortured to death to set an example to everyone else of what would happen if anyone tried to revolt again—those people weren't so lucky. Argonox had an appetite for that kind of violence. He liked it, I think. Torturing people. Especially the women and girls. I think he enjoyed the power he had over them. I think he liked watching them suffer."

Her usually joyful demeanor faded, like the light in her eyes had been snuffed out. "It's good you lot killed him. But sometimes I wonder, out of all the women he tortured and abused, if there's any chance he might have a child somewhere. A son or daughter that could continue his bloodline. An heir to his violent appetite." Garnett shuddered and looked down. "Stones, I pray not. I can't imagine what that would mean if someone tried to take up his banner and fight in his name again."

"Not much," I said confidently. "Because Jaevid Broadfeather would have something to say about that. A lot of people would, I think—maybe even a lot of former Tibrans, like you."

One corner of her mouth tugged back into a smile as she glanced my way. "I suppose you're right about that."

"So, you really never saw Phoebe before this? Not even once?"

She shrugged. "No. I heard of her some, though. But you have to remember, Argonox commanded legions of thousands of soldiers. And I didn't get to see more than the hundred or so people I worked with to make the tunnels. Seems like she's nice enough, though. Scared out of her mind, but nice."

I hesitated, trying to decide how much I should tell her. She was working for a crime lord, after all. Even if she was nice, giving away all our big bad secrets to her might be, well, stupid. But if she was going to keep working with us, then she'd probably figure all this out on her own anyway.

"Yeah, she's sort of having a rough time with all this lately, I think," I muttered at last as I scratched at one of my ears. My outburst had made my hair fall out of its usual, stubby ponytail, so it tickled my ears and the side of my neck. "First it was her trial in the Court of Crowns, and then it was working with Prince Reigh. He absolutely hates her."

"Why?" She sounded surprised.

"I don't know all the details, but it's got something to do with what happened when he was being held prisoner by the Tibrans. I think she was forced to experiment on him, but Reigh won't talk about it much. Not in any detail, anyway." A few more locks escaped and fell right into my eyes. With a huff, I reached back to untie my hair completely and shake it out some before I wrestled it into another sloppy, short ponytail at the base of my neck. Arggh. Maybe I should just cut it off short.

"Ah. Well, that would do it, I guess," she said. "Arlan mentioned the young prince was injured during your last little skirmish with the Ulfrangar. I guess that's why he missed our meeting. And she came from upstairs all speckled in blood. Has she been helping to treat his injuries?"

My mouth clamped in a tense line as I nodded. "She hasn't stopped to eat or rest since we arrived, and we still haven't heard how he's doing. They said the arrows the Ulfrangar shot him with were poisoned."

"I see," she mused thoughtfully. Then she stood up and walked around Fornax's head to stand behind me. Before I knew what was happening, I felt her tug at the piece of string I used to tie back my hair. I didn't dare move a muscle. Not an inch. I barely even breathed as she tugged it free and began whistling to herself while she ran her hands through my hair. Her fingers combed lightly at my scalp as she pulled it back into a much neater, tighter ponytail.

"There," she announced proudly. "Much better."

I was too busy still trying to stay conscious to even say anything.

"We ought to go in, yeah?" she asked as she leaned around, putting her face close to mine as she peered down at me. "I don't know about you, but I'm starving. Think we could get some dinner?"

Words. I needed words. Out-loud words. Now! But now my head felt like it was on fire again, and all the places where she'd touched my scalp tingled. Never, in my entire life, had a girl *ever* done something like that.

"Y-Yeah. I, uh, I think so. Sure," I managed to squeak hoarsely.

"Okay, then. Let's go." She smiled and patted the top of my head, then stood back to offer a hand to help me up.

Her grip was steady and strong when I took it. She practically yanked me all the way up with one tug. It made me laugh a little as I dusted off the rear of my pants. "Please don't take this the wrong way, but you're not at all what I had pictured when Prince Judan mentioned he had a secret connection to a crime lord. I've never met a dwarf before. You're, uh, you're pretty ... amazing, actually."

She squared her shoulders a bit and smirked, giving a teasing wink up at me. "You've got no idea, human. Just you wait—if things get messy and we all end up in another skirmish with your assassin friends or even Duke Phillip, I'm ready to show them all what a little dwarven rage looks like. So just make sure you're standing well clear."

"I'll consider myself warned." I stood back, trying to ignore the nagging urge that ached deep in my chest—the urge to keep a hold of her hand as we started walking out of the barn. I couldn't do that, though.

Not yet. But ... maybe next time.

Definitely next time.

18

CHAPTER EIGHTEEN

The inviting aromas of food wafted in from the open door as Garnett and I made our way inside. Light ebbed from the open doorways to the kitchen and the front sitting room where the hearths were lit, filling the lower level with warmth. The sounds of pots and dishes clinking carried down the hall as we made our way to the kitchen.

Passing the sitting room, I spotted Prince Judan and Isandri sitting by the fire. They talked in hushed voices, their expressions stony and somber. Probably going over the battle plan for tomorrow. Two of Ms. Lin's children sat on the floor playing with a familiar game board—the same two little girls who'd whipped me thoroughly at every game we played. They looked up in unison as we passed by, smiling and waving.

I waved back.

The kitchen was a riot of activity with Ms. Lin right at the center like someone trying to conduct a hurricane. She wore one of the smaller toddlers in a knitted sling wrapped around her so the child rested against her hip as she cooked and called orders to Jondar. All her jet-black hair was tied up in a loose bun and her dress had a few spots of flour around the waist.

Glancing around the room, my stomach twisted and cramped as I searched every dark corner and chair. But Murdoc wasn't here. Neither were Phoebe or Jaevid, actually. I let out a slow shaking breath of relief. I wasn't ready to face him again. But almost instantly, my relief shattered to the realization and worry that ... he might have left. What if he'd been so upset and angry that he just decided to cut his losses and go? Gods, would he really do that? Disappear into the night without telling anyone?

My throat tightened and my chest thrummed with a slow, throbbing pain at the idea that I might never see him again. That interaction—that exchange—might be our last. I bit down hard, trying to tame the frenzy of confused, tangled emotions that tore at my mind. Should I even care that he'd gone? Should I want him to leave?

I ... still didn't know. There were a thousand questions twisting in my brain and not a single answer that felt right.

"Ah. You must be the boy from Thornbend I've heard so much about," an unfamiliar voice spoke up in a heavy Gray Elven accent.

Sitting at the far end of the kitchen's long wooden table, an older, Gray elf man I'd almost overlooked completely sat by himself. His multi-hued eyes gleamed in the light as he studied Garnett and me for a few seconds before he went back to cleaning a set of tiny, differently-shaped knives. He was slipping each one from a divided leather kit and wiping them down thoroughly before setting them out to dry on a clean white cloth. Surgical tools?

Wait a minute—was this the healer who'd been taking care of Reigh? It was, wasn't it?

"I've heard quite a lot about you. Have a seat. I'll take a look at that hand," he said, his long white hair spilling over his shoulders and down to his chest as he tipped his head to the empty chair beside him.

I glanced down at my battered knuckles and cringed. "Oh. I-It's not a big deal. Thank you, though."

His slightly crinkled features flashed from a look of calm indifference to a sort of silent, cold, ominous stare that sent a little thrill of panic through my stomach. Like crossing this guy or refusing his medical advice might be a very bad idea. It sort of reminded me of the look my father gave me any time I smarted off at him, actually. Yikes.

"Okay, um, sure. Yes, sir," I stammered as I eased down into the seat next to him and put my hand on the table. "Are you Reigh's—well not his father, but, um, he was raised in Luntharda, so I just wondered ... "

"Yes. I raised him." The man picked up another clean cloth and unfolded it carefully before putting my hand on it. "My Lady Lin, if you wouldn't mind?"

She practically materialized at the table with a bowl of hot water. She slipped a quick glance at him through her dark eyelashes, her cheekbones seeming to flush slightly as she quickly tucked some of her flyaway bangs behind her ears. "Kiran, please, I've asked you to call me Lin. No need to be so formal."

His brows creased into a slight, almost determined furrow. "And I have reminded you that I am a guest in your home, and owe you every due respect. You are the lady of this house."

Jondar groaned and rolled his eyes as he trundled by, carrying a big platter piled with sliced vegetables—like this was a conversation he'd been forced to endure several times already.

Ms. Lin didn't protest again, although I noticed her eyeing him over as she bit lightly at her bottom lip. Huh. Weird. What was that look about?

I looked over at Garnett, who'd settled into the chair on the other side of Kiran, for a clue. But she was too busy glancing between the two of them with a little smug, knowing grin to notice. Her eyes sparkled as she watched them, and I even noticed Kiran stealing looks at Ms. Lin when she went back to cooking dinner. They were similar in age, I guess. Although it was harder to tell with Gray elves exactly how old they were. They aged much more gracefully and slowly than humans.

Whatever was or wasn't happening between them, I had to fill the silence. It was painfully awkward to just sit there—even after Kiran went to work cleaning the dried blood off my hand. "How is Reigh? Is he awake? You're down here now so that's a good sign, right?"

Kiran's lips thinned. "He's stable now. He regained consciousness for a few minutes earlier today, but he needs to rest. The remedies took some time to begin counteracting the poisons, but the worst is over. He will recover."

Garnett leaned onto the table, resting her chin in her palm as she watched us. "It's lucky you were here to help."

"Ah, well, not so much luck as prudent emergency planning. But fortunate, nonetheless. I was returning from Halfax where I've been attending to the health of several members of the royal household there. Jaevid sent word that he might require additional medical assistance—depending on how things transpired with Phillip. He asked me to stay here for a few days, just in case things went badly and you required some additional aid," Kiran said as he leaned down to examine the tops of my knuckles.

Fortunately, they didn't look as bad now that they weren't caked in blood. Bruised and swollen, mostly. I guess none of that blood had been mine after all.

"My medical clinic in Luntharda has become something of a training school for new healers to learn their craft, and I've been indirectly forced to take on the role of an instructor for them. I suspect this is some manner of dual-conspiracy by the royals in Maldobar and Luntharda. I've worked as a healer in both kingdoms for a great many years. Now, I suppose, they want to expand the knowledge and methods I've developed to open more clinics like mine." Kiran puffed a heavy sigh, as though the thought alone was exhausting. "A good idea, but I've neither the time nor the space for it—my clinic is small and I'm frequently called away to personally handle medical emergencies in the royal households."

"And by 'members of the royal household' I take it you're talking about Queen Jenna?" Garnett asked, her bemused smile sobering some. "And the new prince, of course."

Kiran suddenly shot her an alarmed glare. "How do you know of this?"

She tipped her head to the side a little. "We've got eyes in the castle. We've got eyes everywhere, though. Don't take it personally."

His mouth pinched up furiously as he stared her down. Finally, he licked his teeth behind his lips and panned his focus back to my hand. "Yes. Well. That information wasn't meant to be made public. I hope you'll offer her majesty some mercy and discretion."

Garnett sat up straight in her chair, all traces of humor and teasing gone from her soft features. "Of course! Stones, after what that poor woman went through? Arlan immediately restricted that information as soon as it was brought to him. It won't be circulated beyond the highest tier of his informants—Violet, Howlan, and myself."

Kiran didn't comment, although his severe, scowling expression suggested maybe he wasn't buying that. He avoided looking her way again as he felt each of my knuckles and moved my fingers around like he was testing to see if anything was broken. I tried not to cringe whenever he found a tender spot, but under the table I curled my toes up in my boots. Now was not the time to look like a big baby. Not while Garnett was sitting there.

I'd already cried in front of her once. No way was I doing it again. Especially not twice in the same day.

After probing around my hand, twisting my fingers back and forth, and kneading the joints of my knuckles, Kiran finally let me go and gave a satisfied nod. "Seems you've only bruised it. Nothing to be worried about."

"Oh, uh, thank you." I forced a smile and quickly pulled my arm off the table. "So, um, where is everyone else?"

"Jae took that dear girl, Phoebe, with him to the city—he said something about using a forge or workshop to finish her project?" Ms. Lin said as she stirred a large iron pot of rich vegetable stew.

Even from across the room, the aroma of the slowly roasted onions, potatoes, beans, peppers, and spices all stirred together in a thick, creamy broth made my stomach twist and ache like it might cave in at any moment. It'd been a while since I'd stopped to eat anything, and I was quickly becoming a fan of Ms. Lin's hearty cooking. She'd made small loaves of the dark bread stuffed with thinly diced lamb and herbs baked into the center. They steamed where they sat cooling in a basket in the middle of the table, taunting me like little pockets of delicious perfection.

"The rest are off making their own preparations, I suppose," Ms. Lin continued as she handed her spoon off to Jondar and began pulling out old clay dishware from one of the shelves. The toddler on her hip cooed and shrieked, fussing as she wiped each dish off before placing it on the table. When the child flailed again, Ms. Lin stumbled and nearly dropped one of the bowls.

Without a word, Kiran stood and stepped quickly over to her, unwrapping the thick sash that held the little boy against her. He took the squirming toddler and gave Ms. Lin a small nod before carrying him off down the hall toward the front sitting room. The toddler babbled excitedly, holding fistfuls of Kiran's long silvery white hair. But if it bothered the older Gray elf man, it never showed. In fact, he looked weirdly content as he strode away, talking quietly to the child in the elven language.

Their voices faded into the next room, leaving Ms. Lin standing there with a blank look of shock, still holding her empty sash. Her cheeks shone as pink as ripe strawberries and her mouth hung open a little, staring after him even long after he'd gone. Finally, she snapped her mouth shut and whirled around, ducking her head as she began busily wiping dishes again.

Interesting. She didn't ... I mean, they weren't ... you know, like *that* ... were they?

I glanced over at Garnett and found her grinning wolfishly again, as though she were savoring every second of their exchange. When our eyes met from across the table, she winked one of her lavender eyes.

Whoa—did that mean? Was I right? Ms. Lin and Kiran were ... ?

There wasn't time to work it out. As the dinner table before me filled with dishes, food, and lit candles, more and more people wandered in to see what smelled so good. Eventually, all of Ms. Lin's adopted children, Kiran, Judan, and Isandri made their way to chairs around the table with Garnett and me. Only Phoebe, Jaevid, and Murdoc were absent as we all settled in. Well, and Reigh, too, of course.

I couldn't stop from staring at the empty chair next to me where Murdoc probably would've sat. Guilt and quiet anger still churned in my brain. Where did he go? Was he just off sulking somewhere? Brooding on the rooftop?

Or had he left altogether?

Part of me wanted to go look for him, maybe even yell at him if I actually managed to find him. But I couldn't bring myself to move from my chair because another part of me didn't want to see him at all. That feeling still smoldered deep in my chest like a quiet ember, angry and sparking.

I kept my head down and stayed quiet through dinner, listening to the others going over plans for tomorrow with Garnett. Sometimes they branched off to other topics—like what things were like in the Gray elven kingdom of Luntharda, or where Garnett had traveled before coming to Maldobar. It kept things lively and relaxed.

And once again, I found myself wondering what my father would've thought about all this—about me sitting at a table with a prince, a dwarf, a Lunostri priestess, a couple of Broadfeather relatives, and former Tibrans. Somehow, I doubted he would have believed a word of it. It seemed a little too bizarre to be true, even to me, especially when Jaevid and Phoebe returned and took their seats.

No. Father probably wouldn't have believed any of this. But here I was, staring around at all of them, wondering for the thousandth time why I'd been chosen to have a seat at this table. Why was I chosen to be Ishaleon? Why was I chosen to be a dragonrider? Why was I chosen to be of any importance at all?

I still had no answers for any of those questions. But the minutes were ticking down. There wasn't much time left to prepare. Tomorrow, we'd try to catch Phillip and break Devana's hold over him.

I just prayed I could muster some more of that divine power to help us before it was too late.

CHAPTER NINETEEN

Standing alone beside Fornax, I checked my saddle over one last time. I ran my hand over the sword belted at my hip—the xiphos Murdoc had given me. It'd been almost a full day since our exchange in the barn, and I still hadn't seen him even once. That tingle of panic in my gut grew stronger with each passing hour, wondering if he'd really just left me, er, *us* behind. No one else said a single word about him, either. Surely Jaevid would tell me if Murdoc decided to go, wouldn't he? Or someone would have at least mentioned it in passing?

I didn't know. And the longer it went on like that, the harder it was to focus. I could've sworn my bruised knuckles throbbed more whenever I caught myself looking around for some sign of him. Gods and Fates, where was Murdoc?

I glanced back at the old farmhouse. Warm golden light glowed from many of the windows. Inside, Kiran was still taking care of Reigh and working with Ms. Lin and Jondar to prepare the house in case we returned with severe injuries. Everyone else had already departed, though.

Now it was my turn.

I'd just climbed up into the saddle and pulled my goggles down over my eyes when Jaevid came striding over, dressed out in battle armor with his long, blue dragonrider cloak licking at his boot heels. He'd probably come to give me a final pep talk, but I couldn't take it anymore.

"Where is he?" I demanded.

I sort of doubted I needed to specify whom I was asking about.

Jaevid's already tense expression creased with a solemn frown as he stared up at me. "Thatcher, now really isn't the time to—"

"Just tell me," I snapped. "I deserve to know. Did he leave? Did he go back to the Ulfrangar? Or just run away again?"

His jawline hardened and he took a step back, giving us room for takeoff. "He's in the city, making his own preparations for tonight. We all agreed that having him here made this place more of a target for the Ulfrangar, which we cannot risk considering who else is staying at this house. He'll rejoin us once it's over ... unless, of course, we decide we'd rather not have him with our company any longer. But that choice is not mine to make."

I swallowed hard. Was he asking me whether or not I wanted to send Murdoc away? My brain scrambled at that thought. Why was that my decision? I wasn't the leader of this group—company—whatever we were. Reigh was the one in charge, wasn't he? He'd been chosen to lead the Queen's Hunters, not me! Letting Murdoc stay with us was his choice.

Sooo ... why was Jaevid still looking at me like he was silently willing me to hurry up and make up my mind?

Ugh. I hated it—I hated that expectant look on his face. Something about it made me feel like a bratty little kid about to be scolded. Or like I'd done something to disappoint him and he was waiting for me to apologize.

"You think I should just forgive him? Pretend like it never happened?" I muttered bitterly.

Jaevid shook his head. "I'm not going to tell you what to do one way or the other, Thatcher."

"Why not? You seem to really like giving people advice about this kind of thing. Why not now?"

He shot me an ominous glare. "Because *my* father wasn't the one who died that night, *boy*. And my opinion about this is biased because I've already known one former Ulfrangar who seized his second chance at life and became one of the finest men I've ever known. So, I can't look at Murdoc without seeing that same scenario and wanting him to succeed. And quite honestly, I think there's a bit of blame on your side, too."

"*My* side?" I balked. "How is any of this my fault?!"

"You knew what he was. Murdoc told you himself he's done terrible things and murdered people under the command of the Ulfrangar. Surely by now, you had also put it together that, on the night you two met in Thornbend, he'd come there under their orders and killed people before he found you. Either you've been intentionally ignoring the possibility that he might've been involved in your father's death, or you've chosen now to suddenly be upset because he's confessed it to you. Regardless, no one—not even Murdoc—knows for sure if he was actually present when your father was murdered." Jaevid crossed his arms and scowled dangerously. "Right now, Murdoc is standing at a crossroads, and his position is far more precarious than maybe you realize. Behind him lies his old life and everything he's ever known, but his choices of where he can go from here are limited. He can continue to choose to become something better, but only if he's also willing to face the repercussions of what he was before. That was why I insisted he tell you about your father—because I've seen firsthand how secrets like that can eat away at a person's soul. And Murdoc is carrying enough guilt already. He can't continue down this path unless he's willing to face some of these ugly truths and finally let them go. But, Thatcher, it's your choice what you are going to do with this information now. Forgive him or don't. Just be sure it's a choice you can live with."

I glared back at him, my heart thundering in my ears as I bit back anger that crackled over my tongue like hot cinders. But I couldn't decide if it was anger at him ... or at myself. What he said made sense. And he was probably right about me not acknowledging the fact that Murdoc was somehow involved in my father's death sooner. I'd never stopped to think about it that hard because, well, remembering that night at all was agony.

Now, I sort of wished I had.

Jaevid's shoulders dropped some as he rubbed the bridge of his nose before finally looking up at me again. "We can continue this later. Right now, let's try to focus on the mission at hand. Ride hard. Keep to the plan. I have every confidence in you." He gave me a thumb's up as he took another step away from my dragon's side.

I couldn't look at him again as I leaned down to grip the saddle handles. He had every confidence, sure. But it felt like someone had punched a big hole right through the center of my chest.

Everyone was counting on me for this to work. I couldn't mess it up. I couldn't let more people get hurt. We had to catch Phillip, and this might be our only shot.

Shutting my eyes tightly, I tried to focus on the feel of my dragon shifting beneath the saddle where I sat. His powerful shoulders flexed as he spread his wings. His sides swelled against my legs with every breath he took. Fornax was still with me. I wasn't alone. I ... I could do this.

We would do it.

Opening my eyes, I gave the saddle handles a twist and leaned down closer to his neck. Fornax kicked away from the earth with a mighty roar and rush of wind off his wings. Together, we charged across the horizon toward the city of Dayrise. The sun had already begun to set, sinking slowly beyond the distant mountain peaks. Not long now.

And no turning back.

"Okay, big guy," I gasped shakily. "Let's show Devana what we're really made of."

He gave another low, booming cry in response and pumped his wings harder. We zoomed low, skimming only a few hundred feet off the ground straight for the city center. Phillip was hiding somewhere down there, waiting for me to step back out into the open again.

But I was about to give him more than he ever bargained for.

FORNAX and I did about ten low passes over the city, flying slowly enough that people on the ground got a good look, and making enough racket that we definitely got noticed. On our last lap, Fornax circled back to the broad city square where we'd last faced Phillip. A few workers and city folk still clearing debris and repairing the damaged buildings scattered at the sight of us. They cleared a path for my big orange dragon as he flared his wings and stretched out his hind legs, landing as smoothly as a swan on a pond right next to the fountain in the center.

As soon as Fornax lowered himself to the ground, I hurried through climbing out of the saddle and scrambling off his back. I gave his side a pat before I pulled my goggles down around my neck. "Good job, buddy. Now, be good for a little while, okay? Vexi will be here soon to help you find us. Just sit tight for a few minutes."

His ears perked at the sound of my voice, and he made a low whining, murring sound as he pushed his snout against my chest.

"I know," I whispered as I gave his bony brow one last rub. "I'm nervous, too. But we don't have a choice. So let's just do the best we can, okay?"

He whined again, his ears slicking back and his nostrils flaring with a big snort, as though he wasn't convinced in the least that our insane plan would work.

Stepping back from him, I reached for the hood of my cloak and pulled it over my head. A few of the city folk had begun to wander over, whispering and staring at me as though I were an invader. I guess simply arriving on a dragon didn't make me all that trustworthy anymore. Fair enough. Last time we'd been here, he had burned down the block, after all.

I let my hand rest on the pommel of my blade as I walked quickly across the square, keeping my head down and ducking along one of the side streets that had already been cleared of debris. I turned down the first alley and started at a speedy pace for the next small intersection. The gathering dusk draped every narrow avenue and alleyway in heavy shadows, and the farther I walked, the fewer people I saw. But Judan had advised me that this was a very indirect way to the docks. I wouldn't see many people moving around this part of town at night—well, apart from pickpockets, thieves, and hopefully one giant beastly man who had seen my not-so-discreet landing earlier.

The farther I went, the darker it became as the sun finally set. Chilly wind blew in from the harbor, bringing with it a thick curling fog that swirled in my wake as I sped along another narrow side street. It'd been more than ten minutes since I'd last seen another person. The windows of all the buildings I passed were dark, and their doors shut tight for the night. Now and then, I heard the distant sound of voices calling or laughing, a bottle breaking, or the bark of a dog. But there wasn't a soul anywhere in sight.

I set my jaw. *Come on, Phillip.* Gods, where was he? This had to look like his golden opportunity. I was alone in the dark, making my way through a dodgy side of town. What more could he possibly want unless I went ahead and tied myself up for him?

As I ducked sideways down another narrow, trash-strewn street, the sudden, soft *thud* of something landing in the road behind me made me lurch to a halt. My breath caught. A rush of terror poured over my body like a bucket of cold water as a soft growl rumbled in the dark at my back.

Then I remembered: if our plan wasn't working and Phillip didn't make his move, Isandri was supposed to come find me.

I cursed under my breath and turned around. "Come on, it hasn't been that long ye—"

I froze.

Standing before me on six powerful legs, less than ten feet away, was a creature I didn't have a name for. The creature was every bit as big as Isandri in her feline form, and even looked a little like a large cat, but its wide white eyes glowed like bog fires in the gloom with pure malice. All four of its front shoulders flexed, muscles rippling under a thin hide of sparse coal-black fur as it prowled closer. Its thin legs and bony, angular body was so gaunt it looked almost skeletal, and a jagged row of black spines ran down its back all the way to the end of its long, whipping tail.

My heart hit the back of my throat, throttling the breath from my lungs as I stared at the monster. G-Gods ... what was that thing?!

Then another stepped from the dark right behind it, seeming to practically materialize out of nothing but the pure darkness. They hissed, tall pointed ears pinned back as they bared hundreds of shock-white teeth as thin as fish bones.

I took a staggering step back, nearly tripping over my own feet and smacking into something solid.

A person standing right behind me.

"What do you think of my brothers?" A deep voice cackled right in my ear a second before a hand closed around my throat like the iron jaws of a vice. "They do so love the hunt. And tonight, you've made yourself easy prey. Foolish, boy."

My body went cold and numb. I couldn't even see him, but by now I knew his voice just as I knew that incredible, inhuman strength.

Phillip had found me.

20

CHAPTER TWENTY

Phillip held me by my throat, squeezing so hard I thought my neck might break. I gasped and twisted, clawing at his hand while trying to keep my eyes on the two feline beasts that slowly prowled closer and closer to us. Their pupil-less eyes blinked, tiny black noses sniffing as their mouths gaped hungrily. Each one must have stood nearly five feet to the head, with massive paws tipped in jagged curled claws.

"The Tibrans called them switchbeasts. It was their venom that made me into this. Their power became mine. Their instincts and senses are now fused into my body. I hunt as they do, think as they do." Phillip's deep voice chuckled. "Do they frighten you?"

One of the monsters came close enough to sniff at me, flicking out a long, forked black tongue as though tasting the air like a snake.

I held still, my vision going gray as I struggled for even one tiny breath of air. Gods—was he going to feed me to them? No! I wasn't going down like this. Not without a fight.

With a sudden, desperate flail, I managed to suck in a small gulp of air. My vision cleared, and I reached for my blade. But the instant my fingers wrapped around the hilt, the beast before me hissed again, baring all those needle-like teeth as it coiled back.

"Oh, I wouldn't do that," he warned, his grip on my throat tightening. "One tiny puncture of those teeth and you'll be joining my little family here. It only takes a few drops of their venom coursing through your veins and you become one of them—one of us—forever."

I slowly let go of the hilt and held still again. My lungs spasmed and burned. Air ... I-I needed air!

"That's better. Don't worry, little godling," Phillip mused. "You're to be delivered whole and unspoiled. For now."

"P-Phillip," I managed to wheeze out weakly. "Please ... stop this. Jenna sent m-me to—"

A sudden, sharp pain on the back of my head made my body go limp. I sagged in his grip as the world seemed to spin wildly. Then it all faded to complete darkness. Oh Gods. Had he stabbed me? Broken my neck? Was this the end?

Was I ... dying?

No. That wasn't it. I could still hear the faint sounds of footsteps and the rush of the wind—even before my vision slowly began to fade back into focus. My whole head ached like, well, like someone very strong had just whacked me hard enough to knock me out.

Which is exactly what Phillip had done, I guess.

I hung limp, dangling over his huge, powerful shoulder like a sack of potatoes, and flopped around with the jostling of his inhumanly fast gait. It was enough to shake me awake, though. My head throbbed, but I didn't dare groan or make a sound. I set my jaw and tried to focus. This was it. I couldn't lose it now.

Calm—I had to stay calm. This was all part of the plan and I needed to use my power again soon. Oh Fates, I just prayed I could. If Jaevid and the others weren't able to pin Phillip down long enough to break Devana's hold on him, I might be the only one who could.

Hanging over Phillip's shoulder while he ran, I couldn't tell much about where we were going. He moved fast, leaping through the night on his bizarre bare feet, and I didn't see any sign of the other two monsters anywhere. My pulse pounded at the thought of those creatures—switchbeasts, he'd called them. We hadn't planned on going up against anything like that. And now I had no way of warning the others. Phillip had always acted alone before. Sure, I couldn't see those monsters now, but that didn't mean they weren't somewhere close by, following from the shadows.

This was definitely going to complicate things.

The street rushed by along with the shadowed silhouettes of buildings standing against a starlit sky. The smell of the sea filled my nose more strongly with every breath, and the faint rumble and rush of the surf seemed to come from everywhere at once. We were getting close. Not much longer now.

Garnett had explained that her informants spotted him using one of the tunnel entrances on the cliffs by the coastline—one that was a bit more hidden, difficult to get to, but still in close proximity to the city so he could monitor our movements easily. So far, it looked like they were right.

Phillip darted as fast and nimble as a stag as he made his way down a twisting path that led along the steep cliff face. Hanging there over his shoulder like that, I got a horrifying view of the massive rock face that plummeted from the top of the plateau down to the churning black ocean far below. It took everything I had not to yell and flail. But any sudden moves might throw him off balance and send us both plummeting to the frigid, foaming ocean depths.

I squeezed my eyes shut, clenched my teeth, and waited for it to be over. Hang on. Just a bit longer. I could do this. Come on, divine power, don't fail me now.

Minutes passed like an eternity, and at last Phillip's pace slowed to a walk. Then he stopped. The cold, misty sea wind blasted us both, but even dressed in his sparse, tattered rags, Phillip didn't shiver. He didn't seem fazed by it.

He was focused on something dead ahead.

Phillip stood, totally motionless except for his fast, panting breaths. My mind whirled like a cyclone. What was he doing? Why had he stopped? Were we at the tunnel? Draped over his shoulder like that, I couldn't see what lay ahead.

Then he dropped me.

WHACK—I hit the ground like a newborn foal and lay there, groaning as I tried to get up. A big, paw-like foot crushed down onto my chest suddenly, pinning me to the ground. I wheezed and shakily lifted my head, squinting ahead at the entrance to a large sea cave that loomed before us like a gaping maw.

Phillip was staring that way, too. He hadn't moved a muscle except to pin me under his giant foot. His expression slowly drew into a vicious snarl. He bared his teeth like an animal, nose wrinkled and lips curled, as he leered straight ahead with his eerie platinum-colored eyes. But he wasn't looking at the cave.

He was looking at the man standing in front of it.

Jaevid Broadfeather already held his scimitar in one hand as he stared back at us. The fierce wind teased through his shaggy ash-colored hair and rippled the lengths of his long blue cloak. His sharp features stayed hauntingly calm, even when the two switchbeasts emerged from the shadows again to stand on either side of Phillip.

"This has to stop," Jaevid said, his tone surprisingly gentle. "You have to remember who you really are, Phillip. And this time, I can't help you—not like before. You have to do this on your own. You have to do it for *her*."

One of Phillip's eerie silver eyes twitched.

"Jenna needs you."

Both of Phillip's eyes went wide then. His jawline went solid and tense, and his hands clenched into shaking fists at his sides that made all the thick muscles of his arms and back ripple under stone-gray skin. His whole body seemed to quake as he lowered his head, body flexing hard under every slow, forceful breath.

Was he ... trying to resist Devana's hold on him? Could he even fight it on his own? Or was she trying to break his mind already?

I glanced between him and Jaevid, not daring to move or make a sound.

Then, Phillip's powerful form relaxed. "*You don't speak for Paligno anymore. You have no power over me, mortal,*" he snickered—but the voice that left his lips wasn't his. It didn't sound like him at all. It sounded feminine and light ... almost *childish*. Like the spiteful tone of a rebellious little girl instead of a huge, beastly man.

He slowly lifted his head, revealing the vicious sneer that curled across his lips. He flexed his claw-tipped fingers and took a threatening step closer, his eyes now glowing an ethereal shade of blue.

My stomach dropped. My pulse skipped and stalled. Gods and fates, why did that smile look so familiar?

There wasn't time to figure it out.

Jaevid's expression cooled. His gaze narrowed ominously, and his grip on his scimitar tightened. "You're right. I don't speak for Paligno any longer," he agreed. "But I think you'll find I still hold my own well enough, even as a mortal."

I sucked in a breath, every muscle drawing tense with a fresh wave of adrenaline that hit me like a boiling tidal wave. Jaevid gave a subtle gesture with his hand—the dragonrider signal to attack.

And in an instant, the night filled with utter chaos.

A DOUBLE-HEADED hand axe howled through the night, flying straight for one of the switchbeasts out of nowhere. It caught the beast right in the haunches, cutting deep into its thin, grayish-black hide. The monster yowled and spun, but didn't make it a single step before the second axe whizzed by and lodged right in the middle of the ugly creature's head. It hit the ground with a smack and didn't even twitch—dead before it ever touched the ground.

Somewhere nearby, I heard Garnett give a whoop of victory.

But the second switchbeast was now on full alert.

The creature dove at Jaevid with a screeching yowl, and he immediately threw up a parry to block its snapping jaws. The twang of a bowstring hummed in the air as Judan stepped into view where he'd been hiding on a narrow ledge nearby. He nocked arrow after arrow in his ornate, Gray elven bow, striking the second switchbeast's side dead-on. Each one should've been a kill shot. But the monster whipped around, snarling up at him and letting out an ear-splitting screech of fury.

I saw it half a second before it happened.

The moonlight glimmered off the ghostly graphite hide of a third switchbeast, slinking along that same ledge, moving straight for him. It sprang like a grasshopper, all six of its long, sinewy legs working in unison, and smacked right into him. Judan let out a shout as he threw up his forearm to block the monster's snapping jaws.

I yelled in warning.

But it was too late.

The switchbeast sank its teeth into his arm at the wrist, all those needle-thin teeth punching through his leather armor like warm butter. He cried out as he tried to jerk back and lost his footing on the narrow ledge. Prince Judan fell, taking the switchbeast with him. They tumbled and rolled down the cliff face, probably fifty feet, and finally hit the ground nearby with a *THUD*.

I squirmed under Phillip's foot, fighting to wrench myself free. Judan—I had to get to Judan! He needed help!

Phillip's gaze snapped down to me, his face twisted into a look of pure rage. He stepped off my chest and reached down like he was going to snatch me up again. Or grab me by the throat. Either way, that wasn't going to happen.

Not this time.

I ripped my sword free of its sheath and made a desperate slash at his leg. He howled in pain, jerking away as the tip of my xiphos sliced in deep across his calf. Phillip staggered back and hissed, his eyes still glowing that eerie blue as he glared down at me. His long tail whipped as he slowly stood straight again, flexing his shoulders as his toothy snarl slowly morphed into another chilling smile.

As I scrambled to my feet, two more switchbeasts materialized from the shadowed ledges and crevices of the cliff side. They prowled in, flanking me on both sides as sounds of Jaevid shouting out orders, Murdoc answering, Judan crying out in pain, and the slashing of blades filled the night. Jaevid had managed to force the beast he still fought away from the entrance to the cavern, and Garnett was ripping her hand axes free of the first one to begin another assault.

This was it—my chance.

Gripping my sword tightly, I leveled what I hoped was a challenging glare at Phillip and growled, "You want to take me to Devana? Then you're gonna have to catch me first." And I whipped around and ran full steam toward the open entrance of the sea cave.

Pumping my legs as fast as possible, I darted into the cavern. The darkness immediately engulfed me, as though a giant whale had just swallowed me whole. I couldn't see anything—but I didn't dare stop.

Behind me, Phillip let out a booming roar of frustration. He'd come after me. But with his leg now crippled some, he wouldn't be able to move as fast as before.

Or so I hoped.

The faintest glimmer of something metal on the floor caught my eye as I ran headlong through the tunnel. I sprinted past it, but didn't stop. Faster—I had to go faster! My head swam, eyes wide but seeing nothing in the dark.

Then I heard it:

TWANG—SNAP-SNAP-SNAP!

A metallic sound pierced the thick gloom, followed by a screeching yowl and frantic, manic roar.

I skidded to a halt and whirled around, just in time to see the crystal at the top of Isandri's staff light up the darkness like a star. She and Phoebe stepped from their hiding places on either side of the tunnel, not saying a word as they watched. The brilliant sterling light filled the air and revealed Phillip writhing on the ground between them. He was completely ensnared in a net of thick, golden metal cables that wrapped around his body like a fly caught in a spider's web. Each cable was attached to what looked like three large bear traps covered in tiny, gleaming runes. One had clamped down onto his foot, while the other two were locked onto his shoulder and side.

He bellowed and fought, but every time he twisted against the bonds, the cables around him would tighten even more. The more he struggled, the harder they held. Gods and Fates—we'd done it!

I dared to hope, but one glance at Phoebe's haunted face made my heart sink and my gut clench. This wasn't going to hold him for long.

I had to act now.

"Stand back!" I shouted over Phillip's roaring as I rushed back over, still gripping my sword. Looking down at him, my head spun as I tried to focus. My heartbeat clashed in my ears. I-I didn't know what to do. I didn't know how to use my power. And even if I did, would it help him? A magical shield wasn't going to fix anything. What could a God of Mercy possibly do to help him?

"Devana!" Isandri stepped to my side suddenly, calling out over his rumbling cries. "Devana, listen to me! It is Adiana—and I have come here with Ishaleon. Please, you must let this man go!"

His struggling stopped.

Silence fell over us, filled only by his deep panting breaths.

Then he laughed. It started as a light chuckle, and grew until he was cackling like a maniac on the ground. "*Well, well, look what we have here. Both my darling siblings have come to pay me a visit. So kind of you. And so stupid,*" the soft, female's voice hissed from his mouth again as he stared up at us, his eyes glowing chilling blue. "*I only wanted one of you. But, you know, I think I like this even better. So let's play a little game, shall we? It's quite simple. The rules are: You two do exactly as I say, and maybe I won't scramble this big lummox's brains into mush! You all seem to care an awful lot about him—not that I'd expect any less. You always were a sap for a bad-luck case, weren't you, Ishaleon? And this fellow's had all the worst of it—luck, that is. Just your type! But you'd better play along nicely, little brother. I'd hate to have to leave him a drooling lump for the rest of his life because you tried to be clever.*"

Isandri stiffened beside me, her expression like cold steel in the light of her staff's crystal. Her throat moved as she swallowed hard, jawline going rigid, and brows drawing into a look of wild confusion. "This isn't right," she whispered faintly. "Thatcher, this ... doesn't feel like her. That isn't her voice."

What? This wasn't Devana? But ... but it had to be. She was using divine magic to control Phillip—to brainwash him—and had just threatened to do the same thing she'd done to the Tibran officers. It *had* to be her.

Didn't it?

Oh, Gods and Fates, what if it wasn't?

The eerie blue light in Phillip's eyes dimmed. His entire, heavily muscled body went rigid in his bonds, hands clenching at his sides and face contorting with a look of twisted agony. It only lasted a second or two. Long enough for him to scream out one desperate, garbled word: "*JENNA!*"

Phoebe gasped, flinching back and covering her mouth with her hand as tears welled in her eyes.

I bit down fiercely, watching as a crazed smile curled over his lips returned to his features and the blue glow rekindled in his eyes. "*Now, then, do you see? I could break him so easily. He'd sing a lovely tune while I tore his feeble mind to shreds. So, let's play. Release my faithful pet immediately. We've so much to do!*"

CHAPTER TWENTY-ONE

"*NO!*" The word tore from my throat, and I was helpless to stop it. Heat like the molten depths of a roaring forge filled my chest, swelling and growing with every breath. My pulse slowed and seemed to stop altogether, leaving behind a strange, tranquil silence in my mind. My palm tingled and buzzed as snapping, crackling tongues of golden energy sizzled between my fingers—as though I'd grabbed a fistful of pure lightning.

I stepped forward, stretching out a hand to him with all my fingers spread wide. Immediately, all the heavy cables that held Phillip began to radiate golden light that filled the dark of the cave like a tangled knot of raw power. He cried out, body shaking and skin shining with a fresh sheen of sweat as the blue light in his eyes glowed brighter and brighter.

On either side of me, Isandri and Phoebe gasped and moved away. They watched me with gaping stares as I strode toward Phillip, the palm of my outstretched hand thrumming and pulsing with power. Phoebe's mouth moved, maybe calling out my name, but I couldn't hear it. I couldn't hear anything in that silence.

I wasn't scared, though. Something about it felt ... safe. Comfortable. Familiar. Right.

I walked calmly to stand right beside Phillip's head, my hand still outstretched to him. Looking down at him, a sense of knowing rose up from that warm center in my chest. It buzzed through every muscle and shivered up and down my spine. He convulsed again, the cords around him crackling with power.

"*Ishaleon!*" The female voice hissed in my head, echoing like the ragged edge of a torn and tattered memory. "*You dare challenge me?*"

I slowly got down on one knee, my open hand hovering right over his face. "Either you leave him now of your own free will," I warned in a low growl, "or I will drag you out by force."

Phillip's expression twisted—half agony and half that mad, laughing grin. "*Hah! Such *arrogance from mother's favorite sniveling little whelp! Why don't you make me, little brother? Let's see if you can save him before I rend every last shred of thought and memory from his mind."*

I narrowed my eyes. "So be it."

Tears leaked from the corners of Phillip's eyes as the light in them dimmed again. His expression contorted in confused agony, body shaking so violently he couldn't even speak.

He didn't need to, though.

I could see it in my mind—the powerful presence that had invaded his consciousness and twisted around his every thought like a poisonous briar. I could feel his emotions, caught between terror and a force that shook me down to the marrow. Not divine power or that invading presence, though. This was something else. Something stronger. Something that, as soon as I placed my hand on his forehead, latched onto my presence and clung to it like someone gripping a raft in a stormy sea.

Love.

The image of a familiar face filled my mind; a young woman with hair like bolts of wavy golden silk and eyes of stormy blue. She smiled warmly, the warm sunlight on her face and the wind stirring in her hair as she looked up at me—at *him*—and reached out like she was going to touch his face. And that feeling swelled, making my lips part and my eyes roll closed.

Queen Jenna.

His love for her hit my brain like someone tossing a bucket of dragon venom on a fire. It roared in my veins and sent a surge of power through my touch. Pushing and pulling, I used that rush of energy and strength to latch onto the invading presence that tried to tear at the seams of his thoughts. It tried to choke out his memories and splinter his sanity.

I set my jaw. My lungs burned with every breath. Sweat ran down the bridge of my nose and my hand shook against his forehead. No way was I letting that happen. I wouldn't give up. He would see Jenna again. I'd make sure of it.

A steady hand came to rest on my shoulder, and I didn't even need to look to see whom it was. I felt Isandri's presence like a cool breeze at my back. Her power kindled my own, twisting and mingling as it shivered through my body and all the way down my arm.

Phillip's body went completely stiff, his mouth open like he was trying to scream. But no sound left his throat.

The invading presence in his mind cracked like a porcelain bowl smashing on a stone floor.

All those grasping thorny briars suddenly burst into fine blue mist as I snatched my hand back, wheezing and stumbling. Isandri caught me by the shoulders, holding me steady as we both stared straight ahead ... at *her*.

With her feet planted on either side of Phillip and her shoulders hunched angrily, the wavering image of a little girl in an oversized tunic and leggings glared back at us. Her flickering form filled the cave with brilliant sapphire light, translucent like a ghostly reflection. She didn't look any older than ten or eleven, with hair bobbed at her chin and wide eyes shining like stars.

"*I see you like to cheat! Taking outside help like that—pfft. Pathetic. But two can play that way.*" She wrinkled her nose in a huff and tipped her chin up proudly as she crossed her arms. "*I've got lots of other new friends and pets far better than this one. Just wait till you meet them all, little brother. What fun we'll have!*"

My stomach dropped. Other friends? Other pets? What did that mean? Had this person—whoever she was—taken more people captive? Gods and Fates, who was this girl? Why was she doing this?!

I didn't get a chance to ask. With a giggle, she flipped her hair and gave a teasing wink. Her form burst into a shining blue mist that quickly faded away, leaving nothing behind but the haunting echo of her laugh ringing through the dark cavern.

"T-Thatcher?" Phoebe whimpered as she took cautious steps toward Phillip. "Is he ... ?"

Oh, gods, I'd nearly forgotten.

Phillip didn't move as I crouched back down next to him. He lay limp on the cavern floor, still bound up in the enchanted traps and cables Phoebe had crafted. I put my hand on his chest and let out a ragged sigh of relief as I felt it rise and fall. Alive—he was still alive. "He's all right. Quick, let's get this off him. We need to get out of here."

Phoebe hesitated, shifting her weight and glancing over Phillip with uncertainty before she finally hedged in closer. Not that I didn't get it—he was enormous already, and compared to someone so petite like her? Gods, he must have looked like an absolute monster.

But he wasn't under anyone's control now. And Jaevid had said he was a good person before. I had to believe that.

Phoebe pulled a tiny gold key from her belt and fit it into each of the traps. A soft *click* and the runes engraved on them went dark. The jaws released, and one by one, they clattered to the stone floor. The cables wrapped around him went slack. He lay between us, bloodied and bruised, but alive.

Alive and free.

"Phillip?" I asked, patting his cheek some to try and rouse him. "Can you hear me? Duke Phillip?"

No response.

Uh oh. Well, this meant we had to drag him out. Not ideal, since he was enormous. But maybe with Isandri's feline form we could somehow—

The cavern shuddered around us, quaking and nearly knocking me off my feet. From somewhere far away in the dark, a sound rumbled in the deep. Deep, low, and loud enough to shake bits of rock off the ceiling.

Merciful Fates, was that ... a roar?

All the color drained from Phoebe's face. My heart froze in my chest. Isandri's expression went slack with alarm.

Yep. Time to go.

"Go, go, go!" I shouted as I seized Phillip under one of his arms. Isandri hefted the other one, and together we dragged him down the tunnel toward the distant glow of starlight at the entrance.

The cavern shuddered again, sending another shower of rocks and dust over us. I stumbled again, and barely managed to catch myself against the cavern wall without dropping Phillip.

"What is that?!" Isandri yelled, her eyes wide and panicked.

I didn't know, of course. But I was willing to make a guess that it was big, terrible, and probably wanted to hurt us. That seemed to be the trend lately, after all.

We shambled toward the mouth of the cavern, moving as fast as we could while lugging Phillip's weight along. But roughly fifty yards from the exit, another tremor knocked us to our knees. Phoebe cried out in alarm and ran back, trying to help us as hunks of rock smashed to the ground all around us.

All of a sudden, Phillip's eyes flew open. His catlike pupils narrowed to hair-thin slits. His huge form went solid and tense an instant before he landed in a crouch, long tail lashing and pointed ears perked to whatever was bellowing far down the cavern.

I kicked back across the ground, panic flooding my veins like ice water. Isandri held perfectly still, and Phoebe let out a little yelp of alarm before she stood, paralyzed in fear.

O-Oh, gods, was he ... really okay? Had we actually freed him? Oh Fates, what if I'd been wrong? What if he wasn't himself—or he didn't remember anything from before? Would he attack us?

Phillip's ears drooped and his mouth fell open in horror as recognition dawned on his bizarre features. Whatever was making that sound, he seemed to know what it was. And I guess he didn't like it anymore than we did.

He took one look around at all of us, shot to his feet, and yelled. "Don't just stand there—run!"

That was all the encouragement I needed. Isandri, too, apparently. We took off running behind him without a single hesitation. I seized Phoebe by the hand as we sprinted past and dragged her along. Together, we bolted for the exit with Phillip in the lead, leaping and bounding over the uneven floor like a massive lemur.

Less than twenty feet from the entrance, the cavern rocked with another tremor, shaking free a massive boulder that smashed into the ground right in front of me, missing crushing me to jelly by less than a foot. I let out a curse and Phoebe screamed. No time to stop, though. I hauled her around the huge rock to keep going, but Phillip appeared right in our path.

He took one look at us and immediately swept Phoebe up into his arms. She squeaked again, but didn't resist too much as he held her against his chest protectively. Then he gave me a look of wild-eyed panic and shouted over the noise, "Come on, kid—move your rear!"

We ran like mad, dodging falling boulders and squinting through the debris, all the way to the tunnel exit. Whatever was stirring down in the cavern, I had no idea what it might be. But I didn't want to be anywhere nearby when it finally broke the surface.

Not without my dragon, anyway.

PART THREE
MURDOC

CHAPTER TWENTY-TWO

Nowhere, in any of the hours of planning and preparation we'd done getting ready for this mission, had anyone said *anything* about switchbeasts. The Ulfrangar hadn't offered us much in the way of training in regard to how we should deal with them in a fight. Oh, except that they should be avoided at all costs. They had mentioned that briefly.

Watching the beasts scale the cliff sides like giant, feline-esque spiders, and leap forty feet in the blink of an eye—I was beginning to appreciate why. I was also becoming increasingly aware that we stood no chance whatsoever against this many of them. Sure, I'd managed to bring down a pair of them. And Garnett, despite having the temperament of a squirrel that'd been fed too much sugar, was lethal with her axes. She'd cut through three with a brutal efficiency I couldn't help but admire. If not for the perpetual happiness in the face of certain death, she might've made a good assassin.

But the giggling would've been an issue.

Jaevid was holding his own quite well—not that I expected any less of Maldobar's resident legendary hero. But Judan was down. We were spread thin. And every time we cut down one of those hellish monsters, it seemed like more would appear to take its place. We weren't going to hold out much longer. Not without some major reinforcements.

The narrow shelf where we fought was too small for a dragon Mavrik's size to land. He couldn't bathe it in flame because we'd get caught in the crossfire—literally. Fornax couldn't orient without Thatcher, and Vexi was occupied acting as his guide.

That only left one, suitably small, and annoyingly eager option.

Ugggh.

I sprang back, bracing for another assault from a switchbeast coiling to spring from the cliff before me. Its massive shoulders rolled, pumping in preparation to lunge. But as soon as it leapt out into the open air, a blur of black and red hit it with a gory smack. The young dragon bore the monster all the way to the ground, landing with it pinned beneath his hind legs like an eagle with a freshly caught mouse. One crunch of his mighty jaws and the shrieking, writhing switchbeast went limp.

Then he looked up at me, little ears perked and chirping musically as he glided over to crouch down right before me. Once again, he'd saved my life. And I ... I was running out of reasons to turn him away. With every battle, more of those inhibitions fell away. All my excuses sounded more and more pathetic—save for one. The most important one. The one I couldn't escape.

I was still a murderer.

And murderers didn't deserve to sit in a dragonrider's saddle.

I wiped the sweat from my brow on my sleeve before I prowled forward again, spinning my blades over my hands as two more switchbeasts slunk from the dark, jaws snapping and wide eyes focused squarely on me. The sight of the young dragon at my back made them pause, however. They recoiled, uncertain as he snarled and bristled, stamping his winged forelegs challengingly.

I flicked him a sideways glance. "I'm going after Judan. You got this?"

He slicked his little ears back, snapping his jaws, and gave a snort.

I took that as a yes.

With a burst of flame from his jaws aimed right at the two monsters, I broke to the left and made a headlong sprint to the base of the steep cliff face where Judan had fallen. He lay motionless; his body tangled up in that of the switchbeast that'd knocked him from his perch. I hadn't seen the fall itself, but the way he lay—still half pinned beneath the creature and crying out in agony—wasn't a good sign. He hadn't tried to push the monster off or get free.

Ten paces from his side, another switchbeast dropped from the dark, hissing and baring a maw bristling with a thousand needle-like teeth. It lunged to bite at his head, and I immediately ripped the dagger from the side of my boot and hurled it. The blade hummed through the air, glimmering in the night as it spun and lodged into the beast's head, right between its eyes.

It toppled sideways away from him and lay still, but I still kicked its corpse farther away as I slid to a halt at Judan's side.

He stared up at me, face ashen and lips blue, as he gulped in shallow breaths. His pupils were blown, and his hair and skin were drenched with sweat. Not good.

"Calm down, Judan. Try to slow your breathing. I've got you," I growled through my teeth as I seized the switchbeast lying over him by some of its legs and dragged it off. He gave another sharp, frantic scream of pain.

"M-My hand! Gods! It's got my hand!" he yelled desperately.

His hand? Why would that stop him from getting up? I checked his right one, but nothing about it looked abnormal. Granted, all of his skin was looking a little dusky now.

Then I checked his left.

A massive bite right through the soft flesh around his thumb and wrist had left behind hundreds of those tiny needle-like teeth. They stuck out of his skin like quills from a porcupine, white and hair-thin. But the skin around where they were embedded was ... Gods and Fates, it was hugely swollen and turning a sickly black.

What the—?

"I-It burns!" He screamed as I carefully lifted his wrist. Just that tiny movement made his back arch as he cried out, spine curling. He prayed in elven as I slowly and delicately turned it. The veins along his forearm were already turning black, making the skin around them look purplish, as though whatever venom was in those teeth was spreading fast.

My thoughts raced and scrambled. Should I try taking the teeth out? Would that make it worse? Curse it all, I wasn't a medic. I'd never had any training in healing. Gods —I didn't know!

"*JAEVID!*" I shouted at the top of my lungs.

He might not even hear me over the fray. But I didn't know who else to call for. It'd only been a few minutes, three or four at most since he'd been bitten, and Judan was already shaking as though he were going into shock. How long would he last like this?

On impulse, I reached to unfasten the strap that held his quiver against his back. I ripped the long, thin leather belt out of it and wrapped it around his wrist close to his hand. Bearing down as hard as I could, I used the point of my dagger to punch a new hole through the leather so that the belt would close and form a makeshift tourniquet. If there was venom in the bite, maybe this would slow the spread and buy him some time.

"Just hold on," I panted as I reached for his discarded bow and swiped an arrow from the quiver. I'd never spent much time refining my skills with a traditional Gray elven longbow. Ulfrangar preferred the ease and speed of a crossbow. But I needed a ranged weapon until reinforcements arrived.

"You've got to try to calm down," I said. "Control your breaths. Focus. You can do this —you're a scout. You've trained for worse than this, so concentrate."

He didn't answer. Lying with his face as pale as a corpse and his eyes wide and fixed, he gasped in shallow, fast puffs. Sweat ran in rivers down his face and neck.

He was fading fast.

Suddenly, a dark shape appeared right before us, moving so fast it practically materialized straight from the shadows. Six powerful legs. A long, whipping tail. Two massive, grapefruit sized eyes. A mouth full of teeth.

I raised the bow and took aim, but the switchbeast didn't retreat.

Out of the corner of my eye, I spotted another one stalking in on my right flank.

And then another on the left.

We were surrounded.

Too late, I realized ... it was already over.

PART of me knew that someday, probably sooner rather than later, I would meet a gruesome death in battle. I had just assumed that it would come at the hands and blades of the Ulfrangar after they'd finally hunted me down—not by being torn apart by a pack of hell-born Tibran monsters. I couldn't decide which was worse, honestly. But either way, I had no intention of going down quietly.

Taking aim at the switchbeast before me, I sucked in a breath and prepared to fire. One arrow to the center of the skull would bring it down, and at least I'd die knowing I'd taken one of these cursed creatures with me.

My finger sat poised on the arrow's shaft, and my pulse raced like mad. Once I let it loose, they'd attack. Nowhere to run. No way out. Just death by a thousand venom-laced needles and razor-sharp claws.

All of a sudden, the ground beneath me gave a violent shudder. It rattled and shook, making the loose stones dance and clatter across the ground around us. What the—an earthquake?!

The switchbeast before me rose up and screeched, pitching like mad. My hand slipped on the bow, sending the arrow flying wide and missing him entirely. Curse it!

The switchbeast squirmed and pawed the air, rearing onto its hind legs like a wild horse.

Wait—no. It wasn't rearing.

Something was picking it up.

I lowered the bow, and my mouth fell open as Phillip unfurled from a crouch and stood to his full height, gripping the beast by the scruff of the neck like a kitten and holding it off the ground. Looming before me like a vengeful demon king, Phillip turned his pointed ears back, bared his fang-like incisors, and let out a bone-rattling roar.

Immediately, all the switchbeasts froze in place. Their hissing and growling went silent. Even the one still dangling in his grip stopped struggling and hung there with its tail curled up between its legs. One by one, all of the monsters withdrew back into the darkness. Some of them retreated into the cavern. Others shuffled away back up the cliffsides.

At last, Phillip released the one in his hand. It hit the ground with a *thud* and quickly scurried away. Duke Phillip Derrick stood there, considering us with his eerie platinum eyes. Fear burrowed deep into my gut, twisting like a cold knife. If he attacked, I knew that would be the end. I'd faced him once already, and his strength and speed were too much. I stood no chance. He'd kill me and probably Judan, too.

But then his sharply chiseled features creased with worry. His powerful shoulders relaxed and dropped as he crouched down, looking Judan over. His gaze halted at the shoddy tourniquet I'd put on Judan's wrist and the bite on his hand. His vertical pupils widened.

Gods—they'd ... they'd actually done it. Thatcher and Isandri had actually managed to free him from Devana's mental hold.

"We need to get him to a healer," I said. "He's fading fast."

Phillip shook his head. "Not fading. Changing. I don't know if a healer can do anything about this. Their bite is what made me like this. It changes you from the inside out and turns you into one of them."

I swallowed, trying not to let my horror show. Gods, how was that even possible? "Is there anything we can do to stop it?"

Phillip didn't answer. Maybe he didn't know. But the look on his face—fractured and utterly anguished—didn't inspire much hope.

"D-Don't ... look at m-me ... like that, idiot," Judan gasped weakly, a faint smile tugging at his lips. "T-This is ... y-your fault, y-you know."

Phillip frowned and shut his eyes tightly. "I know, my friend. I—gods, I am so sorry."

Judan sat up a little, just long enough to seize the front of Phillip's tattered shirt with his good hand. He jerked the big man down closer, a bit of ferocity kindling in his glare as he growled through his teeth. "D-Don't ... you *ever* l-let her down like this again. You w-won her heart ... but if y-you break it ... I-I'll come back and b-break you!"

Phillip stared back at him, expression blank for a second or two, before somber realization settled over his strange features. He nodded once and looked away, mouth mashed into a skewed line, as though he were trying to keep his emotions in check.

Judan flopped back onto the ground with a ragged, broken groan. His body shook, still pouring sweat as he blinked owlishly up at the sky.

"Snap out of it and concentrate, Judan. You're not dying here," I urged, then I snapped a glare up at Phillip. "Where's Jaevid? Maybe we can—"

"Murdoc!" Phoebe's voice cried out. Looking up, I spotted her running over the scattered remains of switchbeasts with her mane of red curls flying. Thatcher, Garnett, Isandri, and Jaevid were right behind her.

"We gotta go! Right now!" Garnett shouted, "You felt that tremor, right? There's an underbeast headed this way!"

Great. Just freaking great.

"How long until it makes the surface?" I demanded as soon as they all staggered to a halt around us.

"Not ... sure." Garnett panted as she leaned over to rest her hands on her knees. "They're fast as anything underground, but it might not be able to track us on the surface at all. I don't know—but trust me, you do *not* want to fight one. We've gotta get out of here. Unless ... hmmm."

I stared at her, waiting for her to finish that thought.

"Can you have your little beastie bathe that tunnel entrance in a good bit of venom? As much as it can to block the entrance? The underbeasts despise the smell of it and, of course, the fire. It might deter it from coming any closer."

I flicked a glance over at the small drake—or beastie, as she so lovingly phrased it—and nodded. "I think so. He understands speech fairly well. Or at least, only when it's not direct orders to go away."

The drake gave an indignant snort.

"Okay!" Garnett bounded toward him. "This way, love. We need a bit of that fire."

While I turned my focus back to Judan, the dragon lumbered off with her toward the cavern's entrance, swishing his tail and swiveling his ears at her chattering. It didn't take her long to get the point across. Four or five deep breaths and sprays of acrid, burning venom coated the first hundred yards or so of the tunnel. Hopefully that would be enough to turn the underbeast.

Phoebe stepped closer, stretching out one of her small hands to touch my shoulder. "Are you all right?"

I turned my face away quickly, hoping none of them would see me flushing as I answered, "Fine. But Judan's been bitten."

Phoebe paled. "By a switchbeast? Oh, Fates! No!"

"Where?" Isandri demanded suddenly. She practically blurred the few feet between us and quickly crouched down next to me, close to Judan's side. Her vibrant yellow-green eyes darted over him, locking onto his hand and immediately lifting his arm to look at it carefully.

"Can you help him?" Phillip asked, considering her with obvious uncertainty. I guess he'd never seen a Lunostri elf until now.

Isandri's expression sharpened, her gaze like a razor's edge as she carefully turned his hand over. Every movement made him whimper through gritted teeth. "No," she said at last. Then she snapped a forceful gaze to Garnett as she returned to stand beside me. "But she can. The venom is spreading. We cannot delay. The only way to save him now is to remove it."

"Remove what?" Jaevid questioned.

Isandri's expression hardened as she carefully placed Judan's arm on the ground out away from his side. "The hand."

"You want to *cut off his hand*?" Jaevid protested, scowling and finally taking an assertive stride closer. "He's already been bitten, what good will that do? Isn't it too late?"

Isandri shot our resident god-slaying war hero a punishing glare. "Switchbeasts were brought here from Nar'Haleen—*my* homeland. I have seen such bites many times. It is true, after a certain time, there is nothing that can be done for a bite, but we have caught it early, and the tourniquet has slowed the spread of the venom. If it were possible to remove all the teeth, perhaps it would not be necessary. But there is no time, and even a tiny fragment of a tooth left behind would seal his fate. Either we remove the hand, or the venom will overtake him. In three day's time, he will either perish ... or be changed into a switchbeast himself."

A heavy silence fell over our group as we all stared down at Judan. There was no clean way to do it. If Isandri was right, though, we had minutes to get this done or his fate would be sealed.

Fine. So be it.

I held a hand out to Garnett. "Give me an axe."

The dwarven girl gaped at me. Then, reluctantly, she slipped one of her hand axes from her belt and passed it over. "You don't have to do this. My arm is stronger. I can do it in one swing," she offered.

"So can I," I countered. "And I need you to help hold him still. If he flinches, I might not get a clean cut straight through. Phillip, you help her, too. Make sure he doesn't move."

Phillip nodded and moved in closer, working with Garnett to pin Judan to the ground with his arm stretched out and held firmly in place.

I gripped the axe hard and took a few practice swipes through the air, testing the weight. It was small—made to fit Garnett's hand—but it'd been crafted of one piece of solid bronze and the edge was lethally sharp. It would do.

"Jaevid, be ready with some bandaging—a piece of cloth, anything we've got on hand. The tourniquet will help with controlling the bleeding, but we need to wrap it and get him back to Kiran as soon as possible once it's done."

I sucked in a breath, steeling myself before I glanced over at Thatcher. He was staring right at me, not saying anything, but I couldn't bring myself to look at him long enough to read his expression. "Call in the dragons. Mavrik is too big to land here, but Fornax might be able to manage it long enough to get Judan and another rider in the saddle."

Thatcher didn't answer, and a few seconds later, I heard the shrill call of his whistle. My stomach twisted and writhed, aching deep in my gut like I'd swallowed a mouthful of acid.

Thatcher didn't want me here. I didn't need any divine magic to be able to tell that much. He just didn't have the nerve to say it. That was fine, though. I'd told myself I would see this through—I'd help them complete this mission and get Phillip back. Then they'd have another good fighter working on their side. And I could grant his wish and go.

It was ... the right thing to do, even if Jaevid disagreed.

He'd already given me an earful about it. But my mind was set. I couldn't stay here with them any longer. My presence would continue to draw the Ulfrangar. Their attacks would intensify even further. Reigh had nearly died because of my presence in their little band of hunters, and now Thatcher had finally acknowledged the truth of what I really was.

I had no choice. I had to go.

First, though, I could bear this final burden for them. No one should have to cut off the hand of one of their comrades. But hurting people wasn't exactly a new concept for me.

"Hold him steady," I ordered, keeping my tone quiet and as calm as possible. Judan had already begun to struggle some—not that he could help it, I'm sure. Even if cutting his hand off would ultimately save his life, primal instinct would force his flight instinct. He'd want to get away. He'd want to resist.

We just couldn't allow him to.

Phoebe gasped quietly, turning away and sobbing into her hand as I aligned the hand axe and prepared for the swing. One stroke, fast and clean. Through-and-through. I couldn't miss or falter. To spare him any more suffering, I had to sever it in one hit.

I tightened my grip on the axe's padded leather handle. My pulse clashed in my ears as I set my jaw. Every shred of thought and reason in my brain told me to stop—don't do it—find some other way. Don't freaking do this!

Judan stared up at me, his face twitching as he shivered and his eyes wide but intense with focus. His jawline went rigid as he managed one, weak nod and growled through his teeth, "D-Do ... i-it."

I nodded back, held my breath, and swung down with all my strength.

23

CHAPTER TWENTY-THREE

Standing at the top of the cliff, my heart still pounding and my clothes damp with sweat after running up the treacherous path, I watched Thatcher sail away into the early dawn on the back of his orange dragon. We'd rushed up the cliff side as fast as possible with Phillip in the lead, carrying Judan on his back the entire way. Then it was a matter of getting Judan loaded onto the back of Thatcher's saddle and stable enough that they could take off—not an easy task when he was barely conscious and couldn't sit up on his own. But in the end, we'd managed to tether him securely to his seat. He would make it.

He had to.

I watched Fornax's silhouette fade in the distance. He seemed to melt into the field of twilight stars, heading toward the old farmhouse far on the outskirts of Dayrise. Mavrik took off right after him, carrying Jaevid and Garnett in that same direction. It wouldn't take them long to reach it.

Eventually, their thunderous wing beats faded to silence, and I was left standing alongside Isandri, Phillip, and Phoebe at the top of the cliff. The strong sea wind blasted at my back, stirring in my hair and blowing my bangs over my eyes. It chilled me to the marrow.

Or maybe that was just the crippling realization that my work was done.

Phillip was back safe, standing beside me like a tower of stone-gray muscle and otherworldly strangeness. His silver eyes tracked the movement of the two dragons as they skimmed low over the city. There was no mistaking the look of worry that drew his dark brow into a deep furrow and mashed his mouth into a thin, tight line.

"Judan was your friend?" I dared to guess as I looked away again.

"Yes," he replied quietly. "Since we were children. He, Aubren, and I, well, we practically grew up together."

I almost didn't ask. It wasn't any of my business. The affairs of royals, princes, and kingdoms were far beyond someone of my circumstances. But after the little chat I'd had with Judan in Port Marlowe, and hearing what he'd said to Phillip only minutes ago ... I couldn't help myself. "Before, when Judan talked about 'breaking her heart,' he was talking about Queen Jenna, wasn't he?"

Seconds passed, and Phillip didn't answer.

I stole another look up at him. The blasting sea wind blew through his lengthy black hair, teasing it around his monstrous form and nearly hiding his face altogether. His expression twisted, skewing with anguish as he shut his eyes tightly and bowed his head.

Phillip never replied. But he didn't need to. That look was enough. They'd loved the same woman—and Phillip must have been the one to ultimately win her affection in the end. I had to wonder if that'd come before or after he'd been turned into this beastly mutation of man and monster. That wasn't any of my business either, though. And I didn't dare to ask this time.

"Isandri, can you guide Phillip back to where we're taking refuge?" I murmured as I reached for the hood of my cloak and pulled it up.

"I can," she said, giving our newest companion a wary side-eyed look.

Not that I blamed her. It was hard not to flinch whenever he made a sudden move—probably because I'd been on the receiving end of some of his attacks before. I knew the strength in his hands and had felt the brunt of his uninhibited rage.

"Good. You should get moving. Kiran might want to consult you about Judan's care since you seem to know a great deal about switchbeasts," I reminded her. "You think he'll really pull through this?"

Her slender shoulders rose and fell in a small shrug. "I've never professed to be an expert at medical treatment. Switchbeast bites were not completely unheard of in the village where I lived as a young child—especially during the dry season when such animals became more desperate for food. But I would venture to say that he has a good chance at surviving now, yes. He's strong."

Well, that was good enough for me. "Watch your backs, then. And keep Phoebe between you as you go. She wanders ... and occasionally runs into things."

Phoebe immediately shot me a worried look with her soft, raindrop-blue eyes wide. "You're coming back with us, aren't you? Murdoc, please, you have to—"

"It's better if I don't. At least for now," I interrupted and turned away. I couldn't do this and look at her at the same time. She might see right through my lies and deflections, and I couldn't risk that. I didn't want this to turn into a scene right here in front of Isandri and Phillip. "Being there draws the focus of the Ulfrangar. It puts the rest of you in danger. It's better if I stay in the city, keep a low profile, and wait until you're ready to mount a strike against Devana."

"Murdoc ... " Gods, it sent a shiver like warm current over my skin when she said my name like that—like a quiet prayer breathed in candlelight. "Please, don't leave us."

She said "us," but the word sounded wrong. As though it wasn't the one she really wanted to use.

It took every bit of self-control I had not to look back at her. Not to give in. We still hadn't spoken about what happened, about why she'd kissed me before. And as more time passed, the more I found my mind slipping back to that moment again and again. Trying to recall it more clearly. Trying to remember what it had felt like.

And wishing I was brave enough to be honest with her.

If I looked back now, I might change my mind. I might do what she wanted. I might try to stay with them.

But I couldn't.

"Go safely," I murmured. Lowering my head, I forged toward the dark of the rugged landscape that lay between the edge of the plateau and the city's northeastern limits. It was less than a mile to cross back into the city proper. I still had time to get there and find a place to lie low during the daylight hours.

I didn't make it even half that far, though.

A huge, dragon-shaped mound of scales dropped from the sky and landed right before me. The young dragon craned his neck down and peered at me with his massive blue eyes blinking. He tilted his head to the side and chirped curiously, then gave a disapproving huff and bumped his snout against the center of my chest—as though telling me to go back to the others.

I stretched out a hand to grab ahold of one of his sweeping black horns firmly, intending to yank his big head out of my way. But as my fingers ran over the smooth surface of his hide, my heart sank all the way to the very soles of my boots. Every breath made my chest ache as though my lungs had been stretched beyond their limits. My face throbbed where Thatcher's hits had left my nose, cheek, and right eye bruised.

I ... I didn't know what I was doing anymore. Where was I meant to be? What was I meant to do? Why did everything I did, every choice I made, feel so ... wrong? Was my entire life going to be like this? Like one giant, spiraling sequence of mistakes—fleeing from one shadow to the next—until I found death waiting for me somewhere in the dark?

Was that really all that destiny had for me? Even if it was probably what I deserved. I'd done terrible things—worse than even Thatcher or Jaevid knew about. I'd become the monster the Ulfrangar wanted me to be.

So what kind of life was I fit for now?

My hand slid off the dragon's horn, grazing the side of his head along his bony brow and cheek before it fell back to my side.

"Why?" I asked, my voice sounding as pathetic and broken as I felt right then. "Why do you keep choosing me? Why do you keep fighting for me? Why do you keep protecting me?" I whispered. "Don't you know there are so many other good people out there that could be your rider? What about Jondar? Or Ezran? Or Garnett? You have to know any one of them would be so much better for you than I'll ever be."

The dragon made a low, rumbling, murring sound deep in his chest as he scooted in closer, blasting snorts through his nostrils as he wrapped his big black wings and long tail around me. I stood engulfed and completely hidden by his strong form, as he dipped his head until his massive forehead bumped against mine.

Hidden there by his mighty wings, his warm brow pushing against mine, I ... I couldn't stop it. My vision blurred, swallowed up by tears, as every tense, shaking muscle in my body gradually went slack. I shut my eyes tightly and bit down hard, pushing my forehead back against his.

"You're never going to give up, are you?" I asked shakily.

He grunted and blasted another stubborn snort through his nose. I took that to be a firm, dragon-ish "No."

It made me smile a little as I reached up to run my hand along the powerful arch of his neck. "I don't understand it—why you want me for your rider. I don't know how to start over. I don't know how to be like them. And you're asking me to walk in the footsteps of the greatest men this world has ever known, to be the successor of their mighty legacy. I don't know if I can do that," I confessed. My voice hitched as I sucked in a deep, steadying breath. "But ... if you're really sure about this, then ... then I'll try."

The dragon made another low, rumbling sound and rubbed his head against mine like a cat cheek-marking on the corner of a chair. The force of it nearly knocked me backward, and I laughed weakly and pushed his head away.

"You're still a menace, though. A regular plague that won't go away," I said as I stepped around, letting my palm drag along the smooth, wide scales that adorned his neck. I stopped when I reached that place on his back where I could sit and ride. The sight of it made my chest seize with a thrill of anxiety and something else.

Something wild and fearless.

Something like freedom, calling me home.

I couldn't hold back a smile as I reached for it, gripping the horns that ran down his spine and pulling myself up onto his back. My pulse beat in my eardrums like thunder, sending that frenzied energy through every part of me, as he rose up and spread his wings to the fierce night wind.

"Blite," I decided and patted his side firmly. "That's your name. Sound good?"

He lashed his tail and snapped his jaws, the blaze of red scales on his head catching in the first light of dawn as he let out a satisfied, shattering roar.

I leaned down against his neck, feeling every bit of his strength as he coiled for take-off. "Good. Now let's go back and get the others. We've got a Tibran witch to catch."

My weight was a lot for Blite to manage in flight, and I could tell he wasn't used to having anyone sitting there. It made every stroke of his dark crimson wings rougher and more forceful in flight. Whether that was something he'd get used to in time, or something we'd have to work on as he grew and got bigger, I didn't know.

I knew someone who did, though, and he stared at me like I'd grown a second head as we circled the farmhouse and finally landed right next to his massive blue king drake. Jaevid studied me wordlessly, his pale, glacier-hued eyes narrowed some as I looked back at him. I tipped my head to the side in a half-shrug and scratched the back of Blite's horned head. He chirped a musical, almost smugly satisfied greeting to Mavrik.

What could I say? I'd never known anyone more stubborn than I was—until I'd met this dragon.

Jaevid's lips pursed a little, as though he were choosing his words very carefully.

"That touchdown was sloppy," he said at last, and there was a challenging, almost daring edge in his tone. "You'll need to work on that before you start your formal training."

"I'll need an actual saddle, too," I fired back as I swung myself down from Blite's back. "And my dragon will need to grow several more feet so we can take off without wobbling like a dizzy goose."

Blite puffed defiantly and nipped at the back of my cloak, almost jerking me to a halt by my neck as I walked by.

"But we've got time for all that—providing the Ulfrangar or this Tibran witch doesn't kill me first." I sighed as I looked at the farmhouse before us. All the windows were lit and the front door had been left cracked open. The others had already gone inside.

So what was Jaevid doing out here by himself? Waiting for Phillip and the rest of us to arrive? Hmm.

"The others won't be far behind," I told him. "Isandri couldn't carry someone Phillip's size, and he can't fly. So they're on foot, but making good time. It shouldn't take them more than an hour to get here."

Jaevid gave a small nod, his gaze now fixed upon the house. "Good. We need to gather everyone and go over what happened." His tone had gone deep, somber, and heavy with the same concern I saw settling over his sharp features like a gathering storm front. "We need to know what Phillip saw—what he's witnessed in Northwatch—as soon as possible. We've now got three confirmed deities among us and Fates only know what else. It was never my intention to drag you all into the midst of a feud between godlings, but if that's truly what we're up against, I shudder to think of what we may face next."

"You've dealt with worse things than this, though, haven't you?" I crossed my arms, watching the dark shapes of figures move past some of the windows on the second floor of the farmhouse. It was probably an absolute frenzy in there dealing with Judan. All the more reason to keep out of the way for now.

Jaevid cleared his throat. "Yes, well, I've always had lots of help before. Somehow, it seems that bit keeps getting left out of all those grand stories everyone likes to tell about me."

"You've got lots of help this time, too. Granted, most of it's probably mediocre by comparison to what you had previously. But we'll do what we can."

He chuckled some. "I take it this means you're staying."

"Unless you tell me to go."

His expression softened with a small, slightly nostalgic grin. "Well, then I'd be down to only one decent swordsman, wouldn't I?"

I winced. "Eh, well, Isandri isn't technically a swordsman, but she's very handy in a fight. Phillip will be, too, I'm sure. I don't know how he fares with a blade, though. We might be better off just to let him punch things—he seems to do that well enough." I rubbed my chin as I strolled over to stand next to his dragon's side. "And maybe we can bribe Garnett into sticking around a little longer. We already owe a certain crime lord one favor, however. I doubt he'll just lend us one of his best agents out of the goodness of his heart."

"I can't let Phillip stay here and fight with us," Jaevid muttered as that thin smile slipped quickly from his features. "Even if we need his help, he's been lost to Devana once already. I can't allow him to be lost like that again. He has to go back to Halfax—back to Jenna—immediately. She's in a fragile state, and needs him far more than we do. I mean to take him there myself as soon as we've heard everything he can tell us about what Devana is plotting in Northwatch."

I flicked him a meaningful look. "And what do we do? Sit here and wait for you to return?"

His jaw stiffened and he bowed his head some, never taking his eyes off the light glowing from the farmhouse's open door. "I ... don't know, Murdoc. But with Reigh and Judan now trying to recover, the Ulfrangar still posing a threat, and this much divine power running around, we're more vulnerable than ever. I think now might be the time to seek out some new reinforcements." His chest heaved with a deep, resigned breath. "I just hope they'll be willing to help."

24
CHAPTER TWENTY-FOUR

I could hear Reigh squawking like an angry crow in the front sitting room of the house long before we ever darkened the doorway. Jaevid, Isandri, and Phoebe had gone in ahead of us soon after they arrived, but Phillip and I elected to stay back for a moment longer. Jaevid had suggested he might need to forewarn the rest of them about our new giant ally's arrival. Understandable, considering his appearance alone probably sent people fleeing in terror a lot. It was probably better if Ms. Lin's children weren't there to see him come striding in, covered in blood, and looking like a creature straight out of the abyss.

One crisis at a time.

When we finally walked in, the entire house seemed to go completely silent. Phillip's massive frame filled the entryway like a tower of gray and black muscle. If his monstrous features weren't horrifying enough, the fact that he was dressed in tattered, blood-soaked rags and had several large wounds from Phoebe's trap on his body were probably enough to seal it. The warm light from the lamps burning around the room made the tiny speckles of silver on his graphite-colored skin sparkle like miniature constellations down his arms, legs, and across his face. The end of his tail flicked anxiously, and his large, paw-like feet flexed as he shifted uncomfortably.

He looked like an actual living, breathing nightmare.

Ms. Lin sucked in a sharp breath. Jondar froze up like a deer caught out in the open—as though he couldn't decide if he should sit there and not move, or make a break for it before the fighting started.

The only person who didn't go at least a little pasty at the sight of him was Reigh. He glared up at the towering man from where he sat on the sofa, still a little ashen in the face, but looking more like himself than he had when we left. He was conscious now, at least. And I guess he'd recovered enough to hobble down the stairs.

"You big, stupid, pig-headed, rump-sniffing *moron*!" Reigh thundered as he thrust an accusing finger at Phillip, his voice slipping with that Gray elven accent as he ranted. "Do you have any idea what you've put us through? What you've put my sister through? Gods, Fates, and all things holy—I almost *died* because of you! Judan, too, apparently. And all because you decided to go sporting around Northwatch like a half-wit by yourself!"

"Reigh," Ms. Lin protested weakly, her terrified gaze never leaving Phillip, as though she were afraid he might suddenly lunge for us. She stood right next to the sofa, gripping the tray of empty dinner dishes in her hands like she might try to use it as a weapon if Phillip made a wrong move. "You're barely on your feet. You really shouldn't get yourself all worked up right now—"

Reigh wasn't listening. He staggered to his feet, cringing and biting elven curses through his teeth as he limped toward Phillip. "You were going to leave Jaevid and me to be the ones to tell my sister! After she's just had the baby! You miserable idiot!"

With his torso almost completely wrapped in thick layers of bandaging, Reigh could barely stand up straight let alone walk. He managed to reach Phillip, though, shoving a few of us out of his path on the way, and reared back to take one well-aimed swing at the giant man's chest. The hit didn't even make Phillip flinch. Reigh might as well have tickled him with a feather. But Phillip stared down at his much smaller, sort-of brother-in-law with his features locked in a look of mute horror.

Silence crushed in over the room as the rest of our returning party filed in, then suddenly stopped to stare at the two of them. Reigh stood weaving on his feet, glaring fiercely up at Phillip, who seemed to have stopped breathing entirely.

Finally, Phillip managed to rasp out one quiet, broken word. "Ba ... baby?" His gaze panned the room, seeming lost and catatonic, until he spotted Jaevid.

No one made a sound.

"The baby?" he asked again.

"Yes, Phillip. Jenna had the baby," Jaevid confirmed, keeping his tone controlled and calm as he stepped closer to our new, giant ally. "A boy. She's all right. They're both all right. And I know you need to go to her—*soon*. Trust me, I'll take you there. But first, you've got to tell us everything you can about what happened at Northwatch. We know about Devana. We know she had you under some sort of mind control, and that's why you've been running around doing her bidding. We've got to stop her before she does the same thing to more people, or worse."

Phillip blinked hard and shook his head, still looking around at all of us like he was struggling to shrug off his shock and take everything in at once. Then his brows snapped together into a deeply confused frown. He turned, fixing Jaevid with a hard stare. "Devana? What do you mean?"

"The one who did this to you," Reigh pressed, still glowering at him. Although, now, the faintest hints of worry had begun to seep into his expression. "You found her at Northwatch, didn't you? She was the one who took control of your mind?"

Phillip took a step back, his wide chest heaving as he blinked hard again, wincing each time and rubbing at his forehead with the heel of his hand. His shoulders hunched forward as he bent, seeming to cave in on himself as he buried his face in his palms. "No! No—i-it wasn't—it wasn't—"

"Let's take a breath here," Jaevid insisted suddenly. He stepped over to Phillip, putting a hand on his arm as he studied the big man earnestly—probably worried that all this might be too much for him at once. And after what Phillip had just been through? Yeah. That was more than a valid concern. His mind was undoubtedly still recovering. No need to drop kick him back into madness right away.

"You've been through a lot, too," Jaevid consoled him. "Let's get you cleaned up first. Then we can talk."

No one argued as he ushered Phillip back out of the room and up the stairs, but the collective tense silence only intensified. Yes, Phillip had been through a lot. More than we knew about, probably. And it probably wasn't a bad idea to at least get his wounds bandaged up and give him a few seconds to breathe. But we didn't have much time. Ready or not, we had to get this information out of him soon.

A lot of lives were depending on it—and not just our own.

"Come now, Reigh, you must sit down. You're not healed enough to be moving around so much," Ms. Lin urged. "Don't make me go up and report this to Kiran."

Reigh grumbled a few more elven curses on his way back to sit on the sofa. Relief broke over his rumpled, grimacing features as he finally sank down into it. I guess he hadn't healed up as much as we'd hoped.

From across the room, I met Phoebe's worried stare. She stood, wringing her hands in her tunic with her delicate features crinkled in distress. Hmm. Something wasn't right. I'd figured out weeks ago that, thanks to her extremely transparent expressions, Phoebe was nearly incapable of deception. She knew something the rest of us didn't.

Or *most* of us, I should say.

I looked over at Thatcher and Isandri. They stood right next to Phoebe, side-by-side, with their deeply pensive gazes fixed on the floor as though they were both lost in thought. Thatcher had that telltale look of fretful concern on his soft features, like he was hard at work doing that annoying, overthinking thing again.

Isandri, on the other hand, was a lot harder to read. She kept everything more closely guarded behind those dazzling, other-worldly eyes. But her gaze occasionally darted to the side, stealing fast glances at Thatcher, like she wanted to say something to him. Whatever it was, though, it never left her lips.

I frowned. Those three knew more than they were sharing now. What had happened while she, Isandri, and Thatcher were catching Phillip? What were they holding back? Now was not the time to be biting back secrets—not with so much at stake.

"I, um, I really should send word to my employer about what's happened," Garnett spoke up, her voice quiet and hesitant as she brushed some of her loose golden bangs away from her face. "I'd like to get more information about what's going on in the tunnels with the underbeasts. It's not like them to come so close to the surface, let alone causing a ruckus like that."

Thatcher tensed some, his gaze slowly rising from the floor to meet mine. From across the room, I could see it on his face as plain as day: He definitely knew something important that he hadn't shared yet, and it had to do with the underbeasts.

Fantastic.

"Underbeast? Employer?" Reigh asked suddenly, glancing Garnett over with an eyebrow arched. "Wait, are you one of Arlan the Kinslayer's people?"

Oh. Right. He hadn't exactly been aware of her joining our ranks for this particular mission.

"Yes. Garnett, at your service, Your Highness," she said cheerily as she hopped forward and offered a small bow.

Reigh's gaze traveled around the room, looking between the rest of us in bewilderment. Finally, he sighed and rolled his eyes, leaning forward to rest his face in his hands and scratch at his scalp. "Gods and Fates," he groaned. "I fall out for a few days and you lot nearly burn down another city, start beating the crap out of each other, and almost turn Prince Judan into a switchbeast. Jenna is never going to let me hear the end of it this time."

"We did manage to get Phillip back, though," Thatcher added.

Reigh glowered at him through his fingers. He sighed and ran his hands all the way through his unruly mop of auburn red hair to the back of his neck. "Right. There is that, I guess. I, uh, I also hear I owe you my thanks. They said you saved my life."

"No," Thatcher corrected quickly, his face the picture of childish determination. "I mean, yes, I did help some. But Phoebe was the one who started counteracting the poison. If she hadn't been there, I'm not sure anything else we did to help you would've mattered."

Phoebe's face flushed almost as bright as her coppery hair. She cringed back, shoulders slowly drawing up to her ears as she looked at the floor, the ceiling, anywhere except at Reigh. Her hands fidgeted in the hem of her tunic again, wringing it over and over like someone trying to squeeze water out of a dishrag.

He, on the other hand, leveled a strange expression at her. His throat jumped as he swallowed hard, gaze earnest and mouth mashed up as though he were struggling to keep his composure in front of the rest of us.

What? I could've sworn that look was ... *remorse.*

No. Surely not. Not from Reigh. The Goddess of Death herself might apologize before he ever did.

With his body still shaking and unsteady, Reigh hauled himself back to his feet again. He crossed the room with a few staggering steps and stopped right before Phoebe and stood, staring down into her face for nearly a minute. His expression flickered between regret, pain, and his usual storm of intense frustration until, at last, he bowed his head a little. "I ... I know I owe you my thanks, as well." He faltered, stumbling over his quietly muttered words. "But before I can offer that, I need to ask for your forgiveness. I know I've been ... unfair with you. Horribly, I guess. But I'm not all that good of a person, sometimes, and ... I know that. But, I-I, uh, I—"

Phoebe seized one of his hands, her big blue eyes blinking back tears and her freckled cheeks dimpling as she smiled. "It's okay, Reigh. I'm just so glad you're all right."

His wavering, half-hearted smile spoke volumes. He wasn't all right—not really. And I suppose Phoebe could sense that, too.

She stood on her toes and wrapped her arms around his neck, pulling him gently into a hug. "I know it was so bad before—what you went through. I know I hurt you and, gods, I am ... *so sorry* for that, Reigh. But please understand; I couldn't let you give up. I still can't. Not when there's so much you've got to live for. So many people that love you and need you. You've got to keep living for them. Promise me you will—and then I'll forgive you. Okay?"

Reigh's eyes went wide for an instant as he stood, caught up in her embrace. Then he squeezed his eyes shut and threw his arms around her, too. He hugged her fiercely, never saying a word.

Ms. Lin sniffled loudly, wiping at her eyes and fanning her face. Isandri and Garnett exchanged a knowing smile, as though they found this moment adorable.

But Thatcher just stared at them.

He just stood there, as still as a dried-out corpse. He didn't blink or make a single sound. Slowly, his gaze panned over to meet mine from across the room. His mouth opened as though he were going to speak.

Then it all shattered. His mouth clamped shut and his jaw clenched hard. His brow furrowed into a hard, focused frown down at the floor between us.

I looked away, too.

Somehow, in the silence, it felt like the ground before me had cracked open and caved in, tearing apart and leaving behind a massive rift. That chasm between us might as well have been a vast abyss—a divide neither of us could ever hope to cross.

And honestly, I didn't even know how to begin trying.

25

CHAPTER TWENTY-FIVE

Once Phoebe and I had helped Reigh back up the stairs to lie down in one of the guest rooms, the house grew quiet again. Ms. Lin had lunch on downstairs, and a few of the others had retreated to the kitchen to wait out the hours until Phillip was ready to talk.

Between dressing Judan's arm and trying to purge whatever switchbeast venom still remained in his system, patching up Phillip, and looking after Reigh's progress—our resident Gray elven healer had quite the workload now. Phoebe was all too eager to help, though, and darted around to follow his orders in bringing clean bandages, dressings, and medicinal potions from a large leather bag he'd brought along.

Not long after cleaning her lunch plate, Garnett asked about getting a lift back to the city so she could rendezvous with her contacts and deliver all her information to Kinslayer. Jaevid quickly agreed to take her there straight away. Apparently, Kiran was running low on a few of his supplies, and had already asked him to retrieve more from a healing house in Dayrise, anyway. I didn't mention it, but to me, it seemed more like Jaevid was on the verge of a nervous breakdown and simply wanted a few minutes to himself to process. Understandable.

Or, then again, maybe he also wanted to reach out to those reinforcements he'd mentioned earlier.

Whatever the case, by early afternoon, I found myself sitting in the open doorway of the old barn's hayloft. My feet dangled over the drop to the ground below as I stared out across the sweeping landscape. The sun slid overhead and began to set off to the west, shrouded in clouds that cast large shadows across the low, rolling hills. Unbuckling all my weaponry and slipping off my boots, I tossed them into a pile and unbuttoned the neck of my tunic a little. I closed my eyes as the cool evening air caressed my skin with the sweet smell of the prairie grass. It teased in my hair and filled my lungs, making my shoulders sag. That smell, so clean and crisp, spoke to some far-flung corner of my soul in a way I didn't understand. Somehow, it reminded me of a home I'd never had.

Then again, that was probably just the fatigue talking. I hadn't slept in several days. Maybe this was a good time to try.

"Murdoc?"

I glanced back to see a familiar crown of wild red curls peering over the top of the ladder that led from the first floor of the barn to the hayloft. Phoebe popped up like a prairie dog, eyeing me anxiously as she climbed the rest of the way up. "Are you busy?"

Busy? I glanced down at myself, now half-dressed, and wondered how in the world I looked busy. "Not exactly."

She stumbled forward, almost tripping over her own feet on her way over to stand beside me. "Oh. Good. I mean, um, everyone's beginning to gather to talk to Phillip as soon as Jaevid returns, so I just thought you would … " She stopped suddenly, her petite form going stiff as she whirled around to face where I sat. With her hands in fists at her sides and her expression distinctly terrified, she announced, "Murdoc, I want to talk about what I did before. At Ms. Lin's house. When the Ulfrangar attacked and I, um, well I kissed you."

I blinked, trying to scrape together enough sense to answer as my breath hung in my throat.

She didn't give me much of a chance, though. With her next breath, she crossed her arms around her middle and turned away some, her cheeks and nose bright pink and her delicate features riddled with embarrassment. "I didn't mean to—well, I mean I *did* —but what I didn't mean to do was put you in a position where you felt like you owed me some kind of answer or … or a response." She rambled faster and faster, seeming to quickly lose whatever nerve she'd mustered before. "That isn't, um, it's not what I wanted at all. I didn't want anything, really. Well, except for you to live. I was afraid I might never see you again or that you'd die and then I'd never get a chance to—Ah! No! What I meant to say was that I'm very sorry if you got the impression I wanted you to do or say something back. Because I don't. I mean, of course it's okay if you do, but I'm not expecting anything. Honestly, nothing at all. And that I shouldn't have been so reckless when you're already—"

"Phoebe?" I interrupted.

She cringed and peered at me out of the corner of her eye like she was bracing herself for my response.

"I'm not upset about it."

She perked up some. "O-Oh. You're not? I just, um, well, it sort of seemed like you'd been avoiding me and … " Her voice trailed off as she drew her bottom lip into her mouth, still angling herself away from me as though she were ready to dash away at any moment.

I found myself turning away some, too. "Not because I was angry with you." Rubbing my jaw, I sighed and struggled to come up with the right words. I couldn't. There were no *right* words. And even the ones I could think of were tangled, lost amidst the fast, frantic pounding of my pulse in my head. My chest felt too tight. My head spun around what I had to do—what I had to tell her. There was no good or easy way to say it, no getting around it, or softening it. Not really, anyway.

So I might as well get it over with quickly.

"I can't give you what you want, Phoebe," I admitted, the words burning on my tongue as I kept my gaze locked upon the ground. If I looked at her—if I saw brokenness or sorrow in her eyes—I'd lose my nerve. I'd do something reckless. I couldn't do that to her.

I couldn't subject her to ... me.

"I'm not someone you want in your life like that. You see what merely being friends has gotten Thatcher. But it's more than that," I explained. "I have absolutely nothing to offer you. I have no relatives. No home. I don't even have a family name. I can't give you anything you'd want, Phoebe. A home, safety, the security of a good living—I don't know that I'll ever have any of those things. Being with me, choosing me like that, would be ... pointless. And painful." I hesitate, gathering every scattered remnant of my nerve before I dared to look at her. "And you deserve better than that. Better than me."

Phoebe stared up at me, slender brows drawn together in confusion as those lovely, light blue eyes searched my face. My pulse skipped and stalled, alarms ringing my head like tolling tower bells as she faced me with a little scowl of determination. "Murdoc, I—"

A booming roar broke over the barn, rattling it all the way down to the foundations. The low WHOOM—WHOOM—WHOOM of dragon wing beats followed, and the shadow of a massive dragon passed over the ground and circled around the farmhouse. Leaning out the hayloft door, I spotted the glint of the sun off radiant blue scales and the silhouette of the massive king drake as he briefly eclipsed the evening sun.

I'd never seen Mavrik move that fast, though. Why was Jaevid pushing him so hard? He'd been gone more than three hours—more than long enough to drop off Garnett and do a supply run to the healing house, too. Had something happened? Or gone wrong?

Cursing under my breath, I seized my boots and crammed them back on as quickly as possible. As soon as I was back on my feet, gripping my cross sheath in one hand, I reached to take her arm with the other and drag her with me toward the ladder. "Come on. We need to get down there. Something's not right."

SOMETHING, indeed.

As soon as the mighty king drake touched down, Jaevid and Garnett dismounted and took off toward the house without looking back. Phoebe and I followed and hit the door less than five seconds behind them—just in time to see them disappear through the kitchen doorway at the far end of the narrow entry hall.

I hesitated at the threshold, and Phoebe gripped my arm like a frightened child.

"We should go in, shouldn't we?" she whimpered.

I frowned. A nagging pull at the back of my mind, like the tiniest prick of a needle, made me glance back out the front door. Mavrik still crouched there, his big yellow eyes watching us like a massive crouching cat as he sniffed the air. His ears swiveled and the tip of his long tail swished anxiously. All seemed fine. There was nothing and no one else in sight—and if there had been, surely the giant dragon would've known about it.

So why did it feel like I was being watched?

I tried to shake it off. Let it go. Now wasn't the time. I was probably still on edge from the night before. Too many close calls with switchbeasts had me jumpy. Or I was still recovering from talking to Phoebe about feelings and kissing and all that stuff that made my brain feel like a gooey bowl of scrambled eggs. Fates preserve me.

"Let's go," I urged and jostled her some to coax her on ahead of me. She stumbled forward, reluctant and stalling until we reached the kitchen doorway. Then she darted off to find a seat at the long table where most of our group was already waiting.

Or rather, they were busy helping Garnett wrestle a series of large, yellowed scrolls onto the table. They pinned down the corners with cups and bowls—whatever they could find to hold each one in place. I leaned over Garnett's head to get a better look.

All around the table, Isandri, Thatcher, Phoebe, Reigh, Jaevid, and I gathered close to peer at the series of maps she'd brought along. From a distance, they appeared to be maps of Maldobar, which I'd seen many times before. But some of them were ... slightly off. Or rather, they had different things marked on them in stark red ink. Lines connecting cities like webs or streams. It took me a second to work out what that was exactly. Then it hit me: All those red lines stemmed in from the coast, and nearly all of them led to Northwatch.

My jaw dropped. Gods—these were maps of the Tibran tunnel systems!

The Ulfrangar, countless royals, and Fates only knew who else would've paid handsomely for even a glimpse of these. How on earth had she gotten ahold of them? From Kinslayer?

Garnett's hands trembled and she muttered under her breath in dwarven as she fiddled with more papers, letters I could see written in code. Her lavender eyes darted quickly from the letters to the maps, back and forth, until at last she sank back into a chair with a slow, quaking exhale.

"Are they authentic?" Jaevid demanded sharply.

Garnett slowly bobbed her head. "I think so. It's difficult to be sure, of course. Lord Argonox was very strict about how information like this was supposed to be handled within his ranks. Even I was never privy to maps with this much detail. I was permitted only what I needed to build the next section, nothing more. But the areas I remember seem to be correct." She leaned forward again, staring at the letters and chewing on the inside of her cheek.

"How did you get these?" Reigh asked, his tone and the arch to his brow obviously suspicious. "I thought you went to deliver information."

"I did. But some of my contacts were already waiting for me with these. You see, I had them monitoring a lot of the known tunnel surface entrances in the area. Watching for your man, Phillip, since we needed to know his precise movements and which tunnels he was using to move about unseen. After we found the one he preferred, Arlan gave those agents orders to keep watching some of the other areas, just in case. And now it appears as though they've stumbled across something bizarre ... and very unsettling." Garnett leaned over a section of the map where the red lines circled and ensnared the city of Dayrise, connecting it to Osbran and Northwatch to the west. "Groups of armed men moving in and out of the tunnel systems. Some with up to twenty or so in their company."

"Former Tibrans?" Reigh guessed. "Or thieves?"

Garnett shook her head. "They seem too organized to be common thugs. My contacts said some of them are packing significant and refined weaponry—far beyond the capability of your usual cutthroat. But they carry no banner and wear no symbol, so it's not clear if they're former Tibran or not."

"How do we know these groups are even related?" Isandri leaned down, some of her long hair spilling over her shoulder to brush the tabletop as she inspected the map closely. "They might be separate entities."

Garnett sank back again, staring out across the collection of maps with a fretful frown. "That's what I thought, too. But my contacts have managed to lift a few of their belongings ... including these."

Reigh glanced up. "You mean these didn't all come from the same group?"

"No. Not one. These were collected from four different individuals, and none of them were traveling with the same group. But they're all coded the same way. Whoever these people are, they're mapping the tunnel systems—specifically, the ones spanning out from Northwatch." Garnett tapped a finger on the spot where the old city stood, nearly on the boundary of Maldobar and Luntharda. "I can't think of a single good reason to try to secretly map those tunnels. Stones, some of them are still raw-cut. They could cave in at any moment. But I doubt whoever's wanting them mapped knows that. Someone's up to no good there, and worse, it looks like they're recruiting."

"Devana?" Jaevid guessed, looking at Isandri and Thatcher like they might have the answer.

But the answer came from the doorway in a deep, ominous voice. "No. It's not Devana." Phillip stepped into the kitchen, his silver eyes focused on the maps like he was watching a horrible nightmare replay right before him. His expression closed, darkening into a look of grim concentration ... or perhaps remembrance.

Jaevid stood straighter and leveled a worried frown at the towering man. "What do you mean?"

Phillip took in a deep, steadying breath before he slowly panned those chilling, silver eyes around the room. "My friends, I'm afraid you've all been misled. It's true, I went to Northwatch on my own. Word coming out of that city was that every effort by the local guard to reestablish law and order had been futile. It's overrun—a literal hive of bloodthirsty vagrants and criminals. We'd been trying to reestablish solid trade routes between Dayrise, Osbran, and Barrowton for months, but couldn't get any traction because every caravan that dared to cross within even ten miles of Northwatch fell victim to the scum hiding there. I thought if I could get inside and move through the city undetected just long enough to evaluate some good points where we could bring in soldiers and make a proper stand to retake it ... maybe it would help. Jae, you know I'm no soldier. But I have the benefit of looking like the enemy. I thought I could manage it. I *was* managing."

Phillip stopped short, mouth clamping shut as his pointed ears turned back some.

His gaze drifted back to that place on the map where Northwatch stood on the boundary between our kingdom and Luntharda.

"Then I found my way into the tower where the dragonriders used to reside," he continued, his tone going quiet and careful. "The people there were ... different. Their eyes all glowed blue. They stood around, not moving much or speaking, like ships left to drift out in the open sea. Directionless and empty, but still alive. I didn't understand it. I thought it might be some kind of sickness." His nose wrinkled some, lip curling into a snarl on one side as memories danced like sterling flames in his eyes. "Then *she* found me."

"Let me guess," Thatcher spoke up suddenly, muttering from where he stood on the other side of the table. "A little girl that looked like she was made of rippling blue light?"

Phillip did a double take. "H-How did you know?"

Now all eyes were on Thatcher. And for once, he didn't seem at all nervous or even surprised about that. "Because I've seen her, too. Twice, actually. The first time was when we fought the Ulfrangar outside the King's Cross. The second time ... was when I pulled her out of *your* mind last night. I don't know who she is, but she's not Devana, even if she can control other people's minds."

"No, she used a different name," Phillip agreed.

Jaevid's expression had gone as cold as an arctic wind. "And what name is that?" he demanded. "Clysiros?"

Lowering his somber gaze back to the map, Phillip's expression shifted from that small, bitter snarl. Hints of guarded fear seeped into the corners of his face. His hands shook a little until he clenched them into fists. "I heard her voice in my head, digging so deep and fast, like a worm into an apple. I couldn't shake it. I couldn't resist it. She ... she called herself Iksoli."

CHAPTER TWENTY-SIX

I'd been taught a lot under the Ulfrangar, and not just the quickest and quietest ways to kill someone. The Ulfrangar prided themselves in producing assassins that could blend into the fabric of nearly any community, if needed. We could vanish like phantoms into a crowd in any kingdom around the world. So from a young age, I'd been taught languages, customs, and cultures that spanned far beyond the boundaries of Maldobar. I'd been tutored thoroughly in religious and traditional rituals from as far away as Nar'Haleen and Rienka.

But out of all the knowledge that'd been crammed into my mind since childhood, Iksoli was not a name I recognized.

And one quick glance around the room made me suspect I wasn't alone in that. Everyone else stood eerily still, their faces a mixture of confusion and worry. Who, by all the Fates, was Iksoli?

"To wield such power, she must be something of divine origin," Jaevid reasoned as he rubbed his chin.

"Or something the Tibrans made?" Reigh suggested. "I mean, look what they did to Phillip. What's to say they couldn't do worse things? Maybe this Iksoli is another slave or captive that's been experimented on."

"I, um, ... believe I *might* have heard this name before," Phoebe piped up suddenly. Her face flushed so pink it made most of her freckles disappear entirely as she ducked her head and shrank back. "It was, um, well, it was in regards to that artifact—the Thieving Mask, Lord Argonox called it. He claimed it had been derived from a goddess with that name, I think."

"A *goddess*?" Isandri gasped quietly. "Are you certain? I've not heard of any deity with that namesake."

Phoebe didn't answer except to shrug her trembling shoulders a little, as though she were too anxious to confirm it one way or another.

"I'll see what Arlan can dig up for us," Garnett offered. "I'm certain he'd be interested. He works as an archivist and historian as a front to the royal court."

Reigh's eyebrows rose. "You've got to be kidding me. The most notorious crime lord in Maldobar disguises himself as a *librarian*?"

Her lips bowed into a cheeky little grin. "Clever, eh? Anyway, if this Iksoli person is of any divine historical note, I'm sure he would know."

"We can only hope," Jaevid murmured. He took a step back from the table, looking no more reassured than when he'd first arrived. "What else can you tell us about her, Phillip? Did she need to make physical contact to cast this magic on you? Did you glimpse any of her motives, or did she tell you why she's so fixated on capturing Thatcher?"

Phillip hesitated, seeming lost in thought for a few minutes until, at last, he moved over to sit down in a chair next to Garnett. It creaked a little under his weight as he leaned forward to rest his elbows on the tabletop. "I-I'm sorry. It's all so muddied. I'm trying to remember, but it's like trying to peer through foggy glass." He rubbed his face with both hands and growled quietly. "The last thing I can recall clearly was running through the lowest levels of Northwatch tower. It was pitch black down there, but you know my eyes work far better in the darkness, so I could make my way easily. I found a series of cells that were set apart from the others. Each one was reinforced with a massive door covered in strange markings all around geometric designs. I'd never seen anything like it. And then I heard a sound—like a young woman weeping behind one of those doors."

Isandri's expression went disturbingly blank. Her lips parted and her arms dropped slackly at her sides. She barely seemed to be breathing as he continued.

"I tried to find her. But it was difficult to tell which door she might be locked behind. And when I tried to open one of them, those marks etched onto it lit up like a sunrise and sent a shot of pain through me. I couldn't even grip the handle," Phillip recalled. "I tried calling out to her—asking her if she knew how to open the door or if there was a key I could find. She didn't answer. Not really, anyway. She kept repeating '*Ishaleon. Find me, Ishaleon.*' I don't know what that meant, but she sounded so desperate and terrified. I thought maybe some of the thugs from the city had locked her there. I just wanted to help her escape."

He halted, voice catching as he cringed and turned his face away from us. "I-I turned around, and there was ... someone else there. She was standing right there behind me like she'd been watching the entire time, but she never made a sound. I didn't hear her approach. I couldn't smell her, or sense her presence at all. Her whole being radiated light, just like you said. And she looked up at me with this smile—Gods, I-I couldn't look away. I couldn't move. Everything went dark."

No one spoke for what felt like an eternity as we all stared at him. My mind churned over each detail, measuring his every word. By the sound of it, he'd likely stumbled upon the place where Devana had been imprisoned by the Tibrans beneath Northwatch tower. But how could she still be alive after all this time? Simple, really. Someone had to be holding her prisoner there, giving her food and water, but not allowing her to leave that magical cell. This Iksoli person, most likely—*whoever* or *whatever* she was.

The question was ... why?

Phillip's broad chest heaved in deep, rapid breaths. "I ... I'm so sorry, Jae. I don't remember anything else after that. I was lost in that darkness, and the only thing I could hear was her voice. It seemed to cut right through me like a cold knife. I couldn't avoid it. I couldn't force it away. That's how I learned her name."

"But she didn't tell you anything about herself?" Reigh asked quietly, studying him with a reluctant sort of empathy.

"No," Phillip responded somberly. "Every now and then I could hear something else, something familiar that would find me in the dark; your voices, the sounds of the city, or the sea. But it was all so faint and garbled, like I was eavesdropping through a door. Then I heard you." He looked up suddenly, staring straight at Thatcher with his expression raw as he managed a trembling smile.

Thatcher ducked his head, rubbing at his forearms and picking at his leather vambraces. "I'm just glad I could help. I wasn't sure if I could. But hearing her threaten you like that—I just couldn't take it. She was toying with us, treating your life like it was just a pawn she could sacrifice for fun. She made it all sound like this is one big game to her. She kept calling me her little brother. That, uh, that would make her a godling, too, wouldn't it?"

"Not necessarily," Reigh muttered. He scratched at one corner of his mouth as he studied Thatcher. Then his sharp, light amber eyes darted up to Isandri. "Was there ever a fourth godling in this arrangement?"

She shook her head firmly. "No. Never. I'm certain."

"Well, crap," he sank back in his seat with a slow, shaky exhale. "So, here's what I'm thinking. If this Iksoli-person-maybe-a-goddess is throwing around that kind of magical power, calling you her siblings, and we know for a fact there's no way she's another godling related to you through that legend—that pretty much only leaves one option. Right, Jae?"

Our resident war hero hadn't moved or spoken in a while. He stood as still and catatonic as one of his numerous statues, staring back at Reigh with a haunted expression that chilled me right to the core. "You're thinking this Iksoli truly is a goddess," he breathed in quiet horror.

"Worst case scenario, yes. I mean, it makes sense," Reigh confirmed. "Best case scenario? Maybe she's a different spirit of some kind. Either way, it doesn't matter. We're dealing with something ancient, powerful, and up to no good—and it's recruiting." He bowed his head and pinched the bridge of his nose. "I guess we did this, didn't we? By breaking the law that kept the gods from being able to walk among mortals here?"

Jaevid didn't answer. And for a few long, agonizing moments, everyone stood locked in complete silence. My pounding, racing pulse beat hard at my ribs as I leveled a hard look across the table at Thatcher. This could be bad, far worse than he probably realized.

Then again, he'd been there on the battlefield outside of Halfax right alongside me, cleaning up the charred corpses left behind from the last time a deity had meddled in the lives of mortals. If that was really what we were facing now—the kindling of another war with an insane goddess at the helm—then, Gods and Fates, we had to get out in front of it *now*. This Iksoli had to be dealt with, banished, or whatever was required to defuse the situation. After all, you couldn't reason with gods and goddesses like normal people. They always had a motive, a secret card to play, or an agenda to push.

It hit me so suddenly I nearly choked out loud. Realization burst into my brain like an orb of exploding dragon venom. I ... I knew why Iksoli wanted Thatcher. I knew why she was holding Devana captive.

I knew why she was determined to have them both.

It was so simple, it almost seemed ridiculous. Why hadn't I seen it before? Why didn't anyone else see it? Was I mistaken? No, this had to be it. Nothing else made sense.

"You said Ishaleon is the God of Mercy," I spoke up quickly. "And Devana is actually Eno, the Goddess of Love."

Isandri tilted her head to the side slightly. "Yes, why?"

I took a quick, steadying breath. "We've been thinking about this the wrong way around. We need to be asking ourselves why would someone—even a deity—want to cage and control the forces of mercy and love? What would they possibly stand to gain from that?"

"Chaos?" Reigh guessed.

I pointed it at him. "Exactly. Pandemonium. Reckless dissent and unbridled anarchy. And from that, potentially power. Without mercy there's apathy and slaughter. Without love there's hatred and selfish cruelty." It was only a theory. An educated guess on my part. But as I folded my arms over my chest and cut my gaze over to Jaevid, I couldn't keep from sounding certain. "If I were placing bets, I'd say that's the sort of deity you're dealing with. The nature of the universe has always been achieving balance. It's safe to assume it works that way with the gods and goddesses, as well. For every god of life, there's one of death. So, for every god of mercy and love, we have to assume there's one of chaos and malice. We assumed that Devana was the one responsible for what happened to Phillip because of the nature of her power. But what if that's why this Iksoli is holding her prisoner? What if that's why she wants Thatcher, too? Because with their powers chained to her command—if she were somehow able to bend them to her will or even use their abilities herself—she could easily achieve the mayhem she desires."

"Well, um, Lord Argonox did say something about her being a Goddess of Mischief. At least, I'm pretty sure he did. It was a long time ago," Phoebe confessed, her voice still faltering and afraid. "Is there a goddess like that?"

Realization dawned over Isandri's lovely, oval face. "There must be. That's why she hasn't pursued me. My powers would not lend well to her agenda. I don't have the abilities that permit me to influence others."

"And I do?" Thatcher didn't sound convinced.

"No, no. I think he's right. Thatcher, that is." Reigh motioned to him. "You pulled Iksoli from Phillip's mind. You compelled her to do your bidding out of a desire to spare him from her destroying his mind. You tamed a feral dragon with absolutely no experience because you willed him to trust you." Reigh paused, his light amber eyes suddenly flickering in my direction. He didn't say it out loud, probably in an effort to spare whatever remained of mine and Thatcher's friendship, but it didn't matter. I could practically read the thoughts as though he'd tattooed them across his own forehead.

He suspected that I'd been willed to spare Thatcher's life because of that same divine power.

And ... he might've been right. Everything below my neck went numb as that new information took root in my mind. I'd wanted to leave the Ulfrangar before I met Thatcher that night. I'd hungered for something more, something beyond their cruelty and malic. I'd even searched for my family.

But what if Thatcher's divine magic was what had finally tipped the scale that night? What if he'd unintentionally manipulated me into sparing him? What if I'd never had a choice?

"You're saying you think I can *force* people to do merciful things?" Thatcher objected, and I could feel the pressure of his stare on me. "That's ... that's ridiculous!"

"Maybe it is, maybe it isn't. The fact is, we don't know for sure, so we can't rule anything out. Maybe she wants you for your fancy light-shields. Or maybe she'd like to use your abilities to persuade prison guards to be merciful and let all their inmates go so they can become her mind-slaves, too," Reigh reasoned. "Whatever it is, I think Murdoc has a point. This Iksoli being—goddess or not—is sewing chaos in Northwatch. She's building a force there for something, and using Devana and the Tibran tunnels to do it."

Jaevid's eyes had gone as wide as saucers as he gaped back at me. "Sweet Fates," he gasped hoarsely as his haunted stare slowly drifted down to Reigh. "What have we unleashed?"

OUR WELCOME at Ms. Lin's new house had officially run out. Jaevid wouldn't entertain the idea of sticking around for one second longer than necessary. Having a goddess on our heels wasn't something he was prepared to bring into this home, I guess. Not that I blamed him. We'd burned down one building too many, and knowing that we were undoubtedly going to continue to be targeted by her and the Ulfrangar was more than enough reason for us to keep moving.

I waited outside the door while the others gathered the last of their things and said their final farewells. There wasn't much for me to pack, since I'd always traveled light. Ulfrangar habit, I suppose. We were never permitted many personal items.

"I've got to report this to Jenna and get her take on it. What we do from here to resolve this is ultimately her decision. She may be prepared to commit soldiers to it," Jaevid muttered as he lingered in the front doorway, cramming a few more things into his saddlebag. "You'll stay here with my sister, won't you? To keep looking after them until this is over?"

Standing over him, Kiran looked on with his thin mouth set into a pensive frown. He had all his long white hair pulled back into a ponytail, and his sleeves rolled up to his elbows. "If you wish. Do you foresee this place being targeted even after you've departed?"

"I don't know. Gods, I hope not." Jaevid groaned as he stood up, hefting his bag over his shoulder. "I don't know what to do about any of this, Kiran. I wanted to recall them all to Halfax, but Reigh won't stand for it. He wants to see this through. And he may be right—bringing in more soldiers might only give Iksoli more recruits if she can take control of them. There's only a handful of people I trust to assist them, but with the Ulfrangar still posing a threat, I'm running out of places to send them where they can wait in safety for that help to arrive."

"If there's something more you need from me, you need only to name it." Kiran cast him a knowing, and somewhat concerned look.

"Tell Jace where they'll be, and offer him my deepest apologies for what's happened to Judan." Jaevid sighed. "Maybe light a candle for Phillip and me, too. Jenna is not going to be pleased. It seems my lot now is to be a professional bearer of bad news."

The Gray elf nodded, and the two men exchanged a handshake before Jaevid sped out the door, headed for his dragon.

Hmm. So the great hero Jaevid Broadfeather was running out of ideas. Not a good sign. For once, I agreed with Reigh, though. Retreating wasn't an option now. This wasn't something we could just leave to sort itself out.

And we still only had one decent swordsman left standing.

It took less than an hour for the rest of us to pack our few belongings and prepare to depart. Judan wasn't well enough to be rejoining our efforts, yet, but that didn't stop him from staggering downstairs to find out what was going on. If the angry Gray elven yelling wasn't clue enough, his haggard scowl made it pretty clear he wasn't pleased at all to be left behind.

While we loaded our gear, weapons, and a few days' worth of rations onto our dragons, Judan shuffled around, sweating and cradling his injured arm against his chest, as he tried to reason with Jaevid. It didn't get him very far, though. Whether from the lingering effects of the switchbeast venom or the pain of having his hand crudely amputated, Judan was not ready to ride anywhere—especially not into combat.

At first, Jaevid seemed sympathetic. But after a few minutes of furious yelling from the one-handed prince, his patience ran thin. He spun on Judan and threw his hands up in exasperation. "I said *NO*! I hate to be the one to point this out to you, truly I do, but you are very-recently missing an entire part of your body! Merciful Fates, I can see you sweating with fever right now. Go back inside and lie down, as Kiran has requested, before you collapse. You are not ready for this. When you're well enough to stand without looking like you might faint, I'll be more than happy to welcome your assistance."

Judan's mouth screwed up in a bitter scowl, staring Jaevid down for a few seconds before he finally spun on a heel and stormed back toward the farmhouse.

Jaevid sank back on his heels, shaking his head and muttering under his breath. I couldn't make out most of what he said, but I could have sworn I heard him mutter something like " ... just like his father ... "

Ah. So that stubbornness and pride was a family trait.

At least Reigh appeared to be a bit more solid on his feet now. That, or he was putting up an excellent front so that Jaevid wouldn't make him stay behind, as well. Probably the latter. Idiot.

He went slinking by like a spooked cat, doing his level best not to limp or flinch as he moved. When he caught me staring at him, his eyes narrowed and he made a cutting gesture under his neck, demanding that I keep my mouth shut. Whatever. It was his funeral, I guess. I hadn't come on this venture to babysit *him*, after all.

"You're sure you don't want a lift back to Dayrise?" Thatcher offered as he and Garnett went past. "It's a long way to walk."

She beamed up at him, skipping along with her hands clasped at her back and the breeze bouncing her thick, gingery-gold braids. "Nah. Thanks, love, but I'll be fine! As fun as it is to go joyriding around with you lot, it's better if I go more discreetly this time. Arlan doesn't want us drawing a lot of attention to him, you know. And, well, dragons tend to draw that and more."

He gave a squeaky, nervous chuckle as they stopped next to Fornax. "Heh, uh, yeah. That's true, I guess."

Scratching at the back of his neck, I watched Thatcher alternating his weight from one foot to the other and gnawing on the inside of his cheek as they smiled at one another. Holy gods, this was painful to watch. Why didn't he say something? Talk, idiot. Don't just stand there.

"S-So, um, do you ... uh, do you think I—er—*we* will get to see you again?" he finally managed to croak.

Wow. Well, at least he hadn't passed out or thrown up at her feet.

Garnett shrugged and tossed one of her long braids over her muscular shoulder. "Oh? Hmm, yeah, I'm pretty sure you will. Master Jaevid already gave me the details on where you'll be next when I gave him a few of the maps. I'll be passing along new information as we get it. Maybe it'll help you stay a step ahead of this Iksoli person. And if it looks bad enough, you might need a spare axe or two, yeah?"

Thatcher's face blushed deep scarlet as he nodded. "Uh, d-definitely. I mean, yes. I, um, well ... maybe next time we can ... talk some more."

Ugggh. This was agony. I couldn't stand to watch anymore.

Turning to Blite, I watched Phoebe adjusting the straps on the makeshift saddle she had pieced together from ropes and a few scraps of leather. It wasn't much, but at least it would keep me from plummeting to my death if we had to make any sharp, banking turns.

"I can come up with something better once I've got the right materials," she promised as she stood back, scowling disapprovingly at the contraption. "He's so much smaller—I'll have to work on distributing the weight for him so his flight is smoother."

"We appreciate it," I murmured as I gave the dragon a pat on the shoulder. He chirped in agreement.

Phoebe kept herself angled away, avoiding my gaze as she packed up her little bundle of tools and started away. "Of course. I'm happy to help."

Hmm. She didn't sound very happy. And I'd known her long enough now to be able to tell the difference. But as much as I wanted to catch her by the elbow, pull her back, and find out what the problem was ... part of me already knew.

The obvious truth sat in the pit of my stomach like a cold stone. I'd rejected her feelings. She had every right to withdraw. And I shouldn't try to stop her.

Whatever I wanted, whatever I felt—it didn't matter. I had no right to stand in her way if she chose to turn away from me now.

When Phillip emerged, dressed in new clothes that were probably Jondar's since they almost fit his massive form, everyone began mounting up. He climbed onto Mavrik's back, waiting while Jaevid muttered a few parting words to Reigh. They exchanged a dragonrider salute, clasping a fist across their chests and nodding. Then Jaevid and Phillip were off, headed for Halfax.

As Mavrik took to the air, sending up clouds of dust and dirt with his huge wings, Phoebe settled into the back of the saddle with Thatcher. They ascended quickly, surging skyward and leaving us in another flurry of dust. Reigh and his green dragoness, Vexi, took off next, followed by Isandri—although, she didn't need a dragon to make her exit. Shifting forms mid-stride, her billowing robes of deep purple and green morphed, changing into magnificent feathered wings of the same hue. The staff in her hand dissolved to silver mist as her lithe form changed into a large black feline the size of a tiger. With a silky black hide striped in shimmering silver markings, she bounded forward and beat her wings in strong, smooth strokes until she took flight.

Now it was our turn.

My throat tightened as I gripped the two rope loops tied around my dragon's neck. Watching Thatcher and Fornax wheel away, flying west along the rolling grassland that stretched all the way to the distant foothills, my heart gave a painful wrench. Once again, I had to ask myself what I was doing. Why was I still following them? Putting them all in danger? Thinking I could actually do this *normal life* thing? It wasn't going to work out. I would keep hurting them and putting them in danger.

And maybe I shouldn't even be here to begin with. If Thatcher had used his divine power to compel me to spare him, was any of this even authentic? Had I ever truly belonged here, with them, at all?

Blite swung his head around sideways to peer at me out of the corner of one big, brilliant blue eye. He made confused, anxious chirping sounds as he wiggled his haunches, as though urging me to give him the signal to take off. We were falling behind.

"Give him some time, love. He'll come around," a female voice spoke up suddenly.

I whipped around, looking down to where Garnett still stood close by, her hands resting on top of the axes buckled on her hips. Her broad, knowing smile made her soft lavender eyes gleam and her freckled cheeks dimple as she tipped her chin in Thatcher's direction.

I frowned. "I'm not sure time is going to make much of a difference in this situation," I muttered as I leaned down against Blite's neck and prepared for takeoff.

"It will. He's upset, yes. But you should see the faces he makes when he thinks you're not looking. Like it or not, and regardless of whatever divine magic might have been at play initially, you're family now." She laughed quietly and gave Blite's rump an encouraging pat. "He wants to fix it. He just doesn't know how."

My chest seized with another flourish of pain. I didn't understand that feeling. Was it regret? Sorrow? Or something else? All these things, emotions I didn't have names for, seemed to pull at me from all sides.

"I don't know how to fix it, either," I admitted. "I can't. I took something from him that can't be replaced. There's nothing to be done for it."

"True," she agreed. "But sometimes it's not up to us to do the fixing, you know. Sometimes, for the big hurts, you have to wait for the fixing to happen all on its own. Just be ready when it happens; you won't want to let that opportunity pass you by." Garnett gave me a wink before she twirled on a heel and began sauntering away toward Dayrise, her thick braids bouncing with every step she made. "Until we meet again, dragonrider."

PART FOUR
THATCHER

CHAPTER TWENTY-SEVEN

I was officially, without a doubt, the biggest loser in the entire world when it came to flirting. I couldn't do it. Not successfully, anyway. It didn't matter how hard I tried—all that smooth, suave, mysterious confidence that seemed to come so easily to other guys might as well have been a foreign language to me. Even with a dragon, I didn't have a prayer. Sure, Garnett smiled and laughed when we talked, but I couldn't tell that she looked at me any differently than she did everyone else.

I was supposedly a reborn deity, and I didn't stand a chance with her.

I tried to convince myself that it really didn't make much difference. It wasn't like I had a lot of spare time to court anyone right now. And there were a lot of other things I needed to focus on.

But just a tiny hint that she might've liked me would've been nice. Or maybe she had given me a hint like that and I was just too dumb to tell the difference.

Ugggh. Oh well.

Looking back over my dragon's left side, I spotted Isandri's feline form skimming the clouds nearby. She darted and dove like a falcon on beautiful, tapered feathered wings. It was a completely different sort of flight than a dragon's.

Farther behind, Murdoc and his dragon kept in sight but stayed back. My heart thumped hard and my stomach dropped at the sight of him. The possibility that I'd used my divine power to manipulate his mind made my insides bind up and cramp. I hadn't even considered I might be capable of something like that. If I'd really done it—if I'd stripped away his ability to choose his destiny freely—then I was responsible for everything that happened to him now, wasn't I?

My throat burned as I swallowed hard. I didn't like that idea; the notion that I'd robbed him or anyone else of their free will. I didn't want to be that kind of, er, god, I guess. But, then again, if I hadn't used my power, Phillip wouldn't be on his way back to Jenna and their new baby right now.

Nothing made sense about any of this, and the more I thought about it, the more my brain tangled with questions I knew I'd never be able to answer. Right and wrong blurred into a mashed up mess. I didn't know what to think anymore.

I didn't feel very god-like at all.

Looking forward again, I focused my gaze down Fornax's snout through the lenses of my goggles. Phoebe sat close behind me in the saddle, her arms wrapped around my middle. We soared just above the thin line of clouds, stirring them up in our wake like a boat sailing on a smooth lake. Occasionally, the cloud cover broke long enough that we could glimpse the ground hundreds of feet below. But there was no sign of our destination, yet.

Jaevid had promised to arrange for a suitable place where we could stay. What that meant, exactly, I still wasn't sure. But he'd written out a long letter and given it to Reigh before we left Ms. Lin's house, insisting that we deliver it right away when we arrived at our destination. I guess Reigh knew more specifically where that was. All I'd been able to figure out was that it was somewhere right outside the city of Osbran.

I just hoped this wasn't another one of his relatives' houses. Surely by now, Jaevid had learned not to send us anywhere like that ever again. Any place we stayed was more than likely to be drawn into a fight where it got blown up, burned down, or demolished by a giant underbeast-thing. Okay, so that last one was less likely, according to Garnett. But I wasn't ruling anything out, just yet. Not with the luck I'd been having lately.

The sun sank lower and lower as we continued west, following a thin rise of rocky hilltops a little south. As the moon rose, the clouds seemed to all but melt away and the distant glimmer of city lights danced amidst the clear night. My body sagged in relief. There it was.

Osbran beckoned us in like a lighthouse.

Overall, it was a much smaller city than Dayrise—more of a village, actually. And as we began our final descent, I got a clear view of the stoic old stone walls that flanked three sides of it. The southernmost one seemed to have caved in over the centuries, leaving the rest to form a slightly crooked C-shape with all the larger buildings clustered inside. Beyond the wall, the scattered lights of farms and smaller houses dotted the dark like a field of stars. I guess over time, the city had expanded beyond the borders of its old walls.

Reigh didn't lead us right to Osbran or any of those farms nearby. As we swept in low, making a wide pass around the city, he gestured to what looked like a sizable military camp about three miles to the north. The complex was surrounded by a tall fence made of pointed logs. Watchtowers stood at all four corners of it, lit with torches, and I could barely make out the sounds of alert horns blaring in the night as we flared for landing.

Memories of my time in the prison camp outside of Halfax blazed like wildfire in my brain as we made our final pass to land. Gods and Fates—Jaevid hadn't sent us to a place like that, had he? No. Surely not.

My answer came in a rush of lime green and electric yellow scales that blurred out of the dark and landed right in front us with a *BOOM*. Another dragon!?

Fornax flailed back, flapping his wings frantically and letting out a shriek of dismay, floundering and hitting the ground awkwardly. Phoebe squeezed me harder and whimpered. I let out an angry shout. What the heck was going on?

The green and yellow dragon bristled, whipping around to hiss and bare her teeth. Without the big dewclaws on the back of her hind legs, I could tell it was a female like Vexi, and a much older one, too. She was nearly Fornax's size, with a muscular frame of stark yellow stripes over rich green and black scales. A big yellow blaze ran down from her snout to her tail, and under her belly and the backs of her legs. She eyed us distrustfully, making low grumbling, chattering sounds like an angry sparrow as she hedged in closer and sniffed the air. Her intelligent golden eyes studied Fornax, nostrils puffing and tail swishing.

My dragon stood tall, his strong body tense and his snout wrinkled in a snarl like an aggressive dog bristling before an attack. He didn't move while she smelled him, but his hide shivered with anxious energy under my hands.

Then the green dragoness's head popped up. Her ears perked forward. Her deep, growling sounds immediately changed to curious, conversational pops and chirps as she stretched out her neck to sniff at him more closely.

Fornax sniffed her back, gradually relaxing and sinking lower. With a sudden, almost relieved groan, he pushed his head against hers and made that deep purring sound in his throat.

Huh? Did they ... know each other?

Isandri and Murdoc landed behind us just as Vexi crawled over to investigate, too. She joined in the dragon sniffing fest, and all three of them rubbed their heads against one another and purred like a bunch of giant, fire-breathing cats.

"Shani! Stand down, girl!" someone shouted through the night.

Looking back to the torch lit camp ahead of us, I spotted the figure of a man walking out through the now-open front gate. A few other figures followed from a distance, most of them dressed out in armor. But it wasn't until they got closer that I could see the details. These weren't your everyday Maldobarian guards. Each one of the men wore a different style of armor, adorned and intricate, with a helmet under his arm and large gauntlets on their hands. Their long, royal blue cloaks rippled in the wind, the collars lined with a mane of white fox fur, and the edges trimmed in gold.

I sucked in a sharp breath. Whoa.

Those were ... dragonriders.

The man at the front walked up to our group of dragons without a bit of hesitation. His dark eyes studied us, focused on Fornax and me first with a puzzled frown, before he glanced over at Reigh and Vexi. His eyebrows shot up and his young, squared features went slack in surprise.

"Reigh? Is that you?" he shouted over the ambient sounds of dragon-purring.

Reigh gaped down at him with a similar look of shock. "Eirik Lachlan?" he called back. "What are you doing here?"

The man threw his head back and laughed. "I was about to ask you that! Fates, kid, do you have any idea what kind of hellhole you just dropped into?"

"Nope, But after a while, they all start to look the same," Reigh countered. "Jaevid sent us. I've got a letter for you."

"Is that so? And what does the honorable commander say?" Eirik asked.

"Oh, you know. The world is ending, the gods are stirring up trouble, and there's giant monsters that might level entire cities on the prowl—same old thing."

Eirik's brows rose again. "Oh. Is that all? Well, then ... " He waved a hand, motioning for us to follow as he turned and started back toward the camp. "Come on in. We don't have much, but you're welcome to it."

Passing through the tall, makeshift gateway, I stared around at all the large canvas tents and slapped-together log buildings that lined either side of the complex. It was clean and organized, at least. But clearly this wasn't a place anyone had intended to be a permanent fixture.

Dragons of all colors lounged around in the open areas between tents or did low, swooping passes overhead like massive bats. Men in armor or fine blue and black uniforms walked past. A few of them tripped and nearly fell over when Isandri shifted back into her elven form mid-stride. They stared after us, mouths hanging open.

Isandri didn't seem to notice their reactions, but it made me smirk a little. Maybe she was just used to getting that kind of response, though.

"I thought you lost your dragon in the war?" Reigh asked as he walked alongside our new host into the camp.

"Yeah. I did," Eirik Lachlan replied as he glanced over our ragtag group, his mouth still quirked in confusion. "But you know Jaevid would never let me off that easy. There were a lot of riders without mounts, and mounts without riders after the war ended. He found Shani for me and arranged for me to become her new rider. Not a chosen one like you, of course, but it's worked out well enough. Nice to be back in the saddle and being useful again, anyway."

"I thought you were going to be teaching at the academy, too." Reigh's expression twitched some, tinged with pain as he struggled to keep pace. His halting, staggering gait was a dead giveaway—he was not healed enough for this.

Eirik shrugged his stocky shoulders and motioned ahead. "Eventually yes. Until then, I'm here. The dragonriders that are supposed to be stationed at Northwatch are now displaced because the city is uninhabitable. We can't even launch a formal effort to retake it without basically leveling the place and rendering it unusable. So, here we sit, trying to figure out how to run the rats out of our tower so we can get back to work."

Reigh winced and shot me a look. "Yeah ... I, uh, may have heard something about that."

Eirik shook his head. "It's a nightmare. I've got thirty-three dragonriders here sitting on their hands. Every now and then, we're able to make a small, tactical strike, or act as security escorts to vital merchant caravans trying to make their way to Barrowton, but our forces aren't meant for operations like that. We run the risk of lighting merchant wagons on fire right along with the thieves attacking them. I know Her Majesty is dealing with a whole gaggle of problems these days, but the sooner we can get that city cleaned out and the tower restored, the better."

We stopped as we reached a far corner of the camp where a much larger canvas tent stood off by itself, the door guarded by two dragonriders in full battle dress. They saluted as we entered, and Eirik showed us into what must have been the officers' quarters. Er, well, most of us. Murdoc hung back, standing alongside his young dragon and eyeing the camp around us with his usual broody, sullen scowl. It took him a minute or two of reasoning with his dragon to persuade him that he wasn't going to fit through that door and he should sit outside and wait for us. The red and black beast puffed and snorted sulkily before he sat back on his haunches with a *thud*.

Murdoc rolled his eyes and jogged over to rejoin us as we ducked into the large tent. It had been divided into several rooms, each one outfitted with a few bits of furniture and stockpiles of gear and materials. Rugs stretched across the floor and glass lamps hung from the ceiling to give the place a warm, soft feel.

Rounding a large desk at the back of the first room, Eirik lit another lamp and held a hand out to Reigh. "You said there was a letter?"

Reigh nodded grimly and handed it over. "Do me a favor and ... try to think happy thoughts while you're reading it," he mumbled.

Eirik's wide-eyed stare darted back and forth between Reigh and the letter a few times before he finally sank down into the chair at the desk and began to open it. Jaevid had written out several pages, and as Eirik gave them a quick glance over, he sighed and waved a hand at us. "Right. Well, it looks like this will take me a few minutes. Go ahead and make yourselves comfortable. There's food around the fire rings outside if you're hungry, and rooms in the back you can take if you mean to stay the night."

"Thank you. We'll try to stay out of trouble." Reigh bowed his head slowly before he cast me a meaningful look and tipped his head toward the back like he wanted me to follow.

Oh no. What was this about?

CHAPTER TWENTY-EIGHT

While Murdoc made his way back outside, and Phoebe and Isandri hung close together, I followed Reigh farther into the tent until we came to one of the rooms at the very back. The more distance we put between the rest of our group and ourselves, the more lurching and wobbly Reigh's strides became. He gasped and hissed curses through his teeth, barely managing to stagger beyond the cover of the room's door-flap before he dropped his bag and fell against a nearby washstand. He clung to it with a white-knuckled grip just to stay on his feet.

"Reigh?!" I rushed over to try and take his arm, but he brushed me off, shaking his head as he wheezed and gasped.

"I-Just give me a second," he rasped as he wiped the sweat from his brow onto his sleeve and shut his eyes. "See if you can find some hot water, okay?"

"Right. Yeah. I'll be right back." I darted from the room and scoured the tent, finding plenty of other supplies stockpiled along the walls and hall. When I came into the room directly next to ours, though, I spotted a miniature wood-burning stove in a corner, surrounded by pots and pans. Cinders still smoldered inside it, and a kettle perched on the top. I put a hand against the side of it. Still warm. Perfect.

Snatching up the kettle and another spare, empty pot, just in case, I ran back to the room where Reigh still stood leaning against the washstand. He'd already stripped off his belt, tunic, and was struggling to unravel the many layers of bandaging Kiran had wrapped around his chest and back. His hands trembled, faltering and losing their grip whenever he tried to reach behind to loosen the long strips of white cloth. Some of them were dotted with the faintest hints of blood that'd seeped through from underneath. Not good.

He really had overdone it.

"Here, I found this." I said quietly as I poured some of the hot water into the empty pot and set it on the stand beside him.

"Good. I-I ... I need your help," he managed shakily. "P-Please."

"Just tell me what to do." I stepped over quickly, taking the end of the bandage he'd been wrestling with and continuing to slowly unwrap it from his torso.

The more layers I peeled back, the bigger the blood-soaked stains became. Oh, this couldn't be good. Had he reopened all his wounds? Should I go and find a real medic to help him?

"O-Okay," he rasped as he put both hands on the washstand and steadied himself, his breathing hard between every word. "There's a few clean rags in my bag there. You gotta get them wet and wipe off the old herbal mixture and the blood. Get them as clean as you can."

"Reigh, I think you've ripped some of these back open. You might need someone to stitch them up again." I hurried through rinsing the washcloth and wringing it out, wiping at the coin-sized spots on his back where the three arrows had pierced his body. The areas around them were badly bruised and swollen, still. Fates, he shouldn't have been trying to move around or fly yet. He should have been resting back at Ms. Lin's.

I was so distracted by the most recent wounds on his back, I almost missed it—the massive, horrible scar that covered his back from his neck nearly all the way down to his waist. It was faded, so maybe it wasn't too recent, but the sheer size of it and the raised, gnarled edges that resembled continents drawn onto a map, caught me off guard. Whatever had happened there, it must've been bad. A large wound that had covered almost his entire back. A burn, maybe?

Reigh shook his head, making his mop of dark red hair swish. "No. It's not that bad," he wheezed. "Just pulled a stitch or two. It'll be fine. Clean the wounds out as best you can, but don't rub or wipe too roughly or you'll rip the stitches out. Then I've got more healing salve in that small metal tin there. Put a good-sized glob on each of the puncture sites. Then you can wrap it back up with the gauze and bandages."

I stayed quiet as I followed his instructions, trying to move carefully so I didn't cause him any more pain than necessary. I re-dressed each wound one at a time and bound his torso back up with layers of new, clean bandages before I moved down to do the same thing to the puncture on his leg. It took a while, but I didn't dare rush it. He was still so weak from the poison—I doubted his body could handle an infection, too.

"There. Done." I stood back as I finished re-wrapping his leg and sliding his thick wool sock up over it for an added cushion. "Now, come on. There's a cot and some blankets over here. You're going to lie down. And I'm going to see if I can find a medic somewhere that can give you something for the pain. Or at the very least, something that'll knock you out so you have to rest for a while."

He chuckled weakly. "Heh. You sound like Jae. Bunch of fussing nannies, you two."

I frowned. "Call me whatever you want. You're not in any shape to be doing this, Reigh. I know it's a matter of pride. You want to prove yourself to your sister. But you won't last five seconds if we get into a real fight."

His delirious grin faded as he stared me down. Hanging his head, his mouth mashed up bitterly as he muttered a quiet agreement. He let me help him limp over to where a few low cots stood along the wall and settle into one. I handed him a few blankets and stood back, faltering between insisting he at least talk to a medic and keeping my mouth shut.

"Stop it with the puppy eyes, would you? I'll be fine." Reigh growled as he relaxed back onto a pillow and closed his eyes. "Geez, you might actually be worse than Jae, you know? I've had worse than this."

I didn't doubt that—not after seeing that burn scar on his back. "Just don't push yourself too hard," I said, trying to sound casual. "If you died, I'm pretty sure I'm the one Queen Jenna will blame, and I'd rather not be on her bad side, if it's all the same to you."

He laughed weakly and wafted a hand at me. "Fiiine. Gimme a few hours and I'll be ready to dive headlong into Jaevid's next suicidal scheme. If you've got any sense, you'll try to get some sleep, too. I've played this game before already—I know how it usually ends. If I know Jaevid and his habit of getting us lodged right in the middle of world-ending problems, we're not even to the *real* fun yet."

I TRIED NOT to let that comment freak me out as I left Reigh alone to rest. *Real* fun? He was joking, right? Because literally none of this had been any fun at all. Okay, maybe some of the flying had been pretty fun, but still. The rest had been downright horrible.

Eirik didn't look up from where he sat, frowning down into the many pages of Jaevid's letter as I passed back through the central room of the tent. I made a speedy break for the exit, just in case he happened to get to the part where Jaevid told him I was a reincarnated deity while I was passing through. Yikes.

As soon as I stepped out into the brisk night air, the sounds of the camp rushed me at once. The voices of the dragonriders laughing and talking while they gathered around the big campfires lit between some of the clusters of tents. The dragons squawking or chirping at one another as they gathered together to groom one another and bask in the starlight. The crackle of flames, the clinking of metal armor, and the faintest humming buzz of crickets singing in the grass.

Something about it made me pause and drink it all in. Eventually, if I survived the mess with Iksoli, I might find myself as one of these dragonriders at a camp like this one. Or a watchtower, I guess. I'd be one of those men dressed in armor. The idea made my skin prickle and my heart skip a beat. I'd never imagined I'd be anything more than a half-decent farrier, running the family shop in Thornbend. That I was even standing here, with a dragon of my own and a chance to join these people and be counted as one of them, was just ... unfathomable. It still felt too good to be true. Like a dream I might suddenly wake up from.

It took a few minutes of walking around from one campfire to the next before I found Phoebe, Isandri, and Murdoc. They'd settled in with a small group of dragonriders, most of which were staring at Isandri with expressions of absolute mystification. She did stick out a little. If her long, pointed ears and smooth ebony complexion adorned in shining silver marks weren't enough to get everyone's attention, then her billowing, silken robes and tall crystal-tipped staff were.

Eventually, one of them worked up the nerve to ask her where she was from, and that prompted the others to scoot in a little closer so they could hear. Isandri gave them gentle, knowing smiles as she explained. That was really all it took to get the conversation rolling, and soon Isandri and Phoebe were chatting merrily with the dragonriders while Murdoc sat back, ate some of the camp stew they'd been cooking over the fire, and watched. He hadn't said much at all since ...

My stomach twisted and I looked away. Jaevid's words still echoed in my head like an out-of-tune chorus. What was I supposed to do? What was I supposed to say? Apologizing didn't ... it wasn't ... Argh! I didn't want to do that, even if a part of me knew I should.

And then there was the matter of why he was here in the first place. Maybe it'd never been his choice because I had accidentally forced this on him. But if that was the case, then why was he still here now? If he had never truly wanted this path, he could've left. Not that the Ulfrangar were ever going to take him back, but still—he had other options. And now he had a dragon, too. I couldn't tell if he'd finally accepted the beast or not, and I didn't dare ask while things were still uncomfortable and wrong between us.

I'd barely settled into a seat next to Phoebe when another chorus of horns went up around the compound. The men up on the watchtowers shouted down and used the dragonrider code of hand signals. They did it so fast I could only catch a few of the gestures. But one sequence in particular made my blood go ice-cold in my veins:

... dressed in black armor.

Oh gods.

My gaze immediately flashed to Murdoc, who was still frowning around at the dragonriders hurrying by, mustering and moving toward the front gate of the compound. A few of them were saddling up, checking their weapons, and preparing to take off.

No—no, no, no! This couldn't happen! Not now! We'd only just gotten here. How could the Ulfrangar possibly know where we were?

Without a word, I bolted off to join the crowd gathering at the gate. There were already a dozen of them standing there to watch, fixated on something happening just outside the camp. Whatever it was, I couldn't see through all the big armored bodies in my path. Curse it—I had to know! I had to see! I needed to be sure!

"Move! I have to get through!" I shouted, pushing and shoving through the armored men until I managed to work my way to the front.

Then I saw them.

A company of no less than fifty Ulfrangar assassins stood like a legion of shadow-soldiers right before the doorway of the dragonrider camp. They all wore identical ensembles of black leather armor, cloaks, and silver cuffs. Black silk masks covered their noses and mouths, and a swipe of black war paint had been smeared across their eyes. It was the exact same way Murdoc had been dressed the night we met in Thornbend.

My heart pounded like a war drum, threatening to punch right out of my chest as one of the Ulfrangar prowled forward and stood, solemn, still, and silent. Almost like he was waiting for something.

But what?

"What, by all the gods, is the meaning of this?" Eirik's familiar voice shouted nearby. "Out of the way—stand aside, I said!"

He appeared through the crowd of dragonriders, shoving the last two out of his path and halting abruptly at the sight of the Ulfrangar. His eyes went round for an instant. Then his rugged features drew into a glare like the furious glower of an angry lion. He stepped out of the line of riders, the night wind whipping in the end of his cloak.

"There'd better be a fantastic explanation for this," Eirik warned in an ominous growl as soon as he got close. "Who are you? What is your business here?"

The Ulfrangar who'd come forward away from the rest of their group, stretched out a hand without a word, offering him an envelope of black-dyed parchment sealed with a silver glob of wax.

Eirik took it, staring between the assassin and the envelope in baffled silence. Then he broke the seal and opened it.

The howling night wind filled the eerie silence as no one moved—as though everyone standing there were holding their breath. My pulse kicked and raced wildly, making my body go numb. What was going on? Why had the Ulfrangar given him a letter? Fates, what was happening?!

Eirik lifted his head to look back up at the assassin. His mouth clamped into a bitter, uncertain line. But he didn't say anything, and slowly turned around to walk back into the compound with that black letter still in his hand. I caught the glimmer of silver ink scribbled onto one side of it, but I couldn't make out any of the words.

The Ulfrangar didn't move or retreat, even after the gate shut behind Eirik and we were all sealed back inside the high wooden walls. Were they just going to stay out there? Why? What were they waiting for?

By then, Isandri, Phoebe, and Murdoc had made their way to the front of the gathering, as well. They all stared at Eirik with the same expressions of pale shock—probably a lot like the one on my face, too—as he approached and stopped right in front of us.

The dragonrider officer panned his gaze across our company slowly, carefully, before settling squarely onto me. His voice was quiet and controlled, like he was deliberately keeping all emotion in check, as he asked, "Which one of you is Murdoc?"

My stomach dropped. Every nerve fired at once as panic took my brain like a hurricane, scattering all my better sense and reason. "Why?" I demanded.

Eirik glanced down to the letter in his hand, seeming to hesitate before he finally replied, "Because it seems the army of assassins on my doorstep are willing to spare us a very costly battle ... in exchange for his immediate surrender."

GODLING

THE DRAGONRIDER HERITAGE BOOK FOUR

PART ONE
THATCHER

CHAPTER ONE

The Ulfrangar had come for Murdoc again.

We'd been dodging those murderous assassins basically since Murdoc and I had first met. They had come after us at the Cromwell estate in Eastwatch, and then again twice in Dayrise. They'd kidnapped me, and nearly killed Reigh by shooting him full of poisoned arrows. They had burned down Ms. Lin's house and left us all running like scared rabbits from one place to the next, fighting tooth and nail just to stay ahead of them.

I guess I should've realized this couldn't go on forever. Sooner or later, we'd run out of places to hide, or they'd finally get us backed into a corner. I just hadn't expected it to happen like this—smack in the middle of a military compound full of dragonriders.

Before, the Ulfrangar had always struck from the shadows. They made stealthy attacks, or used poisoned arrows in the cover of night—usually when we were least expecting it. Not this time, though. There were no combusting dragon-venom bombs, no sudden ambushes, and no explosions of flames. This time, they had come with a blatant threat. An ultimatum:

Murdoc's life or an all-out bloodbath.

It wasn't hard to believe they would make good on that threat. Not when roughly fifty assassins clad in black leather armor and cloaks stood before us, armed and ready. They all wore those signature silver bracers as they remained motionless, blocking the way beyond the gate of the small, slapped-together military fort where Jaevid had sent us.

"Which one of you is Murdoc?" Seasoned Lieutenant Eirik Lachlan demanded again, his gaze panning across the crowd gathered around him at the gate.

My heart hit the pit of my stomach like I'd swallowed a brick of solid iron. My head spun, and my hands instinctively curled into sweaty, shaking fists at my sides. I didn't dare to move, speak, or even glance around to see where Murdoc was. Somehow, doing that felt like I might betray his position. He had to be somewhere nearby, though. He'd come with us to the gate. I knew that much. But what would he do? Was he going to step forward? Give himself up? And if he did, how would Lieutenant Eirik respond? Was he seriously just going to hand him over to the Ulfrangar to be killed?

No, surely not. We'd only just met the lieutenant an hour or so ago, but he didn't seem like the kind of guy to just lie down and submit to the threats of assassins. He was a dragonrider, after all. Not to mention, he had a compound full of his comrades waiting right here, didn't he? We didn't have to give in to the Ulfrangar's demands—not when we could fight. The Ulfrangar were strong, but they were no match for a bunch of dragonriders.

Unless ... there was something else going on here, something I was missing.

That idea closed around my mind like an icy fist, making my head pound with sudden pressure as I stared at all the Ulfrangar waiting there like dark specters in the night until the gate boomed shut. Even with that barrier between us, I didn't feel any safer.

My thoughts tangled like thorny vines, painful and pricking, as I tried to figure out what I should do. The Ulfrangar agents weren't stupid. They wouldn't do something like this unless they were certain they had the upper hand. I didn't know much about them, but I was sure about that much.

I flinched, every muscle locking solid, as a tall figure stepped forward from our group.

Then I couldn't help but look right at him.

"I'm Murdoc," he replied quietly, his tone strangely calm—almost like he'd already decided he wasn't going to fight this at all. Even his expression, with his head slightly bowed and his gaze fixed vacantly ahead, was all wrong. I'd never seen him make that face before.

I'd never seen him look ... defeated.

Eirik made a thoughtful sound in his throat and studied Murdoc for a long, silent moment. Every heartbeat in my chest made my head throb and my breath come in fast, frantic pants. I couldn't let this happen. I couldn't let Murdoc give himself up. Not like this. Not when things were still so wrong between us. I didn't want to forgive him for being involved with my father's death. Whatever role he'd played in that, I didn't want to let it go. Not yet.

But I didn't want him to die, either.

"Very well," Eirik murmured, flicking a look at the rest of us before nodding back toward his tent. "It seems we have until dawn to sort this out. All of you, come with me."

What? Until *dawn*? That was it? How long was that? A few hours?

My heart gave a painful, wrenching thud in the back of my throat.

I took off right behind Eirik and Murdoc, following them back through the compound quickly and quietly. The eyes of every dragonrider standing on either side of the rows of tents and campfires followed us the entire way. It took everything I had not to glare back at them. Not out of anger, though. This didn't have anything to do with them. It was frustration, I guess. Humiliation that we were back in the same position once again. I hated this—being cornered by those soulless murderers over and over. Running like scared rabbits from one place to the next. We couldn't keep doing this.

It had to stop.

ONE BY ONE, our entire group filed back into Eirik's private tent and stood around his desk, solemn faced and completely silent. Isandri, Phoebe, Murdoc, and I waited while Eirik went to go retrieve Reigh from one of the partitioned rooms where he'd been resting. Boy, was he in for a rude awakening.

The tension hung thick and heavy over us, and no one dared to speak. I couldn't even bring myself to look any of them in the eye. Not when my face was still flushed with anger, and my heart was pounding like a war drum in my ears.

Reigh was still fastening his sword belt around his hips as he shambled in behind Eirik, groggy-eyed and scowling with all his red hair mussed up. He limped a little with every other step, as though his injuries were still causing him pain. Based on what I'd seen earlier when I helped him change bandages, I knew Reigh was still in no shape to fight. He'd barely survived from our last encounter with these brutal assassins. They'd shot him full of poison arrows and nearly killed him, and it was only the fast work of Phoebe and Kiran that had saved him. No way was he ready to take them on again.

"What have you guys done now? We haven't even been here three hours yet," Reigh grumbled as he rubbed at his face. He muttered elven curses under his breath as he staggered over to stand next to me.

Thankfully, I wasn't the one who had to break the bad news to him.

"Seems some of that trouble you mentioned before has already followed you here in the form of a company of assassins camping outside my gate." Eirik's wooden chair creaked as he sat down and placed the black parchment letter from the Ulfrangar on his desk in front of him. He sat and stared at it for a few agonizing, quiet seconds. Then, at last, he looked up at us and sighed. "It's barely four hours until sunrise. That isn't long enough to call for reinforcements, or obtain Her Majesty's permission to strike against those people, even if I sent my fastest riders right now. But you are a Prince of Maldobar, Reigh. Technically, your word is all I need. Assassins or not, I've got dragons enough to scorch them to soot, if that's what you want me to do. All you have to do is say the word."

Reigh's expression darkened, his jawline going tense as every trace of bleariness vanished from his features. He opened his mouth like he might be about to give that order, but Murdoc spoke first.

"Doing that would get a lot, if not all, of your men killed."

"Hah! They can't possibly hope to take this compound with only a few foot soldiers," Eirik balked as he sat back in his chair. He cut his earthy, light brown eyes around at all of us and frowned suspiciously. "Unless you know something you haven't told me."

"The agents outside were likely only sent to get your attention. It's the ones you don't see that are the ones meant to do the real work here. The ones standing at your side, wearing the armor of your comrades, are the Ulfrangar you should fear," Murdoc insisted, his voice far emptier and more monotone than usual. Something about that look in his eyes, like his soul had already separated from the rest of him, set alarm bells tolling in my head. I'd never seen that look before, and it chilled me right down to the marrow.

"Are you suggesting there are Ulfrangar agents hiding within *my* ranks?" Eirik growled through his teeth, as though that suggestion was way over the line.

"No, I'm not *suggesting* anything. I'm *telling* you Ulfrangar do not make empty threats. They don't usually make threats at all. If they've bothered to offer us a chance to avoid bloodshed, you can be certain there are Ulfrangar somewhere in this compound already." Murdoc flicked a glance past me to Reigh, something almost pleading in his eyes. "You don't have a choice. Having me in your company has already caused a lot of people pain and hardship. But I can't live with the knowledge that I've caused the deaths of these men. I am *not* worth the lives of thirty-three dragonriders, and you know it."

Reigh crossed his arms, meeting Murdoc's desperate expression with a stubborn scowl. "I didn't take you for the type to be a martyr."

"I'm not," he snapped, his eyes wide and nearly crazed with urgency. His voice stayed hushed, and he spoke quickly as he took a step closer to square off with Reigh face-to-face. "I'm being realistic. There's no running from this. There's no fighting it. This is their final solution. I've told you all from the start that they would never let me go, and you were the one who barely walked away from it the last time they came for me. Now they'll do what they have to in order to see that my oath is kept, even if that means making an example of every soul in this camp."

"Except that you took no oath," a man's deep, familiar voice interrupted from the doorway.

We all turned to look, gaping in unison at the two, very recognizable figures standing together in the entryway to Eirik's private tent. An aging human man with graying hair, a neatly trimmed white beard, and cold amber eyes glowered back at us like he'd just caught us all doing something heinous. Right beside him, a petite, staggeringly beautiful woman with long pointed ears studied us, as well. Granted, she didn't look as angry. More curious, I guess. Her silvery-white hair hung in a thick braid far past her waist, and she had one hand on her hip while the other gripped an ornate longbow.

My stomach gave a frantic flip, and I blinked hard a few times just to make sure I wasn't hallucinating. Nope. Definitely not.

King Jace Rordin and Queen Araxie of Luntharda had found us.

2

CHAPTER TWO

King Jace had mentioned something about going to get his wife when he left our company back in Dayrise. Honestly, at the time, I'd just assumed he was referencing some old, inside joke between Jaevid and him. They teased one another a lot like that.

Staring at the breathtaking elven woman, my brain scrambled at the realization that, no, he hadn't been joking about that at all. Queen Araxie cast her shimmering, multi-hued eyes around the room at us. Her controlled expression was impossible to read, and her fine robes of vividly colored silks and ornate leather armor marked her as royalty. She didn't look nearly as old as Jace did. But, then again, it was honestly hard to tell. Gray elves didn't show their age like humans did. Er, well, not physically anyway. Their lifespans were supposedly about the same as ours, but their physical bodies didn't wrinkle and sag with time quite as much as they got older. The queen was an excellent example of that. There were a few fine lines around her mouth and in the corners of her eyes, a sort of diminishing thinness to her frame, and a knobbiness to her hands—but none of that took away from her beauty ... or the keen look of suspicion in her eyes when she considered Murdoc.

"Your Majesties, please forgive me, I had no idea you were coming here." Eirik snapped to his feet, stumbling all over himself as he gave a brisk salute.

The old king came closer, and immediately waved him off. "Which is precisely what I intended. I may be past my prime, but I still know how to sneak past Ulfrangar and dragonrider surveillance. What do you think I've spent the last thirty years teaching my sons?" He gave a dry, throaty chuckle. "You've got quite a problem on your doorstep, haven't you, Lieutenant?"

Eirik deflated some and sank back on his heels. "So it would seem. And not much time to fix it. We have until dawn to deliver Murdoc to them."

"Until dawn? She's being generous, then." King Jace kept his piercing stare fixed on Murdoc with purpose as he stepped farther into the tent. "You were still a pup earning back your patronage price. The debt of your defection is not yours to repay. That was why they sent Rook after you. He was your handler. It was his responsibility to hunt you down and punish you for your defection. You were his mistake to correct."

Murdoc stiffened, his face going paler in the warm light of the lamps flickering around the tent. "Rook is dead," he managed in a shaking whisper. "I have no handler. And even if I did, it wouldn't matter. My life is forfeit either way. The punishment for defection is death, even for a pup."

"True," Jace conceded with a knowing smirk. "But it may not be that simple. By the laws of the pack, you should be my heirling now. That status complicates things a great deal—likely far more than you realize. There are great powers at work all around you, pup. This has become far larger than a mere struggle to save your life. Wheels are now in motion that you cannot even fathom, and that dark destiny waiting for you beyond the gates of this modest fort is not even aware of it."

Murdoc's hazel eyes went wide. His mouth fell open, but he didn't make a sound.

What? Great powers? What was Jace talking about? Did this have something to do with Jaevid? He definitely qualified as a great power, but he wasn't even here.

"Make no mistake, your situation is dire. There's no denying that. I'm just not sure you fully grasp what is truly at stake." Jace flicked his gaze back to Eirik. "The boy speaks the truth, though. You shouldn't assume everyone within the walls of this compound is your ally. The Ulfrangar have spent thousands of years perfecting the art of infiltrating every possible court, guild, legion, and tier of society around the world. Normally, they wouldn't want to compromise their agents working within the ranks of an organization as exclusive as the Dragonriders of Maldobar. It's costly and risky to get them there in the first place. Exposing them would mean compromising those individuals that undoubtedly feed them valuable information. But the task of punishing this pup has become a matter of pride now. Their leader, the Zuer, has been shamed in her failed attempts to bring him in. Her reputation now hangs in the balance. Failing this time would call into question her effectiveness as their leader. For those within the pack, weakness is unacceptable."

"You think she's coming here to deal with me personally." Murdoc's voice was barely more than a trembling whisper.

Jace nodded slowly, memories like dark flames dancing in his eyes. "With a gesture like this, demanding your life or an outright battle against a company of dragonriders out in the open? Yes. I do believe the Zuer herself will come for you at dawn. To say that she is acting desperately would be correct, because now her life and station within the Ulfrangar hang in the balance, as well. If she fails to kill you this time, she will have brought great shame upon the Ulfrangar. She will have to endure rivals attempting to drag her from her throne, revolts within her ranks, and eventually her own demise. To get out of this mess with her pride and position intact, she must make a public example of you to the rest of her order."

Murdoc's throat jumped as he swallowed, and once again, I saw real fear seep into the corners of his face. It made my chest go tight, my lungs squeezing around a rising surge of panic that left me numb. That was the same look he'd given me right before he'd told me about his possible involvement with my father's death.

And it filled me with the same cold bite of dread it had then.

Nothing frightened Murdoc—not when it came to fighting. At least, not that I'd seen. We had been up against some pretty terrible odds before, and I'd witnessed him face down our enemies with a defiant sneer even when things seemed hopeless. So if the idea of this woman, the Zuer, coming here was something that scared him … then we should all be terrified.

THIS NEW REALIZATION about what we might really be up against settled through the room like a toxic vapor. The Zuer was probably coming here—right to this compound—to kill Murdoc herself at dawn. That meant it was also a fair bet that those Ulfrangar she'd posted outside the gate were probably the best she had. Fighting them would be more dangerous than ever. People would die.

"Running isn't an option. You can be certain they're watching for that. And fighting them head-on will end in a bloodbath." King Jace leveled a harrowing stare upon Murdoc, all the intensity of those memories still flickering in his steely eyes. "Fortunately, the only question remaining is actually fairly simple, but it's one you'll have to answer for yourself, just as I did. There was a time when I saw my death as a final sort of release from a lifetime of shame, murder, deceit, and cowardice. I ran from the Ulfrangar, and only escaped because a monster in a crown found some use for me as his hired killer. I wanted to die. But when I thought that time had finally come …" Jace paused, his gaze drawn to the elven woman at his side as though by gravity. The smile that softened all his hard, chiseled features seemed to melt past every cold word that had left his lips. "I was given a new path, instead. A rebirth. A chance to become something better. I didn't know if I would be successful, and I certainly didn't count myself worthy. But it was better to try and fail, than to die in shame."

Queen Araxie smiled back, bumping her arm against his coyly.

Jace leaned down, pressing a kiss against her hair before he cleared his throat and looked back at Murdoc. "I don't envy where you stand now. What lies before you is going to hurt. But I think you've known that all along. And now you must answer that one, simple question. Do you want us to save you? You cannot save yourself from the Zuer's wrath this time—not without significant help." Jace cocked an eyebrow, tilting his head to one side as his expression became curious and pensive, as though he were picking apart every tiny move Murdoc made. "Would you have us hand you over to your certain death? Or are you willing to tempt fate once again, pup?"

I almost missed it. Standing across from Murdoc, I barely caught the flicker of his glance darting in my direction for the briefest instant. I tensed. A hard knot lodged in my throat, making it difficult to breathe. Was he expecting me to say something? To object? Or demand that he continue to fight this?

I tried. But every time I reached for the right words, everything in my mind became so loud I couldn't even hear myself think. That anger and grief welled up too fast, roaring through my head like a tidal wave I couldn't escape. I didn't know what I wanted or how I felt.

I just ... didn't want Murdoc to die.

King Jace seemed to sense the awkward tension rising between us. He cleared his throat again and raised a hand, as though to pause the discussion altogether. "Perhaps we should have the rest of this conversation privately," he suggested. "My dear, why don't you take the rest of Jenna's distinguished hunters outside to ready themselves. Whatever happens next, I think we should all be prepared."

The elven woman cast him a quick, knowing smile before she motioned for us to go with her back outside. Phoebe, Isandri, and Reigh followed wordlessly.

But my feet wouldn't budge.

I stood there, staring at Murdoc as my heartbeat thundered in my ears. He wouldn't even meet my gaze, and kept his face turned down at the ground between us. With his features still swollen and bruised where I'd punched him, his quivering jaw clenched hard, and his broad shoulders curled forward as though he were folding in on himself, I couldn't remember him ever looking so small.

I didn't recognize him at all.

But I knew deep down, like someone had carved it into my brain, that this meant he was giving up. He was going to surrender to those monsters, trembling in fear before them like a scared little kid. Where was the bloody-knuckled brawler I'd known from the prison camp—the one who had beat down any thug who tried to take advantage of us? Where was the coldly defiant warrior who had fought Rook? The strong and capable duelist who'd taught me to fight?

I couldn't find that person anywhere as I studied his face.

And I hated it.

Words burned through my chest, confused and angry like a tangled rat's nest of red-hot wire. I sucked in deep, furious breaths. I wouldn't let him do this. Murdoc would *not* just give up. Not now.

But before I could say anything, Jace's voice growled my name like a warning. "Thatcher. You need to step outside."

I cast the old king what was probably an extremely inappropriate glare of defiance. Step outside? But this wasn't—

"Go, Thatcher," Murdoc muttered, his voice tight and shaking as he glared up at me suddenly. "This has *nothing* to do with you."

3
CHAPTER THREE

I stood outside Lieutenant Eirik's tent, staring at the closed flap. It was just a piece of heavy canvas, but it felt like a door that had just been slammed right in my face. Now I was on the outside, cut off from even being a part of the conversation that would decide Murdoc's fate.

And I didn't know what to do. I didn't know what to say, or think, or feel. Jaevid's words burned through my memory. No one knew for sure if Murdoc had really been the one to kill my father that night in Thornbend. I should've guessed it was a possibility long before Murdoc ever brought it up. But did that really absolve him of being involved in it at all? Should I just let it go? Act like it didn't matter? Should I even want him to live?

Boot steps approached, crunching over the ground and finally stopping right next to me. "Thatcher?" Reigh asked. "You all right?"

I bowed my head some. "No."

"Afraid Murdoc's going to give up and turn himself in?" he guessed.

My head hung lower, and I couldn't even muster up the nerve to answer. I guess I didn't have to, though.

Reigh clapped a hand on my shoulder and gave me a small shove. "Come on. You can mope all you want over there with the rest of us."

I followed him around to the side of Eirik's tent where Isandri, Phoebe, and Queen Araxie were gathered around a campfire ring. They sat on a few wooden crates and boxes that had been dragged close to the fire's edge as makeshift chairs, their faces lit by the warm glow of the flickering flames. Phoebe looked every bit as miserable as I felt, and Isandri had a crease of worry in her brow. Only Queen Araxie seemed calm and unconcerned as she used a long metal poker to stoke the flames.

They all looked up as we approached and sank down into the two remaining seats, but no one said a word. Nothing but the crackle and pop of the campfire, and the occasional distant sound of growling dragons or voices of soldiers, filled the heavy silence. Minutes passed, maybe longer, and all I could do was sit there, numb and motionless. I stared into the glowing embers while my thoughts ran wild, imagining every terrible thing that might happen in the next few hours. What was going on back in the tent? What was Jace saying to Murdoc? Would anything the old king said change his mind at this point? Or was Murdoc too far gone to be convinced to fight the Ulfrangar again?

Was ... was it my fault? Because of the fight we'd had? Because I hadn't talked to him so we could try and fix this?

We sat that way, the atmosphere thick with anxiety, until at last, Queen Araxie gave a heavy sigh. "My, my. I've been told so much about the tenacity and courage of Jenna's hunters, but you are all rather grim."

"There's not much to be tenacious about until we know what's going to happen with Murdoc," Reigh grumbled, sitting slumped forward with his cheek resting on his fist.

"I see. And you truly believe it's his choice to make?" The queen's opaline eyes shone in the firelight, reflecting in colors of silver, purple, blue, and green as she studied me.

"Well, it is certainly not ours." Isandri scowled disapprovingly. "We cannot force him to continue fighting this fate if he does not wish to."

"Is that so?" Araxie's smile was cryptic and still aimed directly at me. "It is my belief that we all need a little forcing every now and then, should we begin to lose our way. That is the function of friendship, I think. To help keep one another on the right path when our courage fails and our hope withers."

My mouth scrunched, screwing up involuntarily, and I looked away. I didn't want her to see me gnashing my teeth so my conflicted emotions wouldn't show.

"Jace has told me a great deal about you all. You've been through a lot in quite a short time. You've endured much," she continued quietly, her tone gentler. "I know it is not common in Maldobar for children to be taught about the ancient gods. We have tried to keep such beliefs and practices alive in my homeland, but as I'm sure you now know, some things have diminished over the years. I had never heard the tales of the godling children until now, and if it weren't my own husband telling me, I'm not sure I would have believed it."

I didn't dare to meet her stare as I rubbed at the back of my neck and mumbled, "I'm still not sure I even believe it."

She gave a light, melodic laugh. "You sound so much like him."

"Like who?"

"Jaevid."

I stiffened, my gaze snapping up to lock with hers just in time to see a warm, almost motherly grin spread over her features. What? She thought *I* was like Jaevid? No—no way. He was the greatest hero Maldobar had ever known. There was no way I'd ever be anything like him.

"He was about your age when I first met him. Maybe a little older. But every bit as unsure of himself as you are now," she recalled fondly. "He doubted his birthright, too. He worried that his power would not be enough. And yet, he made everyone around him want to be better. I wonder if that is how Murdoc has felt, if being around all of you has made him desire to become better?"

My mouth clamped shut and I had to look away again as my heart gave a painful twist deep in my chest.

"I see great pain in your eyes, young man. Sorrow and betrayal. And in that way, I see myself in you, as well." There was a strange, cryptic edge to her tone as she gradually panned her eyes back down to the fire between us. "Did you not know about your friend's past?"

"No, he knew. But they had a pretty intense fight a few days ago, apparently," Reigh piped up, and I'd never wanted to hit him more in my entire life. "They haven't spoken since."

My mouth pinched up and I shot him a glare of warning. He didn't even know what our fight was about, right? He'd still been out of it thanks to getting shot full of poisoned Ulfrangar crossbow bolts. So Jaevid must have told him about it. Or Phoebe. Or Isandri. Ugh!! I didn't know who'd run tattling to him, and it didn't matter. It wasn't his story to tell to Queen Araxie.

"Ahhh, I see." Her shimmering, multihued eyes narrowed a little. "You must be asking yourself if you want him to live or not, then."

Every muscle in my body went stiff as I sat, biting down hard against the urge to storm off. I didn't want to sit here and listen to them try to pick me apart. Queen Araxie didn't even know me. We didn't have anything in common. She'd been born royalty, trained as a powerful warrior, and ultimately been a champion to her people in the Gray War.

I'd shoveled a lot of horse manure. Nothing about our paths were the same.

"I know *exactly* how you feel, Thatcher," she insisted as though she could somehow read my mind. "This might come as a surprise to you all. You're all too young to remember the Gray War when Maldobar fought my homeland of Luntharda. It was a brutal and devasting time. And when I first met Jace, all those years ago, I hated every breath he took. I wanted him to die. I wanted to be the one to end his life for all the pain he'd caused my family." Her expression had gone distant, as if the storm of battles past had carried her mind far away.

"Why?" Phoebe asked, her voice hushed and anxious.

"Because he nearly destroyed my entire family," the queen answered matter-of-factly. "He came with Jaevid to Luntharda, standing at the lapiloque's side as though he were a trusted friend. I couldn't understand it. How could Jaevid—the one sent from the god of all life to deliver us from decades of evil—choose the man who had murdered all of my brothers to be his ally? How could I be expected to help that man, too?"

"You mean ... Jace *murdered* your brothers?" Reigh's mouth hung open. I guess he hadn't heard this story before, either. Maybe it wasn't one they liked to share beyond the members of the royal family.

I couldn't believe it. Was that something Jace had done while he was still an Ulfrangar assassin? Or had it happened after he'd already defected and joined the dragonriders? Either way, how in the world had she wound up marrying the guy who killed members of her own family?

The queen leaned back in her seat some, her long white braid swishing at her waist as she nodded. "Yes. And it filled my heart with anger and resentment for many years. I hated Jace. We fought many times on the battlefield before I actually spoke with him, or even saw his face beneath his helmet. That day he spoke of, the day he nearly died, *I* was the one who had cut him down. It was in the midst of a fierce battle. I shot his dragon down. I avenged my family." Her lips pursed some, seeming to pinch sourly at that particular memory. "But it did not fill me with the peace and satisfaction I had hoped for. And when I finally saw his face—when I looked into his eyes—I didn't find the monster I wanted so desperately to see. I saw a profoundly broken and empty man who had never known happiness or hope. I saw that he hated himself far more than I ever could. He didn't expect me to change my mind, or accept him in any way. He didn't want me to see him for anything except the murderous beast he believed he was."

My mouth twisted to one side as I thought that over. It definitely sounded a lot like the situation I was in with Murdoc now. Well, sort of. I hadn't hated him right away. But there were some eerie similarities. I was asking myself constantly if I wanted him to die or not, and what kind of relationship we should have. Could I ever call him a friend again? Should I? I didn't know.

That's why I had to ask her, "Why did you forgive him?"

Queen Araxie cast me a wistful, misty-eyed smile, almost as though she were staring at a version of herself from years ago. "Out of spite, at first," she answered with a soft little laugh. "Jaevid insisted that I spare him, so I was forced to tolerate his presence. Jace wanted me to hate him, and it seemed to bother him a lot more if I acted indifferent about his presence than if I lashed out at him. But the more I got to know him, the more I began to see glimpses of his true heart. He claimed to be this disgusting monster, but where before I'd only seen the actions of a bloodthirsty murderer, I began to recognize a man's desperate and misguided attempts to stay alive. I saw how a lifetime of violence and hatred had nearly crushed him down to nothing. He didn't think his life had any value at all anymore. But more than anything else, I saw sorrow unlike anything I'd ever witnessed in his eyes—just endless, spiraling, confused anguish. And it broke my heart. I felt truly sorry for him."

I stared back at her, trying to process all that. I couldn't do it—not without picturing Murdoc in my mind. I knew that expression she was talking about. I'd seen that exact same look in Murdoc's eyes many times. Hopeless sorrow. Hatred for himself. An endless spinning vortex of shame that might consume him completely.

"I had grown up with a beautiful family that loved and cherished one another. I had lived in a palace, surrounded by fine things, and never known hunger or true fear until I was much older. The war was a faraway thing my parents worried about," the queen went on, finally glancing away to the rest of my friends. "But even Jace's life before the Ulfrangar was difficult. He was orphaned young, raised by an elder brother who was killed in the crossfire of the same war we would eventually fight one another in. It's as though our paths were destined to intertwine. The more I began to realize that, the easier it was to start letting go. He'd done terrible things, yes. But the world had done terrible things to him, as well. Standing before me was this shattered husk of a man who probably wouldn't even fight back if I decided to take my revenge and kill him once and for all. I decided ... I didn't want that. I found myself enjoying his clumsy attempts at kindness. I liked his crooked smile, and sarcastic laugh. I liked how easy it was to fluster him with any hint of flirting, and I couldn't ignore how my soul felt drawn to his. And when I saw him start to hope for the first time, to trust in me like no one else had, I knew ... I didn't want to hate him at all. I loved him."

Phoebe shifted uncomfortably, her cheeks flushing bright pink as Araxie's stare now settled on her. She kept her eyes fixed down at the toes of her shoes as she wound a lock of her bright red curls around her finger over and over.

"You're all quite young, but I learned long ago not to doubt the strength or heart of those destiny has chosen, regardless of their age. You must understand, though. Families, friends, lovers—all are structures built upon the same foundation. Trusting one another. Understanding that we are all imperfect and broken. Communicating our feelings. Forgiving each other our faults, but holding one another accountable to be better in the future. That is how we make each other stronger and more certain going forward. That is the only thing that will save Murdoc's life, and none of it is his to choose."

Queen Araxie looked over to the front of Lieutenant Eirik's tent, the light from the fires wavering over her face in a way that made her seem timeless, the sculpture of a long-forgotten goddess. "My husband does not understand this. He can't understand it because he sees things only from his side of the situation. I don't fault him for it, though. And I'm not saying that you must forgive Murdoc even if you don't want to. But believing that his path forward is his to choose without consequence to anyone else isn't necessarily true. Becoming a part of this group, your friend and brother in arms, means Murdoc's life is no longer his alone. His actions impact all of you, and he needs to be reminded of that—gently, of course."

Araxie spoke like she was still talking to all of us. She hadn't even mentioned my name specifically during that little speech. Even so, I got the impression there was only one person she believed should be the one to go in there and talk to Murdoc.

I frowned down at the campfire again, anger still prickling through my chest with every breath. Why did I have to be the one to go? Wasn't Phoebe, you know, in love with him or something? They'd done a lot of weird hand-holding recently, and with all the blushing, it seemed like a fair guess that something was up between them. She should do it, right?

And wasn't Reigh supposed to be the one in charge of our group? He'd let Murdoc come with us in the first place. They argued a lot, sure, but Murdoc had always deferred to Reigh as our leader. Shouldn't he be the one demanding Murdoc stay alive until the job was done?

Okay. Fine. I knew why it had to be me. I just ... wasn't ready. Not yet. Murdoc might not even listen to me at all. He'd already told me this wasn't any of my business—that it had nothing to do with me.

"If you are feeling as conflicted as I once did about letting go of those past hurts, then it might be good for you to hear from someone who has been through the same thing: I have not once regretted offering forgiveness. But there are many times when I have regretted holding grudges." Queen Araxie whispered, a somber heaviness in her voice that made me shiver. I didn't even have to look to know that she was staring straight at me again. "It's the words not spoken that haunt us, young hunters. It's the things we wish we had been brave enough to say to the people we hold most dear that follow us like dark shadows all the way to our graves."

4
CHAPTER FOUR

My heart sat like a heavy, cold stone in my chest as I looked toward the canvas-flap door to Eirik's tent. My thoughts had been so scrambled and chaotic before, like snowflakes whipping around in a blizzard's fierce winds. Now it was as though the storm had cleared. All those worries and frustrations slowly drifted to quiet stillness in my mind.

And in that silence, I was lost.

I knew what I had to do, but that didn't make it any less terrifying to think about. That ominous voice screamed in the back of my mind, telling me I wasn't ready to talk to, fight with, or even look Murdoc in the eye yet. Just the thought of doing any of those things made my stomach bind up and wrench like I might throw up. I couldn't decide if it was from anger, terror, or a scorching mixture of both.

I still wanted to hate him. I wanted him to hate me back. I wanted us to yell at one another and maybe even exchange a few more punches. Maybe then that smothering pressure would break.

It didn't make any sense. But I didn't have a choice now. There wasn't time to hesitate. I needed to go into that tent, right now, and figure out what was going on. I'd never even heard what Murdoc's answer was. Had he really decided to surrender? Or was he going to try something else, something that might save him from the Ulfrangar's wrath?

Whatever it was, I needed to find out. I needed to hear it straight from Murdoc's mouth. After everything we'd been through, he owed me that much, at least, didn't he? And I owed him, too.

I owed him some honesty.

Sucking in a deep breath, I stood up and squared my shoulders.

Everyone around the campfire stared at me, but none of them spoke or tried to stop me as I walked away.

When I reached the door to the tent, I almost smacked right into Jace and Eirik.

They emerged suddenly, their expressions grim and cold with focus. I scrambled to move aside, letting them storm past. They didn't even glance my way as they started for the front gate of the compound.

Oh no. What was happening? Where was Murdoc? Why wasn't he with them?

My skin crawled as a cold sweat ran down the sides of my face. My muscles flinched hard at every sound or movement as I looked at the tent's door again. Was he still inside? Or had he left? Had Jace and Eirik sent him away? Just what the heck was going on here?!

Storming into the tent, I stopped short in the main room where Eirik's desk stood, still bathed in the weak glow of the lantern light. The room was empty. There was no sign of Murdoc anywhere. Panic jabbed at the pit of my stomach and my pulse throbbed in my throat as I rushed from room to room, searching for any sign of him.

Bursting into a partitioned room at the back of the tent, I finally found him. Murdoc sat alone on the edge of a cot before one of the small wooden stoves, his cross-sheath already buckled across his back and his head hung low toward his chest. His black hair fell down almost to his chin now, hiding most of his face from view, but I could still see his jaw clench some as my footsteps crunched over the ground toward him.

"Murdoc?" I asked hoarsely.

He didn't look up.

"Look, we ... we really need to talk." My voice cracked a little, probably betraying the fact that I was a complete nervous wreck. My stomach gave a queasy twist like I might be sick.

He still didn't reply. He didn't acknowledge me at all, like I might as well have been invisible.

Like he didn't care.

And that—Gods and Fates, it stoked the flames of my anger back to life full force. I couldn't stop it then. The words poured out as I took an angry step closer to him. Every bitter word I'd wanted to yell at his back. Every stupid worry that kept pricking at my brain like thorns. It all broke past my lips in a rush. "I won't forgive you, Murdoc. Not if you do this. If you go out there and give yourself up to the Ulfrangar, if you let the Zuer kill you, I will *never* forgive you for anything ever again. I'll hate you till the day I die. I'll tell everyone what a coward you were to just lie down before them like a dog. And someday, in the afterlife, I will hunt you down and hit you again. I swear it."

Murdoc's head slowly raised and turned, his gaze panning up to meet mine. His eyes twitched with a mixture of shock and anger. He opened his mouth as though he might try to argue, but I didn't give him the chance.

"Maybe you did kill my father. Maybe you didn't. No one seems to know, and ... and I can't live the rest of my life wondering. So, I've decided to believe it *wasn't* you. As far as I'm concerned, it was someone else who murdered my father. And I don't ever want to hear you say anything different," I growled, my face flushed so hot it made my lips feel numb. "You probably think that's stupid and naïve, but I don't care. It's my choice, just like my decision to count you as my family now. You're my brother. And I need you to freaking act like it."

Murdoc's mouth snapped shut and his eyes went wide.

"I need my brother to stay alive. And whatever I have to do, whoever we have to fight to make sure that happens, I'll do it." My voice shook some, and I looked down as the ground seemed to spin from all the rage and pain that had burst to the surface at once. "I can't lose you, too. Don't you get that? We've come this far because we stayed together and watched out for one another. Don't throw it all away now. Don't bow to them. Because if you do, I'll have no choice but to stand alone."

The cot creaked, and I glanced up to find Murdoc standing before me, his expression still tense and his brow knitted with uncertainty. He stepped closer, a full four or five inches taller than me. Once again, it made me feel like a pathetic little kid sniffling before him. Great.

"Thatcher, I—" He hesitated, seeming at a loss for words. Then his hand fell onto my shoulder and squeezed it some. "I am so sorry. For whatever part I played in what happened to your father, for betraying your trust and not telling you sooner, for letting you down over and over ... please forgive me."

I shrugged away from him and turned my back. I didn't want him to see my face screw up as I asked, "Does this mean you're going to surrender to the Ulfrangar?"

Murdoc didn't answer right away. I could feel his gaze on me, watching my every move like a lion sizing up an injured fawn.

"It's not that simple," he answered quietly. "Not anymore."

"What's that supposed to mean?"

His broad shoulders moved, flexing with a heavy breath. "It means, according to King Jace, there's someone else who has a claim on my life, too. Any decision I make might be irrelevant."

"But that's what you want, right?" I spun to face him again. "After everything we've been through, after how hard everyone has worked to keep the Ulfrangar from getting to you—you'd really just walk out there and surrender to them?!" My voice grew louder as my clenched hands shook at my sides. "We've been looking out for each other for almost a year now, right? You know you've been like family to me. I've told you that over and over. I've fought for you—Reigh, Isandri, Judan, and even Jaevid have, too. But it's like it all means nothing to you, and I really hate the way things are now. I really hate *you*. Or, no, maybe just the old you that did all those awful things before we met. And the worst part is, I don't know if you changed because you wanted to, or because I did some godling magical stuff to twist your thoughts and force you. I-I ... I never meant to do that. I never meant to warp your mind, o-or—"

He didn't make a sound as he surged toward me like a lunging wolf, grabbing my arm and forcing me to look him square in the eye. "Curse it, Thatcher! Just shut up! You have no idea how long I wanted to run, how many times I watched chances slip through my fingers when I might be able to escape them. I let the fear of what they might do keep me there," he snarled, bearing down harder as I tried to pull away. "It was you that night, Thatcher. You did make me defect, but it wasn't because of any stupid divine magic. You were just ... the first one who had ever talked to me like I was a person and not a monster."

I IMMEDIATELY STOPPED STRUGGLING and stared back at him. Wait—really? Was he serious? No one had talked to him like he was a regular person? Even in the Ulfrangar? Hadn't Rook been, er, well, as nice as a handler could be to him?

I did recall overhearing some of the conversation between him and the other assassin on the night we'd first met. That guy hadn't called him anything except "pup." He'd shouted commands at Murdoc like he was an attack dog. Until now, I hadn't thought about what that might mean.

"I guess I never told you that before. I was embarrassed. Ashamed, too. You talking to me like that was bizarre, and yet, it was all I'd ever wanted for as long as I could remember. I'd worked, suffered, and killed to be treated like a person by the other members of the pack. I wasn't considered worthy of being treated as anything other than a semi-conscious blunt object. Pups aren't people. They're raw clay. Crude weapons still being honed for the kill. Nothing more. Then you came along and did it on impulse, like it was nothing, while I still had a blade to your neck." Murdoc's expression fell, his own frustration seeming to fizzle as he slowly released his hold on my arm. Then I saw it again—that same look Queen Araxie had talked about. That hollow stare of an empty, broken man who had nothing left to hope for.

"You talked to me. You trusted me. You listened to me. You defended me before Queen Jenna, even though you barely knew anything about me," he said quietly. "You treated me like someone who had value, even though I was the last person in the world who deserved it."

"Well, there's no way I would have gotten out of Thornbend alive without you. And in the prison camp, you saved my life more times than I could count. It wasn't like I was going to just kick you aside the first chance I got and go on my merry way," I muttered.

"I know. But you could have, and no one would have blamed you for it. You didn't owe me anything. I was—am still—a criminal on the run. It's okay if you hate me, Thatcher."

I hung my head, taking a step back and rubbing my arm. Fates, he had a grip like a vice. I'd probably have a nice big bruise there. "I-I ... I don't. I'm sorry, I didn't mean that. When I get upset, I say stupid things. I just don't want you to give up. We got into this mess together. That's how I want to end it."

Murdoc stepped back, too. With his head bowed so low, all his shaggy, black bangs hid most of his face. "I-I don't want to die." His voice scraped and halted, like he was fighting to keep it together.

I froze.

"I don't know why you and the others want me around. I don't understand why you keep giving me second chances. Over and over," he rasped, biting hard at each word. "I haven't brought you anything but pain and suffering. I'm not worth it. I don't deserve that sort of...."

"Mercy?" I guessed when his voice faded to silence.

Murdoc nodded.

I crossed my arms, taking a few seconds to consider my next words a little more carefully. "No. You don't," I decided aloud. "But I'm not sure anyone does, honestly. When it boils down to it, we're all jerks sometimes, so just get over it already. You don't get to decide if you're worth it or not. The people doing the fighting to keep you alive, the ones who care about you, that's something *we* decide."

He made an annoyed sputtering sound like he was choking on his own spit. "H-How can you—"

"No! I'm serious, Murdoc. You may be a big, brooding, grumpy, violent, stubborn pile of horse flop sometimes," I paused, just for effect, and shrugged. "But you're *our* big, brooding, grumpy, violent, stubborn pile of horse flop. Never forget that."

Murdoc finally lifted his head, giving me one of his classic, blood-chilling scowls. "Oh, trust me, I won't."

I got a little thrill of terror up my spine when he narrowed his eyes slightly.

Oops. Too much?

Oh well. He did owe me a few punches, after all. I figured he'd settle that score sooner or later. "Come on. You need to tell me and everyone else what's really going on here. I saw King Jace and Lieutenant Eirik leave. I take it they have a plan of some kind?"

His brow creased, expression becoming distant and thoughtful again, like he was silently trying to figure out what was wrong with me. Good luck with that one, buddy. If not even Jaevid could figure that out, I doubted anyone could.

"Not a plan," he corrected. "More like a desperate idea."

I deflated. Right. Well, desperate ideas were sort of our specialty at this point. I guess I shouldn't have been surprised. "Your face looks awful, by the way," I added as he followed me from the room. I made extra sure I was moving along at a healthy distance when I made my jabs at him this time. If he came at me for revenge, I wanted a head start.

Not that it would help much, but a guy could try.

"I'm sure," he grumbled. "You hit *decently* for once."

"Yeah, well, this jerk I know has been teaching me some stuff," I baited again as I stopped at the tent's main door and held the flap back so he could go out first. I made sure to stay well out of arm's reach, though.

"I didn't think it was possible, but you're even more obnoxious than usual today," he muttered as he stomped by.

"There's that horse flop charm."

He gave me another squinty, wrathful glare over his shoulder. "This ends badly for you, you do realize that, right?"

"Yep."

"Good," he grunted, and I could have sworn I saw one corner of his mouth twitch into a smirk. "As long as you're aware."

CHAPTER FIVE

I made a point not to glance up at the sky as Murdoc and I stepped out into the chilly night air. My stomach clenched and cramped with dread, too afraid of spotting traces of scarlet sunlight blooming on the horizon to even dare looking. I knew it had to be getting close to sunrise. We'd flown for a while just to get here in the first place. How long did we have left until the Ulfrangar decided to make good on their threat? Hours? Minutes?

The commotion in the compound made for a good distraction, though.

Everywhere I looked, dragonriders were mustering arms, collecting their gear, and assembling in front of their tents in full armor. Their mounts gathered in, too, occasionally growling and snapping at one another as they assembled in the middle of the compound. Had Eirik given them orders to prepare for battle? Were they really going to fight the Ulfrangar? What did that mean for us?

I glanced sideways at Murdoc, but he didn't say anything and kept his grim scowl trained ahead to where the rest of our companions were still sitting around the campfire.

"Oi! Look there, I told you! That's him!" a voice called out suddenly. We both turned to look as a pair of younger dragonriders walked up, waving to get our attention. Both of them seemed to be a little older than Murdoc, maybe in their early twenties, and they smiled broadly at him. "Hey there! Fancy seeing you here! Been a while, yeah? Are you working for the royal court these days?"

Murdoc's eyes narrowed suspiciously. His hand edged toward the hilt of one of the longswords strapped across his back. "Who are you?"

"It's Sam and Kellan. Don't you remember? We saw you come in earlier, but didn't get a chance to say hello before the lieutenant dragged you off." The taller of the two men stopped abruptly, seeming to sense our apprehension. That, or he'd noticed the ominous and slightly terrifying scowl on Murdoc's face. "You're Fenn, aren't you? Fenn Porter? It's been a while!"

Murdoc hesitated, his scowl becoming more of a confused frown. "No. I think you have me confused for someone else."

"See, Kellan? I told you, dummy," the other rider snorted. "He's far too young. Just looks a bit like him, that's all."

The first rider, Kellan, flushed and waved his hands apologetically. "Ah. I see. My mistake. Gods and Fates, you do look like him though. The spitting image! You some relation to them? The Porters, I mean."

"Don't be daft! How would he even know who they are?" The second rider, Sam apparently, scoffed and gave his friend an elbow to the side. "Come off it. The boy obviously has no idea what you're talking about, and we're supposed to be mounting up. Let's go."

Murdoc's face paled a little, watching them walk away with his mouth hanging open some. A haunted sort of shock slowly crept over his sharp features like a fog bank drifting in from across the sea. It seemed to douse any hint of light in his eyes. For a moment, I thought he might run after them. Or start screaming.

But he didn't. Murdoc just stood there, slack-jawed, as more and more of that stunned uncertainty creased his brow and drew his thin mouth into a tense, hard line.

Maybe I shouldn't have been so surprised. Murdoc didn't have a family—at least not one he'd ever been able to find. It must've been like ripping open an old wound to have someone ask him that, especially when he was already reeling from the situation we were in now.

I bumped him with my elbow, trying to break his trance. "That was kinda weird, huh? You okay, Murdoc?"

His mouth clamped shut. "Y-Yeah," he answered quietly.

"Were they talking about the same Porters that we had stayed with?" I wondered aloud, not really expecting him to have an answer. There must've been hundreds of people in the kingdom with that family name, right? What were the odds?

Murdoc's broken whisper was so faint I barely heard him at all. "I ... I don't know."

REIGH WAS ON HIS FEET, still limping a little as he paced back and forth near the campfire. He stopped when he noticed us approaching, his expression going blank in surprise. I guess he hadn't expected I would actually get Murdoc to come out and face us again. Bravo to me, I suppose. Too bad I didn't feel very proud of that fact. Yeah, Murdoc and I were back on speaking terms. For now, at least. But things were still tense between us. Worse than tense, really. Weird. Uncomfortable. Painfully awkward. And I didn't know how long that would last, or if it would eventually go away. Maybe it wouldn't.

I frowned and looked away, silently hoping Reigh and the others would be able to pick up on all that without me having to explain it. We had bigger problems to deal with at the moment.

"What's the plan here, Murdoc? Where are Jace and Eirik?" Reigh questioned as soon as we stopped at the fireside. The rest of our friends, along with Queen Araxie, stood up and gathered in closer to listen.

All I could do was shrug.

Next to me, Murdoc slowly shook his head and muttered quietly, "I don't know. He asked Eirik to divert attention by calling the camp to arms so he could make a stealthy escape by shrike without the Ulfrangar taking notice. I don't know why, or where he's going. King Jace was ... unusually cryptic. Probably afraid of who else might be listening in on our discussions."

"A wise decision considering you both believe there are Ulfrangar hidden within the ranks here," Isandri said approvingly. "We must assume everything we do and say is being watched."

"Right, fair enough, but that still doesn't answer my first question." Reigh flinched some, his voice hitching when he crossed his arms. His injuries were still severe. I'd seen that much firsthand. But he seemed determined not to let anyone else see how much pain he was still in. "I'm not sure if you've noticed, but we don't have a lot of time left here."

"I just said I don't know," Murdoc growled through his teeth. He cut a wrathful look up at the rest of our group through his lengthy bangs. "He made it sound like me walking out there to surrender wasn't an option because ... because there are other figures, powerful people, claiming ownership of my life now. I don't know what he meant, but if you're wanting me to make wild guesses, I'd assume that's who he's gone to talk to."

"*Other* powerful people?" Phoebe echoed, her delicate features creased with bewilderment. "Is he talking about Jaevid, maybe?"

"Possibly," Reigh mused as he rubbed his jaw. "He'd certainly qualify as powerful. But I'm not sure he'd ever declare ownership over anyone's life."

"I would agree." Queen Araxie ran a thoughtful hand along the arc of her bow. "It is not like my beloved cousin to make such claims."

"Queen Jenna?" Isandri guessed.

Reigh's mouth scrunched and he shook his head. "I doubt it. But, then again, she might be willing to make a few drastic claims in order to get the Ulfrangar off our backs. And we are technically in her personal service right now, so ... maybe?"

There was something distinctly dissatisfied in Queen Araxie's expression as she studied Murdoc. She went on rubbing her fingers along the intricate engravings on her bow, her lips pursed and multihued eyes as sharp as razors. "It is too far to reach the royal city before dawn, even on a shrike. They are faster than a dragon, yes. But the distance is too great. There are only a few places my husband might go and be able to return here before the sun rises."

Murdoc's shoulders trembled some as his gaze slowly panned up to meet hers, but he didn't say a word.

"Back to Dayrise, if he pushed it," Reigh mumbled. "Osbran isn't that far away. Port Marlowe, as well, but I don't know who he'd want to see there. Barrowton is too far. He could probably get there, but he'd be hard pressed to make it back in time."

Great. I couldn't think of anyone in those places King Jace might be going after. At least, no one who might also put a claim on Murdoc's life. Of all the likely candidates,

Jenna seemed the most plausible. But Jaevid might be the only one in the area—if he hadn't already departed for Halfax with Phillip, that is.

"I don't guess you have any idea who he's going after? Someone powerful enough to give the Ulfrangar pause? Someone close by?" Reigh eyed the elven queen, his tone edged with suspicion, like maybe he thought she was holding out on us. "No creeping suspicions whatsoever?"

The queen straightened some and cast him an admonishing glare. "My husband has many secrets, young prince, and I've never pressed him for them. He has always told me when he was ready, I very much prefer to let him do it on his own than trying to pry it from him against his will."

"You trust him that much?" Murdoc sounded genuinely surprised. "Even knowing he was an Ulfrangar?"

Her smile was as cryptic as it was enchanting, making her strange eyes reflect the light of the campfire in hues of yellow, deep blue, and radiant red. "What is love if it has no trust? My faith in him far surpasses any uncertainty I might feel."

Murdoc's eyes widened and his mouth mashed into a crooked, bitter line. It only lasted a second, maybe less, but I definitely saw his gaze dart away toward Phoebe for an instant. He drew back slightly, shoulders curling in and jaw clenching hard as he turned his face away. "Look, I know what you all want from me. But I-I ... I can't let Lieutenant Eirik send his men out there to fight the Ulfrangar," he faltered, seeming to force every halting word. "If you choose to stand with me before them, I can't stop you, but I also can't be responsible for the deaths of more innocent people. I can't live with knowing the finest soldiers in Maldobar sacrificed themselves for my sake. Please, Reigh, don't ... don't let them do that. Not for my sake. Order Eirik to call them off and let me go out alone. If King Jace makes it back in time with someone he thinks can force the Ulfrangar to spare my life, then ... so be it. But these are good men with families and children. They shouldn't be led to slaughter for me."

Reigh arched an eyebrow, giving an exaggerated slow blink and small shake of his head in surprise. "Wow. I'm so glad I wasn't the only one standing here for that display. Jaevid might not believe me later if there weren't lots of witnesses to back me up."

"What?" Murdoc's scowl was desperate as he glared back at Reigh in defiance. "Are you mocking me?"

"Not at all." Reigh chuckled and stepped forward to clap a hand onto his shoulder. "It's just all that 'don't let these people die in vain' self-sacrificing talk—I think that might be the most dragonrider-sounding speech I've ever heard!"

"I agree," Queen Araxie chimed in, grinning fondly. "If I didn't know better, I might have assumed it came from the lips of Jaevid himself."

Murdoc's head bowed lower and lower until most of his face was hidden by his lengthy bangs. His ears gave him away, though. They'd turned bright red. "I-I ... no, I'm nothing like him."

Queen Araxie stepped closer and stretched out a hand, lifting his chin with two of her fingers so that he was forced to look her in the eye. "No, you aren't. Not yet. But give yourself this chance to try, young one. Who knows, perhaps a destiny tied to the wings of a dragon will lift you higher than you have dared to imagine."

"Remember, the name of the game is shock and awe. If King Jace is correct, then we'll only have one shot at this." Lieutenant Eirik spoke quickly as he led the way through the compound.

Huddled behind him like a flock of ducklings, Isandri, Reigh, Murdoc, and I passed the rows of armored dragonriders and their snarling mounts. Some of them were already taking off into the night in pairs of two, disappearing like massive scaled phantoms into the star-speckled sky. With any luck, the Ulfrangar would take notice that there weren't any dragonriders left here.

Well, except for us, of course.

My sweaty hand stayed clamped around the hilt of my xiphos blade as I tried not to look too hard at any of the men we passed. If I stared too long, I might start to wonder if they were one of the hidden Ulfrangar spies or not. I couldn't bear to let my mind go racing out of control down that road right now.

Focus, Thatch. Now wasn't the time to get queasy. I had to keep my eyes on our goal. All that mattered was clearing the Ulfrangar's potential battlefield—removing the dragonriders from the equation so they couldn't be used against us. That's why Eirik had given them all the order to go to Osbran immediately. There, they'd be too far for any of the Ulfrangar agents that might be hiding in their ranks to be of any use against us.

Or so we hoped.

"Queen Araxie and your artificer, Phoebe, are already in the towers. I suspect they'll have better range from there," Eirik continued. He kept a fierce pace until we reached the large gate that led out of the compound. The gate was still closed, giving us a small barrier between ourselves and the Ulfrangar forces waiting just on the other side.

"Reigh, you and Vexi are with me so we can make our move from the air. We will put down a perimeter of flame to contain the Ulfrangar within the area and prevent their escape." He turned to face us with a fiercely determined expression. "The rest of you, stall for as long as you can. We'll be watching for your signal."

"Assassins. Poisoned arrows. Slimy scumbag traitors hidden in our own ranks," Reigh fumed under his breath and spat on the ground. "You know, I actually miss when it was just crazy Tibran invaders. At least then you knew who your enemies were. They even had the decency to form nice, organized lines. Made them a lot easier to roast with dragon fire, too. Ah, the good old days."

"Yes, well, the nature of our enemy tends to change with the times. Welcome to life on the frontlines, Your Highness. Say your farewells quickly. We're out of time." Eirik cracked a smirk before he took the helmet from under his arm and slid it down over his head. He gave a hand signal to a few other riders who were waiting nearby, motioning for them to open the gate, and then started walking away toward his dragon.

Reigh faced us, giving me a long, reluctant stare with his mouth skewed to one side.

What? Was there something he wanted to say to me? Or was he just standing there thinking I wasn't up to this fight?

Uggh. Probably the last one.

He wasn't wrong, of course. But I was counting on a little divine magic to even the odds, or at the very least, buy us some valuable time.

"I'm no good at goodbyes, so let's just say good luck for now and leave it at that, okay? Watch your backs. Try not to die," Reigh mumbled at last. His gaze drifted between us and finally settled on Isandri. There was something strangely tense and apprehensive in his expression as he watched her, but I couldn't even begin to guess what he was thinking then.

There wasn't time to try, either.

Reigh gave a nod and turned away, crossing the short distance to climb into Vexi's saddle. It took him a minute to pull her away from Fornax and Shalni. They'd been snuggled up close to one another basically since we'd arrived, preening their scales and making deep purring sounds. Lieutenant Eirik had mentioned that his dragoness, Shalni, had lost her rider in battle just like Fornax had. That thought made my heart twist painfully. What if they had been together in the final battle? What if they'd been partners or related somehow? Maybe it was better not to know.

Raising my whistle to my lips, I called Fornax over long enough to give him a parting scratch under his chin and to give Reigh and Eirik a chance to get airborne. My big orange dragon's scaly ears swiveled forward at the sound of my voice, and his sightless, milky jade eyes looked all around as he lumbered forward. The tension in the air, all the clinking of armor and shouts of the riders preparing for flight, must've been familiar—and not in a good way. Poor guy.

"Just keep to the plan, buddy. I know you want to fight right alongside me, but you have to hang back and watch over Phoebe. If anything goes wrong, I'll call for you." I gave his bony, horned brow a pat. "But remember, don't leave her behind. She's not like the rest of us. She doesn't know how to fight, so you've got to protect her. Think you can handle that?"

He smacked his jaws grumpily and blasted a snort right in my face. It blew my hair back and made me smile. I didn't blame him for being sulky about it. I would much rather try scorching all those Ulfrangar from the safety of his saddle. But we'd already tried that—several times in fact. And, yeah, it had worked in the moment. But it had almost gotten Reigh killed, burned down buildings, and ultimately only encouraged the Ulfrangar to hit us with even more brutal attacks.

This was the end-game. If we really were going to finish this once and for all, then we needed the Zuer to make an appearance. And if we were waiting for her with dragons ready to light her up on sight, we all felt pretty certain she wouldn't be dumb enough to storm straight into the fray. We had to play this *very* carefully.

"All right, just be ready. There's only one door in and out of this tower, so don't let anyone else get in there. If you smell or hear someone getting close, you've got my permission to toast them good." I gave his saddle one last, quick check before I patted the side of his strong neck and backed away. "Stay safe, big guy."

Fornax gave a low whine and dipped his head some, curling his tail around his legs. Next to him, Murdoc's much younger dragon scooted in closer and rubbed his head along Fornax's side as though trying to console him. Lieutenant Eirik had insisted on keeping the smaller dragon hidden here, as well. His hide might not be thick enough to stop Ulfrangar bolts from close range. Best to keep him tucked away safely unless we got desperate for reinforcements.

I had to look away. I hated this—being separated from him when we were both about to be in real danger. What if he needed me? What if I needed him?

My gaze snapped upward, sucking in a sharp breath as a deep rumbling filled the night air. It seemed to shake the entire compound and made the earth shudder under my boots. All at once, every dragonrider still lingering there under Lieutenant Eirik's command surged skyward. They took off like a flock of massive, scaled eagles, wings spreading to the early dawn. After doing one slow circle, I watched in tense silence as they veered away to the south—toward Osbran.

Then we were alone. Three of us on foot, two in the sky, and two in the tower against fifty armed-to-the-teeth Ulfrangar assassins and the Zuer. We did have a few dragons at our disposal. No problem, right?

Gods and Fates, we were going to die.

CHAPTER SIX

The sky burned deep scarlet as the first sliver of the sun peeked over the far mountains. It melted away the stars and offered just enough light to see as Murdoc, Isandri, and I stood at the gate of the dragonrider compound. Our time was up. And our answer to the Ulfrangar's threat would be crystal clear:

If they wanted Murdoc's life, they'd have to fight us to the last breath for it.

"Leave the Zuer to me," Murdoc warned as the gate before us groaned open. "Keep the rest of her forces back for as long as you can. If I can kill her, they will lay down arms and surrender to me. The law of the pack demands that anyone who defeats the Zuer has the sole right to claim the seat of power." His chest rose and fell with a deep, steadying breath. "I was only a pup, so they might decide I'm unworthy. But I don't think a pup has ever challenged a Zuer like this before, so I don't know for certain what they'll do."

"You really want to become the next leader of the Ulfrangar?" Isandri asked with a snort and devious grin.

"No—although it might be convenient for as long as it takes to order them to stop trying to kill me," he sighed like he'd seen that question coming a mile away. "After that, I'll happily leave them for Her Majesty to sort out."

She gave a breathy chuckle and sank lower into an aggressive stance, brandishing her gleaming staff. "Regardless, we are at your side."

I drew my xiphos and glared straight ahead as the opening gate revealed the line of ominous dark figures waiting on the other side. I couldn't tell that any of them had moved an inch all night. Creepy. Were they in some kind of trance? Or was it just another part of Ulfrangar training to be able to stand in one spot for hours on end without even scratching your nose?

"One way or another, we're ending this today." Murdoc's voice thrummed with a deep growl as he took a step forward.

The hiss of the wind through the prairie grass filled the silence as we stood, tense and ready, and glared straight ahead at all the Ulfrangar. With their faces mostly covered by black shawls and cowls, only their eyes were visible. The wash of the crimson light from the rising sun reflected off their silver cuffs, making them seem to glow deep red. Not a single one of them moved or made a sound. They didn't so much as blink. Fates, it's like they weren't even alive—like they might as well have been made of stone.

A tingle of fresh terror prickled up my spine as we waited. Seconds passed. Then minutes. My chest ached from how my heart thrashed hard against my ribs. What were they waiting for? For us to make the first attack?

At last, Murdoc called out across the distance between us, his shout echoing over the dew-laden grass. "You came here with an ultimatum—my surrender or a fight to the death. Now you have my answer. I will not ask the dragonriders to fight on my behalf, but make no mistake, I will *not* go peacefully. I will not surrender. If you want my life, you'll have to rip it from me here and now."

A cold gust of wind made my skin prickle. It rippled through the Ulfrangar's dark cloaks and carried in a bank of low fog, making them seem like a legion of dark spirits hovering not fifty yards away from us. Not one of them moved or made a sound.

Dread squeezed at my heart like the jaws of a steel trap, growing tighter and tighter until I could hardly breathe. I stole a sideways glance at Murdoc. He stood tense, one of his longswords already drawn, with his jawline went solid and his gaze narrowed straight ahead. Sweat drizzled down the sides of his face and his brow twitched some, as though he might snap at any moment and surge forward to attack.

Then, on the very back row of the Ulfrangar's ranks, something moved in the dim morning light. A shadow blurred through the mist, making it curl and shift. One by one, the lines of assassins before us began to part, stepping aside to make way for one figure to approach. Tall and slender, I couldn't tell anything about the individual that slowly approached thanks to the long cloak they wore. But it wasn't like the uniform the rest of the Ulfrangar had on. This cloak had been fashioned from a wolf's pelt, with fur as black as pitch and the head fashioned into the cowl. A single silver eye had been painted into the center of the wolf's head, and beneath it, a slender chin, black-painted lips, and stark pale skin were all I could see.

My stomach dropped to the soles of my boots. Was this really the Zuer?

"Well, well, well. When I saw all of your dragonrider friends depart, I assumed you might try to run again. Color me impressed. You've more audacity than I expected." A smooth, feminine voice cooed from beneath the cowl. Those dark-painted lips bowed into a cunning sneer as she stopped ahead of the rest of her hunting party. "What a waste. I saw your potential from the beginning. You might have gone far under my tutelage, pup. But now your fate is sealed. Step forward and die with whatever honor you may have left. There is no need for these fools to suffer for your betrayal."

Murdoc's chest seized with a shaking breath. His body gave a jerking flinch and his face went pale, as though just the sound of her voice caused him physical pain. Doubt fractured over his features, and in an instant, I knew.

He wasn't going to be able to do this. Not on his own. I didn't know this woman, or what she might have done to him in some wicked, twisted past he'd buried deep. But it was as though she had a hook set deep in his mind, and she could use it to pull him wherever she wanted.

"Hey!" I snarled suddenly, stepping forward and ripping my xiphos free of its sheath to aim the point straight at her. "Don't you dare dismiss me. You're the one whose fate has now been sealed. Ishaleon, God of Mercy, stands for this pup!"

"Adiana, Goddess of the Moon, stands for him as well!" Isandri hissed as she sprang forward, spinning her staff and cracking it off the ground once. The impact sent out a bolt of crackling, sizzling power that lit up the pale dawn with a radiant silver glow.

The Zuer's dark lips parted in a wide, delighted smile. "Ah, yes. The godlings have rallied around you, I see. Such passion. Such devotion. And yet, all in vain. Do you think my pack has not felled gods before?" She stretched out an arm from beneath her heavy, wolf-pelt cloak. The black, oiled leather armor shone as she raised a hand out to the side. "Allow us to demonstrate."

A snap of her fingers cracked through the cold morning air.

And in an instant, all hell broke loose.

Blood ran down the side of my face and seeped past my clenched teeth, thick and warm. My pulse kicked fiercely in my chest, keeping rhythm with the swing of my blade as I pulled from every combat lesson Murdoc, Reigh, and Jaevid had ever given me. Parry up. Defensive stance. Press in for strike one. Sidestep. Dip low and strike two. Parry left. Now make the kill.

Back-to-back with Murdoc, Ulfrangar closed in from every side. Crossbow bolts howled through the red twilight. One punched through my crude armor at my shoulder, making my vision go white with pain for a second. But I didn't stop. Focus. Control. I couldn't lose it now.

Three Ulfrangar fell. Then two more.

Murdoc spun in a blur of deadly motion, every strike flawless and precise. Isandri flipped and wove through her enemy's assaults, jabbing the brutal, tri-dagger tip of her staff easily through the Ulfrangar's leather armor. Another crack of her weapon off the ground sent out a blast of divine energy that blew a few of them off their feet.

Before me, an Ulfrangar surged in, dipping under one of his comrades as fast as a shadow. He lifted a crossbow and leveled it right at my head. I tensed. Curse it! I'd let him get in too close!

TWANG!

The Ulfrangar's eyes went wide over his face-wrap. His body lurched and went stiff, then dropped right where he stood. A slender arrow, fletched with colorful feathers, stuck out of his back.

I chanced a look up at the tower, barely able to make out the silhouette of a woman standing in the small window. Queen Araxie. W-Wow. I guess those stories from the Gray War about her deadly aim were all true, after all.

A pang of pain sizzled down my arm suddenly, making my fingers go numb so that I nearly lost my grip on my blade. I sucked in a sharp breath, biting down hard and taking a tactical step back. Was that arrow in my shoulder poisoned? Was it starting to take effect? Phoebe had said before that the toxins they used would cause paralysis. How much time did I have until I couldn't even move anymore?

I blinked hard and shook my head, trying to clear the fog that made my thoughts go hazy and my ears ring. No—I wouldn't lose focus. Not now!

"Flip parry!" Murdoc shouted suddenly over the clang and clash of his longswords.

I set my jaw and dropped to a knee, immediately making a sideways swing. My xiphos smashed against an enemy blade howling in from my left just as Murdoc leapt into an aerial backflip and landed in front of me, slicing through another assassin to my right. We moved in unison, me scrambling to keep up with Murdoc's lethally efficient pace, as we kept the Ulfrangar at bay. But I could feel each of my swings slowing. My grip faltered as my hand went numb. The poison was spreading. I couldn't even feel the bolt of the arrow embedded deep in my shoulder now.

"I-I'm hit," I managed to wheeze as I forced another whirling strike. "Call it down."

Murdoc turned and our gazes locked for an instant, then he shouted up toward the sky, "LIGHT IT UP!"

Isandri let out a yowl of affirmation that pierced the dawn like the screech of an eagle. A flash of sterling light exploded from amidst the throngs of Ulfrangar, and she broke skyward through a hailstorm of crossbow bolts in her winged feline form.

With a final deadly jab to an Ulfrangar, dropping the assassin where he stood, Murdoc leapt toward me and landed on a knee right at my side. I gulped in a deep breath, pulling all the frayed threads of my focus inward as I squeezed my eyes shut. I stretched out a hand over us, a groan of pain leaking past my lips as the sudden rush of divine power burst from somewhere deep inside me. It hit like I'd been struck by lightning, blowing through all my mental fortifications immediately, and radiating outward in a rush like wind in a wildfire. A wavering globe of golden light bloomed outward from my hand, closing around us like a dome of raw energy.

My body shook. My lungs spasmed for every tiny, desperate breath as it felt like my mind was being stretched inside out. But I couldn't let that shield drop. Not yet.

WHOOOOM!

Fire exploded into the air, pouring from the sky in two plumes that encircled the area around us. Flames, arrows, and swords smashed against my divine shield, making it ripple and waver. But nothing broke through. Ulfrangar screamed, catching sprays of burning dragon venom and trying desperately to douse it before it ate through their armor. More of Araxie's arrows from the tower rained down two and three at a time, dropping one assassin right after another.

I let out another rasping cry of pain as my palm burned like I'd dipped it in molten metal. My vision doubled and went blurry. A little longer—I just had to hold it for a little bit longer. The more Ulfrangar they could take out without having to worry about hitting one of us, the easier the fight would be. We might actually stand a chance. I could do this. I wouldn't fail. Not when I'd already come this far.

Out of nowhere, the burning in my hand stopped. I blinked, my vision suddenly clearing.

"THATCHER!" Murdoc shouted my name, but it sounded strange. Or maybe that was just the ringing in my ears growing louder. His blood-spattered face had gone white with horror as he stared at me.

Wh-What? What was happening?

Behind him, my shield of divine energy melted away like snow in sunlight, seeming to break down around something long, dark, and spear-shaped that had punctured straight through it.

But ... how? Nothing had been able to pierce my divine shield before. What was happening?

Murdoc bared his teeth in fury and growled a curse, looping an arm around my shoulders as my legs suddenly buckled. He thrust his sword up in a frantic parry, barely managing to block an incoming sword point as he slowly let me down to sit on the ground. "Stay with me, Thatcher! I've got you! Just hang on!"

Stay? What did that mean? I looked down as he reached for my stomach. That's when I saw it—the point of that dark spear that had rammed through my divine barrier was now buried deep into my gut.

Oh ... oh no.

The pain hit me so abruptly I couldn't even react. I couldn't scream. I couldn't breathe. Bitter cold washed over me like I'd been shoved beneath the surface of an icy river. I stared at the deep crimson blood soaking through my breastplate in shock. My hands trembled as I reached for the shaft of the spear. As soon as my fingers brushed the surface of it, the entire weapon dissolved into a curling black mist and disappeared, leaving nothing but an empty hole in my armor behind.

Still sitting on the ground, I struggled to look up again. My head bobbed as tremors of agony made every muscle in my body spasm. Standing not even twenty yards away, the Zuer curled her fingers in a gesture that summoned a wisp of dark smoke. One jerk of her wrist made the mist solidify, and the spear appeared in her grasp. One corner of her dark-painted lips twisted up into a pleased grin.

"What a mighty gift you have, little godling. But I have mighty allies, as well. You are not the only ones with godling power at your disposal." she cooed with a voice like warm venom. "Iksoli sends her love."

7
CHAPTER SEVEN

Iksoli? This was her doing? But how?

It didn't make any sense. How had the Zuer managed to pierce my shield? How had she survived Eirik and Reigh showering everything in dragon fire? Was she telling the truth—was it really a manifestation of Iksoli's divine power? Did this mean they'd been working together all along? Or was this some new deal they'd struck?

I scrambled to make sense of the storm of questions whirling through my head as everything around me grew dim. I slumped back and hit the ground next to Murdoc, as my breaths came in shallow, desperate puffs. Everything seemed to grow colder and farther away, as though I were looking at the world through frosted glass. Voices echoed around me. Shouts of panic and rage. The Zuer's wicked laughter.

Oh gods, was I ... dying?

No! I couldn't die! Not now—not like this! I couldn't let everyone down. What if they needed my help?

And Murdoc. He still stood over me, his arms and legs now marred with deep cuts and slashes and crossbow bolts bristling from his leather armor. He snarled like a beast as he forced the Ulfrangar to back away from me with wild swings of his swords. That idiot. If I died, he might do something really stupid and get himself killed, too. He might stand there over me, defending my lifeless body until the Ulfrangar cut him down, as well. Then who would be left to fight Iksoli? Isandri couldn't handle it all by herself. She'd need his help.

No. Murdoc wouldn't die here. I wouldn't let that happen. My hand shook as I reached for the whistle buried beneath my breastplate and tunic and put it to my lips. My vision swerved and dimmed as I blew hard blasts into it, sending up a shrill call above the chaos.

An answering roar like a low roll of thunder resounded over the battle.

Through the wall of flames glowing in the early dawn, a massive dark shape rose up over the wall of the compound, stretching leathery wings wide to the scarlet sky. Fornax bounded over the wall with one beat of his wings, landing with a boom on the other side and baring rows of jagged fangs. His green eyes glowed in the light of the fire as his ears swiveled, tracking the sound of my call.

Four Ulfrangar standing close whirled to face him and raised their crossbows, taking aim at my dragon's head. Even standing so close, Fornax couldn't see them to know he was in danger. I started to blow another signal on the whistle, but before I could even catch my breath, another dark shape dropped from the sky with a *BOOM!*

A second dragon landed right in the fray, crushing one of the Ulfrangar under his weight and snatching another in his jaws. Murdoc's young drake, Blite, flared his spines and flung the assassin around like a rag doll before slamming him into the ground with a gory *crunch*.

Ouch.

The remaining two Ulfrangar fired their crossbow bolts at the younger dragon, one catching him in the side and making the dragon screech in pain. Fornax dove in suddenly, making wild snaps with his jaws and ripping another assassin off his feet.

Glancing back to the tower, I could barely make out the flash of coppery red hair fluttering in the wind through my daze. It was enough, though. Phoebe was there, and she had my goggles. A little aerial sight-assistance was all Fornax needed.

"Enough!" The Zuer's voice snapped out across what remained of her minions like the crack of a whip.

Everything stopped.

The Ulfrangar rushing in to attack Fornax and Blite withdrew immediately at her command. The ones battling against Murdoc bounded back and froze in defensive positions. The flurry of crossbow bolts buzzing through the air stopped. In an instant there was an eerie silence, filled with nothing but the crackle, hiss, and pop of the burning dragon venom.

Through the curling smoke and dancing flames, the Zuer's dark silhouette emerged like a prowling demoness. She spun that magical spear over her hand again and again, her face angled straight at Murdoc. Lifting her empty hand, she made a taunting, curling motion with her fingers as though to call him forward. One small, upward tilt of her head revealed a staggeringly beautiful face. Gods and Fates, she seemed a lot younger than I expected. And her eyes—they *glowed*.

My breath caught, and I winced. Was I seeing things? That couldn't be. But ... I'd seen eyes like that somewhere before, hadn't I?

Murdoc stood over me with a crazed look of fury twisted over his features. He still gripped a longsword in each hand, the blades dripping with blood, and turned to face the Zuer. His chest heaved with every ragged, growling breath as he stared her down like a cornered feral wolf.

"I am pleased, pup. The tales of your strength and defiance were not merely fanciful exaggerations, but I've tolerated more than enough arrogance and defiance from you," she seethed as she whirled that wicked black spear. "I have not come this far to be undone by some pathetic human whelp."

Murdoc's hazel eyes flashed with reflections of the flames as he gave each of his longswords a similar flourishing spin over his hands. "Then why don't you stop playing games and fight me yourself?"

There was something ancient and ethereal about the way she gazed across the distance at Murdoc, like a dark goddess stepping from beyond the Vale to meet him. "As you wish," she purred delightedly.

DARK BLOOD RAN through my fingers and out onto the grass as I gripped my stomach. The world spun and swirled, dimming in and out of focus. Every heartbeat ached, thudding slower with each second. But I couldn't look away. Murdoc was right, I had to hold on. I had to stay awake.

I-I ... had to ...

Before me, Murdoc and the Zuer dueled like something from an ancient fable of gods and heroes. She moved with inhuman speed, seeming to blur from one place to another like a phantom, all while brandishing that spear. Sometimes it would vanish into smoke, only to reappear in her other hand. Other times, I could have sworn she could make herself vanish for an instant, too.

Murdoc bore in hard, his teeth bared and his body drenched with sweat and blood as he matched her every move. His swords hummed through the air, ringing in a dark deadly melody as they clashed with her spear, her reinforced bracers, and glanced off her armor. He snarled and barked cries of frustration, ducking and weaving around her relentless assaults.

The way they pitched, dodged, spun, and leapt at one another with flawless, lethal grace—it almost seemed like a dance they'd rehearsed a thousand times.

The coppery warmth of blood filled my mouth as I coughed. Wiping my chin, I stared in horror at the smear of fresh crimson on my palm. My chest gave a shudder, and all of a sudden, I couldn't breathe. I sputtered and wheezed, falling forward as the coldness paralyzed me.

I barely managed to catch myself with one elbow, fighting to keep my head up. Gods, no! Not like this! I couldn't die—not yet. Not until I knew Murdoc would be okay. I needed to see him end this, to see him win his freedom. I needed to know he'd be okay, and that someone would be able to take care of Fornax.

"Thatcher!" Murdoc's desperate shout pierced the air as he suddenly looked my way just in time to see me flop limply onto my side. His guard dropped for an instant.

And that was all the opportunity she needed.

The Zuer smirked as she rushed him with a brutal assault, using the shaft of her spear to crack him across the face. The blow sent him staggering back, and she swept his feet with another whirling strike.

Murdoc landed flat on his back at her feet. The impact knocked one of his blades from his grasp, sending it sliding over the ground, far out of reach. He let out a yell of rage as he raised the other one, barely managing to put up a frantic parry and deflect another strike of her spear.

The Zuer laughed, her eyes shining with vicious pleasure as she stood over him like a cat over a caught mouse. She rained down blow after blow, toying with him, and preventing him from even trying to get to his feet again. "Rook taught you well," she snickered. "But make no mistake, your life is *mine*. Now, do as you're told and die."

Rearing back her spear suddenly, she took aim right at his chest. The brutal, barbed tip gleamed in the light of the rising sun.

Murdoc's eyes went wide.

I reached a shaking, blood-smeared hand toward him. N-NO!

WOOOSH!

Out of nowhere, a violent rush of wind kicked up around us. It howled through the battle like a stormfront, making all the flames swirl higher and higher. But they didn't spread. Instead, it almost seemed like the fire's flickering was growing *slower*. But why? How was that even possible?

With a deafening *WHOOM,* all the flames surrounding us suddenly froze in place and turned gray, like curled statues of silver glass.

The Zuer stopped mid-attack, the point of her spear less than an inch above Murdoc's heart. Her head snapped up, looking straight at me. No, not me. Her glowing gaze peered farther, focusing on something *beside* me.

I could barely lift my head enough to see the shape of a tall figure in a long, hooded cloak stepping past me across the grass. With wide shoulders flexed, the figure made a gesture with each hand that sent out another burst of wind.

SMASH!

It shattered every one of the frozen, silver flames like someone hurling rocks into a field of glass sculptures. Glittering shards peppered the grass and began to melt away.

The Zuer straightened, her gaze narrowing upon the figure with no traces of a smile anymore. "You," she seethed accusingly. "I might have known."

The figure didn't stop, the lengths of that long cloak twisting and billowing in the crisp wind with every precise step toward her.

Was this another Ulfrangar? Someone else they'd brought to ensure their victory? With the cowl pulled down low and the figure's face pointed back at the Zuer, I couldn't tell.

Every assassin it passed took a calculated step back, but never dropped their guard. They kept their bowstrings taut and blades raised, their heads slowly moving to watch the figure stride by like a shark gliding silently past a reef.

Then the figure stopped. Its head turned some to consider Murdoc lying there on his back, gaping in shock. Even from a distance, I spotted two eyes glowing like tiny specks of candlelight underneath the hood. Locks of golden hair like bolts of satin hung down to the figure's chest. A narrow face and pointed chin appeared as it turned slightly to consider me, as well.

My stomach dropped.

Was that …? No, it couldn't be. I was seeing things. Or maybe I was already dead, and this was some sort of weird hallucination I was having in the afterlife. It couldn't possibly be real—because there was absolutely no reason Arlan the Kinslayer would ever come here to fight for us.

Right?

No. Absolutely not. Everyone had insisted that Arlan didn't want any conflict with the Ulfrangar. He'd even said something like that himself when we'd met him in Dayrise. He didn't want to get involved with assassins. He didn't deal in murder.

So ... what was he doing here? How had he even known where to find us in the first place? Just what the heck was going on?!

Arlan gave me a brief, unconcerned glance before looking toward the Zuer again. The wind billowed in the lengths of his cloak and blew through his hair, but his smooth, ageless features never moved. He never made any expression at all, almost as though he were staring at her through a mask.

"Zarvan," the Zuer snapped from beneath her own hood, her voice spitting the name as though it were something foul.

Uhh, what? Zarvan? Who was Zarvan?

One corner of Arlan's mouth curled into a smirk. "I see you've not forgotten me, Sadeera. Good. Then you know why I've come."

The Zuer stood eerily still, studying him carefully. Her chest rose and fell, each breath deeper and faster than the one before. Her leather gloves squeaked as she clenched her hands into fists around the shaft of her spear.

I bit back a shout of alarm as she suddenly snapped her head back toward where Murdoc still lay at her feet. Wrath warped her beautiful features, as though she were silently weighing the option to end his life now or not. Oh gods, if she did, there was no one close enough to stop her!

"Pathetic," she seethed, "And here I had given you sole credit for masterminding such elaborate and convenient escapes from my pack again and again. I assumed Rook's training was to thank for it. Now I understand. You've had *help*. Clever. And yet immensely disappointing."

"You assume too much," Arlan countered, his tone still chillingly indifferent. "Do not mistake me for one who meddles in the mire of your barbaric pack. I did not come here for his life, dear sister." His brows drew together, and he slowly raised his hands. Currents of silver energy licked like sterling flames around his fingers as he narrowed his eyes, "I came for yours."

The Zuer brushed back her cowl, revealing a smooth, pale face as flawless as a fine porcelain mask. Hair like bolts of fine white satin hung down her back, and had been braided up over her long, pointed ears on either side of her head. Her black-painted lips pressed together bitterly, and her golden eyes shone like embers in the weak light of the dawn as she stared straight at Arlan.

Wait—did he say *sister*? Gods and Fates—the Zuer was an Avoran elf just like Arlan? And they were ... *brother and sister*?!

"What an interesting sentiment," she sneered, matching the cold hatred of his tone. "You know, I did wonder which slimy rock you'd hidden yourself under. Tell me, little brother, how long have you been down here wallowing in the affairs of these mortals? You look positively awful."

"I might ask the same of you." Arlan's tone cut with a venomous edge. "But, then again, the rags of lowland murderers suit you so well. Perhaps you should consider wearing them at court."

The Zuer's veneer of calm indifference shattered. In an instant, her features twisted into a look of pure wrath and she sprang over Murdoc, hurling her spear at Arlan in one lethal, fluid motion. The weapon streaked over the blood-spattered grass, aimed straight for his head, and leaving a trail of curling black smoke behind it.

Arlan didn't flinch. He didn't even blink. Standing tall and composed, his expression sharpened as his chin tilted slowly down to level a dominating snarl upon the Zuer. As fast as a viper's strike, he snapped a hand forward with his fingers spread wide.

The spear froze right before his open palm, suddenly halting in midair. Silver light crackled around it, shimmering like it'd been caught in an invisible forcefield.

Holy. Gods.

Arlan glared past the weapon as it hovered before him, slowly rotating. His eyes smoldered, but they weren't gold like they'd been before. Now, they shone with the same eerie, sterling light as that strange magic he used. "Do not toy with me, Sadeera," he warned. His lip twitched, curling into a snarl as he gave a gesture with his outstretched hand. "I am not one of your mindless pups."

CRACK!

The spear burst into a shower of silver light with a concussive pop.

"*You*," she seethed, her face twitching with fury.

"Yes, dear sister." Arlan licked his teeth like a dragon preparing to feast. "Come, let us finish what we started all those years ago."

PART TWO
MURDOC

CHAPTER EIGHT

I'd heard many stories of the Avoran elves, their incredible magical power, and their floating glass kingdoms throughout my life. All of those tales, usually whispered by merchant caravans around campfires, or woven by storytellers in tavern halls, had sounded a lot more like fables or myths than anything that might actually be true. After all, the Ulfrangar had not taught me much about them beyond a loose grasp of their language and strong advice to avoid them at all costs.

Now, shambling to my feet to watch the two ancient elven beings duel in the scarlet light of the rising sun, I could better understand why. This was why no one dared to cross the Zuer. This was why Arlan had been able to move with such obscurity and ease through society. The Avoran elves never left their homeland unless they were forced to—and that was a good thing. Normal weapons were nothing but a joke to them. Child's play compared to the force of their magical explosions and arcing beams of ancient power.

My heart pounded in my throat as I struggled to keep up with their blurring movements, both figures weaving and dancing around one another like striking serpents. The crackle and hum of each spell sent a current of power through the air that made every hair on my body prickle. I stumbled back as a bolt like a tongue of silver lightning snapped off the ground less than ten feet from me. One of my boots snagged across the body of a fallen Ulfrangar, and I flailed my arms to try to keep from falling.

"Watch it, pup," a gruff voice barked as a strong hand grabbed my arm to steady me.

I yanked away on pure instinct and whirled around, dropping into a defensive position with my longsword raised. Adrenaline poured over me like molten metal as I braced for combat, preparing to face another Ulfrangar assassin bent on killing me.

It wasn't.

King Jace frowned down at me from the back of a shrike, one of his eyebrows arched in a completely unimpressed expression.

What the—what was he doing here? When had he come back? Was he the one who'd brought Arlan here?

"Go get your dragon," he ordered. "This is our chance. We need to clear out while we can."

Another bolt of raw magical power sizzled through the sky and cracked off the ground behind him. It made the shrike screech in panic and flutter its translucent wings.

"Hurry it up, kid!" Jace yelled. "Unless you want to stand here and die on principle!"

Right. Good point.

I started for Blite at a sprint, but I only made it a few steps. Realization hit me like a kick to the face. Wait. No. I couldn't go yet.

Where was Thatcher?

Whirling around, I searched the area where I'd see him fall. Curse it all, he'd been struck by the Zuer's spear. I didn't know how bad it was, but I was willing to bet he couldn't get up on his own dragon without some help.

And I was not about to leave him in this hell hole by himself.

"Blite! Follow me!" I shouted as I forged back into the chaos, ducking stray bolts of magical power and scattering Ulfrangar who had begun trying to take cover, as well. Not that there was anywhere to go. I slashed my sword through one that dashed too close, giving it a brutal jerk and yank before I turned to squint against the glare of the magical battle raging between Arlan and the Zuer.

They clashed like two angels, bodies glowing with radiant power as they hurled their scorching assaults back and forth. At this rate, they'd leave this whole place nothing but a field of ash and bones.

I had to hurry. I had to find Thatcher—*now*.

Blite appeared at my side, cupping one of his wings over me and whining. Behind us, Fornax let out a string of panicked, barking cries and swung his head around. His big, sightless eyes blinked and swiveled, searching as his nostrils puffed. He was looking for Thatcher, too. Calling to him.

I scanned the battlefield, looking for any sign of him. His cloak. That mess of hay-colored hair. Anything.

The flashing light of another magical explosion shone off his armor. There! Thatcher lay only twenty yards away or so, resting on his side, and not moving or flinching even when the sky erupted with the force of those magical assaults around him.

Not good.

"Go back!" I shouted to Blite. "Get Fornax out of here! He can't navigate without your help!"

He growled disapprovingly and nipped at my cloak, trying to drag me away.

I shoved his head away and glared at him. Now wasn't the time for this. "Do as I say! Go!"

Blite's ears drooped. He blinked and gave a low whine, then turned away to bound back across the battlefield toward Fornax, making urgent, cawing sounds the whole way. Good enough. If he could get Fornax clear, maybe Phoebe and Araxie would be able to evacuate with Jace. Isandri, Reigh, and Lieutenant Eirik were already clear.

That just left the two Avoran sorcerers and a few dozen panicked Ulfrangar standing between Thatcher and me.

Better odds than I'd had all day.

"THATCHER!!" I yelled his name at the top of my lungs, pumping my legs as fast as possible to cross that distance. I hit the ground on my knees beside him, taking him by the shoulders and carefully rolling him onto his back.

He coughed and choked, blood oozing from the corners of his mouth, as he lay limp on the ground. He stared back at me, his face already ashen and his eyes glazed. "M-Mur ... Murdoc." He coughed again as he tried to speak.

"It's okay. You're going to be just fine, Thatcher," I rasped as I looked him over. Merciful gods. The ground before me was soaked with blood—*his* blood.

Gods and Fates. He wasn't going to last much longer. I had to hurry. I had to do something—anything!

I looked around for someone, anyone, who might be able to help. A blinding light bloomed over the battlefield suddenly, forcing me to shield my eyes and turn away. When I dared to squint back in the direction of Arlan and the Zuer, I found both standing nearly nose to nose, wreathed in a rippling, crackling globe of power. Arlan snarled as he held the Zuer off her feet, gripping her by the throat and yelling in his native tongue. There was no mistaking the twisted look of rage, like a man crazed by the need to make her suffer, as another blast of power sent out a low, concussive shockwave.

The Zuer's form burst into a cloud of silver mist, vaporizing her before she could even scream. I threw myself over Thatcher to shield him as the wind and humming force of power washed over us like a pounding ocean wave. It lit up every nerve in my body with a rush of stinging pain like the prick of a thousand needles.

Then ... silence.

I sat up again, gritting my teeth as the lingering ache from that final blast throbbed all the way to my bones. Was it finally over? Was she gone?

"F-Fornax ..." Thatcher sputtered weakly. "Wh-Where's ..."

Oh gods. I had to get him out of here. I had to find some way to stabilize him.

"He's fine, I promise. But you have to stay awake, okay? Focus on the sound of my voice. Concentrate. What's your full name?" Panic took my mind like a pond freezing at the first breath of winter. My hands shook as I scrambled to drag his upper body into my lap and wrestled to unbuckle his breastplate. That spear, whatever it was, had punched straight through the steel of his armor and into his abdomen like it was nothing. The wound was deep, and had obviously nicked something crucial.

"Th-Tha ... Thatcher R-Ren ... ley." his voice slurred until he coughed again. Staring up at me, his expression pale but strangely calm, he gave a faint, delirious smile. "W-We won ... right?"

I put a hand over the wound and tried applying pressure—anything to slow the bleeding. "Yeah. We did."

"G-Good." His body relaxed some, arms and legs going slack as he blinked owlishly up at the sky. "I ... I'm c-cold."

I bit down fiercely, trying to keep my emotions in check. Trying to hold it together. "I know, just hold on. Help is coming. Keep talking to me, okay? You need to stay awake." I gulped against the rising knot of heat and pain in my throat. It made my chest ache and my eyes well up. "How old are you? What's my name? You remember it, right?"

"S-Six ... teen," he rasped faintly. His eyes fixed suddenly, and his pupils dilated. "I-I ... I don't ... p-please take c-care ... of ..."

His expression went distant. His chest gave a weak shudder and went still.

"Thatcher?! Thatcher!" I shook him. I smacked his cheek. I yelled in his face and jostled him. Anything to get a response.

Nothing.

O-Oh gods. Gods, no. No. *NO!!*

"HELP! SOMEBODY HELP HIM!" My throat burned as I screamed. "SOMEBODY PLEASE!"

Everything seemed to stop as I sat there on my knees with Thatcher lying limp against me, yelling to the calm morning sky as loudly as I could. It was as though the whole world had gone still and silent. And I was alone.

Completely and totally alone.

Thatcher had been my friend when I didn't deserve it. He'd been my little brother when I had no family.

If he was gone ... I had no one.

"Thatcher," I begged, grabbing fistfuls of the front of his tunic and bowing my head so that my forehead rested against his. "You can't leave. Not now. Not after all this. Where am I supposed to go? What am I supposed to do? Please ... please don't leave me."

"Move aside, boy," a deep voice spoke over me.

I looked up, clutching at Thatcher's body with one arm and snatching up my longsword with the other as that primal, protective instinct took over. "Get back! Don't you dare touch him!"

"Take care what you do with that blade. You've no enemies here now." Arlan the Kinslayer glowered down from where he stood right over me, his long pale golden hair blowing loosely around his broad shoulders. He winced and hissed an elven curse through his teeth, staggering a bit as he knelt down right at my side.

No enemies? What about the other Ulfrangar?

One glance around answered that question. The grassy prairie outside the dragonrider's temporary compound was now littered with motionless bodies dressed in black and silver. Merciful Fates, he'd ... killed them all. And he'd done it so quickly, cleanly, and without a single weapon of his own.

A chill of primal fear stirred in my chest and tingled up my spine. This man—whoever or whatever he was—held power unlike anything I'd ever imagined could be possible.

Arlan's brow shone with sweat and his sharp jawline went rigid as he stretched out a hand toward Thatcher's body. His nostrils flared some, as though he were fighting to keep his composure.

"Stop. Can't you see it's too late?" My voice shook, cracking as I forced out the words. "H-He's ... he's gone."

"Not quite," Arlan murmured, his scowl sharpening as he sucked in a deep, preparatory breath and rested his palm over the wound on Thatcher's stomach. "Be ready."

Be ready? Ready for wha—?

A flare of silver light glowed from beneath Arlan's hand, shocking the air around us with a strange gust of stark, bitter cold. The usually golden rings of his irises shifted, matching that sterling light as he bared his teeth and furrowed his brow. A grunt of pain leaked through his clenched teeth as he leaned into his hand.

"Come on. Do not fail me now," he snapped angrily, but I couldn't tell if he was fuming at Thatcher or himself. He made another low, agonized sound as his knuckles blanched and the veins stood out against the side of his neck.

"Arlan!" A frantic, female voice called out suddenly.

I looked up just in time to see Garnett running for us over the body-strewn battlefield. Flushed and breathless, she gripped an axe in each hand as she jogged to a stop. Her face paled as soon as she spotted Thatcher, and she let out a shriek of horror. "Oh, stones, no! Thatcher! What happened?!" Both her axes hit the ground at her sides and she clapped a hand over her mouth.

"Garnett, you must pull it out," Arlan barked through his teeth, never looking away from where he still forced his hand down against Thatcher's body. "Now!"

Garnett didn't hesitate. She fell to her knees and grabbed the crossbow bolt still lodged in Thatcher's shoulder, giving it a twist before she ripped it free. I cringed back as a beam of radiant, sterling light streamed from the wound, lighting up the dreary dawn.

What the—?!

The light grew brighter, and the flesh around the arrow wound turned a strange shade of ashen, stony gray. Then, little by little, it began to heal. No—not heal. This was something else. It's as though the wound was disappearing completely.

I gaped at Arlan, trying to make sense of it. I'd heard stories of healing magic, mostly in stories about Jaevid Broadfeather. He'd been the chosen champion of the God of Life, and had been gifted with powerful healing abilities because of it. I'd also heard tales and legends of the might of the Avoran elves. Their kingdom was said to be steeped in ancient, pure magics beyond anything the lower kingdoms could even begin to fathom. But this was ... I-I didn't even know what to call it.

I flinched back, nearly coming out of my own skin in surprise as Thatcher's body suddenly tensed and seized once. His mouth opened and he sucked in a deep gulp of air. He blinked hard a few times, almost like he was trying to clear his vision. Then his eyes rolled back and he slumped against me, still wheezing in slow, steady breaths as though he'd fallen asleep.

H-Holy ... gods. He was alive!

As soon as Thatcher took that breath, Arlan jerked back and pulled his hand away. His palm smoked like he'd lit it on fire, and he cradled it to his chest as he doubled over and groaned in pain. Rocking back and forth, I heard him muttering faint words in the Avoran tongue. I wasn't as fluent in that language, but I caught enough to be able to tell he was spitting strings of curses that might have made a demon blush.

"Arlan! By the stones, man, what did you do?" Garnett whispered brokenly. Her expression was still blank with shock as she gingerly touched Thatcher's neck to take his pulse. "Did you bring him back from the dead?"

"No," he managed weakly. He let out another sharp, hissing curse of pain and fell back to sit on the grass beside us. "Nothing so grand as that. He had not yet passed into the Vale, but his spirit was fading. A few more seconds and he would have been beyond all help. I cannot bring anyone back from the dead. It is, however, still within my abilities to alter the threads of time in a very limited capacity."

Oh. Right. Because there was nothing grand at all about manipulating *time*.

"You mean … you altered time around Thatcher's body to undo his wounds?" I guessed, trying to make sense of what I'd just witnessed. When I said it out loud like that, it sounded even more ridiculous.

"In simplest terms, yes," Arlan confirmed. He kept his face angled away from us, but I could still see his cheek moving as he winced in discomfort. Whatever he'd done, time-altering power or not, it had clearly taken a toll on him.

"He will be all right, then?" Garnett asked worriedly as she scooted in closer, now running her hand across Thatcher's cheek. She nibbled at her bottom lip as she brushed some of his bangs out of his eyes.

Heh. Too bad he was unconscious for all that. He might've thrown up from anxiety if he'd known the girl he liked was petting him like that.

Arlan nodded and rubbed his forehead and the bridge of his nose with his good hand. He still held the other one close to his chest, his hand clenched into a shaking fist as though he'd burned it. "Yes, the boy will recover. The wounds are gone, but he's lost a significant amount of blood. He will need to be taken somewhere secure to rest and recover." His voice hitched as he finally held out the hand he'd used to cast his magic and tried extending his fingers. His controlled, calm demeanor cracked again, his expression twisting in pain. He let out another low, agonized moan and shut his eyes tightly. "A-As will I, it seems."

"You've gone and used too much of that high elf power, haven't you?" Garnett scolded quietly. "Can you walk? Or do I need to send for Howlan and Violet?"

He shook his head, making a few smooth locks of his light golden hair swish loose from where he'd tucked them behind his pointed ears. "I'll manage. Send word for the others to wait for us in Osbran. I suspect a certain dragonrider commander will have a long list of questions for me as soon as he arrives there. Perhaps I'll indulge him a little."

Garnett pursed her lips unhappily, her soft violet eyes studying him carefully as he slowly got to his feet. "Pardon me for speaking out of turn, but in light of all this, I'm not so sure toying with Jaevid Broadfeather is such a good idea."

"You're absolutely correct, dear Garnett." Arlan's thin mouth curled slightly at one corner, briefly giving her a bemused half-smile. Then he turned and began staggering away toward the compound's open gate. "That's why I intend to be easily found and completely hospitable."

"And what if he wants to have you arrested?" she called after him.

I could have sworn I heard the strange elven man chuckle, as though he found that idea adorable. "He can certainly try."

CHAPTER NINE

Arlan, Garnett, and I sat sat outside the gate of the former dragonrider compound, staring at the smoldering field of Ulfrangar corpses. Thatcher was still unconscious, so I had to carry him down to the gate on my back. Not so easy given my own injuries, and the fact that the surge of battle-fueled adrenaline had left me weak and unsteady on my feet. Still, as I sat there, I had to wonder how, by all the gods, I was even breathing at all. Destiny? Divine providence? Sheer dumb luck?

A little of all three?

Thankfully, after only a few minutes, King Jace arrived with a cavalry in the form of eight Gray elven scouts all riding shrikes. They picked us up right outside the compound, and immediately took off for Osbran like a formation of speedy, mirror-scaled dragonflies.

Before noon, we'd landed outside a decent-sized tavern on the edge of the small, rural city. Compared to somewhere like Dayrise, Osbran was barely more than a collection of thatch-roofed buildings smashed into the crumbling ruins of an old fortified city. One of the walls had fallen probably hundreds of years ago, and the city had apparently begun to spill over the old boundary there to extend a little bit beyond. It looked a little like a bowl that was cracked open on one side, so the contents of houses, shops, farms, and fields poured out over the sweeping prairie between the knobby, bare-rock hilltops.

I didn't know much about the place, except that it was small and mostly made up of folk who lived off the weaving industry. The farms around it tended flocks of sheep and goats, and many of the businesses within it catered to that by making fabrics and threads that could be supplied to merchant caravans moving across the kingdom. It was supposed to be a quiet, quaint place. Not somewhere you'd expect to find trouble.

Not until we arrived, anyway.

As we landed in the muddy street in front of the tavern, I spotted several groups of locals—farm hands and shepherds, most likely—watching with mixed expressions of worry and fear. Older men scratched at their beards and leaned together to whisper, eyeing us and keeping a firm grip on their staffs. Not that I didn't understand their concern. These people probably hadn't seen a company of elven warriors on shrikes since the Gray War, and I doubted it called back fond memories.

"Take him inside," King Jace instructed as he stepped over to help me unfasten Thatcher's limp body from the back of another shrike. "The others are already here waiting, and a healer is on the way."

"What about the dragons?" I asked as I jostled Thatcher some, trying to get his weight balanced on my back again.

"I'll see to that next. Most of the dragonriders formerly at the compound are scattered throughout the surrounding farmland, taking shelter where they can for now. There's no fort or tower to house them here, but the common folk have been accommodating so far. Hopefully that luck holds out until we can come up with a better plan. I'll return tonight with more information."

"And what about him?" I asked, lowering my voice and tipping my chin toward where Arlan was also dismounting from a back of a shrike.

King Jace joined me in staring distrustfully at the elven man who, ironically, had just saved mine and Thatcher's lives. I didn't expect that grace to be given freely, though. He was still a crime lord, and I wasn't stupid enough to believe for one single second that he didn't have an ulterior motive for intervening on our behalf. He was up to something. I just hoped, whatever it was, it wouldn't require me to sell my soul to yet another wicked entity in this gods-forsaken kingdom.

"I've no right to detain him here. In Luntharda, I might try to hold him long enough to question him about who and what, exactly, he is. But I can't do that here in Maldobar, and I'm not sure that killing the Zuer qualifies as a crime in anyone's book. So, he's not done anything that even warrants me even alerting the local officials," Jace sighed and sank back onto his heels some. "We have no choice but to let him go, for now."

The old king rubbed at his short, white beard as we watched Arlan speak a few words to Garnett, then he strode off into the city without ever looking back. Every step he took away from us made my toes curl inside my boots and my stomach writhe in apprehension. It felt wrong to just let him slither out of sight like that. Then again, he'd mentioned he intended to stay in Osbran, at least long enough to talk to Jaevid. Maybe we'd get some real answers out of him, after all.

"Rest while you can, Murdoc," Jace warned as he flashed me another critical, appraising glance. "You should be safe here for a few days, at least. The city's overseen by Count Wilmot. A good man, by all accounts, but I don't know him personally. You would do well to tread lightly and not burn anything to the ground, if you can manage it."

I snorted and started shuffling off toward the front steps of the tavern, lugging Thatcher along like a scrawny backpack. "No promises." I only made it a few paces before something burrowed deep into the pit of my gut, twisting and gnawing, and forcing me to stop. I turned to give the king one last look.

"Thank you," I murmured, and lowered my gaze in submission.

He gave a squinty, puzzled frown.

"I don't know how or why, but I know you were the one who brought Kinslayer there.

If you hadn't, the Zuer would have killed me. She would have killed all of us. So ... thank you."

"Ah." He gave a stiff nod and quickly looked away. "Don't take this the wrong way, but I didn't do it for you. You're not the only one who's been watching the shadows since the day you left the pack behind, and to be perfectly honest, I owed Rook the courtesy of finishing what he'd started. By taking the risk and trying to get you out of their grasp, he did what I never had the courage to even try to do for him. I wasn't about to let his dying effort be in vain."

I studied Jace's profile for a few seconds, watching the way his brow puckered as his frown deepened, and the way his eyes went steely as though he were trying to keep the memories at bay. Finally, I turned and started for the tavern again, leaving him in that heavy silence.

I did understand why he'd done it. I knew full well what kind of hell he'd lived through all these years, dreading that every step he took might be the wrong one that led him back into the path of the pack. Time didn't make it easier. It didn't make the fear go away. He'd spent a lifetime held hostage by that dread and quiet suffering.

Now, we were both free. Well, hopefully, anyway. Time would tell.

Now, thanks to Arlan the Kinslayer, time was something we had on our side.

I HIT the front door of the run-down old tavern and inn with a sigh that made my chest ache and my back throb under Thatcher's weight. Just a little farther. Then I could put him down and let him get proper treatment and rest. I might even be able to steal a little of both for myself, as well.

The wooden boards of the front porch creaked under my weight, and I had to balance Thatcher's weight just right in order to get an arm free so I could try opening the door.

Another smaller and much faster hand beat me to it.

"I got you, love," Garnett announced as she held the door open so I could stagger inside.

"Not going with Arlan?" I murmured, wondering if I should even be using his name or not.

"He prefers to be on his own. Not that we don't try to help him, but he's a stubborn one." She shrugged, and I could have sworn I saw a hint of worry crinkle her features as she stole a glance up at Thatcher.

Ahhh, so that was it. The *real* reason she'd stayed behind. Miss Crime-Lord-Informant had a new tell of her own, and his name was Thatcher Renley.

Ugh. Why did that sort of make me want to throw up?

The tavern-keeper met us just inside the door, flustered and looking like he might be a heartbeat away from fainting. The short, heavyset man had more hair in his bristly red mustache and thick eyebrows than he did on the rest of his entire head. He stammered through an explanation of which rooms upstairs had been prepared for us, looking concerned when he noticed Thatcher was still unconscious and flung over my back like a caught goat. "They paid for four rooms, but I've opened up an extra just in case. Then you're on a mission for Her Majesty? To retake Northwatch? Gods and Fates, isn't that dangerous? You're hardly more than children!" He fretted and dabbed at his sweat beading on his brow with a handkerchief.

"We appreciate the hospitality." I nodded and started for the wide staircase at the far end of the bar.

"Of course, no trouble at all! We're always happy to assist Her Majesty in any way," the man continued to ramble, following us all the way to the bottom of the stairs. "My daughter, Evie, should be somewhere up there helping, and the healer should be here any moment. I'll send him right up when he arrives, don't you worry."

Garnett did a much better job of thanking him profusely before she bounded after me up the stairs to the second floor. She certainly had a knack for handling people. A useful skill, and not one I possessed in any capacity whatsoever. Well, unless they came at me with a blade. That I could handle proficiently enough.

But according to Thatcher, I needed to try "smiling more." Hah.

The tavern itself wasn't all that large, with only two floors in all. Overall, it had a much more modest and rustic feel, but it was clean and smelled of fresh cut pine logs, spiced ales, and something delicious baking in the kitchen behind the long, high-top bar. The floor above had eight rooms for rent, and it was easy enough to track down which ones had been opened for our use. As usual, I just had to follow the ambient sounds of chaos and arguing.

"Reigh Farrow! Are you even listening to me? You're in no shape to be walking anywhere! I can't believe Kiran even let you leave Ms. Lin's house like this. You've torn nearly all your stitches and you're bleeding all over your clothes." Phoebe fussed like an angry sparrow, her voice echoing down the hallway before I even got to the top of the stairs. "Go back and lie down right now. So help me, I know where you keep your chaser root tea, and I *will* sedate you if that's what it takes—HEY! Don't make that face at me; I'm just trying to keep you alive! Isandri didn't put up any fuss at all, but you're acting like a big baby."

"Lively, isn't she?" Garnett giggled as we made it to the landing.

I just smirked. Phoebe had always been excitable, but now that she and Reigh had arrived at a mutual understanding, she'd been much less cautious around him. A good thing, too. That bratty, stubborn kid needed someone to thump him upside the head now and again. Not that it helped much. It was entertaining to watch, though.

As soon as we rounded the corner, I spotted that familiar mane of wild red curls at the other end of the hall. For whatever reason, the sight made all the muscles in my body want to go slack and the last little bit of my energy fizzle away. My head and shoulders drooped, and I practically had to drag my feet like someone had filled my boots with lead.

We were all here. We were all safe.

That was all that mattered.

"Murdoc!" Phoebe gasped when she saw us. Tears welled in her eyes as she ran to meet me. "You're alive!" She reached out like she might embrace me, then stopped short. Her expression tensed, closing up as she quickly looked away, like she was afraid I might lash out at her or something if she touched me. Then she noticed Thatcher where he lay, still unconscious, and draped over my back. Her wide blue eyes glanced between us like she couldn't decide what to panic over first.

"He's okay," I tried to calm her before she jumped to the wrong conclusion. "Just unconscious."

"O-Okay," she gasped, still blinking back tears as her cheeks flushed pink. "Oh gods, he just looks so pale. Are you sure he's all right?"

I nodded. "It might take him a few days to get back on his feet, but he should be fine. Just tell me where I can put him down. He's supposed to rest."

Phoebe led us farther down the hall, to a room across from the one where I spotted Reigh stretched out on a small bed. With his torso wrapped in fresh bandaging, he lay on his back and scowled up at the ceiling with his arms crossed. Isandri stood over him, one of her biceps also wrapped in bandaging, and frowned down at him as though she were daring him to try and get up again. I guess Phoebe had her working as reinforcements to make sure he stayed put.

"They're, um, they're bringing us some more clean hot water, rags, and bandages," Phoebe rambled as she rushed in ahead of us to pull back all the blankets on the bed, except for one white sheet. A good call, since getting Thatcher cleaned up was going to require dealing with his blood-drenched clothes. It'd make a mess everywhere. "They said the healer should be here soon, too. But, um, I'm not sure how long he'll take. Kiran showed me a few things while I was helping him take care of Reigh and Judan before, so I can at least get everyone ready and—"

"You're doing a great job," Garnett consoled, patting Phoebe on the back and smiling broadly. "And now I'm here to help, too. Just tell me what you want me to do."

Phoebe's smile was still teary and twitchy, like she might break down crying at any moment. I guess it'd been hard for her to watch everything from that tower—too far to do much except fire from Thatcher's crossbow whenever she got a clear shot. Thatcher had also given her his goggles, hoping she could at least help Fornax orient if things got dire. In the end, none of that had helped much. I'd known from the start that once the battle started, regardless of whether or not the dragonriders were removed from the equation, we were going to be in for a bloodbath. Mostly, I think positioning Phoebe in the tower like that was Reigh and Eirik's way of putting her as far out of harm's way as she would allow. She had flat out refused to evacuate with the rest of the dragonriders.

"O-Okay, yes, thank you," she managed in a trembling voice. Her gaze met mine for an instant before she quickly looked away again.

My heart twisted painfully. I didn't understand why—why was it so hard to look at her now?

Turning around, I sat on the edge of the bed and leaned back so Garnett and Phoebe could help slide Thatcher's limp body up onto the mattress. Once they had him sprawled out, they immediately got to work removing the rest of his armor and bloody clothes. Once again, I was a little sad he wasn't conscious enough to be aware of it. He would have blushed as red as a beet if he'd known Garnett and Phoebe were stripping him down to his smallclothes like that.

I'd have to remember to tease him about that later.

"Is the room next door one of ours, as well?" I asked as I stood and started to leave. I wasn't much use here now, after all. Might as well give them some space to work.

"Oh, um, yes. And there's a washroom at the end of the hall." Phoebe looked up from where she'd been wrestling one of Thatcher's boots off. "It's not very big, but they said we could use it. I-I, um, I asked Queen Araxie if she would go and find some new, clean clothes for everyone. She should be back any moment. Oh! And I asked if they could bring us up something to eat. You know, because I sort of thought everyone might be too tired to sit downstairs."

"I'll pass on the food for now. Thanks, though." I looked back long enough to cast her what might have been the world's most pathetic excuse for a smile.

It must've looked as half-hearted, exhausted, and pained as it felt, because Phoebe's expression immediately shifted from that reluctant, evasive anxiety to concern. "Murdoc ...?" She said my name in that soft voice again—the one that passed through my body like a tingling heat and made every corner of my mind go silent.

Great. No way I could keep a straight face now. Or a smiling one, in this case.

I waved a hand, hoping she'd take that as assurance that I really was fine. Seriously, I was. But it didn't seem like she was buying that, either. Her little eyebrows rumpled together suspiciously.

"Let me know if you need any more help," I sighed.

Turning away I let the door close behind me as I stepped back out into the hall. I rubbed my face with my hands, massaging my temples as I tried to shake off that feeling. What was wrong with me, anyway? She'd said my name a thousand times since we'd met. Why was it different now? It was getting harder and harder just to have simple conversations with her. Was I losing my mind?

Urggh. I didn't know. The only thing I was certain of was if she kept on doing that, looking at me with those sad doe eyes and whispering my name in that tone, sooner or later ... I might do something stupid. As in, completely irresponsible, recklessly selfish, Reigh-level stupid.

And no one was prepared for that kind of disaster—not even me.

10

CHAPTER TEN

I almost smacked right into a young woman carrying a big bucket of steaming hot water when I stepped into the tavern's small washroom. She gave a yelp of alarm and froze like a spooked squirrel, staring with wide eyes at my slashed-up, blood-spattered state. Right, so, I probably did look somewhat horrifying like this. Hence the trip to the washroom.

"Sorry," I muttered and moved out of her way.

"Not at all! You just ... surprised me a little. My apologies." She hurried past, still giving me a wary side-eye as she carried the bucket away in the direction of Thatcher's room.

The tavernkeeper's daughter? The one he'd mentioned was named Evie? Seemed like a fair guess. And with those slightly pointed ears peeking out of long, ash-colored hair ... she must've been a halfbreed like Jaevid. Interesting.

Now that I had the washroom to myself, I took my time stripping off my own tattered, bloodstained tunic, pants, armor, and even my socks and smallclothes. Blood oozed from the open slices and gashes I'd gotten in the fight. Fortunately, thanks to my armor, none of the crossbow bolts had managed to pierce through all the way to my skin. The rest of my injuries were minor. A few stitches and some bandages after I'd rinsed myself clean, and I'd be fine.

A large copper basin sat waiting in the corner of the small, dimly lit space. It was already filled with fragrant, steaming water, and I hissed through my teeth as I sank down into it. I cursed when the water washed over a much deeper cut that sliced across my upper back. It stung a lot worse than the rest, although it was hard to tell just how bad it might be. If it hurt that much, though, I'd probably need more than few stitches to close it up.

I rinsed myself off as best I could and dunked my head under a few times, trying to scrub the grit out of my scalp and the grime from my skin, before I finally climbed out.

Godling

There were a few clean but well-worn towels set on a shelf behind the basin, and I swiped one to dry off and ruffle some of the water out of my hair. I didn't have any new clothes to change into—not that I wanted to since I still had injuries slowly oozing blood —so I pulled my smallclothes back on and wrapped the towel around my waist. Good enough.

Poking my head outside the washroom to check, I waited until I was certain everyone else was otherwise occupied to gather the rest of my stuff and make a speedy dash down the hall. I speedily made my way into the room next to Thatcher's and shut the door. Now maybe I could rest some while I waited for the healer to show up.

I dropped my stuff at the foot of one of the two untouched beds, and let out a deep breath. The narrow room itself wasn't anything grand or lavish, which suited me fine. A window on the longest wall let in a few rays of weak midday sun, and two small beds were set on opposite ends of the space with a washstand, little table, and two chairs in between them. It smelled faintly of soap, like someone had scrubbed the floors recently, and the quilts folded neatly on each bed looked a little threadbare, but also clean.

A small round mirror hung behind the washstand, and a glimpse of my reflection in that old glass made me freeze in place. I didn't remember how I'd looked before we left Halfax months ago. I didn't usually pay attention to that sort of thing. Even so, I was willing to bet it wasn't this bad. Dark circles hung under my eyes, and my hair had grown out so long it covered my ears and came down to my neck. A few more weeks and I'd either have to cut it or tie it back like Thatcher did.

Eh. Definitely cut it.

There were still a few green-and-yellow-colored bruises on my face from where Thatcher had punched me. I'd gotten a little thicker through the chest, and a dusting of dark stubble flecked my chin, neck, and jaw. It made me look older, and not in a good way. That combined with everything else—my ragged hair, weary drooping eyelids, and body slashed with fresh and recently stitched wounds from our other encounters with the Ulfrangar—made me look like I'd just crawled out of a gutter somewhere.

It wasn't so far from the truth, I guess.

Standing in nothing but my smallclothes and the towel, I let my gaze wander from one horrific scar to the next that marred nearly every inch of my skin. I couldn't remember how I'd gotten some of them. The worst ones, though—the thick, raised, gnarled, scars on my wrists and neck—I knew all too well where those had come from.

My heartbeat slowed to deep, aching, hard thumps as I stared at those marks. Somehow, now that the Zuer was dead and the Ulfrangar had no reason to hunt me any longer, I expected to feel something. Free, I guess. Or relieved. Maybe even happy.

But now, looking at those marks on my body, I didn't feel any of those things. I only saw the truth of what I was still etched into my being forever. The Zuer was gone. The pack wouldn't pursue me now. And yet, I didn't feel anything except ... lost.

I shivered as a strange numbness like lukewarm water settled through my mind, leaving me adrift and wondering what I was supposed to do with my life now. Who was I supposed to be? Where should I go? I'd done the impossible and escaped the Ulfrangar. I'd gotten my freedom. Now, I just wasn't sure what I was meant to do with it.

The obvious answers were that I'd go to the dragonrider academy and follow

Thatcher wherever else he went. But part of me knew that couldn't last forever. He wasn't like me. Sure, he was gawky and awkward now, but he'd grow into himself. He'd eventually stumble across a girl who found his baby-face and bumbling, naïve kindness endearing. Then he wouldn't need a brother-figure staring over his shoulder all the time. I'd have to move on, too. I'd need to build a life of my own somewhere.

For now, the fact that I was even standing here still felt unreal—like a dream I'd suddenly wake up from at any moment. I still didn't understand most of what had happened. I couldn't begin to comprehend why Arlan the Kinslayer had actually shown up to fight the woman who was apparently his sister. I didn't even know how he'd gotten there in the first place. Had King Jace brought him? Or had he used some of that magical power to somehow cross the distance? Had he simply agreed to help us for the chance of fighting the Zuer? Or had he and Jace struck their own, separate bargain? How was it that an Avoran elf had become the leader of the Ulfrangar? And if she was really dead, did that make Arlan the new Zuer?

All were excellent questions that I had no hope of answering at the moment. Right then, I didn't even have the will to try. I wandered to the bed farthest from the door and sank down onto it, letting my elbows rest on my knees. I didn't want to think anymore. My head swam every time I closed my eyes, as though my brain was bobbing and bouncing around in my skull like a rowboat on a stormy sea. Sleep—I just wanted to sleep. And to know that when I woke up, the world wouldn't be burning down around me again.

Hah. Fat chance, right? If I'd learned anything over the last several months, it's that wherever Thatcher Renley went, disaster was bound to follow at an alarming speed. And, naturally, I'd wind up caught right in the thick of it.

Still, even knowing all that, ... I couldn't think of anywhere else in the world I'd rather be.

I DON'T KNOW how long I sat there like that, tossed amidst my reckless thoughts and trying to decide if it was worth it to try sleeping. I wasn't sure if I could, or if I'd just wind up lying there for hours, worrying over things I had absolutely no control over, and thinking about everything I should have been doing right then. Ugh. Maybe a sleeping remedy was in order, after all. I wondered if Reigh had any packed away in his bag of medicinal tricks.

A soft knock on the door made me look up.

"Murdoc?" Phoebe's quiet voice called from the hall. "Are you, um, is it okay if I come in?"

"Yeah. It's okay," I answered on pure reflex, without really thinking at all.

And by the time Phoebe cracked the door open and peeked inside, it was way too late. As soon as she realized I was sitting there in basically just my underwear, her face blushed almost as red as her wild storm of curls and she immediately slapped a hand over her eyes. "O-Oh! I'm so sorry, I-I didn't know you were still—ah!"

Crap. What the heck was wrong with me? "S-Sorry!" I quickly snatched my pants off the pile of filthy clothes on the floor and pulled them on.

"No! No, I should have realized you were—gods, I'm really sorry!" She panicked, her eyes still pinched shut as she floundered not to drop the armload of bandages and medical supplies she'd been carrying.

"It's fine. Totally my fault. I wasn't paying attention." Great. Now my whole head felt like it was on fire. "I, uh, I'm decent now." Sinking back down on the edge of the bed, I buried my face in my hands so hopefully she wouldn't see me blushing like a moron.

Her light footsteps approached and stopped before me. "Murdoc?" she asked softly. "Are you okay?"

I rubbed at my cheeks still finding a few tender spots from those bruises around my nose and cheekbones. "Yeah," I lied. It didn't seem right to burden her with any of my issues.

She didn't answer for a moment, and I had to wonder if she could tell I was bluffing. "The healer's here. He's, um, he's checking on Reigh and Thatcher first," she said at last. "You got hurt, too, didn't you? Can I take a look? I'm not a healer, but Kiran was teaching me a little about it before."

I lifted my head, meeting her worried, raindrop-blue gaze. She had her bottom lip drawn into her mouth, nibbling at it, and her little ginger eyebrows were drawn up in concern.

"Okay," I surrendered.

Neither of us spoke as she began looking over the new cuts and wounds I'd gotten during our battle. Lucky for me, most of them were trivial. The injuries I'd sustained while taking that godsgrave potion were a little more worrisome. They'd been deeper, and despite Reigh constantly funneling those healing remedies down my throat, they were healing a lot more slowly. The one on my side stung when she lifted my arm and carefully prodded it with her fingers. It made my breath catch and I gave a small grunt of pain.

"That hurts?" she asked, leaning around to peer into my face as though trying to detect whether or not I was fibbing this time.

"Y-Yeah. A little."

There was no mistaking the worry in her face as she ducked back around me and tested the area around it with her fingers. "It's hot to the touch, too. I think it's getting infected. We should ask the healer for some medicines, and you need to rest."

"Well, I'll be happy to as soon as people stop trying to kill me every few hours," I chuckled weakly.

She didn't seem to find that as funny. The bed jostled as she climbed around behind me, examining my back. Knowing what she'd find back there made me cringe and I shut my eyes tightly. I bowed my head as embarrassed heat bloomed in my cheeks again.

"Oh, Murdoc. This cut across your shoulders, it's ... it's really deep. I'm so sorry, we'll definitely need to stitch it, but I don't have any way to numb it." Her voice trembled a bit as she pushed the cloth against it again. "We should wait for the healer. Maybe he has something for the pain, so it won't hurt as much."

"It's fine, Phoebe," I said, trying to keep my tone as gentle as I knew how.

"But, no, Murdoc, it isn't!" she protested, beginning to sound a little panicked now. "It's got to be almost half an inch deep, and—"

"It's okay. Really. I ... I don't have much feeling left back there now, anyway," I murmured.

She didn't make a sound for nearly a minute, but I could barely sense the tickle of her fingertips moving across my back. She traced the old stripes left by years of whelpers' and handlers' whips. Sword cuts and blade marks from training duels, many of which I didn't even remember. After a while, it all ran together, blending into one long tapestry of violence and agony I'd assumed I would never escape. The layers upon layers of scarring there had made the skin rough and thick, and I'd lost a lot of the sensation there because of it.

Finally, I heard Phoebe whimper, "The Ulfrangar did this to you?"

"Yes."

She went quiet again. Her hand moved to my shoulders, then up into my neck. I couldn't resist the urge to let my eyes roll back when she combed her fingers through my hair. No one had ever done that before. But it felt so ... *good*.

A little too good, I guess, because a deep sigh left my chest.

I heard her laugh softly. "You scared me a little, at first, you know. When we first met, I mean."

I frowned. I had scared her? Why? It's not like she'd known who and what I was then. And as far as I could recall, I'd never raised a hand against her before.

"Why?" I dared to ask.

"I don't know. Maybe because you were so quiet and serious all the time. Also, in case you hadn't noticed, you're about twice my size, so ..." She let her voice trail off, as though she were thinking. "But I guess most people are a lot taller than me, so maybe that's not exactly fair to say. Well, other than Garnett. I can't believe I'm taller than her! I've never been taller than anyone except, you know, little kids."

I bowed my head to hide my smirk. "Some people assume you're a little kid, too, probably."

She swatted the back of my head and stormed off the bed, coming back around to stand in front of me with her arms crossed and her cheeks puffed like an angry chipmunk. "Don't be rude! I'll have you know, I am *seventeen* years old! Everyone just assumes I'm a lot younger because I'm short. I know I'm not as tall or mature-looking as other girls my age, but I—"

"Not so scared of me now, are you?" I teased.

She put her hands on her hips. "No, I'm not. Not even a little," she declared. It was hard not to find that fiery little glare of hers amusing. And cute.

"Good," I chuckled.

"Also ... I know you now," she added, her tone softening some again as she scrunched her mouth and looked down. "I know you'd never hurt any of us."

My heart did that squeezing, fluttering thing that made my body tense again. She didn't sound so certain about that last part, maybe because ... I'd already hurt her once. Not physically, of course. But still.

I'd pushed her away. I'd rejected her feelings. I had lots of good reasons for it, of course. And not all of those reasons had changed. I still had nothing to offer any girl that might be interested in me. Didn't that matter to her? Didn't she want a normal life with someone who could secure a good living, provide a safe home, and offer her a future she could rely on? Sure, I might wind up a dragonrider at the end of all this. All that promised was a decent salary and the assurance that I would be traveling under military orders around the kingdom for a while. And not even that future was guaranteed.

I was still a former Ulfrangar pup, a murderer in the eyes of the kingdom, and I wasn't stupid enough to think there wouldn't be some punishment in store for everything I'd done in their name. Unlike Jace, I hadn't wound up a king who was far beyond the grasp of the normal legal system. Jaevid might be able to keep me out of prison, but I wasn't counting on that. Not when Queen Jenna heard about all the people who'd died and the homes that had been damaged during all this.

I mean, gods, Thatcher had almost *died* because of me.

Thinking about that, about those few seconds when I'd thought he was gone, hit me like an iron fist to the chest. My body tensed, and my head bowed lower. All that confusion, frustration, panic, and pure terror surged through my brain like flood waters cracking through a dam. I couldn't stop it.

"Murdoc?" She did it again—said my name in that small, breathless whisper.

I looked up at her, and that last feeble thread of my sanity snapped.

"Are you okay?" she asked, her tone insistent. "And don't brush me off this time."

My mouth screwed up. I wanted to look away, but I couldn't. Her expression of genuine worry held me captive. She wanted to know how I really was … and I didn't have the mental fortitude to even try lying to her right now.

"I-I, I don't know," my voice shook and I sucked in a sharp breath, trying to steel myself. It didn't work. "I almost killed him, Phoebe. I thought I did. Thatcher, he was dying right there in front of me and I couldn't do anything. I couldn't save him. If Arlan hadn't—I-I don't know what I …" I stopped short, my mouth clamping down hard against the rising lump of pain and grief that lodged at the back of my throat. It made every word burn like dragon venom. My eyes welled. I bowed my head lower, praying she wouldn't see. "Now I don't know what's going to happen. I don't know if I owe my life to Arlan as payment, or Jace for arranging all this, or both. I don't understand why any of them wanted to help me. I don't know if I've just traded one form of slavery for another."

"Murdoc, I—"

"Don't." I cut her off immediately.

"Don't what?"

"Don't tell me you're sorry," I snapped hoarsely. "Don't tell me that it wasn't my fault, or that I did the best I could, or that it's going to be fine. Just *don't!*" The words just kept coming. The more I tried to stop, the louder and more broken my voice became. "Thatcher, he … he wouldn't have even been out there if it wasn't for me. He never would have gotten hurt—none of you would have!"

My hands drew into fists, clenching so hard it made my whole body shudder and my knuckles go white. Tears ran down the end of my nose and dripped onto the wood floor at my feet. It should have been me. If anyone had deserved to be lying there on that battlefield, bleeding out, it was me, not Thatcher. I'd almost lost my best friend. I'd almost watched him take the fall for my sake. And I'd been completely helpless to stop it.

My voice caught, strangled by a sob as I buried my face in my hands. "I-I can't do this. I can't be like the rest of you. I don't deserve ... I ... I-I'm ... not worthy of ..."

Phoebe hugged me.

She wrapped her arms around my head, burying my face against her soft purple tunic, and held me tightly against her. "I wasn't either. Don't you remember? I was a Tibran. I did terrible things, too, Murdoc. But you were the one who taught me how to start moving on," she murmured against my hair. "Now you have to try, just like I did. You can't give up—not when you're so close."

I dragged her in closer, squeezing her back as hard as I could. "I-I'm ... I'm scared," I admitted, the low, rasping words like poison on my tongue. Not so long ago, saying something like that would've gotten me beaten within an inch of my life.

Ulfrangar were not allowed to be afraid.

"Shhh. You're safe now, Murdoc," she cooed gently and pressed her lips against my temple. "It's over. Everyone's okay, and you're safe right here with us."

My eyes closed as I relaxed into her embrace, taking in deep breaths of her scent. It reminded me of the soothing, cozy smells in Ms. Lin's house—of warm cinnamon, nutmeg, honey, and sweet cream. Cozy. Inviting. Safe. Comfortable. Phoebe was all those things ... and so much more.

I didn't know when it had happened. I guess it wasn't something that had come about suddenly. It must have grown gradually, little by little, since the moment I'd first met her. But somewhere along the way, I'd ... fallen for this girl.

She was all the happiness I'd ever wanted and couldn't have. She was more resilient than I'd ever be, stronger than I'd ever given her credit for, smarter than anyone else I knew. I'd never deserve her.

But I had never wanted anything more than to call her mine.

Grasping my face in her small hands, she turned my head back so I was forced to look at her. She smiled as she brushed her thumbs along my cheeks and wiped my eyes. "You need to rest. I'll go and speak to the healer. Maybe he has something that will help you relax so you can get some sleep."

I nodded—unconvincingly, I guess, because she scowled and pursed her lips.

"I mean it, Murdoc. How long has it been since you had a decent night's rest?" She fussed and continued to pet my face, brushing my bangs away from my eyes, and running her fingers along my brow and cheeks.

I would've kept on arguing with her all afternoon if it meant she'd keep doing that. Soft, gentle touches like that were still so ... strange. But I liked them.

Or *her*, I guess was a better way of putting it. I liked *her*. A lot. Too much.

"Go ahead and lie down," she went on scolding me. "Not on your back, though. We still need to have a look at that cut on your shoulders. Probably the one on your side, too, I think. I really do think it's getting infected. Fates, between you, Thatcher, and Reigh, we'll be stuck here for a week trying to get you all put back together."

I didn't have the willpower or the energy to protest. Crawling the rest of the way up onto the bed, I collapsed on my stomach with a heavy grunt and lay still. All those clean sheets and soft blankets seemed to swallow me whole, and for a moment, I couldn't think about anything except sleep. Sleep, and Phoebe. I wanted to ask her to stay here, with me. Then I'd know she was safe.

But regardless of how unfathomably kind she was to me, I had no right to ask her for anything like that. Just wanting her to be close—wanting her to be mine—wasn't enough. Phoebe was, without a doubt, the most beautiful person I had ever met in my entire life. Inside and out, there wasn't a single part of her that didn't resonate with goodness and light. She deserved the absolute best that the world could give her.

... And even if she'd never admit it, even if she didn't want to hear me say it, I knew that was never going to be me.

CHAPTER ELEVEN

The Gray elf spy network from Luntharda had done a fantastic job getting us set up with everything we needed in Osbran. At King Jace's request, they had arranged for us to have a place to stay at the tavern, as well as all the supplies we would require in terms of medicines, food, and gear. Honestly, I was surprised at how thorough they'd been in their preparations. They'd even arranged for Blite and Fornax to stay in a farmer's barn, scarcely a quarter mile away from our tavern. It wasn't ideal, but the farmer seemed eager to take in dragonriders—either for bragging rights, or for a little extra coin. Perhaps both.

Somehow, though, I doubted the now one-handed prince would be very thrilled to hear that things were going so well with his network in his absence. He hadn't liked being left behind in the first place, and knowing he'd missed out on all this—a grand battle with the Ulfrangar, the Zuer, and seeing Kinslayer wage magical battle. Well, I wasn't about to volunteer to be the one to fill him in about it later, that's for sure.

Hmm. Actually, that sounded exactly like something Reigh should do while I watched from the opposite side of the room, well out of arm's reach.

The healer, an elderly man with distinctly half-elven features, hobbled between our rooms while Phoebe fluttered around him nervously like a scarlet butterfly. He cleaned and redressed Reigh's wounds, stitched up the places where Isandri and I had a few fresh gashes from sword cuts, gave me a few herbal remedies for infection, and gave Phoebe instructions on how to look after all of us—which essentially boiled down to "don't let them do anything else stupid."

Talk about an exercise in futility.

There wasn't much the old man could do about Thatcher's condition, though. Thanks to Arlan, there weren't any visible wounds on his body to treat anymore. He'd lost a significant and nearly lethal amount of blood, though. The only treatment for that, apart from a few herbal concoctions and a few food choices that would help speed things along, was making sure he stayed off his feet for a few days.

Easier said than done, though.

Thatcher awoke late the next morning, delirious and asking about his dragon. He fretted over me, too, and wouldn't lie down and be still until I came in to prove I wasn't actually dead. I guess the last thing he remembered clearly was the Zuer standing over me with that spear. Ridiculous kid. *He* was the one who'd almost died. Couldn't he worry about himself for once?

The only thing that kept him in the bed, where he was supposed to be, was Garnett. Not that she forced him. But since he was still only wearing his smallclothes under the blankets, he didn't dare to get up while she was sitting in there with him. I had to wonder if not fully redressing him was a tactical move on her part. After all, Queen Araxie had come by at some point early in the morning with fresh changes of clothes for all of us. So, was this her passive-aggressive way of making sure he followed the healer's orders and didn't go wandering off? If so, it was working brilliantly.

She stayed around the tavern for several days, mostly helping Phoebe and the healer. But after two nights, and the growing confidence that none of us were going to die, she finally confessed that she needed to return to her duties. Arlan was still in the area, and there was a lot of loose ends to tie off after what he'd done at the dragonrider compound. What those loose ends were, exactly, she didn't say. I knew better than to ask, though. I might not have been as keen as she was when it came to reading people, but I could tell from her shifty demeanor and reluctant mumbling that something wasn't quite right.

"I'll be in touch as soon as I can," she promised on her way out the door, casting one last, distinctly sad smile in Thatcher's direction. "I know Arlan will be wanting to speak with you all once Lord Jaevid has arrived and you're all up to it. Just try to stay out of trouble till then, eh?"

"Heh, yeah, well, no promises," Thatcher called back. His forced chuckle sounded more like the despairing squeak of a mouse getting stepped on.

I guess that meant he still hadn't worked up the nerve to tell her how he so obviously felt about her. Ugh. At this rate, he never would.

Not that it was any of my business, I guess. I still hadn't spoken to Thatcher beyond a few, muttered passing words since, well, those few, slurred words we'd exchanged when he nearly died right in front of me. I didn't know what to say to him now.

Before the battle, when he came to clear the air and insist that I not surrender to the Zuer outright, I'd known it wasn't the end of that conversation. There was a lot more that needed to be said—a lot more I should be able to tell him now. But just the thought drove me farther and farther away from everyone as the days dragged on. I didn't know how angry he still was, or what he wanted from me anymore. I didn't know if we were still friends like we had been before, or if he wanted space.

And based on the pasty, wild-eyed way he looked at me from a distance, like someone about two seconds away from throwing up, either he felt the same way ... or he was dealing with some extreme food poisoning. He didn't demand that I leave his room whenever I wandered in to see how he was doing, though. I wondered if that might be a good sign ... Hmm.

The next few days passed slowly, bringing with them another storm that choked the sky with thick, gray clouds. Low rolls of thunder and occasional gusts of howling wind stirred over the bleak landscape, and cold rain ran in rivers down the muddy streets outside the tavern. After nearly five days of it, however, I found myself growing restless. There wasn't much space to escape the ambient noise of the tavern and the rest of our group, who'd gone back to their normal antics now that everyone was on the mend. But the foul weather had also forced the gathering audience of locals who hung around outside, hoping to spot a dragonrider or a member of the royal family, back to their homes. That was probably for the best. We were supposed to be meeting with a certain famous war hero any day now, and I doubted he would want to stop and sign autographs on his way inside.

Sitting beneath the shelter of the tavern's slumped-roofed front porch, I took my time cleaning all the pieces of my leather armor and weaponry. Most of what I had was still stained with dried blood, but I'd been able to find a small bottle of oil and a few rags so I could begin getting everything polished back to pristine condition. On the far end of the roof, a dozen or so little copper cups hung on a thin chain. The rain spilling over them made an odd noise, and after a while, I decided I sort of liked it. Something about it was almost musical, and strangely soothing.

The front door creaked open, but I didn't need to look up to know who came tromping out to stand over me. I knew Reigh's restless, frustrated sigh right away. "Still no word from Jaevid," he muttered.

"It's a long flight here from Halfax," I reminded him. "Even for a dragon. The weather will likely slow him down, too."

"Yeah. True. But I'd thought he might at least send a letter ahead if he got delayed, or that we'd hear something from Jace by now." He strolled over to stand in front of me and lean back against the porch's rickety railing. "You, uh, you doing okay? After everything that happened, I mean."

I glanced up, arching an eyebrow. What was this? Concern for my wellbeing? Since when? "Fine," I said, looking back down at one of my now mostly-clean longswords. "You?"

"Relieved, I guess. Confused, but I'm betting we all are," he admitted. "It's easier knowing the Ulfrangar are finally off our backs now. But Kinslayer showing up to fight like that? I knew Jace was up to something, but Gods and Fates, I had no idea he'd go that far." The young prince shuddered, as though the memory of that battle still made him uneasy. "I saw some incredible things in the Tibran War, you know. I guess I did some of them myself while I was Clysiros's harbinger. But I've never seen *anyone* use power like that before. I didn't even know it was possible. I mean, he killed her without even drawing a weapon. Is that something all Avoran elves can do?"

I frowned down at the freshly polished blade of my sword, scrutinizing it while I mulled that question over. "I don't know. The Ulfrangar don't teach much about them, except that they are an ancient, powerful, and highly secretive people. They don't welcome outsiders, and they usually don't leave their own borders, which makes their social circles extremely difficult to penetrate. I've heard stories that suggest they can live for thousands of years, and can perform feats of magic thought to be impossible everywhere else, but many people here in Maldobar still dismiss that sort of thing as nothing but fairy tales. It makes it difficult to discern what's a real account, and what's just someone's imagination running wild."

"Well, I dunno about you, but it seemed pretty real to me." Reigh shook his head, making his thick mop of dark red hair swish over his brow. "I thought it was strange that Kinslayer didn't have any guards or lookouts when we first met him in Dayrise. Isandri and I kept expecting to spot people posted outside, keeping watch for him. But there was no one. Now it all makes sense. He didn't need any backup, just like he didn't need a weapon the other night."

I had to agree. And the more I thought about it, the more I found myself questioning if getting involved with Kinslayer had been a smart move, after all. I wasn't stupid enough to think he'd intervened like that out of the goodness of his heart. He had a motive—a reason. We just hadn't figured it out yet.

"Congratulations, by the way," Reigh said with that smug little grin that always made me want to punch him in the face.

"For what?" I snorted and went back to polishing the hilt of my sword.

"Your sudden career change," he said evenly, giving a flourish of his hand. "You're officially not an assassin anymore, and I also hear you've finally accepted that drake as your mount. From cold-blooded killer to dragonrider—it's so appropriately *dramatic* for you."

I stopped, slowly letting my glare settle on him. "What is that supposed to mean?"

He snickered. "Oh, you know, because you're always walking around with this ominous scowl, lurking in the shadows, and doing that whole 'me-against-the-world' silent brooding thing. Guess you'll have to leave all that behind for a dragonrider's cloak, right? Ahh, when I picture you, standing there in formation with the rest of us as a fledgling in dragonrider training ... I just get all warm and fuzzy inside." He gave a little mocking, fake sniffle and pretended to wipe a tear away.

I blinked, staring at him as I tried to remember a time when I'd wanted to hit him more than I did right now. Hmmm. Nope. This was it. This was the closest he'd ever come to having my fist through his front teeth. I looked away and considered my next words carefully. He was a prince, after all, even if he was a complete idiot.

"I suppose you're right." I managed to keep my tone controlled and casual. "And you know what else?"

He was still giving me that stupid little smirk. "What?"

I let a cold, calculating, and brutally vicious smile curl across my face as I stared at him, doing everything I could to channel all the excitement of a fox entering a coop of sleeping chickens. "I'm *really* looking forward to the first time I get to spar against you."

Reigh's smile vanished, his expression going slack with sudden realization.

My smile widened. "I think it'll be a really *educational* experience for everyone, don't you?"

Jaevid Broadfeather finally arrived early the next afternoon. By then, the storm that had settled over the city had intensified. The air had turned bitter cold, and the rain that still fell in buckets across the prairie had now turned to sleet.

The low WHOOM, WHOOM, WHOOM of dragon wingbeats drew everyone out of their rooms and into the hall. I stole a peek out one of the second-floor windows just in time to see the massive blue king drake touch down right outside. Finally. Perhaps now we would find out what our next move should be.

Mavrik shook himself, snapping his jaws and squinting through the falling slurry as Jaevid quickly climbed down from the saddle and sent him off with a pat on the neck. The massive dragon spread his wings and gave a low growl as he launched skyward again, soaring away until he disappeared above the cloud cover.

It was probably a good idea not to have a dragon that size hanging around close by. The locals would absolutely recognize him, which was bound to draw even more attention to our current location. Not to mention, I doubted there was a barn in the city big enough to accommodate a beast that big. Maybe he'd made other arrangements elsewhere for him?

By the time we all got downstairs, Jaevid was already stepping in the front door. He shook the ice off his shoulders and slid off his helmet, raking his shoulder-length gray hair away from his face with a weary exhale. Tired lines creased the corners of his eyes as he stared around at all of us, hesitating a moment like he was trying to remember why he'd come in the first place.

I did feel a little sorry for him. If rumors were true, he'd left his wife and a new baby at home to go soaring around the kingdom, trying to clean up the messes we left behind while we pursued this so-called hunt for Queen Jenna. Then there was the mess in Halfax where he was basically functioning as crowd control for the Court of Crowns, and the fact that he was supposed to be the Academy Commander at Blybrig. The poor guy couldn't catch a break, it seemed. The true plight of being a kingdom's most famous war hero—everyone expected you to solve any new problems that popped up.

"I'm glad to see you're all on your feet," he said at last. "Some of Eirik's men flagged me down a few miles outside the city. They're preparing to move back to the compound once the storm lifts. I understand there was some trouble there?"

"You didn't get the details?" Reigh asked in surprise.

Jaevid's expression tightened with suspicion. "Not a lot of them, no. Why? What happened?"

Thatcher and I exchanged a tense, sideways glance.

"Oooh boy," Reigh grumbled and shuffled over to one of the dining tables set closest to the tavern's hearth. "Might as well get settled in, Jae. You're gonna want to be sitting down for this one. In fact, let's see if we can't just get some dinner and drinks over here, yeah? This may take a while."

It took about three hours, actually. Jaevid had already been told that there was an altercation with the Ulfrangar at the compound, but since he had yet to speak with King Jace about it, he didn't know the gritty details. I couldn't bring myself to meet his gaze as Reigh explained what'd happened. Or, at least, he tried. There were a lot of gaps since we still didn't fully understand what we'd seen go down between Arlan and the Zuer. It was a safe guess that they had known each other, and might even be related. But what that actually meant in terms of who they were, and what Arlan's real motives were for wanting her dead, was a mystery.

At the end of it all, Jaevid sat back in his seat and stared dejectedly straight ahead. He didn't say a word for a few minutes, and we all sat in uncomfortable silence while the flames crackled and popped in the hearth nearby. I didn't envy his position one bit.

"So, the Zuer is dead," he surmised, glancing in my direction as though looking for verification.

I didn't dare to say a word. Whatever had happened on that battlefield between Arlan and the Zuer was far beyond my understanding. Yes, I wanted to believe she really was gone and my days of being stalked by the pack were over. But I also knew hope like that could be dangerous—especially for someone like me.

"Yeah, as far as we know," Reigh confirmed. "But at this point, what can we say we really know about Kinslayer at all?"

A fair point, and one Jaevid seemed to appreciate as well. His chair creaked some as he leaned forward to rest his elbows on the table and rub at his eyes. "And you believe Jace had something to do with Kinslayer interfering in this battle?"

Reigh gave a flustered snort. "Well, *we* certainly didn't call for him."

"I see." Jaevid sat for a moment, the firelight flickering off the polished pauldrons of his armor. His tight frown made the scar slashing over his eye from his brow to his cheek crinkle some. His mouth pursed and quirked to one side, as though he were chewing on the inside of his cheek while he thought.

To be honest, I'd never studied him all that closely. I'd seen his face a thousand times in statues, mosaics, and tapestries throughout the kingdom. But sitting across from him at the table, watching as he massaged his temples and kept his eerily pale, silver-blue eyes focused on the half-empty ale mug in front of him, I wondered what he must be feeling about all this. He didn't look nearly as old as I'd assumed. In fact, it seemed like he might only be a few years older than I was—well, physically anyway.

But that was another, very long story.

"How are things in Halfax? Is Jenna doing okay?" Reigh asked in a not-so-discreet attempt to lighten the mood.

It didn't work.

Jaevid groaned and sat back in his chair, beginning to unlace his vambraces and pieces of interlocking plate armor and toss them into a pile next to his chair. "They're ... no less complicated than before, although tensions have eased a bit now that Phillip has come home and the Court of Crowns is on a temporary hiatus while she recovers," he replied. "But you know your sister. Her Majesty was less than thrilled to hear about what's been happening with all of you, and especially with the complications coming from Northwatch and nearly losing Judan to the switchbeasts. In light of the rising threat, and the need to have dragonriders properly stationed in that part of the kingdom, she's ready to handle the situation a little more aggressively."

"*More* aggressively?" I blurted. What the heck was that supposed to mean?

Jaevid dropped his pauldrons into the growing pile of armor at his feet with a *thunk* and sighed. "That's the main reason I rushed here so quickly. Queen Jenna would like to send her thanks for your assistance, but she now believes this problem is too big for you to solve. She doesn't want you getting hurt any more than you already have. Two days ago, a decree was sent out from Halfax calling on dragonriders from the other three watches to send a portion of their forces here. They'll be gathering at the compound two nights from now to stage an all-out aerial assault upon Northwatch. The intent is to take it back, even if that means razing it to the ground."

Phoebe covered her mouth to stifle a horrified gasp.

Isandri's expression blanked, her mouth falling open as she stared at Jaevid.

"They're going to burn all of Northwatch to the ground? But what about the people in the city?" Thatcher protested. "They can't all be criminals and thieves, can they?"

"By all accounts, they are," Jaevid replied somberly. "Phillip's account of what he saw there was most distressing. Some of Judan's agents have verified it, too. There's no other option at this point. Allowing the city to be controlled by mercenaries, murderers, and thieves is not an option."

Isandri's chair gave a sharp squeal across the stone floor as she suddenly snapped to her feet. "Devana is no mercenary! She is not a thief! And she is still being held captive there! Would the queen also sentence her to death? To leave her to burn along with the rest of the filth that has tortured her for so long? Is that what serves as justice in Maldobar?"

No one said a word.

Standing with her shoulders flexing as she took in rapid, furious breaths, Isandri's eyes shone with welling tears that sparkled in the firelight. Her ebony cheeks flushed deep scarlet, and her face twitched with a raw frenzy of emotion.

Next to her, Reigh reached out to gently grasp one of her wrists. It made her flinch, at first. Then her leanly muscled frame seemed to relax a little.

I couldn't help but narrow my eyes, watching her chin tremble and her strange, lime-and-yellow-colored eyes search Jaevid with chaotic determination. This wasn't the first time she'd gone leaping to Devana's defense, as though she'd known her personally somehow. In Dayrise, she'd had a similarly emotional response. Sure, there was the connection of both her and Devana being godlings. This seemed more intense than that, though. After all, she hadn't been quite that attached to Thatcher.

No, this seemed ... personal. *Extremely* personal.

Hmm.

Jaevid gave her a sympathetic nod. "I understand all that, Isandri. Truly, I do. But Devana is also locked in a nearly impenetrable tower designed to be a war fortress that is now, as best we can guess, controlled by either a devious goddess or a similarly powerful sorceress calling herself Iksoli. I cannot, in good conscience, send all of you to that place to even attempt a rescue ..." his voice trailed off, becoming meaningfully quiet as his glacier-hued eyes slowly panned around at all of us with purpose. "But I also can't stop you if you decide to try it anyway."

CHAPTER TWELVE

"This is unfathomable," Isandri hissed angrily. Sitting with her arms crossed, tucked into the bell sleeves of her silken robes, she glared down at the tabletop with her cheeks and tips of her long, pointed ears still flushed in anger.

Jaevid had left us sitting alone at the table long enough to take his belongings upstairs to a room. Or, at least, that's the excuse he'd given. I had a feeling his intention was more along the lines of plausible deniability when it came to whatever stupid, reckless, and poorly-thought-out plan we came up with in the next few hours.

"It's far too dangerous," Phoebe worried.

"It's basically suicide," Thatcher whispered in agreement.

"It's typical Jaevid-level insanity," Reigh muttered, his chin resting on his fist. "Not that I'd expect anything less. He's right, though. This is on us now. We don't have a lot of time to figure it out. If we want to try to get into Northwatch and rescue Devana, we need to be ready to go by tomorrow night at the latest. That'll give us one full day to get there, find her, free her, and get out before the dragonriders unleash all hell on that place."

"It's doable," I decided aloud. "Risky. There won't be any room for mistakes or detours. But it's doable, providing we get the right information beforehand. How familiar are you with the layout of that tower?"

I looked up, waiting for one or all of them to reply. At one point or another, Isandri, Reigh, and Phoebe had all been in Northwatch's dragonrider tower before. We already had a description of where she was, thanks to Phillip. But actually navigating there would be the crucial key. We needed someone who knew the fastest, most discreet way in and out.

"I was not permitted much time outside of my cell," Isandri said, her expression still riddled with distress. "They kept prisoners like myself and Devana under extremely tight security. Whenever we were moved, we were blindfolded, so I've no recollection of where we were within the tower."

"I wasn't free to roam without a security officer," Phoebe murmured. "And I was only allowed in certain areas of the tower, even with that supervision. I might be able to find my way back to that cell block, if I had to. Maybe."

"I can," Reigh said, his voice low and heavy.

Thatcher shot him a meaningful look. "I don't know if that's a good—"

"It's fine," Reigh snapped, keeping his face angled down so none of us could read his expression. It didn't matter, though. I could still see how his knuckles blanched as his hands closed into fists. "I've been through the high security cell blocks from the outside. I remember the way. I can get us there."

"You're sure?" I pressed. If this was his stubbornness and pride talking again, he needed to understand that all our lives hung in the balance.

Reigh's light amber eyes burned with quiet wrath as he shot me a scathing glare. "Considering I've had nightmares about it every night for the last year—yeah, I'm pretty freaking sure." Several tense seconds ticked by before his posture finally relaxed. His mouth twisted to one side as he sank lower in his seat and let out a shaking exhale through his nose. When he spoke again, his voice had lost all its fire and venom. "It's basically burned into my brain at this point, whether I like it or not. So don't worry about it; I can get us there."

"Okay," I said, before anyone else could object. If he was determined to do this, I wasn't about to try to discredit his ability—not when we had no other alternatives.

"Then there's just the matter of actually reaching the tower," Isandri reasoned, tapping her chin thoughtfully. "A dangerous endeavor, even with the cover of darkness."

"They'll spot dragons from miles away, and that might tip them off to the dragonriders' coming, so that's out," Reigh agreed.

"Oh, well, I think I can probably help with that." A merry, sing-song voice giggled from behind our table, nearly making Thatcher shoot straight out of his boots as he scrambled to stand up.

We all turned to find Garnett standing right behind us, her hands planted confidently on her hips and her violet eyes glinting with excitement. "Look at you lot! Like a bunch of kittens caught in the cream! Up to no good, I take it?"

Thatcher's face lit up and he immediately straightened in his chair, staring at her like a blind man seeing his first sunrise. Or a starving puppy seeing a freshly grilled sausage.

Yeah, more like the latter.

A smile stretched from one of his cheeks to the other, and I had to actively resist the urge to bury my face in my palm as he eagerly scooted to the edge of his chair. "Garnett! You're back!" he practically cheered.

Gods preserve me.

"I am. And look at you—back on your feet where you belong, I see," she said, matching his enthusiasm in a way that made me a little sick to my stomach.

If Thatcher had a tail, it would've been wagging fast enough to start a whirlwind. "O-Oh. Yeah, I'm feeling much better now."

"Good. Not a moment too soon. Now that everything's calmed down a bit, there's quite a lot we need to talk about. Arlan's requested a meeting with you all—and Lord Jaevid, of course," she announced merrily. "Tonight, preferably, if that suits you."

ARLAN THE KINSLAYER wanted to meet with us tonight? Hmm. I couldn't help but shift uncomfortably at the thought. He certainly hadn't wasted any time.

The scar across Reigh's nose crinkled as his expression tightened into a squinty, suspicious frown. "That didn't take long. Jaevid's barely been here a few hours. Spying on us?"

Garnett's grin was as sheepish as it was prickly, as though she didn't appreciate that brazen accusation. "Yes, well, I like to think I can be as sneaky as the next person, if the occasion calls for it. But a massive blue dragon flying over isn't exactly a secret, now is it? Doesn't take much spying to pick up on that."

Reigh pursed his lips sourly. I guess he didn't have a witty retort for that.

"You really think you can help us get into the tower?" Thatcher pressed, momentarily stunning me with his ability to stay focused on the problem at hand. Wow. Maybe he was growing into this role of being the underdog, dragonrider hero, after all?

Naah. Not a chance.

"I absolutely can!" Her thick braided pigtails swished as she bobbed her head. "Engineered every one of those tunnels myself. Providing no one has gone back and messed up all my fine work, they should be easy enough to access."

"The tunnels?" Reigh's eyebrows rose. "You can't be serious. They're a death trap—especially now. They're bound to be riddled with—"

"—Nothing you lot can't handle, I'm sure," she interrupted, waggling a finger at him. "Besides, you said it yourself, going in above ground stands a greater risk of being spotted and tipping off the whole city—and this Iksoli person—about what's coming their way. This is the fastest and most discreet option, and there's an access entrance not three hours' flight from here. I've been studying all those lovely maps my agents got ahold of. I know this territory backward and forward."

Hmm. She did have a point. Moving underground meant that, even if we were met with some kind of resistance or conflict, we could still keep it quiet. We could snuff out any opposing forces, be they mercenaries or common bandits, without compromising our position. But still ... something nagged at the back of my mind.

"And Kinslayer is willing to allow you to go skipping off to help us like that?" I dared to ask. After all, she seemed to be one of his more valuable agents. I wondered if he'd really be willing to let her do something that dangerous.

Garnett's cheery demeanor dimmed and she fidgeted with one of the ends of her pigtails. "It's not really his decision to make. I'm his employee, not his slave. He doesn't claim any ownership over the people who work for him, and he's always been very clear about that. He protects his workers and contacts, and pays us well, but he isn't going to try to stop us from doing what we want unless it harms his business."

Ahh, so that was it. He'd positioned himself more as a benevolent, understanding figure to his agents, then. A curious choice from a man who dealt in the illegal trade of secrets, information, and illicit goods. No wonder they were so loyal to him. The Ulfrangar had used fear as their unseen tether to force the loyalty of their members. Apparently, Arlan had a different theory about how to ensure his people did as they were told. Interesting.

"I'd like to help you, if I can. And it sounds as though you need it," Garnett continued. "You're not wrong, the tunnels can be quite dangerous. It's easy to get lost if you don't know the right way, and stones only know what or who is hiding down there now."

"Like underbeasts?" Phoebe asked with a shudder.

"Or more of those switchbeasts," Reigh agreed.

There were a lot more problems to consider, things that I wasn't sure Reigh or anyone else standing there in our midst had even considered yet. Dangers that had stared us in the face already. But before I brought any of that up, I wanted to hear what Arlan the Kinslayer had to say. He might be able to solve some of them. More than anything, though, I wondered if he would bother mentioning them at all, or if he was happy to let our little band go stumbling off to our doom in ignorance.

I wanted to see who's side he was really on, and maybe even figure out which angle he was playing. I had a lot to thank him for, and he might even claim ownership over my life—which I undoubtedly owed him—but I also knew his reputation in the criminal underworld.

And it wasn't nearly as generous and understanding as Garnett seemed to think.

"We need to plan to leave tomorrow night, just after nightfall. We can take the dragons to the tunnel entrance," Reigh decided, keeping his voice hushed. "With so many dragons already in the area, I doubt anyone will even notice."

"I take it we are not going to mention any of this to Lord Jaevid?" Isandri asked, an edge of concern in her tone.

Reigh shook his head. "Absolutely not. He'd be duty-bound to try and stop us—he knows that as well as I do. Jenna would never approve of this. Lucky for us, I'm betting he'll have his hands full when all those dragonriders start arriving. We can slip out, no problem."

Garnett clapped her hands, looking pleased as she rocked up onto her toes. Reaching into her belt, she took out a single piece of crisply-folded parchment and handed it to Thatcher. "Right, then. Please pass the word on to Lord Jaevid, if you don't mind. We'll be expecting you later this evening."

Thatcher blushed like an idiot as he took it. He stammered and choked, looking like he might suddenly faint and drop right where he was standing from pure anxiety. "I, uh, yes. Okay. See you later then."

I could spot the silent panic in Thatcher's eyes from ten paces away. Unbelievable. Ugggh. Gods. Send this kid some help, please.

"Watch yourselves, yeah? And don't you go running off to have all the fun without me." Garnett said, giving us all another broad grin and wink as she patted one of the axes hanging at her hips. "If there's gonna be any more beast and baddie-slaying, I want more than just a few test swings this time."

Reigh arched an eyebrow and flicked a disconcerted sideways glance in my direction. "Riiight. Yeah, we'll try to, uh, refrain from ... all the ... *fun*."

I turned away, trying to stifle a laugh by covering my mouth. Instead, I somehow managed to choke on my own spit while I snorted and nearly gagged myself. Fantastic. Well, at least as far as stupid antics and general idiocy went, I was in good company. That was more than I'd ever been able to say about the people I lived with before all of this.

So, for whatever it was worth, I'd take it.

PART THREE
THATCHER

CHAPTER THIRTEEN

As soon as the tavern door shut behind her, I thought of about fifty things I should've said to Garnett. Like how she looked really pretty today, and how I loved that her smile made that rune tattooed under her eye crinkle a little, and that she told the funniest stories I'd ever heard. Now that she was gone, it felt like all the warmth and light had been sucked out of the room.

I sank back in my chair, ignoring the lingering hint of tightness in my chest whenever I took a deep breath. It was the only thing still holding me back after … well, after everything that'd happened in that fight with the Ulfrangar. To be honest, so much of that night felt like a muddied, hazy blur of pain, confusion, and fear. I had a hard time figuring out what was real, and what was just a nightmare.

I wanted to ask. But the only person who would know for sure, was standing a few feet away, his arms crossed and his expression drawn into a forbidding, thoughtful scowl as he stared at the door Garnett had just gone through. Murdoc was keeping his distance. Even I could tell that. Things were better-ish between us, although I still didn't know where we stood, exactly. I'd said a lot of things to him before that battle with the Ulfrangar. And then I'd nearly died, I guess. It was a lot to process, and we hadn't gotten a chance to talk about it alone.

Maybe tonight, before we got started on this mission to rescue Devana, I could find a good opportunity to pull him aside and we could … I don't know … talk.

Frowning down at the clean, neatly folded piece of parchment in my hand, I winced against that pain in my chest as I sighed deeply. "I'll go give this to Jaevid and break the news," I volunteered as I stood, forcing what I really hoped was a believable smile back at everyone.

I guess it wasn't, though, because they all frowned back at me.

Great.

"I can do it, if you'd rather not," Reigh offered glumly, leaning into his elbows and letting his head drop some.

"No, it's fine. I'm not much use when it comes to battle planning anyway, right?" I waved a hand dismissively. "Be right back."

Okay, so maybe it was an excuse to get some air. I hadn't been left on my own much so I could think things over since we'd gotten back from the compound. Or, well, since way before that, actually. Everything was moving so fast. We blurred from one crisis to the next, and I could barely keep up. We had one problem solved now, yes. Er, well, hopefully, anyway. But there were still so many unanswered questions about Devana, Iksoli, what was happening in Northwatch, and myself.

And to make it all worse, we now had a very fixed deadline before it was all bathed in dragon flame.

It made my brain throb as I climbed the steps back to the hall where our rooms were reserved. Tracking down Jaevid's room took a few minutes. I expected to find him busily working to arrange his gear or checking weaponry. Instead, I found all of that piled in the hall outside like he'd dropped it and gone inside. Strange.

I knocked on his door. "Um, Jaevid? Sir? It's Thatcher. I have a letter for you."

No answer.

Oh no. This couldn't be good. Was he hurt? Had something happened? Immediately, memories of how I'd been abducted by the Ulfrangar flashed through my mind. I couldn't let anyone do that to him, too.

"Jaevid?!" I whipped the door open and stormed in, realizing halfway into the room that I didn't even have a weapon.

It didn't matter, though.

Sitting on the foot of the bed, leaned over with his face in his hands, Jaevid didn't even look up when I suddenly burst in. "Yes, Thatcher?" he muttered, his voice low and so muffled by his hands I barely heard him. "What is it?"

"S-Sorry, I-I … you didn't answer, so I thought you might be in trouble or something," I stammered.

"I'm fine." He still didn't look up.

Fine? He didn't sound fine. I mean, he wasn't hurt anywhere that I could see, but he also looked like he might be in the middle of a mental breakdown, so …

I closed the door behind me, giving us a little privacy before I walked over to stand next to him. "I'm sorry if this is way out of line, sir, but you don't *seem* fine. Sort of the opposite, actually. Is there, um, is there anything I can do?"

He let out a long, heavy sigh that made his broad shoulders flex and relax. "No, Thatcher."

I glanced down at the letter in my hand. Now definitely didn't seem like a good time to hand him this. It could wait a few more minutes—or a few hours, if he needed it.

"I'm sorry none of this went according to plan." Hedging a little closer, I sat down beside him on the edge of the bed. "You and Queen Jenna put your faith in us, and we made a real mess of things."

Jaevid lifted his head some, his chin now resting in his palms. At least now I could see his eyes, though. Too bad they looked droopy, bloodshot, and every bit as miserable as I'd feared. The creases around them were deep and weary, like he'd spent the majority of the last few months scowling more than sleeping.

"Please ... don't. I'm the one who should be apologizing to you, Thatcher," he murmured.

"O-Oh! No, I'm fine now, really. And the stuff with the Ulfrangar wasn't really you're fault anyway—"

"I don't mean about that," he said quietly. His eyes fell closed and his dark brows knitted deeply. "I hate that I'm here. I hate every step I take, everything I must do. Every second that passes feels worse than the one before. But I can't do anything about it. I can't leave."

Huh? He didn't want to be here? I leaned over some, trying to get a better look at his expression—to understand what he really meant. "Why?"

A look of anguish ghosted across his sharp features an instant before he bowed his head again. "I had to fly past my home twice. Once carrying Phillip to Halfax. A second time coming here. Both times, all I could think about was how badly I wanted to turn back. My wife is there, with our baby, and ... I can't go to her," he confessed, his tone utterly broken. "I keep remembering how, many years ago, she told me that her own mother had warned her against marrying a dragonrider. That it would only lead to pain and separation. I wanted so badly to prove her wrong. But where am I? Sitting here, repeating the mistakes of hundreds of dragonriders before me."

"Then go home, idiot," a deep, grouchy voice huffed from the doorway.

Jaevid and I both looked up to find King Jace standing there, dressed out in the colorful silken ensemble of a Gray elf scout, with his arms crossed and one shoulder leaned against the doorframe. The old king's disapproving scowl made my insides cringe up with that same sort of feeling I got whenever my father caught me slacking off during my chores. Yikes.

"You know it's not that simple," Jaevid grumbled back.

"Isn't it, though?" Jace countered. He pushed away from the door and ambled in, stopping only when he stood right in front of us. "I seem to have forgotten the moment when you were told to solve every single problem that arises in this kingdom, Jae. You're one, very young man. And you need to go home. Now."

Jaevid's tone tightened, snapping with anger as he glared up at him. "How can you say that? You know as well as I do that the dragonriders—"

"—will be just fine in your absence," Jace cut him off, matching his angry tone with a similar growl. "Look at you. Your head's not in this fight, anyway. What good are you? You and Jenna chose the men to place in command over the dragonrider ranks, but as best I can tell, you don't trust them to actually do their jobs. If the Dragonriders of Maldobar can't handle taking one city without you holding their hands like a nanny, then what good are they?"

Jaevid's mouth snapped shut, but his lips pinched and mashed together as though he were fighting to keep his temper in check.

After what was probably the most uncomfortable few seconds of heated silence I'd ever experienced in my life, King Jace finally shook his head. "Listen, if you're really worried about it, take my shrike back to your estate, lend Mavrik to me, and I'll see this done. You seem to have forgotten you're not the only dragonrider standing in this room. You at least trust me to handle it, don't you?"

All the anger seemed to fizzle from Jaevid's face at once. His posture relaxed, becoming almost defeated as his shoulders dropped and his arms relaxed. "I can't ask you to do that."

Jace cast him a knowing, half-cocked smile. "You don't have to. That's the beauty of me still technically being your senior officer. Granted, I'm an unseated one. But I'm old enough now to be able to tell you with all certainty when you're making a big mistake. Take it from a father who has already made his share of them—the moments you let slip by because you chose your job over your family cannot be replaced. The job won't mourn you when you're gone, Jae. There'll be a new Academy Commander to take your seat before it even gets cold. But the people you love will be the ones laying flowers on your grave and speaking your name for generations." He stepped closer and leaned down, putting a hand on Jaevid's shoulder. "So go pack your things, go home, kiss your wife, and hold your baby."

I WAITED out in the hall, still holding that letter from Arlan the Kinslayer, so the two men could talk a little more while Jaevid packed up his belongings and redressed in his armor. Giving them some space seemed like the right thing to do, especially after seeing Jaevid so broken down. I'd grown up hearing stories and legends about Jaevid's adventures—about all his incredible feats to save Maldobar from not one but two deadly wars. Somehow, seeing him that way, stirred up a courage in my chest I hadn't felt since he'd given me that necklace. I fiddled with it, wondering at the things he had done and witnessed while he wore it, and feeling much less ridiculous about all my fears and worries.

After all, if the great Jaevid Broadfeather got homesick, maybe it wasn't so bad for me to be nervous about storming a tower full of mercenaries and cutthroats under the mind control of a crazed goddess.

"Give Beckah our love. And I apologize in advance if I mention this to Araxie in a way that even *hints* you might need help with the baby. I think we both know she will be knocking down your door within hours if it means getting to play grandmother again," Jace said as the door opened again and he and Jaevid came out into the hall, too. "And be sure to leave a word with that dragon of yours to go easy on me. It's been a while since I was in the saddle."

Jaevid gave a tired laugh. "I'll try. But you know he won't."

They went on saying their farewells and exchanging a handshake before Jaevid dipped his head at me, ruffling my hair some on his way past as he headed for the stairs. I watched him go, wondering if there was anything else I could or should have said to him. Maybe I needed to go thank him before—

King Jace cleared his throat. "Well, well, well. Looks like you're *my* problem now."

I winced and turned to face him. "Uh, y-yeah. I guess so."

"Is that for me?" He held out a hand for the letter.

"Um, well, technically it was for Jaevid, but I guess … yes?" I quickly passed it over and took a *big* step back. You know, just in case he wasn't nearly as calm about receiving word from Arlan the Kinslayer as Jaevid had been before.

Also, he terrified me a little.

Okay, a *lot*.

It only took him about two minutes to read it, his sharp, light amber eyes scanning the page as his eyebrows rumpled together and his lips pursed thoughtfully. When he'd finished, he folded the letter up again and tucked it into the fine leather breastplate fitted over his colorful robes. "Very well, then. Seems Kinslayer wants to hold audience with us at sunset. Does the rest of your merry band know about this already?"

I nodded.

"Good. Then I suggest you get some rest while you can," he said as though it were a warning. "Whether you realize it or not, every time you cross paths with that man, you're going into the lion's den. Now isn't the time to be sluggish or distracted."

"Sir—um, I mean—Your Majesty … sir," I managed to squeak. "Can I ask you something?"

His eyes narrowed dangerously. "As long as it's not something stupid. And just call me Jace. Got more than enough people clucking around here like a yard full of hens calling me that. Makes me twitchy."

"Right. Um, Jace … sir," I tried again, a little less squeaky this time. "You were the one who went to get Arlan, weren't you? You told him what was happening between Murdoc and the Zuer, right?"

He blinked, his scrutinizing expression seeming to size me up like someone trying to select which pig they were going to butcher for dinner. "And if I was? Is that a problem for you?"

"N-No! Not really, I just … wondered how you knew where to find him, and … well, um, … why you did it." I floundered and waved my hands, stealing another quick step back. "Before, at Eastwatch, you were ready to have Murdoc executed. Then you went to all that trouble to save him. I guess I'm just confused."

The king stared me down for what felt like a terrifying eternity during which I sweated rivers down my back and couldn't keep my stomach from feeling like a spinning whirlpool. Gods and Fates. I shouldn't have said anything at all.

"I supposed I'm confused, too, kid. But I've watched you all rally around that kid, one after another. Rook died for him. A dragon chose him. So, I guess all of that combined tends to sway a person's mind." He rubbed the back of his neck and looked away, still frowning thoughtfully. "That, and it's hard not to look at him now and not see a much younger version of myself. He's come a long way. But make no mistake, he still has a long way to go. The life he had before—it's not something you just slough off and forget. He'll be recovering from it for the rest of his life. Make sure you don't forget that."

I swallowed hard. "I won't, sir."

"Jace," he corrected with an irritated growl.

"Oh! Right. I mean, Jace, sir."

He groaned and rolled his eyes. "No wonder Jae was at his wit's end. Fates preserve me."

14

CHAPTER FOURTEEN

Thanks to the miserable weather and pouring, sleety rain, it was difficult to tell when, exactly, sunset was. But as the sky grew dim, and everyone grew more anxious, we all gathered in the tavern downstairs and prepared to go meet Arlan the Kinslayer once again.

Murdoc grumbled quietly, standing near the door and helping Phoebe tie on her cloak so that it hid the small dagger belted to her hip. Reigh and Isandri sat near the hearth, already dressed to go and muttering to one another in low voices. She flicked me a meaningful look when I came downstairs, as though silently asking if I was all right. I forced a smile that probably wasn't fooling anyone.

I'd wanted to try talking to Isandri before we left, to find out if she was all right after that sort of heated moment when she found out what was going to happen to Northwatch. But there hadn't been a good chance. Or, rather, there hadn't been an opportunity when Reigh wasn't lurking somewhere nearby her. Whether it was just friendship or something else budding between them, they definitely seemed to be spending a lot more time talking.

And I wasn't even going to try to guess what was happening between Murdoc and Phoebe. Nope. No way.

Glancing between each pair, I found myself standing awkwardly at the bottom of the stairs ... alone. I'd almost made up my mind to sit down on the bottom step and wait when the door swung open and Jace came in wearing a long rain-drenched cloak. He stuck his head inside long enough to glare around at all of us and give one solemn nod.

"Time to go."

With my insides frantically tying themselves up into a thousand knots, I pulled on my own cloak and followed behind everyone else out into the frigid rain. Mud squished under my boots and the bitter wind stung at my face. I wished immediately I'd bundled up with more clothes. I could only hope we weren't walking all that far.

The feel of my teeth chattering and my fingers going stiff as my nose went numb brought back flashes of memory like splinters in my mind. It'd been a storm a lot like this one when Rook and the Ulfrangar had marched me out of Dayrise. I'd almost died then, er, well, the first time. Reigh had said I was severely hypothermic. I would've died of exposure in another hour or two if Isandri hadn't found me in the back of that upturned wagon.

I stumbled, almost tripping as those distracting thoughts overtook me. Gods, I had to pull it together. I couldn't go into a meeting with Arlan like this. Confidence—I had to project confidence!

Jace led the way as the night closed in, driving the few villagers and commonfolk who were willing to brave the weather back into the warmth and safety of their homes. We passed empty, muddy streets, closed shops, and windows lit by soft golden light. Smoke drifted up from the tall chimneys, and muffled laughter echoed from beyond bar and tavern doors.

We trudged along for nearly a mile before Jace finally threw up a hand, signaling us to stop. At a crossroads on the far eastern edge of the city, we squinted through the pouring rain. The cottage stood on a busy corner only about a block off Osbran's main road. The stacked stone sides were mottled with frozen moss, slimy mushrooms, and splotches of brown lichen, and the thatched roof shed the frigid rainfall into a growing moat around the outside.

At first brush, it looked every bit as run down, soggy, and miserable as the rest of the city. But looking more closely, I noticed that its windows also shone with inviting light, smoke curled from its crooked chimney, and a little wooden placard hanging on one of the porch posts read "Bookseller – Inquire Within" in curling green letters. Bookseller? I'd never heard of a shop that only sold books before, but something about it made me smile.

Everyone began to cross, making their way up the weathered stone steps and under the low porch roof to the front door. An old copper bell hanging over the door jangled as we entered, and the heavy smells of ink, old parchment, and dried herbs seemed to wrap around me like a friendly hug. Warmth radiated from the large, raised hearth on the far wall, and an iron kettle whistled where it hung over the low embers.

"Fates. It's incredible," Phoebe whispered in awe as she turned in a slow circle, drinking in the walls that were lined from floor to ceiling in bookshelves and cubbies. Every single one was crammed with tomes, scrolls, stacks of clean parchment, or ink bottles.

"It is, isn't it?" An older human woman in a long, billowy dark purple dress laughed merrily from behind a long counter set up right next to the crackling fireplace. With large round spectacles perched on the end of her nose and her long, somewhat wild golden hair beginning to turn a frosty white around her temples, she leaned against the counter and stroked the back of a black kitten with large, oddly yellow eyes. Portions of her hair was braided with colorful beads, charms, little feathers, and flowers woven into it. More trinkets like that, including a few more pairs of those large glasses and even a few tiny bottles of what looked like ink hung on beaded strings around her neck.

Her skirt fluttered as she whirled around the counter, sky blue eyes looking us over one at a time as she fished through one of the many pockets of her long white apron. "My, aren't you all a proper mess? Here to see Arlan, I take it?"

"We are," Jace confirmed, seeming a little tense at the sight of her rummaging through her pockets like that ... until she pulled out what looked suspiciously like a cookie.

Yep. Definitely a cookie.

"Very well, then. Wipe your boots and take off those drippy cloaks, if you don't mind," she said before taking a bite. "Then it's the fourth book on the far shelf just over there."

Wait, what? Fourth book? What was that supposed to mean? Who was this lady? And did she have any more cookies or was that the last one?

And why was her cat staring at us like that? Its eyes followed every move we made, and its ears perked curiously, almost like it could understand everything we said. Weird ...

After we'd all shrugged out of our rain-soaked cloaks and wiped our muddy shoes off on the small rug right outside the door, everyone followed Jace down the long shelves of books to a narrow one squished in the corner of the room on the other side of the hearth. He counted down four spines until he arrived at one particularly thick tome bound in dark burgundy leather. He and Murdoc exchanged a dubious glance before he grasped the spine and began to pull. Something clicked inside the shelf, like the heavy metal *thunk* and clack of a door lock.

The shelf swung in like a big, thick, book-laden door, groaning on old hinges.

Whoa.

Phoebe was practically convulsing with excitement as she squirmed her way to the front of our group so she could peer through into the next room. It made Jace grumble in disapproval, but he didn't try to stop her. Or maybe he couldn't.

She was pretty fast, after all.

"Well, then," the familiar tone of Arlan the Kinslayer carried in from the dim space beyond. "Don't just gather at the door. Come in. You're right on time."

THE INSIDE OF ARLAN'S, er, secret office was definitely not what I'd been expecting from a guy who supposedly made his living doing bad, illegal things. Granted, that was beginning to become sort of a theme with him. It made me wonder who he really was, exactly. Was all of this a disarming front meant to put us at ease? Or was this his true personality, and all the crime stuff was just something he did to make money?

Regardless, as I stumbled along after the rest of our group into his hidden room behind the bookcase, I once again stared around in amazement at every crowded corner. His room shared the same fireplace as the storefront, although you couldn't see through it to the other side. Pretty clever. A long velvet sofa and several fancy-looking chairs with clawed feet and big, intricately embroidered cushions were pulled close to it. A low, marble-top coffee table was stacked high with books and papers, some of which were held open with weights that looked suspiciously like enormous gemstones. Those weren't real, right? No way. They couldn't be.

More overloaded bookshelves covered most of the walls, but there were a few empty spaces packed with framed maps, oil portraits, and iron sconces lit with flickering candles in colored glass globes. A chaise lounge with a blanket and a pillow had been pushed to one corner of the room like an afterthought, and a large mahogany desk was set to face into the room with a wingback chair pulled up to it.

Like before when we'd met Arlan in Dayrise, his desk was also covered in stacks of books, scrolls, quills, and ink bottles. Some of the tomes lay open, while others had been set aside with twenty or so strips of ribbon slipped between the pages to mark certain passages. A few empty bottles of wine were scattered here and there, and an untouched plate of sliced bread, cheese, and grapes sat on a little round pedestal table next to his desk.

Arlan himself stood at one of the far shelves, perusing the spines of some of the books before he plucked one from the collection and turned around. "I'm pleased to see you've all recovered," he said without ever looking up. Opening the book, he thumbed through the pages as he strode right past our group and sat back down at his desk. "Although, I can't help but notice the esteemed Academy Commander has elected not to join you. I trust he's in good health? Or has Her Majesty's most recent call to action concerning the fate of Northwatch summoned him away?"

Geez. He already knew about that? How? Had Garnett told him?

I glanced around, taking in the cluttered, dimly lit room again. But I didn't see her anywhere.

"Neither, actually. He's gone home. It's long overdue," King Jace announced. "Hopefully, you'll accept my presence as a substitute."

Arlan finally looked up, his peculiar eyes glowing just as brightly as the coals smoldering in his fireplace. "Jace Rordin, formerly known as Rift among the ranks of the Ulfrangar, although much more recently a Seasoned Lieutenant for the dragonriders, who now sits enthroned as Luntharda's king. I suppose you'll suffice, since I'm also told you are the one who brought warning to my agents of the Ulfrangar's movements."

Jace tilted his chin up, a defiant smirk playing over his features. "Well-informed, aren't you?"

Arlan looked back down at his open book as though he'd already lost interest. "Frighteningly so, My King. Now, if you would be so kind, move whatever might be in the way and have a seat at the hearth. I'll be with you momentarily."

It took some light stepping and awkward shuffling to get through all his stuff—the stacks of papers and books on the floor, random artifacts, stone figures, and a folded-up painting easel—to get back to the sitting area. I took one of the chairs closest to the fireside and watched, chewing on my cheek, while Arlan took up his quill and scribbled a few things onto a piece of parchment he had spread out on his desk. The feather tip scratching on the paper and the soft crackle and hiss of the fire filled the awkward silence while we waited. Finally, he closed the book, folded up the parchment neatly, and sealed it with a drop of red wax. His long golden hair swished at his back as he strode by, opening the bookshelf just long enough to pass the letter to the merry, cookie-eating woman outside.

"See that Violet takes this directly to the Zuer, Larisse," he ordered.

She answered, confirming his request around what sounded like another mouthful of food. Probably another cookie. Not fair.

Then it hit me so suddenly I choked and wheezed—did he just say ... *Zuer?!*

No. No way. Not possible. I was hearing things, I had to be.

Looking around, I found all my companions staring straight ahead with blank looks of absolute shock. Oh gods ... I wasn't just hearing things. He'd really said Zuer—as though that was a person who was still *alive*.

My gaze immediately locked onto Murdoc. All the color had drained from his face, and he sat eerily motionless, not blinking or breathing at all. What did this mean? Was the Ulfrangar going to continue to hunt him? Was he still in danger? Had they seen us come here? They'd attacked us the last time we met with Arlan, so I sort of doubted his presence was going to deter them. Or maybe it would after what had happened a little over a week ago? Gods, I didn't know.

My stomach cramped and my hands clenched at the arms of the chair as I bit back the urge to yell—to demand to know just what the heck was going on here.

Calm—we had to stay calm. Now wasn't the time to freak out. Deep breaths. Control the panic.

Arlan had just begun to pour himself another glass of wine when Jace suddenly snapped up from his seat and spun to face him, teeth bared in anger like a bristling wolf. "You spared the Zuer? After all that?" he growled.

The elven man swirled his glass, studying it with a keen, scrutinizing frown before he finally came over to sit down in our midst as though nothing were wrong. "No. I simply appointed a new one."

"You ... *WHAT?!*" Jace thundered.

Arlan took a sip before he finally glanced up at the raging king. "If you don't mind, sit down, and we will discuss this at length. It was not a decision I arrived at lightly, and with some contemplation, I think you will agree it was the appropriate course of action."

Jace licked his teeth behind his lips and slowly shook his head. "Oh, I very much doubt that."

"Do you?" Arlan arched an eyebrow, looking wholly unimpressed. And after what I'd seen him do with his magic on that battlefield, I could appreciate why. Arlan's gaze fixed upon Jace, a hint of disapproval crinkling his ethereally perfect features. "I understand your concern, Your Majesty. Truly, I do. But I would like to invite you to consider the situation a bit more deeply. On the surface, yes, the Ulfrangar are a consistently malevolent presence. They deal in death and contracted murder as a specialty," he said, his tone as collected and precise as ever. "But as an organization, you know as well as I do that the Ulfrangar have been in existence for many centuries. Their network spans kingdoms and empires far beyond these borders. They're interwoven into cultures and communities that are otherwise closed to the outside world. Yes, their treatment of their initiates is harsh and violent. Their purpose is no less unsavory. But they are profoundly structured, and can be reasoned with, when necessary."

Reigh spoke up, matching Arlan's expression with a frosty glare of his own. "Make your point."

Arlan's mouth pressed into a tense, dissatisfied line. "My point, Your Highness, is very simple. Dismantling the Ulfrangar will not eradicate the demand for the services they provide. Right now, they are a superior force in that world. An apex predator, if you will. And one that we now have the ability to communicate openly with and, to a degree, influence. If you remove them from play, others will seek to take their place. New organizations that we have no understanding of or influence over will arise to seize the opportunity of controlling that market. Currently, we know who and what the Ulfrangar are. We know how they operate. We can anticipate their movements and actions, with a tactical choice of successor to the Zuer, we can even sway them if needed. A known enemy can be an effective tool if used properly."

"A choice of successor? So, then, ... you don't intend to take on that role yourself?" Reigh sputtered. "Not in *any* capacity?"

Arlan made a scoffing sound and wafted a hand. "Of course not. I've no interest in the business of paid assassination, lucrative though it may be. And they have no desire to be led by someone who is not a true member of their pack. That is why I summoned the remaining elder hunters of the Ulfrangar here this morning, to strike this bargain with them. In exchange for advocating my position and passing the role of Zuer on to another, I made a few simple requests. They found my terms agreeable, and so the deal was struck."

"And what terms were those?" Jace snapped bitterly, his face still flushed.

"First, that the claims against yours and Murdoc's, lives would be forever forfeited. You are, as they say, free men henceforth," he explained with a satisfied smile. "Second, that *I* would be the one to decide the successor to the role of Zuer, that being my right as the one who has slain their previous one. And lastly, that the existing understanding of the boundaries between our two organizations would now be more defined and solidified. I will not encroach upon their work or hinder their agents, and they will show me the same respect and never target my affiliates or interfere with subjects of my business dealings. Should they receive a contract for someone of interest to me, I reserve the right to declare that person off limits—within reason, of course."

"And they agreed to this?" Murdoc asked, his voice shaking and hushed.

Not that I didn't get why. Out of all of us, he undoubtedly felt the sting of this situation more than anyone. It seemed like Arlan had a handle on it, though. In fact, by the sound of things, he had the whole pack sitting and rolling over like trained dogs now. Impressive.

And ... sort of terrifying.

My stomach fluttered a little, realizing probably way too late the sheer magnitude of the power this man now had. He had friends in all the most critical and convenient places, and was well on his way to making himself untouchable. He had the Ulfrangar underfoot. He had connections in every noble house and court.

Gods and Fates, he might even be more powerful than Queen Jenna.

"They did," he confirmed evenly. "They are happy not to have an outsider presiding over their organization. And I'm equally pleased to finally have the relations between us crystallized and mutually understood."

I guess Murdoc couldn't take it anymore. He sat forward in his seat, staring Arlan down with an expression of absolute terror, like he was just waiting for the axe to drop. "You expect me to believe that's it? That I'm walking out of here a free man? We both know I owe you my life. But you're letting go of your claim over me? Just like that?"

Arlan's cold stare made my stomach flip and twist up again. That look, like the mysterious, unpredictable gaze of a tiger lurking in our midst, chilled me to the marrow. At any moment, he might snap. He could destroy every last one of us with a snap of his fingers.

But he didn't.

"Trust me, the exchange was more than fair. By luring one of Sadeera's aspects into the open where I might dispel it, you've more than compensated me for any claim I might have over you," he replied. "My own agents have not been able to accomplish that very task despite trying for a great many years."

"Sadeera?" Jace crossed his arms. "You're referring to the former Zuer?"

Arlan dipped his head slightly, his golden eyes shining just as brightly as the flames flickering in the hearth. "Yes ... and no. She was posing as the Zuer of the Ulfrangar, and likely has been for quite some time. But what you saw to be a physical woman was, in fact, a very complex manifestation of magical power. A duplicate, if you will. She's conjured a great many of them—no small feat, even for an individual of our heritage. The amount of magical power required, along with the rare artifact necessary to accomplish the ritual, is staggering." He took a long sip from his wine glass and slowly licked his lips. "Because of that, she is very careful with them, and luring one of them out into the open so that I might destroy it has been frustratingly difficult."

"So this aspect ... it wasn't a real person? Just a duplicate of someone else? This Sadeera person?" Murdoc pressed.

His quiet answer was barely more than a whisper over the rim of his wine glass. "Yes."

15
CHAPTER FIFTEEN

I frowned as my mind raced, trying to quickly assemble all the pieces to this puzzle. The Zuer had been a woman named Sadeera—another Avoran elf. Er, well, sort of. According to Arlan, she wasn't even a real person at all. She was something he called an aspect, which as best I could tell, meant she was some sort of magical duplicate. I guess she was able to give those aspects commands, or control them somehow, even from far away. Was the actual Sadeera even in Maldobar? Or was she still in Avora?

Fates, this was a lot more complicated and involved than I'd ever imagined.

"And this Sadeera person, the real one, you're related to her? You called her 'sister' before," I recalled.

Arlan's eyes flicked up, catching the firelight like two golden mirrors, although the rest of him never moved. He stared at me as he answered, "She is, indeed, my sister."

"She called you by a different name," Murdoc added. "Zarvan."

The elven man shuddered some, looking away and sucking his teeth, as though the sound of that name left a bitter taste in his mouth. "I'd thank you never to speak that name again. The life attached to it ended a very long time ago—long before any of you were ever born," he snapped coldly. "My personal history is irrelevant, and entirely beside the point. I called you here to discuss another matter. A business opportunity, if you will. Garnett has informed me that you hope to infiltrate Northwatch tower and rescue Devana before the proverbial hammer drops. No small task."

Jace shook his head and pinched at the bridge of his nose right between his eyes. "Are you kidding me, Reigh? You're going in there after that woman? Have you lost your mind?"

"We got a clear account from Phillip about her situation in there. She's being held prisoner by this Iksoli person," Reigh reasoned, his expression softening as his gaze drifted over to Isandri. "It's important."

"It better be," Jace snorted. "Since you'll likely get yourselves killed trying it."

Arlan gave a deep, bemused chuckle. "Now, now. Perhaps not. Garnett has expressed her intentions to go along with you, and I've suggested that I might be able to provide some additional assistance to you, as well ... for a price, of course."

Murdoc's eyes narrowed. "What kind of assistance?"

"Information, primarily." Arlan gave a sweeping gesture to the cluttered room around him. "It is, as they say, power. And I've quite a lot of it at my disposal. You've neglected to ask some very significant questions regarding the individual who calls herself Iksoli. What I know would give you an edge—a degree of assurance to your success, as well as caution to prevent any unfortunate casualties."

"What is it you want in exchange?" Jace asked, shifting to stand with his arms crossed over his chest.

Arlan took another sip from his wine glass. "There is a certain artifact located in that tower, one brought there by the Tibran Empire, that I would like to collect. It has immense significance to my people, and power that no person outside Avora would be able to utilize without killing themselves."

Jace's forbidding frown deepened. "And ... that would be?"

"The lowlanders, such as yourselves, call it the Mirror of Truth. It has a different name in Avora, naturally. I would like to have it secured so that my people can go in and extract it," he replied.

Reigh made a sputtering sound. His eyes went wide, face going nearly as pale as milk. He sank back in his seat, staring at Arlan like he was seeing a phantom. "What, by all the gods, would you want with that thing?"

"Ahh, so you've seen it, have you?" Arlan's expression softened, becoming somewhat intrigued.

"Yeah," he rasped, his voice quaking some as he breathed in hard puffs through his nose. "Yeah, I've seen it. I've seen it suck the souls right out of people if they try to tell a lie while looking into it. Is that what you'll do? Interrogate people with it?"

"Rest assured, young prince, I've no interest in using it in the same, barbaric manner the Tibrans did," Arlan assured, his nose wrinkling as though he found the idea disgusting. "They defiled it with their blundering attempts to wield it's true power. The Mirror of Truth, as you call it, is not a mirror at all. It is a means of contact, a holy relic used to commune with one of our patron deities. There are three, all identical in make, and each one is tethered to a separate entity—beings that your people here, in the lowlands, refer to as the foregods. The one you know as the Mirror of Truth is tethered to Itanus,"

Arlan stopped, taking a final drink from his glass and setting it aside. He wafted his hand, as though brushing the subject aside. "There's no point in explaining it further. Not at the moment, anyhow. I realize the object is far too large for you to remove yourselves. I would merely like to have it located so that my people can go in and extract it later. All I require of you is your assurance that you will move it to a securable location, and then relay that to my network. Easy enough, wouldn't you agree?"

"Yeah, except the part where we're on a time crunch in case the dragonriders decide to make their strike early and douse the whole place in dragon venom," Murdoc muttered. "Will the mirror even survive being burned if it gets caught in the crossfire?"

Once again, Arlan's cold smile curled over his thin lips, and sent a fresh jolt of terrified chills up my spine. "Absolutely."

No one spoke for almost a minute, each second passing with the weight of a brick being stacked on my head. Making another deal with Arlan, especially one like this, left a bitter taste in my mouth. I didn't know anything about this Mirror of Truth, but it sounded like something dangerous. What did Arlan want to do with it? Probably something bad, right?

Jace finally puffed a growling sigh. "This is your call, Reigh. You know what you're up against in that tower. I hate to lay it all at your feet, but it's your life you're gambling with by going in there in the first place."

"We'll do it," Reigh blurted suddenly.

Everyone stared at him.

Arlan's eyebrows rose. "Oh?"

Sitting tense and stiff in his chair, Reigh kept his gaze locked onto the floor as his chest heaved in slow, furious breaths. "Yeah. We'll secure the mirror. Now, tell us what you know about Iksoli."

"To understand Iksoli, you must understand what, precisely, the gods are," Arlan began. Setting his wine glass aside, he shuffled through some of the books and loose pieces of parchment scattered across the coffee table until he tugged one small, slim tome bound in faded green leather. The golden leafing upon the cover had all but been worn away, making it pretty much illegible.

His thin lips pursed thoughtfully as he flipped through it, his vibrant eyes scanning each page with startling speed. Was he really able to read that fast? No way—that was impossible, right?

"Ah, yes. Here it is." He opened the book to a page with an intricately drawn diagram. It looked sort of like a ladder, or maybe a lattice, with little scribbled words and tiny pictures all around. But the language wasn't one I recognized.

"The divine hierarchy," Murdoc muttered as he leaned over to steal a look.

I stared at him. Wait a second, he could actually read whatever language this was? How? Had the Ulfrangar taught him that?

Arlan's smile was cryptic again, and it made my skin crawl. "Indeed. I realize this is not something commonly studied by the lowland kingdoms. But perhaps now you can all see the importance," he said smoothly. "Those with a limited understanding of the divine realm often lump all of the gods together, as though they are all of the same power and presence. But in truth, there is a very distinct recurrent evolution to their essences. They are a separate race unto themselves, although their life cycles are much different than what we experience as mortals. They begin as godlings, juvenile beings of limited divine power, still struggling to establish their place and define their essence. As they grow over the ages, they mature, expanding and assuming the mantle of their true power."

"You mean, the gods all began, as sort of people? Like us?" I asked.

Arlan shook his head. "Not precisely, but it is comparable. Your situation, being bound completely within a mortal body, is slightly different. But the essence you possess, your spirit, is that of a godling. A young deity still sorting himself out."

"O-Oh," I managed to wheeze. "I get it."

I absolutely did *not* get it.

"With the passing millennia, godlings like you are expanded even further. Their interest in the toils and ventures of mortals wanes, until, at last, they are stretched even into the fabric of reality—existing far beyond the realm of mortal understanding. Instead of a powerful being with relatable sentiments, reactions, and comparable feelings, they become a cold, indifferent, and distant presence that cares nothing for the mortal world. They exist above it, beyond it, and through it, even unto the farthest reaches of the universe."

I had to remind myself how to breathe and blink at the same time. That was going to happen to me? I was going to ... expand into ancient, omnipresence god-form? Just the idea made my brain scramble. I stared at Isandri, who looked similarly overwhelmed and mildly panicked. She gnawed at the inside of her cheek, her vivid eyes darting back and forth as though she were frantically trying to process all this.

"Taking that into consideration, what you are dealing with now from the entity calling herself Iksoli, is another godling of the same caliber as you," Arlan said, staring straight at me for a few seconds before shifting his focus to Isandri. "Devana, as well. You are the next generation of your species. There is one other, but he has not yet made himself known to the world. I have my people watching him closely, however. It won't be long, I'm certain."

"You mean, Iksoli ... she's a godling, too?" I just had to be sure I was hearing all this correctly.

"Precisely," Arlan confirmed. "But an unfettered one. While you, Isandri, and Devana have found yourselves bound in mortal flesh, Iksoli has no such constraint. Her powers have become more affirmed, as well, and I suspect your time spent in mortal flesh is to blame for your delayed progress in that regard." He gestured to Isandri and me with a sweep of his hand. "Devana, also, has likely suffered some difficulty in controlling and calling forth her abilities. The tyrant Argonox attempted to forcefully expidite this process, and in so doing may have fractured her very essence. Now Iksoli has preyed upon her, as well."

"Not that I'm not enjoying story time, but how does any of this help us fight Iksoli?" Reigh demanded.

"Have patience, young prince. It is because you rush so recklessly through life, and do not take time to know your enemy before you engage it, that you have suffered so much already." Arlan's expression cooled, obviously not pleased to be rushed, and he raised a finger. "First, now knowing that you are dealing with a rival godling, you can be assured that her powers are likewise limited to the constraints that would hinder any deity. It has long been understood that one god cannot use their power to injure another. They are impervious to that sort of harm, but rather struggle for dominance in a space. It's not unlike the struggle between two children trying to shove one another out of a chair. The one who earns the seat is dominant, and the other is forced out."

"Then how is it that Iksoli is controlling Devana?" Reigh countered. "If she's holding her prisoner, and using her power to control other people's minds—"

"Not *using*," Arlan interrupted to correct him. "Mimicking. That is the basis for all of Iksoli's divine power. She is, as best my research can establish, a goddess of mischief and chaos. Her power lies in deception, illusions, and mimicry."

"It makes sense," I murmured, talking more to myself than to the rest of them. But when I looked up, even Arlan was staring at me with a puzzled expression. "I-I mean, just based on what Duke Phillip told us about his encounter with her. He said she touched him in order to get control over him. So maybe that's how she does it? Maybe she has to make physical contact to copy someone's power and that's why she's keeping Devana prisoner?"

Arlan tapped his pointed chin. "A worthy guess. I would advise you to take special care, then, not to let her touch you, or she may turn your own powers against you, as well."

Wow. Now there was a terrifying thought. Not really because of mine, honestly, but Isandri's powers were pretty incredible.

"One touch, and she could turn any one of us," Murdoc pointed out, panning his gaze around at our group in solemn realization.

My stomach dropped. Gods—he was right! What if Iksoli turned Murdoc on us? Or Reigh? I'd only barely managed to drive her out of Phillip's mind. The longer I thought about it, the more this felt like a mission doomed to failure. Now I understood why Queen Jenna was ready to just burn the whole place and call it a day.

"This will be dangerous," Isandri whispered. "Far more than we anticipated. Reigh, you needn't endanger yourselves for this. Going there—freeing Devana—is my responsibility. I can go alone."

My heart gave a furious jolt. "*Your* responsibility? I'm a godling, too. Not to mention, I'm the one Devana has been calling for this whole time. I'm all for minimizing risk, but why is this all on you?"

Isandri snapped a wrathful glare in my direction, all those frantic emotions bursting back to the surface just like they had the last time we'd discussed Devana's fate. But this time, she didn't shout. She didn't storm away. Her head bowed some, and her gaze drifted to the staff in her hand as her features fell into a look of quiet anguish. "Because ... she was my sister." Her eyes closed and her brow wrinkled, as though each word stung. "Not by blood. And not just by divine connection. It was more than that. We ... grew up together. Devana was brought to the temple seven or eight years before me. The priestesses had raised and taught her after her parents left her there, as well. Her abilities were much different—softer, I suppose. At first, the priestesses let us study together. But when it became clear that my own abilities would be more aggressive, more suitable for battle, they separated us. I didn't see her very often after that. Only once a month, on a full moon, when I could make myself invisible. I could sneak through the temple grounds to visit her."

"Then the Tibrans invaded your kingdom," Murdoc guessed.

Isandri nodded, making her long black hair swish where it fell to her waist. "They burned our temple and killed the priestesses. I nearly died as well, trying to defend it.

They must have thought me dead. That's the only reason I can fathom they didn't take me captive like they did Devana." Her shoulders rose and fell with a deep, unsteady breath. "For a while, I followed the Tibran movements as they conquered. I tried several times to rescue her, but eventually, they captured me, as well."

Reigh tilted his head to one side, studying her with a fractured expression. "That's why I found you in that prison cell," he murmured quietly.

She stared back at him, tears welling in her strange, lime-and-yellow eyes. "Yes." She sniffled some, her lips thinning as she turned her face away and wiped her cheeks with a shaking hand, as though she didn't want anyone to see her that way. "I should have been able to protect Devana. Instead, I failed her and the rest of the people who had cared for and raised me. Now you understand why I must set her free. I will not give up. I will not abandon her."

"Neither will we," I promised. "We started this together. That's how we should finish it. Right, Reigh?"

His crooked grin never quite reached his eyes as his gaze stayed fixed on Isandri. "Yeah. You're right. So, no more of these rogue warrior antics. If anyone here is going to die doing something insanely dangerous on their own, it's gonna be me. Got it?"

Isandri flicked him an exasperated look, then smiled faintly as she rolled her eyes and shook her head. "Very well, Reigh. If you insist."

16
CHAPTER SIXTEEN

We sat with Arlan for a long time, probably hours, going over as much information as we could about the specifics of divine magic, Iksoli's identity, and what we could do to get Devana out of her grasp. Bottom line? Yeah. It wasn't going to be easy. But with some preparation, it might be possible. We just couldn't afford to make any wrong turns—literally.

There were a lot of "don'ts" that we had to consider. Don't get lost in the tunnels, obviously. Don't let any of the cutthroats or vagabonds we might come across live long enough to tell the tale about our arrival. Don't get sidetracked. Don't let Iksoli touch us. Don't get lost in the tower. And, most importantly, don't die.

"We'll have to split off into two teams once we get inside the tower," Reigh considered aloud. "That's the only way to get this done as fast as possible and with the least confrontation. One team will be focused on getting Devana, the other on securing the mirror. Crap. I hate irony."

Murdoc arched an eyebrow, as though silently asking what he meant by that.

Reigh just shrugged. "Trust me, the last time I split up with my allies in that place, it did *not* go well. But it's not like we have a choice."

"I can take a group to secure the mirror." Murdoc insisted. "Phoebe, can you get us to where that thing is kept?"

She flinched in her chair, suddenly sitting up straighter as she stammered, "I-I, um, yes. Yes, I think so. The divine artifacts were kept in the same area, under tight security, but I did have access a few times. I think I can find it again."

Murdoc nodded, then glanced back to Reigh. "Garnett can come with us, too, so we have enough muscle to move the mirror if we need to. That'll put you, Thatcher, and Isandri headed for the cell block where Devana is. Phillip said he came across her in the cells near the base of the tower, right? That should help to narrow your search."

My heart gave a painful throb and twist in my chest, feeling like a soggy sponge being squeezed in someone's fist. Murdoc was going with Garnett? In a separate group? What if something went wrong? What if they were attacked? I'd be too far away to help them—I might not even know they were in trouble at all.

My mouth screwed up and I looked down, biting back everything I wanted to yell in protest. I didn't like it. Not one bit. But what could I do? Deep down, I knew Murdoc and Reigh were right. We couldn't go running all over the tower in one big group. We'd get spotted, overwhelmed by Iksoli's mind-controlled army, and probably killed without finding the mirror or Devana. Splitting up really was the best option.

I just ... didn't like it *at all*.

"Once we've accomplished what we came for, the fastest point to evacuate from is the passage on the roof of the tower. That's where we can call down the dragons to airlift us to safety before the rest of the dragonriders come in for their assault." Reigh rubbed at his chin and jaw, his gaze distant as he stared into the flames flickering in Arlan's hearth. "Gods and Fates, I can't believe I'm about to do this again. This is either the most severe form of divine punishment or ... I don't even know what. Torture, I guess? Someone remind me to punch Jaevid later for ducking out right before we do this."

Murdoc looked to me, somehow managing not to look the least bit worried about any of it as he spoke. "Blite won't be able to take any additional weight apart from mine. Fornax can carry two, right? Vexi, as well. And Isandri can fly on her own. So we should be set for departure if you can take Devana as your passenger. We don't know what state she'll be in, so we need to pair her with someone who can hold her in the saddle, if necessary. Reigh, you can take Garnett. Isa can take Phoebe, since she's the smallest and lightest—that way carrying her doesn't slow us down. I think we can anticipate some pushback. By that point, the word will be out and the whole tower will know we're there, so we need to be prepared for a fight. Unless, of course, liberating Devana eliminates Iksoli's control over her minions. That would be ideal."

"Yeah, but let's face it, we are *not* that lucky," Reigh snorted.

Nope. Definitely not. I had to agree with him there.

"There's only one access point to the roof, so it should be easy to bottleneck there if you are pursued," Jace mused. "As far as I know, there haven't been any altercations with aerial forces coming from the tower. I'll try to confirm that for you before you depart tomorrow night. No promises, though. Asking too many questions may give you away."

A few seconds of heavy, suffocating silence passed before Reigh finally slapped his knees and stood. "Well, then. Not to rush out, but I've got a lot to prepare—a few panic attacks and mental breakdowns to have—before we make this grand suicidal gesture. You understand."

Arlan smirked as he settled back into his seat, crossing his legs and giving a flourish of his hand. "Of course. I wish you all the greatest success in your mission. And do look after Garnett. She tends to get a bit carried away, and I would be greatly displeased to hear of her coming to any harm."

"We won't let anything happen to her," I promised as I stood up, too. Ugh. It sounded stupid even as the words left my mouth. I wasn't even going to be in the same group with her. How could I guarantee she would be okay?

Thankfully, no one called me out on that as we all prepared to leave. Stepping back through the door hidden behind the bookcase, the smell of the bookseller's shop and the cold rain, mingling with the ambient aroma of freshly brewed tea, washed over me. It made my soul feel calmer and heavier all at the same time.

I almost didn't notice the cookie-eating woman leaning on her countertop, talking to someone else and petting the black kitten. A much shorter, gingery-blonde someone else who made my heartbeat skip and stall like it might suddenly launch right out of my chest.

"Oi! There they are!" Garnett called out cheerily and practically skipped over to greet us. "And with such long faces. Not good news, then?"

"Oh, you know, nothing any more hopeless, dangerous, and totally mad than usual," Reigh grumbled as he skulked by on his way to collect his cloak.

Garnett clapped him on the back as he passed. "Oh, now, it can't be all that bad. Besides, you've got me to help this time!" She stroked one of her axes and grinned, making that rune under her eye crinkle and her lavender eyes sparkle. "I only got a few good swings in last time, and you weren't even there to see them. Just wait, young prince, I'll have those odds evened right up for you."

I wasn't sure if he was just dreading going back to Northwatch tower, or tired from trying to keep up with Arlan's mind games for so long, but Reigh did *not* look convinced.

I tried not to dwell on the fact that Garnett didn't say anything to me, or even glance in my direction, as we made our way out of the shop and back into the gusting storm. Maybe that was for the best, though. My head was a mess, trying to sort through all the information Arlan had given us about the gods, what it meant to be a godling, and what we might expect from Iksoli if we encountered her. We were the same thing, basically. Godlings. The only difference was, being trapped in a mortal body limited what I could do with my powers. Iksoli didn't have those same limitations, and that put Isandri and me at a definite disadvantage.

Not a great way to start out.

But I told myself that wasn't the point. We didn't have to beat or destroy Iksoli. We just had to maneuver around her, slip free of her grasp, and be gone before she could stop us. An open fight was not the goal. Simple, right?

Oh, gods help us.

I COULDN'T FIGHT that sinking, secluded feeling as my steps slowed and I fell to the back of our group. Looking ahead, I watched the rest of my companions forging on ahead through the stormy night, braving the wind and pouring rain, toward the tavern. Murdoc and Jace walked together in the front, muttering quietly. Most likely going over plans, or Ulfrangar stuff, or ... well, who knew, honestly. They had a lot in common, I guess. Part of me was glad to see Murdoc interacting with someone who'd successfully made the transition from assassin to normality. It might be good for him. But another part wondered if that lingering strangeness between us was permanent, and a few indifferent conversations were as close to friendship as we'd ever get now.

Behind them, Reigh and Isandri strode along silently, side-by-side, but didn't seem to be saying a word to one another. It seemed like they did that a lot, now. Isa usually hung around not far from his side ever since he'd nearly been killed by the Ulfrangar's poisoned arrows. I wondered if that was out of guilt, or if she was just worried about him. Both, maybe.

Phoebe and Garnett, on the other hand, were chattering away as happily as two songbirds. A few locks of Phoebe's wild red curls had escaped the cowl of her cloak and blew around her face as she smiled down at Garnett. She went on and on about her ideas for ... well, everything. New weapons for Murdoc. New dragon saddle designs. Something about a replacement hand for Judan. She raved about Arlan's collections of books and artifacts, and Garnett agreed to take her back sometime so she could chat with him more casually about some of the things he had in his office.

By the time we got back to the tavern, I'd fallen several paces behind everyone else. The rain had soaked through my cloak and ran down my neck and back, making me shiver. I wanted a hot bath, something to eat, and to sleep for the next week. But that wasn't going to happen. And there was something else I wanted even more.

As everyone else went inside, I stopped at the base of the front steps and stared at the open door. My mouth pinched up, and I stole a glance back over my shoulder at the dark silhouette of the old barn nearby. It was barely visible through the gusting sleet and darkness. A single lantern hung over the door, it's faint yellow light shining through the gale like a guiding star.

Before I could even think about it, I started walking there. I probably should have ducked inside just long enough to tell someone where I was going. But, then again, they might not even notice. Everyone had been pretty distracted before. Besides, I didn't want to have to explain myself. I just wanted a few minutes to think. And more than anything, I wanted to see my dragon.

I hurried through the darkness, my boots sloshing in the mud all the way to the barn door. The big lantern creaked as it swung back and forth, blown in the angry winds. It gave me plenty of light to see as I unlatched the barn's side door and ducked inside. Pulling the door closed behind me, I took a moment to catch my breath. Water dripped from my cloak and hood, pattering on the stone floor. I took in a deep breath, drinking in the smells of old hay, grain, and the familiar musk of horses.

The inside of the barn was nearly pitch black, with only one small, glass lantern hanging on another hook just inside. I brushed back the cowl of my drenched cloak and took the lantern down, holding it ahead as I made my way farther inside. It didn't take long to find where the dragons were roosting. This barn wasn't as big as the one we'd used at Ms. Lin's new farmhouse, and it barely had enough open space in the center for Fornax and Blite to curl up together. It did seem a lot cleaner, though. The floor was patched together from large, flat stones that had been filled in with sand around the edges, and a fine layer of hay was scattered about. Big sacks of grain were stacked along one wall, and barrels were arranged in a far corner. A small workbench was set up with basic farrier's tools—nothing fancy, but enough to trim and clean hooves, brush down horses, and maybe do some light repairs to saddlery or wagons.

All of it brought back my own private storm of memories as I walked forward and finally stopped right in front of the small mountain of black, orange, and red scales.

Fornax lifted his head and his scaly ears perked at the sound of my footsteps. His big nostrils puffed in deep breaths, probably able to tell it was me just by my scent alone.

"Hey, big guy," I said as I stretched out a hand to rub the end of his snout. "Are you doing okay, in here?"

He gave a low, satisfied grumbling noise as he snuffled through my hair and along the front of my tunic.

I leaned forward and let my forehead rest against his. "I'm sorry I didn't come sooner. It's been a little ... complicated," I whispered. "I guess I almost died again. And this time, it didn't scare me as much as it did before. I haven't told anyone, but it almost felt ... okay. I don't know why. I guess it could be because I'm not supposed to be in a mortal body in the first place, but to be honest, that just sounds really weird and ridiculous. So maybe I'm just getting tired of constantly being in survival mode. Or I'm getting jaded. I don't know."

I sighed deeply, stepping back and setting the lantern down on the floor nearby. I'd hoped saying that out loud, to someone who wasn't going to yell at me for it, would make me feel a little better about it. Nope. No such luck.

Unbuckling my soggy cloak, I dropped it next to the lantern and tried to shake some of the water out of my hair. My damp tunic stuck to my skin and left me shivering. I let out a totally undignified yelp as a big scaly tail suddenly snaked around my legs and dragged me forward. I stumbled and fell, landing on my hands and knees in the hay right against Fornax's big, scaly chest. He lowered his head, curling his neck around me and sandwiching me in that space between his neck and shoulder.

Then he started to purr.

His big, milky jade eyes rolled closed and he let out a blasting, snort of a sigh that stirred up the hay in front of him.

It was kinda hard to argue with that—mostly because he was squishing me and preventing my escape. I didn't struggle for long, though. Not when his scaly hide was so warm compared to the cold night air and all my soggy, rain-drenched clothes. The thrumming rhythm of his purr against my ear made every tense muscle in my body relax. I didn't feel so squished, then. More like ... embraced. Or aggressively cuddled.

Yeah, definitely that.

I let my head loll back against his chest as I stared up into the barn's wooden rafters and beams. The whoosh of the storm outside seemed to grow farther and farther away as my eyelids drooped. I rubbed my fingers along Fornax's smooth, warm scales.

"I don't want to be a god," I whispered to myself. It was easier to say it knowing none of my friends—Murdoc and the others—were around to hear it. "I have all these questions now, and no one to answer them. If this is the last time Ishaleon is going to be reborn, then what happens after I die? Will I even remember my mortal life? Or any of my other mortal lives? Or will I just wake up somewhere as a god and not remember anything about who I was before?"

I hoped not. Gods, I hated that idea. But it wasn't like I had much choice in the matter.

A long, exhausted sigh slipped past my lips and I closed my eyes. "I wanted to ask Arlan. He seems like the kind of guy who might actually know. He knows a lot about the divine stuff. But asking in front of everyone like that—I just couldn't. Everything still feels so weird and wrong. Murdoc's avoiding me. I act like an idiot every time I try to talk to Garnett." My voice slurred as the exhaustion overtook me, dragging me under to the deep rumble of Fornax's purring.

Maybe tomorrow would be better. Maybe I'd wake up feeling clearer and more confident. Talking to Arlan always seemed to shake me up, mostly because he knew things that, quite honestly, terrified me. Things about the gods, the past, and the fate I seemed to be hurtling toward. I didn't like that idea—that feeling like I had no real control over what happened to me. Like it was all decided and I was just following along. I just wasn't sure how to change it. All I could do right now was take the next step, and hope for the best.

Even if all those steps seemed to be leading me straight for disaster.

17
CHAPTER SEVENTEEN

"**THERE YOU ARE!**" I jolted awake, floundering on my bed of hay and dragon scales as an angry voice boomed through the barn. Oh dear sweet gods, what was happening?

"Wh-What is it? Iksoli? Are we being attacked?" I rasped groggily, scrambling backward over the ground. I backed right into one of Fornax's horns and doubled over, whimpering and clutching the back of my head.

Murdoc loomed over me like a tower of wrath, his hair and clothes soaked, and one of his eyes twitching. "You stupid, air-headed, little—what the heck is wrong with you?! You came out here and fell asleep without telling anyone where you were going? Do you have any idea how long we've been looking for you, you idiot?" he shouted.

"What?" I winced, the back of my head still throbbing. "O-Oh. Oh, fates, I … I'm sorry. I didn't think anyone would notice if I—"

"You didn't think anyone would notice if you, the reason most of us wound up involved in this mess in the first place, decided to go missing in the middle of the night on the eve of the fight for our lives?" he finished for me. "Thatcher, by all the gods, you better stay down because if you stand up right now, I will punch your face inside out and break every bone in your body." He shut his eyes tightly and slowly shook his head, licking his teeth behind his lips like he could already taste blood.

I did not dare move a muscle, mostly because I'd seen him do that to someone while we were in that prison camp. No way was I ready to volunteer for a repeat of that performance. "I-I really am sorry, Murdoc. I … well, everyone seemed busy. And I've kind of been in the way, lately. I'm not much good for battle planning anyway, so I honestly didn't think it would matter if I came out here for a little while," I confessed, probably sounding even more pathetic than I felt. Ugh. He was right. I should have at least mentioned it.

His eyes popped open suddenly and he stared down at me with an accusing scowl. "What do you mean you've been 'in the way?'"

Great. Why did I have to say it like that? Why did I have to say anything at all?

"Nothing. Just forget it. I didn't intend to cause any more problems. I'll come back in," I checked my hand to make sure the back of my head wasn't bleeding. "Just give me a few minutes to—"

"Thatcher," Murdoc growled my name like a curse through his teeth.

I sat, backed up against Fornax's side, and glared straight ahead so I didn't have to look him in the eye. What more did he want me to say? I'd apologized, hadn't I? Did he want to fight again—is that why he was pushing this?

We stayed that way for what felt like a few centuries, with him glaring at me and me glaring at the toes of his boots because I was too big of a coward to look him in the eye. Finally, Murdoc let out another deep, growling noise and stepped forward. He shoved a hand down into my face like he was going to help me up.

"Look, we ... we need to have a conversation. And it sucks, because I'm exquisitely terrible at this kind of thing, as you well know. But I can't keep tiptoeing around, not knowing where I really stand."

Oh no. Not this. Not now. Reluctantly, I seized his hand and let him drag me back up to my feet. I tensed up a little, you know, just in case he did decide to hit me.

He didn't, though.

"I don't know what's going on here anymore, Thatcher, and my head hurts from trying to figure it out," he said, blurting it out like the words had been hung in his throat for days. "All I know is that I hate this. I hate the way you've been slinking around like a nervous cat whenever I'm in the room, keeping your distance, being so quiet, and giving me all those weird looks. I hate that we can't just talk about things anymore, and you're acting like you're alone in this mess. Maybe you'll never trust me again, not like before, and I get that. I don't blame you for it at all. But I at least need to know if you hate me still. I need to know what *this* is." He motioned to the empty space between us. "You said I was like a brother to you, but do you actually mean that? Or was that just the adrenaline talking? Are we friends? Acquaintances? What?"

I opened my mouth, but nothing except a few panicked, squeaky choking sounds would come out at first. "I-I don't hate you," I sputtered at last. "Really, I don't. I know I've been sort of ... withdrawing. I don't know why, except that the whole godling thing is just really ... overwhelming. My power didn't stop the Zuer from almost killing me. What if it doesn't protect us from Iksoli, either? What if someone else gets hurt or killed?"

Murdoc looked down, his wet bangs falling so that I couldn't see his face. I could still hear the frustration in his sharp, quiet tone, though. "Yeah. I've been thinking about that some, too. You're right. You almost died. And if it wasn't for Arlan showing up like that, having the powers he does, you might be gone. But, Thatcher, none of that is within our control. One or both of us might die in that tower, your powers might be enough, or they might not. We don't know." His shoulders rose and fell with a heavy breath. "Fortunately, this all boils down to one, very simple question: do you want to go in there and try to save Devana or not? Cause with or without us, Isandri is going. And if she goes, Reigh goes. But their choices don't have to impact ours. We can leave, if that's what you want. So, what's it going to be?"

I hesitated, my thoughts racing as I pieced all that together. Before I could really understand it, however, my head bobbed and words spilled out. "Yes. I want to go with them."

"Why? Just because they're your friends and you don't want them to go alone?"

"No," I realized aloud. "I want to see her. Or, them, I guess. Devana's been crying out for me this whole time. Iksoli's been targeting me. I want to know why. I want to stop whatever plan this is she's trying to concoct in that tower. I don't want her to hurt anyone else."

Murdoc looked up at me again, seeming satisfied. "Then we go. And maybe we die, maybe we don't. We can try to be prepared, take precautions, and play this as smart as we possibly can, but it's going to be risky. There's no way around that."

"I know."

"Good." He pursed his lips and shrugged. "So, what does this mean for us? Where do we stand? Are *we* good, or not?"

An uncertain, twitchy smile spread over my face. "Yeah. We're good."

"All right, then." He made a popping sound with his lips and turned around, waving a hand for me to follow. "Come on. We've got work to do, and you get to apologize to everyone else for making them freak out and think you'd been kidnapped or something."

I cringed as I jogged over to catch up, stopping only to grab my cloak off the floor. "R-Right."

"Reigh's probably going to hit you, so prepare yourself."

I chuckled as I fell in step beside him. "I bet it doesn't hurt nearly as bad as when you punch people."

"Nope."

Hesitating at the barn door, I glanced back at Fornax. He'd already gone back to sleep. "You know what I think when I look around a place like this?" I realized aloud. "That I would give anything to have nothing more to worry about than Master Godfrey yelling at me to muck stalls faster."

Murdoc gave a low chuckle. "Yeah. That guy was a jerk."

"I kinda liked him, though."

He rolled his eyes. "You like everyone."

"Not everyone," I corrected.

Murdoc flashed me a challenging smirk. "Oh yeah? Name one—*one* person—that you don't like."

It didn't take me even two seconds to come up with that answer. "I don't like Arlan."

Murdoc's brows rose in surprise. "Is that so? Why not?"

My mouth scrunched as I looked away. "He gives me a bad feeling, I guess. I can't really explain it. Maybe that's wrong to say, since he's the one who saved my life. But something about him just ... I don't know, it's like that feeling you get when you're standing in a dark room by yourself, and you think someone might be watching you."

"Fair enough," Murdoc agreed with another soft laugh. "For the record, he creeps me out, too."

REIGH DIDN'T HIT me when I got back to the tavern. He did yell a lot, though. Nothing new there. Granted, he did come up with some pretty creative names to call me.

Isandri and Jace just smoldered ominously in a corner, dripping wet and eyeing me like they might both try to corner me in a dark alley when I least expected it. Yikes.

The person who actually hit me was Phoebe—which I wasn't expecting. She smacked me upside the back of the head, and glared so hard it made a little wrinkle pop up between her eyebrows.

"Do you have any idea how upset you made everyone? All night we've been searching while you just snoozed away in that barn," she fumed, jabbing an accusing finger in the center of my chest. "The nerve. You had us all thinking Iksoli had come for you or you'd been abducted again! Garnett's still out there looking for you in this horrible weather! She was beside herself with worry, and now we don't—"

Everyone, even Murdoc, jumped as the tavern door flung open and cracked off the wall with a *BANG!*

Garnett stood in the doorway, breathless, wide-eyed, and absolutely drenched from head to foot. Her wet hair stuck to her cheeks and shoulders as she sucked in panting breaths. Our gazes locked, and I knew right away.

Ooh no. Trouble. I was in trouble.

So. Much. Trouble.

I'd only just begun to realize that this was my one and only opportunity to start running so maybe I'd get a head start when she hit me like a charging bull. Garnett moved incredibly fast, like a blur of dwarven fury, and she wrapped her arms around my waist and tackled me straight to the ground. I hit the floor with a "OOF!" that knocked the wind from my lungs and left my vision spotting.

I expected to get smacked again—much more painfully this time since, you know, Garnett was probably stronger than Murdoc and basically everyone else I knew. I tensed up, shutting my eyes tightly, and bracing for it. Would it be my face? Stomach? Surely, she wouldn't go for the groin. I mean, she was probably really angry, but that was—

"You stupid, *stupid* man," Garnett gasped suddenly.

Oh gods. This was it.

She grabbed my face in her hands, practically sitting on me as she leaned down and pressed her mouth against mine.

My eyes popped open wide. My arms and legs went stiff. I didn't dare to move, breathe, or do anything at all.

Wh ... What? She, uh, she was ... really? No. No way. This had to be a dream, or a hallucination. Or maybe Murdoc had actually hit me back when we were standing in the barn, and I was now dead. Or he'd punched me so hard I'd been knocked into a different reality altogether. Yeah. That was probably it.

I mean, because she'd also called me a *man*, and literally no one had ever called me that before.

Kid? Yep.

Brat? Definitely.

Idiot? At least five thousand times, probably.

But never a man.

"Careful, Garnett," Murdoc snickered as he strode past, stepping over my legs on his way to the stairs. "We need him alive, remember? Don't send him into a heart attack."

She snatched back, still mashing my cheeks with her hands as her rain-soaked hair and clothes dripped all over me. I was honestly surprised every drop didn't sizzle when it hit my face because ... well, it felt like someone had lit my entire head on fire. Gods and Fates. Had she really just ... kissed me?

"Don't you ever do that again, you hear me? Honestly! You scared us all half to death. I was ready to have Arlan's entire network scouring every gutter in the kingdom trying to find you," she scolded.

"Ahm shorree," I tried to apologize, but she still had my face all smooshed.

"Oh, I'll bet you are. We ought to have you wearing a bell like a goat from now on. Honestly, what—" Garnett stopped and snapped her mouth shut, seeming to suddenly realize the, uh, several other people in the room who were staring at us. She jerked her hands back, releasing my face and quickly scooting off me to get back to her feet.

I just lay there for a few more seconds, still wondering if this was a dream or not. If it wasn't, then for the first time in my entire life, a girl had just kissed me. On purpose. In front of witnesses.

I don't know what it was—fear of the fact that I might be about to die tonight, a sudden boost of confidence and courage, or just sheer panic—but as I got to my feet, I felt a heat rise in my chest like a roaring forge. If today really was the last day of my life, and we got ourselves killed tonight when we tried to sneak into that tower, then by the Fates, I was going to make it count.

I turned to face Garnett, who was still dripping a puddle on the floor and frowning sourly up at me. Her nose wrinkled some, mouth pinching up like she might be about to start yelling at me again.

Nope. She'd thrown down the gauntlet. Now I was picking it up.

I stepped toward her and snagged my arms around her, drawing her in before she could protest, and planted a returning kiss against her lips.

When I finally drew back, Garnett blinked up at me with her face flushing bright pink and her eyes as big as two lilac moons. She didn't say a word, which suited me fine. There was something I had to say first.

"I am really sorry for ducking out last night without telling everyone," I panted, my head swimming a little from adrenaline. Oh gods, I wasn't about to pass out, was I? Better do this quickly, then. "And also, I like you—a lot. And not just as a friend. I think you're beautiful, and amazing, and I *romantically* like you. So ... yeah. I just wanted to make sure that was ... you know, clear."

"Wow," Reigh blurted, almost like he hadn't meant to say that out loud.

"All right, you kids, knock it off with that," Jace grumbled from the corner. "Just because Jaevid's gone doesn't mean you get to act like a bunch of rabbits in springtime. Break it up."

Murdoc gave a suppressed, snorting laugh. He held a hand out to Reigh and wiggled his fingers.

"Ugh, you've got to be kidding me." Reigh growled elven curses under his breath as he reached into his pockets and took out a few coins, smacking them angrily into Murdoc's palm.

Wait a second, were they *betting* on me? For what?

Before I could ask, Garnett slipped out of my grasp and darted for the stairs. Phoebe immediately bounded after her, practically glowing with excitement as she dashed by. Footsteps thumped rapidly along the hall. Then a door slammed somewhere upstairs. I stood in awkward silence, staring up at the ceiling, as I heard the muffled sound of voices ... followed by a chorus of two girlish squeals of delight.

18

CHAPTER EIGHTEEN

There wasn't much time to relish in the victory of my very first, successful, attempt at kissing a girl. Sinking down into the nearest chair, I tried to breathe through the shock of what I'd just done. Gods and Fates, what had I done?

"We'll set out just before nightfall," I overheard Reigh muttering quietly to Jace as they walked past, Murdoc and Isandri close behind them. "Anything you can do to make sure no one questions our movements through the area would be appreciated. With any luck, maybe this storm will lift and then we won't be flying in slop."

Jace shifted the weight of the bag he had slung over one of his shoulders as he made his way toward the door. "I'll do what I can, but I wouldn't count on the weather easing any. This time of year, slop is about all we get. Count it as a blessing, though. It'll make you harder to spot from the ground." The old king paused at the door, glancing back at me and smirking some. "Watch out for one another. I don't know how long it might take for me to be able to meet with you again once it's done and the siege of the city begins, but I would suggest not lingering anywhere near Northwatch. I'll come looking for you here."

Jace and Reigh went on talking even as they headed out the door. Murdoc and Isandri followed, listening, but not saying much. Finally, the tavern grew quiet and still. It must have been very early in the morning. I couldn't tell, exactly, because of the weather. The lingering storm made everything seem so bleak, gray, and dim. But after a while, the tavernkeeper came down from their private quarters on the top floor, along with his daughter, and they began opening up their business and making preparations for the day. They offered to serve breakfast for us, but with nerves making my stomach churn and my thoughts tangle up like old fishing nets, for once, I didn't feel much like eating. No one else did, either, although Phoebe gratefully accepted some tea with honey.

Most everyone took a few hours upstairs to rest since, you know, they'd spent most of the night running around in the storm looking for me. Oops. But with all our plans made, and a decently clear idea of what we had to do, there wasn't much else to prepare. All my weapons were ready. I had two cartridges of bolts for my crossbow, my xiphos was cleaned, I'd checked over Fornax's saddle, and had almost thrown up from anxiety a few times—so I was ready to go. Now, all that was left was to wait for the perfect time to make our move.

Murdoc had already cleaned all his weaponry and checked over his leather armor, making sure it all fit perfectly into place, before he took a seat by the fire with his feet kicked up on a tabletop and sat, staring into the flames and rubbing his fingers together anxiously. Isandri settled into the chair next to his, her arms folded into the big, bell sleeves of her robes as usual. The light from the fire danced in her eyes as she ran one hand along the smooth, wooden pole of her staff.

Nearby, Phoebe pored over the tiny little bits and pieces of something new she was crafting. Some of the parts looked suspiciously like they'd come from the trap she had made for Phillip. I guess she was repurposing them? It didn't seem like a good time to ask, though. She'd pulled all her wild red curls into a massive bun on the back of her head and leaned in close, fidgeting with tiny tools as she squinted at her work.

Reigh slept for a few hours, then got up and began feverishly writing out a few letters. He quietly passed them off to the tavernkeeper when he thought no one was paying attention. Farewell letters in case we died? I wondered if I should do that, too. Except, I didn't really have anyone to write to. Pretty much anyone I knew who would have cared if I died or not was already sitting in the room.

Speaking of which, Garnett was the last to come down stairs. By the look of it, she'd spent some time brushing out and re-braiding her hair and had changed into a different set of much more complex and hardy leathers. She'd buckled on pieces of plate armor that fit the curves and contours of her frame, and had her two double-headed hand axes belted to her hips.

Her cheeks still seemed a little rosy when she glanced my way. That look in her eyes, like there was something she wanted to say but wasn't sure how, stirred up a fresh wave of panic in my gut. It took everything I had not to let it show. Cool—I had to play it cool. Confidence. Dragonrider-level confidence.

I managed a somewhat-twitchy smile at her, which only made her duck her head and blush harder.

Great. I'd probably embarrassed her by doing all that and saying those things in public. But, to be fair, she'd started it. She had kissed *me* first. Was I not supposed to react to that kind of thing?

Uggghhh. None of this girl-stuff made any sense to me at all.

As the hours passed, the mood got heavier. The already faint light outside grew dimmer. Low rumbles of thunder sounded in the distance like the growl of a beast. Cold shivers ran through my body, making me shudder and my skin prickle. At last, I looked up and locked gazes with Reigh from across the room. He didn't say a word. He didn't have to. I could tell just by the look on his face, like a somber finality had settled over his brow.

It was time.

I nodded once, and slowly stood up. Buckling on my now only slightly damp cloak, I pulled the hood down low and fastened my crossbow to the holster Phoebe had made that fit against my hip and leg. Then I started for the door. Murdoc was at my side before I could blink, and Isandri and the others weren't far behind. We gathered by the front door of the tavern, greeted by a blast of icy, frigid wind and the howl of the storm.

While everyone waited under the shelter of the porch, Murdoc and I struck out for the barn where I'd spent last night sleeping. The freezing rain lashed at my face and stung my eyes, but I barely felt the cold now. All I could feel was my heart pumping hard and fast, throbbing in my fingertips as I helped him roll the barn's big door open far enough that the dragons could exit. Then I pulled my whistle out from under my tunic where it hung, still strung on the resin cord of Jaevid's necklace. I blew a few signaling blasts.

Fornax answered with a deep roar. The ground shook under my boots as he lumbered forward, snarling into the sleet and blasting a snort of disapproval at being forced out into the weather. Murdoc's smaller drake made a similar squawk of distaste and hunkered back, squinting out through the gale at us reluctantly.

"I know it's lousy, guys. Sorry about that," I said. Rubbing my hands along Fornax's horned head, I stole a sideways look at Murdoc as he did the same to his dragon.

The young drake scooted toward him sideways like an eager puppy, whining and dipping his head in submissive excitement. He sniffed through Murdoc's hair and nipped at the end of his cloak, swishing his tail and keeping his small ears pinned back.

"Blite, right?" I'd heard Murdoc call his dragon that in passing.

My sulky friend shrugged. "Yeah. I'm not good with names."

"No, I think it's a good one." I patted Fornax's neck and sighed. "Time to go, huh?"

He sighed, too. "Yeah. I think it is."

"Hey, Murdoc?"

"Yeah?"

"Try not to die, okay? I know we won't be together for this mission. I probably won't have any clue where you are in that tower. Do me a favor, and don't get killed. We're supposed to go to the dragonrider academy together after all this is done, and I'm not doing that without you."

He turned to face me, his features locked in a stubborn glare. "On one condition—you don't die, either. I mean it. I already watched you almost die right in front of me one time. Don't do it again. Got it?" He stuck a hand out like he wanted to shake on it.

I grinned and grasped his hand as tightly as I could. "Deal."

Progress was slow through the rough air, and flying in the failing light did not make it any easier. Hunkered low against Fornax's back, I was only able to see thanks to the goggles Phoebe had made for us. They shielded my eyes and let me get a clearer look around at everyone in our formation. To my right, Reigh and Phoebe sat astride Vexi. The sleek, green dragoness had come soaring in as soon as she heard the commotion with Fornax and Blite. According to Reigh, she'd been wild before she chose him, and so it wasn't uncommon for her to prefer roaming over being cooped up in barns and tight spots for long periods of time. She never went far, though, and always kept an ear turned his way.

On my left, Murdoc and Blite soared in close enough to draft off my wing, which helped the smaller dragon keep up with our greater speed through the storm. Isandri did the same, streaking through the wind and slurry on her graceful dark wings like a diving falcon. And Garnett, well ...

I looked down, feeling that knot of excited heat in the center of my chest at the way she had her arms wrapped tightly around my waist while she sat in the saddle behind me. I'd, um, made a few suggestions when it came to our passenger assignments. I mean, it made sense that Fornax and I should be the ones to carry her. We had the better saddle set up and Fornax was bigger and stronger than the other two dragons. Plus, Garnett was the one showing us where to go to find this hidden access tunnel, so she needed to be sure she was in the lead and could give directions to everyone else.

Yes. It all made perfect sense.

Okay, fine. Vexi probably could have carried her, instead. But a girl wanting to sit next to me in any circumstance was kind of a first for me, so I wasn't about to let this opportunity slip by.

So here we were, me sitting in front gripping the saddle handles to steer my big orange and black dragon, and her pressed right up against my back. Her arms hugged me around the middle, warm and sturdy. Part of me wished I could reach down and take one of her hands in mine.

Buuut now did not seem like the right time for that. Later, though. Definitely later.

We zoomed low over the rolling farmland outside of Osbran as darkness took the kingdom like the grip of an iron fist. Heading west as fast as we dared, the dark shapes of the exposed, dark rock clusters passed by like phantoms in the whiteout of the falling sleet. Thunder rolled in the stormy sky overhead, making my heartbeat skip every time. I bit down hard to keep my teeth from chattering, and tried to keep my gaze focused on the path ahead. Sometimes the ghostly shapes of other dragons would appear through the low clouds, soaring by but never coming close enough to make out any detail. According to King Jace, there would be more and more of them as the night went on. The riders were departing in waves, making their way from all corners of the kingdom to rally at the military outpost nearby. That's where they would launch their assault tomorrow.

There wasn't a single minute to waste.

I urged Fornax on, pushing him to pump his large wings faster as we dropped down to soar less than two hundred feet off the ground. We had to be getting close. We'd been at this for almost three hours. How much farther would it be? With the wind in my face, I couldn't ask. Garnett probably wouldn't be able to understand a word I said in this weather.

I knew she had to be getting anxious, too, though. Every now and then, she would lean to peek around, looking around at the landscape and features in the area. Finally, I felt her give me a little squeeze and pat on my shoulder to get my attention. I looked down, my gaze tracking the direction where she pointed to a cluster of large, black boulders piled in a crude C-shape. It didn't look any different than any of the others we'd passed already, but if she was sure this was the right spot, then I was willing to take her word for it.

I threw up a signal to the others and started a steep turn, arcing around the hilltop. Fornax flared his wings, coming in for a swift landing and catching the ground with his clawed hind legs. Vexi touched down in perfect formation right beside us, and Blite touched down a little behind. The smaller dragon shook himself and growled, lashing his tail and flexing his shoulders as though Murdoc's added weight was still difficult for him to manage. Hopefully that would improve as he got older.

Isandri bounded in front of us, shifting forms mid-stride and brandishing her staff as her brightly-hued eyes scanned all around for any signs of danger. Even in her human shape, there was something distinctly feline about how she prowled around on the balls of her bare feet, her dark purple and green robes billowing around her lithe frame. She stood poised, waiting while the rest of us climbed down from the saddles and unloaded our gear. We didn't have much to take apart from our weaponry—a few rations, a bundle of torches, and some small packs of medical gear for each group.

Garnett didn't wait for me to help her down from the saddle. She unbuckled herself and bounded off, landing in a crouch and slowly rising to fix a focused glare upon the cluster of boulders before us. "All right, then. Everyone keep a distance and I'll give it a look. No telling what might come popping out of there once we throw the hatch."

Gathering before our dragons, the rest of us watched in silence while she forged ahead to the base of the rock formation. It didn't take her even two minutes of digging around in the mud and moss to find a small crevice between two of the rocks. Reaching her arm inside all the way to her shoulders, she quirked her mouth, sticking her tongue out to one side while she felt around.

Something gave a loud, metallic *CLUNK*.

Murdoc and I exchanged a glance.

"Hah! There it is," Garnett announced proudly as she pulled her arm out of the hole and bounded over to a mossy slope on the other side of the cluster of boulders. She hooked her fingers along the bottom of a narrow hatch door hidden seamlessly amongst the rocks, roots, moss, and mud. She gave a little grunt as she lifted it, her impressively muscular shoulders flexing as she hefted it upward until a stabilizing mechanism caught it and held the door ajar.

Whoa.

It wasn't all that big of a door. Maybe five feet wide and seven feet tall. Somehow, I'd pictured it being a lot larger—big enough to fit a monster or war machine through. But this was a lot more discreet, almost as though it'd been placed here for something other than just moving Tibran military forces around. Spies, maybe? Or infiltration behind enemy lines?

"It was meant to be a sort of emergency exit," Garnett explained, as though she could easily read the confusion on my face. "A smaller offshoot passage leading to one of the main tunnels. It could be easily collapsed if needed. We didn't build too many of them, though. Argonox wasn't a fan of wasting time and materials on things that would make things safer for his forces. I managed to convince him that, in the areas where our tunnel construction was rushed and I wasn't able to take the necessary precautions to ensure they wouldn't collapse, having a few pathways out might spare him the lives of his key engineers—namely me. I refused to dig one more foot until he started allowing at least a few emergency safeguards for my teams."

"I can imagine how well he took that," Reigh muttered as he stepped past her and leaned in to peer down into the tunnel beyond the hatch.

"Oh, stones, it made him furious! He was ready to have me strung up and tortured for my insolence. But I was in the rare position of having a teensy bit of leverage against the madman, since he saw fit to murder the rest of my people. He didn't have a Plan B to take over the construction of his tunnels, and they were supposed to be the key to overtaking Maldobar and avoiding open conflict with the dragonriders—a fight he must have known he would ultimately lose. Hard to match that kind of air power." She grinned up at Fornax, something softly affectionate in her expression. "I've never been so glad to have all my plans made useless."

"Is this going to be secure for us to move through?" Murdoc asked, shuffling over with the others to peer through the gaping, dark maw of that open hatch.

"As safe as any other. According to the maps my people lifted off Iksoli's forces, the main tunnel this passage connects to is still open and operational. If it's lasted this long, it should be fine," she explained. "Now, then, I suppose we should light a torch or two, yeah? My eyes are keen to the deep places of the world, but I rather doubt the rest of you will fare so well."

Reigh made a face as he followed her instructions, ducking under the cover of the open hatch door and pulling one of the torches from our bundle. "For the record, I hate everything about this," he complained as he lit it.

"Just let me take the lead and stay close and quiet," Garnett warned, already disappearing down into the darkness of the tunnel. "This isn't the sort of place you want to go strolling around without your guard up and your wits about you."

19
CHAPTER NINETEEN

Stepping through that passage into the deep, smothering darkness of the Tibran tunnels felt like we'd all just been swallowed whole by a giant serpent. The walls were muddy and slimy at first, and the temperature plummeted as the tunnel delved down farther and farther into the earth. It twisted and seemed to wind back on itself so that I lost all sense of direction immediately.

Fortunately, Garnett didn't seem the least bit unnerved by it. She walked along at the head of our group, Reigh following close behind her with a torch raised to cast a warm yellow glow around so the rest of us could see. With Isandri, Phoebe, and I in the middle, Murdoc brought up the rear of the group with another torch—just in case. The wavering light revealed an exposed smooth dirt ceiling, reinforced every now and then by a wooden frame. I'd expected to see roots poking through, or even a worm here and there. But there was no sign of life anywhere. The hard-packed floor was barren and the longer we walked, the less moisture seemed to hang in the air. I guess that meant we were traveling down a lot deeper than the rain could soak through.

Somehow, that wasn't exactly comforting.

The smell of rich, moist earth changed the farther we went. I caught the wafting scents of something almost mineral-like, sort of like the inside of an old well. The air grew colder still, until I could see my breath, and the tunnel didn't twist or curve quite as much. With my thoughts racing and my heart beating wildly, I couldn't tell how long we had been walking before Garnett threw up a hand in a signal for us stop.

Dead ahead, the tunnel came to what looked like another heavy hatch door made of thick wooden beams bound together with iron plates. Jogging the distance, Garnett left us standing and waiting for her signal while she checked the door over thoroughly. Then she motioned for us to follow.

"This should take us into the main tunnel system," she whispered. "Once we're inside, we need to be on our highest guard. Stay very close. No noise. No talking. Eyes and ears open. If you even think you see something odd, get my attention. All right?"

We all nodded.

"Good. Now, wait here. I'll scout ahead a bit and make sure it's clear." She took in a deep breath, seeming to collect her nerve before she turned back and slowly began to unlatch the door. She pressed against it little by little, easing it ajar an inch at a time, before she finally dared to poke her head out and take a look around.

Slipping through the door, Garnett disappeared into the dark beyond without a sound. I gripped the handle of my crossbow, ready to draw in a moment's notice. Or run. Whatever the occasion called for.

Minutes passed. Or maybe it was only a few seconds. I couldn't keep focused when every faint noise of a boot on the stone or someone swallowing made me flinch. My chest hurt thanks to how my pulse kept thrashing hard, and my hands shook, although I couldn't tell if it was from the cold or the adrenaline. Both, probably.

I almost came out of my skin as Garnett's head suddenly popped back through the doorway, glancing around at all of us and giving a quick, silent nod. All was clear. So far, so good.

We emerged out into the main tunnel one at a time, moving as quickly as we dared without running the risk of making too much noise. As soon as my boots hit the solid stone of the main tunnel, I couldn't stop my mouth from falling open as my gaze drifted up to the tall, cavernous ceiling overhead. Fates, it must have been thirty feet or more. And judging by the almost patterned-looking slashes and cuts in the rock on every side of the passage, it looked like it had been made by something ... *chewing* the stone.

My stomach dropped.

An underbeast? That was the only thing my panicked brain could come up with. Not a lot of animals spent time chewing their way through solid rock. At least, not that I knew of.

Garnett had talked a lot about the underbeasts, and how Argonox had stolen them from her homeland and brought them here to dig these tunnels. She'd described them as big, brutish, strong, and without any eyes. They could apparently dig very fast, and I guess I'd pictured something a tad smaller than ... whatever behemoth of a monster had left this kind of a tunnel behind. No wonder the one we'd stirred up while we were rescuing Phillip had sounded so massive. It had nearly shaken down the entire cavern right on top of us, and we'd never even glimpsed it.

I prayed we never would.

We walked in the near dark of the tunnel, keeping to one side and picking our way very carefully. Garnett's demeanor seemed to grow colder and more distant with every step, her usually smiling face now sealed in a look of determined focus. Her jaw stayed set, and she already had one of her hand axes out and clenched tightly in her fist as she moved ahead of us as quiet as a fox. Every movement was calculated and precise, as though she'd slipped into survival mode and was only focused on the way ahead. Her forehead shone with a sheen of fresh sweat, and it made a few stray locks of her hair stick to her brow and cheeks. Every few yards, she panned her gaze methodically all around, searching every dark corner that our torchlight didn't reach.

But so far, nothing raised any alarm.

I dared to hope. If we could do this—if we could make it all the way to Northwatch tower without being detected or running into any of Iksoli's forces—then maybe we stood a chance of pulling off this rescue without any catastrophes. We could get this done and be long gone by the time the dragonriders decided to incinerate that place.

I should have known better, I guess. Things never went that well for me. And down here, miles away from the surface and any form of help or rescue, we were far more vulnerable.

This deep underground, if something did go wrong, no one would be able to hear us scream.

Hours dragged on as we trekked through the darkness until, at last, Murdoc jogged to the front of our group to catch up to where Garnett was still in the lead. He took her arm to get her attention and tipped his head back down the line to the rest of us. "Let's take a breather," he whispered. "We're no good to anyone if we show up with everyone dead on their feet."

Oh, thank the gods.

I sagged on my feet, wiping sweat from my brow onto my sleeve. I would've given anything to sit down long enough to peel my boots off and rub at my sore heels. Keeping this pace was hard enough in armor and carrying all our gear, but after the surges of adrenaline had left my muscles shaky and cold, it was getting harder and harder to keep my senses sharp to anything that might be around us, hiding in the dark. Thankfully, I wasn't the only one losing steam. Phoebe blinked owlishly, leaning against me a little as she panted. Of all of us, she was probably the least physically prepared for it. Hiking into battle hadn't exactly been one of her hobbies before all this.

"It'll be okay," I whispered to her. "We've got to be getting close now, right? Just a little farther."

"How close are we to the tower?" Isa asked, dropping into a crouch to run her hands along the rough stone floor as though she were trying to get a sense of her surroundings. Her brow scrunched sourly as she shook her head and flicked a meaningful glance up in my direction. I guess whatever abilities she might have been able to use on the surface wouldn't work down here. Were we too far from the moon? Would she be able to use any of her powers as long as we were down here?

Garnett glanced down our line, her expression a mixture of apprehension and worry, as though she didn't like the idea of staying in one place for too long. "The emergency access tunnel we entered through is a good twenty miles from Northwatch," she whispered back, shifting her focus back to Murdoc. "Of course, the paths themselves aren't a straight shot, but I would guess we're still a good three or four miles from the tower itself. Maybe a touch more."

Twenty miles? Gods and Fates. No wonder my back and feet were killing me.

"It doesn't get any safer from here," she warned as she spun her axe over her hand a few times. "You can bet there'll be a lot more of Iksoli's mind-controlled minions the nearer we get to the city. She's smart, keeping her forces in close. She must be on guard since we took the Zuer out of play. I'm betting she'll have things locked down nice and tight around the tower."

Great. Well, that sounded ... fun.

I helped Phoebe ease down to sit on the floor so she could rest. Reigh spoke to her quietly, seeming to notice that of all of us, she seemed to be struggling the most to keep up the pace. He and Isandri hovered over her, offering her a few sips from a waterskin, while Murdoc stood over them like he was supervising.

I glanced at Garnett, but she still stood facing away down the tunnel ahead, bristled and gripping her axe like she was ready to hurl it at a second's notice. Probably not a good time to check on her. Not while she was this focused, anyway.

Picking up Reigh's torch, I wandered a few feet away—not too far—and held it up to get a better look at the area around us. The sheer scale was still staggering, and my brain boggled at the idea that the Tibrans had built all of this in such a short amount of time. The looming ceiling was still thirty to forty feet tall, and the tunnel must have been twenty feet wide. Big enough to march a line of soldiers through, even on horseback. Granted, I imagined getting horses through the dark on this uneven ground would've been a challenge. Unless they'd been thoroughly conditioned not to spook.

I stopped, squinting across the width of the tunnel as the torchlight glimmered off something metallic. Weird. What was that?

I stole a look over my shoulder at my companions. They all seemed pretty occupied. I probably should have been resting, as well. But my curiosity got the better of me. Just one quick look, then I'd go back and sit down. Besides, it's not like the rest of them couldn't see where I was with the big burning torch in my hand, right?

Right.

I picked my steps carefully as I crossed the width of the tunnel, making my way toward that metallic object shining and reflecting the torchlight. Was that gold? Or brass?

I stopped when the dark shapes surrounding it came into view. My mouth opened slightly and I stared in silent awe at the cluster of skeletons dressed in Tibran armor lying around something that looked like a huge crossbow on wheels. Or, at least, it had been once. My torchlight had caught off one of the brass fixtures on the arms, and now that I stood much closer, I could see that the back half of it was smashed to splinters. Likewise, some of the skeletons looked like they'd been crunched, as well. Their armor was bent and cracked, like something huge had mashed it underfoot.

"The Tibrans used those to shoot down dragons," Reigh explained in a low whisper as he suddenly appeared at my side like a phantom from the dark.

I gasped and flinched away, biting back the urge to hit him for sneaking up on me like that. Geez. "I-I ... figured," I managed to wheeze quietly.

"We should go back and get the others ready to ..." his voice trailed off as his eyes narrowed, head tilting to one side. He stepped away toward one of the fallen skeletons sprawled nearby, still dressed in its rotting clothes and dinged-up bronze armor. Crouching down, he pulled something from around its neck. A necklace?

"Weird," he murmured as he held it up into the light of the torch in my hand.

Hanging on a thin gold chain, the small emblem in the shape of a hand with an eye in the center, sparkled and glittered.

"What symbol is that?" I asked quietly.

Reigh just shrugged. "Never seen it before. No telling, though. The Tibrans took people from kingdoms all across the world. It could have come from anywhere."

My mouth scrunched as I watched Reigh tuck the necklace into his pocket. Something about that symbol put an uneasy shiver up my spine. Even if I was sure I'd never seen it before, it gave me a bad feeling. Like maybe we shouldn't take it with us.

I didn't say anything, though. After all, if that symbol meant something bad, maybe it was a good idea to let someone like Arlan look at it and tell us what, exactly, it was. He seemed like the person who might actually know that kind of thing, especially if it came from somewhere far away from Maldobar.

"Let's go," Reigh urged, still keeping his tone quiet as he nudged me with his elbow and gestured for me to pass the torch back over. "And, uh, hey ... good luck. You know, in case I don't get a chance to say it later."

I stared at him. Why did this sound so much like one of those deathbed speeches? Like maybe he thought he wasn't going to make it out of that tower, so we might as well end things on a nice note with everyone?

"Yeah, well, good luck to you, too." I frowned and looked away. "I'm not sure luck has anything to do with this, though."

He gave a faint, humorless chuckle and started walking ahead of me. "You're probably right. It's good, though, `cause when it comes to luck, I've never had any."

I was about to remind him that I didn't, either. My hometown got burned to a crisp by Tibrans, my father had died, I'd wound up being best friends with an assassin, had found out I was actually some kind of reborn deity who really sucked at using my powers, had almost died several times, and now I was about to try and sneak into an enemy-occupied death tower with no idea whether or not I could count on my divine powers to protect me and everyone else in my group. Talk about no luck.

Before I could even get a word out, a sudden sound made both of us pause halfway across the tunnel. It started out distant. Faint. Like maybe it was far away. But as we both stood there, my blood rushing and all my extremities going numb, it grew louder.

And louder.

Oh gods, was that ... people screaming?

"Hide!" Reigh barked through his teeth, dropping his torch and seizing my arm. He dragged me back to that heap of skeletons and we dove in, hiding as best we could against the bones and debris.

Across the tunnel, the rest of our group scrambled to their feet at the noise. Garnett and Isandri ducked into a small crevice in the wall, all but vanishing from sight. Murdoc doused his torch and grabbed Phoebe, sprinting for a large fallen boulder we'd passed a few yards back and leaping behind it.

I held my breath.

The screaming grew louder, intermingled with the sounds of footsteps and the clunk and clatter of armor. The light of our abandoned torch flickered and wavered, illuminating a crowd of people dressed in patched-together mixtures of armor. They ran past, tripping and falling over one another like startled sheep.

Merciful Fates. What was happening? What were they running from?

I clamped a hand over my mouth to keep myself from making a sound as one of them fell right in front of my hiding place. The man let out a garbled yell, pitching and flailing, as something big landed right on top of him and bit down into his shoulder. I recognized the creature's pitch-black fur, bulbous white eyes, six powerful legs, and long, whip-like tail.

Every muscle in my body froze solid. I didn't dare to move, breathe, or even blink.

That was a switchbeast.

CHAPTER TWENTY

No—not just one. There were more switchbeasts running after the group, taking them down one at a time like lions on the hunt.

They sprang and latched onto the fleeing fighters, gripping them in razor-sharp talons, and sinking their quill-like teeth into them. Some of the monsters crawled along the cavern walls, able to move as easily as they did on the ground.

Sprawled on his belly next to me, Reigh's face drew into a fierce scowl. His hands slid slowly down his sides, moving to the hilts of his two elven-styled blades. I shot him a desperate look, barely managing to shake my head once. No. We couldn't attack them. We had to stay still and silent. They might continue on without even noticing us.

My heart kicked at my ribs, like a horse bucking in a stall, as the switchbeast not even six feet away from us tore into the man it had pinned down, then looked up. In the wavering light of our discarded torch, I got a clear look as the monster panned its gaze around, long tail slowly swishing as its many shoulders flexed under short, silky black fur. Its jaggedly pointed ears swiveled and flicked, nose wrinkling as it sniffed the air.

I held perfectly still.

Next to me, Reigh seemed to have stopped breathing completely.

No sound. No movement.

The switchbeast let out a sudden, piercing yowl and darted forward to continue the chase. It disappeared into the dark, scrambling up the walls and forging after the rest of the fleeing fighters—mercenaries, or whoever they were.

I dared to let out a slow, shaking breath.

Reigh made a gesture over his mouth, signaling for me to stay silent, as he slowly began to move out of our hiding spot amidst all the bones and bits of armor. I watched down the tunnel, straining to see any sign of the switchbeasts in case one of them had fallen behind or was doubling back our way. Nothing. Just darkness and the fading echoes of screams.

"Come on, we have to get out of here—*now*," Reigh urged, his voice barely audible thanks to the thrashing of my pulse in my ears as he helped me wriggle free of the bone pile.

Across the tunnel, Garnett and Isandri were already emerging from their hiding spot, staying completely soundless as they waved us over frantically. I could barely make out the blanched look of terror on Phoebe's face as she and Murdoc peeked over their boulder and immediately began running to rejoin, too.

I stopped and bent down to grab the torch as we ran by. We still needed at least one to make sure we didn't trip over any of the rubble or uneven places on the tunnel floor.

Just as I seized the wooden handle, something dark dripped onto the floor right next to the flame's flickering light. Three dark splotches dotted the stony ground. Huh? Was that water?

I dipped my fingertips into them near the light

No. Not water.

It was clear, but sticky almost like sap or snot. And it reeked with a sharp, musky odor. Was that ... drool? It reminded me a little of dragon venom except it didn't burn when air touched it.

I looked up, trying to peer through the dark to see where on the ceiling of the tunnel it might be coming from.

I almost didn't see it. But my one quick glance overhead and the sparkle of the torch's glow off the stone must have coalesced at just the right instant. Something shifted in the dark and then held perfectly still.

I froze, my gaze now locked onto a large, dark shape on the ceiling. The glimmer of the torchlight briefly reflected over what I could have sworn looked like two big eyeballs.

Then a maw bristling with thousands of needle-like teeth appeared.

Oh gods.

Reigh stopped a few feet away and whirled back to stare me down with a crazed expression, like he was ready to drag me along if I didn't start moving. He hadn't seen it. He didn't know. But I guess he could read the terror on my face even from a distance.

Immediately, Reigh's gaze darted upward, following my line of sight. Then his eyes went wide, too. His mouth twisted into a snarl. Moving slowly, he sank down into a defensive position and reached back to the two, curved blades sheathed at his hips. The metallic hum and scrape of the scythe-like weapons leaving their sheaths made the rest of our group stop and turn, just in time to hear him growl in a quiet, low voice, "No. Sudden. Moves."

He was right. I didn't know how intelligent those creatures were. Maybe it didn't realize we'd spotted it, yet. I clenched my teeth, keeping my eyes fixed on that spot—the pair of big white eyes staring down at me. *Think, Thatcher. You can do this. No panicking.*

It was too far up. None of us could make a successful swipe at it with a sword. And if it sprang, it might take a bite at one of us. One tiny prick of one of those fangs is all it would take. My hand drifted slowly to my crossbow.

I'd have to take a shot.

My mind seemed to go strangely quiet, as though every racing, terrified thought had been dissolved away like mist in the morning sun. Reigh's pupils narrowed, going as tiny as pinpricks in terror as I set my jaw and unhooked the leather strap that held my crossbow to my hip. One movement. One shot. That's all I'd get.

No time to second guess it.

Overhead, the switchbeast gave a low, probably suspicious hiss.

I sucked in a sharp breath and held it.

Now or never.

I dropped to a knee and ripped the crossbow free, finger already poised on the trigger as I leaned back and aimed for the darkness right between those two eyes. My finger squeezed against the warm metal of the trigger. The thick, taut bowstring fired with a *THUNK*, sending the bolt howling through the gloom.

THERE WASN'T time to make sure that I'd actually hit it. I turned and ran, seizing Reigh by the collar on the way by and dragging him along as I sprinted for the rest of our group.

A piercing yowl and *THUD* from behind sent a fresh wave of terror through me, giving me a new burst of speed. When I finally dared to look back, I found the switchbeast pitching and flailing on the ground, making sickly gurgling sounds until it went still.

"Nice shot," Reigh gasped as he stopped next to me, still gripping his weapons. "For a moment there, I thought for sure we were—"

A low, answering chorus of eerie yowls echoed from down the passage.

Oh no.

We ... we had to ...

"RUN!" Garnett shouted, already sprinting ahead as fast as she could.

Was she serious? Run where?! We couldn't possibly beat those things on foot!

We didn't have much of a choice, though.

I bit back a curse as I took off after her. Everyone else followed, dashing as fast as we could along the tunnel. Isandri's form shimmered as she changed into her feline form, her feathered wings unfurling and giving off a radiant silver light that was not stealthy at all. That ship had sort of sailed now, though. The evil, venomous, six-legged cat was out of the bag, and it definitely knew we were here.

Isandri dipped her head, performing a maneuver she'd used on me once before at the Cromwell estate. She scooped up Phoebe with her snout and tossed her up on to her strong, feline back. Bounding forward, Isandri gave a low growl of frustration as another split in the massive tunnel came into view ahead.

"Left!" Garnett shouted.

We all headed for the path to the left, scrambling over a place where the floor had buckled and left big boulders and chunks of uneven stone cracked upward. We passed more skeletal remains of Tibran soldiers in the rubble. More smashed war machines.

And all the while, the screeching and hissing of the switchbeasts grew louder at our heels. They were gaining fast. We wouldn't make it. We had to—

A sharp pain shot up through my leg and I fell, my head cracking off the stone floor as something dragged me backward. I kicked and fought, rolling over to find a switchbeast with its claws embedded in my calf. Curse it! Without thinking, I raised my crossbow and fired three bolts right at the monster.

THUNK—THUNK—THUNK

The switchbeast shrieked and let me go, scrambling back and pawing at where my arrows had lodged into its chest. Then its head snapped up, baring those needle-like fangs and coiling its muscular shoulders for a vengeful lunge.

THUNK!

The final bolt lodged deep into its open mouth and the switchbeast dropped right where it stood.

I spat at it and started to stagger up, biting back a cry of pain as blood oozed from the deep claw-punctures in my boot.

"Thatcher!" Murdoc shouted, running at me with his longswords already drawn. His expression went blank suddenly, a primal sort of fear draining all the color from his features as he stared past me.

I looked back down the tunnel behind us. There, just beyond the range of Isandri's celestial light, the glow of dozens of more eyes winked in the gloom. More climbed along the wall and skittered across the ceiling.

My blood seemed to freeze solid in my veins as I squeezed my crossbow desperately. There were ... more. A *lot* more than before. The noise must have attracted them. Now there were too many for us to fight like this. Not without one or several of us being bitten.

As the hoard of switchbeasts closed in, we grouped together around Isandri. She spread her gleaming wings over us, Phoebe still clinging to her back as she snarled and bared her fangs at the encroaching monsters. Murdoc took a defensive stance on my left. Reigh stood at my back, and Garnett held her axes at the ready on my right. We could make a stand—but it wouldn't last long. We'd be overwhelmed in seconds. We didn't stand a chance.

"How far to the tower?" Reigh shouted.

"A mile and a half, at least!" Garnett called back.

"Good. Thatcher, you and Isa take Phoebe and go! We'll hold them off!" Reigh ordered. "Go!"

Was he freaking kidding? That would never work!

"I'm not leaving you here!" I snarled.

"Listen, you idiot, either you go now, or we all—"

BOOOOM...

A low, concussive sound like the heartbeat of the earth itself made the ground rumble and shake under us. Even after the sound faded, the vibrations still shivered all the way up from my feet to the top of my head. The writhing hoard of switchbeasts all went eerily silent. They froze, their big white eyes blinking and their bodies shifting uneasily.

"Wh-What ... was that?" Reigh gasped hoarsely.

BOOOOM...

A second tremor hit, nearly knocking me off my feet this time. I slammed into

Garnett, faltering on my injured leg. She looped an arm around my waist and held me up, her expression closed and grim as she stared ahead at the hesitating swarm of switchbeasts. Her throat tensed as she swallowed.

There was no denying the look of pure, mortal dread in her eyes as she looked up at me and whispered one, breathless word.

"Underbeast."

CHAPTER TWENTY-ONE

U*nderbeast.*
That word cut through my mind like a blade through warm butter. I stared back at Garnett, waiting for some clue or indication of what to do. Why were we just standing here? Wasn't this our chance to run for it?

BOOOOM ...

Another tremor, louder and more violent than the rest, shook rubble and dust from the ceiling that fell in a clacking shower around us. Murdoc coughed. I had to shield my eyes. Not even fifty yards away, the writhing, twisting hoard of switchbeasts still hesitated. The shuddering of the tunnel shook a few of them off the ceiling, sending them crashing into the ones below. A few of the ones on the walls scurried away, running like startled lizards back down the tunnel they'd come out of.

"It's coming!" Garnett cried, hauling me along as she whirled around to the rest of our group. "Run! Go, go, go!"

Pushing away from her, I hobbled as fast as I could, wincing and cursing with every step. Murdoc tried seizing my other arm and looping it around his shoulders, but I shrugged him off, too. We didn't have time for that. Either I made it or I didn't. I wasn't going to risk slowing anyone else down because of it.

Behind us, a cacophony of dismayed yowling broke through the tunnel. Oh gods, were some of the switchbeasts still willing to chase us? We'd never be able to outrun them like thi—

CRACK—BOOM!!

We all staggered to a halt and scrambled back as another massive tremor dislodged a huge chunk of rock from the ceiling and sent it smashing down in front of us like a small moon. It blocked the way ahead and choked the air with dust.

Then the rock *moved*.

No. Not a rock. This was ... something else. Something enormous.

It rose up, unfurling before us like a colossal god, wreathed in the swirling clouds of dust. A blasting snort like a gust of wind blew the dust clear enough for a massive snout to appear, followed by a head and body covered in thick, leathery hide. Huge jaws snapped with four muscular mandibles, each one lined with jagged teeth as big as my arm. There were no eyes on its flat bony skull, and its hulking body had only two arms as thick around as tree trunks. Each arm had a big, paddle-like paw with thick claws caked with dirt and rock. The ground shook as it crawled forward dragging its long, eel-like lower half behind it.

Garnett stood in front of us, her arms spread out wide with her axes still gripped firmly in her hands. She gaped up at the towering behemoth, but it only lasted a second. She glanced back at us, locking gazes with me ... and then Murdoc. She nodded at him slowly, and something came over her features—a grim sense of resolve I didn't understand—and Garnett stepped forward with her strong shoulders tensed.

A shrill note went up through the cavernous tunnel, echoing off the stone walls like an eerie melody. Was she ... whistling? She was! It was the same sort of method I'd developed to communicate with Fornax.

Garnett made the sound again, stepping closer to the underbeast with her axes still at the ready. Its huge head swung down in her direction, blasts of its breath whipping in her hair and sending all the loose dirt and pebbles around her skittering away.

"That's right, you big beastie," she growled bitterly. "You remember who I am."

The underbeast let out another booming cry that made my brain scramble and my vision spot. Its slithery hind quarters writhed, bashing against the sides of the tunnel as it reared back and opened its jaws. Garnett bolted forward as fast as a flash of lightning, diving into a spin with both of her axes primed for an attack as the creature's giant head descended toward her like it meant to swallow her whole.

Reigh let out a yell and charged in, too.

Murdoc snarled, baring his teeth and flashing me a quick, determined glare. "This is where we part ways. We'll hold it off as long as we can! *GO!*"

What?! No! I wouldn't leave him to be—

"We must hurry!" Isandri yowled. With Phoebe still clinging to her back, she bounded forward and spread her wings, letting out a grunt of effort as she seized the back of my cloak in her teeth and broke for the open air. Our weight slowed her down and made her flight erratic, but she managed to zoom around the monster's bashing head, dodging flying boulders and sprays of rock and rubble. She zipped over the underbeast's shoulder and darted down its back, barely making it to the tunnel beyond before my cloak ripped and I fell.

My arms and legs flailed as I plummeted about eight feet and landed with a *thud* on the tunnel floor. I rolled a few feet, finally stopping flat on my stomach and wheezing for breath.

"Get up! Now! We must make it to the tower before it is too late," Isandri hissed as she landed beside me.

"W-Working ... on ... it," I rasped as I staggered back to my feet and began to shamble along beside her down the dark tunnel ahead. A mile and a half—maybe. We could make it there.

I glanced back over my shoulder, unable to see anything except the massive pitching creature moving like a writhing worm, cracking down more hunks of rock as it bellowed. I couldn't spot any sign of Murdoc or any of the others. I didn't know if they'd make it. Even if they somehow managed to get past the underbeast—what about the switch-beasts? Would they all flee the much larger predator or not?

Tears welled in my eyes as I turned away and continued on, biting down hard against the coppery flavor of rage that burned over my tongue. They *would* make it. They had to. Garnett knew those monsters better than anyone. Murdoc was the strongest person and the best fighter I knew. Reigh never gave up—ever—even when all the odds in the world were stacked against him. He was way too stubborn to die.

They would all make it to the tower, too.

I refused to believe anything else.

This wasn't how it was supposed to go.

Phoebe was meant to go with Murdoc's group in search of the mirror. Reigh was supposed to be with us, looking for Devana. He'd been through those base level tunnels before. He had a much better idea of where to go. Now we had it backwards, and I didn't know what that might mean for our plan. Did Phoebe even know where to take us once we got into the tower? I wanted to ask, but as I jogged on, gritting my teeth against the shooting pain from the wound on my leg, it didn't seem like a priority just yet. First, we had to actually reach the tower. Then we could worry about where to go inside of it.

One crisis at a time, as Murdoc liked to say.

The sounds of combat slowly faded behind us, replaced by our panting breaths and the scuffle of our footsteps over the stone. Sweat made my clothes feel damp and heavy and my bangs stuck to my forehead. My head pounded, and I'd probably cracked a rib or something when I fell from Isandri's grasp. Small problems, though. Well, comparatively, anyway.

Still in her feline form, Isandri didn't seem much better off. Her wings slumped and her feline mouth gaped as she panted. Maybe staying in that form for so long was exhausting to her, as well.

"Isa, please, just put me down. I can run on my own. You need to conserve your strength," Phoebe insisted after we'd been stumbling along for almost an hour. "We must be getting close now, right?"

She was right. It shouldn't take this long to walk a mile and a half, even if the terrain was rough and the tunnel zig-zagged some. We should be getting close. Gods and Fates, without Garnett, we really had no idea where we were going now. What if we passed the entrance and didn't even realize it?

"Let's stop, take another breather for a minute, and think this through," I suggested, stumbling to a halt and doubling over to try and catch my breath.

"There is no time," Isandri objected, snapping her jaws angrily.

"Then we will *make* time," I fired back. Trudging over to the side of the tunnel, I leaned back against it for support as I slowly sank down to the floor to sit. "I need to do something about my leg or I'm not going to be any use running around Northwatch. And Isa, if you need to rest ... you've got to do it right now. We're gonna need all our power once we get inside."

She sent me what I can only describe as a scowl of utter feline disapproval. She slicked her ears back and snorted, looking away and swishing her long tail before she finally came stalking over. She folded her luminescent wings in tight to her sides and crouched down close beside me long enough for Phoebe to slip down from her back.

While Phoebe pulled another torch from our supply bag and lit it, Isandri stomped over and plopped down close by. Her form shimmered, giving off a shower of sterling light as she resumed her elven form, sitting beside me, with her knees drawn up to her chest and her arms wrapped around her legs. Her staff lay on the ground beside her and she glared straight ahead—but it wasn't a pouting or sulky look. The creases in her brow were drawn upward, and her eyes darted quickly back and forth as though in silent desperation.

I guess I wasn't the only one worrying about the rest of our friends. I couldn't imagine what she must be thinking, although I was willing to guess it had a lot to do with a certain redheaded prince. She'd left him behind once before, in a situation sort of like this one, I gathered. He'd stayed behind to fight. She'd gone ahead and escaped.

I wondered if, for her, this was like reliving a nightmare.

"Here, I can take a look at your leg," Phoebe offered. She scooted over close and took out one of the emergency medical kits we'd brought along.

"It was a scratch, not a bite. It just hurts a little," I told her, trying not to wince as she unlaced my boot and rolled up my pantleg to get a better look. "No time for stitches."

"I'll just bandage it tightly, then." Phoebe's lips pressed together, obviously not liking that she couldn't be more thorough in her treatment.

"Phoebe?" I cleared my throat some, already hating that I even had to ask this question. There was no way around it, though. Of the three of us, she was the only one who knew anything about Northwatch. "Do you know what the entrance to the tower looks like from, um, *underground*?"

She winced some, brows crinkling up into a look of distress. "I-I ... no, I never saw it from underground before. I'm sorry. I don't know where we are, or how to get there from here."

Great. Well, that wasn't the news I'd been hoping for.

"What about if we get inside? I know you were supposed to go with Murdoc and the others, but do you think you can take us to the place where Iksoli is holding Devana? Cell doors with those symbols on them?" I tried again. "They were supposedly near the bottom of the tower, right? So, we don't have too far to go once we get inside ... hopefully."

Her head raised slowly to look me in the eye. She drew her bottom lip into her mouth, her gaze distant as though she were thinking hard. "I ... maybe. I went down there a few times. Not for Devana, of course. Lord Argonox had me examine a few other magically gifted people he had captured. He was always wanting us to find ways to extract their abilities or harness them somehow. But it was only twice—once for a man and then ... once for Reigh."

"But it was the same place?" I pressed. "The cell block that Phillip talked about?"

She nodded slowly. "I think so. But I only ever went there from my workshop, not from other places inside the tower. If I found my old workshop, I might be able to navigate there. But it's hard when I'm starting at a different point. Lord Argonox didn't let us have free range. I lived in my workshop almost all the time. Every now and then I got to go down to the manufacturing levels to inspect progress on the machines I'd designed, critique them, and watch tests. Except for the few times I was sent to the cell block to examine Reigh and that other man, I didn't get to go out. And even when I did, there were armed guards chaperoning me."

"So, if we find your old workshop, you can probably find the cell block we need," I surmised aloud.

Phoebe nodded again. "Yes."

"How far up the tower is it?" Isandri asked. "We don't have time to take a long trip out of the way."

Good point.

"Um. Not that far, I don't think. Maybe two or three floors up?" Phoebe guessed, fidgeting nervously as she glanced between us. "The higher levels were reserved for officers, experimentation rooms, and other things I didn't have access to."

"Okay, then. That's our first goal." I looked over at Isandri, who had leaned forward some to rest her chin on her kneecaps. "Now we just have to find that tower entrance, somehow slip inside without anyone noticing, and not get attacked and killed on our way through it."

Uggh. If I was the one trying to come up with plans, we really were in trouble. Maybe if we sat here for a few minutes, caught our breath, and let Isandri rest while Phoebe patched up my leg, the others would catch up to us.

A guy could hope, anyway.

Glancing across the tunnel, I caught another glint of metal sparkling in the light from our torch. More Tibran skeletons dressed in armor, no doubt. There were a lot more of them scattered around now that we were getting closer to the tower. I wondered what would happen to all of the gear and weapons that were just lying around. There must have been hundreds of suits of armor, swords, shields, and all kinds of stuff the Tibrans had left behind.

An idea hit me like someone had slapped me in the face with a dead fish.

Sweet Fates. I knew how we were going to sneak into that tower. I knew how we were going to pass through it unnoticed. It was an awful, truly terrible idea. But I knew it would work—

Because I'd seen it work before … on the night my village burned.

22
CHAPTER TWENTY-TWO

"This is not going to work," Isandri muttered as she buckled the Tibran breastplate on over her robes.

Rummaging through the pile of bones and armor, I tossed her a set of greaves and vambraces, too. "It did last time. Plus, if the people here fighting for Iksoli are really under her mind control, they're probably not going to look too closely. Did you see the ones who ran past us during that switchbeast attack? Most of them were wearing patched-together bits of old Tibran stuff, too."

"He does have a point." Phoebe's voice echoed from under the helmet she'd pulled down over head. It fit her about as well as an empty bucket. Honestly, she was so petite that all of the armor was bound to be hilariously too big for her, but we didn't have a lot of time to be choosy. Hopefully, no one would look at her closely enough to notice.

"Last time? You've disguised yourself this way before?" Isandri arched an eyebrow as she held up the vambraces.

I turned my face away just in case I couldn't keep it together. I didn't want either of them to see any signs of weakness right now. "Yeah." I cleared my throat a little. "Murdoc, he, uh, he had us dress in Tibran armor to escape my village. It worked, mostly."

I could feel Isandri's probing stare without ever having to look her way. "Mostly?" she pressed.

"Well, right up until the tide of the battle turned and the dragonriders arrested us because we looked like Tibrans." I forced a chuckle that seemed to snag in my throat. "Look, I know it's not fool-proof. But it's the best we can do right now."

A warm hand touched mine. "Thatcher." Isandri said quietly. "You don't have to do this. I can go on alone. This was never meant to be your burden. Devana has called out for you, yes. But you are not responsible. Not like I am. You can take Phoebe and be—."

"And be a coward?" My mouth screwed up and I lifted a defiant glare up at her. "I've been running ever since this all started, Isandri. I ran from my home and left my father to die. I ran from Phillip. From the Ulfrangar. From the underbeast. I've stood behind stronger people like Jaevid, Murdoc, Reigh, and even you, letting you all fight my battles for me. I ... I'm not doing it anymore. Iksoli has wanted to get to me from the beginning. I'm going to grant that wish and give her all of my attention she can stand."

Somber understanding shone in the depths of Isa's otherworldly eyes. She seemed to look through me—past my flesh and down into my soul—and sank back onto her heels with a small, relinquishing sigh. "Very well."

"If it helps, in the event that I get killed doing this, you can say you tried to talk me out of it, right?" I forced a half-grin.

She shook her head and turned away, going back to fastening on the old Tibran armor.

No one said much else as we finished strapping on all the bits and pieces we found among the bones. I had to help Phoebe tighten hers up a little, and I found a light short-sword she could easily carry. Now, if no one paid much attention to the fact that she was about the size of a fourteen-year-old, we'd be fine. Honestly, I didn't know how old she actually was, but now wasn't the time to ask her about it.

Striking back out down the tunnel, I held the torch aloft to light the way as we took off as quickly and quietly as we could. Keeping Phoebe between us, Isa prowled along behind us with her staff at the ready, eyes narrowed keenly through the slit in her helmet's visor. I kept a hand on my crossbow, just in case.

We'd been going for less than an hour before more noise echoed down from the passage ahead. I threw up a hand and motioned for everyone to get against the wall. This time, it wasn't screaming or yowling. This sounded like ... conversation. People talking loudly. Shouting commands to one another. Footsteps on the stone and the clunk and clatter of armor.

Isa and I exchanged a look.

Roughly two minutes passed and the noise didn't seem to be getting any closer—more like it was focused in one spot, dead ahead. An outpost? Or a mercenary camp? Or were we at the base of the tower?

Only one way to be sure.

I gave Isa a slow nod, handing off the torch and motioning for her and Phoebe to stay put. Her eyes squinted up in a disapproving glare, so I gave my very best "no seriously, I've got this" look with my eyes widened and made the stay here gesture again.

She took the torch and growled something softly under her breath—probably a curse in her elven language.

I crouched down, moving as carefully and silently as possible with one hand on the wall to keep track of my location as I crept away from the wavering torchlight. As soon as I was back in the pitch black of the tunnel, I spotted it—the faintest glow in the distance. If it weren't so dark, I never would have noticed. Ahead, the passage curved to the right rather sharply, and around that bend there seemed to be some sort of light source. The closer I got, the brighter it was. The voices grew louder, too.

At last, at a point where the ground made a sharp angle upward, I went down on my belly and crawled up the incline. Peering over the edge, I kept myself crammed into the shadows as much as possible as I gaped in awe at the open chamber ahead of me. It must have been a hundred feet across, at least, with a ceiling that spanned upward nearly as high. Four other tunnels met here, all leading off in different directions. But that wasn't what made my breath catch and my toes curl up inside my boots.

The chamber was filled with at least fifty armed men. They were separated out into smaller groups, almost like they were trying to organize themselves into hunting parties or something. Crap—did that mean Iksoli already knew we were here? Or had the commotion with the underbeast just drawn their attention enough to try and hunt the thing down themselves? Either, way it was a big problem—because also in the middle of the chamber was a large rectangular wooden structure like scaffolding that spanned from floor to ceiling. Cables ran down the sides of it on massive ironwork gears, and the top part disappeared into a large shaft cut into the ceiling overhead.

Wait a second ... I'd seen something like this before, hadn't I? Yes! In Eastwatch tower. There had been an elevator made of wood and metal with a broad platform that could be raised and lowered through the entirety of the tower. Jaevid had warned us about it—that being careless around it was a fantastic way to get killed. It was for moving crates and gear, not people, so it wasn't exactly made with safety in mind. But that's exactly what these guys were using this one for.

As the platform appeared from the dark open shaft overhead, slowly descending the wooden framework to the ground, I could make out the shapes of more people wearing hodgepodge assortments of armor standing inside it.

Okay. Well. We'd found the way into the tower, so that was one problem solved. This new issue, however, was going to require a change of plans.

Oh, and an insane amount of luck.

I BEGAN SCOOTING BACK down the incline, finally daring to get on my feet and make a dash back to where Isandri and Phoebe were waiting once I was sure I was out of sight. It took a few seconds of panicked gasping before I was able to explain to them what we were up against. Meanwhile, Phoebe's face went ghostly white and she chewed on her bottom lip, looking like she might faint on the spot as I described everything.

"So they did extend the elevator shaft, after all," she whimpered. "I told them it was dangerous until the tunnels were completed in the surrounding areas. Any tremors or explosions might cause the framework to become compromised. But Argonox didn't like hearing any of my suggestions when it came to the safety of his workers and soldiers. They were all just expendable to him."

"How are we going to get past all those mercenaries?" I asked, looking to Isandri in hopes that she would have an idea.

"I could transform and fly you both up there," Isandri suggested. "If your estimation is correct, it is a long way up, but I can manage it."

"Except everyone will definitely see that," Phoebe pointed out. "They'll be trying to shoot us down. And then the entire tower will know we're there."

Hmm. She was right. Simply storming in there and making a run for it wasn't going to work, even through the air. Isandri was fast, but not when she was loaded down with passengers.

"We look like them now, don't we? Dressed like this, how do we know they wouldn't overlook us entirely if we simply walked in?" Isandri glanced between us, as though expecting someone to object.

Only, I didn't have a good reason right off the top of my head for why that *wouldn't* work. That had been sort of my idea from the start. But it felt a teensy bit riskier now that I knew we would be standing amongst at least fifty-or-so armed fighters under ambient light where one of them might notice that, you know, we were definitely *not* part of their ranks.

Yeah. This felt like one of those moments where Murdoc would have called me an idiot.

"What if ... we don't try to hide it when we enter?" Phoebe said suddenly.

"I'm not sure we could hide it, even if we wanted to," I reminded her.

She waved a hand. "No, no. I mean, what if we try to get their attention on purpose. You said it yourself, we just saw a bunch of switchbeasts hunting down people dressed like us. What if we ran in, screaming and warning them that there's been an attack and there's an underbeast in the tunnel? Draw their attention that way?"

"And if the others are following us farther behind? We might be sending enemies straight into their path," Isandri warned.

Phoebe glanced fretfully back down the way we'd come. "I know. But maybe they can hide just like we did before."

Isandri did not look convinced *at all*.

"I don't like it any more than you do," I muttered as I bent over and began pulling off the bandaging from inside my boot where Phoebe had wrapped up my leg. "But this is the best chance we've got. We have to get to that elevator, and I'm fresh out of ideas."

"If you can get us onto it, I'm sure I can get it to work. The mechanics are fairly basic," Phoebe said, as though hoping to give Isandri a little hope that we weren't completely out of our minds.

I held up the bloody strips of gauze. "Sounds like all we need now is to make some makeup adjustments."

I HAD NEVER IMAGINED that acting in any capacity might be one of my finer skills. I couldn't even recall having ever tried it before now. But as I ran headlong up the incline again, screaming my head off while dressed in Tibran armor smeared with my own blood, and sporting an extremely authentic and convincing leg wound from a switchbeast, I realized I might actually pull this off. If being a dragonrider didn't work out, maybe I could give stage performances a try.

I reached the top of the tunnel's incline, stopping with Phoebe and Isandri right behind me, and yelled, "THE UNDERBEAST IS IN THE TUNNEL!"

Every single swordsman, cutthroat, and mercenary assembling in that chamber stopped dead in their tracks and stared at me in stunned silence.

I took that opportunity to limp dramatically forward and stumble, collapsing into a heap. Isa and Phoebe rushed forward to catch me, hauling me back up and looping my arms around their shoulders to begin dragging me away toward the elevator.

That's when they all began to converge upon us—drawing blades, nocking arrows into bowstrings, raising shields, and storming straight in our direction.

I braced. On both sides of me, Isa and Phoebe stiffened and squeezed harder at my arms. I held my breath.

The armored mob ran past us, clambering down the passageway and off into the tunnel beyond. Nearly half the chamber emptied out, and as we staggered for the elevator, no one tried to stop us. I added in a few groans and wails—just to really sell it. Phoebe and Isandri laid me down slowly on the platform and motioned to the guy operating the crank system to begin lifting us up.

I dared to let out a shaky exhale.

So far, so good. But we weren't clear, yet. There was still a lot of ground to cover between us and Phoebe's workshop.

As soon as I was sure we were high enough up that no one on the ground might see, I sat up and got busy wiping as much of the blood off my armor as I could. Isandri crouched down next to me, eyeing the rickety elevator distrustfully. Not that I blamed her in the slightest. The way the thing lurched and rattled, chains groaning and clanking loudly as we slowly climbed higher and higher toward the open dark chasm above, didn't inspire much confidence.

"This should take us to the base subterranean floor of the tower," Phoebe whispered, her voice trembling. "Th-There, um, there were some cells down there. But they were mostly for high-profile prisoners, not the magically-gifted ones, I think." She pinched her eyes shut and took a few deep, shaking breaths. "I-I'm trying to remember, I'm sorry."

"How do we get to your workshop from there?" I asked, reaching out to grasp one of her hands to give it a reassuring squeeze. "You can do this, Phoebe. Just try to remember."

"I-I ... well, there was a window in my workshop. A small one. I needed some ventilation for some of the things I had to work on. I could see out. It was a long way to the top from there—I-I only went up a few times. I think my workshop was ... on the second floor." She opened her eyes again and stared at me, anguish drawing her features tense. "I'm sorry, I just keep thinking about Murdoc and the others. Gods, what if we sent all those mercenaries straight at them? What if they were injured and ... and we just got them killed!"

I gave her hand another firm squeeze. "Phoebe, if there's one thing I know for sure, it's that no one is better at killing things than Murdoc. I once saw him kill a man with one punch. Literally—it was one hit to the face that broke the guy's jaw and I guess gave him brain damage or something. It was horrible, but at the time it also sort of kept us from being beaten to a pulp in a prison camp. Anyway, my point is, injured or not, I don't think the people who just ran down there can take him down. And he's got Garnett and Reigh with him. They're going to make it."

She stared at me through the visor of her helmet with her big blue eyes rimmed with tears. Bobbing her head a little, she sniffled and lifted it long enough to wipe her eyes on her sleeve. "O-Okay. You're right. He's ... stronger than anyone else I know."

"Yeah, he is." I looked back to Isandri, who was staring up at the slowly encroaching dark hole as our platform ascended into it. "Now, what do we do when we get to the subterranean floor?"

"There should be a staircase leading upward. It's part of the original tower," Phoebe explained.

"Yes," Isandri growled low. "I am familiar with it."

I blinked in surprise. "You are?"

"I was held there for a time. That is where I first met Reigh. Our area of cells were different. The doors did not have runes or marks upon them. They were secluded, and there were no guard patrols watching us. I think it was where they sent the prisoners they either intended to execute ... or allow to die slowly of their injuries or neglect. I was relocated there after Argonox concluded that my powers would not be useful to him, and my will could not be broken to his will. I was blindfolded for my transport, however. I don't remember how to navigate those halls."

"We won't have to," Phoebe assured us. "We just need to get to the stairs, and that shouldn't be so hard to find. We go up and start searching at the second floor. I'll know right away if it's the one where my workshop was."

Getting to my feet, I pulled my crossbow from its resting place, belted at my hip, and held it at the ready. "Good. Let's do this as fast as we can. In and out."

"And when we encounter Iksoli?" Isa flicked me a wary look.

I spun the cartridge on my crossbow, making sure it was already primed with a bolt ready to fire. "Then we give her the reunion she's been waiting for, and a whole lot more."

PART FOUR
MURDOC

23
CHAPTER TWENTY-THREE

I'd imagined my death a thousand times. Being caught in the dark at the end of an Ulfrangar blade. Being beheaded in a city square by an executioner's axe. Being shot full of arrows by a city guard. Being incinerated by a dragonrider's flame. And more recently, being cut down in a duel against the Zuer.

But I had never imagined it might go like this—miles underground in a Tibran tunnel, overrun with switchbeasts crawling the walls like cockroaches, and ducking the body slams and the snapping maw of an underbeast.

Never let it be said that the Fates aren't creative with their destinies.

I kicked into a side roll, ducking another sweep of the underbeast's lashing tail. The thing crawled along like a salamander missing its hind legs, bellowing and threatening to shake the entire tunnel down on top of us. Boulders the size of buildings broke loose from the ceiling and smashed down into the crawling onslaught of switchbeasts. Most of them had fled in the presence of this monster, but the few that remained made lunging strikes at us whenever they got the chance.

I dipped and dodged, weaving around the hailstorm of flying debris, snapping switchbeast jaws, and the thundering crash of the underbeast slamming its head into the ground. It made wild snaps at Reigh, Garnett, and anything else that got too close. Without eyes, I could only guess it oriented by sound or maybe smell, although the latter seemed less likely for a creature that lived underground.

A squeal and crunch made me look back, just in time to watch a switchbeast that had come too close disappear down the monster's throat, crushed in those four mandible jaws.

My pulse raced, and I made another driving strike with my swords, scrambling through the underbeast's tree-trunk-sized stomping legs. I cursed, feeling the steel of my weapons glance off the monster's thick, leathery hide. Gods and Fates, it must have had skin five inches thick. I couldn't get through to pierce anything vital. And by the look of things, Reigh and Garnett weren't having much luck, either.

Garnett screamed dwarven curses as she hurled one of her axes, sending the weapon howling through the air and catching the underbeast in the soft meat of its throat. It sliced through the thick hide, but not deep enough to even make the monster bleed. Curse it.

I set my jaw and tried again, angling my blades in a frantic downward thrust with all my strength against the beast's hide. My strike stuck in less than an inch before the blade slid askew and sent me floundering backward. Mashed against the stone, I cringed as the underbeast slammed into the tunnel wall, barely missing me with its massive leg. Curse it all to the abyss! Nothing made a spit's worth of difference! Was there any way to kill this thing before it caused a cave in or smashed us all to jelly?

"Murdoc!" Reigh shouted suddenly.

I spun to see him standing atop a fallen switchbeast, his elven kafki blades still jabbed deep into its back. He glared past me at the underbeast, blood dribbling from what I sincerely hoped was a claw-swipe and not a bite mark across his forehead.

"Ever heard tales of my sister fighting in the Tibran War?" He growled as he prowled closer, his chest heaving with panting breaths.

I arched a brow. Now really wasn't the time for—

He spun his blades over his hands once, giving them a testing flourish before he flicked me a meaningful look. "I'm gonna give it the bitter bite. Cover me."

The bitter—oh gods, no.

"Reigh!" I shouted after him. That idiot! Was he completely insane? Did he *want* to die?

He took off toward the monster at a sprint, spinning and weaving through its roiling fit, until he came to a skidding halt right in front of it. The underbeast's massive head cranked around, nostrils flaring and four jaw-arms opening wide. Reigh dropped down into a crouch, curling his body into a ball with his arms and legs tucked in tight.

I ran for him. No way would I let him try this. There was stupid, and then there was—

My body flew backward through the air, tossed end over end as the underbeast's head slammed down into the ground before me. I hit the ground yards away, my blades knocked from my grasp. Flat on my back, I wheezed and groaned. My vision swerved and tunneled, spots like fairy lights dancing before my eyes as I tried to move. My head lolled as I dragged myself to my hands and knees, looking up just in time to see the underbeast gulp down the idiot prince whole.

"REIGH!" I shouted, my voice broken and hoarse.

Nearby, Garnett's face went white with terror. She'd seen it, too.

A thousand thoughts took my mind like a winter storm. Gods, how would we tell Jenna? Could we even recover his body? Or were we all about to meet a similar fate?

The underbeast rose up, rearing back with its jaws snapping with another shattering cry. Its mighty claws raked trenches in the earth, crushing more switchbeasts underfoot. It floundered like a beached fish, suddenly pitching into a mad frenzy. What the—?

BOOOOM!

A thrash of its body sent a shower of rocks and earth plummeting from the ceiling directly before it. Garnett dove toward me, and I surged forward to catch her hand and drag her out of the way as the passage caved in. I yanked her behind me, trying to shield her with my body as rubble showered over us. The beast bellowed, rattling the earth and slamming its head back and forth between the sides of the tunnel.

BAM—BAM—BAM!

Gods, what was it doing?

With another deafening bellow, the monster threw its head back as a gurgling spray of something black spewed from its mouth. Its mandibles opened wide as its body jerked erratically. I tucked my head down and shut my eyes tightly, curling as closely as I could against Garnett, as it suddenly pitched forward and hit the ground with bone-rattling force. One of its passive paws crashed into the stone wall right next to us, missing us by only a foot or two.

Then silence.

A second past, and I couldn't hear anything except the hiss and rattle of bits of rock and dirt still showering down from the ceiling. No angry roars. No thrashing. No shrieks of switchbeasts. Just my own heartbeat still pounding like a war drum in my ears.

I slowly lifted my head and squinted back over my shoulder. There, amidst the debris and curling plumes of dust, the underbeast lay on its side ... motionless. Its jaws were splayed open, a long prickly tongue lolled out amidst rivers of that black stuff. Its blood?

Pulling away from the wall, I dared to face it. I didn't have my weapons—they were lying somewhere in the chaos—so I bent down to slide the dagger free from where I always kept it tucked in the side of my boot. Prowling forward, one cautious, slow step at a time, I watched the creature for any signs of stirring. Its sides didn't heave with any breaths. Its hide didn't so much as twitch.

Was it ... dead?

I scrambled back, nearly tripping over my own feet as a sudden spray of that black blood spewed from the underbeast's neck with a sickly, slapping burble. Its throat split open like an orange peel as something sharp poked through from the inside. I gripped my dagger harder, ready to fling it at a moment's notice.

Prince Reigh Farrow crawled out of the underbeast's throat, soaked with black blood, and gasping for breath like a newborn calf. He wrenched himself free, still gripping his blades in his fists.

Holy. Gods.

"Reigh!" Garnett shrieked. She bounded past me and seized him by the elbow, helping him squirm the rest of the way out of the monster's corpse. "Are you all right?"

Reigh sat, a dripping, slimy mess, and panted for a few seconds with a look of catatonic shock on his face like he couldn't believe he'd survived. That made three of us, I guess.

Finally, he let go of his weapons just so he could try wiping some of the bloody slop away from his eyes. "That ... was ... so much ... worse ... than Jenna ... made it sound," he coughed and spat out mouthfuls of the blood. "Have I mentioned ... I really *hate* ... Northwatch?"

Garnett doubled over, catching her weight with her hands on her knees as she laughed. "Stones, man! Who does something like that? You are one reckless fool, Reigh Farrow."

He flopped back onto the ground with a sticky slapping sound and lay there, arms and legs sprawled wide, and slowly shook his head. "You ... have no idea."

"Maybe they'll stop and wait for us farther down the tunnel?" Garnett suggested as we all sat, staring across the now barricaded exit behind us. Not that we'd planned on making a retreat that way when all this was done, but now it wasn't even an option.

"I doubt it. They were running with the fear that either the underbeast or some of the switchbeasts might be right on their heels. I doubt they would stop unless they had no other choice," Reigh said, still trying to wipe the monster's blood from his face and hands.

Rummaging through the debris, I unearthed my longswords from where they'd been knocked from my grasp. One of them had been pinned under a good-sized rock and was now bent enough it wouldn't slide into the sheath on my back again. Ugh. Useless. I tossed it down and put the other one away. Fortunately, that one was only slightly dinged, so at least I wasn't empty-handed now.

"Is the entrance to the tower something they'll be able to find on their own?" I asked as I turned to rejoin them.

Garnett grunted, her foot planted on the underbeast's neck for leverage as she wrenched her second axe free of its leather hide. "Probably," she huffed as she tugged. "It's not like there are signs with big arrows pointing the way. But five tunnels converge there in a fairly large chamber. I'm sure that ought to tip them off."

"We can only hope," I muttered.

"Regardless, we now have a problem. They're traveling with Phoebe. She knows the tower better than I do, probably. Maybe she can get them to the cell block where Devana is—which is good news for them. The bad news is, I don't have a clue where the Mirror of Truth would be held in that place." Reigh grunted as he stood, combing some of his now slimy hair away from his face. "I've seen the mirror once, but it was in an underground chamber or something. Hilleddi was using it to interrogate people."

Garnett nodded like that made sense. "Argonox didn't like to move his more precious captured artifacts out in the open. He moved them underground, where they were less likely to be stolen or damaged if there was an attack."

"Any chance it might still be down here somewhere?" Reigh guessed, his tone hopeful.

She sighed as she clipped her axes back into place on her belt. "I doubt it. On the eve of the battle at Halfax, Arognox wanted everything locked down inside the tower and secured—artifacts, valuable prisoners, and people he considered especially useful assets like me. I guess he knew the tunnels could be collapsed or infiltrated, but the Maldobarian architects who designed the watches built them with the intention that they would be difficult to siege."

"And you have no idea where he would've wanted these artifacts secured inside the tower, then?" I pressed. "Think, Garnett. Because the only other choice we have is searching the tower from top to bottom on foot, which will take more time than we have. I'm not sure how your boss deals with not receiving payments he wants, but I'm willing to bet it's unpleasant."

Her mouth mashed up sourly and she crossed her arms, beginning to pace back and forth. "I'm thinking, I'm thinking. Just give me a moment, will you?"

"Think while you walk. Or better yet, run. We've got to try to catch up to them if we can," Reigh urged.

I had to agree. If there was any chance at all of catching up to them and swapping back to our original groups, we had to seize it while we could. Unless Garnett had a sudden stroke of genius about how we could find the mirror in this rat's nest of a city, we were going to be kicking in doors up and down that tower until we found the right one. Not ideal.

Pulling another torch from our supplies—one of the only two I had left—I took a second to light it before we all took off at a jog. Garnett led while Reigh and I matched pace behind her, keeping our eyes and ears attuned as best we could for the approach of anything else that might want to eat, bite, or kill us. Not an easy task, considering the way Reigh's blood-drenched boots sloshed with every step. There was nothing stealthy about our approach whatsoever.

And suddenly, that didn't matter.

Light appeared ahead of us down the tunnel, coming closer—fast. The sound of footsteps echoed over the walls, along with a ruckus of angry shouts and the metallic clanking of armor.

Oh no. What now?

Reigh growled an elven curse and motioned for us to hide. Only, where the heck were we supposed to hide? Looking around, there weren't any convenient crevices or piles of Tibran rubble. No boulders or shards of old war machines.

I spun back to face him. "There's nowhere to—"

Reigh was gone.

I looked around for Garnett.

She'd vanished, too.

What the—?

My pulse roared in my ears as I whirled in a circle, searching every dark shadow. But there was no sign of them. How …? Where …?

I opened my mouth to call out for them, but something clamped down around my face, gagging me before I could make a sound. I dropped my torch as two large, hairy legs tipped in shiny black claws snatched me up and spun me like a sausage on a spit, wrapping my middle with something stringy and sticky as I wrenched and fought. I couldn't even yell out as I was yanked upward to the ceiling of the tunnel and held there.

Looking to my left, I finally spotted Reigh and Garnett. They'd been bound up just like I was, their mouths gagged and arms pinned with what looked like … was that spider silk?

My head snapped to the other side, looking to my right as something enormous, black, and covered in glossy hairs clung to the ceiling right next to me on eight long legs. The biggest spider I had ever seen stared directly at me like something straight out of a nightmare. Fates, it must have been the size of a horse. It peered at me with two big, dinner-plate-sized yellow eyeballs facing front, and numerous ones along the side. They blinked in a sort of rippling pattern, seeming to consider me curiously.

Then the massive spider took one of its legs and held it over its mouth.

Wait a second—was it gesturing for me to be quiet?

No. Not possible. I was imagining things. I had to be. There were no spiders this size in Maldobar. Not that the Ulfrangar had ever told me about. I hadn't heard anything about Argonox bringing giant spiders along with his forces, either.

Even if he had, and one had taken up residence down here in these tunnels ... as far as I knew, spiders of any size did not *shush* people.

My gaze snapped back downward as light bloomed through the tunnel, growing brighter and closer as the voices became louder. A mob of mercenaries roughly twenty or thirty men strong stormed by, their weapons already primed and as they called to one another, barking orders for forming ranks. They stormed past right below us, but never looked up in our direction.

Dread poured through my body, leaving me breathless and limp as I hung, suspended by the spider's silk. Had those mercenaries already found Thatcher and the others? Had they killed them and now they were coming for the rest of us? Or taken them prisoner? Gods, what if Iksoli already had them? What would happen to them? Would she torture them?

I shut my eyes tightly, fury like molten metal surging through me at the thought. No. I wouldn't accept any of that. Not until I'd seen their bodies myself. They were still alive. They were somewhere ahead of us. They were fine.

They had to be.

CHAPTER TWENTY-FOUR

"Lukani! You put us down this instant!" Garnett's voice hissed angrily. Somehow, she'd managed to work that spider silk gag out of her mouth. She glared at the creature, her violet eyes practically glowing with wrath. "I mean it! What are you even doing here?"

The spider made a sound sort of like a sad puppy's whimper, coiling back and rubbing two of its front legs together sheepishly.

"Don't you dare make that face at me," Garnett growled. "Put us down right now. Arlan is going to be ready to spit fire when he finds out you've snuck off again. Honestly, who do you think he'll blame for this?"

The spider went on making sad, squeaky sounds as it slowly lowered us to the tunnel floor one by one. I stared in complete awe as the creature scurried down the wall and stepped onto the ground before me, changing shape mid-stride. Its outline wavered, rippling and warping like a reflection through curved glass, until it took the shape of a young boy. Or, rather, he appeared young. Maybe twelve or thirteen at most, with a lithe build and boyish face. But since his features weren't of any race I could name or remember from all my Ulfrangar training, I didn't dare assume.

His skin was a strange, emerald green hue, and his large ears sloped to sharp, knife-like points. Similar to an elf's, but much more ... exaggerated. He wiggled them like a fox as he crept closer to me on bare feet, dressed in nothing but a pair of dark purple silk breeches and a broad, woven leather belt. He pulled a curved dagger and bent over me, studying me with bizarre yellow eyes and feline-like vertical pupils.

I drew back on instinct, panting through my nose as my gaze flicked between him and the blade.

He smiled broadly, tilting his head to one side and tossing some of his long black hair away from his face in the process. "It's okay. I won't hurt you, human," he announced, his accent strong and a little similar to others I'd heard from Damaria. He spun the blade through his fingers with an effortless speed I had to admire. Then he cut down the front of the spider silk that still held my arms in place before quickly bounding over to do the same to Reigh and Garnett.

"What are you?" I demanded as soon as I could pull the sticky, silken gag out of my mouth.

Lukani flicked a long, lion-like tail tipped in a tuft of black fur that emerged from a slit cut in the back of his pants. He opened his mouth, a haughty grin already curling over his childlike face, but Garnett cut him off.

"He's a menace, that's what he is," she grumbled as she snatched the silk away from her arms. "Wildshapers is what people call them outside of Damaria. But in their homeland, they're called Rajinna. They seldom ever leave their cave-cities, let alone make it all the way to other kingdoms. But Arlan stumbled across Lukani being trafficked by slavers. We've been trying to get safe passage back to Damaria, and the location of a Rajinna tribe to take him in, but it's not been easy now that the Tibrans have stirred everything up in a nasty way."

Reigh frowned at the boy ... or whatever he was. "How did you get down here?"

"Oh! That wasn't so hard. I just had to blend in a little," Lukani rocked back on his heels, swishing his tail while he spun his dagger around his hand a few more times. His form wavered again, rippling and warping into the shape of a switchbeast. He gave a convincing hiss that sent Reigh scrambling backward and ripping one of his kafki blades out.

"You stop that," Garnett scolded as she picked more spider webbing out of her hair. "Scaring folk with your clever shapes. It's just rude."

"He can shapeshift like Isandri?" I asked, studying his new form for any clue that he wasn't authentically a switchbeast. There wasn't any—not that I could see. Impressive.

"No, not exactly," Garnett sighed. "Isandri can take one alternate form because of her godling powers. Lukani, and every other Rajinna, can change into an animal they've seen before. Some especially clever ones can also change into people, but only ones they've already seen. It's a good trick, but it's gotten them into a lot of trouble in their time. That's why Arlan says their tribes have become so reclusive and wary of outsiders —they fear being abused for their power."

Lukani's image flickered again, blurring back into his green-skinned, somewhat elven-looking form. He sat in a squat, lips pursed unhappily as he crossed his arms. "Are you going to send me back?"

"Now, I can't very well do that, can I? The tunnel's caved in so there's no going back that way." Garnett put her hands on her hips and stared him down like an angry mother hen. "You've got to stick with us. If anything happens to you, Arlan will have my head on a pike. Stones, and after all the trouble he's gone to finding you a way back to Damaria. Why would you want to follow me down into this pit?"

"You said you were going to the tunnels," the boy sulked, looking down. "I wanted to see them. Besides, you would've gotten seen if I didn't come, right? I saved you from those people!"

Garnett threw her hands up and rolled her eyes, muttering angrily in dwarven as she stomped off down the tunnel.

Right. Well, I guess that meant we were dragging this kid along with us. Fantastic.

Snatching up my torch again, I started after her. Reigh wasn't far behind.

Aaand neither was Lukani. He bounded ahead, fast as a cat on his bare feet, and swishing his long, lion-like tail, grinning proudly to himself the whole way. I tried not to reflect too deeply on the fact that we'd just been forced to babysit, as well. At least his shapeshifting ability might come in handy, and he seemed fairly competent with that dagger.

We pressed on, taking up a faster pace as we trekked the tunnel toward the tower. After only a few minutes, Reigh gave a whistle to call our attention over to one side of the tunnel. We'd been passing more and more Tibran ruins, long forgotten down here in the dark. The remains of soldiers, their skeletons still dressed in armor and gripping weapons or clinging to the rotting remains of war machines. Not unexpected, but a harrowing reminder of where we were headed, nonetheless.

Off to the left, Reigh crouched down over a pile of gray bones clustered together. I held the torch higher, trying to get a better look on my way over. Then he held up a very familiar breastplate. I stopped dead in my tracks. That was ... Thatcher's.

My pulse raced for a moment, sending a fresh wave of panic through my body. My thoughts raced, trying to make sense of it.

Then Reigh held up other pieces of his armor. And the Tibran bones, they weren't lying neatly in their skeletal arrangements anymore—as though they'd been disturbed. Many of them were missing pieces of armor. Three helmets. Three breastplates, sets of greaves, vambraces, and belts.

It clicked in my mind and sent a smirk curling across my face. Aaah. So *that's* what he'd done.

"Why would Thatcher take off his armor? Or do you think those mercenaries took him and stripped him of it?" Reigh guessed as he stood again.

"No," I corrected. "He changed. He and the others have dressed themselves in Tibran armor to try and blend in."

"Clever," Garnett said approvingly. "They might be able to sneak their way in."

I wasn't ready to start jumping to that conclusion just yet. After all, this was Thatcher we were talking about. Sneaking into anything was not his strong suit. "Maybe. It'll help. But we'll have to see. Something sent those fighters our way—tipped them off to our presence. We need to assume they know we're here and move with caution."

"Agreed." Reigh stepped back and rubbed the back of his neck. "Fates, I still don't know how we can even find the mirror. That tower's going to be a hive of terrible things that all want to gut us alive."

Garnett raised a finger. "Actually, I've been thinking on that. I might have an idea. Granted, it's not a great one. But it's worth a shot, I think."

I made a sweeping motion with my hand. "By all means."

"When Argonox began restructuring portions of the tower, turning the former soldier bunk rooms into prison cells and the like, he had blueprints made for the builders. Diagrams of what he wanted in the new constructions inside. If we can find those, we can narrow our search."

"Makes sense," Reigh murmured, his demeanor becoming grim and focused as he stared at the armor scattered on the ground before us. "I don't remember a lot from when I was in there. I was ... in and out of consciousness most of the time. But on the eve of the last battle for Halfax, I know Argonox was doling out orders to lock down the tower, like Garnett said. The vaults are going to be our best bet."

"You're sure about that?" I pressed, not entirely convinced. I knew a little about the state he'd been in during that battle—the kinds of torture the Tibrans subjected their captured enemies to. He was probably in agony and drugged out of his mind.

Reigh fixed me with a harrowing glare like the soul had been sucked straight out of him and left nothing behind but hate and venom. "Yeah. I'm sure."

Hmm. Good enough for me, then. "All right. So, we find these blueprints. Then we find whatever vault Argonox might have wanted his divine artifacts placed in."

"Finding the blueprints should be easy enough. Argonox didn't trust anyone, not even his own people. He kept all sensitive information under lock and key, where no one could have access to it without his supervision. I'd bet my life they'll be in his old office," Garnett pointed straight up. "At the top of the tower."

"Well, this is going to complicate things," Reigh grumbled softly as we crouched at the edge of a steep incline in the tunnel path.

Peeking over the edge, the chamber ahead of us was slightly less populated now, probably, thanks to that group that had gone storming down the passage earlier. But there was still a gathering of twenty or thirty armed men between us and the freight elevator that led from the tunnels up into the tower itself. Not to mention, based on what I could see from this distance, it didn't look like the elevator was even down here now. They must have raised it up. That presented its own problem, since we didn't exactly have time to sit around waiting for them to decide to lower it again. Maybe they never would. What then? We had to get up into that tower soon.

"We can take them. There's not that many." Garnett wiggled with excitement where she lay next to me, her purple eyes sparkling.

She was probably right about that. But fighting them would draw attention—specifically, Iksoli's attention. We needed to move in shadow and silence for as long as possible. Once she knew we were here, I had no doubt she'd dedicate every sorry soul in this place to killing us. Not ideal.

On the other hand, the right kind of distraction might be just what we needed.

"What's at the top of that elevator shaft?" I asked, looking to Garnett. "Do you know?"

Her mouth mashed into a thoughtful line. "It goes to the base level of the tower. It's still underground, but it was part of the original structure. A dungeon, I suppose. Or something like it. I went up there a few times, and best I can remember, the room is, mmm, probably less than half the size of this one. Circular with some halls leading off of it, but I never went down those. The central staircase that spans the length of the tower ends there, as well."

"She's right," Reigh answered darkly. "The elevator goes up the full height of the tower, too. Just like it did at Eastwatch. In fact, the dungeon where they had you imprisoned there isn't unlike the room that tunnel opens up into. The watch towers are all designed basically the same way."

Perfect.

"How long can that kid hold one of his shapeshifting forms?" I whispered.

Lukani popped up between us like a daisy, beaming proudly as he whispered back, "Depends on the size. Bigger ones are harder. I can't hold those shapes for more than a few minutes. Small ones are easy, though. I can stay that way for almost a full day now."

I ignored the seething look of absolute rage Garnett was giving me from behind him as I asked, "What about a dragon?"

Lukani's eyes went wide, practically sparkling with enthusiasm as his mouth made an O-shape like he hadn't thought about that before.

"Absolutely not—are you mad? You can't send him in there! He'll be shot full of arrows in seconds!" Garnett fussed like an angry squirrel.

"Which would be a problem for most things, but not a dragon. Regular arrows won't pierce their hide. Crossbows might, but only at close range. He won't need to get that close," I reasoned.

Her eyes narrowed suspiciously. "That close for what?"

"To fly us up that elevator shaft ... and light this place up with dragon fire on the way so no one follows."

Garnett's mouth fell open.

It wasn't the most discreet approach, true. But we were running out of options in that respect. As long as we were going to send up an alarm through Northwatch of our arrival, we might as well make sure we closed this area off so we weren't dealing with more of Iksoli's fighters pouring out of here like ants from an anthill.

Dragon fire was, essentially, the best way to be sure of that.

"Oh, please, Auntie G. Oh, please, oh please, oh please," the boy whirled to face Garnett, his long, pointed ears drooping as he begged. "I've never gotten to do a dragon shape before!"

Garnett cast me another smoldering, withering glare. Hmm. I might have to watch my back for a little while, until she cooled off. Otherwise, she might try planting an axe in it when I wasn't paying attention.

"Fine," she snapped sharply. "But if something happens to him and he's injured, you'd better believe I'll be telling Arlan it was *your* fault."

I smirked and panned my gaze back across the chamber before us. "Fair enough."

CHAPTER TWENTY-FIVE

We took the room in a flurry of shining golden scales and blistering flames. Clinging to the back of Lukani's dragon form, we tore through the air and headed straight for the elevator shaft. Men scrambled beneath us, screaming in panic and running for cover as he bathed the ground with sprays of burning venom. Arrows zipped past us, humming through the air and glancing off his scales. Flat against his back, I wasn't sure if anyone on the ground would even look closely enough to see us. Hopefully, they'd been a little too worried about burning to death to notice.

Flaring his wings wide, Lukani landed on the scaffolding like a bat on the wall of a cave. The wooden framework creaked and cracked, beginning to list dangerously to one side. I clenched my teeth, gripping the scales and horns of his back as his body flexed and moved, beginning the awkward climb upward. Below us, the scaffolding broke away and shattered, wooden beams falling like tree trunks to smash on the stone floor far below. Flames roared high and choked the air with smoke and heat.

Reigh snarled a curse as Lukani floundered to one side, barely managing to hang on as we climbed up to the opening of the elevator shaft above. It wasn't much more than a hole cut into the stone overhead, but it was our only way out of this hell pit and into the tower.

As Lukani's clawed front legs struck solid stone, finding purchase and sparking over the dark rock, the rest of the wooden framework cracked and broke away below, landing with a *SMASH* and shower of sparks. No one would be following us now. Not this way.

"This was a bad idea!" Reigh shouted over the chaos, keeping his own white knuckled grip on the dragon's hide as we slowly ascended.

Lukani crawled through the vertical elevator tunnel, his wings tucked in tight and his jaws still dripping with burning venom that lit the path ahead. Chancing a look up, I could spot the round hole where the passage opened up overhead. It wasn't far. Maybe a hundred more yards. We would make it.

Bursting out of the passage like a demon crawling up from the abyss, a volley of arrows pinged and clattered off Lukani's scales again as he hauled himself out of that hole. He roared and threw his head back, plated chest heaving in a deep breath before he sent out another blistering spray of acrid, burning venom around the much smaller stone chamber.

Men screamed as flames filled the tighter space, catching most of them in the initial blast. We'd barely managed to scramble off Lukani's back when his form wavered and he shrank back down to his normal, childlike size. He wobbled on the edge of the open pit, arms flailing and barely managing a small yelp of alarm before I lunged and seized one of his arms to drag him back onto solid ground.

"Make for the stairs!" Garnett shouted, already sprinting for a passage to the right.

There wasn't time to question it. We were now fully relying on hers and Reigh's ability to navigate this place. That didn't inspire a lot of confidence, and I silently wished I'd been paying more attention to the layout of Eastwatch tower when we'd been there. At the time, I'd had other things on my mind.

With Garnett in the lead, we dashed for the stairwell and charged headlong up it, taking the steps two and three at a time. But after about ten floors, we began to lose steam. Especially Garnett, who thanks to her dwarven ancestry, was at a slight disadvantage when it came to leg and step length. We'd already been sprinting for hours now. Sooner or later, we were all going to reach our limit.

Garnett slowed and finally came to a stop, resting her weight against the wall as she struggled for breath.

We didn't get to stand around wheezing for long, though. Reigh and I had barely jogged to a halt behind Lukani, when the door at the next landing burst open ahead of us with a *BANG!*

More men dressed in patched together pieces of armor stormed out into the stairwell. They stumbled some, seeming shocked to see us. Then they raised their blades and charged.

I didn't hesitate for a second. Drawing my only remaining longsword, I surged over the distance to meet them halfway. My lips drew back into a snarl as I spun through a sequence of assaults, cutting through the first two before I locked blades with a third.

It took Reigh a few seconds longer to react. Typical. But he appeared at my side with his twin, scythe-like blades whirling. Garnett stormed in last, yelling as she hurled one of her axes ahead of her. It hummed as it spun end over end, lodging dead center in one of the fighters and dropping him like a tree immediately.

A hauntingly familiar, piercing shriek sent a shiver of primal terror up my spine. I hesitated and looked back—just in time to see a switchbeast bound over my head and pounce onto another one of our enemies, bearing him to the ground with its fangs already clamped onto his neck.

The sound of a switchbeast's cry sent several of the swordsmen fleeing back the way they'd come, and I could have sworn I saw Lukani's toothy, feline mouth grinning as he sprang after them.

Okay. Garnett could fuss all she wanted about having him here, but that kid had been more useful in the last ten minutes than anyone I'd ever met. As far as I was concerned, he could follow us around for as long as he wanted.

We cut through the ten or so swordsmen like harvesters reaping wheat, leaving nothing but broken bodies behind. Garnett gave a shrill whistle to call Lukani back, and he loped along behind us in his yellow-eyed switchbeast form with his massive, six-legged body easily scaling the stairs. Four more floors. Then six. Sweat soaked through my tunic and ran down my face, drenching me completely as we forged ahead. I hadn't asked how tall the tower was in all, but after a while I lost count of what floor we were on anyway.

More fighters appeared, bursting through doorways along the stairwell and storming for us. Most of them took one look at us, blood spattered and yelling in fury with a switchbeast behind us, and immediately ran screaming in the opposite direction. The ones who didn't and held their ground, didn't last long. We were going to make it. The odds were in our favor now. We had the momentum. We had the advantage. We could do this.

We ran until my feet went numb, winding around the tower as the stairs seemed to spiral up and up for an eternity. It was a blur of mad running, desperate fighting, and the constant slow burn of rage in my blood.

Glimpsing an occasional barred window, I caught hints of daylight outside. This was it, the day of Queen Jenna's attempt to retake the city. At sundown, this place would be nothing but flames and carnage.

Faster—we had to go faster. We had to get this done.

"There!" Reigh shouted suddenly.

Up the stairs ahead of us, a larger landing led to an open, arched doorway. Or, at least, it had been open. An iron-gated door now blocked it, appearing to have been bolted into place as a security measure after the Tibrans had taken occupation of the tower. Beyond it, the dim hallway looked abandoned. I guess if this door had been shut and locked since the war, no one had been able to get inside. A good thing for us. It meant the rooms beyond wouldn't have been looted or ransacked already by the thieves and cutthroats living here.

"Great." Reigh growled as he seized the iron bars in his hands and shook them. The door rattled some, but held firm. "What now? If Argonox was using the former Colonel's office here for his own, it's at the end of this hall."

"Stand aside, Your Highness. Let me show you how it's done." Garnett muscled her way to the front of our group and put her hands on two of the bars. Widening her stance, she clenched her jaw and her gaze went steely with focus. Her sturdy shoulders flexed, hard muscles going solid on her arms as she let out a low, grunting exhale. The metal groaned under her hands, creaking and slowly bowing outward as she pulled the two bars apart like she was parting a curtain. She pulled them far enough apart that we'd easily be able to slip through now.

Sweet Fates. Maybe I didn't want her putting axes in my back, after all.

Standing back, she dusted her hands off and gave a little bow. "Princes first."

Reigh snorted. "You're a little terrifying, you know that?" he quipped as he stooped over and slid sideways through the freshly-bent bars.

"I do know, actually." She chuckled and hopped through the gap next. "Keeps all you human folk from pushing me around, though. Handy for a young dwarven woman just trying to make her way here. Now, which way did you say it was?"

Reigh motioned to the left. "End of the hall. There's probably an even bigger locked door there, too, so maybe do some stretches and limber up. Don't want you pulling any muscles out here."

Garnett just laughed as she trotted proudly on.

Lukani slipped through the bars next, and I waited until he was well clear, taking a second to check down the stairwell both ways, before I followed. Something nagged at the back of my mind—a whisper that made me hesitate. My skin prickled with that eerie feeling, as though I was being watched by someone—someone I couldn't see.

We'd come through the entire tower, up every flight of those god-forsaken stairs, but we hadn't seen any sign of Thatcher and the others. Shouldn't we have seen something? Some sign? Or heard them? I'd expected to meet with more resistance than this, or at the very least, to detect some sign that the others had passed us or gone the same way.

"Murdoc, come on!" Reigh shouted down the hall.

I shook my head, trying to clear those thoughts. I couldn't get distracted. Not now—when we were this close. Once we knew the location of the mirror and had it secured, then finding Thatcher and the others was priority number one.

I couldn't speak for the others. I knew the plan was to meet at the top of the tower and leave before the dragonriders came to destroy this city and everyone in it. But I wasn't going anywhere without the rest of my ... family.

CHAPTER TWENTY-SIX

CRACK!

With one mighty swing of her axe, Garnett easily cut through the door lock on Lord Argonox's private quarters. We all crowded in close, weapons at the ready, as the hinges creaked and the massive door slowly swung open. The cool air rushed out, and I winced at the smell of old, rotted blood that hung thick in the air. A smell I knew all too well.

All the little hairs on the back of my neck stood on end as I stepped across the threshold, my boots leaving prints in the fine layer of dust. So … this was what the personal quarters of a tyrant looked like. Not what I expected.

Everything about the room was a contradiction. The fine furnishings stained with dark splotches—probably the source of the smell. Porcelain teacups, crystal goblets, empty bottles of liquors and wines lay aside shackles, torture implements hung on gilded pedestals on the walls, and an array of different sized skulls displayed on shelves. An oil-painted portrait of the man himself dominated an entire wall, hanging in a massive golden frame, and flanked on either side by gold-plated sconces.

I'd never seen Argonox in the flesh before, but the painting didn't look at all how I'd imagined him. He was a lot younger, clean-cut, and better looking than I'd imagined someone who had conquered and devastated nearly every known kingdom in the world would be. If the picture was accurate, he must have been somewhere in his early thirties, at most. His dark black hair was cut short and efficient, he was clean shaven, and there was something strangely disarming about his deeply set blue eyes. I would have assumed he was a prince or some royal, not a soulless murderer.

"He was a monster unlike any other," Garnett whispered.

I flinched, looking down from my trance to find her standing right beside me, staring up at the portrait, as well. Her violet eyes studied the image, her expression closing up like a flower folding in on itself at nightfall.

"You hear stories of wicked people, but it's a much different experience to actually look one of them in the eye. One moment he'd be smiling, talking in such a friendly way. And he was charming, so you ... you forgot who he really was. He could do that—manipulate people so easily. Make them drop their guard. Make them relax and trust him. Then in an instant, he would ... change." Her eyebrows drew up, expression tensing with fear. Her eyes went wide, as though the memory of that man was still all too real for her. "It's like he became someone else. Someone evil. He would snuff out a life, listen to the screams of people begging him for mercy, and never stop smiling. I used to wonder where he came from. How does a person become that way? What has to go wrong in their lives for them to feel ... nothing? No pity. No empathy. No reaction to brutality and violence at all."

"It starts when you're young," I murmured. "Someone has to break those things in your soul, and what grows back is twisted and wrong."

"Like the Ulfrangar do to their people?" she asked.

I swallowed hard.

Her strong hand reached out to grasp mine firmly. "I know you've been worried that Thatcher's power compelled you to spare him. That it wasn't a choice you made on your own. But I don't think that's true. I think his power healed everything in you that the Ulfrangar had broken before. Those things in your soul that had grown back wrong. He made them right again, so now you can do good and be the man you were meant to be from the start. That's what a God of Mercy would do, don't you think?"

"Found it!" Reigh called from where he'd been digging through a small cabinet in the corner of the room. Each of its drawers had been locked, so it had taken him a while to pick each one and work his way through.

The rest of us looked up from where we'd been scouring the other corners of the room for some sign of the blueprints like prairie dogs.

"You're sure?" Garnett rushed over, vaulting over the sofa on her way to check the roll of papers he held up.

Lukani ... well, he hadn't really been helping all that much. He had gotten distracted by the collection of skulls, and was looking over each one of them curiously. He glanced over from where he'd been busy poking his fingers through the eyehole sockets, seeing the papers, and giving a snort of disinterest.

Crowding together, Garnett, Reigh, and I carefully unrolled the thin, weathered papers and spread them out across the desk.

"You're right," Garnett confirmed, her voice shaking a bit with nervous excitement. "This is them—the plans for restructuring the tower. Look there, you can see where the experimental wing was. There are the high security cells, too. That's probably where Devana is being held. Stones, it's a long way from that central chamber where we first popped out of the elevator shaft. I hope they can find their way that far."

I leaned in to get a better look, noting where she pointed to a rough sketch of the tower and all the modifications Argonox had made. It looked like he'd transformed what once had been small, closed off armament storage rooms into cells, installing those large, rune-infused doors and blocking off several of the passages leading to them with more barred gates to prevent breakouts. Judging by the scale and the markers for stairwells, Garnett was correct. Those high-security, magically reinforced prison cells were far beneath our feet now.

So ... had we passed by it on our way here? Had we gone by Thatcher and the others when Lukani set fire to that central chamber and not even known it? Gods, what if we'd cut off their exit point? What if they couldn't escape now because of the fire? Or the rush of enemy forces to that area?

"Looks like the floor below this one has some of the vaults." Reigh muttered under his breath as he ran his fingers over the pages, skimming them for details. "There's more down closer to the level where the elevator used to stop. I guess it was easier to have them there, in case he needed to remove them from the tower quickly. Hmm. You know, I'm betting that's where the mirror will be—close to the unloading dock where crates and supplies were taken off that elevator. The Mirror of Truth was huge. They had it on this rolling frame just to move it, and so they wouldn't be able to transport it up the stairs."

He went on, rambling about possible locations, but it was only muffled noise. My thoughts wouldn't stop racing, and I couldn't tear my eyes away from that place where Garnett had suggested Devana might be held. I wracked my brain, trying to remember what we'd encountered down that far. Had there been fighters pouring out of those doorways? Were they having to fight their way to the holding cells to find Devana? Or had they all just burned alive?

"Murdoc?"

I jerked at the sound of my name, looking up to find all three of them staring at me. O-Oh. What had I missed? I should have been paying attention. I needed to—

"Go find them," Garnett said suddenly. Reaching across the desk, she pointed to that spot on the map ... the one I'd been staring at.

The place where Thatcher, Phoebe, and Isandri might be.

I took a step back from the desk. "I-I can't, I have to—"

"Listen, love. We can take it from here. It's a simple matter now," she insisted. "But those three ... I think we both know that if things should go badly, sweet Phoebe is going to be caught up in a battle between gods. And if she or Thatcher get hurt, Isandri can't get them out on her own. They need you more than we do."

My mouth clamped shut as my throat seemed to close around everything I should say—all the reasons I shouldn't just abandon the three of them to handle this on their own. But, Gods and Fates, she was right. Thatcher had come a long way with combat training, but he was far from being ready to take on the brunt of a long battle by himself. Phoebe couldn't fight at all. Isandri handled herself well, but she couldn't protect all of them.

Reigh crossed his arms and gave me one of those smug, know-it-all looks that made me want to punch him in the neck. "She's right and we all know it. We got this. It's just moving some furniture around right? Go, Murdoc. We'll see you at the top of the tower."

I stumbled a little as I took another step back—another step toward the door. They weren't serious, were they? What if something happened here? I looked between the three of them, searching for anyone who might object or have second thoughts.

No one did.

Grabbing the hilt of my longsword, I pulled it free again and ran for the door. My focus narrowed straight ahead as every corner of my mind went silent, every sense and instinct drawing as taut as bowstrings. That hunting instinct quickened in my blood, stripping away every shred of doubt as I bolted back out into the hallway without ever looking back.

PART FIVE
THATCHER

CHAPTER TWENTY-SEVEN

"This ... this is it," Phoebe whispered brokenly, standing before an arched doorway at one of the floor landings in the tower. "My workshop was this way."

Behind us, the echoes of combat and the bellowing of what I could have sworn sounded like a dragon made my stomach spin like a whirlpool. That wasn't possible, though. There couldn't be a dragon anywhere in this tower. How would it have gotten in? And why? Unless Queen Jenna had launched her attack early, in which case, we were all going to be incinerated long before we ever found Devana.

I panted and wheezed, barely making it to the landing right behind Isandri. We must've run up four flights of stairs and zig-sagged down a dozen halls, only to slip along some smaller flights of spiraling steps just to get here. We'd gotten rid of most of our armor a long time ago, though. It made running this far a little easier, and a lot less noisy. So far, we'd managed to duck and dodge our way past the groups of armed men moving through the tower. Most of them seemed normal enough and were headed down to whatever commotion was happening below. But others moved strangely. Their eyes glowed blue, and they didn't speak to one another, or even react to anyone around them. Their expressions were empty of all emotion. It was just like Phillip had said before—they were in some kind of trance.

And I had a good idea who was responsible for it.

"Come! We cannot stop now," Isandri urged, her tone becoming more frantic as she darted past Phoebe into the hall beyond the doorway. It curved in a broad circle, just like all the other floors had. But the Tibrans had altered so much of the interior of the tower, it was difficult to tell what it might have been before the war. Barracks? Or a training area? Gods only knew.

It didn't matter now, though.

We moved fast and low, sneaking along the halls while Phoebe peered at every door, her lips moving as though she were quietly talking to herself. I tried not to focus on the petrified, almost catatonic look in her eyes, or the way she'd begun to shake like she was freezing, as we came to the far end of one of the halls. A large black door made of solid iron loomed before us. There was no handle, just a hole where it should have been, and a tiny window with a sliding panel over it that sort of reminded me of the slot I'd had to feed dragons through in the Deck back in Halfax.

Phoebe's face drained of all color as she stared up at it, seeming to shrink before it as though it were a looming beast about to devour her whole.

She didn't have to say it out loud. That look of petrification was enough.

This had been her workshop.

Only, it didn't look at all how I'd expected. I'd assumed it might look something like the Porter's workshop—open and inviting—where everyone could see whoever was working the forge and bellows, crafting new weapons, and meeting with customers.

This was a glorified cell.

"There is no handle?" Isandri asked, narrowing her eyes at the triangular-shaped hole.

"No," Phoebe whispered, her voice still shaking as she curled back away from it with her hands in fists against her chest. "I was not ... free to leave. The guard who was charged with supervising me had the knob. Only he could put it in and open the door. It was something Argonox asked me to make."

I stared at her, totally bewildered. "He forced you to make a lock for your own door? Just so he could trap you inside?"

Her mouth mashed up as her expression skewed with grief. Tears welled in her eyes as her chin trembled. "Y-Yes."

Something warm thrummed in the back of my mind. A heat like the comforting glow of firelight in a cold night. It spread over my brain and buzzed through my chest, bringing with it a sense of calm I couldn't understand. It didn't matter what it was or where it came from, though. It just felt ... right.

"Do we need to go in?" I asked her, keeping my tone soft and gentle as I put a hand on her shoulder. "Phoebe, do you need to see it?"

Right here, right now might be her only chance, and if this was the closure she needed, we could make time for that. Isandri could go on ahead of us if she didn't want to wait. But Phoebe's peace mattered, too.

"No," she answered softly. Closing her eyes sent fresh tears spilling down her cheeks. "It's enough to stand here ... on *this* side of the door."

I gave her shoulder a reassuring little squeeze. "Okay. Let's go, then. It's time to get this done, and go home."

"Okay." The corners of her mouth twitched upward, tugging into an exhausted and strangely relieved smile. As though she had waited a lifetime for this moment. To walk away from that room on her own, without a Tibran guard on her heels like a guard dog, or the threat of death and torture in the back of her mind.

She'd been free before we ever set foot in this place, thanks to Queen Jenna absolving her at the Court of Crowns. But somehow, deep in my heart—the same place where all that buzzing, radiating warmth seemed to resonate from—I knew this was the first time she had actually felt free.

"*Ishaleon ...*"

I stiffened, my breath hitching as a voice, faint and fleeting, filled my mind like a rush of cool water. A swell of cold tingles shivered over me, starting at my toes and climbing all the way to the top of my head.

I whipped around, looking down the hall behind us. But there was no one there. No movement. No sound of anyone or anything coming closer.

But how was that possible. It had sounded so close, like someone leaning in to whisper right against my ear.

"Devana?" I heard myself ask, but it sounded so far away. Like I was hearing myself through a long tube or muffled beyond a door.

Isandri's head snapped around to stare at me, eyes wide. At first, I thought maybe she had heard it, too. But then she rushed toward me, searching my face with a frantic urgency. "What is it, Thatcher? Are you hearing her? Is she calling out to you?"

"I-I think so," I stammered, still barely able to hear my own voice.

Phoebe sucked in an alarmed gasp. "Isa, what's wrong with his eyes? Why are they glowing like that?"

What? My eyes were ... *glowing*?

"Listen to her, Thatcher," Isandri pleaded. "Perhaps she can help us find her."

I didn't know about that. If it really was Devana calling out to me, her voice had been so weak. Was she suffering? Was Iksoli doing something to her?

I turned away some and closed my eyes, trying to pull my focus back in away from everything else. My consciousness drifted, skirting the edge of that thrumming warmth that seemed to resonate from somewhere deep in my chest. Closer—I needed to get closer to it. To focus on that. I drew all my concentration there, trying to gather in around that buzzing heat like someone hugging the edge of a campfire.

"*Devana?*" I called to her—not out loud. I tried to do it in my mind, with my thoughts, the same way she did. My pulse gave an excited skip when it didn't sound muffled and distant like it did when I spoke out loud.

No answer.

I frowned. Why wasn't this working? It felt like it should. It felt right. So why didn't she answer me?

Oh ... maybe *that* was why.

In all the time I'd been aware of her, the times before when I'd heard her call my name, and the things Phillip had said about her calling out for me as well, she never once called me Thatcher. She never used my mortal name.

She had only ever called me by my divine name.

"*Eno?*" I tried again.

"*Ishaleon.*" Her answer was immediate, and a lot louder than before. I could feel it, the answering echo of her divine presence close by, like ripples on a pond spanning outward. Her voice shook with emotion, halting and catching as though she were crying. "*Ishaleon, please ... please find me.*"

I opened my eyes slowly, sensing the direction of those ripples of divine power. My gaze fixed downward, focusing on that point. And somehow, I just knew.

Two floors down. The hallway to the left. Two right turns. Then a sharp left at the place where the corridor split. There—a door in the dark, covered in runes.

That's where Devana was.

"I'm coming," I told her in my mind. *"Just hang on a little longer."*

"Ishaleon," she begged, her tone growing higher and more frantic. "Hurry—hurry, please! She is ... she is coming!"

BAM!

Everything snapped back into focus suddenly as a crash made all three of us jump and look up just in time to see every doorway up and down the hallway behind us burst open at once.

In a matter of seconds, a company of men in full battle armor, brandishing swords, scimitars, and spears, blocked our only exit. They stood shoulder-to-shoulder, staring straight ahead with eerily blank expressions, and their eyes glowing with an unnatural bluish light.

My stomach dropped and I lifted my crossbow, staring in horror at the small army blocking the passage. Gods and Fates, had they all just been standing in those rooms waiting this whole time? They hadn't made a single sound!

All their mouths moved in perfect unison, the crowd of fighters all speaking together like one, loud, disharmonious voice. "We meet again, my darling little brother. Let's play again, shall we?"

I set my jaw. Iksoli. So, this is what she'd been planning all along—to pin us down without a way to escape. I'd expected a fight. Sooner or later, I knew we'd have to cross blades with someone in this tower. That was a fact we all knew going in. But this wasn't at all what I had hoped for. And worse?

The person we'd come here to fight wasn't even in the crowd of armored fighters in front of us. Not really. Iksoli was hiding, as usual. Pulling her strings and making her puppets dance from afar.

It had to stop.

I spat on the ground, lowering my crossbow and shouting, "Why don't you face me yourself? Or did losing last time make you even more of a coward?"

All the soldiers suddenly erupted with laughter, leaning on one another and chuckling. They slapped each other as they cackled and pointed at me, then immediately snapped back to attention. Their expressions went totally blank again and they spoke as one, *"Ishaleon, my dear, you always were my favorite fool. I have dreamed of nothing else since last we met. Came to rescue our sweet sister, did you? Very well. Let's see if you are truly worthy."*

I ripped my xiphos free of its sheath and held it out, that heat roaring from my chest in waves down my arms, back, and across my face. I heaved in slow, heavy breaths as I sank down into a defensive stance.

"I will take the ones on the left," Isandri purred, stepping in next to me with a flourish of her hand. A flash of silver light lit up the hall as her staff materialized in her hand and she whipped it into a blurring spin and held it firmly out before her. "You can handle the ones on the right?"

I nodded once. "Absolutely."

Blood roared in my ears as I clenched the hilt of my sword, bearing in hard with every strike and parry Murdoc had ever taught me. My heart pounded, throbbing in my palms and kicking fiercely against my ribs, as I surged through the swarming soldiers with Isandri right at my back.

I dove forward, dropping to a knee and thrusting my blade in a blitzing slice across one of the soldier's legs. He staggered, immediately crumpling. I pitched backward just as Isandri's staff whirled over my head and smash his helmet to bring him the rest of the way down.

Isa and I kept up the pace, carving our way forward, and moving in perfect unison. All the while, that radiant heat swelled in my chest. It sizzled through my veins, making my mind go completely silent and everything around me seem to slow down. I didn't have to think. I didn't have to worry about whether or not I could pull off that strike or handle parrying that blow. The impact of my blade locking with another didn't make me flinch. I felt no fear. No hesitation.

Only primal instinct ... and the heat of divine power.

"Shield!" Isa shouted.

I sprang backward, throwing up my empty hand and calling down a rush of that divine energy. A globe of golden light spread from my palm, enclosing me and Phoebe inside it an instant before Isandri cracked the crystalline head of her staff on the floor before us.

VOOOOM!

A shockwave of her power like a tidal wave of sterling light spread out from that point in every direction. The force of it sizzled against my shield and blew soldiers off their feet, sending them all flying back like ragdolls.

"Crossbow," I called back to Phoebe, keeping the shield up long enough for her to scramble in closer and unclip it from my belt. She had pretty good aim with it, after all. It'd serve her better than that Tibran sword she still had on her belt.

Isandri wasted no time. She rushed forward, stabbing her way through as many of the fallen soldiers as possible before they could get back to their feet. Once Phoebe had my crossbow in hand, I sprang in to help.

Six more down. Then ten. The hallway rang with the clash and clang of blades, the concussive booms of Isandri's divine attacks, the thunk of crossbow fire, and the gurgling cries of the soldiers as they fell one-by-one.

I whirled through another parry, kicking forward into a roll and coming up behind two more. A speedy stab to the place where their breastplate met their helmet put them on the ground fast. Isandri let out a yowl nearby as she sprang forward, shifting into her feline form and pouncing on another one like a furious winged tiger.

Then I could see it—the way through. We'd nearly cut through the entire crowd of

Iksoli's fighters. I spun to the side, narrowly stepping around the swing of an enemy's blade as it hummed past my head. Gritting my teeth, I set my gaze on that exit point.

A shout of pain tore past my lips as something suddenly jabbed against my side. My vision went white and I staggered, reaching for whatever had hit me. Before I could find it, a soldier ripped the end of his spear free of my side with a gory yank. Leering at me with his eyes gleaming that ominous, misty blue hue, he bared his teeth and reared back as though to make another strike.

"Thatcher!" Phoebe cried out in alarm.

But everything went strangely ... dim. I couldn't feel it—any pain from the wound. It vanished in an instant as I stood, watching him advance on me again. He moved so slowly it was almost funny. The flutter of his clothes and hair, it all wavered in slow motion as he drove the point of his weapon in my direction again for another stab.

I blinked, watching it slowly inch toward me in amazement. Weird. What was happening? Had I done this? And why wasn't there any blood on the tip of his spear? Something about his posture, the way he moved as he thrust that weapon toward me, was like watching time repeat itself—only very slowly.

I looked down, realizing that I could still move normally. The world hadn't grown dim. I was ... *glowing*. My body radiated golden light like a beacon, and when I reached out to touch the slowly advancing spear, it lit up, too.

The spear shattered into a thousand tiny shining sparks. Immediately, everything sped back to its normal pace. The soldier staggered and nearly fell, floundering away as his weapon exploded in his hands and vanished in a flash of golden light. He didn't even have time to be confused, though. The tri-dagger end of Isandri's spear suddenly punched through his torso, making him go stiff and fall limp as she stabbed him through from behind.

She looked at me, half in shock and half in concern that I might be mortally wounded now.

I reached down to my side, touching the place where the spear had stabbed me. But there was no wound. No blood. No evidence that I'd been struck at all. Wait, had that actually happened? Or ... had I just ... known it would? Had I glimpsed the future somehow? Had I known what that soldier was going to do before he did it? Was that even possible?

I had no idea, and right then, I didn't have time to figure it out.

"Go!" Isandri called, motioning for Phoebe to make her dash past the few remaining soldiers.

I fell in step beside her, seizing Phoebe's hand and pulling her close to my side to make sure no one made an easy slash at her as she dashed by. Isandri, her beautiful robes now torn and spattered with blood, ran up behind us in her human shape again. With her staff clenched firmly in hand, she stole a sideways glance at me, and I could have sworn there was the tiniest hint of bewildered fear in her eyes.

That's when I knew—whatever I'd just done, Isandri had seen it.

And she had no idea what it meant, either.

28

CHAPTER TWENTY-EIGHT

"Are you kidding me? Is that *dragon fire?!*" I yelled as we approached the bottom of the stairs in the tower's base level.

Yep. It definitely was. I'd been around dragons long enough now to know that dragon venom, burning or not, put off a very acrid stench that stung my eyes and throat. No mistaking it.

"Has the attack started?" Isandri said, throwing out an arm protectively in front of Phoebe as we all smashed together in the stairwell, staring out into the crackling furnace that was the base level of the tower.

I didn't know. Maybe it had. I'd lost all track of time while we were underground in those tunnels. And this tower was a little short on windows to the outside in order to check.

"It doesn't matter," I decided. "We've come this far. I'm not turning back now. You don't have to come with me, though. You can go up to the top of the tower and wait for the others."

I knew that wouldn't fly far with Isandri. She wasn't about to turn heel and run now.

"We're with you, Thatcher," Phoebe insisted.

Isandri's lips thinned with a determined glare and she nodded. She was coming, too.

All right, then. Only one way to do this.

I sucked in a steadying breath before I shut my eyes tightly and stoked the coals of that heat still simmering in my soul. Stretching out a hand, I unleashed that globe of energy again, letting it stretched down around us like a translucent curtain of golden light. Then, I started to walk forward.

"Stay close to me," I warned, taking it slow as I descended the last few steps into the smoldering dragon flames. I didn't know if this would work, or even how long I could sustain it. The effort made that heat in my chest grow more intense, like someone slowly pressing a hot branding iron against my clothes. It started out as just ambient warmth, then it grew more and more uncomfortable as we stepped into the crackling flames and made our way through the inferno. Bodies lay strewn, smoldering and melting under the heat and acidity of the burning venom.

I tried not to look at them too closely. What if I'd been wrong about thinking I heard a dragon down here? What if it had been an explosion, or some sort of Tibran weapon that had detonated? I knew they liked to use dragon venom—they'd filled orbs with it and fired them from catapults during the war.

Gods, what if Murdoc and the others had gotten caught in the blast.

No. I clenched my teeth and tore my gaze away, back toward our goal. I couldn't think about that. They weren't here. They were somewhere safe, maybe even already waiting for us at the top of the tower.

They had to be.

Sweat drizzled down my face as I watched the flames lick the outside of my shield, but none crossed through it. Not even a spark or a whisp of smoke touched us as we descended the stairs and crossed through the chamber to the hallway on the left—the same one I'd sensed before. Up ahead, the flames hadn't spread more than twenty yards or so down the hall. There wasn't much there to burn, after all. The stone floor, walls, and ceiling were bare of anything that might catch fire.

Staggering the last few feet past the flames, my arm dropped to my side and my shield dissolved. I wheezed and caught myself against the wall, fighting for every breath. The heat in my blood subsided, but not as quickly as it had before. It thrummed and pulsed through me, making my muscles draw tense and my lungs constrict like they were shriveling up inside me. I curled my hands into fists and pushed away from the wall, steadying myself before I dared to face Isandri and Phoebe again.

I had to get it together. We were nearly there. Just a little farther.

"Take it easy, Thatcher," Isandri whispered as she stepped over quickly and grasped my arm. She studied me, her expression tinged with worry, as she used the sleeve of her robe to wipe some of the sweat from my face. "You're not used to using your power this much. I spent years at my temple training to withstand the physical strain, but our mortal bodies were not meant to bear it for long."

"I-It's not like we have a choice," I gasped hoarsely. "I'll be okay."

"I, um, I think it's this way." Phoebe ventured a few steps ahead, pointing down the passage. "I remember—yes! It's this way!"

"She's right. We've got to hurry." I stumbled a few steps and had to catch myself against Isandri's side before I felt steadier on my feet. Managing a clumsy jog, I tried not to think about the fact that my feet and hands were tingling and numb. Flexing my fingers helped, a little, but the residual burn of that power left my head throbbing.

Isandri was right. I couldn't afford to push myself too far. Not if I still had Iksoli to contend with.

These tunnels and halls spanning out beneath the tower were smaller, but no less dark and ominous as we sped through them. According to Phoebe, they were all original to the construction of Northwatch tower—a place where the Maldobarian soldiers had stored their armor, weaponry, and other extra supplies. They didn't stretch out terribly far, and they formed almost a grid with numerous interconnecting halls lined with small storage rooms.

Or at least, they had been storage rooms once.

Now, every door was reinforced with iron plating and a heavy locking mechanism. They'd turned rooms meant for storing gear into prison cells, and by the look of things, a lot of those rooms were still shut tight. Gods and Fates, were there still people in every one of those rooms? My heart wrenched, pulsating with that heat at the thought. Surely, after being trapped in there this long, they'd all be dead, right? For their sake, I hoped so. There were hundreds of cells, and we didn't have time to check them.

We jogged to a halt at the end of a long corridor that split off two directions. I glanced to the left, then to the right. Both passages looked equally dark and potentially life-threatening. But I knew which way we had to go.

"I-I don't remember this part," Phoebe confessed, her face flushing as she looked frantically back and forth between the two halls. "I'm so sorry, I don't know which way to go."

"It's this way," I said, nodding to the left.

She stared up at me, eyes wide with amazement. "How do you know that?"

"I, uh, don't know. Just a feeling." I looked down, to the side, up—pretty much anywhere to keep from meeting her mystified gaze. I didn't know if she could tell when I lied, but I wasn't willing to chance it.

"You're hearing her, aren't you?" Isandri asked, her tone accusing.

I winced and nodded. "Before, when Iksoli sent those men in armor to fight us, I could hear her in my head. She knows we're coming for her. But ... obviously, so does Iksoli."

A few seconds of awkward silence passed before I dared to look either of them in the eye again. I turned around again, intending to continue on in awkward silence, but Isandri snapped a hand out, suddenly catching me by the wrist.

"Wait!" she whispered, as she yanked me to a halt. "Listen."

I stood perfectly still.

"What is it?" Phoebe whispered, too. "I don't hear anything."

Isandri's grip on my wrist tightened. She stared straight at me as terror crept over her features like a winter evening's chill. Her lips barely moved as she slowly uncurled a finger, pointing upward as she breathed the word, "Exactly."

I DIDN'T GET it at first. It was quiet down here, yes. Why was that a problem? It just meant we weren't being chased by more mind-controlled men with swords who wanted to kill us, right?

Wait a second.

If Iksoli's mind-puppets weren't down here ... then where were they?

My gaze tracked upward, following Isandri's gesture as the faintest sounds of thuds and thumps resonated from somewhere far overhead. Footsteps? No. They were more distinct and consistent. Rhythmic, almost. A dull *whoomp—whoomp—whomp* sound.

All the feeling drained from my face. Oh. Oh gods. I knew that sound.

Dragon wingbeats.

"Queen Jenna has launched her attack," I realized in horror. The dragonriders were here, right now, flying somewhere far over our heads. They would start burning Northwatch to try and run out all these criminals and cutthroats so they could retake the area.

We ... we were out of time.

"We'll be trapped!" Phoebe whimpered, her eyes welling as she clung closer to my side. "Once they reach the tower, there's no other way out from this level!"

I didn't reply. Seizing her by the hand, I took off down the final, dark hallway. My jaw ached as I clenched my teeth, breathing in hard against the dull pain that pulsed through every muscle as I ran. I could bear it. I wouldn't give up. I wouldn't fail—not when we were this close.

"DEVANA!" I shouted as we ran. No point in keeping quiet now, right? Iksoli knew we were here. "WHERE ARE YOU?!"

No answer.

With Isandri running right alongside me, she gave a crack of her staff off the ground that sent up a current of her power to the crystal affixed at the top of her staff. The big, raw mineral lit up like a small star, lighting the way ahead and revealing the doors we passed. Each one of them had been crafted to look like a thick, metal vault instead of something you might store stuff in. The black iron surfaces were etched with patterns and spiraling designs, just like Phillip had described. Close—we were getting close.

My heart thumped like mad, my eyes searching frantically for the one I'd seen in my vision. The one that felt right. Would I even be able to tell? What if I got it wrong? How were we going to get it open?

"Ishaleon!" That fragile voice cried out in my mind so suddenly I nearly tripped and fell-face first on the stone floor. Skidding to a halt, I stared up at one of the doors. My hand slid out of Phoebe's. Wild energy began to buzz in my fingertips again as my gaze roamed the wicked black surface of the metal. Every inch of it covered with glyphs carved into the metal, like a patchwork of interlocking circles and sharp, jagged lettering in a language I couldn't read. All of it stemmed from one silver, dinner-plate sized, rotating dial right in the center. No handle. No knob.

Fates, it really was like a vault.

Stepping forward, I ran my fingers over the surface to trace along some of those rune marks. The instant my fingertips brushed the cold metal, a sting of pain hit the back of my mind like I'd been bitten by it somehow. I snatched my hand back with a hissing curse. What the—? What was that?

"It is heavily warded against divine magics," Isandri seethed bitterly as she held her staff closer, the light from the crystal giving a much better view of all those runic designs.

"Then how do we open it?" I growled, still shaking the lingering sting from my hand.

"It's a puzzle," Phoebe gasped, her pale blue eyes shining in the light as she stared up at the circular, silver dial in the center. "Look there, see the symbols around the edge of this part? I think the whole thing rotates and you have to find the right combination to deactivate the runes and unlock it."

Hmm. I hadn't noticed the tiny symbols etched around the edge of the silver dial. She was right, though. Gods, I'd never seen anything that complex.

"Can you figure out the combination?" I pressed.

Phoebe nibbled her bottom lip. "I-I—maybe? I did work with these kinds of runes some, but they're extremely complex. It will take me a few minutes, but I think I—"

A shower of dust poured over us as the ceiling shook, rattling the tunnel around us with a low groan like an earthquake. Phoebe shrieked, and I dragged her in close to try and shield her in case the whole place caved in on top of us. After a few seconds, the shaking stopped. Everything went hauntingly still again.

Isandri stood, staring upward again as the blood seemed to drain slowly from her face. "It's just like before," she gasped faintly, her voice shaking with terror.

"Like before?" What was she talking about? What did that even mean?

Isandri crept closer with her staff raised protectively. "The dragonriders attempted to retake the city while I was held captive here, in these very halls. The earth shook and groaned over us, and many prayed that we might be crushed so their suffering would finally end." Her gaze shifted slowly, panning back to look at me with her features drawn tense into a haunted expression. "There is a battle waging."

"A battle?" I barked in disbelief. "Against the dragonriders? No way! There aren't enough people here to wage that kind of resistance ... are there?"

"Oh, little brother. Do you think I would dedicate my efforts simply to trifling with you and your pathetic mortal companions?" A feminine voice giggled. It wasn't just in my head this time, though. Her excited laughter echoed down the hallway behind us, coming from somewhere in the dark beyond the swirling clouds of dust still hanging thick in the air.

My heartbeat skipped. Her name slipped from my lips like a hushed curse. "Iksoli."

Isandri tensed, her lip curling in a snarl. Her knuckles blanched as she gripped her staff harder, her vivid yellow-and-lime eyes searching the gloom for the source of the voice.

I didn't see her, either. Not at first. Then, something moved in the gloom. Squinting down the passage, I could barely make out the silhouette of a figure prowling toward us.

"As if I would ever be so boring," Iksoli snickered again. *"Tibran soldiers stumbling around like sheep with no shepherd, and so many of their delightful war machines—all courtesy of that brilliant little mortal you've got tagging along there, of course. I really should think of a way to thank you, personally, Phoebe. None of this would have been possible without you, now would it? And to think, all of these delightful toys you made were just left to spoil. I couldn't allow that."*

Beside me, Phoebe shrank back and clutched my crossbow tighter to her chest. Her eyes welled, expression twitching as though she were a breath away from a full mental breakdown.

"Stop it," I growled as I drew my blade again. "Leave her and everyone else out of this. You've wanted to lure me here from the beginning, right? Now you've got your wish. So why don't you show yourself?"

Iksoli's laughter was venom. It reverberated off the halls all around us, seeming to come from everywhere at once, as that figure stalked closer. Through the curling wisps of dust still sparkling in the light from Isandri's staff, the figure finally stepped into view, eyes glowing like two blue stars in the gloom.

My heart stopped. My breath froze in my chest.

M-Mur ... Murdoc?

"You know, I've worn a lot of mortals over the eons. Usually, it's so cramped and confining to be packed into their meaty, heavy bodies—like a shoe that's too small." Her voice sighed through his lips with a blissful smile. *"But I rather like this fellow. He fits nicely, wouldn't you agree?"*

My sword slid from my hand and hit the ground at my feet with a clatter. "N-No," I stammered.

"Oh yes," she sneered with delight, manipulating his body into drawing the longsword from the sheath at his back. *"Now then, pick up your little sword, and let's have a rematch, shall we? Winner takes all."*

CHAPTER TWENTY-NINE

A million questions took my mind like a raging winter storm. How had this happened? How had she gotten control of Murdoc? What about the others—Garnett and Reigh? Were they okay? Had she killed them? What was I supposed to do now? How could I fight him?

I tipped my chin down some, never breaking eye contact as I slowly bent to pick up my sword again. "Open the lock," I murmured to Phoebe, trying to keep my voice low enough that Iksoli wouldn't be able to hear.

She gaped at me, still frozen in fear.

I gave Isandri a quick, hard look. Hopefully she would understand. This was their only chance. I didn't know how long I could hold Iksoli off. I didn't even know if it was her I would be fighting, or Murdoc. But as long as I had her attention, that freed them up to get through that door and rescue Devana.

It was now or never.

Stepping forward, I squeezed the hilt of my blade hard to try and get my hand to stop shaking as I stared into the glowing blue eyes of my best friend. I didn't know if he was okay, or if she'd broken his mind already. Surely she needed his thoughts intact to fight, right?

I didn't know—and the not knowing was enough to make my stomach swim and my knees feel weak.

"Why are you doing this?" I demanded, forcing my tone to stay steady. I needed to keep her focus on me so Phoebe and Isandri had time to work.

Murdoc's chest heaved with a bored sigh. *"Oh, you know, family issues. Oh wait, I suppose you don't know—not in this form. You can't remember anything about who you really are, can you? All the lives you've lived. All the things you've done. A shame, really. This is, by far, your least impressive manifestation. If not for the dragon, you'd be downright pathetic."*

"We'll see, won't we?" I growled. My throat burned as I surged forward, my blade swung wide in an assault Murdoc himself had taught me. Straight in, then a fast, sideways feint.

My feet flew, pulse booming as I dipped in a swift sidestep and slashed upward.

CLANG!

Our blades clashed as he blocked my blow without even looking my way.

Oh no.

"Tsk, tsk. You'll have to try harder than that," Iksoli taunted. "*Go on, try again.*"

I gave a frantic shout of frustration and bore in harder, trying to shove him off balance as I moved through another sequence. Parry down, strike to one side, another swift sidestep with a heel hook to try and trip him.

Murdoc moved with me, matching my attacks and parries in perfect form. The clash of our weapons, of metal ringing against metal, resounded through the hall. The weak light from Isandri's staff cast Murdoc's twisted, sneering features in eerie relief. Each slam of our weapons rattled my bones. I could do better. I knew that. I could use my power. But ... but what if I hurt him, by accident? I had to find some way to pin him down, to immobilize him so I could focus and try to pull her out of his mind like I had with Phillip.

But how?

"*Too slow!*" she hissed as Murdoc sliced his sword across my chest. It sparked and scraped off my breastplate—the only piece of Tibran armor I hadn't discarded.

I dropped to a knee and kicked into a sideways roll, trying another fighting sequence he'd only just taught me. Roll sideways, try a flanking strike, interlock hilts, and disarm.

Murdoc was on me before I could even bring my sword around. He lunged like an attacking lion, blocking me immediately and shoving me backward. I lost my balance, arms flailing wide. I rocked back onto my heels, floundering to throw up a protecting parry as he brought his longsword down with bone-crushing force.

I didn't have a choice.

I thrust my empty hand forward, drawing from that raging heat that blazed through my chest and sizzled over my tongue. A flash of golden light burst from my open palm. Iksoli gave a shriek. Murdoc's blade slammed against my shield and the force of my power immediately threw him back. He staggered, barely managing to stay on his feet.

"Better, better," Iksoli seethed excitedly.

My body sagged, feeling the pull of that heat like an anchor had been tied around my heart. Every muscle ached and burned. My pulse throbbed, making my vision go bright with each beat. I was pushing it too far. I knew that.

I dove after him, a frantic grunt leaking through my clenched teeth as I let that power take over again. It surged through every part of me, pulsing down my arms and legs. The blade in my hand began to glow brilliant gold, just like the rest of me. Flames of power crackled between my fingers. Every nerve screamed in protest, like I was slowly being torn apart from the inside.

But I had no other choice.

Just like before, I could see her presence entangled in his mind, ensnaring him like a twisted, gnarled black briar. She'd taken root more deeply, spreading her poisonous roots through his thoughts and emotions, trying to choke out every trace of reluctance and memory associated with me. She wouldn't let him feel anything, except the seeds of hate and bloodlust she'd planted.

"LET HIM GO!" I thundered, wailing my sword down against his as hard as I could.

Light exploded through the hall on impact. She shrieked again, more startled this time. With my free hand I reached for his face, stretching to press my glowing palm against his forehead. One touch. That's all I needed.

"*NO!*" She screeched in rage.

Murdoc drove his knee into my gut.

All the wind rushed out of me and I pitched forward, nearly falling.

He cracked the hilt of his blade across my face and sent me sprawling sideways onto the floor. I hit hard, barely managing to keep my grip on my weapon. Up. I had to get up. I scrambled to my knees as I wheezed in gulps of air.

Murdoc kicked my face again, harder this time.

Everything went white. Blood exploded into my mouth, and I flopped sideways. My body met the cold stone floor with my ears ringing.

"*Did you think this would be easy? That you'd make it here, unlock our dear sister's chains, and simply walk away?*" Murdoc's head rolled back with a deep laugh as his arms spread wide. He gripped a bloodied blade in each one—a longsword and another, much shorter sword I'd never seen him use before. "*I've waited an eternity for this moment! Are you watching, mother? Do you see me yet? Are you proud of your little girl?*"

His head snapped forward again, leveling a wicked grin at us that curled slowly up his lips. His eyes gleamed like azure embers, empty of any sense of the person I'd known before. My stomach cramped and clenched. I couldn't stop myself from searching—hoping—needing to see some trace of his soul still in there, fighting to resist her.

But there was nothing.

Only malice ... and sadistic pleasure.

"*Our parents have spurned me for the last time. Too long they have sneered at me from their lofty thrones. They have called me an instigator. A meddler. An unworthy imposter. She who was born without her own divine magic and can only survive by leeching power from her betters.*" Iksoli's voice boomed, making the hall shudder as Murdoc took a step forward with the blade still held out wide. "*They find me disgusting. They refuse to speak their own daughter's name, and so the mortals do not know me. They build no temples in my name. They make no pleas for my favor. They call me a cautionary tale. A figment of a nervous imagination. But now they will know ... I am all too real. I will carve my name into their history, and they will know that Iksoli is the goddess who broke the strongest of them. They will pray for my favor, and beg for my mercy. And with your power finally mine to wield ... I will give it to them. Their minds will bend to me entirely. Their hearts will love me and crave my attention.*"

"Y-You're ... insane." My voice scraped with agony and my body shook as I sat up again, still holding my sword.

"*No, brother darling,*" she cooed as Murdoc leaned down to touch the point of his blade to my throat. "*I am chaos.*"

PAIN like a white-hot spike drove through my head as something—like a tether forged in the foundations of my soul—suddenly snapped. My mouth opened wide, but I couldn't draw a breath let alone scream. M-My skin, my head, my eyes, e-everything—it ... it burned! Blisters welted upon my skin like I'd been lit on fire, but in place of blood and flesh beneath there was only blinding golden light.

I dropped my sword, clutching my head and trying to make it stop. That heat raged up like an erupting volcano, making my spine curl and every muscle convulse at once.

Murdoc stumbled back, that sneer of amusement faltering as he stared down at me in shock. Then his brows snapped together. His mouth twisted into a vengeful snarl. He swung in with his blade, slashing like he meant to cut my whole head off in one clean stroke.

Everything froze, like time itself had come to a grinding halt. His blade hung in the air, falling a tiny fraction of an inch at a time. I saw it—felt it—like it was a dance I'd already done a thousand times.

My hand snapped forward, catching his weapon in my fingertips. Just like before with the spear, the longsword glowed with that blistering light that traveled from my hand, up the length of the blade, all the way to the hilt. As soon as the light consumed it, the metal dissolved, vanishing into nothing but a cloud of tiny glittering sparks.

"Enough." The voice that came from my mouth wasn't mine. It was older, more mature—deep and smooth with a confidence I'd never had before. It flowed from my lips like a cooling rain upon parched, cracked earth, bringing with it a calm that resonated through every part of me. "You will not have him, nor will you take another mind within this mortal world."

I stood, my form seeming to grow and swell to greater height above him. Reaching down, my hand passed through the surface of Murdoc's physical form as though it were nothing more than an illusion—a mirage. Within it, though, I felt my fingers strike against something solid. I seized it. It writhed and struggled in my grasp, hissing and clawing at my arm as I ripped it free and held it out at arm's length.

A little girl made of shining blue light hung from my grip. Only, I knew she was no child. With my fist clenched hard around her neck, the goddess writhed and hissed like a caught viper. She bared her teeth, her nearly translucent form wavering and flickering as she tried to vanish, to flee again into the shadows of the world.

But I would not let her go. Not this time.

"You cannot do this!" Iksoli screamed in fury. *"You'll die now, you fool! Your mortal body will perish, burned away by divine power. You'll perish here in the dark, and all of your mortal pets along with you!"*

I frowned and tightened my hold on her. She stiffened, eyes going wide with sudden panic and realization. I leaned in closer, holding that look with my own steady, unrelenting glare. "There are things far worse than death that even gods might fear, dear sister. When you meet them, think of me and do not beg for mercy. You will find none."

Fear—whole and final—filled her eyes as the power swelled within me. The heat scorched along my arm, crackling toward her like a tongue of golden lightning. It caught her right between the eyes and Iksoli went rigid in my grasp, letting out a final, shrill scream that hung in the air even after her body began to dissolve into shining mist.

Gone. She was ... finally gone.

The world around me suddenly spun out of control, becoming nothing but a spiraling smear of color as I dropped to my knees. When my body hit the cool stone off the floor, I felt smaller again. Normal-sized, I guess. I couldn't be sure though. I-I couldn't see anything clearly. Everything was blurred and whirling. Every sound was faint and fuzzy, muffled like I was hearing it from underwater.

I didn't want to die. Not here. Not like this. I'd known it was a possibility from the beginning. But I'd hoped, somehow, I'd wind up on the other side of this horrible nightmare alive, wiser, and stronger.

Still, the others—Murdoc, Phoebe, Reigh, Isandri, and Garnett—would all be okay. I still believed they would make it. They would be safe from Iksoli now. No more schemes and dirty mind-control tricks. Northwatch would be reclaimed. Maldobar and the rest of the world would continue to heal. Everything would be right again.

And that ... was more than enough to make it all worth it.

PART SIX
MURDOC

30
CHAPTER THIRTY

My eyes flew open, everything suddenly clearing from the foggy, distant nightmare I'd been trapped in only seconds before. Lying sprawled on the floor in the middle of a dark tunnel, I bolted upright. My head throbbed sharply as I squinted around, trying to figure out where I was. Before, it had all been so ... chaotic and garbled. Flashes of images like shattered bits of a nightmare. How much of it was real? Or had it all been a dream?

I looked over to my right, and a sudden, primal shout ripped from my lungs.

Lying on his side, his body smoking like he'd just been pulled from a furnace, Thatcher lay motionless.

I scrambled over the floor toward him, seizing his shoulder and rolling him on to his back. His skin was pink and pocked with open sores, like he'd been in a fire. His eyes were bloodshot, and his lips were turning blue. He blinked up in my direction, but I could tell by the faraway look on his face that he couldn't actually see me.

Oh no. Not again. What had happened? H-Had I done this? Us fighting, and me cutting him down, and—Gods, had all of that been real?!

"Thatcher!" I called as I tried to prop him up against me. "Don't you dare do this to me again, you idiot! Not again! Why—why do you always push things too far?!"

"M-Murdoc?" His voice crackled dryly. His eyes focused up at me with a little more clarity.

I clenched my teeth and bowed my head. "I'm here, Thatcher."

"D-Devana ... is she?" he croaked.

I looked up, staring through the open door of the cell. All I could see from there was the glow of sterling light from within. "I don't know. Just relax, okay. We'll get you out of here as soon as—"

His jaw stiffened and he started pushing away from me and trying to get up. "I-I have to s-see her."

Seriously? He was an inch from death, and he wanted to go in there? I growled a curse under my breath as I seized his arm suddenly and looped it over my shoulder, hauling him up to his feet. I basically had to drag him the whole way into that cell, his legs trailing behind as limp as overcooked noodles.

Rounding the corner into the tiny, shadowy room, I stopped short when I found them. Crouched on the floor before us, Isandri and Phoebe were wrestling fiercely with the chains connected to an emaciated female figure lying on the floor. She was so thin you could see every rib, joint, and tendon pressing against her ashen skin. Fates. I hadn't seen someone in that state since I'd been with the whelpers in the Ulfrangar. They had her arms and ankles shackled, and she didn't have a stitch of clothing on. If not for the ragged, halting rise and fall of her chest as she breathed, I would have assumed she was already dead.

But that wasn't what made bile rise in my throat as I stared down at the woman in horror.

Her entire head was locked inside some kind of egg-shaped device. It had no eyeholes, no way to see out of it, and only a tiny hatch door where her mouth might have been. Was that ... a mask? Gods, why did they have that on her? How long had it been there? How was she even still alive at all? The tarnished bronze surface of it reflected the light from the crystal on Isandri's staff, revealing a network of odd geometric designs and shapes, adorned in runes, and inlaid with what looked like silver. Powerful warding spells, probably.

"Murdoc!" Phoebe sobbed, looking up at me with tears making clean streaks in the ash and dirt as they rolled down her face. "Please—please help her!"

I carefully lowered Thatcher to the ground and rushed over, taking the small sword she'd been trying to use as leverage to break the chains on the woman's arms. I cracked them off easily, just as Isandri managed to do the same to free her ankles.

But the mask ... that was going to be a problem. There were no holes or places to put in a key that I could detect. No seam where I could wedge a dagger point in and crack it open. I couldn't understand how they'd even gotten it on her to begin with, let alone how to get it off.

"Here." Phoebe pressed something into Isandri's hand, a worried smile ghosting over her features.

Isandri hesitated, staring down at the little, palm-size cylinder made out of the same type of bronze as the mask. The same sort of marks had been etched onto it, inlaid with silver, and arranged in the same way.

"How did you ...?" Isandri's voice faded as her gaze slowly drifted up to stare at Phoebe in mystification.

"I've been working on it since we left Halfax," she said quietly. "I don't know if it's going to work, but it needs a source of divine power to activate it—your divine power, Isa. Then if you hold it close, it should negate the ones keeping the mask locked on."

Ahhh. So that explained all the late nights she'd spent tinkering away on her own. She'd been working on this—the key.

Isandri's hand closed around the key-box. Her eyes shut tightly for a moment. Then she scooted closer to Devana's side, holding it close to the front of the mask. Her brow creased with concentration as all those silver inlaid marks began to ignite across the surface. The closer she held it to the mask, the more of the lines on the mask glowed in the exact same way. The marks sparked to life inch by inch, spreading over the mask and filling the air with gentle, radiant light. Behind us, Thatcher let out a grunt as he sat up to watch.

Click.

I sucked in a sharp breath as one panel of the mask popped ajar like an orange slice and fell away. Then another. And two more. Sliver by sliver, the mask opened up and fell to the floor with a *clang* like a flower bud opening. With every piece gone, more of the woman's head came into view.

Thick hair as black as raven feathers was matted around her neck and slender, pointed ears. Darkly tanned skin without a single freckle bore the same sort of markings that Isandri's did across her forehead. Her cheeks were sunken from malnutrition, and her lips cracked and dusky from dehydration, but her wide eyes of startling turquoise green were clear and lucid.

This was her—the Tibran witch we'd been sent to hunt? The one the Tibrans had struggled to subdue? A Rienkan elf? Those eyes were a dead giveaway. The sea elves of the south all had eyes the same hue of the warm waters that flowed through their homeland. I'd only met one or two before this, when their sleek and beautifully crafted trading ships made port in Saltmarsh.

The woman lay perfectly still and stared up at Isandri. For a moment, neither one of them moved or said a single word. Then Isandri gave a stammering, broken gasp. "D-Devana."

The woman's eyes squinted a little, as though confused. Then a faint, weary smile tugged at her lips. "Isandri ... my sister."

Isandri let out a cry and threw herself down, embracing the woman and sobbing against her. Devana must have been too weak to return the gesture. Not surprising, given her state. Her whole body trembled as she barely managed to lift a hand to touch Isandri's shoulder. "I knew you would come."

"I'm sorry it took me so long. I had to find him, I had to—" Isa pulled back suddenly, looking over at Thatcher who was still sitting close by. Her face paled some when she saw the state he was in.

Devana looked at him, too. Lying on her back, she smiled at him with a warmth and affection I'd never seen before. The hand that'd been resting on Isandri's shoulder now drifted out, reaching toward him. "Ishaleon," she called gently. "The mask held me here. T-Trapped me in this body. But now, I ... I can see you. I can see you and grant her wish."

Thatcher's eyes went wide. "Wh-What?"

She blinked slowly, the words seeming faded and fragile, like an old forgotten prayer, as she murmured, "Please, Ishaleon. I have to give it to you. Th-There isn't much time left ... and I promised her I would."

Isandri's frown was tinged with worry. "Promised who, Devana?"

The woman's smile softened as the clarity and light in her turquoise eyes began to fade. "His mother."

Thatcher's expression went completely blank.

His *mother*? Did she mean his divine mother, or ...?

Thatcher had never spoken about his birth mother. Not to me, anyway. In fact, I'd never heard him say anything about her whatsoever. No fond memories. No off-handed references. Nothing. Until now, I hadn't given it much thought. I'd assumed she had passed away, and the memory of her must be too painful for him to want to speak about it. Thatcher talked almost as constantly as Phoebe, and I reasoned if there was something about his mother he wanted me to know, he would tell me.

Now I had to wonder ... if I should have asked.

I glanced between them, trying to figure out what Devana meant by that, and why it had Thatcher looking pastier than ever. Granted, he did look nearly as awful as she did. Every breath he took made his chest shudder and quake, and he could barely keep himself sitting upright. Dark dusky circles hung under his severely bloodshot eyes, and his skin looked like it was still slowly searing away in places.

"Th-that's not ... she's not ..." he began to object as fear crept over his features. "She's —" He stopped short and looked at me, his mouth clamping down hard as though he didn't want to finish that thought while I was present.

"She's dead?" I guessed.

He didn't answer except to slowly nod.

"It's okay, Ishaleon," Devana murmured. "It wasn't your fault. She wanted you to know that. She didn't want to go. But she had no choice. It wasn't your fault. It was Iksoli. She touched your mother's mind and planted the seed of chaos. Your mother resisted it for years." Her hand opened, thin, nearly skeletal fingers slowly uncurling to reveal two small objects resting in her palm. A tiny scrap of folded paper, and a tiny gemstone that sparkled in the light. "Her love for you burned so brightly. So beautifully. I felt it, even from afar. She pleaded for me to give you this ... and I promised her that I would."

I watched, unable to speak as all the color drained from Thatcher's face. He wasn't close enough to reach out and take those things from her, and his jaw locked as he began trying to move—to crawl closer. His body shook, practically convulsing with every movement.

Isandri snapped her arm out, blocking my path when I started to help him. She slowly turned her face to stare at me, a grim understanding passing over her expression like an encroaching rainstorm. She didn't have to say a word. I understood. Thatcher had to do this on his own. I couldn't interfere.

He let out a groan, half agony and half relief, when he finally got close enough to take those two objects from her palm. As soon as he did, Devana moved with startling speed to grip his fist. All of her fragile, emaciated body trembled with the effort as she gripped his hand fiercely. Urgency took her features as she yanked him down and wrapped her other arm around his neck. She hugged him hard, her eyes suddenly shining a vibrant scarlet as they filled with tears.

"I-I am ... so proud of you." The voice that left her lips and filled the room with a harmony of echoing whispers didn't sound like hers. It sounded much older, and brimming with an emotion that made my heart sit like a lead weight in my chest. The whispers grew, seeming to penetrate my mind and body like arrows through soft cotton. Each heartbeat made my breath catch.

Devana's eyes glowed like two scarlet stars as she stared up, still holding onto Thatcher as though she were in some sort of trance. Her brow drew up, her expression skewing in grief before she turned to press her lips against his cheek with a final, fading murmur in that same, resounding voice, "I will always ... love you."

Devana's arm slipped away and she sank back against the floor, motionless. Her breathing stopped, and her expression became distant as the light faded from her eyes ... and her life along with it. Her skin seemed to rapidly turn ashen as the same sort of burns that had been on Thatcher suddenly bloomed across her. The same dark circles formed under her eyes.

And then everything went perfectly still.

Thatcher still sat, bent over her in shock. He didn't say a word as he gripped that tiny note and gemstone in his fist. Just as those wounds seemed to appear across Devana's body, they slowly faded away from him. The burns on his skin dissolved away. The circles under his eyes faded. He stopped shaking, and took in each deep, slow breath without shuddering or flinching.

Gods and Fates—had she *healed* him?

No. Not healed. She'd taken his injuries on as her own. And that, I could only guess, was more than her already fragile body could withstand. Her last breath given to spare his life.

The truest act of love.

Thatcher stretched out a hand and carefully brushed her forehead, closing her eyes and folding her arms over her chest. Then he slowly got to his feet. Tucking the two objects she'd given him into his pocket, he turned around to face the rest of us. I expected to see anguish and grief when he finally looked up to meet our stares. Sorrow and tears heavy in his eyes. But instead, there was only ... calm. Peace like a morning sunrise over the gently swaying prairies outside of Dayrise.

"Her time imprisoned in the mortal world is over now. She's back as she should be. We'll see her again when it's our time to return," he said as he reached to take Isandri's hand. "But for now, we need to go. The others need our help."

Isandri stared back at him, tears still streaming down her cheeks. She shut her eyes tightly, leaning in briefly to touch her forehead against his. "O-Okay."

31
CHAPTER THIRTY-ONE

It was a mad dash to the top of the tower. My second one, actually. And this time, I was definitely beginning to feel it in my calves and thighs. This would hurt tomorrow.

Phoebe, Isandri, Thatcher and I ran like the hounds of hell were at our heels, me bringing up the rear of the group to make sure we didn't have any stragglers. We dodged past the few lingering heaps of burning dragon venom that hadn't extinguished yet on the sublevel, and made a break for the stairs again. Not ideal, but I wasn't willing to risk taking that elevator when the entire structure rattled and shook, taking blows from whatever was happening outside. The chances of us getting trapped between floors on that thing were substantial.

Phoebe began to lose steam about halfway up, lagging farther and farther behind and finally stopping to lean against the wall. She panted and gasped, clutching her chest. I was willing to bet it was probably a lot more exertion than she was used to. Until we'd met, she'd probably done significantly less long-distance running for her life.

On my way by, I grabbed her around the waist and threw her over my shoulder, carrying her like a caught lamb. She squeaked and clung to my back, protesting a little—but only because she thought it was too much for *me*.

Hah.

The only other person who wasn't used to this much running had that determined scowl on his face like an angry teddy bear as he huffed and puffed. Thatcher began to lag about two-thirds of the way to the top, growling angrily under his breath and cursing himself.

Not that it was his fault, really. Farriers' sons weren't exactly renowned for their endurance sprinting abilities. At least, not that I'd ever heard of.

Isandri didn't miss a beat. Shifting forms mid stride, she seized the back of his tunic in her teeth and basically tossed him up onto her back. She bounded ahead with her glistening wings filling the narrow corridor as it spiraled around the tower, sloping upward to the pinnacle.

"I'm fine!" Thatcher growled. "Put me down, I can run!"

"Yes, but you're too slow," she snapped back.

"Well, excuse me for having shorter legs!"

"It's got nothing to do with your leg length!"

Well. It seemed like they'd worked out the sibling dynamics now. Great.

"Would you both just shut up and run," I shouted up to them.

BOOOOM!

The tower shuddered again, nearly shaking me off my feet. I stumbled and caught myself against the wall, feeling the stones vibrating under my palm from impact. Gods and Fates—what was happening out there?

"Murdoc!" Someone shouted from behind me. "You're not dead yet? I figured you were toast for sure!"

I turned, still carrying Phoebe over my shoulder, and spotted Reigh, Garnett, and Lukani bounding up after us. Or at least, I assumed the grinning shaggy, yellow-eyed dog loping along beside them was him in another one of his animal forms.

I gave him a deadpan stare. "Oh. You're alive, as well. Wonderful. I'm so relieved."

He scowled and made a rude gesture as he ran by.

I smirked. Too easy.

Waiting until the lot of them passed by, I took up the chase and followed again.

BOOOOM!

We all came to another staggering halt as the tower rocked, taking another impact from somewhere outside. Phoebe screamed and gripped me harder. Up ahead, Reigh yelled a string of curses as he lost his footing and nearly fell face-first on the steps.

"What the heck is going on out there?!" he fumed as he stumbled back up and kept going.

"Iksoli's forces are using Tibran war machines—they're trying to shoot down the dragonriders!" Thatcher yelled back.

"How do you even know that?" Reigh shouted.

"I saw it in Iksoli's thoughts! Long story! Let's just go!" Thatcher called.

BOOOOM—BOOOOM!

Isandri screamed over the noise. "I thought you killed her!"

Thatcher braced himself against the wall. "I banished her beyond the Vale, but that doesn't mean the people who actually *chose* to fight for her are just going to give up!"

Right. Some people were wicked enough on their own without any divine encouragement.

"Almost there!" Reigh called back as he rushed ahead, bounding to the front of the group and steering us along until we came to a landing that must have been one or two floors down from the very top. "This way!"

I hesitated, glancing back up the central stairwell we'd been climbing for gods only knew how many floors. I'd lost count at forty this time up. Ugh. Whatever. I'd just have to trust that Reigh knew where we were going. If anyone knew how to get us out of here, it was him.

He led us down a few side passages, smaller halls blocked off by more of those ironwork gates. Garnett made quick work of them, though, and we slipped through easily. At the far end of a cramped side passage, a lone door stood looking like it might be nothing more than a broom closet. Only the door itself was made of solid plate iron, with a pair of heavy crossbars blocking it to prevent anyone or anything from coming through. It took Garnett and Reigh working together to lift the massive bars and toss them aside. Then Reigh pulled the door open with a creak and groan of the old, rusting hinges.

I guess no one had used this exit in quite some time.

The smell of cold, fresh air filled my nose as we plunged into the darkness of the steep, narrow staircase beyond. It sloped up steeply, completely unlit, and ended abruptly at the ceiling where a small hatch-door was also barred closed. I put Phoebe back on her feet and seized her hand, keeping her close at my side. Thatcher climbed down from Isandri's back, as well, and we all clumped together while Garnett and Reigh worked on prying the hatch open.

BANG!

I flinched and Phoebe shrank against my side as the hatch door suddenly caught the fierce wind outside and ripped open. Frigid wind rushed in, as well as the low, droning boom and roar of combat. Fire lit up the night sky, giving off enough of a glow for us to see as we scrambled through the hatch door, one at a time.

As soon as my boots struck the roof of the tower, I stood frozen in shock at the battle that spanned out from around the tower like a roiling, boiling sea of fire. Northwatch burned like the abyss itself as dragonriders sailed low, gliding just above the flames in groups of two and four. Their bellowing cries rumbled like thunder, interrupted now and then by the *SNAP—WHOOSH—BOOM* of a Tibran catapult firing at them.

Men brawled in the streets, appearing as hardly more than ant-sized specks from where we stood as they locked blades with what I could only assume were dragonriders or Maldobarian infantry. Honestly, from this height, it was impossible to tell. Whatever the case, they clearly had the upper hand. The enemy lines were broken and fleeing. All they were dealing with now were the stragglers who refused to surrender.

"Merciful Fates, Jenna," Reigh gasped as he stood next to me, the light from the inferno below reflecting in his light brown eyes.

The shrill note of a whistle made us both turn, spotting Thatcher as he stood right on the edge of the tower's staggering fifty-floor drop. He blew blast after blast into the whistle hung around his neck. I grinned when I saw him pull his goggles out from beneath his shirt collar and slide them on. His hair blew around his face as he looked down, around, and out across the city—giving that dragon of his directions to find us.

I turned, staring back out across the blazing battlefield as the distant sound of a familiar roar rose above the ambient symphony of chaos all around us. Through the plumes of smoke and columns of rising flame, the shape of three dragons flew straight for us, their saddles empty. Vexi led the way, her green scales shimmering electric in the firelight. Fornax flew right off her wing, following her sound and smell through the air as he rushed to answer his rider's call.

Last in line, and smallest of the three, a young drake with scales as black as onyx and a flashing red blaze down his back, steered straight for me. His big, blue eyes were intent and his wings flapped furiously to keep pace with the others. As soon as he spotted me, his mouth opened and his tongue lolled like an excited puppy, his hind legs paddling in the air like he was trying to go faster. Blite gave a few crowing calls of greeting, almost like he was relieved to see me.

I smiled back.

That ridiculous, troublesome beast. What would I ever do without him?

The dragons circled, holding in a pattern above, while one landed at a time on the top of the tower. The space was narrow, and time was short. The battle was already spreading to the base of the tower. Judging by a few dark scorch marks marring the stone, it had either taken some catapult fire, or a few errant blasts of dragon venom. No wonder it had felt like we were being shaken around inside a tin can before.

Fornax landed first and hunkered low as Thatcher rushed through getting himself and Garnett buckled into the saddle. As soon as they took off, Vexi touched down, and Reigh did the same with Phoebe while Isandri paced in her feline form, her wing feathers ruffled anxiously as she eyed the battle below. The only dragon who could manage the landing easily, thanks to his much smaller size, was mine.

Sitting astride Blite, I quickly tethered myself to the makeshift saddle before we took off. After all, my passenger was significantly easier to manage. Lukani wriggled deeper into my pocket, his long mouse-tail poking out. He was having a harder time holding his forms now. Getting tired, I guess. He hadn't been sure he could hold a large animal shape long enough to make it clear of the city. Better safe than sorry. I just hoped he didn't suddenly revert to his normal, boy-sized shape mid-flight and simultaneously cause us to crash while he ripped my pants off.

I might just have to let him plummet to his doom for that.

We took to the air and joined in formation with Vexi and Fornax, rising over the roaring heat of the fires and chaos still boiling far below. We kept in close and stayed far above the fray, well and clear of any of the dragonriders' battle maneuvers going on down below. Halfway across the city, however, a monstrous shape burst from the flames below and surged upward like a comet, beating mighty black wings and sending out a shattering cry that made Blite's hide shudder under my hands. The fire flashed across the king drake's body as he zoomed low, throwing down another incinerating line of flame before veering upward toward us. The orange glow of the lashing flames wavered off his midnight blue scales and obsidian-black horns, and flashed off the polished metal helm of the man riding on his back.

"*You're late.*" King Jace signaled, using the dragonrider code of hand signals to communicate in the air.

"*It's done,*" I signaled back. Naturally, I'd been taught this code as part of my Ulfrangar training, but this was the first time I'd used it while also riding a dragon. "*Going to Osbran.*"

"*Meet you there. Don't die,*" he replied, and then waved us off.

I watched, unable to keep myself from smirking again as he sailed back down into the battle and Mavrik breathed another long, blistering spray of burning venom. It was hard not to envy his speed and strength, and even harder to suppress the childish excitement that stirred in my gut to think that I was doing anything even remotely similar to that. Never in a million years would I have guessed I'd be sitting astride a dragon of my own, destined to follow someone like that upon a road of honor and valor.

But here I was.

And the path before me, a road lit by dragon fire and blazing with purpose, was clearer than ever before.

Dawn lit the horizon, turning it molten red as we prepared to touch down in Osbran, back outside the tavern we'd left behind scarcely a day and a half before. Somehow, it seemed much smaller and more secluded now. Like it might as well have existed in a completely different world compared to the utter pandemonium we'd left behind in Northwatch. Villagers scattered beneath us as our dragons landed one by one, cupping their broad wings and stretching out their hind legs to catch the ground like massive eagles. They cheered when we dismounted, crowding around to help us down and clap us excitedly on the back and shoulders. I knew they were probably just assuming we were official dragonriders returning from glorious battle, and simply didn't know any better, but it still felt ... good.

Granted, a few of them did take some cautious steps back when a mouse crawled out of my pocket and immediately turned into a green-skinned boy with strange yellow eyes. Lukani ducked behind me some, seeming equally unsure about them. I put a hand on his head and ruffled his hair in what was probably a horrible attempt to reassure him. He gave me a nervous smile, though, so maybe it worked.

It didn't take long for other, far more official dragonriders, to land around us. More and more came until there were about ten altogether, forming a circle and forcing the villagers back so we could make our way into the tavern and out of the open. Once we were all inside, and the tavern owner had been ordered to lock down his establishment and not let anyone else in, the dragonriders—probably on orders from Jace—began to question us. Not that they were holding us captive, necessarily. But there was a sense of urgency and concern in the way they spoke. Caution, too, like maybe they were concerned one or all of us might still be under Iksoli's control. They pressed us for information, asking if there was anyone else who'd been left behind that might need help, if any of us were injured and in need of a healer straight away, or if there was anything we'd seen in the tower that should be noted for the soldiers making their way through it.

Garnett and Reigh swapped a meaningful glance at that last question and both shook their heads. Hah. I guess they'd found the mirror, after all.

Luckily, as for the rest of it, there really wasn't much to tell. Most of us had superficial injuries, cuts and shallow sword wounds, and were spattered in varying degrees of filth and blood, but we were alive and whole. Nothing a bath, a few simple stitches, and a long night's rest couldn't fix.

Hmm. For the most part, anyway.

As soon as most of the dragonriders withdrew back outside, keeping a perimeter around the tavern to keep the locals from harassing us further, Isandri drifted away almost immediately. She stared around at the tavern's dining room, her expression utterly lost until, through the anxious company of lingering dragonriders and medics still checking a few of us over, I saw her lock eyes with Reigh. He'd been exchanging hushed words with one of the riders, but as soon as their gazes met, his mouth snapped shut. He started for her with urgency in every step, muscling his way through the people gathered around until he got to her. He caught her in his arms, grasping the back of her head as she seemed to fall against him. With her face buried against his shoulder, I couldn't see her expression. But I didn't need to. Her whole body shook as she clung to him, all of her steely fortifications seeming to dissolve into grief the instant he touched her.

My soul went numb at the sight, and I couldn't tear my gaze away. Reigh gripped her fiercely, turning to guide her into a corner where no one else would see as he whispered something against her ear. Her head bobbed some, but she never looked up, and kept her face hidden against his shoulder as he went on cradling her tight.

We'd walked away from this. We'd stayed alive, and completed the mission just as we'd intended—for the most part. But the price had been great, and the scars would remain. They always did. Long after the battle ended and the embers died, the memory endured, deep and cutting.

Eternal in the hearts of the ones who'd carried the flame.

32
CHAPTER THIRTY-TWO

What happened next was inevitable. It came at the end of every grand heroic tale I'd ever heard. Feasting. Celebrating. Hazardous amounts of drinking followed by a parade of poor life choices. Typical hero stuff, or so they say.

Hah. I suppose the dragonriders likely did those things. But for us, the recovery was much more subdued. Quiet, even. We were alive. We'd completed our mission. But beyond that, there wasn't much else for us to celebrate. We hadn't been able to save Devana. I wasn't even sure that had been possible from the outset. In her state, she was only being kept alive by that gilded helmet they'd locked her in. To free her was to also kill her, but she'd been reunited with Isandri and had made contact with Thatcher before the end. She'd also given him those items—things I hadn't seen since he'd slipped them into his pocket—and a message from his mother. Maybe it was all worth it. Somehow, it didn't feel like my place to be the one to say whether it was or not. Life and death had always seemed like very simple concepts to me before all of this. Now, I wasn't so sure.

King Jace arrived the following morning, still filthy from battle, and looking like he might drop from exhaustion. He and Reigh spoke quietly, occasionally glancing in mine and Thatcher's direction. I guess I could have gone over and demanded to know what they were going on about. We were a little past all that shadow and secrecy nonsense now. Deep down, though, I knew it didn't really matter. The decisions being made now were out of my hands, and sweet Fates, I'd never been more thankful for that.

We spent nearly four days at the tavern getting patched up, under the careful supervision of King Jace—until he couldn't take the public fascination with his presence anymore and departed for Halfax. He said it was to deliver the details to Queen Jenna about our little adventure, but I couldn't help but notice how a little angry vein throbbed in his forehead more prominently with every day that went by. That probably had something to do with all the villagers that thronged around the tavern, peeking in all the windows, and ogling anyone in armor. I didn't know what he'd expected, though. Arriving on the back of the most famous dragon in all of Maldobar in shining armor hadn't exactly been inconspicuous.

A few of the other dragonriders had taken a shine to our tavern, though, and he commanded them to hang around and offer us assistance or security if we needed it until he returned. It made me snort and roll my eyes. Assistance? Security? Why didn't he just call it what it actually was—disaster prevention—and be done with it?

Lucky for him, we were all fairly satisfied with our recent disaster experience and weren't raring for more just yet. Garnett had trotted off to fill Arlan in ... and drag Lukani back by the end of one of his long, pointed ears. Something told me we'd see him again, though. Like it or not, he struck me as the kind of kid that even a man like Arlan would have a hard time containing.

"You think she'll come back?" Thatcher moaned into his cup of cider, leaning against the bar. He'd been moping ever since she left.

"If you want to see her so badly, go to Arlan's place and look for her," I muttered as I sipped at my own mug of spiced ale.

"That just makes me look desperate, though, right?" he grumbled.

I sighed. "Well, right now you look pathetic, so which is worse?"

He didn't reply.

We both looked up as a pair of figures came in from the biting cold, stamping the icy sludge from their boots and throwing back their heavy, fur-trimmed cloaks. A familiar pair of dragonriders wandered in, jabbering loudly and waving when they saw us. I forced a smile and nodded back, if only to at least appear friendly. Maybe they'd leave it at that and go on their way instead of—

Nope. Of course not.

Sam and Kellan, the two dragonriders I'd bumped into at the military compound outside of Osbran, swaggered over and leaned against the bar right next to where I sat. They laughed and pulled off their riding gauntlets, taking turns patting me roughly on the shoulders. "There he is! The Not-Porter!"

"Hey," I managed through my teeth, still forcing that agonizing smile. Ugh. Being social was excruciating. "What brings you two out this far? I thought the dragonriders were working on sifting through the ashes now?"

"Heard there was a nice *restful* babysitting post here in Osbran, but I didn't realize it'd be watching over you," the taller one, Sam, glanced me over with that suspicious look. "You mean you're not even a dragonrider?"

"Not yet," Thatcher piped up, still staring mournfully into his cider. "We both got chosen, but we have to go through training now."

"Aaaah. So that's it," Kellan mused. He leaned on the bar top beside me and waved a hand, trying to get the tavernkeepers attention. "Well, looks like we're going to be watching you lot for the next few days."

"Fantastic," I muttered and looked away.

"I didn't catch your real name before?" Sam pressed. "You sure you're not like a ... Porter cousin? Once removed, or something?"

I took another drink to hide my scowl. "I seriously doubt it."

He leaned in a little, close enough I could see him squinting at me and feel his breath puffing on my cheek. "What's your *real* name, then?"

"Fred," I growled. Putting down my mug, I left a few coins on the bar and turned away. "I'm going upstairs."

Thatcher just nodded, still sighing forlornly and not seeming to notice I'd left him alone with the idiot-brigade, as I retreated up the steps to my room. I'd scarcely made it halfway down the hall before the sound of scuffling beyond Reigh's door made me stop. I listened, almost certain I heard bags or heavy objects thumping against the floor right inside.

I rapped my knuckles on the door. "Reigh? You in there?"

It opened immediately. Reigh paused where he'd been lugging two saddlebags along the floor and stared at me in surprise. "Oh. Hey. I was just on my way down."

I studied the bags. "Going somewhere?"

He dropped them with a thud at his feet and straightened with a groan. "Yeah, actually. Isandri's decided she's ready to go to Halfax and talk to my sister about everything. Seems like the right time to, you know, come clean about what was really going on with Devana in there?"

Ahh. Well, that explained why he'd apparently packed up every bit of his gear like he wasn't planning on coming back. "Right. Where is she? Already gone?"

"No, she's uh, saying her goodbyes to Phoebe." He combed his shaggy mess of dark red hair away from his eyes and let out a heavy breath. "I actually thought about seeing if she wanted a lift back there, as well. It's probably pointless to ask, though. She's not going to want to go anywhere without you."

I stared at him, wondering how many of his bones I could break before he managed to call for help. Hmmm. Probably six. Seven, if I really pushed myself.

Reigh shifted and cleared his throat, almost like he could sense my violent thoughts. He looked away and quickly changed the subject. "So, uh, where will you go next? Back to Halfax, too. Can't stay here forever, right?"

No. I guess I couldn't. "I'll probably head that way with Thatcher when he's ready."

"Back to shoveling horse dung, eh?" He chuckled.

I shrugged. "If no one throws me in prison first."

"Well, in the event no one does, I guess I'll see you at the academy at some point, right?" He arched an eyebrow, as though silently asking me if I was still considering taking that path.

I smirked. "Worried about that little promise I made about sparring, aren't you?"

Reigh balked, "No! Definitely not!"

Suuure. Liar.

I stuck a hand out for him to shake. "See you there, then."

He eyed my outstretched hand like he was afraid I might pull a fast move and punch him in the throat, instead. Not that it wasn't tempting. Finally, he grasped my hand and shook it. "See you there."

Our royal summons arrived four days later. Queen Jenna didn't spare anything on ceremony, and sent a grouchy but familiar face to hand deliver an intricately adorned letter bearing the royal seal. Southern Sky General Haldor graced us with his presence, bearing her invitation to return with him to Halfax and meet with her about what happened in Northwatch ... and what would be happening to us next. Not that I wasn't ready for a change of scenery, and anxious to get this over with, but finding out what the queen planned to do with me put an uneasiness in the pit of my stomach like sea sickness.

"It'll be fine, I'm sure of it," Phoebe coaxed as she followed me down the steps to the front door of the tavern. We'd already packed our things, and now we just had to load them onto Fornax and Haldor's dragon so we could go. Thankfully, between the three of us, Phoebe was the only one who had anything in the way of actual items to carry. I traveled light, and Thatcher could carry everything he owned on his person. Easy.

"I hope you're right," I admitted quietly as I helped tie a few more of her bags of crafting equipment and tools onto Fornax. "But if not, it is what it is. I never expected to walk away from this at all. The fact that I am is ... good. I'll take a lifetime in prison over a lifetime as an Ulfrangar any day."

"You deserve a lot better than that, Murdoc. You *are* better than that." Her smile was as sad as it was worried as she stared up at me, those big raindrop-blue eyes pulling me in like a vortex.

I had to look away. We hadn't spoken much since, um, that conversation after the confrontation with the Ulfrangar. I didn't know what to say to her now. I didn't know what any of that meant. I didn't know where we went from here, or what she expected from me. I knew what I wanted, what I felt, but that was irrelevant. I wasn't in a position to go launching off into personal fantasies about my future when I had no idea what truly awaited me back in Halfax. I'd gotten a hero's welcome here, yes. But I wasn't ready to bet on that same reception when I faced Queen Jenna again. Since the last time I'd seen her, my presence had been the cause of personal injury and nearly death to several people she cared deeply for—including her own brother. Somehow, I doubted that was something she would just brush off.

My gaze drifted over to where Sam and Kellan strolled by, carrying their own bags slung over their shoulders as they laughed. They spotted us and waved, grinning broadly. Heh. They must've been happy to finally get back to doing something useful. A few days of being cooped up with us in that tavern and the luster of getting an "easy babysitting assignment" had worn right off.

As he sauntered by, Sam threw his head back, whistling merrily to the open sky as he made his way toward his dragon.

My heartbeat gave a frantic skip. I froze. Phoebe's bag slipped out of my hands and hit the ground at my feet with a *thud*.

"Murdoc? What's wrong?" Phoebe must have noticed my expression go blank.

I stared at Sam's back. That ... that song. I knew that song. Didn't I? I did. I'd heard it before.

I sprinted away from Phoebe, leaving her standing there with her things as I bolted after him. "Wait!" I shouted, barely managing to catch Sam by the back of his long blue cloak as he began to climb up onto his dragon's back.

He slid his helmet visor up and frowned down at me. "Something wrong there, Fred?"

Oh. Right. Curse it, I'd forgotten about that. Ugh. Never mind—not important.

"That song ... the one you were whistling just now," I panted as I gripped his cloak to keep him from brushing me off and flying away. "What's it called? Where did you hear it?"

He arched an eyebrow. "Oh, that one? It's just an old sailor's tune. Heard it all my life. I expect most people growing up around the docks at Dayrise have, though."

Docks at Dayrise ... Oh. That's where I'd heard it. I must've forgotten. Or just hadn't paid enough attention to it at the time. "R-Right. Oh. I just, uh, it sounded familiar."

He waved a hand dismissively. "Ah, I'm sure it's not uncommon. Funny you should ask, though. Mr. Porter used to have all of us whistling it while we worked the bellows for him as kids. Keeps you on the right rhythm."

What? Mr. Porter had taught him that? But he was a swordsmith, not a sailor, wasn't he?

"Murdoc!" Phoebe called after me, running over with her red curls and skirts flying "Murdoc, what's going on?"

Sam barked a laugh. "Murdoc? I thought you said your name was Fred?"

I scowled and looked at the ground. "It was a joke," I lied.

"Which one was a joke? Fred or Murdoc?" He sounded genuinely confused.

Curse it, this was stupid. I was stupid. Wasting my time over something like this ... "Murdoc," I lied again, purely out of spite and humiliation this time, and let go of his cloak.

He cackled like that was absolutely hilarious. "Thought so! As if anyone would name a kid after that place!"

Every muscle in my body locked up solid. My pulse came to a frantic, hammering halt. Slowly, I lifted my head to stare up at him. "That's ... that's a *real* place?"

"Oh yeah! Course it is! Everyone who grew up around there knew about Mur-dock." He slid his visor back down and shrugged. "At least, that's what the locals call it. The real name is Hamourlow Dock, but the lettering on the sign for it's been worn away for, gods, probably forty years. No one's bothered to fix it, and all that's left of it now is M-U-R-D-O-C-K. The K's starting to look a bit iffy now, too, though. It's sort of a local joke, I guess."

My ears rang, blocking out anything else he might have said as he gave his dragon's neck a pat. My legs shook, wobbling dangerously as I took a few steps back while they took off into the sky. Everything went numb. I dropped to my hands and knees in the cold dirt of the road. Th-There ... there was a place. A place called Murdoc. A place I'd even been to before.

It was where I'd heard that song before, whistled like a lullaby that cut me straight to the core.

It was where a family lived ... the ones Sam and Kellan said looked like me.

A family that was also ... missing a son.

The Porters.

"Murdoc? What happened? Snap out of it and talk to me!" Thatcher's voice shouted right in my face.

I jerked back, falling onto my rear end and blinking at him in shock. My head whipped around, looking for—curse it, where was he—where was Blite?!

Go. I had to go. Right now.

I scrambled up and ran for my dragon, Thatcher and Phoebe still shouting and chasing after me. There wasn't time. I couldn't stop. I couldn't explain it all to them now. Later—I'd tell them everything later. Right now, I just had to go.

"WAIT!" Thatcher hollered, finally grabbing the back of my tunic and dragging me to a halt right at Blite's side. "What is wrong with you? Why won't you talk to me?"

I whipped around to stare at Thatcher with my thoughts spinning out control. Something—I had to tell him something. Words. Speak, curse it! "Murdoc," I managed to sputter. "They knew ... he said ... he knows where it is, Thatcher! He told me! It's ... it's in Dayrise!"

His face paled. "S-Seriously?"

All I could do was nod.

Thatcher let me go and stumbled backward. He blinked a few times, then turned and ran for Fornax, seizing Phoebe by the arm on the way. "GO!" He shouted as he bolted away toward Fornax. "WE'LL CATCH UP!"

CHAPTER THIRTY-THREE

It didn't take long for Fornax and Haldor's large male dragon, Turq, to catch up and fall right into formation on either side of Blite and me. We were at a slight disadvantage when it came to size and speed, after all. For now, anyway.

I pushed my young dragon hard all the way across the open prairies and rolling hilltops to the east, soaring between the towering plumes of clouds until the city of Dayrise appeared far in the distance. Thankfully, we didn't have all that far to go. It was a similar distance from Northwatch to Osbran. We had the wind in our favor this time, too.

As the city appeared before us, glittering in the evening light like a handful of jewels cast upon the dark, craggy shoreline, I looked out beyond it to the dark ocean. It shone and rippled, like a deep midnight blue blanket spread out along the steep sea cliffs. The smell of those cold salty waters carried strong on the wind, even this far away.

I shut my eyes and let that smell wash over me, seeping down into the very foundations of my soul. Gods, no wonder everything about this place felt so familiar. No wonder the sounds and smells of it had felt like I belonged there. It couldn't just be a figment of my imagination or hopeful thinking. No—it had to be real.

The sun had barely slipped beyond the mountains at our backs as we touched down in a large, familiar courtyard where we'd housed our dragons before in a nearby barn. I didn't waste a second. The instant my boots touched the ground, I spun to press my lips against Blite's scaly nose, and took off for the Porter's house like an absolute mad man.

Once again, Thatcher and the others called after me, but there wasn't time to wait around for them to get down. Besides, Thatcher had to be able to guess where I was heading now, right? Yeah. He wasn't a *complete* idiot. He'd figure it out.

My legs wobbled dangerously as I dashed down the sidewalk and onto the avenue that led in front of the Porter's sizable old house. It stood like a grand monument on the street corner, old and distinguished, but not too elaborate to be called noble. Staggering to a halt, I sucked in ragged breaths as I stared up at it. Lights glowed in the windows on every floor, and smoke floated up from both chimneys. They were home. Oh gods, they were home.

Fear took my mind like gnarled, clawed fingers as I started toward the front door. Oh no. I'd ... I'd come all this way. I'd flown all the way here on a whim. And why? Because some doofus thought I looked like a Porter? Because he'd whistled a song I recognized? Because a dock nearby had a name similar to mine?

Gods and Fates, what was I doing?!

Knock, knock, knock.

I hadn't even realized I'd reached for the big, brass knocker on the front door until it was too late. I snatched back, almost tripping over my own feet. Run—I should run. I should go back. This was stupid. I didn't know these people, and they certainly didn't know me. This was madness. I-I was—

The door cracked open just enough for one big, hazel eye to peer up at me. Then, with a creak of the hinges, a familiar young woman pushed it open the rest of the way and sighed. Aria Porter.

"Oh. It's you again." She didn't even try to hide the disappointment on her face as she glanced around, like maybe she was hoping to see someone else standing there with me. "Where's the rest of your friends?"

I shifted some and rubbed the back of my neck. "They're, um, they're not ..." My voice hung in my throat. The suspicious arch in one of her eyebrows almost made me forget why I'd come. "It's just me, for now, actually. Can I come in for a moment?"

Her lovely features sharpened, eyes narrowing some as she gave me a wary look. "I suppose. Is there something you needed?" She pushed the door open a bit farther and stood aside, motioning for me to enter. "The shop isn't open for customers this late if you're wanting work done."

"Oh, I-I ... no. No, that's not why I came," I stammered, unable to keep myself from staring at her. Was this really my—could she actually be my ... *sister*?

I let out a curse of alarm as I tripped over the doorstep on my way inside. Staggering, I barely managed to catch myself on the frame. Fates, what was I even doing? Why had I come here? This was ridiculous. I should go. Right now, before I humiliated myself any further.

"Then did you forget something? We didn't find any gear or personal items left behind after you left," she said, watching me flail with an unmistakable look of subdued bewilderment.

Gods, I must've looked like a complete idiot to her.

"A-Actually, I was wondering if I ... could I speak with your father? Or ... or, um, your mother. E-Either one. If they're available." I went on stumbling over my words, my face flushing as I tried to hold her gaze and force a smile.

I guess it came out as panicked and borderline insane as it felt. Fates preserve me.

She took a cautious step back, as though she expected me to snap at any moment and try to rob her or something. "Ah, well, yes. What for, exactly?"

I let out a heavy sigh and hung my head, rubbing my forehead with the heel of my hand. The longer I stood there, the more idiotic it seemed. I'd come here on a hunch.

That's it. I had no evidence—no good reason at all to think I might be related to these people.

"Look, there's just something I need to ask them. It won't take long. And I already know what the answer will probably be, but if I don't ask it's going to drive me crazy."

Aria glanced me up and down, her eyes narrowing distrustfully. Great. She really did think I was nuts. And I guess she wasn't entirely wrong about that. "Oookay. Wait right here for a moment, then."

I held it together until she had disappeared upstairs, then I threw my head back and groaned. Why—why had I done this?! I'd come all this way on some stupid, totally unfounded hope that two random idiots were right about me looking like these people? Had I completely lost my mind?

Now that I was here, I couldn't even see much resemblance to myself in Aria. Maybe our hair and eyes were a similar color, but there must be thousands of people in Maldobar with black hair and hazel eyes. I mean, yes, there was the name of the dock to consider. I hadn't been able to find anywhere else on any map of Maldobar called Murdoc. But still, that wasn't conclusive. I could have come from anywhere in the kingdom or even other lands beyond it. Not even Rook had known where the Ulfrangar had gotten me, right? Unless he'd gone to great lengths to figure it out somehow—which I doubted. It wasn't like they kept a logbook of it. I shouldn't be here. I should just go, right now, before they came down here and I had to—

"My daughter tells me you've a question?" A deep voice called down as heavy footfalls thumped down the steps.

The tone of it, deep and steady, confident but gentle, made my mind go completely silent. I froze. My heart gave a frantic, painful thud. Slowly, I forced myself to turn around.

I FELT about two inches tall as I met the guarded stare of a much older man coming slowly down the stairs. His dark hair fell loosely over his brow, flecked in silver at his temples, and framed his hard, angular features. His sharp jaw was dusted with silver stubble, and the creases at the corners of his eyes deepened as he looked me over from head to foot. His gaze had the same intensity of a lion inspecting an intruder that had wandered into his domain. It made me tense and take an instinctive step back.

When the man stopped at the base of the stairs, I spotted Aria and another slender woman who looked like she might be somewhere in her forties following close behind him. Mrs. Porter, maybe? I hadn't met either of these people, but the woman looked so much like Aria, it seemed like a decent enough guess. Her long hair hung in a silky black braid over one of her slender shoulders. She gasped at the sight of me, and latched onto the man's arm as though to stabilize herself. Her wide green eyes studied me with a look of silent terror as all the color drained from her soft features.

"Well?" Mr. Porter asked again.

"I, uh, yes. I do." I glanced between him and his wife a few times, scrambling to collect my thoughts. "I-I apologize for the intrusion. I just ... well, I heard about your son. The one that you lost, that is. And I wanted to know ... what happened to him?"

Mr. Porter's eyes narrowed dangerously. "What did you say your name was?"

I hesitated, biting back all the stupid lies I'd used a hundred times before to dodge that question. They were all far more palatable than the truth. But I hadn't come here to skirt honesty again. I hadn't come to deflect and make excuses.

My voice shook some, every word tangling up in all my fear and doubt as I stared back at all three of them. "I-I ... I don't know."

Aria gave a bewildered frown. "What do you mean? Before, you told me you were—"

"I know. I-I ... well, it's sort of complicated. When I was an infant, I was .... taken," I said quickly. "A group of people who called themselves the Ulfrangar stole me and a lot of other kids from our families all over the kingdom. They took us far away, and ... and didn't tell us where they'd gotten us." I tried to explain, to keep my voice calm, but every breath made my chest shudder and my hands shake. "They gave me a name after the place they took me from."

All traces of suspicion and foreboding intensity slowly drained from Mr. Porter's face as he watched me. His scowl softened. His dark brows rose. Beside him, his wife gripped his arm like a lifeline as her lips parted.

"And ... where was that?" he asked softly.

The words hung in my throat, burning and aching as I forced them out. "Somewhere called Murdoc."

Mrs. Porter gasped.

Aria went pale and clapped a hand over her mouth.

But Mr. Porter frowned—not angrily or bitterly, though. The soft furrow to his brow and squint to his eyes, and the way he tilted his head to one side a little, seemed more ... confused. Worried, even. He took a few steps closer and stopped right before me, leaning in to look at me eye-to-eye. "What do you remember?" he asked quietly. "Do you remember anything from before those people took you?"

Staring back at him, it felt like my brain had suddenly tangled into a thousand knots. What did I remember? "For the longest time I thought I didn't. I was really little when the Ulfrangar took me. And everything after that was so ..." My voice trailed off as my gaze wandered, drifting past him to the woman, Mrs. Porter. She stared at me like she was seeing a ghost—as though she might bolt back upstairs at any moment.

A heaviness settled in my chest, like an iron block sat right where my heart should have been. It made every breath a fight as I continued, "But when we came here before, with Jaevid and the others, I ... I heard something. A song. A lullaby, I think. I knew the instant I heard it ... that it wasn't the first time. I've heard it somewhere before, a long time ago. I just can't remember where."

Closing my eyes, I focused on that tune and started to whistle it. I couldn't sing it. I didn't know the name of the song, let alone the actual words. Fates, I didn't even know if it meant anything to them.

But what if it did?

I flinched and stopped whistling when something warm touched my face. Opening my eyes, I looked into the face of a man I knew I'd never seen before. He grasped my chin in his fingers, lifting my head so he could look me over carefully. His brows drew up when he brushed some of my hair away from my face, and his chin trembled as he ran a thumb over a spot on my cheek right below my ear where I knew I had a small dark freckle. Usually my hair hid it, and I'd never given it a second thought before now.

But Mr. Porter's eyes welled at the sight of it.

"Could it be?" he whispered hoarsely. "After eighteen years?"

I held perfectly still. Or, I tried to. I couldn't stop myself from shaking as Mrs. Porter came closer and joined him in studying me. She took one of my hands and began slowly unlacing my vambrace and pushing up the sleeve of my tunic. Her lips parted in another hushed gasp as she touched another place on my elbow where, amidst the dozens of scars that marred my forearm, I had a second small, dark freckle right at my elbow.

H-How had she known about that? Unless ...

"Rylen?" she whimpered, tears already sliding down her cheeks as she cupped my cheek.

I shuddered, unable to keep a sob from breaking past my lips. "M-Mom?"

They never answered.

Mr. and Mrs. Porter dove at me at once, flinging their arms around my neck and nearly dragging me off my feet. Sandwiched between them, I buried my face against my mother's shoulder and squeezed her as hard as I dared. She wept and kissed my cheeks and forehead. My father cried against my hair as he held both of us tightly against his chest.

We stayed that way for a long time. But I could have lived in that moment forever. Finally, my father pulled back long enough to shout to Aria, "Go! Go and get your brothers right now! Fenn is in the workshop. Derrin and Dorian are upstairs. Hurry!" he urged, his voice caught somewhere between tears and laughter. "Tell them Rylen has come home!"

She didn't waste a second, and took off upstairs as fast as a startled doe. I could hear her screaming their names as her footsteps thumped along the floorboards overhead and she opened and slammed doors. Then more voices joined hers, all repeating that name like bewildered echoes throughout the house.

"I-Is ... is that m-my name?" I stammered, my voice quaking as my chest seized with every broken breath.

My mother pressed her lips to my forehead, her eyes shining with the same deep green color as rose leaves. "Yes," she murmured as she went on petting my hair, as though she thought I might suddenly disappear at any moment. "Gods have mercy, you look just like your father."

I did?

Glancing back, I found him smiling proudly. He turned his head to the side a bit and tapped a place right below his ear. A bolt of emotion I didn't have a name for shot through me like cold lightning when I saw he had the same freckle on his cheek that I did. Tears filled my eyes again and I buried my face in my hands. All this time, all the years I'd spent searching, and there it was ... a tiny speck of evidence that no one could refute.

And I looked like my father.

"But you've got your mother's lovely dark hair," he said as he put a comforting arm around my shoulders. "And your grandmother's eyes."

"We all got that much," a voice called from behind us.

Looking back, I stared in silent awe at the four people gathered around the base of the stairs. Aria stood alongside two identical young men who seemed to be close to her age, or maybe a few years older. The sight of them hit me like a punch to the throat. They ... Gods and Fates, they all looked just like me! They had the same black hair, a similar face shape, and even hazel eyes like mine and Aria's. They were a little taller and maybe a little stockier, too. But the family resemblance was unmistakable.

The last man, who seemed to be the oldest, was the only one who had a more brownish hue to his hair. But apart from being somewhere in his thirties, that was the only stark difference I could see. He wore a spot-stained leather smithing apron and gloves, still holding a pair of heavy iron tongs in one hand like he'd ran straight over from the shop. Fenn, then? Did that mean the other two—the twins—were Derrin and Dorian?

My head spun as I gaped at them, leaving me breathless and lightheaded. I stumbled a little, but my father held me on my feet. I-I ... gods, I had *siblings*. I had three brothers, and ...

My eyes locked onto Aria as realization hit me so hard I nearly doubled over. That day in the street—when I'd first met her while she was chasing down her papers—she had been hanging up signs for *me*. She had been trying to find me, even eighteen years after the Ulfrangar had stolen me. Long after everyone else, including me, had stopped daring to hope ... she had still been searching.

My sister had still believed she would find me.

I took a staggering step toward her. I opened my mouth, wanting desperately to say something—to thank her somehow. But nothing would come out. I guess it didn't matter, though. She cried out and rushed for me, throwing her arms around my neck and hugging me frantically.

It didn't take long for everyone else to join in. They all gathered around me, closing me in from every side. My mother and father, three older brothers, and my sister. The family I had searched for, longed for, and thought I would never find again. The Ulfrangar had robbed me of so many things, but taking me from them was the cruelest of all.

But for the first time in my entire life, that past didn't matter. Nothing they'd done to me or forced me to do made any difference. There was only one fact—one truth—that meant anything at all now:

I was Rylen Porter. And I was finally home.

CHAPTER THIRTY-FOUR

There was a lot to figure out. A lot of gaps to fill in. And while I was eager to do whatever I had to in order to find my place here, with my family again, I had to admit ... I didn't really know what that meant. Fortunately, I wasn't alone in that.

Thatcher and the others came in not long after, and everyone moved into the living room and began to do a lot of explaining—including me. After a few hours, when we'd all calmed down a little, reality came crashing in for all of us. The truth of what had happened to me. The day I was taken, stolen from Aria's arms as a baby while she carried me to the market to meet our father, had nearly crushed the Porters. It'd hit her especially hard. She was only six years old at the time.

They'd searched for me for years. They'd scoured every city up and down the coast, and gone as far as Northwatch in search of anyone who knew what might have happened to me. But of course, I was long gone. And then the war had nearly torn the kingdom apart. They'd lost all hope of ever finding me again.

Well, everyone except Aria.

Talking them through my life was doomed to be every bit as difficult. I didn't know how much I should share. Right now, with emotions raw and my parents still in tears, I just ... couldn't tell them. The words hung in my throat like knots of heated metal. Thatcher helped, though. He told them how we'd met, sparing the details of me being an assassin, of course. He told them how we'd been working in Halfax at the royal stable, and that I'd been part of a mission authorized by the queen herself. He prodded me to tell them about Blite, and both my parents sobbed against me again when they heard that they had a dragonrider in the family once more.

They were proud.

But they didn't know the truth, yet.

"Right then. I suppose I should find lodging for our dragons, then. I'll send word to

Jaevid and Queen Jenna to let them know we'll be delayed," Haldor said, standing and excusing himself quickly from the house.

"We should find a place to stay, as well," Phoebe suggested, giving Thatcher a little nudge with her elbow. "Wasn't there an inn nearby?"

"Nonsense! You'll stay here as our honored guests!" My mother protested. "Any friends of Rylen's are friends of ours."

My insides clenched up a little at the name. Would I ever get used to it? My *real* name?

"Thank you, but you would probably like a little privacy right now. We completely understand." Phoebe curtsied and grabbed Thatcher by the arm, practically shoving him out the front door. "We'll drop by in the morning for tea, if that's okay. Just to check in and see how you're all doing?"

"Oh. Oh, yes. We'll look forward to it," my mother agreed. Honestly, in that state, it seemed like she might agree to just about anything.

"I'll go and get your room ready," Aria announced, standing and going to gently take her mother's arm. "Don't you want to help me? We can pick out a quilt for him."

Ah. I could see what this was. They knew there was something I wasn't telling them —information I was holding back. Things that my very delicate and emotionally fragile mother did not need to hear.

My father, brothers, and I sat in silence while Aria escorted my mother upstairs. Once they were well out of earshot, the atmosphere in the room grew heavy. All four of them stared at me, as though silently picking me apart to try and figure out what I might be hiding.

Fear prickled at my insides like spiders crawling around under my skin. I had to tell them. There was no way around it. And when I did, what if they decided maybe they'd rather not have me back? What if they found their long-lost son, only to learn he was going to prison as a murderer? What if they wished they'd never found him at all?

"You said the people that took you were called the Ulfrangar," Mr. Porter said at last, his tone quiet and firm.

"Yes," I answered.

"I've heard stories about them," Fenn spoke up, studying me with his head tilted to one side. He looked like he might be in his late twenties, or maybe very early thirties, at most. He'd taken off his metalworking gloves and apron, and sat with his thickly muscled arms crossed. "Rumors mostly. I always thought they were just something people made up—a drunken sailor's tale."

"No," I murmured. "In fact, they're the ones who set fire to the city square at King's Cross. They were ... trying to hunt me down."

"Hunt you down?" My father leaned in, visibly unsettled. "Why?"

I had no choice then. I had to tell them. Whatever happened, whatever they did about it after—I couldn't keep this ugly truth from them.

So, I fixed my gaze on the floor between my feet, and I started at the beginning.

None of my brothers said a word the entire time. My father only asked a few questions. He wanted to know more about Rook, what specifically had happened in Thornbend when I met Thatcher, and where'd I'd lived while I was with the Ulfrangar. And I told him everything I knew. His brows went up when I mentioned the loose association I had with King Jace—Rook having been his pup, and so on.

Then he leveled a serious, unblinking stare on me that held me like a blade to the throat. "Did you kill people for them, son?"

"Yes." I swallowed hard. That word—*son*—hit me like a hammer to the chest. No one had ever called me that before. Not even Rook.

"How many?"

I bowed my head again. I couldn't look him in the eye as I answered, "Three hundred and forty-one confirmed kills, as commanded by the Zuer."

He sank back in his seat some, eyes going wide. "Sweet Fates."

"Wicked cool. Can you teach me how to fight like that?" one of the twins—I wasn't sure which—whispered excitedly.

Our father cut them both a punishing glare.

Fenn did, too. Then my oldest brother looked back at me again, his pensive expression impossible to read. "What has Jaevid Broadfeather said about all this?"

"He's been supportive of my decision to defect and leave that lifestyle behind," I answered, not really sure what to say beyond that. Jaevid had always chosen his words carefully around me. He had pushed me sometimes, but only so far. I guess in the end, he still wanted it to be my decision to follow this destiny or not. "I think he wants me to choose this path and become a dragonrider. I think he believes I can do it. I want to believe that, too. But ... I know there may be repercussions for what came before."

"Even if you were forced to do it against your will?" My father pressed, sounding more concerned than ever now.

I shook my head. "Murder is still murder."

"Do you think he will plead for you? Jaevid Broadfeather, I mean." Fenn asked.

To be honest, I hadn't really considered that. Maybe he would. He'd done a lot for me so far. King Jace, too. I didn't fully understand why either of those men cared anything at all about what happened to me, but if it came down to it, I had plenty of reasons to suspect they might try to intervene to keep me out of prison.

Even if I knew I didn't deserve that kind of compassion from either of them.

"Maybe?" I wasn't confident enough about that to say anything else. "But I already owe Jaevid a lot. I won't ask him for that kind of favor. I haven't done anything to deserve it."

"We'll just have to wait and see what word he sends back, yeah?" one of the twins piped up again.

"In the meantime, we can't tell Mum about this," Fenn warned as he rubbed at his jaw. "She's been through a lot. This would be too much, especially right now."

"Agreed." The twins nodded in unison.

"Then let's give it a few days," Mr. Porter decided with a heavy sigh. He looked at me, and I could see the weary lines of the years creasing his brow. Like each day spent in grief and worry, wondering where I'd been, had crushed down over him and left those marks. "Whatever happens, Rylen, I don't want you to doubt that we are glad to have you back. I know this is ... complicated. But we'll get it sorted. I have faith. The men you've walked with are world-changers. To have my son counted among them, working alongside them, I am truly proud. Whatever comes next, we'll handle it together, as a family."

I nodded, keeping my head down in hopes of hiding my face. I didn't want him to see how I was hanging by a thread—how desperately I wanted to believe all that. But with my fate now tossed to the wind for royals and powerful figures far beyond this threshold to decide, I had no idea what to expect.

And hope, I knew, was a dangerous thing.

I sat with my father and brothers for several more hours, talking quietly around the fire in the living room. They were eager to share more about their lives, our extended relatives, and the family business. Apparently, the Porters had been swordsmiths for generations, crafting the finest blades and weaponry in Maldobar. Our father, Bram Porter, took his sons to Blybrig Academy in the spring to craft in the dragonrider forges and outfit them for battle. A high honor for any craftsman in the kingdom, I knew. But, unfortunately, not an art I knew anything about—not when it came to the actual process of it, anyway.

My father's eyes twinkled with thought when I told him I preferred to dual-wield longswords. At my height, and with my inclination to agility and acrobatics, the weapons suited me better than most. I'd trained with many, though, and he seemed pleased at my extensive knowledge of the different types of blades and how they were used in combat.

My sister was a sharp mind when it came to the bookkeeping, apparently. She had a finesse for handling the various merchants, navigating intense negotiations, balancing expenses, and acquiring the finest materials. Somehow, that didn't surprise me. She didn't seem like the sort of woman who liked to take no for an answer.

"She keeps us in line." Father chuckled fondly as he rubbed at his chin. "I suppose it's only a matter of time till some fellow is knocking down the door to try and marry her. And may the gods guard him. Any man seeking Aria's hand had better have a will to match hers."

"I'm not sure anyone like that actually exists," Fenn muttered.

The others got a quiet laugh out of that. I couldn't really join in, though. I didn't know her well enough, and ... I had a feeling that iron will of hers had been the only thing that kept her motivated to search for me all this time.

We talked until the embers in the hearth died down, barely glowing amidst the ashes. Fenn stood and excused himself to go back to the workshop and close things up for the night. The twins reluctantly went back upstairs to bed, dragging their feet the entire way. Apparently, it was their duty to open the forge up first thing in the mornings and get things ready for the day.

"Come, I'll show you upstairs to your room," my father offered. He stood, stretching his back a bit before he gestured to the stairs.

My stomach spun and clenched as I climbed the steps, my hand sliding along the smooth wooden railing. The rich scent of clove and dried orange hung in the air. The stairs continued up to a third floor, but Father motioned for me to turn at the landing.

The hall stretched on in either direction. On the right, he explained, was the washroom, study where Aria kept track of their books, and a small parlor. On the left, my room was next to the twins on one side of the hall. Fenn and Aria's rooms were directly across. My heart thumped as I walked along the rug that stretched over the wooden floor. A few brass sconces mounted on the walls illuminated old oil paintings of relatives, more proudly displayed weaponry, a few tapestries that looked like they must be a hundred years old, and some finely mounted antlers. All of it carried the feel of a long, proud family legacy.

"Try to get some rest, son," my father said as he stopped before the bedroom door—the room that was supposedly mine. "Tomorrow, we'll start figuring everything out. For now, let's be glad. It's been eighteen years since all of my children were safe in their beds. Let's be thankful for that."

He put a hand on my shoulder. I flinched some—an old habit. People did that to me a lot these days, and I still wasn't used to it. Kind and friendly touches were ... strange and foreign. No one hugged in the Ulfrangar. No one shook hands, patted one another on the back, or gave playful punches. Any time someone else had touched me before, when I was with them, it was always to inflict harm. To punish. To assert dominance.

Sorrow flickered in my father's eyes, almost like he understood. I didn't see how he possibly could, though. He couldn't have known what it was like to walk with the pack, and I was incredibly glad for that.

Wrapping a hand around the back of my neck, he dragged me in suddenly and pressed his lips against my forehead. "I know this won't be easy. Not for any of us. But I want you to know, that your family is ... very glad to have you back home, Rylen. Your mother and I have never stopped loving you. And we will be here to help you now in any way you need."

Tears welled in my eyes. I bit down hard and tried to blink them away. My father's hand slid away from the back of my head as he studied me carefully, probably noticing how I was fighting to hold it together. I wanted to apologize to him. No father wanted to find out his child was a murderer. But I was a monster shaped for destruction. And I didn't know if I could be anything else. I wanted to try, but that might not be enough. I might disappoint him.

"Goodnight, son." He gave my cheek a soft pat and turned away to go up the stairs to the third floor.

For several minutes, all I could do was stand there while his footsteps faded to silence somewhere overhead. Then my gaze drifted to the door—my bedroom door. I grasped the knob and twisted, pushing it slowly open.

Sterling moonlight bled through the large window directly across the modest, but well-furnished room. An armoire stood against one wall, and a washstand sat beside a tall dressing mirror. A large trunk under the window had blankets folded neatly and stacked on top, and an oil lamp flickered in a glass globe on the nightstand next to a decent-sized bed. When we'd stayed here before, this was the room Isandri and Phoebe had shared.

Now it was mine.

But I wasn't alone.

Aria sat on the foot of the bed, dressed in a long, white nightgown with a thick wool shawl wrapped around her shoulders. Her dark hair was braided over one shoulder like a long satin rope, and she cradled a small candle flickering in a clay bowl.

I hesitated, wondering if I'd come into the wrong room at first. Had Father meant the one on the other side of the hall?

I cleared my throat. "I-I, um, I apologize. I wasn't sure if—"

"Mother wanted me to tell you goodnight for her," Aria murmured without looking up. "I had to put her to bed. She's got a nervous illness. It makes her very weak sometimes and she can't breathe or speak."

"Oh. I didn't realize." I stepped into the room, watching the dancing flicker of the candlelight reflect on her eyes. "Is she alright?"

"She'll be better once she's had some rest." Aria looked up, her expression a mixture of apprehension and sorrow. "She ... she was never the same after you were taken. None of us were. Mother fell ill. Father hardly said a word for years. He drifted from job to job, working when he had to, but seeming almost like his mind had died and it was just his body moving on out of habit. The boys and I ... we had to carry on. We didn't have a choice. Fenn took care of us as best he could, trying to fill in the gaps so Mother and Father could ... grieve. But he was only fourteen."

"I'm ... I'm so sorry, Aria." I said as I sat down on the edge of the bed next to her.

"Don't be. It wasn't your fault," she murmured. "It was ... mine."

I frowned hard. "What do you mean? It wasn't your fault. You were a *child*. You couldn't have fought off the Ulfrangar, even if you'd been an adult." Fates, didn't she understand? She was lucky they hadn't taken her, as well, or killed her just for spite.

"*I* insisted on carrying you to the docks that day," she confessed, turning her face away. "Mother told me it wasn't a good idea. The dockside markets are busy in the middle of the day. But Father was waiting for us there. He'd promised to take us all to buy candied apples. And you were ... *my* baby. That's what everyone joked, because I loved taking care of you. Mother showed me how to wear you in a wrap. I helped her feed you, bathe you, rock you—everything. I could always make you smile and laugh. I taught you how to crawl and you'd just started pulling up and trying to walk. I even made Mother put your crib in my room so we could be close." She paused, her shoulders drawing up some as the hand holding the candle shook slightly. "Then you were just ... gone. They snatched you right out of my arms. They hit me across the face so hard I fell. By the time I got up, they were already getting in a wagon and speeding away. I couldn't stop them. I ran ... for miles. But you were gone. And I couldn't even remember what they looked like."

I held my breath, studying her for a moment. I knew what I had to do. I just, gods, I was no good at this. I steeled my nerve and reached out to rest a hand on her shoulder, the same way Father had when he spoke to me. "Don't blame yourself for someone else's wickedness, Aria. You didn't do anything wrong. What's wrong is that men like that, who do those things, walk free in this kingdom in the first place."

Her head turned slightly, peering at me through falling locks of her long dark bangs like she wasn't buying a word of that. "I missed you so much, Rylen. Every day. And now it feels like I've missed so many other things—parts of your life I should have been there for."

I pulled her in so she could lean against my side. "Sorry I'm not a cute baby anymore," I muttered. "If you've still got that crib, I can try to cram myself back in it."

A faint smile brushed her lips as she leaned her head against my shoulder. "Oh, gods. You've got Father's sense of humor, too, haven't you?"

"Maybe."

She puffed a deep sigh. "Great. Now Fenn and I are outnumbered in that respect."

I smiled back and gave her a little squeeze, hoping that was a consoling gesture. I'd seen other people do it, after all. Maybe it wasn't as awkward as it felt. "Thank you, Aria."

"For what?"

I closed my eyes and let my head lean over to rest on top of hers. "For not giving up."

She sniffled some and wiped at her eyes. "I would have searched for you forever. Every day until the end of time."

"Well, now there's only one thing I want you to do for me."

Her brow crinkled some, studying me with a hint of worry as the candlelight made all the tiny golden flecks in her hazel eyes sparkle. "What?"

I gave her another small squeeze. It'd felt good to hug her like that the first time—the sister who had never given up on me. "Be happy."

35
CHAPTER THIRTY-FIVE

I awoke late the next morning, lying sprawled in a bed that was mine, with sunlight peeking through the heavy drapes over the window. I found a set of new clothes, folded neatly and left on the bedside table. The dark green tunic looked a little worn around some of the hems, but it was clean and well made. The dark pants were, too, and they fit nicely despite my long legs that usually made everything I tried on a few inches too short. I smirked at my reflection in the mirror across the room as I finished lacing up my boots. I'd never had hand-me-downs before. Not like this, anyway. I liked it immediately, and wondered how many of my older brothers had worn these before. Maybe all three of them?

The house downstairs smelled of freshly brewed tea and the lingering aroma of a cooked breakfast. I'd slept in too late—a personal first for me—and had missed it, but Mom had made sure that a plate was set aside for me to have whenever I came downstairs. Mom and Aria sat at the table while I ate, asking me questions about myself that, thankfully, had nothing at all to do with my past as an Ulfrangar. They wanted to know where I'd traveled, what Queen Jenna was like, and if I'd seen Jaevid's wife, Beckah. They prodded carefully around the subject of my own romantic life, hedging at the question of whether or not I was courting anyone or not. I guess they were eager to have another woman in the house to even those odds, as well.

Mom patted my arm soothingly when I told her that, no, I was not courting anyone at the moment. "Don't you worry. My sons will have no trouble at all finding good matches."

My face burned and I looked away, trying to avoid Aria's teasing little grin.

It didn't work.

I could still feel it like the prick of needles on my skin as she very casually commented, "Oh, I know. How about that lovely girl who came along with you yesterday? I think her name was Phoebe, wasn't it? She's quite pretty, isn't she, Mum?"

My mother immediately launched into a hearty agreement, approving thoroughly of Phoebe's manners and how beautiful she thought her red hair and dainty blue tunic were. All the while, I could have sworn my hair was on fire because my head grew hotter and hotter until I knew I must be sweating.

"Sh-She's, uh, she's very nice," I agreed, nearly choking on my own spit.

"Is anyone courting her?" Aria pressed, feeding the fire like her life depended on it. "She seemed awfully attached to that cute, blond-headed boy with her. Are they a couple?"

I licked my teeth behind my lips, feeling that rising urge to inflict some manner of physical pain on Thatcher, purely on principle. "No," I managed stiffly. "They are definitely not a couple."

They'd better not be.

"So, she's available?" Aria was grinning wolfishly.

Gods, please save me from this. "I-I ... don't ... I guess she is, yes."

"Then what are you waiting for?" My mother joined in.

I opened my mouth, but before I could get a word out to defend myself, Aria jumped in again. "Well, if you're not interested in her, maybe Derrin or Dorian will be. I spoke with her a little before, and she seemed quite bright, too. She would be good to have in the family, I think. Mom, we should have her in for afternoon tea, don't you think?"

I could feel my pulse throbbing in my ears as I stared at her, my mouth still hanging open like an idiot. Seriously? Did she ... did she know that I—well, maybe not *loved*. Love is a strong word. But I certainly preferred Phoebe.

A knock at the door spared me from having a full-blown cardiac episode. We all leaned over to peer out into the hall, watching as one of the two servants working for my family answered it. The familiar voices coming from the doorway made me sink down in my chair with relief. Haldor, Thatcher, and Phoebe had come back at last.

But they weren't alone.

As they all filed into the dining room, smiling and greeting us with a mixture of curiosity and hesitance, a much older man in formal Gray elven robes followed at a distance. I'd have known his ominous, focused scowl from miles away. King Jace spoke a few hushed words to the servant, who tripped all over herself to dash away into the house.

I frowned. Why had he come? How had he found us here in the first place?

Oh. Right. He had spies all over this kingdom, thanks to Judan's hard work.

Aria and my mother began to rise when he entered, offering shocked, scrambling curtsies until he waved a hand and offered a gentler smile than I'd ever seen touch his features before. "Please, ladies, it's all right. Continue with your meal. We've come to speak with you and your family." His gaze landed on me with intent, that smile fading from his eyes to let the tiniest bit of cold pressure bleed through. "*All* of your family."

Ah. So that's what this was about. He'd come with word from Jenna, then. Maybe even Jaevid, too. The decision about me had been made.

I tried not to let my apprehension show as I sat alongside my mother, waiting while the servant collected the other members of my family from around the modest estate. Father and Fenn came from the workshop. The twins, Derrin and Dorian, wandered in from the courtyard, each carrying wooden practice swords. They all stared in shock at our new collection of guests sitting around the long dining table.

Not that it was the first time King Jace had been there, but they hadn't shared a meal with him the last time.

While everyone got settled in, Thatcher immediately rushing over to take the seat on my other side like it was some kind of competition, I watched Aria's gaze fix onto Phoebe like an eagle on the hunt. The corners of her mouth curled into a cunning, conspiring little grin, and I could practically see the machinations brewing in her eyes.

Then *he* sat down.

Haldor settled into the chair next to Phoebe, his smile more awkward and uncertain, like he wasn't sure why he'd been invited to this little gathering but was too polite to question it. Dressed in gleaming dragonrider armor, that royal blue cloak trimmed in fox fur clipped to his pauldrons, he sat straight and graciously accepted a servant's trembling offer for tea. I'd only met him in passing—including the night when he'd arrested Thatcher and me in Thornbend—but I'd heard a little about his family. They were rich Damarian merchants with strong holdings in Southwatch, apparently.

I watched the smile gradually dissolve from my sister's face as she stared at him, probably noting those vivid, golden Damarian eyes. He was a bit older than she was, probably in his early or mid-thirties, but with that smooth, light brown complexion, who could tell? Not that I was any kind of judge, but there were probably a lot of women who would find his shoulder length black hair and sharp brow attractive.

Aria did, apparently. I couldn't think of any other reason for her to be blushing like that. Granted, dragonriders tended to have that effect. The flashy armor and reputation as the superior fighting force under the royal banner were considered a very potent and desirable mix among the noblewomen at court.

Hmmm.

Once the rest of my family arrived, taking their seats and staring nervously at their new guests, King Jace cleared his throat. "First, let me dispel any concerns so we're not all sitting here in suspense. Jaevid and Her Majesty won't be coming, although they do send their greetings and gratitude to your family for your support, especially over the last few weeks."

My father gave a nod. "We are honored to serve Her Majesty however we can."

Jace returned the gesture, although I could see him sizing my father up from across the table with that practiced, Ulfrangar speed. "They also wish to extend their condolences for what your family has suffered these many years. As do I. As a father myself, I cannot imagine what you've endured. I must admit, I was shocked to hear that Murdoc had—"

"Rylen," Aria interrupted suddenly. "His name is Rylen."

I stared at her in shock. Had she just ... interrupted a *king*? For my sake?

My reaction was nothing compared to our parents', though, who gaped at her in total mortification.

Even Jace seemed a little surprised. He blinked a few times, then gave a light, snorting chuckle. "Rylen it is, then. At any rate, I was quite shocked to learn he'd located his family. For someone in his situation, I hope you can appreciate how incredibly rare that is. Children who are lost to the Ulfrangar never break free of them, and certainly never reunite with their families. Now, I cannot confirm this as he's no longer with us to speak of it, but I suspect that Rook may have chosen his Ulfrangar name in the hopes that this would happen. To select such a unique name tied so specifically to one location is not typical. I have reason to believe Rook chose it hoping that, eventually, Rylen would find his way back here."

My heart gave a hard, wrenching jerk. Rook had wanted me to come back? He'd been the one to give me that name yet, and until that moment, I hadn't realized ... by calling me that, he'd also given me a clue. The only clue that would lead me straight back home.

My eyes watered as I looked down again, fighting desperately to keep my emotions in check. Not now. I couldn't do this right now. Not in front of everyone.

"Unfortunately, simply locating and reuniting with his family is not enough to absolve Rylen of his past crimes as an Ulfrangar. I know many of you likely have no idea what that means, fully. I'm more than willing to explain it in greater detail, as I have a very ... similar history to your son. Like him, I was brought up within the ranks of the Ulfrangar. I also managed to escape. Granted, my own journey to freedom did not see me finding the trust and loyalty of friends until much later. Your son has been very fortunate to have met so many people who were willing to speak for him and stand at his side." King Jace's expression darkened some, and he tapped his fingers on the table. "But nothing they do or say can erase what was done while he still walked with the pack. Rylen knows this. There is only one person who can truly offer him a clean slate going forward."

I swallowed hard.

Next to me, Thatcher shifted in his seat like he'd sat on a pinecone.

"I've spoken with Queen Jenna at length concerning your history—the same history you know that I share. She was ... reasonably shocked and dismayed. But hearing what you've done since your defection, how you've attempted to alter the course of your life and atone, was also surprising to her. I won't make light of the path you've been forced to walk, Rylen. I told her what pups like us were made to endure, and how we earned our place and survived. I told her plainly when I first met you, I feared what you might do to these people. I didn't believe you could be saved or salvaged from that life. I believed you were well and truly lost to the darkness of the Ulfrangar, and it goes without saying that those who have done what we have to survive their brutality are not worthy of mercy in any form." Jace's gaze shifted, catching on Thatcher who still sat right beside me. "But mercy sometimes finds us anyway. And I have never been so glad to be proven wrong. I put my word before Queen Jenna to vouch for your worthiness. I told her of your dragon, as well. And so, she has passed her judgement."

I stiffened in my chair as he reached into the breast pocket of his robes and pulled out a fine square of golden parchment, sealed with a blue and gold ribbon and the crest of an eagle. He placed it on the tabletop and slid it across to me with a knowing smile.

"Queen Jenna has given you official pardon, young man. But on one condition. You must walk the path I walked to redemption. Your sword must now serve Maldobar, as a Dragonrider formally trained under the supervision of Academy Commander Broadfeather," he said, holding my gaze as I slowly reached out to take the letter. "What do you say?"

My hand halted, still holding the heavy piece of thick, folded parchment. It felt like it might as well have been a lead weight in my hands. My life, my future, was bound to this letter. What I chose now ... it was the path that would define me forever.

I glanced down the table toward my parents, my sister, my three brothers, Thatcher, and Phoebe. They all stared back. No one made a sound.

I looked back to King Jace, his brow now arched expectantly. "Well?"

Sucking in a deep breath, my voice shook as I finally answered, "It would be my greatest honor, Your Majesty."

THE HOUSE WAS pure chaos after that. The good kind, though. My mother was frantic to serve wine and celebrate, even if it was far too early in the day for that. My siblings thronged around Thatcher and Phoebe, curious about the two companions I'd been traveling with all this time. Granted, I had a feeling Aria was still up to no good in terms of Phoebe. I'd have to address that soon.

My father stepped aside with Jace and Haldor, exchanging hushed and likely far more serious words. My father stood with his hands at his back, nodding and rubbing his fingers together in an all too familiar nervous habit. Hmm. So that's where that had come from. He nodded emphatically as he listened to Jace, and I had a feeling there was a lot to be said there—details about me, and what he might expect going forward. I probably needed to hear some of that information at some point.

But right now, there was a much more serious issue at hand.

"You know, Mom, that man there is Southern Sky General Haldor Kal'Sheem," I said as I put a hand on her arm and motioned to the only armor-wearing dragonrider in the room.

Her eyes went wide and misty at the sight of him. "Is that who he is? My, he's quite handsome, isn't he?"

"Oh, sure. And single, too, I've heard," I added quickly. "You know, I could be wrong, but I'm pretty sure his family are the same Kal'Sheems who run that big merchant company out of Southwatch. Big fancy house. Lots of ships. Tons of money and connections. He must be very picky about who he's going to marry, I guess, with that kind of a business to consider. He's probably just biding his time for the right woman with good business sense and an honorable family to come along ..." I let my voice trail off, watching as my mother's eyes went from Haldor straight to Aria.

Bingo.

I made sure I was giving Aria the same wolfish grin she'd given me when our mother went straight to her, seized her by the arm, and basically dragged her over to meet Haldor. Good luck with that, sis. Two could play that little game.

With that little situation sorted, it wasn't hard to drift into the background of all the excitement and chatter in the dining room. The servants brought out tea and snacks, looking more flushed and disheveled than I'd ever seen them.

I took the first chance I got when I was sure no one would notice to slip out of the room. I made my way through the house, running my hands along the walls to feel the bumps in the plaster as I went. I passed through the door on the first floor that led out into the wide courtyard. It was the same place where I'd sparred with Thatcher and taught him more swordplay. I'd also argued with Blite here a few times, which was why it didn't surprise me at all when the little black and red drake came waddling toward me over the cobblestones. He made musical clicking and popping sounds and sniffed through my hair, nibbling at my boots until I pushed his big head away.

"Hey, none of that. These are the only pair I've got left, thanks to you," I reminded him.

Blite's ears perked, his head lifting suddenly as he focused on something right behind me.

"You're missing your own celebration in there, you know," Thatcher said.

I smiled to myself and turned around, studying him with my dragon's big scaly head right next to mine. "Yeah. I guess I am."

"The crowd getting to you?" he guessed.

I shrugged. "A little. Mostly just ... wanted to think."

He wandered closer, grinning up at Blite and offering a hand for my dragon to sniff. "It's pretty great, right? You've got your family back. And we even knew them basically the whole time! I keep trying to wrap my mind around it," he laughed, but it was all wrong. Forced and almost frantic. "I guess you'll be staying here with them now, right? I'm really happy for you."

"Thatcher ..."

"No, I *really* am. I mean, yeah, it's kind of out of the blue. But you've been searching for them for a long time, and ... and they've been trying to find you, too. Your sister was telling us about it. Maybe it's a little weird for you still, though. I'm sure after a few months, once you've had a chance to really settle in, it'll get easier."

"Thatcher ..." I tried again. I wasn't sure who he was trying to convince—me or himself.

"And, you know, we'll still see one another at the academy, right? I know I'm a little younger, but Jaevid seemed to think I could handle it. We'll still—"

"THATCHER." I had to raise my voice to get him to stop.

He cringed and looked down, his mouth screwing up as he studied the toes of his boots like he'd found the meaning of life down there. Or rather, like he was desperately searching for it in a moment of pure and complete panic.

But I got it. He didn't have to say another word. I understood completely.

I had a family now.

And he ... was alone.

His home was still gone. His father was still dead. I'd been the only sliver of familiarity and safety left in his entire life. And now ... all of this had happened.

I couldn't go back to Halfax with him.

His eyes welled as he swallowed. "I'm okay. I'll be okay," he gasped, still sounding like he was trying to convince himself that was really true. "It's good that you're going to be here with them. It's where you should be."

I lunged at him, grabbing that stupid, ridiculous, troublesome kid in my arms and hugging him tight. He was a few years younger than me, a lot shorter and as scrawny as an alley cat—which I'd known from the beginning. But right then, it felt like he might as well have been six years old. A scared orphaned kid who was losing the only fragment of home he had left.

"I'm sorry, Thatcher," I growled through my teeth. "Gods and Fates, I ... I am so sorry."

"I-It ... it's ...o-okay," he started again.

"Shut up. Don't say another word like that," I growled again. "It's not fine. None of this is fine. You're such an idiot, you know that?"

"Y-Yeah ..."

I seized his shoulders and held him out at arm's length. "I'll talk to my father. I'll ask him if you can ... I don't know. It's a big house. They've got plenty of room for ..."

I saw the answer in his face long before he ever spoke. That broken goodbye smile and hollow, quiet voice put a pang of pain through my gut as he murmured, "I don't belong here, Murdoc."

My chest heaved in slow, angry breaths as I gripped his arms harder. "Thatcher?"

"I've wondered a long time what it meant to be a God of Mercy. I worried about using my power to influence people into doing things they didn't really want to do. I've never felt very god-like. I don't even know what that means, really," he looked past me, up at Blite, and his smile widened some. "I think I get it now, though."

What? What was he talking about?

Thatcher took my hands off his arms, then carefully pressed his hand into mine to grasp it tightly. "It isn't about flashy powers or incredible miracles. It never was. It was about finding the lost ... and showing them the way back home. Not because they deserve it, but because deep down, we're all lost people. And we're all just trying to find our way home."

I frowned down at the way he was gripping my hand, almost like he was ... saying goodbye.

Then Thatcher held up his other hand, showing me where he held the tiny crystal between his fingers. It sparkled and shone in the sunlight, no bigger than a sunflower seed. "I've got one more miracle to do. It's waiting for me in Halfax," he said quietly. "I'll wait until you come to visit, okay? Don't take too long, though. I promise, this is one you won't want to miss."

PART SEVEN
THATCHER

CHAPTER THIRTY-SIX

"I think that about does it," I said, groaning as I bent backwards a little to stretch. I'd been helping Phoebe pack up her workshop in the undercrofts of the royal castle for almost a week. Today was the last day, though. Tomorrow, there would be a ship waiting in the port with her name on it.

"Thank you, Thatcher. You won't get in trouble with the stablemaster, will you? I know this took a lot longer than we thought," she worried. "I can go and explain to him personally, if I need to."

"Nah. I'm sure it's fine." I turned around to sit on one of the freshly-packed crates and wipe the sweat from my face with my sleeve.

"Are you going to the ball tonight?" she asked as she came over to offer me a waterskin.

I took it and gulped down as much of it as I could without choking myself before I answered, "Yeah. Queen Jenna invited me, so I can't exactly say no, right?"

She giggled. "No, I guess not. Are you excited? Rylen is coming. And Prince Judan, Kiran, Jondar, and even Duke Cromwell!"

"Yeah. I am actually. It'll be good to see everyone again." Hearing her say it like that made me realize just how long it had been. Three months now, if I was remembering correctly. And in that time, a lot had happened, to say the least.

First, I'd gone back to my old job working for Stablemaster Godfrey. Not because I had to, necessarily. Queen Jenna was allowing me to stay at the castle as her esteemed guest, so I could have loafed around if I wanted to. But sitting on my hands and eating pastries was only fun for a few days. Phoebe had gone immediately back to working down here, designing new things and consulting with all of Maldobar's finest engineers. I wanted something to keep me busy, too.

And, well, stable work always was one of my finer skills.

Granted, the look on Godfrey's face when I told him I wanted to work in the Deck with the dragons was priceless. I guess he hadn't seen that one coming. But it let me be near Fornax so I could keep working with him, perfecting our flying, and using all the new equipment Phoebe had made for us.

Her life had been a lot more interesting, by far, though. Not even a month after we came back, the Court of Crowns was called to a close and all the nobles and royals began making preparations to leave. During that time, a much older woman we'd seen sitting in the court during Phoebe's trial came down to her workshop with Queen Jenna. I remembered her instantly because of her hair. It looked a lot like Phoebe's, although it was turning white around her temples and brow.

The woman had introduced herself as Orna, and explained she was the queen of a kingdom called Noltham, which lay far to the east. She believed Phoebe might be a relative of hers—a niece she'd believed was lost to the Tibran invasion years ago. The rest of her family had been executed, but due to the efforts of her castle guard, they had managed to smuggle some of her youngest relatives out. Many of them had been hunted down and eventually killed. But there had never been any evidence found when it came to her youngest niece, an especially bright little girl with wild red curls.

The whole time, Phoebe looked like she might pass out any second. She didn't say much, which for her, was sort of a big deal. In fact, I couldn't remember a time when she'd been quiet for that long. Eventually, though, she seemed to come to terms with the fact that this elegant, soft-spoken older woman might really be her aunt. Naturally, that made Phoebe a duchess, since she was now her only surviving heir.

And about the time Phoebe realized that, she finally did pass out.

It was a lot to take in. The queen offered to take her back to her homeland, Noltham, and let her see the place where she'd been born, tour the kingdom, and meet the few other members of her family who had managed to escape the Tibrans. There weren't a lot of them, and most were just distant cousins, but the queen sounded hopeful.

I guess finding out she had any close descendants left alive was more than she'd expected to find here.

Initially, Phoebe didn't seem to like that idea at all. She talked me in circles for days, explaining why it wasn't a good idea, that she really didn't want to be nobility, and that she liked her life here in Maldobar. But after a few days, Phoebe finally confessed that she really did want to go. She apologized over and over, almost like she felt bad for leaving. Maybe she thought she had to stay because of me. Like she was supposed to watch over me and keep me company now that everyone else had gone on their separate ways.

Of course, that wasn't true. My life was getting emptier by the day, sure. But ... the silence and calm weren't so bad. There was peace in it. And deep down, I knew it wasn't over. I'd see them all again—hopefully tonight at the farewell ball.

Granted, there weren't a lot of nobles left now. Most of them had been all too eager to go back to their kingdoms and attend to rebuilding their lands and restoring everything the Tibrans had destroyed. But for the ones who had stayed, or were taking a bit longer to make their departures, Queen Jenna was having a grand celebratory ball in the royal castle. People from all across Maldobar and Luntharda would be there, as well. I'd never been one for dancing, but the idea of seeing everyone again, spending the night celebrating, and catching up on what we'd all been doing sounded great.

Also, lots of free extra-delicious food. That was always a bonus.

"You know, I think Jenna is right. I think you've gotten taller," Phoebe mused as she tapped her chin, staring up at me with a broad smile.

I groaned and rubbed my forehead. "Well, it's about time. Maybe everyone will quit assuming I'm twelve now."

She laughed again and petted my head consolingly. "I'm sure Garnett will be very impressed."

Ugggh. There it was. That joke was starting to get old now. I hadn't seen or heard from Garnett since we'd parted ways in Osbran. The fact was, I'd put myself out there in a big, embarrassing, and totally awkward way. I'd told her how I felt. I'd kissed her. And she had said ... nothing. She'd acted like it never even happened. I probably wasn't the most knowledgeable person when it came to girls, sure, but even I knew what that meant. Silence like this was a nice way of saying "no thanks."

"I really don't think she's going to come to something like this, Phoebe," I muttered as I stood. Time to go before she launched into all the reasons why I shouldn't give up hope. I couldn't listen to that again. It was completely humiliating. "I've got to head back to the stable, but I'll see you tonight, okay?"

Phoebe's mouth twisted to one side, looking at me with a heavy sigh and her hands on her hips. For once, though, she didn't argue. She just waved a little and murmured back, "See you tonight, Thatcher."

THE CASTLE WAS LIT up like something straight out of a fairy tale. As the sun set and all the candles along the walkways, white cobblestone drives, and through every window and over every doorway were lit, the whole place sparkled like a field of stars. Wreaths of flowers and evergreen hung everywhere, filling the air with inviting smells. Music filled the night, mingling with the sounds of conversation and laughter as I stood against the wall in one of the massive ballrooms. All four of them were open tonight and filled with people in beautiful clothing. Men wore suits or flowing robes. Women displayed dazzling ball gowns or sleek fashions made of colorful silks embroidered with jewels. Dragonriders and infantrymen walked the halls with their ceremonial armor polished to mirrored perfection, and some of the international guests sported ensembles so elaborate and strange it made everyone stop and marvel.

I smiled as I watched the couples whirling on the dance floor before me, occasionally catching a glimpse of a face I knew. Reigh and Isandri twirled together, laughing and grinning like they were plotting something. They'd spent a lot of time together since they came back, and while they didn't visit as often now that Isa was serving in the court as an ambassador for Nar'Haleen, it was still nice to have them around.

Jaevid stopped by to say hello, introducing me to his wife, Beckah, before they went off to join in the dance, too. Jenna finally agreed to a dance with her fiancée, Phillip, who despite still looking like a monster straight from the darkest pit of the abyss, was a pretty decent dancer. It was easy to spot him, though, since he towered over everyone else and was the only one with a tail.

Judan strolled by with his mother, and they both said hello, too. I didn't spot Jace anywhere, though. Maybe he was hiding out in case someone forced him to dance. Somehow, he didn't seem like the kind of guy who enjoyed this kind of setting much.

"Quite a gathering, isn't it?" Someone bumped my shoulder suddenly to get my attention.

I looked over and up, meeting Ezran Cromwell's familiar roguish grin.

"Oh! Hey," I stammered in surprise. "Yeah, it's, uh, really big. And loud."

He laughed and leaned against the wall next to me, holding a glass of wine I suspected probably wasn't his first. "I always did hate these things," he admitted. "Say, where's that broody friend of yours? The one who stole my *favorite* hatchling right out from under my nose?"

I cringed. "He's ... well, I don't know, exactly. He said he was coming. Maybe he's around here somewhere?"

Ezran made a miserable, growling sound into his goblet. "I owe him a good smack for that. So, Jaevid tells me you've been back to mucking stalls these days? Gods, boy! You're a bloody dragonrider now!"

I laughed, unable to hide the embarrassment that rose like tingling heat in my cheeks. "Yeah, well, I don't have anywhere else to go. And I don't like just sitting around doing nothing."

"Is that so?" He cast me a thoughtful sideways glance. "You like it, then? Living here and mucking stalls all day?"

"I-I mean, it's ... okay," I stuttered. When he said it like that, it did sound kind of miserable.

"I see. You're supposed to go to the academy next year, right? You getting a lot of training in?" he questioned.

Oh boy. Well, this was going to be a disaster. "Not really. I don't have anyone to spar with. Everyone's really busy, and I ..."

My voice died in my throat as Ezran stared me down, his eyebrows scrunching together like two angry little caterpillars. "Unacceptable," he pronounced. "Completely unacceptable. I won't have a rider chosen by a Cromwell dragon going off to the academy and making a fool of himself. Fates, Jaevid said you were out here wasting away, but I had no idea it was this bad. That settles it, then."

My eyes went wide. "Settles what?"

"You," he lifted his wine glass toward me. "You're coming back to the Cromwell estate with me. We'll start training you properly."

My mouth fell open. "But, uh, I have a job here and—"

"And you think someone else can't clean horse dung out of a barn? You're the only one qualified for that?" He scoffed and rolled his eyes, clapping his free hand on my back. "Nonsense. You're coming to stay with me, kid. You're good with dragons, right? Maybe my stable hands can teach you a thing or two that's a bit more to your liking. Place is pretty sparse these days, anyway. Just me and the servants. It'll be nice to have someone else to talk to. And we'll work on that training every day. You'll be fit for it when you start at the academy. Make no mistake, boy, that place is not for the faint of heart."

My whole face flushed as I stared at him, wondering if he really meant all of that ... or if Jaevid had put him up to it. "If, um, if you're really sure you want me there." I managed to rasp.

"I am." He looked back out across the ballroom and let out a deep, resigned breath. "You're not the only one who arrived at the end of all this with nothing to go home to, kid. Guess that means we should band together, right?"

I smiled weakly and nodded. "I'd be honored, then."

"Okay," he grinned back, "Now, let's find that broody friend of yours. I'll never forgive him for taking my hatchling. He owes me at least one free punch, no flinching."

CHAPTER THIRTY-SEVEN

The night dragged on, and I managed to track down nearly everyone I'd wanted to see. I even danced a little with Phoebe, which was a lot more fun than I'd expected. I wasn't completely terrible at it, anyway. That, or she was just lying to make me feel better.

Yeah, probably that.

Murdoc arrived fashionably late, strolling in alongside his sister, Aria. Part of me wanted to run up and meet them, but even from a distance … I could feel that things were different now. Murdoc was different. He was Rylen now.

He'd cut his hair short and wore finer clothes, a ceremonial breastplate, and matching bracers. He carried himself with much more distinction, looking perfectly at ease among the other esteemed nobles in the room. I wondered if that was something he'd learned in the Ulfrangar, or from his new life in Dayrise with his family. I wondered a lot of things, though. First and foremost, I wondered if he'd even want to talk to me at all now. We'd only exchanged a few letters over the last few months. Not that I didn't get it—he had a lot to deal with now. New family. New life. New everything. I wondered if he'd be upset if I accidentally called him Murdoc. It still felt strange to call him anything else. And lastly, I wondered if he was happy or not. It seemed like a weird thing to ask, though. Why wouldn't he be?

Walking in with one arm at his back and the other escorting Aria, he gave a small nod and smirk when he spotted me across the ballroom.

I waved a hand and smiled back. Part of me expected that would be it. He'd go off to mingle, and I might not even see him again for the rest of the night.

But Murdoc started for me at a speed walk, basically dragging his sister along the whole way. She scowled at him when she nearly tripped over her gown, and gave him a punishing elbow to the ribs.

"What's wrong with you?" she hissed. "Fates, Rylen. You planning on dragging me out by my ankles later?"

He snickered and winked. "Why don't you run off and find your beloved Haldor, eh?"

If looks could have killed, Murdoc would've dropped right where he stood. Aria pursed her lips and slowly shook her head, her eyes promising violence, like there were tiny burning villages inside them, as she slowly turned and walked away. Yikes.

"Haldor?" I had to be sure I heard that right.

Murdoc sagged on his feet and groaned. "Yes. Gods, I had no idea when I started that nonsense it would evolve into this. I thought it was just a prank. Just a taunt to pay her back. But they've been courting for three months and it's excruciating to watch. If he doesn't propose soon, we're all going to move out."

I laughed and shook my head. "You set your sister up with Haldor?"

"I didn't think she'd actually like him!" he flailed his arms like an angry puppet.

Well, so much for him not acting the same. Gods, I'd missed this.

"It's good to see you, by the way," I chuckled.

"And you," he sighed and stepped into his usual spot, standing right at my side with his arms crossed, like we'd never been separated. "You look slightly less pathetic than before."

"Phoebe thinks I've gotten taller," I announced proudly, straightening my collar a bit.

"She lied."

I elbowed him in the arm as hard as I could, but it didn't even make him flinch. Ugh. Typical.

We stood in silence for a few minutes, watching the dancing as the conversation of the hundreds of other guests roared on around us. I could tell by that angry little crease in his brow, right between his eyes, that there was something else he wanted to say. I guess he was just trying to figure out the right words.

"By the way, I'm going to stay with Ezran Cromwell for a while. He wants to help get me ready for the academy." I decided to break the awkward silence first. "He also wants to punch you for stealing his dragon, so, you know, be on the lookout."

"He is more than welcome to try." Murdoc's tone was ominous. Then his gaze panned down to study me out of the corner of his eyes. "Do you want to go there? To the Cromwell estate?"

My arms flapped against my sides as I shrugged. "I guess so. He said I could also learn to work with the dragons and hatchlings at his stable."

"Sounds like a good fit for you."

I bowed my head a little, smiling down at the floor. "Yeah. I guess it does."

Shifting where he stood, Murdoc cleared his throat and took in a deep breath. "Have you seen Phoebe?"

Theeere it was. The thing he'd really been wanting to say. I grinned and pretended to pick at my fingernails. "Yeah. Danced with her some. You know, she leaves for Noltham tomorrow."

"Yeah," he replied quietly. "I know."

"She's probably dancing in one of the other ballrooms. You should go say hello," I suggested.

His mouth pinched up bitterly and he tugged at his collar. "Maybe I will. Coming with me?"

I opened my mouth to answer, but someone else beat me to it. "Oh, no. He's got a previous engagement to attend to."

We both turned, looking down in shock to find Garnett standing behind us, beaming and wearing a beautiful emerald green dress with big bell sleeves trimmed in fur. All her ginger-blonde hair was tied up into an intricate plaited bun, and her lips were painted deep red. She flushed a little when she caught me staring, grabbing handfuls of her skirts and giving them a little twirl. "What do you think? Looks decent, yeah?"

"Looks ... beautiful ..." I managed to croak.

Murdoc seemed less enchanted by her beauty, though. "What are you doing here? I didn't think ... someone of your profession would be keen on making public appearances."

She winked one of her violet eyes. "Aye, well, you see that was before my employer suggested I make myself known to Her Majesty as one of the only survivors of my people, and appeal to her to help me find others. After hearing how she pardoned you, and was so avid to intervene for Phoebe, I decided it was worth the risk. So, now I'm officially being given the position as ambassador in her court. She's allowing me to use her resources to see if I can find any other dwarves who might have survived the Tibran scourge."

"And also passing along any other valuable information you happen to find along the way, I assume," Murdoc surmised.

Garnett nibbled her bottom lip innocently. "Only a little, here and there."

Suuure.

"But that's not why I came here tonight," she added quickly. Gathering up her skirts again, she stepped toward me and dipped into a graceful curtsy. "I came to talk to you, Thatcher Renley."

My hands got all sweaty and clammy as I led Garnett out onto the dance floor. I tried not to let how badly my knees were shaking show as I put a hand on her waist and guided her into a smooth, steady waltz around the room. We swayed gently to the rhythm of the music, me staring down at her and trying to balance my internal panic attack with remembering which steps came next.

"You dance pretty well," she sounded genuinely impressed.

"I practiced a little," I confessed.

"It shows." She smiled wider, making those dimples appear in her cheeks and her lavender eyes shine. Fates, I'd never seen anyone so pretty. "I have to admit, I was worried about you being here on your own. I wanted to come sooner to make sure you were okay." Her smile faded a little. "Are you?"

"Yeah," I managed to say without choking or wheezing. "I am. Knowing everyone's found happiness and a place they belong—it helps."

Her smile faded even more. "Everyone except you."

"Maybe so," I agreed. "But I like to think that just means my journey isn't over yet. The best is yet to come."

She laughed softly and moved in closer, dancing so near it made my heartbeat go nuts. "That's why I like you, Thatch. You always see the best in everyone. You see light even in the darkest places of the world. It's a wonderful gift."

"Some people think I'm just being naïve," I pointed out.

Her hand that was resting on my shoulder drifted over to touch my cheek. "Not naïve," she said softly. "Just good. Through and through. The best man I've ever met."

Again—she'd said it *again*. She'd called me a man instead of kid, boy, or any number of slightly dismissive words I'd been called throughout my life. I tried not to read too much into that.

But I wasn't successful.

"I hope you can forgive me for taking this long, but there's something I wanted to tell you. I just had to wait until I'd gotten all my stones in a row," she said as she slowly came to a stop. Still standing in front of me, the light from the chandeliers overhead making all the little pearls woven into her hair shine, Garnett put both hands on my cheeks and stood up on her toes so we were looking eye-to-eye.

Oh. Oh gods. What did this mean? What was she doing right here in front of everyone?

"I like you, too, Thatcher. And not as a friend. I think you're the kindest person I've ever met, and I *romantically* like you, as well." She leaned in and pressed her lips lightly against mine for a brief second. "And I'm only sorry it took me this long to say it, but I wanted to be sure I could be close. You deserve to be with someone who isn't always hiding in the shadows. It was scary for me, you know. I've been so worried about how the people here would receive me—especially the royals who would decide my fate. But you gave me hope, and a reason to want something better. Thank you for that."

All I could manage was a breathless, squeaky, "You're welcome."

She grinned and kissed me again, harder this time. "Let's dance some more, all right? Then let's go find the rest of your friends and see what kind of trouble we can stir up, yeah?"

I nodded. My heart still pumped wildly, making my head spin and my knees wobbly as I stepped in to dance with her again. "I, uh, I actually have a little sort-of trouble I need to, um, stir up."

Her eyebrows rose. "Is that so?"

"Yeah." I leaned down and whispered against her ear, making sure no one dancing around us might hear. "It won't be easy, though. You're a spy, right? How hard do you think it'll be to sneak something into Duke Phillip's wine glass?"

Garnett pulled back slightly, eyeing me with sudden uncertainty. "Like what, exactly?"

I slipped my hand from her waist down into my pocket, pulling out the tiny sparkling stone Devana had given me. "This."

"What's it for?" She sounded worried.

I gave her a wink as I pocketed it again. "Nothing bad, I promise. Let's just say ... I've got one chance to show him the greatest act of mercy the world has ever seen. So I can't afford to mess it up. Understand?"

Her eyes went wide, panning back and forth between my face and my pocket a few times. "You mean ...?!"

I nodded. "Think you can help me pull it off?"

Garnett's face lit with a smile that made her whole being seem to glow. "Without a doubt, love."

CHAPTER THIRTY-EIGHT

It wasn't nearly as difficult as I'd thought it would be. Not with Garnett's added help, anyway. She knew all the right things to say and ways to talk our way around the servants, making our way to the head table where Phillip and Jenna sat together. She made herself quite the spectacle, laughing and complimenting them on how beautiful the evening was, just long enough for me to lean over, using shaking Phillip's hand as an excuse to discretely drop the tiny fragment of crystal into his goblet before I leaned away.

Boom—mission complete.

We scampered off back into the crowds, hand in hand, and found Isandri and Reigh talking to Murdoc and Phoebe. In a matter of seconds, it was like I'd gone back in time. Like we'd never been separated. Like we might as well be right back in that tavern in Osbran, or in Ms. Lin's house near Dayrise. And in that moment, standing in the castle with the air filled with music and laughter, everything was right.

Everything was as it should be.

A few hours later, I noticed Duke Phillip make a face as he drank from his goblet. He smacked his lips and rubbed at his forehead, frowning into his glass before he took another sip. Boy, was he in for a wild night.

A wild rest of his life, actually. But a better one, I hoped.

When Devana had given me that crystal, and the note along with it, I hadn't realized what either of them meant right away. She'd whispered in my mind that this was the Gift of Grace—a fragment of pure love in physical form. It was all my mother had left behind to give me, and using it would allow me to negate one act of cruelty. I could undo something terrible someone else had done. I just didn't know what that should be.

But the note had a name written on it, and that was when I understood.

Phillip Derrick was a good man, too. He was destined to be our king. And what had been done to him by Argonox and the Tibrans was probably the cruelest thing I'd ever seen. He was cursed to live out his life like that—walking among his friends and family as a monster.

Or at least he had been before.

After tonight, all that would change. And by morning, gods willing, his life would be different. I didn't know if he'd go back completely to the way he had been before they experimented on him. I didn't know if that much damage could be repaired. But I believed. And sometimes believing is all you can do ... and all that matters in the end.

As dawn began to break over the kingdom, the ball finally wound to a close. Beautiful carriages rolled up to the front of the castle to carry all the shining guests back off into the night. But the six of us just sat on the front steps, watching the procession, and passing a wine bottle back and forth. It tasted terrible, but maybe that wasn't the point.

One by one, each of us started to break off and say our goodnights. Phoebe had a long day tomorrow, so she went first. Garnett volunteered to help Murdoc's sister find the room in the castle's guest wing where they'd be staying for the night. Isandri slipped away, giving me a wistful smile as she prowled away into the night and disappeared. Reigh went next, grumbling something about having to help with the departure arrangements for some of the vessels tomorrow.

Then it was just Murdoc and me, sitting on the steps, watching the sun rise.

"Hey," he muttered as he nudged my leg with the now empty wine bottle. "You know you can still call me Murdoc, right?"

Somehow, hearing him say that made every last bit of tension in my body about being around him, whether or not we were still friends like before, finally ease. I leaned forward and let my elbows rest on my knees as I drew in a full, calm breath for the first time in three months. "You're sure you're okay with that?"

"Yep."

"Good, cause it's really weird to call you anything else," I coughed a nervous laugh.

"Yeah," he agreed. "It's weird for me, too."

"Do you like it? Your real name, I mean?" I wondered.

He rubbed his fingers together—a nervous habit I'd seen him do probably a thousand times. "It scares me a little. It comes with a lot of expectations. A lot of weight and history, way more than I'd ever expected."

I showed him my best, most confident and resolute grin. "Yeah. It's a heavy name for sure. But you're a pretty strong guy, so I'm sure you can carry it."

"We'll see. I intend to try. By the way ... I saw you kissing Garnett out there again," he taunted with a sly twinkle in his eyes, even if the rest of his expression stayed stone cold and focused ahead. "Does that mean you're courting her?"

"I don't know," I admitted. "I didn't see you kiss Phoebe, though. Kind of running out of time for that, aren't you?"

He shot me the best impression of a shocked and offended stare I'd ever seen. Too bad I knew him better than that.

I snickered and looked back out across the castles front drive. "She's leaving tomorrow, you know. It's now or never."

"I hate you sometimes, you know that?" he growled through his teeth as he bowed his head.

"Nah," I countered. "Only when you know I'm right."

THERE WAS a considerable commotion in the castle early the following morning. Excitement, I guess you could say. Joy, even.

Naturally I knew *absolutely nothing* about the reason for it, or why there would be any cause for the royal family to call all their close relatives to come immediately to Queen Jenna's private wing of the castle.

Nope. No idea at all.

Servants cried tears of joy and whispered excitedly as they dashed through the halls outside the servant's quarters where I'd been given a modest room—at my own insistence, of course. Aubren had offered to put me up in his wing of the castle again. Reigh had even argued with me about it for days. But it felt weird to encroach on their family any more than I already had. Besides the servant quarters were clean and comfortable, so it wasn't like I was suffering at all.

A group of other stable hands went running by to see what was going on. One of them stopped long enough to stick their head in my doorway and ask if I was coming to see what was going on. "Nah, I'm sure I'll hear about it. I've got to talk to Godfrey about something this morning," I said, wafting a hand.

Okay, fine. It was kind of a fib. A really small one, though. I did need to talk to Stablemaster Godfrey at some point about going to the Cromwell's. That could wait, though. I had more important things to attend to, first.

The courtyards were buzzing with activity as I made my way out across the castle grounds with Murdoc and the others. Servants, maids, stable hands, and guards all crowded together or ran around, trying to organize the chaos. Bells began tolling in the city streets of Halfax, and I had to duck my head some to hide my smile.

As soon as I set foot into the castle itself, the excitement intensified. The halls and parlors resounded with the sounds of happy crying and more maids rushed by with tears in their eyes. Halfway through the front vestibule, one of the servant girls who sometimes brought meals out for Stablemaster Godfrey rushed up and seized my hands, squeaking excitedly that Duke Phillip had been healed.

"O-Oh, yeah? Really? That's amazing," I sputtered nervously.

I guess she was too elated to notice my terrible attempt at a genuinely surprised expression, because she just went on shrieking with glee and skipped off out the door. I didn't even get a chance to ask for details.

Ah, well, if everyone was this happy about it, that had to be a good sign, right?

I couldn't hold back a proud smile as I continued down to the undercrofts beneath the castle. We'd all agreed to help Phoebe load the rest of the things into the wagons that would take them down to the royal port. Then, we'd say our goodbyes to her. Just for now, though. She'd promised to come back as soon as she could, repeating over and over that she loved it here in Maldobar, and she didn't want to live anywhere else. She insisted that her aunt understood, and had assured her she could come back whenever she wished. She could even live here if she wanted.

Of course, we all knew that was a lie. Not an intentional one, of course. Phoebe wasn't like that. But once she set foot in her homeland, we all knew she probably wouldn't want to be anywhere else. And who could blame her? There wasn't much tying her here now. We were all friends, yes. But family took precedence. And like Murdoc, she now had a chance to finally experience life with a family.

Who would pass that up?

Speaking of Murdoc ...

As we all gathered to heave the last crate onto the already overloaded wagon bound for the nearby port, he stared at Phoebe with a look like he might suddenly throw up at any second. I made sure I stood clear of him, you know, just in case. Better safe than sorry and covered in puke.

We could have ridden with the wagons down to the port. We could have flown on the dragons, too. But with only a few minutes before everyone went their separate ways for what could be a long time, it felt good to walk together on the long, gently curving road that led across the rocky grassland toward the port a few miles ahead.

Vexi and Blite were circling above us like massive scaly vultures, nipping at one another's tails and growling playfully. Even Fornax seemed to be relaxed and in a good mood as he lumbered along behind me, seeming to prefer sticking close today rather than joining in the aerial tussle. Garnett walked alongside him with her hand on his head, speaking to him like a mother cooing to a baby—a very large, fire-breathing baby that could have eaten her in one bite like a bon-bon. But he purred and seemed to enjoy the attention.

Up ahead, Isandri and Reigh strolled along making swats at one another as they bickered. Reigh was teasing her about her new, courtly robes that were a lot more extravagant than the ones she'd worn before. She wrinkled her nose and reminded him over and over that it was his fault for talking her into it in the first place. Squabbling aside, it was easy to see they were both in a much better place now. Happier, I guess.

"Did you see Duke Phillip?" Phoebe gasped up at Murdoc, who still looked a few breaths away from a full-blown mental breakdown as he walked quietly along with us. "I only caught a glimpse when I went to say farewell to Queen Jenna. Gods! It's incredible! How do you think it happened?"

Garnett and I exchanged a look. Oooh boy.

"I didn't see him," Garnett piped up, somehow executing a perfectly nonchalant and convincingly curious expression. "What happened?"

"He's human again! It's unbelievable, Garnett! It's like nothing ever happened. Every trace of what the switchbeast venom did to him just ... gone!" Phoebe bubbled with happiness and bounced onto her toes. "You should have seen him and Queen Jenna. I've never seen anyone so happy. They're all a bit nervous, too, I think. No one knows how it happened or if it'll last, but the medics were all flabbergasted. It's so wonderful!

"It's true," Reigh added, suddenly glancing back at us. "I saw him before we left. It's like the switchbeast venom never touched him at all. I knew him before all that, and he's completely back to normal."

Murdoc's eyes narrowed slightly, but he never looked my way. "And no one knows how or why it happened?"

Reigh just shook his head. "Nope. He wasn't feeling well after the ball last night, so he went to bed early. We all figured he just had a little too much to drink at dinner. But this morning—poof! It's like a miracle. They're all over the moon about it."

My throat went dry. He still hadn't even looked at me, but I knew just by the way Murdoc's jawline tensed ever so slightly ... Yep. He definitely knew.

CHAPTER THIRTY-NINE

While the rest of our group ran ahead out onto the long, busy dock of the royal port, a powerful hand grabbed the top of my head like someone picking up an apple. Oh gods.

"That was you, wasn't it?" Murdoc demanded in a low, ominous growl. "You did that to Duke Phillip, didn't you?"

I showed him a toothy, wincing smile. "Sorta, yeah, a little bit."

His eyes narrowed.

"I mean, I did tell you I was going to do ... *something*," I panicked.

His expression sagged with what I could only interpret as exasperation and general weariness. He let me go and rubbed at his eyes. "I'm not even going to ask. Plausible deniability. And don't you dare tell anyone I knew anything."

"I won't!" I promised. "Besides, it's not like they'll ever figure out it was me. I was extra-sneaky about it."

He moved his hand just enough to glare at me with one, bloodshot, very exhausted eye. "Thatcher, there is nothing even *remotely* sneaky about you."

I cleared my throat and tried smoothing down my hair. "It was good, though, right? They'll be happy now, don't you think?"

His broad chest heaved in and out with a long, exaggerated exhale. "Yeah," he relented at last. "I think they will be."

Good. That was enough for me.

Looking ahead again, I tipped my head back some at the warmth of the morning sun over the ocean. Gulls floated on the strong winds, and the massive ships rocked gently at their moorings. The swish and rumble of the waves lapping at the shore mixed with the shouts of the sailors and dockhands as they loaded cargo onto one especially robust looking vessel on the farthest end of the docks. With three large masts, windows all down the sides, and a gold-painted figurehead carved in the shape of an owl with its wings spread wide, I wondered at the flags flying proudly that bore that same insignia. The royal symbol of Noltham?

High upon the deck, a familiar older woman with long coppery red hair dressed in a deep purple gown and white cloak stood with a man who, due to his formal uniform and broad-brimmed hat, must have been the captain. She smiled when she noticed us, and Phoebe bounced up onto her toes again and waved excitedly.

We stood by watching while the dockhands rolled loading carts full of Phoebe's things onboard, an awkward silence passing over us almost like we were watching a funeral procession. When it was done and everything was loaded, then she'd have to go. She'd sail away over the eastern seas, and gods only knew when she'd be back.

If ever ...

"Oh! Fates, I nearly forgot!" Phoebe gasped suddenly. She swung her messenger-styled bag around to the front and opened it. Metallic objects clunked and clattered as she dug around inside, and finally pulled out a decent-sized black velvet bag. It was roughly the length of my forearm, and the object hidden inside seemed almost cylindrical as she handled it. Phoebe handed the bag off to Reigh with a secretive little smile, "This is for Judan. It's just a prototype. Tell him I'll send updated versions along very soon, but this ought to get him by until then."

Reigh took the bag cautiously, his eyes wide and a little alarmed as he studied it. "Okay," he agreed finally. "It's not going to explode, right?"

She giggled. "No! Not this one."

No one laughed with her.

She didn't seem to notice, though. "And then there's these," Phoebe continued as she dug around in her bag some more. She pulled out a bunch more velvet bags, each one only about the size of my palm, with a little drawstring tied closed. She handed one to each of us and stood back waiting, smiling from ear to ear.

"Oh, Phoebe," Isandri breathed in reverence as she poured the contents of her bag onto her hand. On a glittering silver chain, a thumb-sized pendant made of silver metal hung and sparkled in the morning light. It was a roundish, almost disk shape, and a tiny shard of a misty, purplish gemstone right in the center. The outside of the round silver disk part had been very intricately engraved with tiny rune marks that looked strangely familiar.

Hmmm. They were similar in style and shape to the ones on my goggles, weren't they?

"What are they?" Reigh asked as he held up an exact duplicate that he'd poured out of his own bag.

There was one for each of us—Garnett, Murdoc, Isandri, Reigh, and me—that were all crafted to be identical.

Phoebe clapped and squealed with delight, then pulled her own out from under the collar of her tunic. "Aren't they lovely? They're all connected! No matter how far apart we are, if any one of us ever needs help, all you have to do is press your thumb over the jewel. If you get it just right, it'll prick your thumb. Nothing too bad, I promise! But the runes need a tiny bit of blood to activate. When they do, they make all the other necklaces glow, so we know someone's in trouble." She calmed a little, her shoulders drawing up sheepishly as she fidgeted with her own pendant. "I just ... wanted to come up with some way for us to all stay connected."

"It's a good idea," Reigh said as he slipped his around his neck. "Thank you, Phoebe."

Everyone stayed quiet as we all did the same, sliding the pendants around our necks and tucking them under our shirt collars. The heaviness in the air was impossible to miss. Grief crept in like a poisonous fog, curling around us and sealing us in that silence. A low horn blared from the ship nearby.

It was time for final boarding.

Phoebe went to each of us one at a time, hugging our necks tightly and kissing our cheeks. She sniffled as she stood back, fidgeting with her hands and looking down at her toes. "I'm going to miss you all so much," she whimpered. "I'll come back as soon as I can, I promise."

"Don't rush, Pheobe," Garnett consoled with a knowing smile. "Enjoy your time with your people and learn about your home. It is a rare gift these days. We wouldn't dare ask you not to savor and treasure it."

We all nodded in agreement.

Well, most of us did. Murdoc stood disturbingly still, staring at her like he was stuck in some kind of trance. It didn't even look like he was breathing. I had to resist the urge to wave a hand in front of his face to make him snap out of it.

He probably would've snapped my wrist for that.

Phoebe's eyes darted up and hesitated on him for a few seconds longer than the rest of us as she gave a final, trembling smile. Then she turned and started walking away.

Garnett slipped her hand into mine and squeezed it, her eyes a bit misty as we all watched Phoebe climb the boarding ramp and make her way onto the ship's deck.

I stole another look at Murdoc. His chest was heaving fast now, drawing in rapid, heavy breaths as all the color drained from his face. His sharp features twisted into a look of pure, uncontrollable panic. But he didn't move. He didn't say a word.

As the sailors up and down the dock began withdrawing all the cargo-loading planks and ramps, untying the moorings from the dock, and raising the anchor, his jawline flexed like he was gnashing his teeth. His hands clenched in shaking fists at his sides. His eyes darted wildly between the dock and the ship.

"Murdoc," I snapped suddenly.

He jolted and stared back at me, almost as pale as a corpse now.

I gave him the very best annoyed glare I could muster. "What the heck are you waiting for?!"

His mouth fell open. That look of quiet terror shattered on his face. He looked back up to where Phoebe now stood next to her aunt near the bow of the ship, just as the last loading ramp was dragged out of reach.

Then, without a word, Murdoc bolted for the ship like a madman.

Reigh barked a laugh as Murdoc sprinted to the edge of the dock and leapt through the air, barely managing to grab onto one of the mooring ropes before the ship drifted out of reach. We all ran to the edge, watching and laughing as he climbed up the rope while the sailors onboard shouted at him, calling him a colorful variety of names that, given what he was doing, were probably deserved.

Murdoc made it to the deck of the ship, basically throwing himself over the rail and landing in a heap. He scrambled up immediately, disheveled but determined, and started shoving his way past the crew members who rushed him in varying degrees of anger and confusion. By then, the whole ship was aware they had an unexpected new passenger on board—including Phoebe. I guess she'd been watching the whole thing, because she started sprinting across the deck toward him. She cried out, but over the ambient noise of frustrated bewilderment now brewing on the dock and ship, I couldn't hear anything she said.

We all heard it when Murdoc shouted "PHOEBE!" at the top of his lungs, though.

They ran to one another across the deck. Phoebe hit him at full speed, her red curls and dainty pink tunic blowing around her wildly as she wrapped her arms and legs around him. He grabbed her out of midair and held her tight, pressing his mouth against hers in a desperate kiss like he couldn't hold it back for another second. The sailors who'd been chasing him began to laugh as they stopped and stayed back.

Murdoc gripped Phoebe tightly, kissing her deeply until she finally pulled back and cradled his face in her hands. I couldn't hear what they said—not from that distance. But I could see happy tears streaming down her face as she nodded and hugged him again with all her strength.

It took a little dragon-shaped help to get Murdoc back to the dock. Hard to turn a ship like that around on a whim, after all. But we all got a good laugh out of watching them sail off into the mid-morning sun a bit, holding each other. Then Blite soared over to pick him up, yipping and crowing excitedly as he zoomed around the ship. The sailors watching the sails and masts didn't seem to find it nearly as amusing, though. Maybe they were concerned about what a playful puff of dragon fire might do to their ship.

A valid concern, really.

Murdoc returned windblown and breathless at the far end of the dock. He stared after the ship, rubbing Blite's neck as the rest of us wandered up to meet him. He didn't look quite so sick and pasty anymore, though. There was a strange smile on his lips and a sadness in his eyes I understood all too well.

"Quite the show," Reigh jabbed with a snort. "All that and she still wouldn't come back with you, eh?"

"I didn't ask her to stay," Murdoc said quietly. "I'd never ask her to do that."

"Then ... what did you say to her?" Isandri asked, a curious arch to her brow.

"I told her that I loved her," he confessed without even the tiniest hint of shame or embarrassment. "And I promised that if she ever dared to set foot in Maldobar again, I'd find her ... and I'd marry her."

Garnett's mouth pinched into a thrilled little O-shape as she looked between the rest of us with wide, delighted eyes.

Reigh made surprised sputtering sounds.

I guess I did, too. Or maybe that was just me trying to breathe through the shock.

"You dashing devil, you," Garnett cheered as she clapped him on the back hard enough to make him stumble some. "How's a woman supposed to say no to that?"

Murdoc bowed his head and laughed under his breath. "She didn't. She said yes." He laughed harder and shook his head like he couldn't believe it. "She actually said yes."

"Well, congratulations then. Could be a while till she does come back, though, you know," Reigh reminded him.

Murdoc lifted his gaze back to the dark, retreating silhouette of the ship as it slowly slipped closer to the glow of the horizon. "I know. It's okay," he murmured. "Like every good thing that's ever happened in my life, I have no doubt ... she's worth the wait."

Almost a week passed like a blur. And like all good things, my time with everyone finally came to an end. Or, rather, a break. Yeah, that sounded better. Besides, it's not like we'd never see each other again. But life was sweeping us all in different directions now, and I'd come to accept that wasn't always a bad thing.

Murdoc went back to Dayrise to live with his family and continue settling in. He had a lot of catching up to do, after all. The Porters were elated to find out he was engaged, especially when they found out it was to Phoebe. I guess they really liked her. Somehow, that made me even happier to think about. I cared so much for both of them. Knowing they'd found happiness together was the best situation I could've ever imagined.

Reigh was probably the busiest of all of us. He and Aubren had taken the helm of handling all the departing dignitaries, making sure everyone was prepared and the exits of each royal and noble back to their homeland went as smoothly as possible. I honestly couldn't tell how much Reigh enjoyed the work, though. His time at the dragonrider academy was looming closer and closer, and maybe that's why he seemed more tense than ever. I didn't understand why he might be worried about it, though. Yes, dragonrider training was supposed to be brutal—mentally and physically. But he'd already undergone a lot of training, and he fought better than most people. Er, well, except for Murdoc, of course. Anyway, I seriously doubted Reigh was going to struggle through dragonrider training. What was he worried about?

Whatever it was, he wouldn't say no matter how many times I asked. Eventually, I just had to let it go. Maybe someday he'd let me in on it, but for now, he was determined to keep his mouth shut.

Isandri and Garnett settled in to their courtly duties well, joining the growing council of international ambassadors who met with Queen Jenna and the soon-to-be King Phillip regularly. It kept them pretty busy, although Garnett always found time to come to the stable to visit. She didn't seem worried at all that I'd turned in my resignation to Stablemaster Godfrey so I could go and live with Duke Cromwell. In fact, she thought it was a great idea. I needed the preparation for the academy, and it wasn't all that far. I could visit her often.

Packing up the last of my few belongings—which amounted to a few changes of clothes, a sword belt, my xiphos, and crossbow—I buttoned up my only saddlebag and stood to look over the small room where I'd been living. The bed was clean and made. Nothing was left to tidy up. In a few hours, it would be like I'd never stayed here at all.

I sighed. Another chapter of my life had closed, and it felt like another one was just beginning. I just didn't know what to expect from this one.

Hopefully less fire and fewer poisoned crossbow bolts.

"Well now, you look ready to go," a deep voice observed from the doorway behind me.

I turned, facing the imposing figure of a tall, broad-shouldered man in a dragonrider's cloak and armor as he leaned in the doorway. Jaevid Broadfeather's smile was strangely cryptic, and maybe even a little nostalgic, as he asked, "Everything okay, Thatcher?"

I nodded. "Yeah. It is."

"Come on, then," he tipped his head toward the hall behind him. "I'll see you out."

We walked together from the servant's quarters, through the modest dining hall where the stable hands and other workers could share meals, and out into the open air of the broad courtyard between the royal stable and the Deck. The fierce wind tugged at Jaevid's long cloak, making the golden trim shine in the sunlight with every step.

"Ezran won't say it, but I think he's very pleased to have company in his house," he said evenly. "He's been alone there for quite some time. He's also a very talented fighter, so try to learn all you can."

"I will," I promised.

His toned quietened, becoming almost careful as he glanced at me briefly. "I must admit, I was concerned for you when I heard Rylen had chosen to stay in Dayrise with his family. I know it wasn't easy to leave him behind there."

"No," I agreed. "It wasn't easy. But ... it wasn't about me. Murdoc—er, Rylen—needs to be there. And he's my friend, so I need to support him. As long as he's okay, I'm okay."

"That's very noble of you."

I scrunched my mouth to one side, not sure if I agreed. Was it noble? Or was it just the right thing to do? Murdoc was still my best friend. Nothing about that had changed just because we lived farther apart. I wanted him to find the peace he'd searched for. Yeah, it hurt not to have him around. It was lonely sometimes. But part of being a friend is accepting that not everything is going to work out equally for both sides all the time. Sometimes, you have to give a little. And demanding that he come back with me, or trying to force my way into his new family, wasn't going to do anything but drive a wedge between us. I didn't want that at all.

I just wanted him to be happy.

As we approached the front of the Deck, Jaevid's pace slowed until he came to stop right outside the big, arched doorway. I stopped, too, and he turned to face me with a much more thoughtful frown. "I realize I should have told you this much sooner, but I wanted to let you know that I am proud of how you handled yourself through that ordeal, Thatcher. And I'd like to apologize for ever doubting you could handle it."

I grinned and jostled my bag some, balancing it over my shoulder. "I'm tougher than I look."

His smile was nostalgic again, almost like he was seeing a reflection of someone else standing in my place. "Yes," he agreed. "Yes, you are."

"I won't let you down in dragonrider training either," I promised. "I'll do my best."

"I know you will." Jaevid stretched a hand out to me, offering to shake. "If you ever need anything, please don't hesitate to contact me. I may be your commander, soon. But I'm also your sponsor. And more than that, I'm your friend."

Hearing that sent a little fluttering tingle of excitement through me. Never, in my wildest dreams, would I have dared to dream that Jaevid Broadfeather would consider me his friend—but he did. And as I grasped his hand and shook it once, I felt that connection like a seal stamped over my heart. I'd always assumed that being a dragonrider meant I'd be walking in the shadow of his incredible legacy, trying desperately to keep up and prove myself worthy.

I'd missed the whole point, though.

It wasn't about walking behind him or trying to match up to the heritage of his greatness. It was about both of us, turning to the same rising sun flung far upon the wild horizon, and walking our own, unique paths toward destiny without hesitation or fear.

"Have a safe journey, Thatcher," he said with a parting smile. "I'll see you soon."

"Until then." I nodded and jostled my bag, balancing it over my shoulder as I walked into the Deck alone. The musky smell of dragon filled my nose as I walked the sloping walkway up to the highest level. Sunlight hit my face with tingling warmth as I rolled open the stall door.

In the far corner of the stall, the huge mound of orange and black scales stirred. Fornax unfurled from where he'd curled himself into a ball, yawning widely and smacking his jaws. He blinked his milky jade-colored eyes in my direction, and purred when I ran a hand along his snout.

"Hey big guy. Ready to go home?"

He gave a deep, earnest snort as he got to his feet and stretched his wing arms one at a time.

"Good." I dropped my bag and walked around to where his saddle sat on a stand in a corner of the stall. A grin stretched over my face as I ran my hands across the smooth, sun-warmed leather.

Fornax's massive, horned head appeared over my shoulder, sniffing curiously.

"It's not going to be easy, you know. Ezran and the others are right—we're not ready for the academy. Not yet. We've got a lot of work to do." I reached up to slide my goggles down over my eyes.

He gave another loud, excited snort and trill of chirping sounds as we shared my sight through those goggles.

It was true, though. The academy was our next challenge. It might even be our greatest one. But whatever happened, whatever we had to face there, Fornax and I were in this together to the bitter end. Our bond was strong. And our strength was growing every day. As long as we held true to that connection, to that soul-deep oath we'd forged together, there was nothing we couldn't handle.

That was the path of the dragonrider.

And it was the only one I'd ever want to take.

THE DARKLING PRINCE

A DRAGONRIDER SHORT STORY

THE DARKLING PRINCE

"AUBREN!!"

My eyes flew open, seeing nothing but darkness as I bolted upright. Dazed and soaked with sweat, I stared around as bright spots winked and danced in my vision. My heart thrashed against my ribs like a caged animal. I clutched the front of my tunic as I fought to breathe against the pressure that crushed over me. Gods, it was like someone was sitting on my chest. Breathe—I just had to keep breathing. It wasn't real. I wasn't there anymore. Just a few more minutes. A few more breaths. It would pass.

Just like all the times it had before.

Minutes dragged by, and every gasp came easier. The tightness in my lungs eased, and I could suck in deep breaths of the cool air. I blinked hard and buried my face in my hands, clearing the stars that still swam around before my eyes. Easy—I had to take it easy. Let it pass.

When I looked up again, the room was calm and dim, barely lit by the glowing red bed of coals still smoldering in the hearth at the foot of the bed. My armor glimmered on the stand in the corner, and my long, regal blue cloak with a white fur-trimmed collar was thrown over the back of a velvet chair by the window. A plush rug of silky soft tigrex hide stretched across the floor, and the heavy drapes were drawn over the tall windows. A set of regal, white faundra stag horns were mounted above the hearth, and plates of my half-eaten dinner sat on the coffee table.

I shivered, rubbing my forehead with the heel of my hand. Nothing helped, though. The visions still replayed every time I closed my eyes. The blur of stone halls crushing in around me as I ran, farther and farther, deeper and deeper, while the snarls of beasts and snickers of men echoed at my heels. Ahead, my older brother called out to me in screaming torment, begging me to help him.

But I never made it there in time.

Usually, I just ran until the light of dawn finally seeped through my curtains and I awoke, tired, sweaty, and aching. Other times, the monsters at my heels caught up to me.

Tonight was one of those times.

It was as though a part of me—a sliver of my soul—was still trapped in Northwatch tower. My sister, Queen Jenna, had made an aggressive move to retake it after it was overrun by remnant hostile Tibran forces, thieves, and cutthroats. Since then, it had been a massive effort to rebuild the city and tower alike. I'd been there several times now, helping to oversee the reconstruction when Jenna wanted an update, but it never got any easier. The memories I had of that place had already seeped down deep into the foundations of my being like a bitter poison. No amount of time dulled that pain. Every detail still cut like a razor through my brain, every bit as sharp and clear as though it had happened yesterday.

That part of me that was still trapped there, running the halls and screaming for help, could never escape.

I sank back into my bed, staring up at the carved wooden beams on the ceiling. The faint light from the hearth draped everything in heavy shadow, and my eyes instinctively searched for any of them that might have moved strangely. They never did, though. Not anymore.

I couldn't believe I actually missed that.

My eyelids grew heavy as every muscle gradually relaxed. I sighed, finally ready to surrender. Then the door creaked.

I went stiff. My heart gave a lurch of white-hot terror. I bolted upright, my hand darting for the dagger hidden securely under the edge of the mattress. Then I spotted a small head with a mop of dark wavy hair, and two big eyes peering at me over the edge of the bed.

Gods and Fates.

"Ronan, what are you doing here? It's late, buddy. Really late." I sagged in relief and blew a ragged breath through my lips.

My nephew was barely three years old, and yet he could be as stealthy as a cat when he wanted to be. This wasn't the first time he'd caught me off guard and successfully scared a few years off my lifespan.

Still peeking over the edge of the bed, his big, cobalt blue eyes blinked drowsily. Half asleep, I guess. He held a stuffed doll shaped like a purple dragon under one arm, and the oversized neck of his white sleeping shirt hung off one of his shoulders.

"You have a bad dream again?" I asked.

Ronan bobbed his head, making his chaotic mop of loose curls swish some.

"Yeah ..." I sighed and rubbed at my eyes again. "Me too."

"I can sweep wiff you?" he asked, but he didn't wait for an answer. Before I could even get a word out, he was already climbing over the edge of the bed and making his way toward me.

I frowned. "Hey now, your mom wants you to stay in your room," I protested, but it was only half-hearted.

The little runt must have been able to tell I didn't have it in me to put up much of a fight. He muscled his way up into my personal space and tucked himself in right against my side, curled up with his thumb in his mouth. He was asleep before I could blink twice.

Great. This was the third time this week. Why did he always come in here? Aubren's room was closer, not that he was home much these days. He was overseeing the rebuilding of Northwatch personally, which took up most of his time and kept him away for weeks on end. Regardless, why did Ronan keep coming to me? I wasn't particularly good with kids. Shouldn't he go to his parents for this kind of thing? Ugh. Whatever. I'd wait and let him get fully back to sleep before I carried him back to his room.

Settling down on my back next to him, I stared up at the ceiling again. My eyes got heavy. Everything grew quiet and still. Some of the cinders in the hearth popped and hissed as they cooled. My body relaxed into the bed. Sleep. I could sleep for a few hours, and then take Ronan back to—

BAM!

My bedroom door banged open again.

I bolted upright, yanking my knife from under my pillow on reflex and holding it up in a defensive pose.

Breathless and only half-dressed, my brother-in-law, and the King of Maldobar, shambled into the room. Phillip spotted Ronan next to me, now awake and halfway hidden behind me, and his shoulders sagged in relief. "I've found him, Jenna! He's in here!" he called back out into the hall.

I lowered my blade. "You could've just knocked, you know," I grumbled drowsily. "Or come in calmly, like a normal person."

"There's no time," Phillip panted as he walked quickly around to the edge of the bed and gathered his son into his arms. "Come, Ronan. We must go right now."

I frowned. "At this hour? Go where?"

Phillip was already on his way out of the room. He paused in the doorway, his jawline hardening and his hand placed protectively on the back of Ronan's small head. "*He* sent word. He can meet us tonight, here in the city, but we must move quickly."

A pang of panic and dread instantly stripped away every bit of warmth from my body. *He?* As in …?

No. No way. Phillip couldn't seriously be considering taking my nephew to Arlan the Kinslayer. It was a terrible idea. The worst of all the bad ideas in the entire history of the world.

We still didn't know much about Arlan, but just the thought of that guy, with his eerie glowing eyes, made my skin crawl. The only thing I disliked more than having him in my blind spot, was seeking him out on purpose. Arlan was brilliant, sure. He was probably the most informed and connected man in the entire kingdom—maybe even the world. And things with Ronan had been complicated from the outset, so I didn't blame Jenna and Phillip for wanting to do whatever they had to in order to find answers. But asking for help from Arlan the Kinslayer?

Nope. Terrible idea.

I started climbing out of bed. "Phillip, wait. Just hold on. You can't do this. Arlan is—"

"I know who he is," Phillip cut me off immediately.

"No, you don't. No one does. That's the whole problem," I argued as I seized my thicker, outer-layer tunic off the back of the sofa on my way over to him. "I know things are complicated with Ronan, but there has to be another way to—"

"THERE ISN'T," Phillip shouted suddenly. He turned on me, his expression drawn into a look of frantic, nearly-mad desperation. "I-I ... forgive me, Reigh. But we have tried everything we possibly can. We've consulted scholars throughout the court. We've met with brine witches and seers from Rienka and Damaria. We've met with high priestesses from Nar'Haleen, and no one could tell us anything. No one can help him. No one even understands what's happening to him." His gaze grew distant, expression filling with the weight of despair, and he looked away. "This man, Arlan ... he is the only one left. The only one who might have answers. Believe me, if there was any other way, any other choice at all, I would take it. But we are running out of time."

I stared back at him for a moment while my thoughts ran wild, picturing every possible horrible outcome to this situation. Everything about my sister's pregnancy had been abnormal, right up to the night when Ronan was finally born. The circumstances that had brought my one and only nephew into the world were ... well, to put it in simplest terms, cursed. Now Jenna and Phillip were afraid. Desperate. And that's when people generally make the worst mistakes.

"Phillip, please, just think about what you're doing right now." I took a step toward him and tried to keep my tone calm and even. I didn't want to scare Ronan any more than necessary. "Arlan doesn't just give away favors. He doesn't do acts of charity. If you go in there expecting him to just help out of the goodness of his heart, that isn't going to happen. He knows how desperate you are. He knows you have no other alternatives. He's going to use that against you. Surely you realize that."

His head bowed some. The hand cradled against the back of Ronan's hand moved, softly petting the boy's unruly mop of dark hair. "I do. But, Reigh, there's nothing I can do about that. I can't go to this man and pretend not to be desperate. I can't possibly convince him I'm not at my wit's end. If he intends to extort me for any hope of saving Ronan from this nightmare, then ... so be it. What other choice do I have? If you've some other alternative to this, please share it, because this is our final hope, and I would treasure the opportunity for Jenna and I not to sell ourselves to this man's whims."

All I could do was stand there, staring into my brother-in-law's eyes, while his entire life seemed to crash down around him like a sandcastle overwhelmed in the roaring surf of an encroaching tide. I knew exactly what this meant for him. He'd already suffered more than most at the hands of the Tibran Empire. After being tortured and transformed into a beast at the command of Argonox, Phillip had been robbed of any chance to have a normal life of his own. He'd been stripped of his humanity—literally. And based on the conversations I'd had with my sister, he'd also lost any chance of having kids of his own.

Then along came Ronan.

Only a few people beyond our family actually knew the details behind Ronan's birth and how my sister had gotten pregnant with him in the first place. Honestly, we had all sort of been expecting her to give him away, or that Phillip might reject him entirely even after he'd been miraculously restored to his former, human self. But he and my sister had done the complete opposite. They decided to keep Ronan and raise him together, as a Prince of Maldobar.

Ronan looked enough like Phillip that no one thought twice about it. No one asked questions or suspected anything might be amiss. Only a very trusted few knew the truth. And for about a year, everything was great. They were a perfectly happy family.

Then, on Ronan's first birthday, it all began to go wrong.

Staring at my nephew, who peered at me over Phillip's shoulder with wise, frightened eyes, made my gut clench into knots like tangled barbs of cold steel. I knew what it was like to be caught in the gaze of a certain goddess. To fall prey to her *special* attention. Hell—that's what it was. I wouldn't have wished that on anyone, least of all an innocent little kid. But I'd never been given a choice ... and neither had he.

"I'm going with you," I decided aloud as I spun around to begin yanking on the rest of my clothes, my boots, and armor.

"Reigh, please, you've already been subject to this man once," Phillip began to protest.

"Exactly," I countered without even looking up. I hurried through lacing up my boots and buckling on my breastplate. Thanks to a few years at Blybrig Academy, I'd learned to do this in record time, even in the dark. "So believe me when I say, Arlan isn't the kind of guy you want to deal with by yourself. So far, Jaevid is the only one this guy hasn't been able to talk circles around. I know I'm not much of a stand in, but you're my family and I won't let you do this alone."

I heard surrender in his voice before I looked up and found it etched hard into the weary lines of his face. He nodded once and turned back to the door. "Very well. Go down to the garden parlor. Arlan's agent is waiting for us there. We will be down as swiftly as we can."

The castle stood, as dim and silent as a crypt, in the dead of night. Not even the servants were awake at this hour, and the only figures lurking at a few of the doorways were the occasional pair of castle guards. Nearly all of the lamps were doused in the sprawling halls, and no sound carried through the vestibules and grand stairwells other than the thud of my heavy footsteps on the marble.

My nerves drew tense as I reached the tall stained-glass doors that led out into the broad garden courtyard. Moonlight poured through a large glass-domed ceiling overhead, making the white cobblestoned floor seem to glow. A tall, feminine figure dressed in dark, form-fitted leathers leaned against the white marble statue in the center. With her arms crossed and head down, I couldn't see her face thanks to the hooded tunic she wore.

This definitely wasn't Garnett, though. Had Arlan sent someone else? Why?

The young woman looked up as I approached, the moonlight catching over her fair cheeks and a few long locks of golden hair that had spilled out of her hood to fall down nearly to her chest. Eyes of shocking, deep scarlet studied me as her lips bowed into an amused little grin.

"Where's Garnett?" I asked without bothering to introduce myself. If she worked for Kinslayer, then I had no doubt she already knew good and well who I was.

Her smile widened as her gaze flickered up and down, like she was sizing me up. "Occupied elsewhere. The boss is concerned she's a little too *emotionally invested* when it comes to you lot, so he sent me."

I gave her the same, appraising up and down glance she'd given me. "And you are?"

"Violet."

"Garnett's mentioned you," I realized aloud.

Her tone stayed coy as she looked away. "Has she? Well, I do hope the tales were complimentary."

"No tales," I corrected quickly, not wanting to give anything else away—just in case there was some rule within Arlan's network about not passing around the names of his other agents. I wasn't out to get Garnett in trouble with her boss. "She just mentioned that you were ... following a similar career path. Are you a former Tibran, too, then?"

Her expression cooled some, that bemused smile fading as her lips pursed slightly. "No. Not exactly."

I arched an eyebrow. "And here I thought that's where Arlan got all his hired talent."

"Only recently. Don't worry, little prince. I promise, I'm just as capable as Garny." She turned her head and winked one of her ruby-colored eyes. More of her hair slipped free of the hood and spilled down over her chest like a river of gold satin. "Love the armor, by the way."

I snorted and shook my head. "Yeah, I'll bet you do."

"I do. Blue really is your color." Violet gave a soft, melodic little laugh. Taunting me, I guess. "It's not very subtle, though."

"Who said I was trying to be subtle?" The pauldrons buckled to my shoulders clunked some as I crossed my arms.

"My instructions were to keep this arrangement as discreet as possible," she replied coolly. "Has that changed?"

"No, it most certainly has not." My sister's voice carried across the courtyard, drawing our focus to where she and Phillip approached.

Dressed in drab commoner's clothing and long dark cloaks with the hoods pulled down low to hide most of their faces, they made their way to meet us in the center of the courtyard. Phillip's face still looked pasty and there was a wild sort of panic in the way his eyes darted all around. Jenna, on the other hand, stood as straight as an old oak tree, steadfast and steely-eyed as she studied Violet. She held my nephew close against her chest, covering him almost entirely with her cloak.

"Your Majesties." Violet gave a small nod of recognition.

Jenna didn't waste a single second on formalities. "Is he here? In the city?"

"He is." Violet's smile faded, her demeanor shifting to something far more guarded as she met my sister's gaze. Interesting.

My sister wasn't some soft-handed damsel. She'd fought as a Dragonrider in the Tibran war, and knew her way around a blade better than most. After all, the same man had instructed both of us in the ways of combat, she'd attended the dragonrider academy, and had even been given some training from Jace when she was younger. I had to wonder if Violet was aware of that, too. Probably, considering who she worked for. No wonder the two of them staring one another down reminded me of a lioness eyeing a fox that had just wandered into her territory.

"Then let's not waste time," Phillip urged, as though he could sense the tension between them prickling in the air. "Lead on. Reigh, can you follow from a distance?"

I set my jaw and gave a Dragonrider salute, clasping a fist over my breastplate and bowing my head for a second. "On your orders. If anything goes wrong, I won't be far behind."

Before tonight, I had never set foot inside a temple in Maldobar. There weren't all that many to be found in the first place. Most were left to ruin, or had been converted to some other purpose. For the most part, Maldobar had slipped from a culture of devout belief in the gods, to more of a lukewarm indifference about them a long time ago. They called that time the Age of the Stones. Complicated story there, but basically after a long and deadly war involving the gods and mortals, those godly beings had withdrawn to the divine realm and left behind sacred artifacts—stones, to be specific—that worked sort of like anchors to keep their essences present in the mortal world.

Like I said—complicated.

Naturally, that time had been a total disaster with people warring over control of the stones, and Jaevid was finally the one to end that nonsense. Well, with my help, anyway. But that was another long story, too.

Standing before the old temple, staring up at the granite columns and chiseled reliefs of dragons intertwined amidst stars, tree branches, waves, and flames, I couldn't help but shudder. Something about its looming shape, draped in heavy shadow and sparse of any decoration, reminded me more of a tomb than a place of worship. This temple had been converted into a private archive for a college of greater learning. Basically, a fancy word for a library attached to a school where people studied to become artificers, linguists, historians, court advisors, and other stuffy jobs like that. Boring.

Finding Arlan here, however, wasn't really a shock. He'd apparently been passing himself off as some sort of scholar for a long time—a ruse that gave him access to all kinds of privileged information and valuable relationships with nobles. He probably came here a lot.

Violet led us around to the back of the building, through a dark courtyard with manicured hedges, and up to a small back door lit only by one small lamp. She held it open, letting my sister and her family go inside first before she waved me over. She slipped in last once we were all inside, and swiftly closed the door again.

The inside of the temple was no warmer or inviting than the outside had been. Our footsteps echoed through the cavernous halls as we followed Violet into a massive library filled with shelves that spanned from floor to the lofty ceiling. Moonlight poured through the tall windows between each shelf, sparkling off the marble floors and massive silver chandeliers.

My hands drifted to the hilt of my blades as we walked on, making our way slowly toward a sweeping staircase that led up to the second floor of the library. I stared down each row of shelves as we passed, my heart pounding in my eardrums and my nerves drawn as taut as bowstrings. But no figures lurked between the rows of books. No one sat at any of the study tables or walked the halls. The place seemed completely empty at this hour.

That is, until we arrived at one of the private study rooms on the far end of the second level. We'd already passed a few of them as we walked. They weren't much more than a small room filled with a broad table in the center for spreading out scrolls and larger documents, a few chairs, and a lamp or two. None of those had been occupied. But light shone through the crack underneath the door of this one.

I drew in a deep breath, my hands still twitching at the ready. Violet paused and glanced back, as though making sure we were all still there. Then she knocked on the door four times.

Footsteps approached in the room beyond. Something eclipsed the light leaking through from under the door a second before the knob twisted and it cracked open a few inches—just enough for a bright, multihued eye to peer out at us.

Wait, was that a Gray elf? It had to be. Kinslayer didn't have eyes like that.

"It's me," Violet whispered. "I've brought them."

The door opened farther and the tall, lean figure of a man with pointed ears and black hair leaned out to take a better look at all of us. The sight of him, about my height and maybe a year or two older, made my head spin a little. I'd grown up in Luntharda and lived among the Gray elves longer than I'd been here in Maldobar. I knew their culture and customs firsthand. I'd spoken their language first, long before I ever learned the common tongue.

But I had *never* seen a Gray elf like this guy before.

First of all, apart from his distinct multihued eyes, he didn't look like a Gray elf at all. Normally, when they entered puberty, it happened very suddenly. They lost the pigment in their hair, leaving it a silvery white color, and grew into their adult bodies practically overnight. Er, well, over the span of a few days, actually. But despite looking mature, this guy still had pitch black hair that was long on one side and shaved close to his scalp on the other. Not a style customary to the people of Luntharda. They never cut their hair. But it only got stranger from there. His deep bronze skin was also covered in tattooed markings. Shapes of swirling, dark brown lines twisted down one of his arms, across his collarbone, and over his forehead. I'd never seen Gray elves wear marks like that, either.

Despite all that, he didn't look particularly frightening. Bizarre, sure, but not threatening. His pointed ears were pierced a few times through on each side, and there were several strings of bone-carved necklaces and little copper and brass pendants hanging against his chest. They clattered some as he leaned out to peek into the hall. The drab, brown and dark green robes he wore were tied only over one shoulder and revealed most of his leanly muscled torso down to a broad leather belt he wore. His baggy, sirwal-style pants were gathered at his ankles, and he wasn't wearing any shoes. He wasn't even carrying any weapons that I could see.

Definitely not a Lunthardan scout.

He stared at me with a dark brow arched and his sharp, symmetrical features crinkled with suspicion. "I thought it was only the three of them?"

Violet huffed and pushed past him unapologetically. "The prince decided to tag along. I doubt the boss will mind. Now, get out of the way, would you? We're in a time crunch, here."

The young elven man didn't protest and stepped back, watching us all move past him into the room with that prickly, guarded stare still fixed right on me.

I was about to ask him what his problem was, but a voice from farther in the room made my blood rush like a cold mountain stream. "Welcome. I do apologize for the abruptness of my invitation. A necessary precaution should anyone be trying to follow you here, you understand."

I looked ahead, squinting into the wavering glow of a few oil lamps burning on the broad table. Another wide-shouldered figure stood silhouetted against the lamplight with his hands resting on the tabletop and his golden eyes glowing like two embers. Arlan the Kinslayer stared at each one of us for a solid ten seconds before a thin smile finally stretched across his lips. Something about that look chilled me right down to the marrow.

"Violet, Howlan, please leave us and wait outside," he commanded smoothly. "This should not take long, but it would be best if we are not disturbed."

I met Violet's scarlet gaze, watching her expression gradually shift from mild tension to concerned disapproval before she nodded and wordlessly slipped from the room. The strange elven guy followed behind her, his bare feet padding softly on the marble floor.

Once the door clicked shut, Phillip's body language seemed to relax some. But I wasn't dropping my guard just yet. Arlan might have dismissed his hired muscle from the room, but I'd seen what he could do on his own. He didn't need any extra help when it came to combat.

"Your Majesties, I'm honored to be of service. I'm certain you would prefer to do this quickly, so let's not delay any further," he offered, his tone cordial. Motioning to my sister, his glowing eyes fixed upon the squirming shape of my nephew still covered by her cloak as she held him close.

Jenna's face went steely. She pulled back slightly, her lips thinning as she placed a hand protectively on the back of Ronan's head. "No one else could do anything for him," she said. "They didn't even know what was happening to him. Why do you think you'll be able to do anything for him? Why should we trust you at all?"

Arlan's sharp stare cooled some, becoming more quizzical as he made his way around the table to stand before her. He still kept a cautious distance, regarding my sister like a foreign specimen he'd rather observe for now.

Strange ... It didn't make any sense to me. Arlan was an incredibly powerful sorcerer. Sure, Jenna was Queen. But she would be no match for his magical abilities. So why was he treading lightly? Why did he seem so hesitant to go any closer to her?

Unless ... *she* wasn't the one who had him so nervous.

"I understand that you have suffered through much, Your Majesty. Pains and torment that others might have succumbed to. You, however, have proven remarkably resilient. But, rest assured, I would not have invited you here tonight if I did not believe I could at least provide some insight into your son's ... situation," he explained, his tone much softer. "I assume you know who and what I am? And where I come from?"

"I only know stories others have told me. But as I'm sure you're aware, the people of Avora are not very open with their culture," she replied. "They send no ambassadors or word to any of the other kingdoms. They welcome no messengers from any court. No one crosses their borders coming or going, and we have very little understanding of their ideals and where their loyalties lie."

Arlan took a few slow steps closer as Jenna spoke. But she didn't blink or back away from him. She was made of tougher stuff than that. "Just the same, no one seems to understand why or how you came to be in Maldobar," she went on. "I was told you're involved in some sort of feud with your sister, and that she is a powerful and dangerous sorcerer, too."

Arlan looked down, shifting his stance some as he folded his arms over his chest and seemed to ponder on that before he spoke again. "Yes, well, it's a rather complicated situation, I'm afraid. And one we might discuss at a later time. For now, I am willing to examine your son, if you wish. While I cannot guarantee that I can resolve his issues, I stand a far better chance of at least identifying his condition. My people have an extensive knowledge of the divine realm and the functions of its power. We have been intertwined with it for more than a millennia."

Jenna opened her mouth, almost like she was preparing to argue or question him further. She was well within her right to, of course. This guy was as slippery as a serpent and he'd been weaving his way through her kingdom for, well, no one really knew how long. According to what I'd heard about Avoran elves, it could have been centuries ... or longer.

Before she could get a word out, Phillip stepped closer and put a hand on her shoulder. "Then, please. Tell us what is happening to Ronan. Tell us how to help him."

Arlan flicked a glance my way so fast I nearly missed it. His features drew into a tense and focused frown. There was a hint of apprehension as he moved in closer again, standing before my sister and gazing down into her wide-eyed look of awe. He looked over her at nearly a foot taller, his sharp features, shining golden eyes, and long pointed ears a stark contrast to her much smaller, softer form. Stretching out a large hand, he murmured, "Let me see him."

My sister's throat jumped. She hesitated, seeming to fight the urge to snatch my nephew back out of reach and run. My pulse skipped as my fingers brushed the hilts of my blades, ready to take up her defense at any instant. But Jenna held firm. Those familiar fires of resolve smoldered in her gaze. We all knew there was no other choice. This might be Ronan's last hope.

Jenna's hands shook as she unwrapped my tiny nephew from where he'd fallen asleep against her shoulder. He grumbled some as she bent down and carefully placed him on his feet before her. Still dressed in his nightshirt with his mop of black hair tousled, Ronan blinked groggily up at Arlan. He used one of his tiny fists to rub at his eyes as he yawned.

Arlan withdrew a step, seeming surprised and even a little baffled at the sight of him.

Granted, his line of work wasn't exactly something you'd want a lot of kids involved in, and he didn't strike me as the kind of guy who enjoyed having his clothes wrinkled.

But as Arlan slowly sank down into a squat and studied my nephew, his expression sharpened from shock to intense focus. His thin mouth straightened, and his brows pulled together until a little wrinkle formed right at the top of the bridge of his nose.

Ronan stared right back at him, his eyes suddenly widening and his soft, cherubic face the picture of startled excitement. Jenna flinched as he took a few steps closer to Arlan, grinning widely. I tensed, too. Ronan wasn't exactly known around the castle as a shy kid. I'd never seen him take to anyone this quickly, though.

"Yes," Ronan said suddenly, almost like he was answering a question. He tilted his head to one side and then the other with a squinty, thoughtful look. "Hmmmm. Nope!"

My mouth fell open. Wait a second ... were they *talking* to each other with their *minds?!* Was that even possible? I mean, yes, there'd been a time when I'd spoken telepathically with Noh and a certain goddess, but I'd never been able to do it with another normal person.

Er, well, not that either of these two were normal. Crap, I had no idea what any of this meant. It was creepy, terrifying, and put dread like a cold fist right in the pit of my stomach—that I was pretty freaking certain about.

Watching it all, Jenna looked every bit as stunned and mortified. Her features hung slack in ashen shock, staring at her son with her chin trembling as though she were caught somewhere between fury and horror.

Arlan's expression remained calm, however. His gleaming eyes narrowed slightly, still saying nothing as he seemed to lean forward a bit closer to Ronan.

"Nuh uh, but I see dem sometimes in my woom," my nephew answered again, his tiny voice still struggling with some of the words. "I can twy I fink." He squeezed his hands into little fists and stared back at Arlan, his expression pinching up like he was, well, trying to force *something* out. I didn't dare ask what.

Suddenly, Arlan drew back. His features went slack and his lips parted slightly. "I would advise all of you to remain very still and say nothing." He froze where he crouched, his gaze tracking something else—something standing *behind* us.

A cold shiver tingled up my spine. Every little hair on my body prickled at once. The gasp that slipped past my lips sent a puff of white fog into the air as I saw a pair of creatures go slinking along the edges of the room. Shadows licked off their jagged, almost humanoid forms like black flame, their eyes of red glowing like smoldering bog fires in the gloom as they considered all of us.

I tried to swallow. To breathe. But it was as though I'd swallowed a mouthful of white-hot cinders. My vision blurred as I stared unblinkingly at my nephew. Gods and Fates. He had *summoned* those things? How?!

My chest seized with a pulse of panic as Ronan crumpled suddenly, making a frantic squeaking sound of pain before he dropped like a newborn faundra. Arlan caught him before he could hit the ground, sweeping my tiny nephew up into his arms and giving a flourish of his hand that filled the air with an abrupt flash of blinding golden light.

Jenna and Phillip let out cries of alarm.

I drew my blade.

The door at the back of the room burst open, cracking off the wall as Violet and Howlan charged back in, weapons drawn.

"*STOP!*" Arlan's voice boomed over us like a clap of thunder as the light faded from the room.

Everyone held perfectly still. My pulse boomed in my ears and throbbed in my palms as I held my kafki blades at the ready, searching for any sign of those two shadow entities. Merciful gods, they'd looked exactly how Noh used to whenever he manifested, only they hadn't looked like wolves.

They'd almost looked ... human. Smaller and squattier, sure. But they'd had the same relative shape.

"They've gone," Arlan announced as he stepped over to Jenna and held Ronan's unconscious body out to her. "Take him. He will recover."

She didn't hesitate for an instant, seizing her son and cradling him against her protectively again. "Recover from *what?*" she demanded, her tone sharp and nearly screaming. "What just happened? What were those things? What is wrong with my baby?!"

That last question hung in the air for what felt like an eternity. All the while, Arlan stared at Ronan, his expression creased and tense, but utterly unreadable. "Lesser ghouls, if my assumption is correct. Some in the lowlands call them imps, however. The soul scavengers. Drawn to places where there has been much death, they enjoy feasting on wandering lost souls." His molten gaze flicked up, locking with Jenna's so suddenly it made her flinch. "According to your son, they follow him occasionally, as well. They also appear in his room, most often at night. I asked if he could call to them, to bring them here at his command. And it seems he can."

Phillip sank into his heels, his expression falling to despair. "He can *summon* ghouls —imps—whatever those things are?"

Arlan nodded. "He is also an innate telepath—but likely only with others who are also attuned to the presence of divine power. A rare gift, and not one I have seen beyond the borders of Avora, let alone inborn to a human."

"What does it *mean?*" Jenna demanded again, her voice far more broken now.

"It is as I suspected. He is a misborn. A darkling. One born under a divine curse," he explained with a hint of what might have been genuine sympathy in his voice. Hard to tell with that guy. "This particular curse seems to have been imparted by Clysiros, the Goddess of Death. Although, I suspect you had already guessed as much."

Jenna squeezed Ronan harder, her eyes glistening with fresh tears.

Phillip moved to her side, placing a hand gently on her shoulder as though to steady her. "If it's a curse, then there must be a way to break it."

"Perhaps." Arlan didn't sound as confident about that. "Though the particular mechanics of how it would need to be done are something only the goddess herself would know, so unfortunately I cannot offer any guidance to that end. What I can be certain of is that as the boy ages, the condition of his curse will surely worsen. I can only speculate as to how, but I believe it would be a safe guess to say that he will be drawn farther and farther away from the world of the living and inevitably into her world. The physical toll, as you've seen, will be a great risk. But the mental toll is far more concerning. Mortal minds are not meant to roam such places."

"You're saying ... he'll go mad?" Jenna whispered. Tears ran freely down her cheeks as she looked down at Ronan, his tiny features slack but peaceful in her embrace.

Arlan didn't reply. He didn't have to. The weight of his silence was more than enough. Nearly a minute passed before he finally took another, bold step toward my sister and took one of Ronan's tiny hands in his. "I will continue to investigate what I can," he murmured, his brow snapping into a grimace of effort as he pinched his eyes shut. Another soft glow of light from between his hands made my skin tingle again. "In the meantime, this might buy him some time. I ... am truly sorry I cannot do more, Your Majesties. But even this small favor may invite Clysiros's wrath against me. They do so hate it when others meddle in their affairs, and she has already marked his soul as her own."

A curling blue rune spread across the top of Ronan's hand like ink spreading over cloth. It gave soft pulses of light, like the rhythm of a heartbeat, before it gradually faded and turned black. Anyone else would've thought it was just a tattoo.

"It will not last forever. Soon, his power will likely overwhelm and shatter it. But for now, consider this a gift to accompany my condolences. The Blessing of Enais will slow the progression of his symptoms."

No one thanked him, although that probably wasn't because my sister and her husband weren't grateful. This was a lot to digest, and their downtrodden expressions as Violet let them out of the room made it clear no one would be sleeping for a few nights.

Or years, maybe.

I slipped my kafki blades back into the sheaths at my hips, preparing to follow them back out into the night ... until Arlan spoke up again.

"Do they intend to tell the prince of his true parentage when he comes of age?"

I stopped. Every muscle in my body seemed to thrum with angry heat at once. I didn't dare look back at him as I growled through my teeth, "I doubt it. What good could possible come from him knowing that?"

Arlan's tone was as soft as it was pensive. "I believe a much better question would be: what harm could come from keeping that knowledge a secret from him? It is kind of King Phillip to claim him, but the truth has a way of finding us past even the gentlest of lies. That boy already has destiny in his blood, perhaps even more strongly than your heroes of old. I would take care not to paint his world with rosy falsehoods and fragile secrets. I would think that you, of all people, would understand this best of all."

I turned to shoot him a glare of warning over my shoulder. "Because Clysiros tried to claim me, too?"

Arlan the Kinslayer dipped his chin in a cryptic smile as the flames from the hearth made the shadows dance and waver around him. "Because the search for hidden truths nearly destroyed you once. In fact, it left you quite fractured, didn't it? You run from those truths even now. Hide from them. Bargain with them. It's most interesting to witness."

My jaw creaked as I gnashed my teeth against everything I wanted to do. Rush him. Stick a blade through his neck. And that was just for starters. "Shut up. You may know a lot about gods and goddesses, but you *don't* know me," I snarled low as I turned and stormed for the door.

"On the contrary, Reigh Farrow," he purred at my back, delight dripping from every word. "I'm quite sure I'm one of the few who truly does. Go carefully now, young prince. I foresee a time very soon when our paths will cross again."

THE ADVENTURE CONTINUES IN

SOJOURNER

Available for Preorder Now!

ABOUT THE AUTHOR

Nicole Conway is a graduate of Auburn University with a lifelong passion for writing teen and children's literature. With over 100,000 books sold in her DRAGONRIDER CHRONICLES series, Nicole has been ranked one of Amazon's Top 100 Teen Authors. A coffee and Netflix addict, she also enjoys spending time with her family, rock climbing, and traveling.

Nicole is represented by Frances Black of Literary Counsel.

Made in the USA
Las Vegas, NV
19 January 2023

65911889R00439